CREATED BY MIKE MIGNOLA

PLAGUE
OF FROGS

VOLUME TWO

BUREAU FOR PARANORMAL RESEARCH AND DEFENSE

CAPTAIN BENJAMIN DAIMIO A United States Marine whose distinguished thirteen-year career ended in June of 2001, when he and the platoon he was leading were all killed during a mission. The details of his death remain classified. Exactly how it was that he came back to life is an outright mystery.

ROGER A homunculus made from human blood and herbs. Discovered in Romania, Roger was first brought to life by Liz's pyrokinetic touch. Whether or not he is actually alive may be up for debate, but his childlike love of that life is not.

ABE SAPIEN An amphibious man discovered in a primitive stasis chamber in a long-forgotten subbasement beneath a Washington, DC, hospital. Abe has served as a B.P.R.D. field agent since shortly after being revived.

LIZ SHERMAN A fire starter since the age of eleven, when she accidentally burned her entire family to death. She has been a ward of the B.P.R.D. since then, learning to control her pyrokinetic abilities and cope with the trauma those abilities have wrought.

DR. KATE CORRIGAN A former professor at New York University, an authority on folklore and occult history. Dr. Corrigan has been a B.P.R.D. consultant for over ten years and now serves as special liaison to the enhanced-talents task force.

JOHANN KRAUS A medium whose physical form was destroyed while his ectoplasmic projection was out of body. His essence now resides in a containment suit. A psychic empath, Johann can create temporary forms for the dead to speak to the living.

COVER MIKE MIGNOLA WITH DAVE STEWART

EDITOR SCOTT ALLIE

PRESIDENT AND PUBLISHER MIKE RICHARDSON

B.P.R.D.

PLAGUE OF FROGS

VOLUME TWO

MIKE MIGNOLA   **JOHN ARCUDI**   **GUY DAVIS**

HERB TRIMPE   **JOHN SEVERIN**   **PETER SNEJBJERG**   **KARL MOLINE**

DAVE STEWART   **BJARNE HANSEN**   **CLEM ROBINS**

DARK HORSE BOOKS®

ASSISTANT EDITORS DANIEL CHABON, MATT DRYER, RACHEL EDIDIN, FREDDYE LINS, and DAVE MARSHALL
COLLECTION DESIGNER AMY ARENDTS

Special thanks to Jason Hvam

Mike Richardson **PRESIDENT AND PUBLISHER** · Neil Hankerson **EXECUTIVE VICE PRESIDENT** Tom Weddle **CHIEF FINANCIAL OFFICER** · Randy Stradley **VICE PRESIDENT OF PUBLISHING** Michael Martens **VICE PRESIDENT OF BOOK TRADE SALES** · Anita Nelson **VICE PRESIDENT OF BUSINESS AFFAIRS** · Micha Hershman **VICE PRESIDENT OF MARKETING** · David Scroggy **VICE PRESIDENT OF PRODUCT DEVELOPMENT** · Dale LaFountain **VICE PRESIDENT OF INFORMATION TECHNOLOGY** · Darlene Vogel **SENIOR DIRECTOR OF PRINT, DESIGN, AND PRODUCTION** Ken Lizzi **GENERAL COUNSEL** · Davey Estrada **EDITORIAL DIRECTOR** · Scott Allie **SENIOR MANAGING EDITOR** · Chris Warner **SENIOR BOOKS EDITOR** · Diana Schutz **EXECUTIVE EDITOR** Cary Grazzini **DIRECTOR OF PRINT AND DEVELOPMENT** · Lia Ribacchi **ART DIRECTOR** · Cara Niece **DIRECTOR OF SCHEDULING**

DarkHorse.com   Hellboy.com

This volume collects "B.P.R.D.: Born Again" from *Hellboy Premiere Edition*; "Revival" from *MySpace Dark Horse Presents*, issues #8–#9; and stories from the comic-book series *B.P.R.D.: The Dead*, issues #1–#5; *B.P.R.D.: War on Frogs*, issues #1–#4; and *B.P.R.D.: The Black Flame*, issues #1–#6; published by Dark Horse Comics.

Published by Dark Horse Books
A division of Dark Horse Comics, Inc.
10956 SE Main Street
Milwaukie, OR 97222

First edition: September 2011
ISBN 978-1-59582-672-5

10 9 8 7 6 5 4 3 2 1
Printed at 1010 Printing International, Ltd., Guangdong Province, China

When we put together the first of these hardcovers, it seemed like a crime not to put John Arcudi's name on the front. As Mike has often said, we think of *B.P.R.D.* as John and Guy's book, but John didn't work on those first three trade paperbacks. This book kicks off his fantastic run on the series.

The one *B.P.R.D.* story Mike wrote on his own, *Plague of Frogs*, had given us our mission statement for an ongoing series, but when we began work on *Plague*, we knew Mike wouldn't continue as the regular writer. The way I remembered it, it was the success of *Plague of Frogs* that made us decide to continue *B.P.R.D.*, but we must have come to the conclusion sooner. While putting this book together, I realized we must have arrived at the choice of John Arcudi as cowriter before *Plague* even came out. I don't remember how we got there, but we had John's script for *The Dead* #1 less than a month after *Plague of Frogs* #1 went on sale.

Plague of Frogs #5 came out in July 2004, and then there was a four-month break before *The Dead* #1 went on sale in November. After *The Dead*, there was a five-month break before *The Black Flame* #1 (August 2005). The breaks grew shorter, until late 2007, when we committed to having a *B.P.R.D.* comic on sale every month.

We wanted every issue to be drawn by Guy, but while he's one of the fastest artists in comics, he couldn't keep up with a monthly schedule and still work on his other projects. Our plan to deliver a monthly *B.P.R.D.* book required fill-ins—drawn by other artists, written by Mike and John, and telling stories set outside regular continuity but still serving the direction of the series.

War on Frogs started as a two-part story in *MySpace Dark Horse Presents* in early 2008, followed by four one-shots between mid-2008 and late 2009. We served the larger *B.P.R.D.* plot by leaping back to 2005, around the beginning of the frog war, fleshing out that turning point in the series. The stories were all written and published well after the six-issue *The Black Flame* series but take place for the most part between *The Black Flame* #1 and #2.

Although *War on Frogs* was supposed to give Guy a break while bringing in other artists, we didn't want Guy to feel left out. The first *War on Frogs* story went to him. Then, when the next one fell behind schedule, Guy came in to ink Herb Trimpe's pencils. That story was conceived to combine Herb's renown on *The Incredible Hulk* with his time on Marvel's *Nick Fury, Agent of S.H.I.E.L.D.* comics, by looking at the relationship between Roger (who could be our Hulk) and Daimio (who *is* our Nick Fury). The next story played to John Severin's legendary work on realistic war comics. John Arcudi wrote the Johann story before the Liz one, but because of Karl Moline and Peter Snejbjerg's schedules, the Liz one-shot came out first. Their order was reversed in the *War on Frogs* trade paperback, to put the Liz one-shot at the end as John had intended. How these five stories relate to the events of the six-issue *The Black Flame* story is even more complicated, leading to a hot debate about how to arrange this book, resulting in *The Black Flame* #1 being moved up to be *War on Frogs* chapter 1, and the Liz *War on Frogs* one-shot to serve as an epilogue to *The Black Flame*.

John's first story as cowriter moves the Bureau's headquarters from Connecticut to Colorado, but that was just the beginning of big changes for these characters. Comics readers are trained to expect things to remain unchanged decade after decade, but the stories in this volume demonstrate to our readers that nothing is sacred here—expect shakeups—and they should be careful about getting too attached to anyone.

Scott Allie

Portland, Oregon, 2011

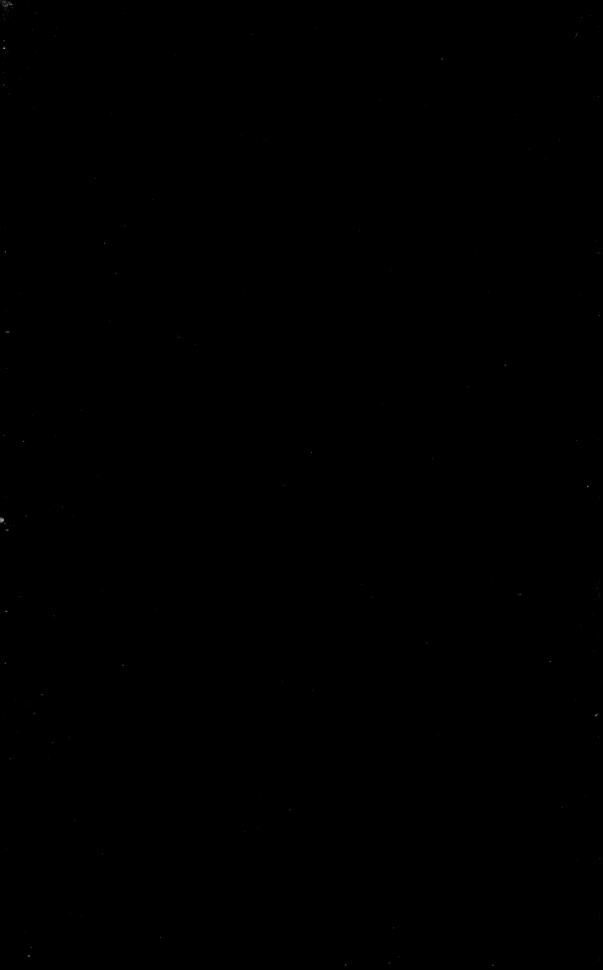

BOOK ONE

THE DEAD

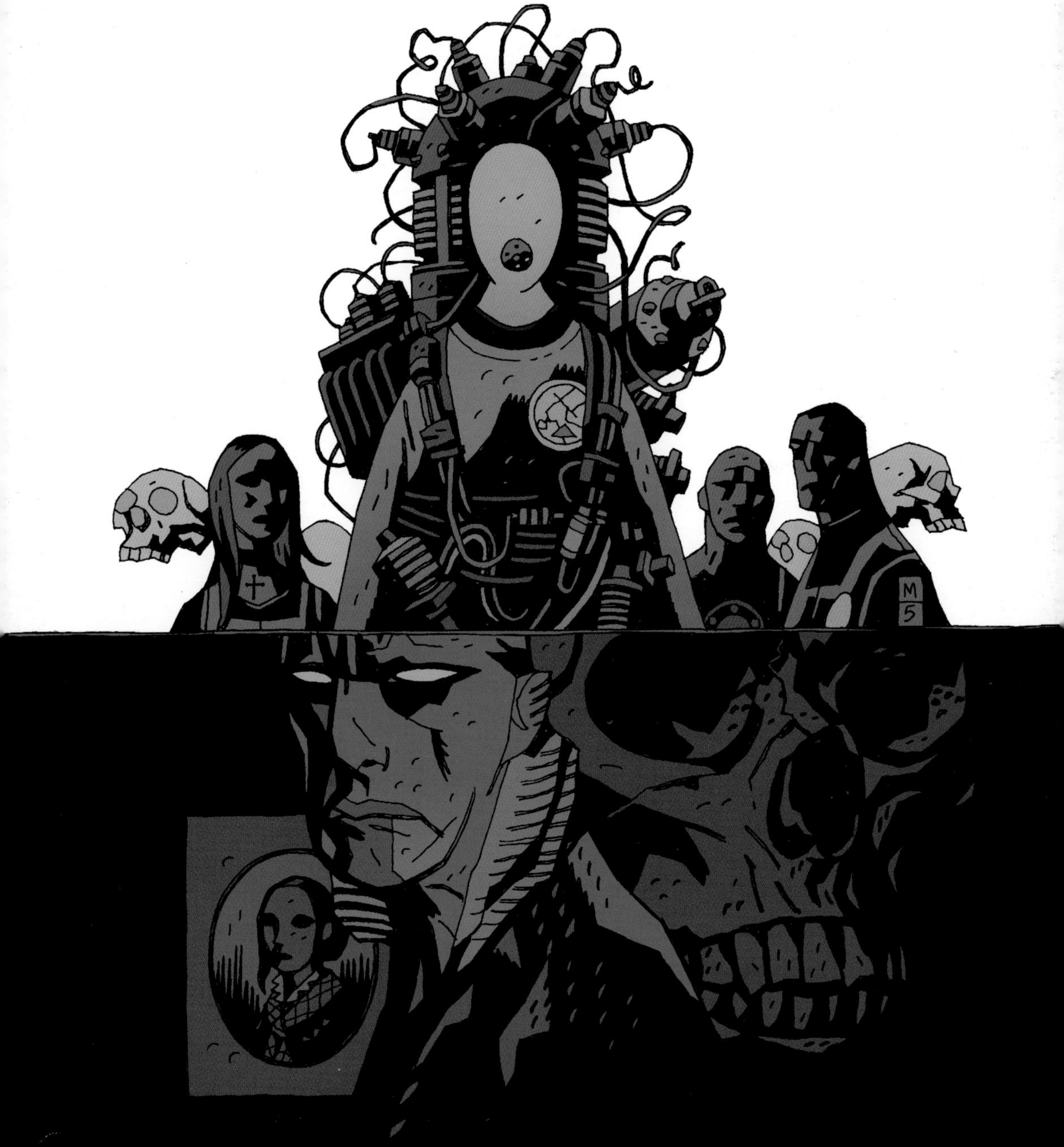

M
5

THE DEAD

STORY BY MIKE MIGNOLA & JOHN ARCUDI

ART BY GUY DAVIS

COLORS BY DAVE STEWART

LETTERS BY CLEM ROBINS

PROLOGUE

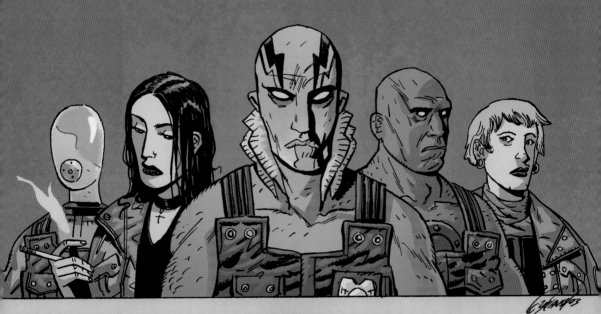

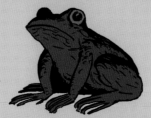

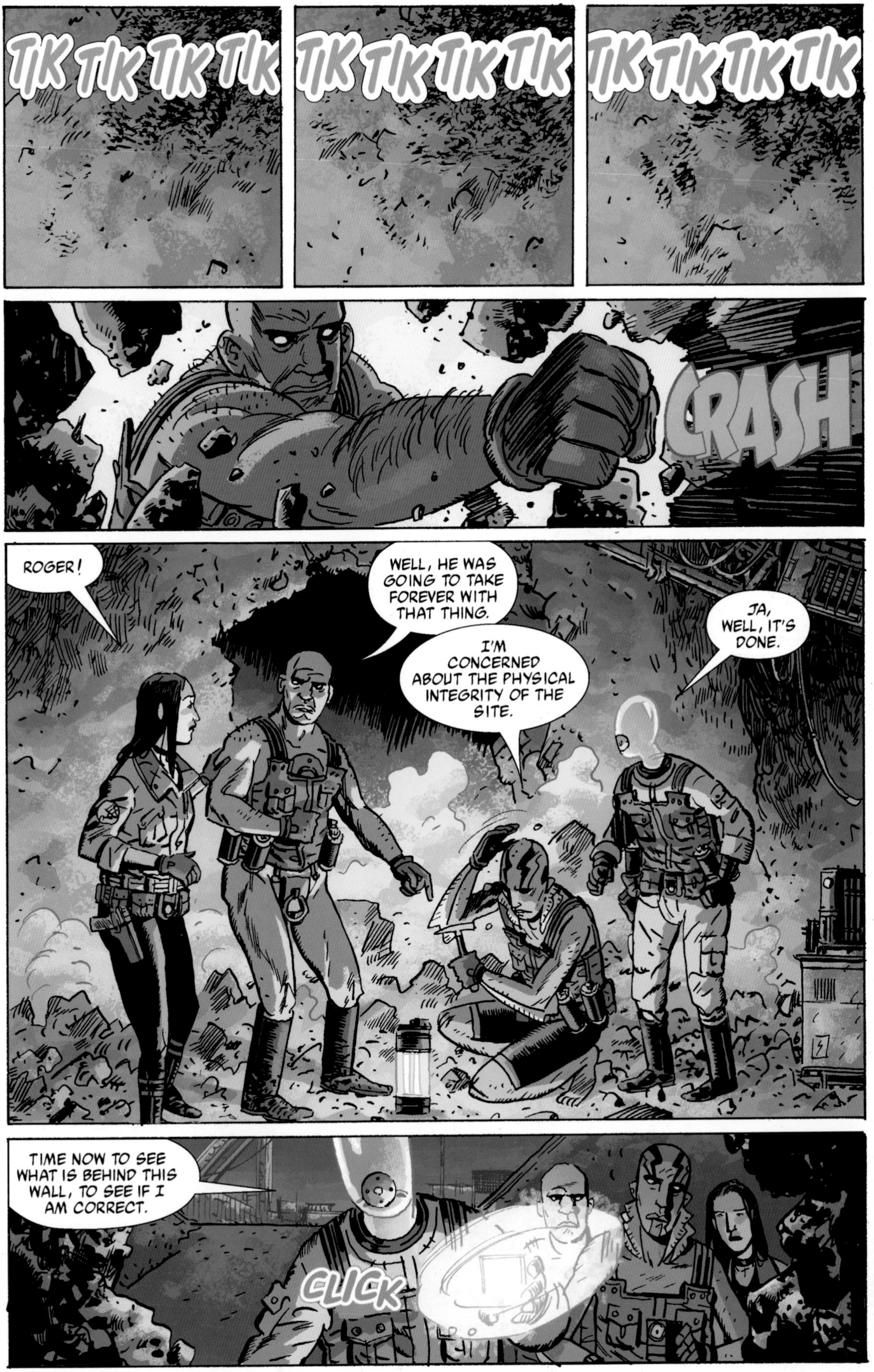
TIK TIK TIK TIK
TIK TIK TIK TIK
TIK TIK TIK TIK
CRASH
ROGER!
WELL, HE WAS GOING TO TAKE FOREVER WITH THAT THING.
I'M CONCERNED ABOUT THE PHYSICAL INTEGRITY OF THE SITE.
JA, WELL, IT'S DONE.
TIME NOW TO SEE WHAT IS BEHIND THIS WALL, TO SEE IF I AM CORRECT.
CLICK

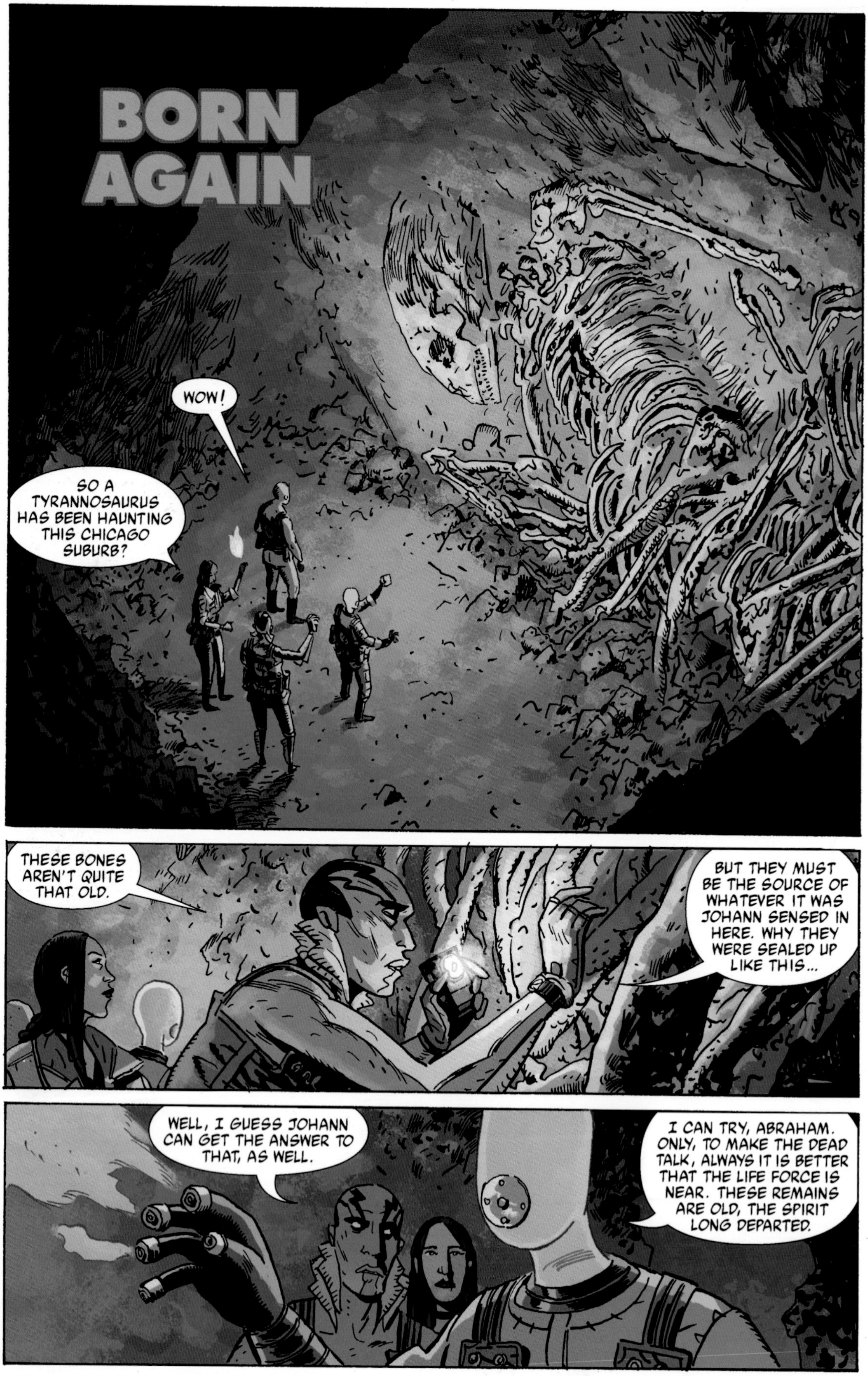
BORN AGAIN
WOW!
SO A TYRANNOSAURUS HAS BEEN HAUNTING THIS CHICAGO SUBURB?
THESE BONES AREN'T QUITE THAT OLD.
BUT THEY MUST BE THE SOURCE OF WHATEVER IT WAS JOHANN SENSED IN HERE. WHY THEY WERE SEALED UP LIKE THIS...
WELL, I GUESS JOHANN CAN GET THE ANSWER TO THAT, AS WELL.
I CAN TRY, ABRAHAM. ONLY, TO MAKE THE DEAD TALK, ALWAYS IT IS BETTER THAT THE LIFE FORCE IS NEAR. THESE REMAINS ARE OLD, THE SPIRIT LONG DEPARTED.

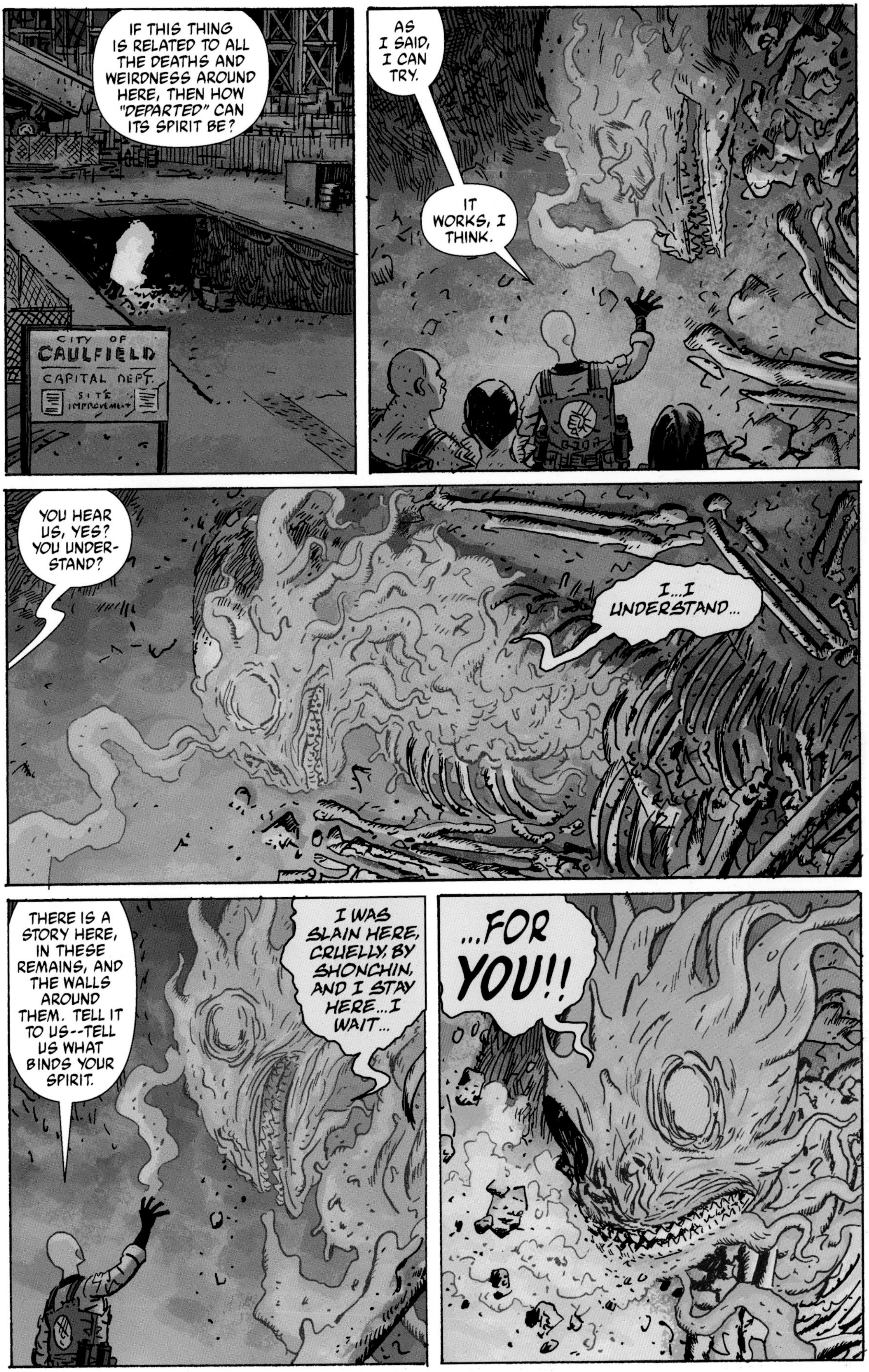
IF THIS THING IS RELATED TO ALL THE DEATHS AND WEIRDNESS AROUND HERE, THEN HOW "DEPARTED" CAN ITS SPIRIT BE?
CITY OF CAULFIELD
CAPITAL DEPT.
SITE IMPROVEMENT
AS I SAID, I CAN TRY.
IT WORKS, I THINK.
YOU HEAR US, YES? YOU UNDER-STAND?
I...I UNDERSTAND...
THERE IS A STORY HERE, IN THESE REMAINS, AND THE WALLS AROUND THEM. TELL IT TO US--TELL US WHAT BINDS YOUR SPIRIT.
I WAS SLAIN HERE, CRUELLY, BY SHONCHIN, AND I STAY HERE...I WAIT...
...FOR YOU!!

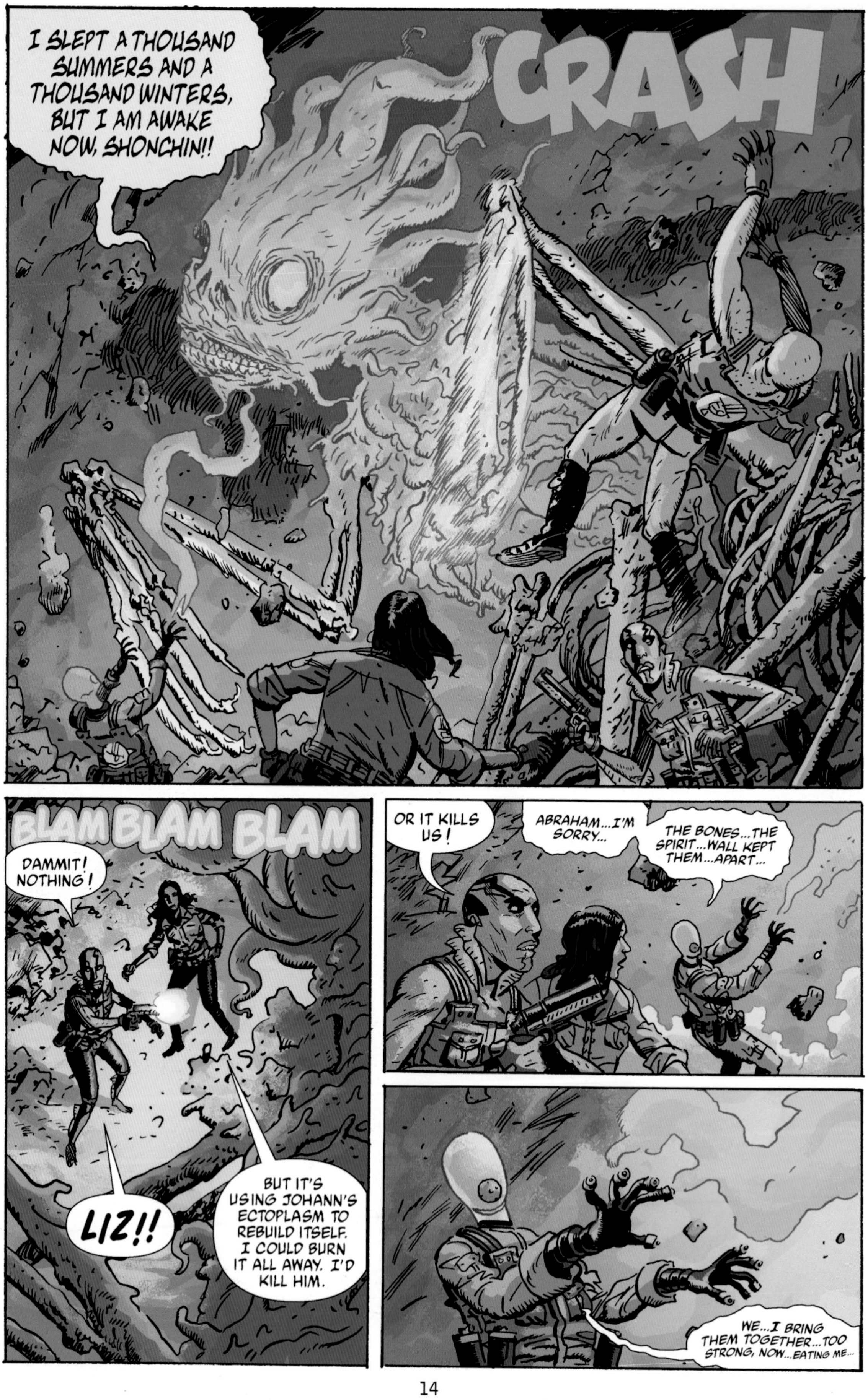
I SLEPT A THOUSAND SUMMERS AND A THOUSAND WINTERS, BUT I AM AWAKE NOW, SHONCHIN!!
CRASH
BLAM BLAM BLAM
DAMMIT! NOTHING!
LIZ!!
BUT IT'S USING JOHANN'S ECTOPLASM TO REBUILD ITSELF. I COULD BURN IT ALL AWAY. I'D KILL HIM.
OR IT KILLS US!
ABRAHAM...I'M SORRY...
THE BONES...THE SPIRIT...WALL KEPT THEM...APART...
WE...I BRING THEM TOGETHER...TOO STRONG, NOW...EATING ME...

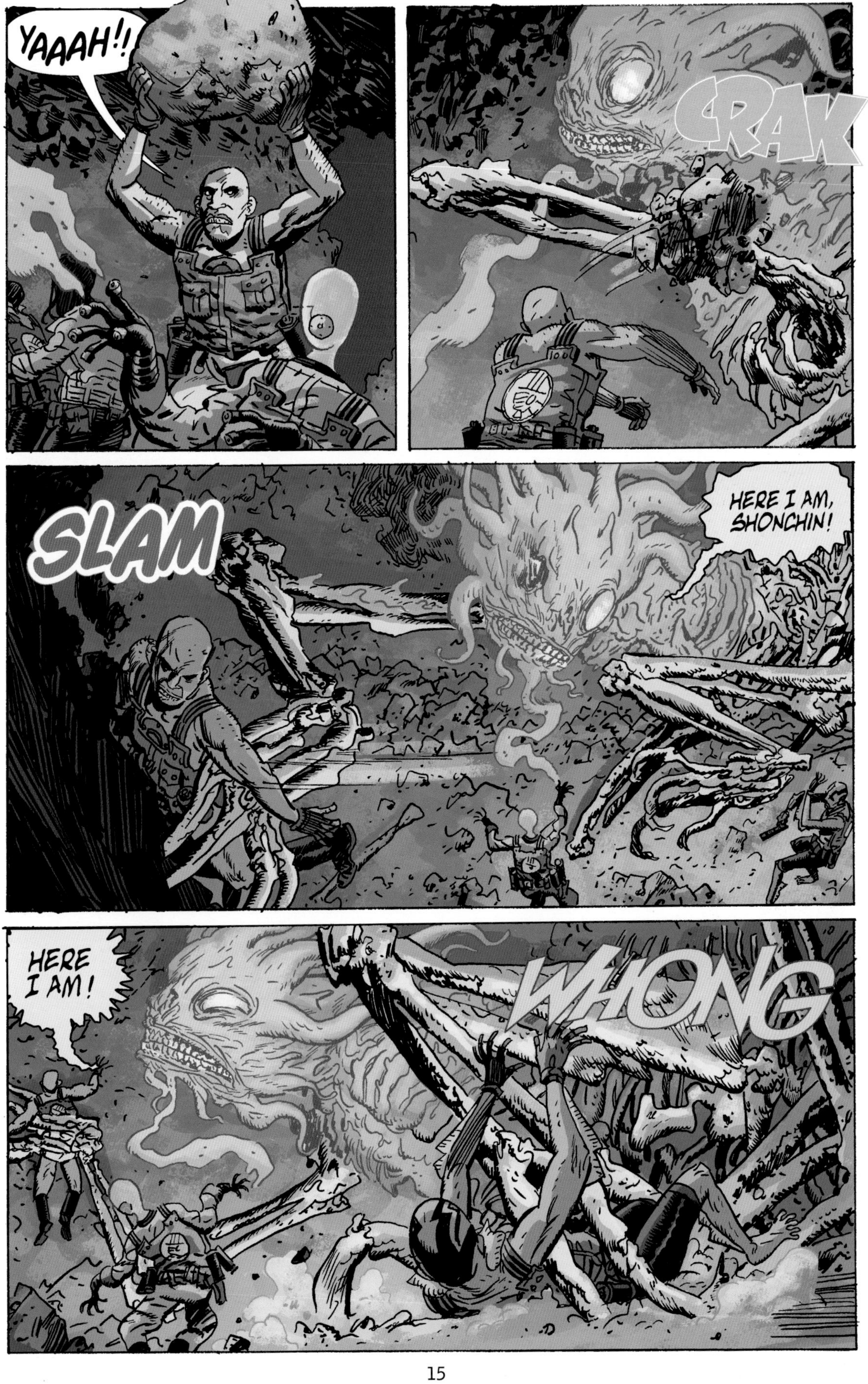
YAAAH!!
CRAK
SLAM
HERE I AM, SHONCHIN!
HERE I AM!
WHONG

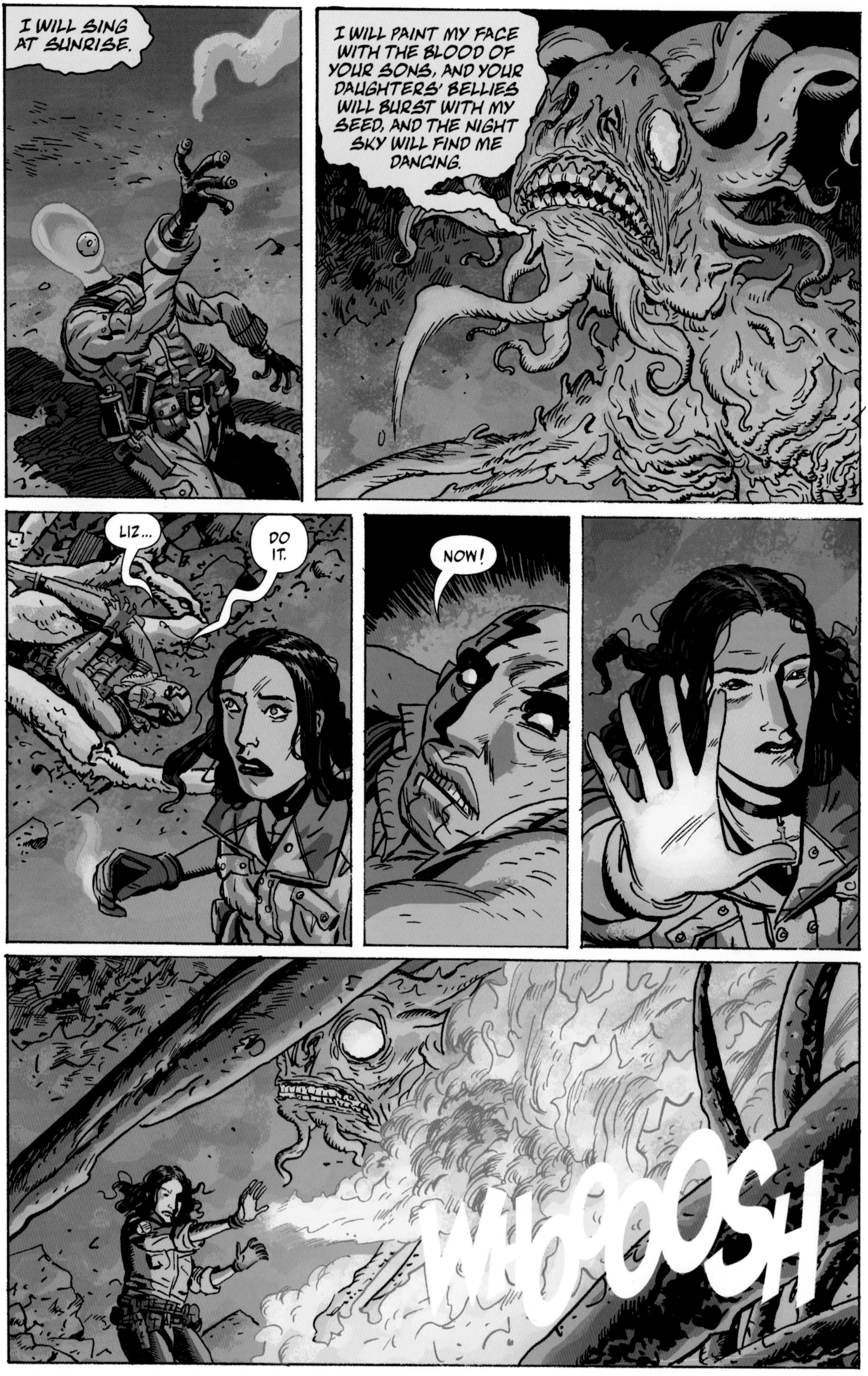
I WILL SING AT SUNRISE.
I WILL PAINT MY FACE WITH THE BLOOD OF YOUR SONS, AND YOUR DAUGHTERS' BELLIES WILL BURST WITH MY SEED, AND THE NIGHT SKY WILL FIND ME DANCING.
LIZ...
DO IT.
NOW!
WHOOOSH

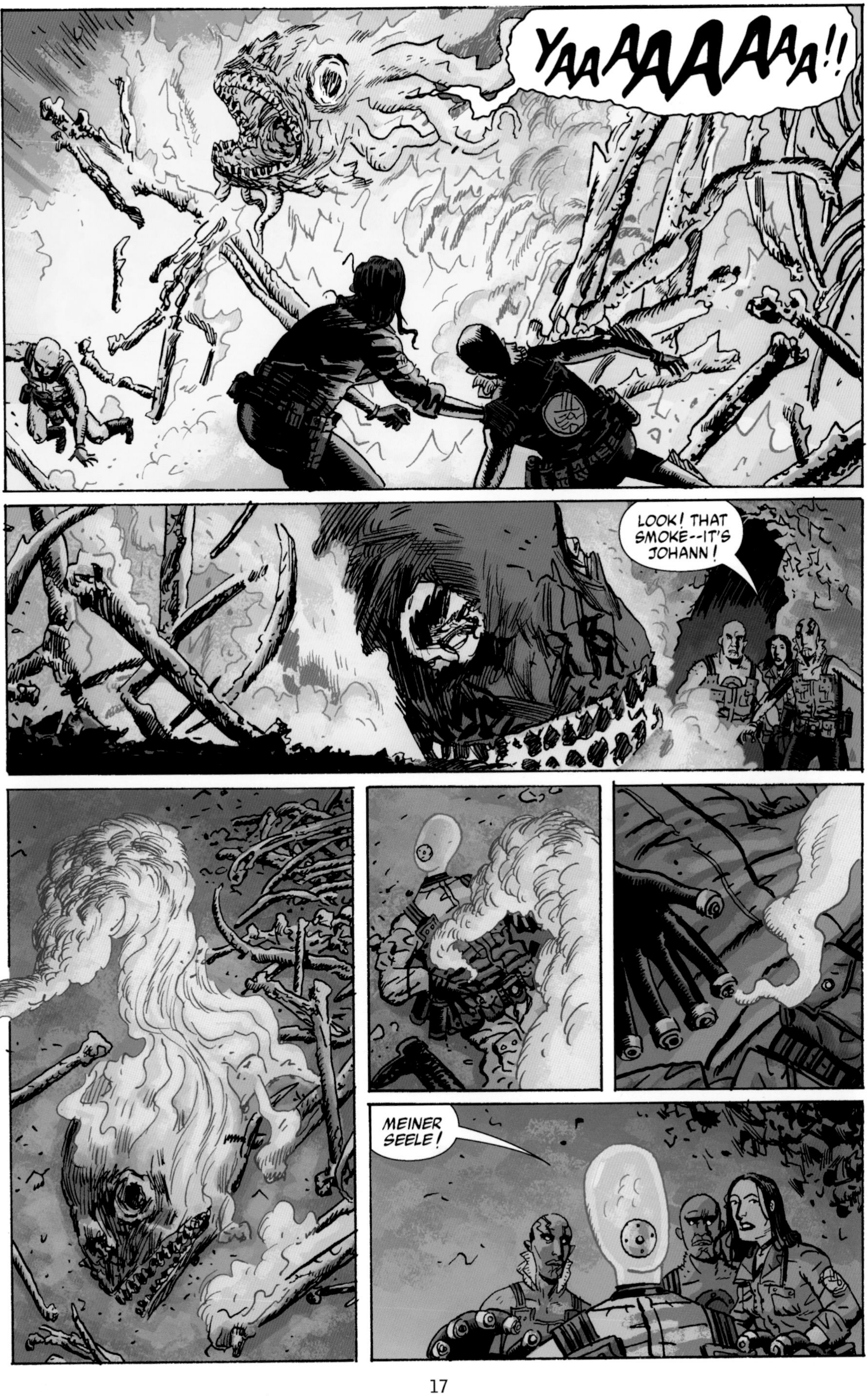
YAAAAAAAAA!!
LOOK! THAT SMOKE--IT'S JOHANN!
MEINER SEELE!

NOT SO HELPFUL, THAT CREATURE.

BUT I THINK THIS SHONCHIN WAS ONE OF YOUR NORTH AMERICAN ABORIGINAL SHAMANS.

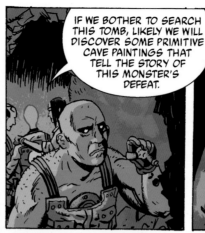

IF WE BOTHER TO SEARCH THIS TOMB, LIKELY WE WILL DISCOVER SOME PRIMITIVE CAVE PAINTINGS THAT TELL THE STORY OF THIS MONSTER'S DEFEAT.

?

COLONEL. YOUR MEN WILL FIND SOME BURNT REMAINS UNDER THE SITE. JUST BAG IT UP. THE BUREAU WILL SEND THE RECOVERY CREW TOMORROW.

YOU GOT IT.

ARE YOU SURE YOU'RE OKAY, JOHANN?

WHAT'S THAT?

YES, GOOD. ONLY I HAVE THIS SENSATION, A FEELING I NEVER THOUGHT I'D HAVE AGAIN.

I'M VERY WARM.

CHAPTER ONE

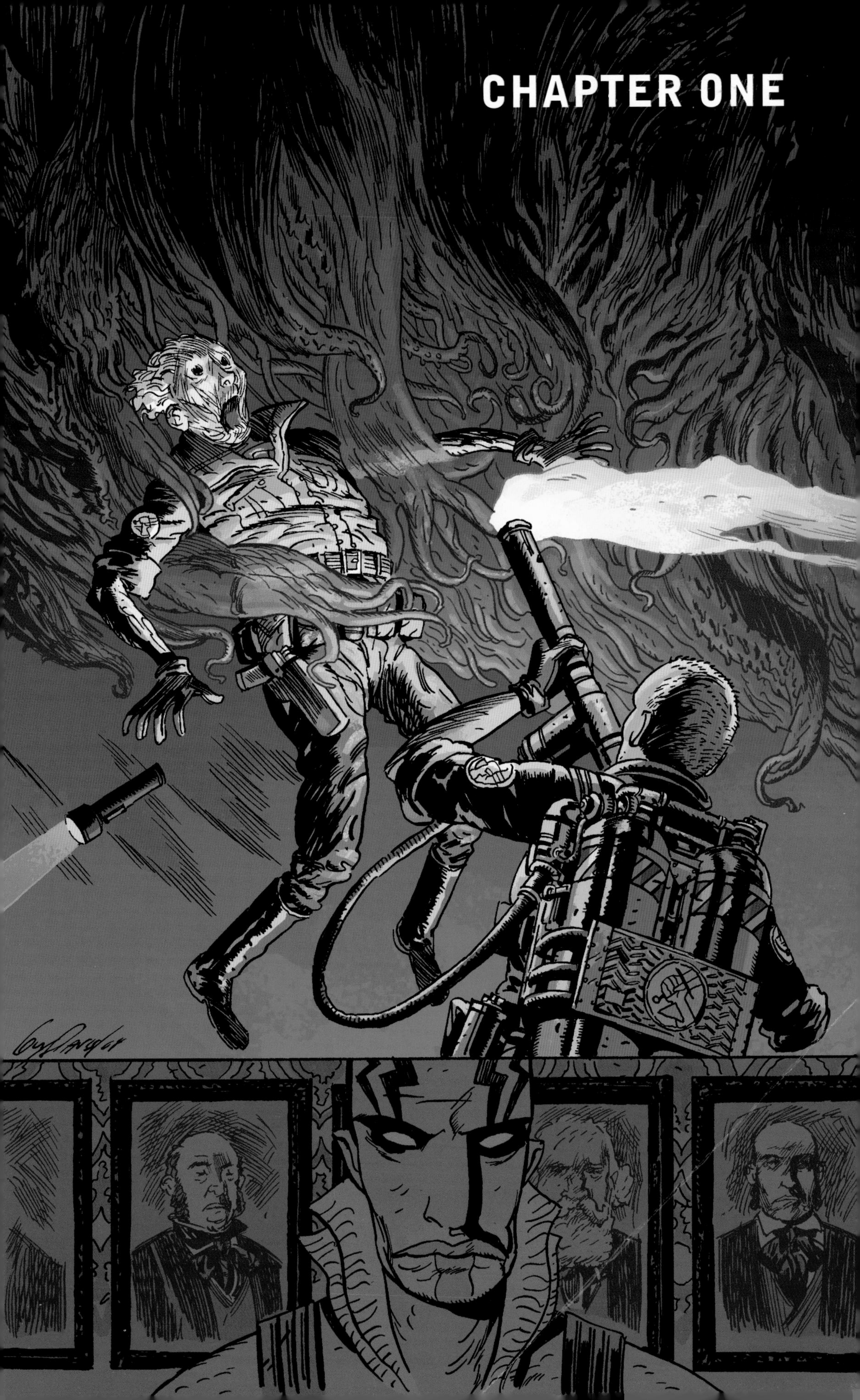

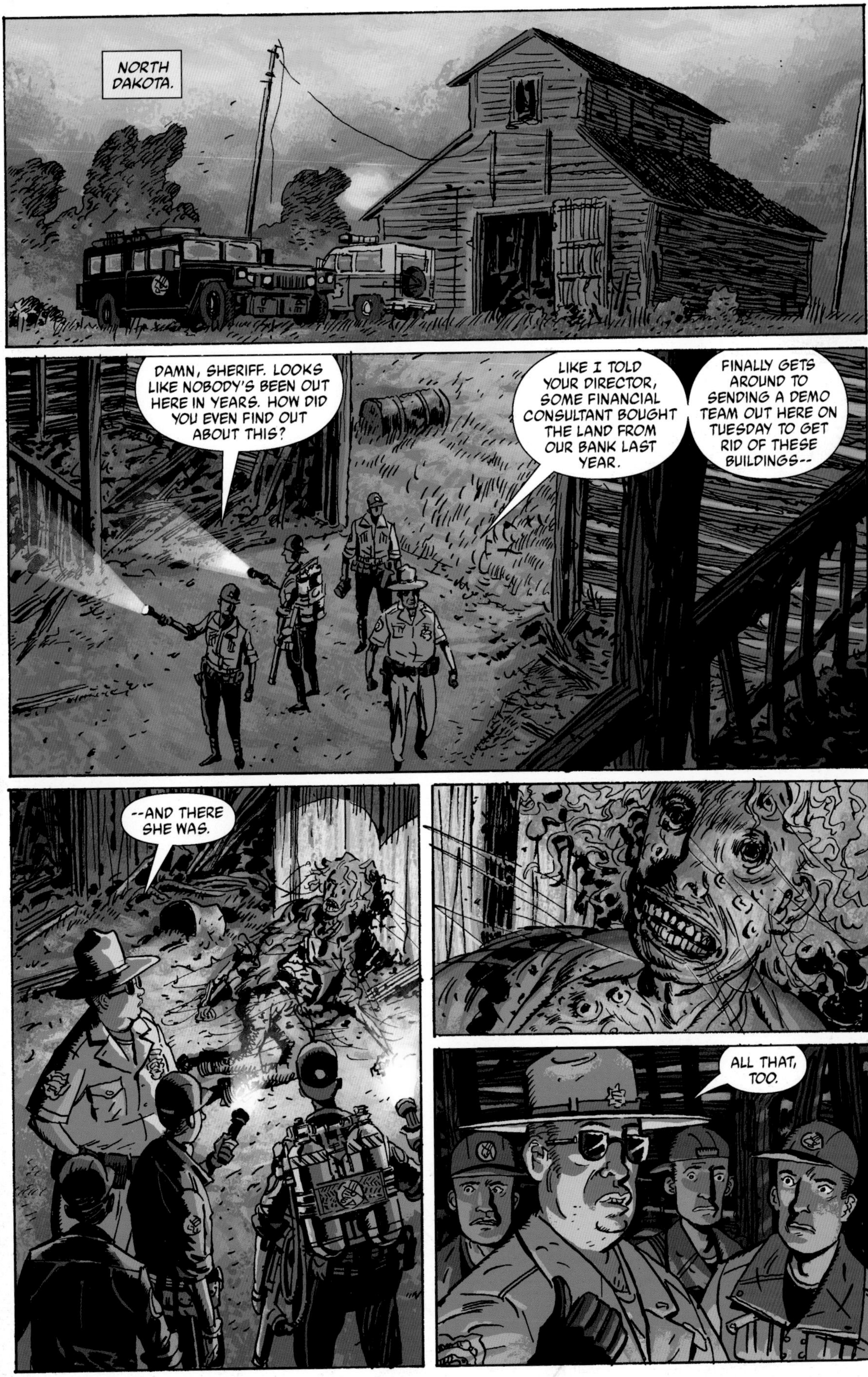
NORTH DAKOTA.
DAMN, SHERIFF. LOOKS LIKE NOBODY'S BEEN OUT HERE IN YEARS. HOW DID YOU EVEN FIND OUT ABOUT THIS?
LIKE I TOLD YOUR DIRECTOR, SOME FINANCIAL CONSULTANT BOUGHT THE LAND FROM OUR BANK LAST YEAR.
FINALLY GETS AROUND TO SENDING A DEMO TEAM OUT HERE ON TUESDAY TO GET RID OF THESE BUILDINGS--
--AND THERE SHE WAS.
ALL THAT, TOO.

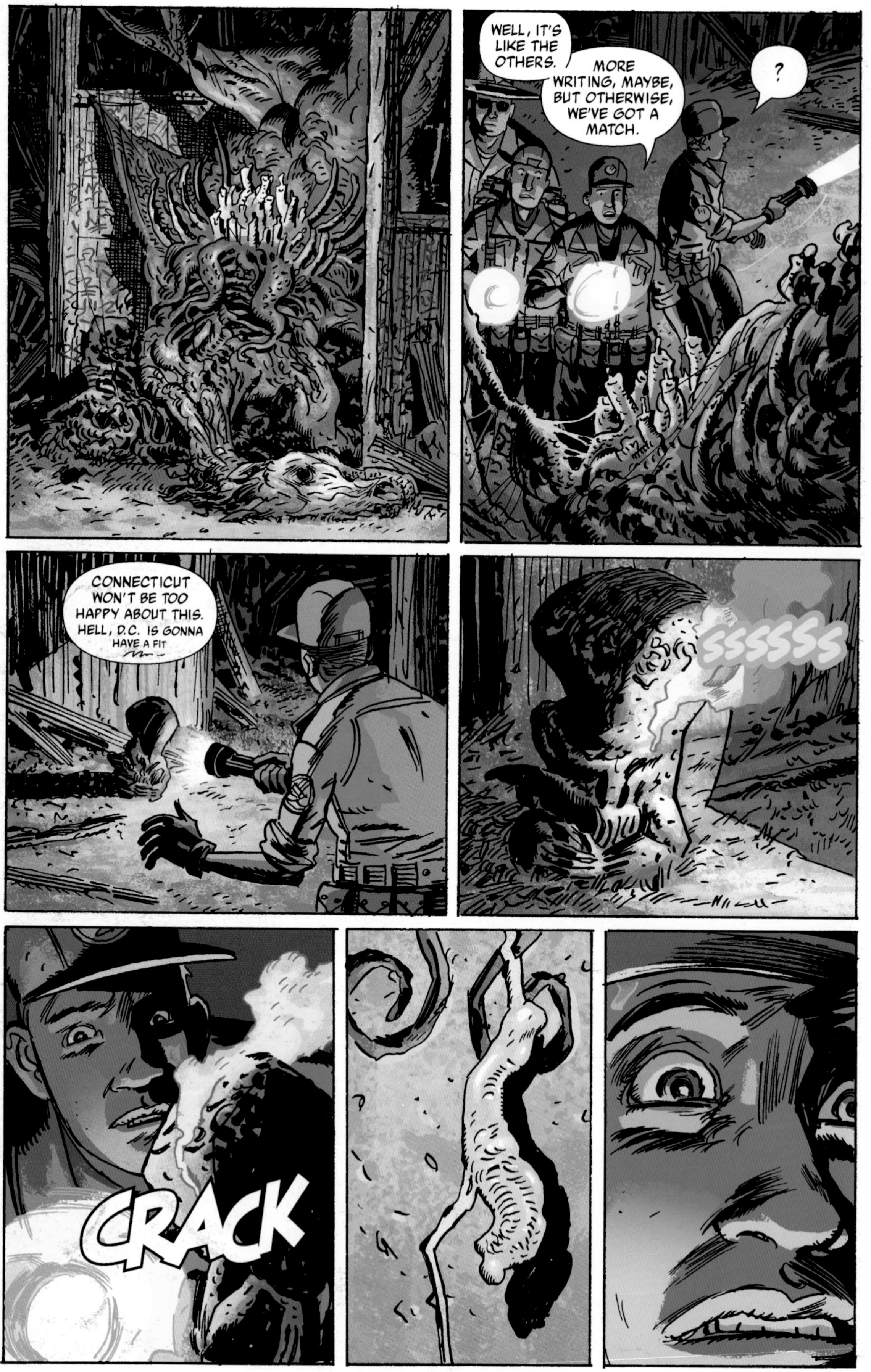

WELL, IT'S LIKE THE OTHERS.
MORE WRITING, MAYBE, BUT OTHERWISE, WE'VE GOT A MATCH.
?
CONNECTICUT WON'T BE TOO HAPPY ABOUT THIS. HELL, D.C. IS GONNA HAVE A FIT
SSSSSS
CRACK

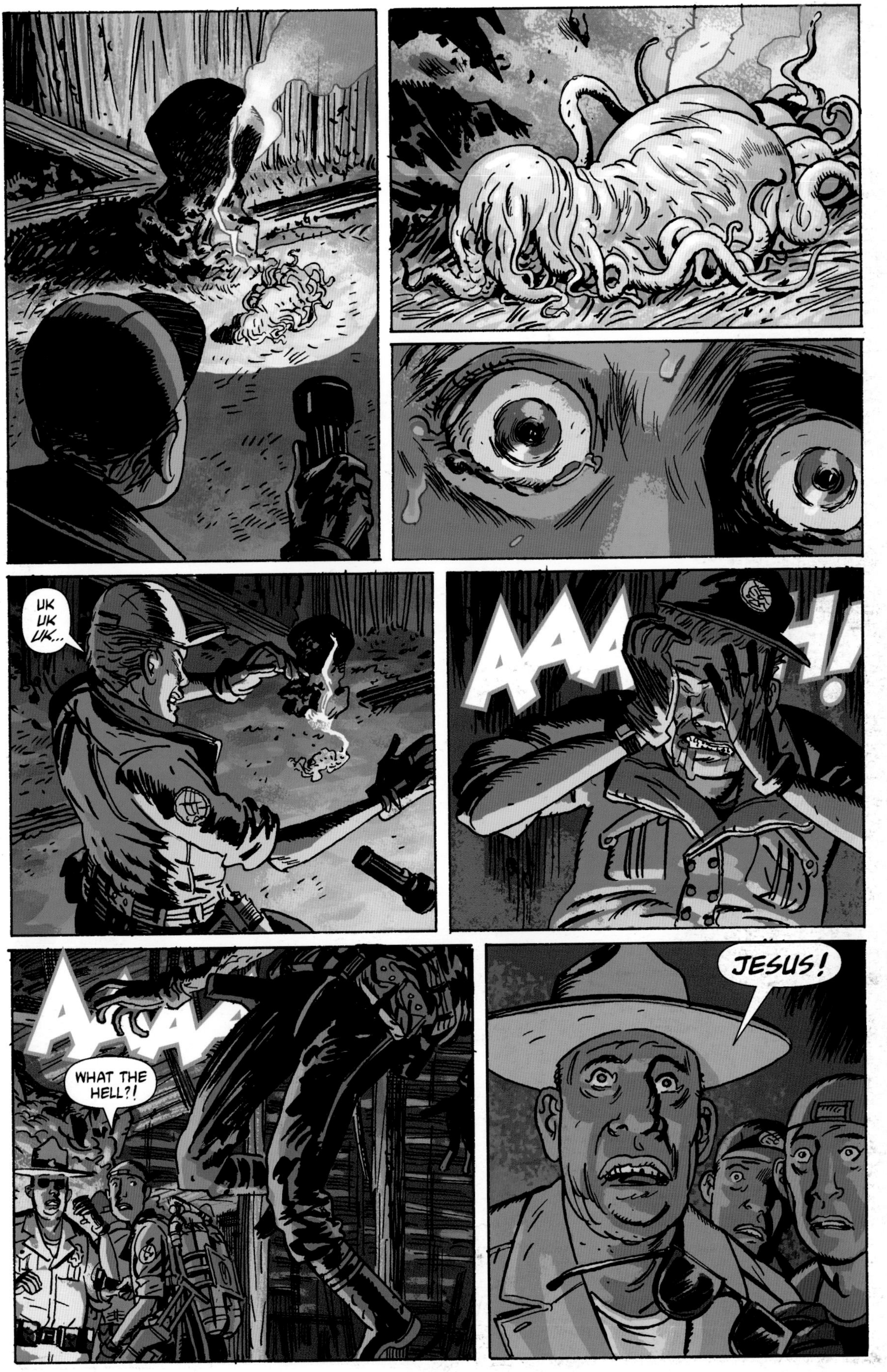
UK
UK
UK...
AAAAGH!
AAA
WHAT THE HELL?!
JESUS!

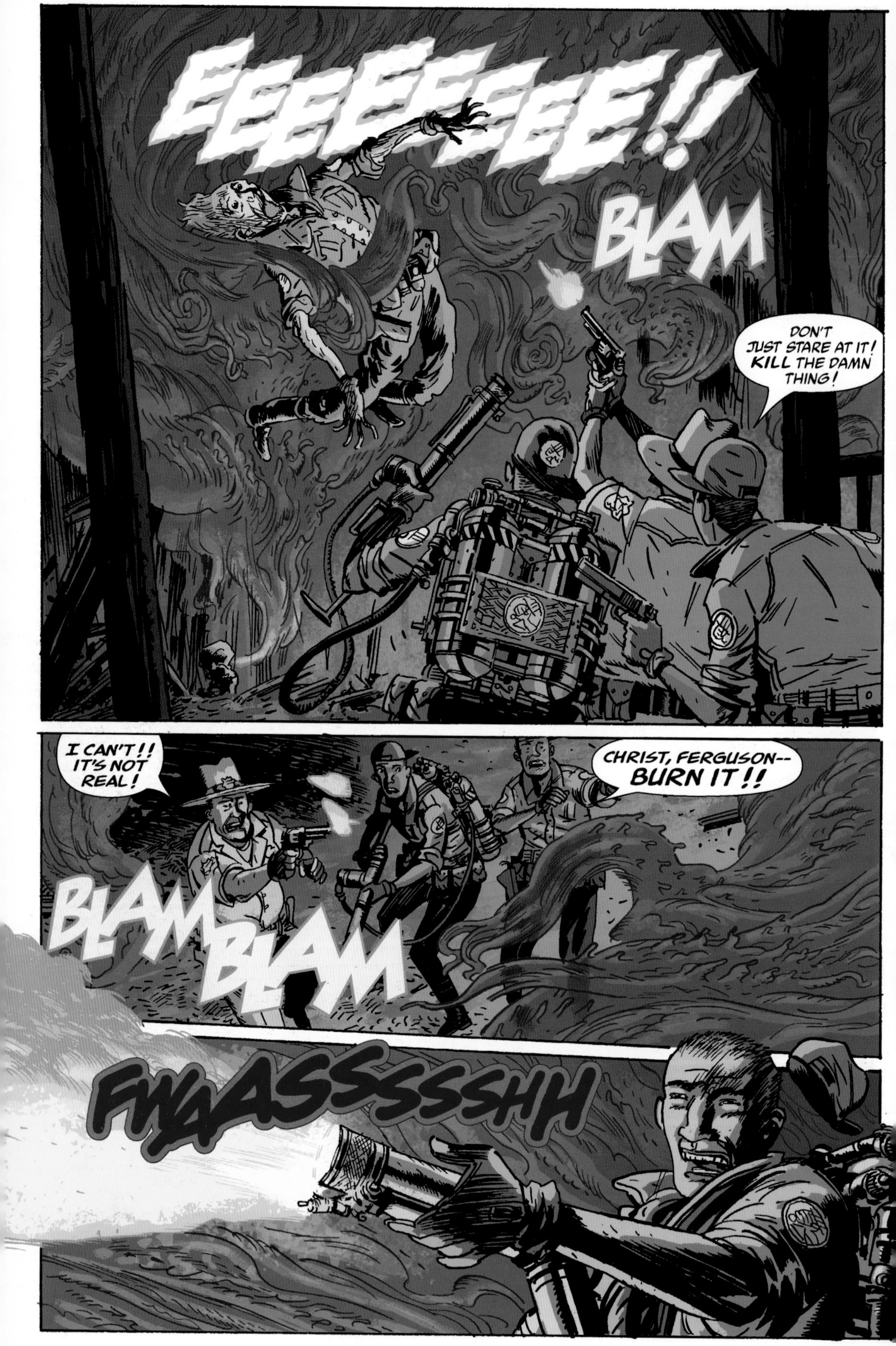
EEEEEEEE!!
BLAM
DON'T JUST STARE AT IT! KILL THE DAMN THING!
I CAN'T!! IT'S NOT REAL!
CHRIST, FERGUSON-- BURN IT!!
BLAM BLAM
FWAASSSSSHH

B.P.R.D. HEADQUARTERS, FAIRFIELD, CONNECTICUT.

--LEAVING EVERYONE BUT THE SHERIFF DEAD.

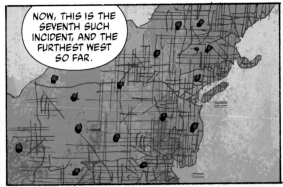

NOW, THIS IS THE SEVENTH SUCH INCIDENT, AND THE FURTHEST WEST SO FAR.

THIS FROG CULT IS SPREADING QUICKLY, AND SOMEHOW, THEY MANAGE TO STAY AHEAD OF US EVERY STEP OF THE WAY.

WE HAVE INTERNATIONAL COOPERATION FROM THE CANADIANS, BUT IT'S NOT ENOUGH. WE'RE LOSING MEN, THEY'RE LOSING MEN, AND THE FROGS, JUDGING FROM THE EVIDENCE, ARE GROWING IN NUMBERS.

ROGER, YOU DON'T HAVE TO RAISE YOUR HAND. WHAT IS IT?

SO, ARE WE STILL FIGHTING THOSE FROG MEN?

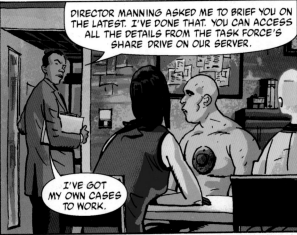

DIRECTOR MANNING ASKED ME TO BRIEF YOU ON THE LATEST. I'VE DONE THAT. YOU CAN ACCESS ALL THE DETAILS FROM THE TASK FORCE'S SHARE DRIVE ON OUR SERVER.

I'VE GOT MY OWN CASES TO WORK.

25

LIKE WE NEED THE DETAILS.

THOSE FROG MONSTERS WILL ESTABLISH POPULATIONS AS FAR AS VANCOUVER BEFORE THE END OF THE YEAR. ONCE THAT HAPPENS...

I WOULD LIKE TO SEE THOSE FILES, ACTUALLY.

I KNOW EACH INCIDENT IS A LITTLE DIFFERENT--

MORE THAN ONLY A LITTLE, ELIZABETH.

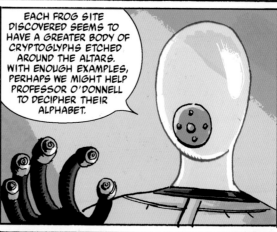

EACH FROG SITE DISCOVERED SEEMS TO HAVE A GREATER BODY OF CRYPTOGLYPHS ETCHED AROUND THE ALTARS. WITH ENOUGH EXAMPLES, PERHAPS WE MIGHT HELP PROFESSOR O'DONNELL TO DECIPHER THEIR ALPHABET.

CODE CRACKING? THAT'S WHAT THE BUREAU'S BEEN REDUCED TO?

THE MIGRATION IS IN THE NATION'S MIDWEST, THE BUREAU HERE IN CONNECTICUT--NOT IDEALLY PLACED TO DO MORE.

FOR NOW.

THAT MEETING WE'RE HAVING WITH OUR ESTEEMED DIRECTOR? I HEARD IT'S ABOUT A POSSIBLE RELOCATION.

IS THAT WHERE KATE AND ABE WENT?

DID THEY ALREADY RELOCATE?

NO, ROGER. NOT EXACTLY.

DON'T WORRY. THEY'LL BE BACK SOON.

THEY BETTER BE.

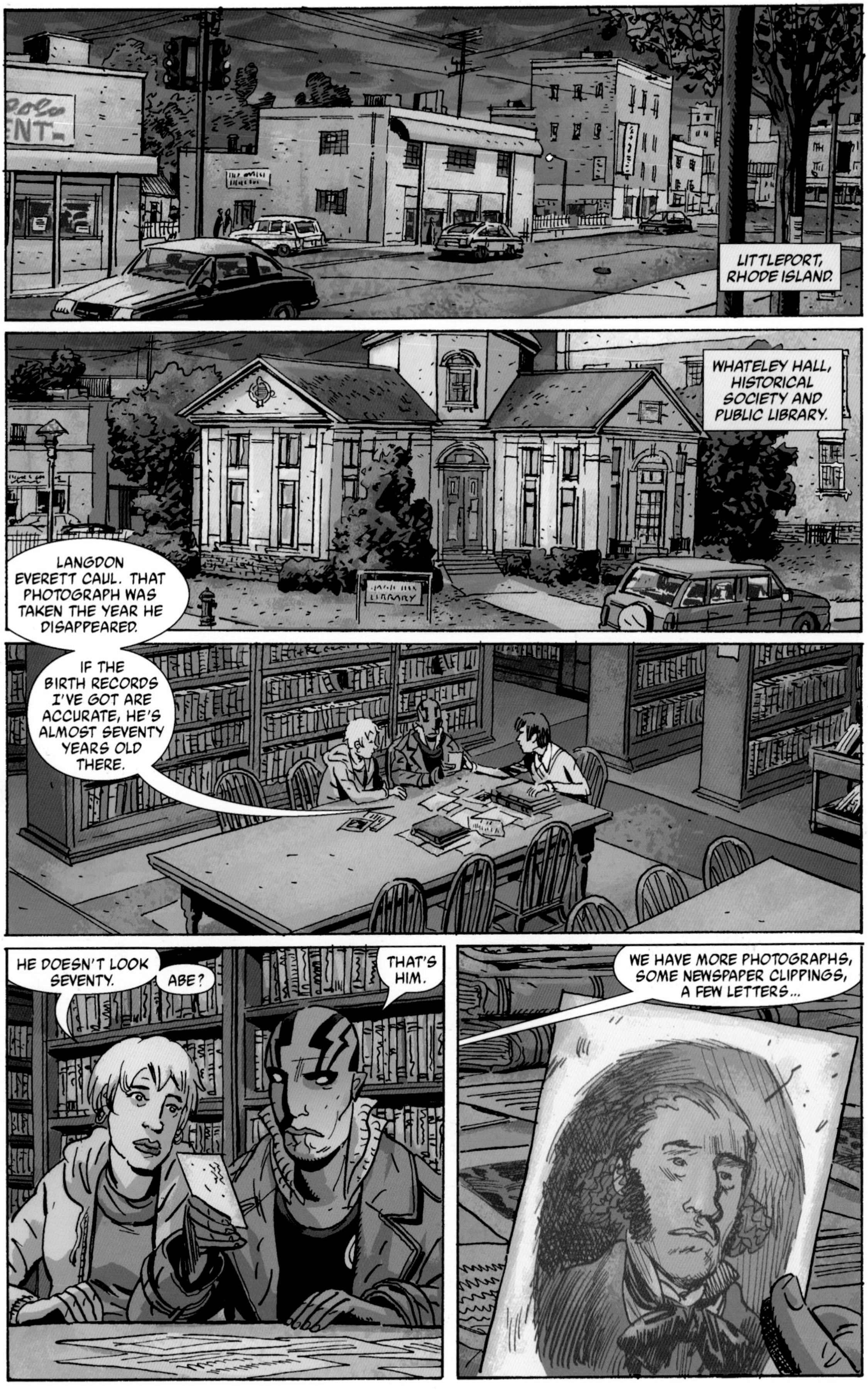

LITTLEPORT, RHODE ISLAND.
WHATELEY HALL, HISTORICAL SOCIETY AND PUBLIC LIBRARY.
LANGDON EVERETT CAUL. THAT PHOTOGRAPH WAS TAKEN THE YEAR HE DISAPPEARED.
IF THE BIRTH RECORDS I'VE GOT ARE ACCURATE, HE'S ALMOST SEVENTY YEARS OLD THERE.
HE DOESN'T LOOK SEVENTY.
ABE?
THAT'S HIM.
WE HAVE MORE PHOTOGRAPHS, SOME NEWSPAPER CLIPPINGS, A FEW LETTERS...

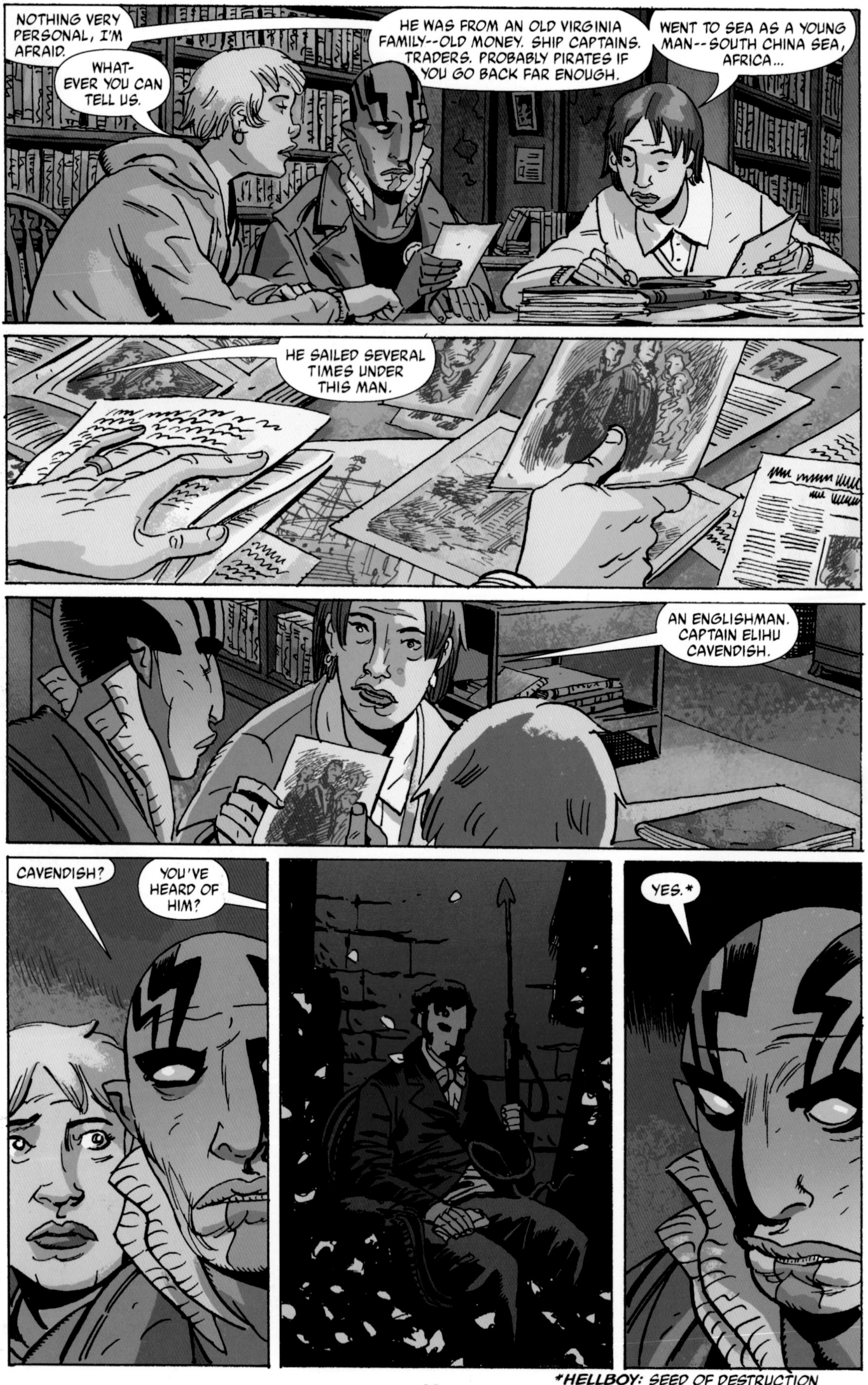
NOTHING VERY PERSONAL, I'M AFRAID.
WHAT-EVER YOU CAN TELL US.
HE WAS FROM AN OLD VIRGINIA FAMILY--OLD MONEY. SHIP CAPTAINS. TRADERS. PROBABLY PIRATES IF YOU GO BACK FAR ENOUGH.
WENT TO SEA AS A YOUNG MAN--SOUTH CHINA SEA, AFRICA...
HE SAILED SEVERAL TIMES UNDER THIS MAN.
AN ENGLISHMAN. CAPTAIN ELIHU CAVENDISH.
CAVENDISH?
YOU'VE HEARD OF HIM?
YES.*

*HELLBOY: SEED OF DESTRUCTION

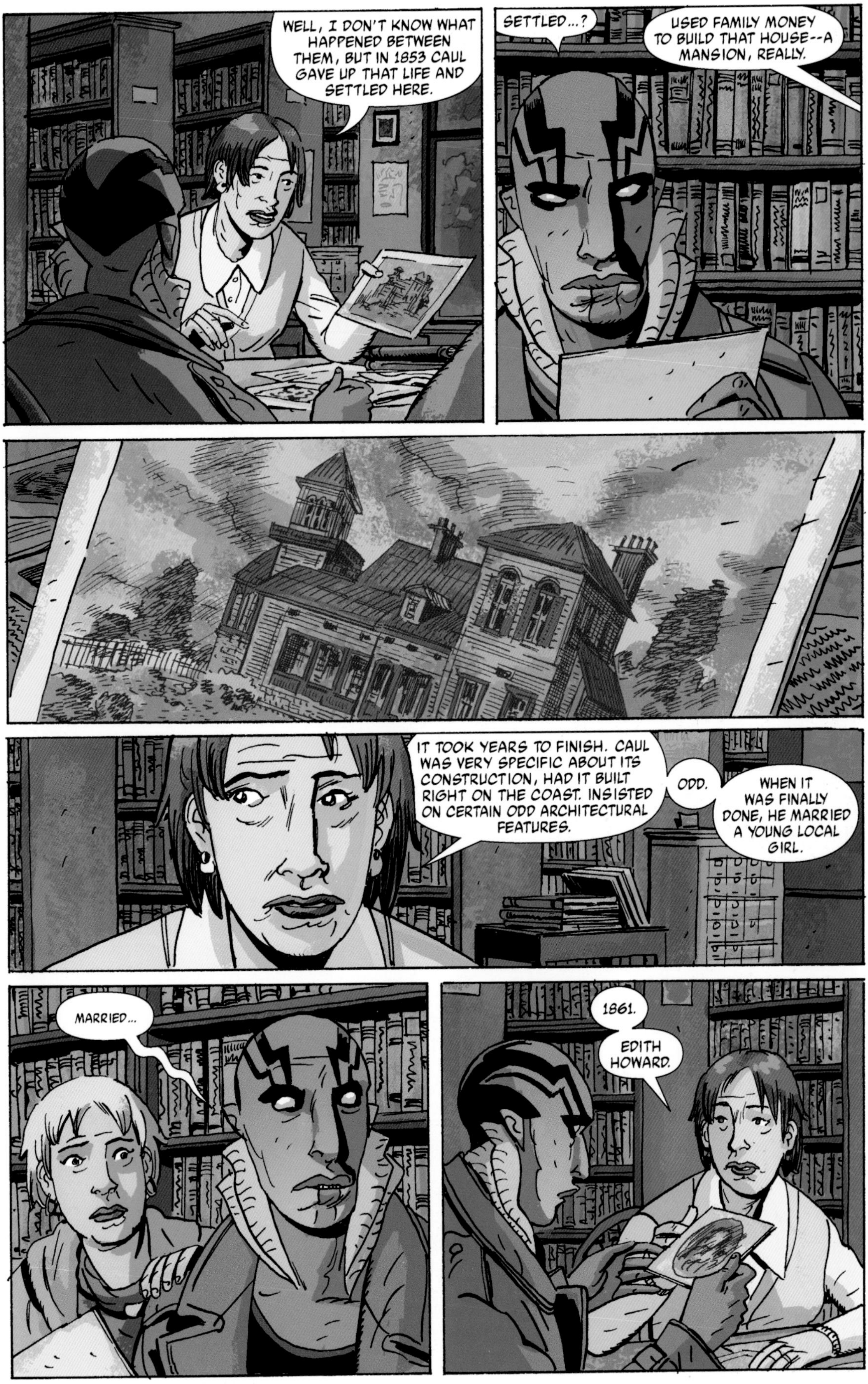
WELL, I DON'T KNOW WHAT HAPPENED BETWEEN THEM, BUT IN 1853 CAUL GAVE UP THAT LIFE AND SETTLED HERE.
SETTLED...?
USED FAMILY MONEY TO BUILD THAT HOUSE--A MANSION, REALLY.
IT TOOK YEARS TO FINISH. CAUL WAS VERY SPECIFIC ABOUT ITS CONSTRUCTION, HAD IT BUILT RIGHT ON THE COAST. INSISTED ON CERTAIN ODD ARCHITECTURAL FEATURES.
ODD.
WHEN IT WAS FINALLY DONE, HE MARRIED A YOUNG LOCAL GIRL.
MARRIED...
1861.
EDITH HOWARD.

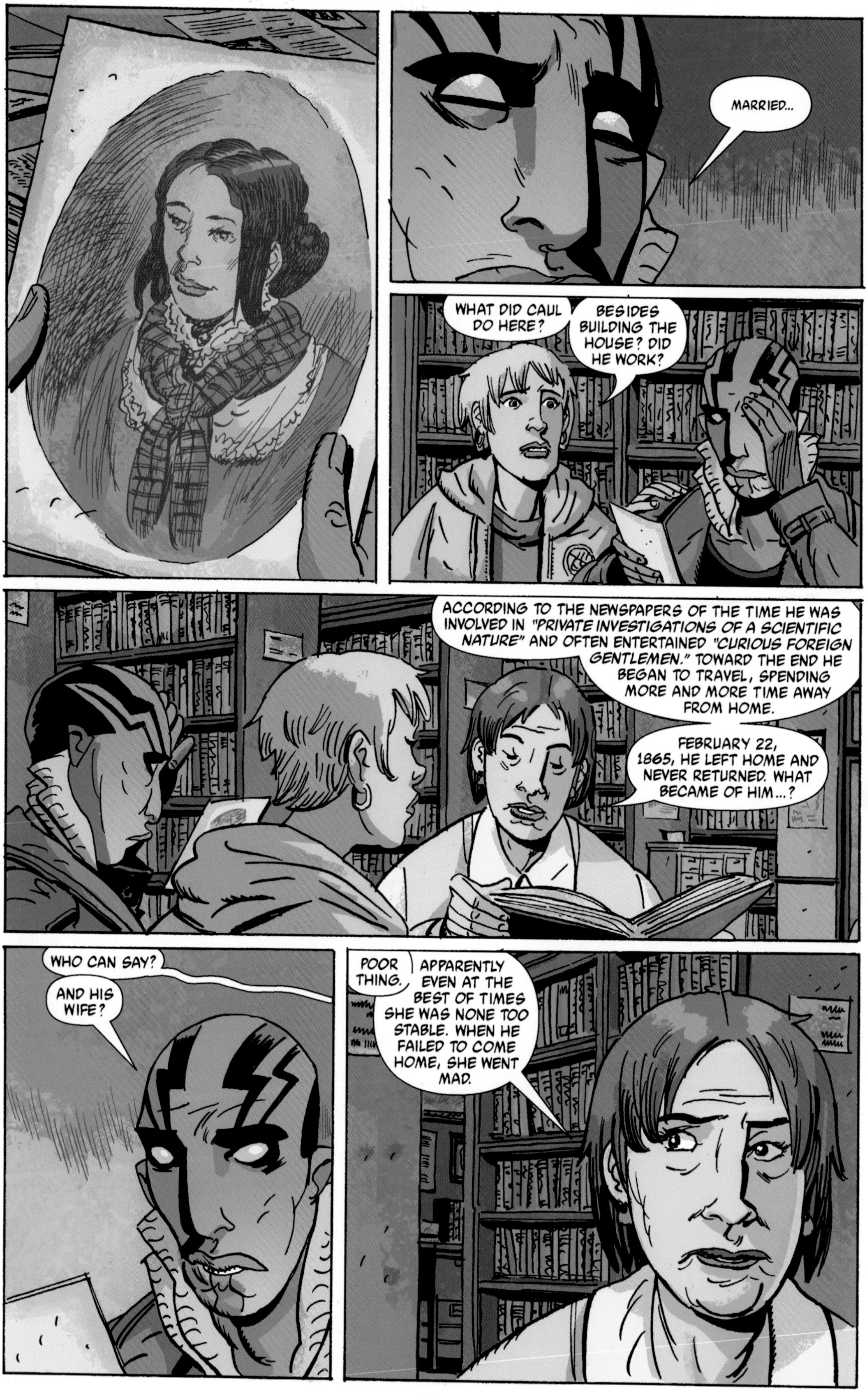
MARRIED...
WHAT DID CAUL DO HERE?
BESIDES BUILDING THE HOUSE? DID HE WORK?
ACCORDING TO THE NEWSPAPERS OF THE TIME HE WAS INVOLVED IN "PRIVATE INVESTIGATIONS OF A SCIENTIFIC NATURE" AND OFTEN ENTERTAINED "CURIOUS FOREIGN GENTLEMEN." TOWARD THE END HE BEGAN TO TRAVEL, SPENDING MORE AND MORE TIME AWAY FROM HOME.
FEBRUARY 22, 1865, HE LEFT HOME AND NEVER RETURNED. WHAT BECAME OF HIM...?
WHO CAN SAY?
AND HIS WIFE?
POOR THING.
APPARENTLY EVEN AT THE BEST OF TIMES SHE WAS NONE TOO STABLE. WHEN HE FAILED TO COME HOME, SHE WENT MAD.

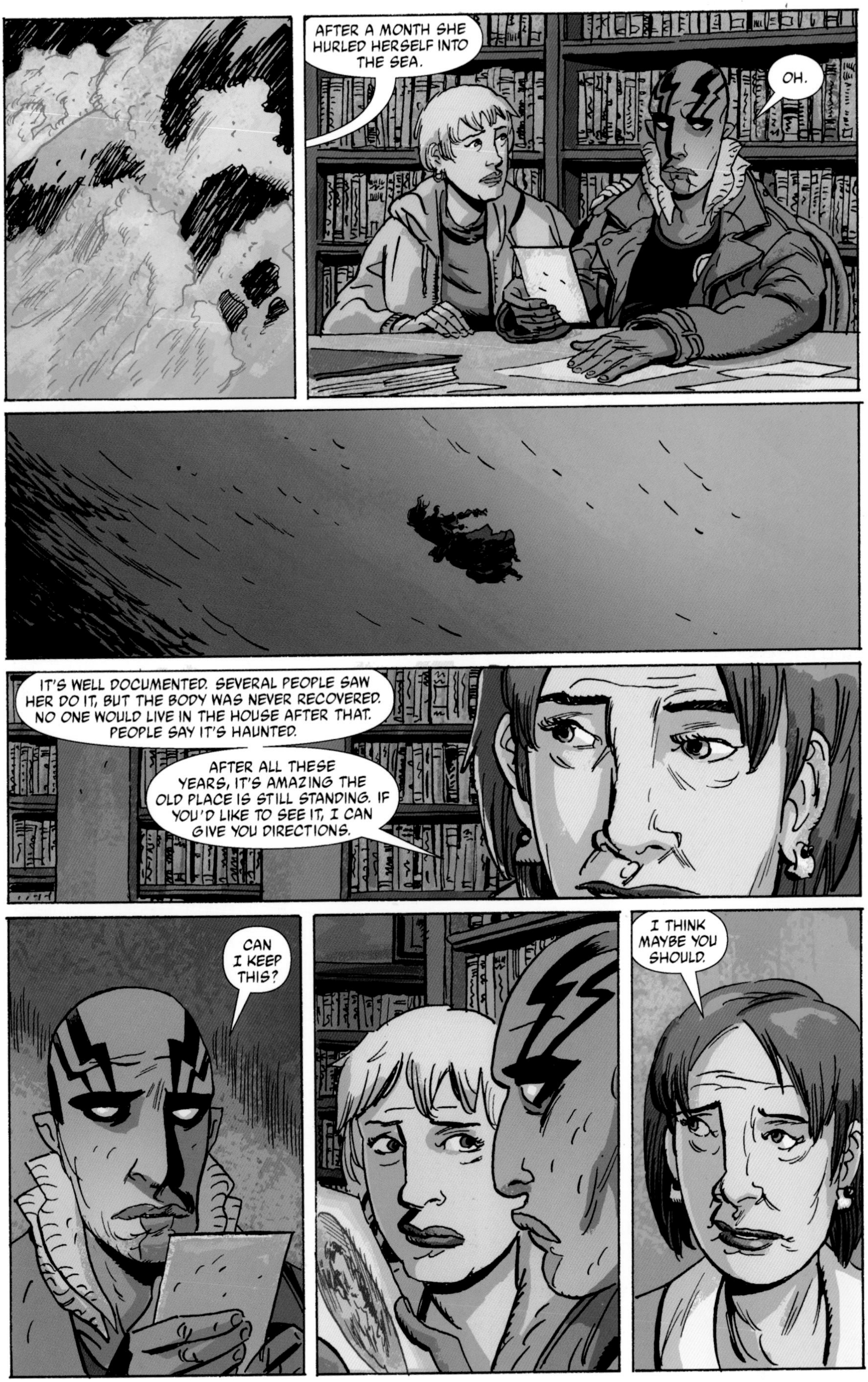
AFTER A MONTH SHE HURLED HERSELF INTO THE SEA.
OH.
IT'S WELL DOCUMENTED. SEVERAL PEOPLE SAW HER DO IT, BUT THE BODY WAS NEVER RECOVERED. NO ONE WOULD LIVE IN THE HOUSE AFTER THAT. PEOPLE SAY IT'S HAUNTED.
AFTER ALL THESE YEARS, IT'S AMAZING THE OLD PLACE IS STILL STANDING. IF YOU'D LIKE TO SEE IT, I CAN GIVE YOU DIRECTIONS.
CAN I KEEP THIS?
I THINK MAYBE YOU SHOULD.

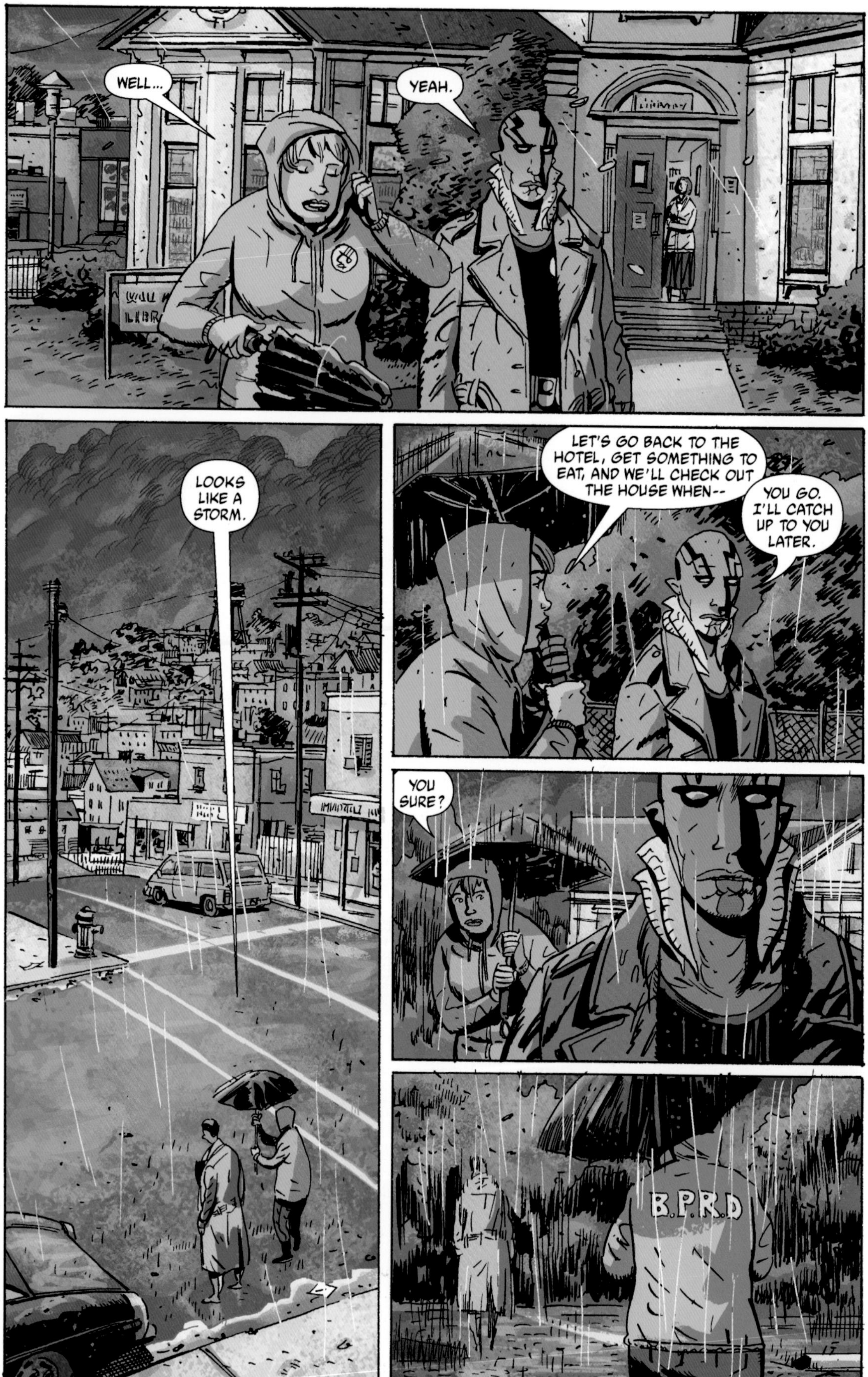
WELL...
YEAH.
LOOKS LIKE A STORM.
LET'S GO BACK TO THE HOTEL, GET SOMETHING TO EAT, AND WE'LL CHECK OUT THE HOUSE WHEN--
YOU GO. I'LL CATCH UP TO YOU LATER.
YOU SURE?
B.P.R.D

WE ARE ABOUT TO BEGIN OUR INITIAL EXAMINATION ON THE REMAINS OF THE FIRST SOLDIER ASSOCIATED WITH MISSION #D16F8-4188.

6/13/01 17

I AM DR. ROLAND WILSON, AND THIS IS THE 13TH DAY OF JUNE, 2001.

ZZIIIPP

6/13/01

THE TIME IS SEVENTEEN HUNDRED THIRTY-SIX HOURS.

THESE ARE THE REMAINS OF CORPORAL STEVEN HARMON.

A CURSORY EXAM OF CORPORAL HARMON REVEALS NO GROSS TRAUMA.

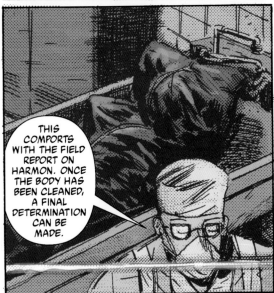

THIS COMPORTS WITH THE FIELD REPORT ON HARMON. ONCE THE BODY HAS BEEN CLEANED, A FINAL DETERMINATION CAN BE MADE.

IF THERE IS ANYTHING REMARKABLE TO NOTE AT THIS TIME, IT IS THE ABSENCE OF ANY LIVIDITY WHATSOEVER.

POP

EH?

RRRIIIPPP

OH MY GOD!! MY GOD!! HELP!! SOMEBODY HELP!!

WHAT THE #$%¢* IS GOING ON HERE, FOUR EYES?!

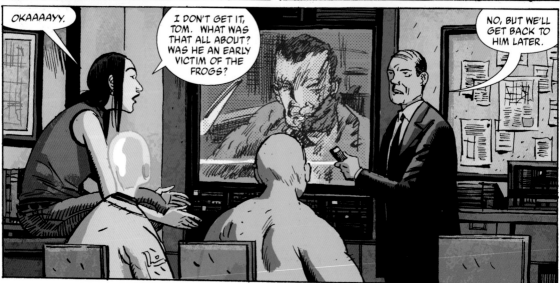

OKAAAAYY.

I DON'T GET IT, TOM. WHAT WAS THAT ALL ABOUT? WAS HE AN EARLY VICTIM OF THE FROGS?

NO, BUT WE'LL GET BACK TO HIM LATER.

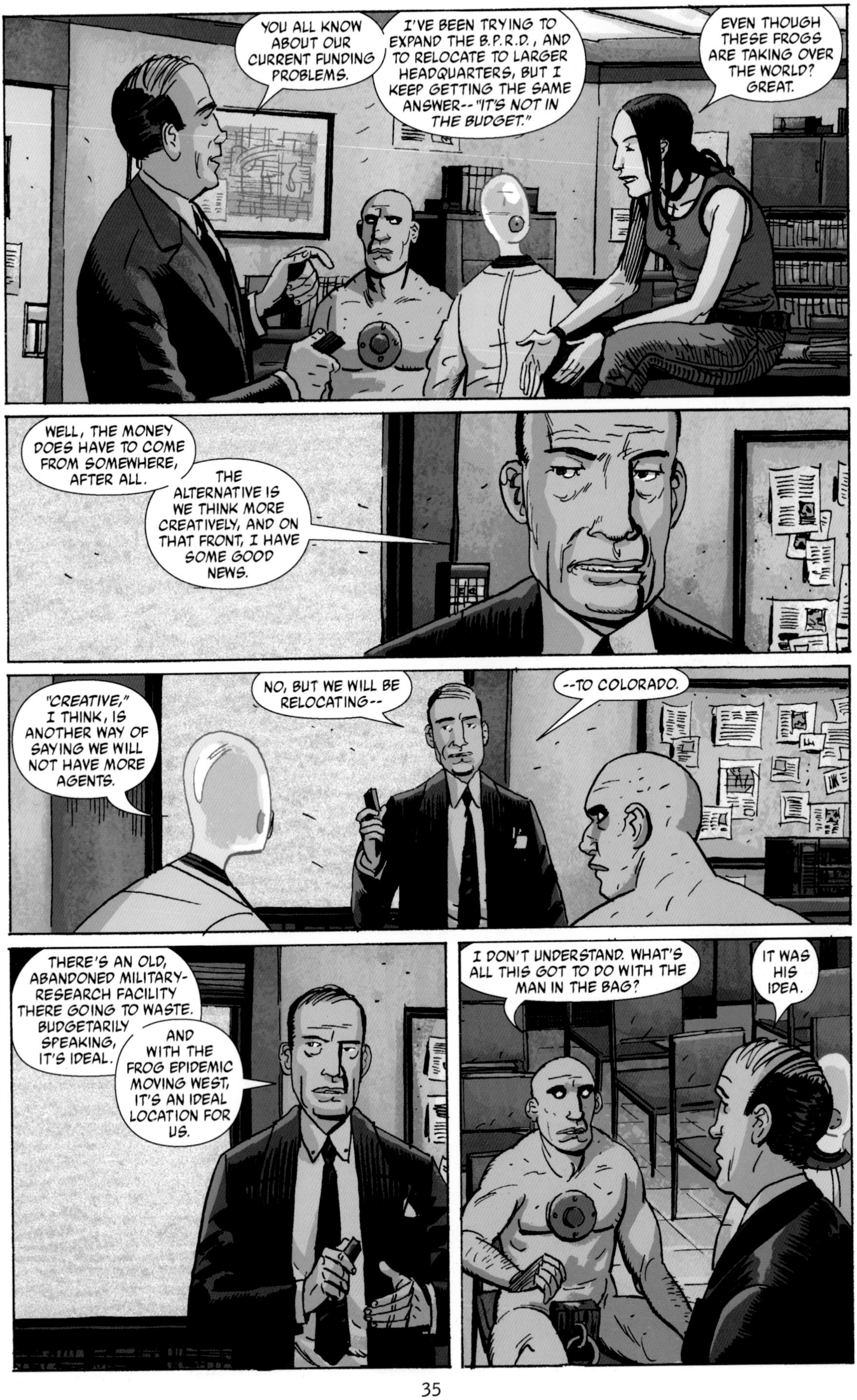
YOU ALL KNOW ABOUT OUR CURRENT FUNDING PROBLEMS.
I'VE BEEN TRYING TO EXPAND THE B.P.R.D., AND TO RELOCATE TO LARGER HEADQUARTERS, BUT I KEEP GETTING THE SAME ANSWER-- "IT'S NOT IN THE BUDGET."
EVEN THOUGH THESE FROGS ARE TAKING OVER THE WORLD? GREAT.
WELL, THE MONEY DOES HAVE TO COME FROM SOMEWHERE, AFTER ALL.
THE ALTERNATIVE IS WE THINK MORE CREATIVELY, AND ON THAT FRONT, I HAVE SOME GOOD NEWS.
"CREATIVE," I THINK, IS ANOTHER WAY OF SAYING WE WILL NOT HAVE MORE AGENTS.
NO, BUT WE WILL BE RELOCATING--
--TO COLORADO.
THERE'S AN OLD, ABANDONED MILITARY-RESEARCH FACILITY THERE GOING TO WASTE. BUDGETARILY SPEAKING, IT'S IDEAL.
AND WITH THE FROG EPIDEMIC MOVING WEST, IT'S AN IDEAL LOCATION FOR US.
I DON'T UNDERSTAND. WHAT'S ALL THIS GOT TO DO WITH THE MAN IN THE BAG?
IT WAS HIS IDEA.

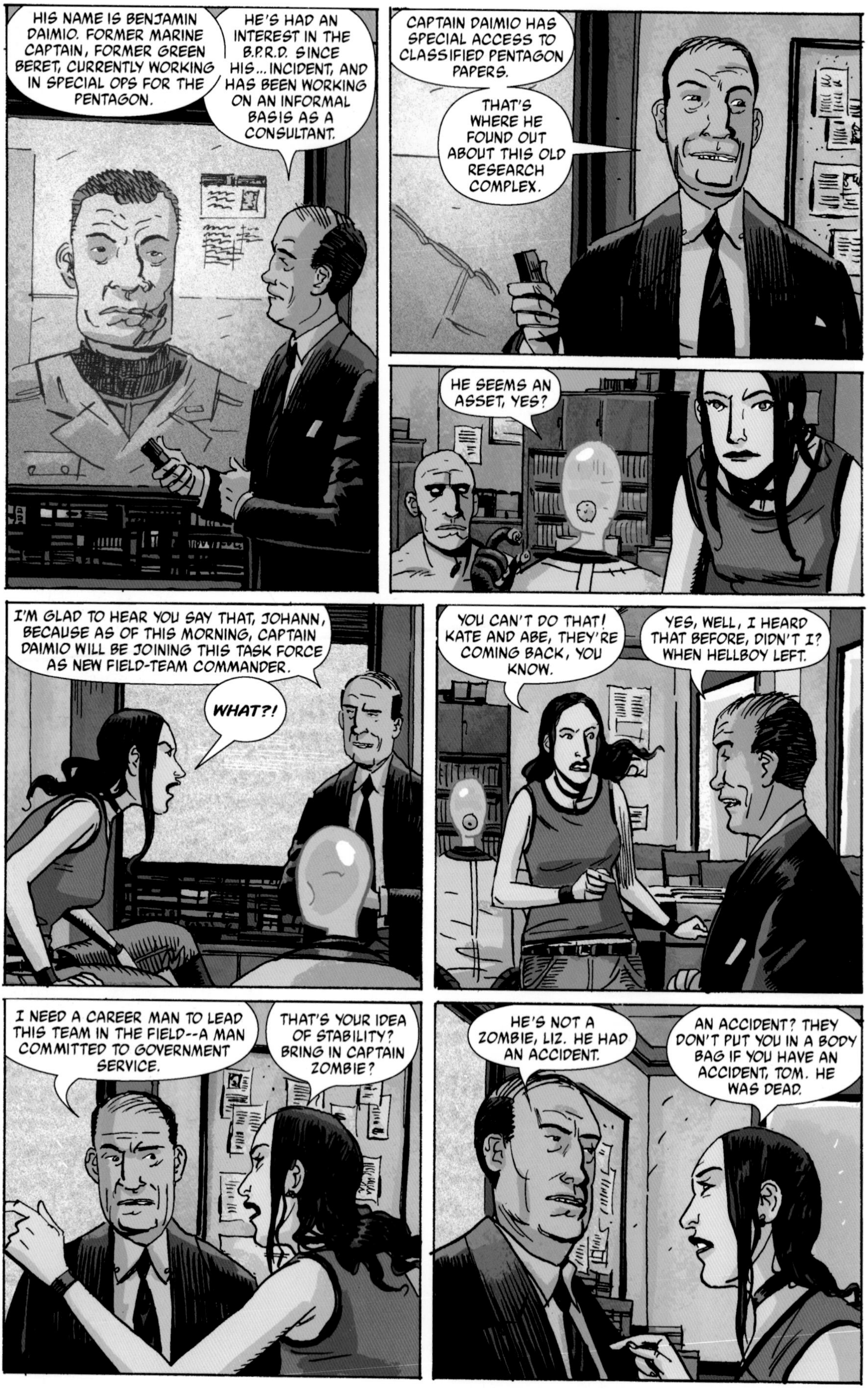
HIS NAME IS BENJAMIN DAIMIO. FORMER MARINE CAPTAIN, FORMER GREEN BERET, CURRENTLY WORKING IN SPECIAL OPS FOR THE PENTAGON.
HE'S HAD AN INTEREST IN THE B.P.R.D. SINCE HIS... INCIDENT, AND HAS BEEN WORKING ON AN INFORMAL BASIS AS A CONSULTANT.
CAPTAIN DAIMIO HAS SPECIAL ACCESS TO CLASSIFIED PENTAGON PAPERS.
THAT'S WHERE HE FOUND OUT ABOUT THIS OLD RESEARCH COMPLEX.
HE SEEMS AN ASSET, YES?
I'M GLAD TO HEAR YOU SAY THAT, JOHANN, BECAUSE AS OF THIS MORNING, CAPTAIN DAIMIO WILL BE JOINING THIS TASK FORCE AS NEW FIELD-TEAM COMMANDER.
WHAT?!
YOU CAN'T DO THAT! KATE AND ABE, THEY'RE COMING BACK, YOU KNOW.
YES, WELL, I HEARD THAT BEFORE, DIDN'T I? WHEN HELLBOY LEFT.
I NEED A CAREER MAN TO LEAD THIS TEAM IN THE FIELD--A MAN COMMITTED TO GOVERNMENT SERVICE.
THAT'S YOUR IDEA OF STABILITY? BRING IN CAPTAIN ZOMBIE?
HE'S NOT A ZOMBIE, LIZ. HE HAD AN ACCIDENT.
AN ACCIDENT? THEY DON'T PUT YOU IN A BODY BAG IF YOU HAVE AN ACCIDENT, TOM. HE WAS DEAD.

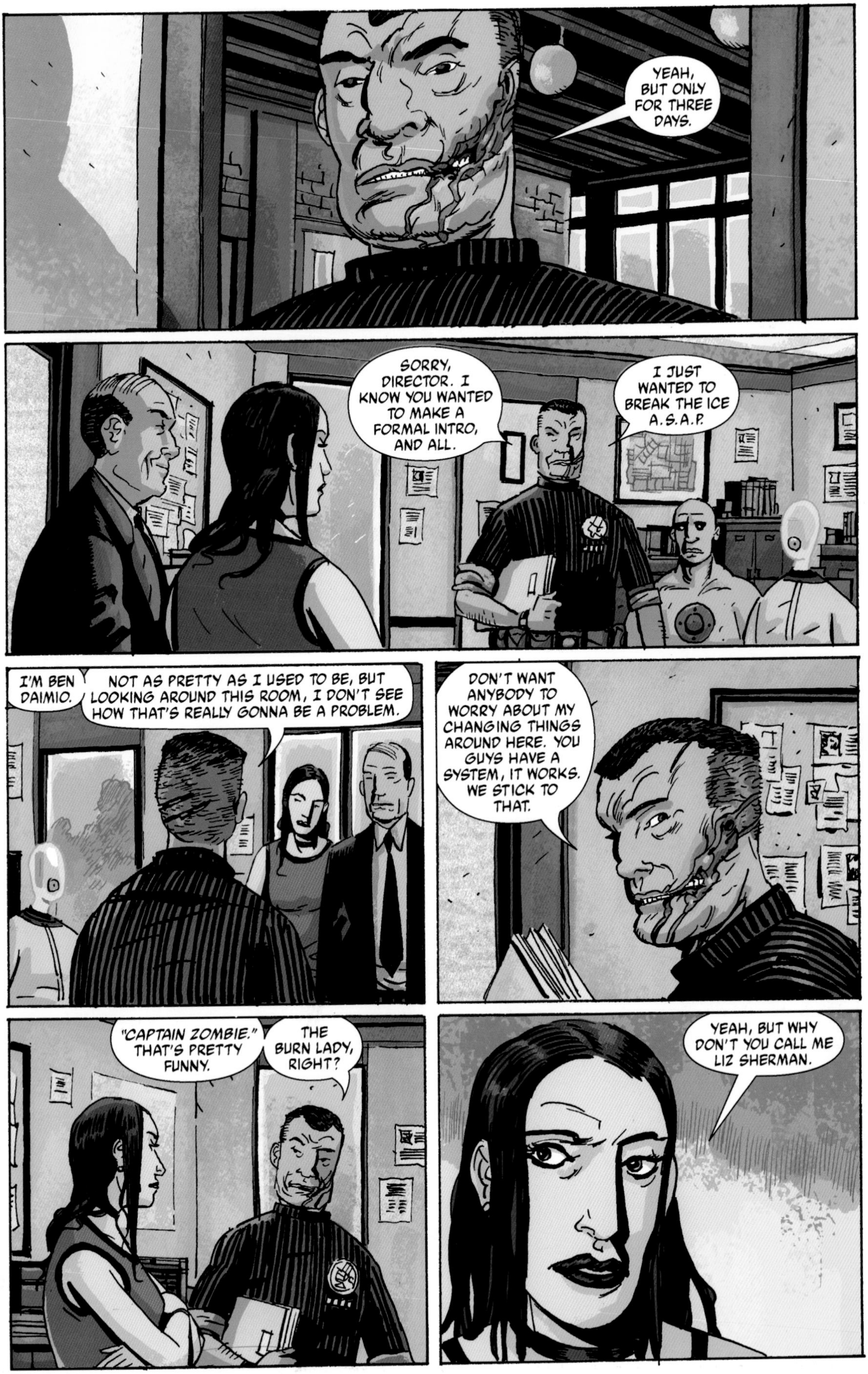
YEAH, BUT ONLY FOR THREE DAYS.
SORRY, DIRECTOR. I KNOW YOU WANTED TO MAKE A FORMAL INTRO, AND ALL.
I JUST WANTED TO BREAK THE ICE A.S.A.P.
I'M BEN DAIMIO.
NOT AS PRETTY AS I USED TO BE, BUT LOOKING AROUND THIS ROOM, I DON'T SEE HOW THAT'S REALLY GONNA BE A PROBLEM.
DON'T WANT ANYBODY TO WORRY ABOUT MY CHANGING THINGS AROUND HERE. YOU GUYS HAVE A SYSTEM, IT WORKS. WE STICK TO THAT.
"CAPTAIN ZOMBIE." THAT'S PRETTY FUNNY.
THE BURN LADY, RIGHT?
YEAH, BUT WHY DON'T YOU CALL ME LIZ SHERMAN.

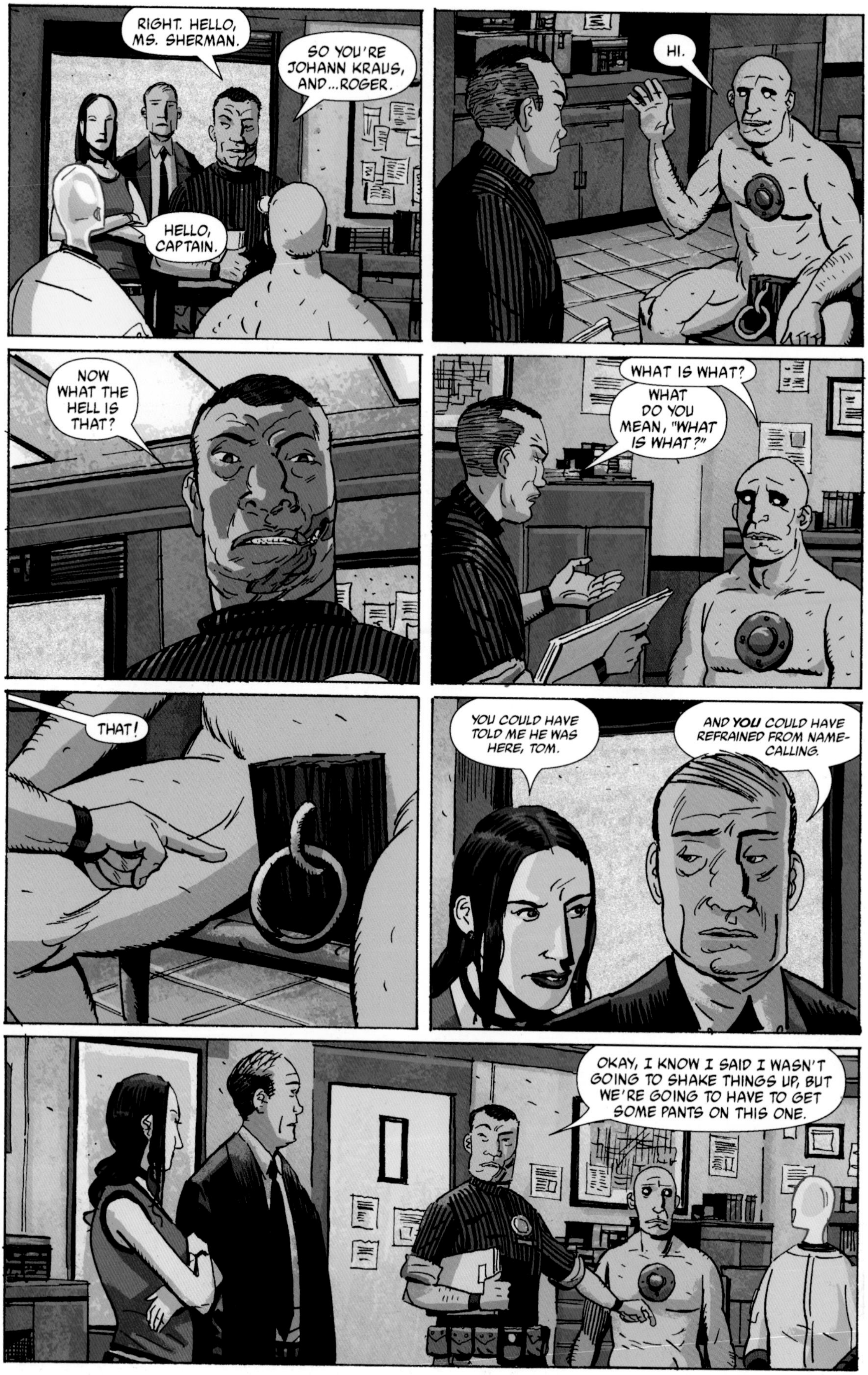
RIGHT. HELLO, MS. SHERMAN.
SO YOU'RE JOHANN KRAUS, AND...ROGER.
HELLO, CAPTAIN.
HI.
NOW WHAT THE HELL IS THAT?
WHAT IS WHAT?
WHAT DO YOU MEAN, "WHAT IS WHAT?"
THAT!
YOU COULD HAVE TOLD ME HE WAS HERE, TOM.
AND YOU COULD HAVE REFRAINED FROM NAME-CALLING.
OKAY, I KNOW I SAID I WASN'T GOING TO SHAKE THINGS UP, BUT WE'RE GOING TO HAVE TO GET SOME PANTS ON THIS ONE.

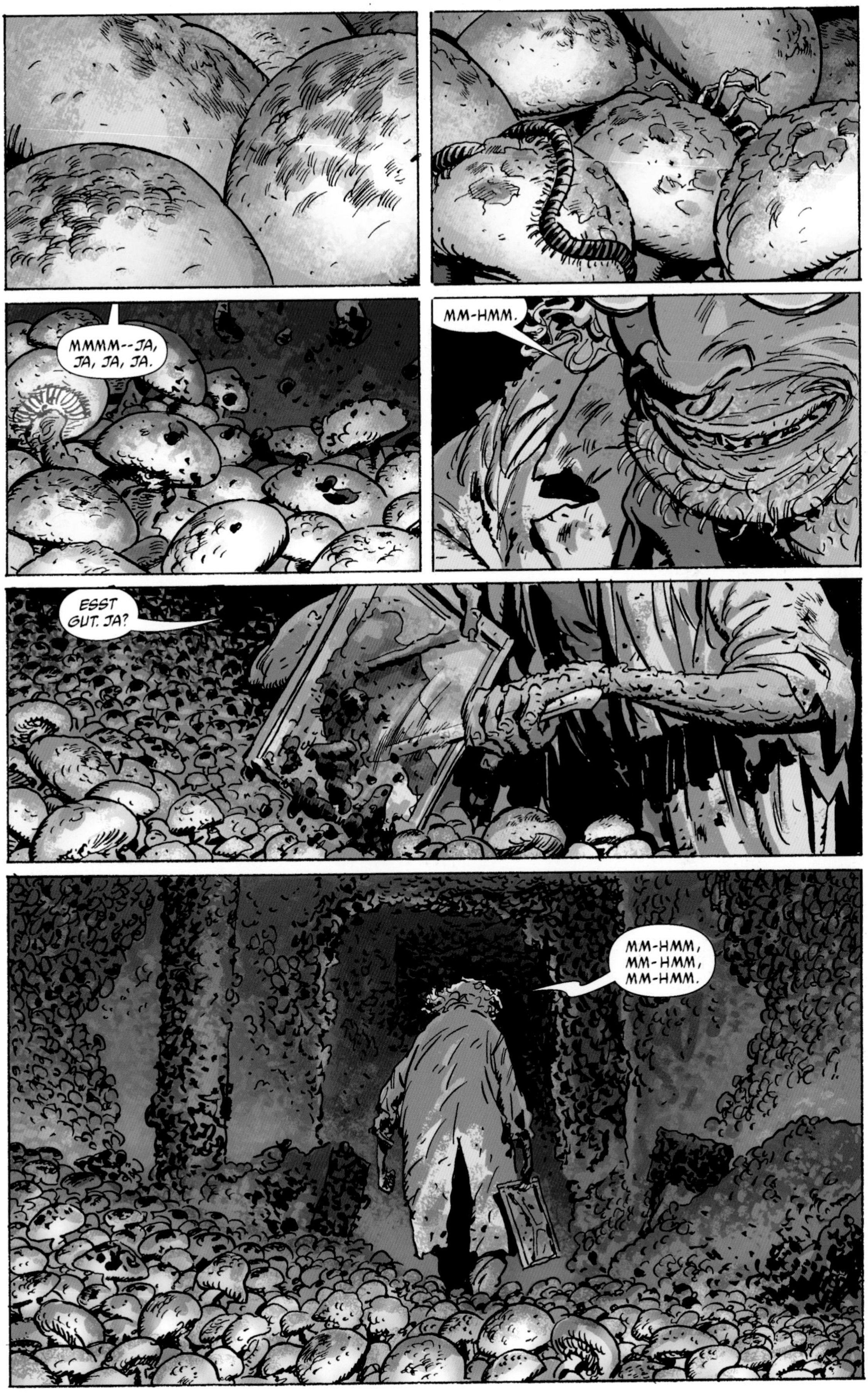
MMMM--JA, JA, JA, JA.
MM-HMM.
ESST GUT. JA?
MM-HMM, MM-HMM, MM-HMM.

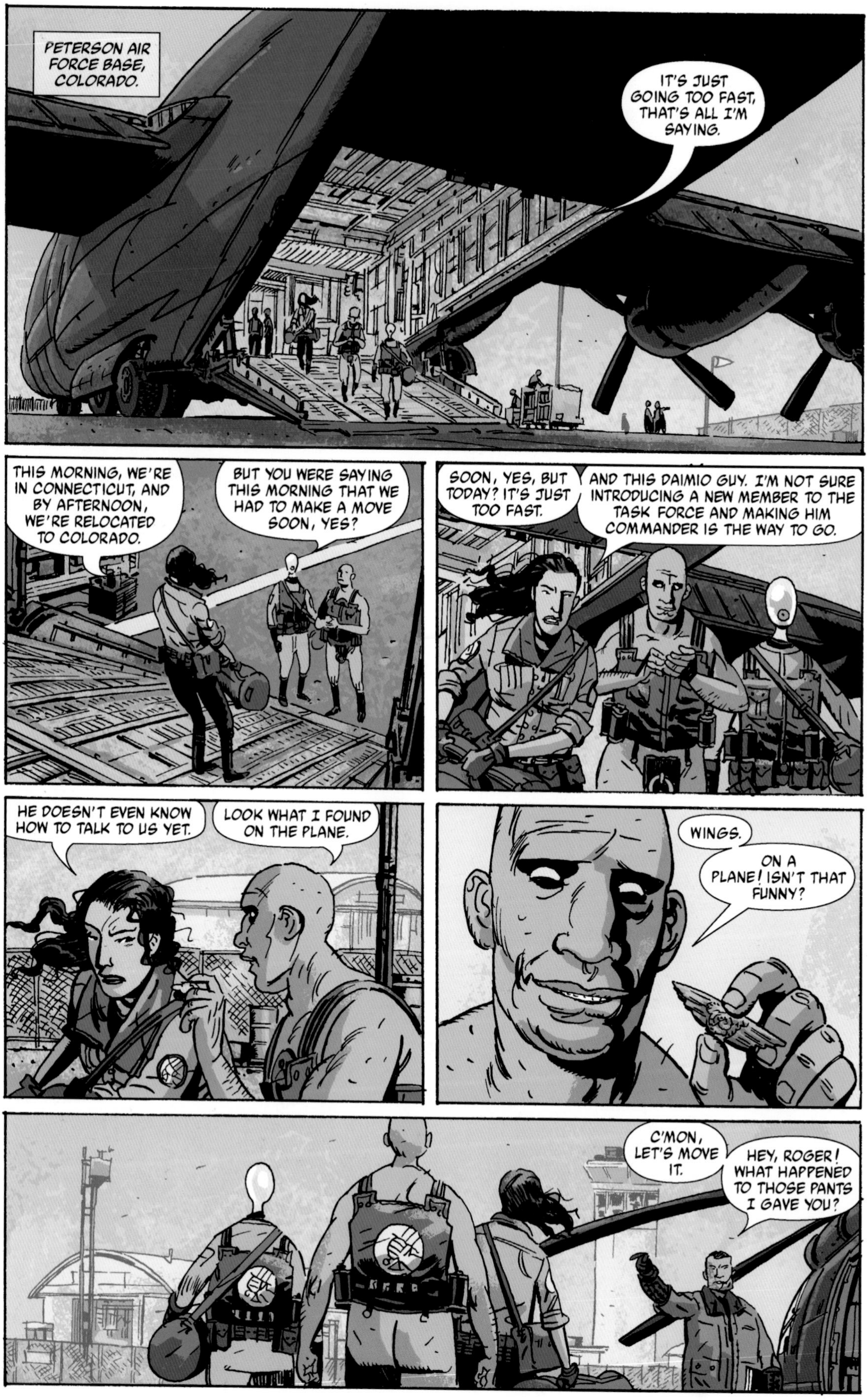
PETERSON AIR FORCE BASE, COLORADO.
IT'S JUST GOING TOO FAST, THAT'S ALL I'M SAYING.
THIS MORNING, WE'RE IN CONNECTICUT, AND BY AFTERNOON, WE'RE RELOCATED TO COLORADO.
BUT YOU WERE SAYING THIS MORNING THAT WE HAD TO MAKE A MOVE SOON, YES?
SOON, YES, BUT TODAY? IT'S JUST TOO FAST.
AND THIS DAIMIO GUY. I'M NOT SURE INTRODUCING A NEW MEMBER TO THE TASK FORCE AND MAKING HIM COMMANDER IS THE WAY TO GO.
HE DOESN'T EVEN KNOW HOW TO TALK TO US YET.
LOOK WHAT I FOUND ON THE PLANE.
WINGS.
ON A PLANE! ISN'T THAT FUNNY?
C'MON, LET'S MOVE IT.
HEY, ROGER! WHAT HAPPENED TO THOSE PANTS I GAVE YOU?

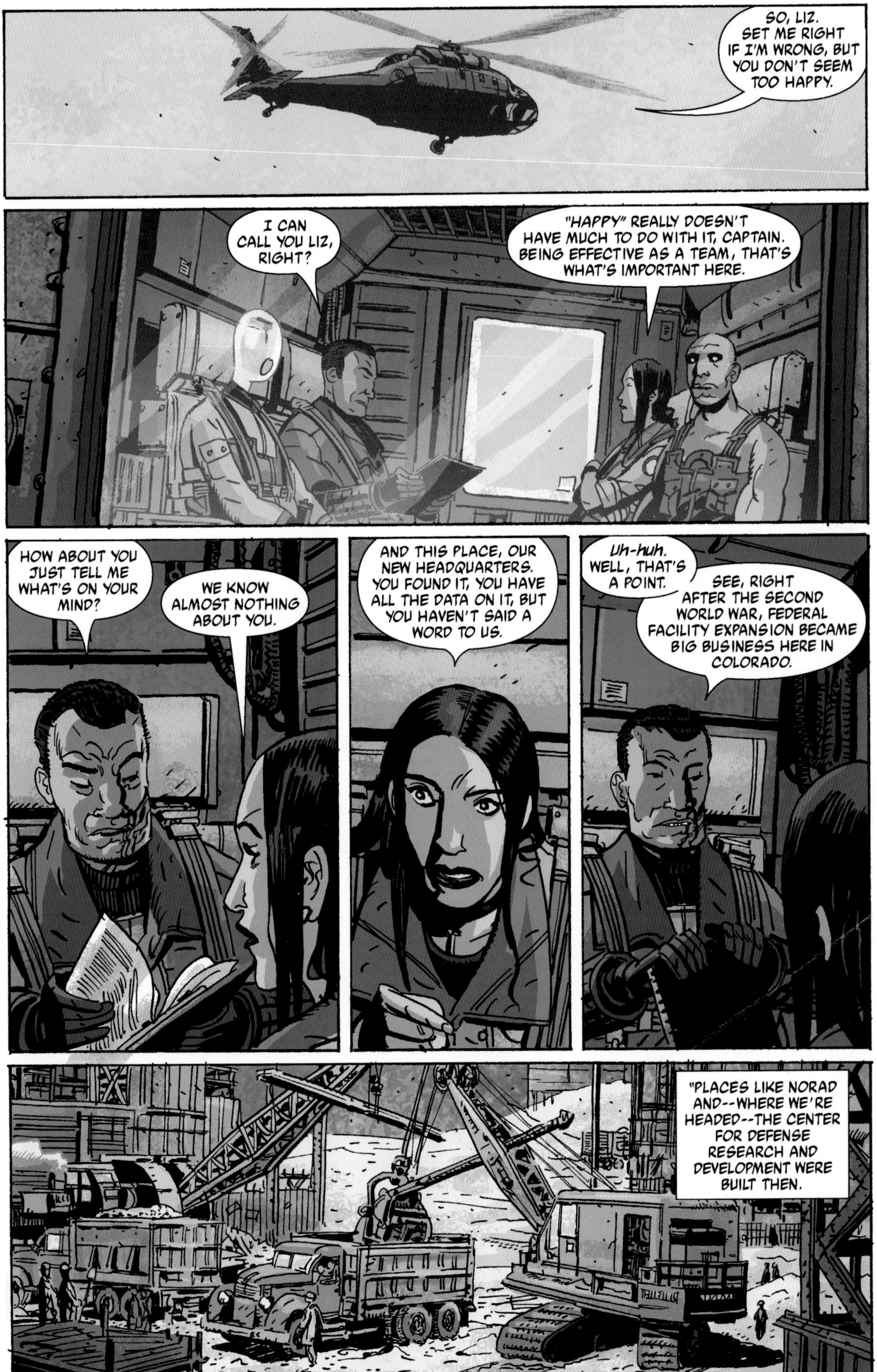
SO, LIZ. SET ME RIGHT IF I'M WRONG, BUT YOU DON'T SEEM TOO HAPPY.
I CAN CALL YOU LIZ, RIGHT?
"HAPPY" REALLY DOESN'T HAVE MUCH TO DO WITH IT, CAPTAIN. BEING EFFECTIVE AS A TEAM, THAT'S WHAT'S IMPORTANT HERE.
HOW ABOUT YOU JUST TELL ME WHAT'S ON YOUR MIND?
WE KNOW ALMOST NOTHING ABOUT YOU.
AND THIS PLACE, OUR NEW HEADQUARTERS. YOU FOUND IT, YOU HAVE ALL THE DATA ON IT, BUT YOU HAVEN'T SAID A WORD TO US.
Uh-huh. WELL, THAT'S A POINT.
SEE, RIGHT AFTER THE SECOND WORLD WAR, FEDERAL FACILITY EXPANSION BECAME BIG BUSINESS HERE IN COLORADO.
"PLACES LIKE NORAD AND--WHERE WE'RE HEADED--THE CENTER FOR DEFENSE RESEARCH AND DEVELOPMENT WERE BUILT THEN.

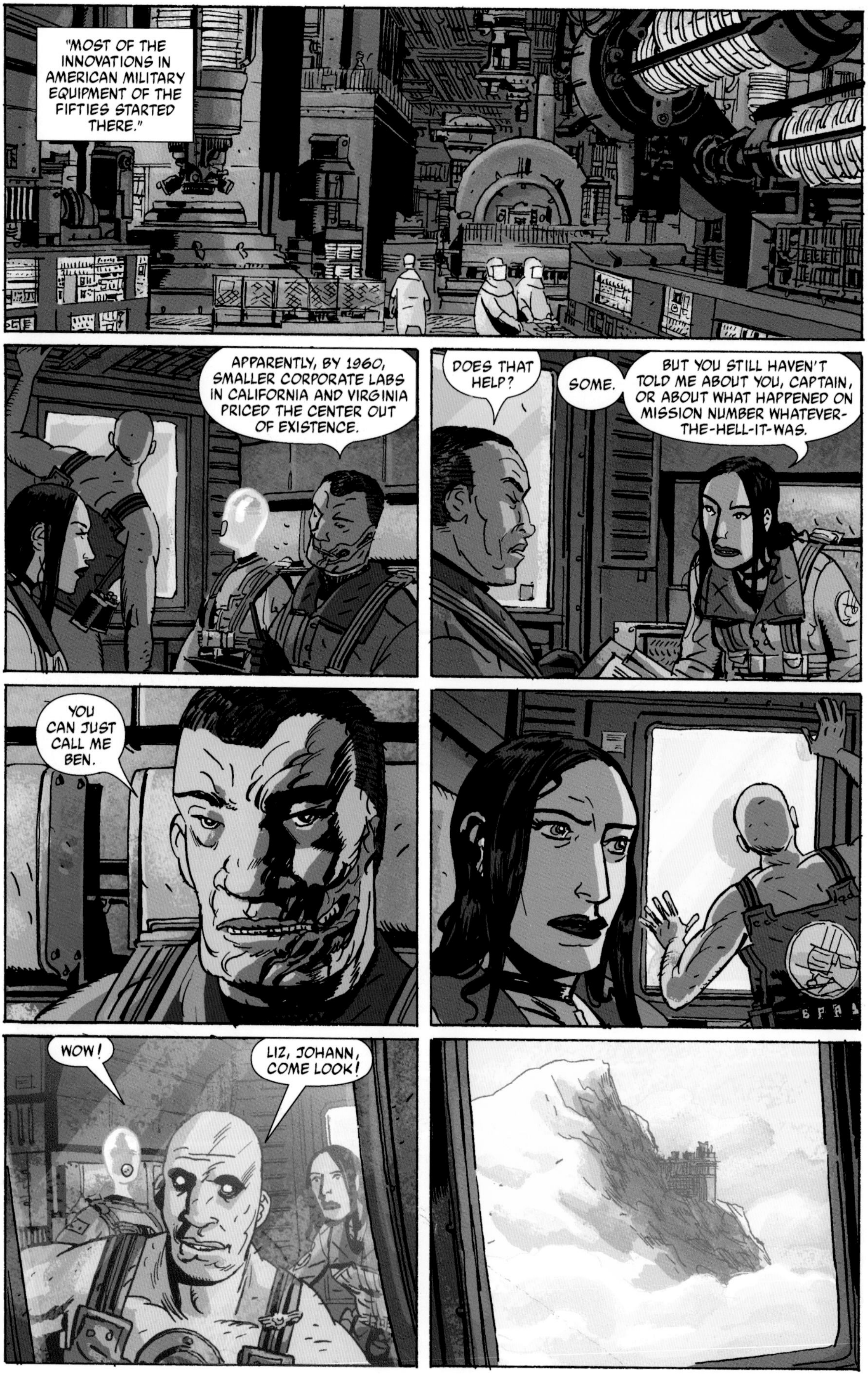

"MOST OF THE INNOVATIONS IN AMERICAN MILITARY EQUIPMENT OF THE FIFTIES STARTED THERE."
APPARENTLY, BY 1960, SMALLER CORPORATE LABS IN CALIFORNIA AND VIRGINIA PRICED THE CENTER OUT OF EXISTENCE.
DOES THAT HELP?
SOME.
BUT YOU STILL HAVEN'T TOLD ME ABOUT YOU, CAPTAIN, OR ABOUT WHAT HAPPENED ON MISSION NUMBER WHATEVER-THE-HELL-IT-WAS.
YOU CAN JUST CALL ME BEN.
WOW!
LIZ, JOHANN, COME LOOK!

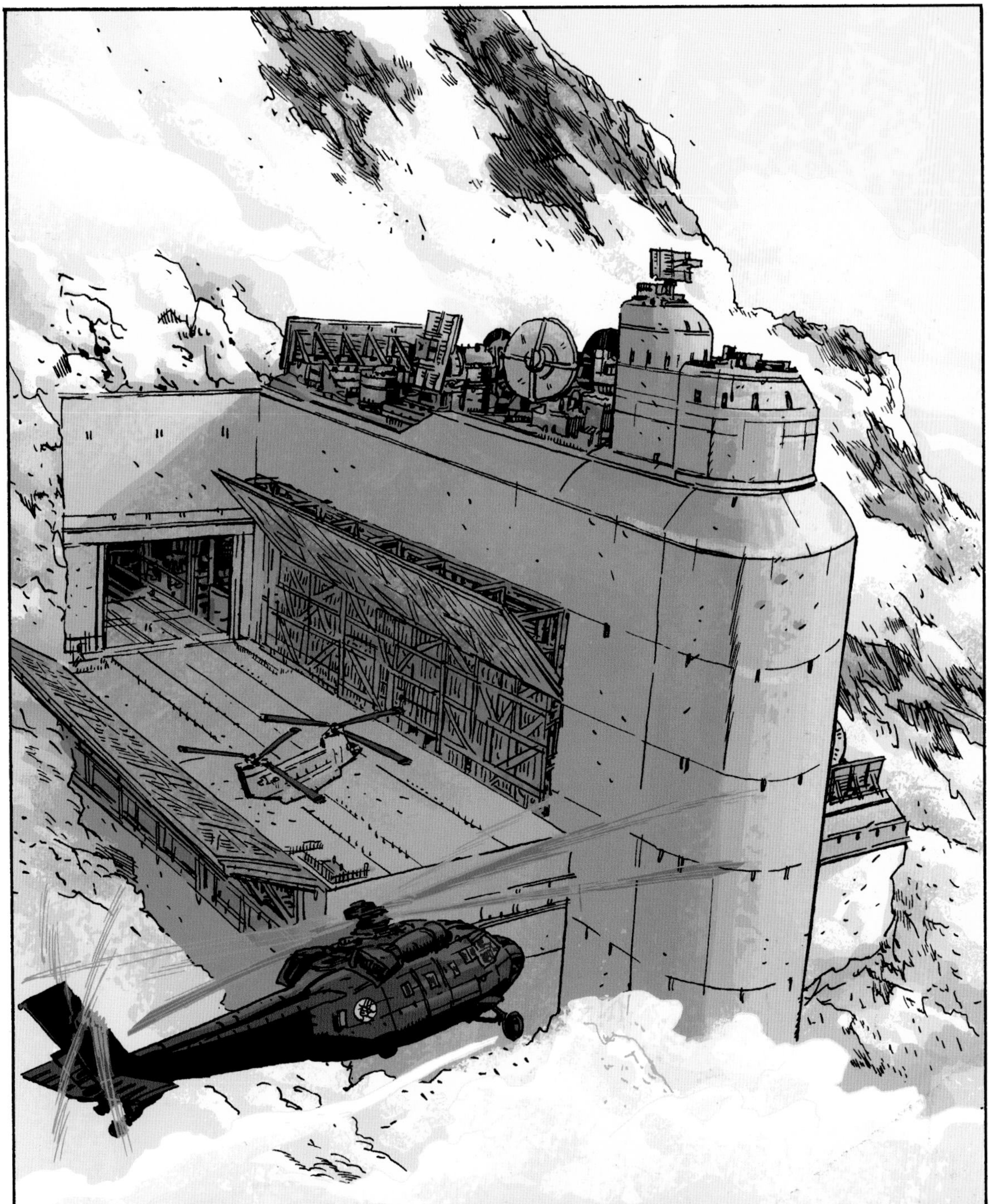

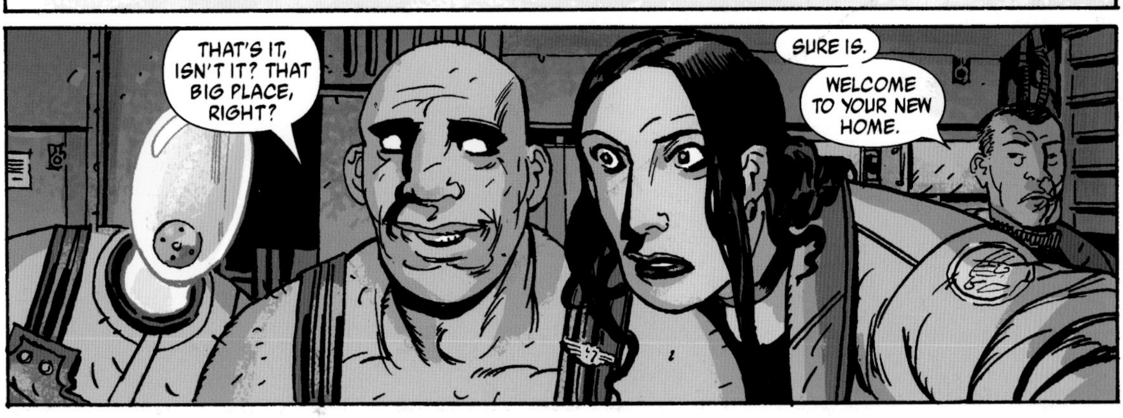
THAT'S IT, ISN'T IT? THAT BIG PLACE, RIGHT?
SURE IS.
WELCOME TO YOUR NEW HOME.

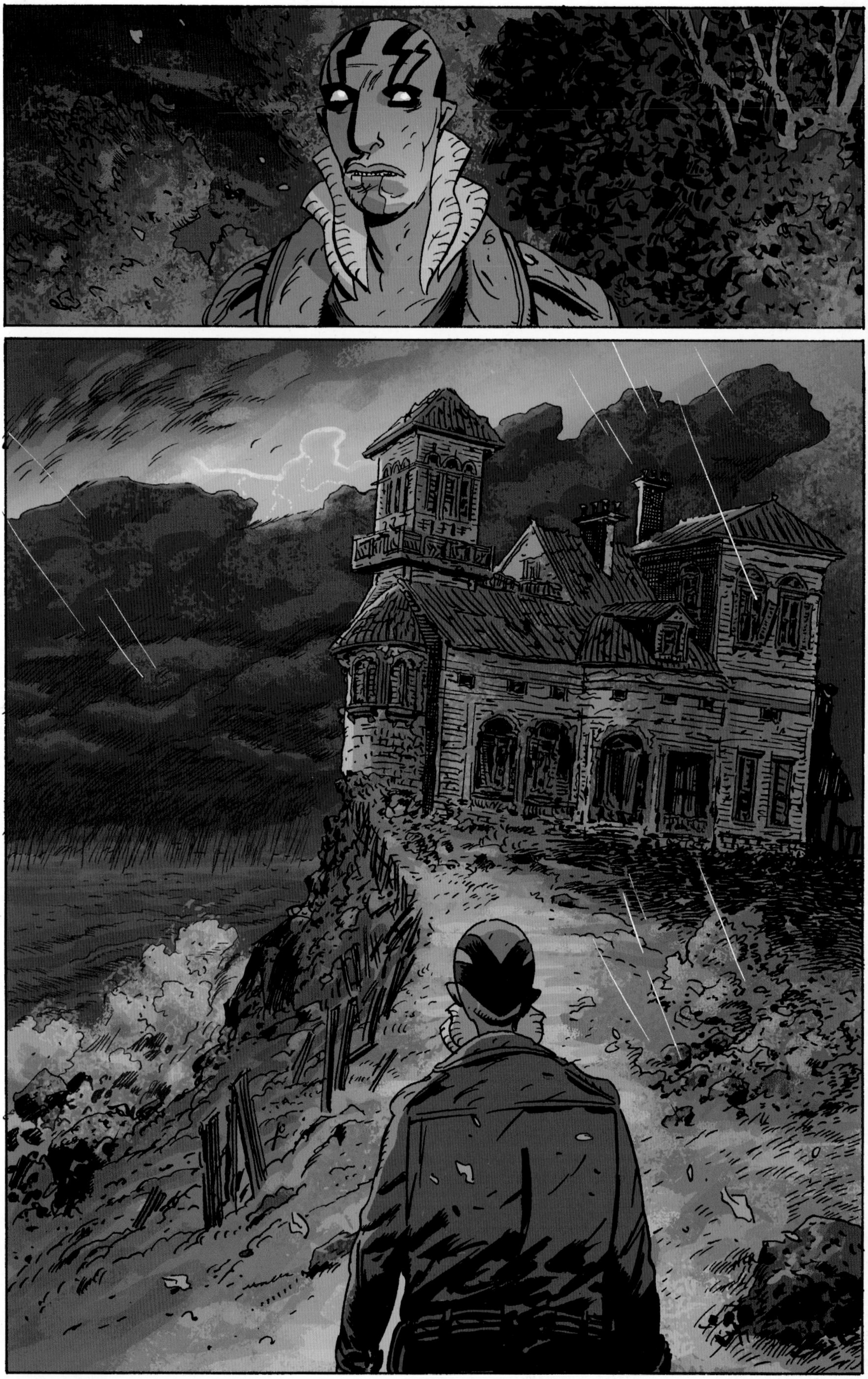

CHAPTER TWO

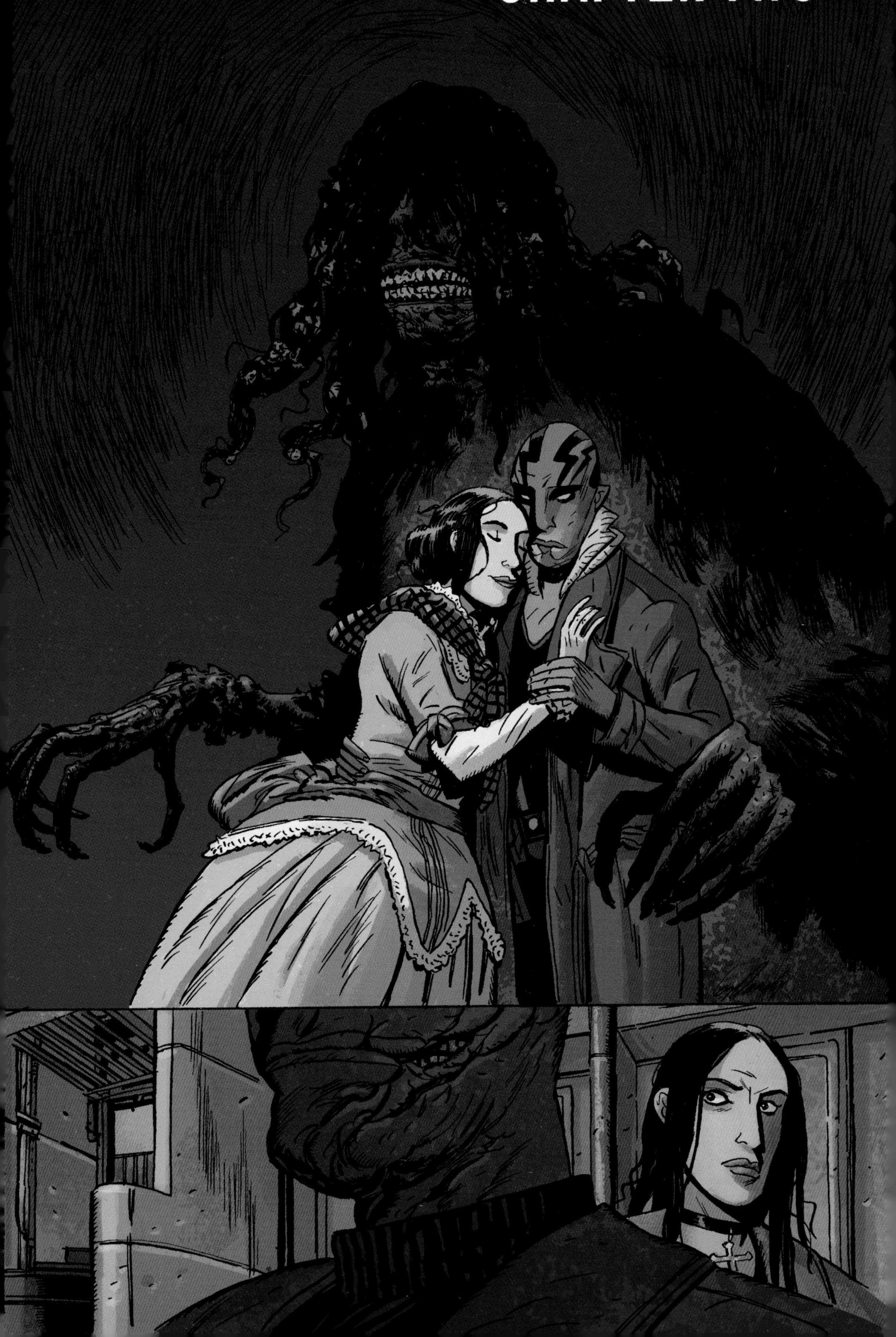

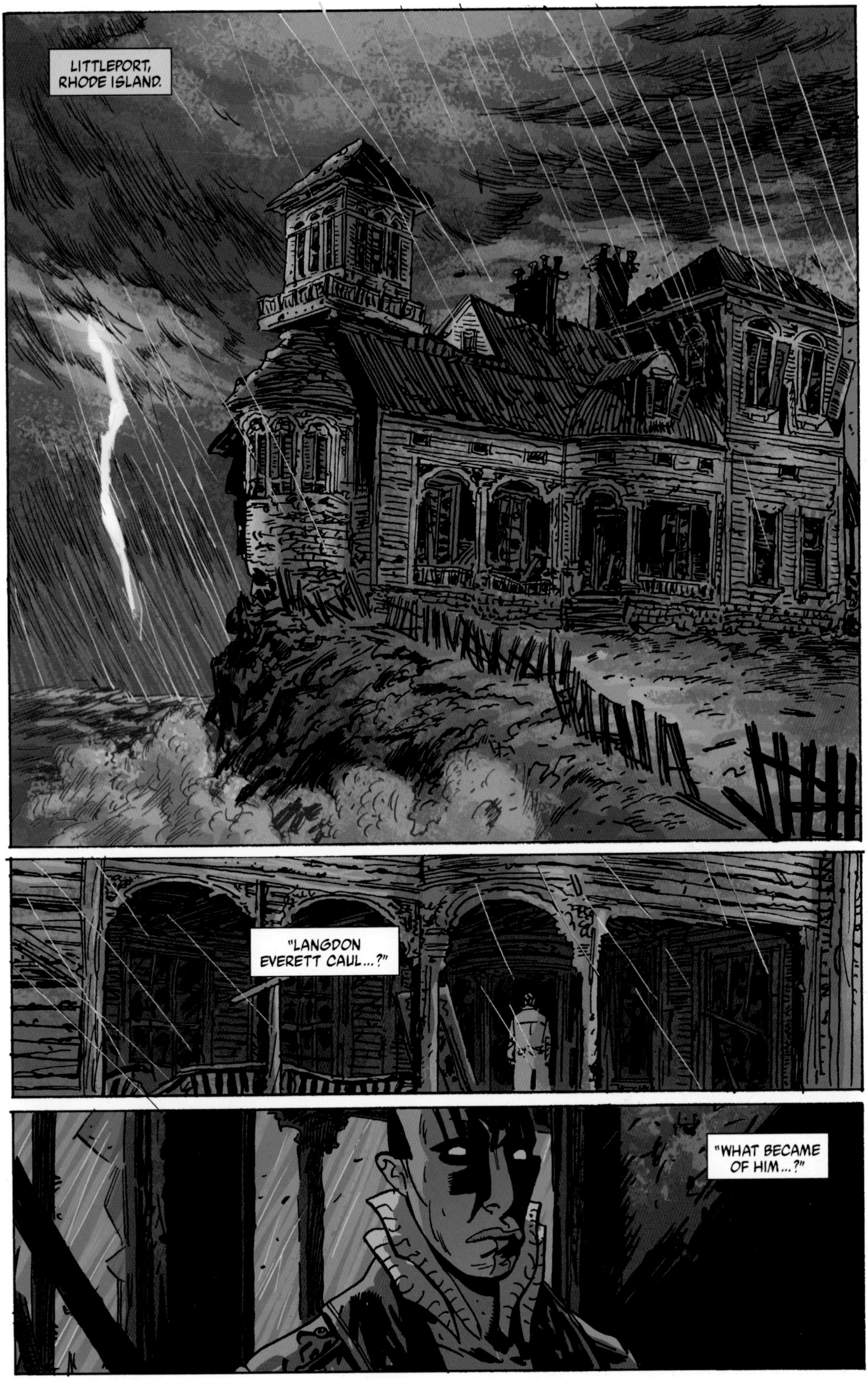
LITTLEPORT, RHODE ISLAND.
"LANGDON EVERETT CAUL...?"
"WHAT BECAME OF HIM...?"

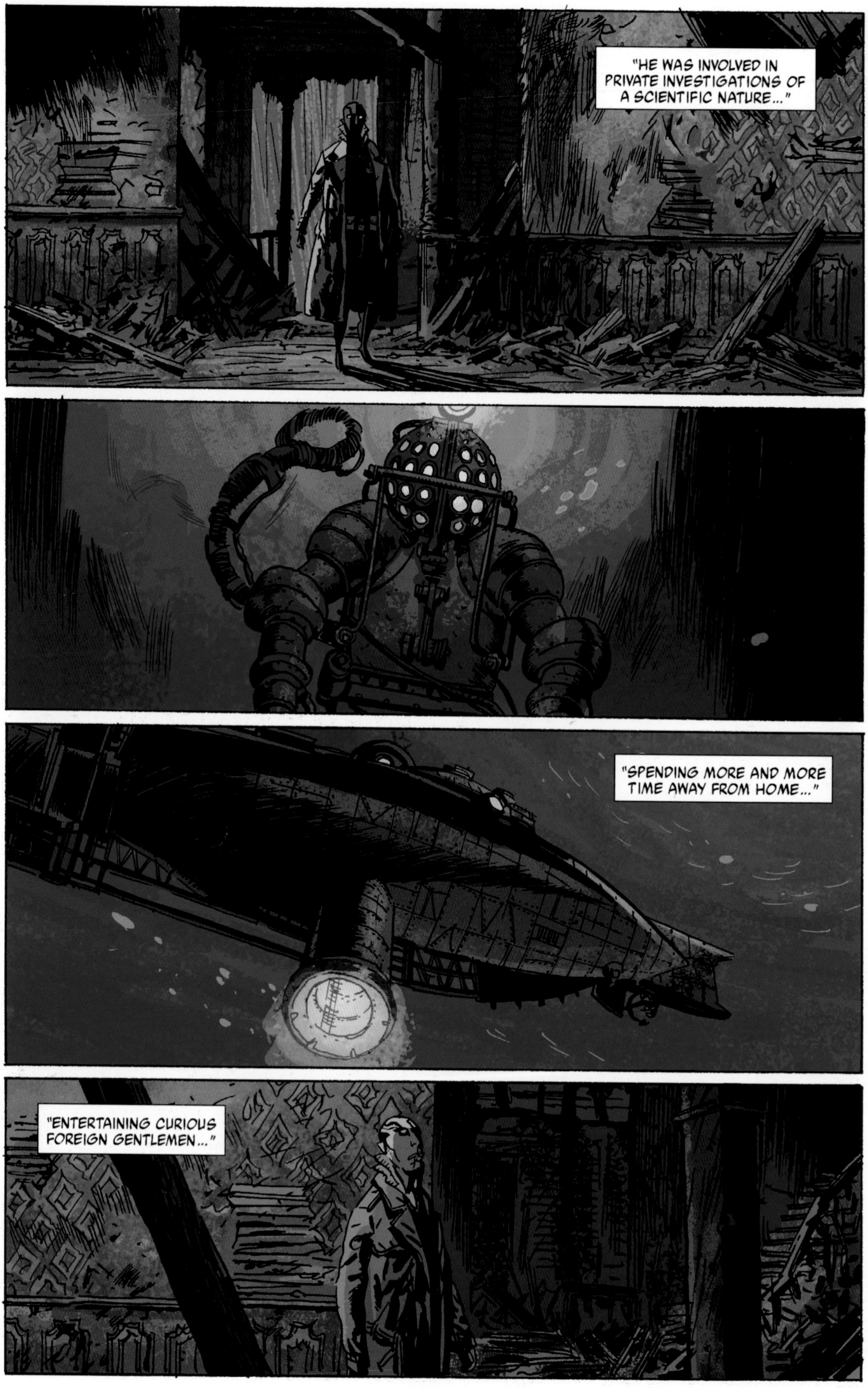
"HE WAS INVOLVED IN PRIVATE INVESTIGATIONS OF A SCIENTIFIC NATURE..."
"SPENDING MORE AND MORE TIME AWAY FROM HOME..."
"ENTERTAINING CURIOUS FOREIGN GENTLEMEN..."

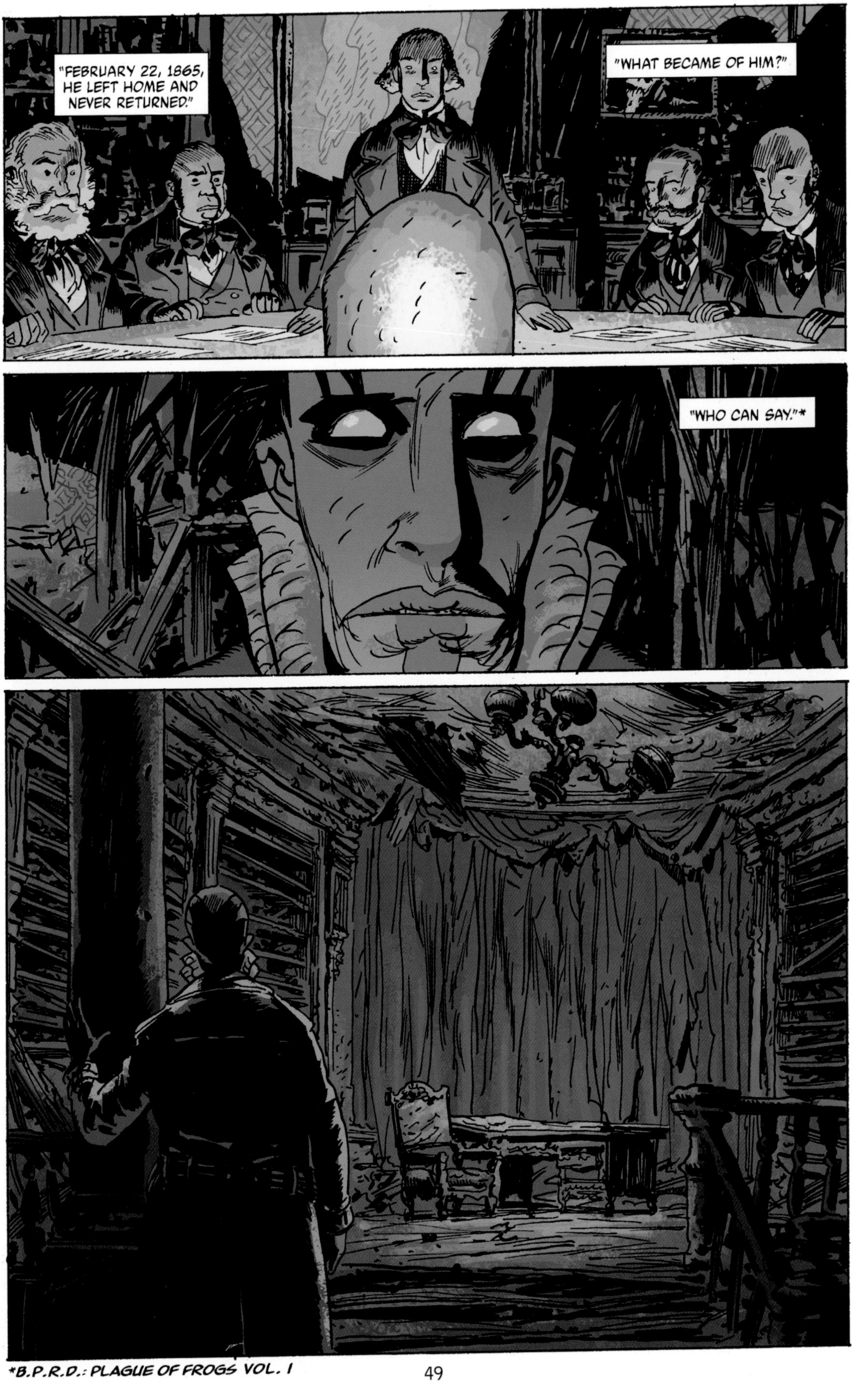
"FEBRUARY 22, 1865, HE LEFT HOME AND NEVER RETURNED."
"WHAT BECAME OF HIM?"
"WHO CAN SAY."*

*B.P.R.D.: PLAGUE OF FROGS VOL. 1

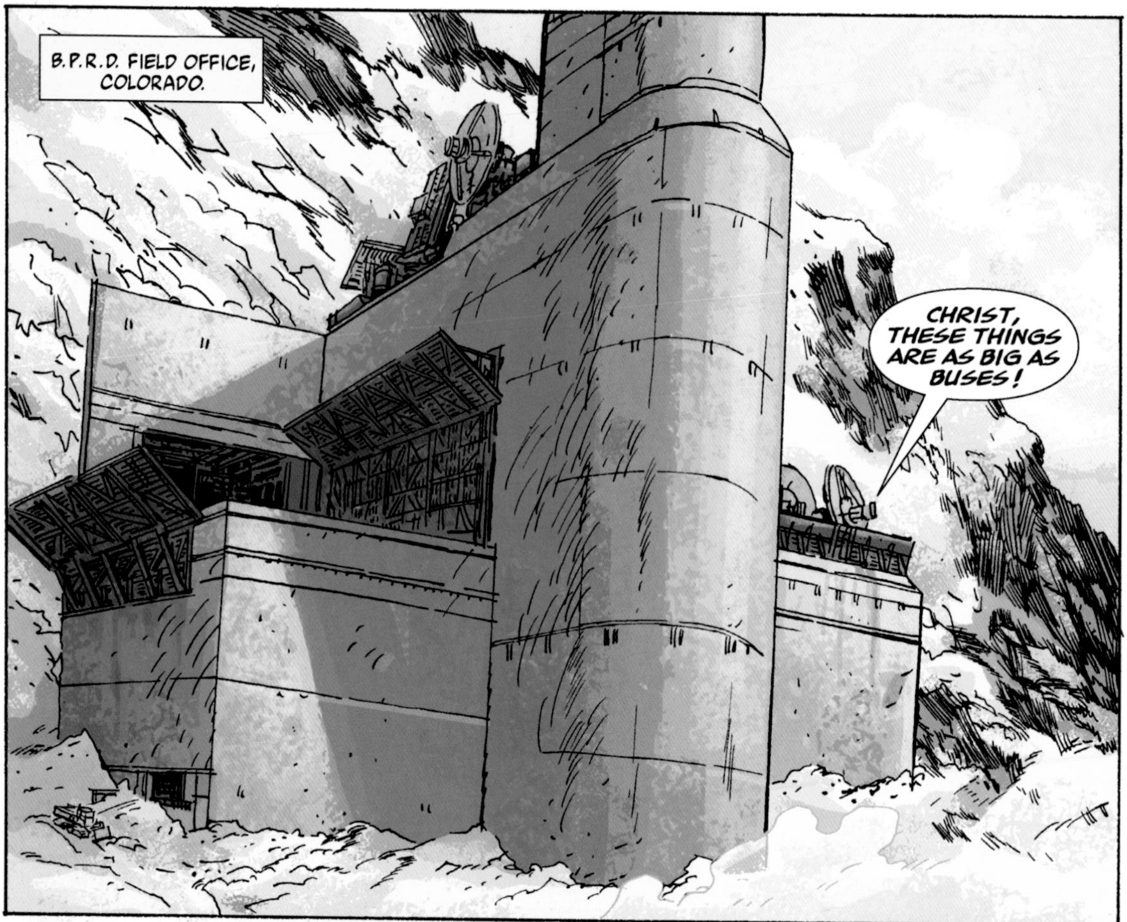
B.P.R.D. FIELD OFFICE, COLORADO.
CHRIST, THESE THINGS ARE AS BIG AS BUSES!

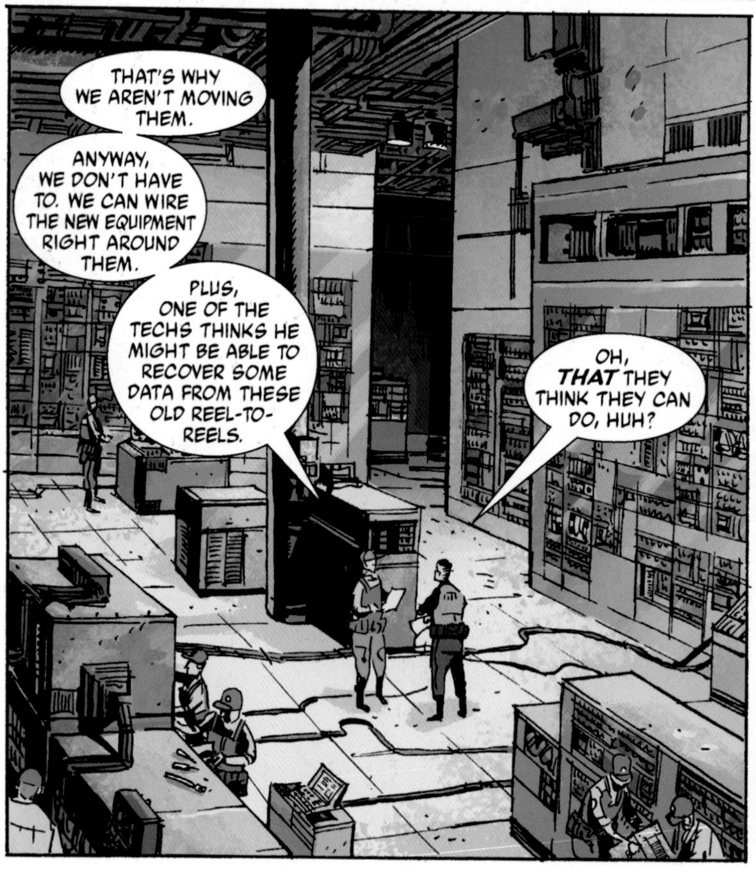
THAT'S WHY WE AREN'T MOVING THEM.
ANYWAY, WE DON'T HAVE TO. WE CAN WIRE THE NEW EQUIPMENT RIGHT AROUND THEM.
PLUS, ONE OF THE TECHS THINKS HE MIGHT BE ABLE TO RECOVER SOME DATA FROM THESE OLD REEL-TO-REELS.
OH, THAT THEY THINK THEY CAN DO, HUH?

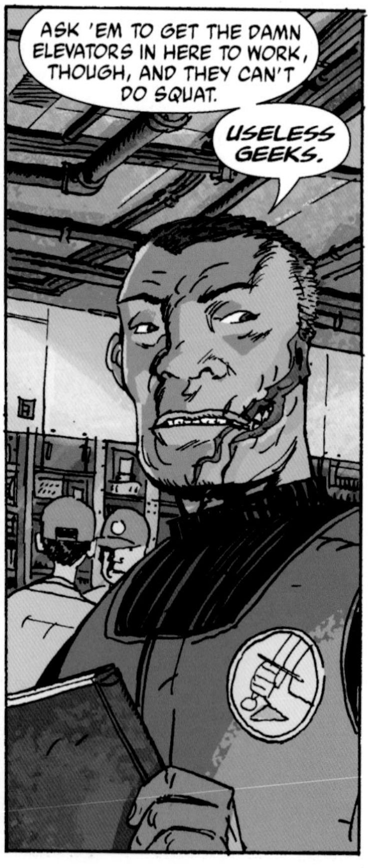
ASK 'EM TO GET THE DAMN ELEVATORS IN HERE TO WORK, THOUGH, AND THEY CAN'T DO SQUAT.
USELESS GEEKS.

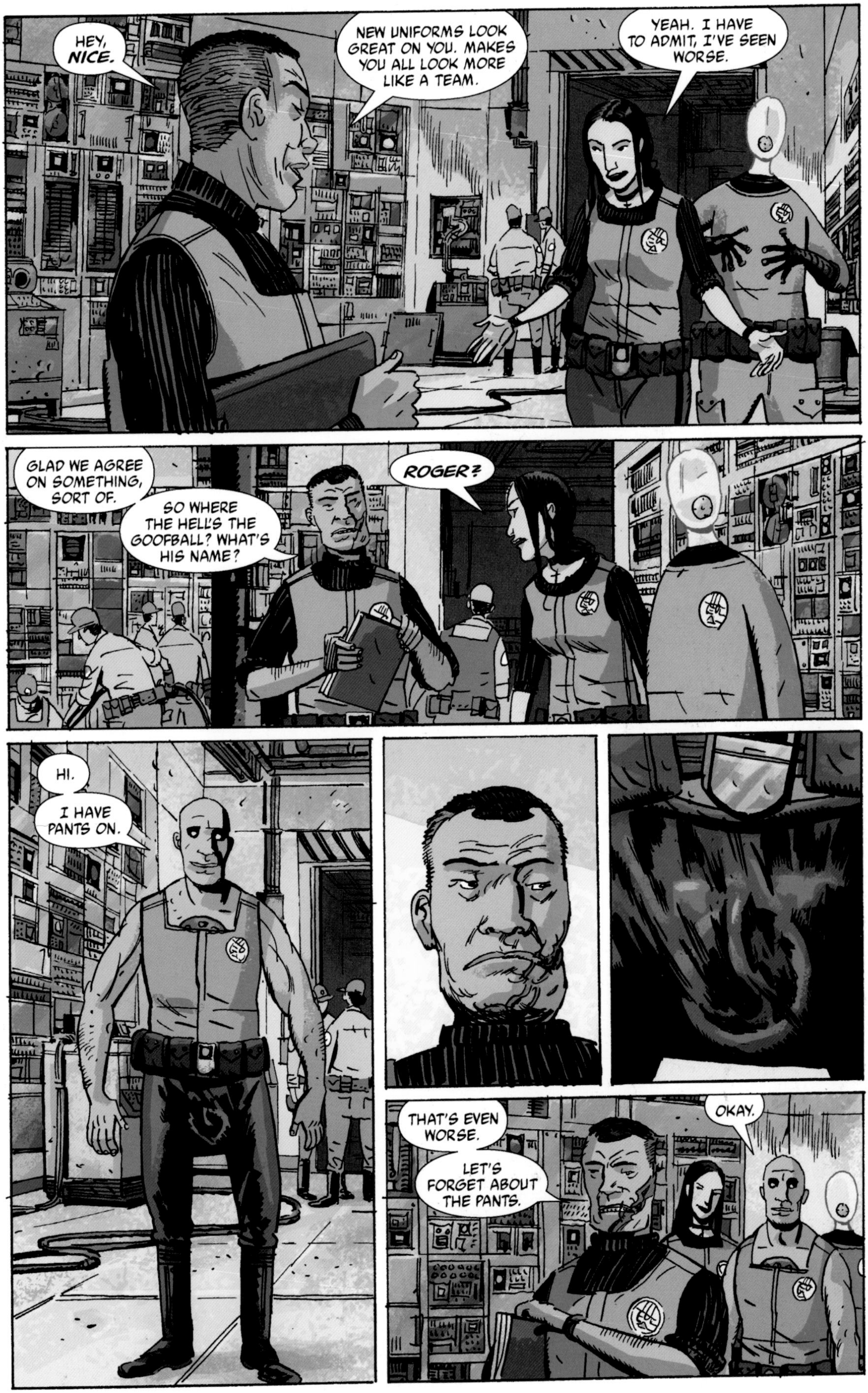
HEY, NICE.
NEW UNIFORMS LOOK GREAT ON YOU. MAKES YOU ALL LOOK MORE LIKE A TEAM.
YEAH. I HAVE TO ADMIT, I'VE SEEN WORSE.
GLAD WE AGREE ON SOMETHING, SORT OF.
SO WHERE THE HELL'S THE GOOFBALL? WHAT'S HIS NAME?
ROGER?
HI.
I HAVE PANTS ON.
THAT'S EVEN WORSE.
LET'S FORGET ABOUT THE PANTS.
OKAY.

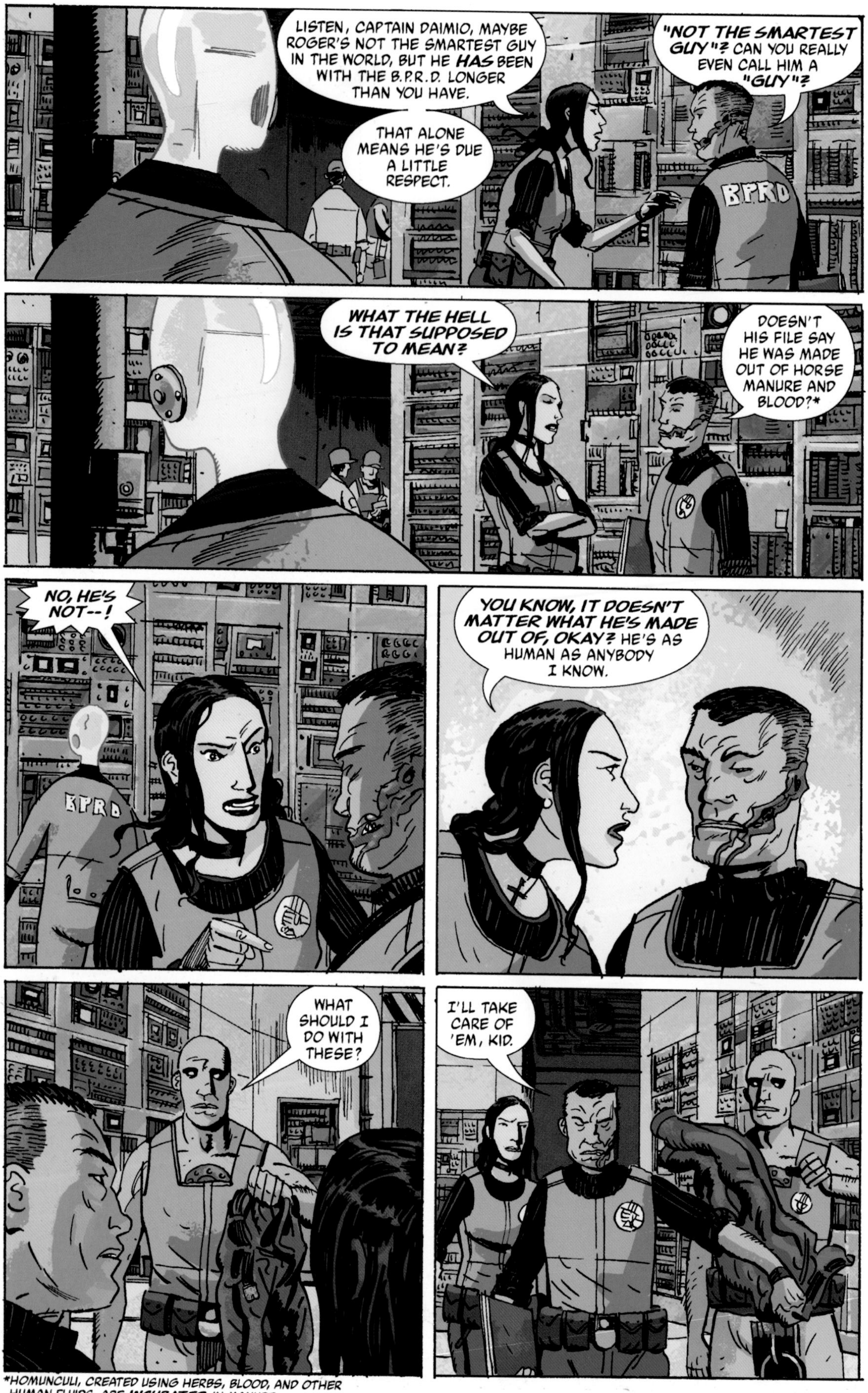
LISTEN, CAPTAIN DAIMIO, MAYBE ROGER'S NOT THE SMARTEST GUY IN THE WORLD, BUT HE HAS BEEN WITH THE B.P.R.D. LONGER THAN YOU HAVE.
THAT ALONE MEANS HE'S DUE A LITTLE RESPECT.
"NOT THE SMARTEST GUY"? CAN YOU REALLY EVEN CALL HIM A "GUY"?
BPRD
WHAT THE HELL IS THAT SUPPOSED TO MEAN?
DOESN'T HIS FILE SAY HE WAS MADE OUT OF HORSE MANURE AND BLOOD?*
NO, HE'S NOT--!
BPRD
YOU KNOW, IT DOESN'T MATTER WHAT HE'S MADE OUT OF, OKAY? HE'S AS HUMAN AS ANYBODY I KNOW.
WHAT SHOULD I DO WITH THESE?
I'LL TAKE CARE OF 'EM, KID.

*HOMUNCULI, CREATED USING HERBS, BLOOD, AND OTHER HUMAN FLUIDS, ARE **INCUBATED** IN MANURE.

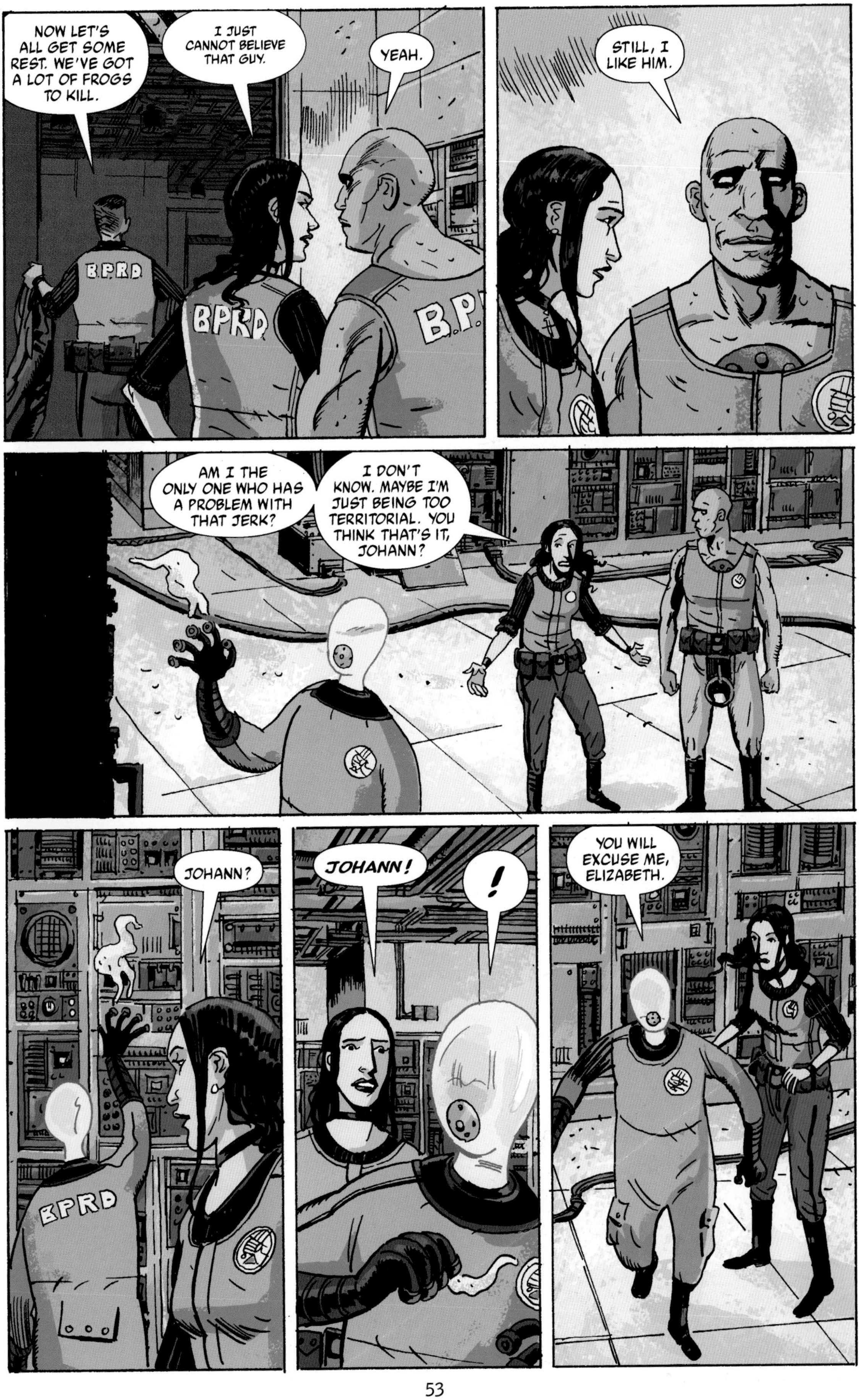
NOW LET'S ALL GET SOME REST. WE'VE GOT A LOT OF FROGS TO KILL.
I JUST CANNOT BELIEVE THAT GUY.
YEAH.
B.P.R.D.
BPRD
B.P.
STILL, I LIKE HIM.
AM I THE ONLY ONE WHO HAS A PROBLEM WITH THAT JERK?
I DON'T KNOW. MAYBE I'M JUST BEING TOO TERRITORIAL. YOU THINK THAT'S IT, JOHANN?
JOHANN?
BPRD
JOHANN!
!
YOU WILL EXCUSE ME, ELIZABETH.

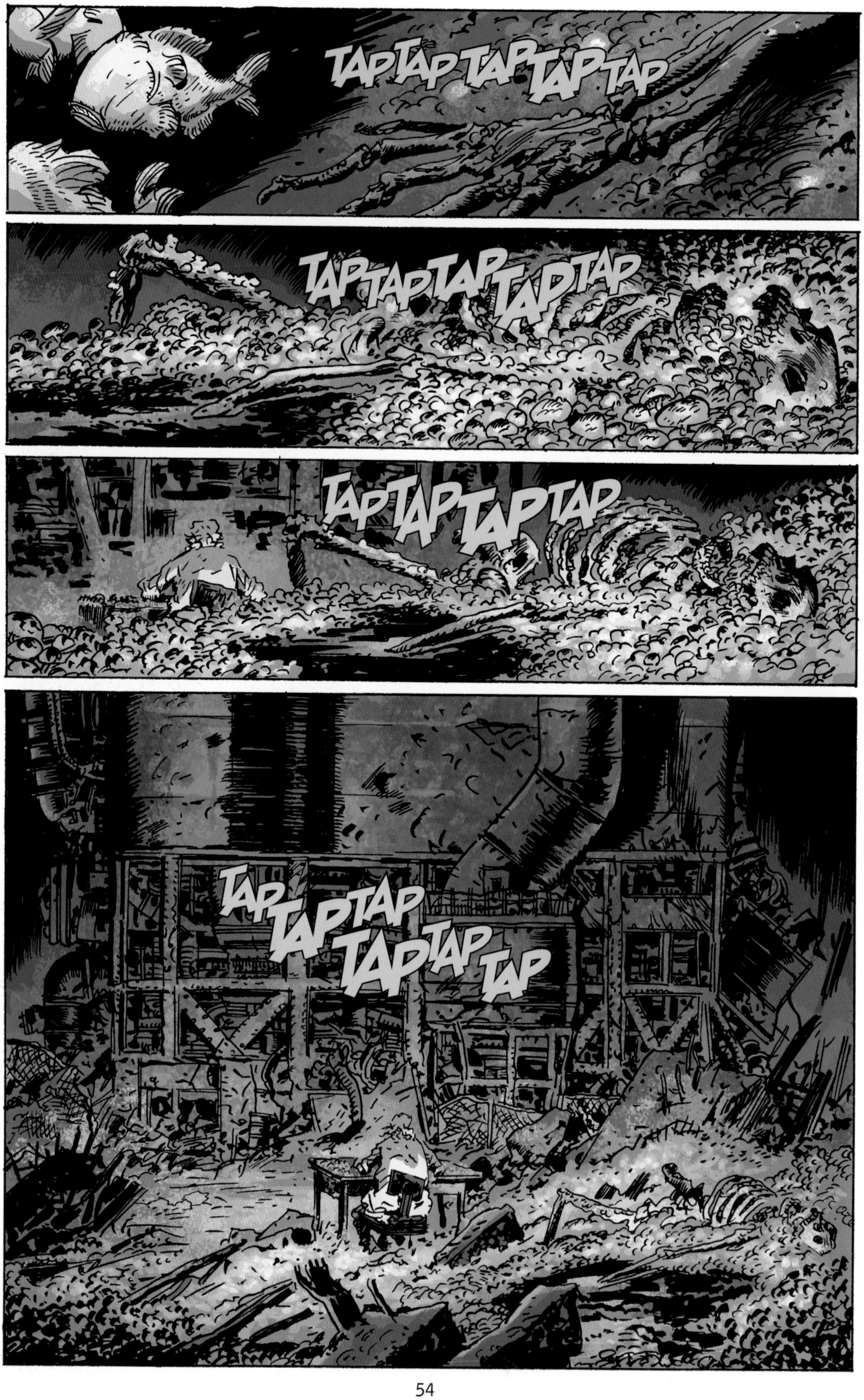
TAP TAP TAP TAP TAP
TAP TAP TAP TAP TAP
TAP TAP TAP TAP
TAP TAP TAP TAP TAP TAP TAP

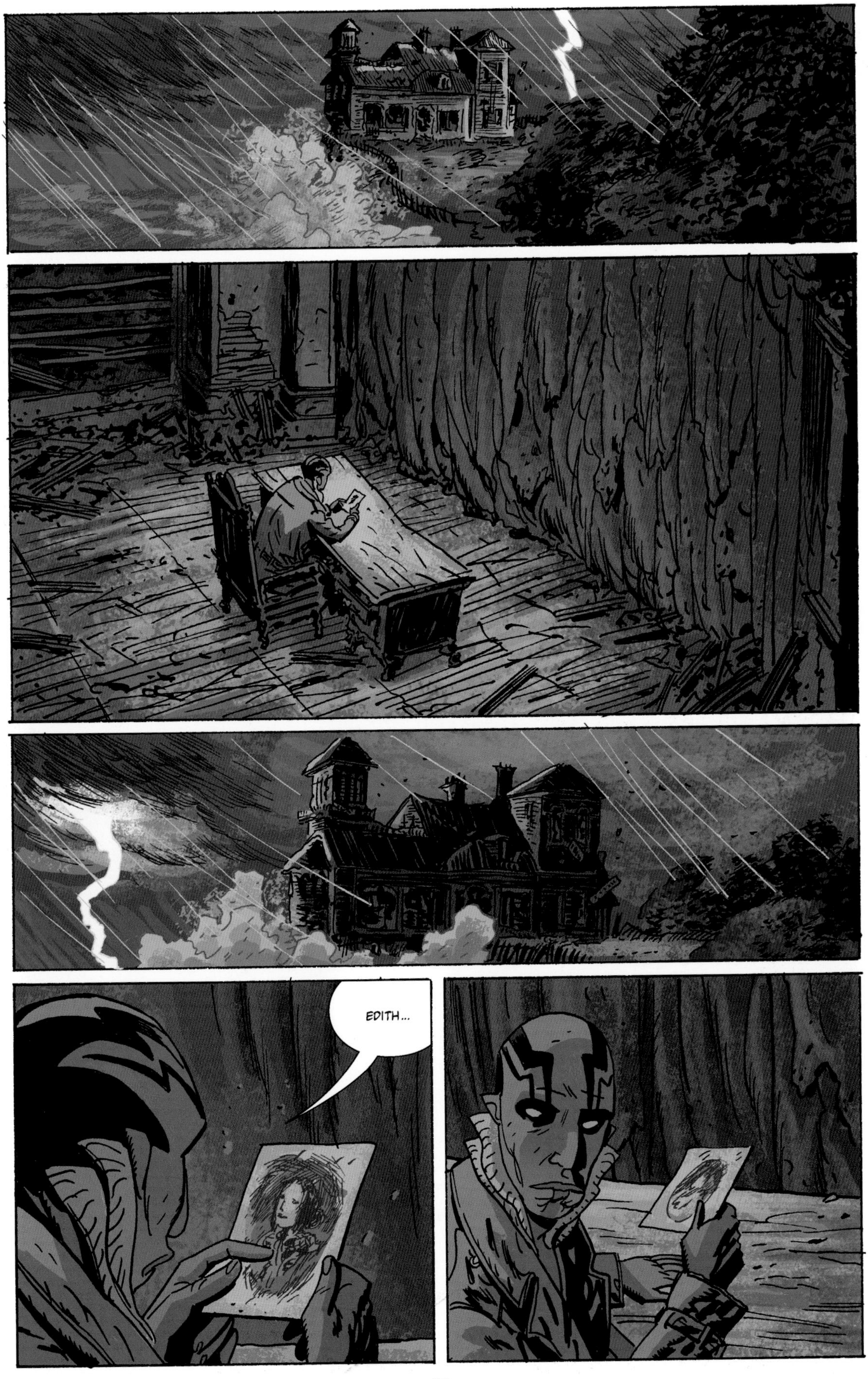
EDITH...

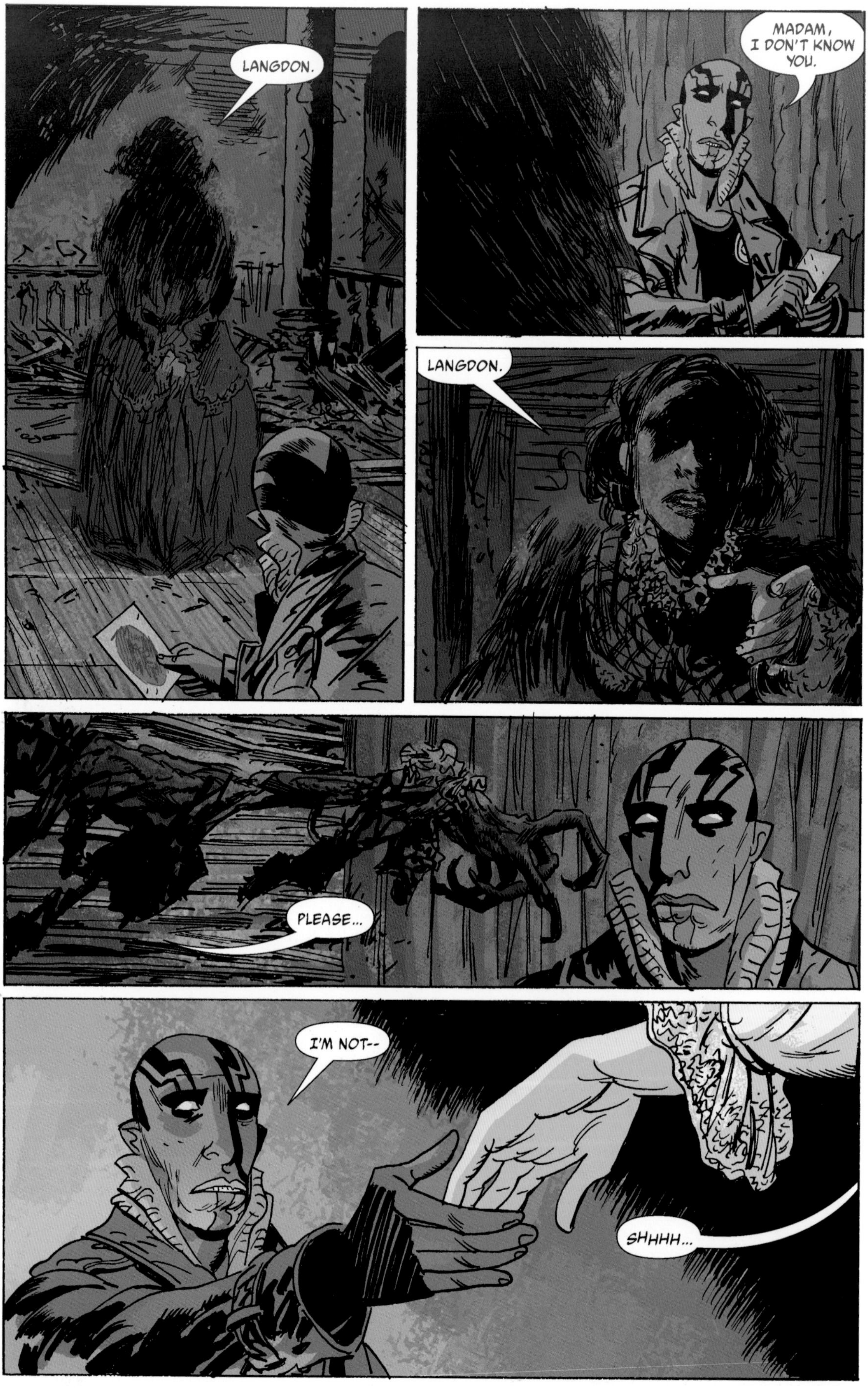
LANGDON.
MADAM, I DON'T KNOW YOU.
LANGDON.
PLEASE...
I'M NOT--
SHHHH...

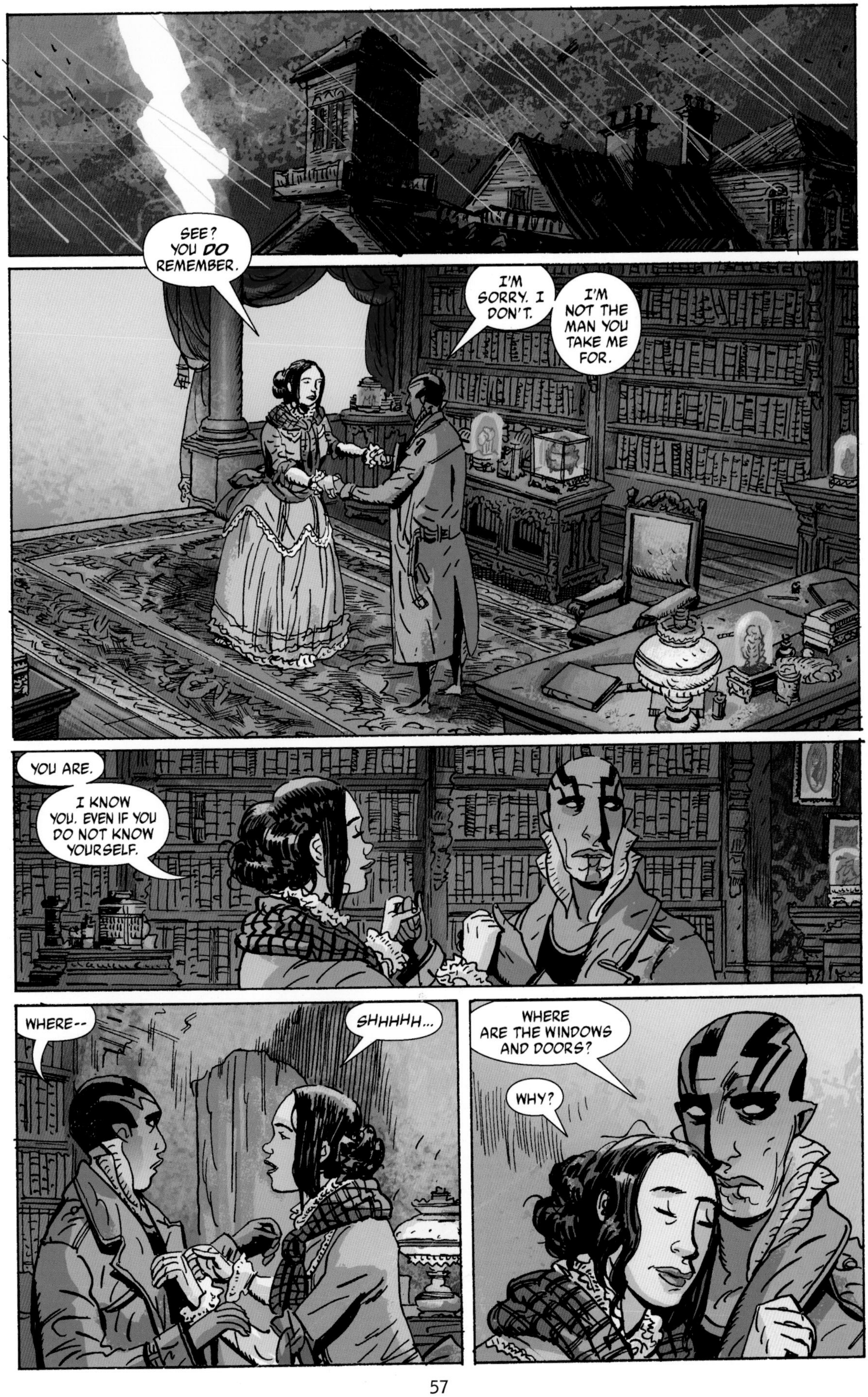
SEE? YOU DO REMEMBER.
I'M SORRY. I DON'T.
I'M NOT THE MAN YOU TAKE ME FOR.
YOU ARE.
I KNOW YOU. EVEN IF YOU DO NOT KNOW YOURSELF.
WHERE--
SHHHHH...
WHERE ARE THE WINDOWS AND DOORS?
WHY?

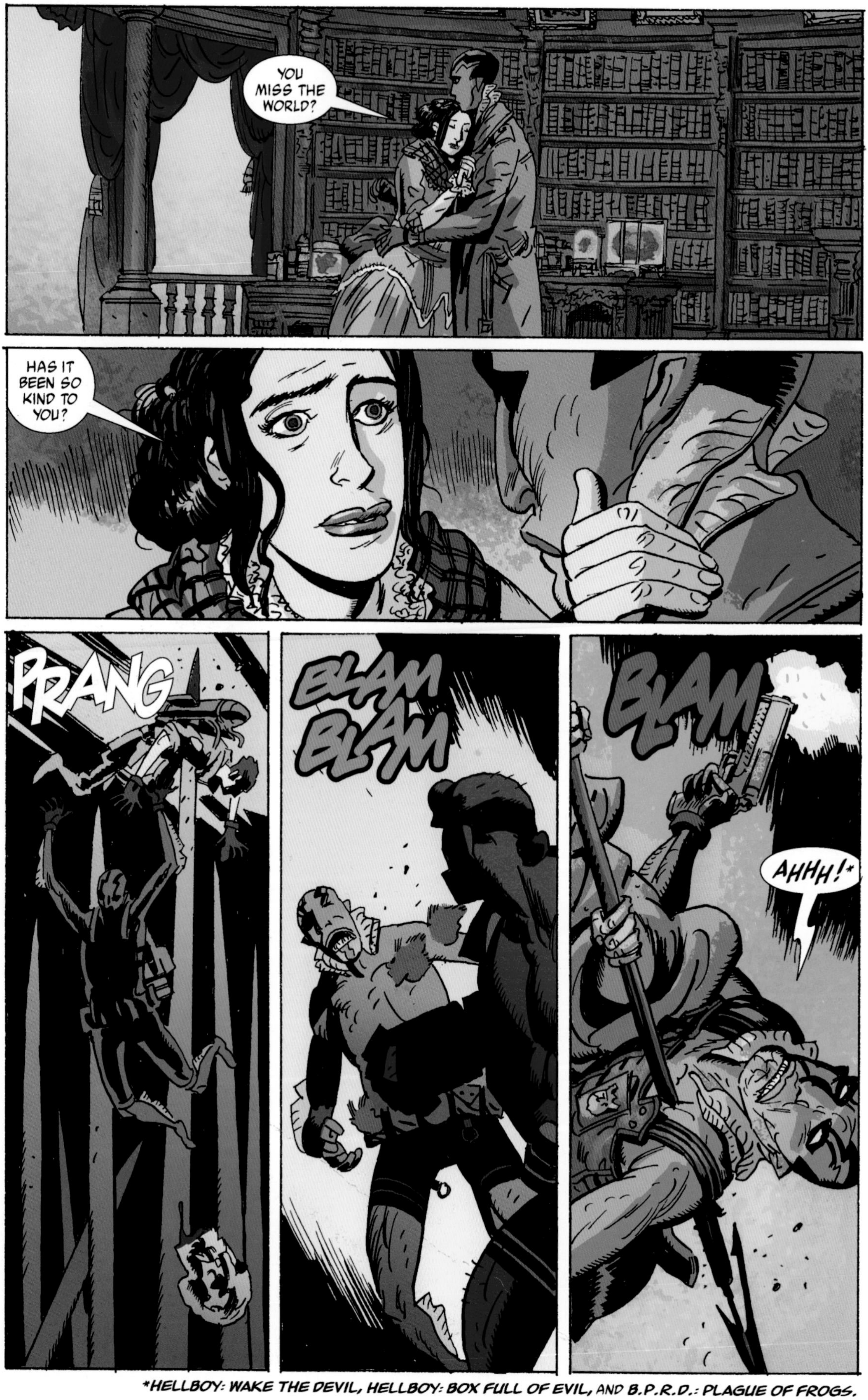
YOU MISS THE WORLD?
HAS IT BEEN SO KIND TO YOU?
PRANG
BLAM BLAM
BLAM
AHHH!*

*HELLBOY: WAKE THE DEVIL, HELLBOY: BOX FULL OF EVIL, AND B.P.R.D.: PLAGUE OF FROGS.

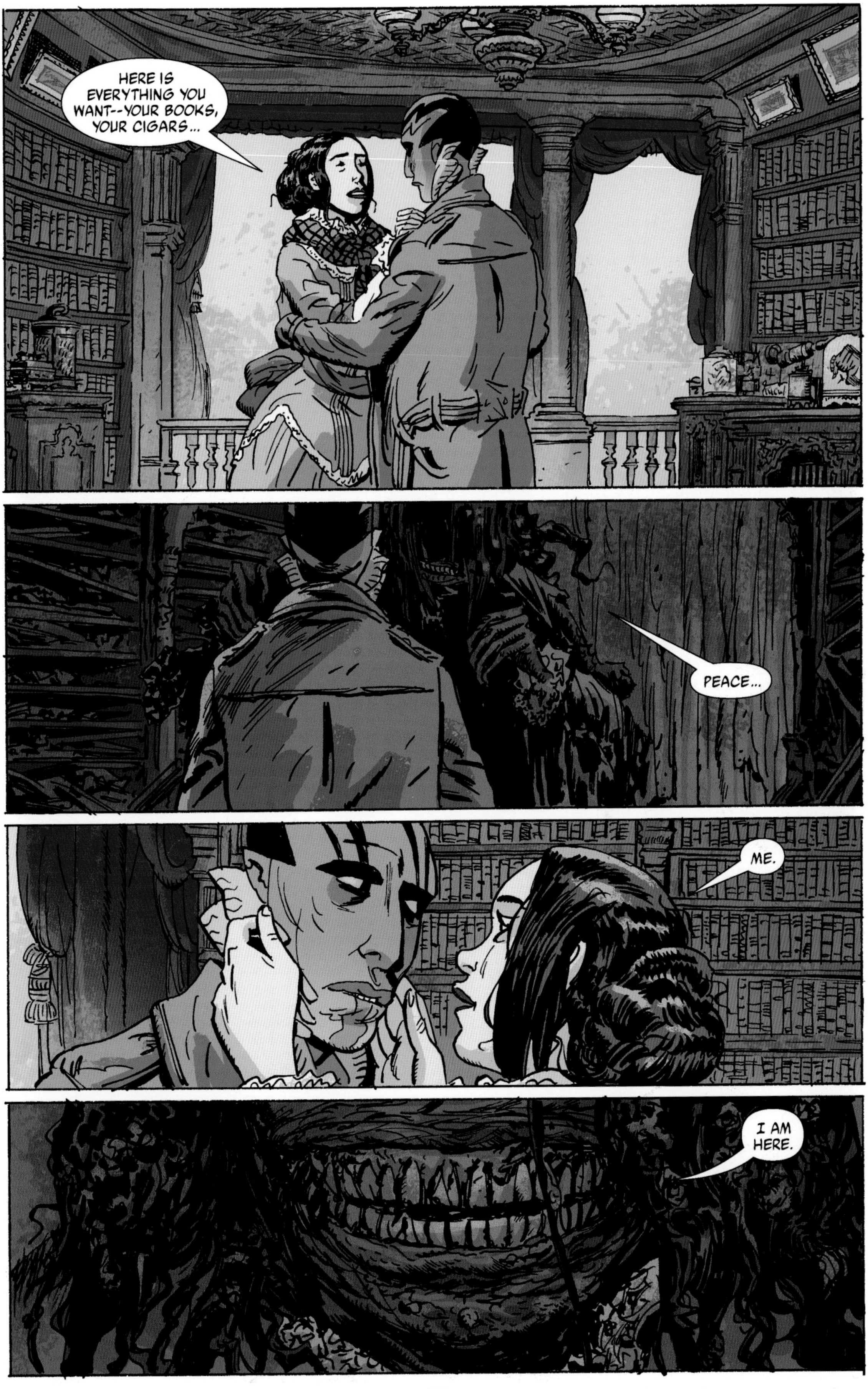
HERE IS EVERYTHING YOU WANT--YOUR BOOKS, YOUR CIGARS...
PEACE...
ME.
I AM HERE.

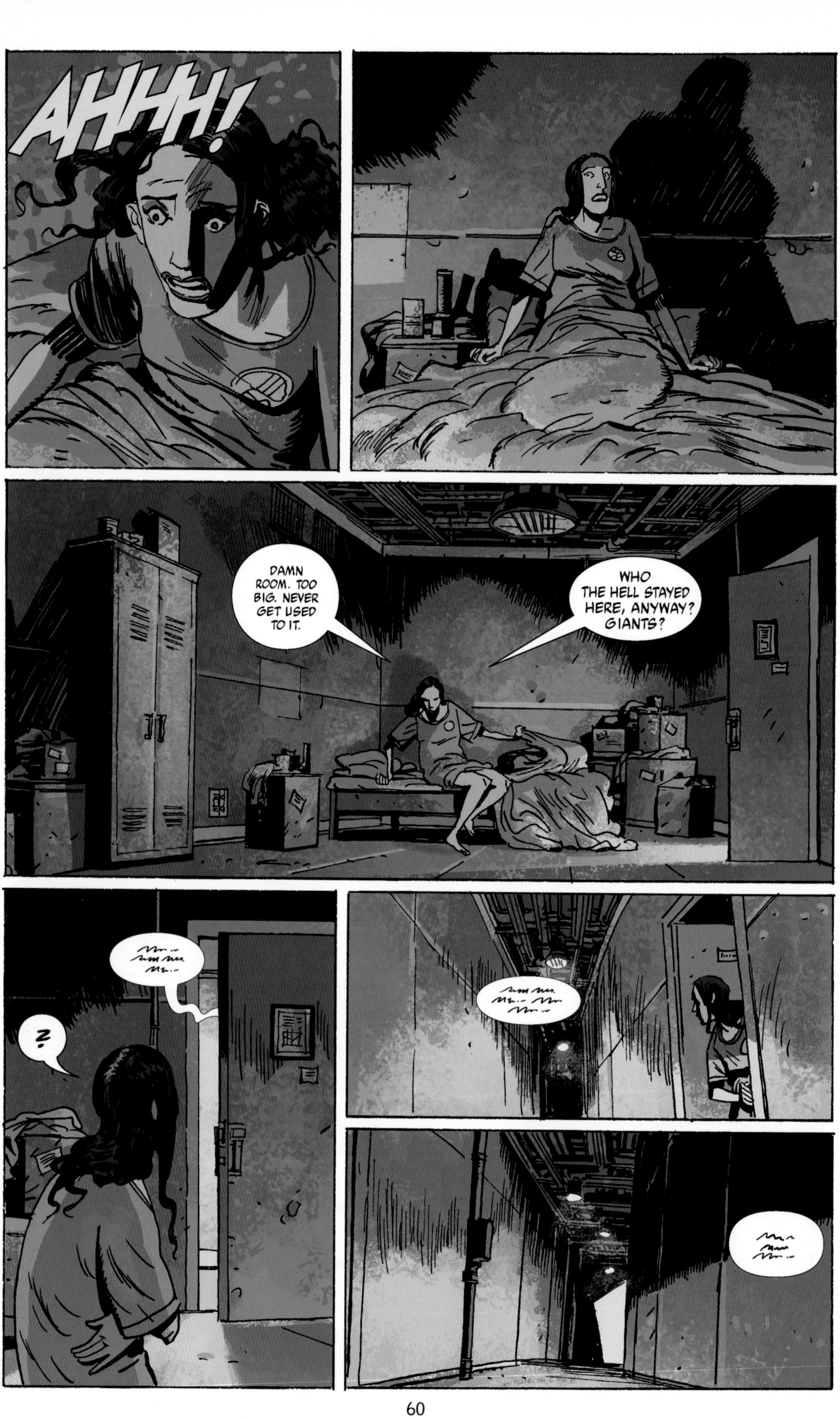
AHHH!
DAMN ROOM. TOO BIG. NEVER GET USED TO IT.
WHO THE HELL STAYED HERE, ANYWAY? GIANTS?
?

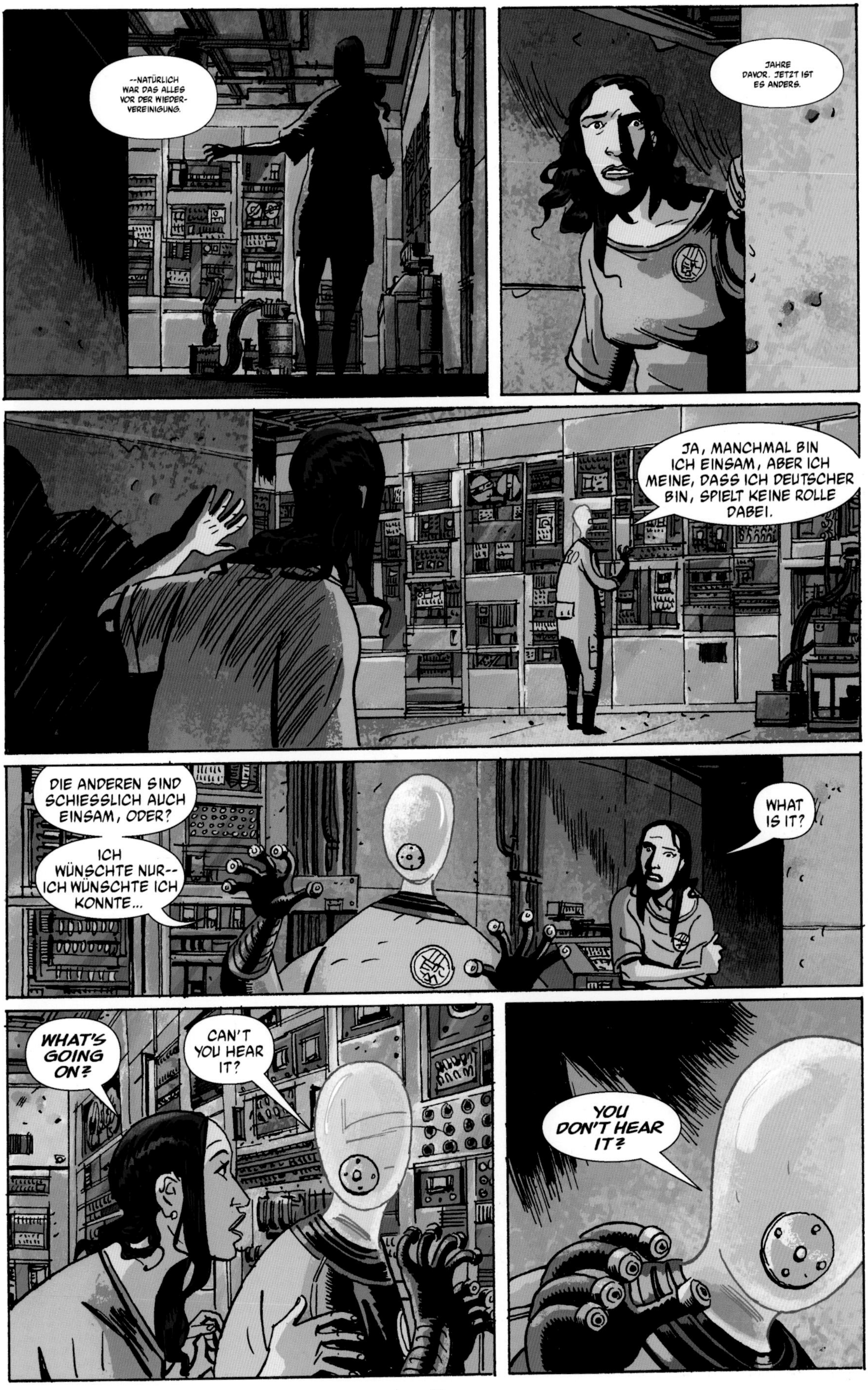
--NATÜRLICH WAR DAS ALLES VOR DER WIEDER-VEREINIGUNG.
JAHRE DAVOR. JETZT IST ES ANDERS.
JA, MANCHMAL BIN ICH EINSAM, ABER ICH MEINE, DASS ICH DEUTSCHER BIN, SPIELT KEINE ROLLE DABEI.
DIE ANDEREN SIND SCHIESSLICH AUCH EINSAM, ODER?
ICH WÜNSCHTE NUR-- ICH WÜNSCHTE ICH KONNTE...
WHAT IS IT?
WHAT'S GOING ON?
CAN'T YOU HEAR IT?
YOU DON'T HEAR IT?

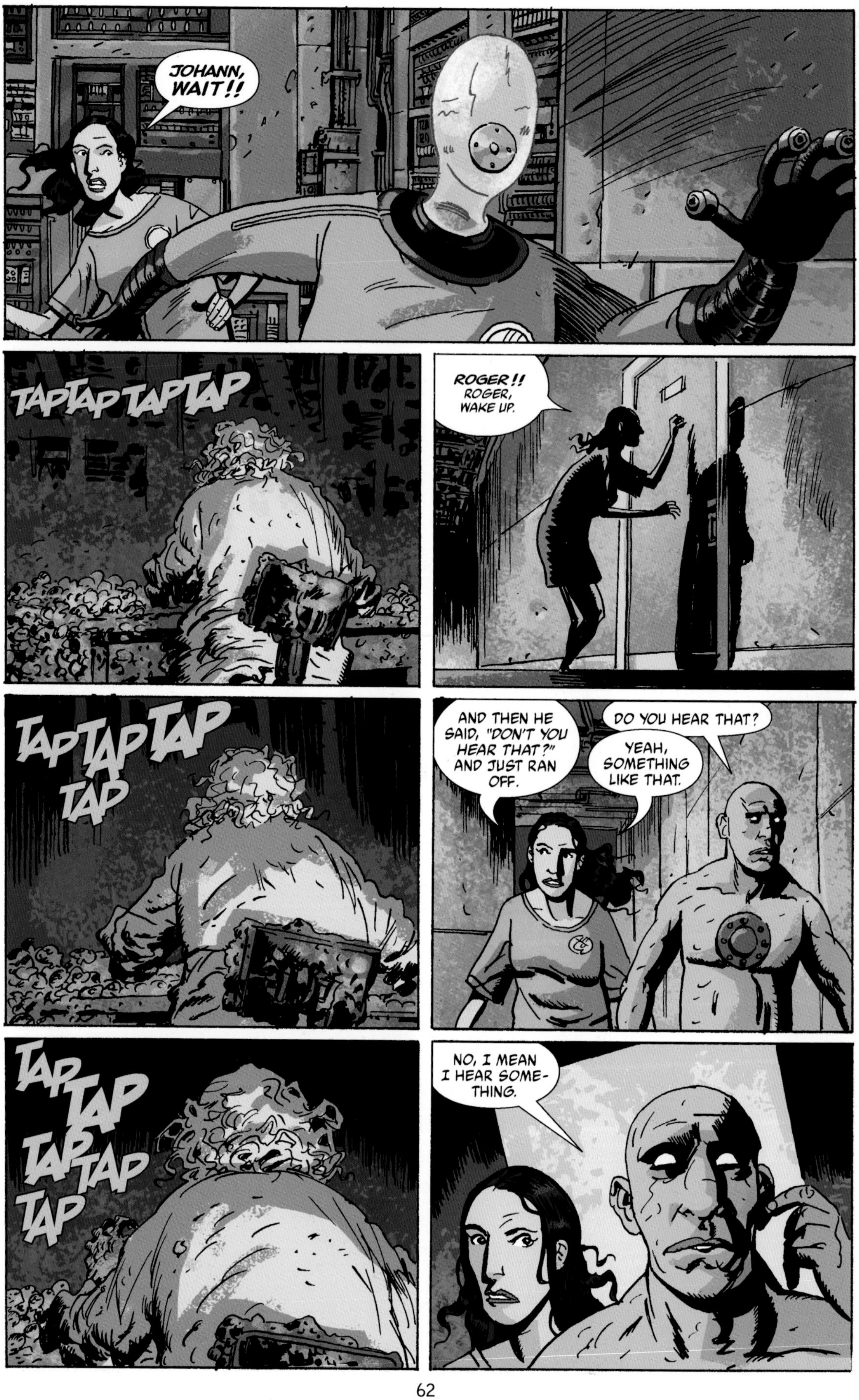
JOHANN, WAIT!!
TAPTAP TAPTAP
ROGER!! ROGER, WAKE UP.
TAPTAPTAP TAP
AND THEN HE SAID, "DON'T YOU HEAR THAT?" AND JUST RAN OFF.
DO YOU HEAR THAT?
YEAH, SOMETHING LIKE THAT.
TAP TAP TAP TAP TAP
NO, I MEAN I HEAR SOME-THING.

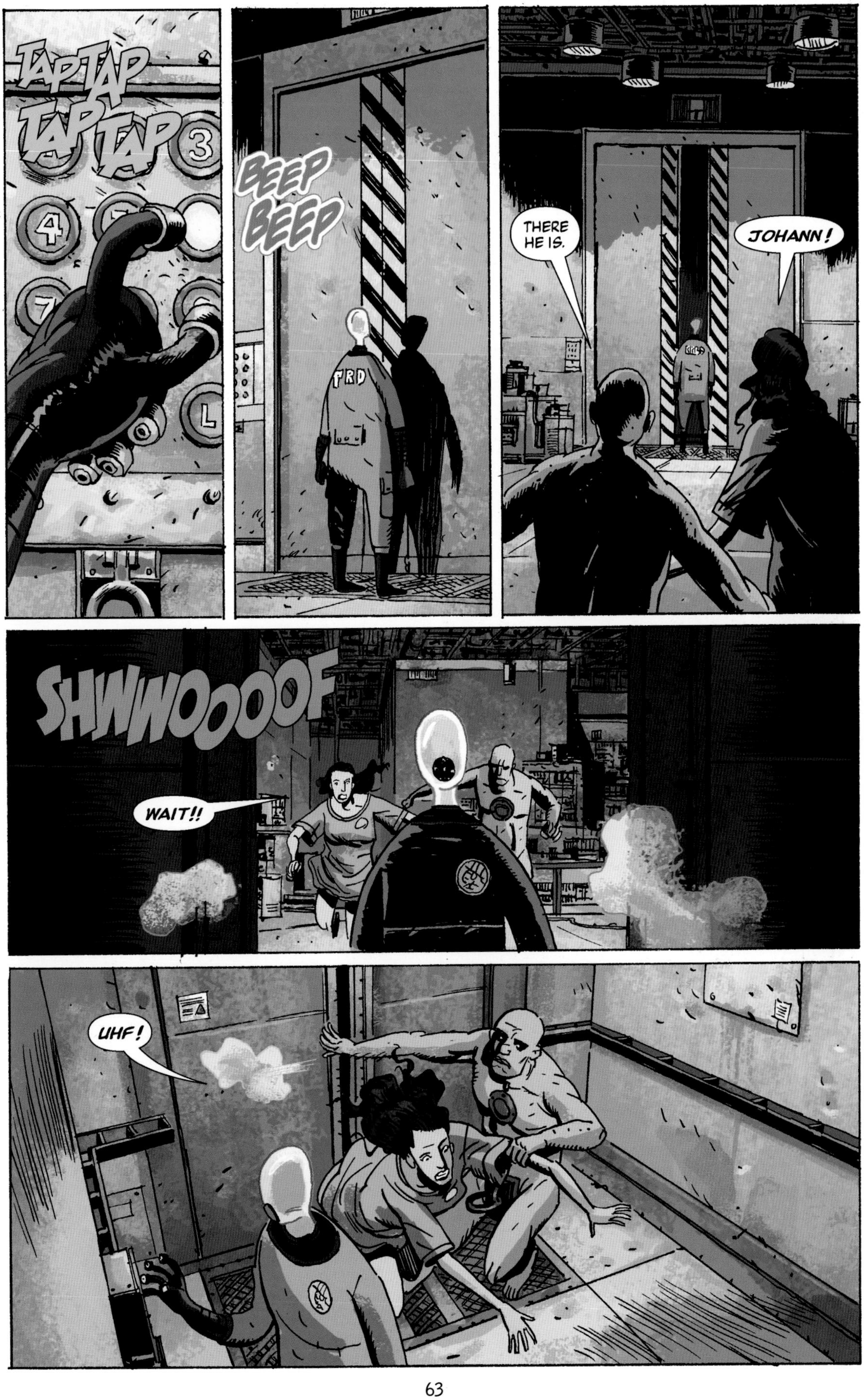
TAP TAP
TAP TAP
BEEP
BEEP
THERE HE IS.
JOHANN!
SHWWOOOOF
WAIT!!
UHF!

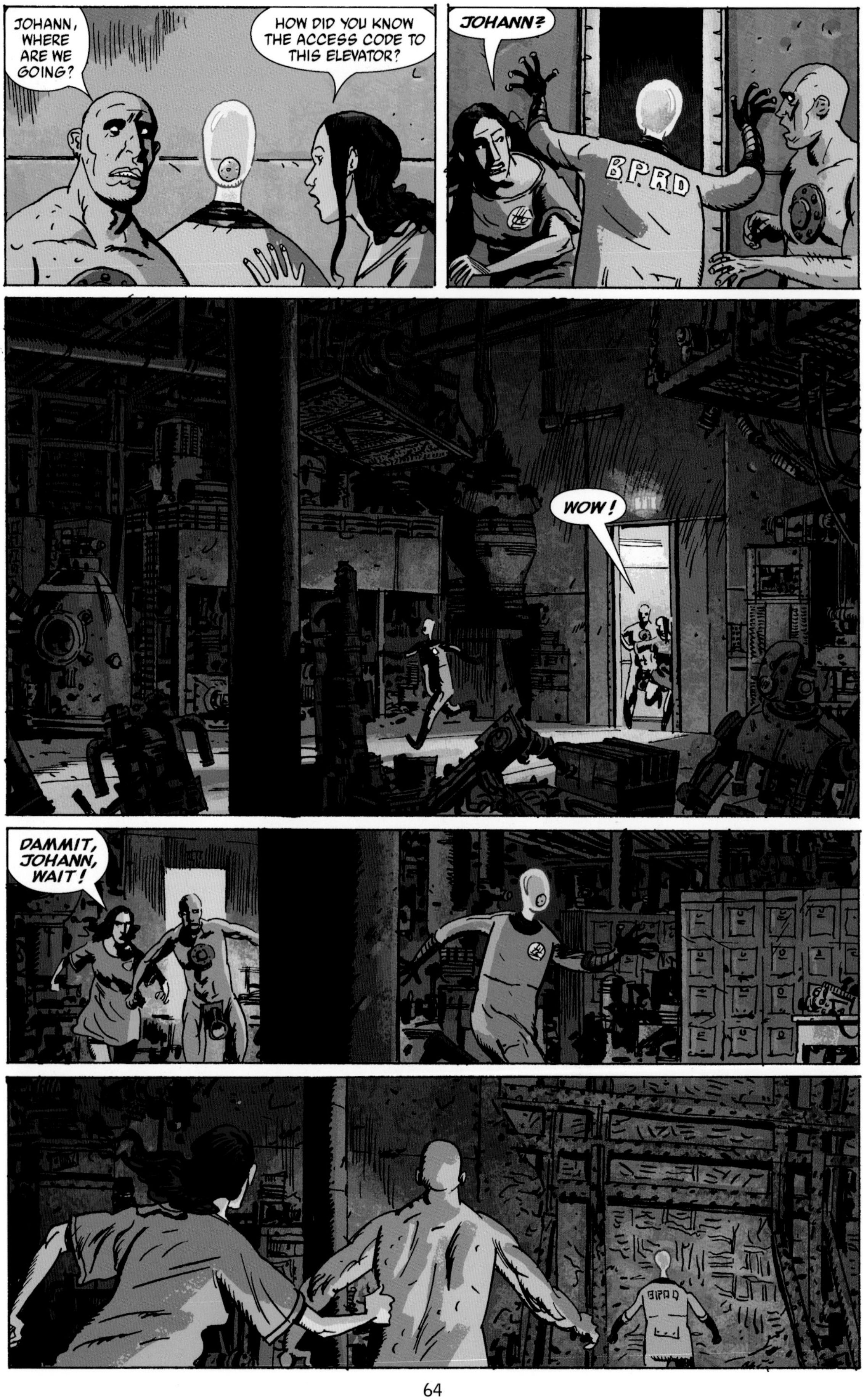
JOHANN, WHERE ARE WE GOING?
HOW DID YOU KNOW THE ACCESS CODE TO THIS ELEVATOR?
JOHANN?
B.P.R.D
WOW!
DAMMIT, JOHANN, WAIT!
BPRD

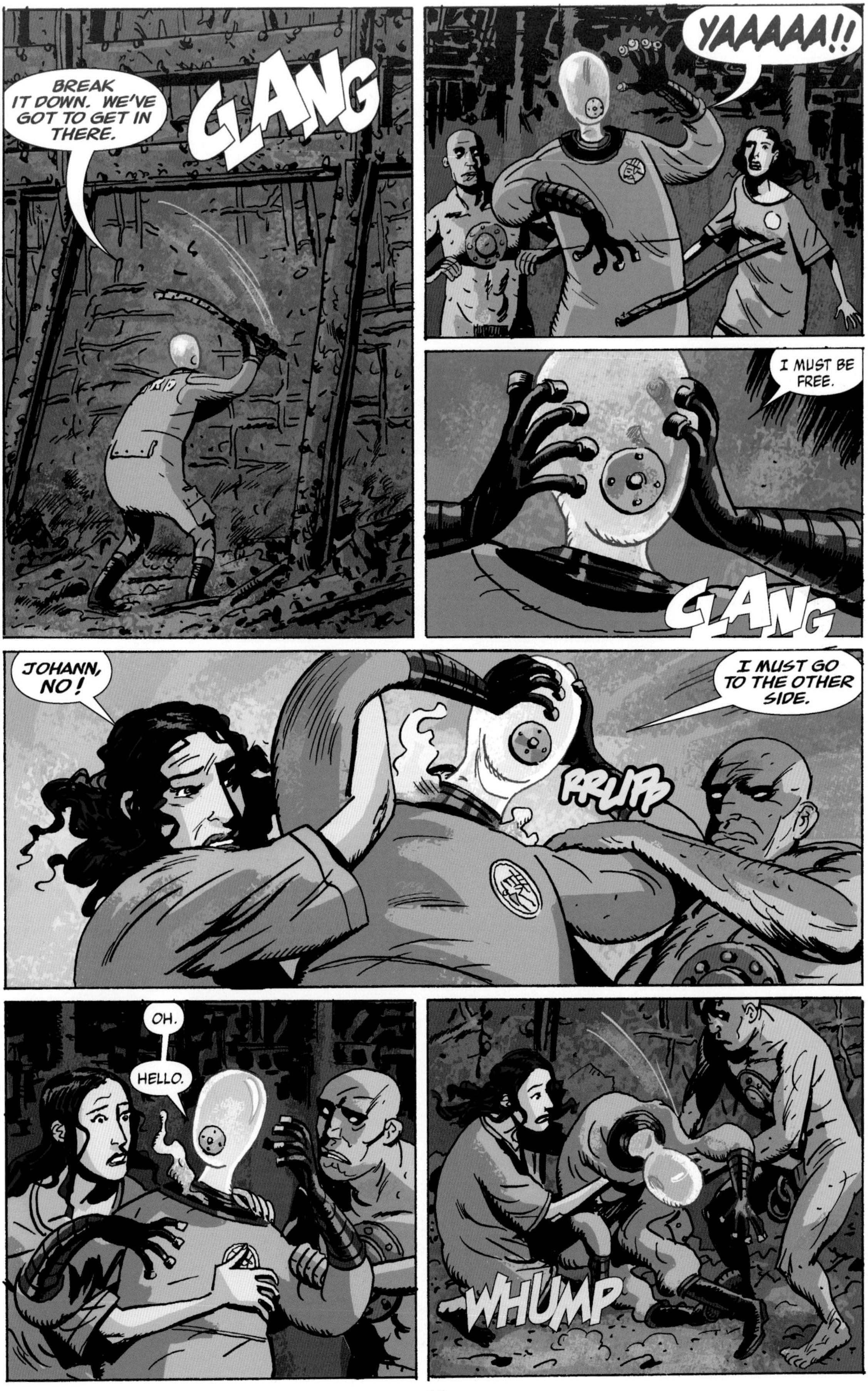
BREAK IT DOWN. WE'VE GOT TO GET IN THERE.
CLANG
YAAAAA!!
I MUST BE FREE.
CLANG
JOHANN, NO!
I MUST GO TO THE OTHER SIDE.
RRUPP
OH.
HELLO.
WHUMP

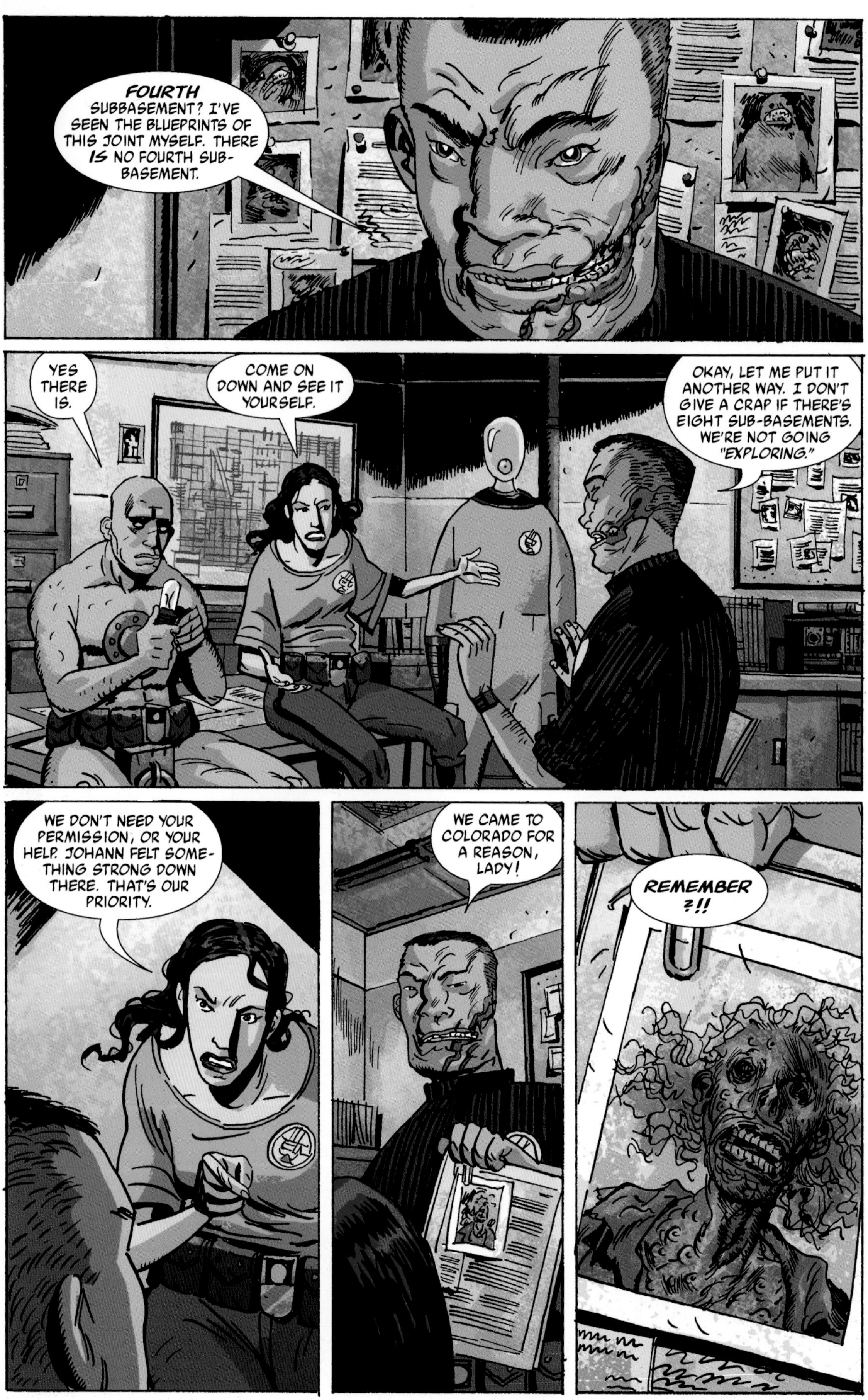
FOURTH SUBBASEMENT? I'VE SEEN THE BLUEPRINTS OF THIS JOINT MYSELF. THERE IS NO FOURTH SUB-BASEMENT.
YES THERE IS.
COME ON DOWN AND SEE IT YOURSELF.
OKAY, LET ME PUT IT ANOTHER WAY. I DON'T GIVE A CRAP IF THERE'S EIGHT SUB-BASEMENTS. WE'RE NOT GOING "EXPLORING."
WE DON'T NEED YOUR PERMISSION, OR YOUR HELP. JOHANN FELT SOME-THING STRONG DOWN THERE. THAT'S OUR PRIORITY.
WE CAME TO COLORADO FOR A REASON, LADY!
REMEMBER ?!!

THOSE THINGS ARE SPREADING ALL OVER.

"MORE OF 'EM EVERY DAY. I DON'T KNOW *HOW* THERE ARE MORE, BUT THERE ARE.

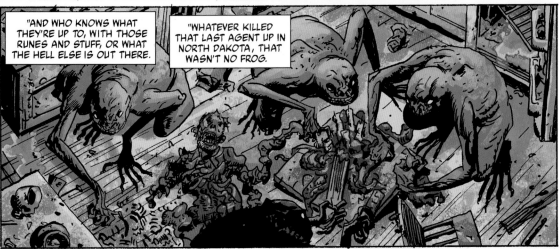

"AND WHO KNOWS WHAT THEY'RE UP TO, WITH THOSE RUNES AND STUFF, OR WHAT THE HELL ELSE IS OUT THERE.

"WHATEVER KILLED THAT LAST AGENT UP IN NORTH DAKOTA, THAT WASN'T NO FROG.

"I DON'T WANNA GET SIDETRACKED, BECAUSE MY JOB--*YOUR* JOB--IS TO STOP THOSE THINGS.

"*NOW.*

"BEFORE IT GETS PLENTY WORSE."

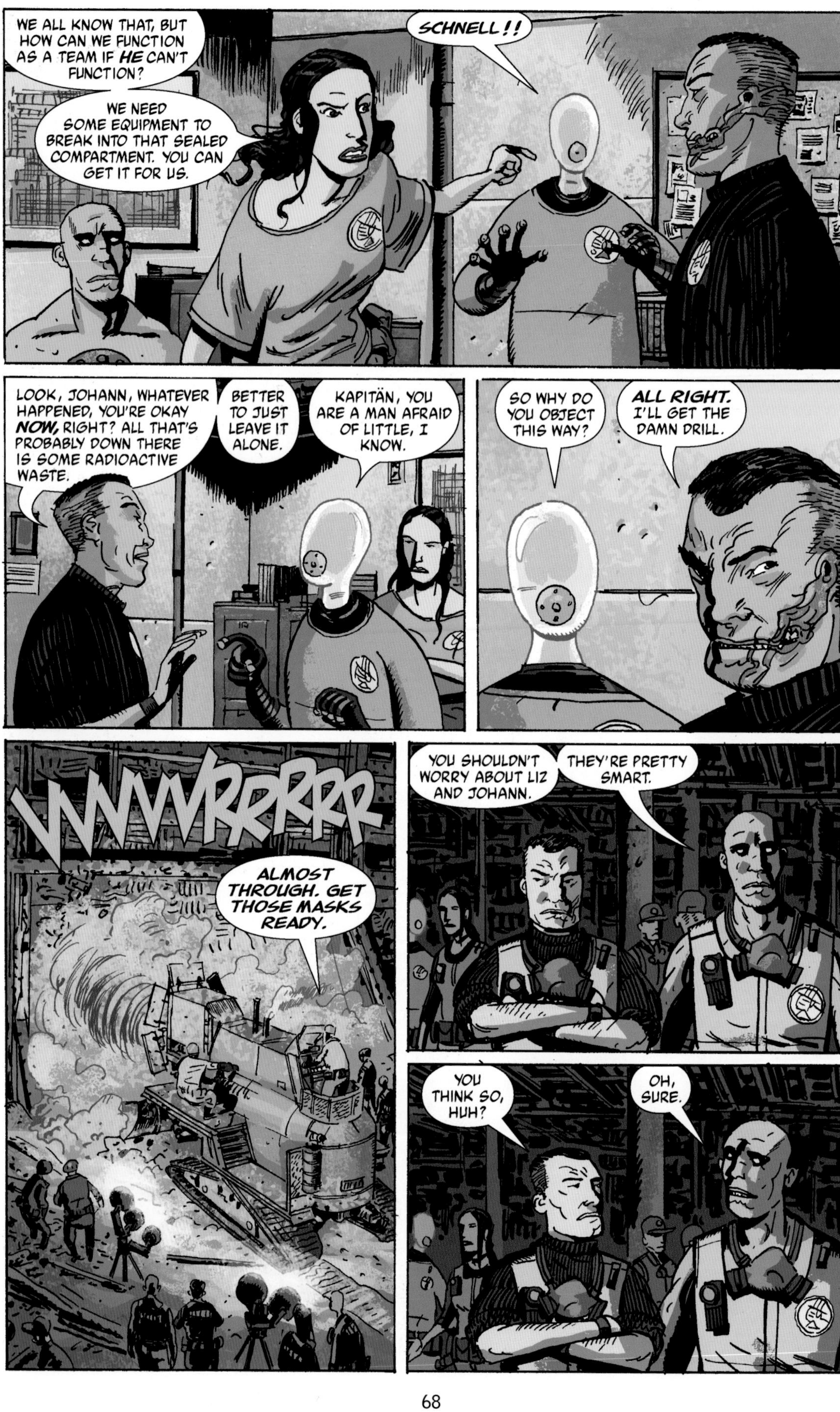
WE ALL KNOW THAT, BUT HOW CAN WE FUNCTION AS A TEAM IF HE CAN'T FUNCTION?
SCHNELL!!
WE NEED SOME EQUIPMENT TO BREAK INTO THAT SEALED COMPARTMENT. YOU CAN GET IT FOR US.
LOOK, JOHANN, WHATEVER HAPPENED, YOU'RE OKAY NOW, RIGHT? ALL THAT'S PROBABLY DOWN THERE IS SOME RADIOACTIVE WASTE.
BETTER TO JUST LEAVE IT ALONE.
KAPITÄN, YOU ARE A MAN AFRAID OF LITTLE, I KNOW.
SO WHY DO YOU OBJECT THIS WAY?
ALL RIGHT. I'LL GET THE DAMN DRILL.
VVVVVRRRRR
ALMOST THROUGH. GET THOSE MASKS READY.
YOU SHOULDN'T WORRY ABOUT LIZ AND JOHANN.
THEY'RE PRETTY SMART.
YOU THINK SO, HUH?
OH, SURE.

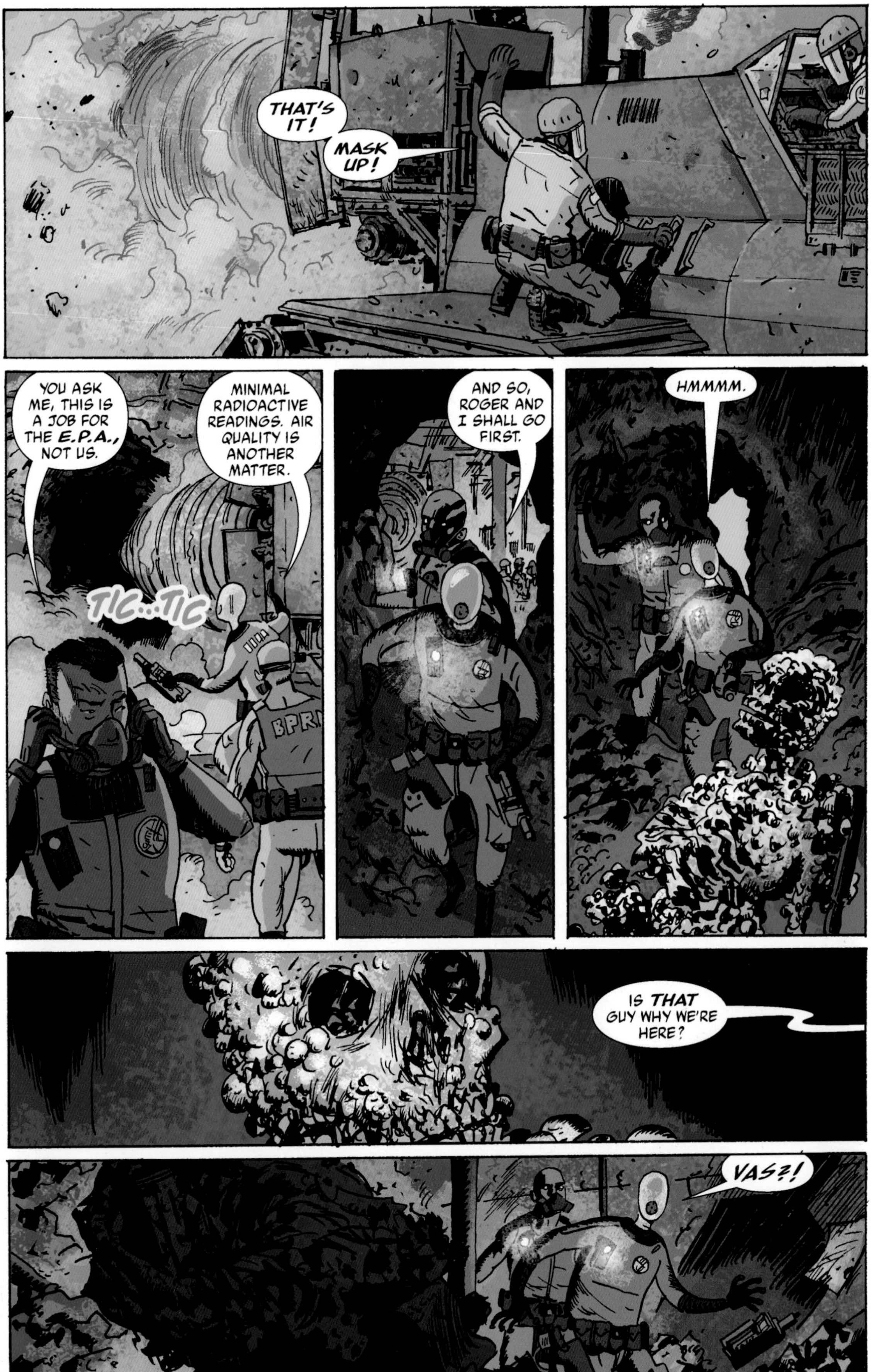
THAT'S IT!
MASK UP!
YOU ASK ME, THIS IS A JOB FOR THE E.P.A., NOT US.
MINIMAL RADIOACTIVE READINGS. AIR QUALITY IS ANOTHER MATTER.
TIC...TIC
BPRD
AND SO, ROGER AND I SHALL GO FIRST.
HMMMM.
IS THAT GUY WHY WE'RE HERE?
VAS?!

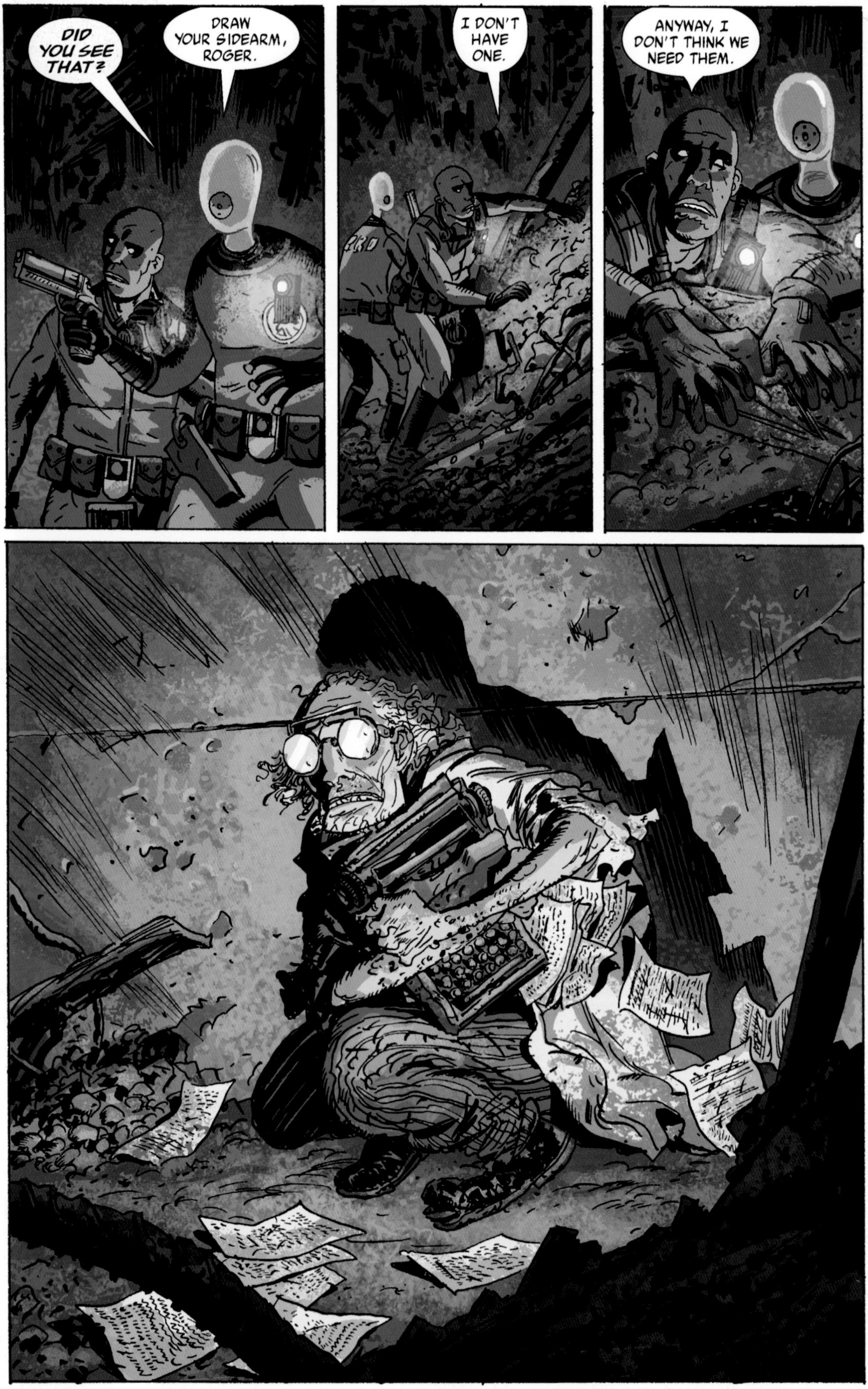
DID YOU SEE THAT?
DRAW YOUR SIDEARM, ROGER.
I DON'T HAVE ONE.
ANYWAY, I DON'T THINK WE NEED THEM.

CHAPTER THREE

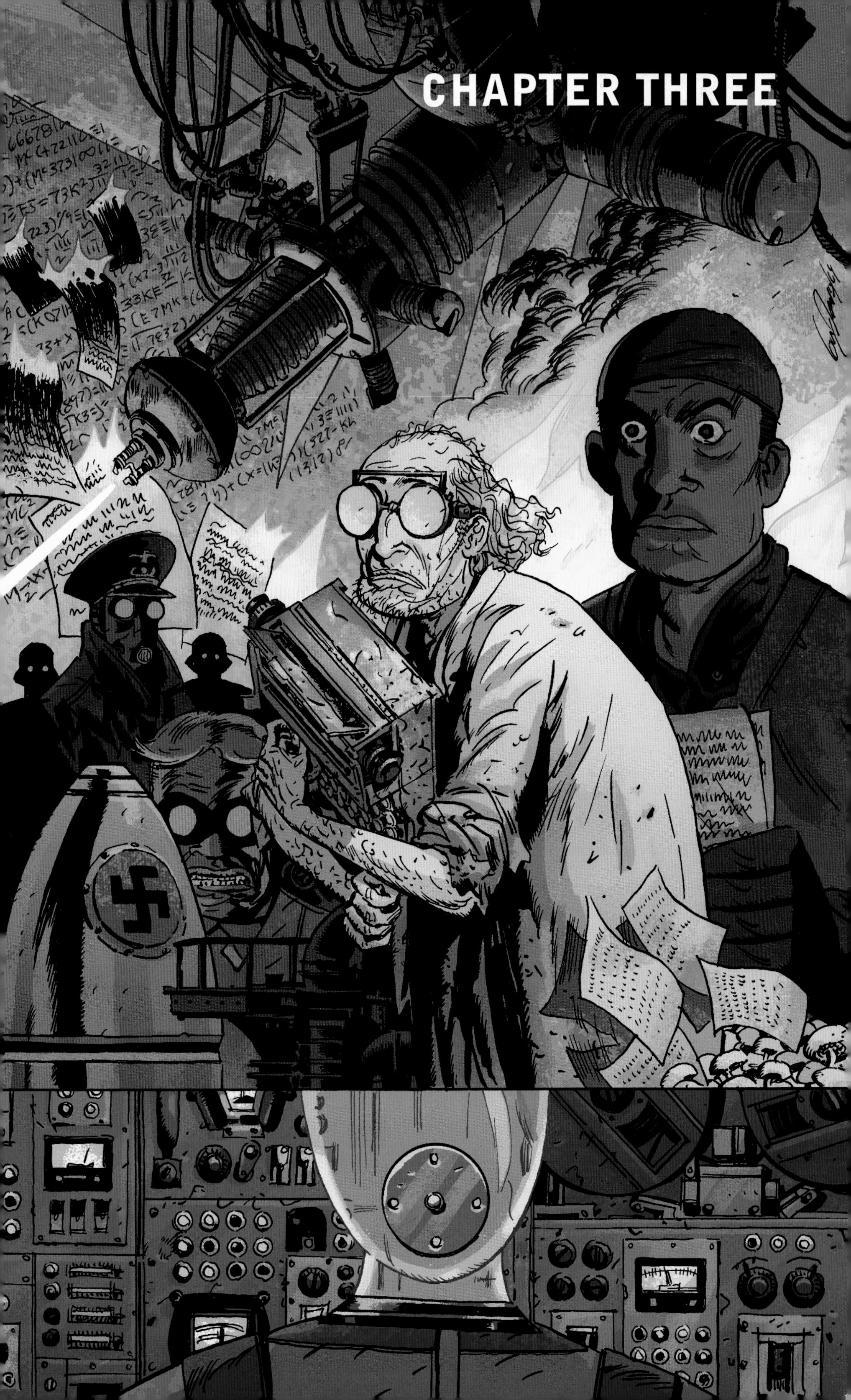

SO WHERE IS JOHANN NOW?

DOWN BELOW, IN THE SUB-BASEMENT, DOING A SITE ASSESSMENT.

WHY?

I MEAN, WE GOT THE GUY OUT, DIDN'T WE? WE'VE GOT SOME FROGS TO KILL, LADY.

YOU SAW THOSE BODIES DOWN THERE. SOMETHING HAPPENED. JOHANN MIGHT BE ABLE TO GET A READING.

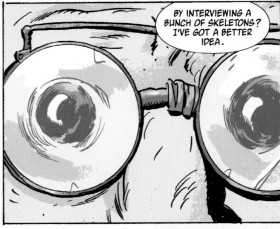

BY INTERVIEWING A BUNCH OF SKELETONS? I'VE GOT A BETTER IDEA.

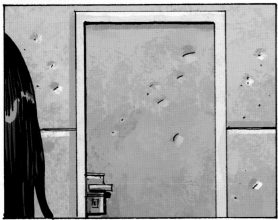

HEY, PAL. HOW YOU DOING?

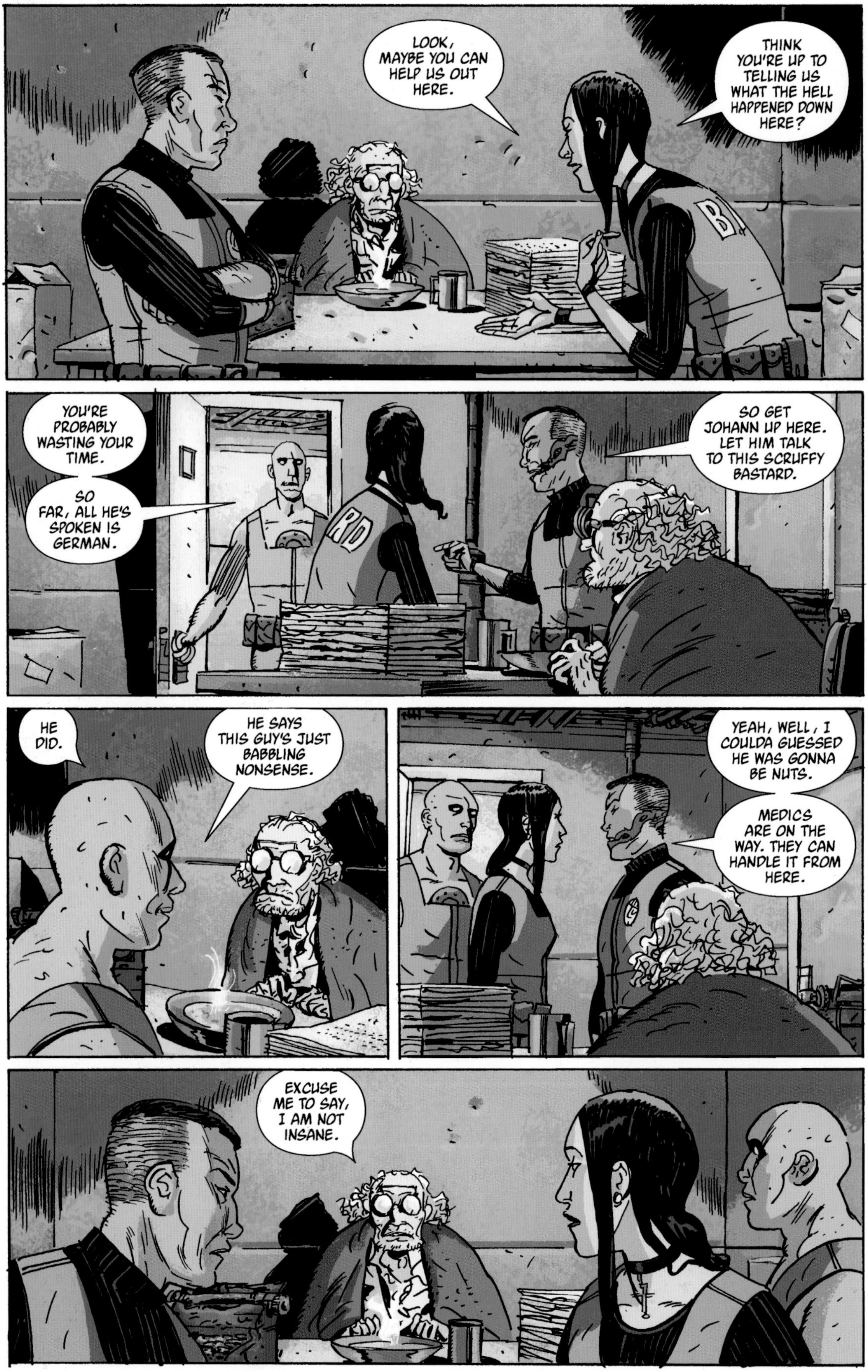
LOOK, MAYBE YOU CAN HELP US OUT HERE.
THINK YOU'RE UP TO TELLING US WHAT THE HELL HAPPENED DOWN HERE?
YOU'RE PROBABLY WASTING YOUR TIME.
SO FAR, ALL HE'S SPOKEN IS GERMAN.
SO GET JOHANN UP HERE. LET HIM TALK TO THIS SCRUFFY BASTARD.
HE DID.
HE SAYS THIS GUY'S JUST BABBLING NONSENSE.
YEAH, WELL, I COULDA GUESSED HE WAS GONNA BE NUTS.
MEDICS ARE ON THE WAY. THEY CAN HANDLE IT FROM HERE.
EXCUSE ME TO SAY, I AM NOT INSANE.

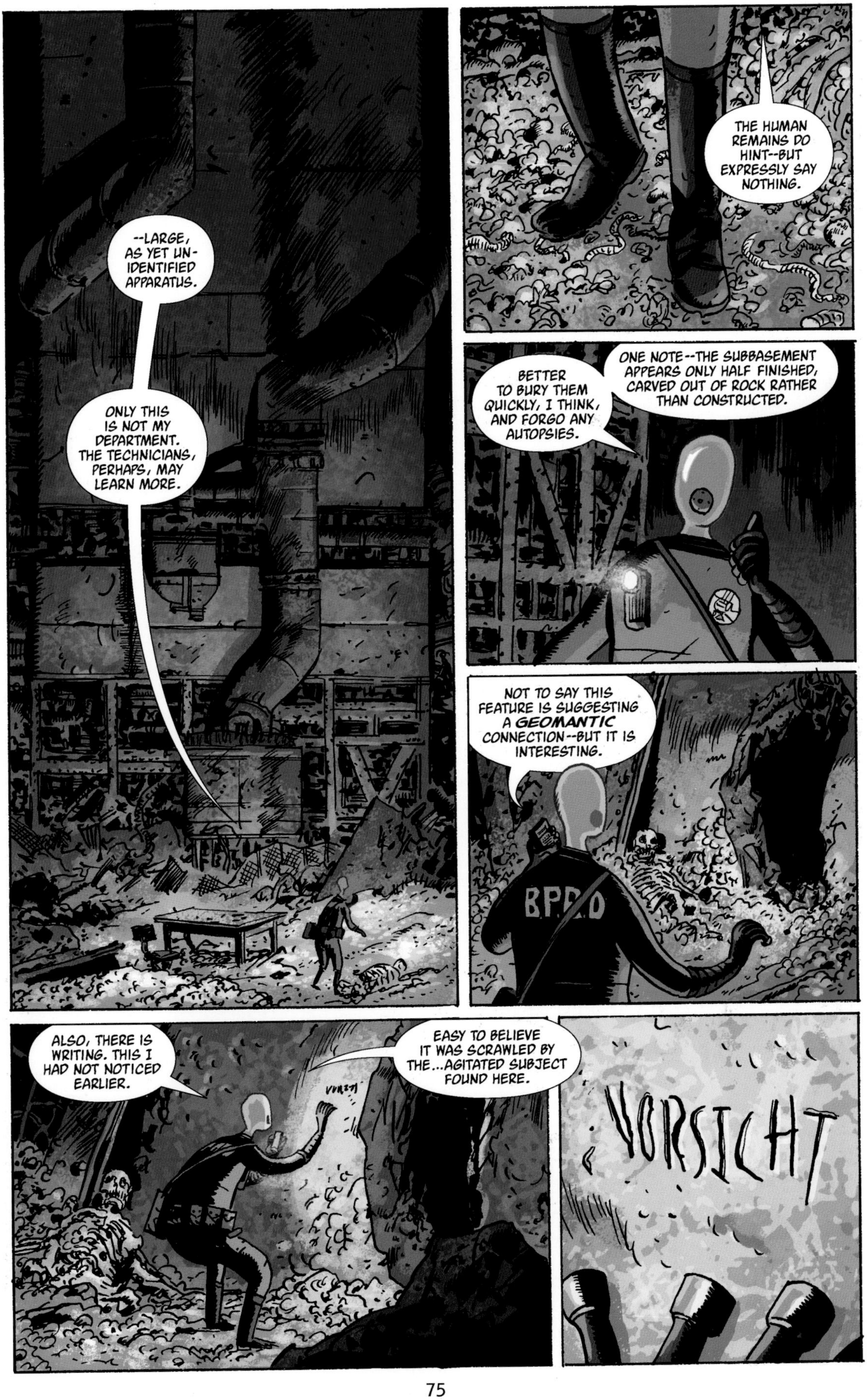
--LARGE, AS YET UN-IDENTIFIED APPARATUS.
ONLY THIS IS NOT MY DEPARTMENT. THE TECHNICIANS, PERHAPS, MAY LEARN MORE.
THE HUMAN REMAINS DO HINT--BUT EXPRESSLY SAY NOTHING.
BETTER TO BURY THEM QUICKLY, I THINK, AND FORGO ANY AUTOPSIES.
ONE NOTE--THE SUBBASEMENT APPEARS ONLY HALF FINISHED, CARVED OUT OF ROCK RATHER THAN CONSTRUCTED.
NOT TO SAY THIS FEATURE IS SUGGESTING A GEOMANTIC CONNECTION--BUT IT IS INTERESTING.
B.P.R.D
ALSO, THERE IS WRITING. THIS I HAD NOT NOTICED EARLIER.
EASY TO BELIEVE IT WAS SCRAWLED BY THE...AGITATED SUBJECT FOUND HERE.
VORSICHT

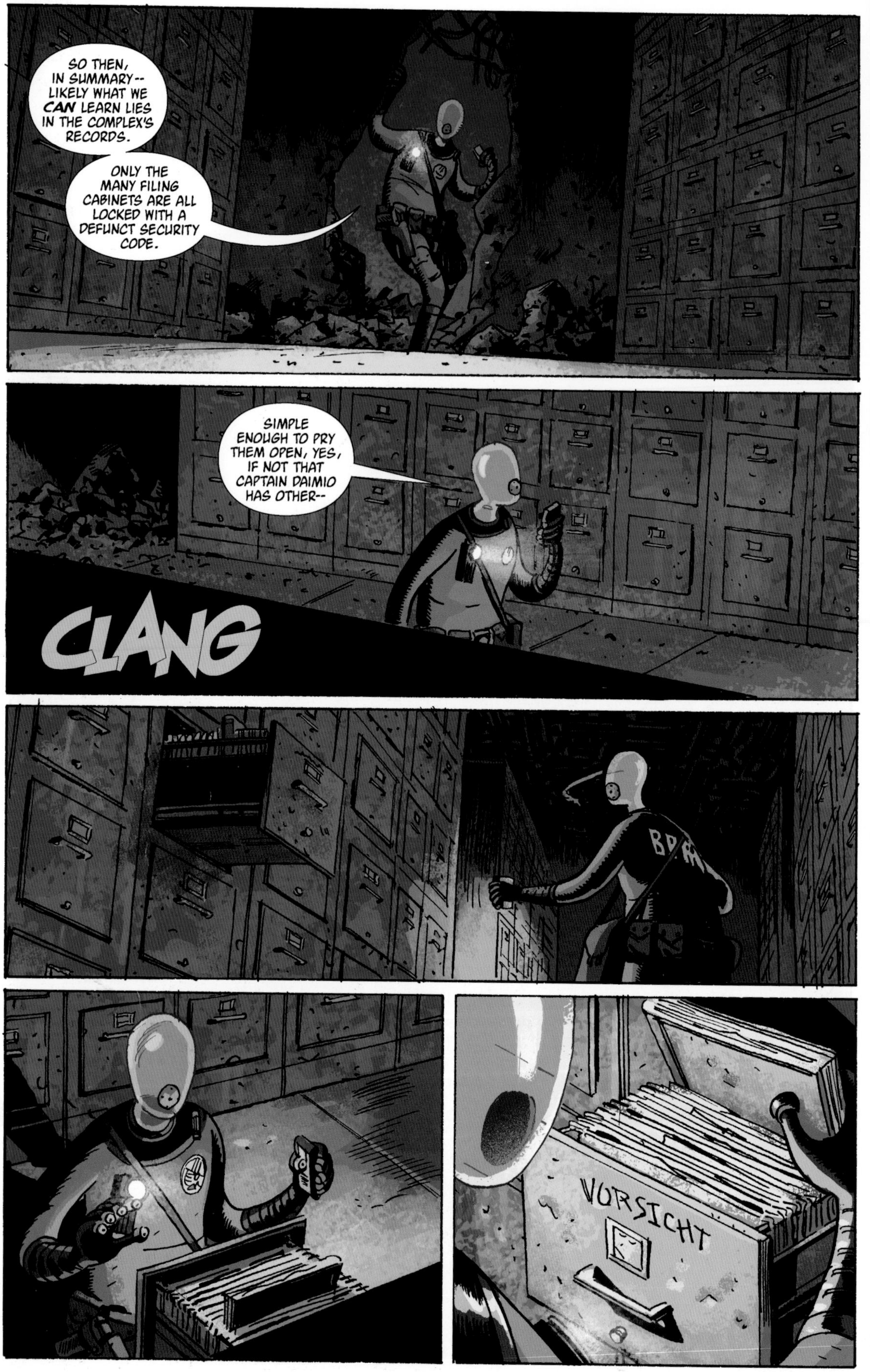
SO THEN, IN SUMMARY-- LIKELY WHAT WE CAN LEARN LIES IN THE COMPLEX'S RECORDS.
ONLY THE MANY FILING CABINETS ARE ALL LOCKED WITH A DEFUNCT SECURITY CODE.
SIMPLE ENOUGH TO PRY THEM OPEN, YES, IF NOT THAT CAPTAIN DAIMIO HAS OTHER--
CLANG
VORSICHT

YOU-- YOU SPEAK ENGLISH?

OF COURSE. HAVEN'T YOU READ MY NOTES?

IT IS ONLY THE LONG ISOLATION WHICH HAS MADE ME... CAUTIOUS.

AND WHEN I SAW *HIM* WITH THE BUBBLE MAN COMING TO GET ME, I THOUGHT THE MONSTERS HAD TAKEN OVER.

THE MONSTERS?

THE CAPTAIN KNOWS WHAT I AM SAYING. HE KNOWS.

?

OKAY, SO YOU'RE NOT NUTS. THEN MAYBE YOU CAN TELL US WHAT WENT ON DOWN THERE IN YOUR LITTLE HIDEY-HOLE.

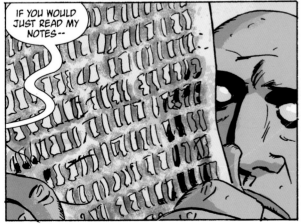

IF YOU WOULD JUST READ MY NOTES--

--BUT VERY WELL.

I AM DR. GUNTER EISS.

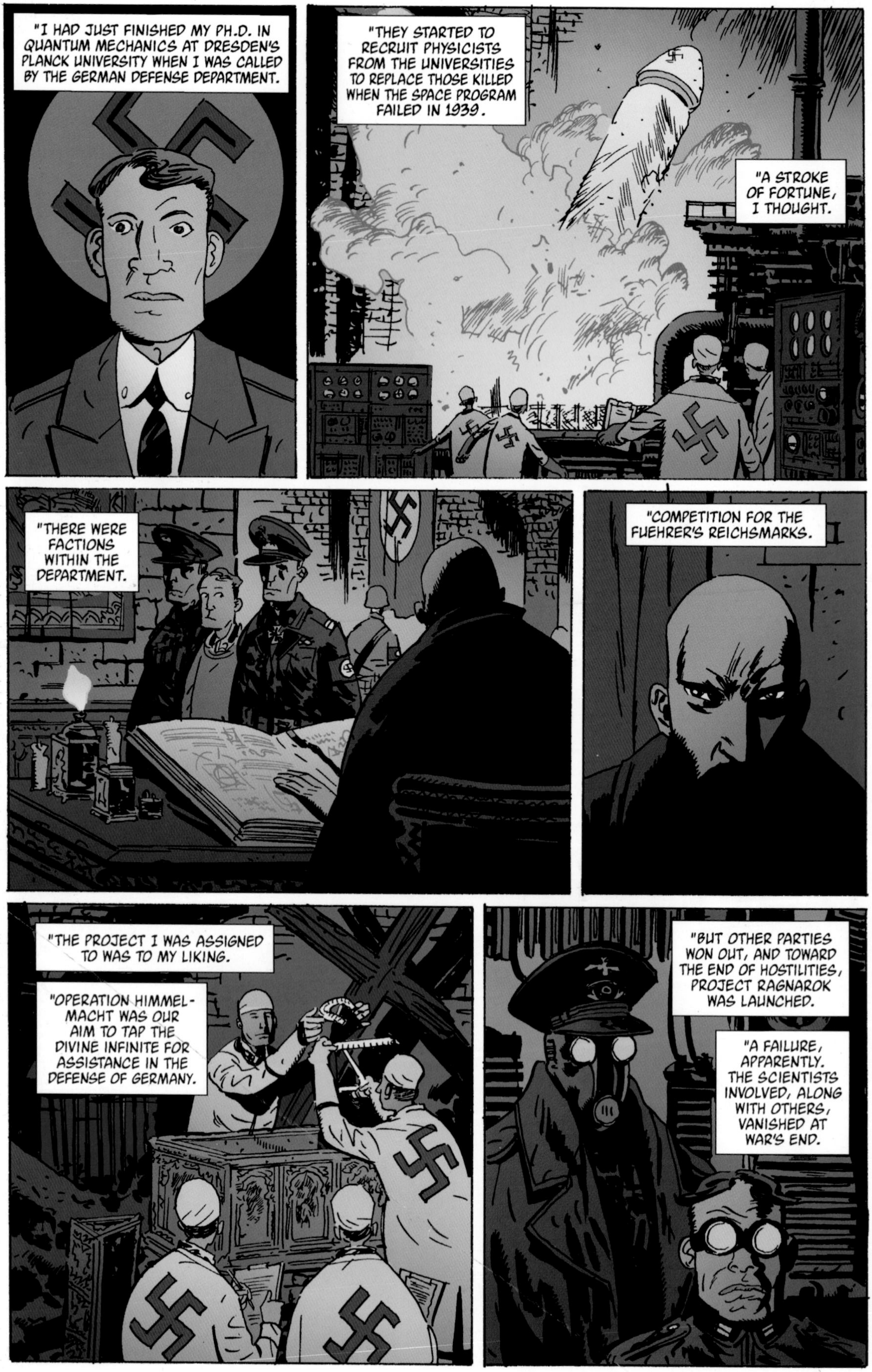
"I HAD JUST FINISHED MY PH.D. IN QUANTUM MECHANICS AT DRESDEN'S PLANCK UNIVERSITY WHEN I WAS CALLED BY THE GERMAN DEFENSE DEPARTMENT.
"THEY STARTED TO RECRUIT PHYSICISTS FROM THE UNIVERSITIES TO REPLACE THOSE KILLED WHEN THE SPACE PROGRAM FAILED IN 1939.
"A STROKE OF FORTUNE, I THOUGHT.
"THERE WERE FACTIONS WITHIN THE DEPARTMENT.
"COMPETITION FOR THE FUEHRER'S REICHSMARKS.
"THE PROJECT I WAS ASSIGNED TO WAS TO MY LIKING.
"OPERATION HIMMEL-MACHT WAS OUR AIM TO TAP THE DIVINE INFINITE FOR ASSISTANCE IN THE DEFENSE OF GERMANY.
"BUT OTHER PARTIES WON OUT, AND TOWARD THE END OF HOSTILITIES, PROJECT RAGNAROK WAS LAUNCHED.
"A FAILURE, APPARENTLY. THE SCIENTISTS INVOLVED, ALONG WITH OTHERS, VANISHED AT WAR'S END.

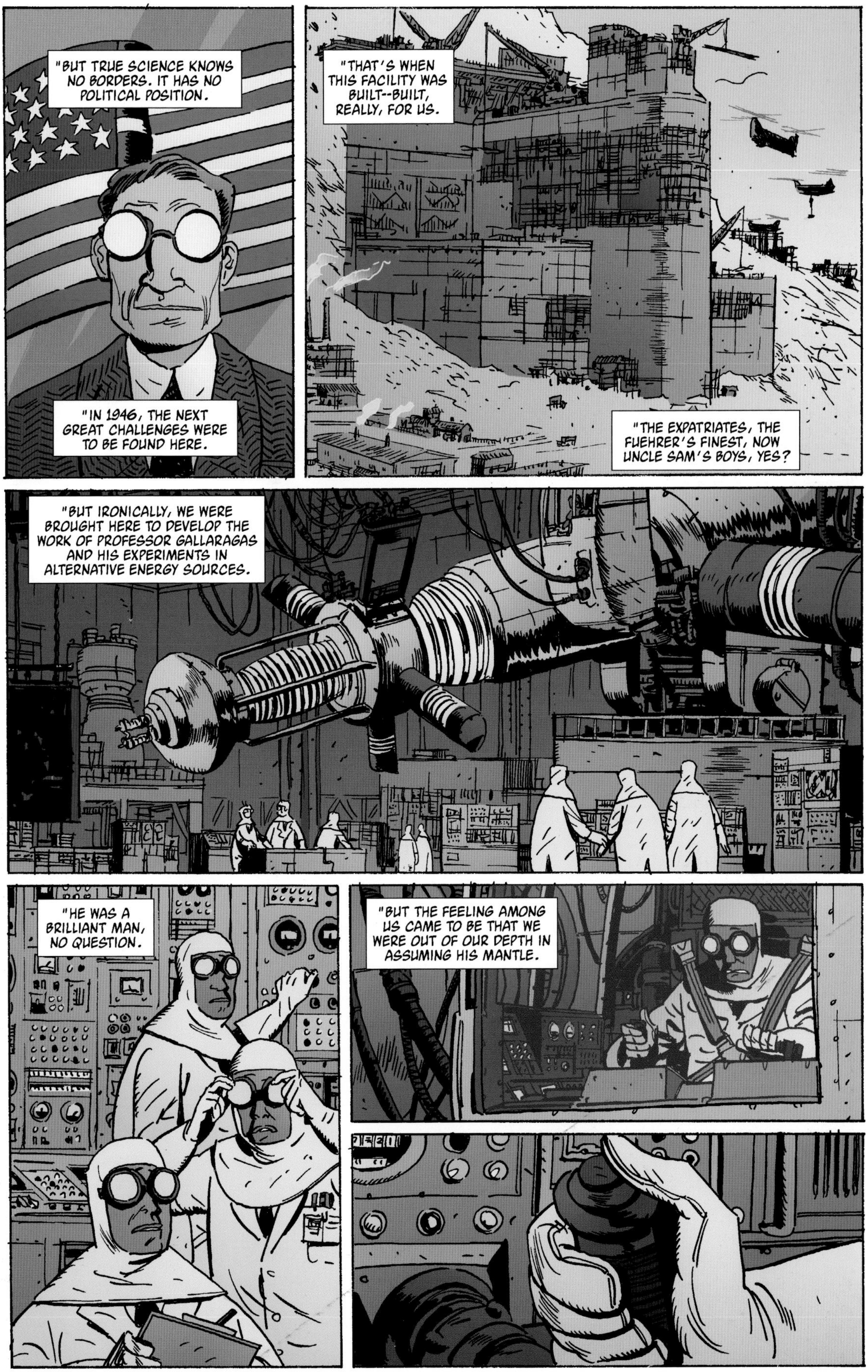
"BUT TRUE SCIENCE KNOWS NO BORDERS. IT HAS NO POLITICAL POSITION.
"IN 1946, THE NEXT GREAT CHALLENGES WERE TO BE FOUND HERE.
"THAT'S WHEN THIS FACILITY WAS BUILT--BUILT, REALLY, FOR US.
"THE EXPATRIATES, THE FUEHRER'S FINEST, NOW UNCLE SAM'S BOYS, YES?
"BUT IRONICALLY, WE WERE BROUGHT HERE TO DEVELOP THE WORK OF PROFESSOR GALLARAGAS AND HIS EXPERIMENTS IN ALTERNATIVE ENERGY SOURCES.
"HE WAS A BRILLIANT MAN, NO QUESTION.
"BUT THE FEELING AMONG US CAME TO BE THAT WE WERE OUT OF OUR DEPTH IN ASSUMING HIS MANTLE.

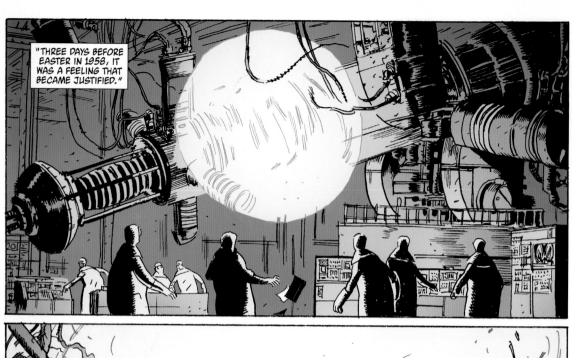

"THREE DAYS BEFORE EASTER IN 1958, IT WAS A FEELING THAT BECAME JUSTIFIED."

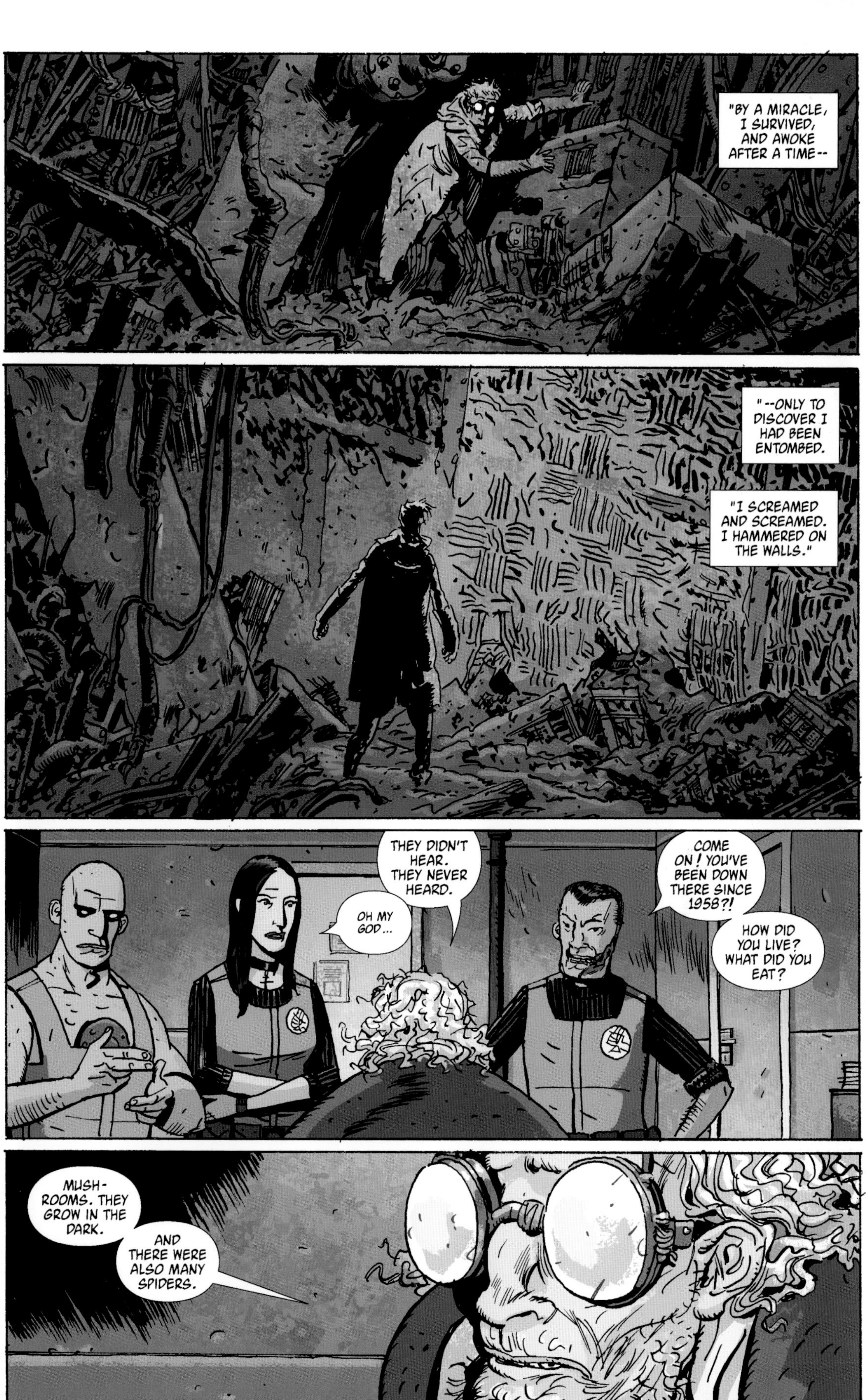
"BY A MIRACLE, I SURVIVED, AND AWOKE AFTER A TIME--
"--ONLY TO DISCOVER I HAD BEEN ENTOMBED.
"I SCREAMED AND SCREAMED. I HAMMERED ON THE WALLS."
THEY DIDN'T HEAR. THEY NEVER HEARD.
OH MY GOD...
COME ON! YOU'VE BEEN DOWN THERE SINCE 1958?!
HOW DID YOU LIVE? WHAT DID YOU EAT?
MUSH-ROOMS. THEY GROW IN THE DARK.
AND THERE WERE ALSO MANY SPIDERS.

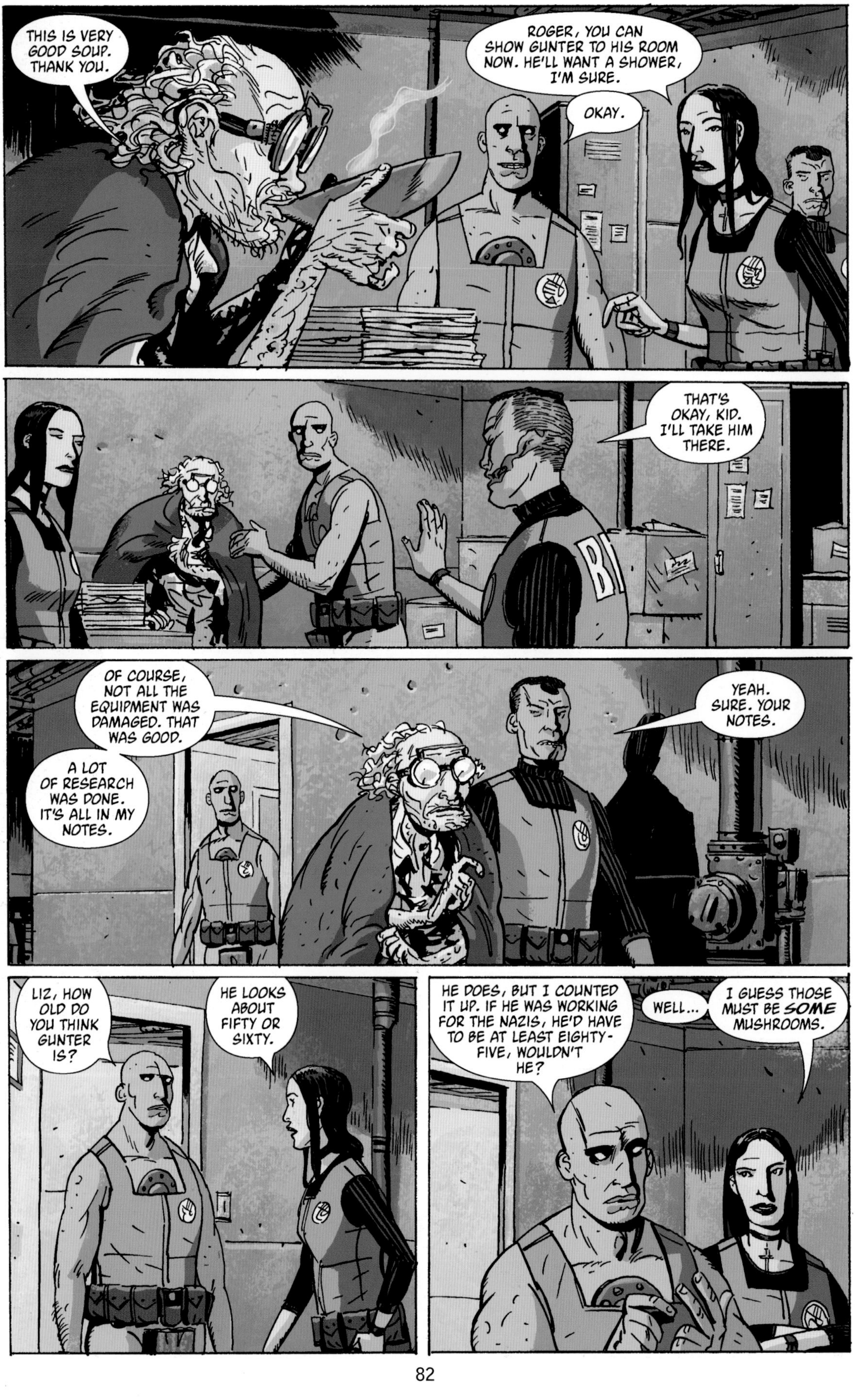
THIS IS VERY GOOD SOUP. THANK YOU.
ROGER, YOU CAN SHOW GUNTER TO HIS ROOM NOW. HE'LL WANT A SHOWER, I'M SURE.
OKAY.
THAT'S OKAY, KID. I'LL TAKE HIM THERE.
OF COURSE, NOT ALL THE EQUIPMENT WAS DAMAGED. THAT WAS GOOD.
A LOT OF RESEARCH WAS DONE. IT'S ALL IN MY NOTES.
YEAH. SURE. YOUR NOTES.
LIZ, HOW OLD DO YOU THINK GUNTER IS?
HE LOOKS ABOUT FIFTY OR SIXTY.
HE DOES, BUT I COUNTED IT UP. IF HE WAS WORKING FOR THE NAZIS, HE'D HAVE TO BE AT LEAST EIGHTY-FIVE, WOULDN'T HE?
WELL...
I GUESS THOSE MUST BE *SOME* MUSHROOMS.

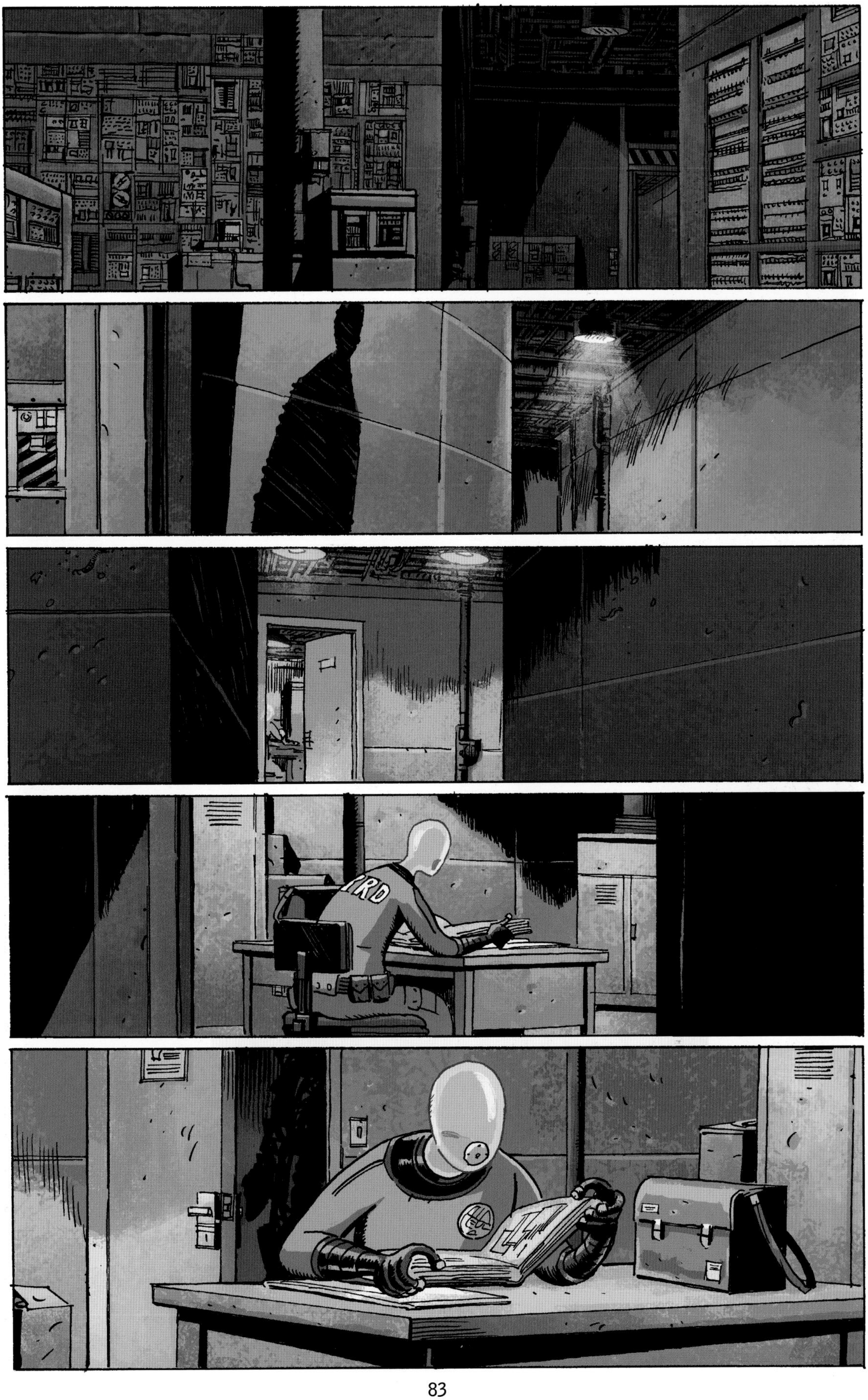

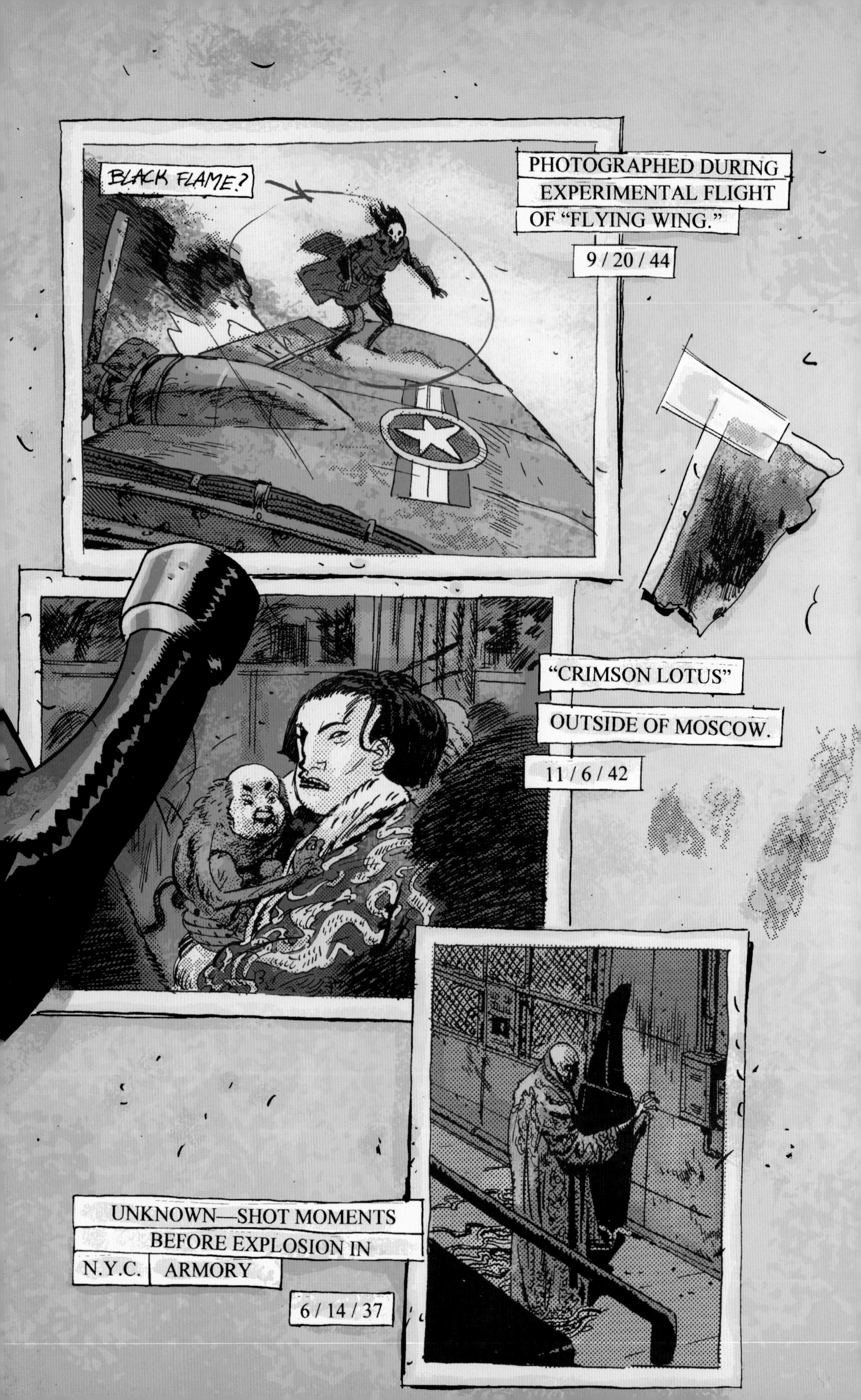
BLACK FLAME?
PHOTOGRAPHED DURING
EXPERIMENTAL FLIGHT
OF "FLYING WING."
9 / 20 / 44
"CRIMSON LOTUS"
OUTSIDE OF MOSCOW.
11 / 6 / 42
UNKNOWN—SHOT MOMENTS
BEFORE EXPLOSION IN
N.Y.C. ARMORY
6 / 14 / 37

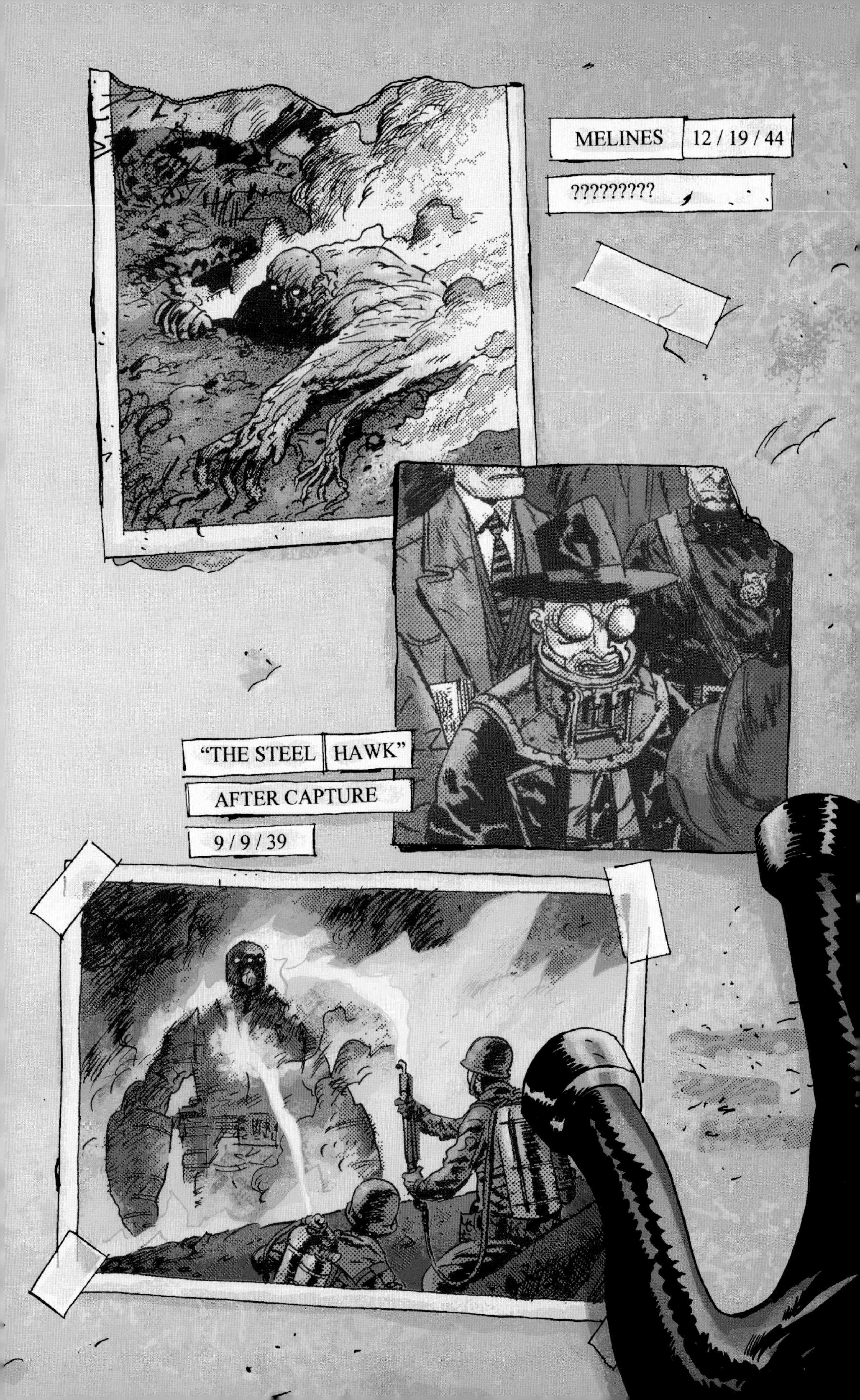
MELINES 12 / 19 / 44
?????????
"THE STEEL HAWK"
AFTER CAPTURE
9 / 9 / 39

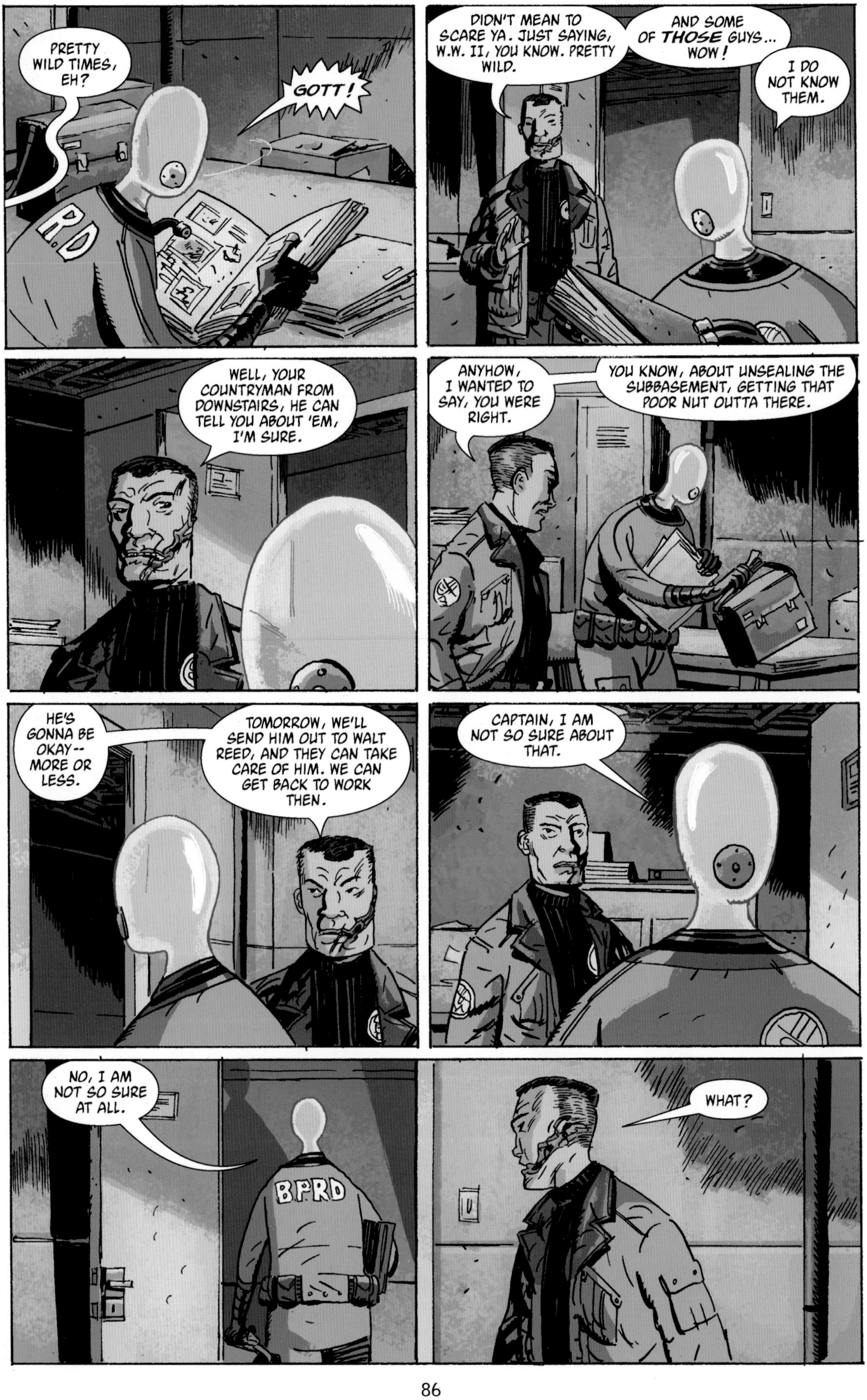
PRETTY WILD TIMES, EH?
GOTT!
DIDN'T MEAN TO SCARE YA. JUST SAYING, W.W. II, YOU KNOW. PRETTY WILD.
AND SOME OF THOSE GUYS... WOW!
I DO NOT KNOW THEM.
WELL, YOUR COUNTRYMAN FROM DOWNSTAIRS, HE CAN TELL YOU ABOUT 'EM, I'M SURE.
ANYHOW, I WANTED TO SAY, YOU WERE RIGHT.
YOU KNOW, ABOUT UNSEALING THE SUBBASEMENT, GETTING THAT POOR NUT OUTTA THERE.
HE'S GONNA BE OKAY-- MORE OR LESS.
TOMORROW, WE'LL SEND HIM OUT TO WALT REED, AND THEY CAN TAKE CARE OF HIM. WE CAN GET BACK TO WORK THEN.
CAPTAIN, I AM NOT SO SURE ABOUT THAT.
NO, I AM NOT SO SURE AT ALL.
B.P.R.D
WHAT?

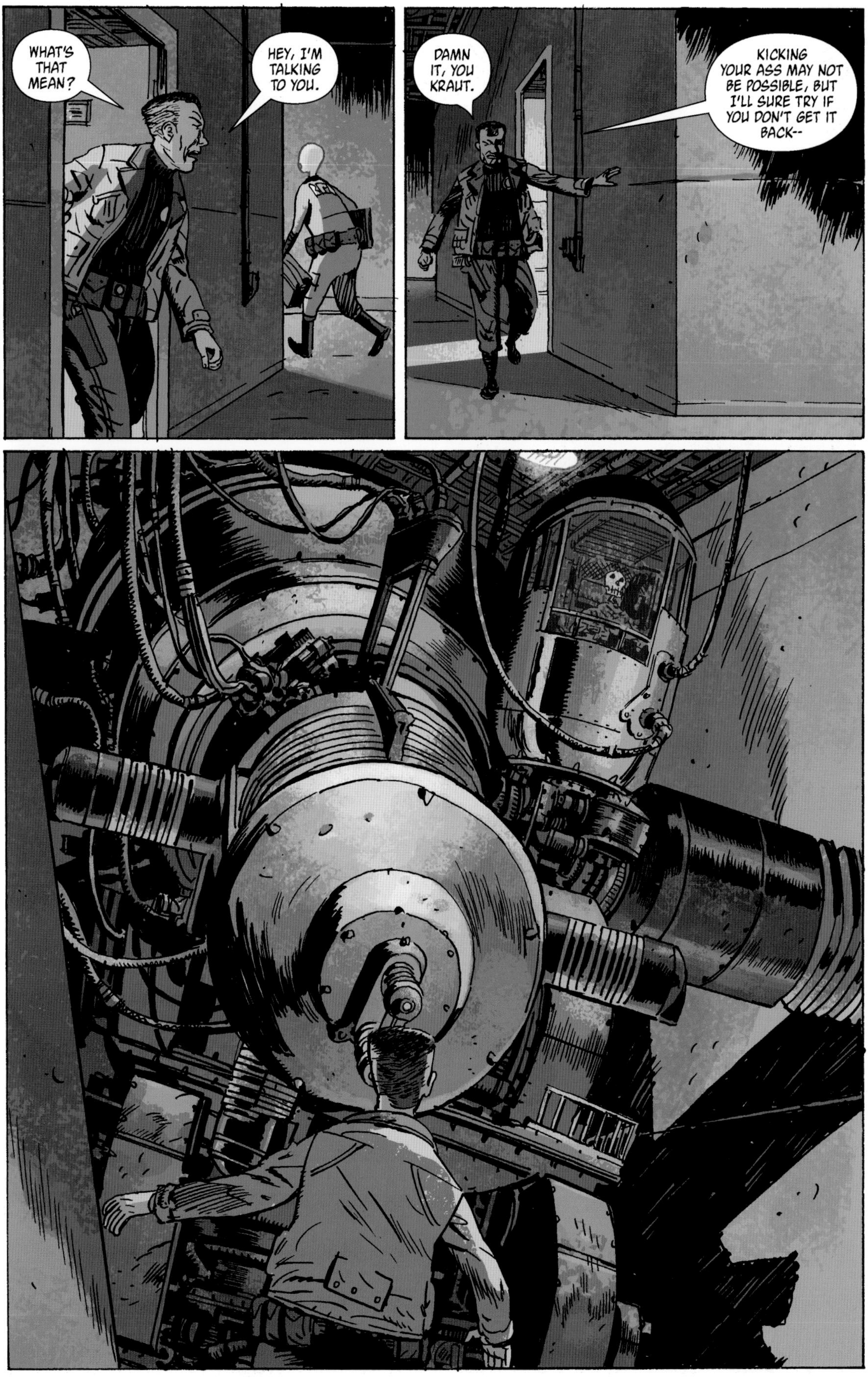
WHAT'S THAT MEAN?
HEY, I'M TALKING TO YOU.
DAMN IT, YOU KRAUT.
KICKING YOUR ASS MAY NOT BE POSSIBLE, BUT I'LL SURE TRY IF YOU DON'T GET IT BACK--

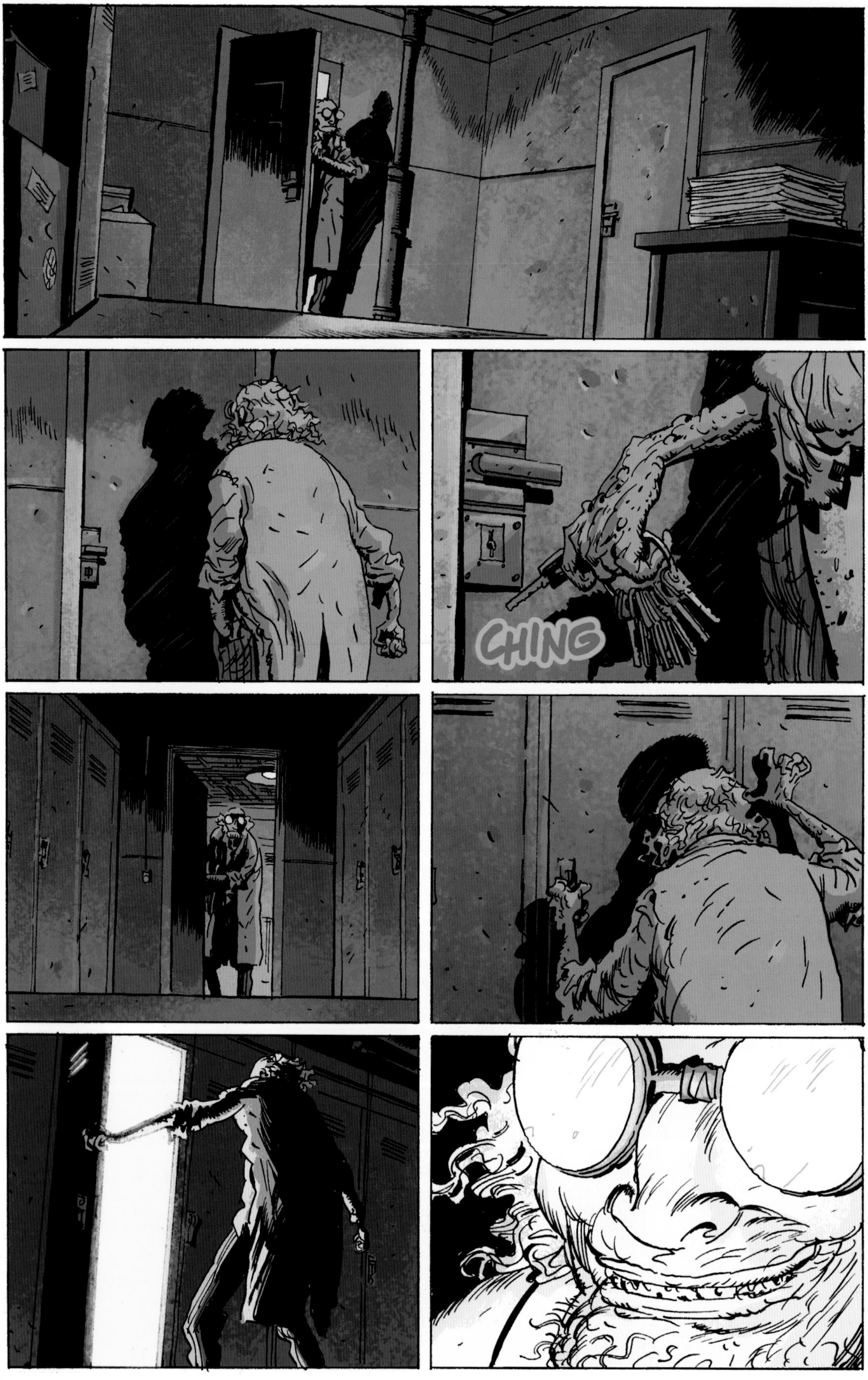
CHING

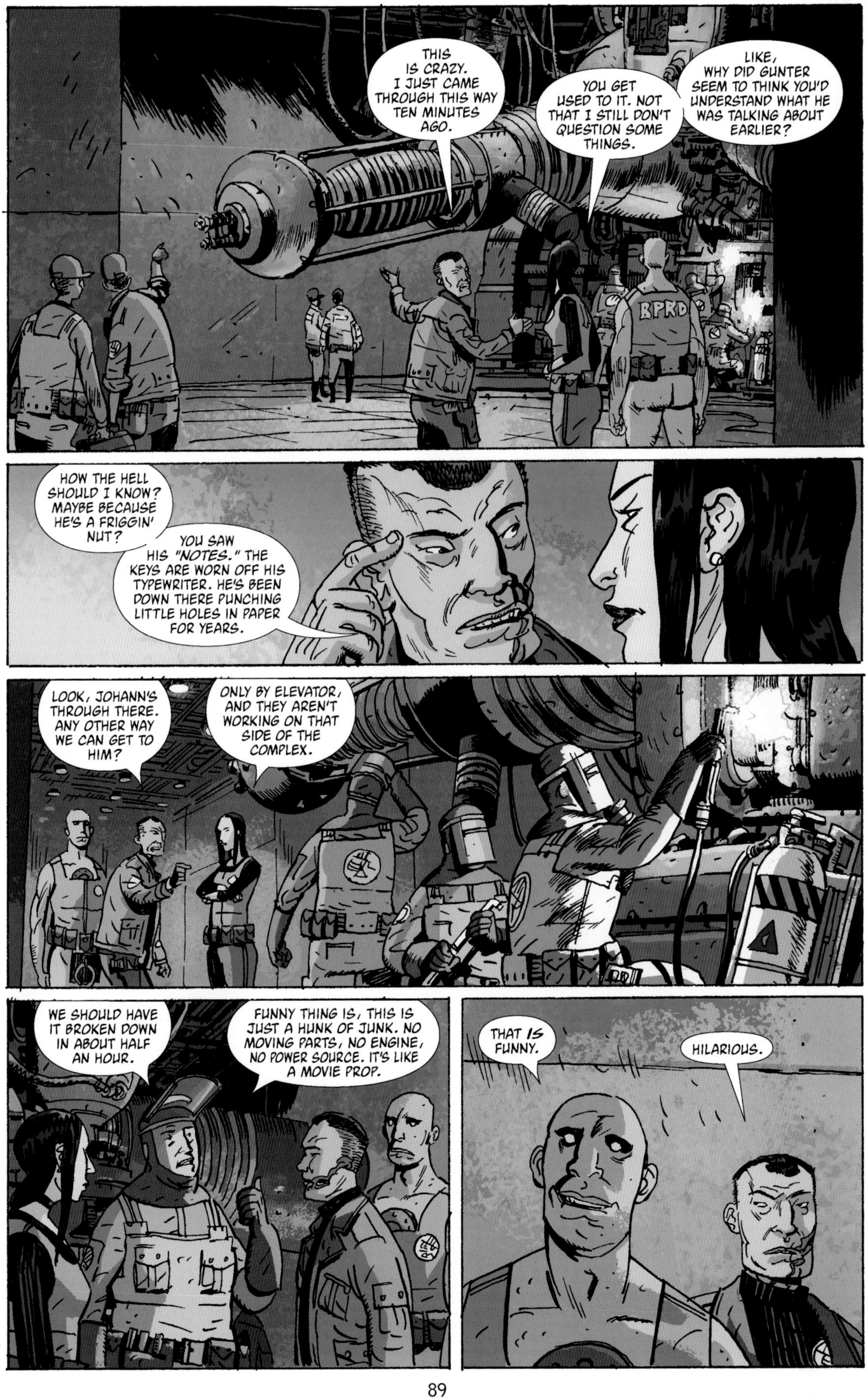
THIS IS CRAZY. I JUST CAME THROUGH THIS WAY TEN MINUTES AGO.
YOU GET USED TO IT. NOT THAT I STILL DON'T QUESTION SOME THINGS.
LIKE, WHY DID GUNTER SEEM TO THINK YOU'D UNDERSTAND WHAT HE WAS TALKING ABOUT EARLIER?
BPRD
HOW THE HELL SHOULD I KNOW? MAYBE BECAUSE HE'S A FRIGGIN' NUT?
YOU SAW HIS "NOTES." THE KEYS ARE WORN OFF HIS TYPEWRITER. HE'S BEEN DOWN THERE PUNCHING LITTLE HOLES IN PAPER FOR YEARS.
LOOK, JOHANN'S THROUGH THERE. ANY OTHER WAY WE CAN GET TO HIM?
ONLY BY ELEVATOR, AND THEY AREN'T WORKING ON THAT SIDE OF THE COMPLEX.
WE SHOULD HAVE IT BROKEN DOWN IN ABOUT HALF AN HOUR.
FUNNY THING IS, THIS IS JUST A HUNK OF JUNK. NO MOVING PARTS, NO ENGINE, NO POWER SOURCE. IT'S LIKE A MOVIE PROP.
THAT IS FUNNY.
HILARIOUS.

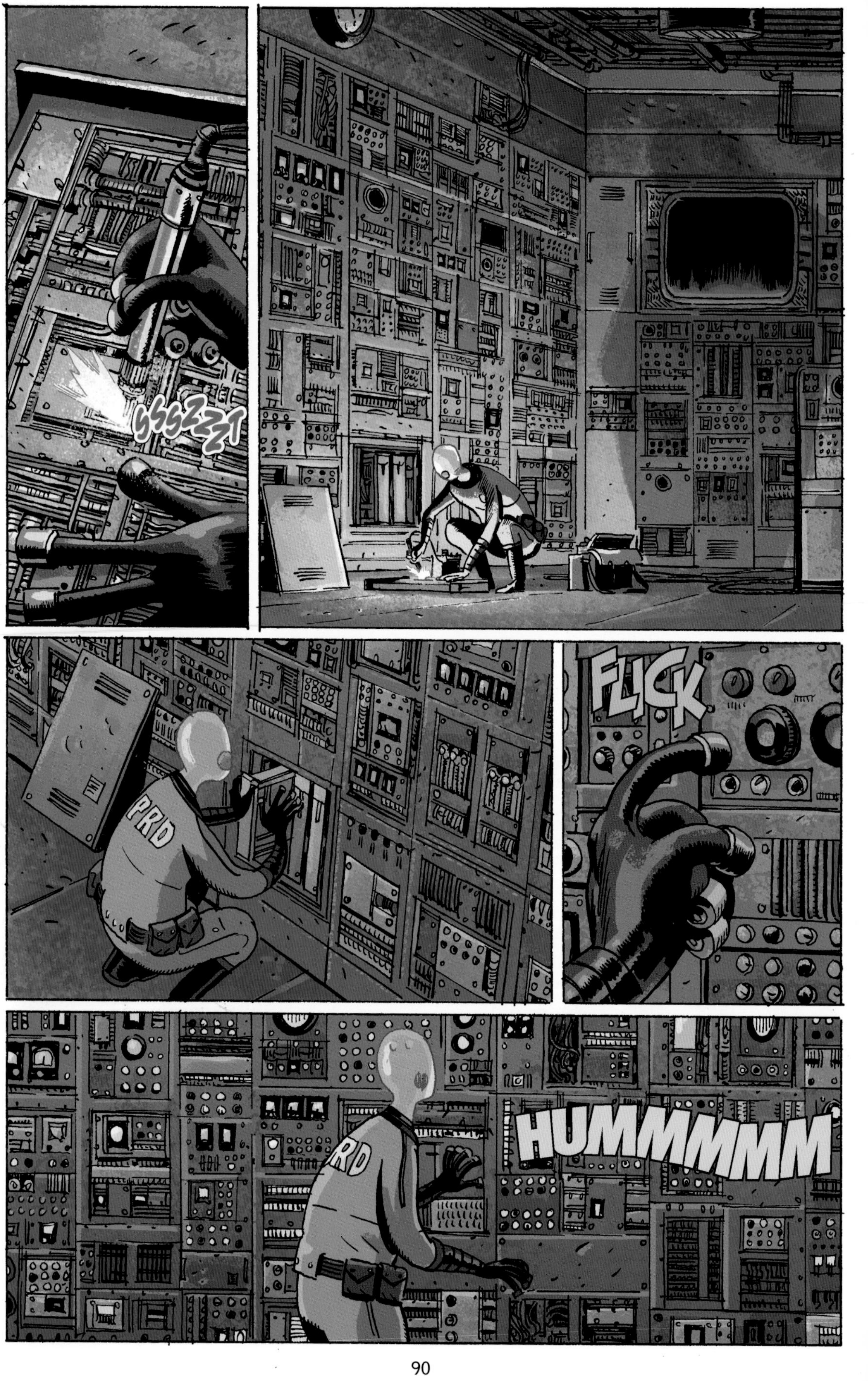
SSSZZZT
FLICK
HUMMMMMM

ClickCLICK CLICK CLICKETY CLICKETY·TICK TICK CLACKETY

TIC

VORSICHT, JOHANN

JA, "BEWARE."
ONLY, BEWARE
OF WHAT?

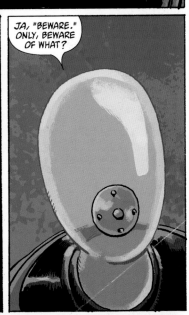

91

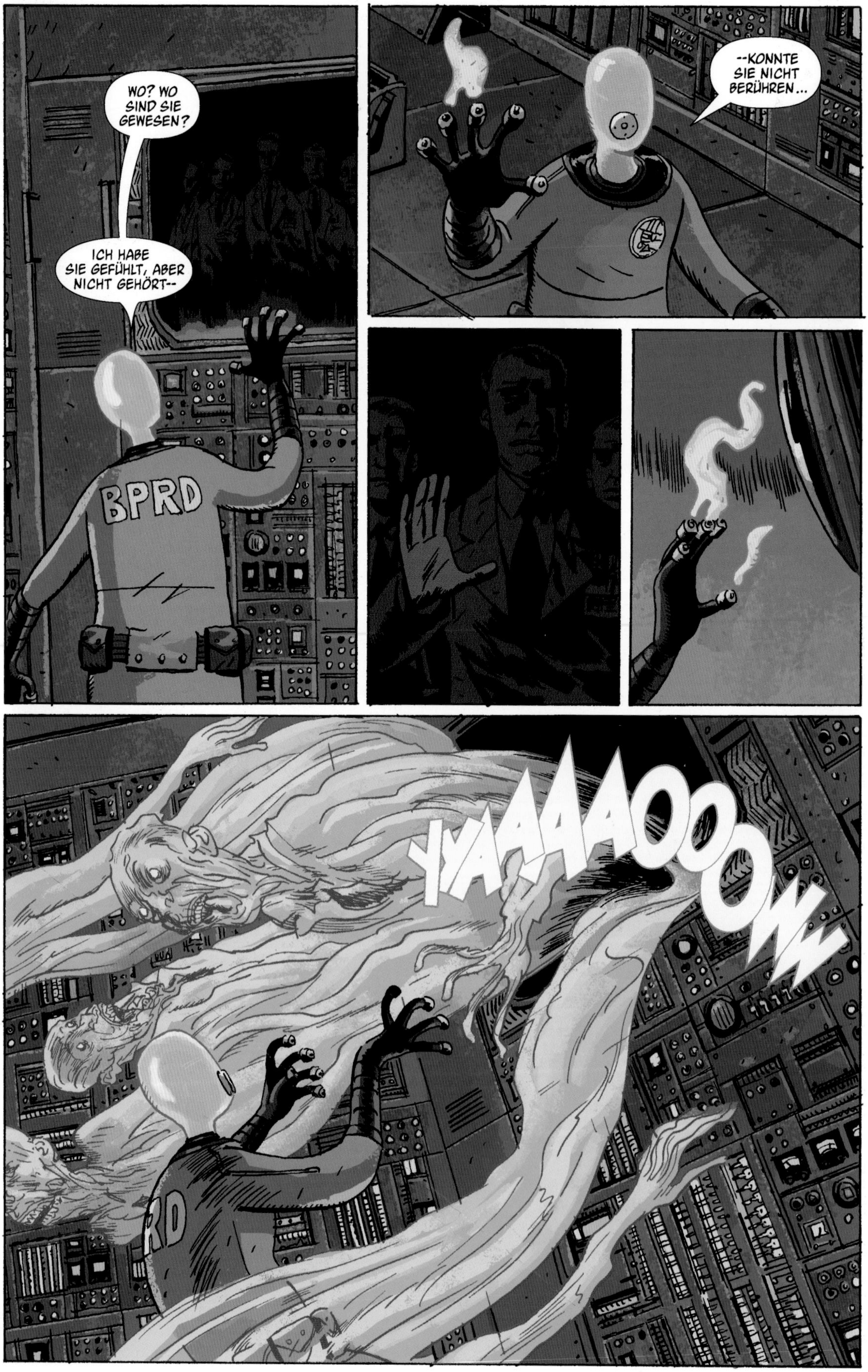
WO? WO SIND SIE GEWESEN?
ICH HABE SIE GEFÜHLT, ABER NICHT GEHÖRT--
--KONNTE SIE NICHT BERÜHREN...
YYAAAAOOOOW

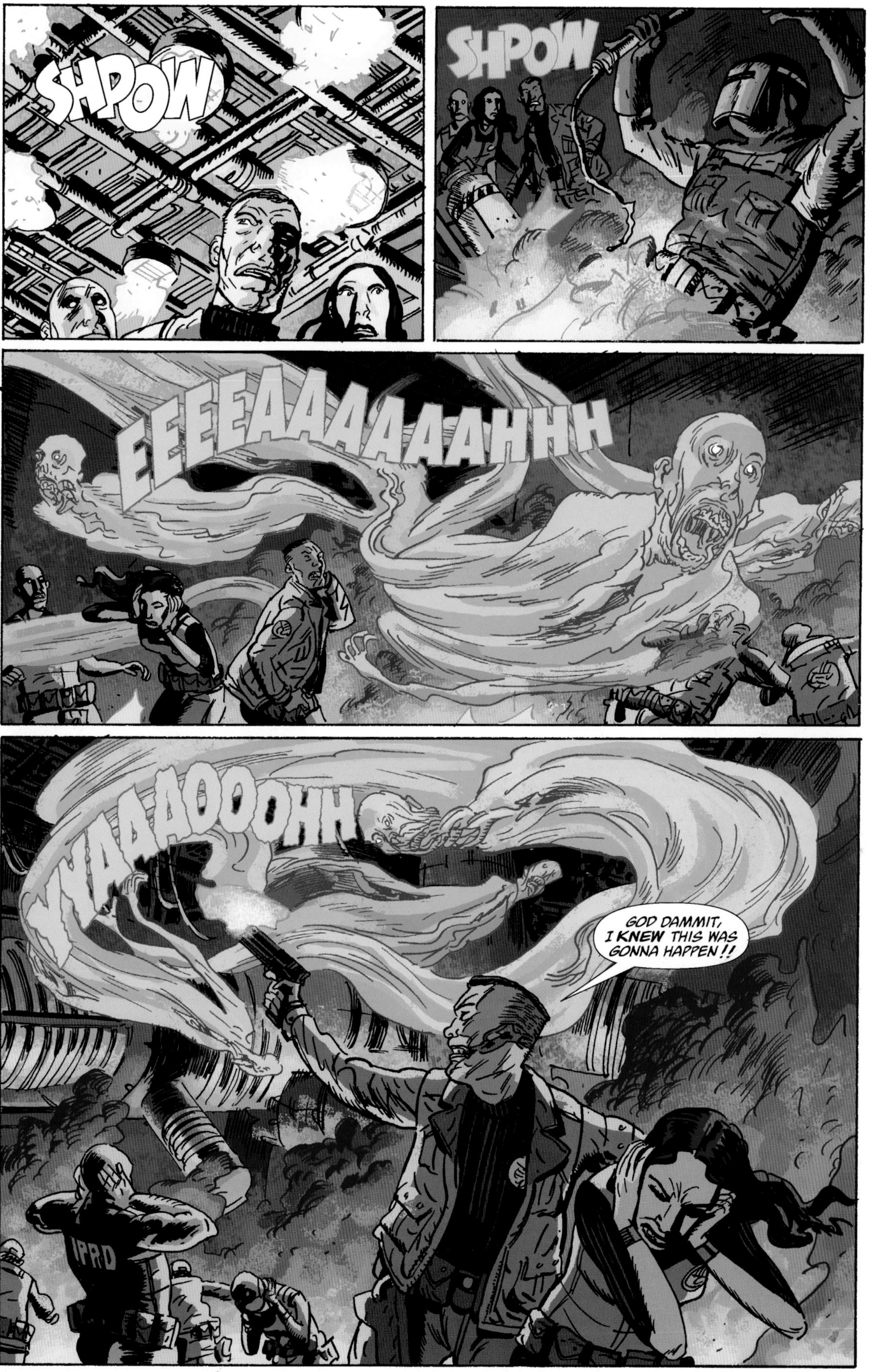
SHPOW
SHPOW
EEEEAAAAAAAHHH
YYAAAOOOOHH
GOD DAMMIT, I KNEW THIS WAS GONNA HAPPEN!!
IPRD

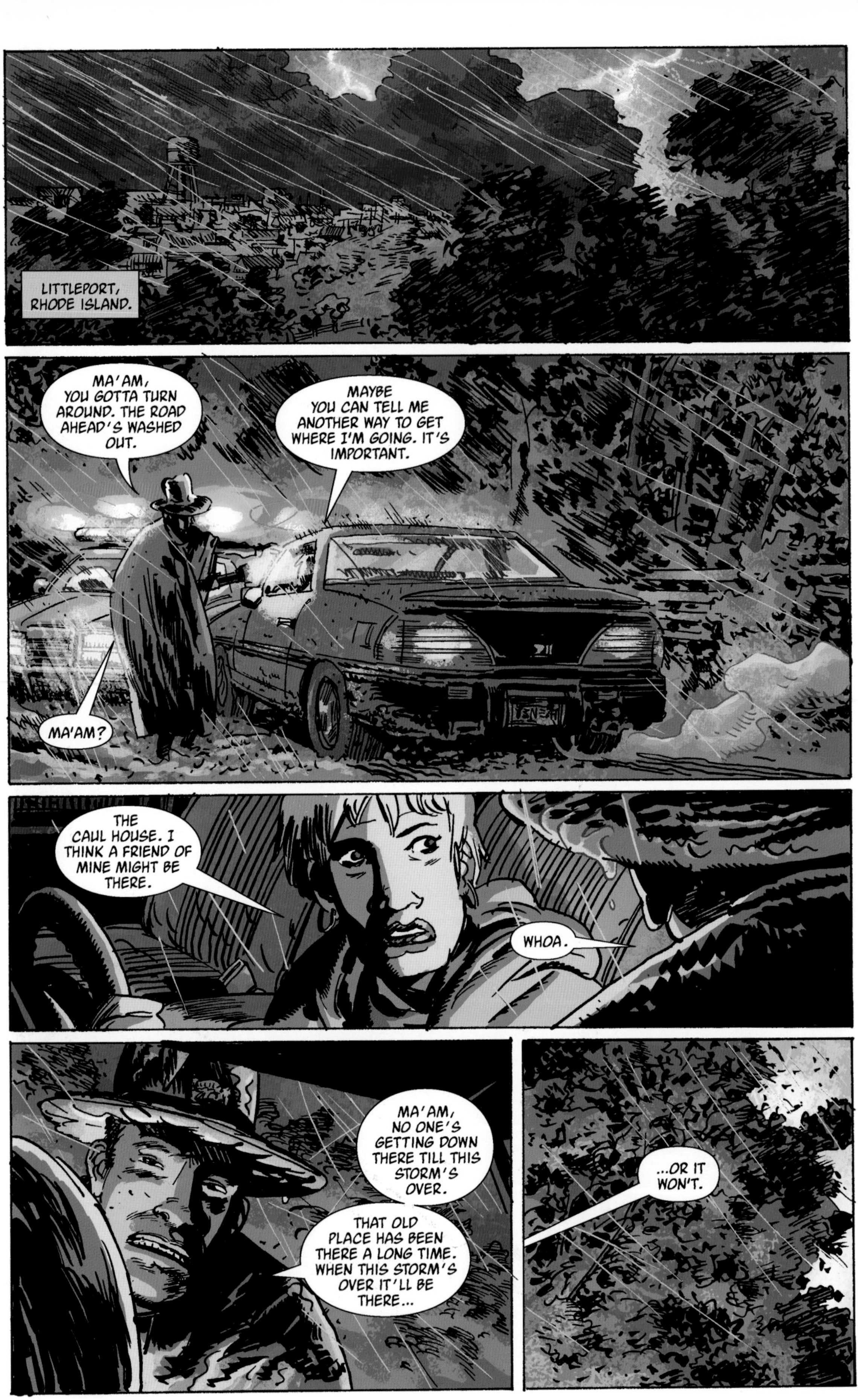
LITTLEPORT, RHODE ISLAND.
MA'AM, YOU GOTTA TURN AROUND. THE ROAD AHEAD'S WASHED OUT.
MAYBE YOU CAN TELL ME ANOTHER WAY TO GET WHERE I'M GOING. IT'S IMPORTANT.
MA'AM?
THE CAUL HOUSE. I THINK A FRIEND OF MINE MIGHT BE THERE.
WHOA.
MA'AM, NO ONE'S GETTING DOWN THERE TILL THIS STORM'S OVER.
THAT OLD PLACE HAS BEEN THERE A LONG TIME. WHEN THIS STORM'S OVER IT'LL BE THERE...
...OR IT WON'T.

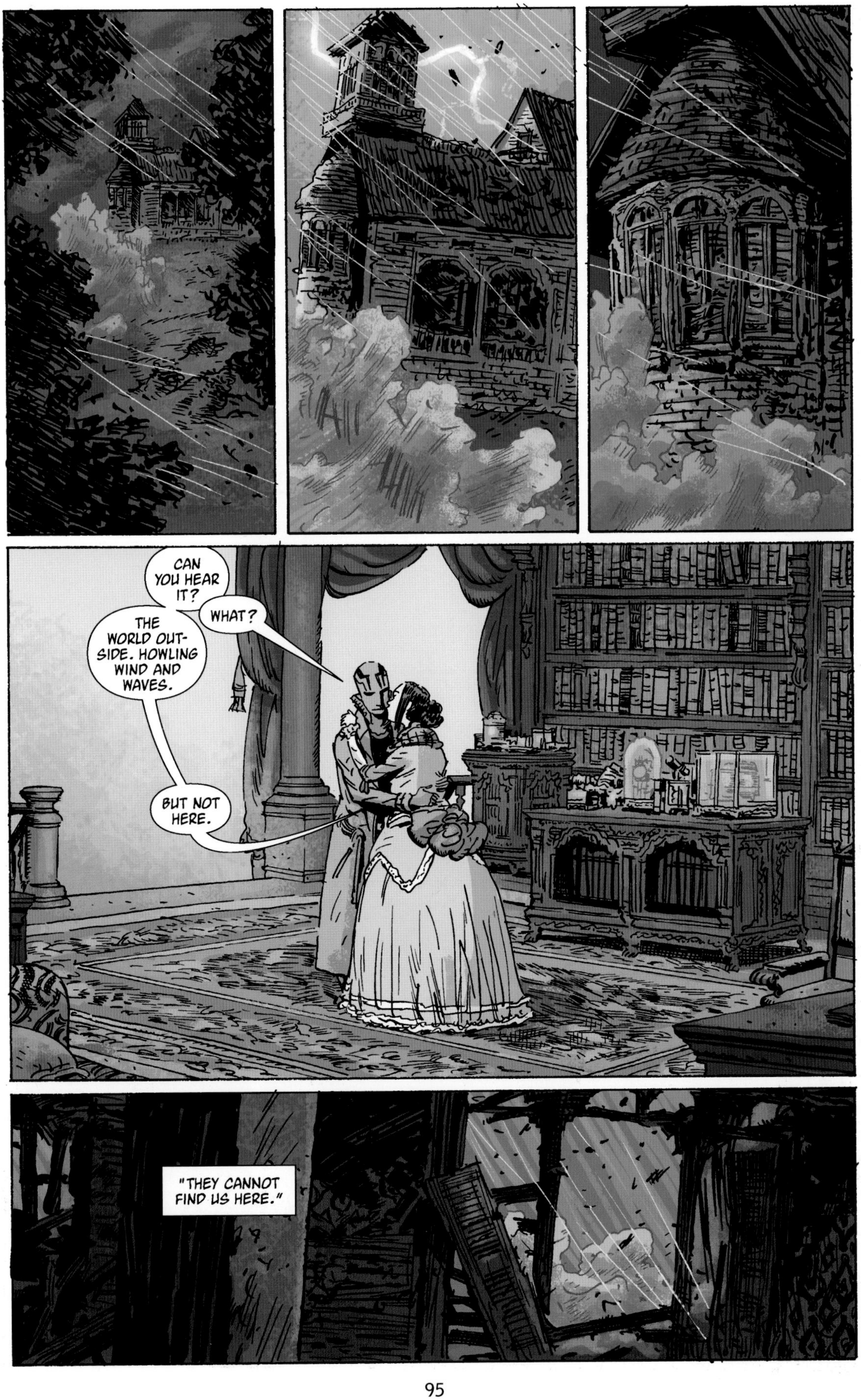
CAN YOU HEAR IT?
WHAT?
THE WORLD OUTSIDE. HOWLING WIND AND WAVES.
BUT NOT HERE.
"THEY CANNOT FIND US HERE."

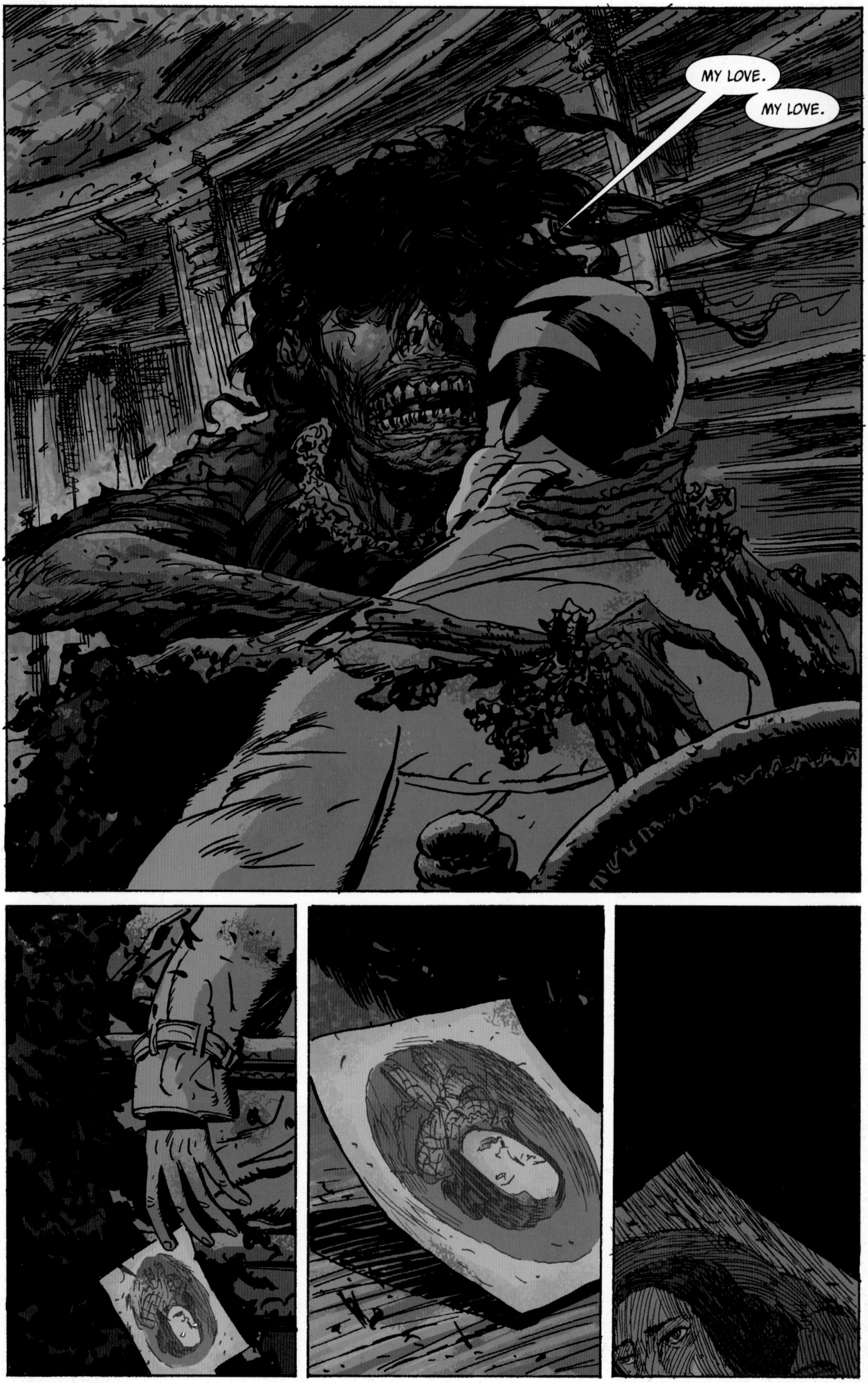
MY LOVE.
MY LOVE.

CHAPTER FOUR

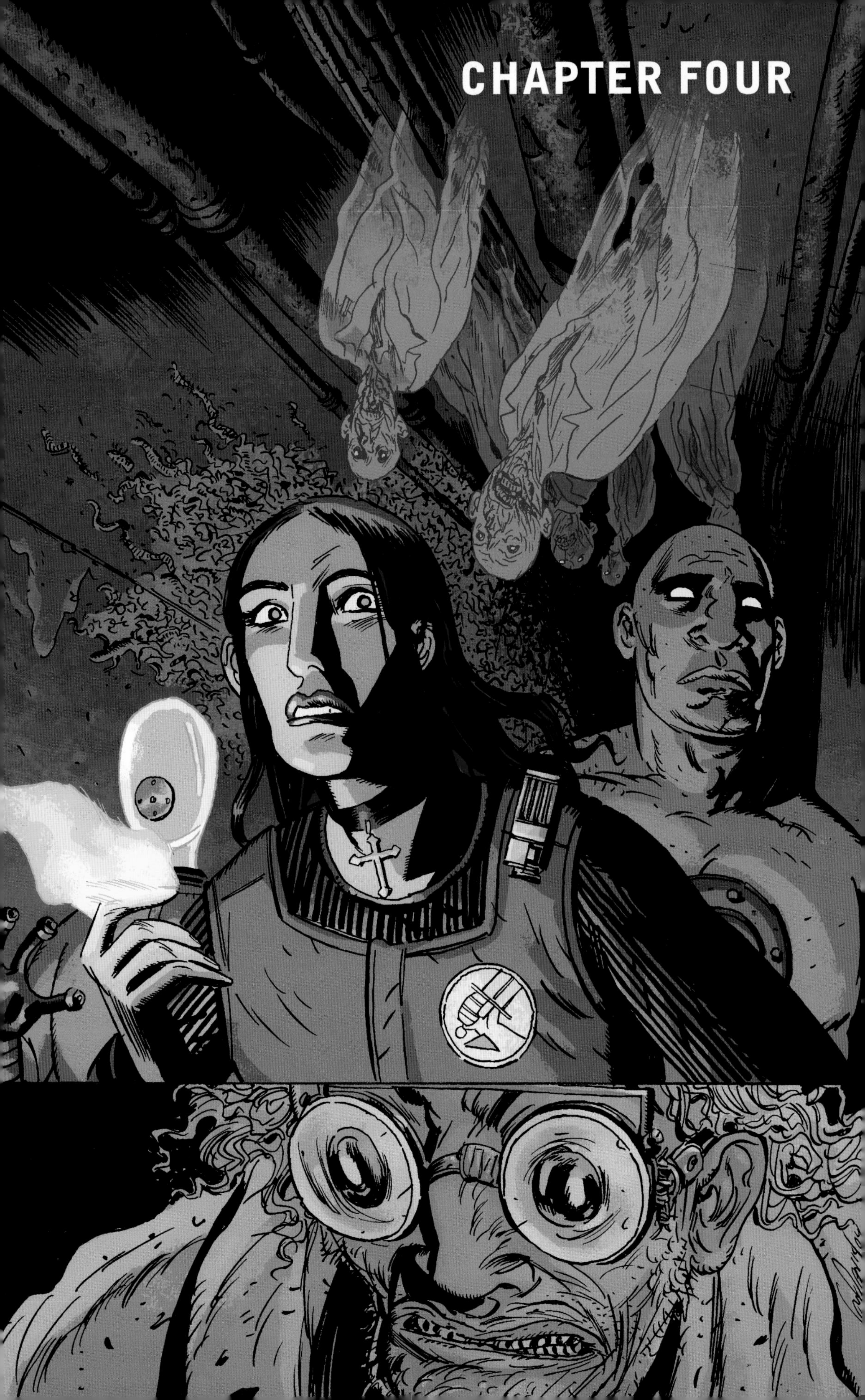

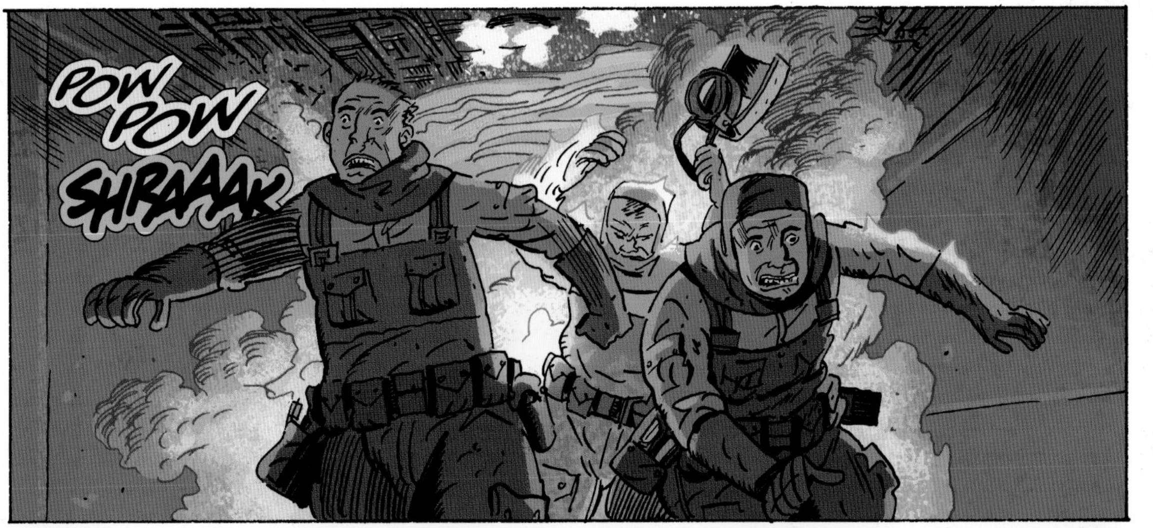
POW POW
SHRAAAK

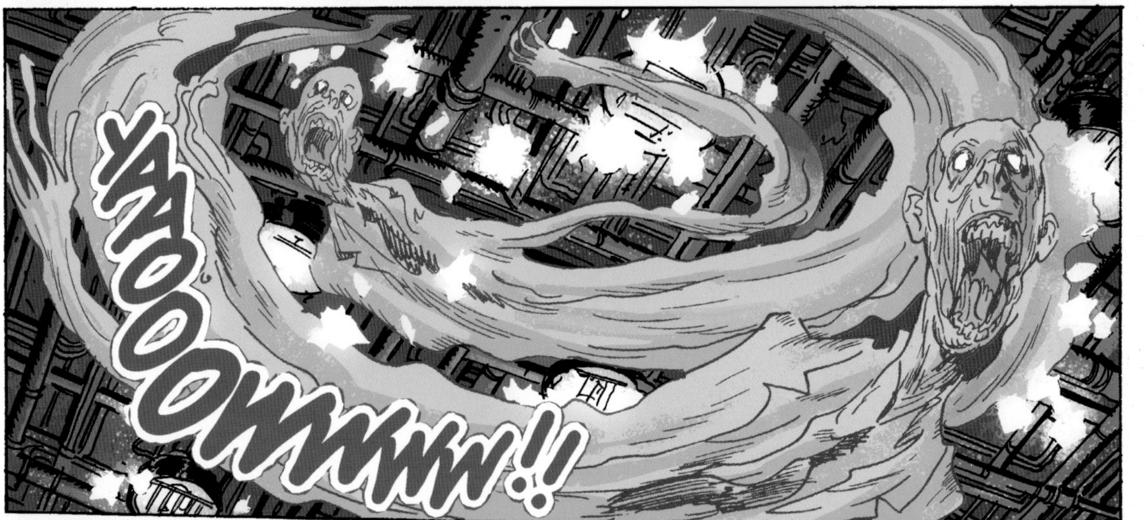
YAAOOOOWWWW!!

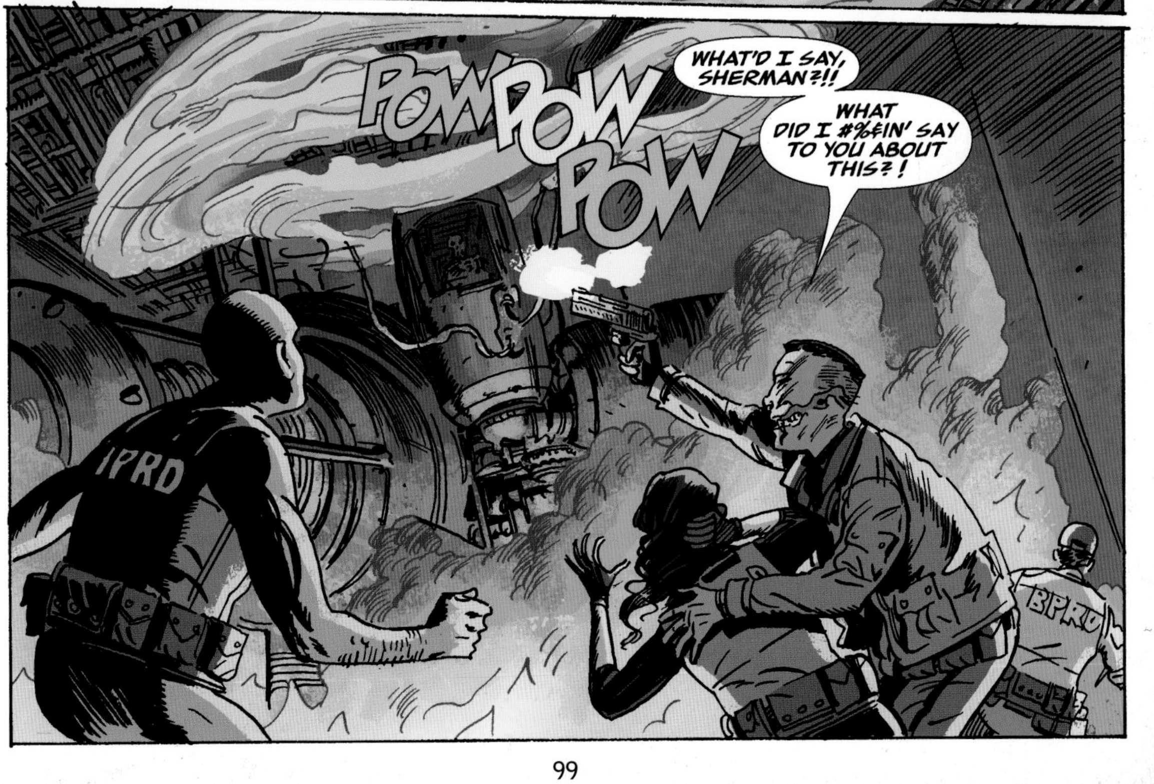
POW POW POW
WHAT'D I SAY, SHERMAN?!!
WHAT DID I #%$IN' SAY TO YOU ABOUT THIS?!
BPRD
BPRD

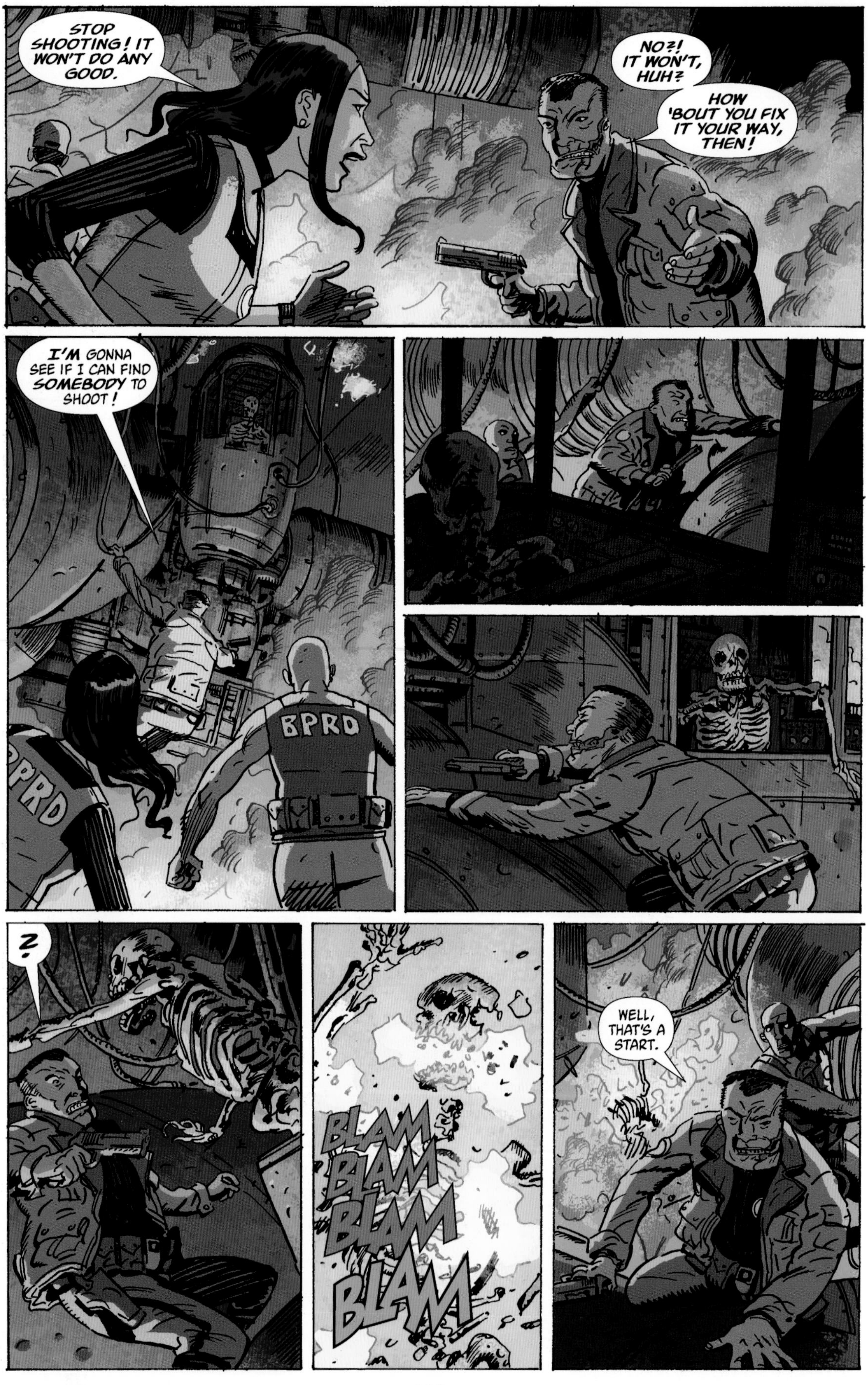
STOP SHOOTING! IT WON'T DO ANY GOOD.
NO?! IT WON'T, HUH?
HOW 'BOUT YOU FIX IT YOUR WAY, THEN!
I'M GONNA SEE IF I CAN FIND SOMEBODY TO SHOOT!
BPRD
BPRD
?
BLAM BLAM BLAM BLAM
WELL, THAT'S A START.

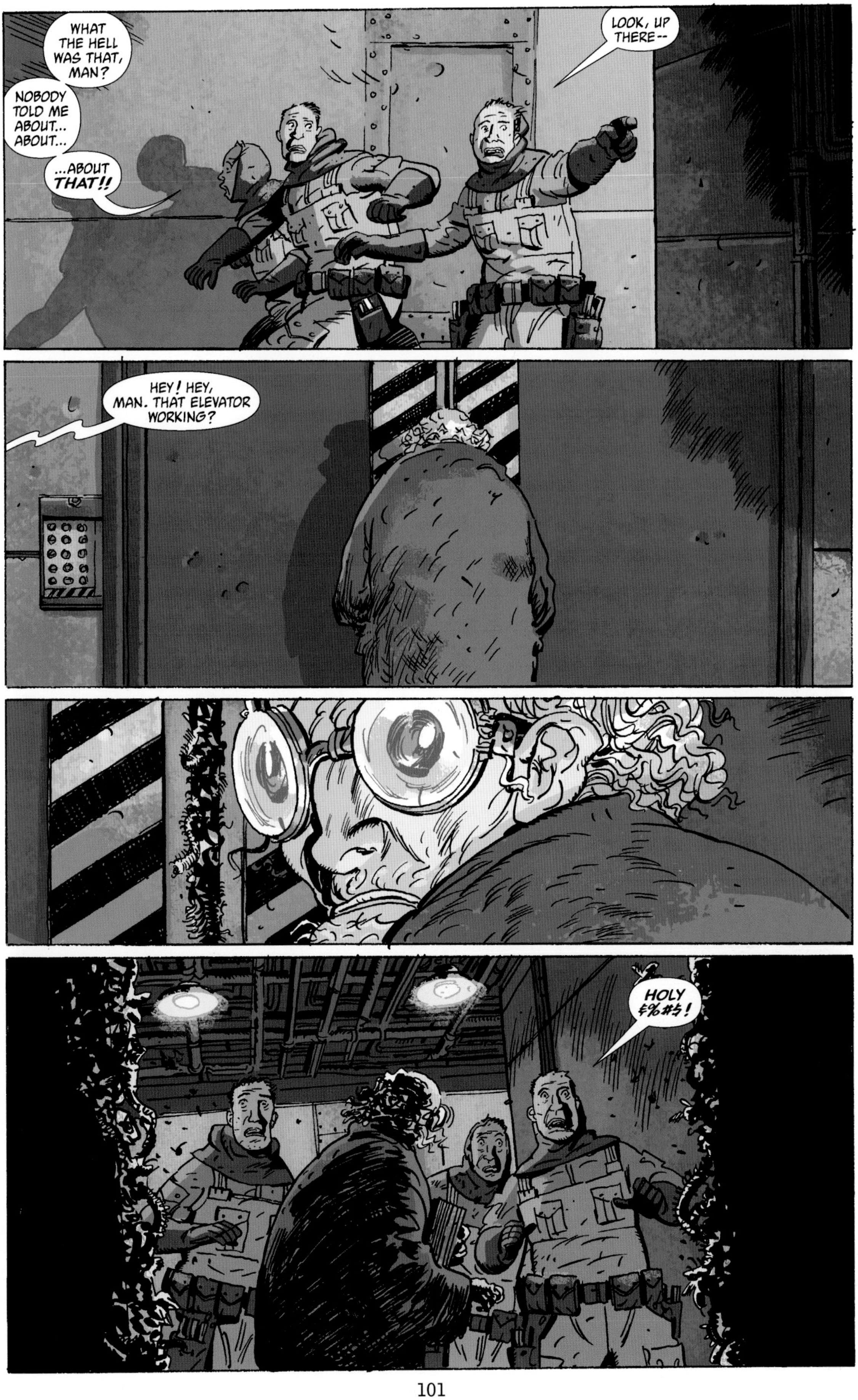
WHAT THE HELL WAS THAT, MAN?
NOBODY TOLD ME ABOUT... ABOUT...
...ABOUT THAT!!
LOOK, UP THERE--
HEY! HEY, MAN. THAT ELEVATOR WORKING?
HOLY £%#$!

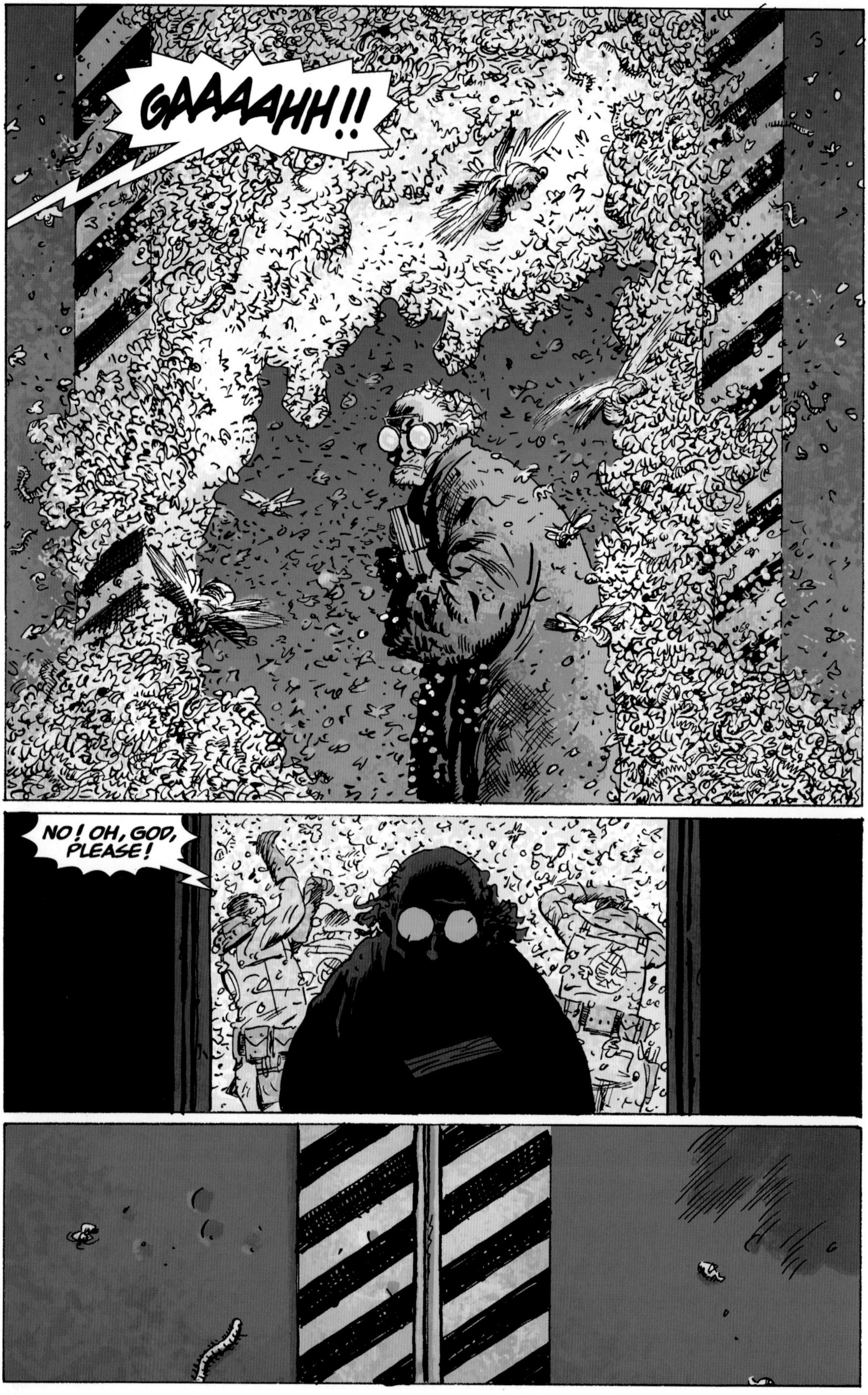
GAAAAHH!!
NO! OH, GOD, PLEASE!

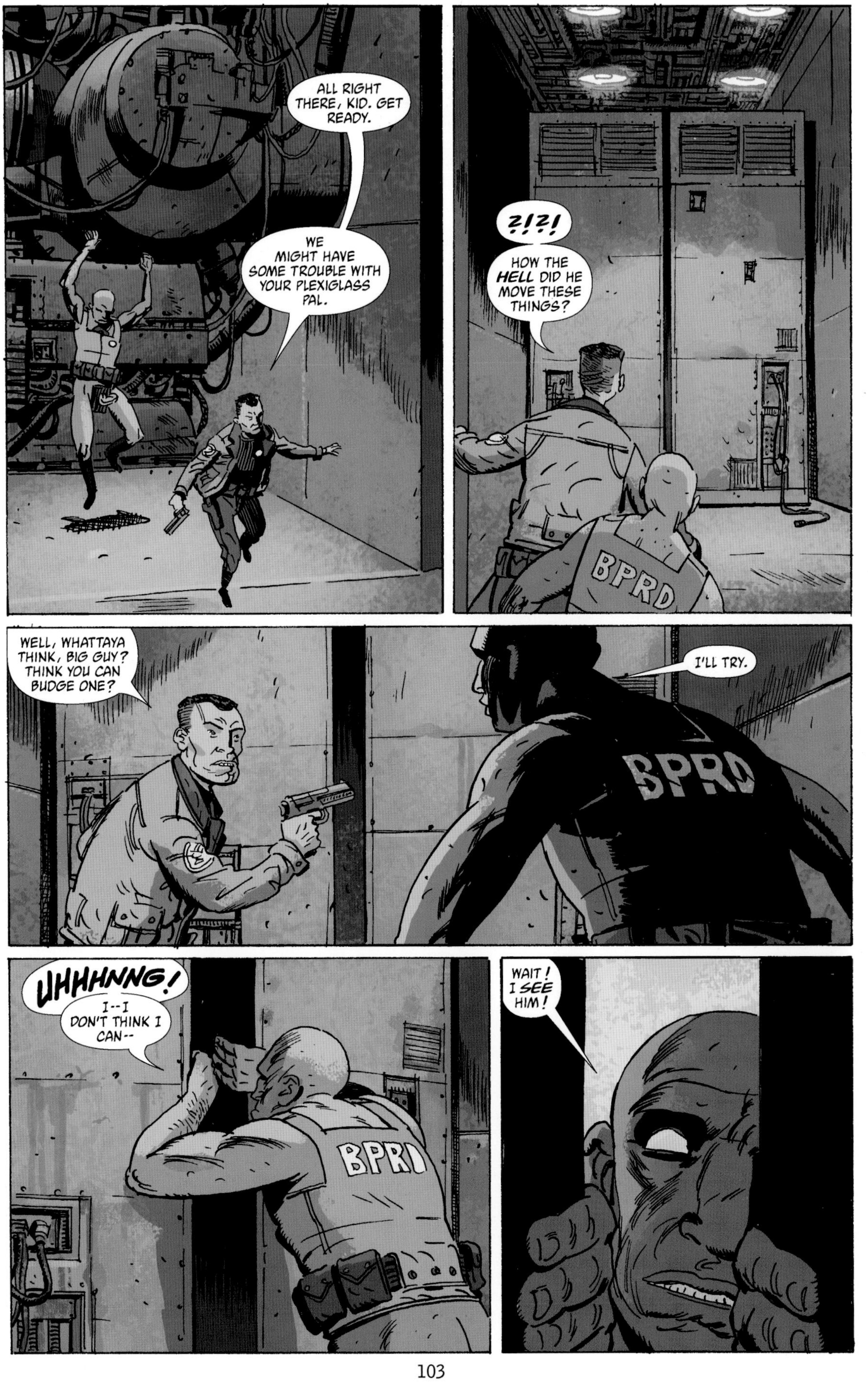
ALL RIGHT THERE, KID. GET READY.
WE MIGHT HAVE SOME TROUBLE WITH YOUR PLEXIGLASS PAL.
?!?!
HOW THE HELL DID HE MOVE THESE THINGS?
BPRD
WELL, WHATTAYA THINK, BIG GUY? THINK YOU CAN BUDGE ONE?
I'LL TRY.
BPRD
UHHHNNG!
I--I DON'T THINK I CAN--
BPRD
WAIT! I SEE HIM!

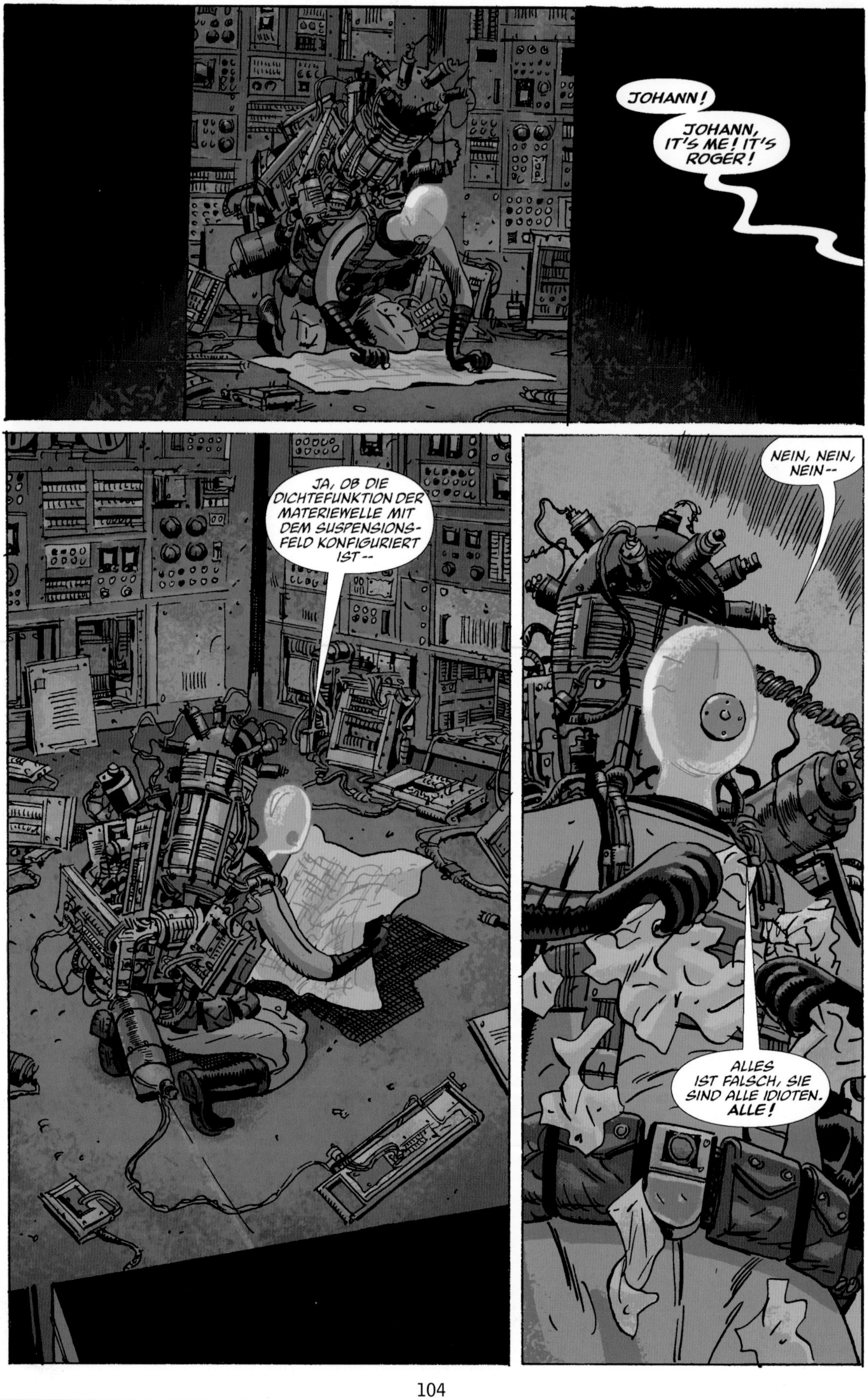
JOHANN!
JOHANN, IT'S ME! IT'S ROGER!
JA, OB DIE DICHTEFUNKTION DER MATERIEWELLE MIT DEM SUSPENSIONS-FELD KONFIGURIERT IST --
NEIN, NEIN, NEIN--
ALLES IST FALSCH, SIE SIND ALLE IDIOTEN. **ALLE!**

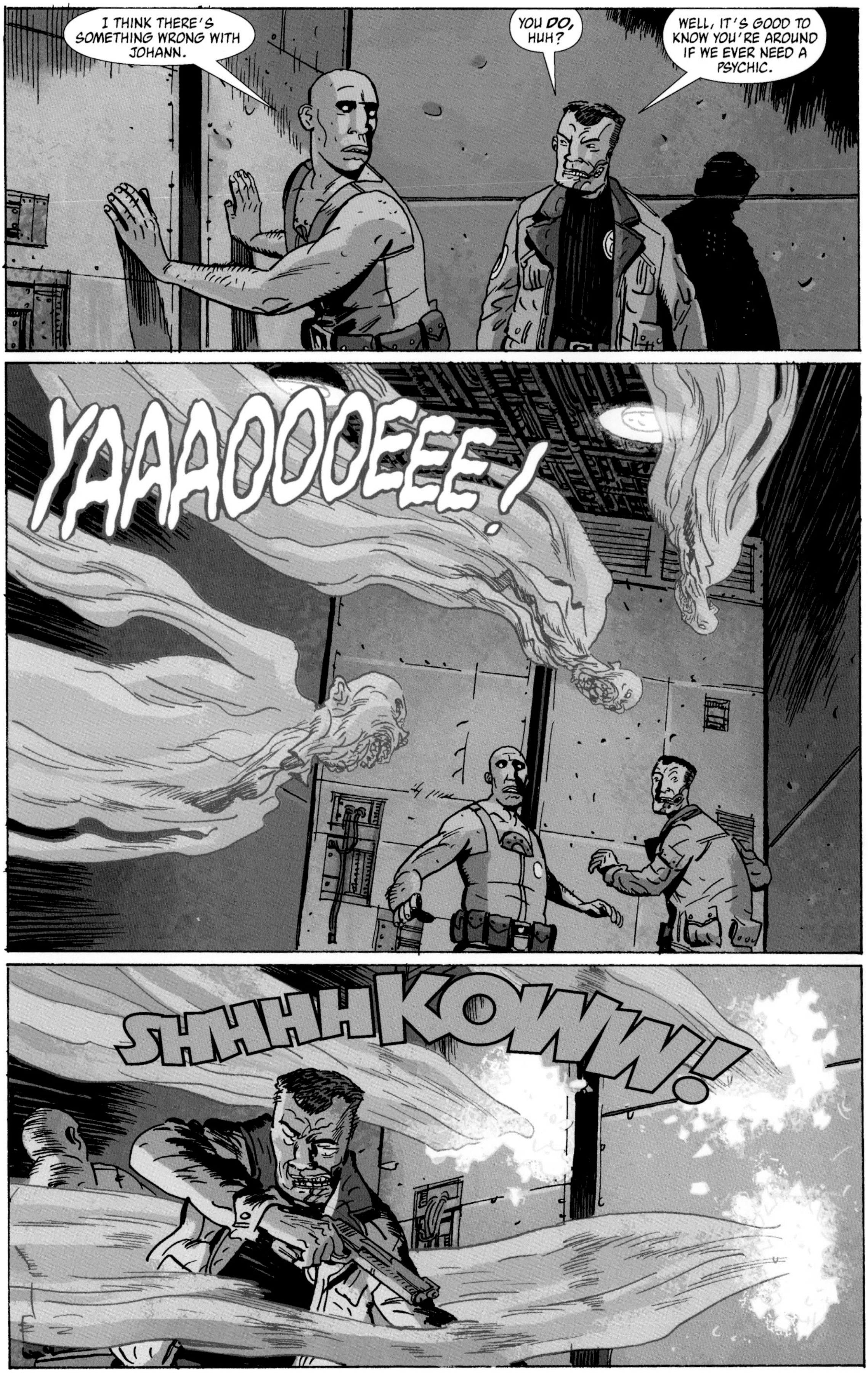
I THINK THERE'S SOMETHING WRONG WITH JOHANN.
YOU DO, HUH?
WELL, IT'S GOOD TO KNOW YOU'RE AROUND IF WE EVER NEED A PSYCHIC.
YAAAOOOEEE!
SHHHHKOWW!

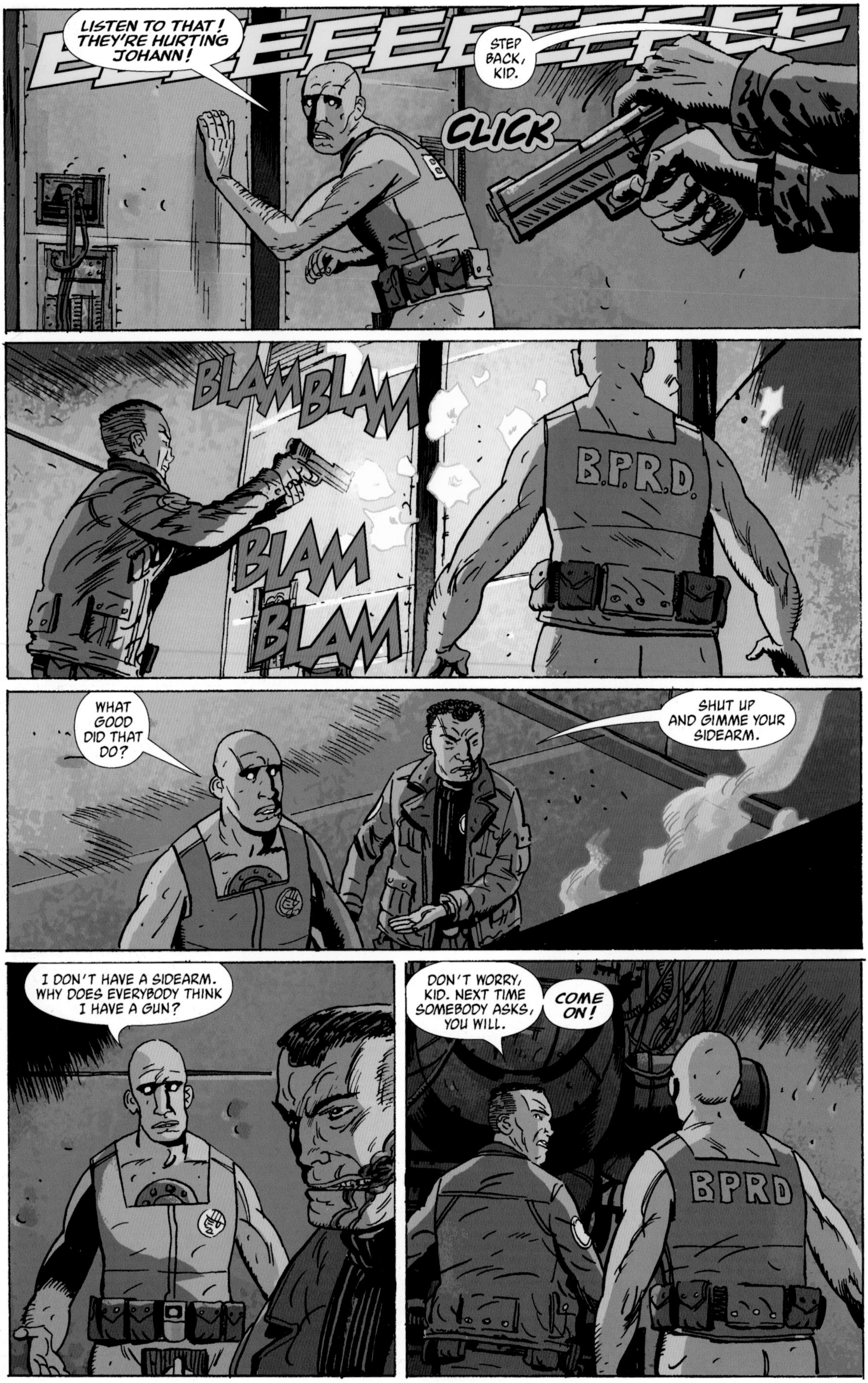
LISTEN TO THAT! THEY'RE HURTING JOHANN!
STEP BACK, KID.
CLICK
BLAMBLAM
BLAM
BLAM
B.P.R.D.
WHAT GOOD DID THAT DO?
SHUT UP AND GIMME YOUR SIDEARM.
I DON'T HAVE A SIDEARM. WHY DOES EVERYBODY THINK I HAVE A GUN?
DON'T WORRY, KID. NEXT TIME SOMEBODY ASKS, YOU WILL.
COME ON!
BPRD

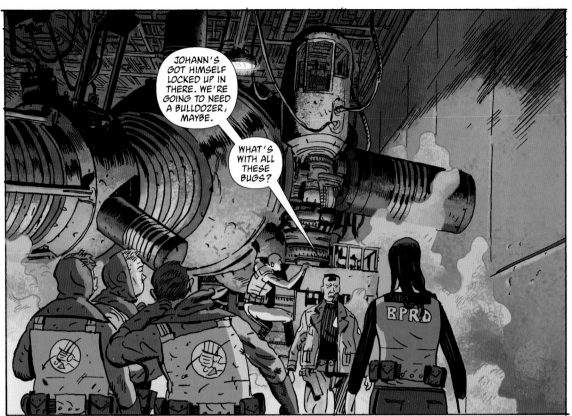

JOHANN'S GOT HIMSELF LOCKED UP IN THERE. WE'RE GOING TO NEED A BULLDOZER, MAYBE.

WHAT'S WITH ALL THESE BUGS?

YEAH, ABOUT THAT--

THE ELEVATOR. THEY CAME UP THROUGH THE ELEVATOR. THOUSANDS AND THOUSANDS OF THEM.

THAT OLD GUY? HE WAS STANDING THERE AT THE ELEVATOR, AND WHEN THE DOORS OPENED...

HE DIDN'T SAY A THING. THEY ALL CAME OUT, AND THEN HE JUST WALKED ONTO THE ELEVATOR--

--LIKE HE WAS JUST BEING POLITE, LIKE HE'D BEEN WAITING FOR THEM TO COME OFF.

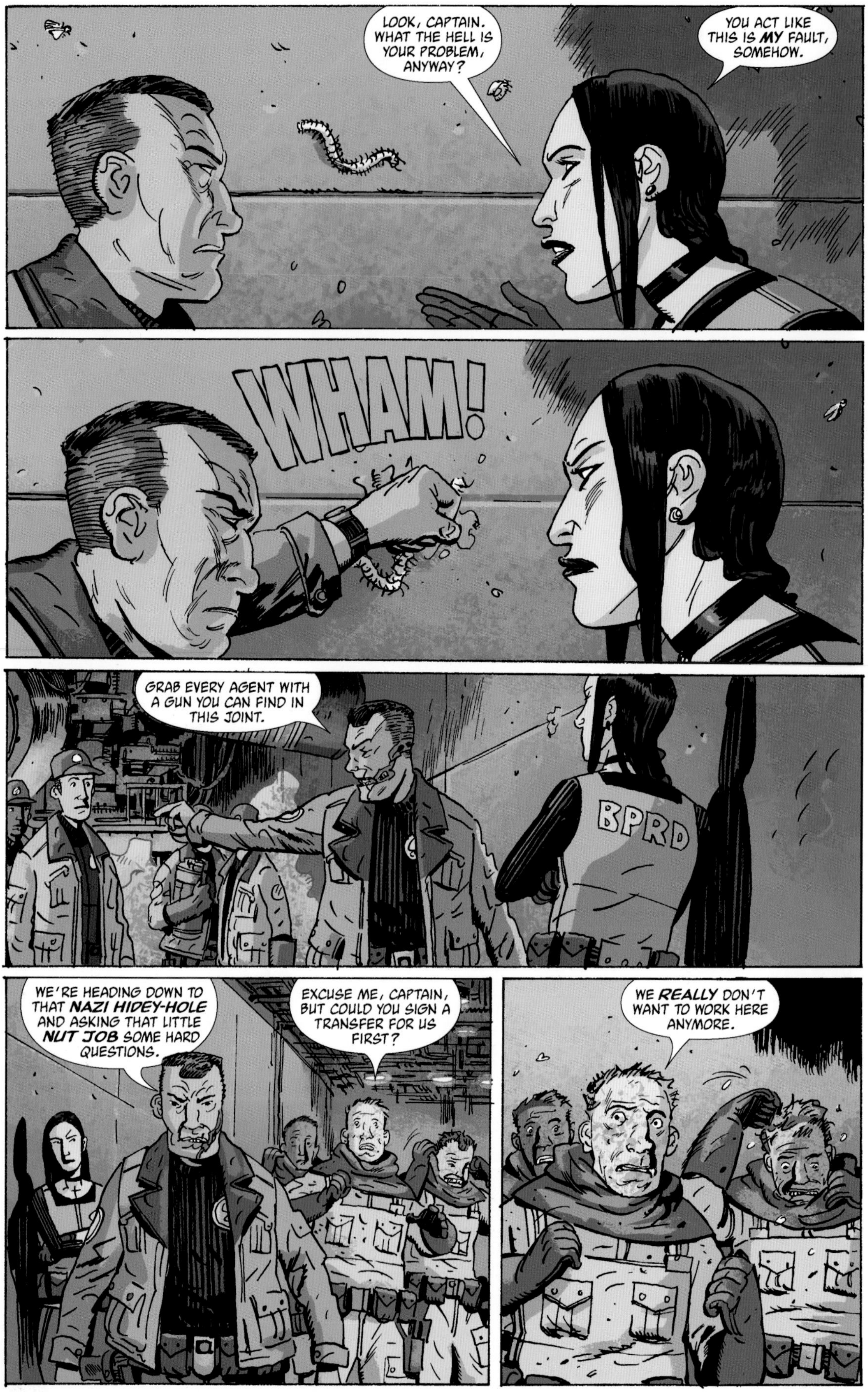
LOOK, CAPTAIN. WHAT THE HELL IS YOUR PROBLEM, ANYWAY?
YOU ACT LIKE THIS IS MY FAULT, SOMEHOW.
WHAM!
GRAB EVERY AGENT WITH A GUN YOU CAN FIND IN THIS JOINT.
BPRD
WE'RE HEADING DOWN TO THAT NAZI HIDEY-HOLE AND ASKING THAT LITTLE NUT JOB SOME HARD QUESTIONS.
EXCUSE ME, CAPTAIN, BUT COULD YOU SIGN A TRANSFER FOR US FIRST?
WE REALLY DON'T WANT TO WORK HERE ANYMORE.

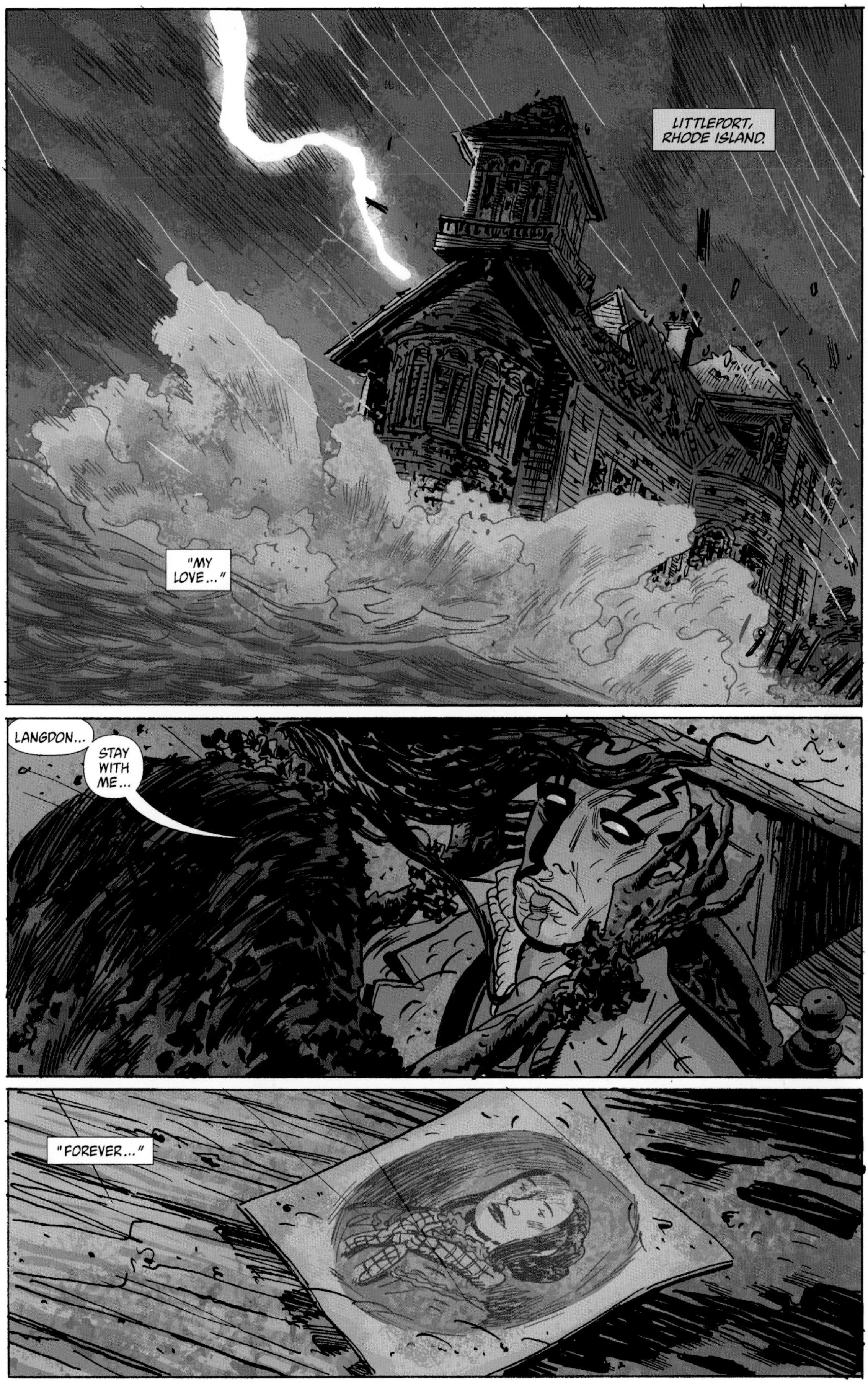
LITTLEPORT, RHODE ISLAND.
"MY LOVE..."
LANGDON...
STAY WITH ME...
"FOREVER..."

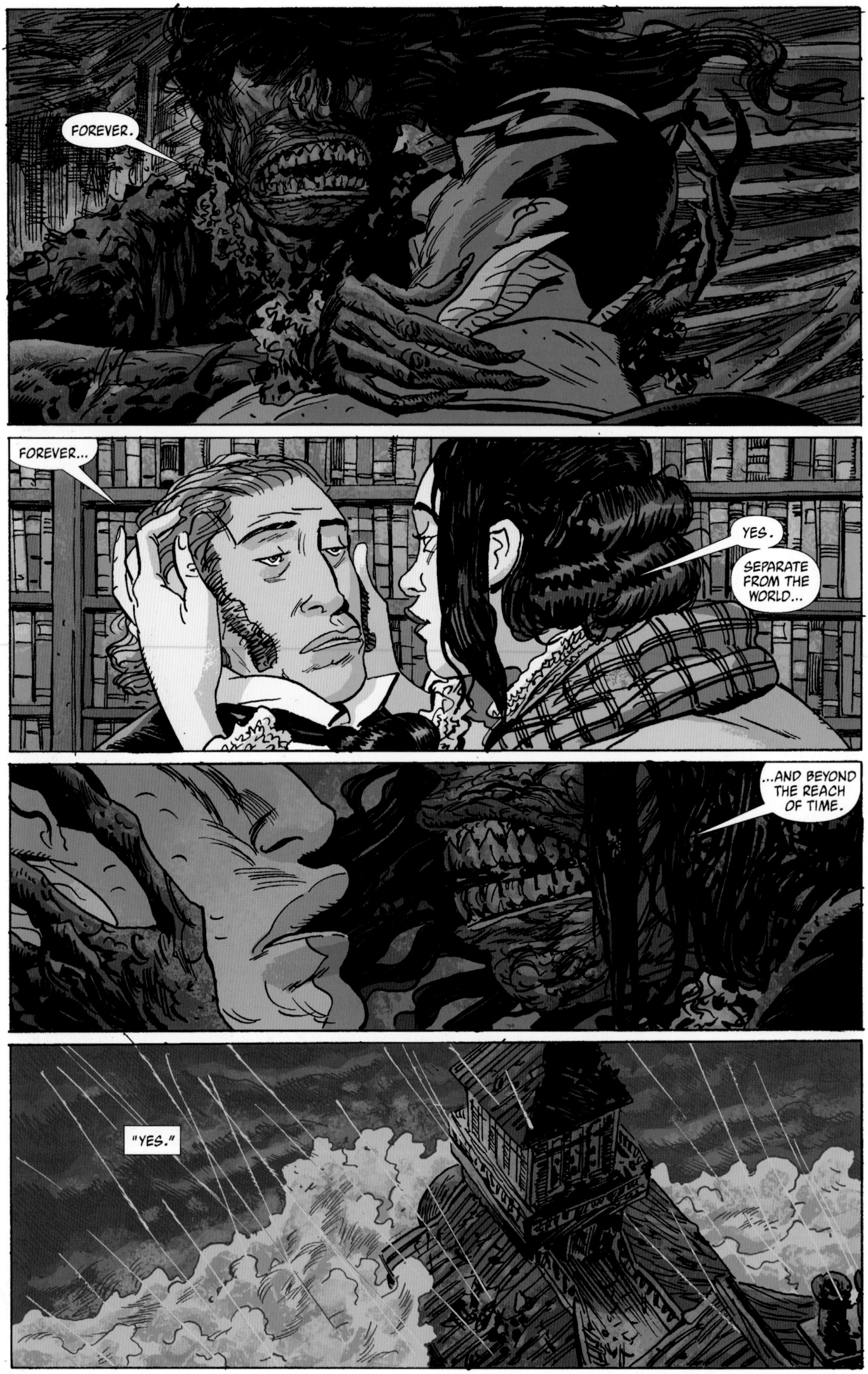
FOREVER.
FOREVER...
YES.
SEPARATE FROM THE WORLD...
...AND BEYOND THE REACH OF TIME.
"YES."

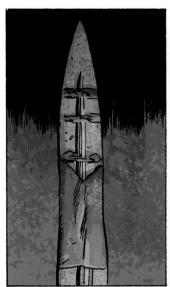

NICE. REAL NICE OUTFIT.

STRANGE THINGS GOING ON HERE, GUNTER.

MY CRAZY BONE TELLS ME *YOU* GOT SOMETHING TO DO WITH ALL THAT.

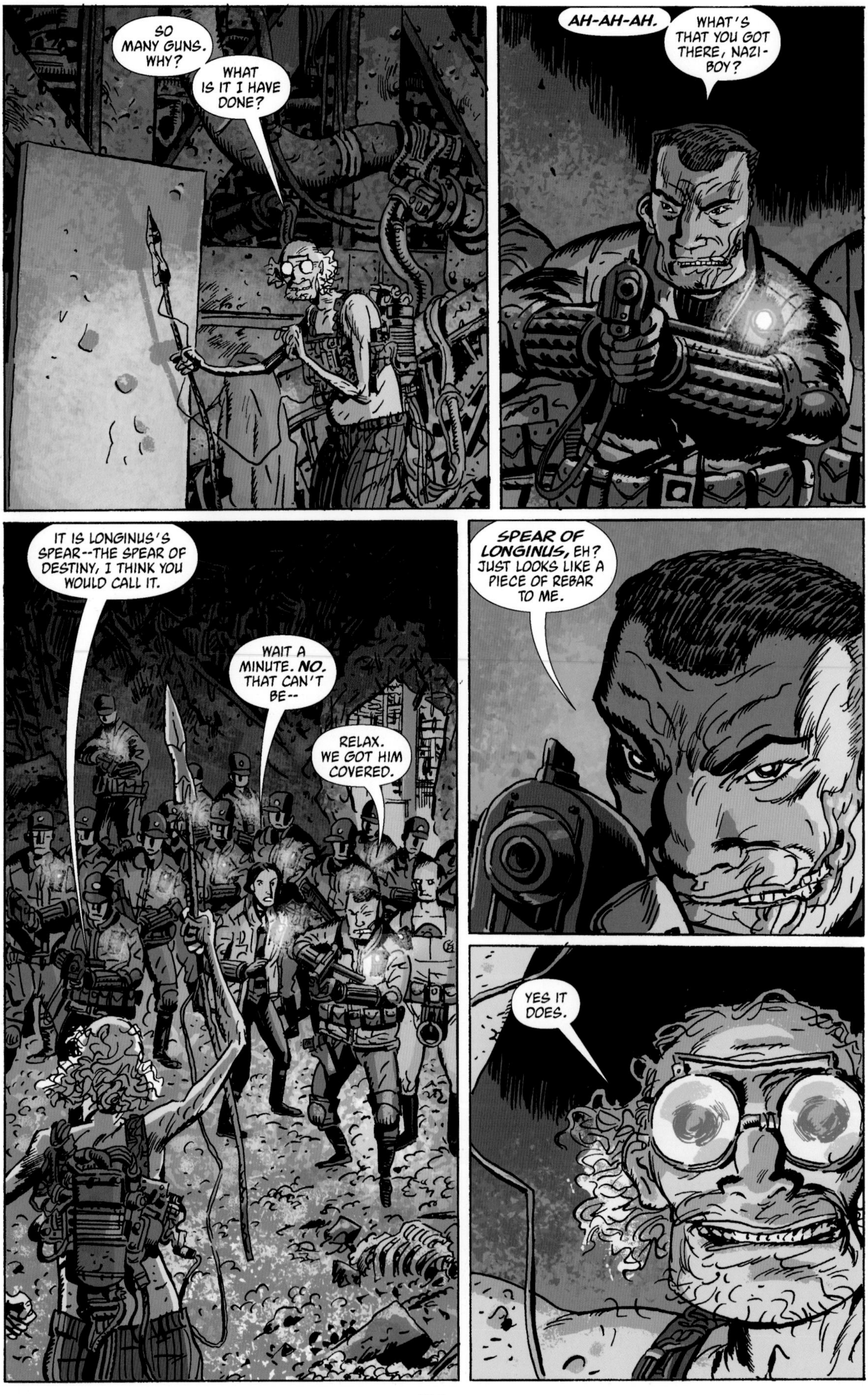
SO MANY GUNS. WHY?
WHAT IS IT I HAVE DONE?
AH-AH-AH.
WHAT'S THAT YOU GOT THERE, NAZI-BOY?
IT IS LONGINUS'S SPEAR--THE SPEAR OF DESTINY, I THINK YOU WOULD CALL IT.
WAIT A MINUTE. NO. THAT CAN'T BE--
RELAX. WE GOT HIM COVERED.
SPEAR OF LONGINUS, EH? JUST LOOKS LIKE A PIECE OF REBAR TO ME.
YES IT DOES.

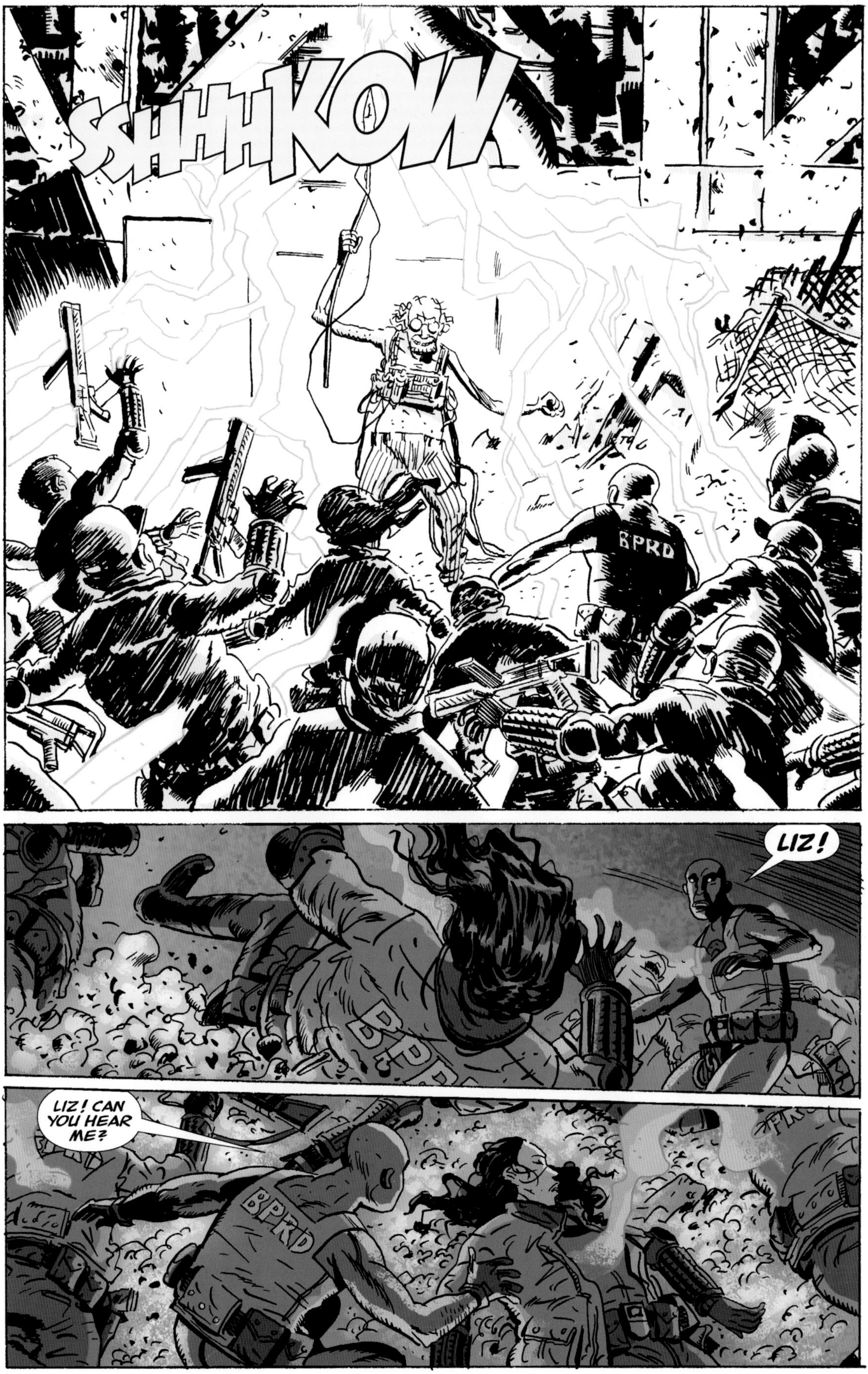
SSHHHKOW
BPRD
LIZ!
LIZ! CAN YOU HEAR ME?
BPRD

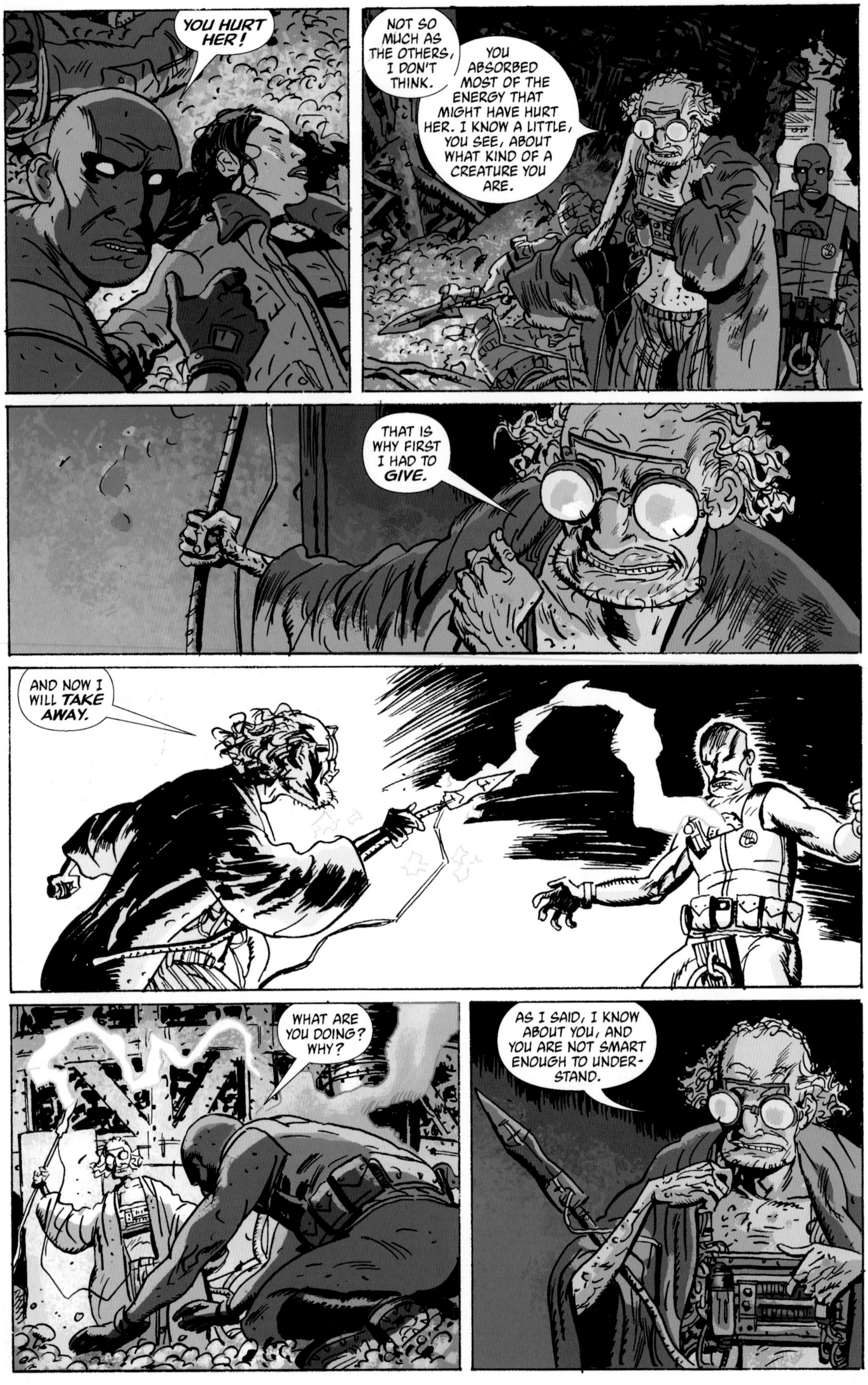
YOU HURT HER!
NOT SO MUCH AS THE OTHERS, I DON'T THINK.
YOU ABSORBED MOST OF THE ENERGY THAT MIGHT HAVE HURT HER. I KNOW A LITTLE, YOU SEE, ABOUT WHAT KIND OF A CREATURE YOU ARE.
THAT IS WHY FIRST I HAD TO GIVE.
AND NOW I WILL TAKE AWAY.
WHAT ARE YOU DOING? WHY?
AS I SAID, I KNOW ABOUT YOU, AND YOU ARE NOT SMART ENOUGH TO UNDER-STAND.

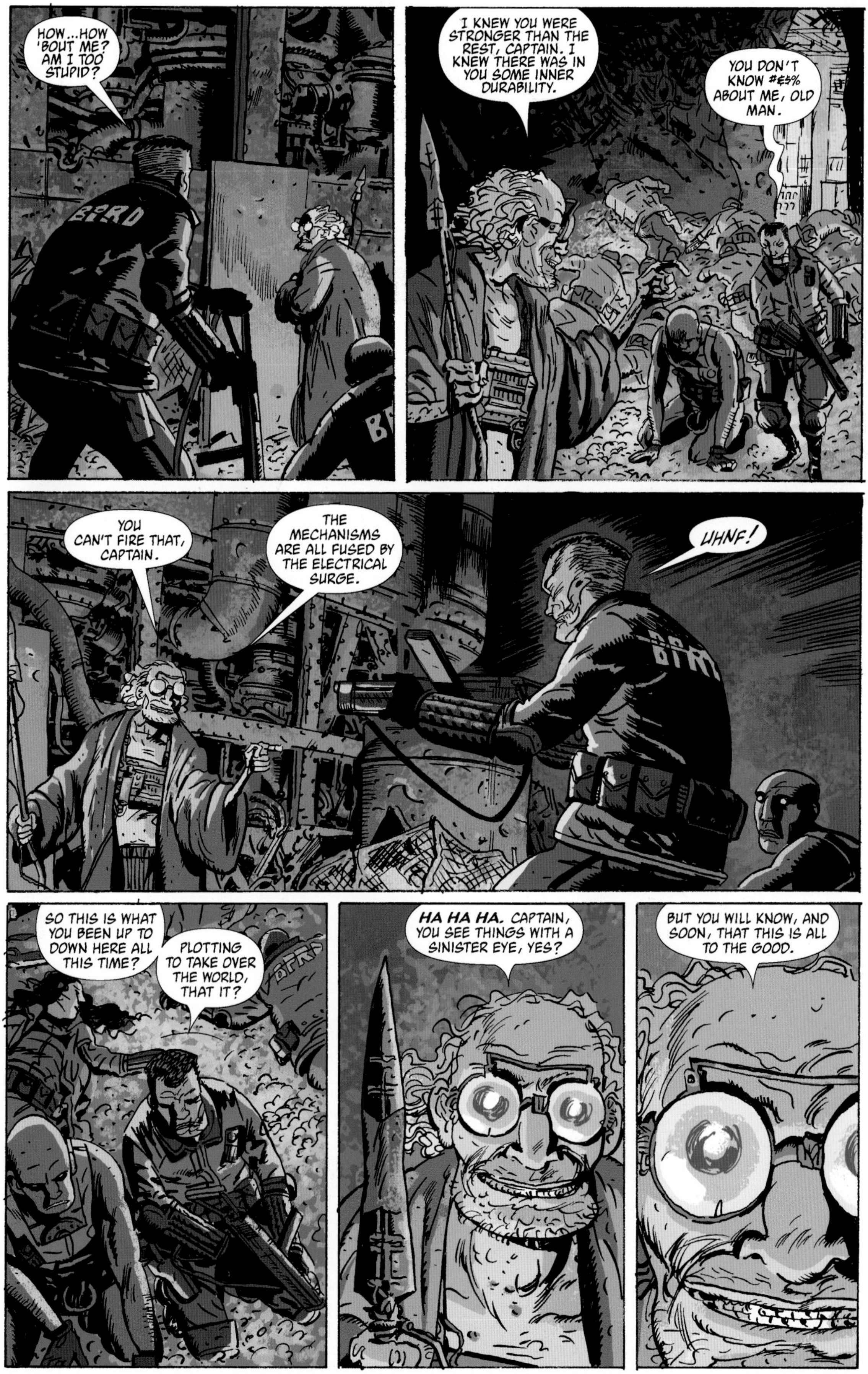
HOW...HOW 'BOUT ME? AM I TOO STUPID?
I KNEW YOU WERE STRONGER THAN THE REST, CAPTAIN. I KNEW THERE WAS IN YOU SOME INNER DURABILITY.
YOU DON'T KNOW #€$% ABOUT ME, OLD MAN.
YOU CAN'T FIRE THAT, CAPTAIN.
THE MECHANISMS ARE ALL FUSED BY THE ELECTRICAL SURGE.
UHNF!
SO THIS IS WHAT YOU BEEN UP TO DOWN HERE ALL THIS TIME?
PLOTTING TO TAKE OVER THE WORLD, THAT IT?
HA HA HA. CAPTAIN, YOU SEE THINGS WITH A SINISTER EYE, YES?
BUT YOU WILL KNOW, AND SOON, THAT THIS IS ALL TO THE GOOD.

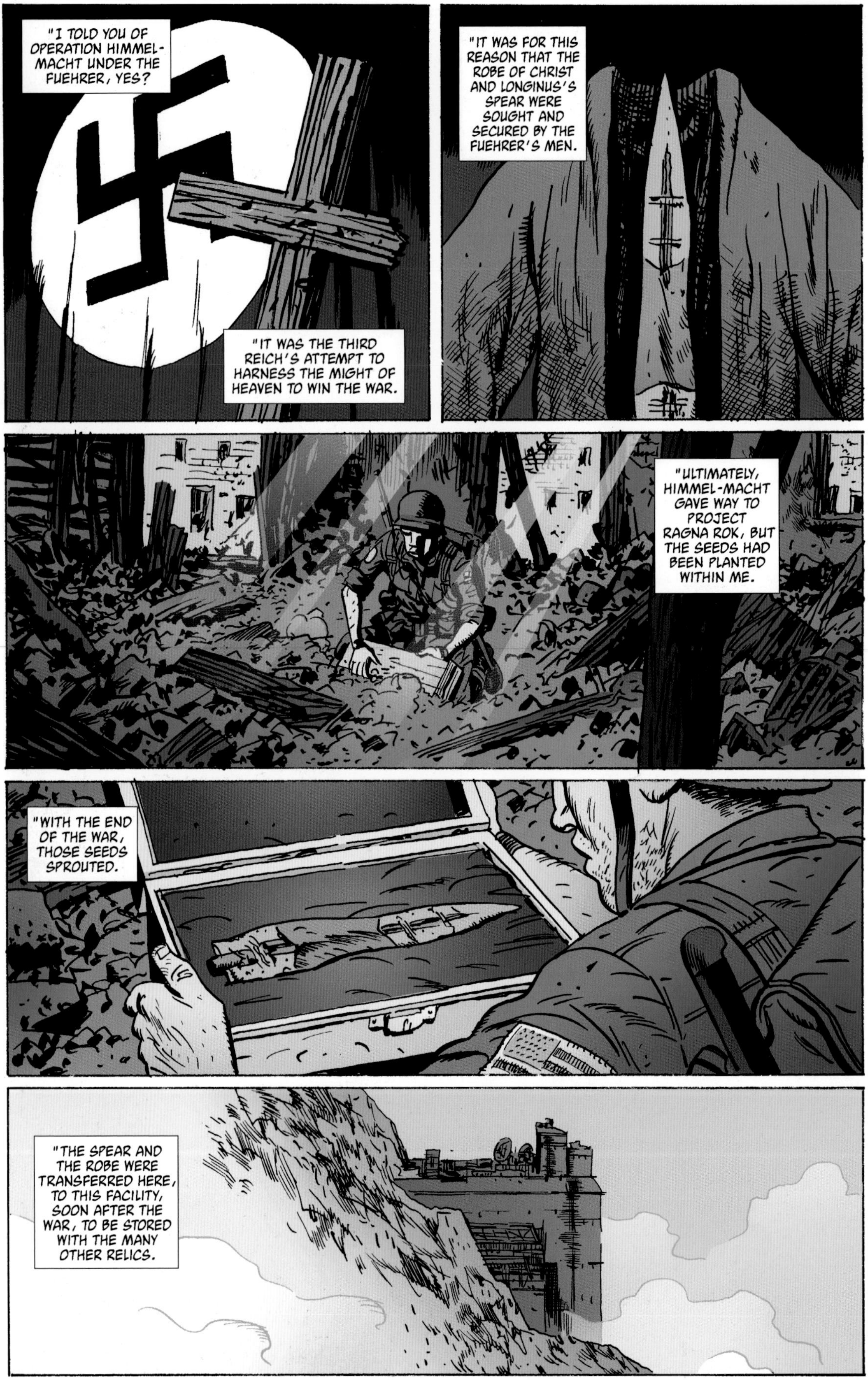
"I TOLD YOU OF OPERATION HIMMEL-MACHT UNDER THE FUEHRER, YES?
"IT WAS THE THIRD REICH'S ATTEMPT TO HARNESS THE MIGHT OF HEAVEN TO WIN THE WAR.
"IT WAS FOR THIS REASON THAT THE ROBE OF CHRIST AND LONGINUS'S SPEAR WERE SOUGHT AND SECURED BY THE FUEHRER'S MEN.
"ULTIMATELY, HIMMEL-MACHT GAVE WAY TO PROJECT RAGNA ROK, BUT THE SEEDS HAD BEEN PLANTED WITHIN ME.
"WITH THE END OF THE WAR, THOSE SEEDS SPROUTED.
"THE SPEAR AND THE ROBE WERE TRANSFERRED HERE, TO THIS FACILITY, SOON AFTER THE WAR, TO BE STORED WITH THE MANY OTHER RELICS.

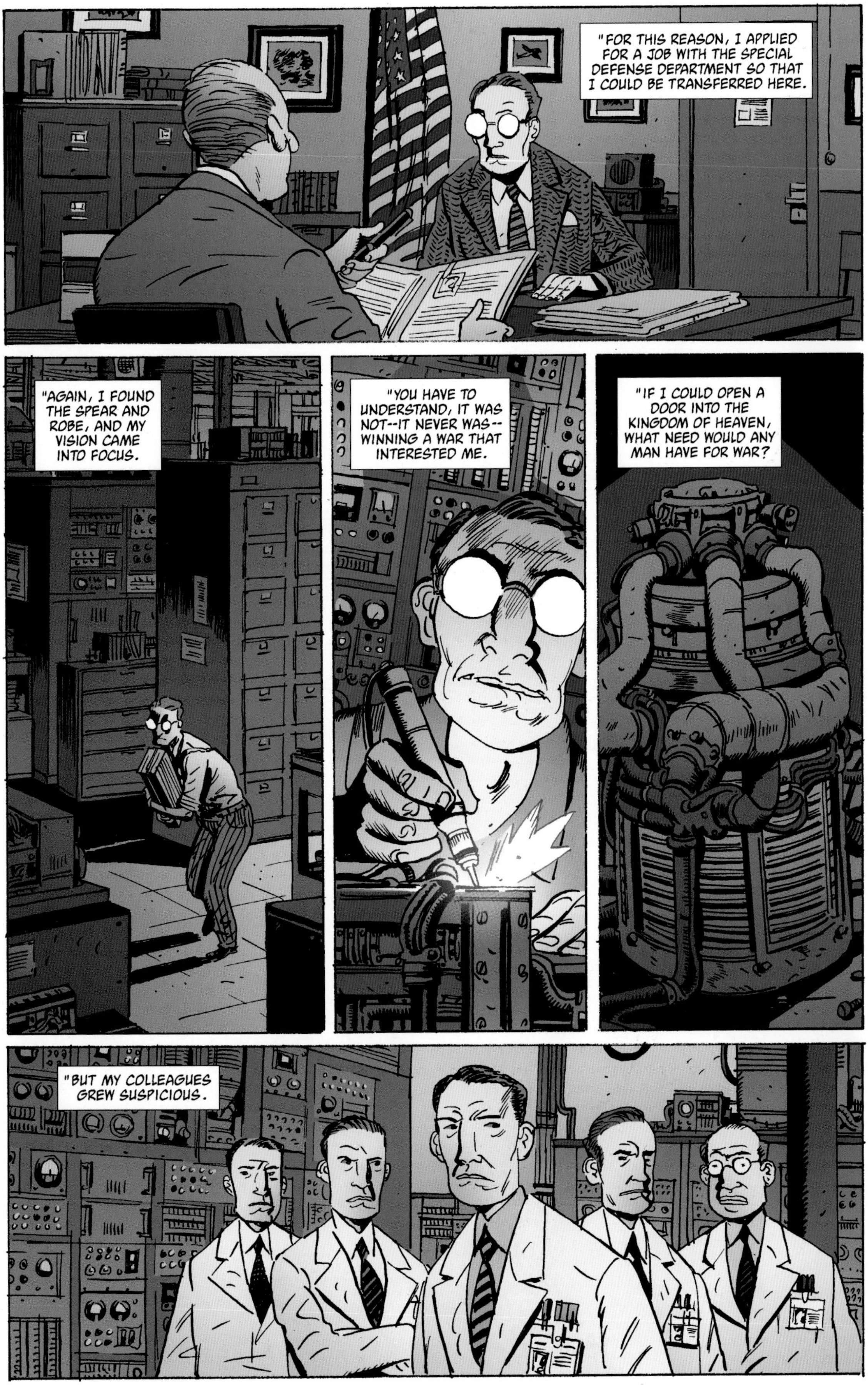
"FOR THIS REASON, I APPLIED FOR A JOB WITH THE SPECIAL DEFENSE DEPARTMENT SO THAT I COULD BE TRANSFERRED HERE.
"AGAIN, I FOUND THE SPEAR AND ROBE, AND MY VISION CAME INTO FOCUS.
"YOU HAVE TO UNDERSTAND, IT WAS NOT--IT NEVER WAS--WINNING A WAR THAT INTERESTED ME.
"IF I COULD OPEN A DOOR INTO THE KINGDOM OF HEAVEN, WHAT NEED WOULD ANY MAN HAVE FOR WAR?
"BUT MY COLLEAGUES GREW SUSPICIOUS.

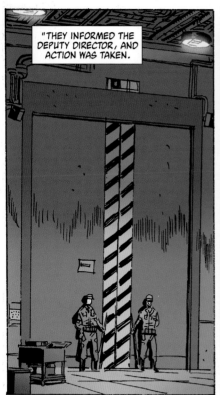

"THEY INFORMED THE DEPUTY DIRECTOR, AND ACTION WAS TAKEN.

"THE WRONG ACTION.

"THEY TRIED TO DISMANTLE MY WORK, BUT I HAD BUILT IN AN ANTITAMPER DEVICE.

"UNFORTUNATELY, TO TINKER WITH THE DEVICE WAS MORE FATAL THAN EVEN I HAD TAKEN INTO ACCOUNT."

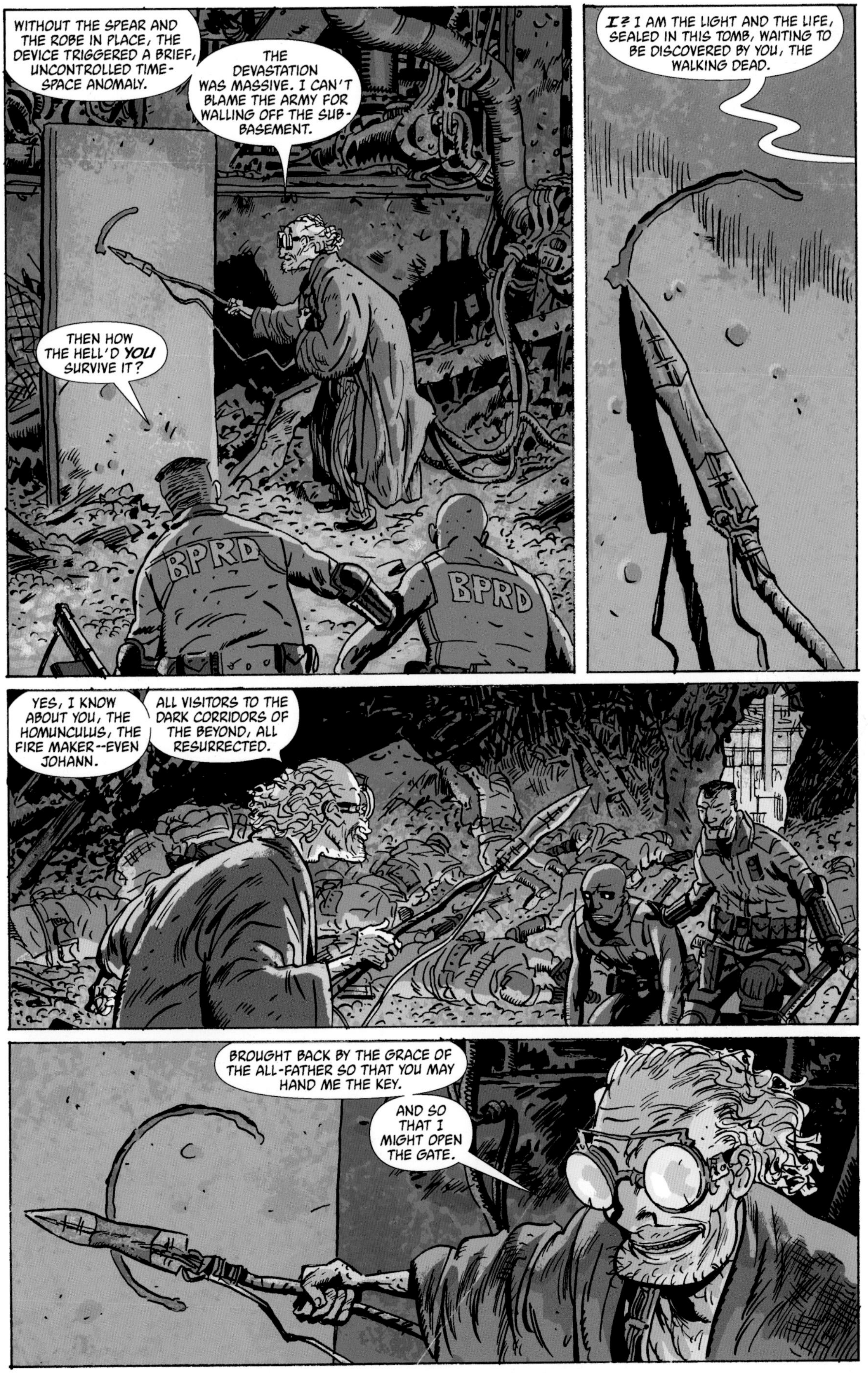
WITHOUT THE SPEAR AND THE ROBE IN PLACE, THE DEVICE TRIGGERED A BRIEF, UNCONTROLLED TIME-SPACE ANOMALY.
THE DEVASTATION WAS MASSIVE. I CAN'T BLAME THE ARMY FOR WALLING OFF THE SUB-BASEMENT.
THEN HOW THE HELL'D YOU SURVIVE IT?
I? I AM THE LIGHT AND THE LIFE, SEALED IN THIS TOMB, WAITING TO BE DISCOVERED BY YOU, THE WALKING DEAD.
YES, I KNOW ABOUT YOU, THE HOMUNCULUS, THE FIRE MAKER--EVEN JOHANN.
ALL VISITORS TO THE DARK CORRIDORS OF THE BEYOND, ALL RESURRECTED.
BROUGHT BACK BY THE GRACE OF THE ALL-FATHER SO THAT YOU MAY HAND ME THE KEY.
AND SO THAT I MIGHT OPEN THE GATE.

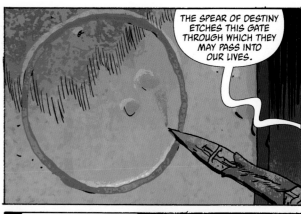

THIS IS NOT A MATTER OF FAITH. THE KINGDOM OF HEAVEN IS A REAL AND KNOWABLE PLACE.

MY CALCULATIONS, AND MY VISIONS, HAVE SHOWN ME *THE ELYSIAN FIELDS*, AND THE *SIX-WINGED SERAPHIM*.

THE SPEAR OF DESTINY ETCHES THIS GATE THROUGH WHICH THEY MAY PASS INTO OUR LIVES.

AND WHEN PARADISE HAS COME TO PASS ON EARTH, CAPTAIN--

CLACK

--YOU WILL *THANK* ME.

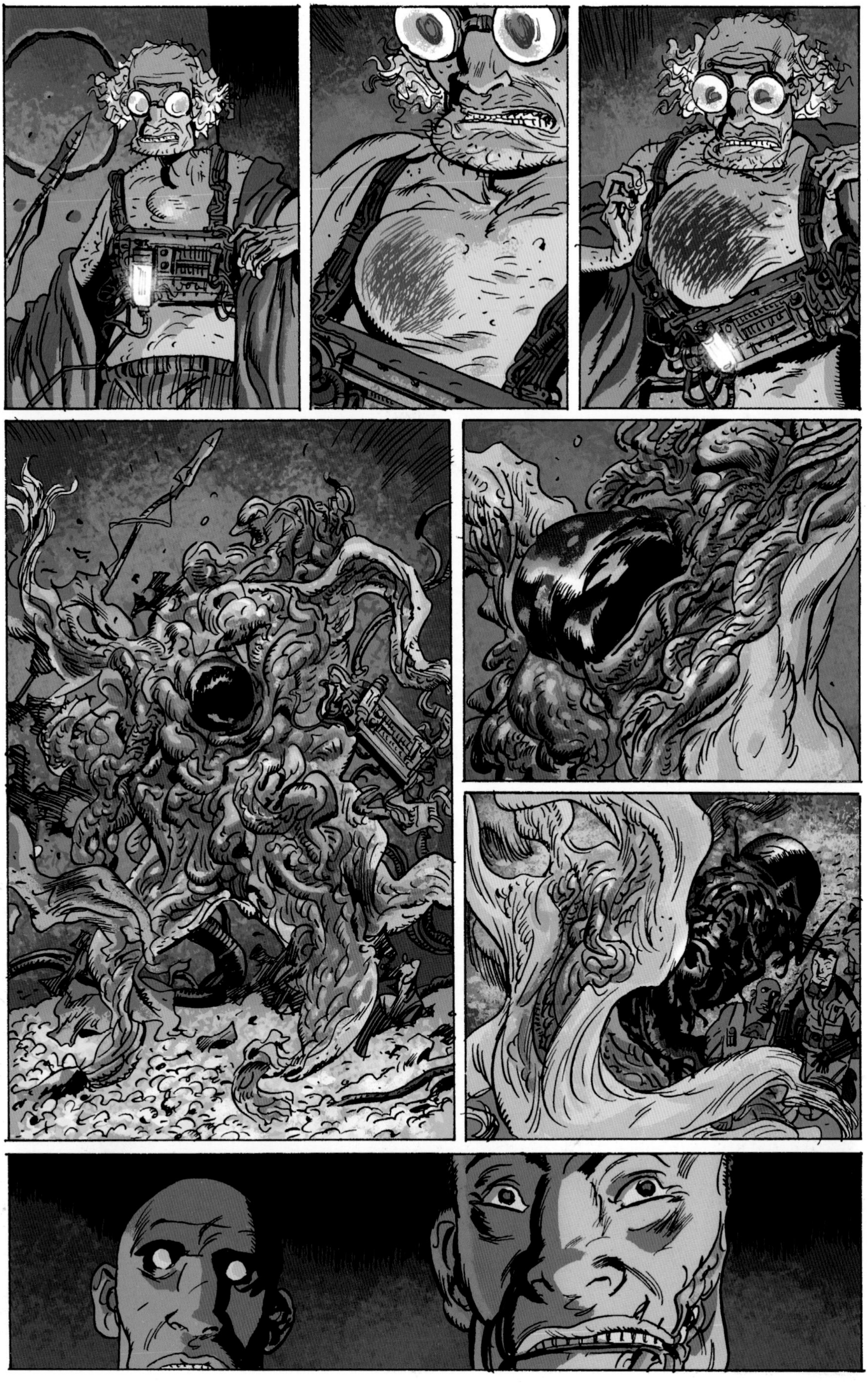

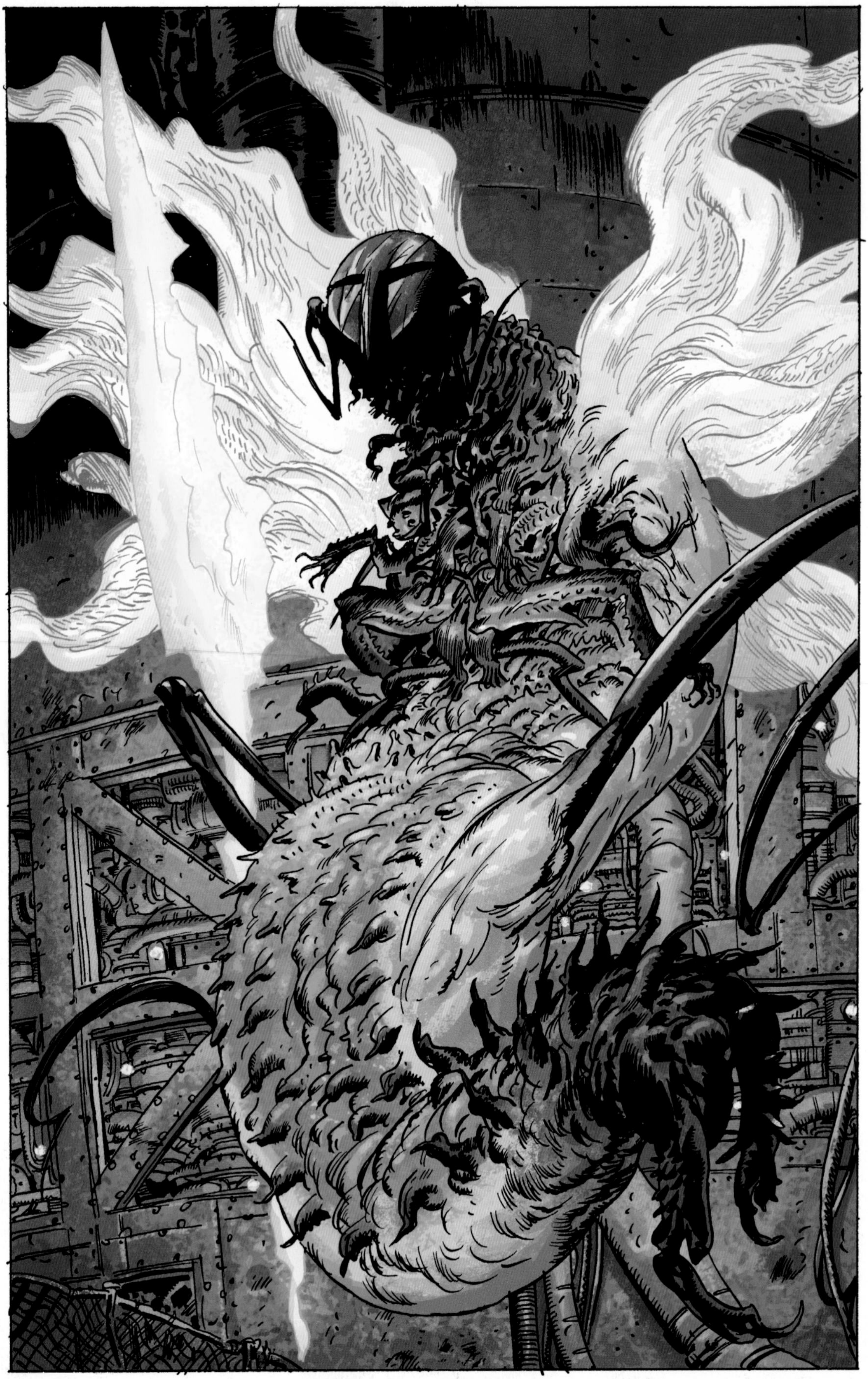

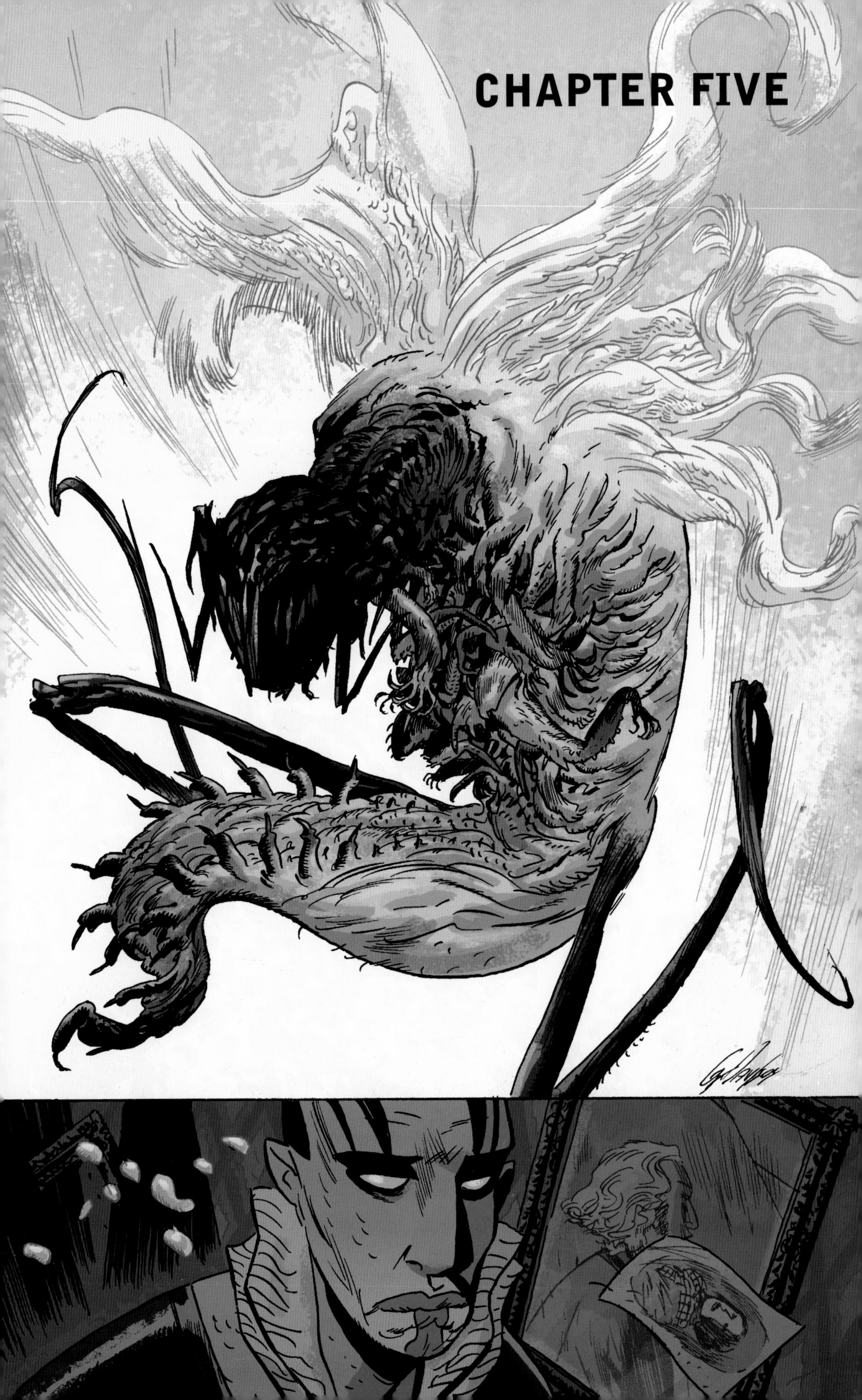
CHAPTER FIVE

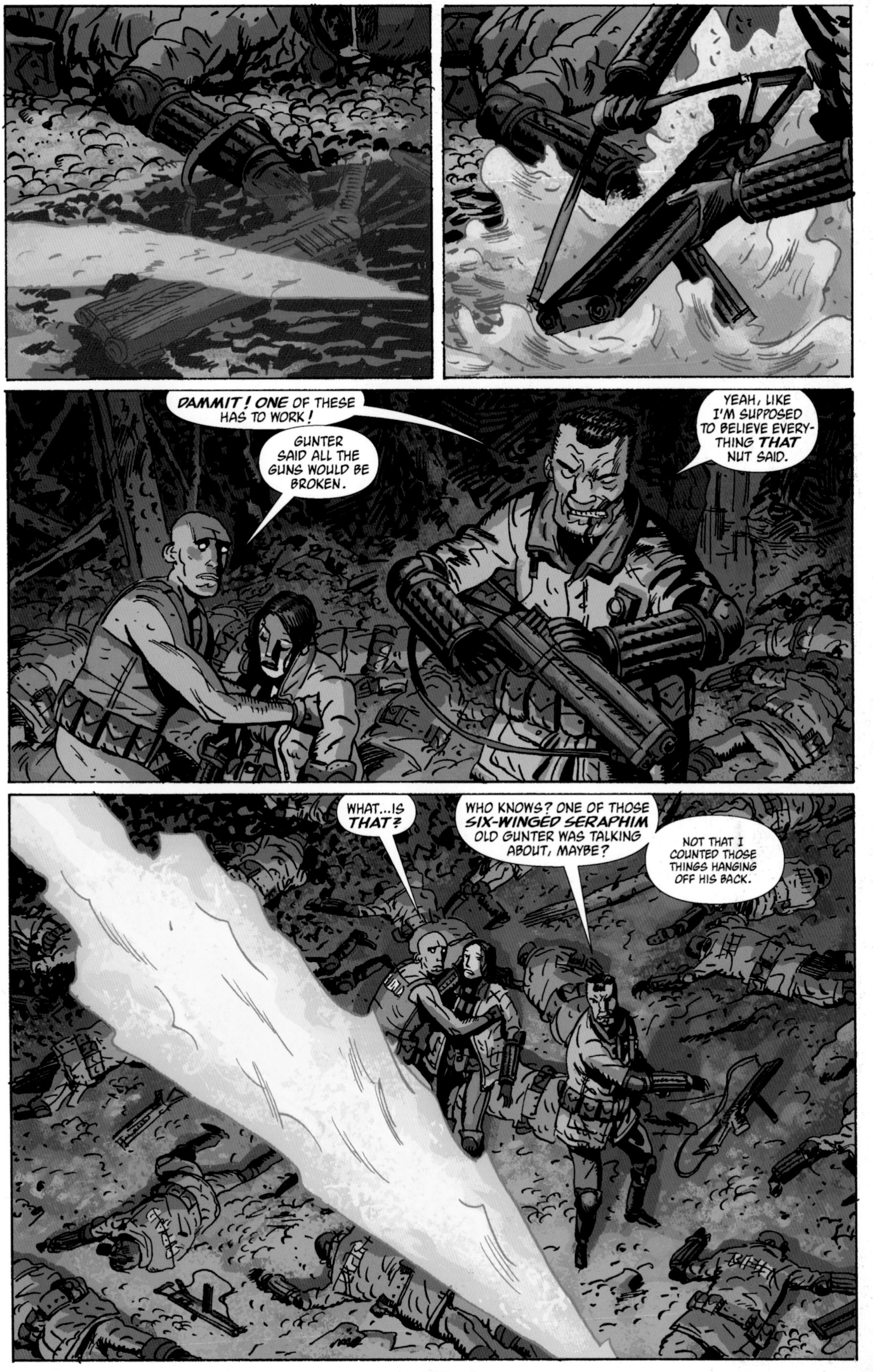
DAMMIT! ONE OF THESE HAS TO WORK!
GUNTER SAID ALL THE GUNS WOULD BE BROKEN.
YEAH, LIKE I'M SUPPOSED TO BELIEVE EVERY-THING THAT NUT SAID.
WHAT...IS THAT?
WHO KNOWS? ONE OF THOSE SIX-WINGED SERAPHIM OLD GUNTER WAS TALKING ABOUT, MAYBE?
NOT THAT I COUNTED THOSE THINGS HANGING OFF HIS BACK.

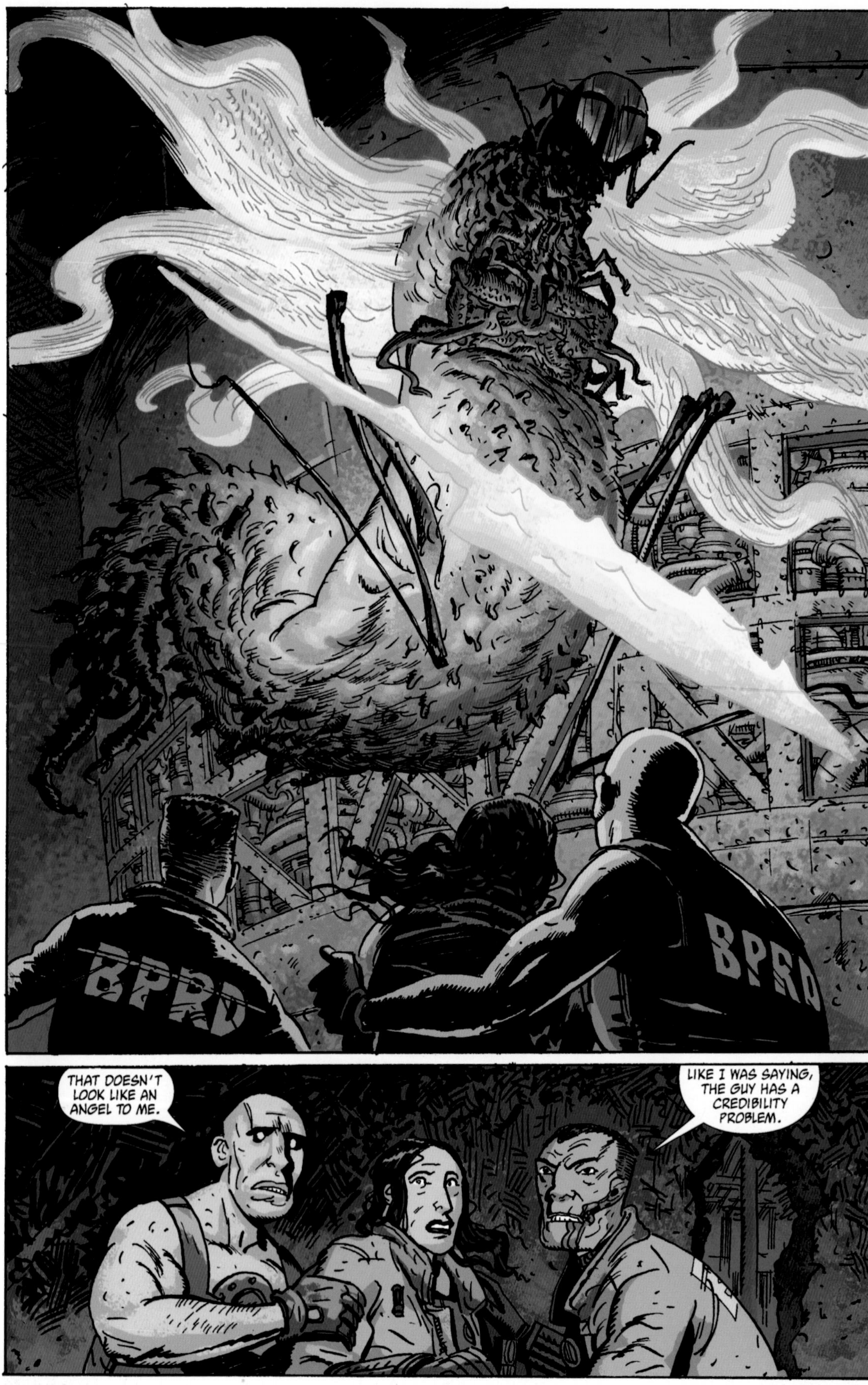
BPRD
BPRD
THAT DOESN'T LOOK LIKE AN ANGEL TO ME.
LIKE I WAS SAYING, THE GUY HAS A CREDIBILITY PROBLEM.

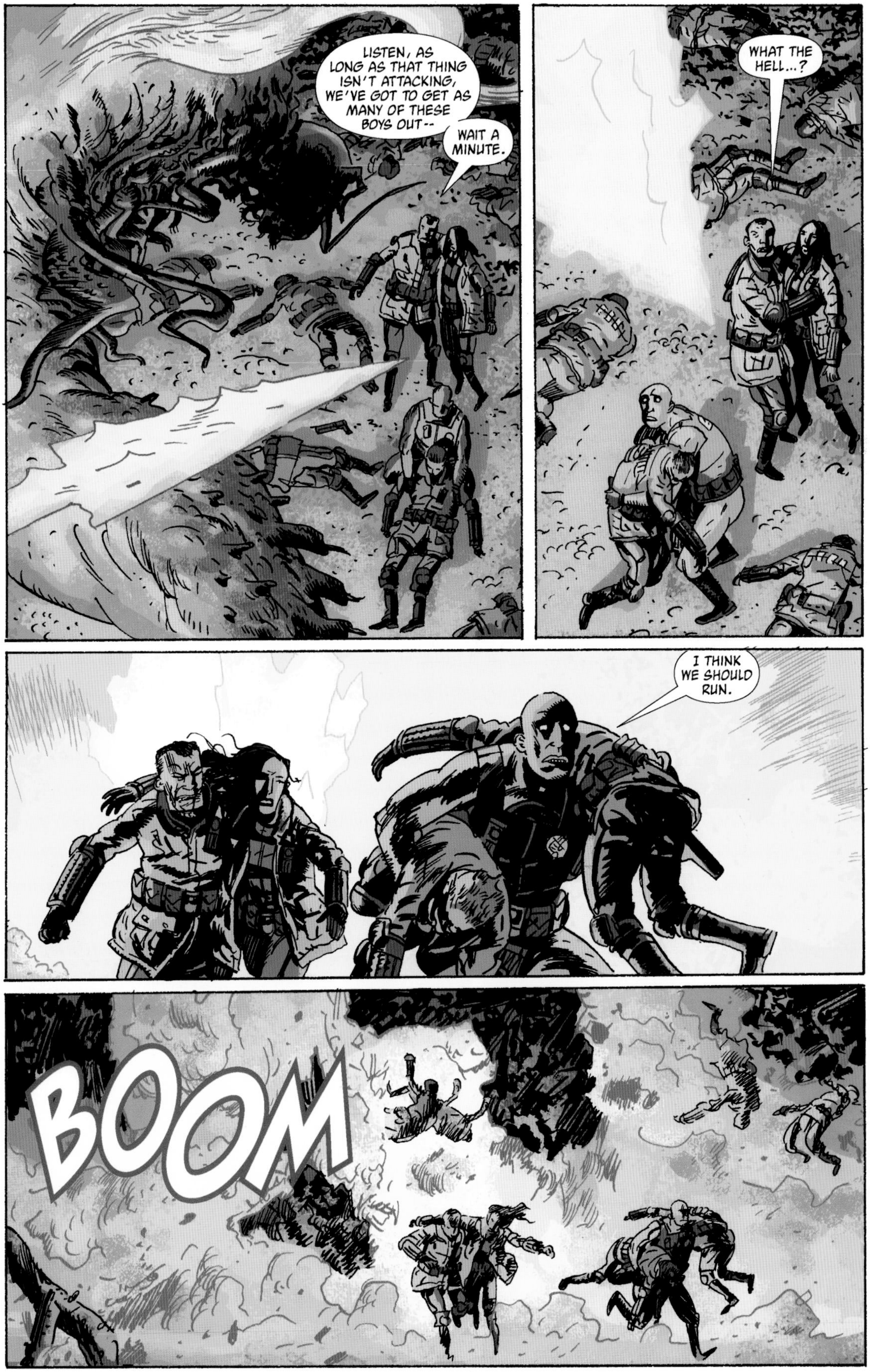
LISTEN, AS LONG AS THAT THING ISN'T ATTACKING, WE'VE GOT TO GET AS MANY OF THESE BOYS OUT--
WAIT A MINUTE.
WHAT THE HELL...?
I THINK WE SHOULD RUN.
BOOM

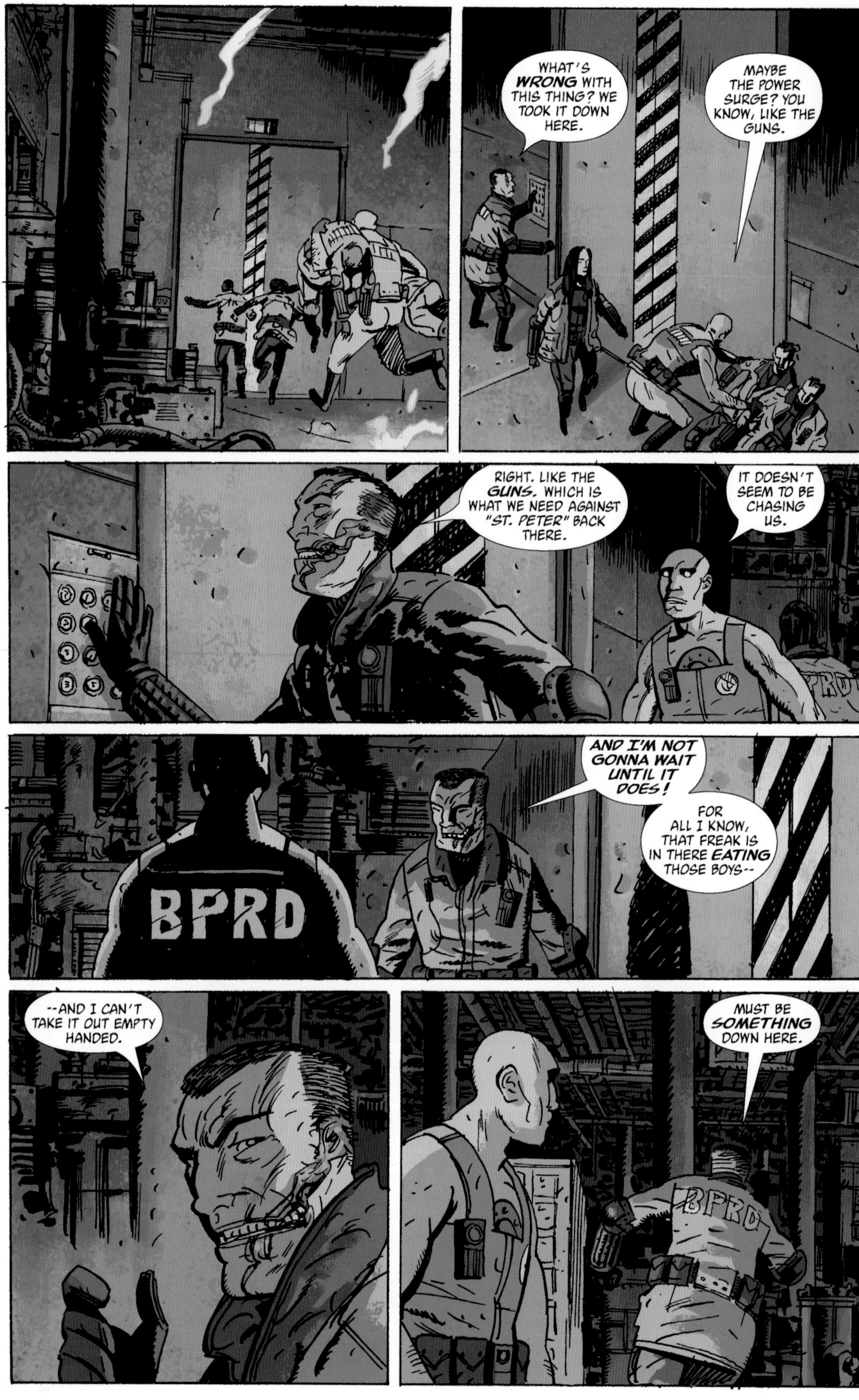

WHAT'S WRONG WITH THIS THING? WE TOOK IT DOWN HERE.
MAYBE THE POWER SURGE? YOU KNOW, LIKE THE GUNS.
RIGHT. LIKE THE GUNS. WHICH IS WHAT WE NEED AGAINST "ST. PETER" BACK THERE.
IT DOESN'T SEEM TO BE CHASING US.
BPRD
AND I'M NOT GONNA WAIT UNTIL IT DOES!
FOR ALL I KNOW, THAT FREAK IS IN THERE EATING THOSE BOYS--
--AND I CAN'T TAKE IT OUT EMPTY HANDED.
MUST BE SOMETHING DOWN HERE.
BPRD

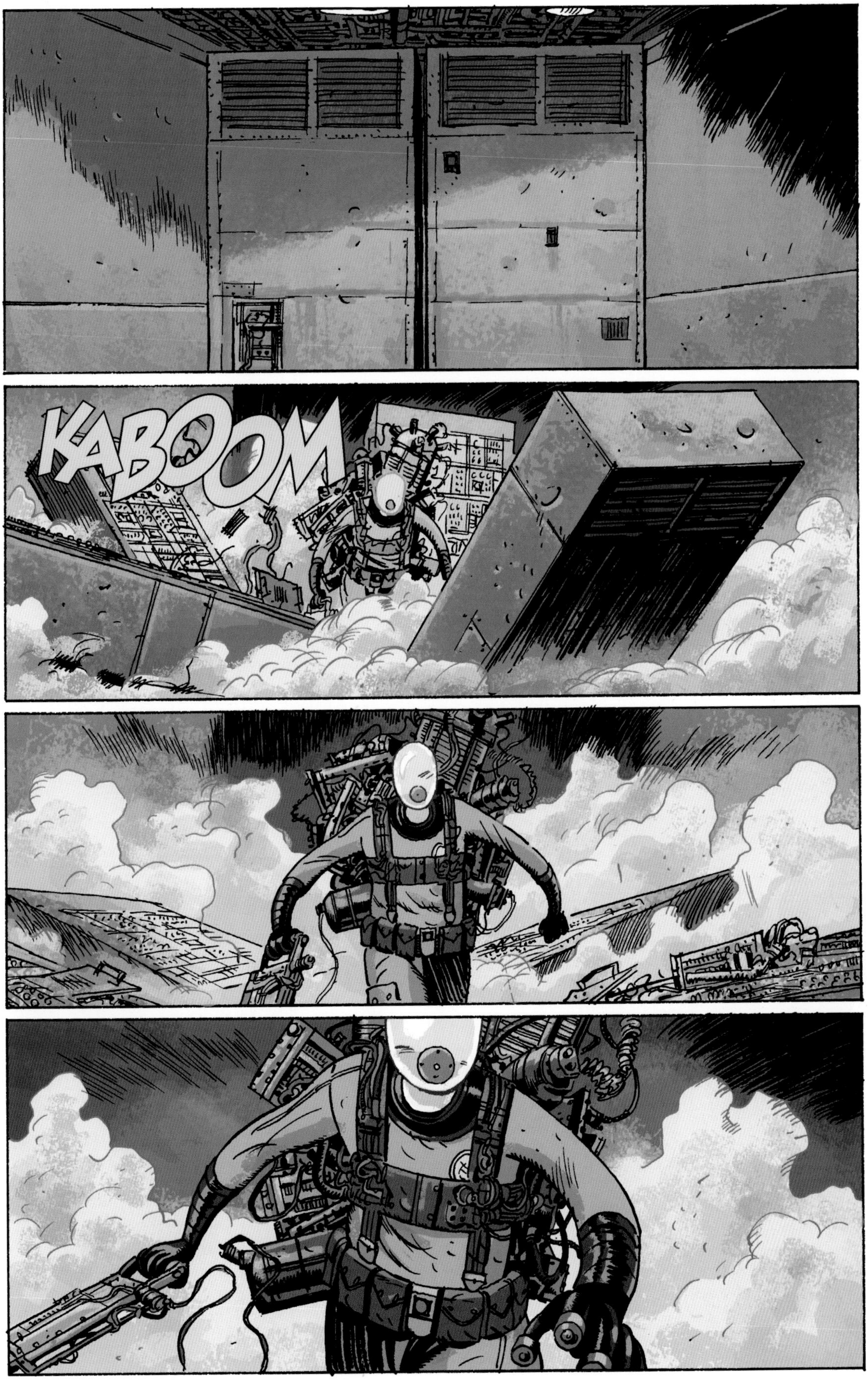
KABOOM

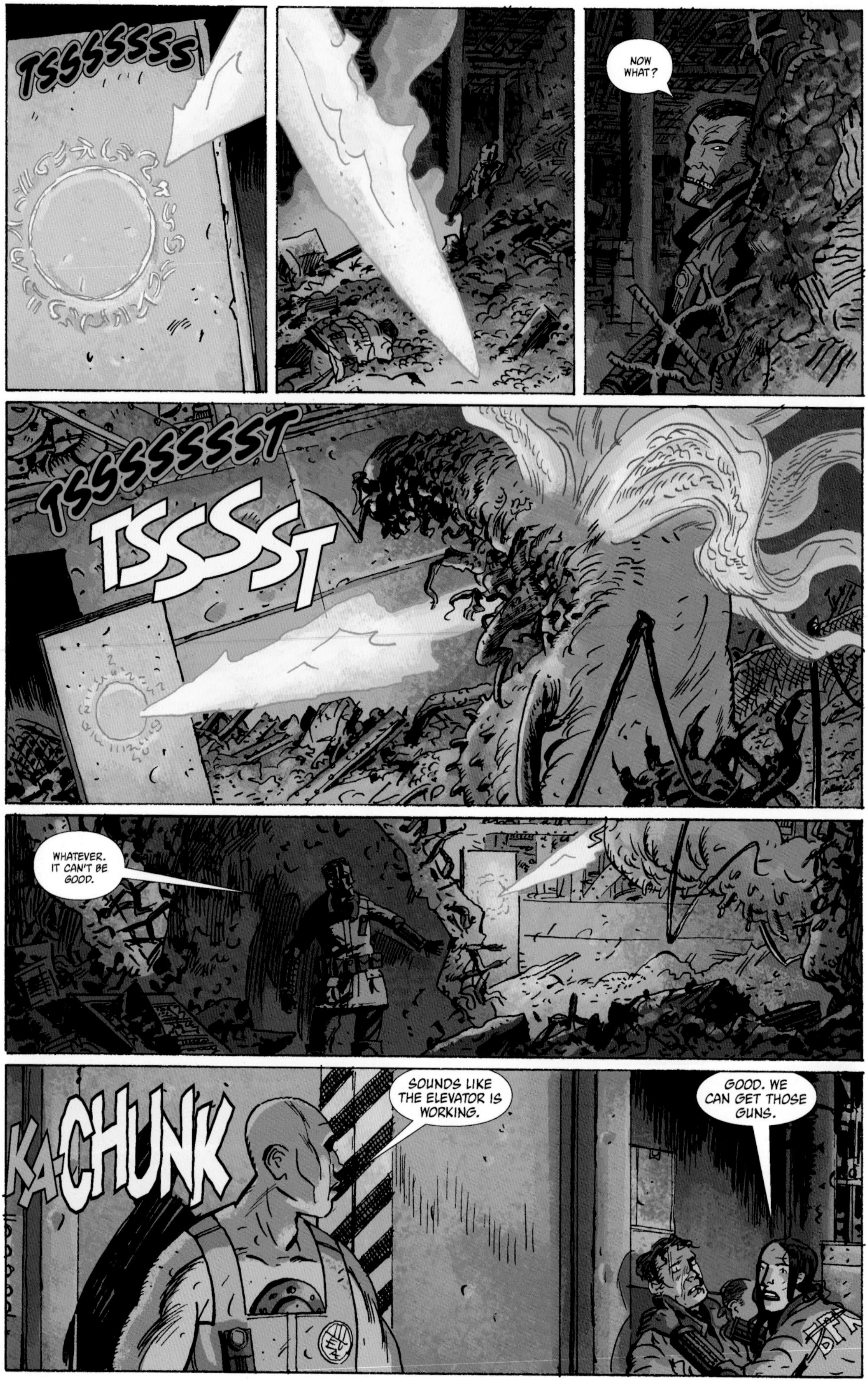
TSSSSSSS
NOW WHAT?
TSSSSSSSST
TSSSST
WHATEVER. IT CAN'T BE GOOD.
KA-CHUNK
SOUNDS LIKE THE ELEVATOR IS WORKING.
GOOD. WE CAN GET THOSE GUNS.

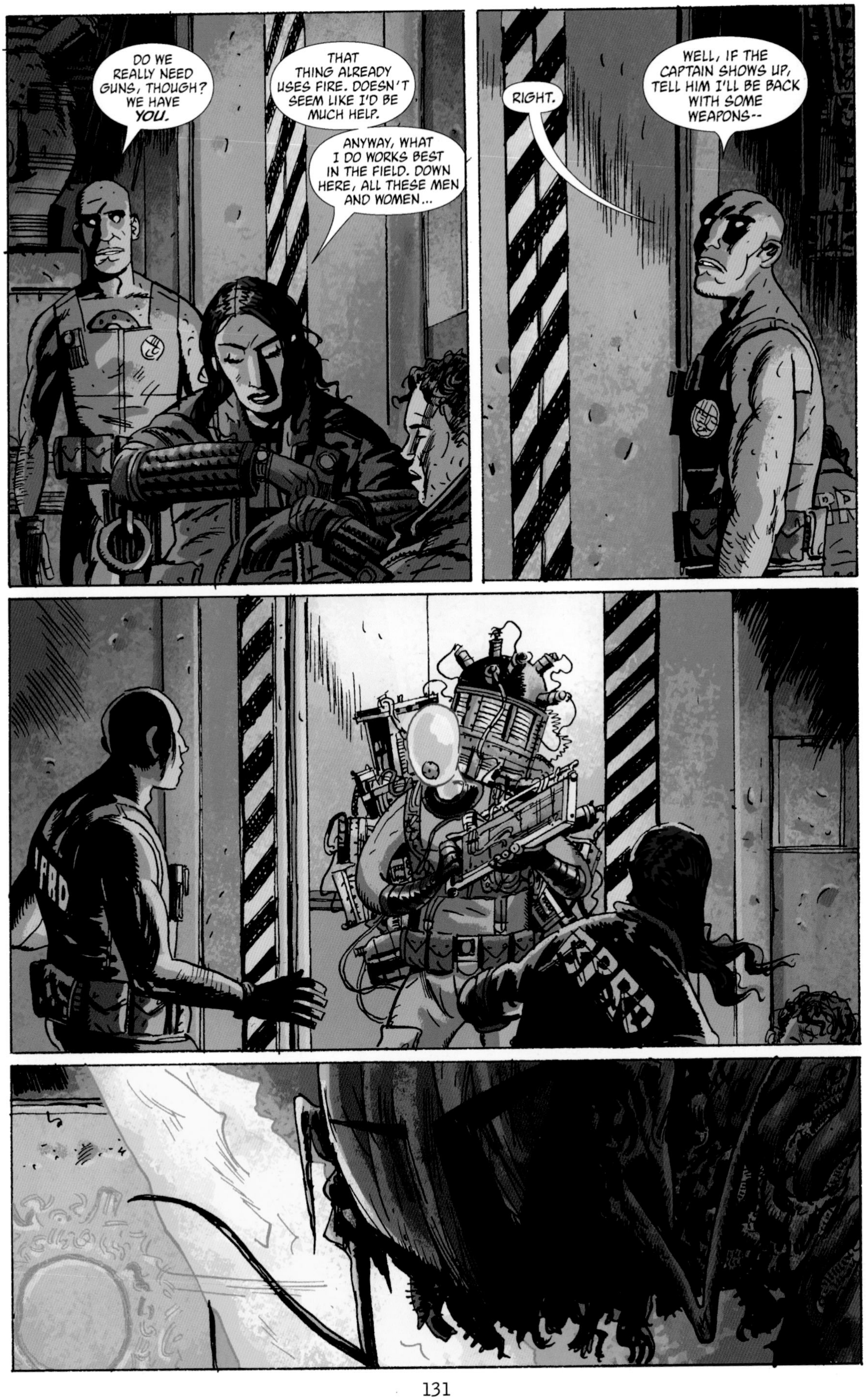
DO WE REALLY NEED GUNS, THOUGH? WE HAVE *YOU.*
THAT THING ALREADY USES FIRE. DOESN'T SEEM LIKE I'D BE MUCH HELP.
ANYWAY, WHAT I DO WORKS BEST IN THE FIELD. DOWN HERE, ALL THESE MEN AND WOMEN...
RIGHT.
WELL, IF THE CAPTAIN SHOWS UP, TELL HIM I'LL BE BACK WITH SOME WEAPONS--

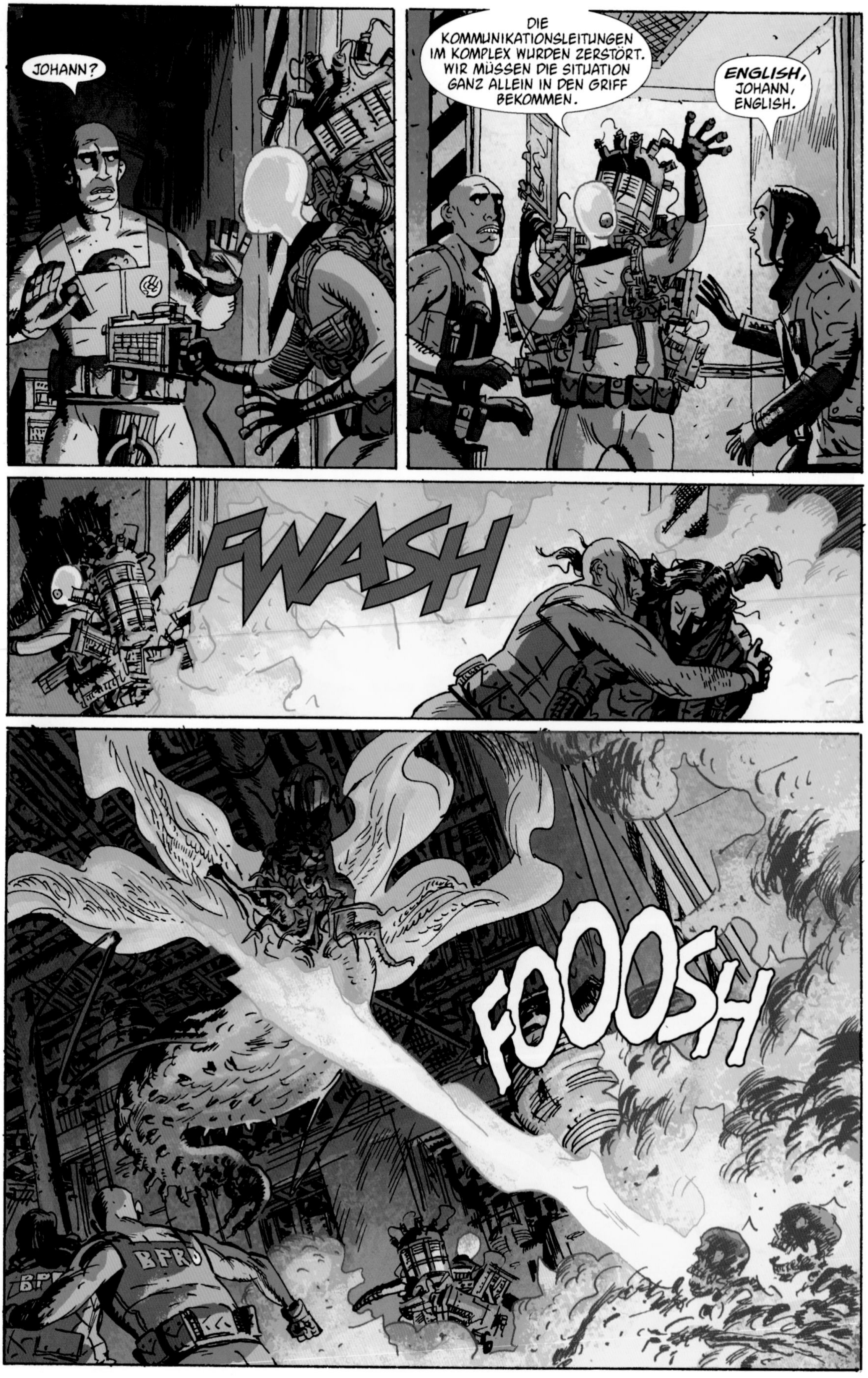
JOHANN?
DIE KOMMUNIKATIONSLEITUNGEN IM KOMPLEX WURDEN ZERSTÖRT. WIR MÜSSEN DIE SITUATION GANZ ALLEIN IN DEN GRIFF BEKOMMEN.
ENGLISH, JOHANN, ENGLISH.
FWASH
FOOOSH
BPRD

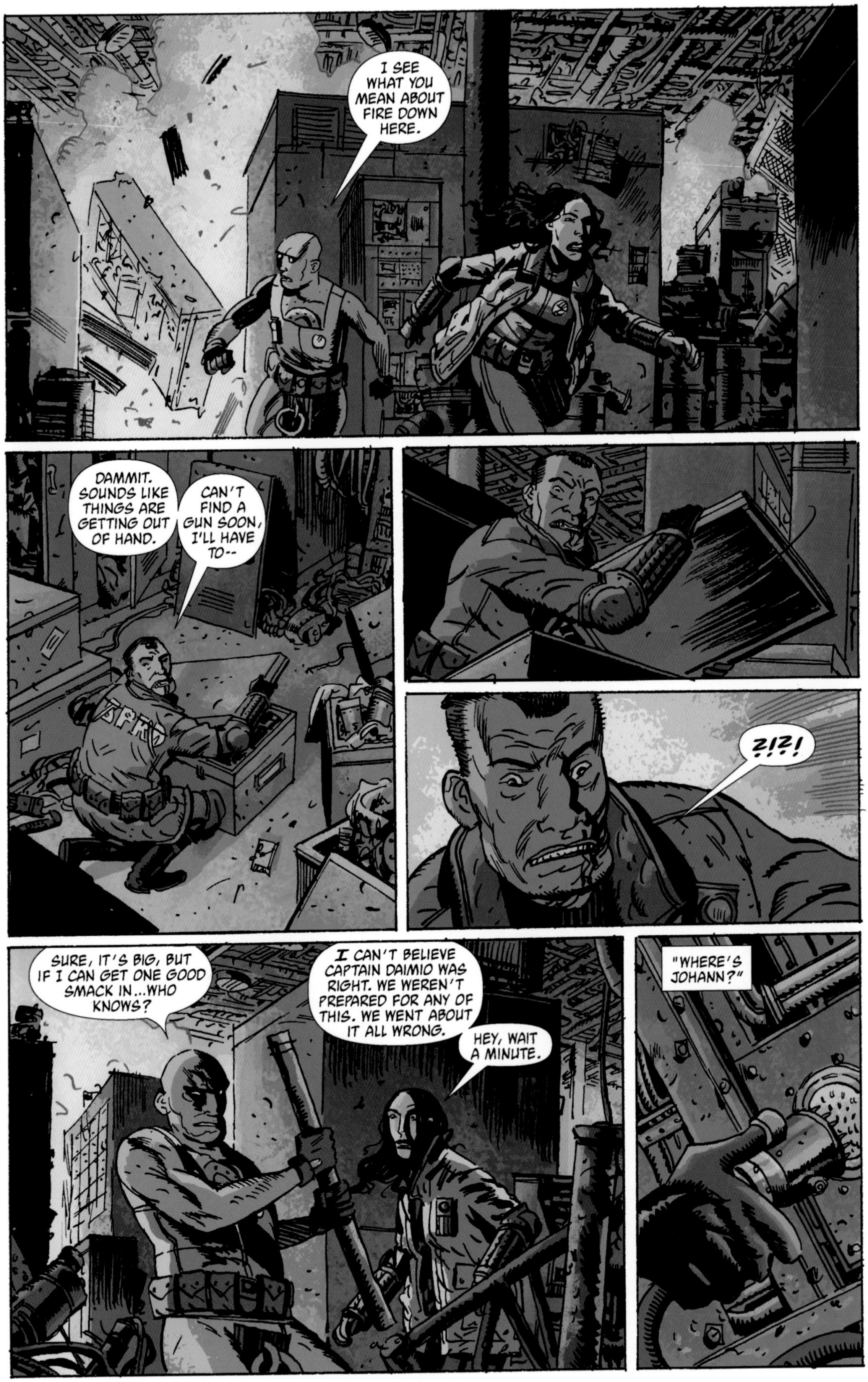
I SEE WHAT YOU MEAN ABOUT FIRE DOWN HERE.
DAMMIT. SOUNDS LIKE THINGS ARE GETTING OUT OF HAND.
CAN'T FIND A GUN SOON, I'LL HAVE TO--
?!?!
SURE, IT'S BIG, BUT IF I CAN GET ONE GOOD SMACK IN...WHO KNOWS?
I CAN'T BELIEVE CAPTAIN DAIMIO WAS RIGHT. WE WEREN'T PREPARED FOR ANY OF THIS. WE WENT ABOUT IT ALL WRONG.
HEY, WAIT A MINUTE.
"WHERE'S JOHANN?"

UND JETZT WOLLEN WIR MAL SEHEN, OB EURE KLEINLICHEN, UNBEDEUTENDEN STREITEREIEN ETWAS GEBRACHT HABEN.

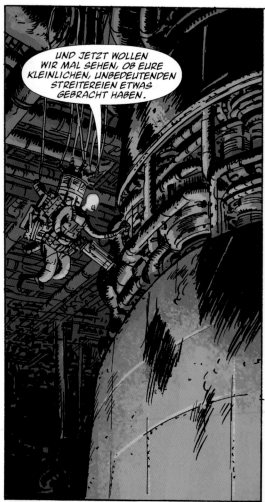

ROGER, MAYBE WE SHOULD WAIT FOR THE CAPTAIN.

THAT THING IS COMING FOR US, LIZ.

ANYWAY, I'M PRETTY TOUGH.

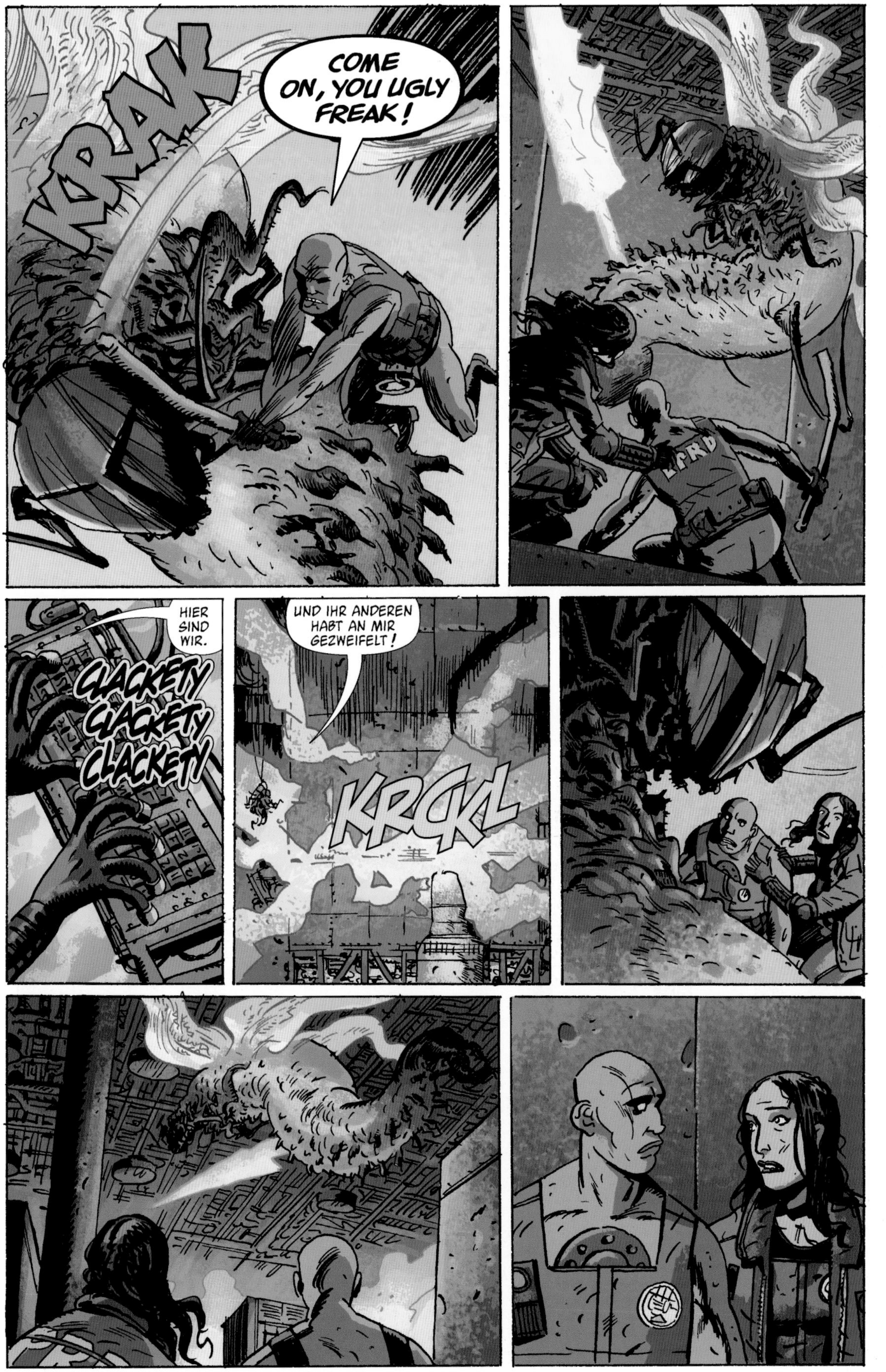
KRAK
COME ON, YOU UGLY FREAK!
HIER SIND WIR.
CLACKETY CLACKETY CLACKETY
UND IHR ANDEREN HABT AN MIR GEZWEIFELT!
KRCKL

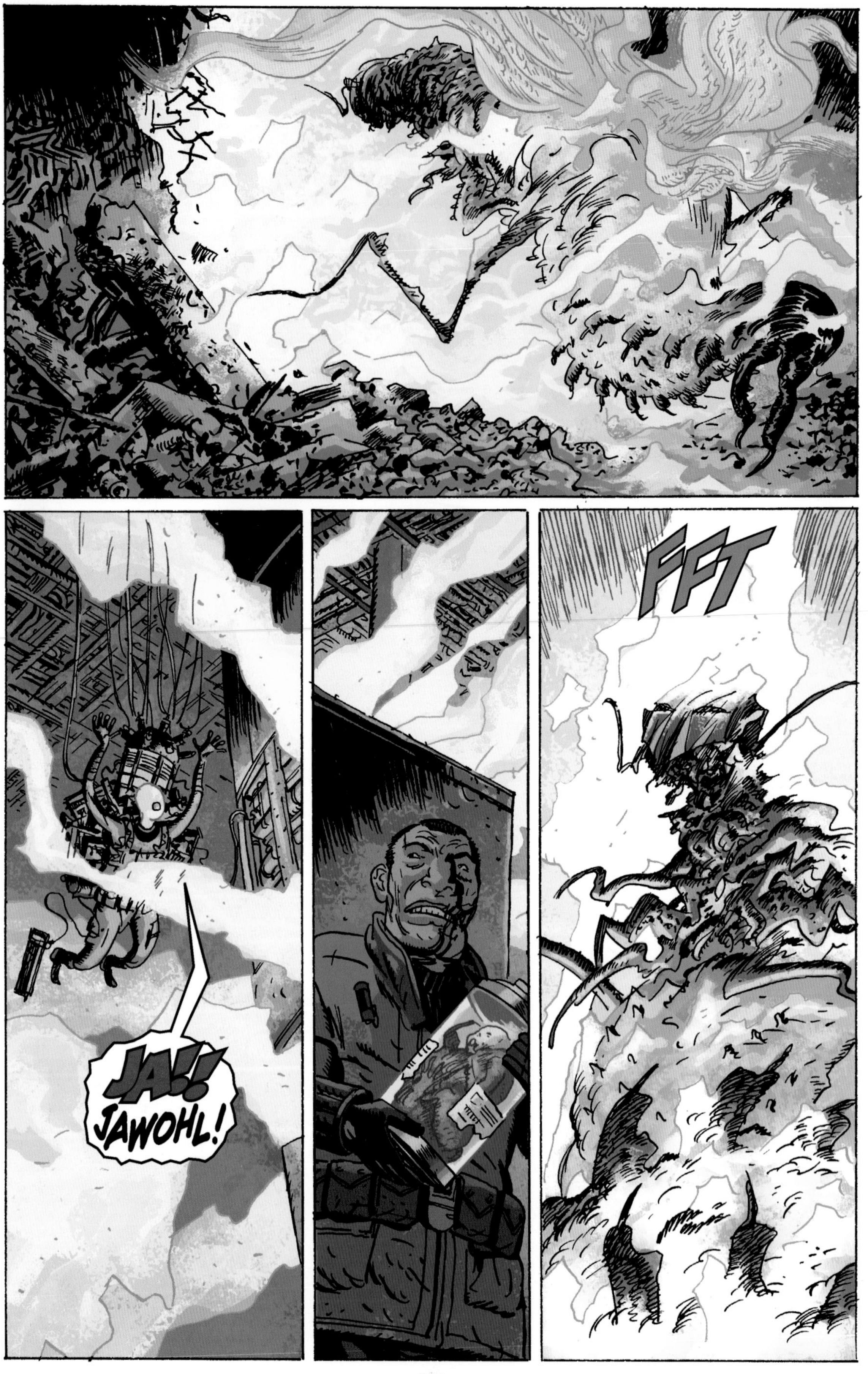
JA!!
JAWOHL!
FFT

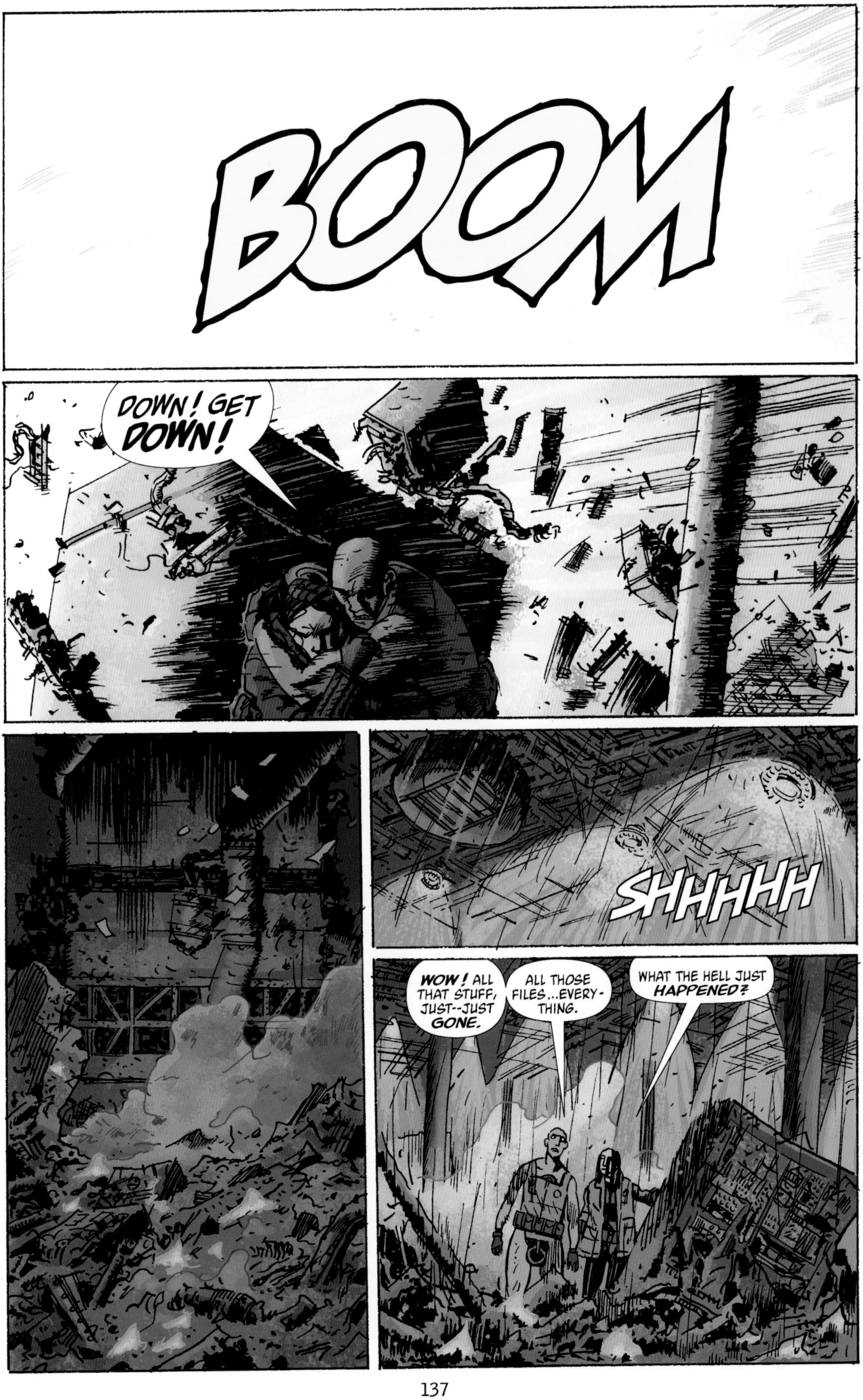
BOOM
DOWN! GET DOWN!
SHHHHH
WOW! ALL THAT STUFF, JUST--JUST GONE.
ALL THOSE FILES...EVERY-THING.
WHAT THE HELL JUST HAPPENED?

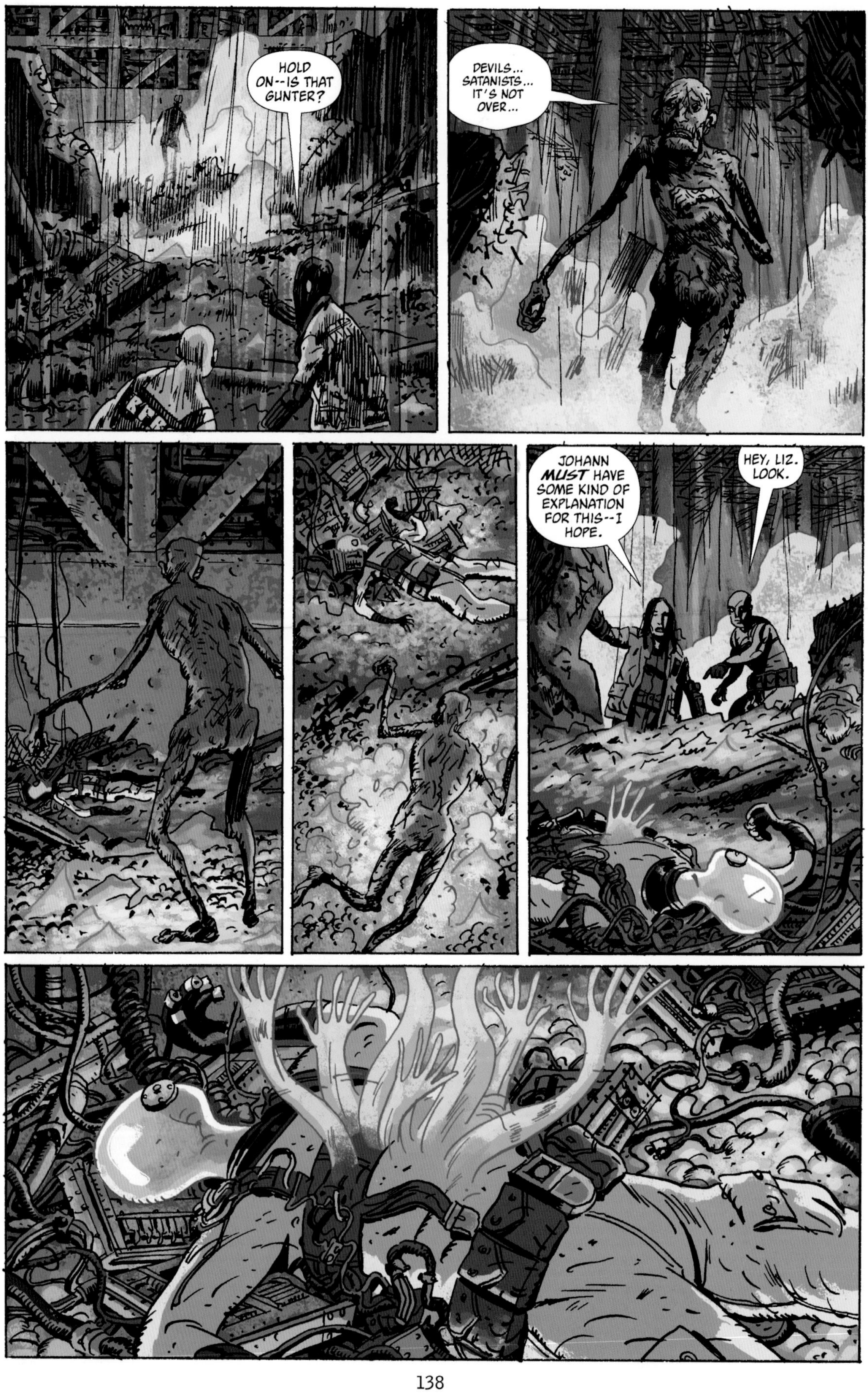
HOLD ON--IS THAT GUNTER?
DEVILS... SATANISTS... IT'S NOT OVER...
JOHANN MUST HAVE SOME KIND OF EXPLANATION FOR THIS--I HOPE.
HEY, LIZ. LOOK.

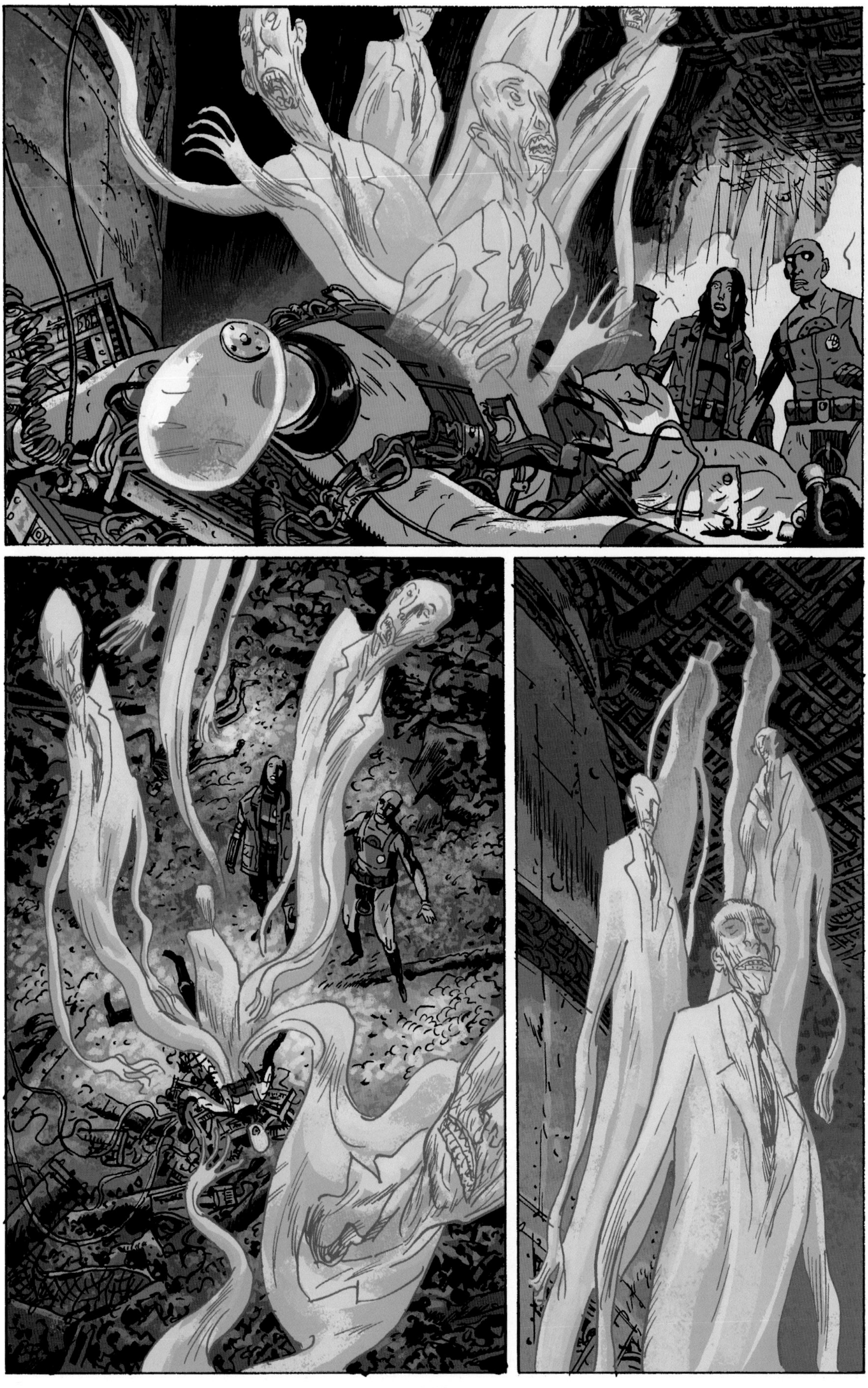

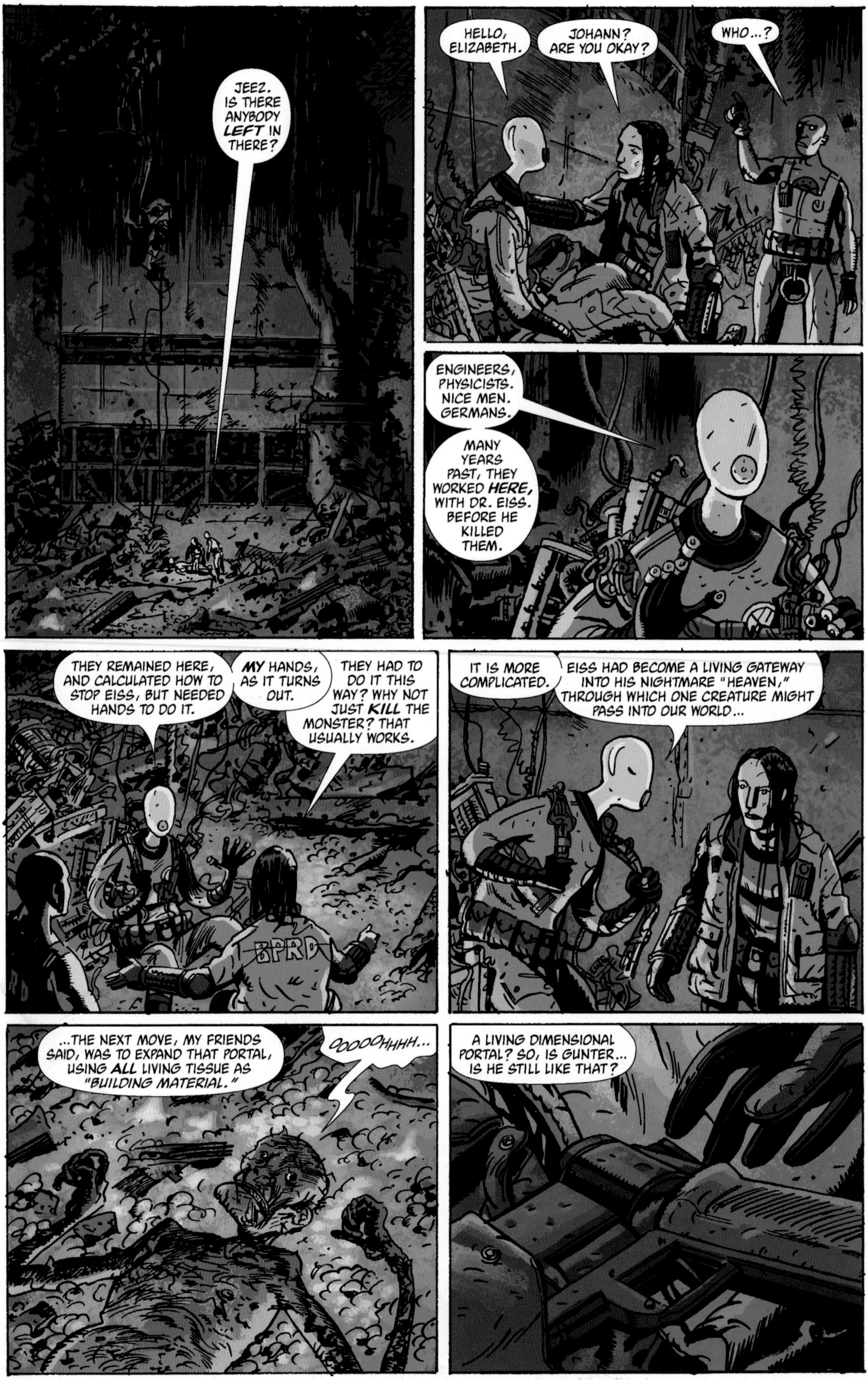
JEEZ. IS THERE ANYBODY LEFT IN THERE?
HELLO, ELIZABETH.
JOHANN? ARE YOU OKAY?
WHO...?
ENGINEERS, PHYSICISTS. NICE MEN. GERMANS.
MANY YEARS PAST, THEY WORKED HERE, WITH DR. EISS. BEFORE HE KILLED THEM.
THEY REMAINED HERE, AND CALCULATED HOW TO STOP EISS, BUT NEEDED HANDS TO DO IT.
MY HANDS, AS IT TURNS OUT.
THEY HAD TO DO IT THIS WAY? WHY NOT JUST KILL THE MONSTER? THAT USUALLY WORKS.
BPRD
IT IS MORE COMPLICATED.
EISS HAD BECOME A LIVING GATEWAY INTO HIS NIGHTMARE "HEAVEN," THROUGH WHICH ONE CREATURE MIGHT PASS INTO OUR WORLD...
...THE NEXT MOVE, MY FRIENDS SAID, WAS TO EXPAND THAT PORTAL, USING ALL LIVING TISSUE AS "BUILDING MATERIAL."
OOOOOHHHH...
A LIVING DIMENSIONAL PORTAL? SO, IS GUNTER... IS HE STILL LIKE THAT?

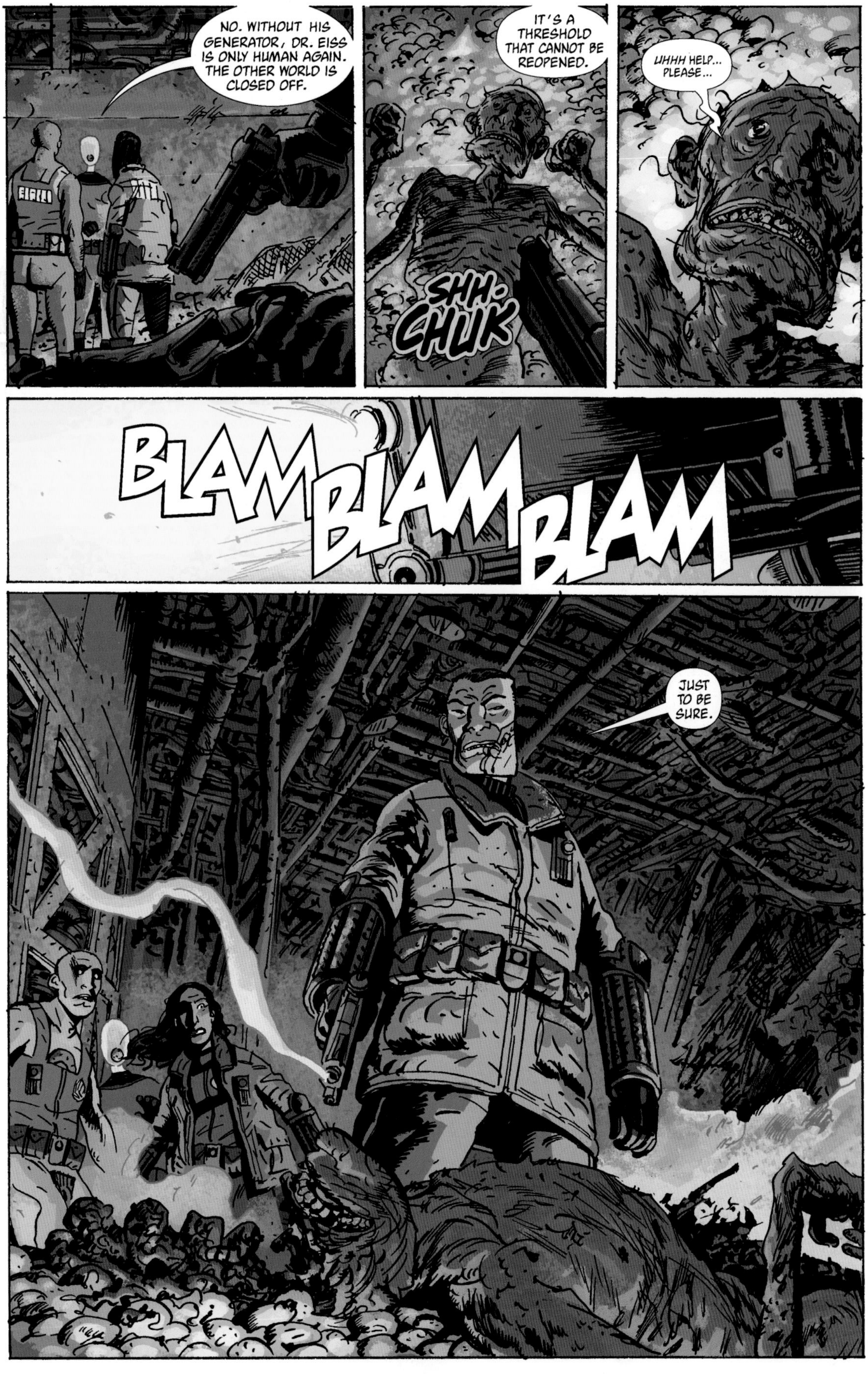
NO. WITHOUT HIS GENERATOR, DR. EISS IS ONLY HUMAN AGAIN. THE OTHER WORLD IS CLOSED OFF.
IT'S A THRESHOLD THAT CANNOT BE REOPENED.
SHH-CHUK
UHHH HELP... PLEASE...
BLAM BLAM BLAM
JUST TO BE SURE.

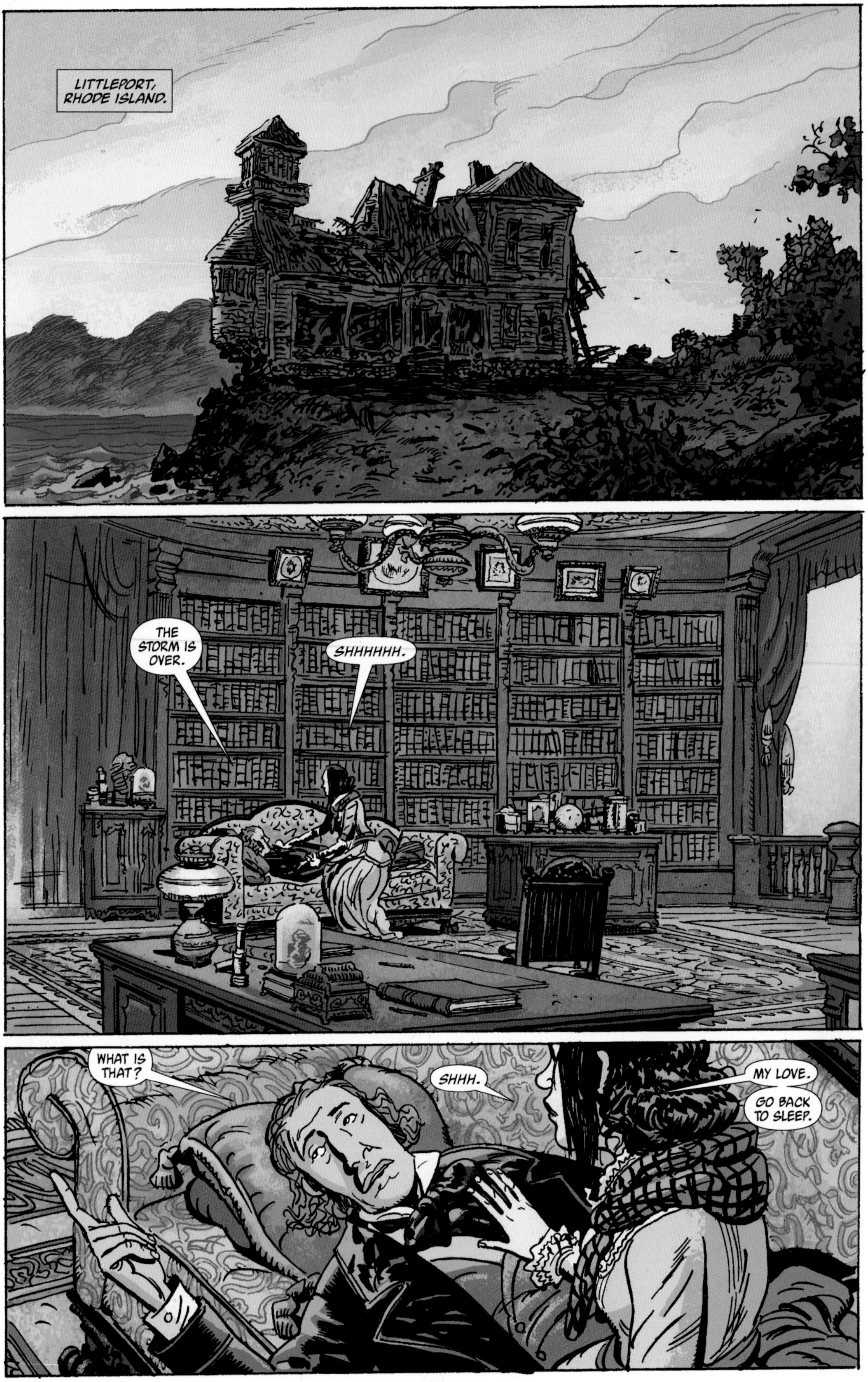
LITTLEPORT, RHODE ISLAND.
THE STORM IS OVER.
SHHHHHH.
WHAT IS THAT?
SHHH.
MY LOVE.
GO BACK TO SLEEP.

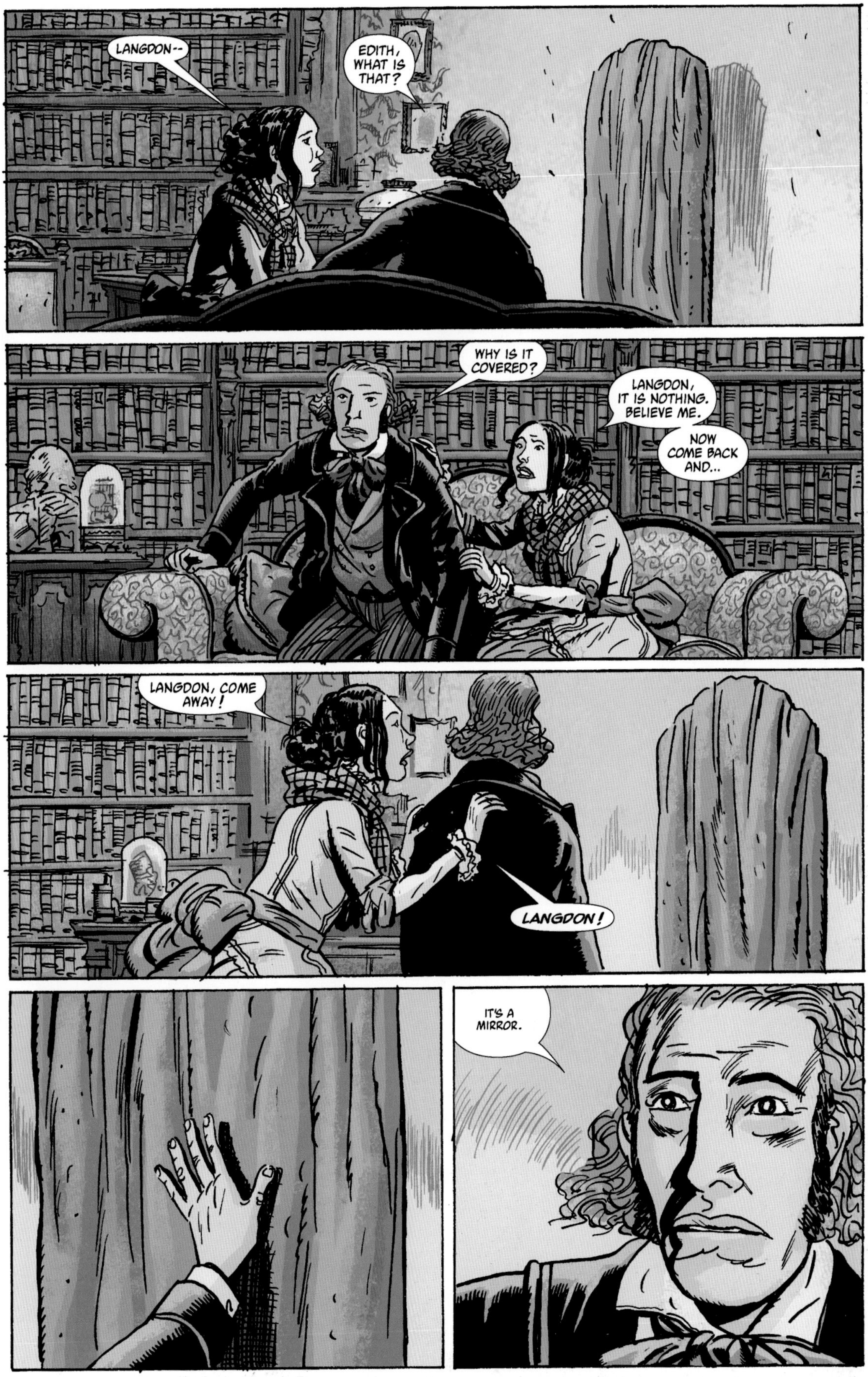
LANGDON--
EDITH, WHAT IS THAT?
WHY IS IT COVERED?
LANGDON, IT IS NOTHING. BELIEVE ME.
NOW COME BACK AND...
LANGDON, COME AWAY!
LANGDON!
IT'S A MIRROR.

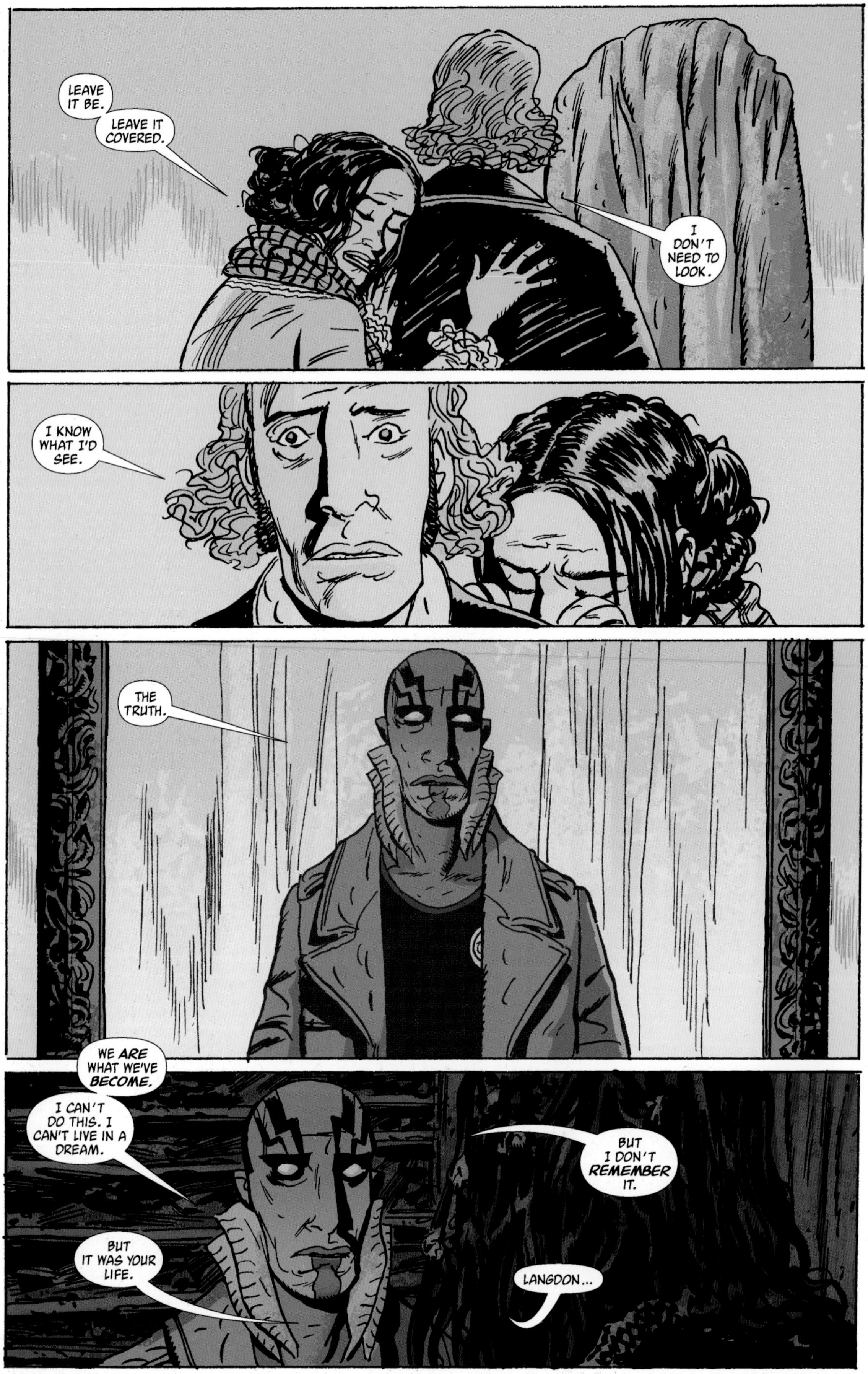
LEAVE IT BE.
LEAVE IT COVERED.
I DON'T NEED TO LOOK.
I KNOW WHAT I'D SEE.
THE TRUTH.
WE ARE WHAT WE'VE BECOME.
I CAN'T DO THIS. I CAN'T LIVE IN A DREAM.
BUT I DON'T REMEMBER IT.
BUT IT WAS YOUR LIFE.
LANGDON...

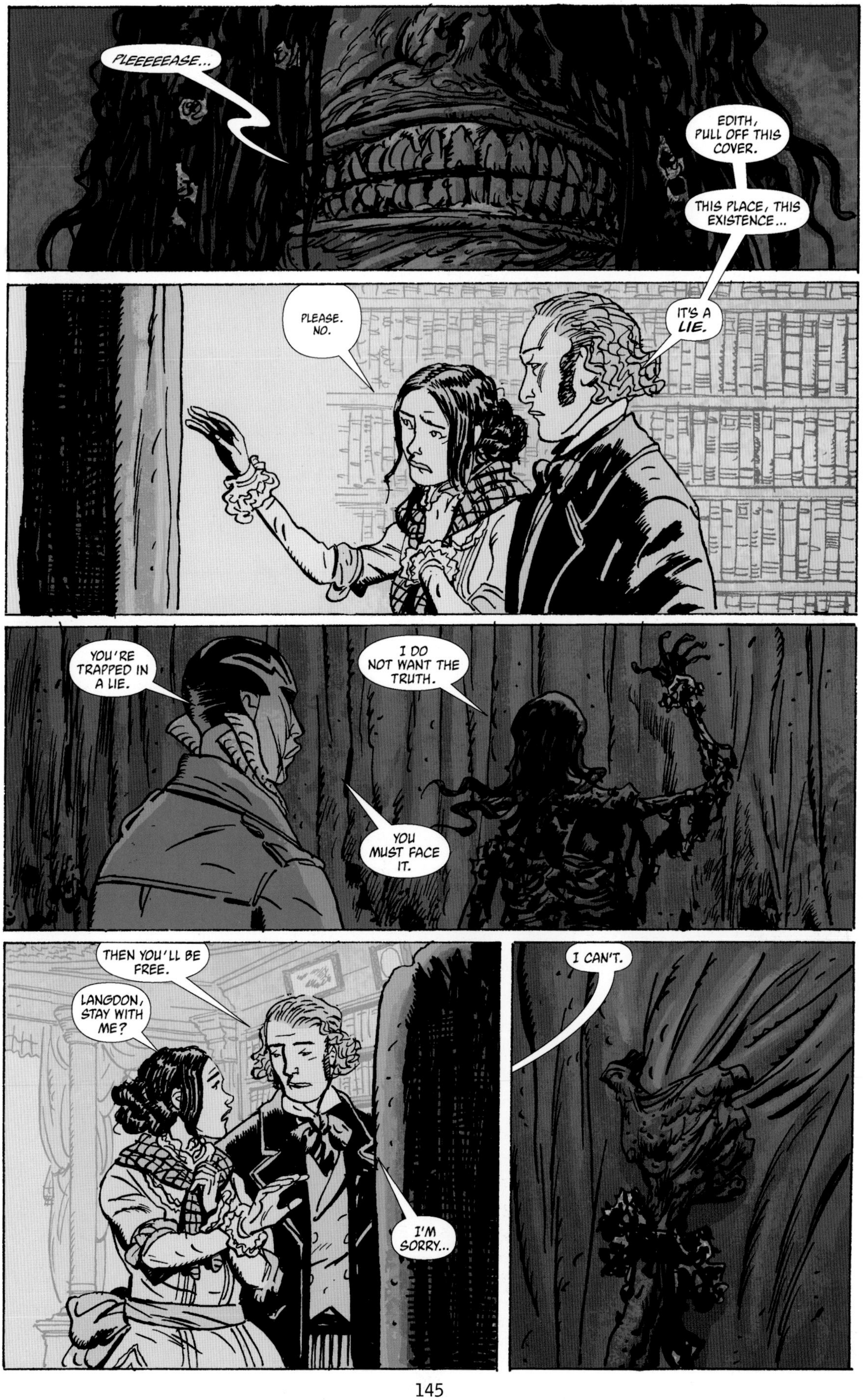
PLEEEEEASE...
EDITH, PULL OFF THIS COVER.
THIS PLACE, THIS EXISTENCE...
IT'S A LIE.
PLEASE. NO.
YOU'RE TRAPPED IN A LIE.
I DO NOT WANT THE TRUTH.
YOU MUST FACE IT.
THEN YOU'LL BE FREE.
LANGDON, STAY WITH ME?
I'M SORRY...
I CAN'T.

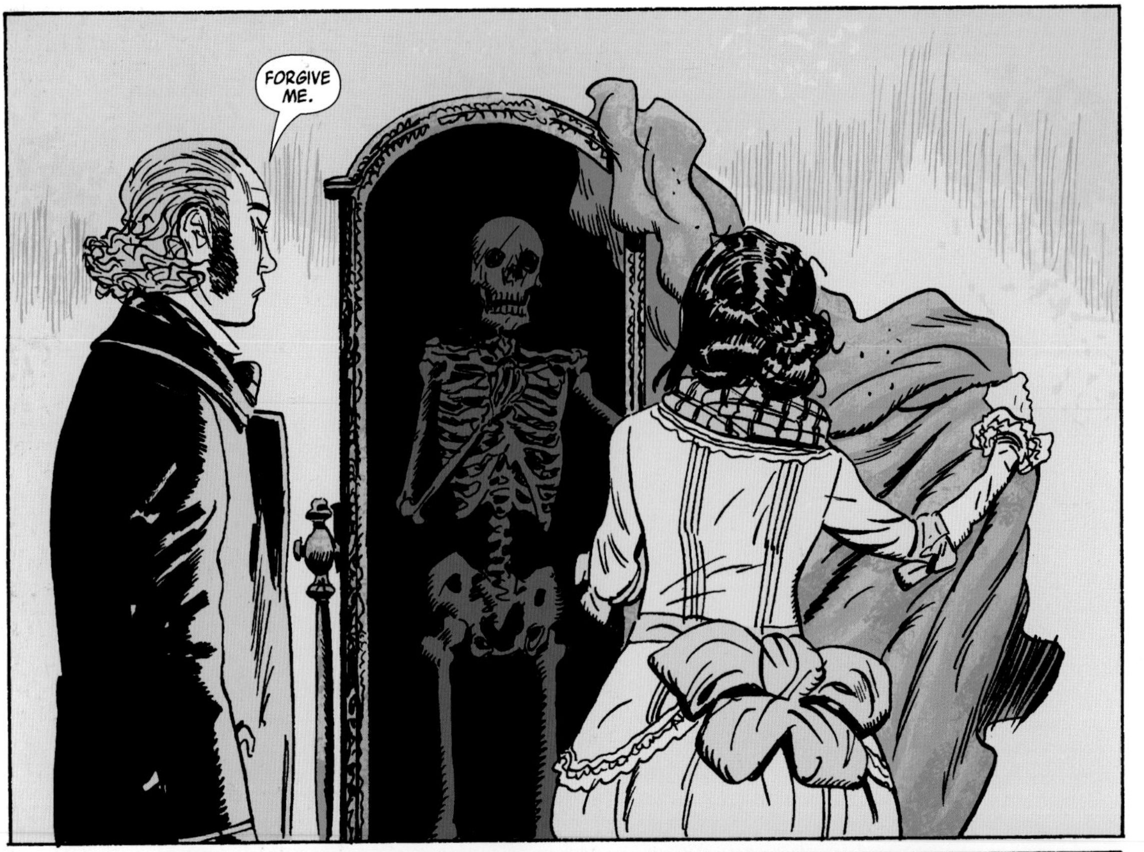
FORGIVE ME.

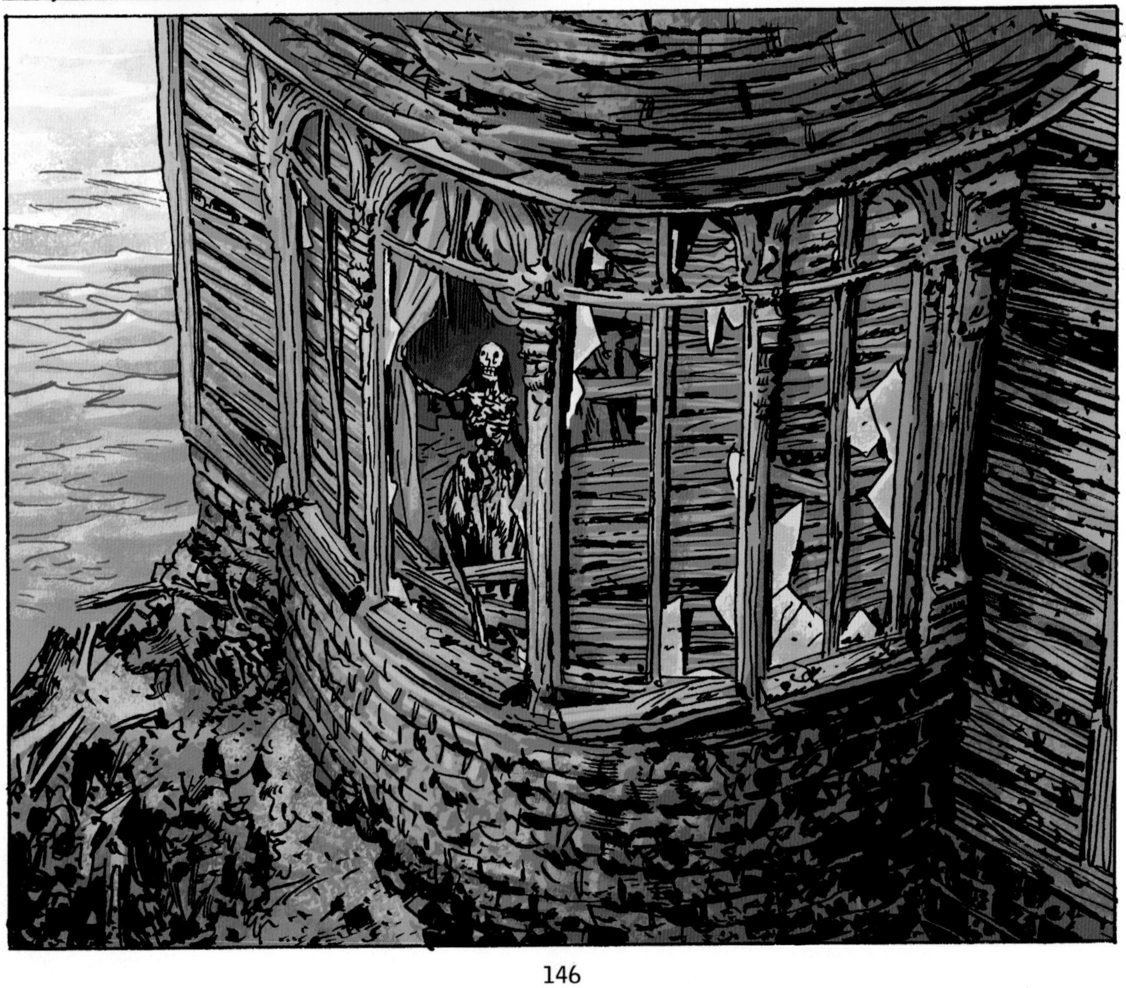

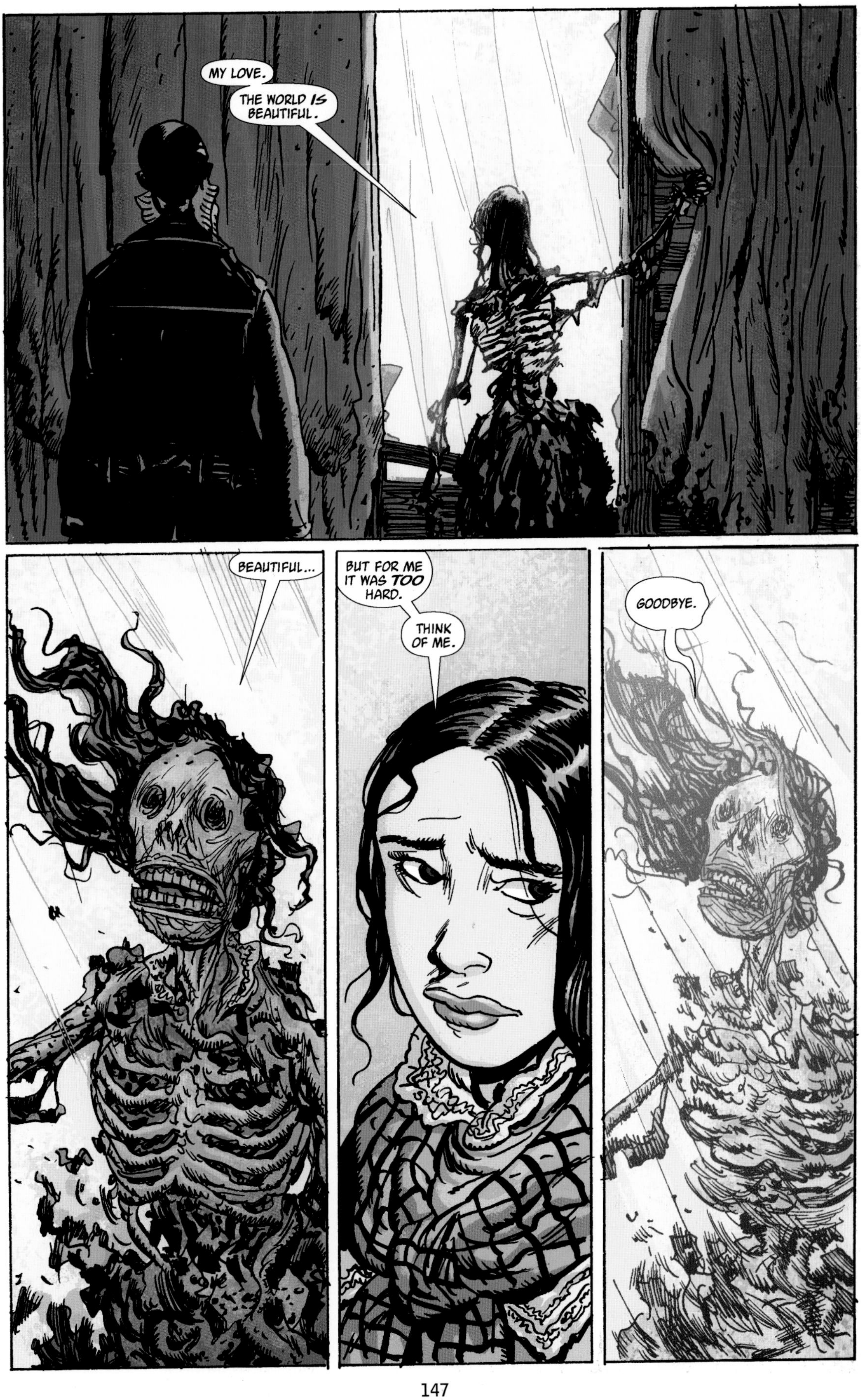
MY LOVE.
THE WORLD IS BEAUTIFUL.
BEAUTIFUL...
BUT FOR ME IT WAS TOO HARD.
THINK OF ME.
GOODBYE.

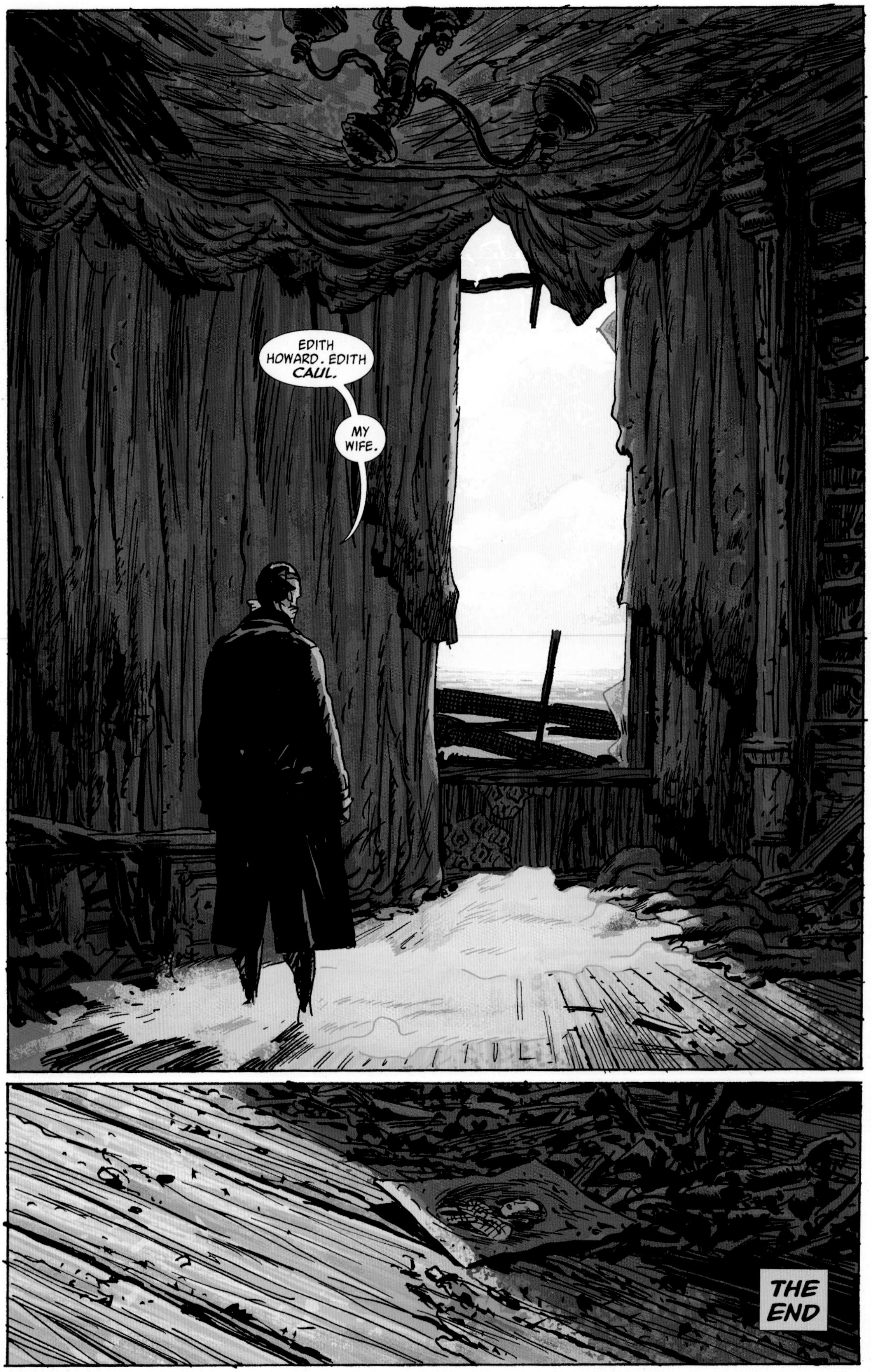
EDITH HOWARD. EDITH CAUL.
MY WIFE.
THE END

BOOK TWO

WAR ON FROGS

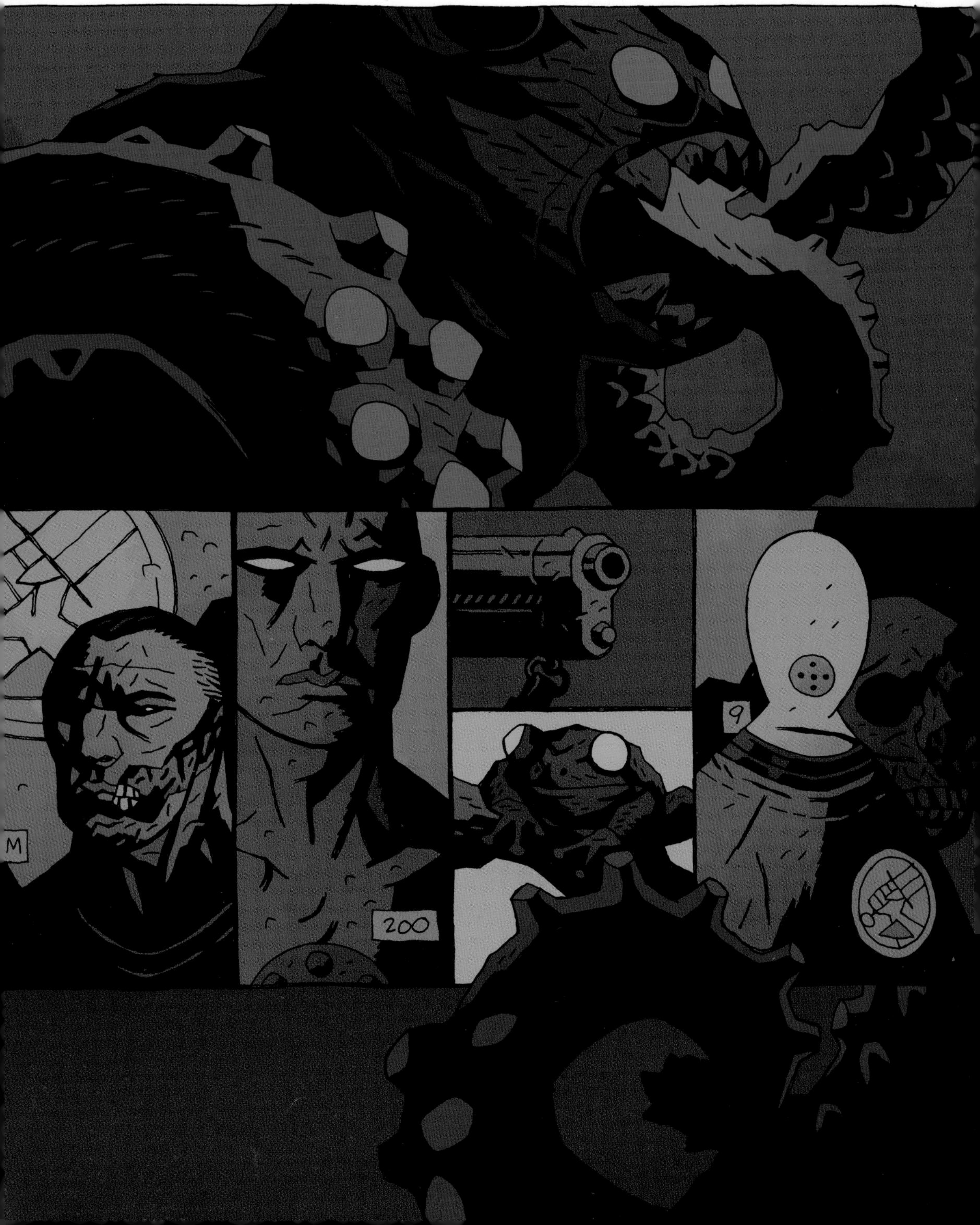
M
200
9

CHAPTER ONE

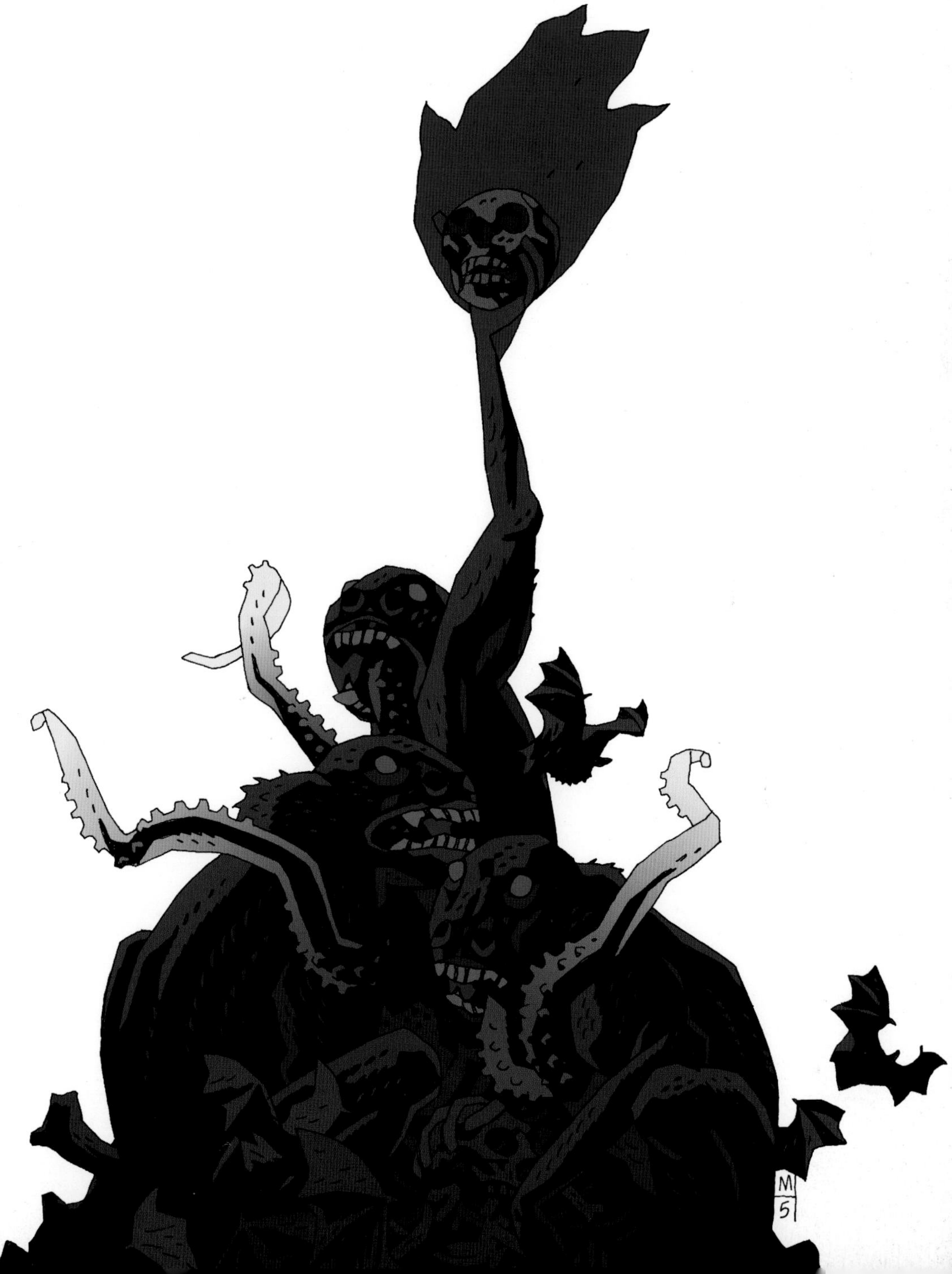

STORY BY MIKE MIGNOLA & JOHN ARCUDI

ART BY GUY DAVIS

COLORS BY DAVE STEWART

LETTERS BY CLEM ROBINS

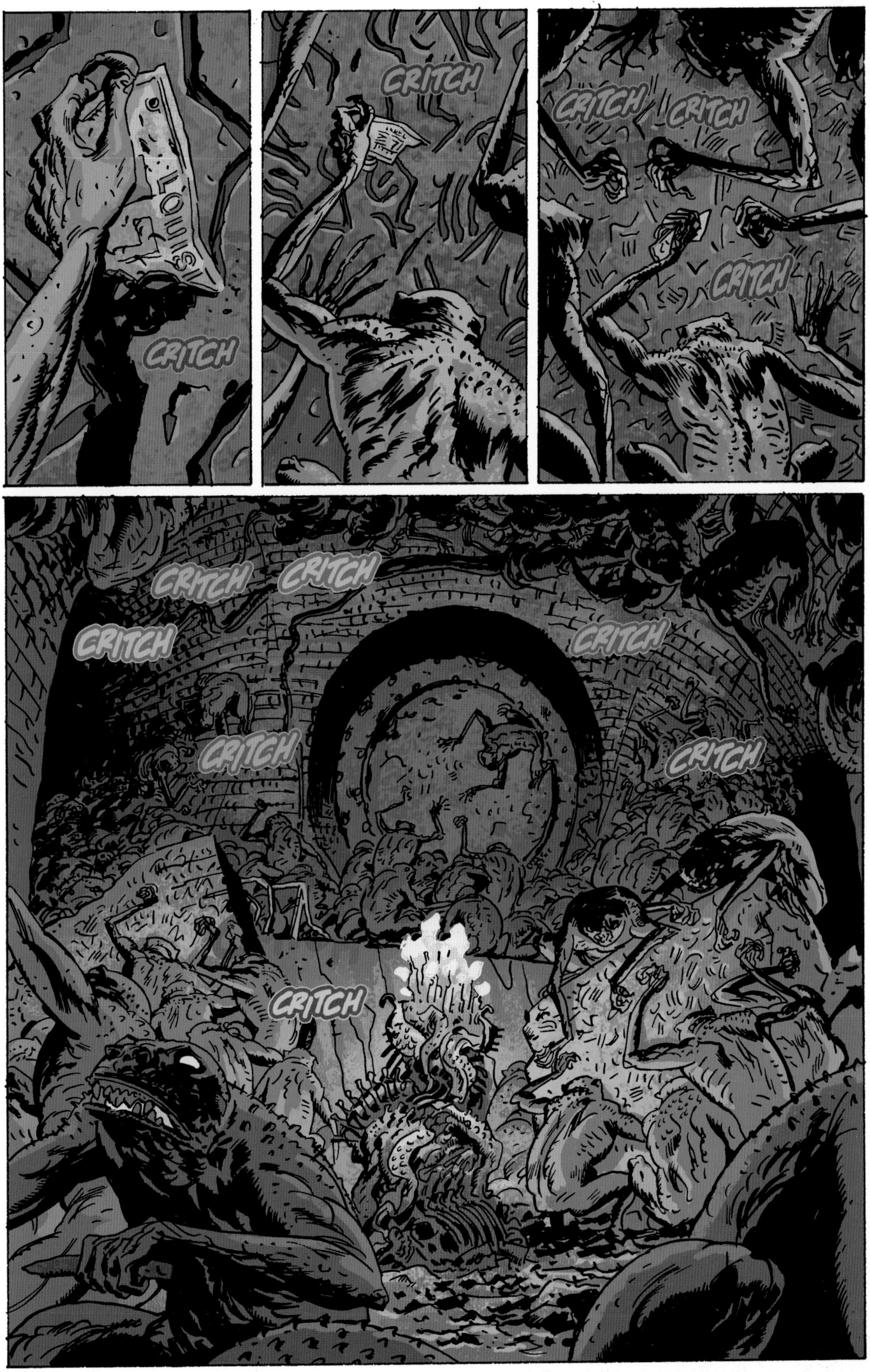
LOUIS
CRITCH
CRITCH
CRITCH
CRITCH
CRITCH
CRITCH
CRITCH
CRITCH
CRITCH
CRITCH
CRITCH
CRITCH
CRITCH

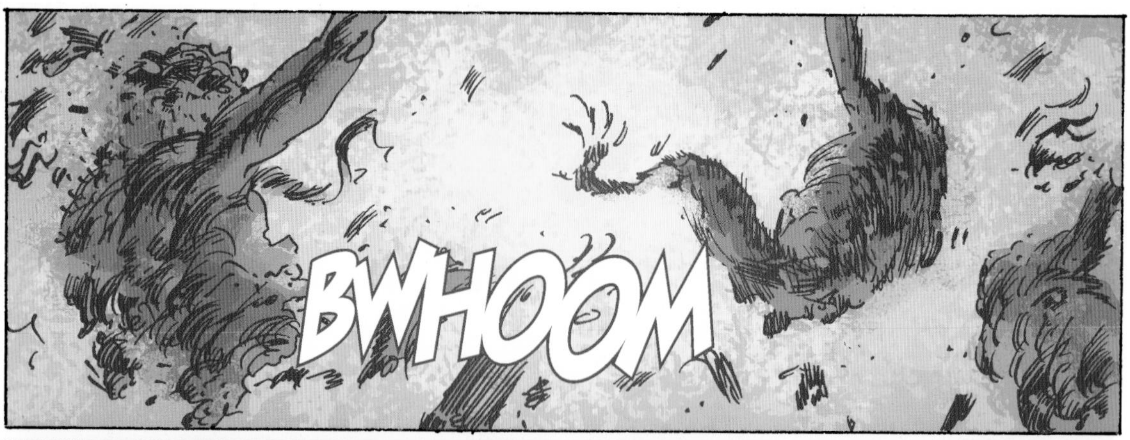
BWHOOM

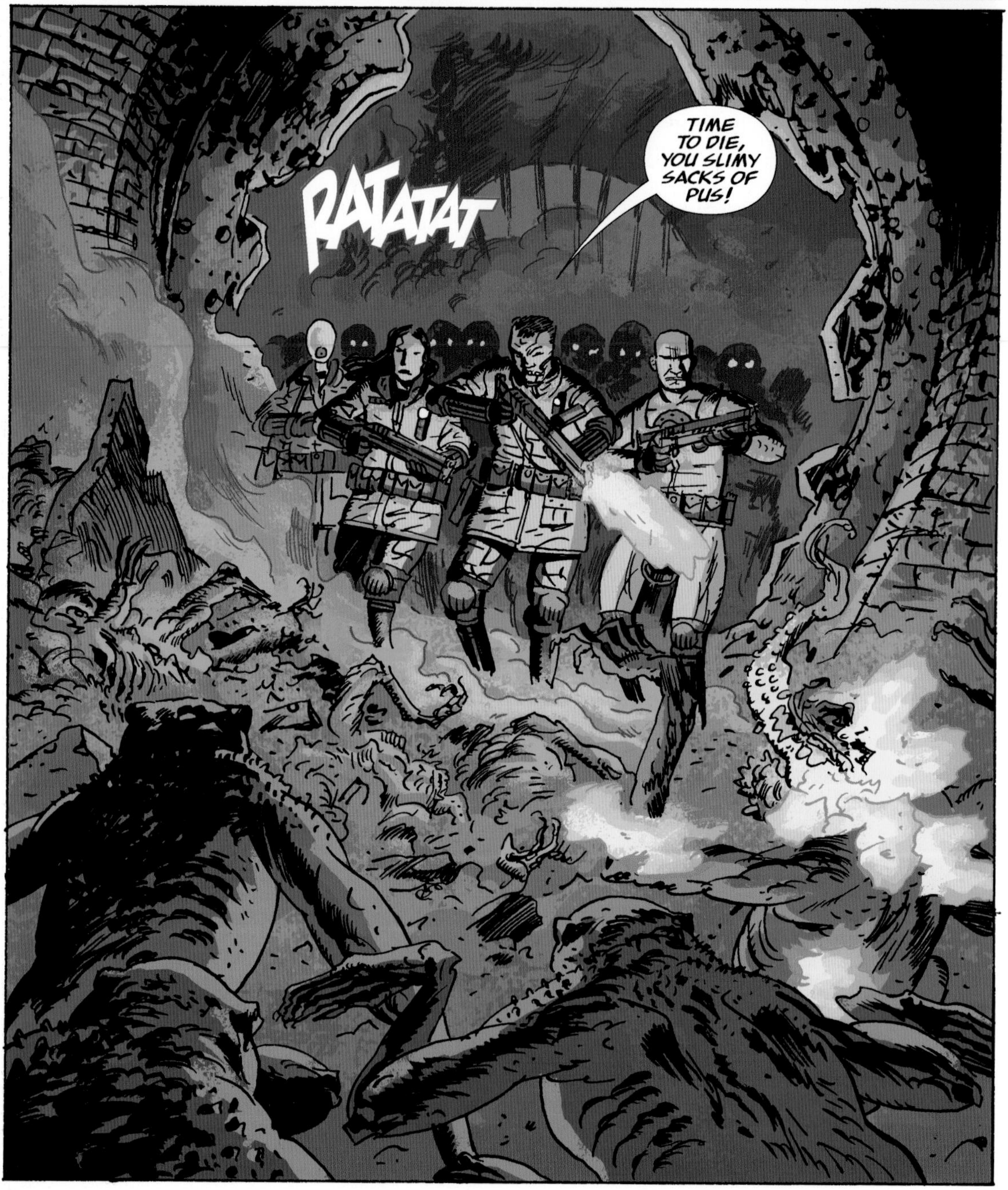
RATATAT
TIME TO DIE, YOU SLIMY SACKS OF PUS!

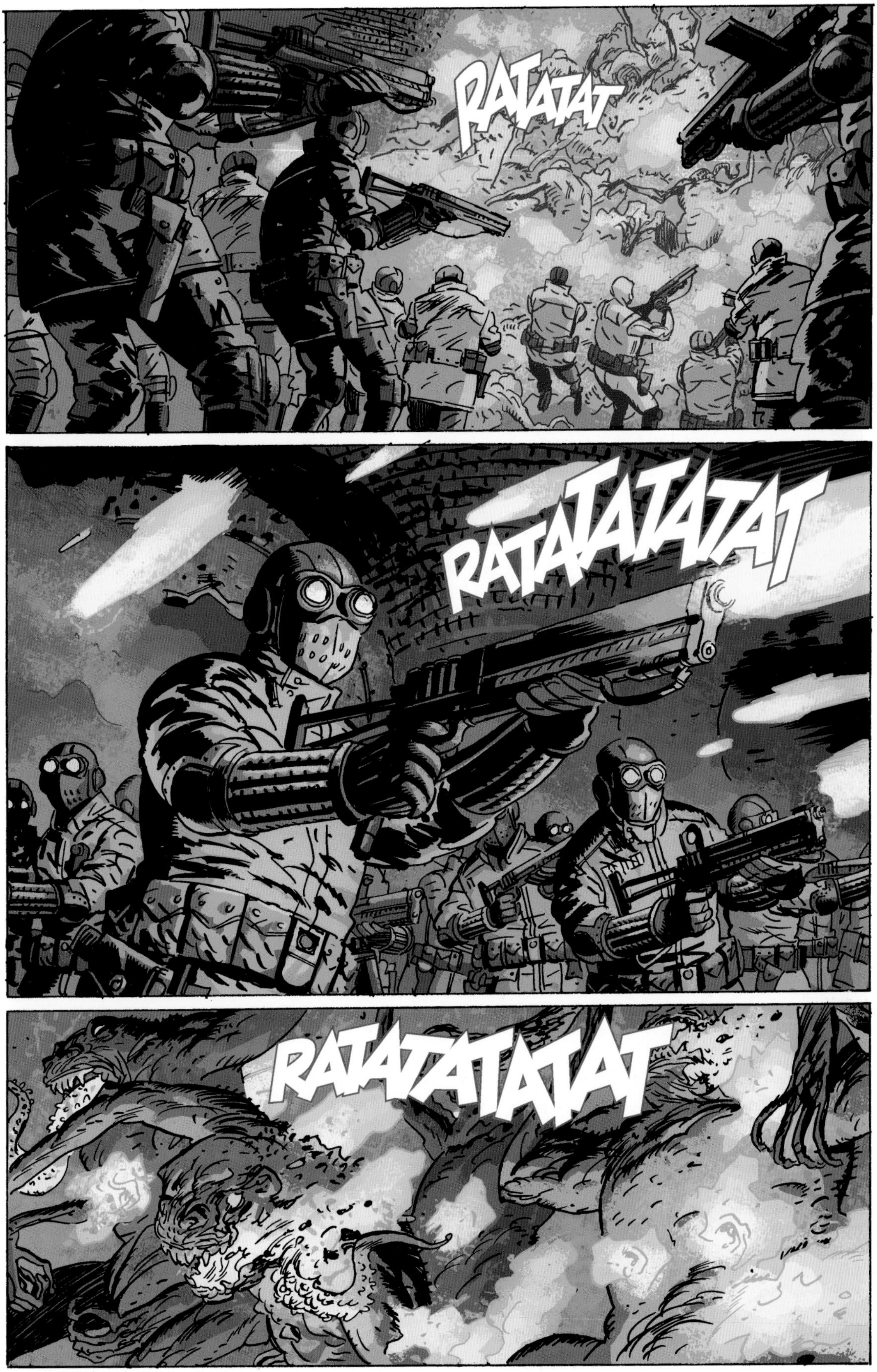
RATATAT
RATATATATAT
RATATATATAT

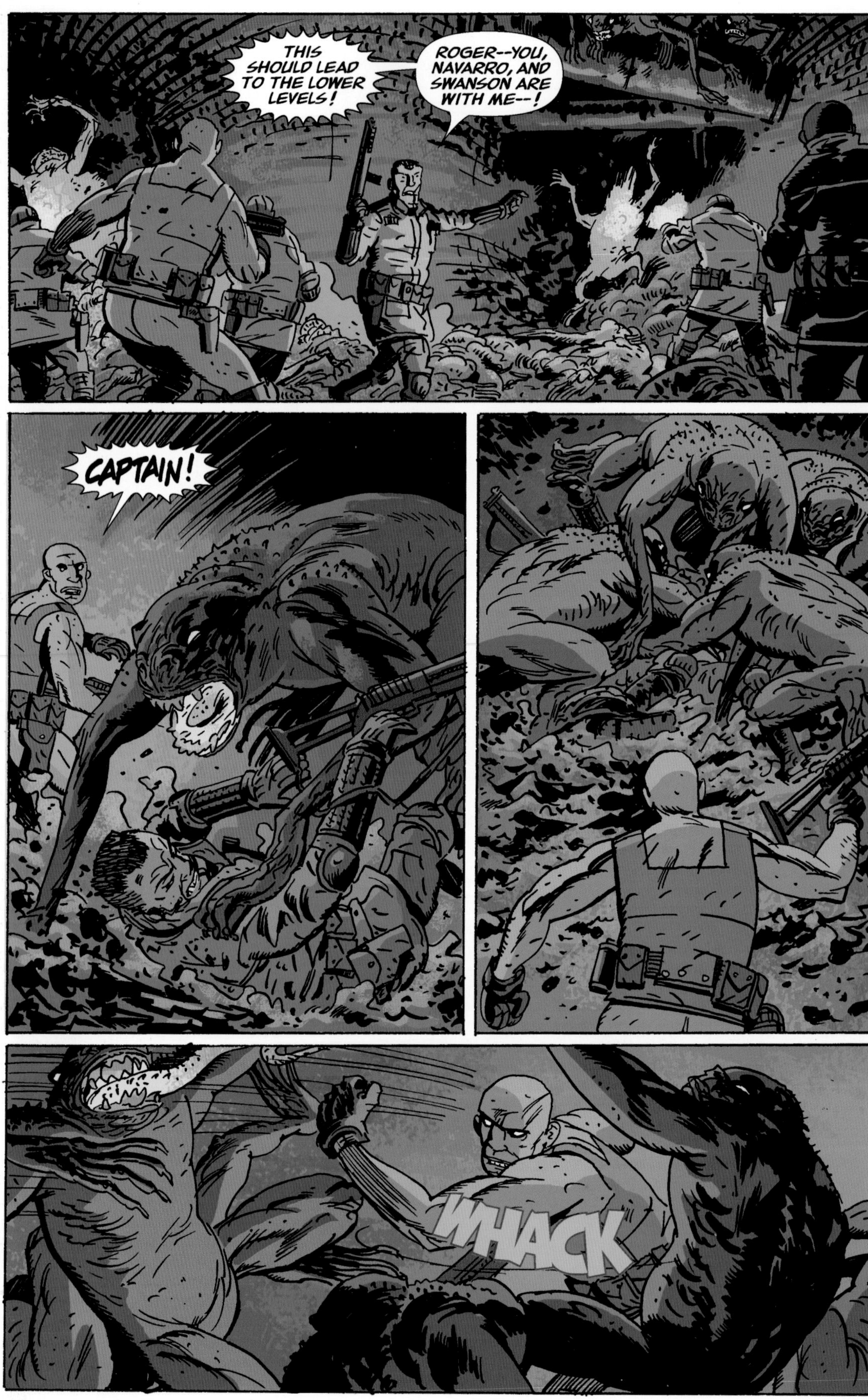
THIS SHOULD LEAD TO THE LOWER LEVELS!
ROGER--YOU, NAVARRO, AND SWANSON ARE WITH ME--!
CAPTAIN!
WHACK

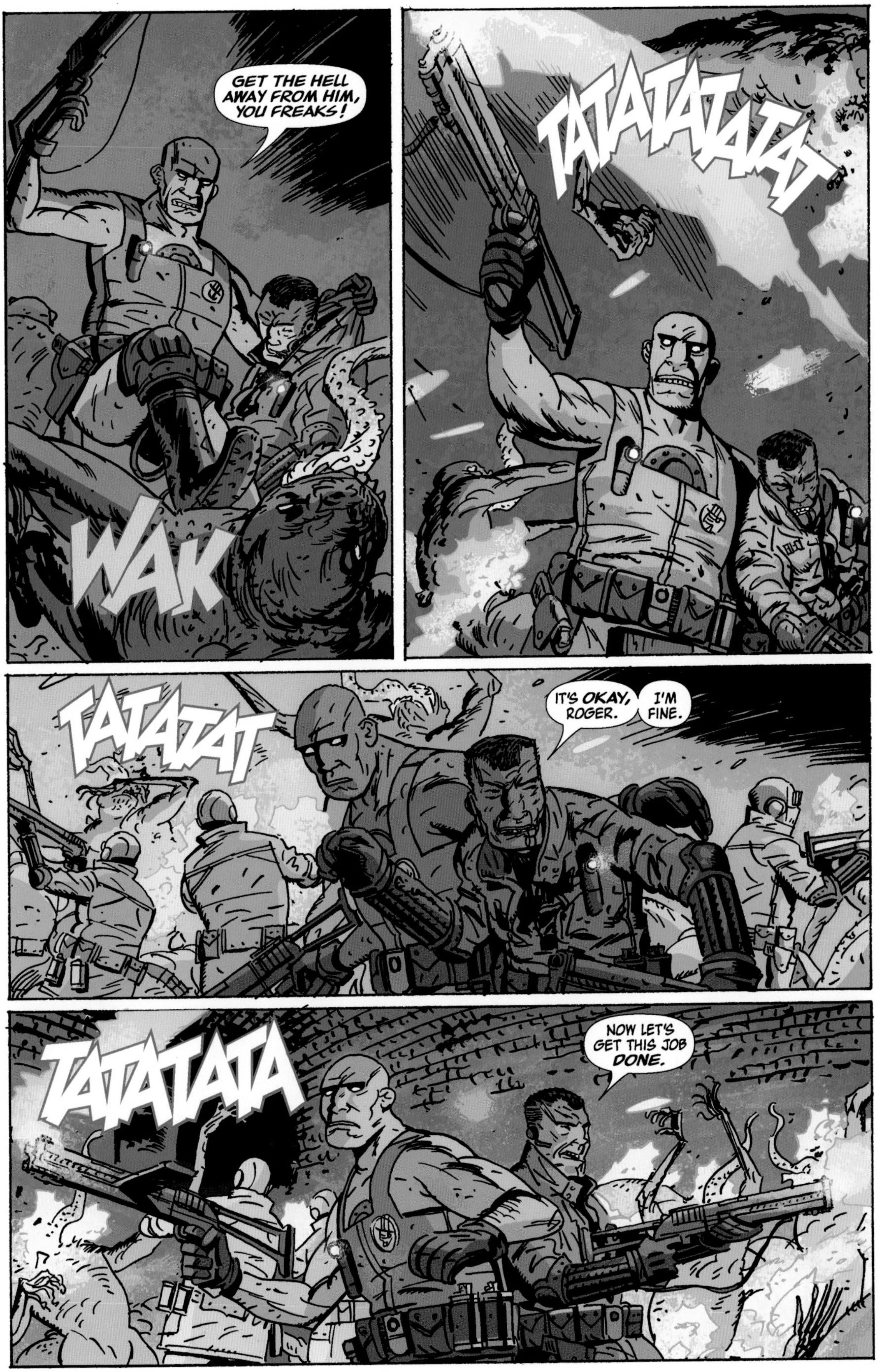
GET THE HELL AWAY FROM HIM, YOU FREAKS!
WAK
TATATATATATAT
TATATAT
IT'S OKAY, ROGER.
I'M FINE.
TATATATA
NOW LET'S GET THIS JOB DONE.

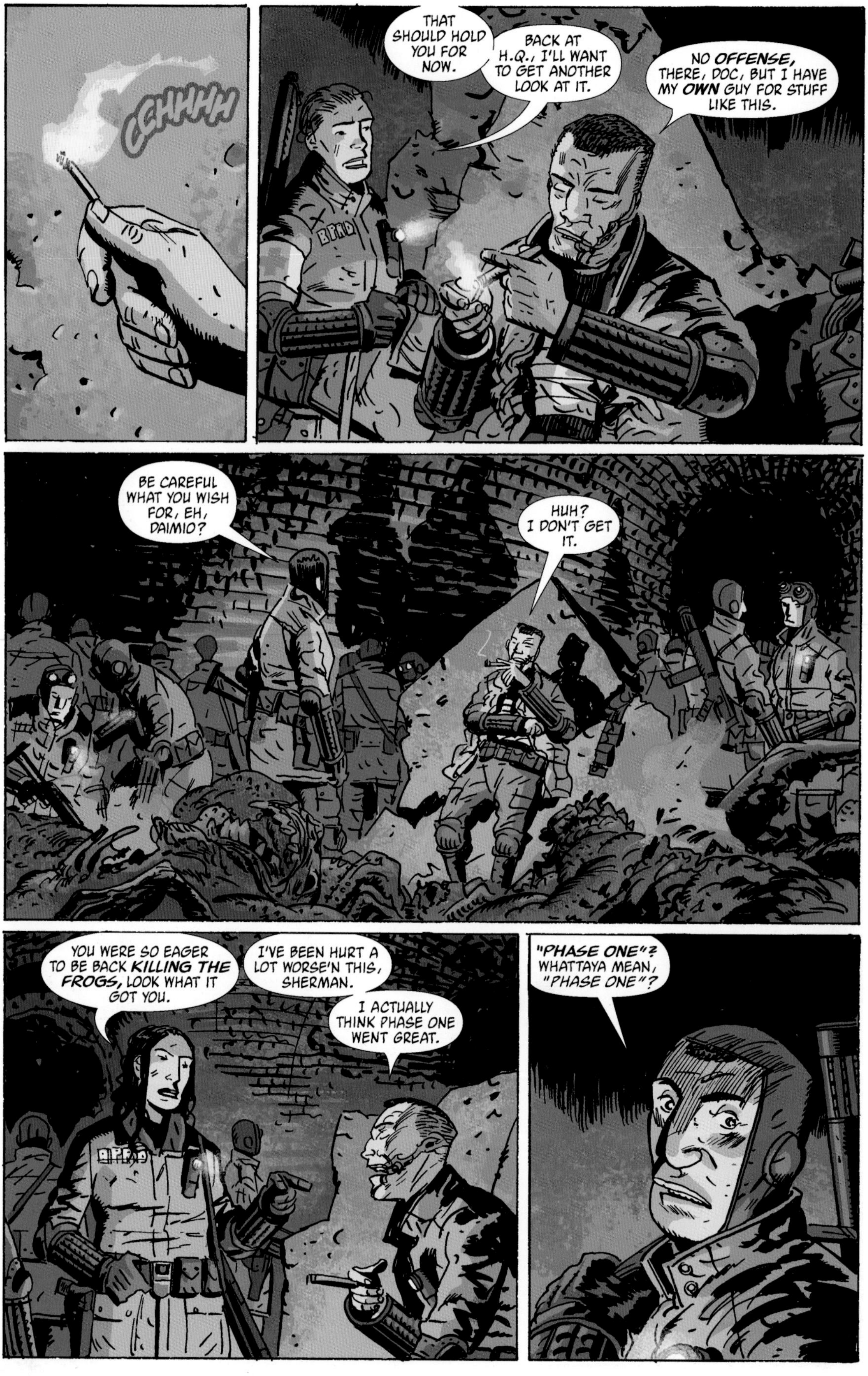
CCHHHH
THAT SHOULD HOLD YOU FOR NOW.
BACK AT H.Q., I'LL WANT TO GET ANOTHER LOOK AT IT.
NO OFFENSE, THERE, DOC, BUT I HAVE MY OWN GUY FOR STUFF LIKE THIS.
BE CAREFUL WHAT YOU WISH FOR, EH, DAIMIO?
HUH? I DON'T GET IT.
YOU WERE SO EAGER TO BE BACK KILLING THE FROGS, LOOK WHAT IT GOT YOU.
I'VE BEEN HURT A LOT WORSE'N THIS, SHERMAN.
I ACTUALLY THINK PHASE ONE WENT GREAT.
"PHASE ONE"? WHATTAYA MEAN, "PHASE ONE"?

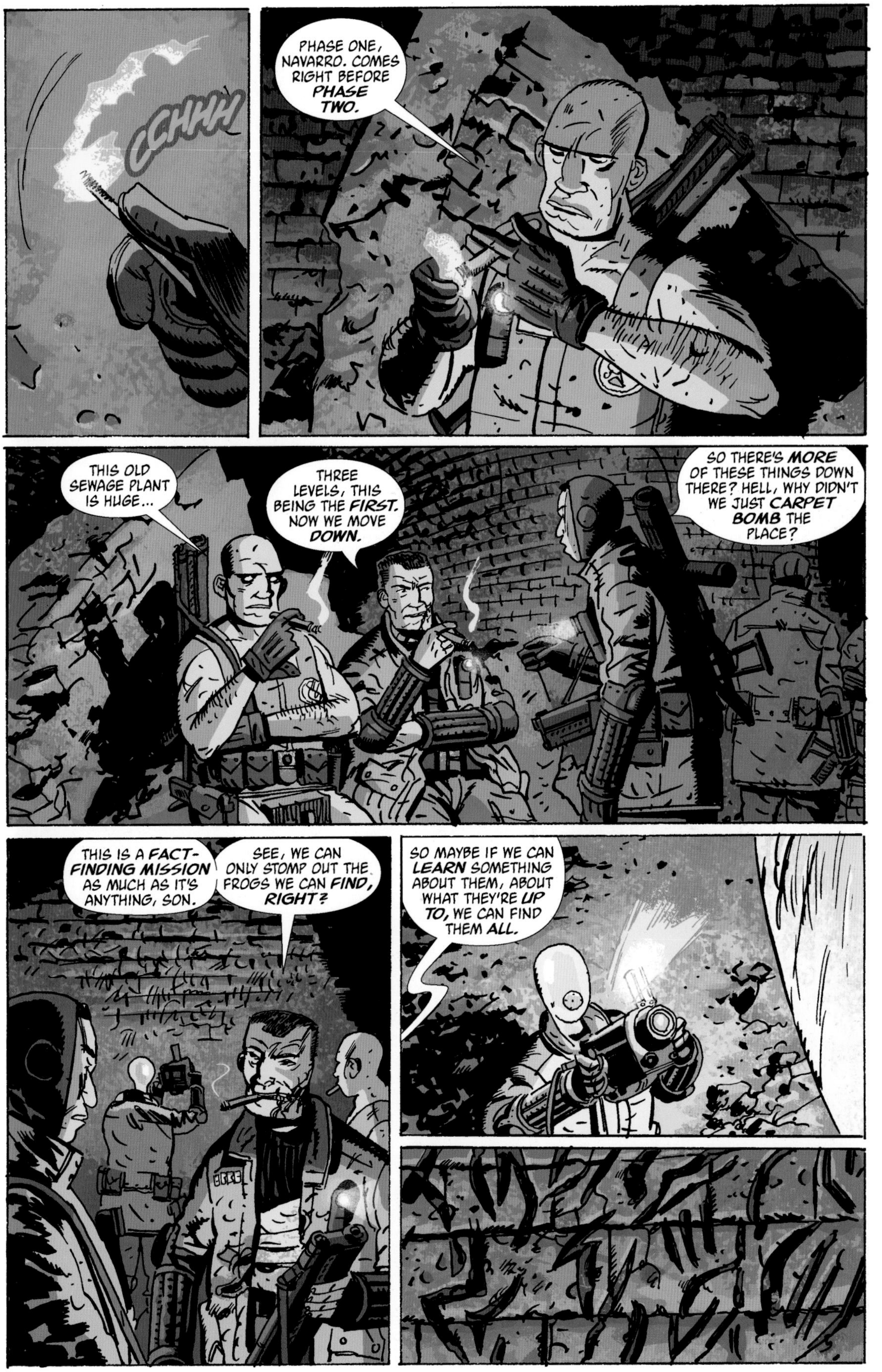
CCHHH
PHASE ONE, NAVARRO. COMES RIGHT BEFORE PHASE TWO.
THIS OLD SEWAGE PLANT IS HUGE...
THREE LEVELS, THIS BEING THE FIRST. NOW WE MOVE DOWN.
SO THERE'S MORE OF THESE THINGS DOWN THERE? HELL, WHY DIDN'T WE JUST CARPET BOMB THE PLACE?
THIS IS A FACT-FINDING MISSION AS MUCH AS IT'S ANYTHING, SON.
SEE, WE CAN ONLY STOMP OUT THE FROGS WE CAN FIND, RIGHT?
SO MAYBE IF WE CAN LEARN SOMETHING ABOUT THEM, ABOUT WHAT THEY'RE UP TO, WE CAN FIND THEM ALL.

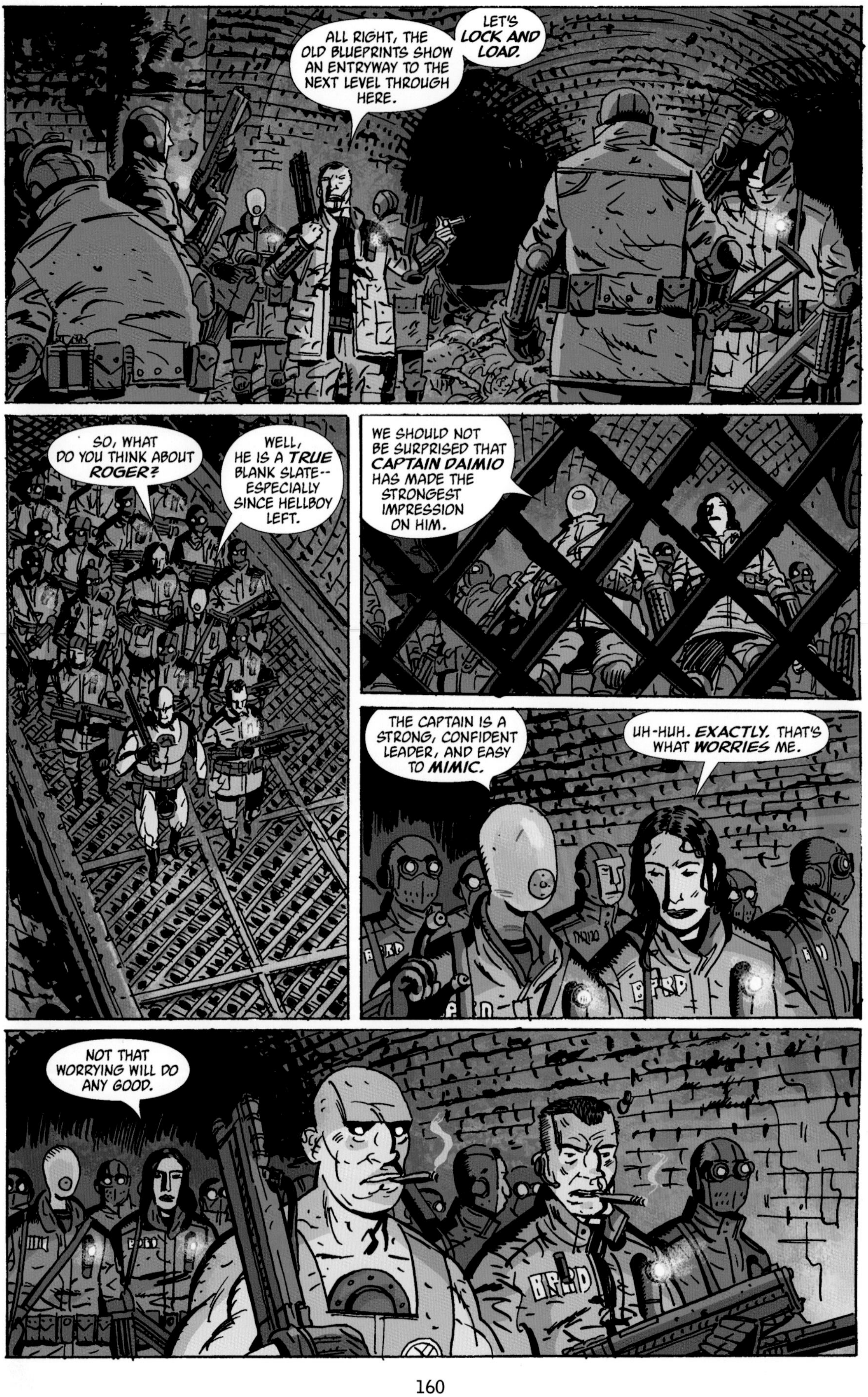
ALL RIGHT, THE OLD BLUEPRINTS SHOW AN ENTRYWAY TO THE NEXT LEVEL THROUGH HERE.
LET'S LOCK AND LOAD.
SO, WHAT DO YOU THINK ABOUT ROGER?
WELL, HE IS A TRUE BLANK SLATE-- ESPECIALLY SINCE HELLBOY LEFT.
WE SHOULD NOT BE SURPRISED THAT CAPTAIN DAIMIO HAS MADE THE STRONGEST IMPRESSION ON HIM.
THE CAPTAIN IS A STRONG, CONFIDENT LEADER, AND EASY TO MIMIC.
UH-HUH. EXACTLY. THAT'S WHAT WORRIES ME.
NOT THAT WORRYING WILL DO ANY GOOD.

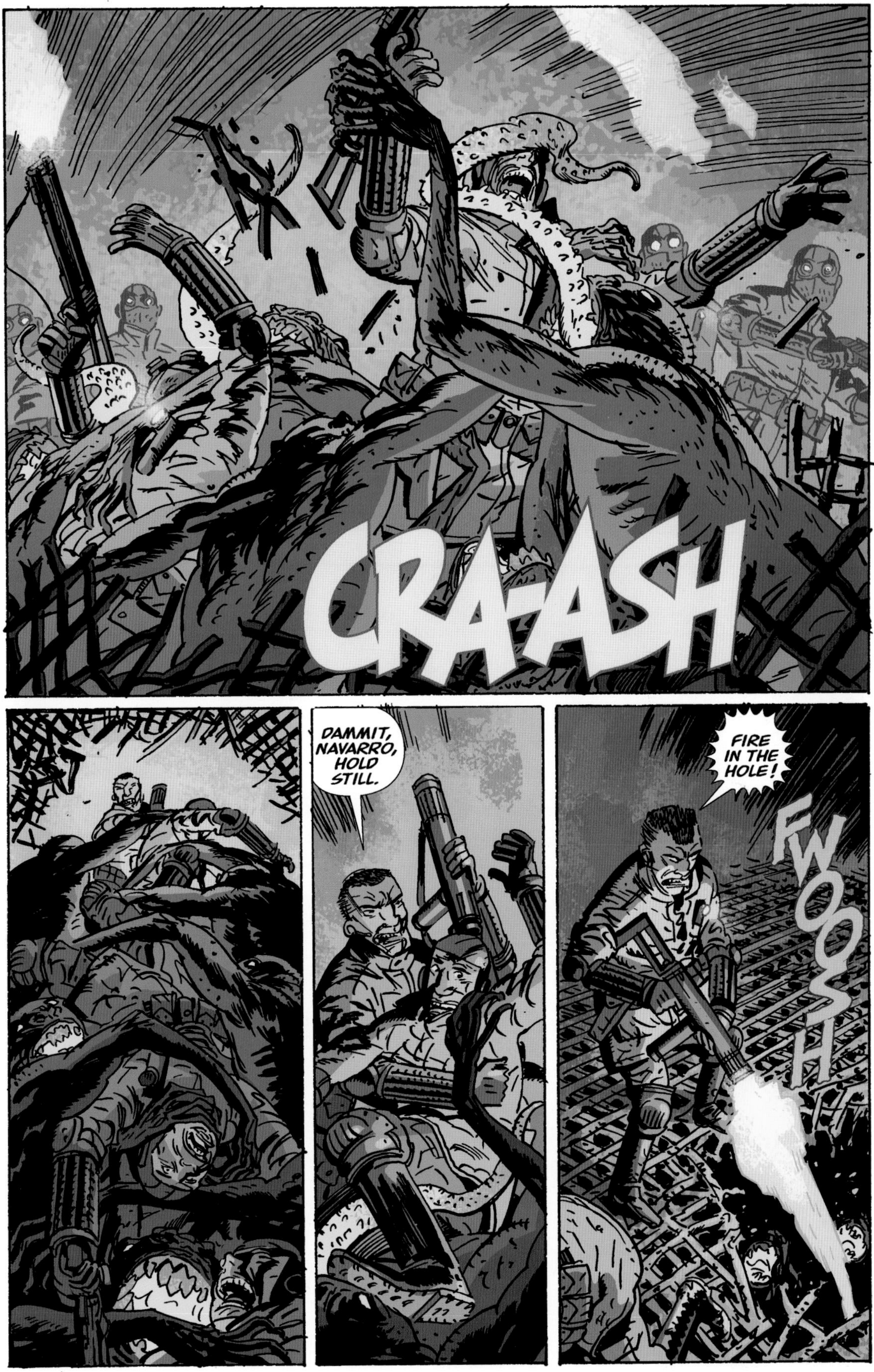
CRA-ASH
DAMMIT, NAVARRO, HOLD STILL.
FIRE IN THE HOLE!
FWOOSH

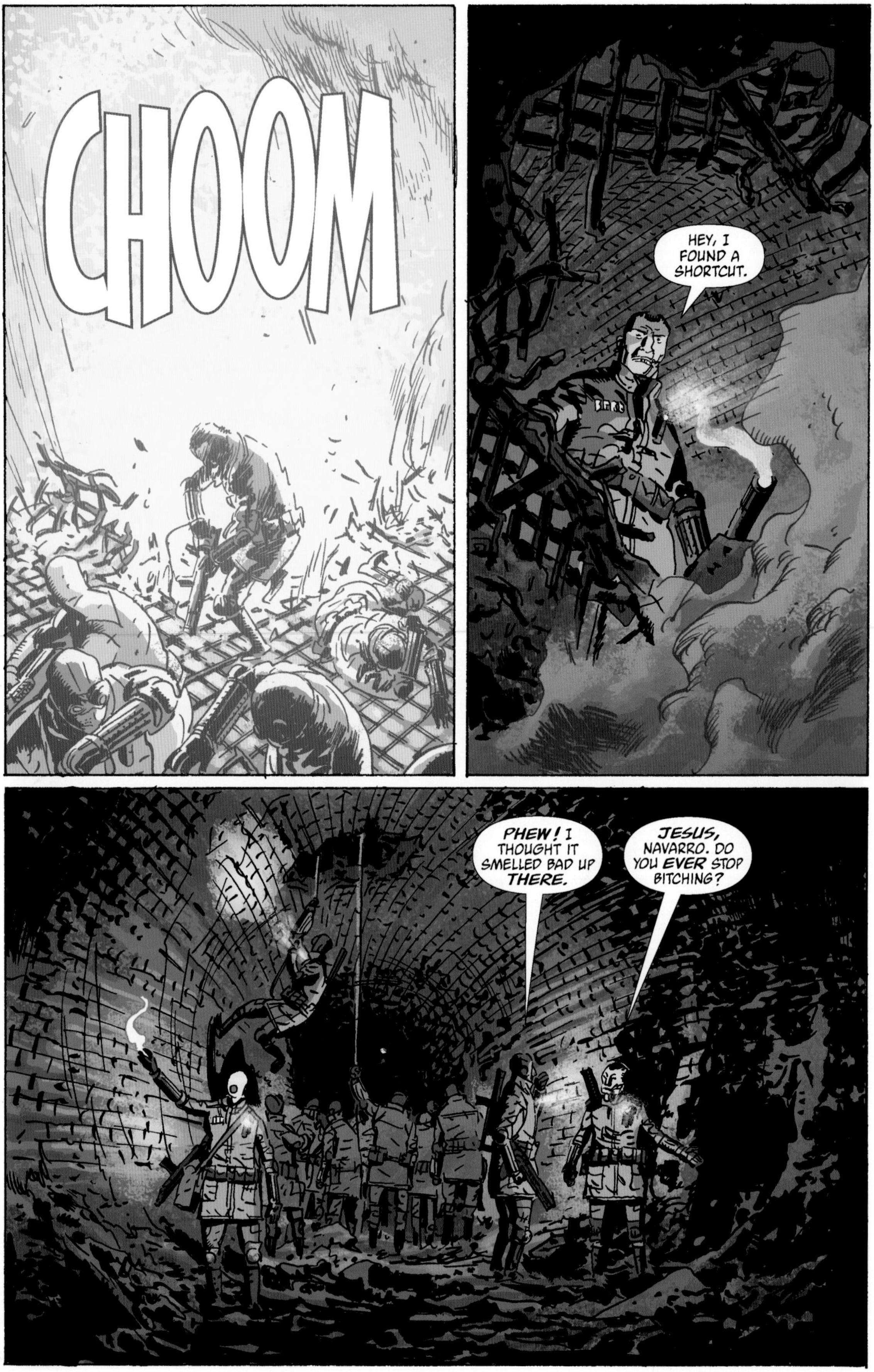
CHOOM
HEY, I FOUND A SHORTCUT.
PHEW! I THOUGHT IT SMELLED BAD UP THERE.
JESUS, NAVARRO. DO YOU EVER STOP BITCHING?

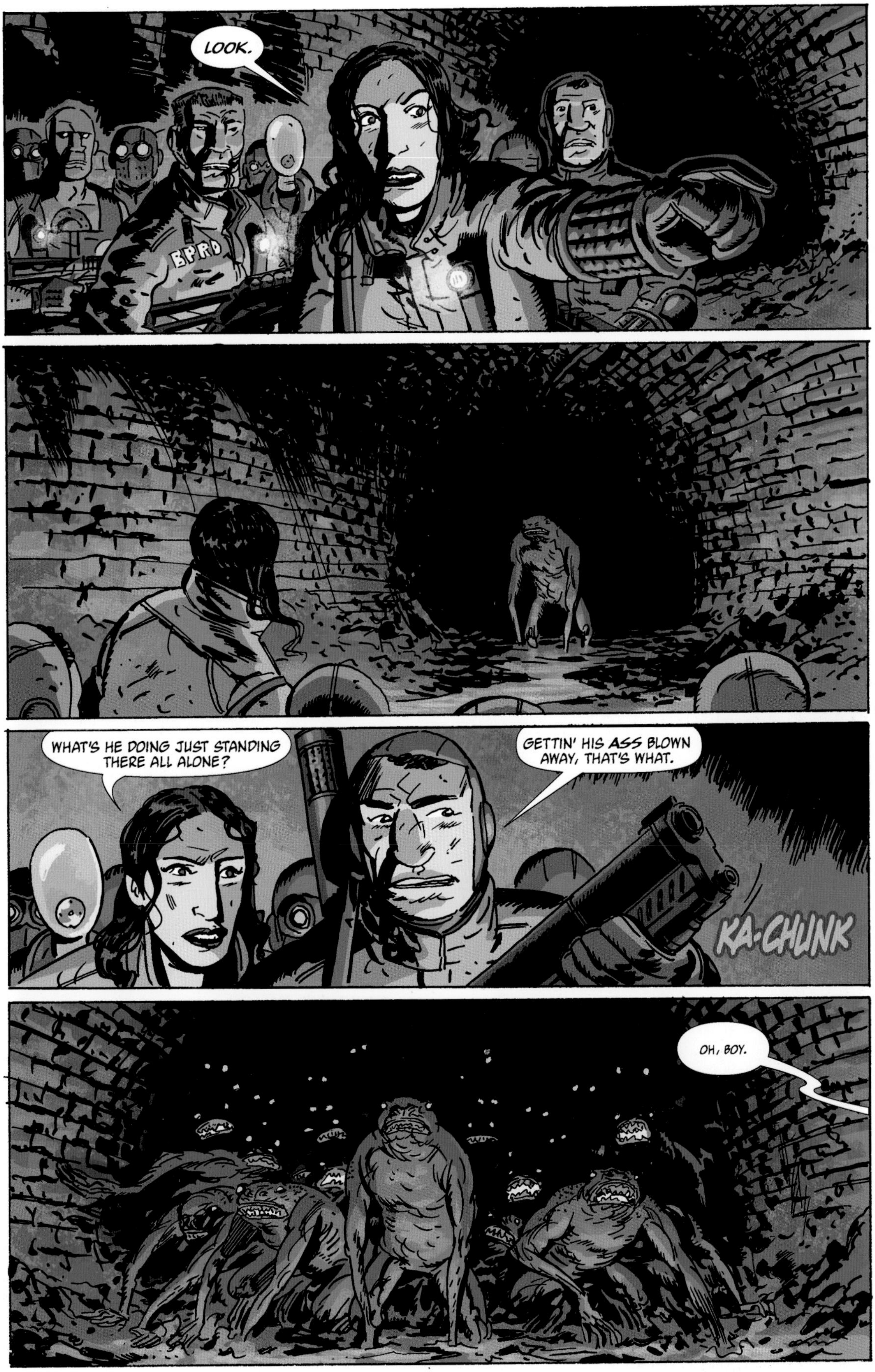
LOOK.
WHAT'S HE DOING JUST STANDING THERE ALL ALONE?
GETTIN' HIS ASS BLOWN AWAY, THAT'S WHAT.
KA-CHUNK
OH, BOY.

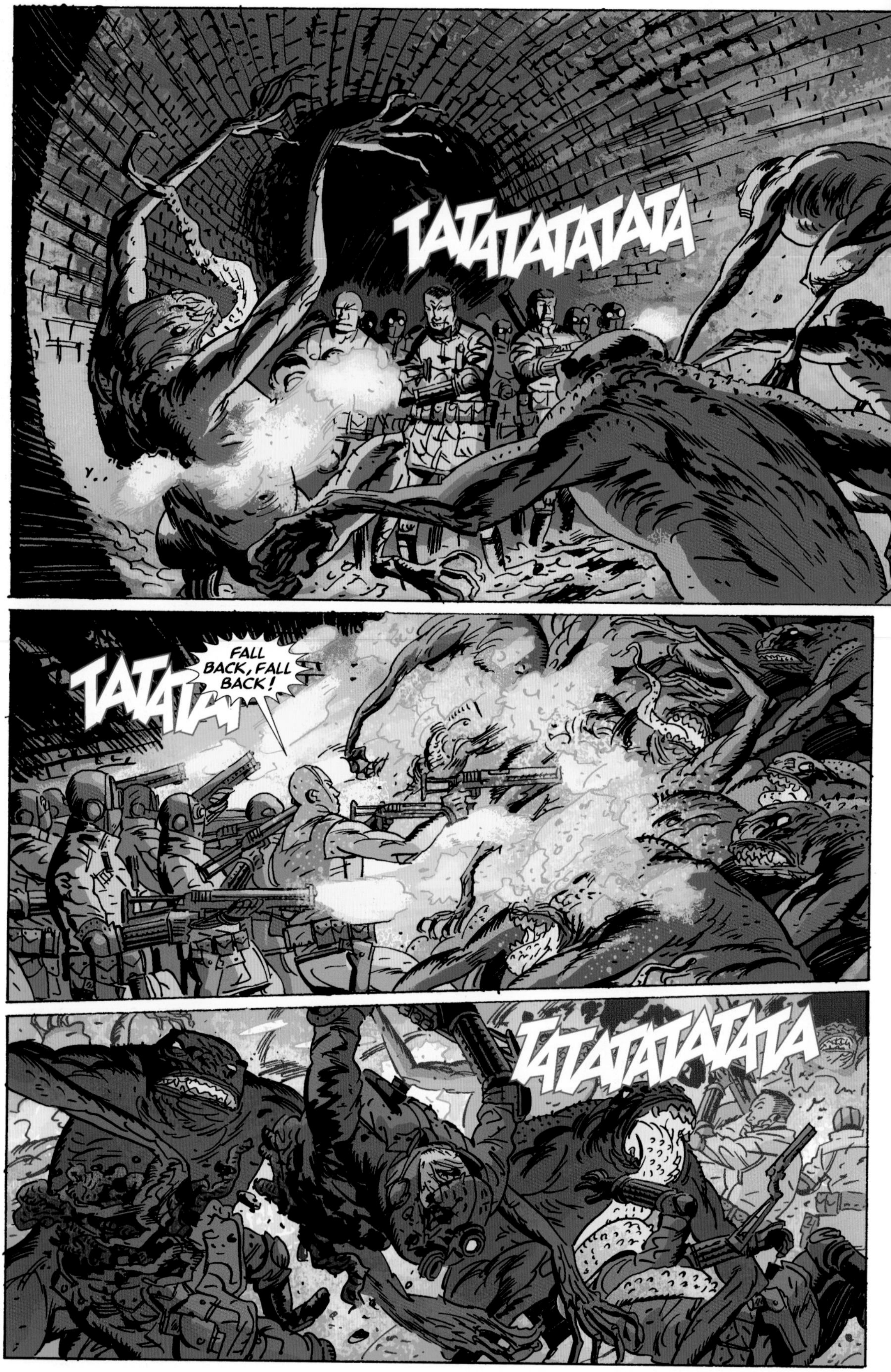
TATATATATATA
TATATA
FALL BACK, FALL BACK!
TATATATATATA

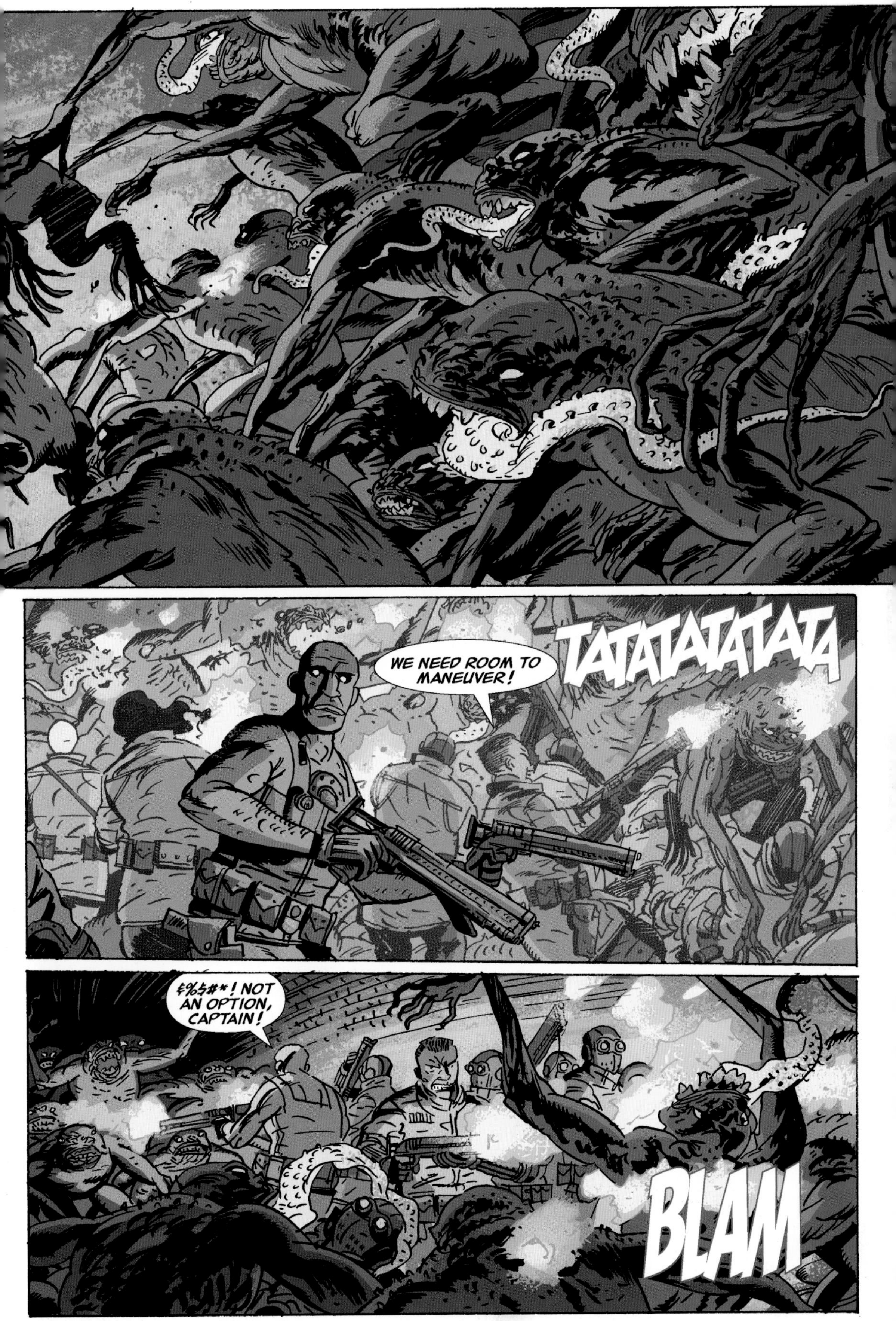
WE NEED ROOM TO MANEUVER!
TATATATATATA
¢%$#*! NOT AN OPTION, CAPTAIN!
BLAM

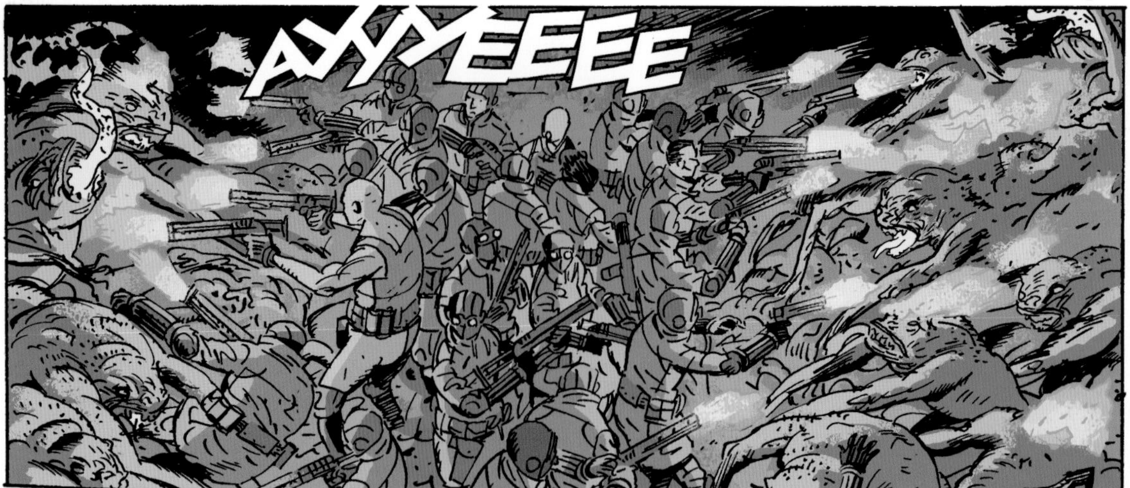
AYYYEEEEE

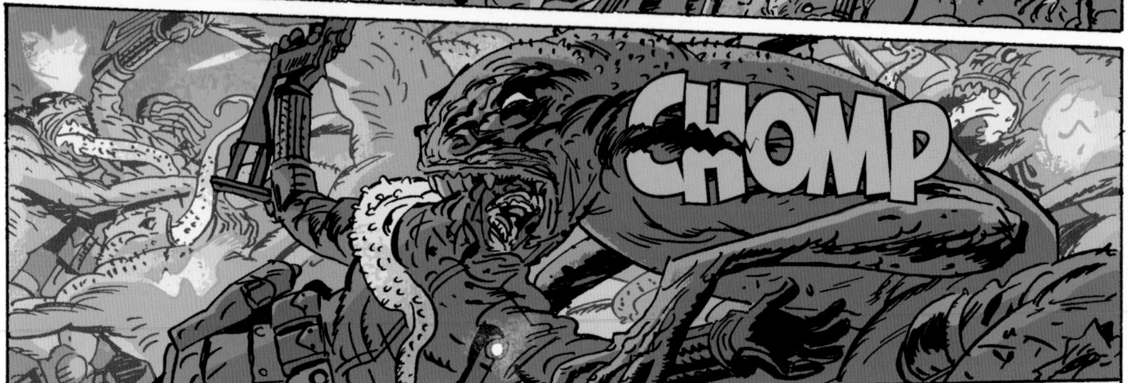
CHOMP

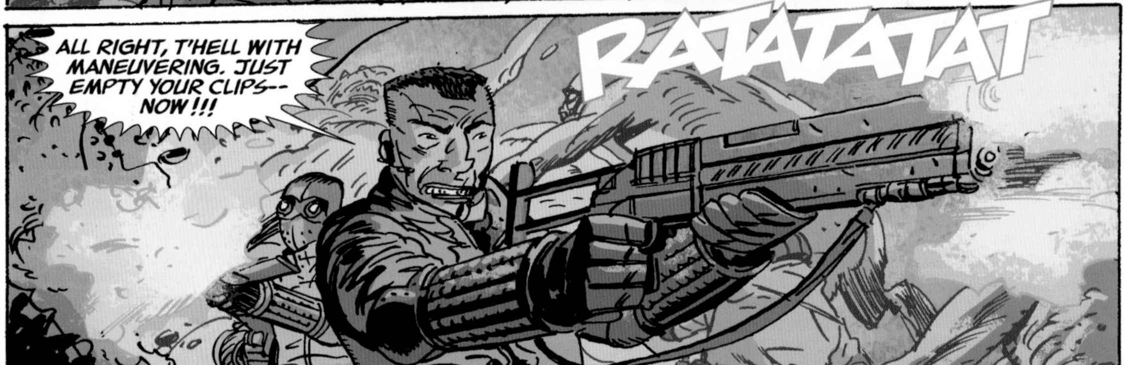
ALL RIGHT, T'HELL WITH MANEUVERING. JUST EMPTY YOUR CLIPS-- NOW!!!
RATATATAT

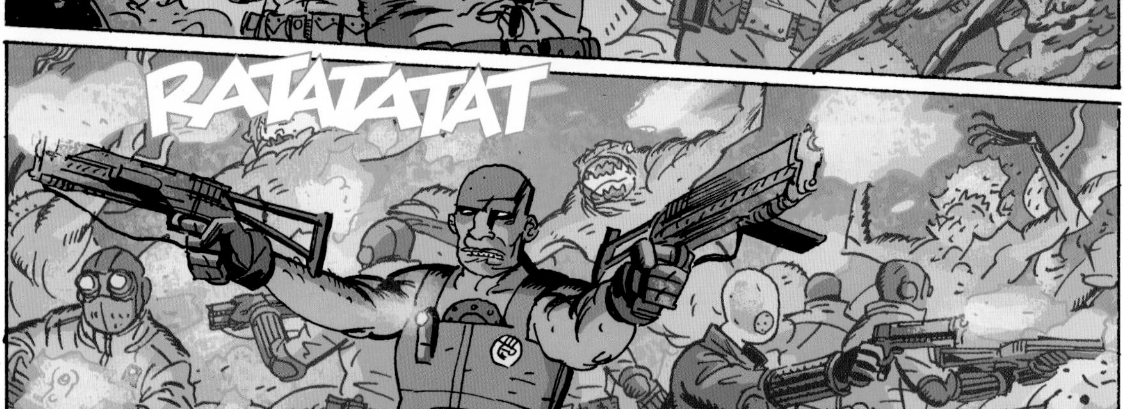
RATATATAT

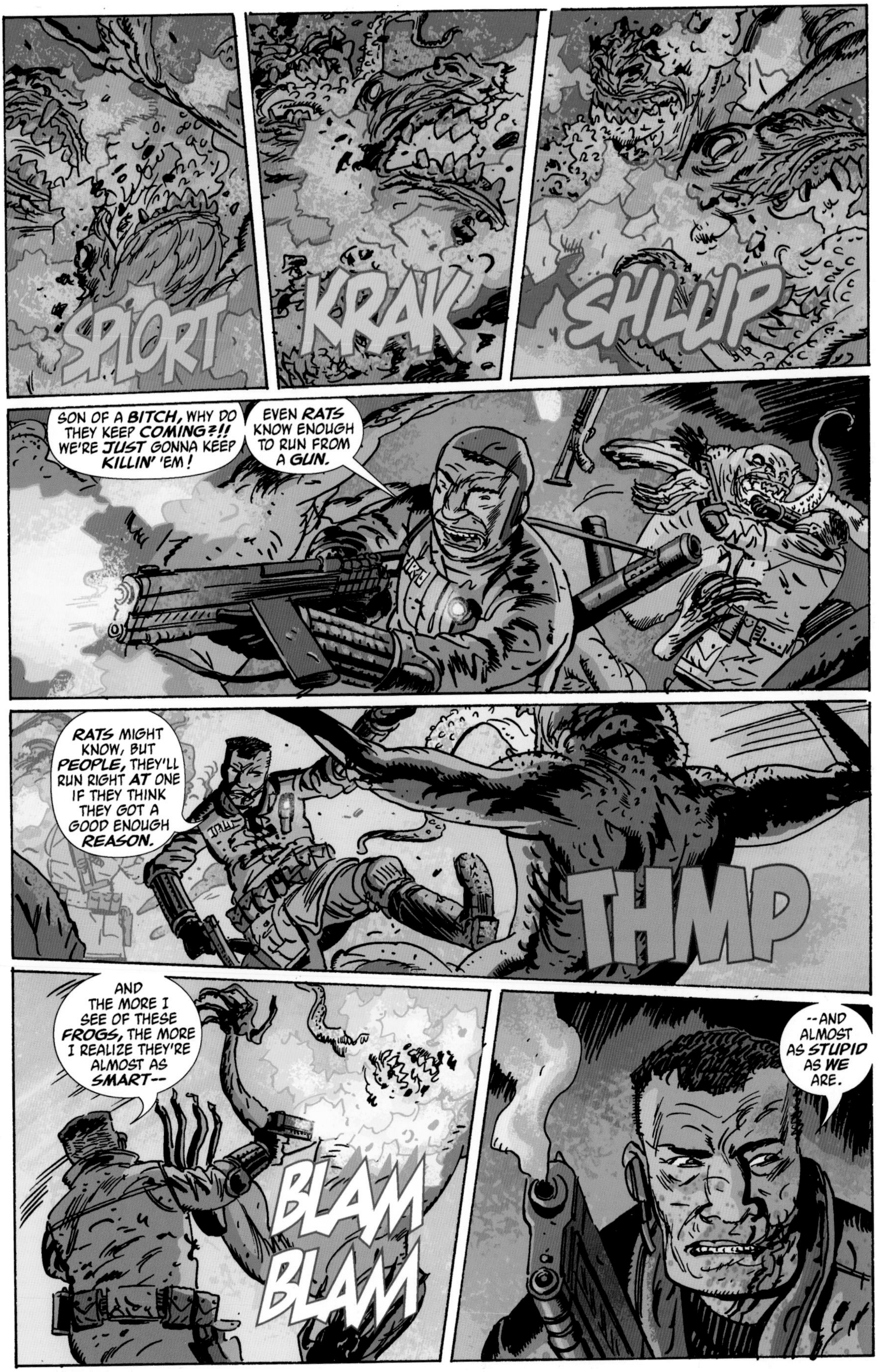
SPLORT
KRAK
SHLUP
SON OF A BITCH, WHY DO THEY KEEP COMING?!! WE'RE JUST GONNA KEEP KILLIN' 'EM!
EVEN RATS KNOW ENOUGH TO RUN FROM A GUN.
RATS MIGHT KNOW, BUT PEOPLE, THEY'LL RUN RIGHT AT ONE IF THEY THINK THEY GOT A GOOD ENOUGH REASON.
THMP
AND THE MORE I SEE OF THESE FROGS, THE MORE I REALIZE THEY'RE ALMOST AS SMART--
BLAM BLAM
--AND ALMOST AS STUPID AS WE ARE.

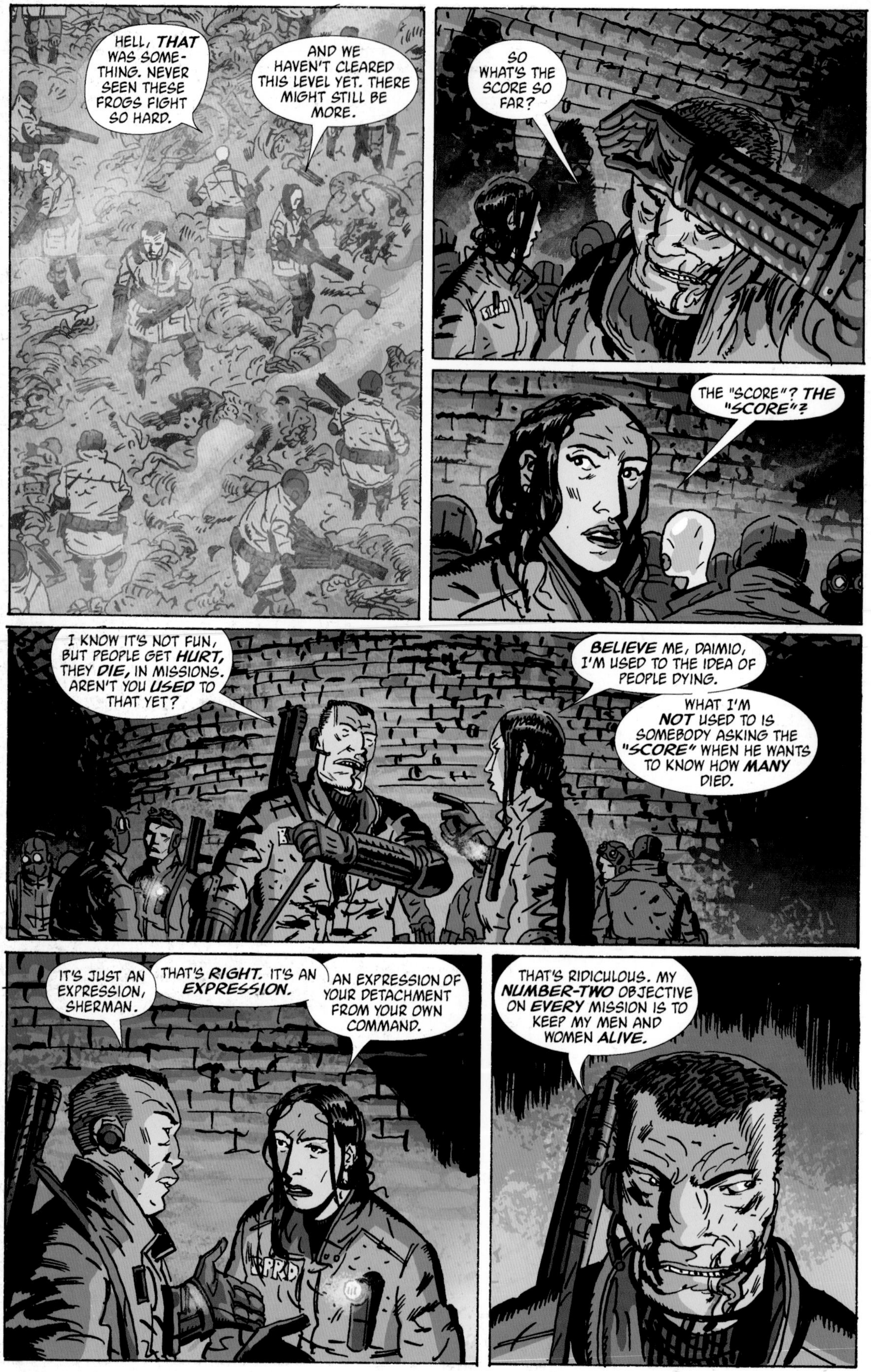
HELL, THAT WAS SOME-THING. NEVER SEEN THESE FROGS FIGHT SO HARD.
AND WE HAVEN'T CLEARED THIS LEVEL YET. THERE MIGHT STILL BE MORE.
SO WHAT'S THE SCORE SO FAR?
THE "SCORE"? THE "SCORE"?
I KNOW IT'S NOT FUN, BUT PEOPLE GET HURT, THEY DIE, IN MISSIONS. AREN'T YOU USED TO THAT YET?
BELIEVE ME, DAIMIO, I'M USED TO THE IDEA OF PEOPLE DYING.
WHAT I'M NOT USED TO IS SOMEBODY ASKING THE "SCORE" WHEN HE WANTS TO KNOW HOW MANY DIED.
IT'S JUST AN EXPRESSION, SHERMAN.
THAT'S RIGHT. IT'S AN EXPRESSION.
AN EXPRESSION OF YOUR DETACHMENT FROM YOUR OWN COMMAND.
THAT'S RIDICULOUS. MY NUMBER-TWO OBJECTIVE ON EVERY MISSION IS TO KEEP MY MEN AND WOMEN ALIVE.

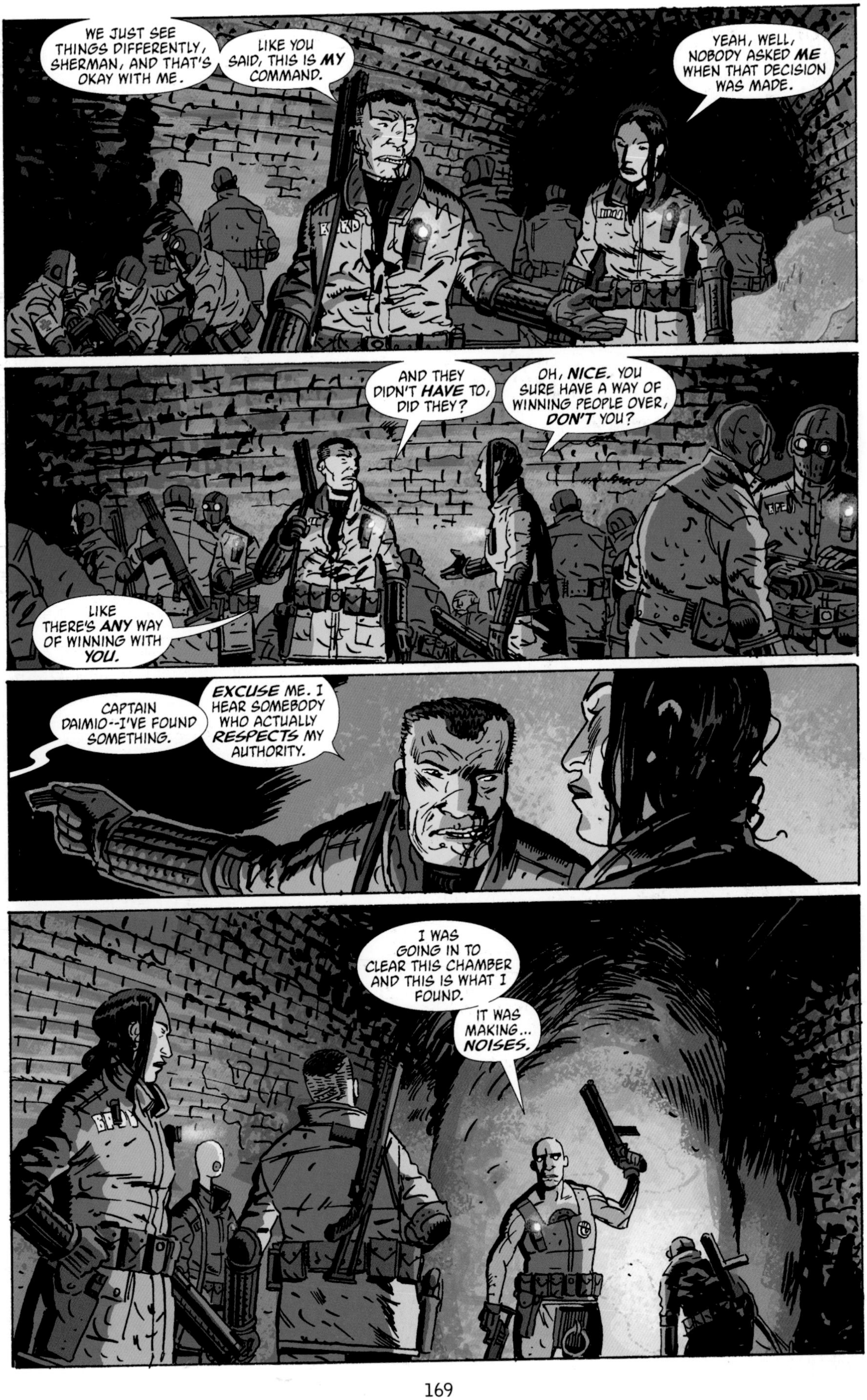

WE JUST SEE THINGS DIFFERENTLY, SHERMAN, AND THAT'S OKAY WITH ME.
LIKE YOU SAID, THIS IS MY COMMAND.
YEAH, WELL, NOBODY ASKED ME WHEN THAT DECISION WAS MADE.
AND THEY DIDN'T HAVE TO, DID THEY?
OH, NICE. YOU SURE HAVE A WAY OF WINNING PEOPLE OVER, DON'T YOU?
LIKE THERE'S ANY WAY OF WINNING WITH YOU.
CAPTAIN DAIMIO--I'VE FOUND SOMETHING.
EXCUSE ME. I HEAR SOMEBODY WHO ACTUALLY RESPECTS MY AUTHORITY.
I WAS GOING IN TO CLEAR THIS CHAMBER AND THIS IS WHAT I FOUND.
IT WAS MAKING... NOISES.

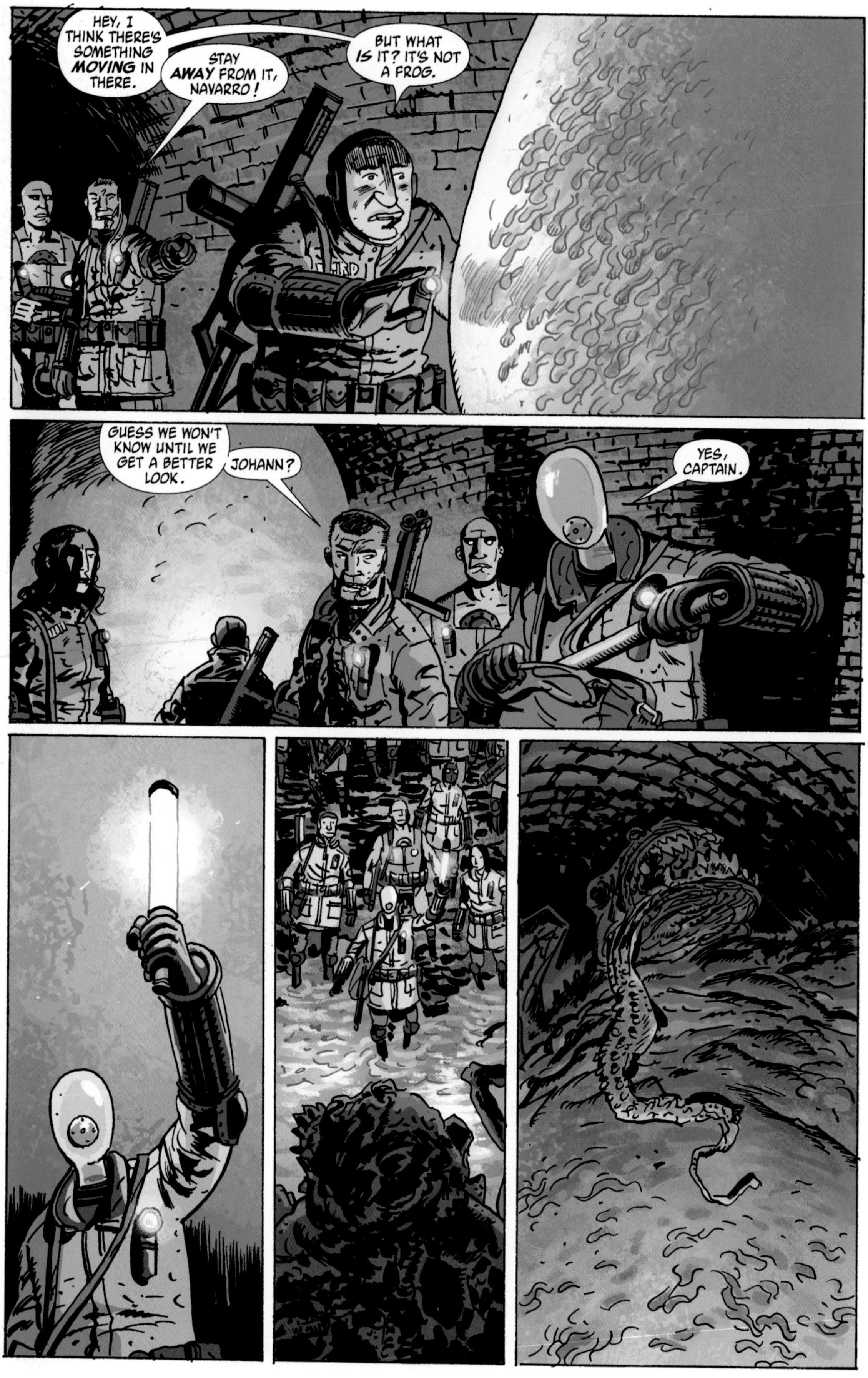
HEY, I THINK THERE'S SOMETHING MOVING IN THERE.
STAY AWAY FROM IT, NAVARRO!
BUT WHAT IS IT? IT'S NOT A FROG.
GUESS WE WON'T KNOW UNTIL WE GET A BETTER LOOK.
JOHANN?
YES, CAPTAIN.

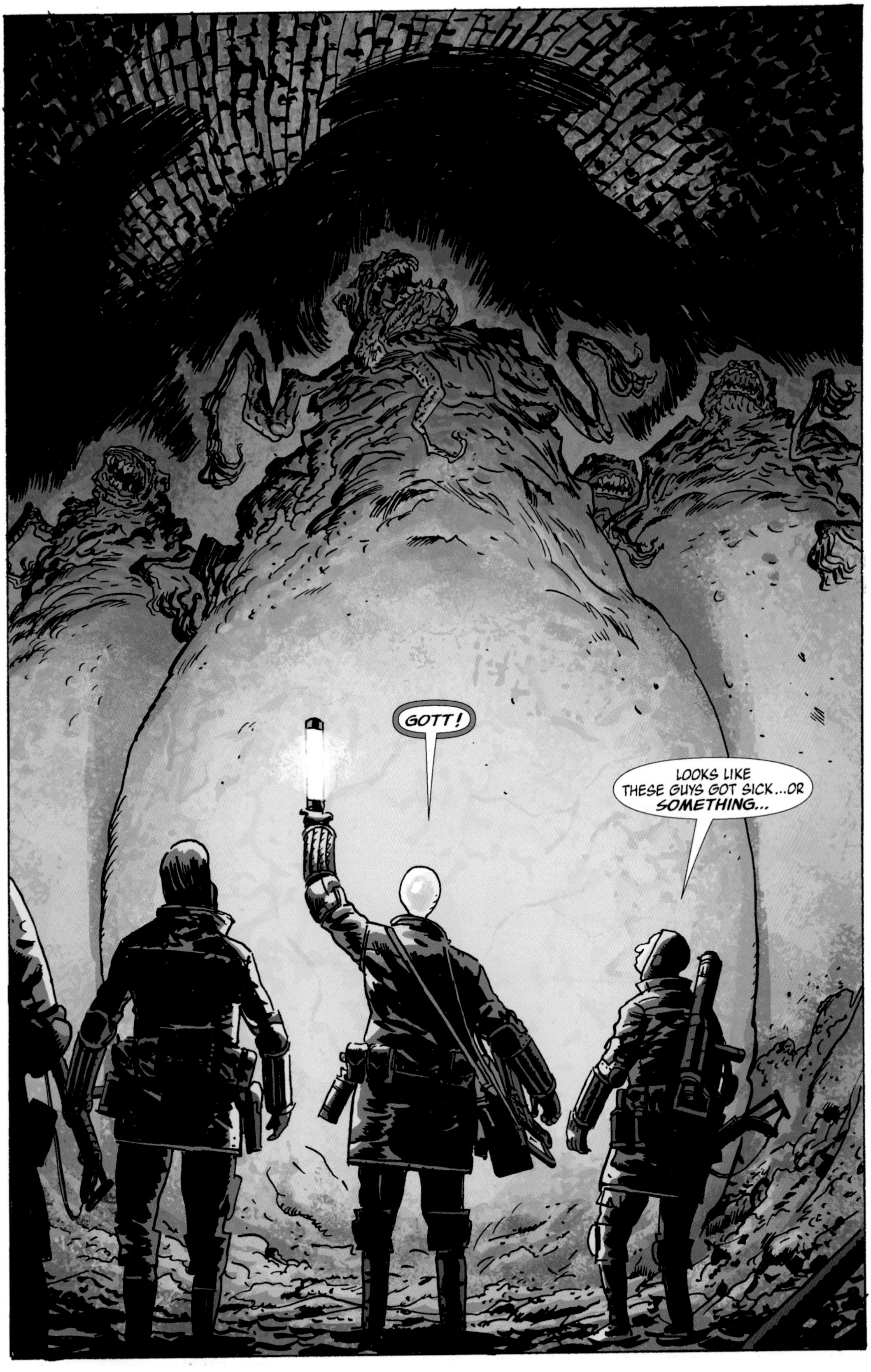
GOTT!
LOOKS LIKE THESE GUYS GOT SICK...OR SOMETHING...

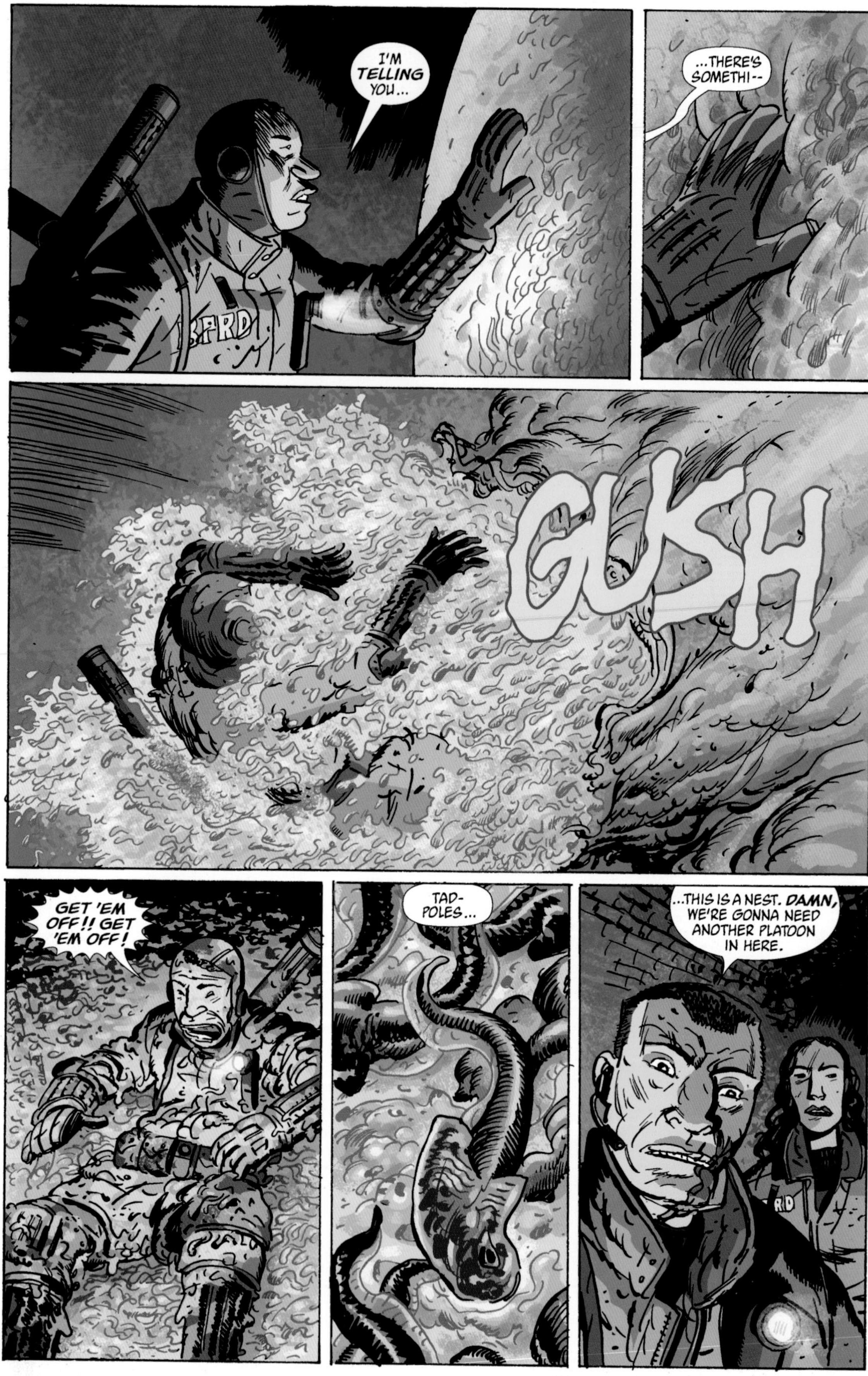
I'M TELLING YOU...
...THERE'S SOMETHI--
BPRD
GUSH
GET 'EM OFF!! GET 'EM OFF!
TAD-POLES...
...THIS IS A NEST. DAMN, WE'RE GONNA NEED ANOTHER PLATOON IN HERE.

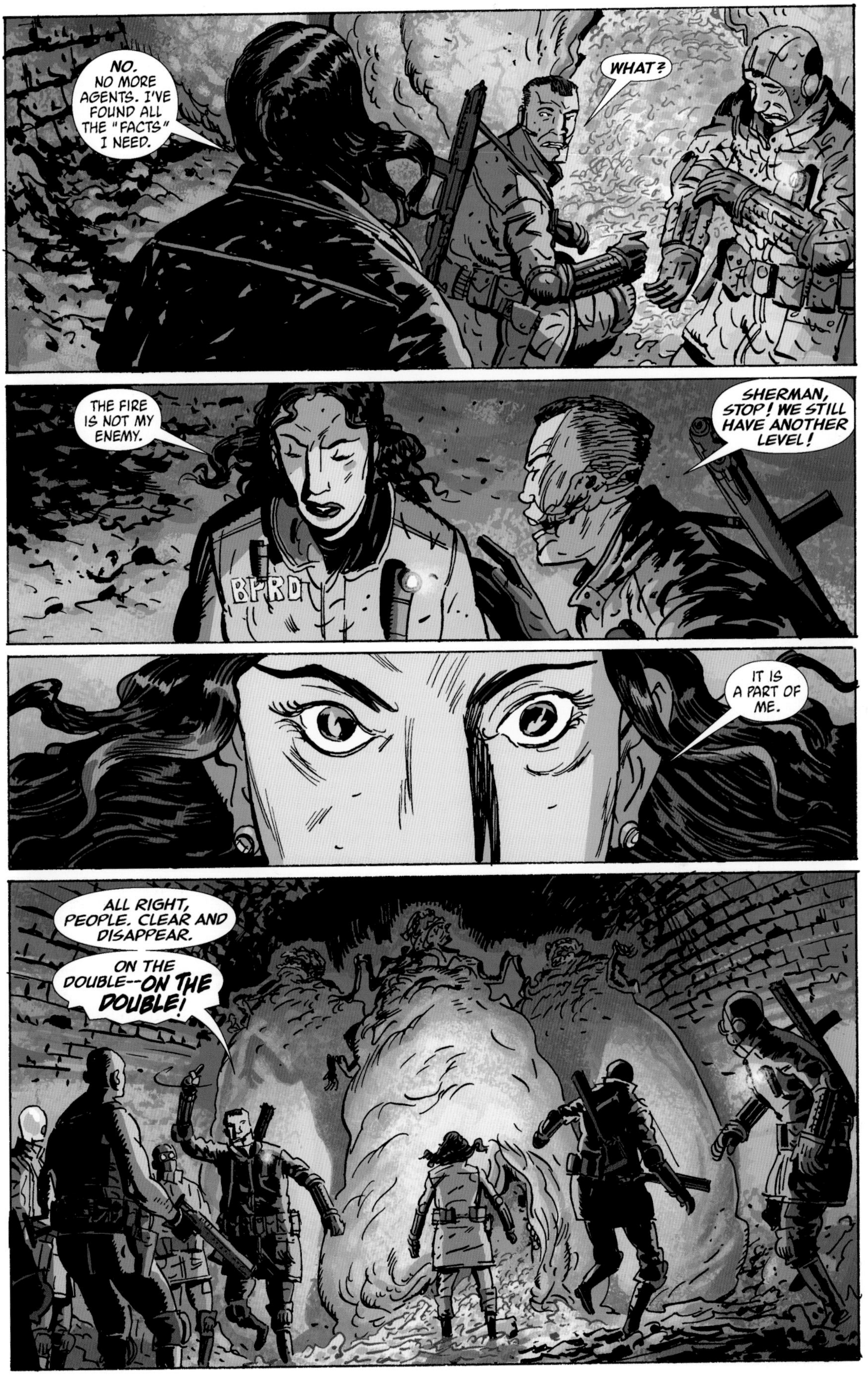
NO. NO MORE AGENTS. I'VE FOUND ALL THE "FACTS" I NEED.
WHAT?
THE FIRE IS NOT MY ENEMY.
SHERMAN, STOP! WE STILL HAVE ANOTHER LEVEL!
BPRD
IT IS A PART OF ME.
ALL RIGHT, PEOPLE. CLEAR AND DISAPPEAR.
ON THE DOUBLE--ON THE DOUBLE!

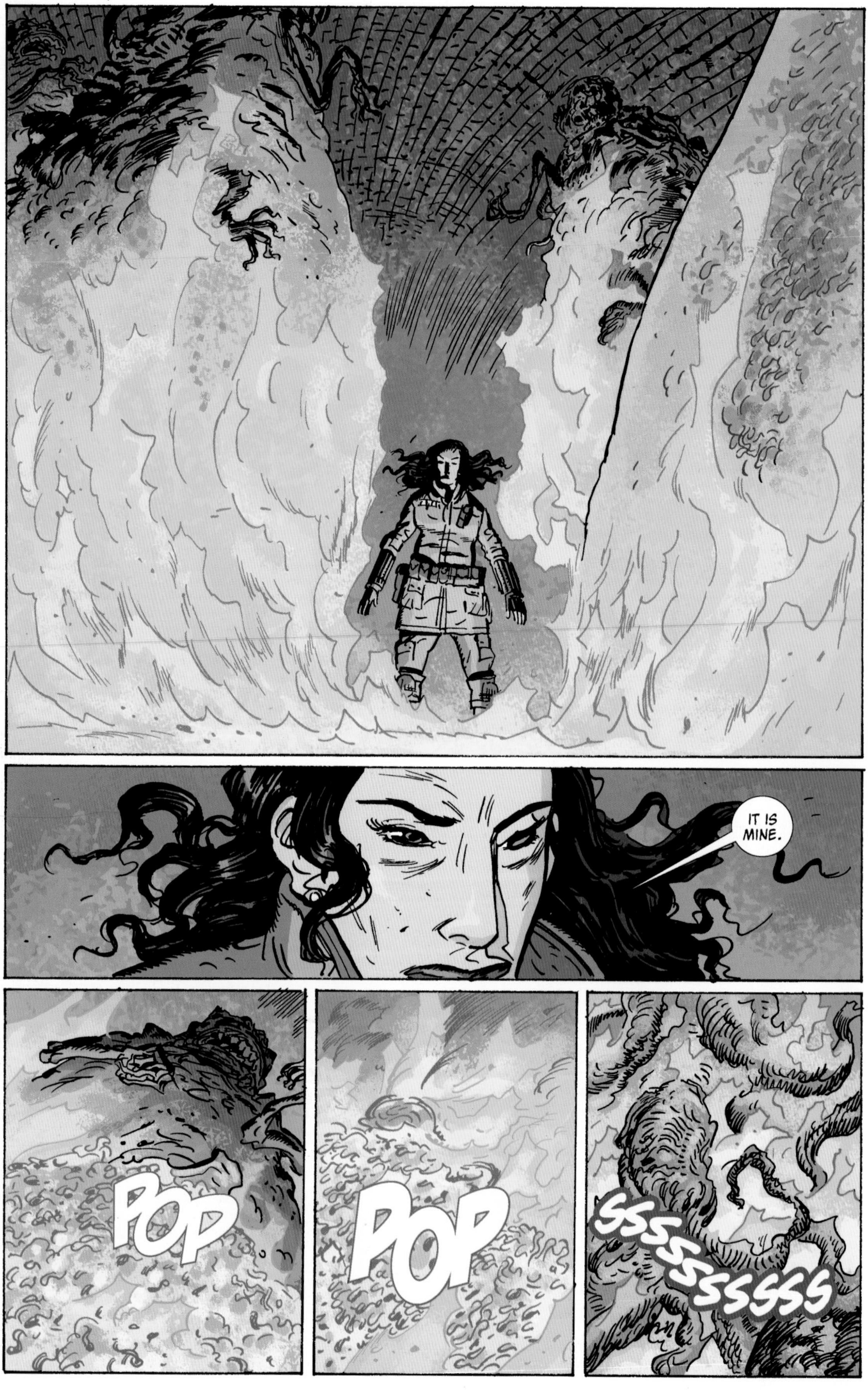
IT IS MINE.
POP
POP
SSSSSSSSSSS

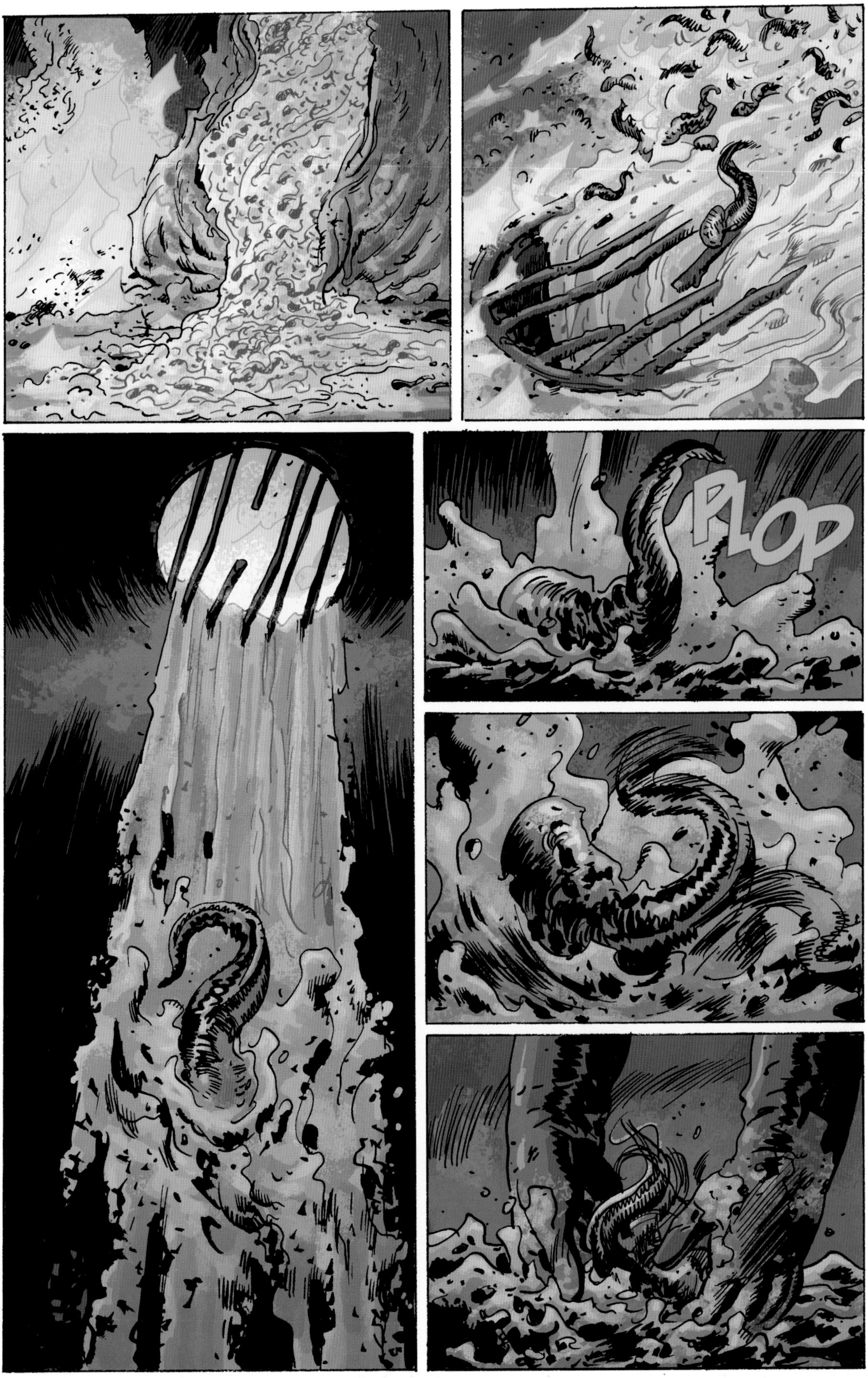
PLOP

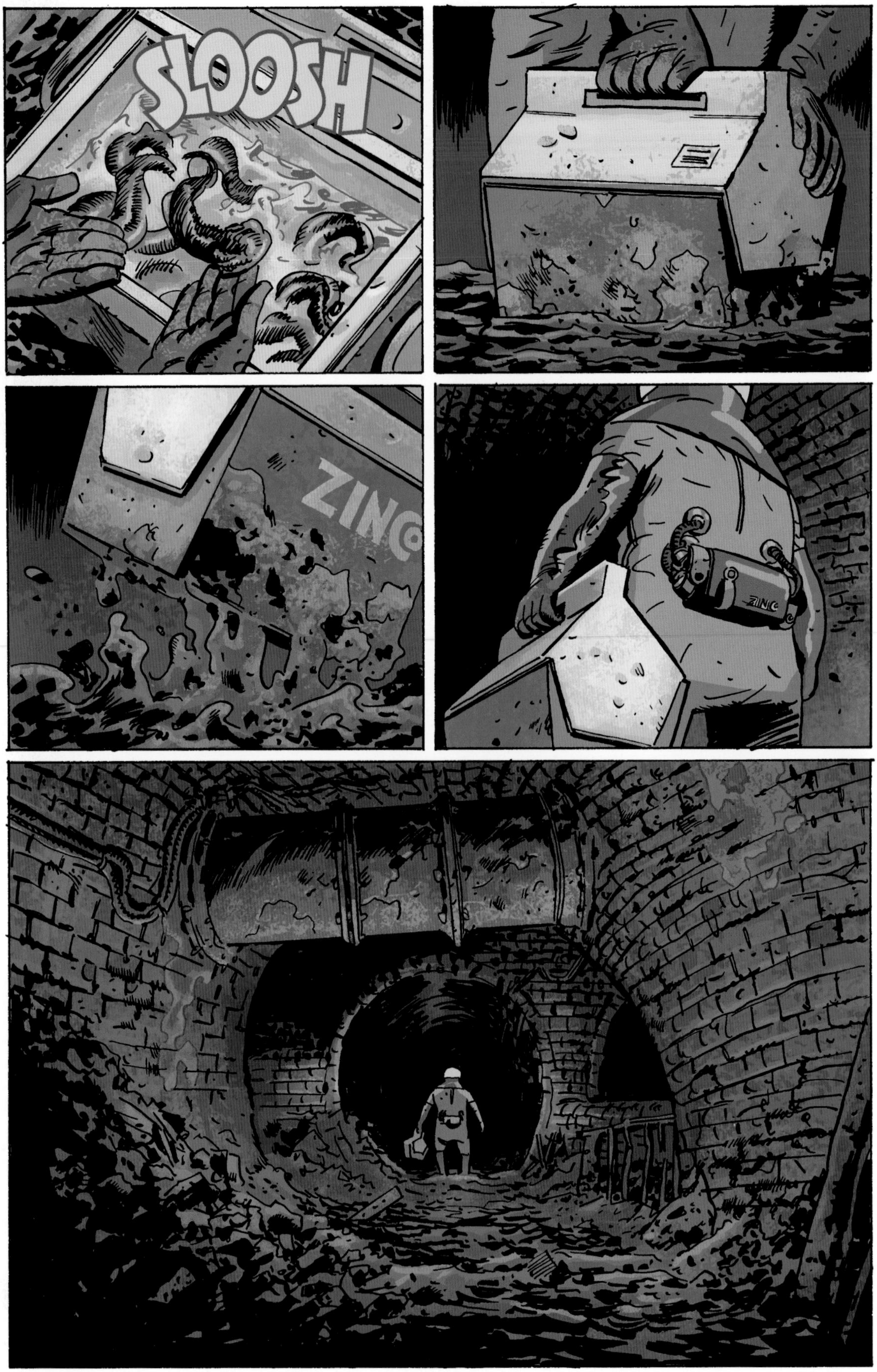
SLOOSH
ZINC
ZINC

CHAPTER TWO

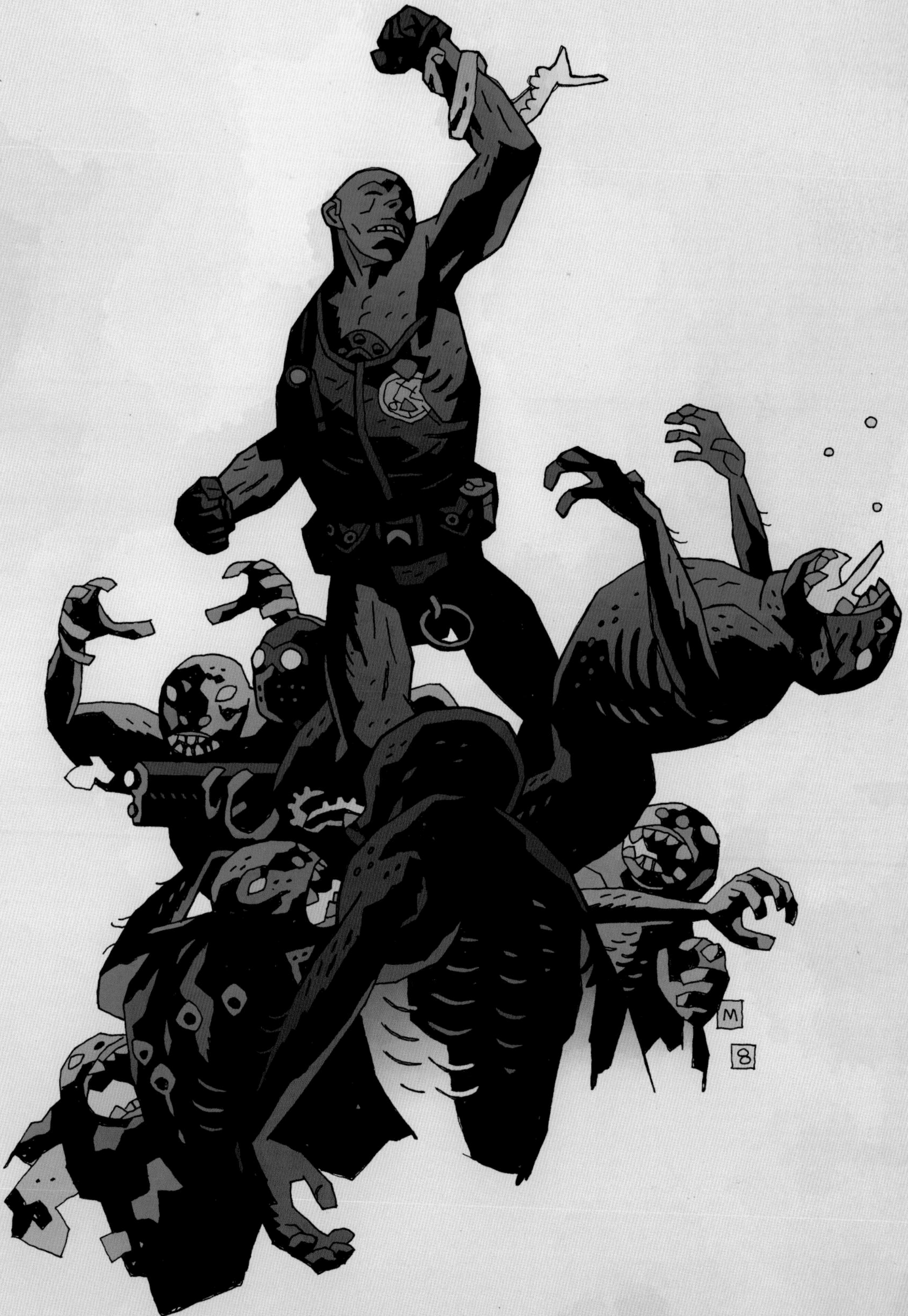

STORY BY JOHN ARCUDI

ART BY HERB TRIMPE & GUY DAVIS

COLORS BY DAVE STEWART

LETTERS BY CLEM ROBINS

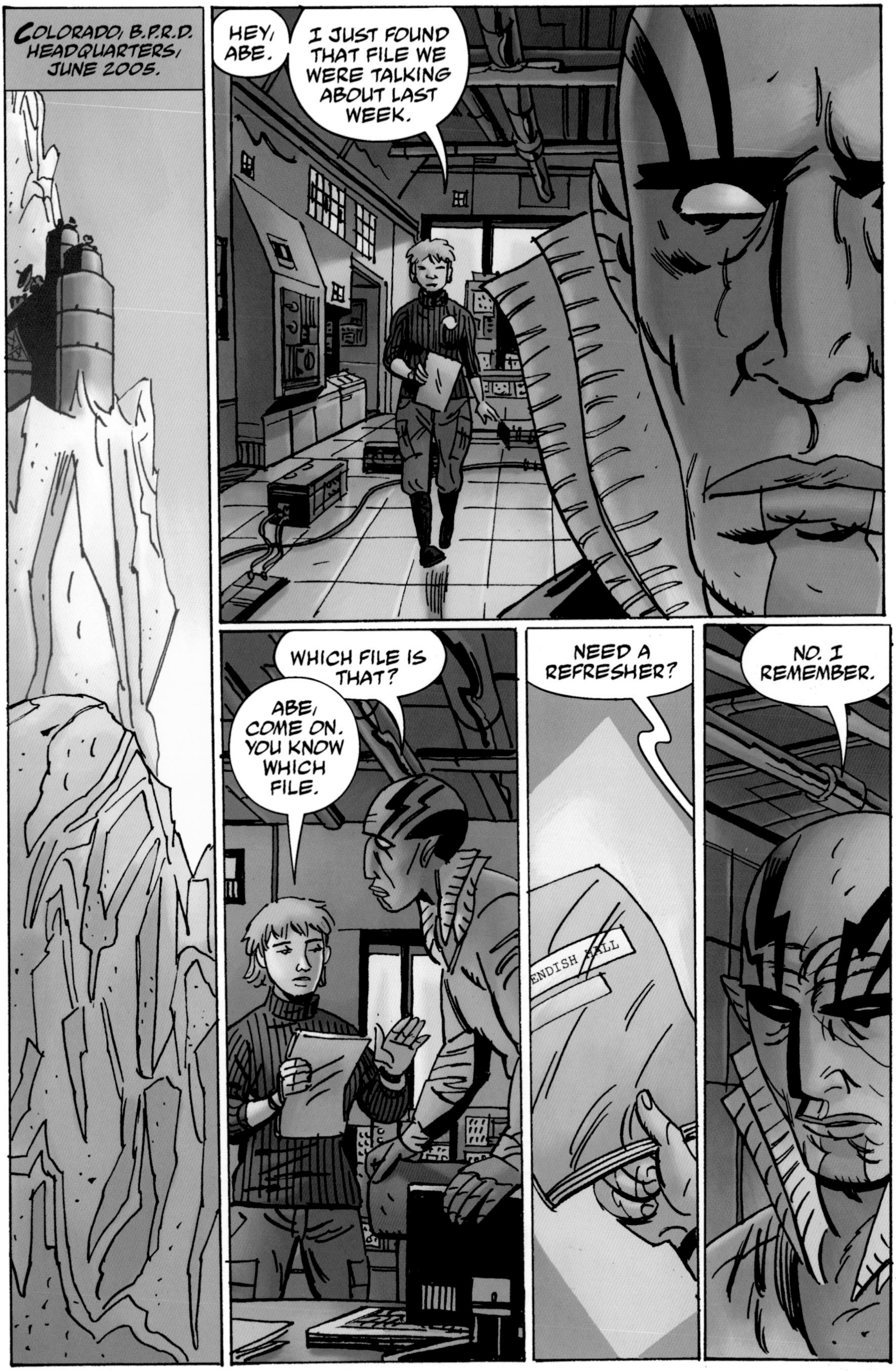
COLORADO, B.P.R.D. HEADQUARTERS, JUNE 2005.
HEY, ABE.
I JUST FOUND THAT FILE WE WERE TALKING ABOUT LAST WEEK.
WHICH FILE IS THAT?
ABE, COME ON. YOU KNOW WHICH FILE.
NEED A REFRESHER?
ENDISH HALL
NO. I REMEMBER.

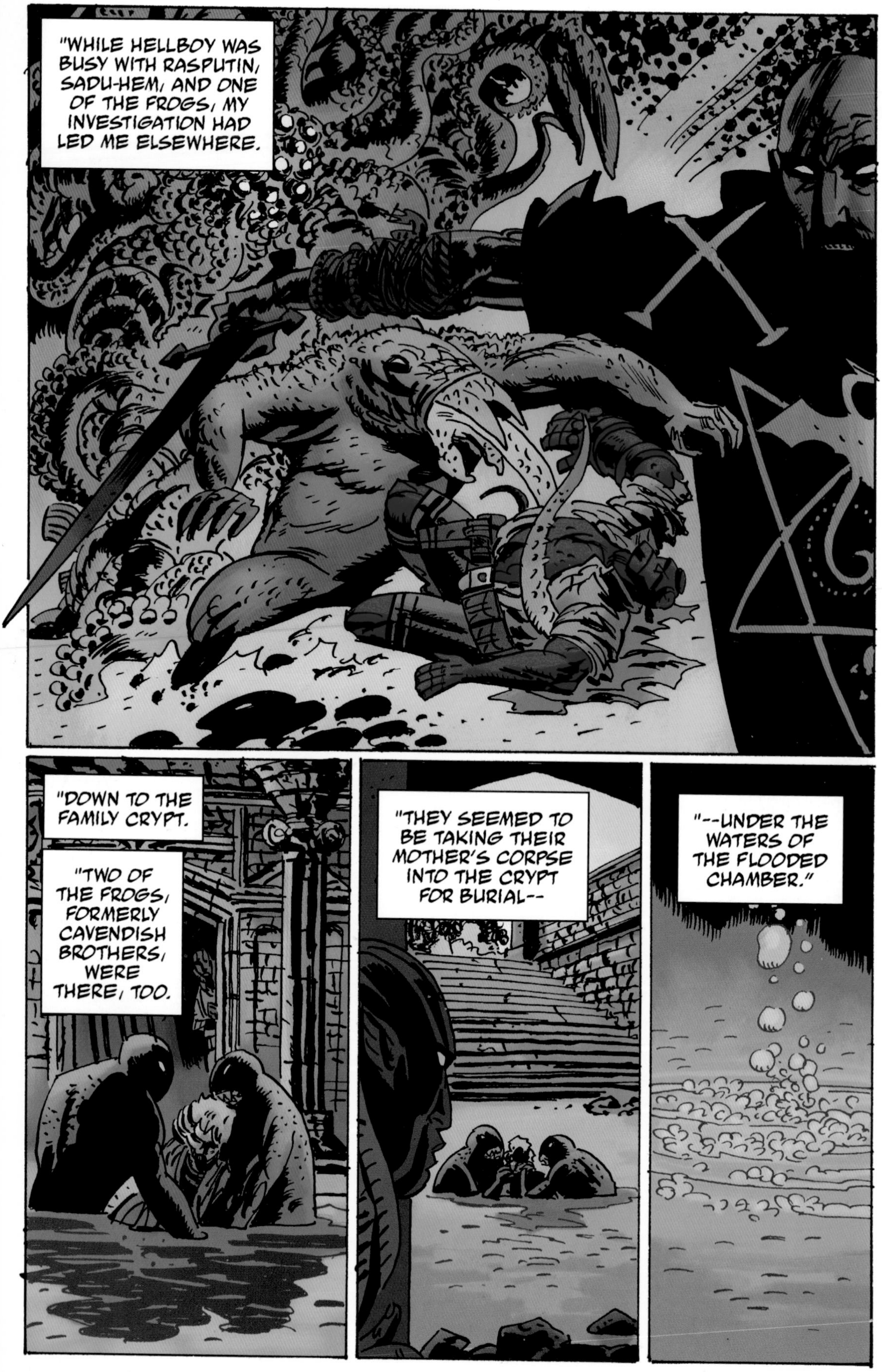
"WHILE HELLBOY WAS BUSY WITH RASPUTIN, SADU-HEM, AND ONE OF THE FROGS, MY INVESTIGATION HAD LED ME ELSEWHERE.
"DOWN TO THE FAMILY CRYPT.
"TWO OF THE FROGS, FORMERLY CAVENDISH BROTHERS, WERE THERE, TOO.
"THEY SEEMED TO BE TAKING THEIR MOTHER'S CORPSE INTO THE CRYPT FOR BURIAL--
"--UNDER THE WATERS OF THE FLOODED CHAMBER."

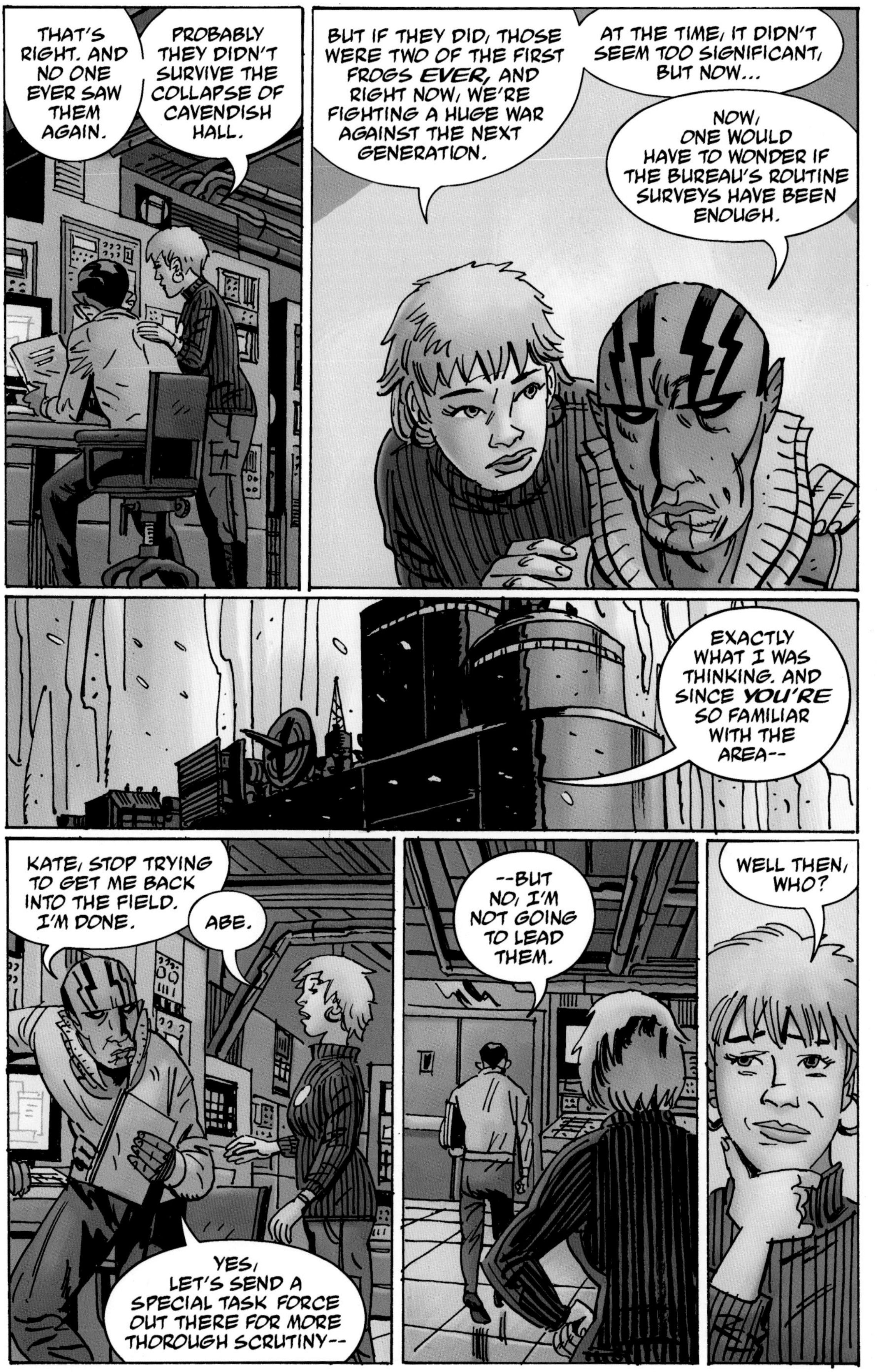
THAT'S RIGHT. AND NO ONE EVER SAW THEM AGAIN.
PROBABLY THEY DIDN'T SURVIVE THE COLLAPSE OF CAVENDISH HALL.
BUT IF THEY DID, THOSE WERE TWO OF THE FIRST FROGS EVER, AND RIGHT NOW, WE'RE FIGHTING A HUGE WAR AGAINST THE NEXT GENERATION.
AT THE TIME, IT DIDN'T SEEM TOO SIGNIFICANT, BUT NOW...
NOW, ONE WOULD HAVE TO WONDER IF THE BUREAU'S ROUTINE SURVEYS HAVE BEEN ENOUGH.
EXACTLY WHAT I WAS THINKING. AND SINCE YOU'RE SO FAMILIAR WITH THE AREA--
KATE, STOP TRYING TO GET ME BACK INTO THE FIELD. I'M DONE.
ABE.
YES, LET'S SEND A SPECIAL TASK FORCE OUT THERE FOR MORE THOROUGH SCRUTINY--
--BUT NO, I'M NOT GOING TO LEAD THEM.
WELL THEN, WHO?

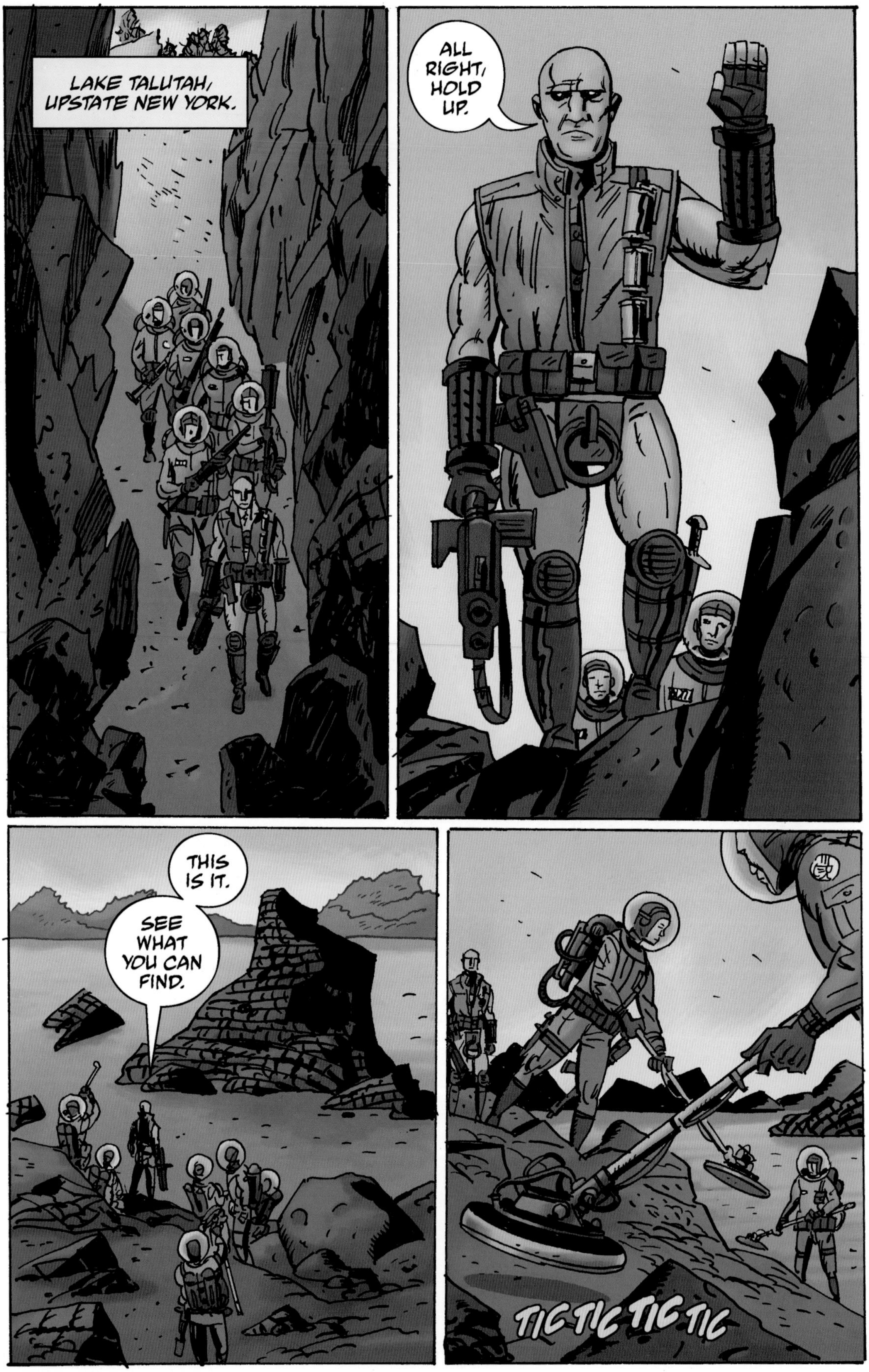
LAKE TALUTAH, UPSTATE NEW YORK.
ALL RIGHT, HOLD UP.
THIS IS IT.
SEE WHAT YOU CAN FIND.
TIC TIC TIC TIC TIC

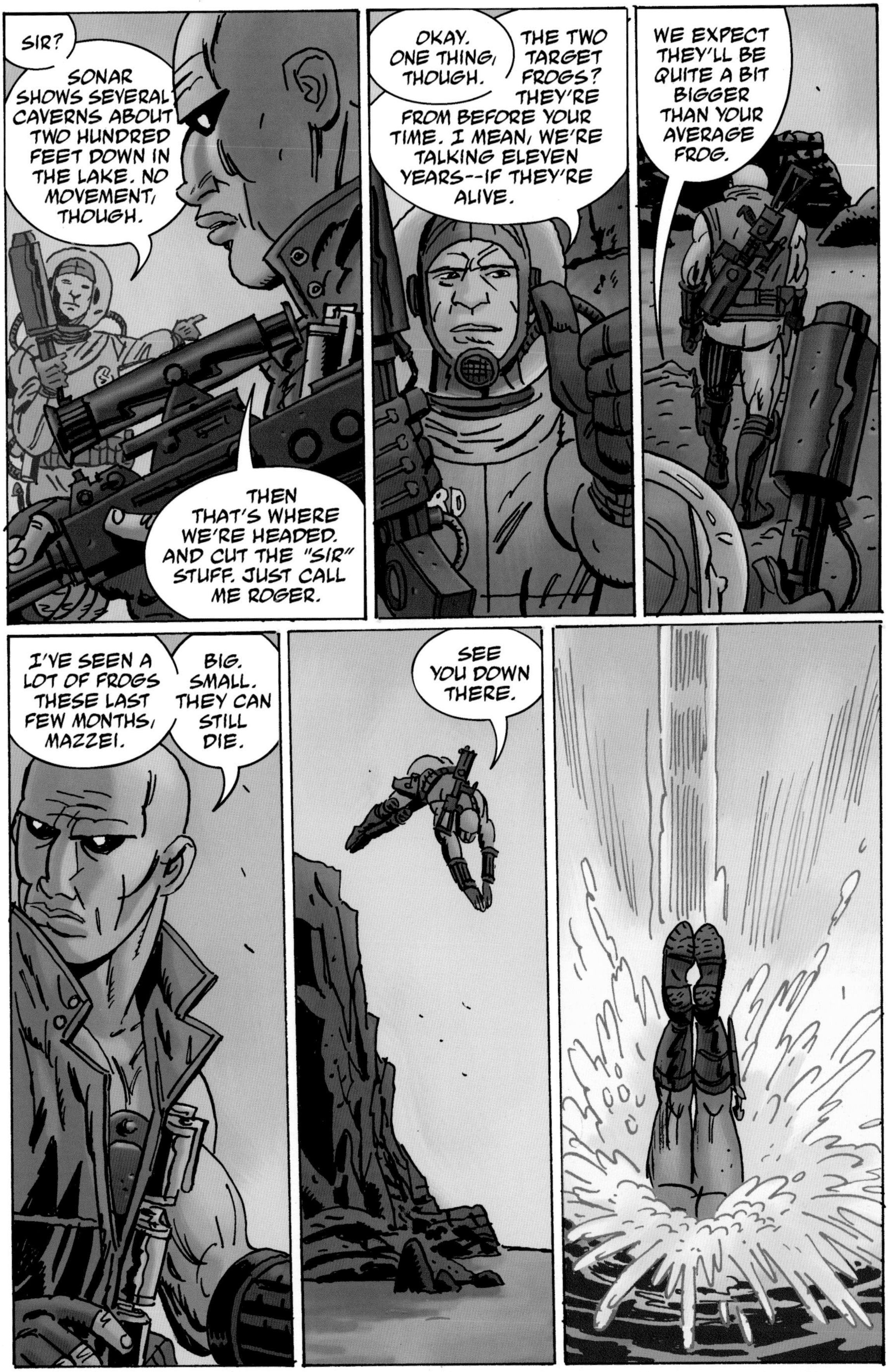
SIR?
SONAR SHOWS SEVERAL CAVERNS ABOUT TWO HUNDRED FEET DOWN IN THE LAKE. NO MOVEMENT, THOUGH.
THEN THAT'S WHERE WE'RE HEADED. AND CUT THE "SIR" STUFF. JUST CALL ME ROGER.
OKAY. ONE THING, THOUGH.
THE TWO TARGET FROGS? THEY'RE FROM BEFORE YOUR TIME. I MEAN, WE'RE TALKING ELEVEN YEARS--IF THEY'RE ALIVE.
WE EXPECT THEY'LL BE QUITE A BIT BIGGER THAN YOUR AVERAGE FROG.
I'VE SEEN A LOT OF FROGS THESE LAST FEW MONTHS, MAZZEI.
BIG. SMALL. THEY CAN STILL DIE.
SEE YOU DOWN THERE.

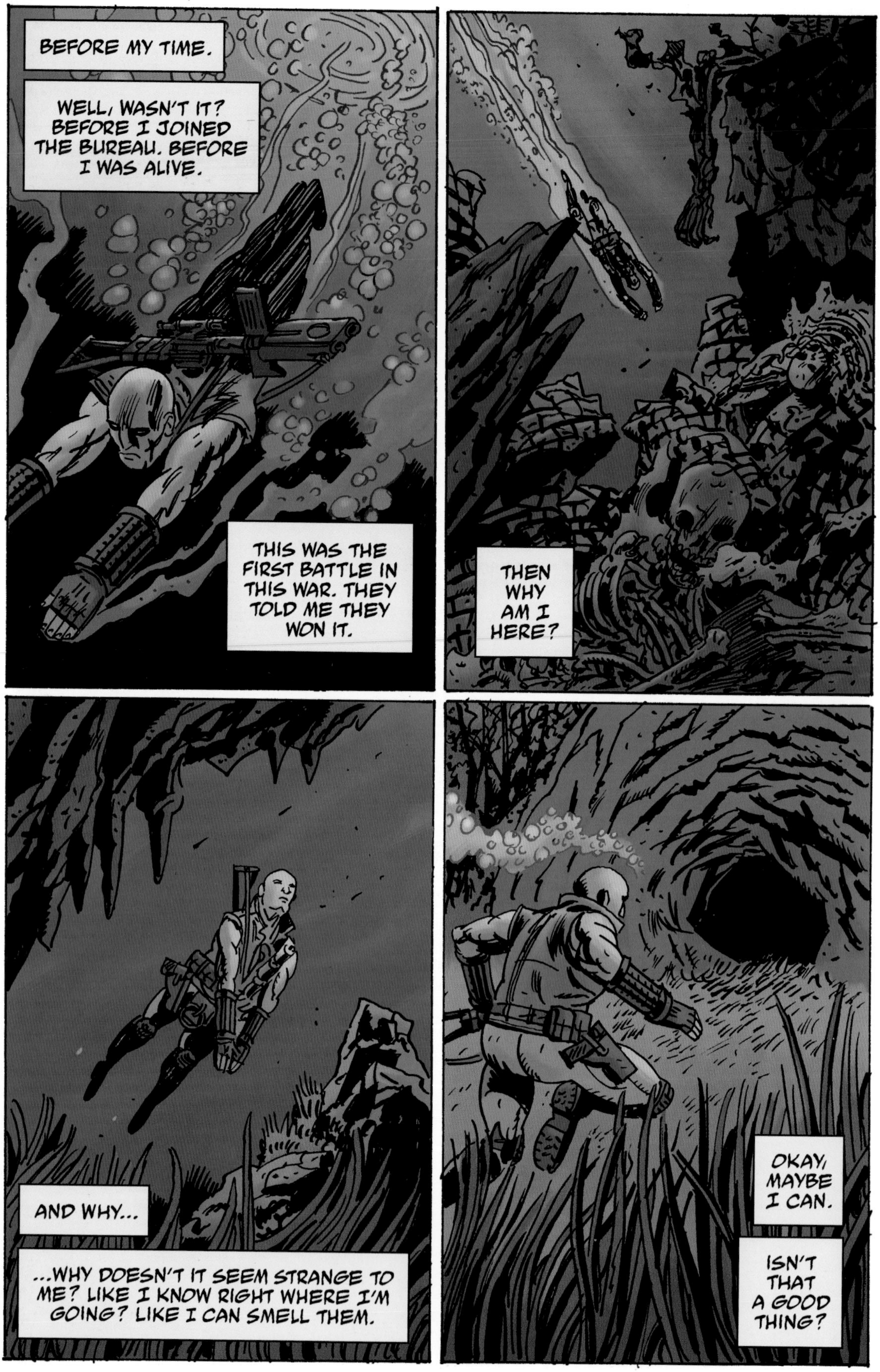
BEFORE MY TIME.
WELL, WASN'T IT? BEFORE I JOINED THE BUREAU. BEFORE I WAS ALIVE.
THIS WAS THE FIRST BATTLE IN THIS WAR. THEY TOLD ME THEY WON IT.
THEN WHY AM I HERE?
AND WHY...
...WHY DOESN'T IT SEEM STRANGE TO ME? LIKE I KNOW RIGHT WHERE I'M GOING? LIKE I CAN SMELL THEM.
OKAY, MAYBE I CAN.
ISN'T THAT A GOOD THING?

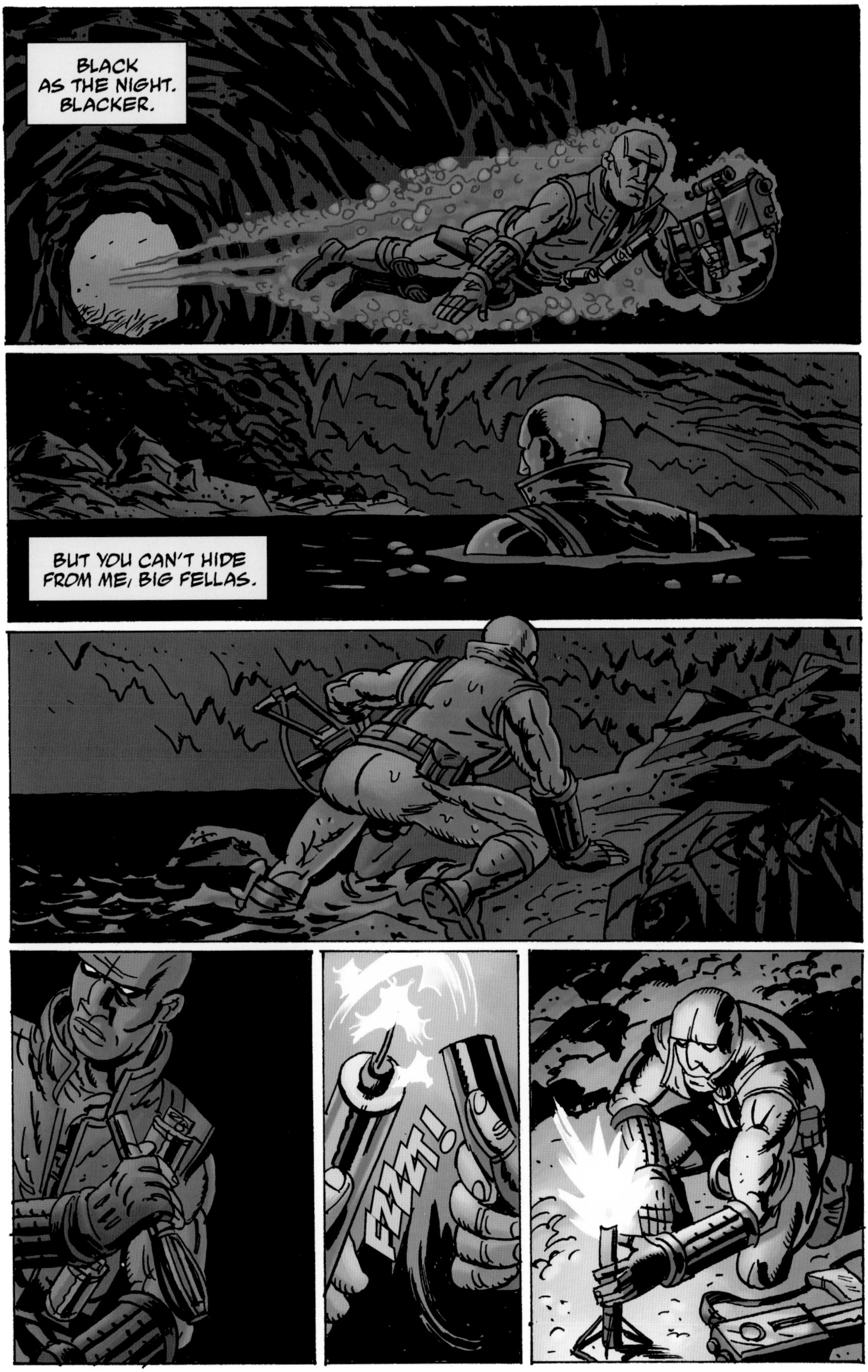
BLACK AS THE NIGHT. BLACKER.
BUT YOU CAN'T HIDE FROM ME, BIG FELLAS.
FZZZT!

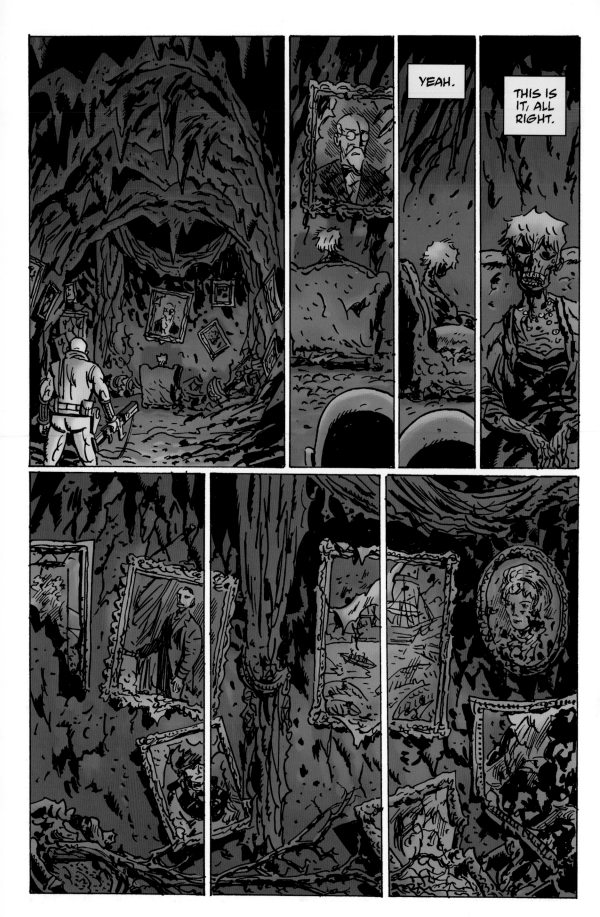

YEAH.

THIS IS IT, ALL RIGHT.

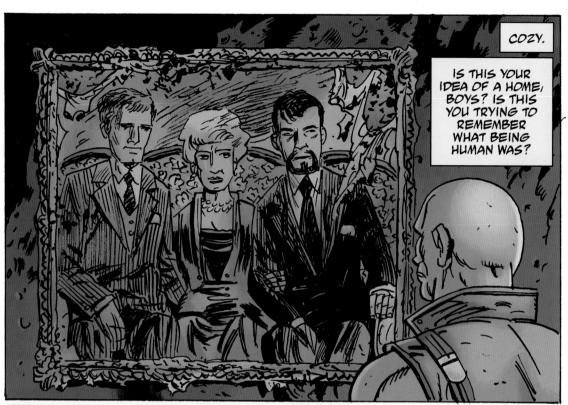

COZY.

IS THIS YOUR IDEA OF A HOME, BOYS? IS THIS YOU TRYING TO REMEMBER WHAT BEING HUMAN WAS?

I SHOULD RADIO THE OTHERS. TELL THEM I HIT THE JACKPOT. HAVE THEM ALL COME RUNNING.

BUT IT'S SO QUIET HERE.

AND YOU?

YOU WOULDN'T HURT ANYBODY.

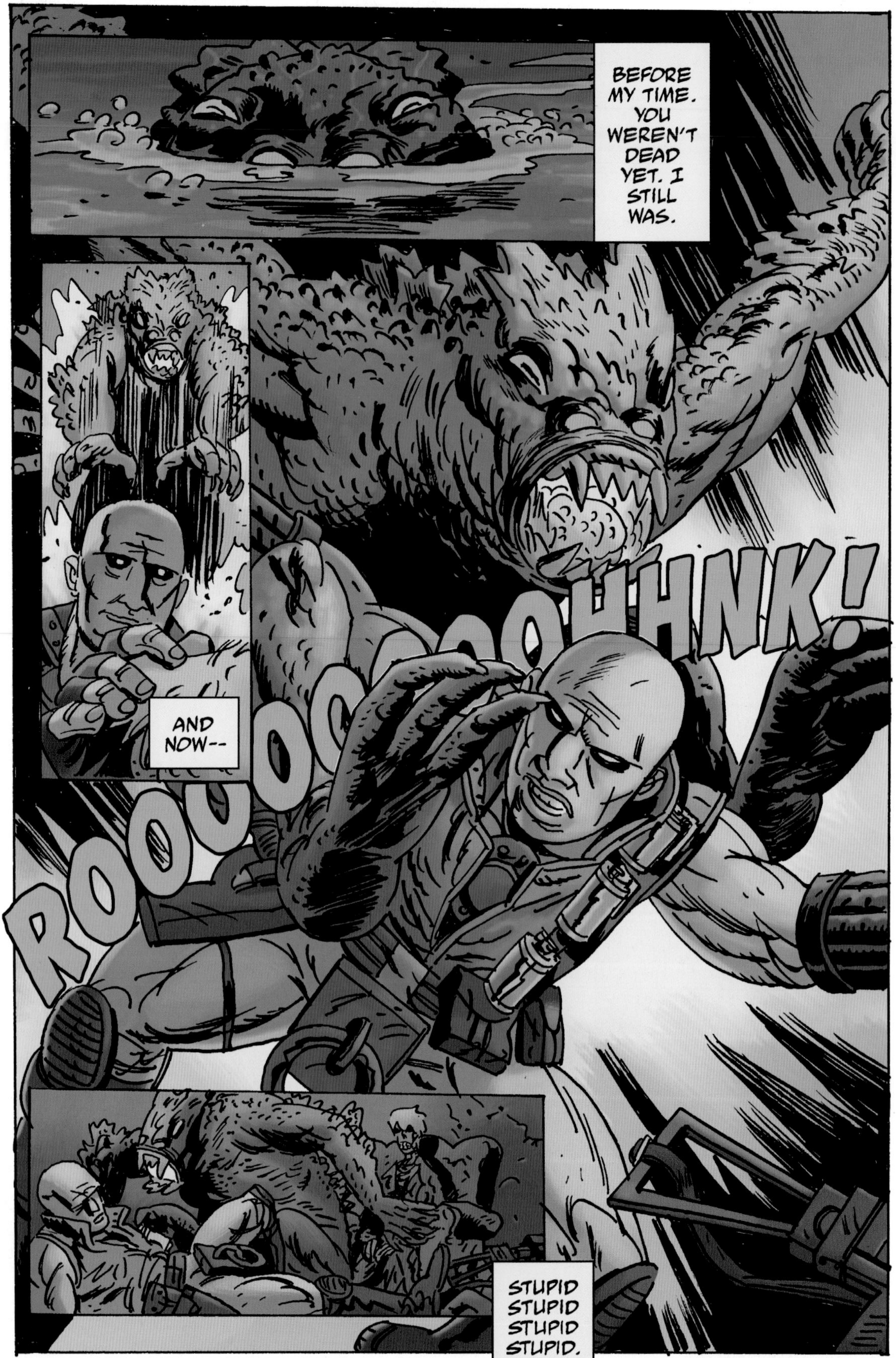
BEFORE MY TIME. YOU WEREN'T DEAD YET. I STILL WAS.
AND NOW--
ROOOOOOOOHHNK!
STUPID STUPID STUPID STUPID.

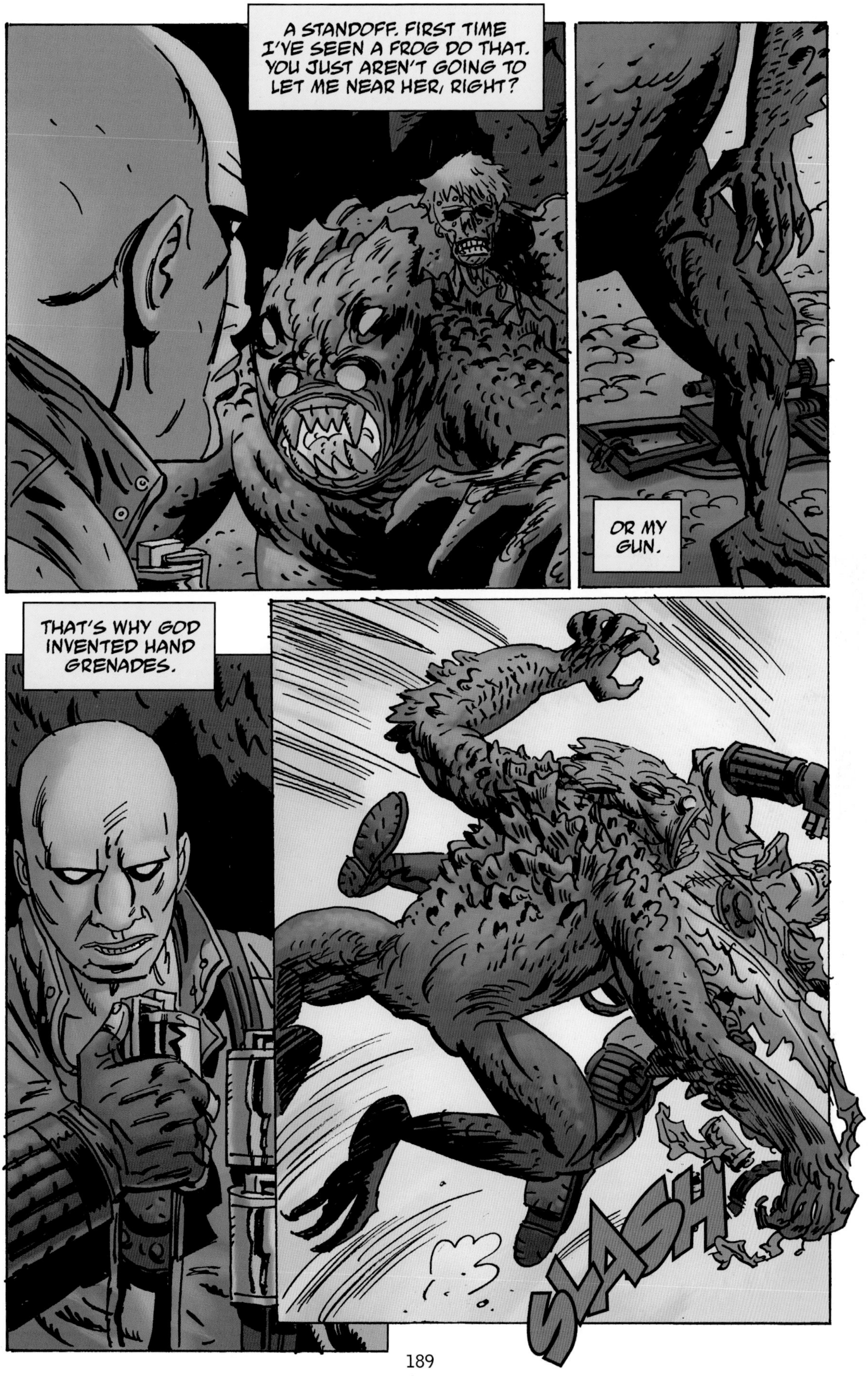
A STANDOFF. FIRST TIME I'VE SEEN A FROG DO THAT. YOU JUST AREN'T GOING TO LET ME NEAR HER, RIGHT?
OR MY GUN.
THAT'S WHY GOD INVENTED HAND GRENADES.
SLASH

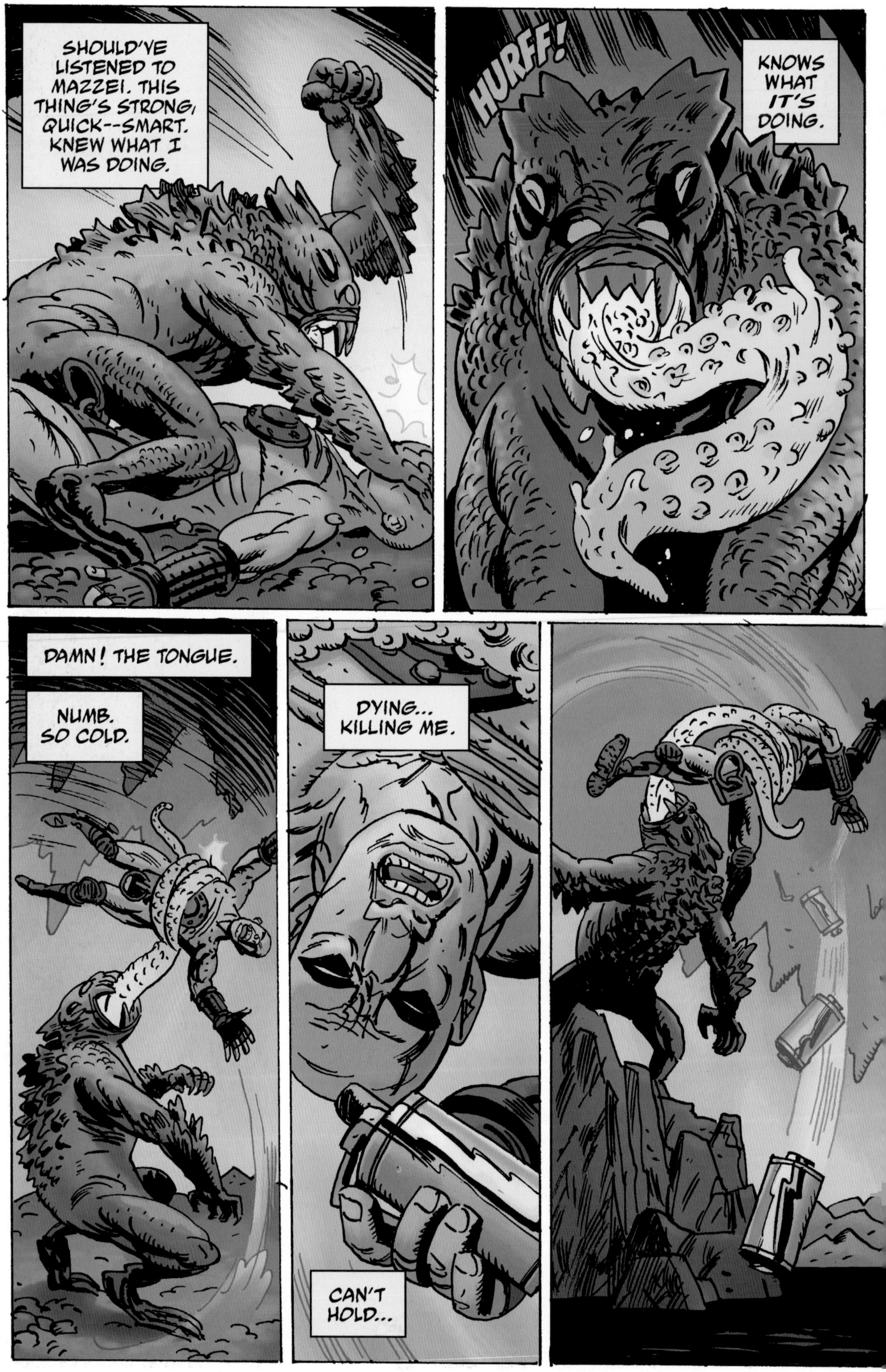
SHOULD'VE LISTENED TO MAZZEI. THIS THING'S STRONG, QUICK--SMART. KNEW WHAT I WAS DOING.
HURFF!
KNOWS WHAT IT'S DOING.
DAMN! THE TONGUE.
NUMB. SO COLD.
DYING... KILLING ME.
CAN'T HOLD...

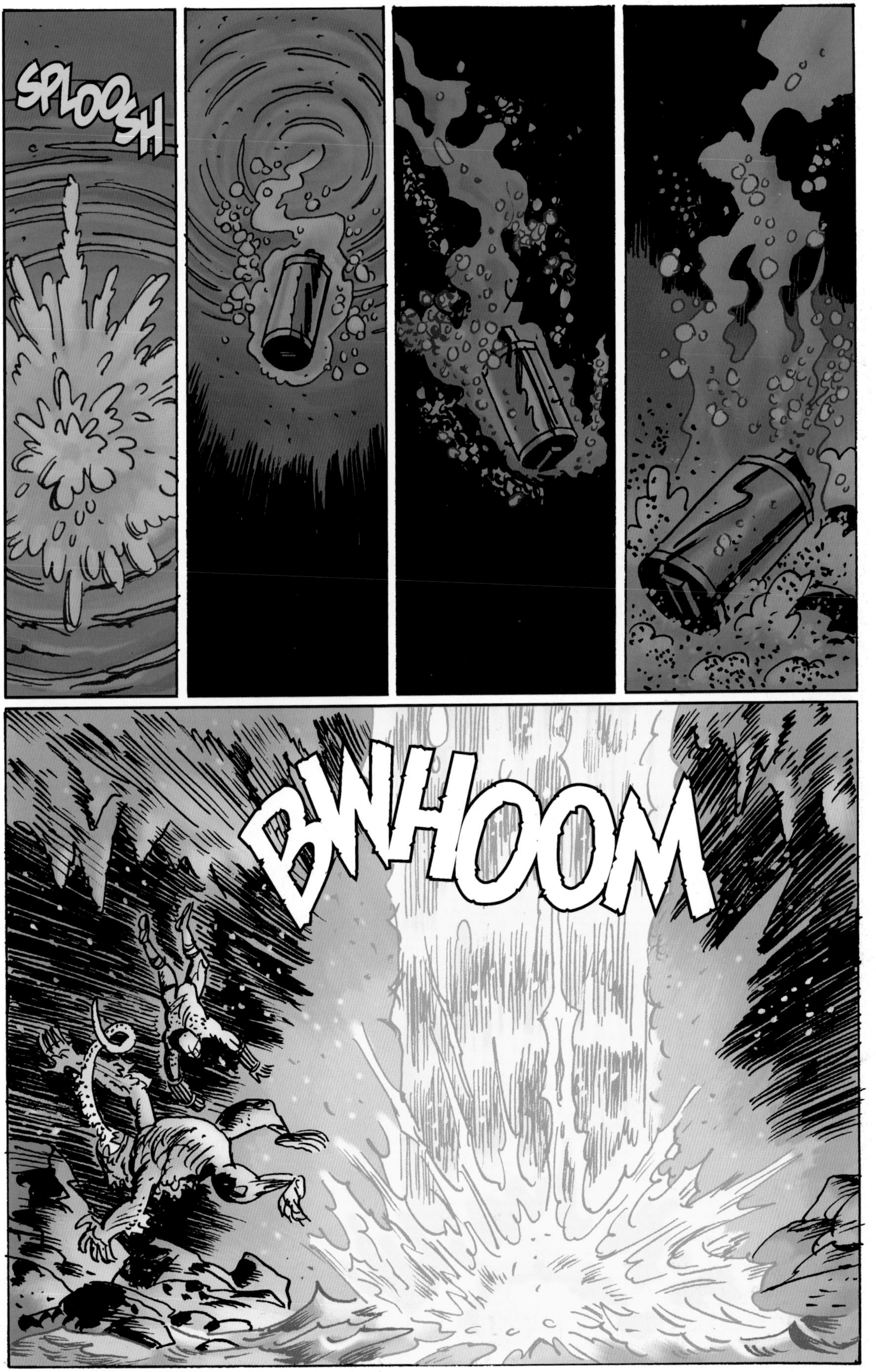
SPLOOSH
BWHOOM

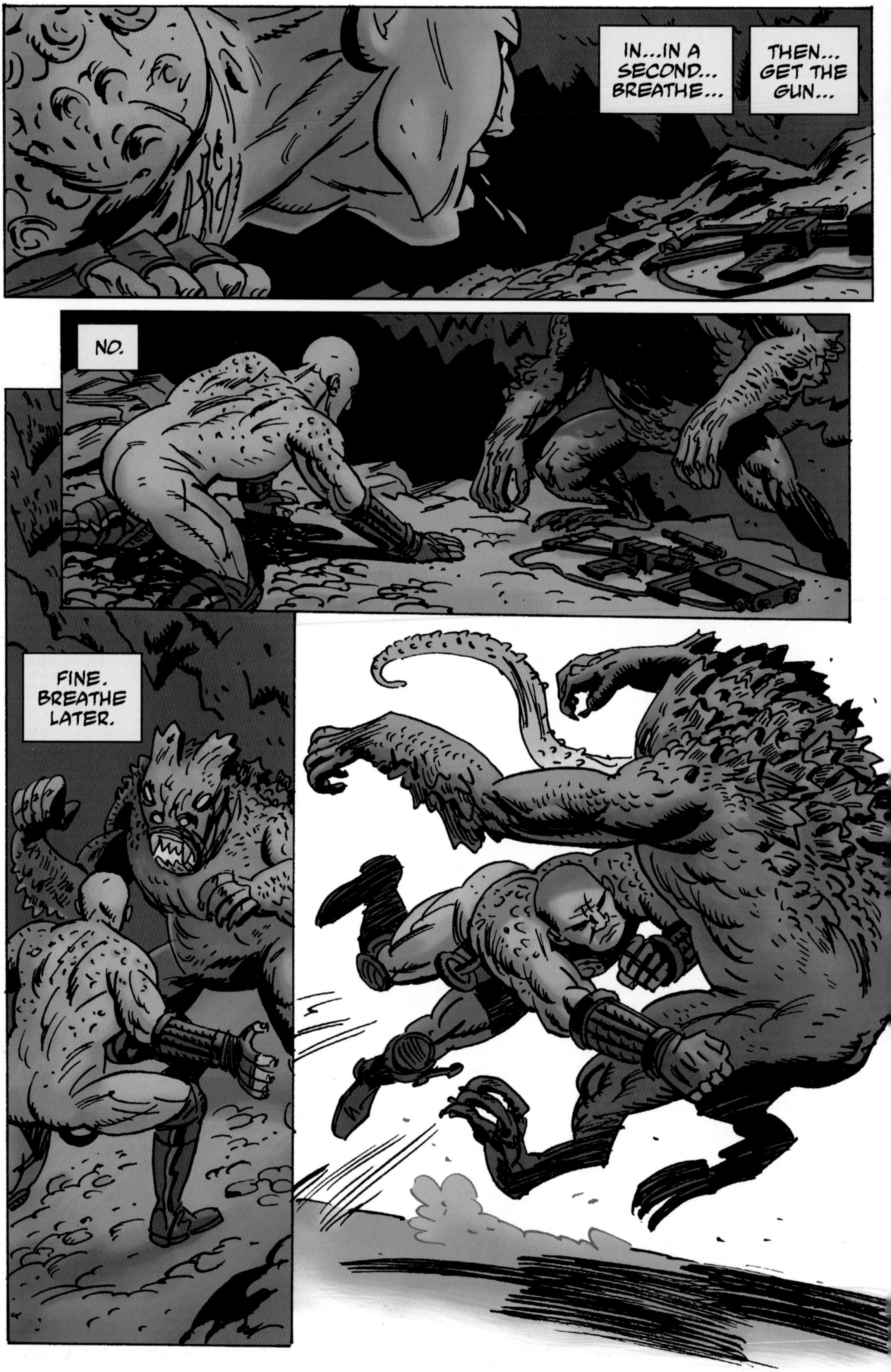
IN...IN A SECOND... BREATHE...
THEN... GET THE GUN...
NO.
FINE. BREATHE LATER.

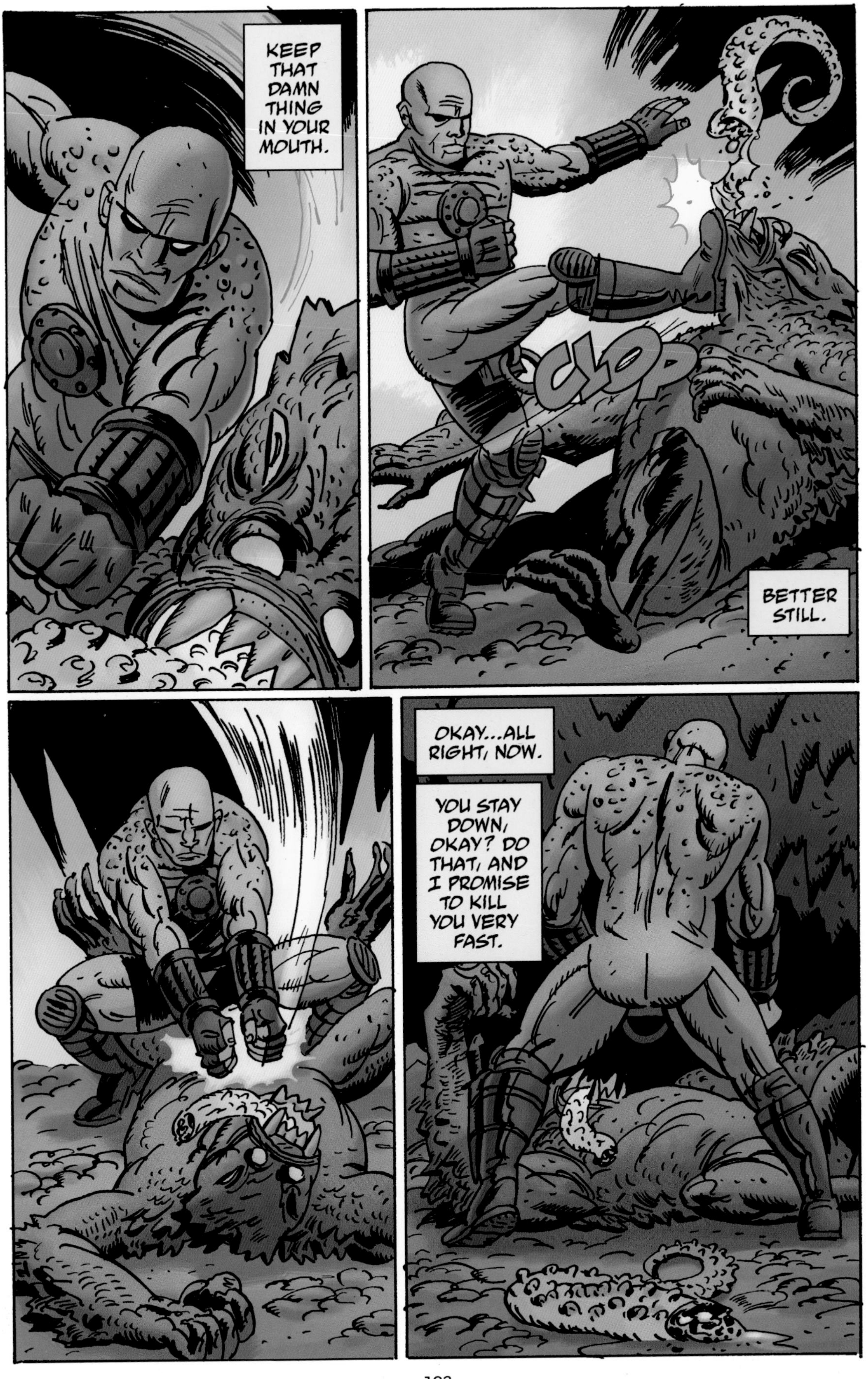
KEEP THAT DAMN THING IN YOUR MOUTH.
CLOP
BETTER STILL.
OKAY...ALL RIGHT, NOW.
YOU STAY DOWN, OKAY? DO THAT, AND I PROMISE TO KILL YOU VERY FAST.

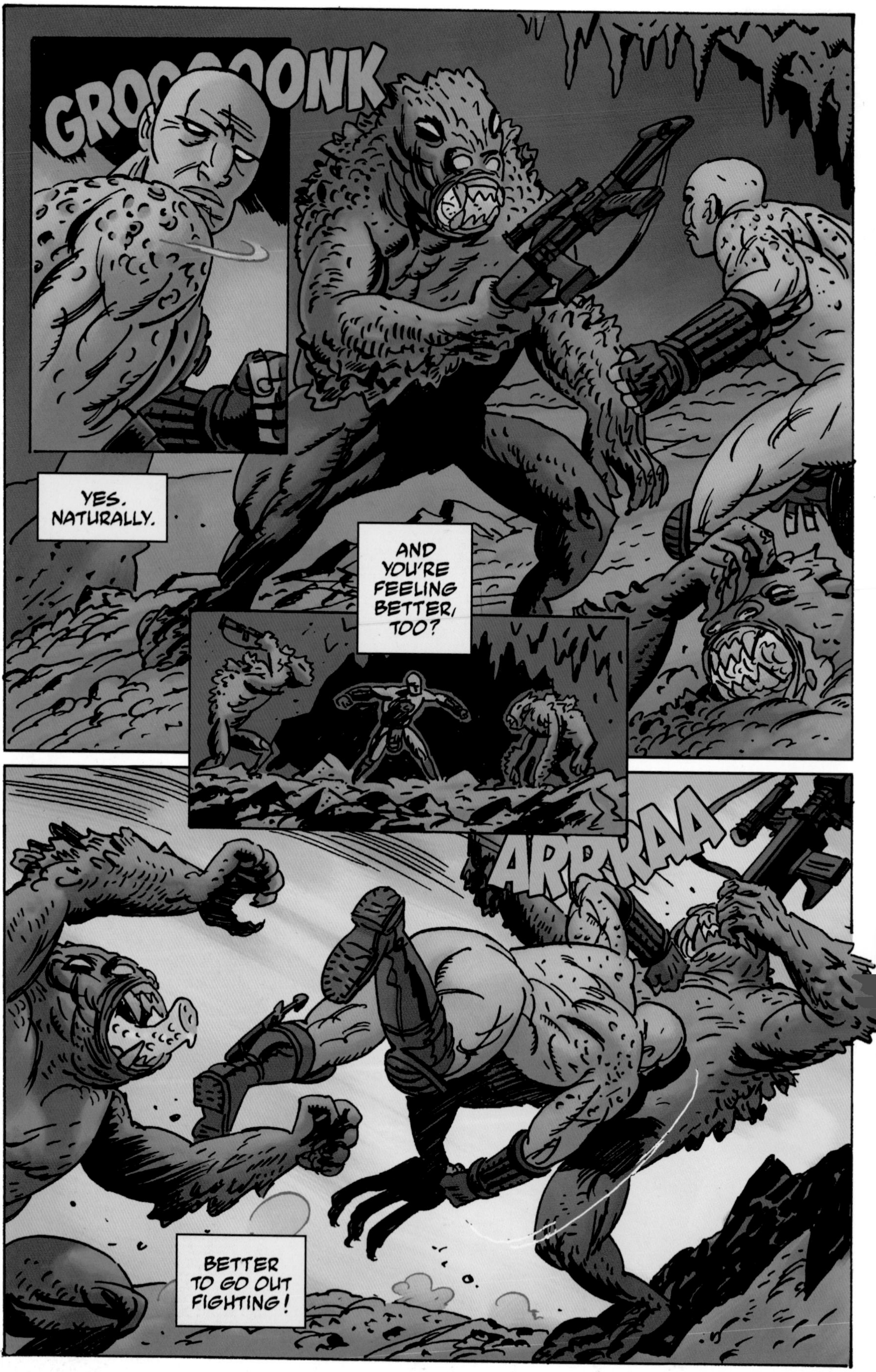
GROOOOONK
YES. NATURALLY.
AND YOU'RE FEELING BETTER, TOO?
ARRRAA
BETTER TO GO OUT FIGHTING!

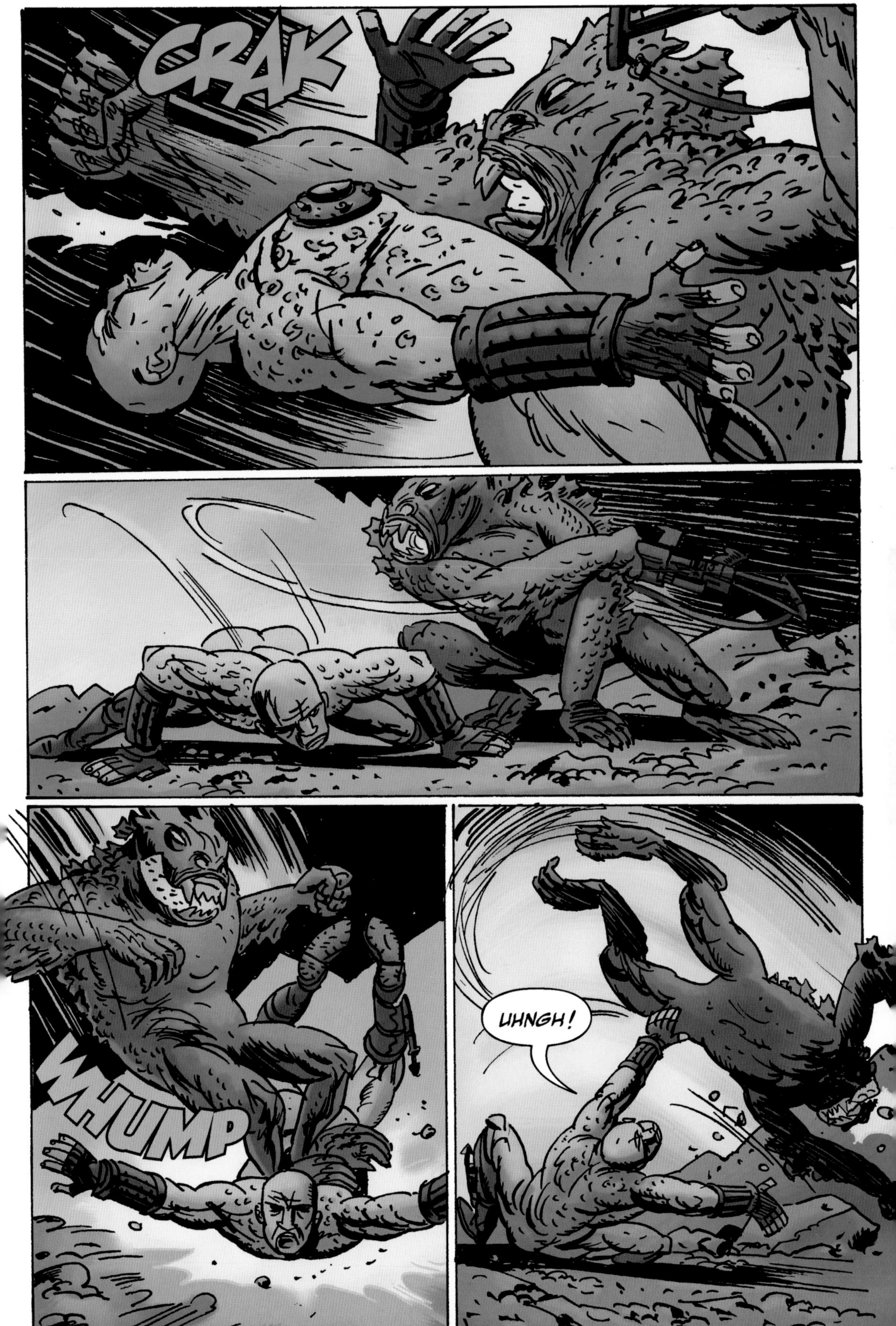
CRAK
WHUMP
UHNGH!

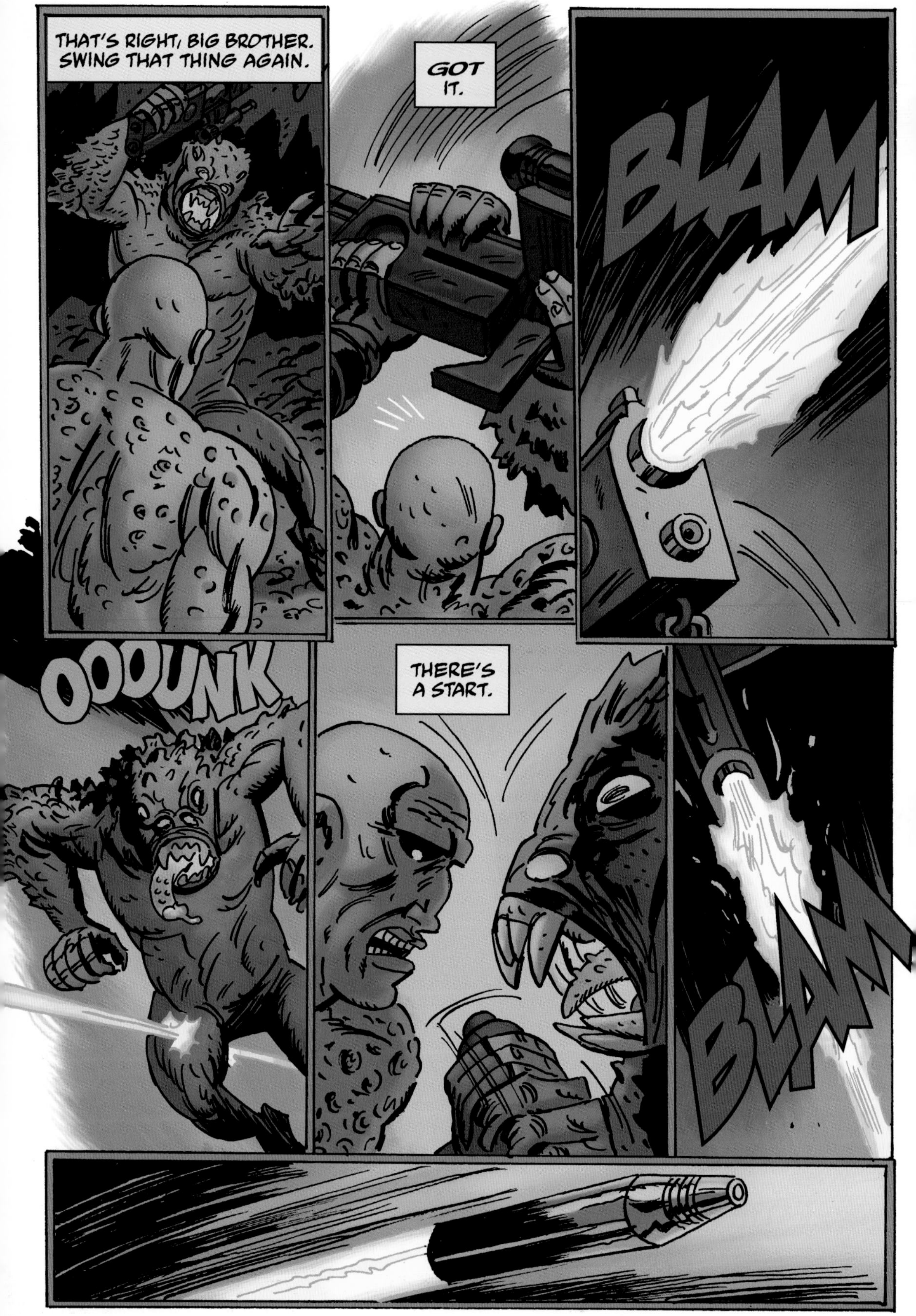
THAT'S RIGHT, BIG BROTHER. SWING THAT THING AGAIN.
GOT IT.
BLAM
OOOUNK
THERE'S A START.
BLAM

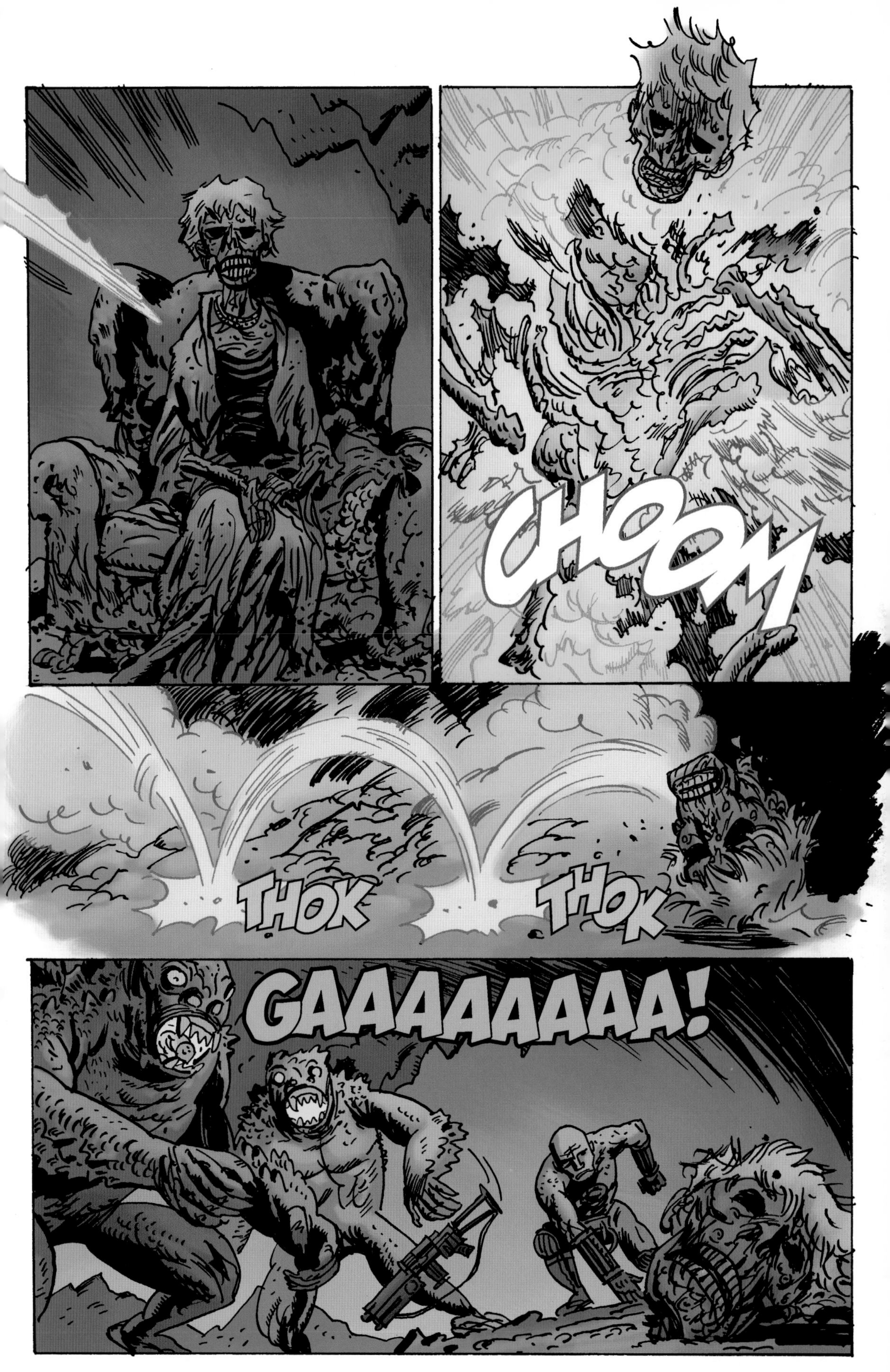
CHOOM
THOK
THOK
GAAAAAAAA!

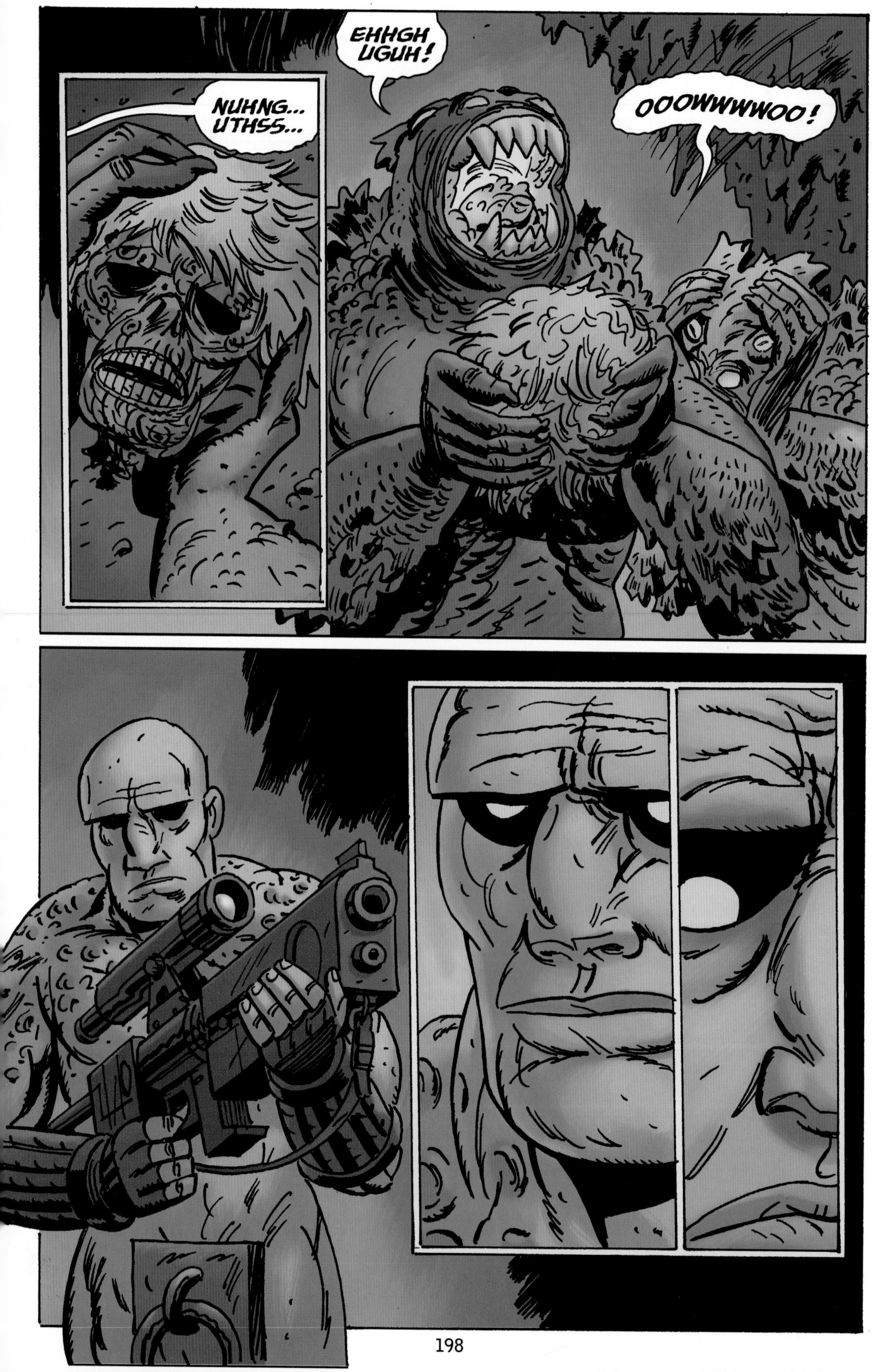
NUHNG... UTHSS...
EHHGH UGUH!
OOOWWWWOO!

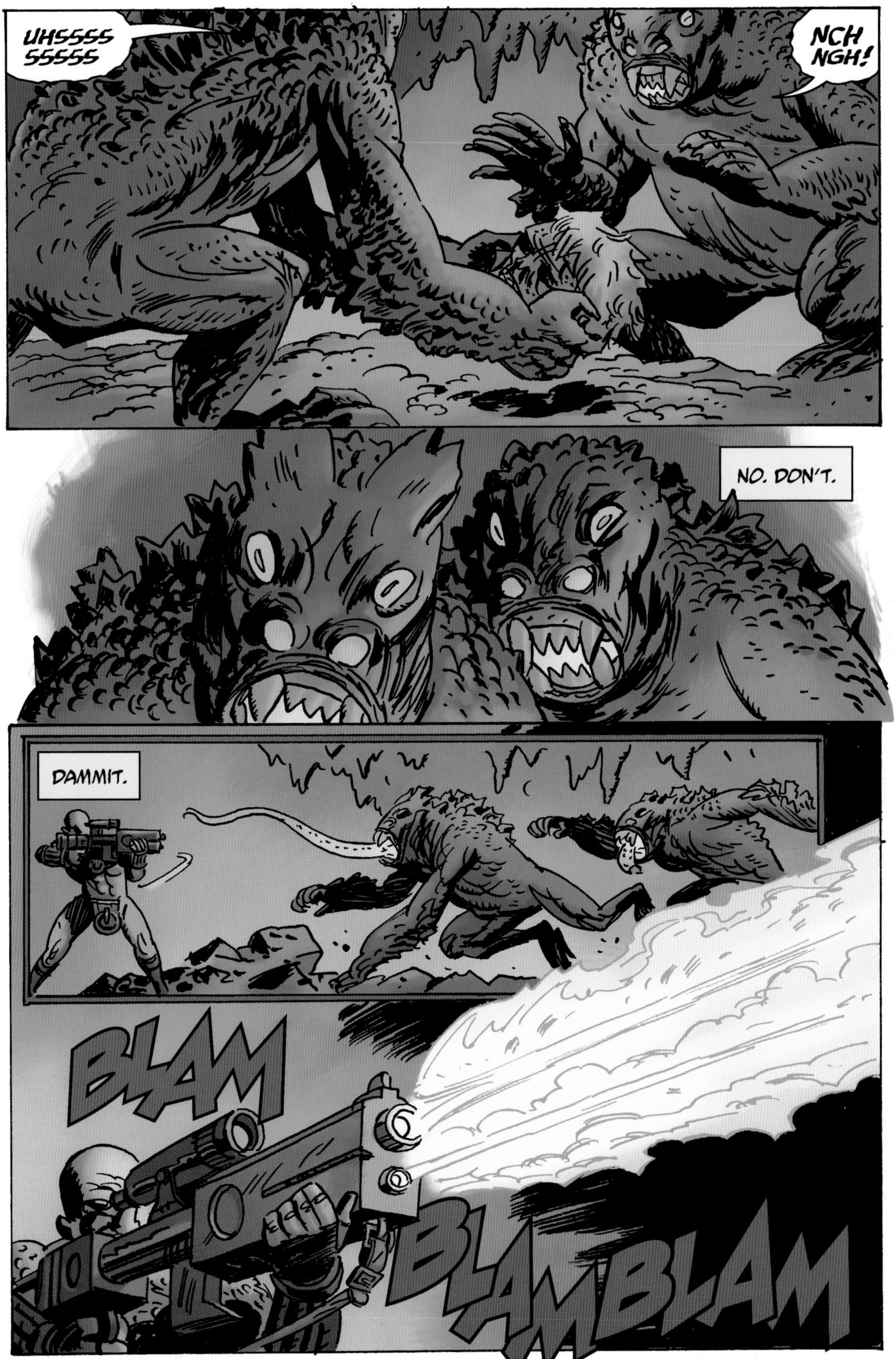
UHSSSSS SSSSS
NCH NGH!
NO. DON'T.
DAMMIT.
BLAM
BLAMBLAM

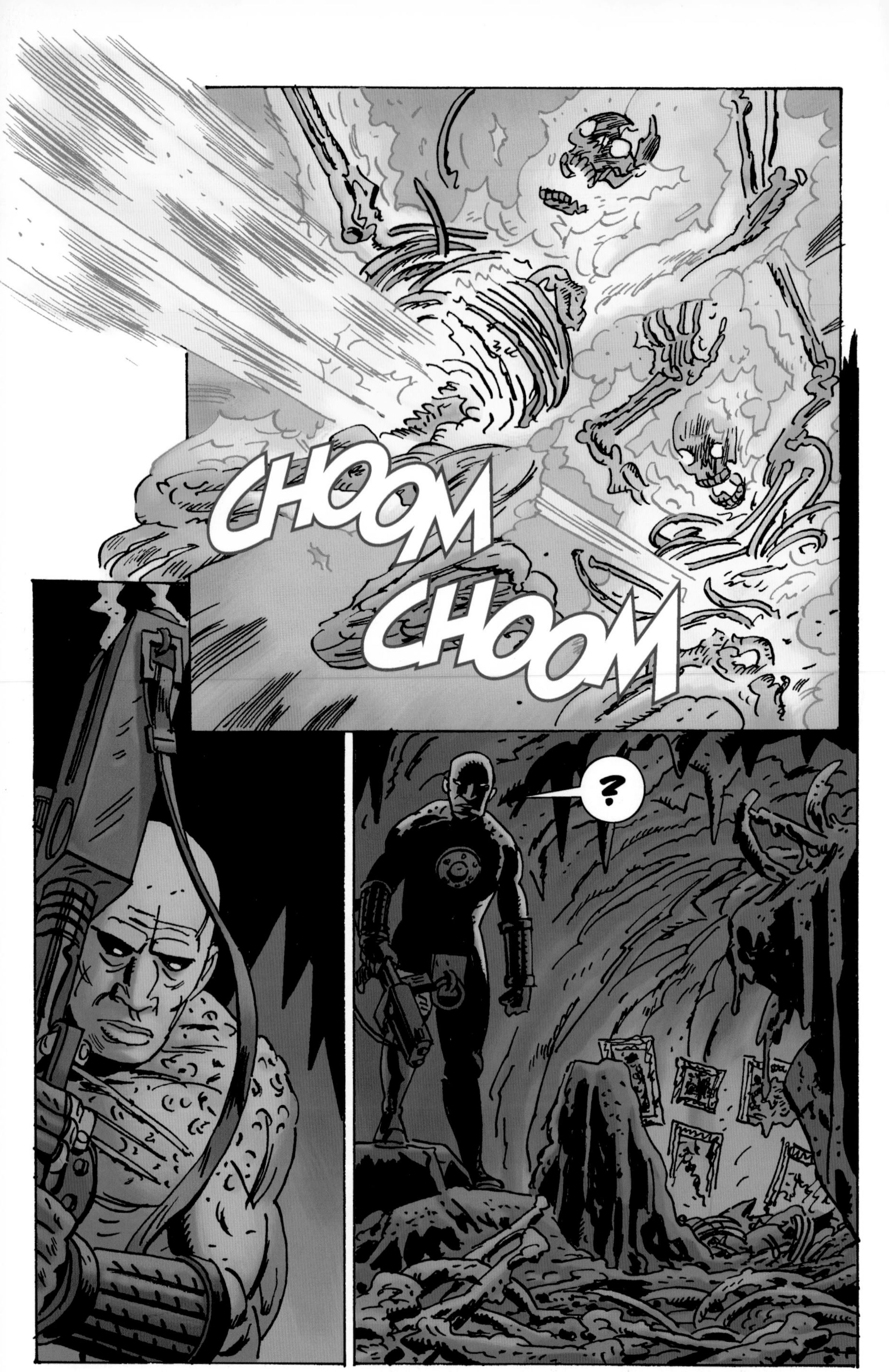
CHOOM
CHOOM
?

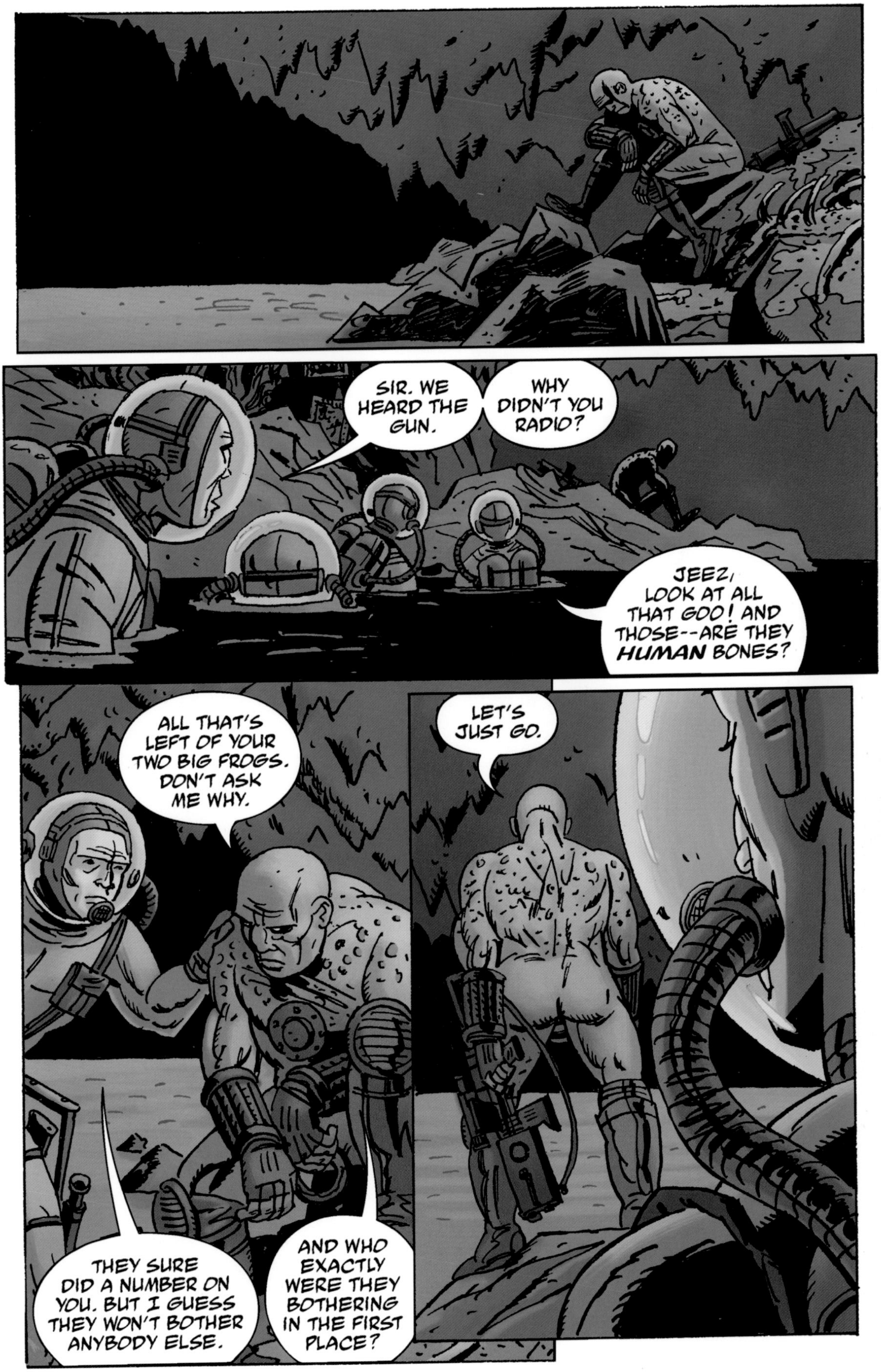
SIR. WE HEARD THE GUN.
WHY DIDN'T YOU RADIO?
JEEZ, LOOK AT ALL THAT GOO! AND THOSE--ARE THEY *HUMAN* BONES?
ALL THAT'S LEFT OF YOUR TWO BIG FROGS. DON'T ASK ME WHY.
THEY SURE DID A NUMBER ON YOU. BUT I GUESS THEY WON'T BOTHER ANYBODY ELSE.
AND WHO EXACTLY WERE THEY BOTHERING IN THE FIRST PLACE?
LET'S JUST GO.

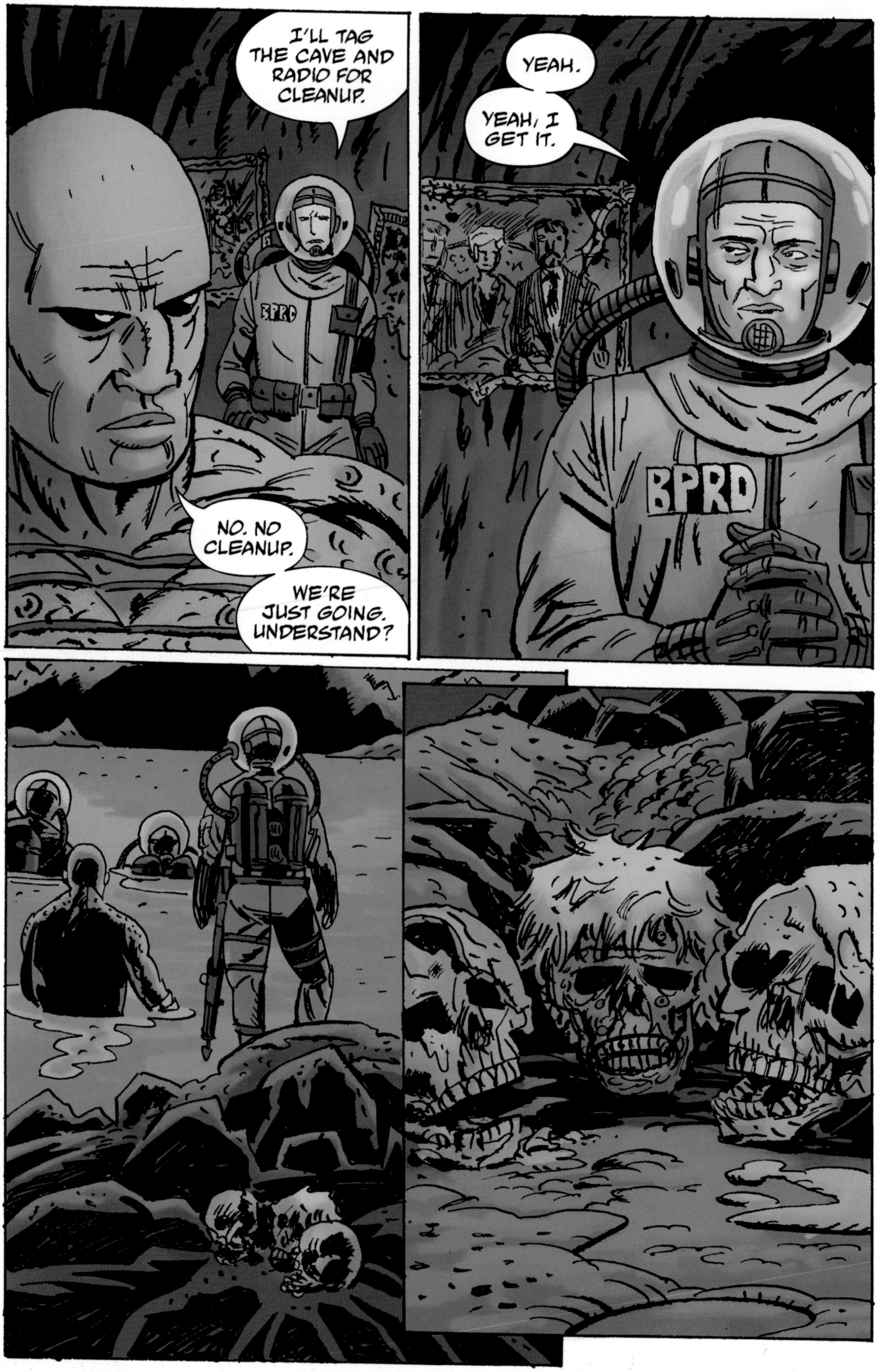

I'LL TAG THE CAVE AND RADIO FOR CLEANUP.
NO. NO CLEANUP.
WE'RE JUST GOING. UNDERSTAND?
YEAH.
YEAH, I GET IT.
BPRD

CHAPTER THREE

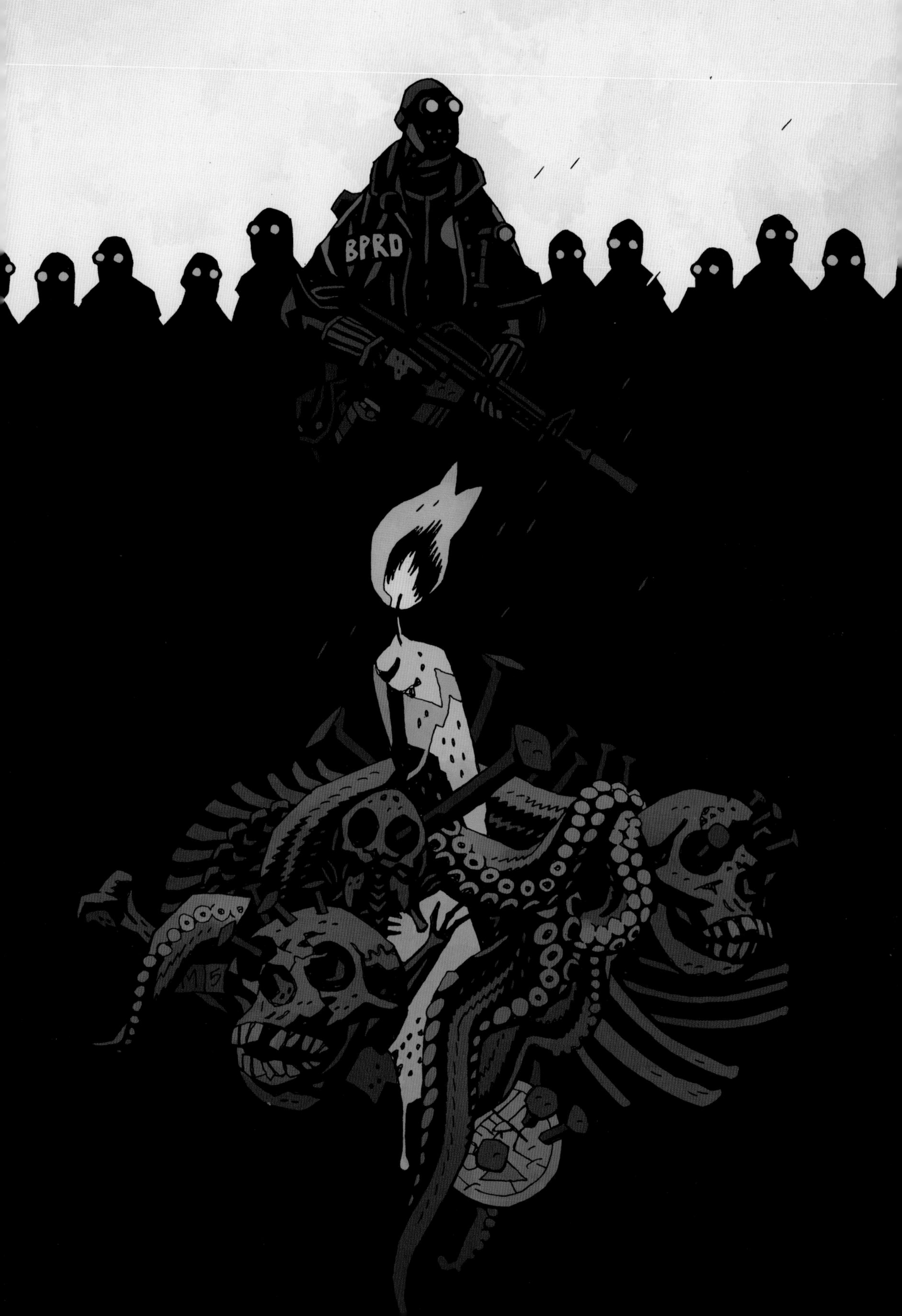
BPRD

STORY BY MIKE MIGNOLA & JOHN ARCUDI

ART BY GUY DAVIS

COLORS BY DAVE STEWART

LETTERS BY CLEM ROBINS

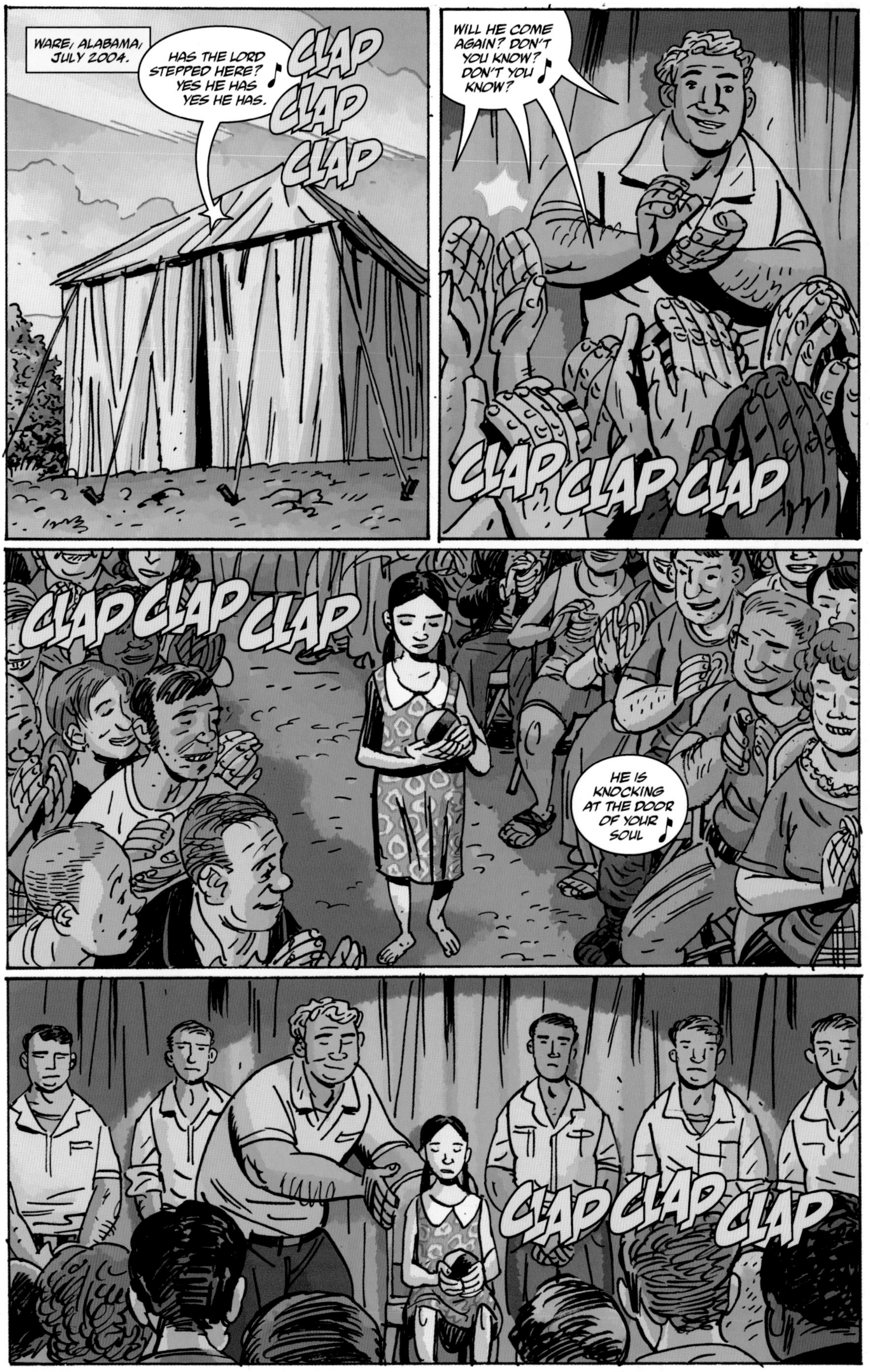
WARE, ALABAMA, JULY 2004.
HAS THE LORD STEPPED HERE? YES HE HAS YES HE HAS.
CLAP CLAP CLAP
WILL HE COME AGAIN? DON'T YOU KNOW? DON'T YOU KNOW?
CLAP CLAP CLAP
CLAP CLAP CLAP
HE IS KNOCKING AT THE DOOR OF YOUR SOUL
CLAP CLAP CLAP

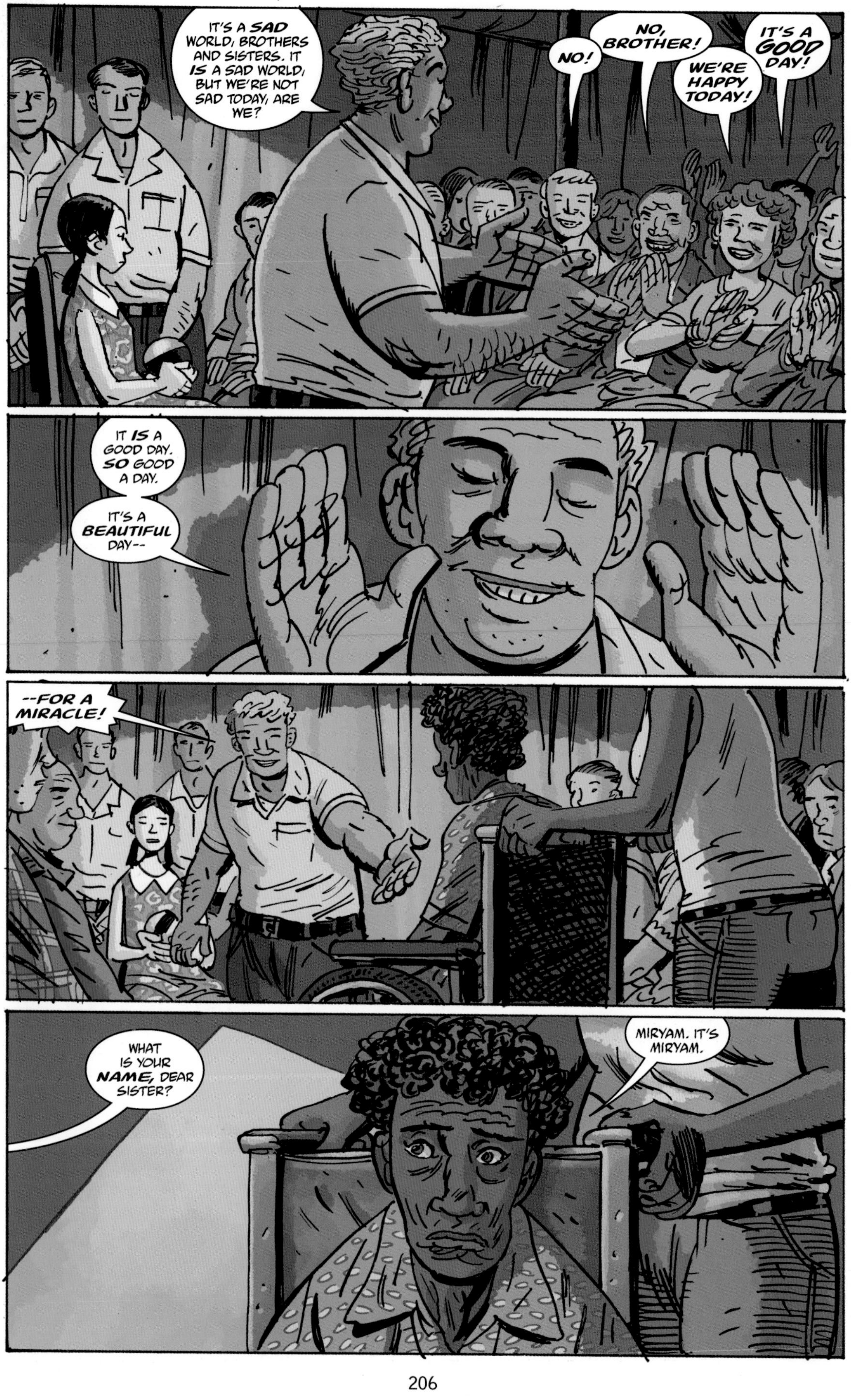
IT'S A SAD WORLD, BROTHERS AND SISTERS. IT IS A SAD WORLD, BUT WE'RE NOT SAD TODAY, ARE WE?
NO!
NO, BROTHER!
WE'RE HAPPY TODAY!
IT'S A GOOD DAY!
IT IS A GOOD DAY. SO GOOD A DAY.
IT'S A BEAUTIFUL DAY--
--FOR A MIRACLE!
WHAT IS YOUR NAME, DEAR SISTER?
MIRYAM. IT'S MIRYAM.

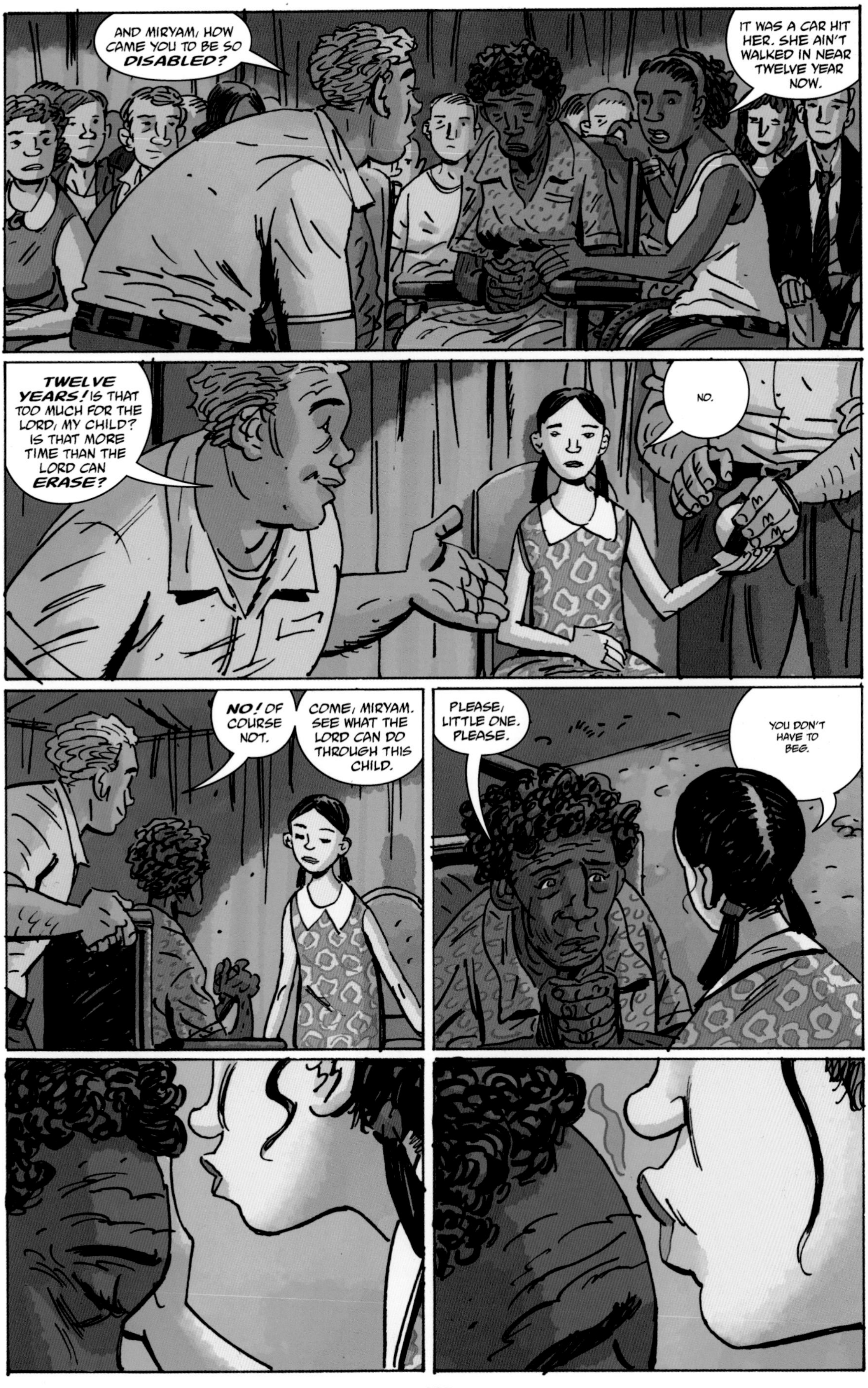

AND MIRYAM, HOW CAME YOU TO BE SO DISABLED?
IT WAS A CAR HIT HER. SHE AIN'T WALKED IN NEAR TWELVE YEAR NOW.
TWELVE YEARS! IS THAT TOO MUCH FOR THE LORD, MY CHILD? IS THAT MORE TIME THAN THE LORD CAN ERASE?
NO.
NO! OF COURSE NOT.
COME, MIRYAM. SEE WHAT THE LORD CAN DO THROUGH THIS CHILD.
PLEASE, LITTLE ONE. PLEASE.
YOU DON'T HAVE TO BEG.

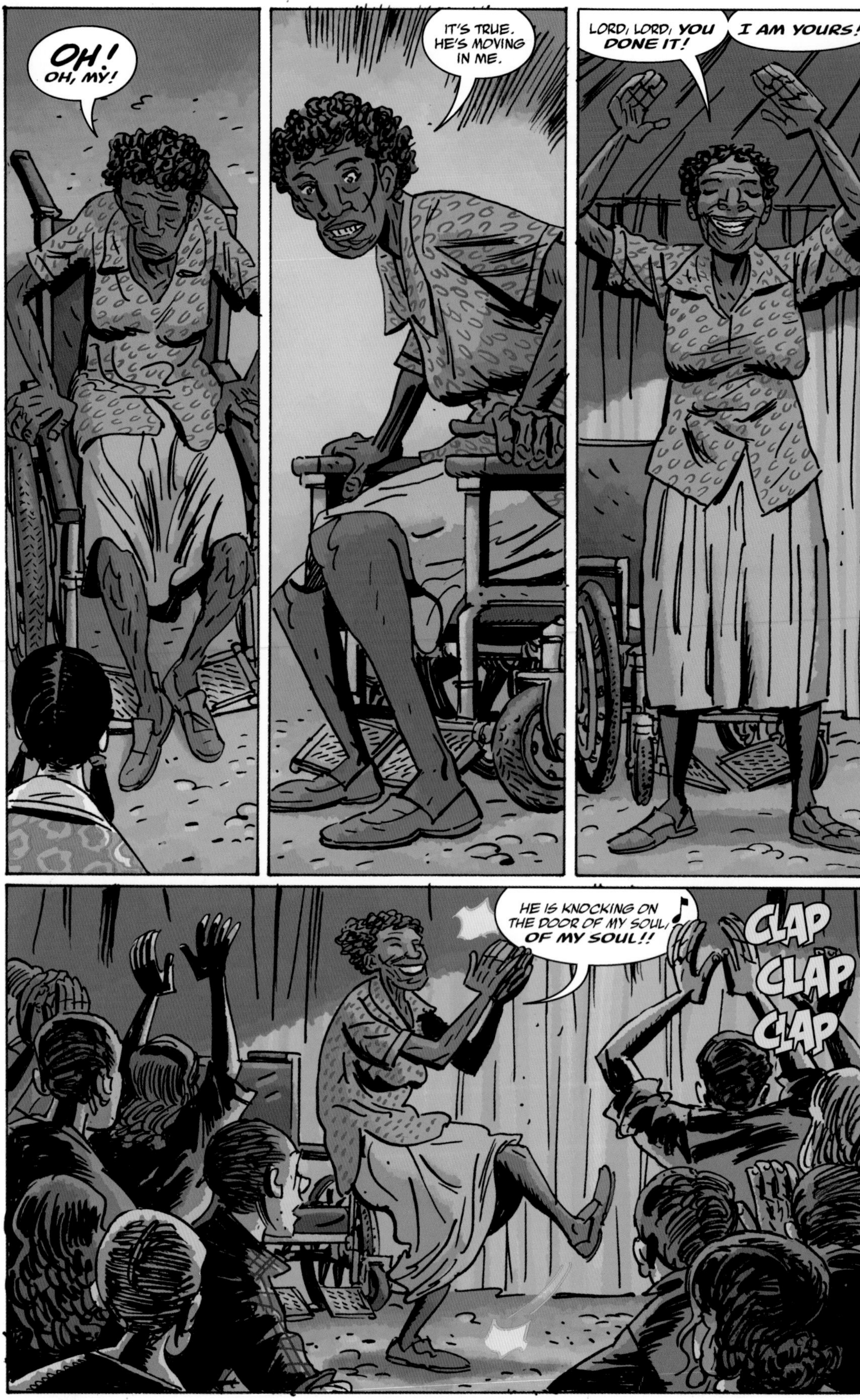
OH! OH, MY!
IT'S TRUE. HE'S MOVING IN ME.
LORD, LORD, YOU DONE IT!
I AM YOURS!
HE IS KNOCKING ON THE DOOR OF MY SOUL, OF MY SOUL!!
CLAP
CLAP
CLAP

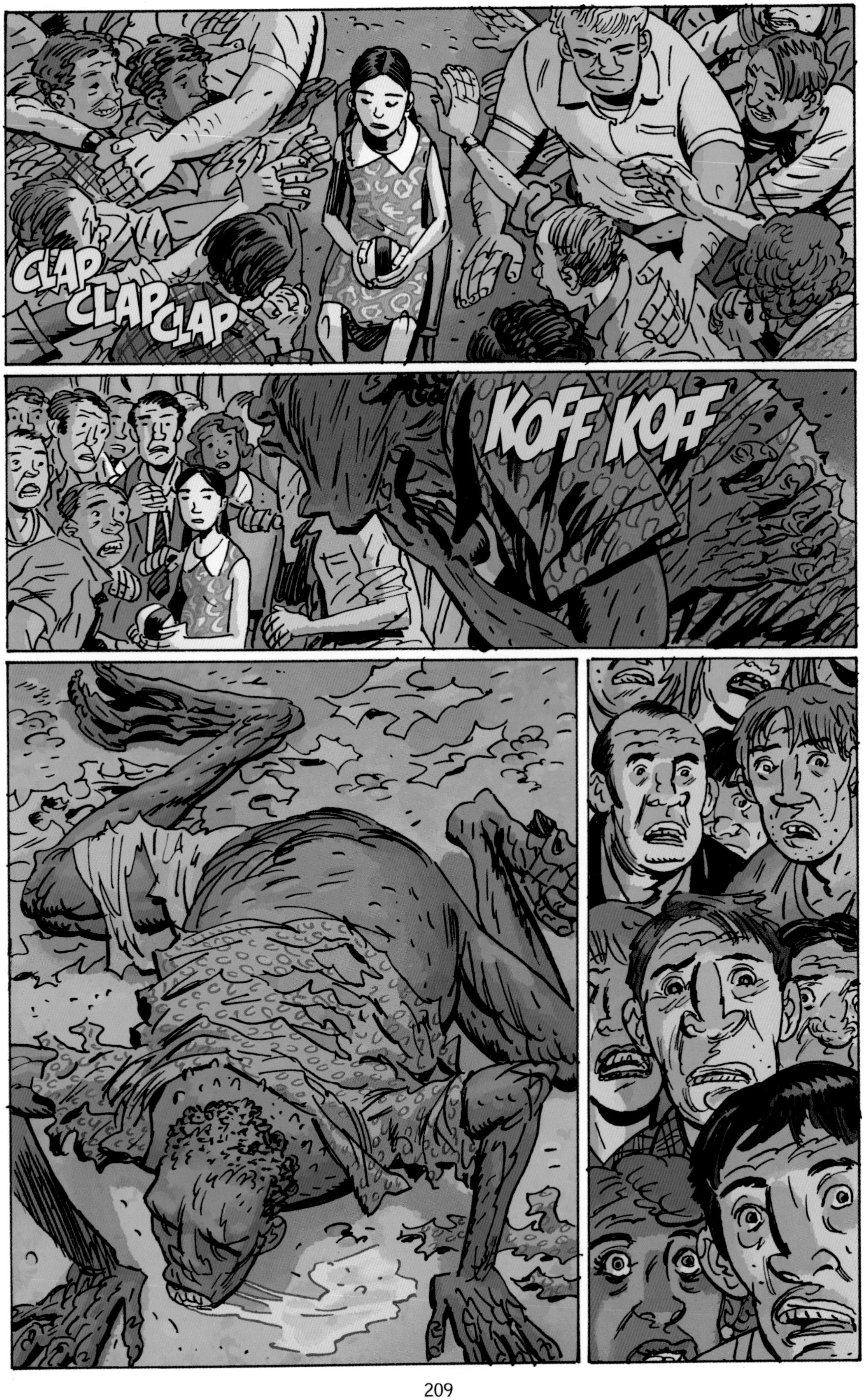
CLAP CLAP CLAP
KOFF KOFF

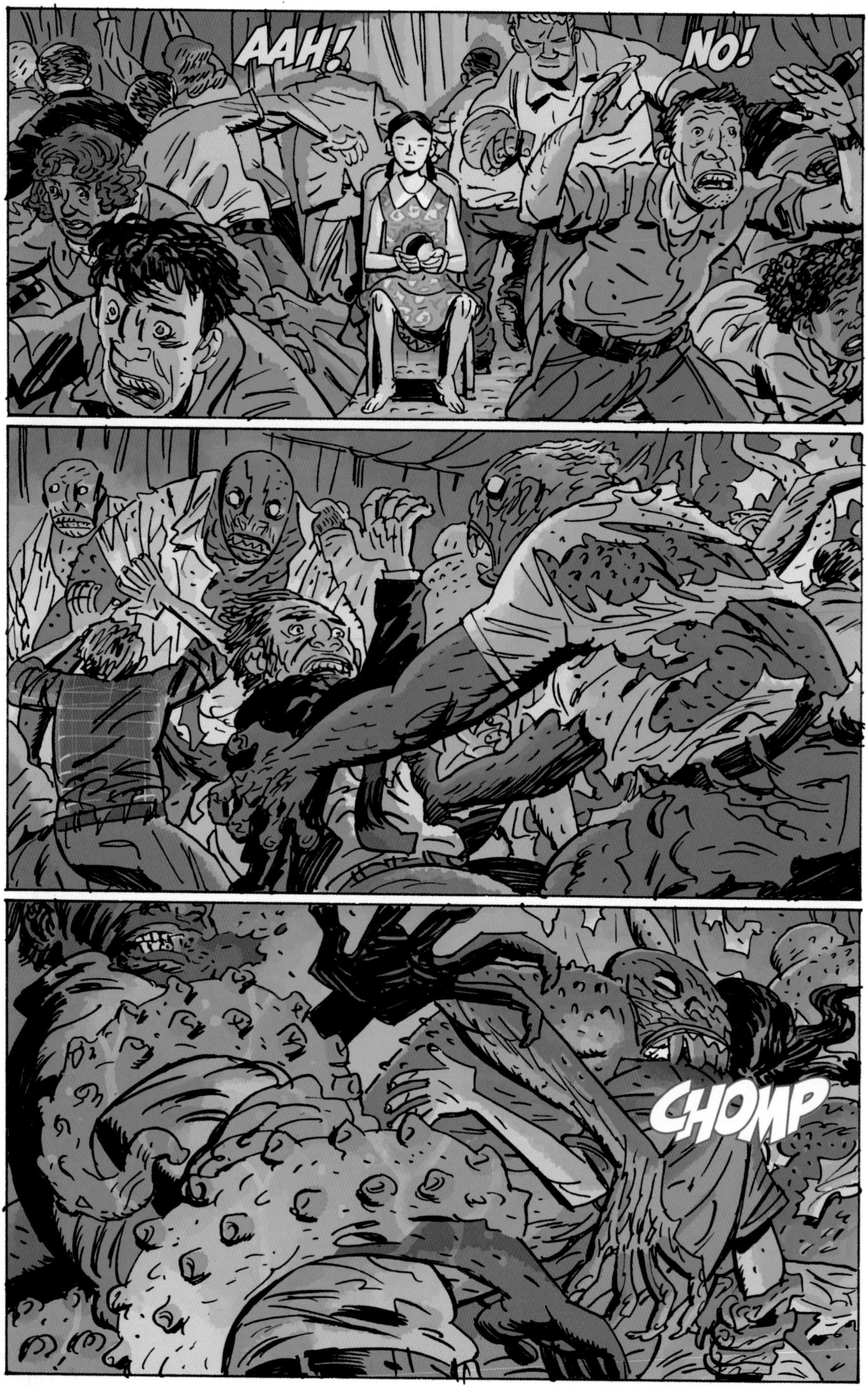
AAH!
NO!
CHOMP

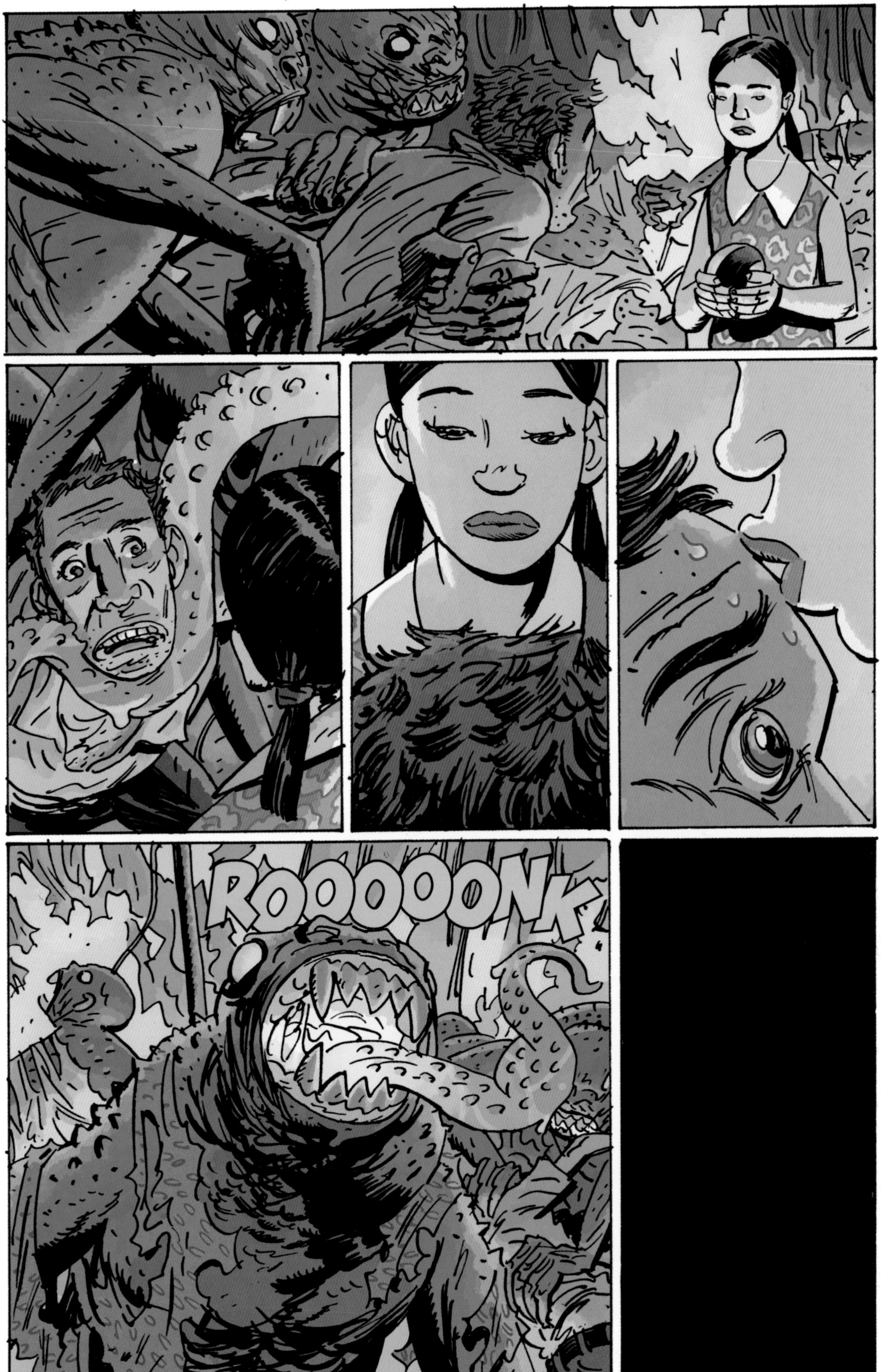
ROOOOONK

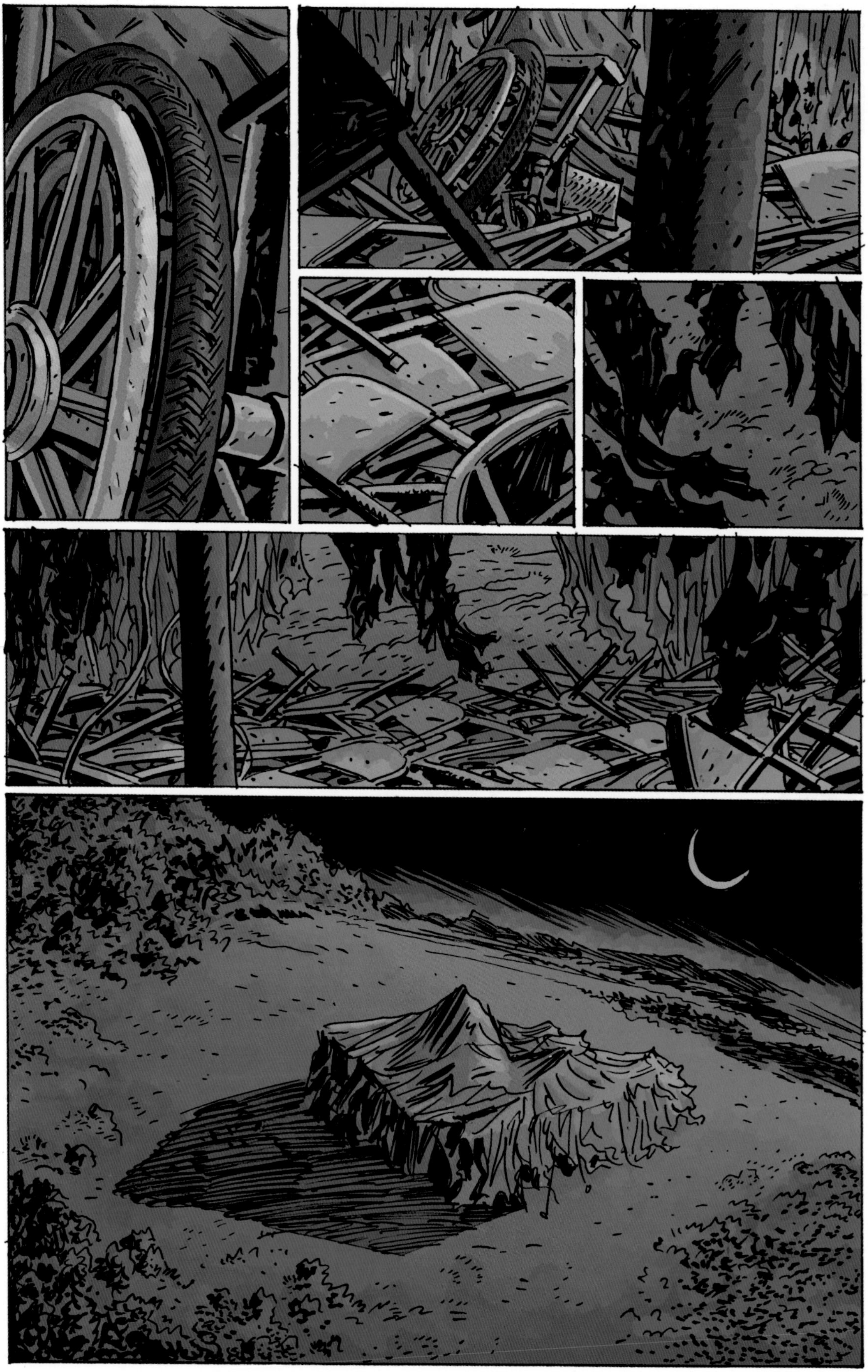

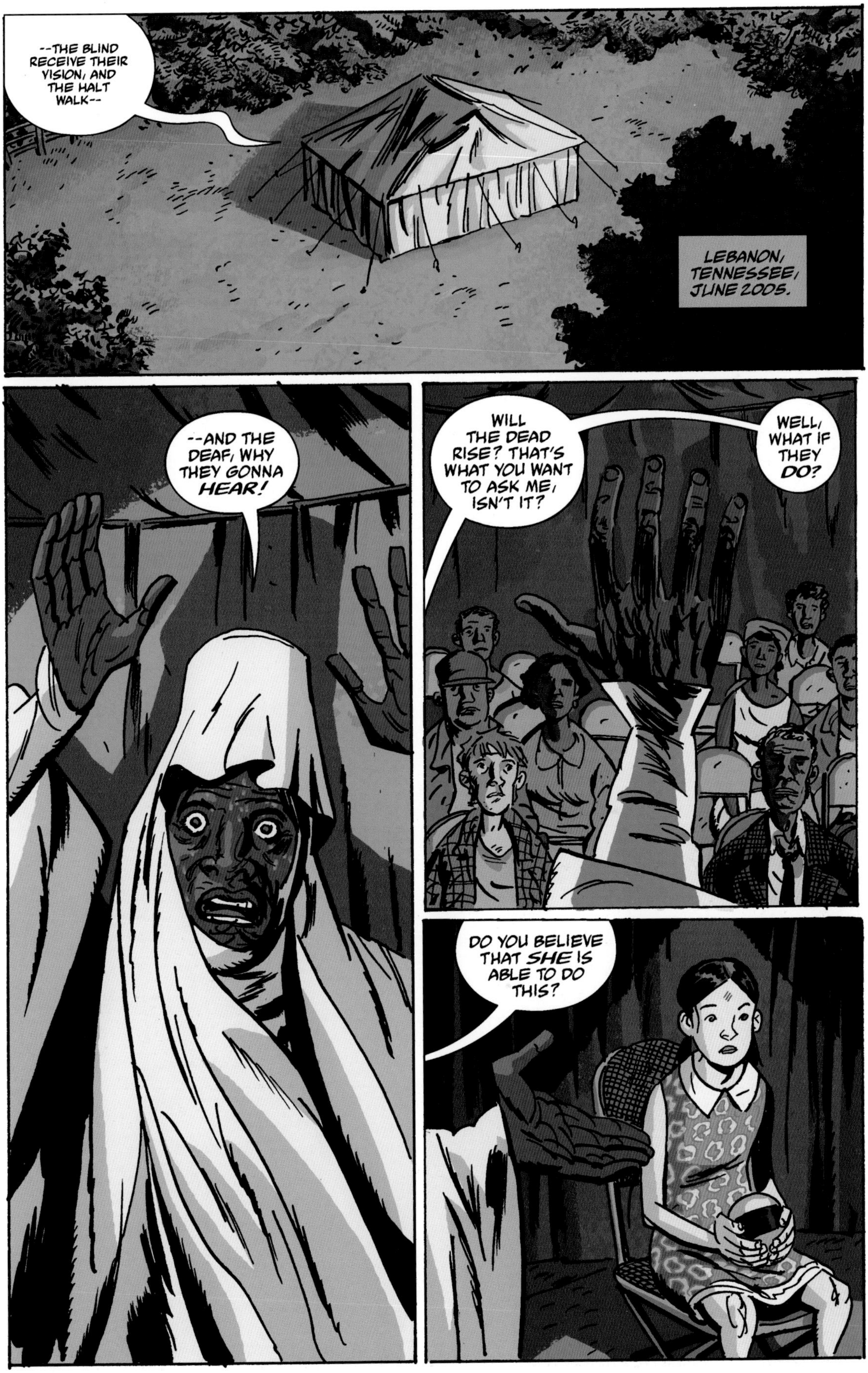
--THE BLIND RECEIVE THEIR VISION, AND THE HALT WALK--
LEBANON, TENNESSEE, JUNE 2005.
--AND THE DEAF, WHY THEY GONNA HEAR!
WILL THE DEAD RISE? THAT'S WHAT YOU WANT TO ASK ME, ISN'T IT?
WELL, WHAT IF THEY DO?
DO YOU BELIEVE THAT SHE IS ABLE TO DO THIS?

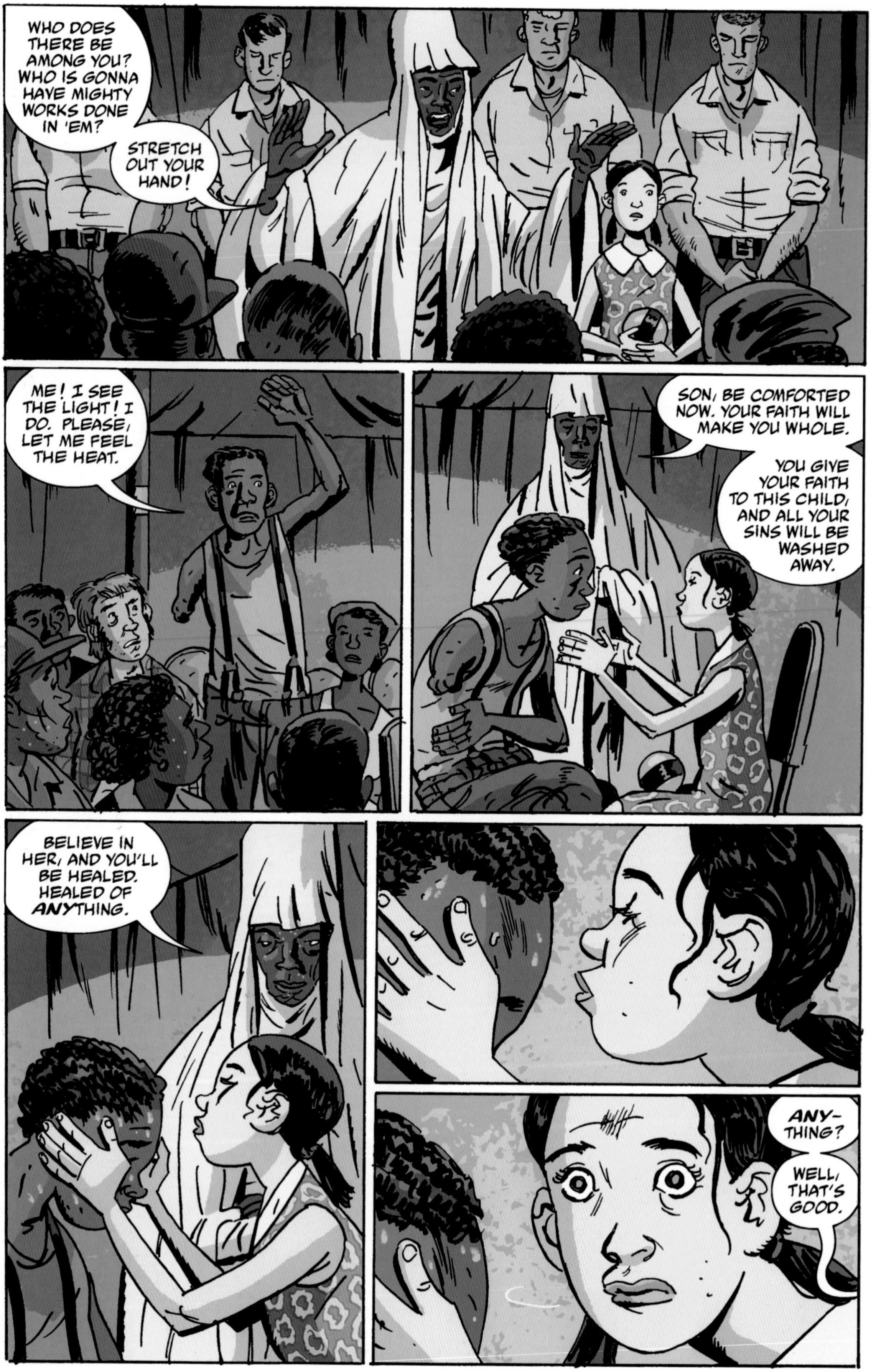
WHO DOES THERE BE AMONG YOU? WHO IS GONNA HAVE MIGHTY WORKS DONE IN 'EM?
STRETCH OUT YOUR HAND!
ME! I SEE THE LIGHT! I DO. PLEASE, LET ME FEEL THE HEAT.
SON, BE COMFORTED NOW. YOUR FAITH WILL MAKE YOU WHOLE.
YOU GIVE YOUR FAITH TO THIS CHILD, AND ALL YOUR SINS WILL BE WASHED AWAY.
BELIEVE IN HER, AND YOU'LL BE HEALED. HEALED OF ANYTHING.
ANY-THING?
WELL, THAT'S GOOD.

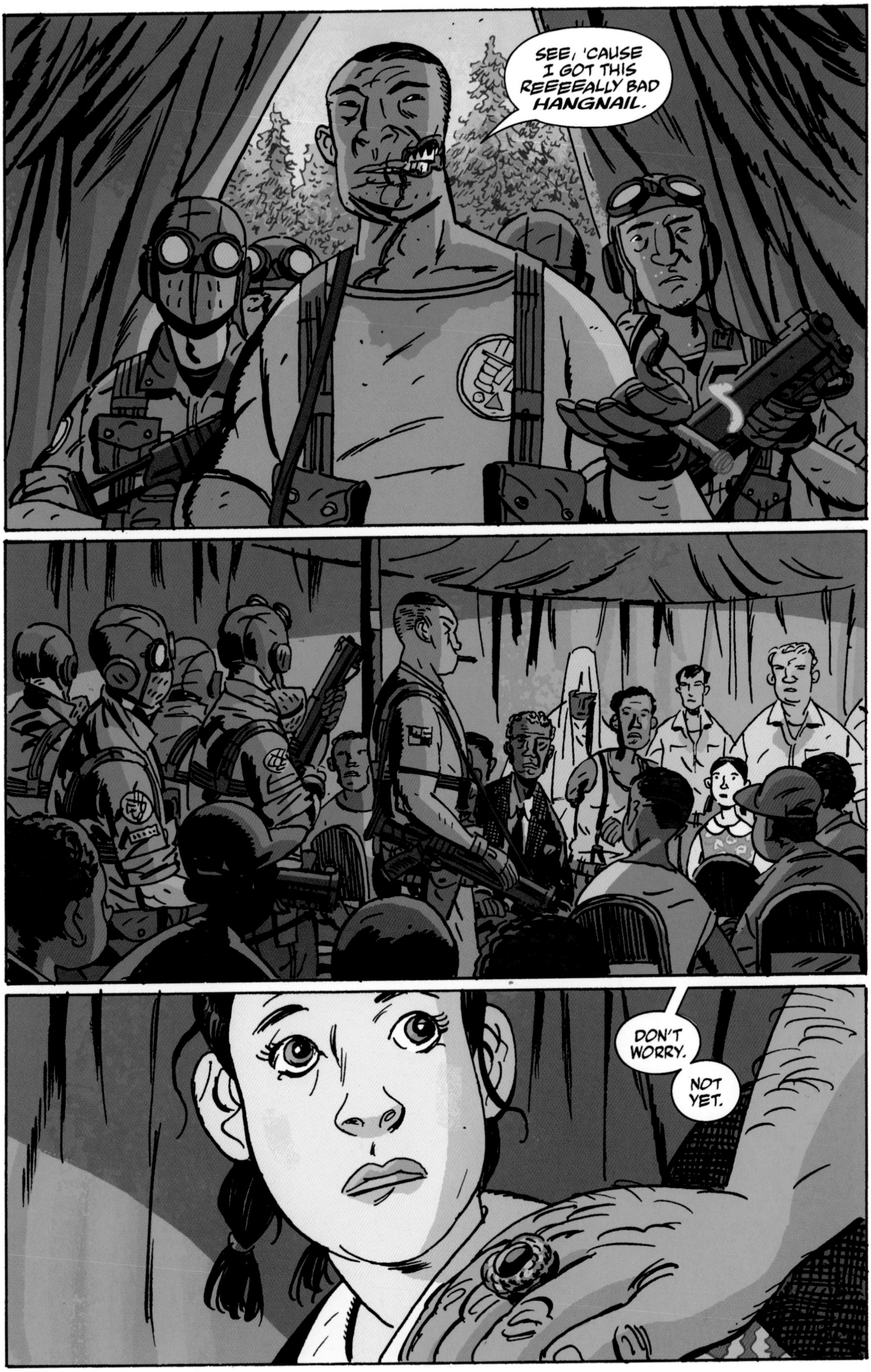
SEE, 'CAUSE I GOT THIS REEEEALLY BAD HANGNAIL.
DON'T WORRY.
NOT YET.

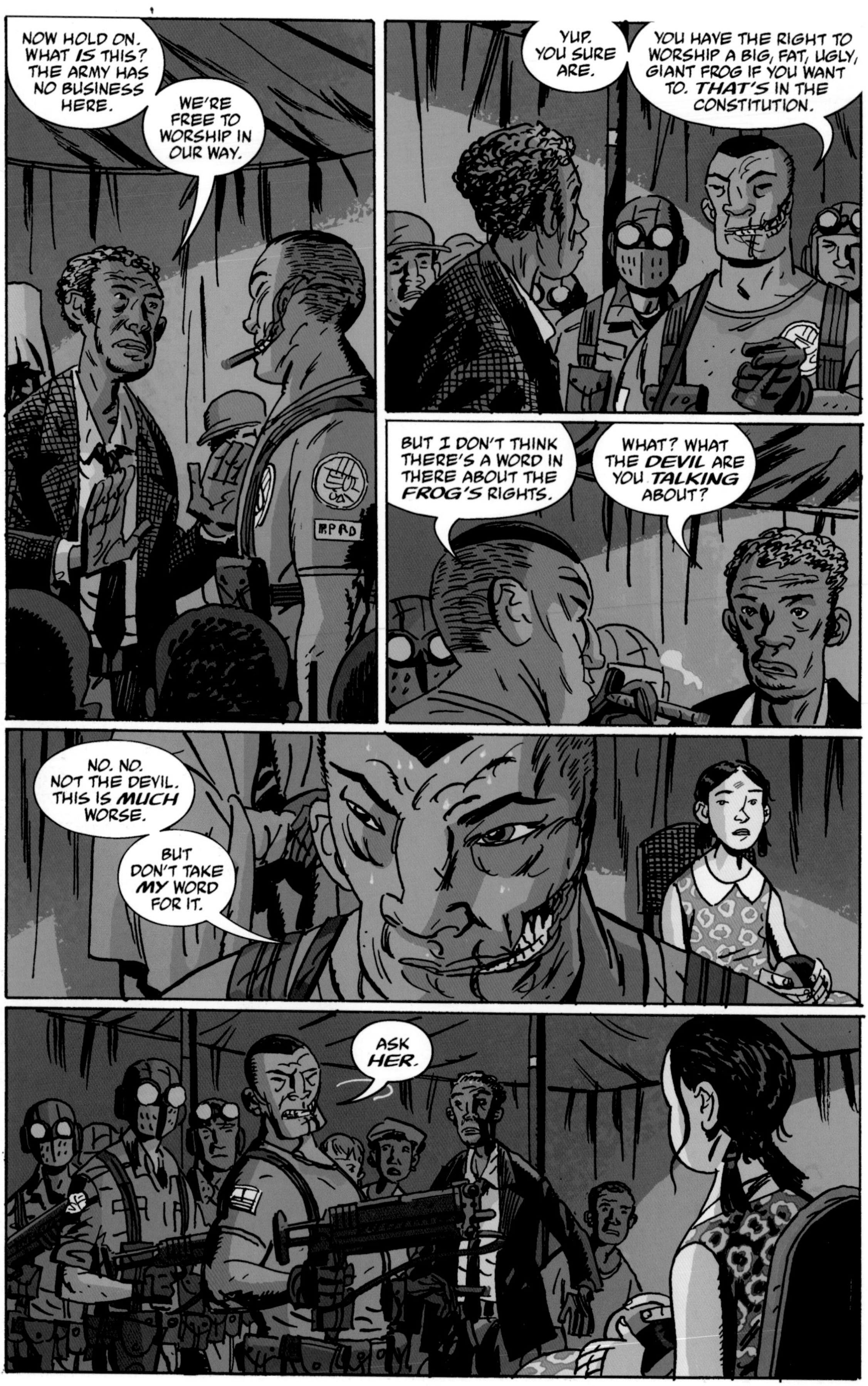
NOW HOLD ON. WHAT *IS* THIS? THE ARMY HAS NO BUSINESS HERE.
WE'RE FREE TO WORSHIP IN OUR WAY.
YUP. YOU SURE ARE.
YOU HAVE THE RIGHT TO WORSHIP A BIG, FAT, UGLY, GIANT FROG IF YOU WANT TO. *THAT'S* IN THE CONSTITUTION.
B.P.R.D.
BUT I DON'T THINK THERE'S A WORD IN THERE ABOUT THE *FROG'S* RIGHTS.
WHAT? WHAT THE *DEVIL* ARE YOU *TALKING* ABOUT?
NO. NO. NOT THE DEVIL. THIS IS *MUCH* WORSE.
BUT DON'T TAKE *MY* WORD FOR IT.
ASK *HER*.

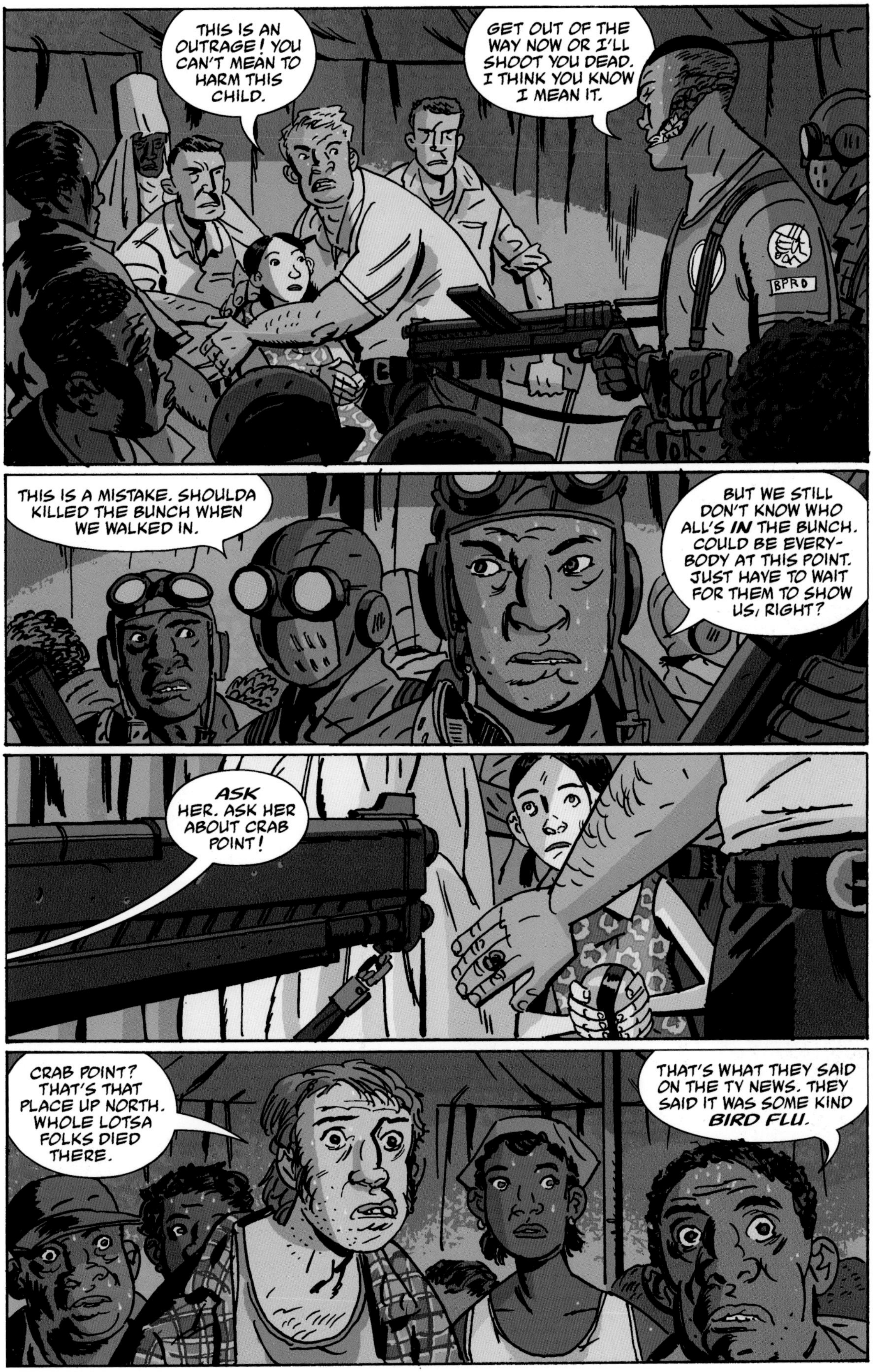
THIS IS AN OUTRAGE! YOU CAN'T MEAN TO HARM THIS CHILD.
GET OUT OF THE WAY NOW OR I'LL SHOOT YOU DEAD. I THINK YOU KNOW I MEAN IT.
BPRD
THIS IS A MISTAKE. SHOULDA KILLED THE BUNCH WHEN WE WALKED IN.
BUT WE STILL DON'T KNOW WHO ALL'S IN THE BUNCH. COULD BE EVERY-BODY AT THIS POINT. JUST HAVE TO WAIT FOR THEM TO SHOW US, RIGHT?
ASK HER. ASK HER ABOUT CRAB POINT!
CRAB POINT? THAT'S THAT PLACE UP NORTH. WHOLE LOTSA FOLKS DIED THERE.
THAT'S WHAT THEY SAID ON THE TV NEWS. THEY SAID IT WAS SOME KIND BIRD FLU.

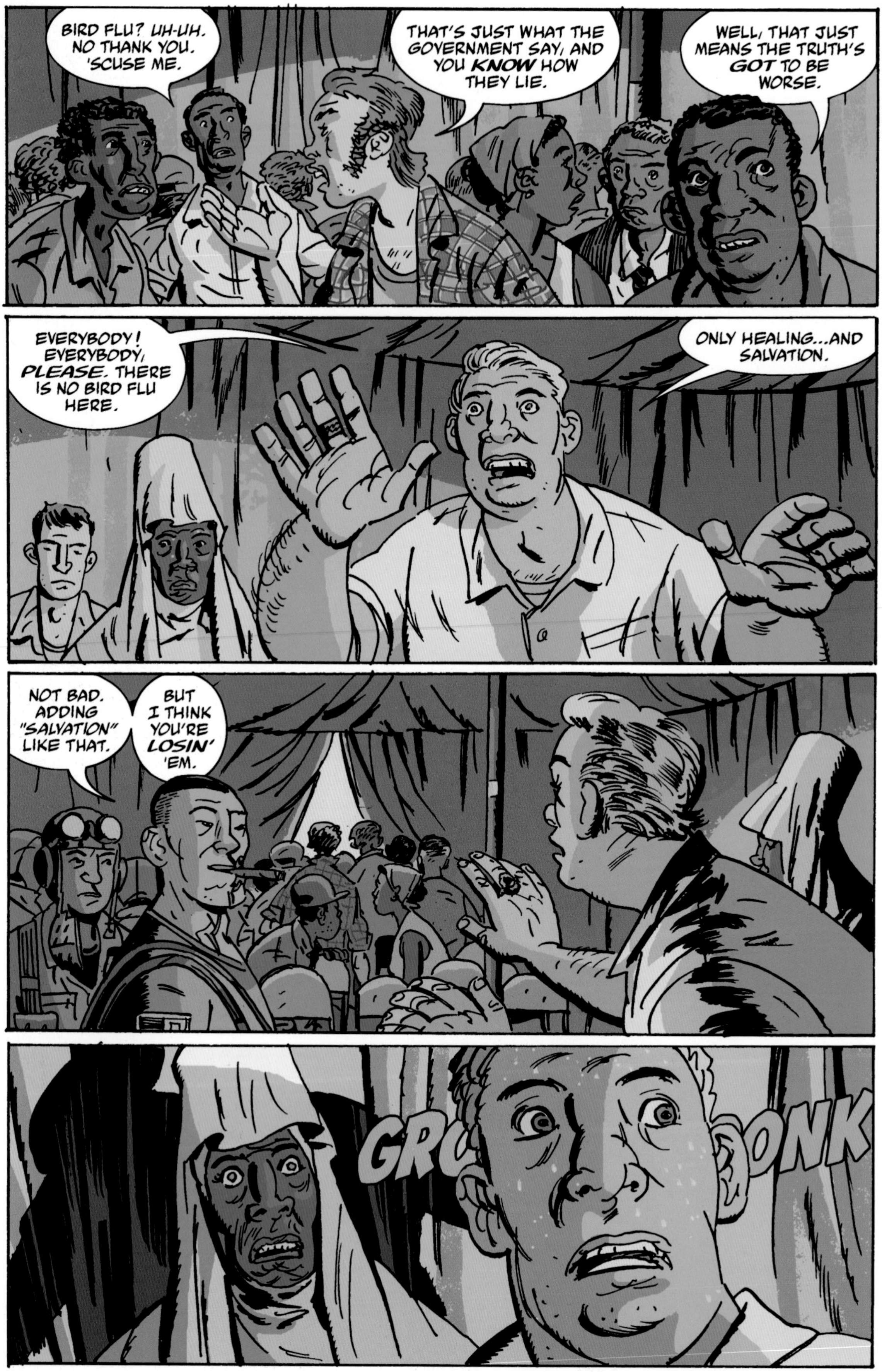
BIRD FLU? UH-UH. NO THANK YOU. 'SCUSE ME.
THAT'S JUST WHAT THE GOVERNMENT SAY, AND YOU KNOW HOW THEY LIE.
WELL, THAT JUST MEANS THE TRUTH'S GOT TO BE WORSE.
EVERYBODY! EVERYBODY, PLEASE. THERE IS NO BIRD FLU HERE.
ONLY HEALING...AND SALVATION.
NOT BAD. ADDING "SALVATION" LIKE THAT.
BUT I THINK YOU'RE LOSIN' 'EM.
GRO
ONK

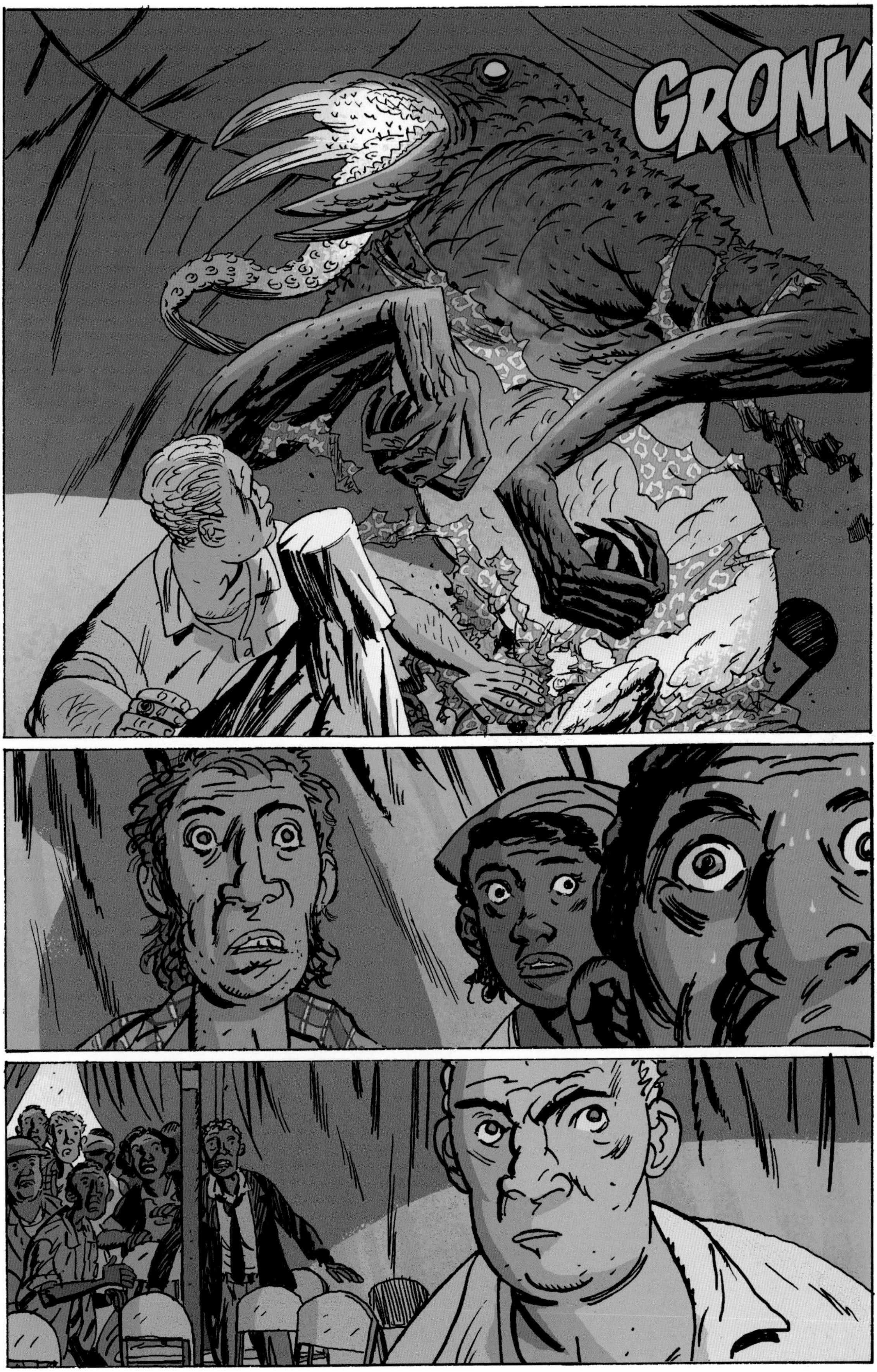
GRONK

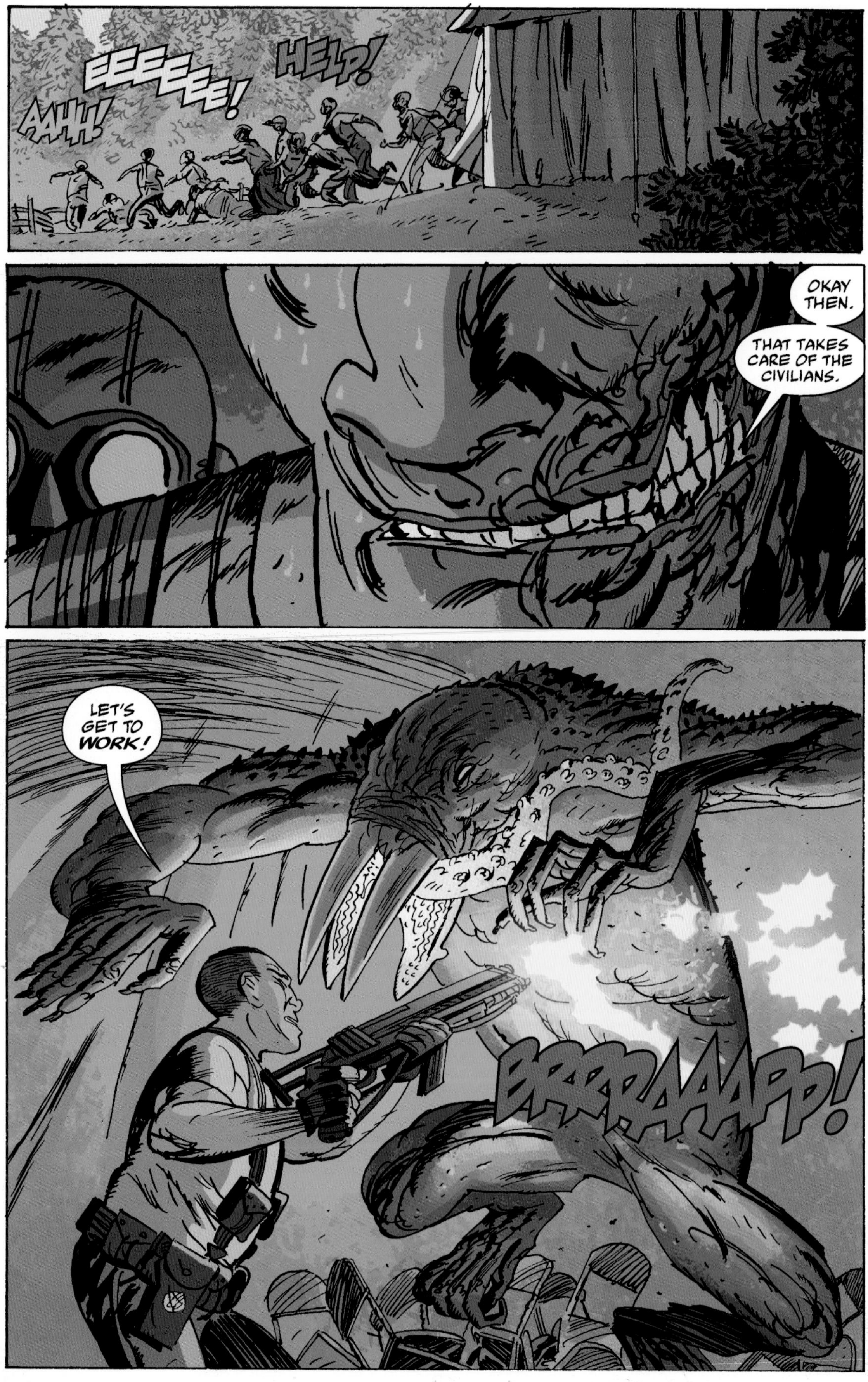
EEEEEEEE!
HELP!
AAHH!
OKAY THEN.
THAT TAKES CARE OF THE CIVILIANS.
LET'S GET TO WORK!
BRRRAAAAPP!

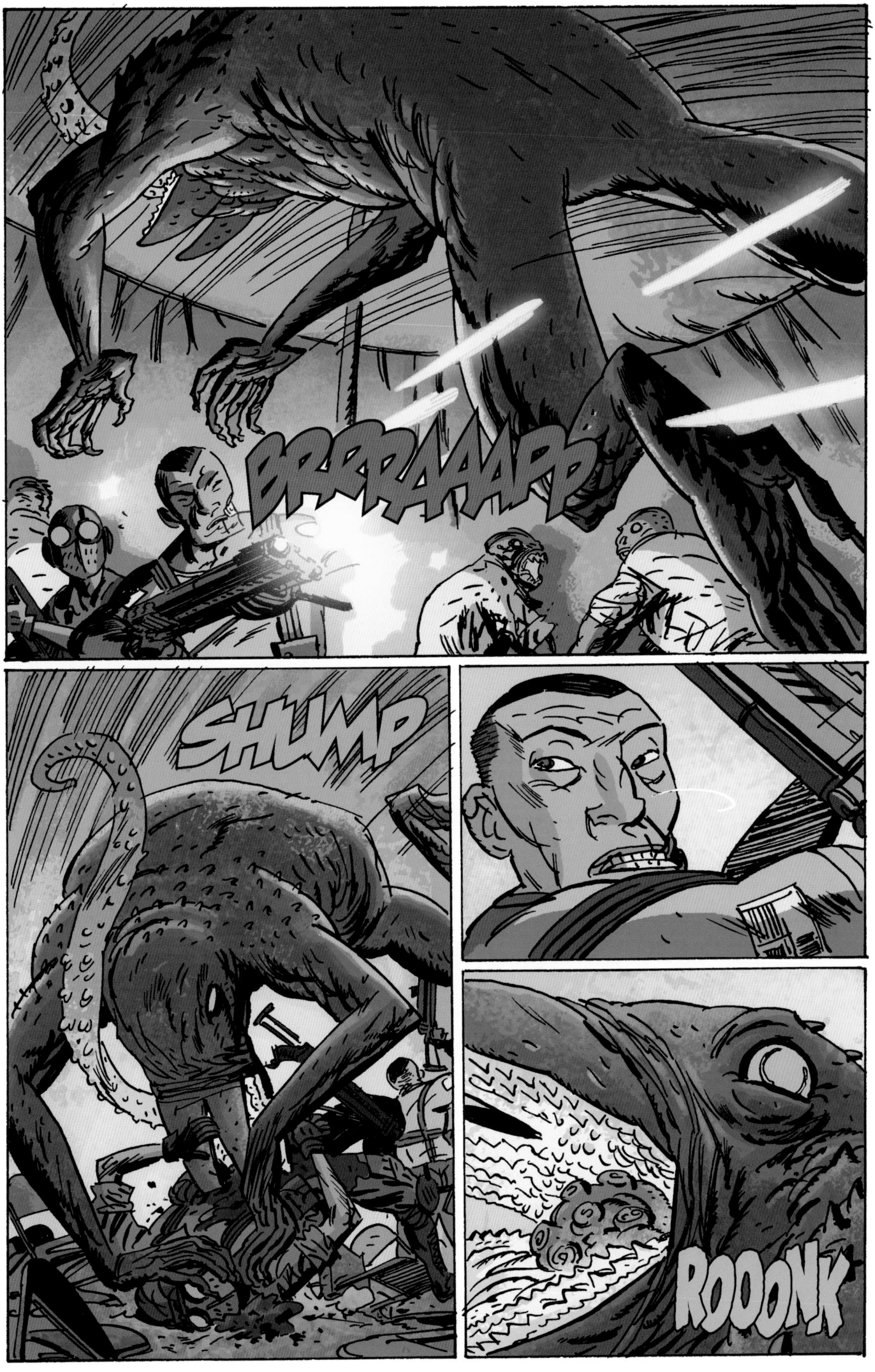
BRRRAAAPP
SHUMP
ROOONK

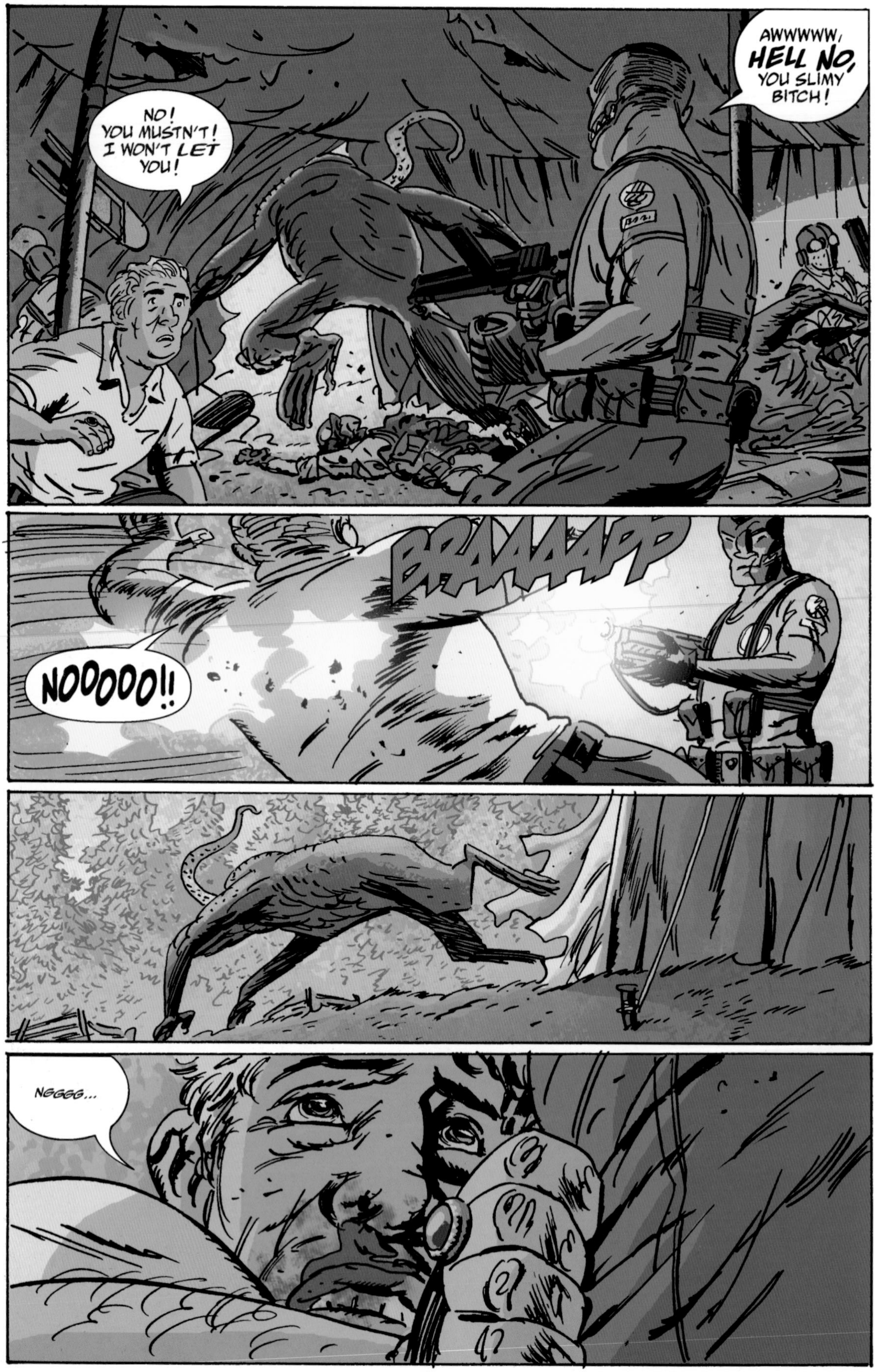
NO! YOU MUSTN'T! I WON'T LET YOU!
AWWWWW, HELL NO, YOU SLIMY BITCH!
BRAAAAPP
NOOOOO!!
NGGGG...

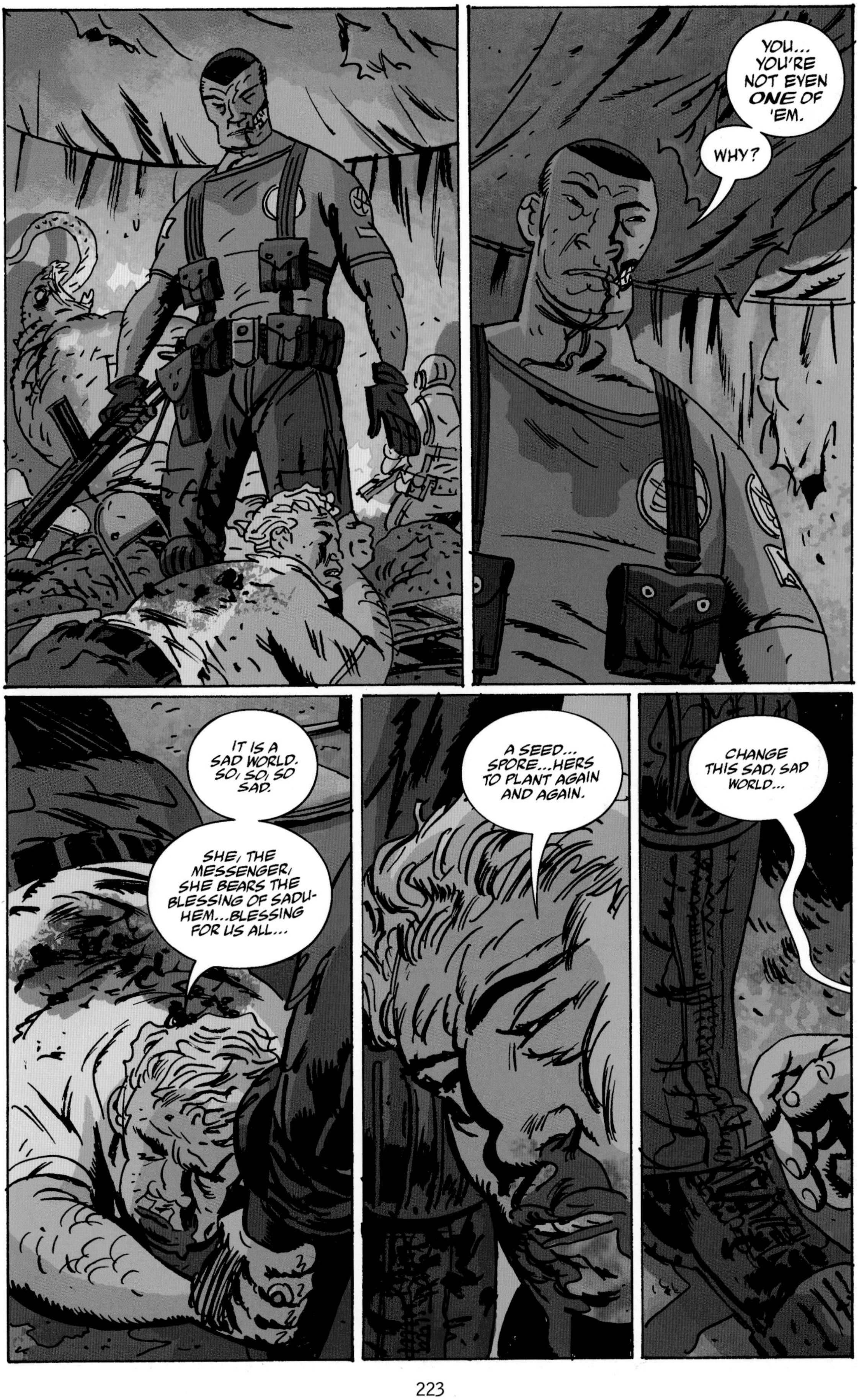
YOU... YOU'RE NOT EVEN ONE OF 'EM.
WHY?
IT IS A SAD WORLD. SO, SO, SO SAD.
SHE, THE MESSENGER, SHE BEARS THE BLESSING OF SADU-HEM...BLESSING FOR US ALL...
A SEED... SPORE...HERS TO PLANT AGAIN AND AGAIN.
CHANGE THIS SAD, SAD WORLD...

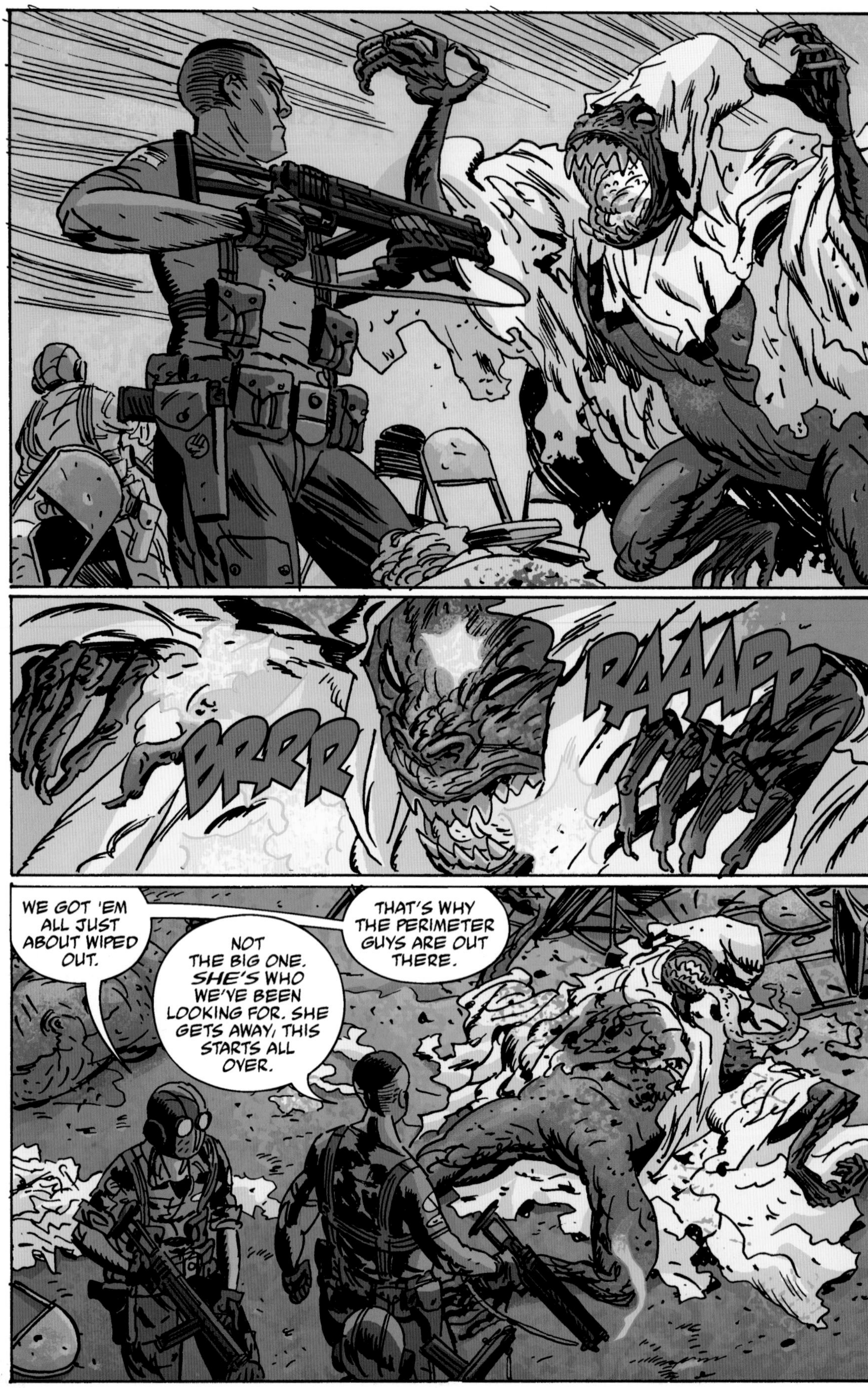
BRRR
RAAAPP
WE GOT 'EM ALL JUST ABOUT WIPED OUT.
THAT'S WHY THE PERIMETER GUYS ARE OUT THERE.
NOT THE BIG ONE. SHE'S WHO WE'VE BEEN LOOKING FOR. SHE GETS AWAY, THIS STARTS ALL OVER.

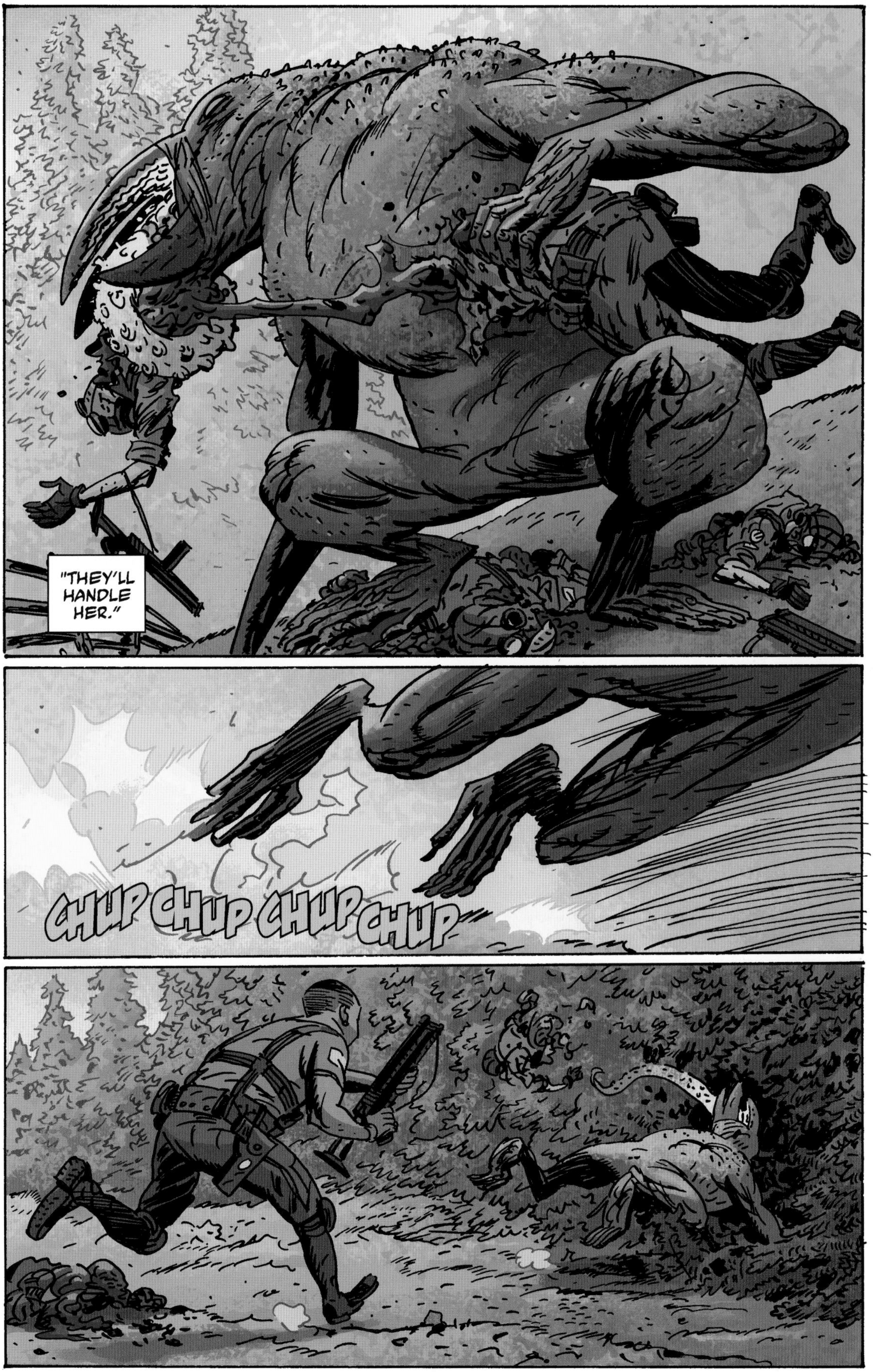
"THEY'LL HANDLE HER."
CHUP CHUP CHUP CHUP

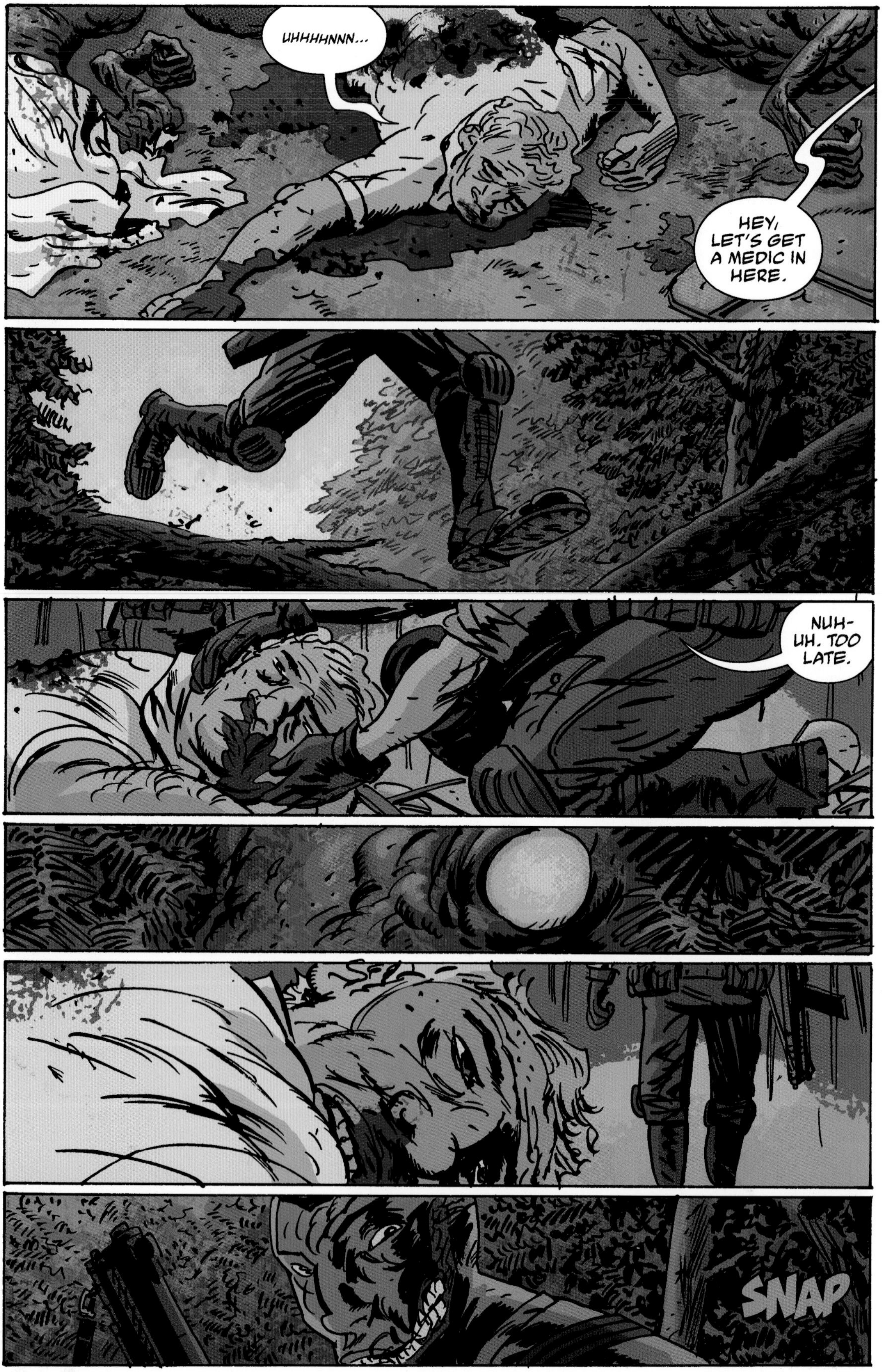
UHHHHNNN...
HEY, LET'S GET A MEDIC IN HERE.
NUH-UH. TOO LATE.
SNAP

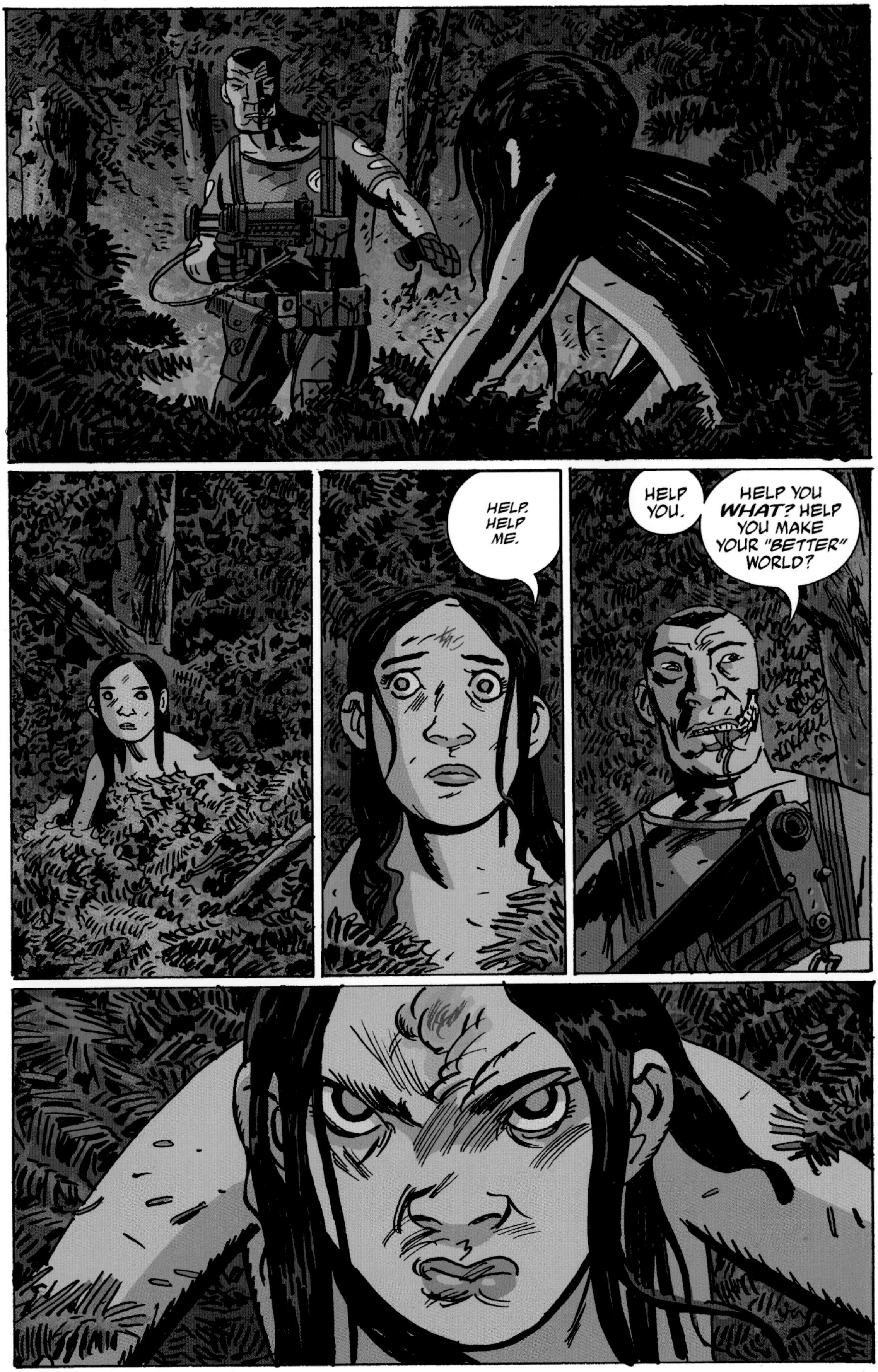
HELP. HELP ME.
HELP YOU.
HELP YOU WHAT? HELP YOU MAKE YOUR "BETTER" WORLD?

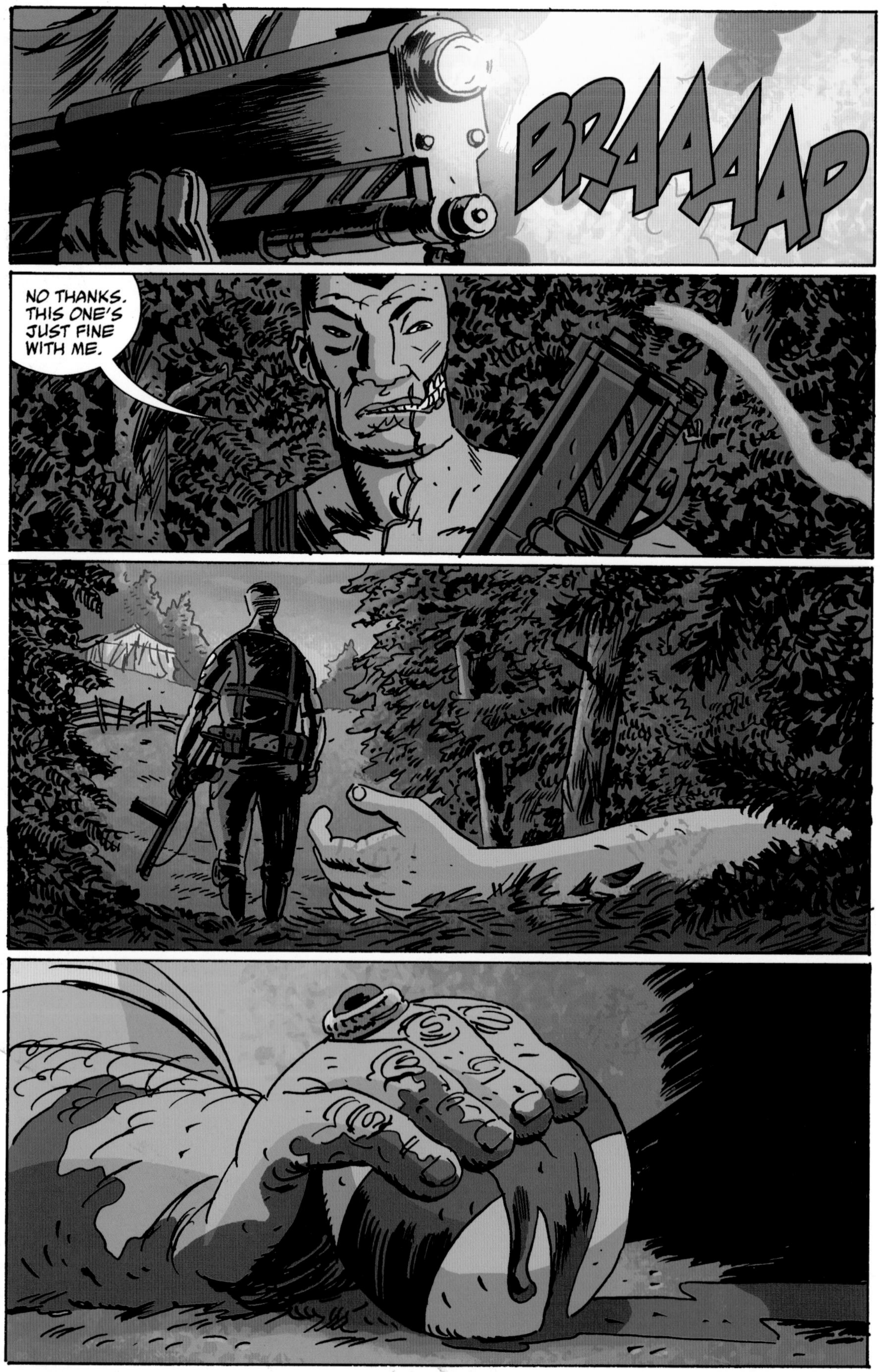
BRAAAAP
NO THANKS. THIS ONE'S JUST FINE WITH ME.

CHAPTER FOUR

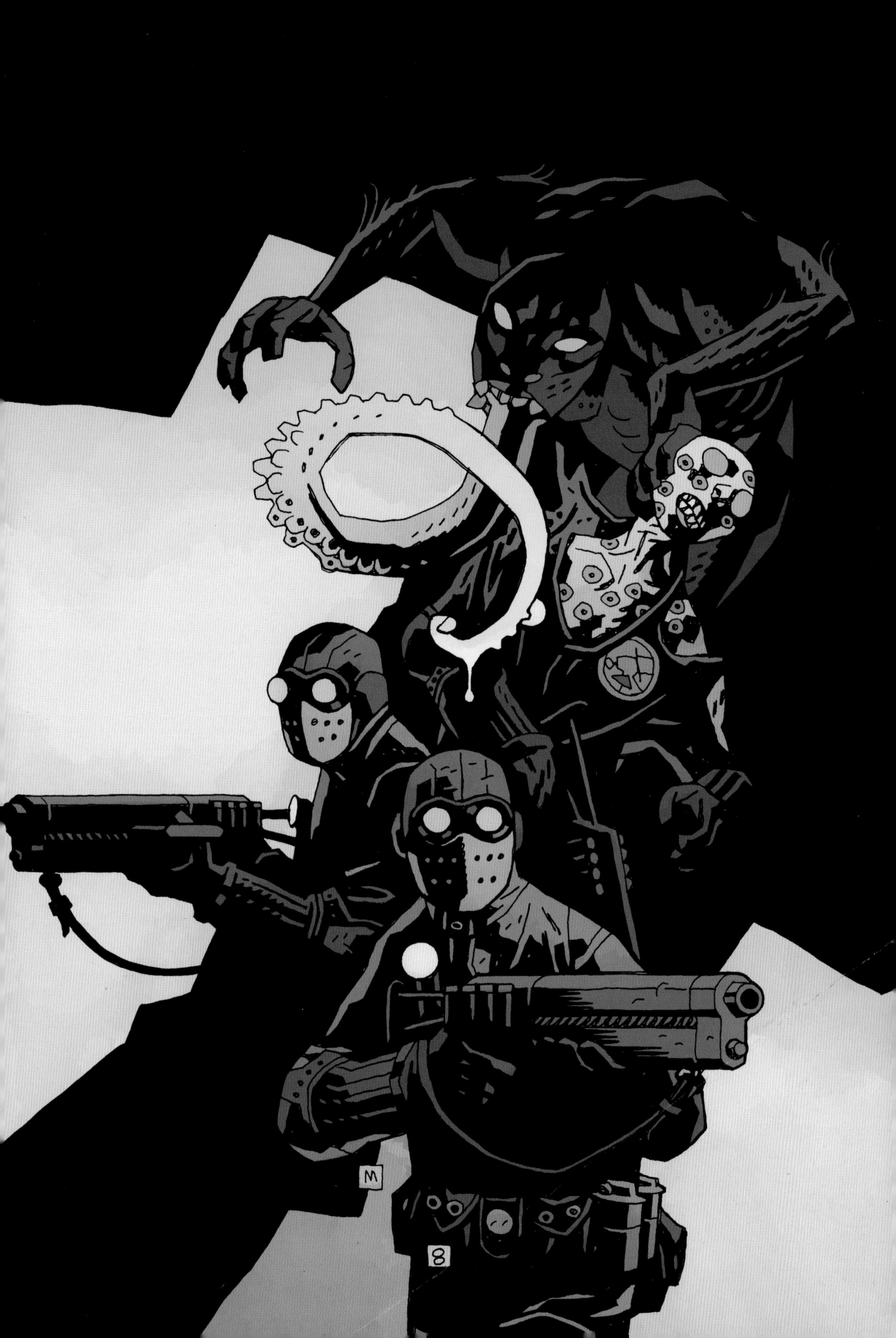

STORY BY JOHN ARCUDI

ART BY JOHN SEVERIN

COLORS BY DAVE STEWART

LETTERS BY CLEM ROBINS

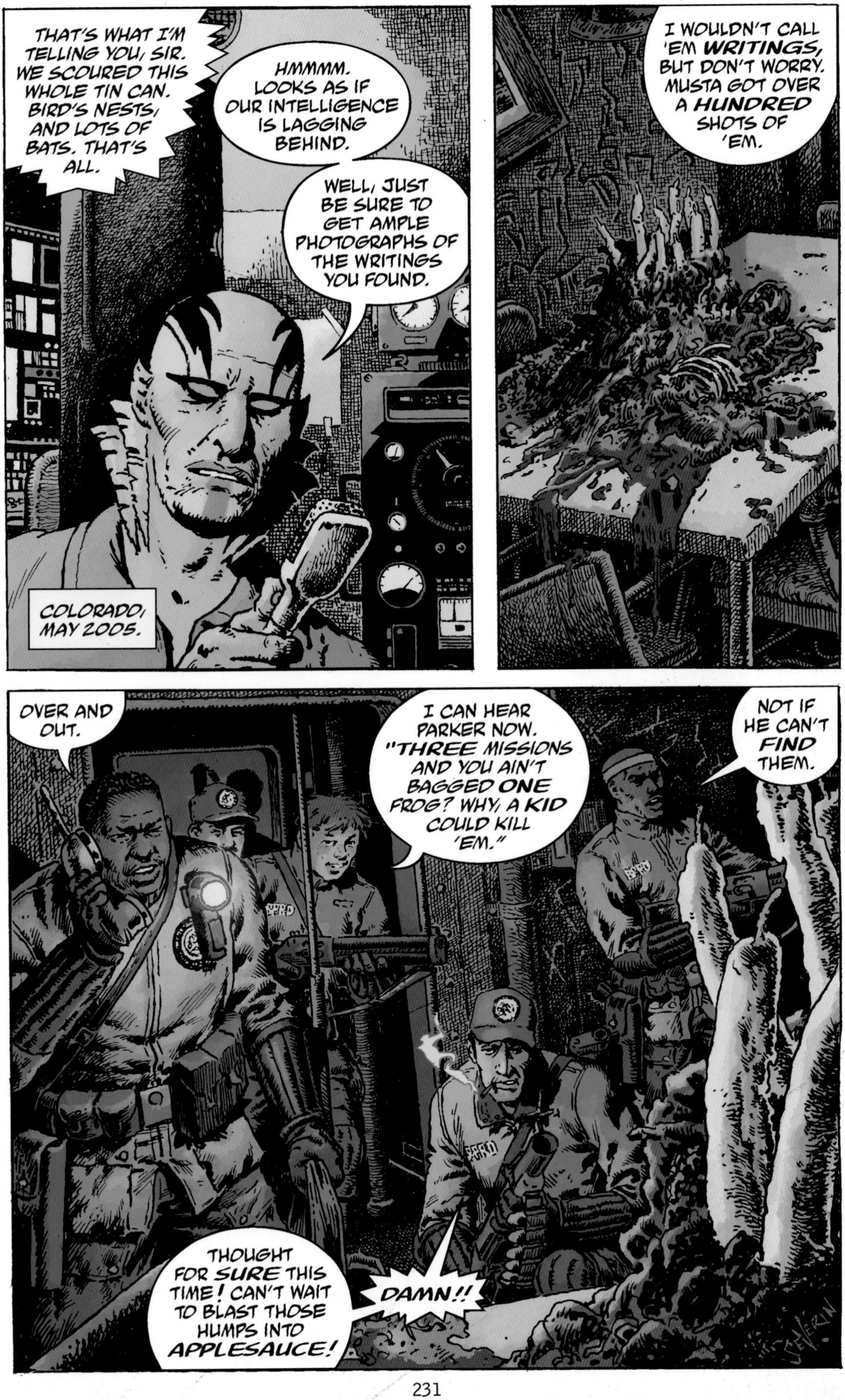
THAT'S WHAT I'M TELLING YOU, SIR. WE SCOURED THIS WHOLE TIN CAN. BIRD'S NESTS, AND LOTS OF BATS. THAT'S ALL.
HMMMM. LOOKS AS IF OUR INTELLIGENCE IS LAGGING BEHIND.
WELL, JUST BE SURE TO GET AMPLE PHOTOGRAPHS OF THE WRITINGS YOU FOUND.
COLORADO, MAY 2005.
I WOULDN'T CALL 'EM WRITINGS, BUT DON'T WORRY. MUSTA GOT OVER A HUNDRED SHOTS OF 'EM.
OVER AND OUT.
I CAN HEAR PARKER NOW. "THREE MISSIONS AND YOU AIN'T BAGGED ONE FROG? WHY, A KID COULD KILL 'EM."
NOT IF HE CAN'T FIND THEM.
THOUGHT FOR SURE THIS TIME! CAN'T WAIT TO BLAST THOSE HUMPS INTO APPLESAUCE!
DAMN!!

COME ON, LADIES.

SAY, WHY ISN'T THAT FISH-GUY OUT HERE IN THE FIELD WITH US? I KNOW HE USED TO BE.

GOT HIS REASONS, NO DOUBT. SOMETHIN' SPOOKED HIM, MAYBE.

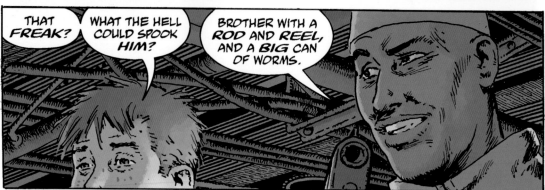

THAT FREAK?

WHAT THE HELL COULD SPOOK HIM?

BROTHER WITH A ROD AND REEL, AND A BIG CAN OF WORMS.

HA HA HA HA

YEAH, FUNNY, BUT I NEVER MET NOBODY WASN'T SCARED OF ONE THING OR ANOTHER.

WELL, EXCEPT I GUESS THE BIG RED GUY.

WAIT. YOU MET HELLBOY?

UH-HUH. REASON I JOINED THE BUREAU.

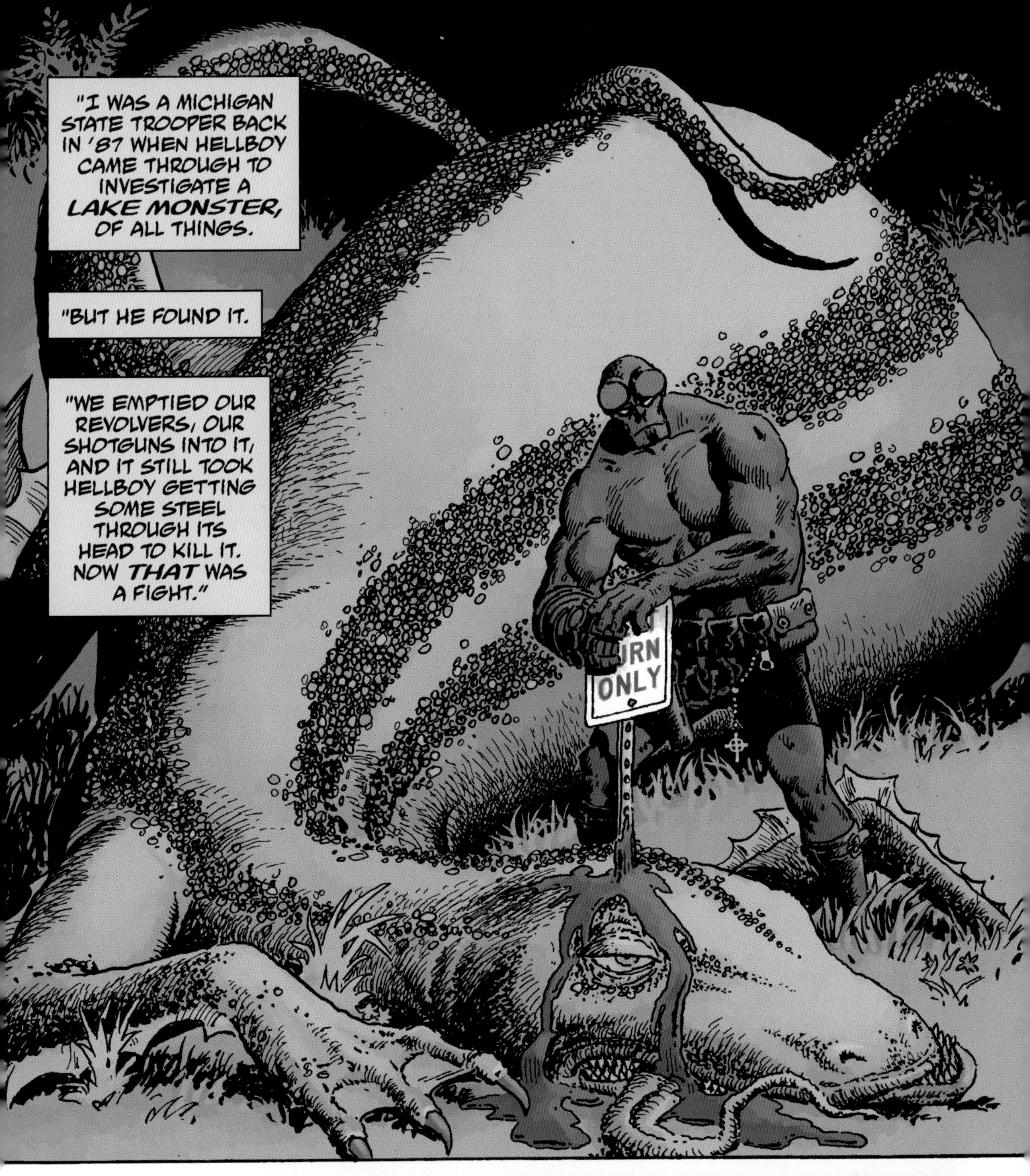
"I WAS A MICHIGAN STATE TROOPER BACK IN '87 WHEN HELLBOY CAME THROUGH TO INVESTIGATE A LAKE MONSTER, OF ALL THINGS.
"BUT HE FOUND IT.
"WE EMPTIED OUR REVOLVERS, OUR SHOTGUNS INTO IT, AND IT STILL TOOK HELLBOY GETTING SOME STEEL THROUGH ITS HEAD TO KILL IT. NOW THAT WAS A FIGHT."
ONLY

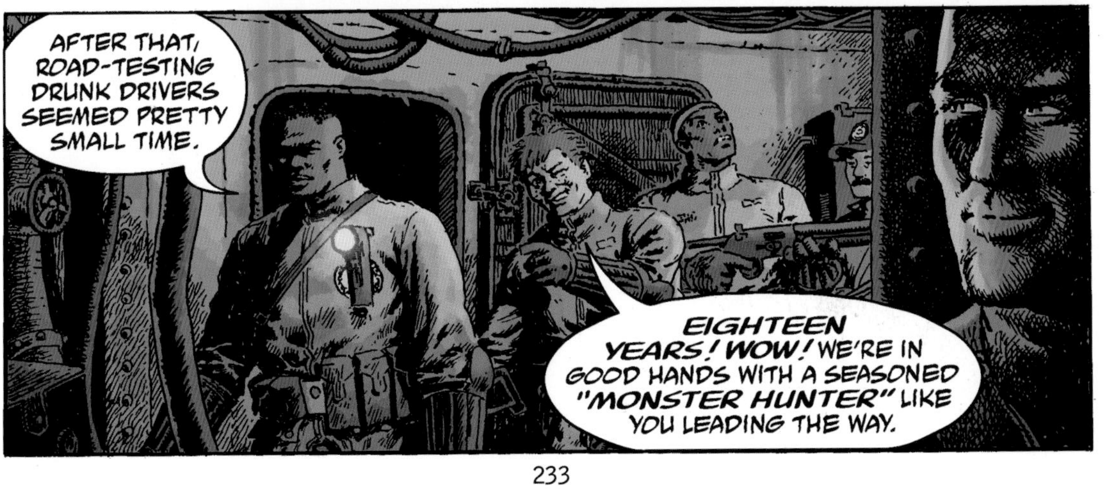
AFTER THAT, ROAD-TESTING DRUNK DRIVERS SEEMED PRETTY SMALL TIME.
EIGHTEEN YEARS! WOW! WE'RE IN GOOD HANDS WITH A SEASONED "MONSTER HUNTER" LIKE YOU LEADING THE WAY.

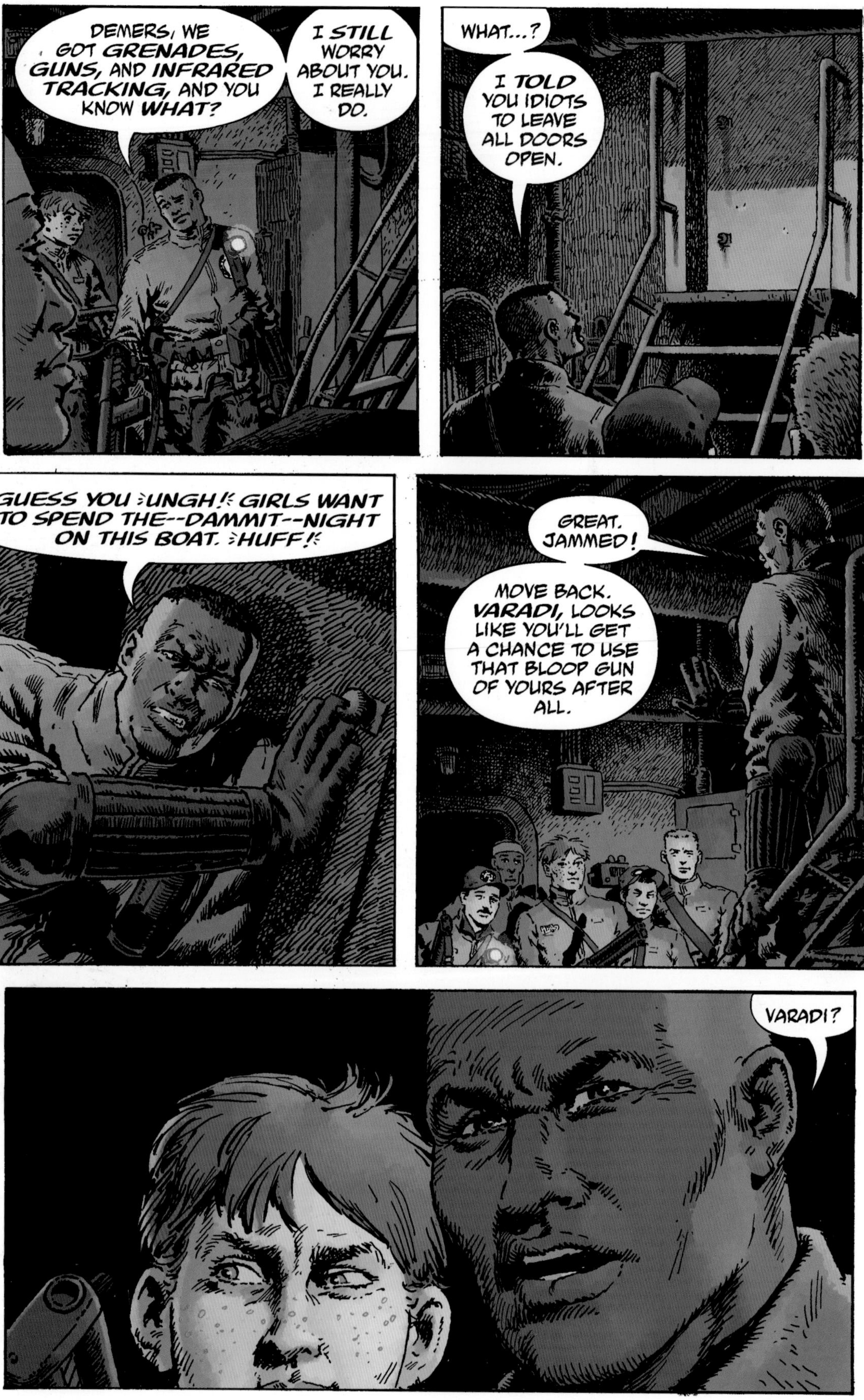
DEMERS, WE GOT GRENADES, GUNS, AND INFRARED TRACKING, AND YOU KNOW WHAT?
I STILL WORRY ABOUT YOU. I REALLY DO.
WHAT...?
I TOLD YOU IDIOTS TO LEAVE ALL DOORS OPEN.
GUESS YOU ›UNGH!‹ GIRLS WANT TO SPEND THE--DAMMIT--NIGHT ON THIS BOAT. ›HUFF!‹
GREAT. JAMMED!
MOVE BACK. VARADI, LOOKS LIKE YOU'LL GET A CHANCE TO USE THAT BLOOP GUN OF YOURS AFTER ALL.
VARADI?

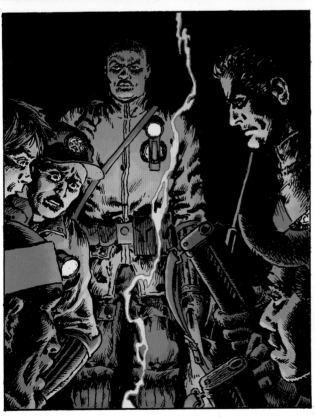

HOW EXACTLY DID ALL THIS HAPPEN, LIEUTENANT BRADLEY?

AHH, THAT BOY WAS ITCHY TO KILL *SOMETHIN'*. MAYBE HE SAW A PIGEON AND WENT AFTER IT.

AS FOR GETTIN' *LOCKED IN*...

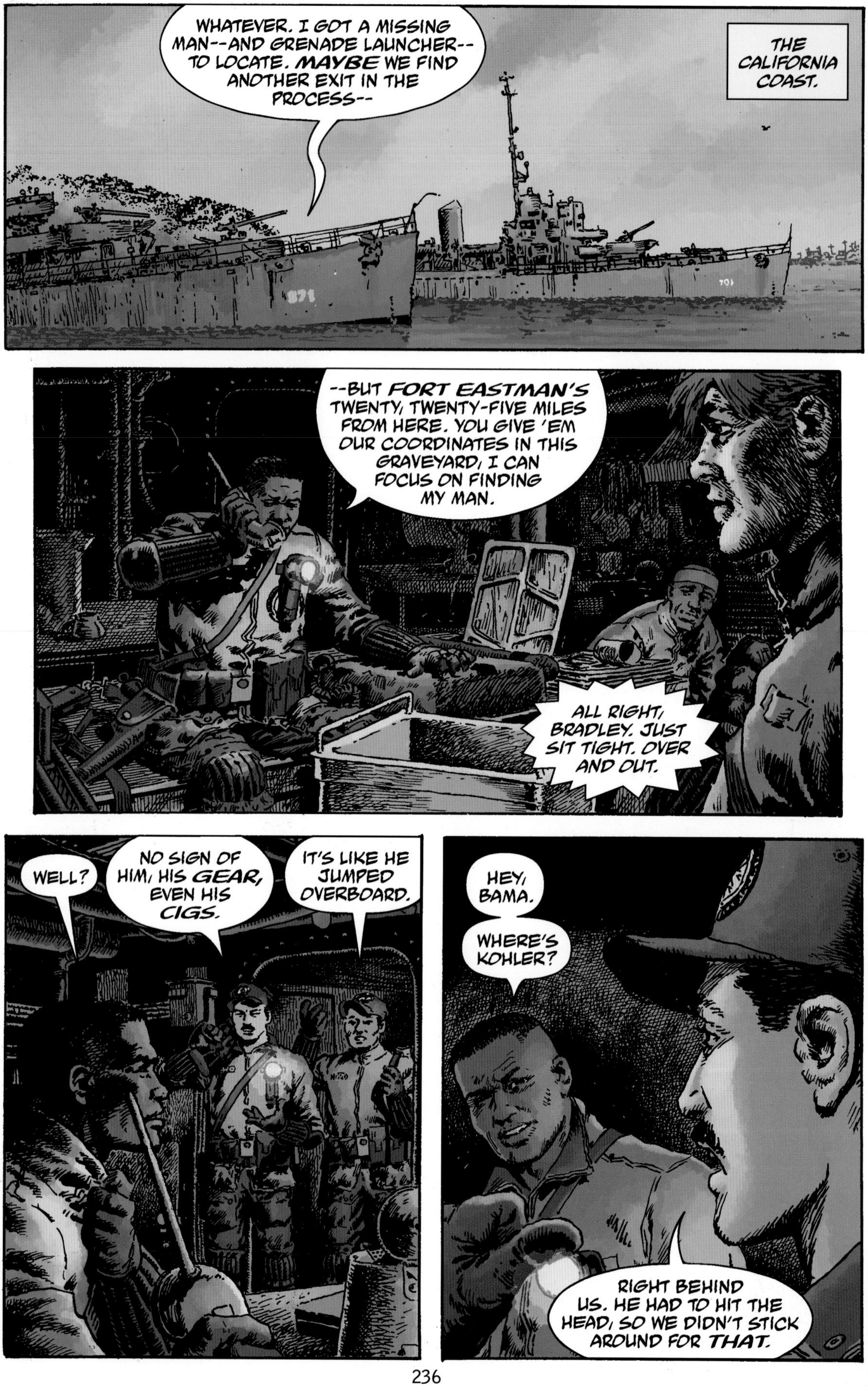
WHATEVER. I GOT A MISSING MAN--AND GRENADE LAUNCHER--TO LOCATE. MAYBE WE FIND ANOTHER EXIT IN THE PROCESS--
THE CALIFORNIA COAST.
--BUT FORT EASTMAN'S TWENTY, TWENTY-FIVE MILES FROM HERE. YOU GIVE 'EM OUR COORDINATES IN THIS GRAVEYARD, I CAN FOCUS ON FINDING MY MAN.
ALL RIGHT, BRADLEY. JUST SIT TIGHT. OVER AND OUT.
WELL?
NO SIGN OF HIM, HIS GEAR, EVEN HIS CIGS.
IT'S LIKE HE JUMPED OVERBOARD.
HEY, BAMA.
WHERE'S KOHLER?
RIGHT BEHIND US. HE HAD TO HIT THE HEAD, SO WE DIDN'T STICK AROUND FOR THAT.

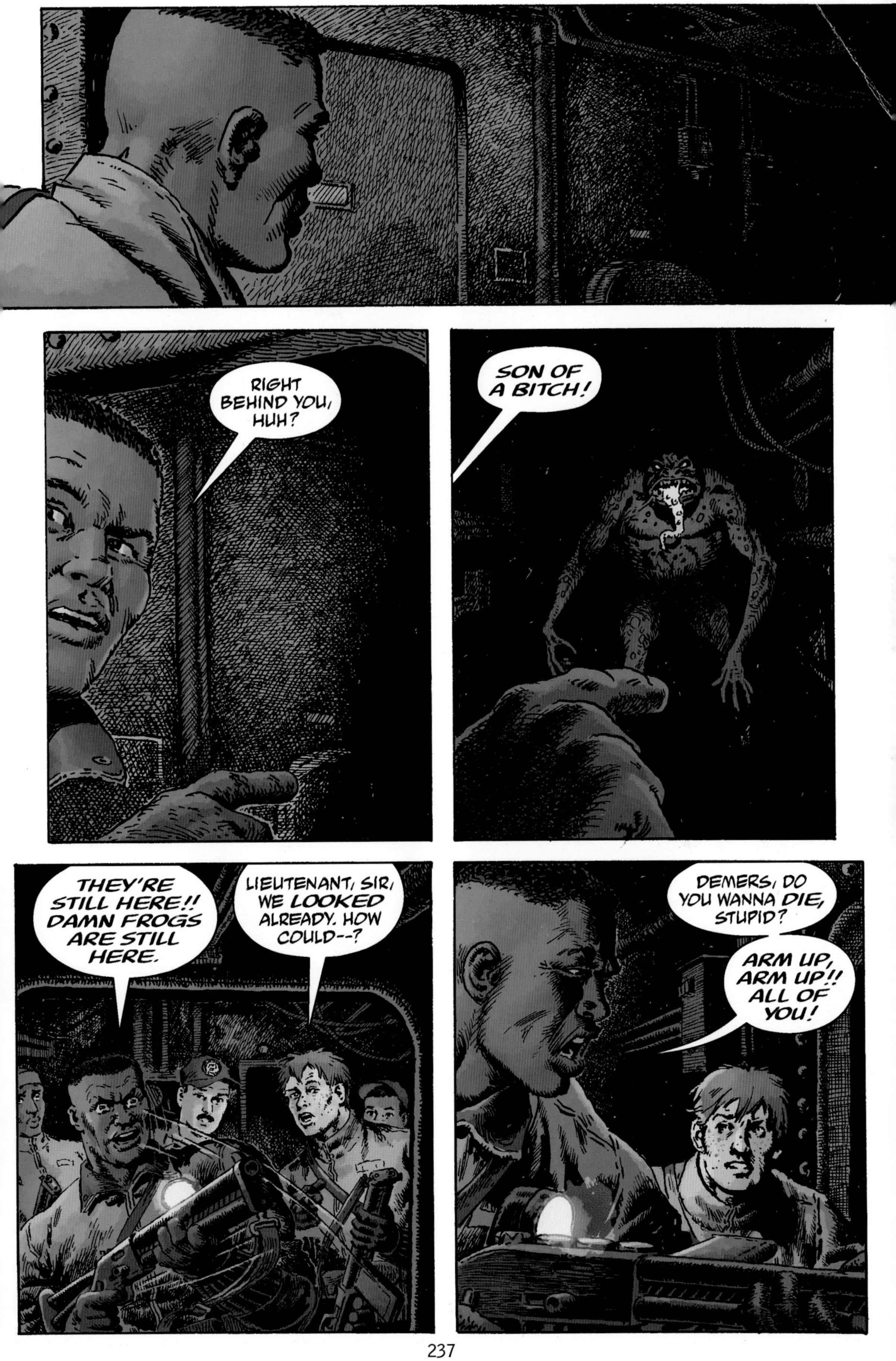
RIGHT BEHIND YOU, HUH?
SON OF A BITCH!
THEY'RE STILL HERE!! DAMN FROGS ARE STILL HERE.
LIEUTENANT, SIR, WE LOOKED ALREADY. HOW COULD--?
DEMERS, DO YOU WANNA DIE, STUPID?
ARM UP, ARM UP!! ALL OF YOU!

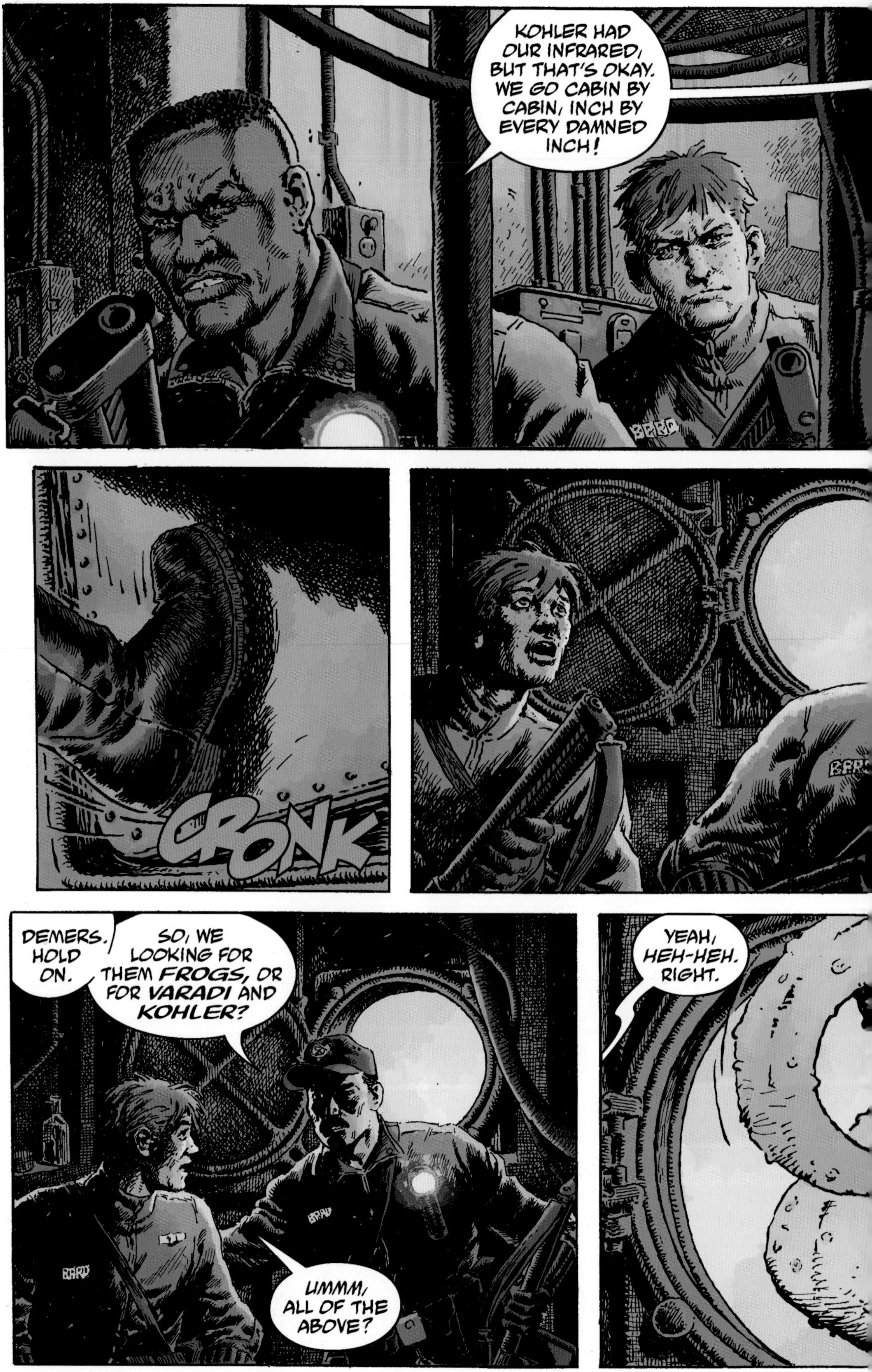
KOHLER HAD OUR INFRARED, BUT THAT'S OKAY. WE GO CABIN BY CABIN, INCH BY EVERY DAMNED INCH!
CRONK
DEMERS. HOLD ON.
SO, WE LOOKING FOR THEM *FROGS*, OR FOR *VARADI* AND *KOHLER?*
UMMM, ALL OF THE ABOVE?
YEAH, HEH-HEH. RIGHT.

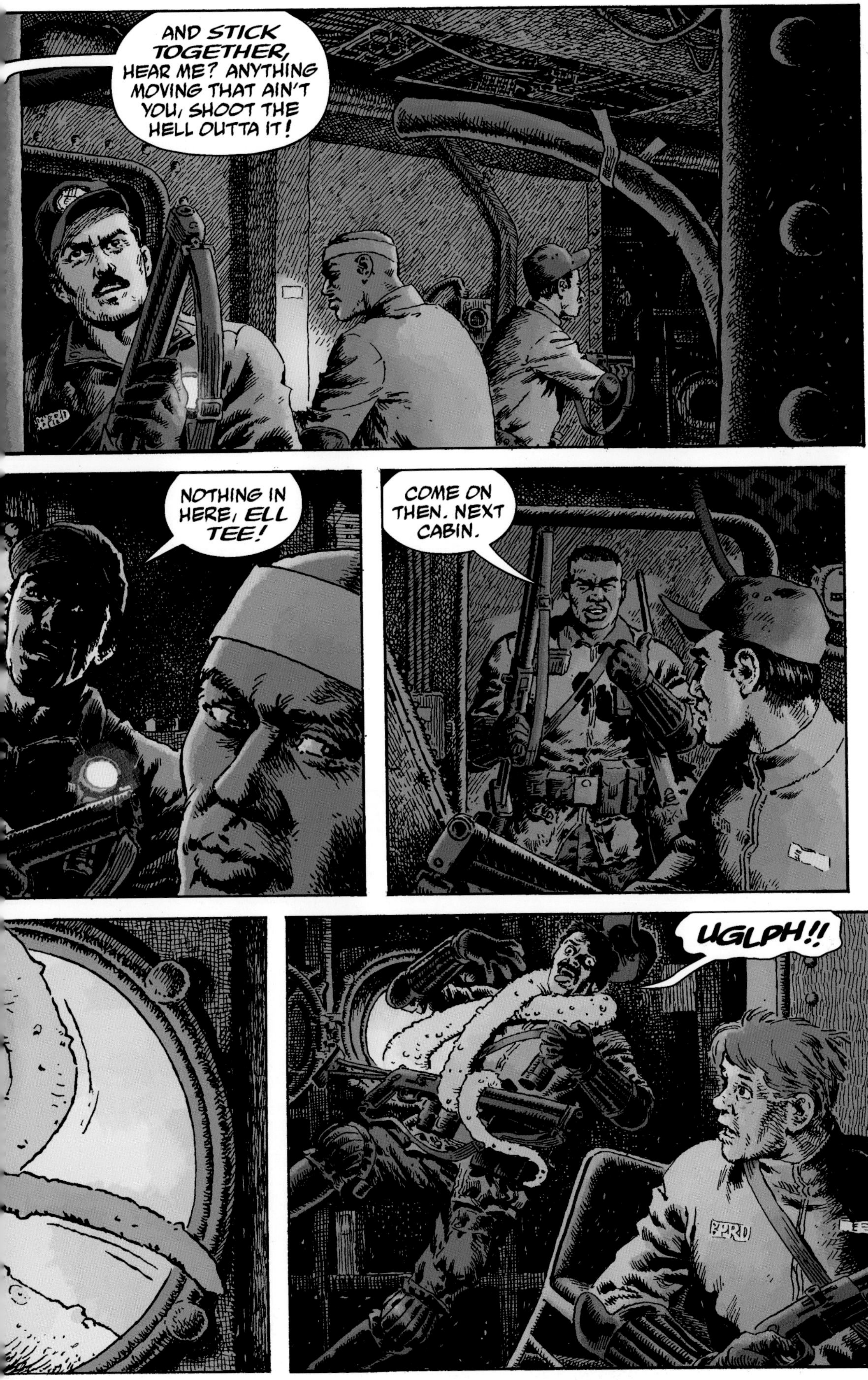
AND STICK TOGETHER, HEAR ME? ANYTHING MOVING THAT AIN'T YOU, SHOOT THE HELL OUTTA IT!
NOTHING IN HERE, ELL TEE!
COME ON THEN. NEXT CABIN.
UGLPH!!

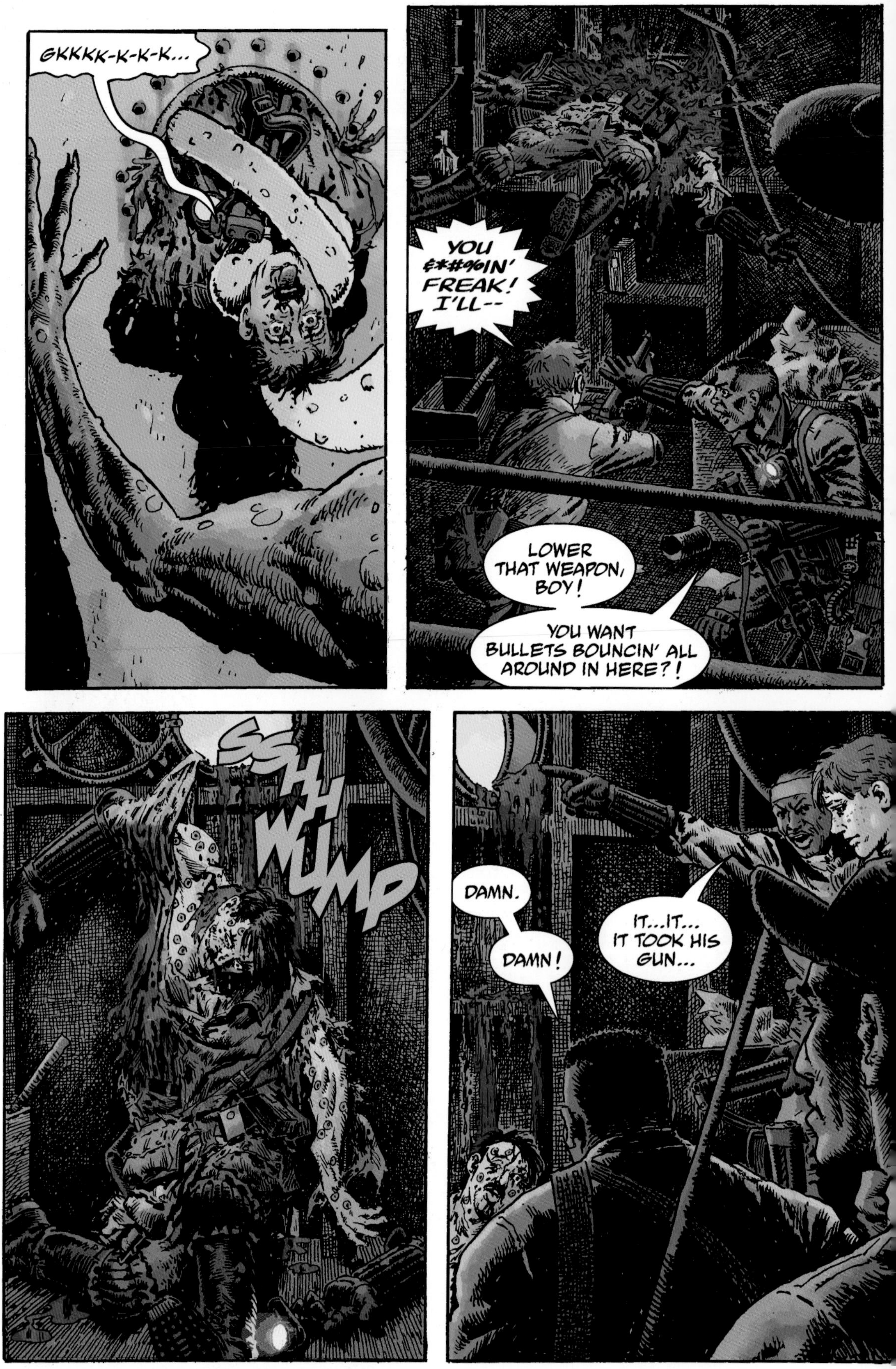
GKKKK-K-K-K...
YOU £*#%IN' FREAK! I'LL--
LOWER THAT WEAPON, BOY!
YOU WANT BULLETS BOUNCIN' ALL AROUND IN HERE?!
SSHHWUMP
DAMN.
DAMN!
IT...IT... IT TOOK HIS GUN...

WHAT I SAY?! WHAT I #*£%IN' SAY TO YOU, BOY?!!

"STICK TOGETHER!" SOUND FAMILIAR?!!

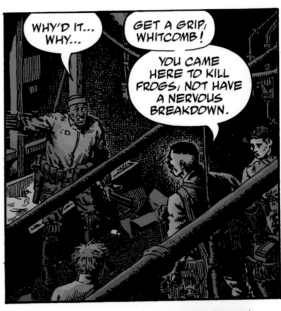

WHY'D IT... WHY...

GET A GRIP, WHITCOMB!

YOU CAME HERE TO KILL FROGS, NOT HAVE A NERVOUS BREAKDOWN.

SO SOMEHOW--OBVIOUSLY-- WE MISSED THE BASTARDS. SMARTER'N WE THOUGHT, BUT A FEW BULLETS'LL CHANGE THAT.

PARKER TOLD ME UP IN CANADA, HIS SQUAD MOWED DOWN ABOUT A HUNDRED. SAYS THEY GO DOWN JUST LIKE TALL GRASS.

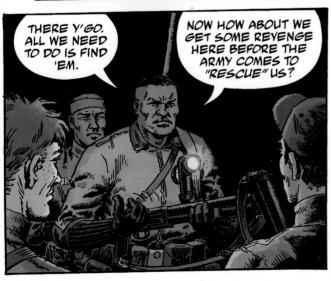

THERE Y'GO. ALL WE NEED TO DO IS FIND 'EM.

NOW HOW ABOUT WE GET SOME REVENGE HERE BEFORE THE ARMY COMES TO "RESCUE" US?

AND FOR GOD'S SAKE, STICK--TO-- GETHER!

241

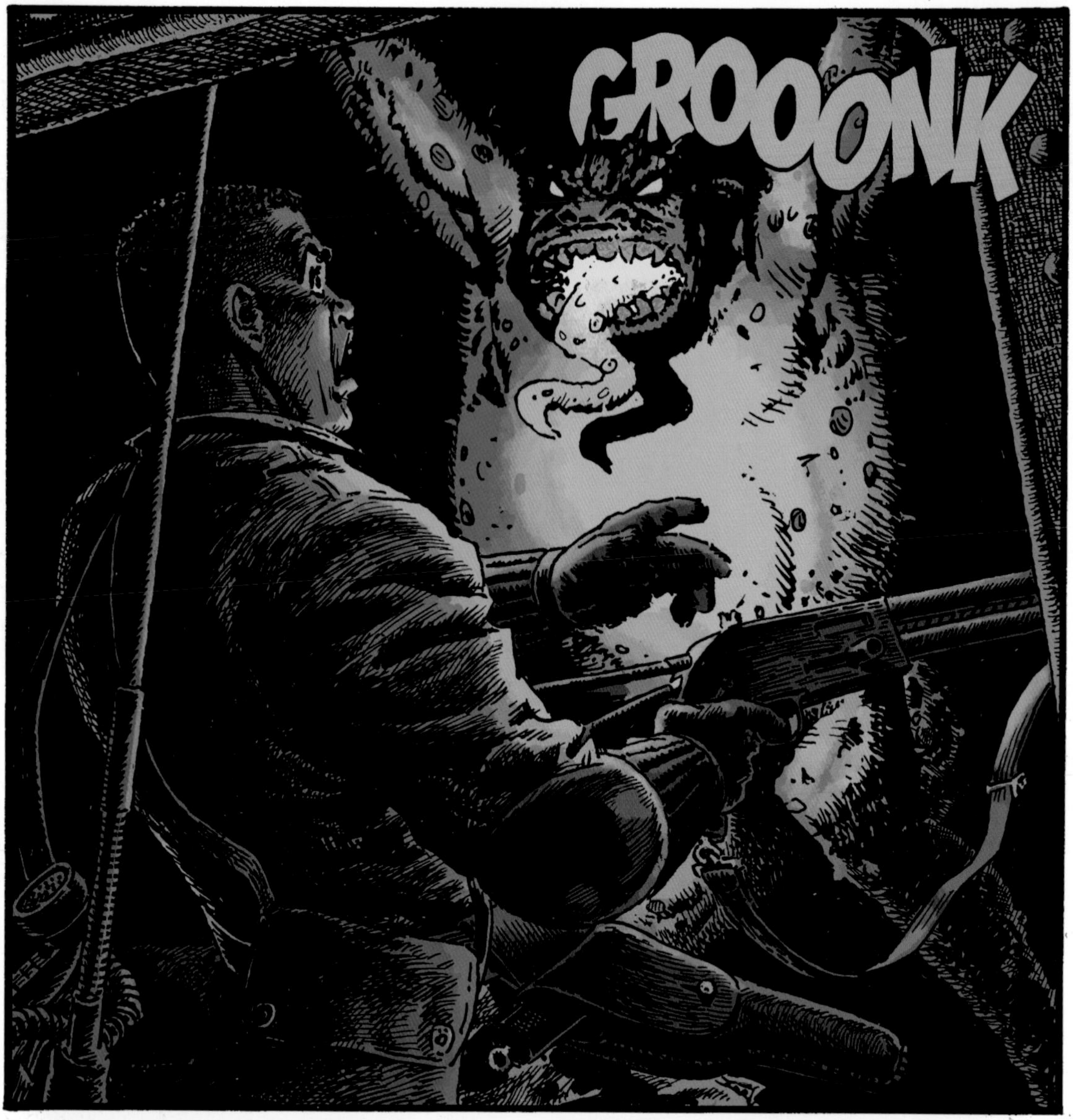
GROOONK

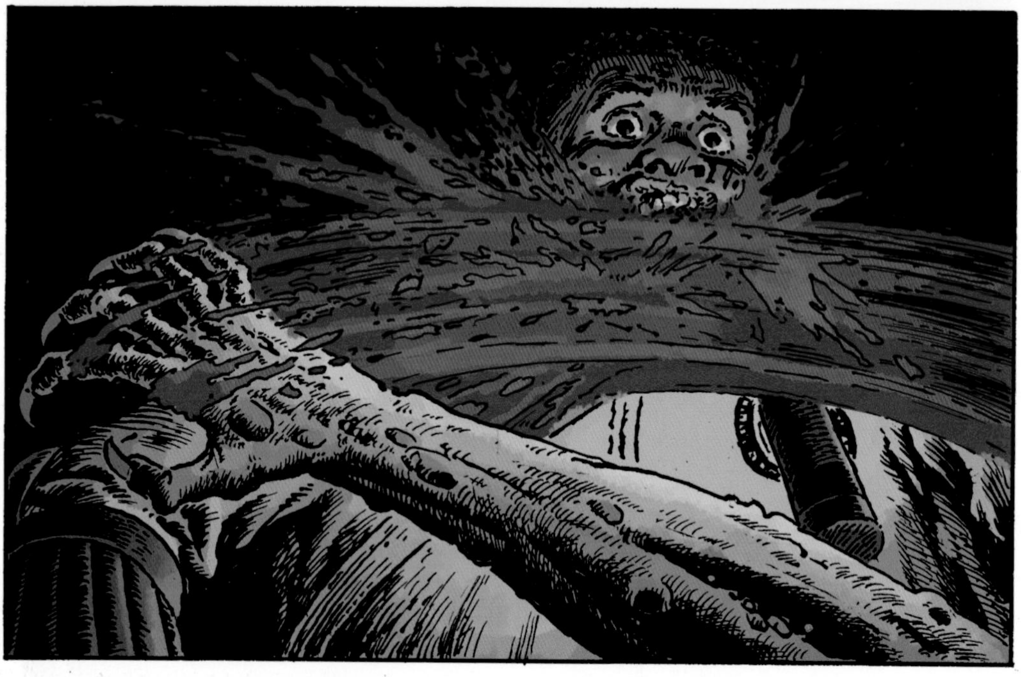

YAAAAA!!
RATATATATA
YOU HIT IT?
IN THE LEG.
THAT'S IT! NO MORE HUNTING. LET'S JUST GET OUT!
FROG SEASON'S OFFICIALLY OVER!

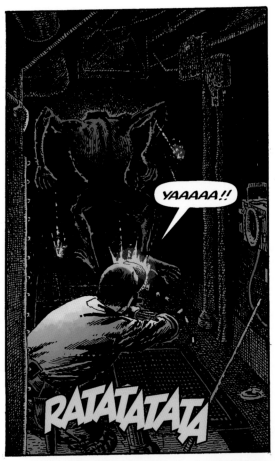

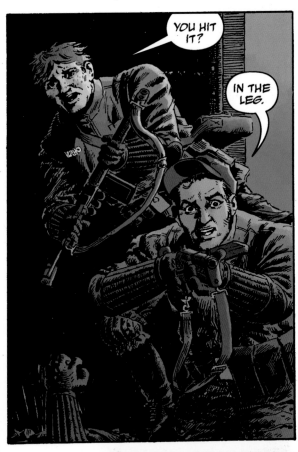

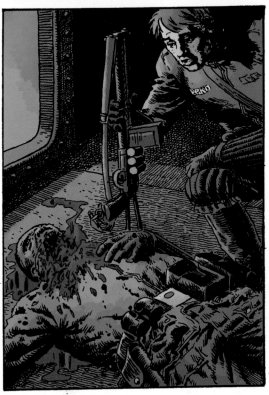

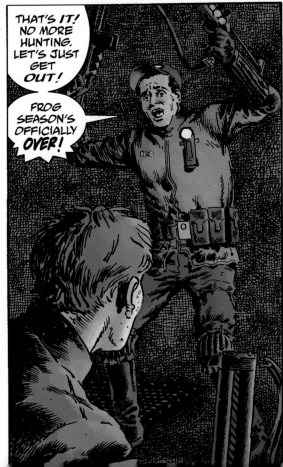

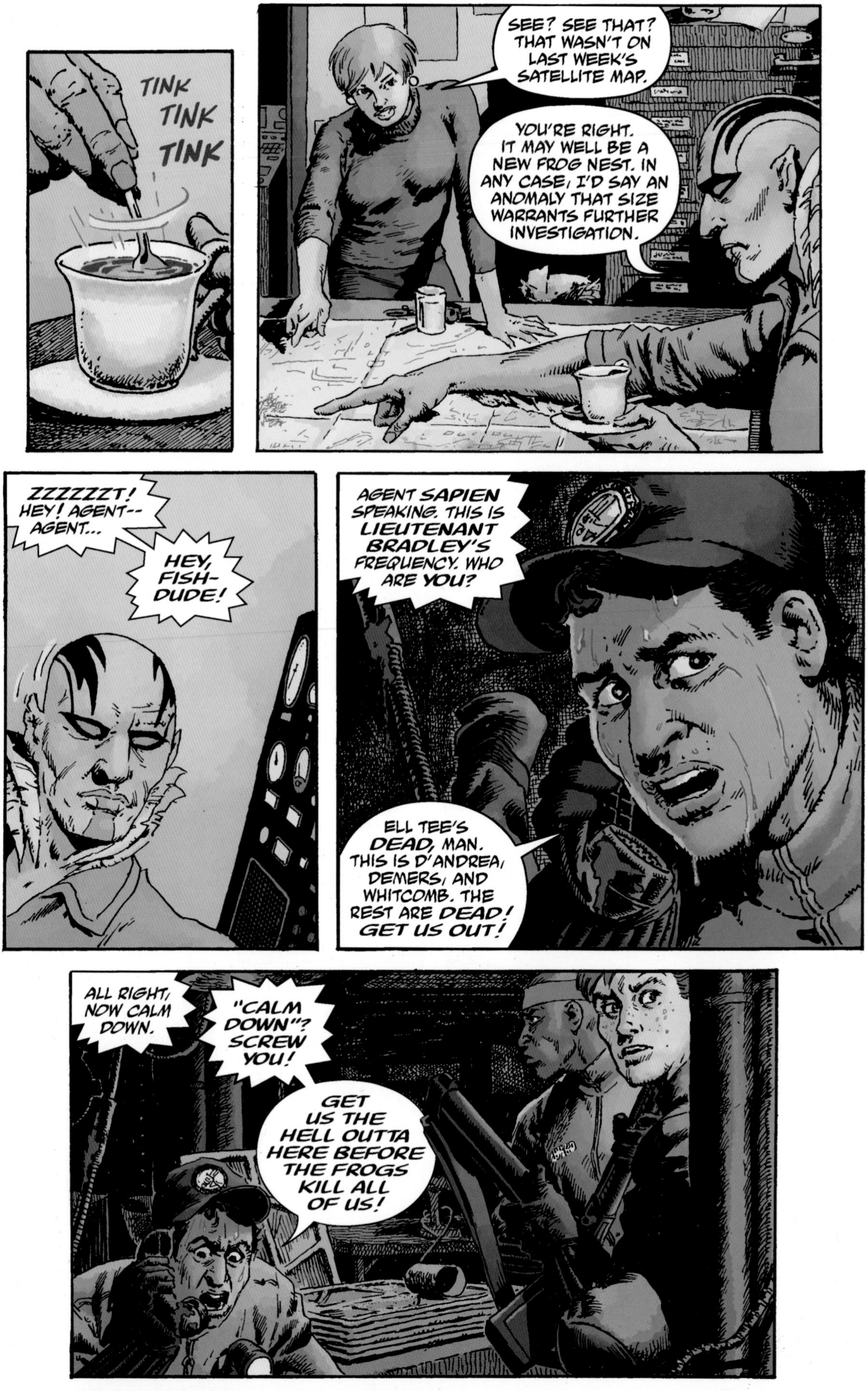
TINK
TINK
TINK
SEE? SEE THAT? THAT WASN'T ON LAST WEEK'S SATELLITE MAP.
YOU'RE RIGHT. IT MAY WELL BE A NEW FROG NEST. IN ANY CASE, I'D SAY AN ANOMALY THAT SIZE WARRANTS FURTHER INVESTIGATION.
ZZZZZZT! HEY! AGENT-- AGENT...
HEY, FISH-DUDE!
AGENT SAPIEN SPEAKING. THIS IS LIEUTENANT BRADLEY'S FREQUENCY. WHO ARE YOU?
ELL TEE'S DEAD, MAN. THIS IS D'ANDREA, DEMERS, AND WHITCOMB. THE REST ARE DEAD! GET US OUT!
ALL RIGHT, NOW CALM DOWN.
"CALM DOWN"? SCREW YOU!
GET US THE HELL OUTTA HERE BEFORE THE FROGS KILL ALL OF US!

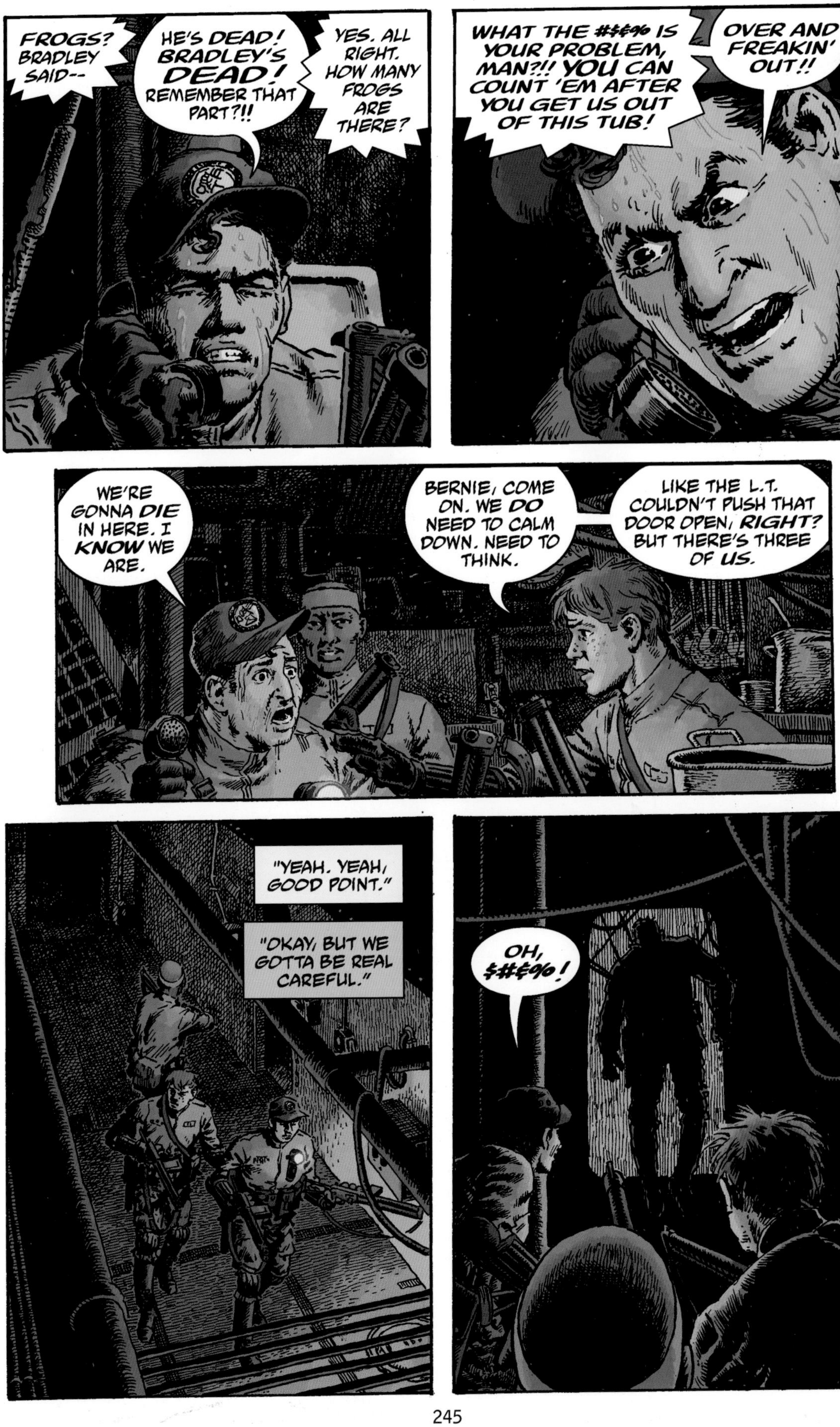
FROGS? BRADLEY SAID--
HE'S DEAD! BRADLEY'S DEAD! REMEMBER THAT PART?!!
YES. ALL RIGHT. HOW MANY FROGS ARE THERE?
WHAT THE #$&% IS YOUR PROBLEM, MAN?!! YOU CAN COUNT 'EM AFTER YOU GET US OUT OF THIS TUB!
OVER AND FREAKIN' OUT!!
WE'RE GONNA DIE IN HERE. I KNOW WE ARE.
BERNIE, COME ON. WE DO NEED TO CALM DOWN. NEED TO THINK.
LIKE THE L.T. COULDN'T PUSH THAT DOOR OPEN, RIGHT? BUT THERE'S THREE OF US.
"YEAH. YEAH, GOOD POINT."
"OKAY, BUT WE GOTTA BE REAL CAREFUL."
OH, $#&%!

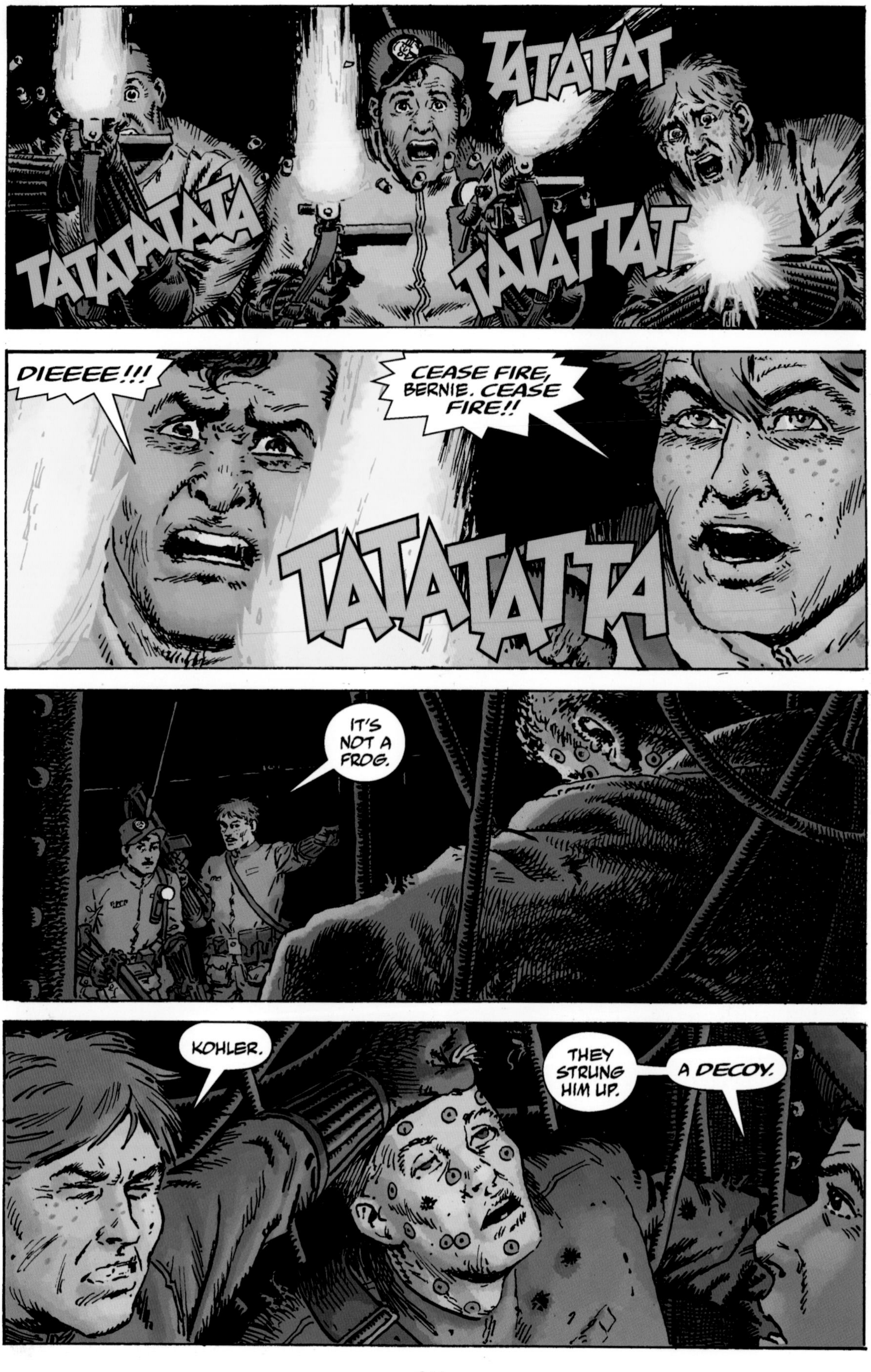
TATATAT
TATATATA
TATATTAT
DIEEEE!!!
CEASE FIRE, BERNIE. CEASE FIRE!!
TATATATTA
IT'S NOT A FROG.
KOHLER.
THEY STRUNG HIM UP.
A DECOY.

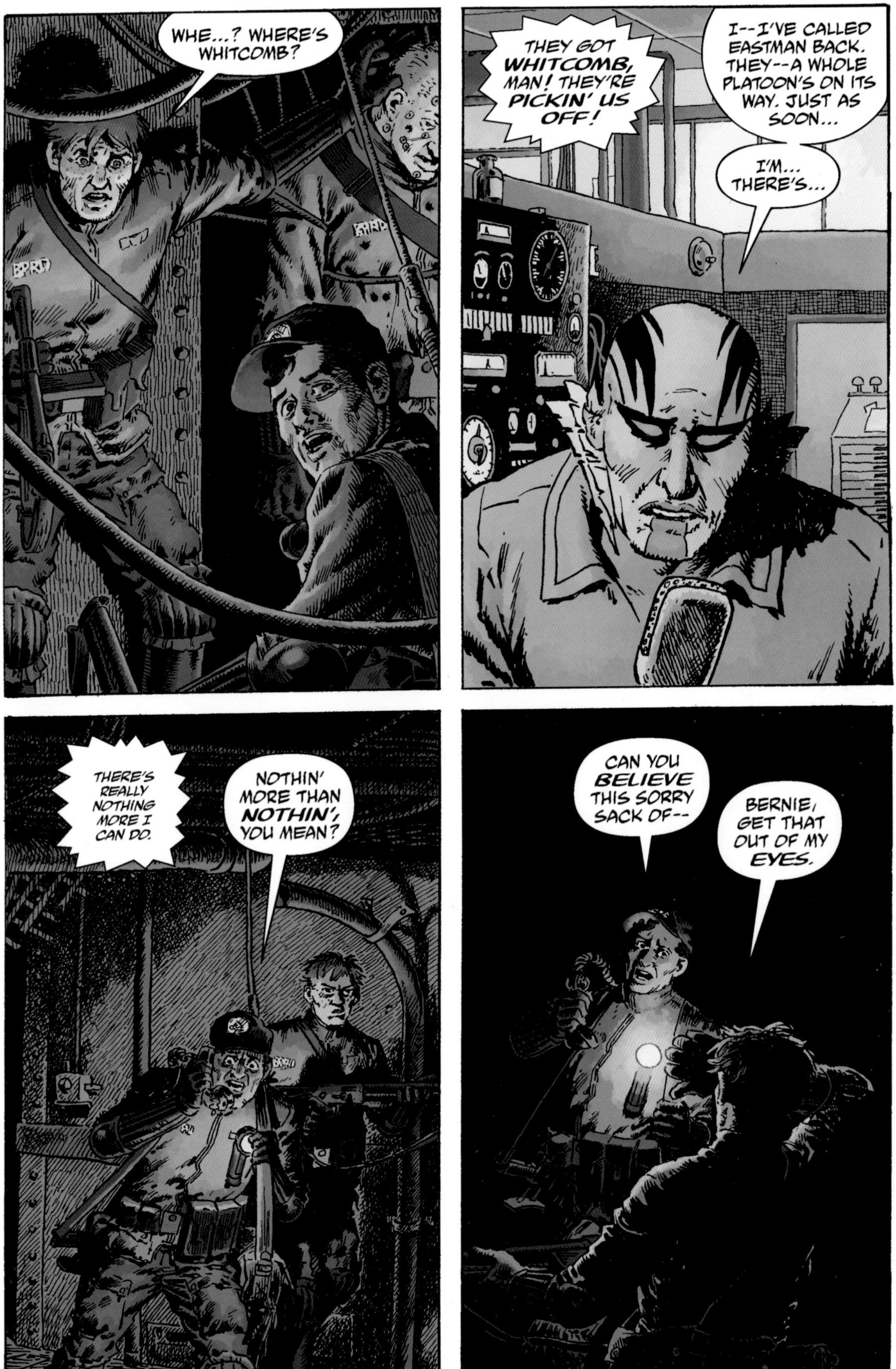
WHE...? WHERE'S WHITCOMB?
THEY GOT WHITCOMB, MAN! THEY'RE PICKIN' US OFF!
I--I'VE CALLED EASTMAN BACK. THEY--A WHOLE PLATOON'S ON ITS WAY. JUST AS SOON...
I'M... THERE'S...
THERE'S REALLY NOTHING MORE I CAN DO.
NOTHIN' MORE THAN NOTHIN', YOU MEAN?
CAN YOU BELIEVE THIS SORRY SACK OF--
BERNIE, GET THAT OUT OF MY EYES.

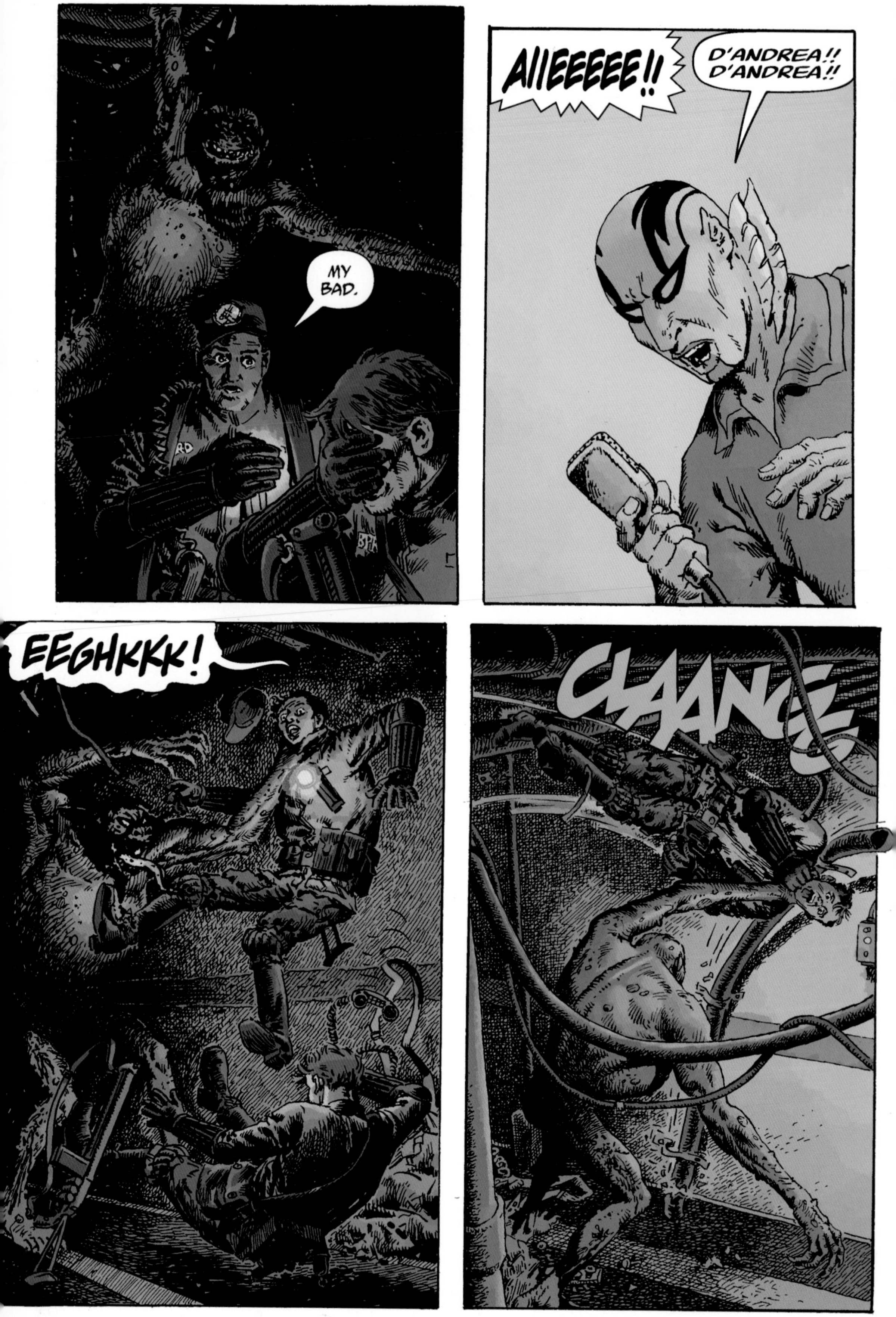
MY BAD.
AIIEEEEE!!
D'ANDREA!! D'ANDREA!!
EEGHKKK!
CLAANG

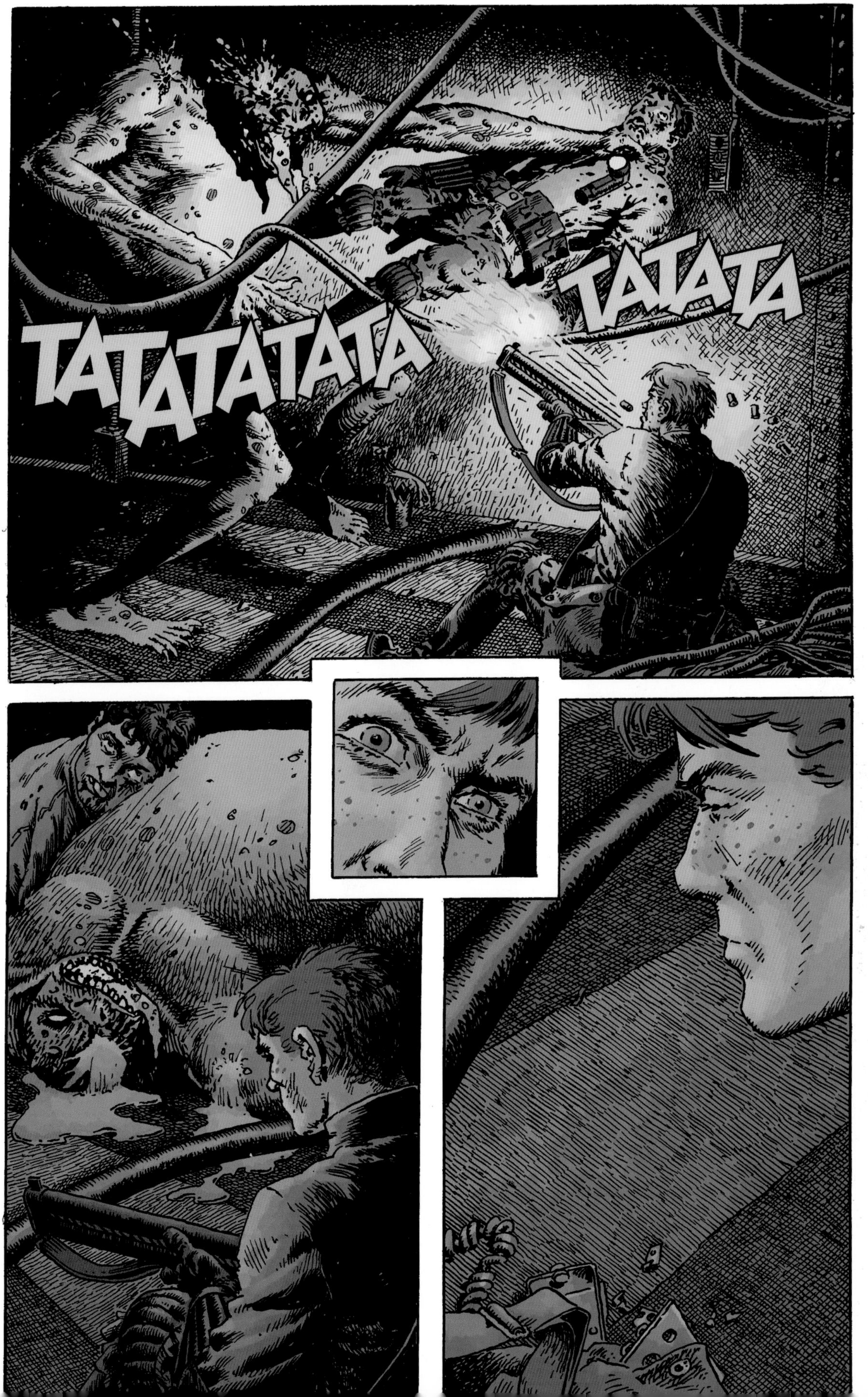
TATATATATA
TATATA

UHHHHNGHH!

UHHHYES YESYESYES YESYES YES!

YES!

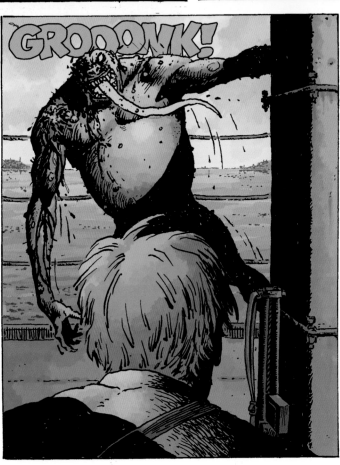

GROOONK!

HIS EYE. I JUST SHOT HIM. SAME ONE. ALIVE.

HOW-- HOW'D HE GET UP...?

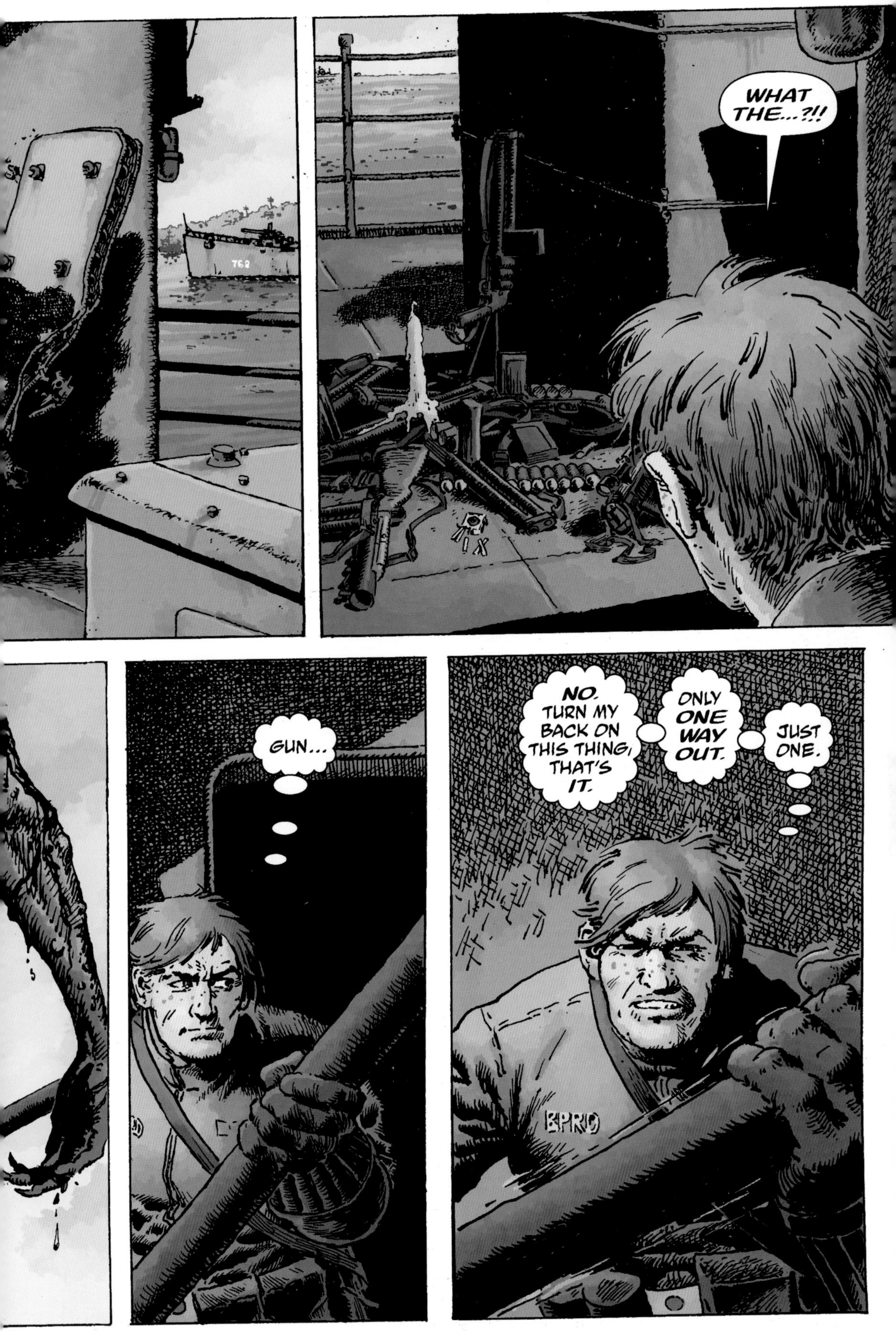
WHAT THE...?!!
GUN...
NO. TURN MY BACK ON THIS THING, THAT'S IT.
ONLY ONE WAY OUT.
JUST ONE.
BPRD

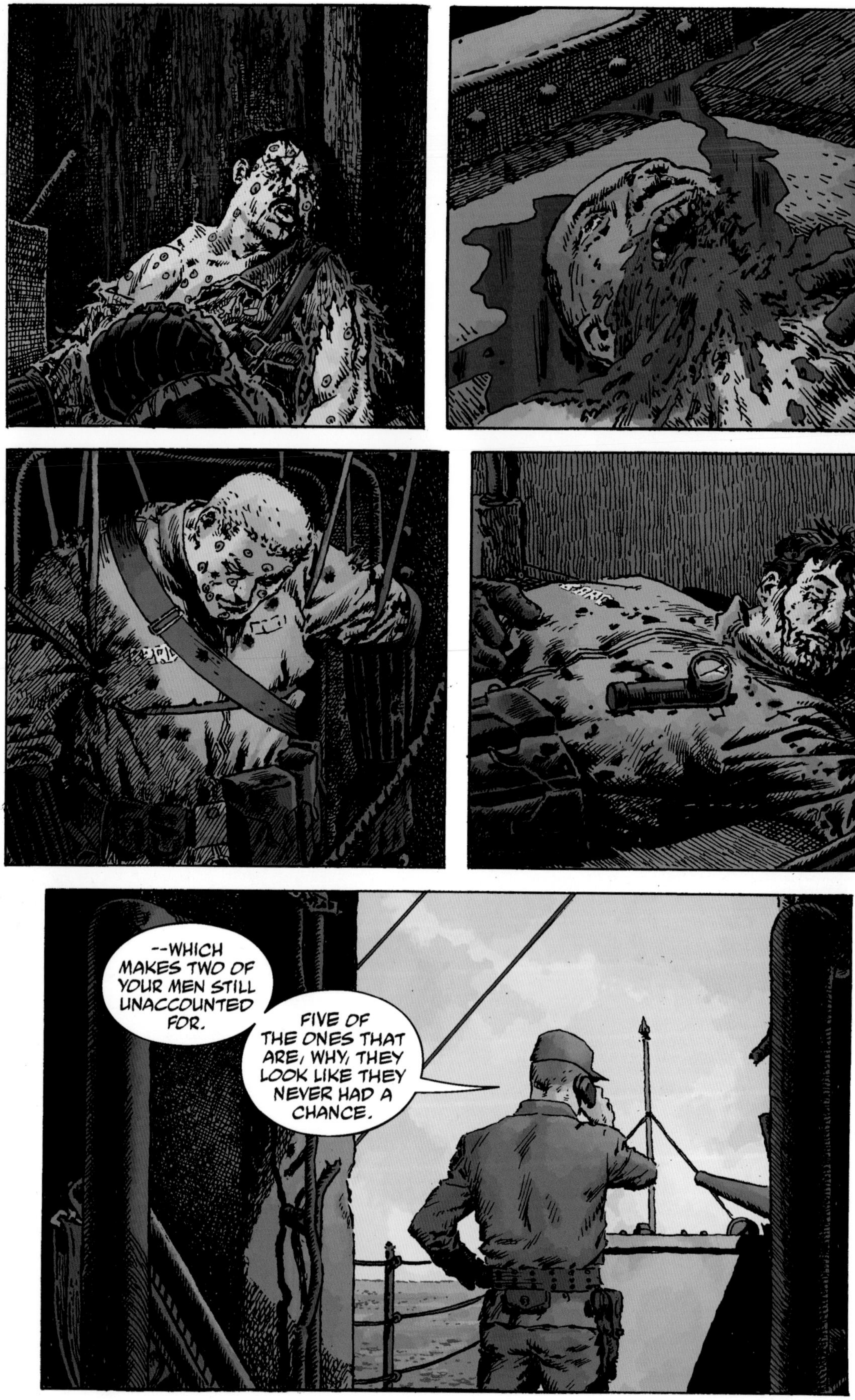
--WHICH MAKES TWO OF YOUR MEN STILL UNACCOUNTED FOR.
FIVE OF THE ONES THAT ARE, WHY, THEY LOOK LIKE THEY NEVER HAD A CHANCE.

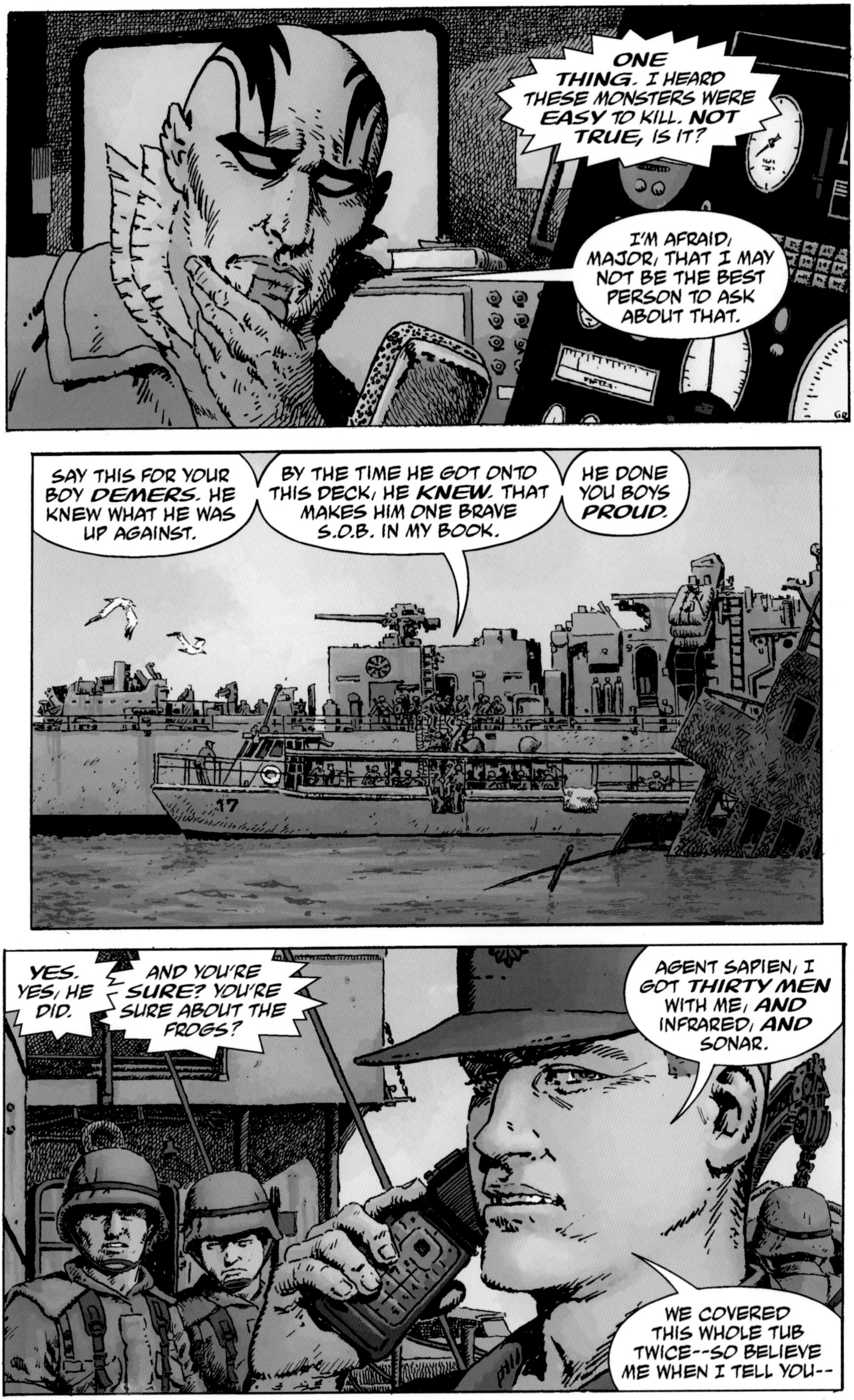
ONE THING. I HEARD THESE MONSTERS WERE EASY TO KILL. NOT TRUE, IS IT?
I'M AFRAID, MAJOR, THAT I MAY NOT BE THE BEST PERSON TO ASK ABOUT THAT.
SAY THIS FOR YOUR BOY DEMERS. HE KNEW WHAT HE WAS UP AGAINST.
BY THE TIME HE GOT ONTO THIS DECK, HE KNEW. THAT MAKES HIM ONE BRAVE S.O.B. IN MY BOOK.
HE DONE YOU BOYS PROUD.
17
YES. YES, HE DID.
AND YOU'RE SURE? YOU'RE SURE ABOUT THE FROGS?
AGENT SAPIEN, I GOT THIRTY MEN WITH ME, AND INFRARED, AND SONAR.
WE COVERED THIS WHOLE TUB TWICE--SO BELIEVE ME WHEN I TELL YOU--

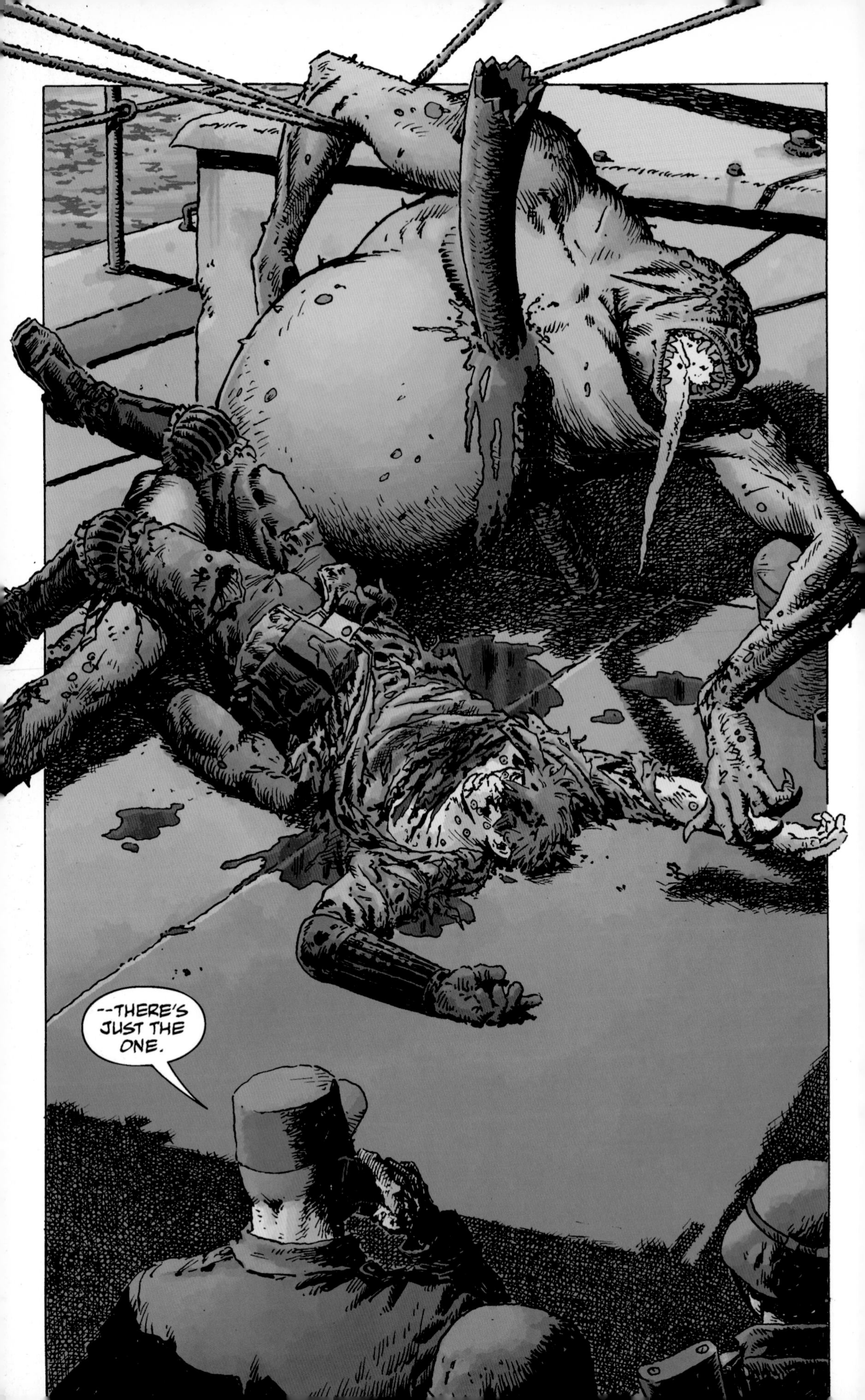
--THERE'S JUST THE ONE.

CHAPTER FIVE

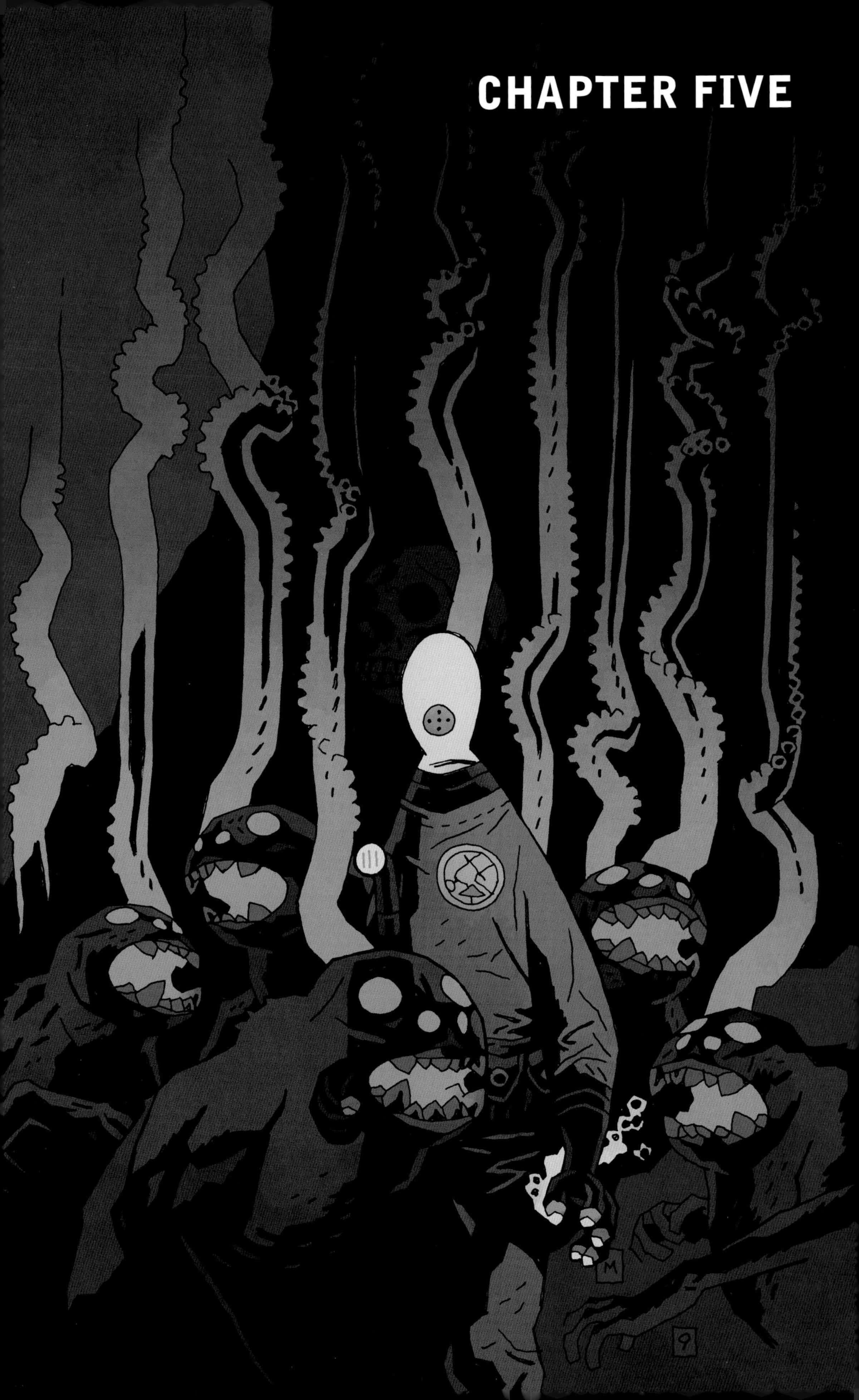

STORY BY JOHN ARCUDI

ART BY PETER SNEJBJERG

COLORS BY BJARNE HANSEN

LETTERS BY CLEM ROBINS

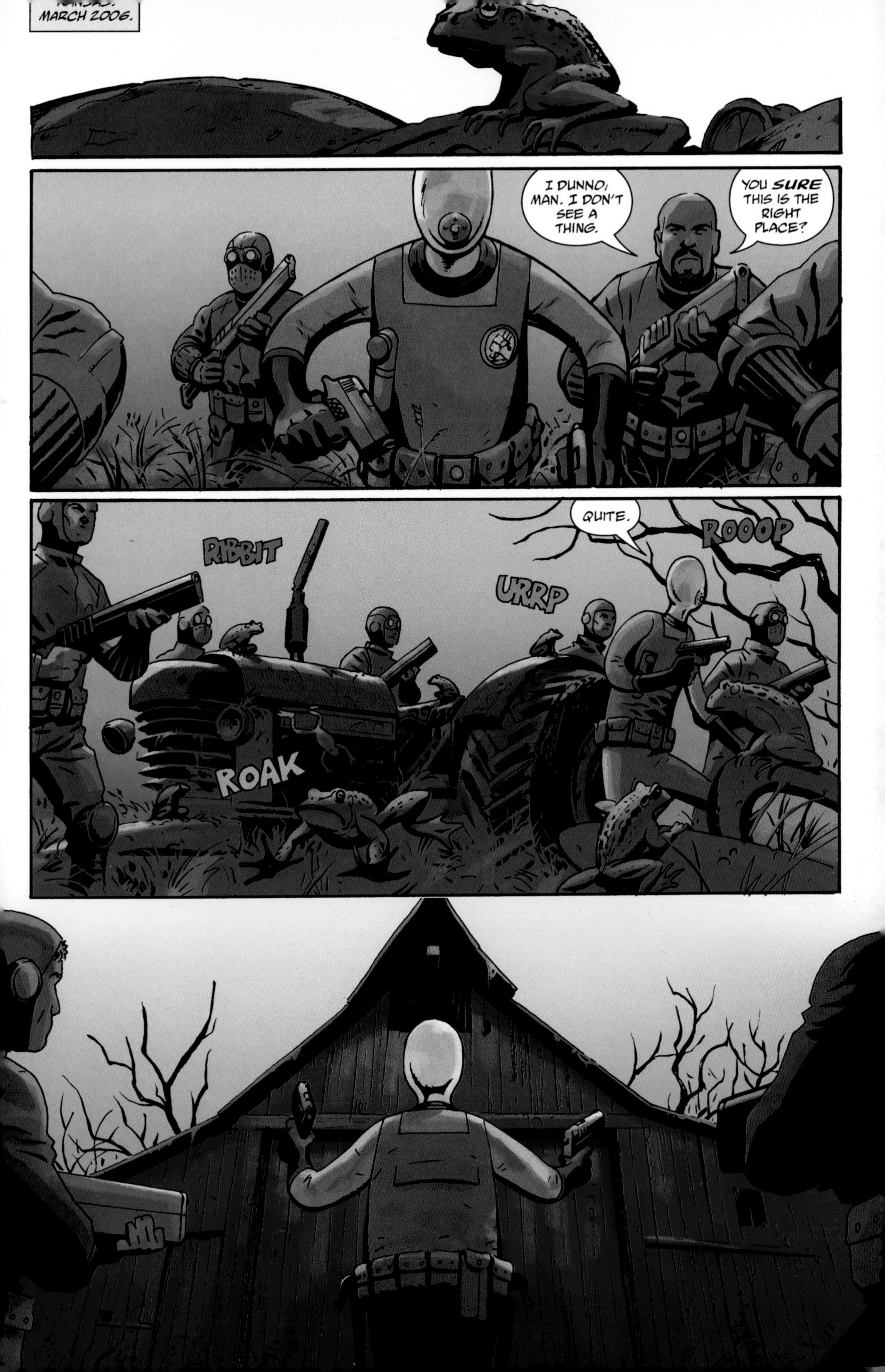
MARCH 2006.
I DUNNO, MAN. I DON'T SEE A THING.
YOU SURE THIS IS THE RIGHT PLACE?
RIBBIT
URRP
QUITE.
ROOOP
ROAK

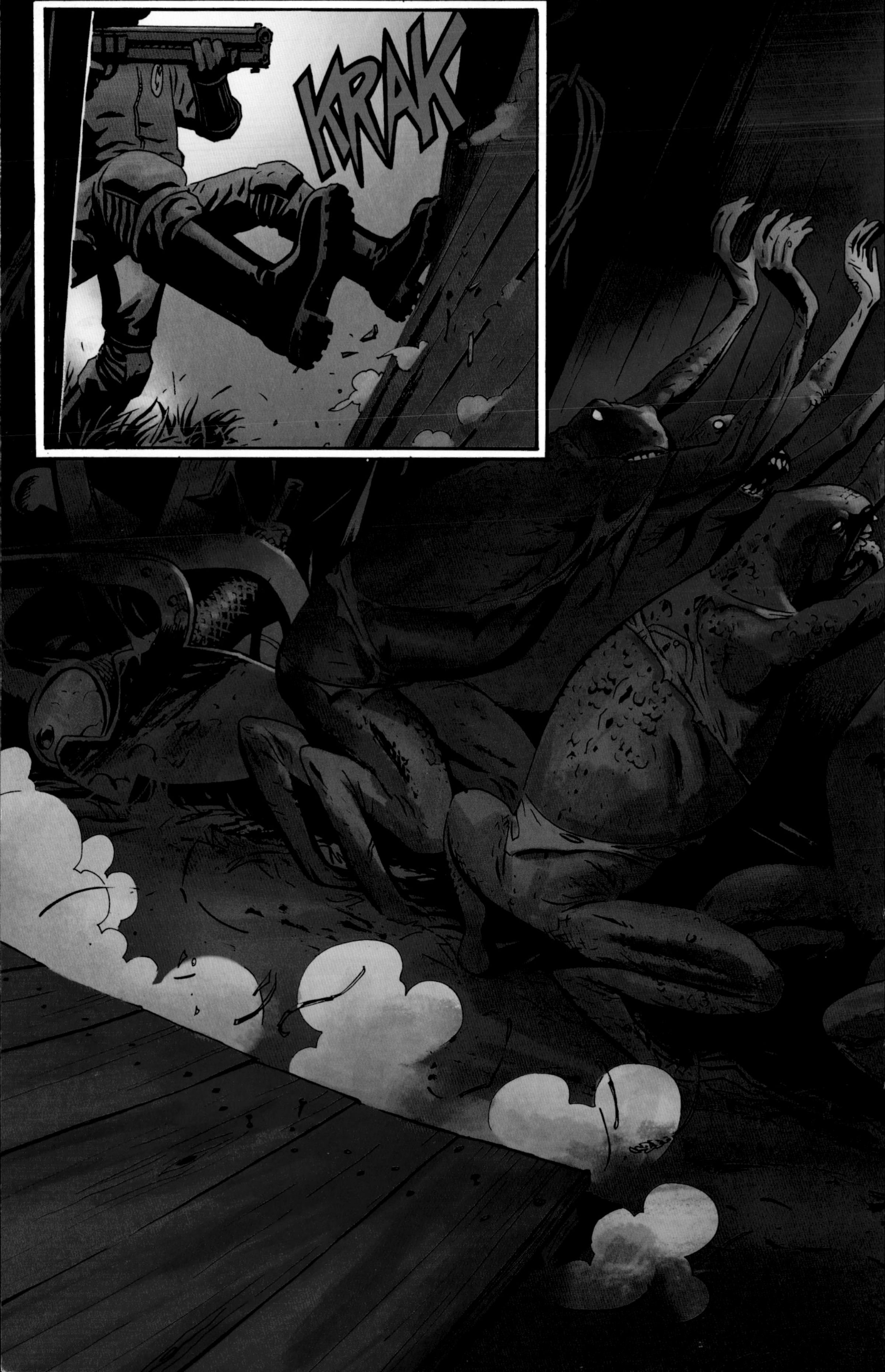
KRAK

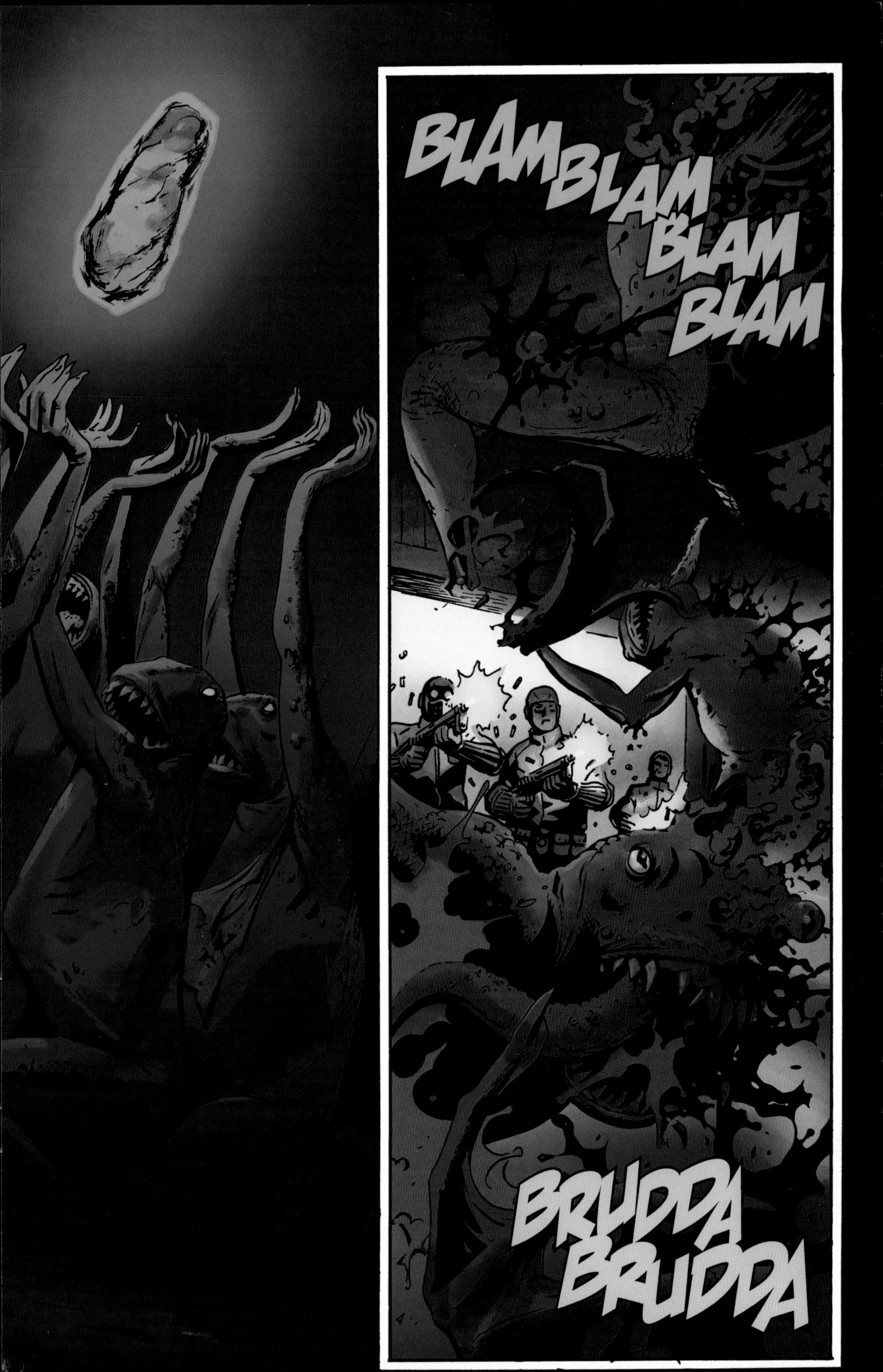
BLAM BLAM BLAM BLAM
BRUDDA BRUDDA

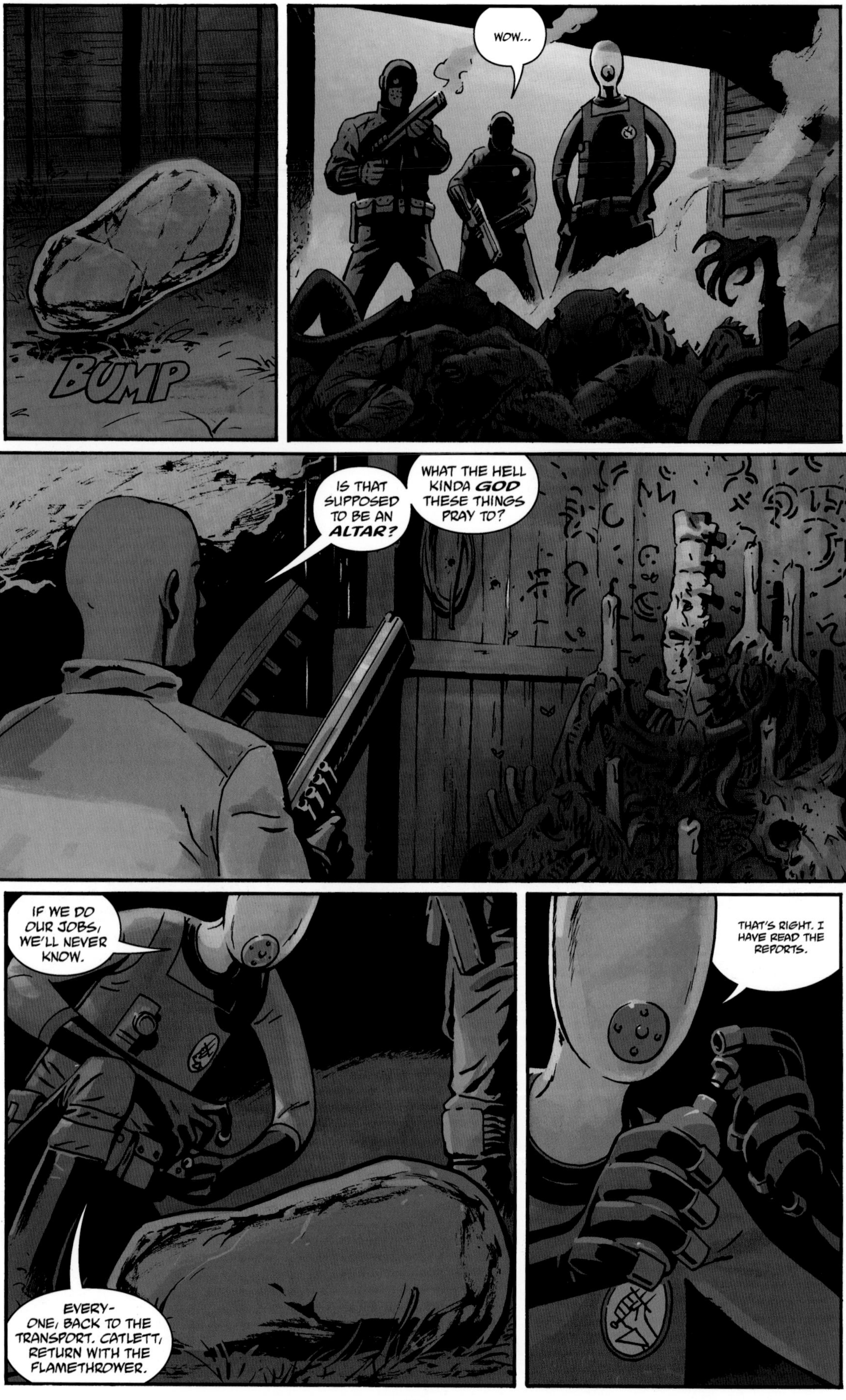
BUMP
WOW...
IS THAT SUPPOSED TO BE AN ALTAR?
WHAT THE HELL KINDA GOD THESE THINGS PRAY TO?
IF WE DO OUR JOBS, WE'LL NEVER KNOW.
EVERY-ONE, BACK TO THE TRANSPORT. CATLETT, RETURN WITH THE FLAMETHROWER.
THAT'S RIGHT. I HAVE READ THE REPORTS.

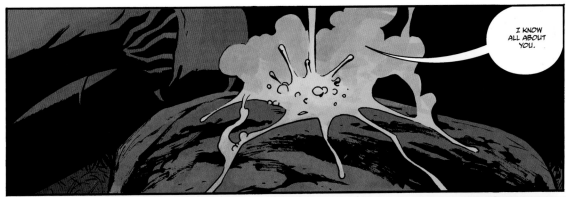

I KNOW ALL ABOUT YOU.

AGENT KRAUS?

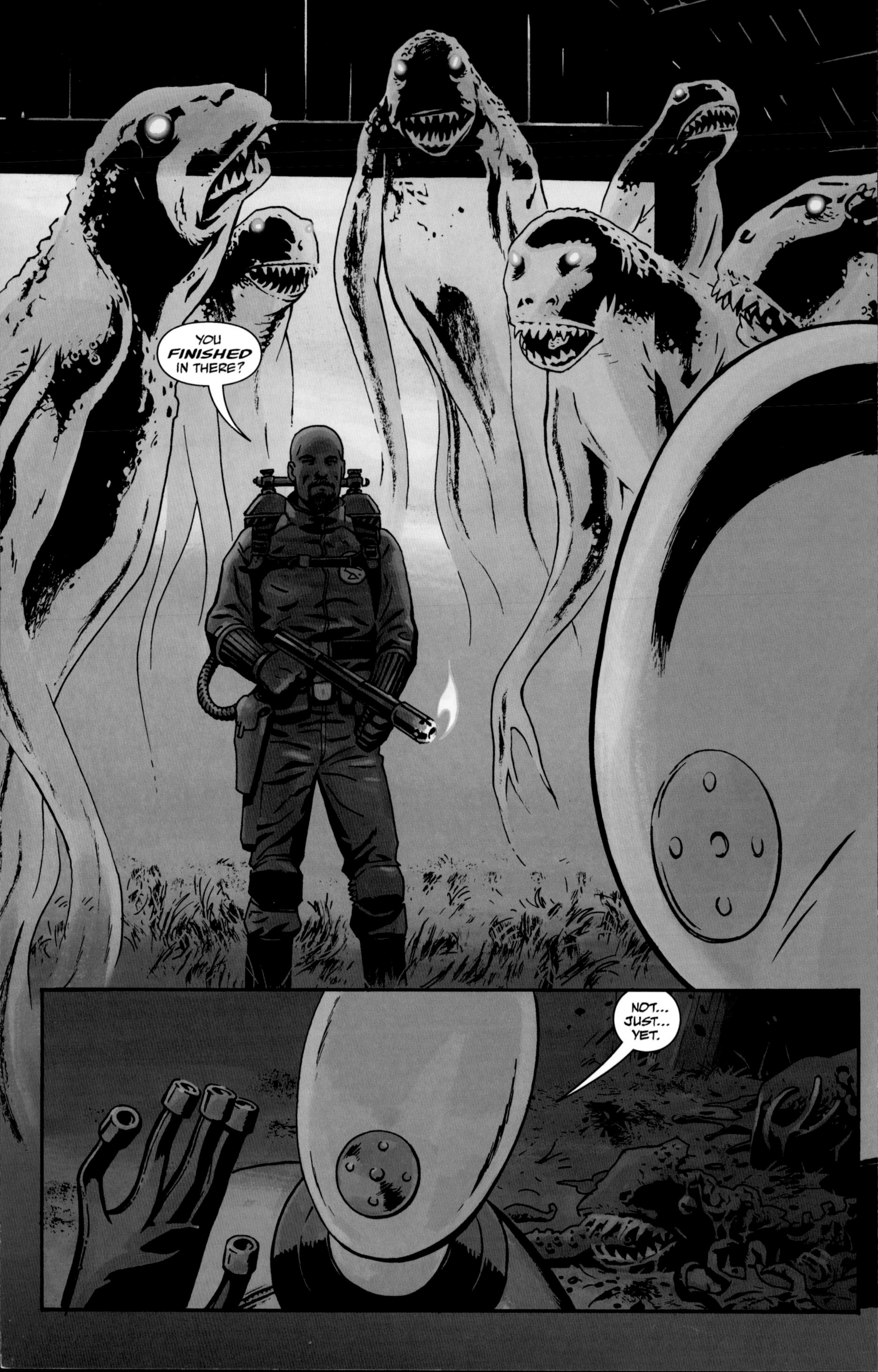
YOU *FINISHED* IN THERE?
NOT... JUST... YET.

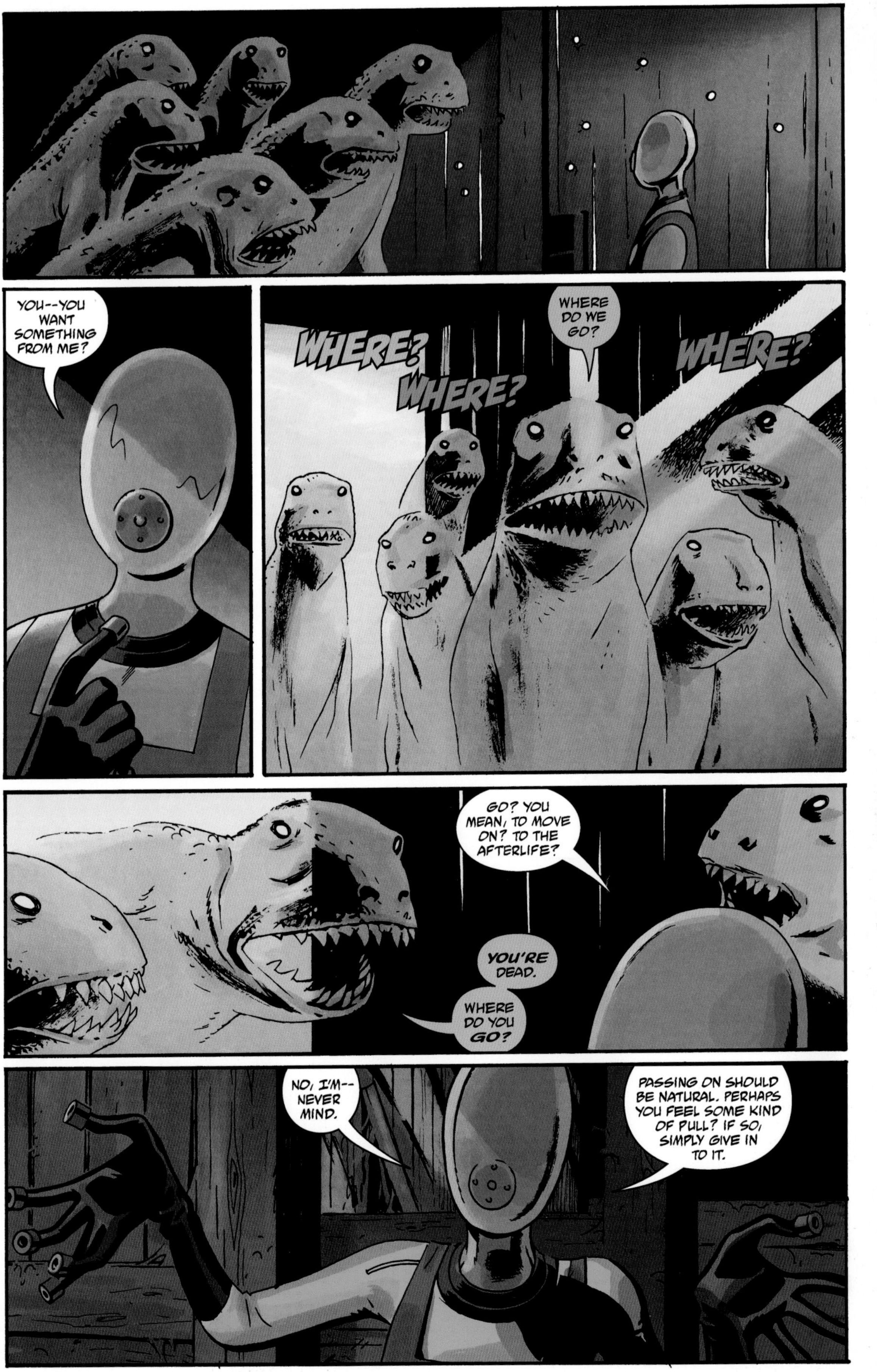
YOU--YOU WANT SOMETHING FROM ME?
WHERE?
WHERE?
WHERE DO WE GO?
WHERE?
GO? YOU MEAN, TO MOVE ON? TO THE AFTERLIFE?
YOU'RE DEAD.
WHERE DO YOU GO?
NO, I'M-- NEVER MIND.
PASSING ON SHOULD BE NATURAL. PERHAPS YOU FEEL SOME KIND OF PULL? IF SO, SIMPLY GIVE IN TO IT.

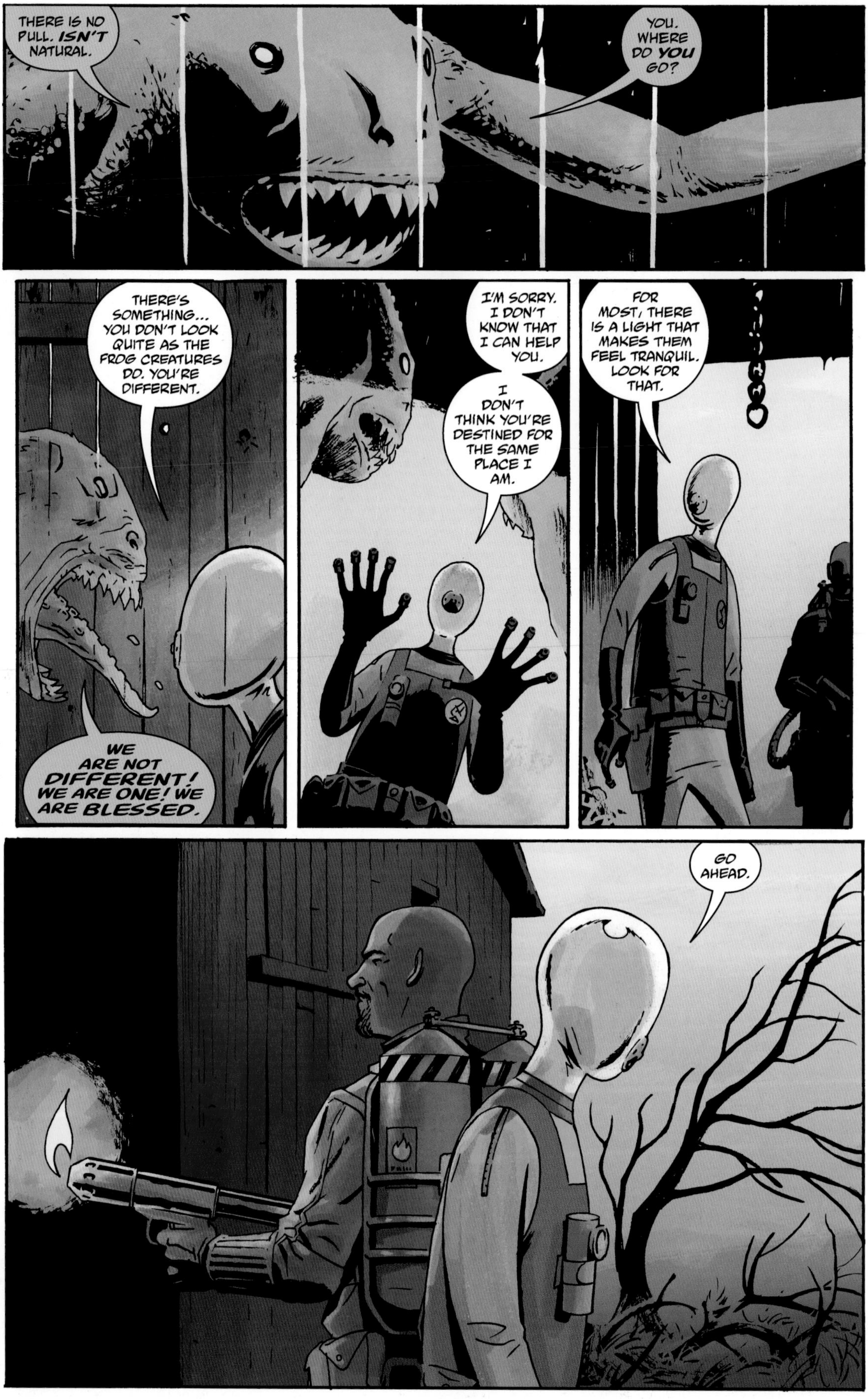
THERE IS NO PULL. ISN'T NATURAL.
YOU. WHERE DO YOU GO?
THERE'S SOMETHING... YOU DON'T LOOK QUITE AS THE FROG CREATURES DO. YOU'RE DIFFERENT.
WE ARE NOT DIFFERENT! WE ARE ONE! WE ARE BLESSED.
I'M SORRY. I DON'T KNOW THAT I CAN HELP YOU.
I DON'T THINK YOU'RE DESTINED FOR THE SAME PLACE I AM.
FOR MOST, THERE IS A LIGHT THAT MAKES THEM FEEL TRANQUIL. LOOK FOR THAT.
GO AHEAD.

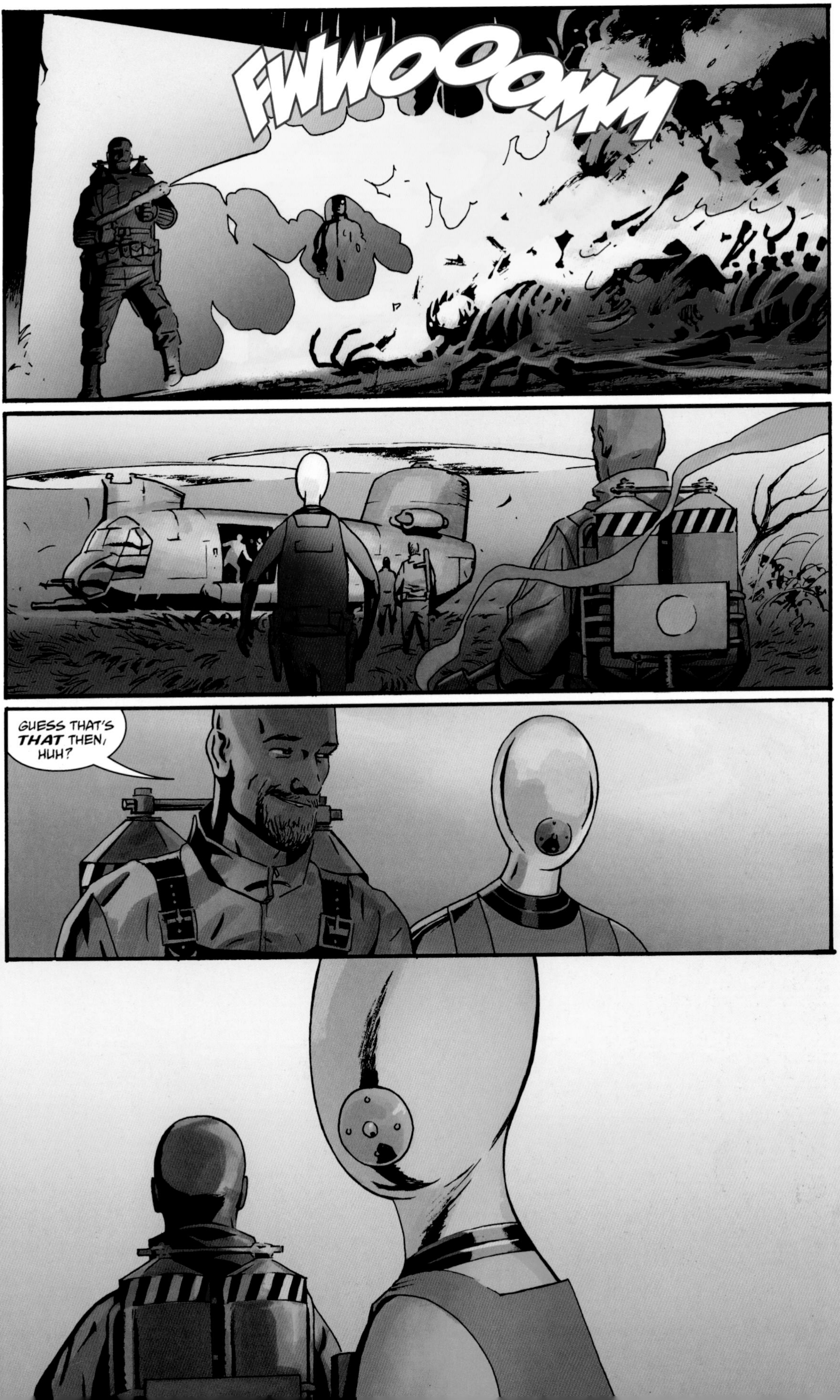
FWWOOOOMM
GUESS THAT'S **THAT** THEN, HUH?

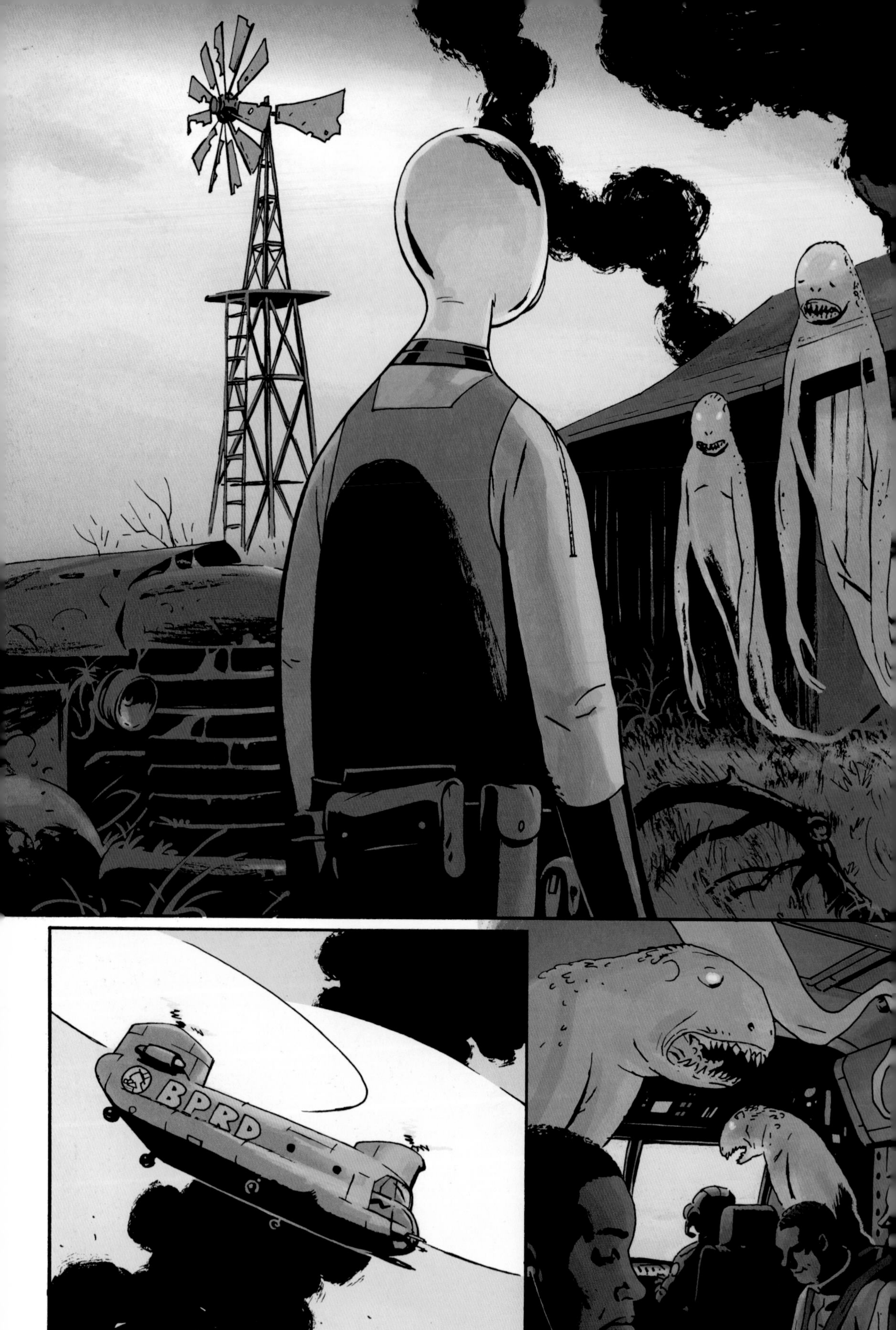
BPRD

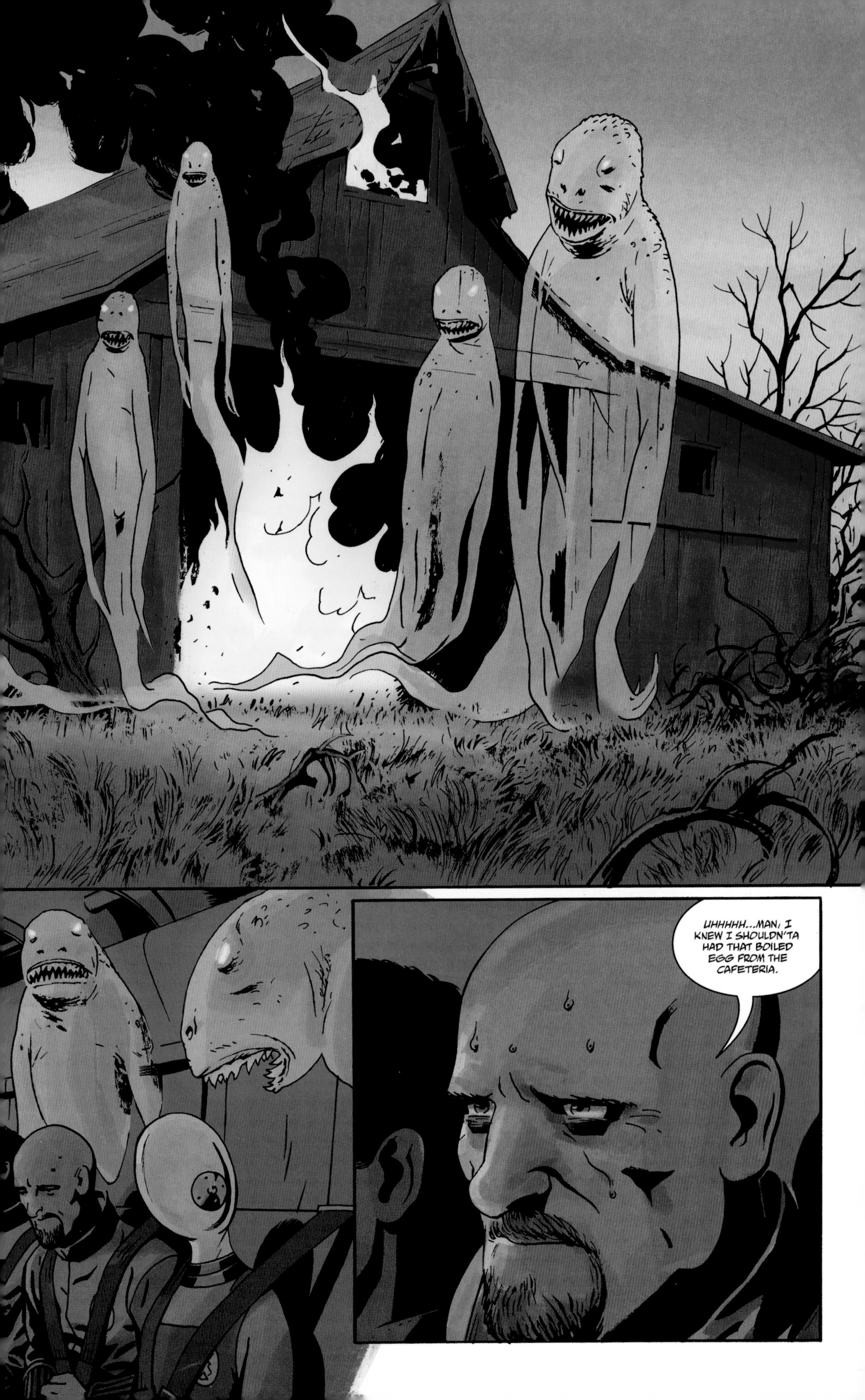
UHHHHH...MAN, I KNEW I SHOULDN'TA HAD THAT BOILED EGG FROM THE CAFETERIA.

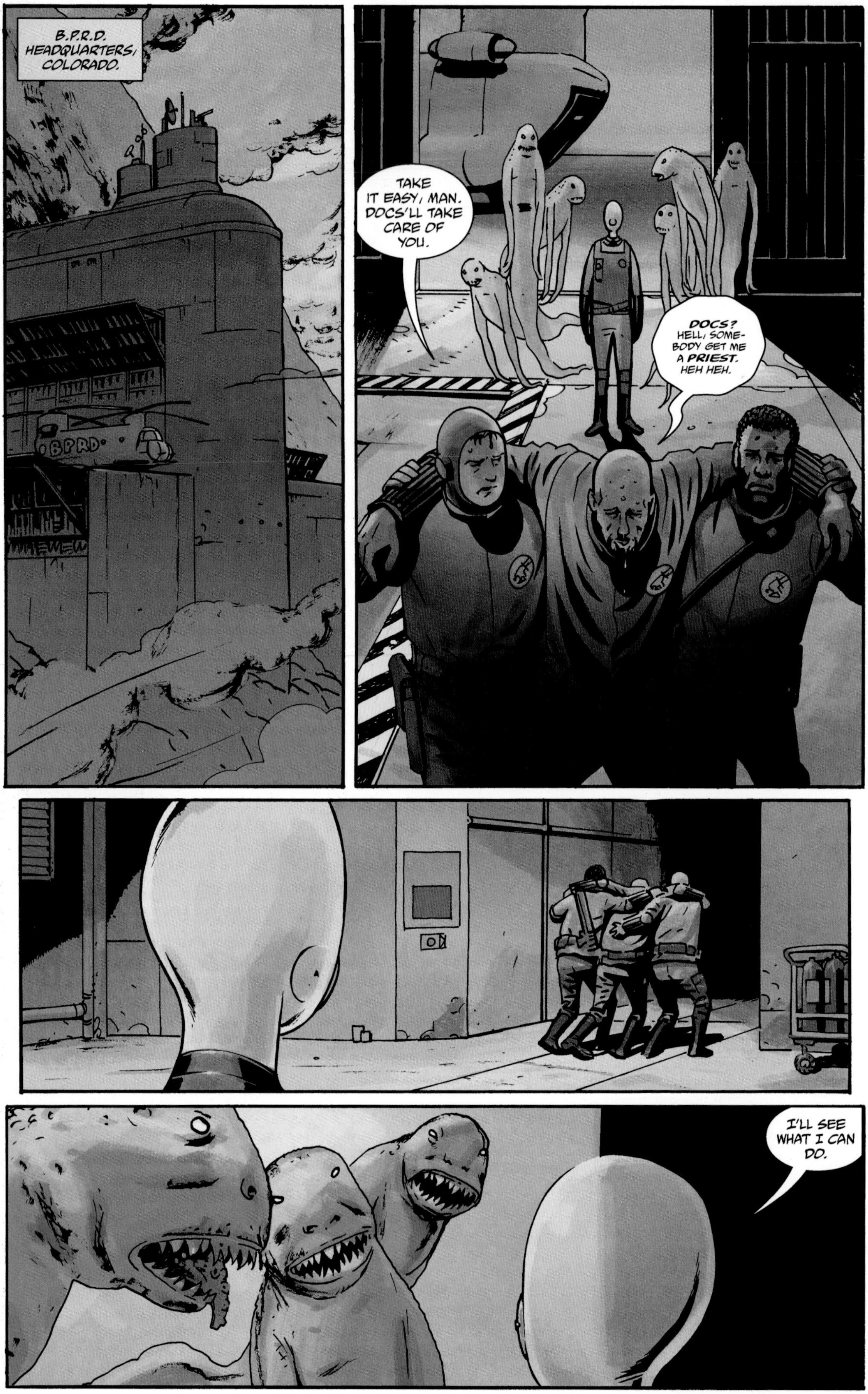
B.P.R.D. HEADQUARTERS, COLORADO.
BPRD
TAKE IT EASY, MAN. DOCS'LL TAKE CARE OF YOU.
DOCS? HELL, SOMEBODY GET ME A PRIEST. HEH HEH.
I'LL SEE WHAT I CAN DO.

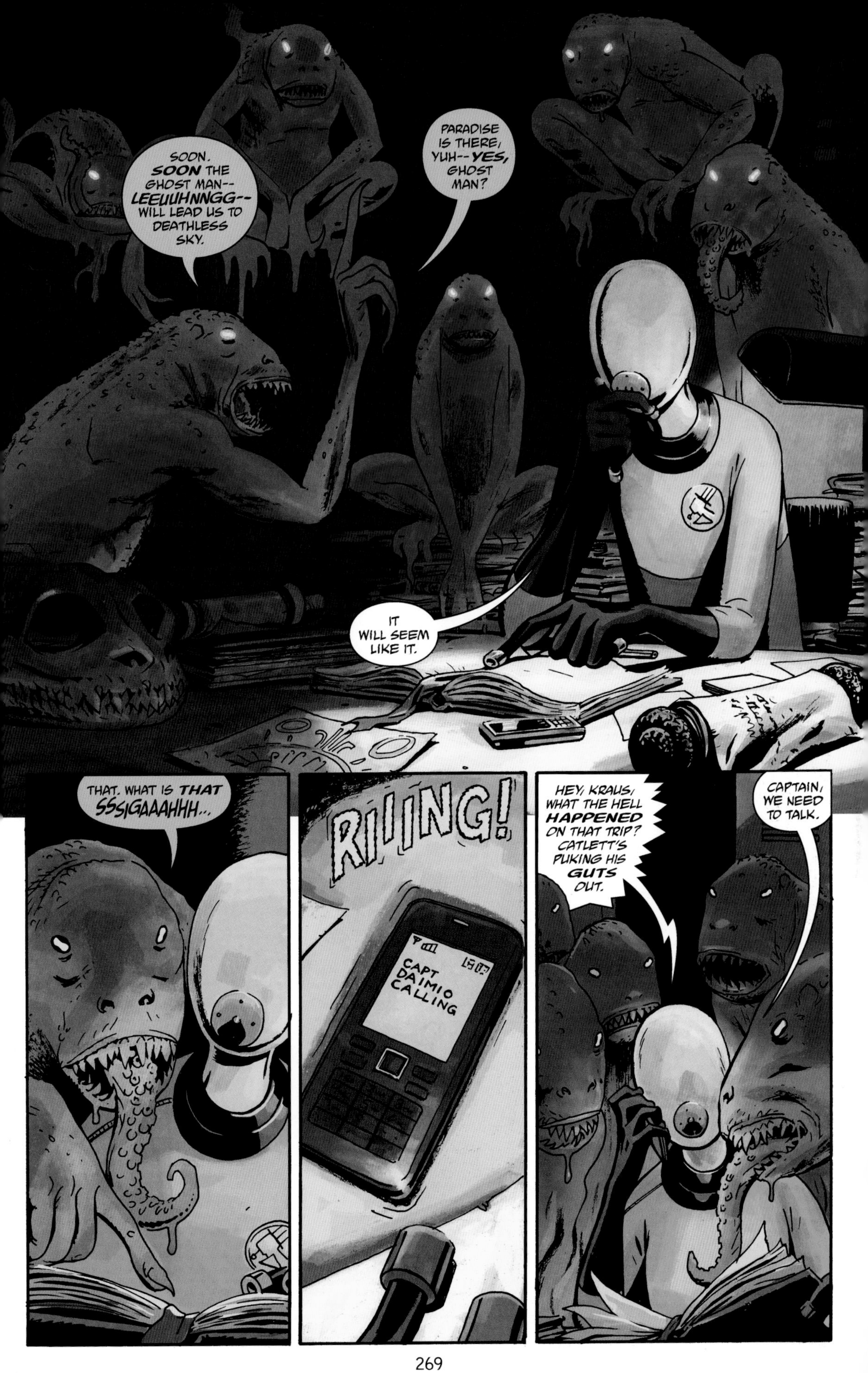
SOON. SOON THE GHOST MAN-- LEEUUHNNGG-- WILL LEAD US TO DEATHLESS SKY.
PARADISE IS THERE, YUH--YES, GHOST MAN?
IT WILL SEEM LIKE IT.
THAT. WHAT IS THAT SSSIGAAAHHH...
RIIING!
CAPT DAIMIO CALLING
HEY, KRAUS, WHAT THE HELL HAPPENED ON THAT TRIP? CATLETT'S PUKING HIS GUTS OUT.
CAPTAIN, WE NEED TO TALK.

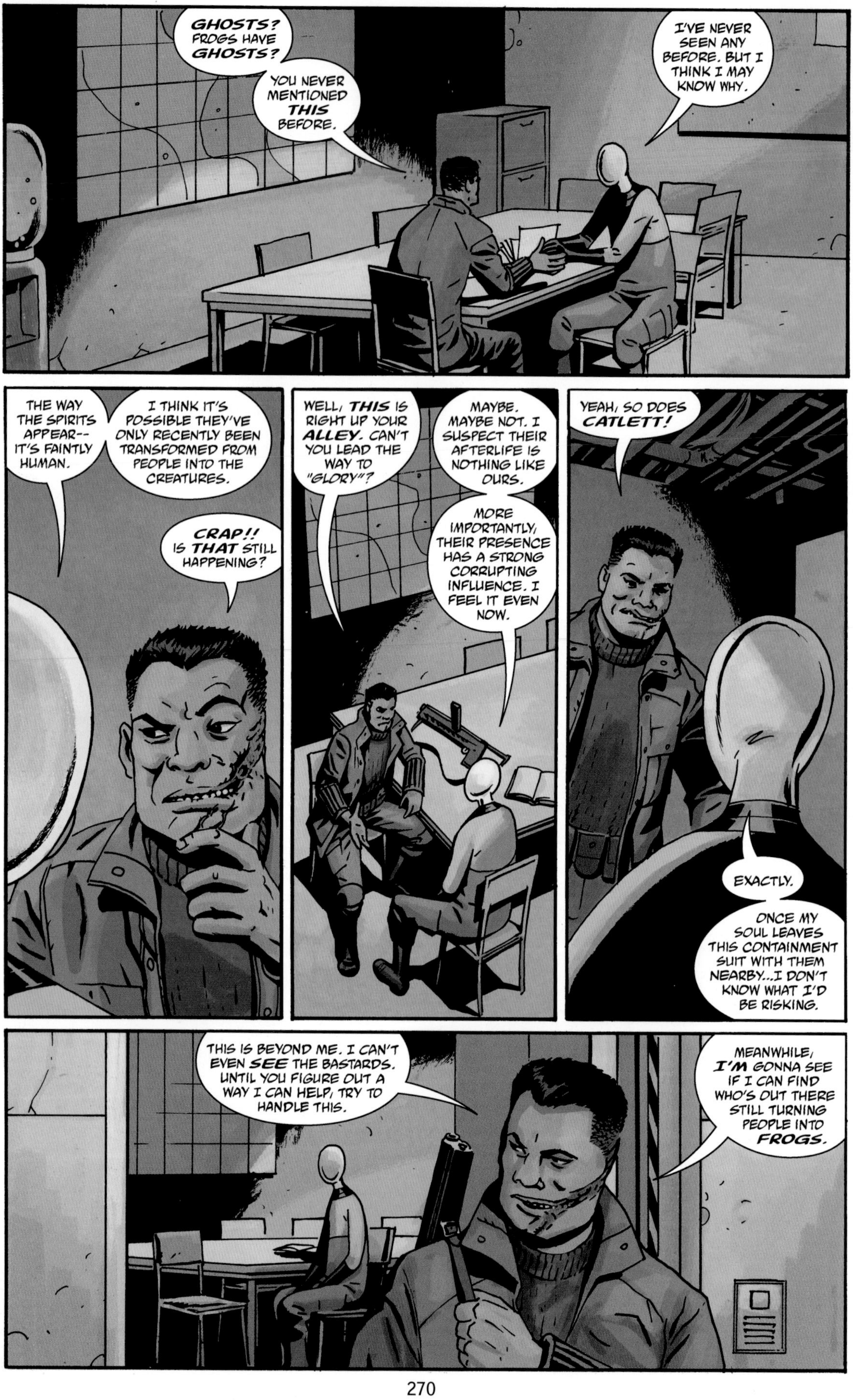
GHOSTS? FROGS HAVE GHOSTS?
YOU NEVER MENTIONED THIS BEFORE.
I'VE NEVER SEEN ANY BEFORE. BUT I THINK I MAY KNOW WHY.
THE WAY THE SPIRITS APPEAR-- IT'S FAINTLY HUMAN.
I THINK IT'S POSSIBLE THEY'VE ONLY RECENTLY BEEN TRANSFORMED FROM PEOPLE INTO THE CREATURES.
CRAP!! IS THAT STILL HAPPENING?
WELL, THIS IS RIGHT UP YOUR ALLEY. CAN'T YOU LEAD THE WAY TO "GLORY"?
MAYBE. MAYBE NOT. I SUSPECT THEIR AFTERLIFE IS NOTHING LIKE OURS.
MORE IMPORTANTLY, THEIR PRESENCE HAS A STRONG CORRUPTING INFLUENCE. I FEEL IT EVEN NOW.
YEAH, SO DOES CATLETT!
EXACTLY.
ONCE MY SOUL LEAVES THIS CONTAINMENT SUIT WITH THEM NEARBY...I DON'T KNOW WHAT I'D BE RISKING.
THIS IS BEYOND ME. I CAN'T EVEN SEE THE BASTARDS. UNTIL YOU FIGURE OUT A WAY I CAN HELP, TRY TO HANDLE THIS.
MEANWHILE, I'M GONNA SEE IF I CAN FIND WHO'S OUT THERE STILL TURNING PEOPLE INTO FROGS.

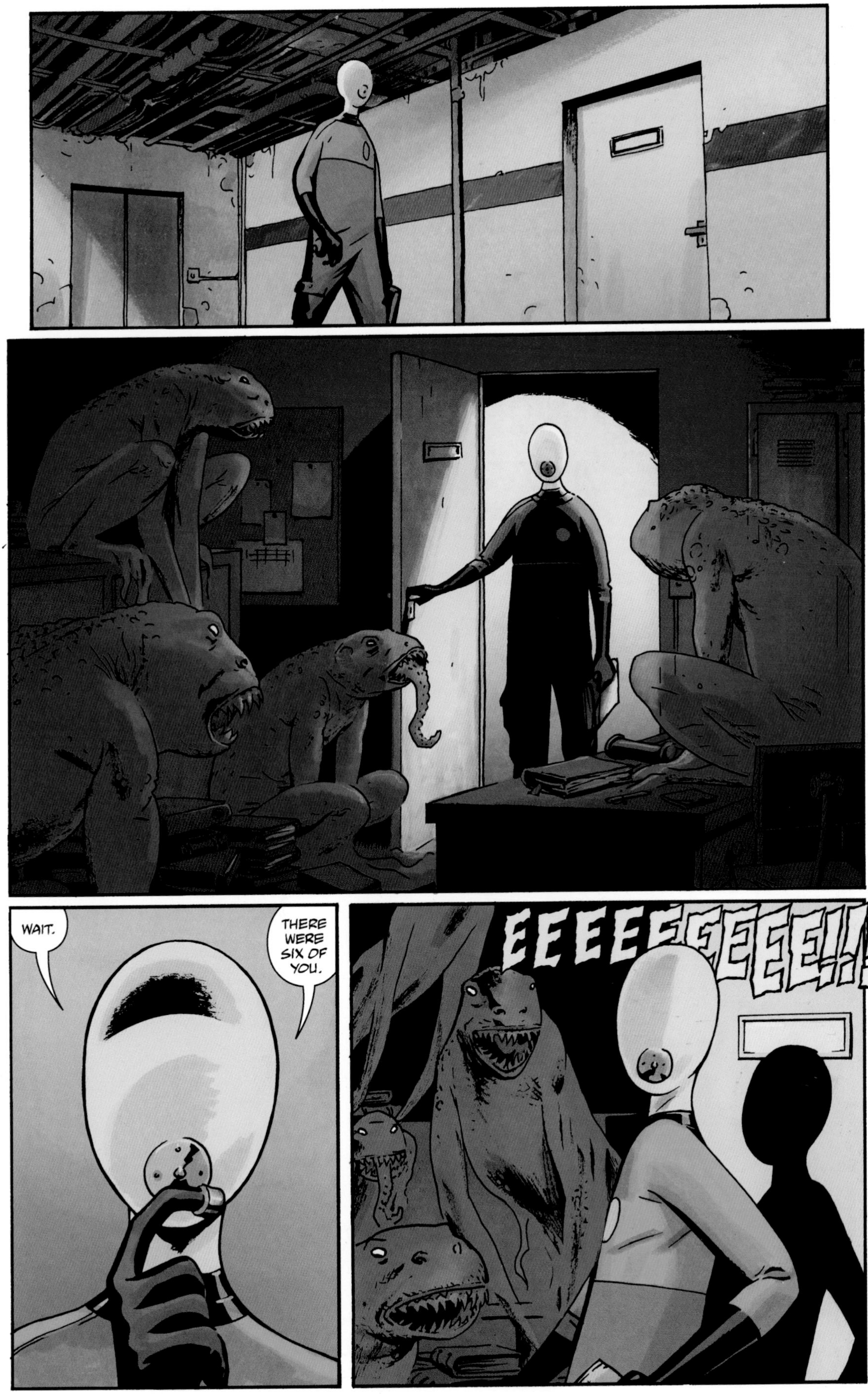
WAIT.
THERE WERE SIX OF YOU.
EEEEEEEEEE!!!

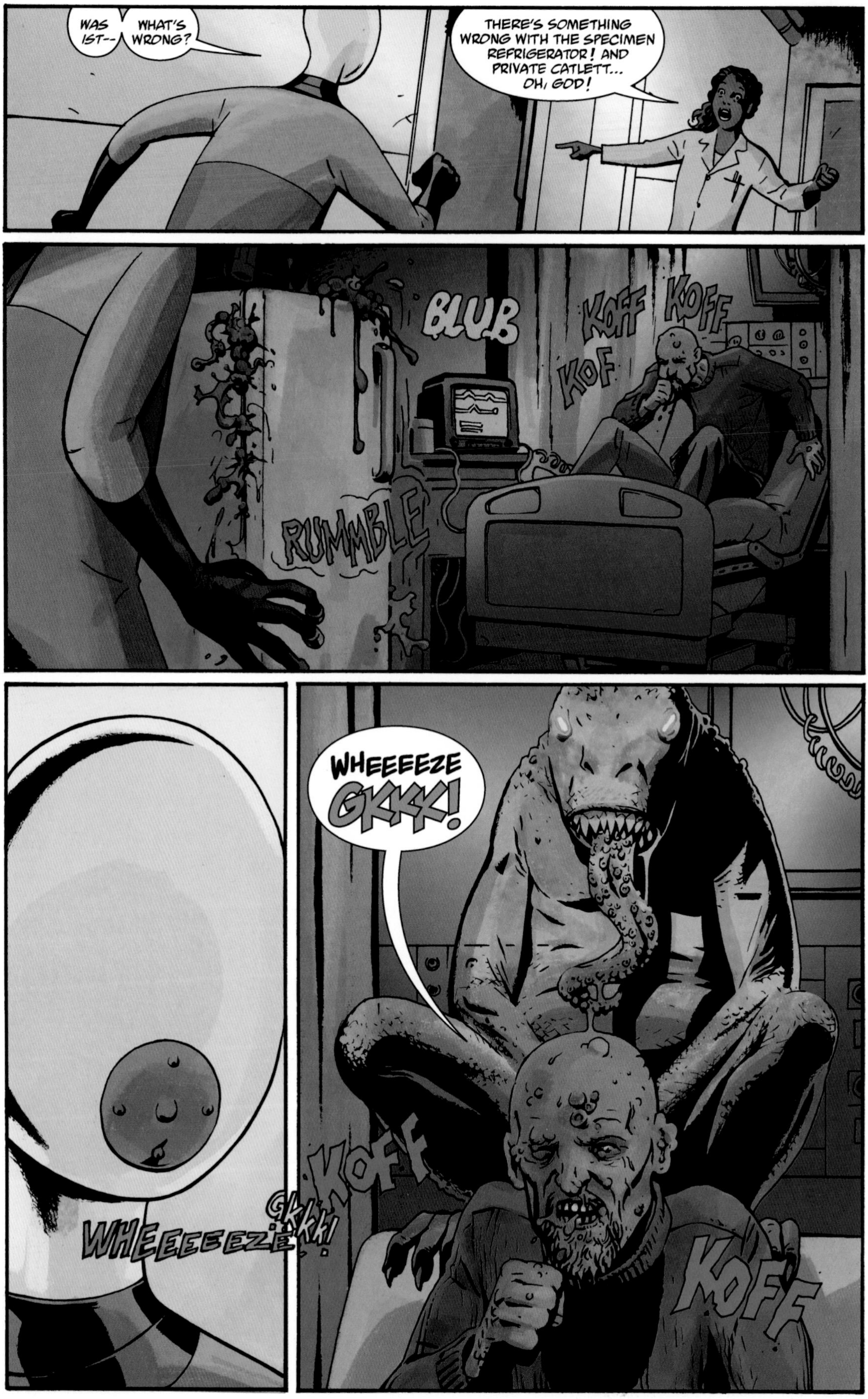
WAS IST--
WHAT'S WRONG?
THERE'S SOMETHING WRONG WITH THE SPECIMEN REFRIGERATOR! AND PRIVATE CATLETT... OH, GOD!
BLUB
KOFF KOFF
KOF
RUMMBLE
WHEEEEZE GKKK!
KOFF
WHEEEEEZE GKKK!
KOFF

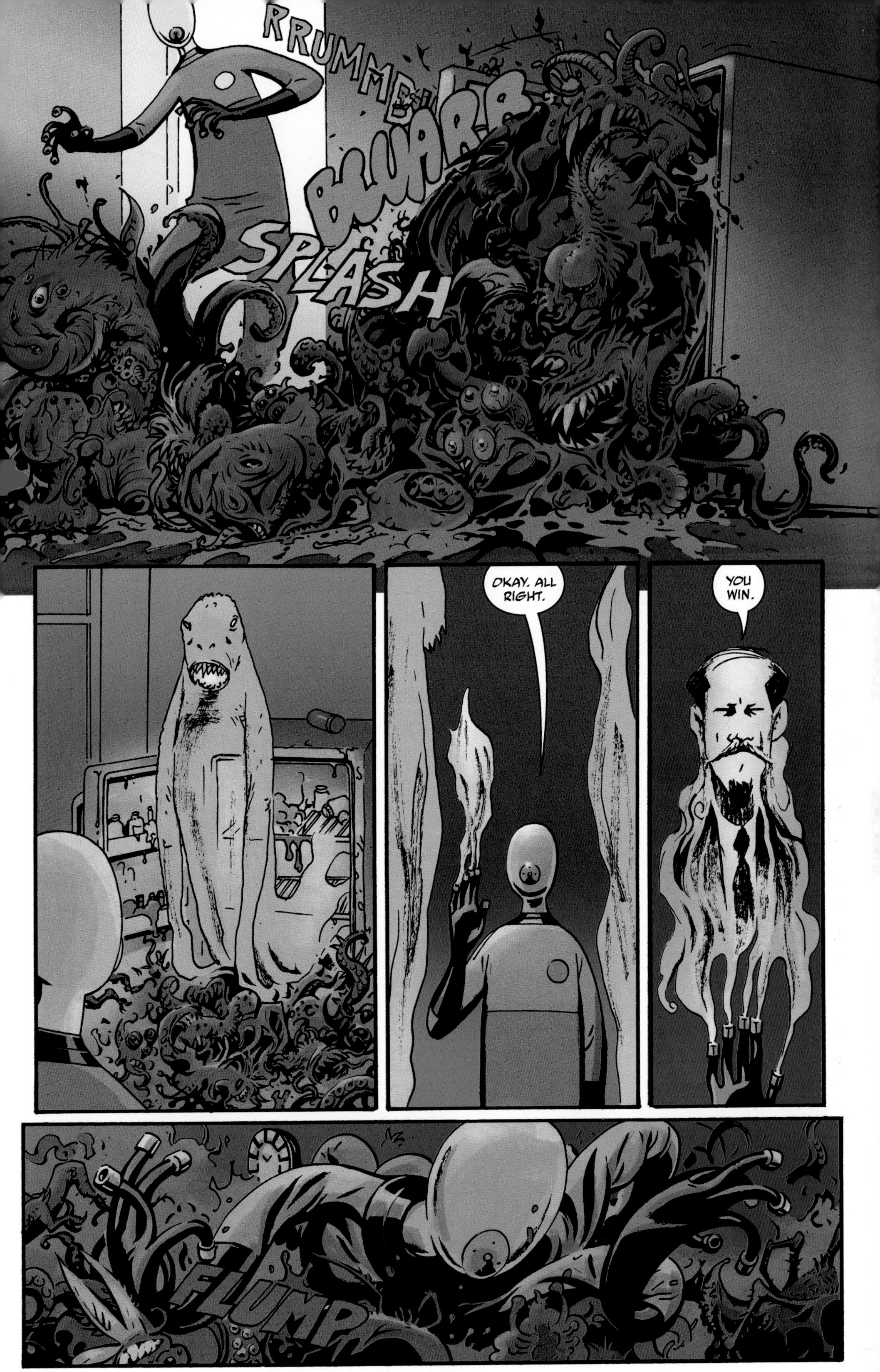
RRUMMBLE
BLUARB
SPLASH
OKAY. ALL RIGHT.
YOU WIN.
FLUMP

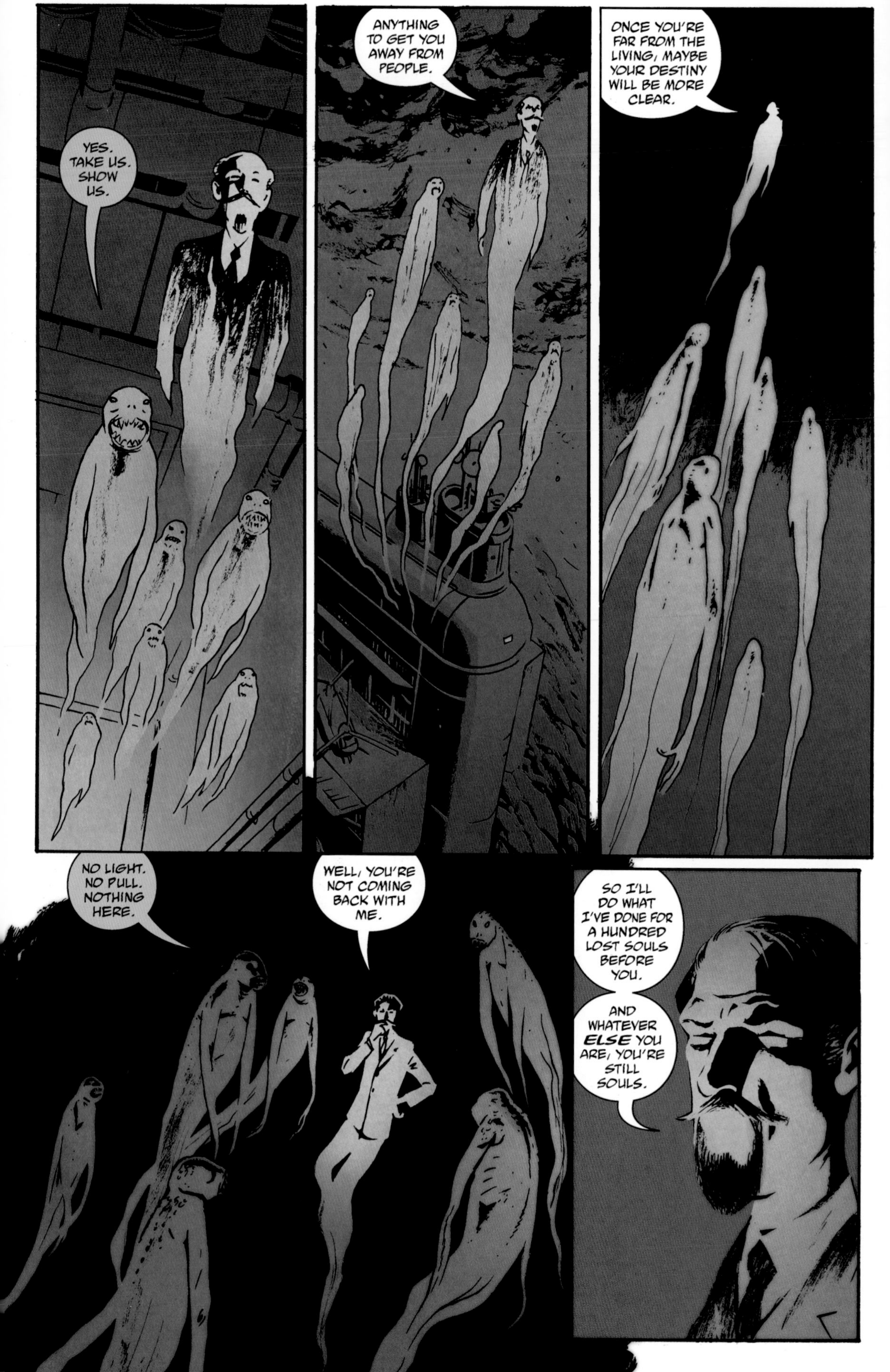
YES. TAKE US. SHOW US.
ANYTHING TO GET YOU AWAY FROM PEOPLE.
ONCE YOU'RE FAR FROM THE LIVING, MAYBE YOUR DESTINY WILL BE MORE CLEAR.
NO LIGHT. NO PULL. NOTHING HERE.
WELL, YOU'RE NOT COMING BACK WITH ME.
SO I'LL DO WHAT I'VE DONE FOR A HUNDRED LOST SOULS BEFORE YOU.
AND WHATEVER ELSE YOU ARE, YOU'RE STILL SOULS.

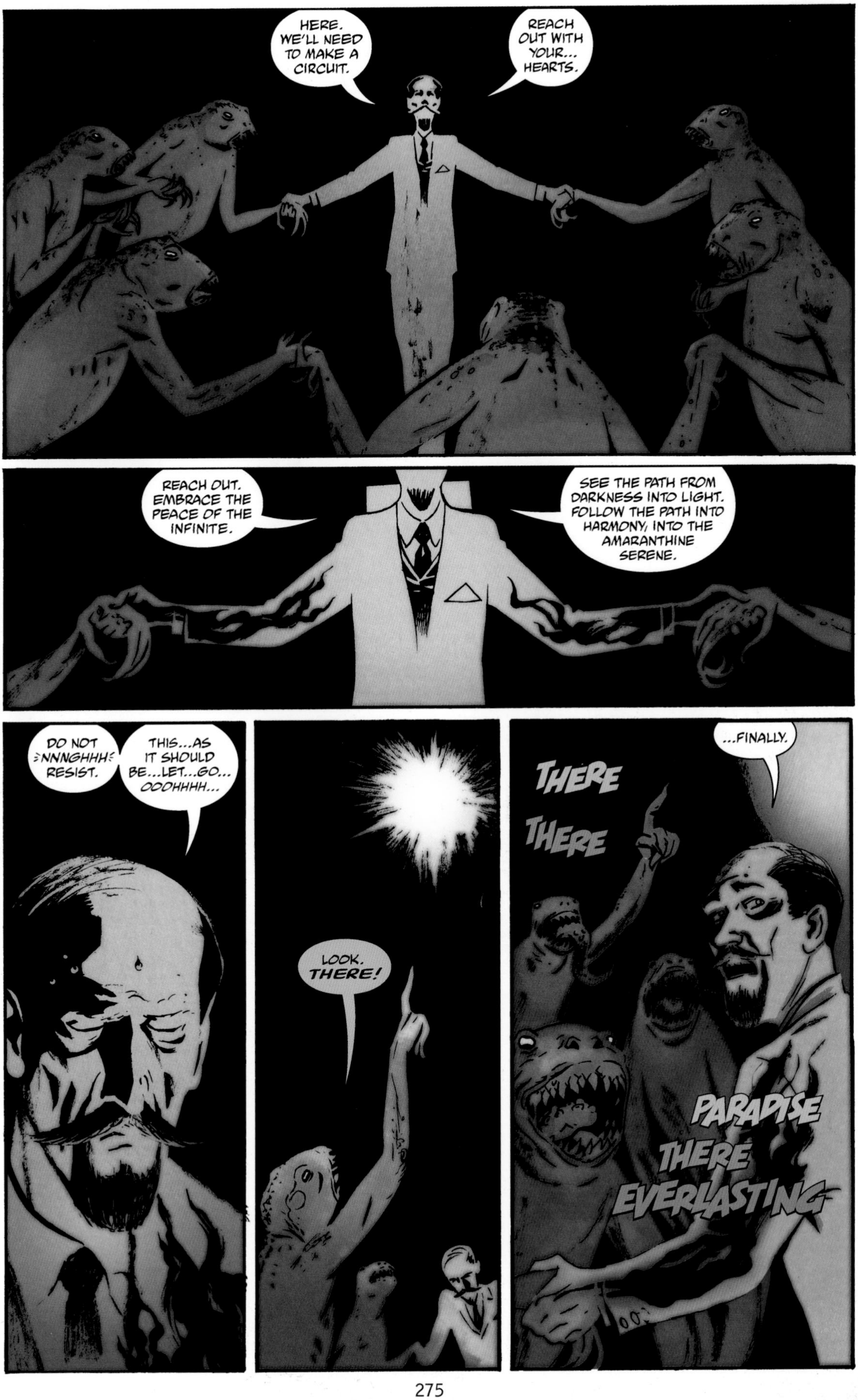
HERE. WE'LL NEED TO MAKE A CIRCUIT.
REACH OUT WITH YOUR... HEARTS.
REACH OUT. EMBRACE THE PEACE OF THE INFINITE.
SEE THE PATH FROM DARKNESS INTO LIGHT. FOLLOW THE PATH INTO HARMONY, INTO THE AMARANTHINE SERENE.
DO NOT NNNGHHH RESIST.
THIS...AS IT SHOULD BE...LET...GO... OOOHHHH...
LOOK. THERE!
THERE
THERE
...FINALLY.
PARADISE
THERE
EVERLASTING

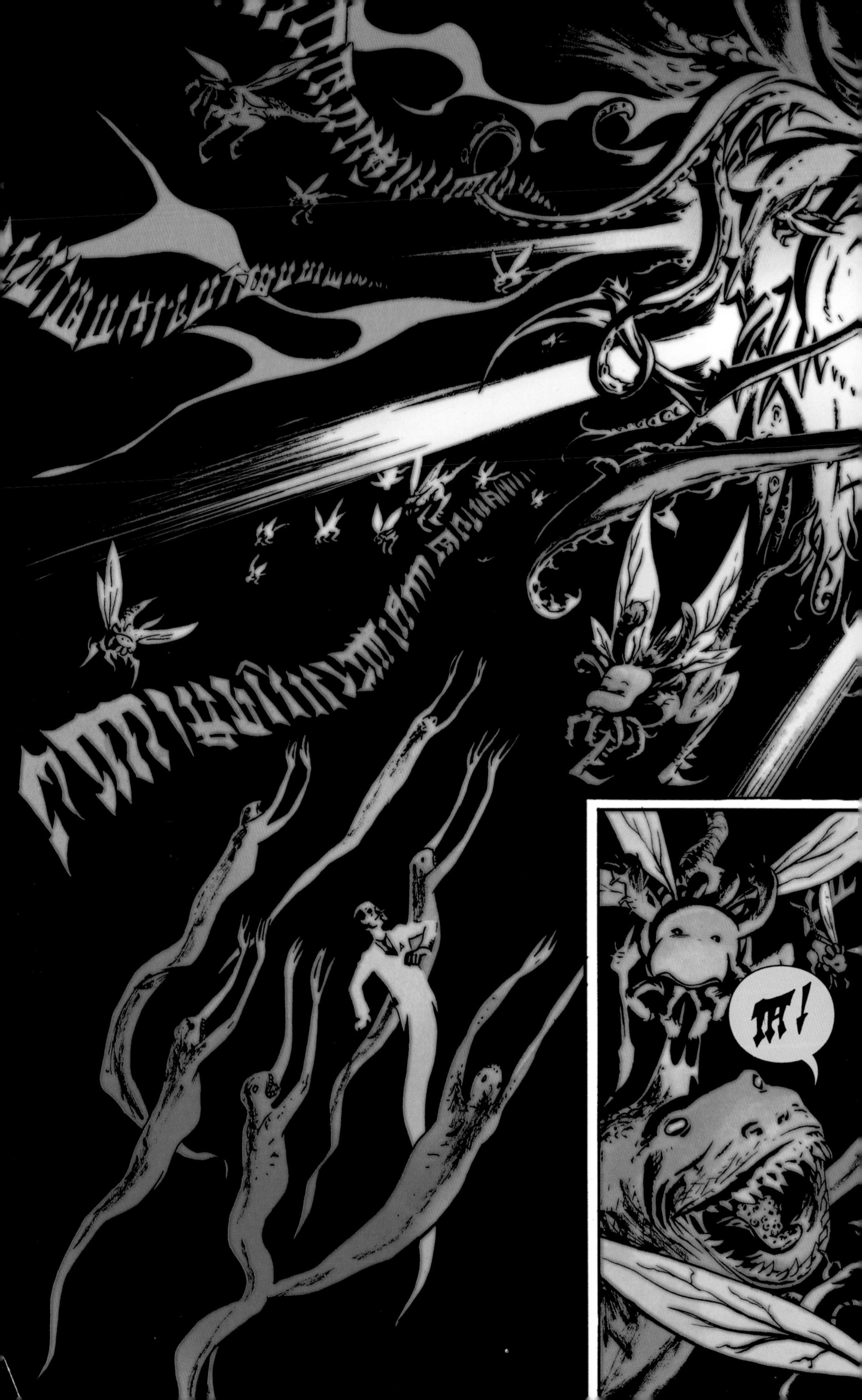
IA!

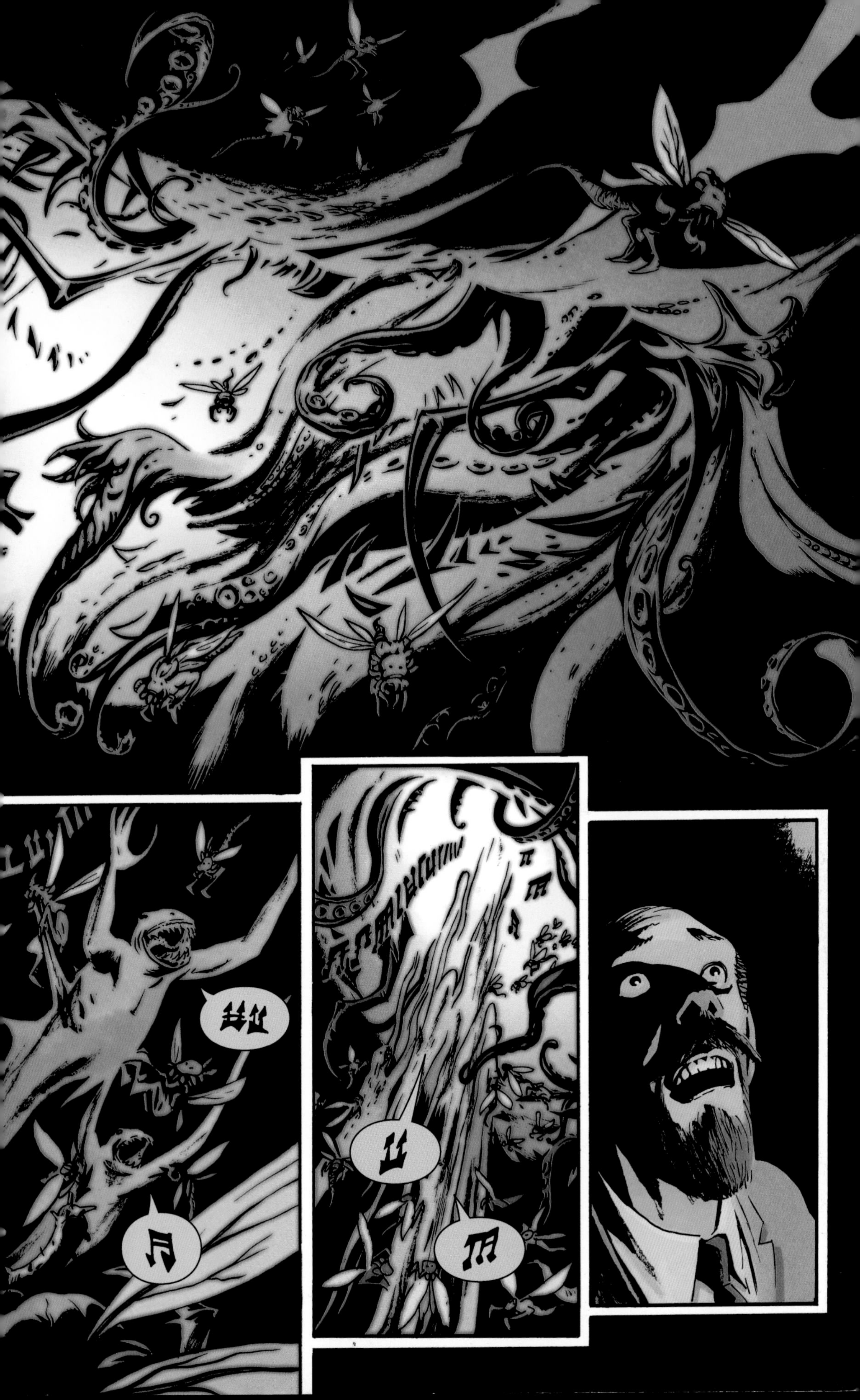

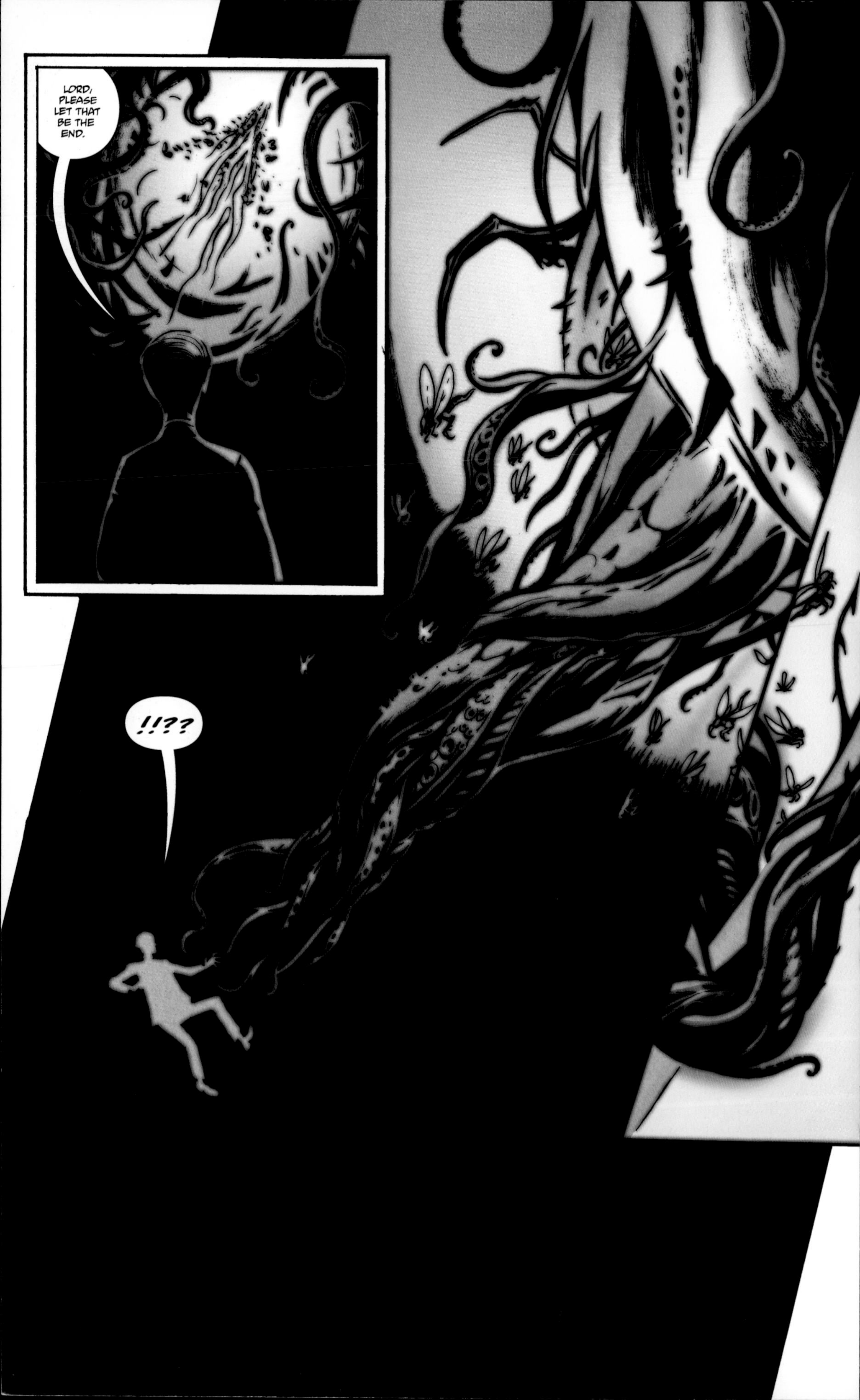
LORD, PLEASE LET THAT BE THE END.
!!??

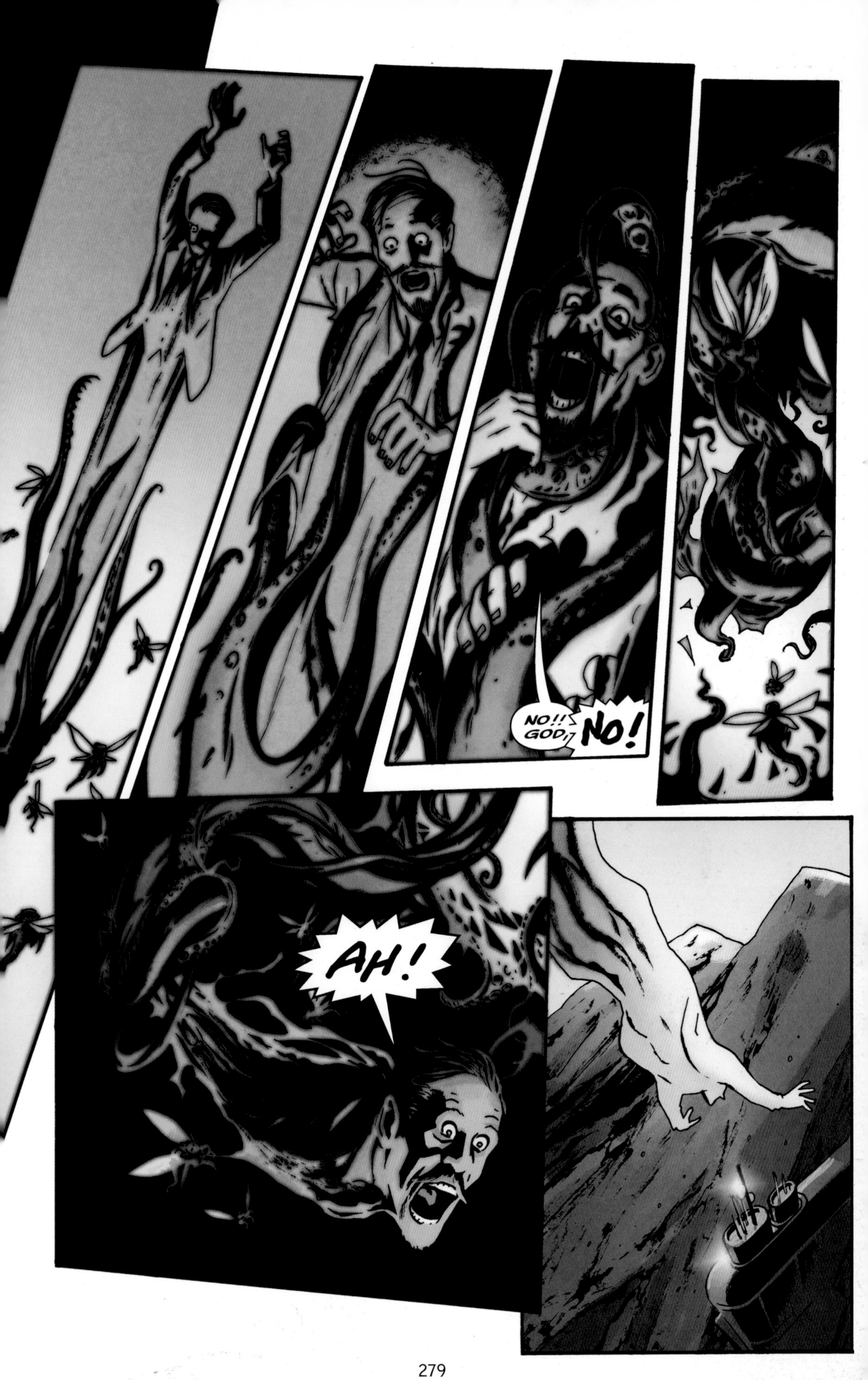
NO!! GOD,
NO!
AH!

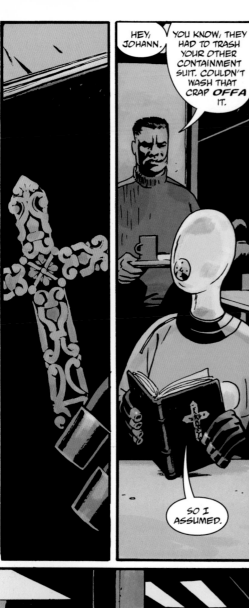

HEY, JOHANN.

YOU KNOW, THEY HAD TO TRASH YOUR OTHER CONTAINMENT SUIT. COULDN'T WASH THAT CRAP *OFFA* IT.

SO I ASSUMED.

AND CATLETT'S DOING MUCH BETTER.

LISTEN, WHAT YOU SAID YESTERDAY ABOUT YOUR SOUL BEING AT RISK. I NEVER *THOUGHT* MUCH ABOUT THAT STUFF IN THE CORPS.

JUST TOOK IT FOR *GRANTED*, I GUESS.

NOT SO EASY TO DO THAT *HERE*, IS IT?

LESS AND LESS SO EVERY DAY, CAPTAIN.

THE END

BOOK THREE

THE BLACK FLAME

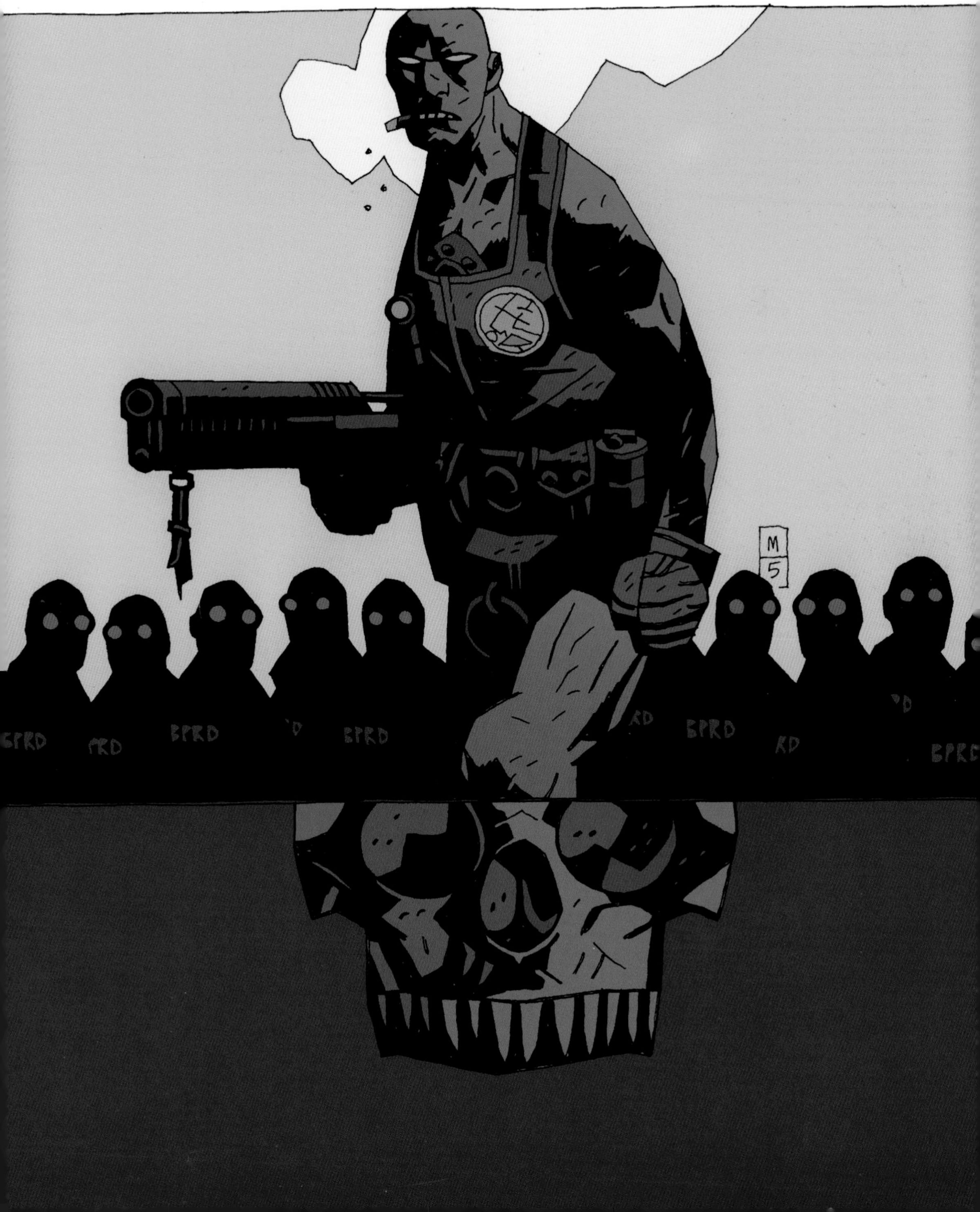
BPRD
BPRD
BPRD

STORY BY MIKE MIGNOLA & JOHN ARCUDI

ART BY GUY DAVIS

COLORS BY DAVE STEWART

LETTERS BY CLEM ROBINS

CHAPTER ONE

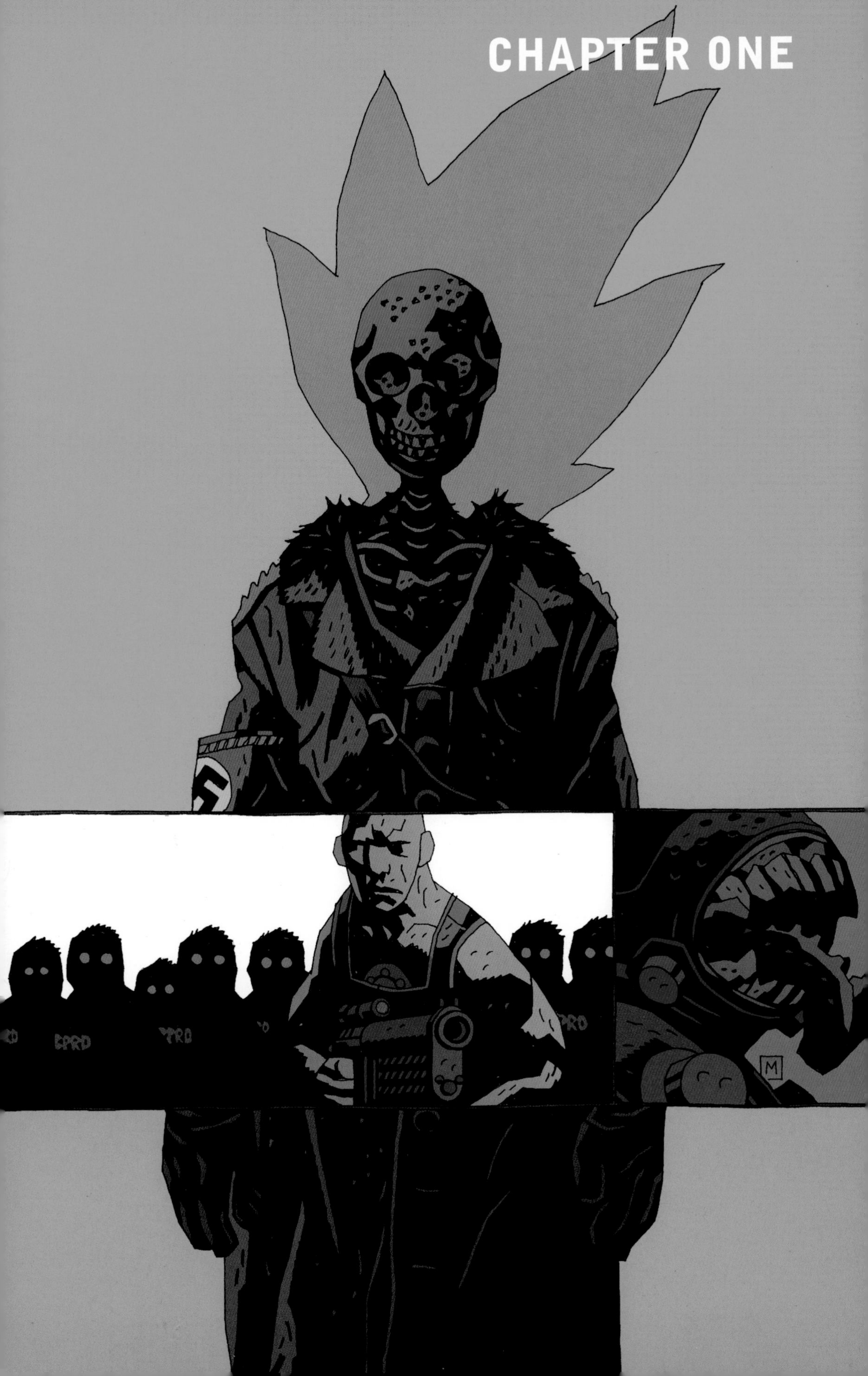
BPRD

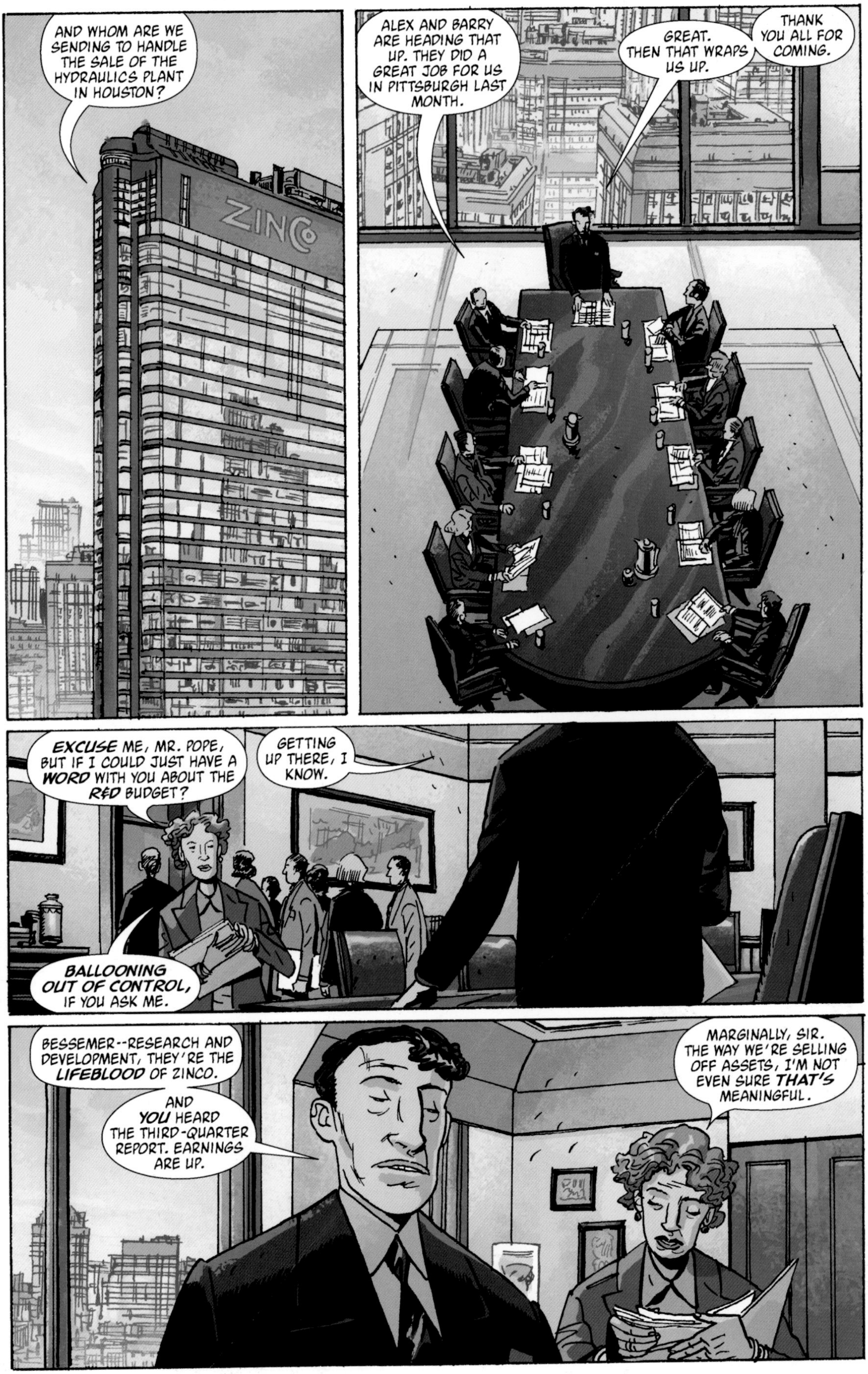
AND WHOM ARE WE SENDING TO HANDLE THE SALE OF THE HYDRAULICS PLANT IN HOUSTON?
ZINCO
ALEX AND BARRY ARE HEADING THAT UP. THEY DID A GREAT JOB FOR US IN PITTSBURGH LAST MONTH.
GREAT. THEN THAT WRAPS US UP.
THANK YOU ALL FOR COMING.
EXCUSE ME, MR. POPE, BUT IF I COULD JUST HAVE A WORD WITH YOU ABOUT THE R&D BUDGET?
GETTING UP THERE, I KNOW.
BALLOONING OUT OF CONTROL, IF YOU ASK ME.
BESSEMER--RESEARCH AND DEVELOPMENT, THEY'RE THE LIFEBLOOD OF ZINCO.
AND YOU HEARD THE THIRD-QUARTER REPORT. EARNINGS ARE UP.
MARGINALLY, SIR. THE WAY WE'RE SELLING OFF ASSETS, I'M NOT EVEN SURE THAT'S MEANINGFUL.

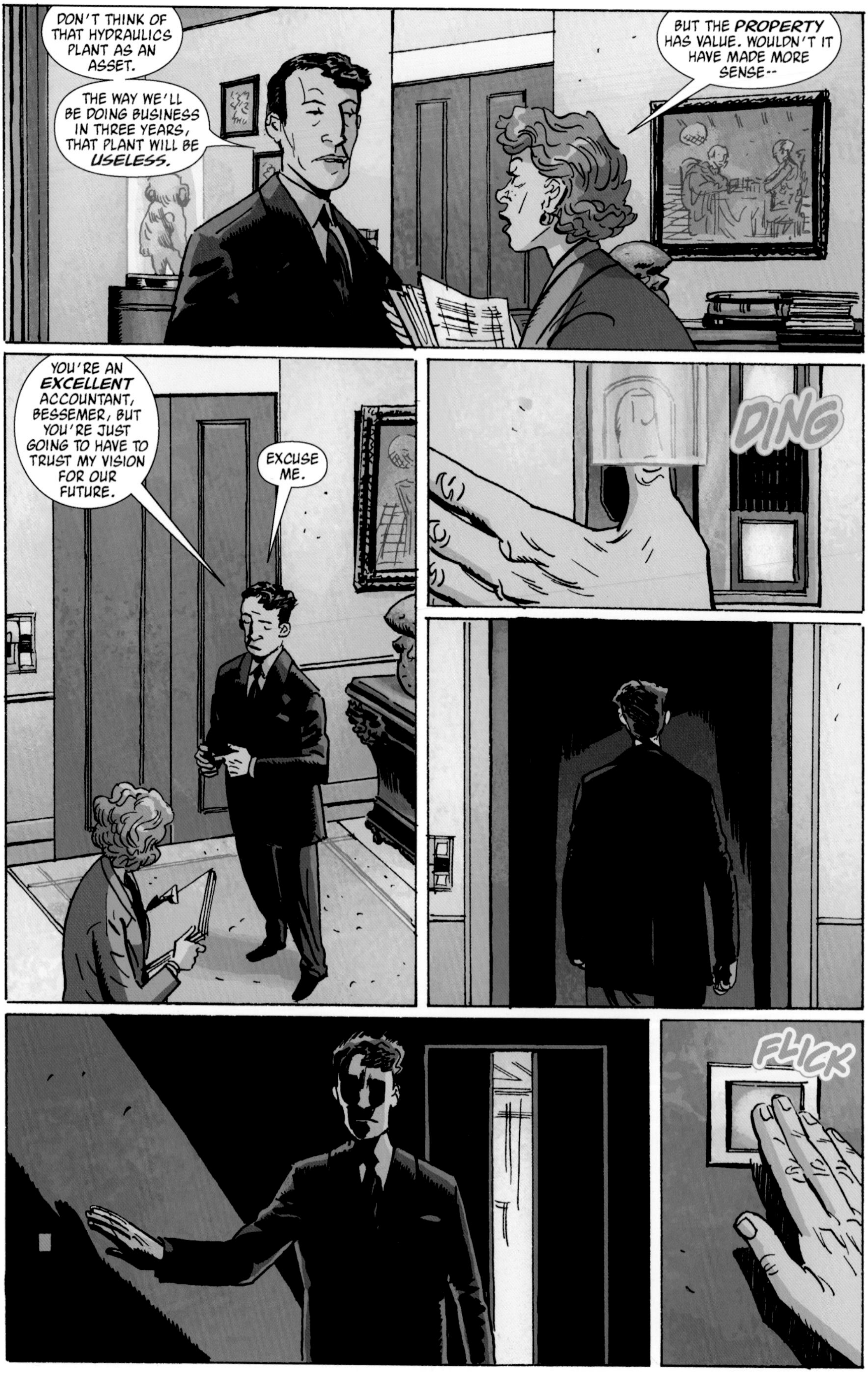
DON'T THINK OF THAT HYDRAULICS PLANT AS AN ASSET.
THE WAY WE'LL BE DOING BUSINESS IN THREE YEARS, THAT PLANT WILL BE USELESS.
BUT THE PROPERTY HAS VALUE. WOULDN'T IT HAVE MADE MORE SENSE--
YOU'RE AN EXCELLENT ACCOUNTANT, BESSEMER, BUT YOU'RE JUST GOING TO HAVE TO TRUST MY VISION FOR OUR FUTURE.
EXCUSE ME.
DING
FLICK

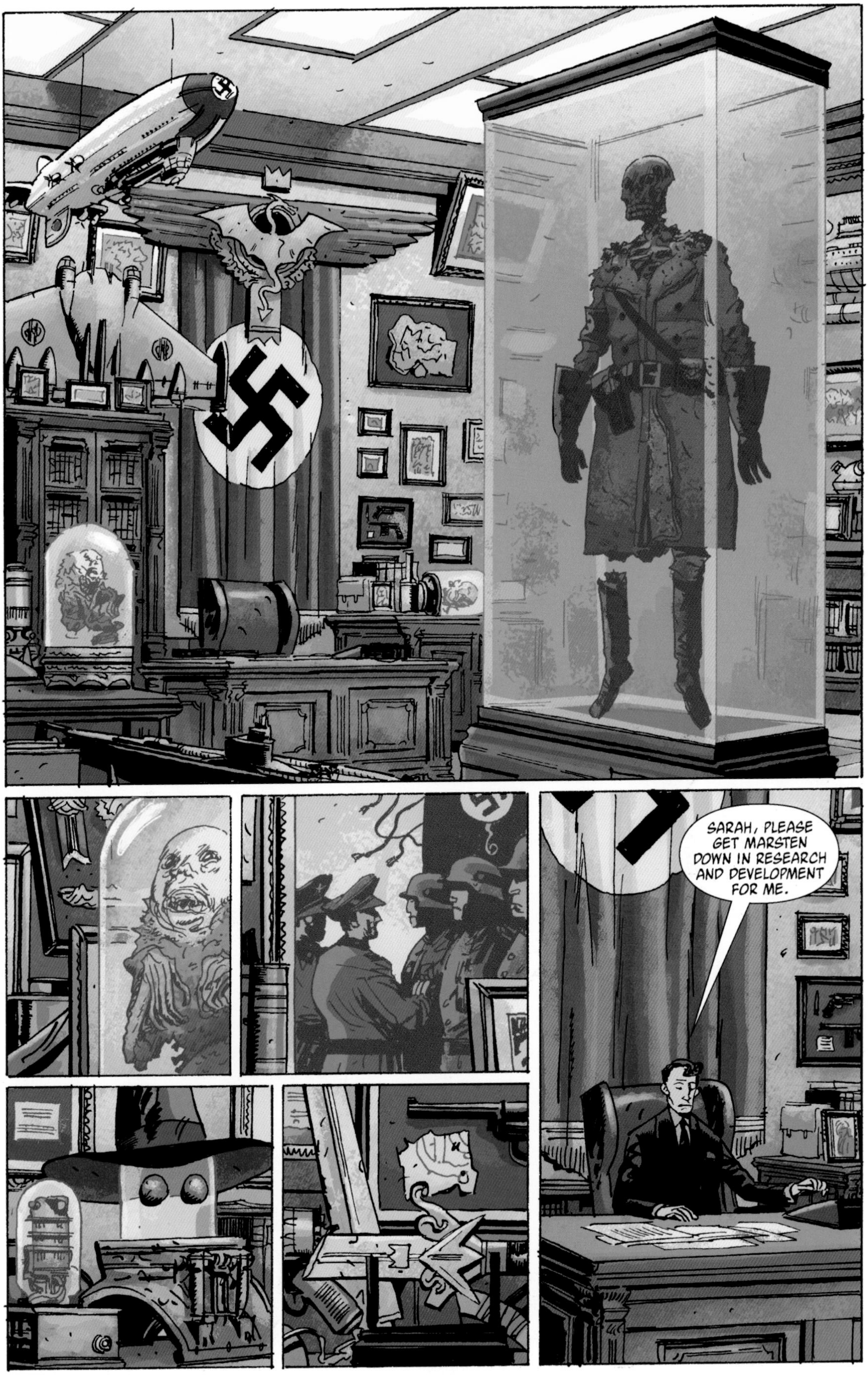
SARAH, PLEASE GET MARSTEN DOWN IN RESEARCH AND DEVELOPMENT FOR ME.

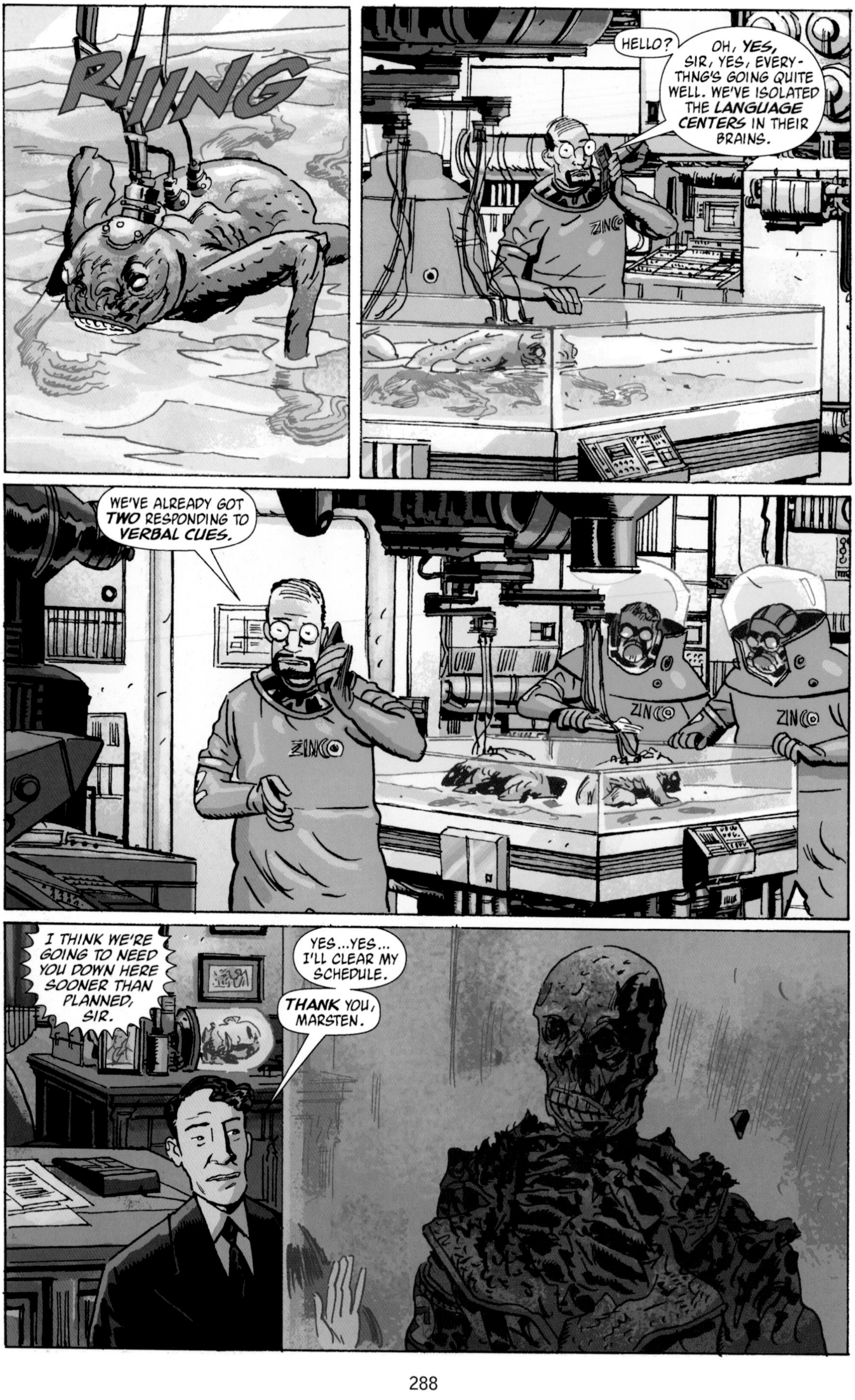
RIIING
HELLO?
OH, YES, SIR, YES, EVERY-THNG'S GOING QUITE WELL. WE'VE ISOLATED THE LANGUAGE CENTERS IN THEIR BRAINS.
ZINCO
WE'VE ALREADY GOT TWO RESPONDING TO VERBAL CUES.
ZINCO
ZINCO
ZINCO
I THINK WE'RE GOING TO NEED YOU DOWN HERE SOONER THAN PLANNED, SIR.
YES...YES... I'LL CLEAR MY SCHEDULE.
THANK YOU, MARSTEN.

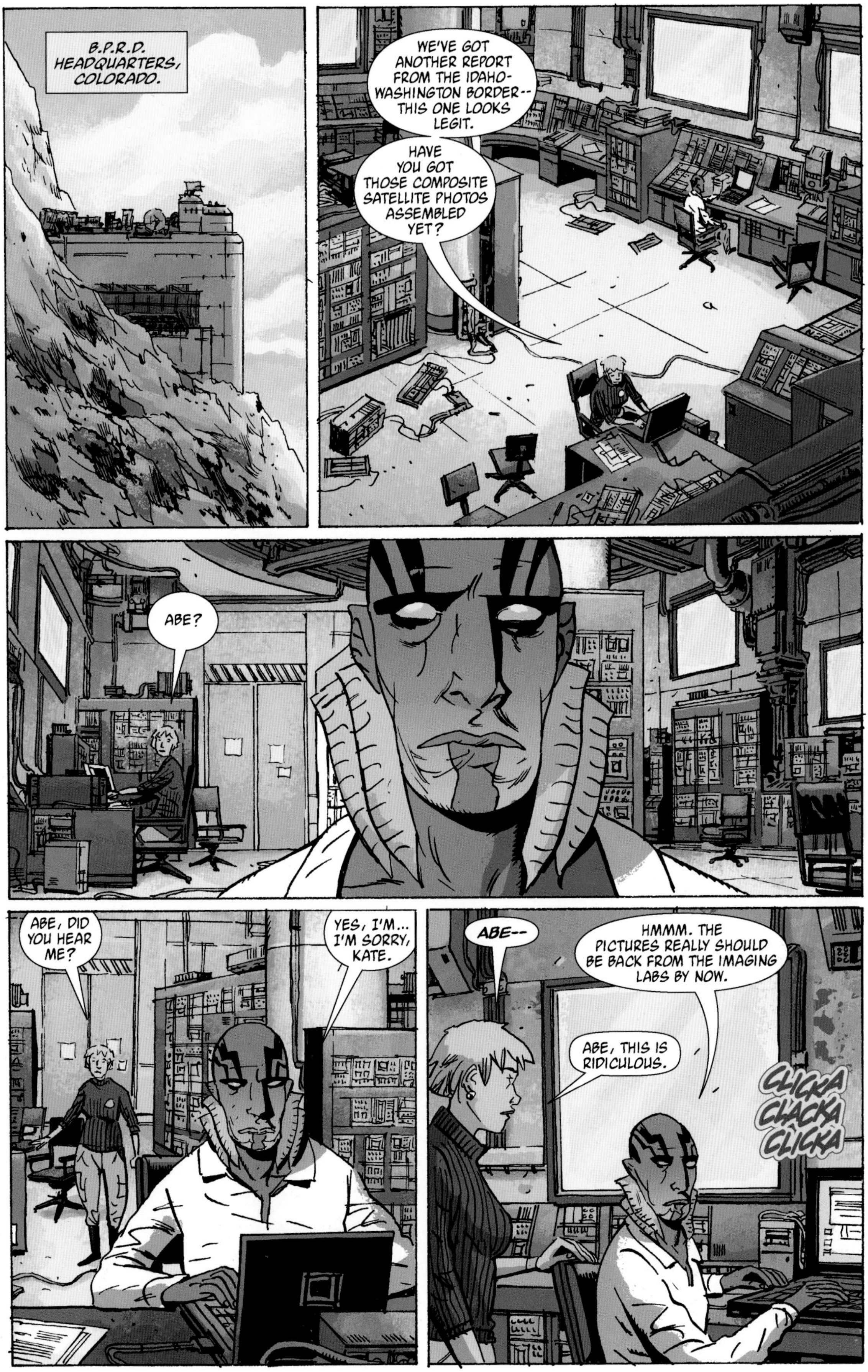
B.P.R.D. HEADQUARTERS, COLORADO.
WE'VE GOT ANOTHER REPORT FROM THE IDAHO-WASHINGTON BORDER--THIS ONE LOOKS LEGIT.
HAVE YOU GOT THOSE COMPOSITE SATELLITE PHOTOS ASSEMBLED YET?
ABE?
ABE, DID YOU HEAR ME?
YES, I'M... I'M SORRY, KATE.
ABE--
HMMM. THE PICTURES REALLY SHOULD BE BACK FROM THE IMAGING LABS BY NOW.
ABE, THIS IS RIDICULOUS.
CLICKA CLACKA CLICKA

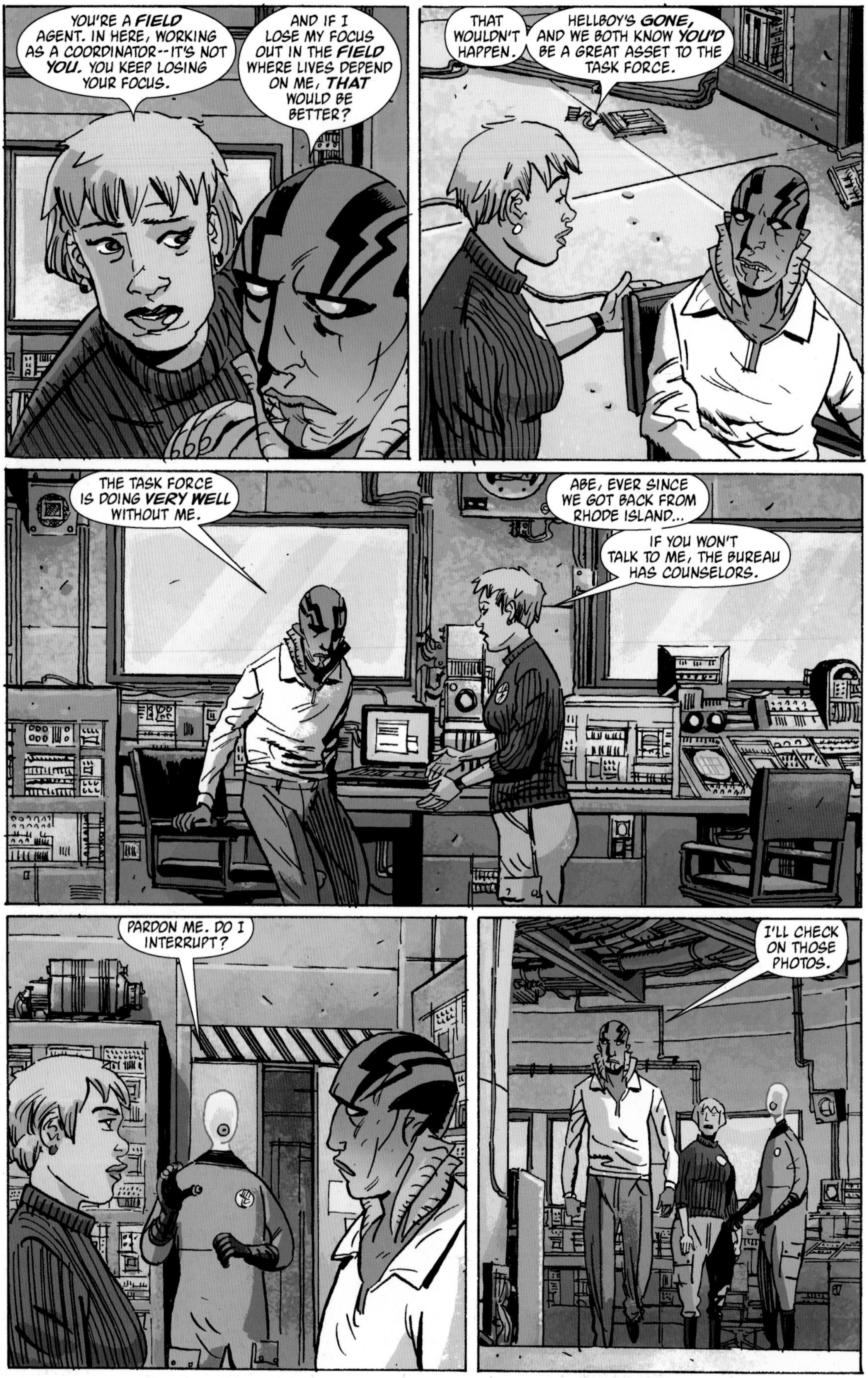
YOU'RE A FIELD AGENT. IN HERE, WORKING AS A COORDINATOR--IT'S NOT YOU. YOU KEEP LOSING YOUR FOCUS.
AND IF I LOSE MY FOCUS OUT IN THE FIELD WHERE LIVES DEPEND ON ME, THAT WOULD BE BETTER?
THAT WOULDN'T HAPPEN.
HELLBOY'S GONE, AND WE BOTH KNOW YOU'D BE A GREAT ASSET TO THE TASK FORCE.
THE TASK FORCE IS DOING VERY WELL WITHOUT ME.
ABE, EVER SINCE WE GOT BACK FROM RHODE ISLAND...
IF YOU WON'T TALK TO ME, THE BUREAU HAS COUNSELORS.
PARDON ME. DO I INTERRUPT?
I'LL CHECK ON THOSE PHOTOS.

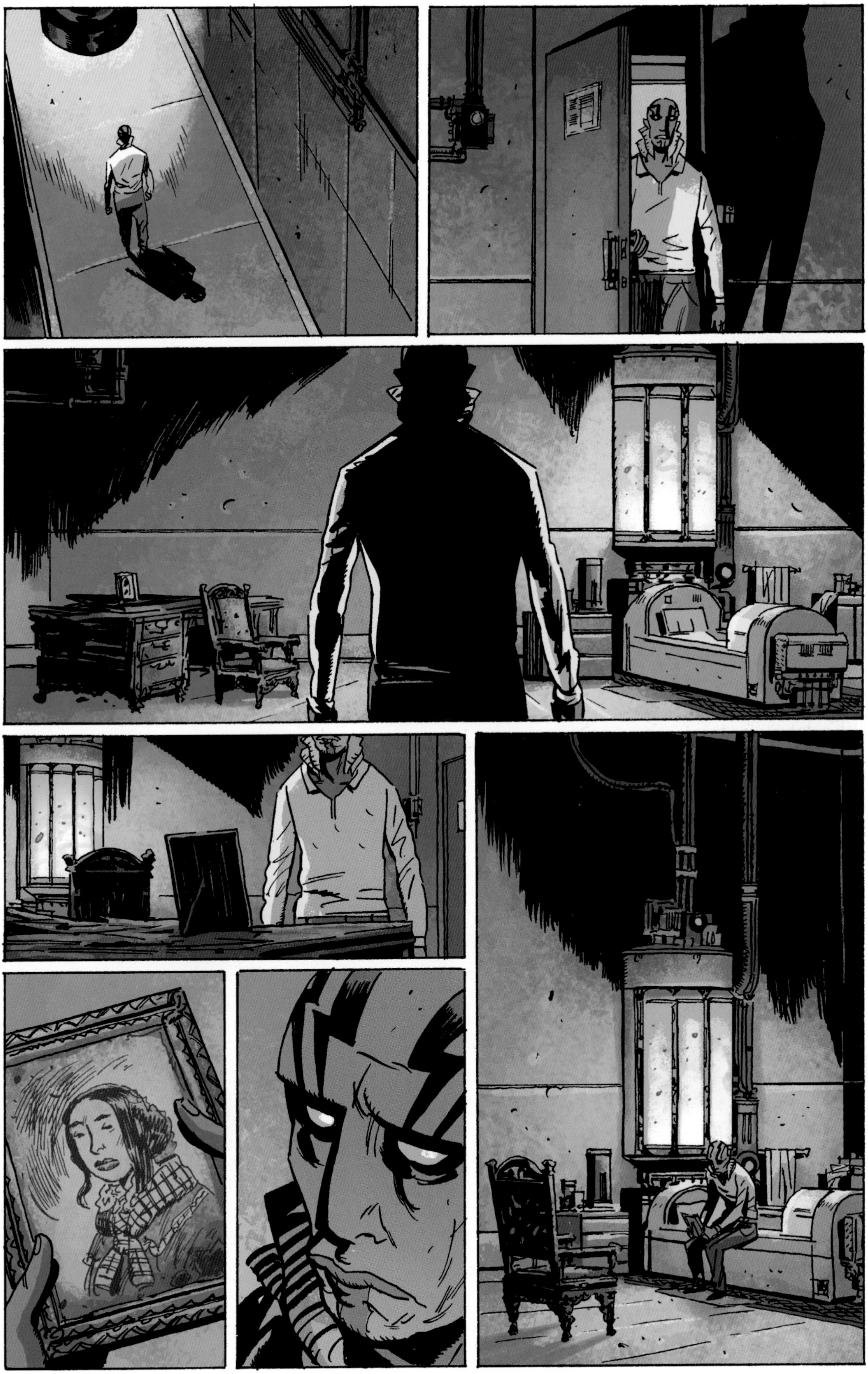

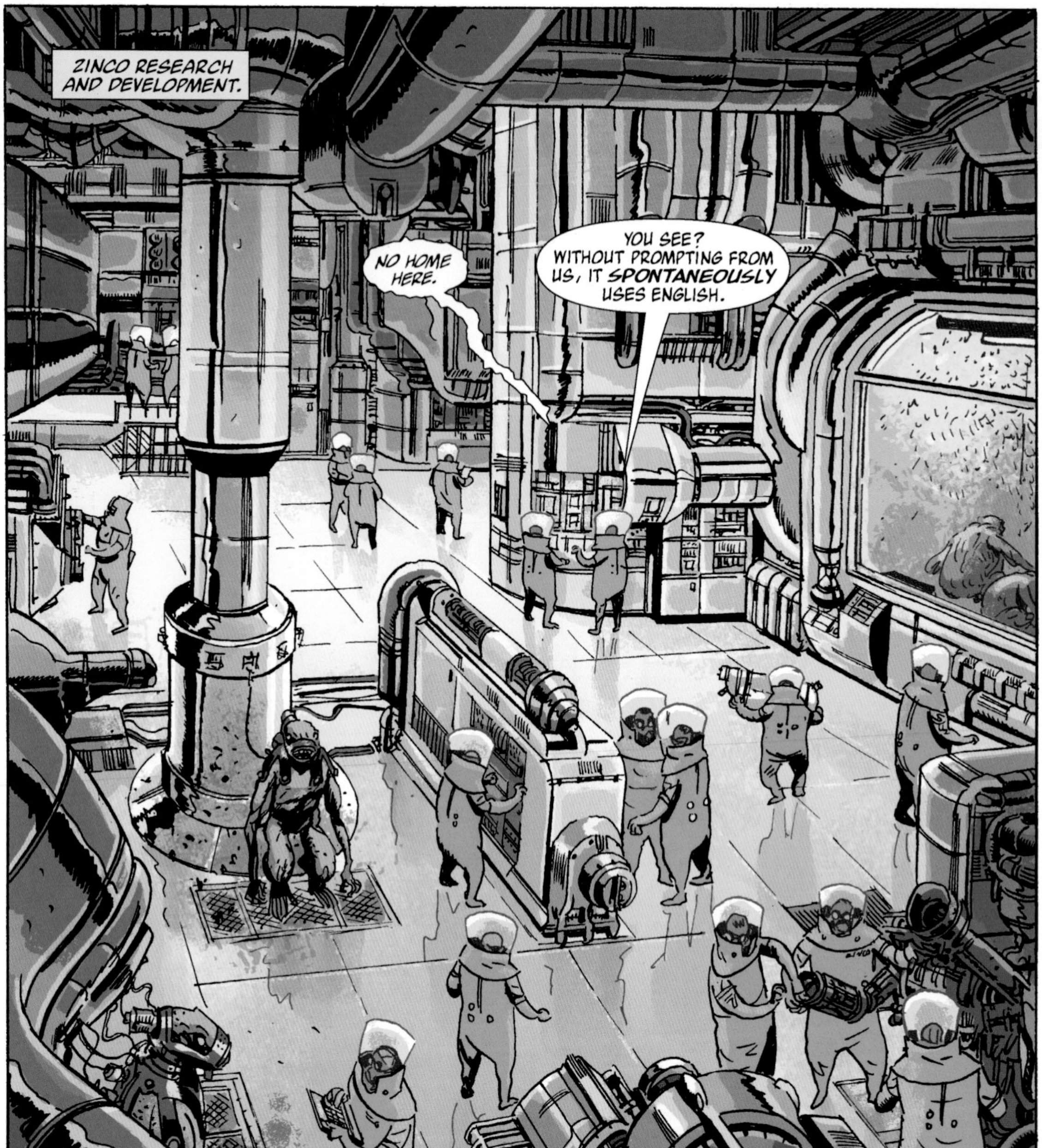
ZINCO RESEARCH AND DEVELOPMENT.
NO HOME HERE.
YOU SEE? WITHOUT PROMPTING FROM US, IT SPONTANEOUSLY USES ENGLISH.

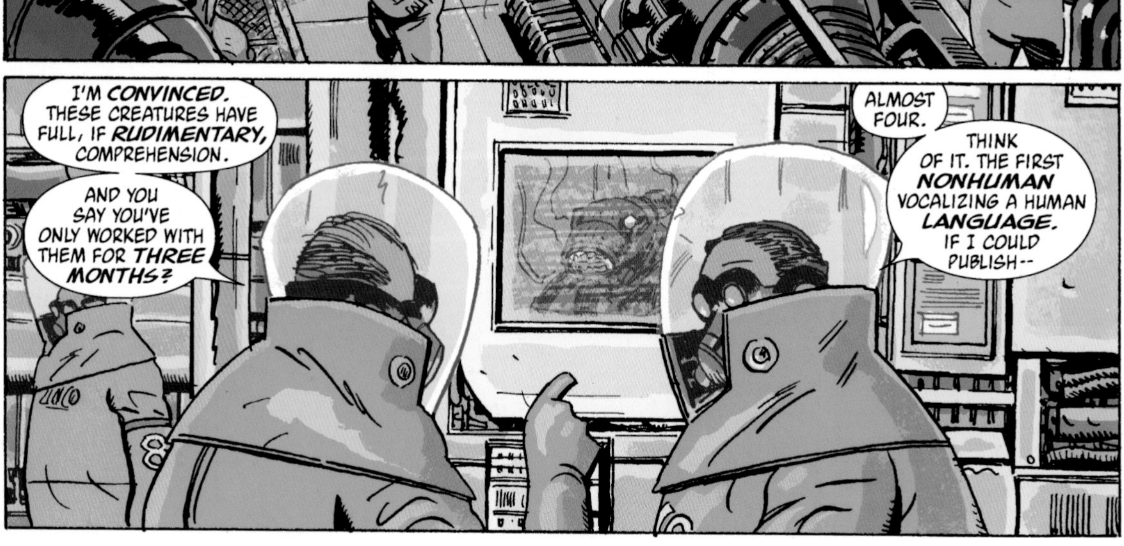
I'M CONVINCED. THESE CREATURES HAVE FULL, IF RUDIMENTARY, COMPREHENSION.
AND YOU SAY YOU'VE ONLY WORKED WITH THEM FOR THREE MONTHS?
ALMOST FOUR.
THINK OF IT. THE FIRST NONHUMAN VOCALIZING A HUMAN LANGUAGE. IF I COULD PUBLISH--

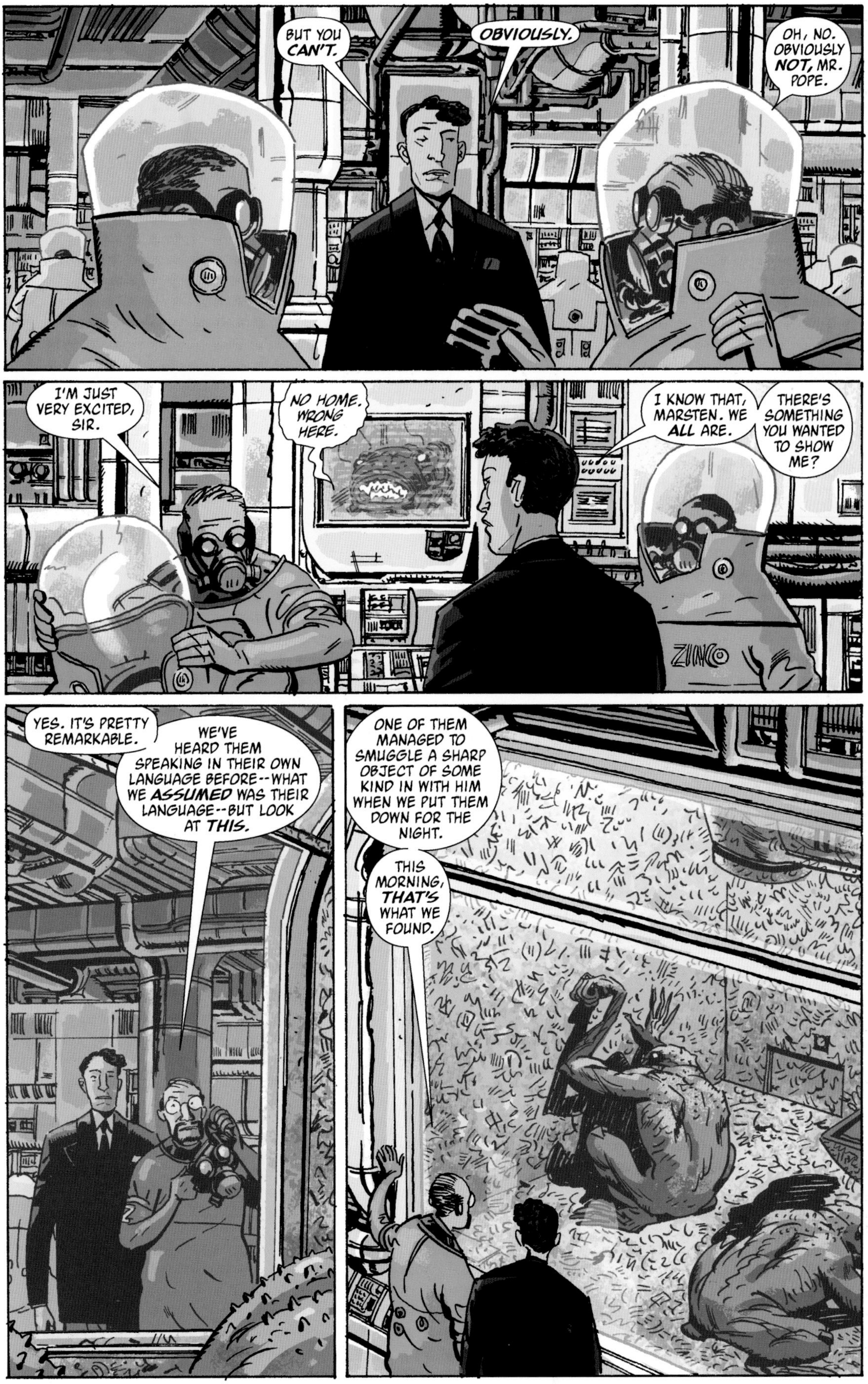
BUT YOU CAN'T.
OBVIOUSLY.
OH, NO. OBVIOUSLY NOT, MR. POPE.
I'M JUST VERY EXCITED, SIR.
NO HOME. WRONG HERE.
I KNOW THAT, MARSTEN. WE ALL ARE.
THERE'S SOMETHING YOU WANTED TO SHOW ME?
ZINCO
YES. IT'S PRETTY REMARKABLE.
WE'VE HEARD THEM SPEAKING IN THEIR OWN LANGUAGE BEFORE--WHAT WE ASSUMED WAS THEIR LANGUAGE--BUT LOOK AT THIS.
ONE OF THEM MANAGED TO SMUGGLE A SHARP OBJECT OF SOME KIND IN WITH HIM WHEN WE PUT THEM DOWN FOR THE NIGHT.
THIS MORNING, THAT'S WHAT WE FOUND.

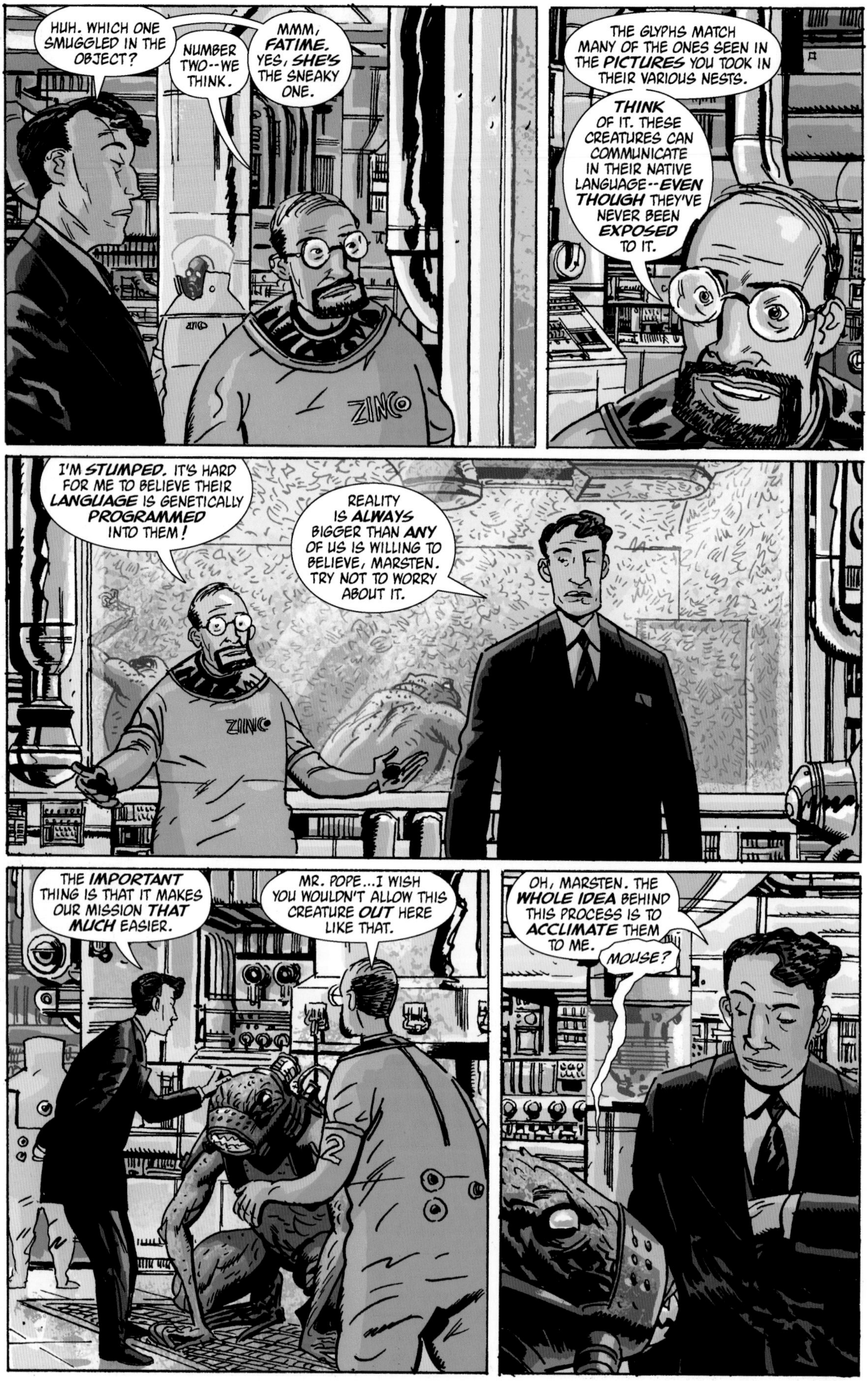
HUH. WHICH ONE SMUGGLED IN THE OBJECT?
NUMBER TWO--WE THINK.
MMM, FATIME. YES, SHE'S THE SNEAKY ONE.
ZINC
THE GLYPHS MATCH MANY OF THE ONES SEEN IN THE PICTURES YOU TOOK IN THEIR VARIOUS NESTS.
THINK OF IT. THESE CREATURES CAN COMMUNICATE IN THEIR NATIVE LANGUAGE--EVEN THOUGH THEY'VE NEVER BEEN EXPOSED TO IT.
I'M STUMPED. IT'S HARD FOR ME TO BELIEVE THEIR LANGUAGE IS GENETICALLY PROGRAMMED INTO THEM!
REALITY IS ALWAYS BIGGER THAN ANY OF US IS WILLING TO BELIEVE, MARSTEN. TRY NOT TO WORRY ABOUT IT.
ZINC
THE IMPORTANT THING IS THAT IT MAKES OUR MISSION THAT MUCH EASIER.
MR. POPE...I WISH YOU WOULDN'T ALLOW THIS CREATURE OUT HERE LIKE THAT.
OH, MARSTEN. THE WHOLE IDEA BEHIND THIS PROCESS IS TO ACCLIMATE THEM TO ME.
MOUSE?

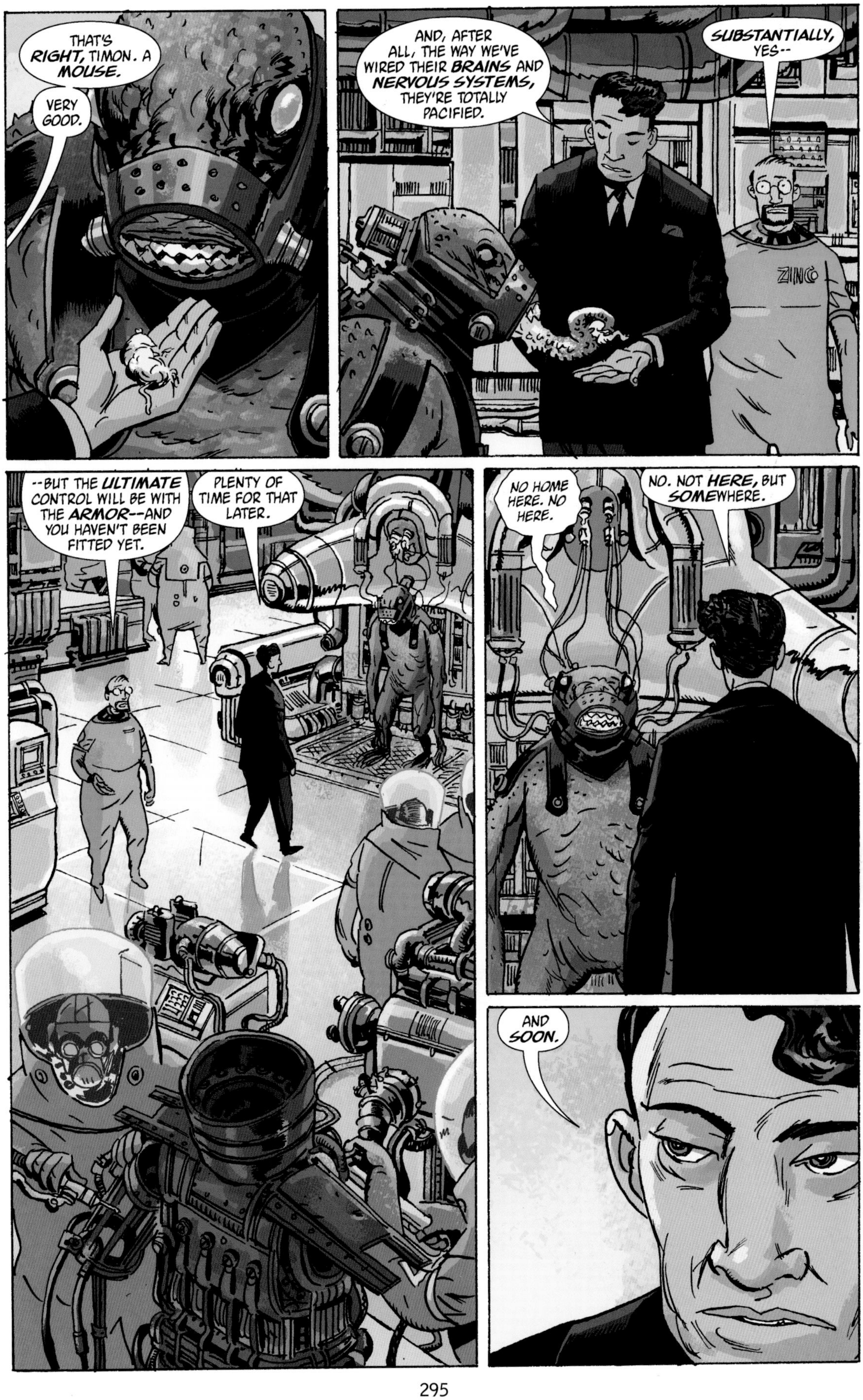
THAT'S RIGHT, TIMON. A MOUSE.
VERY GOOD.
AND, AFTER ALL, THE WAY WE'VE WIRED THEIR BRAINS AND NERVOUS SYSTEMS, THEY'RE TOTALLY PACIFIED.
SUBSTANTIALLY, YES--
ZINCO
--BUT THE ULTIMATE CONTROL WILL BE WITH THE ARMOR--AND YOU HAVEN'T BEEN FITTED YET.
PLENTY OF TIME FOR THAT LATER.
NO HOME HERE. NO HERE.
NO. NOT HERE, BUT SOMEWHERE.
AND SOON.

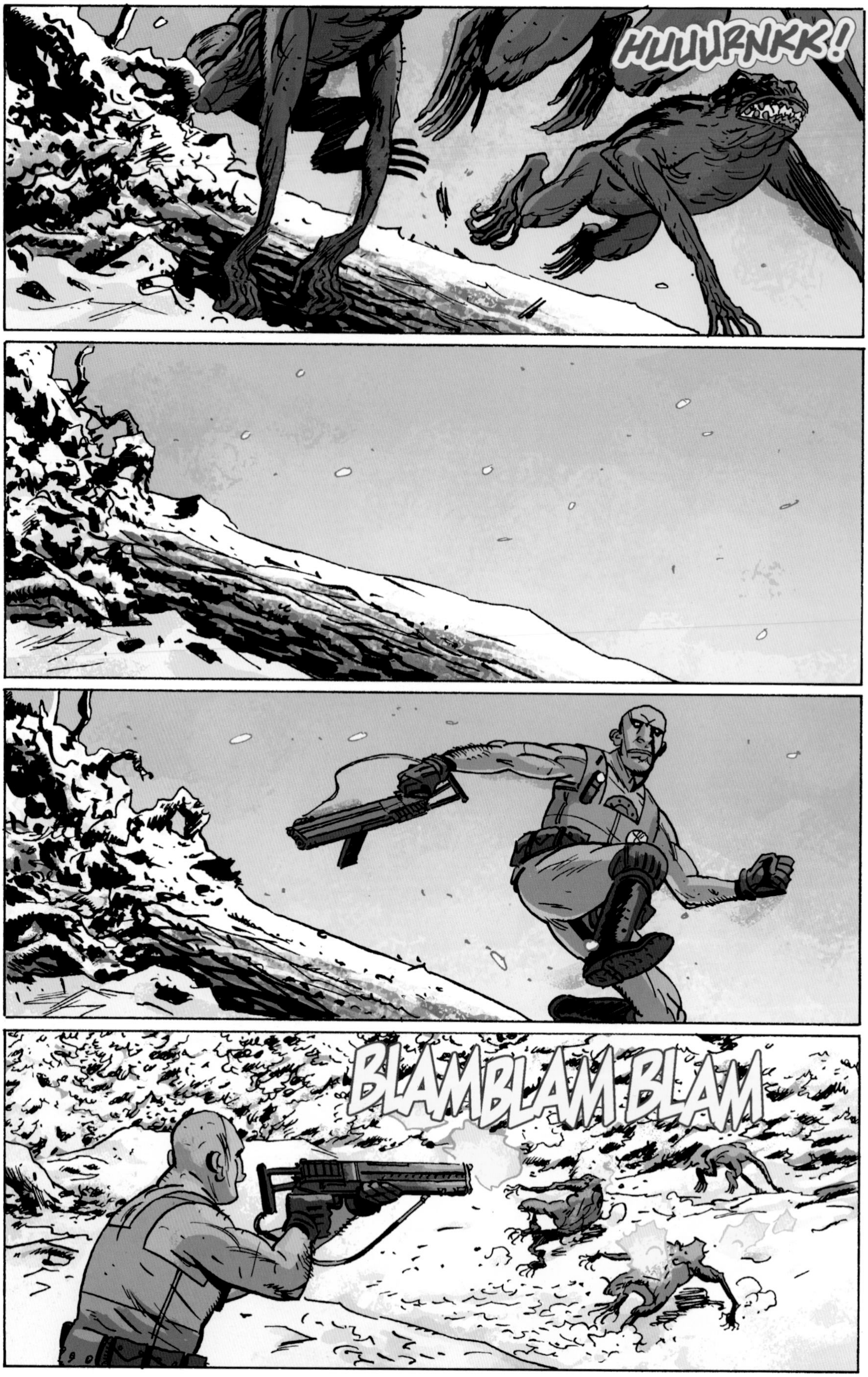
HUUURNKK!
BLAMBLAM BLAM

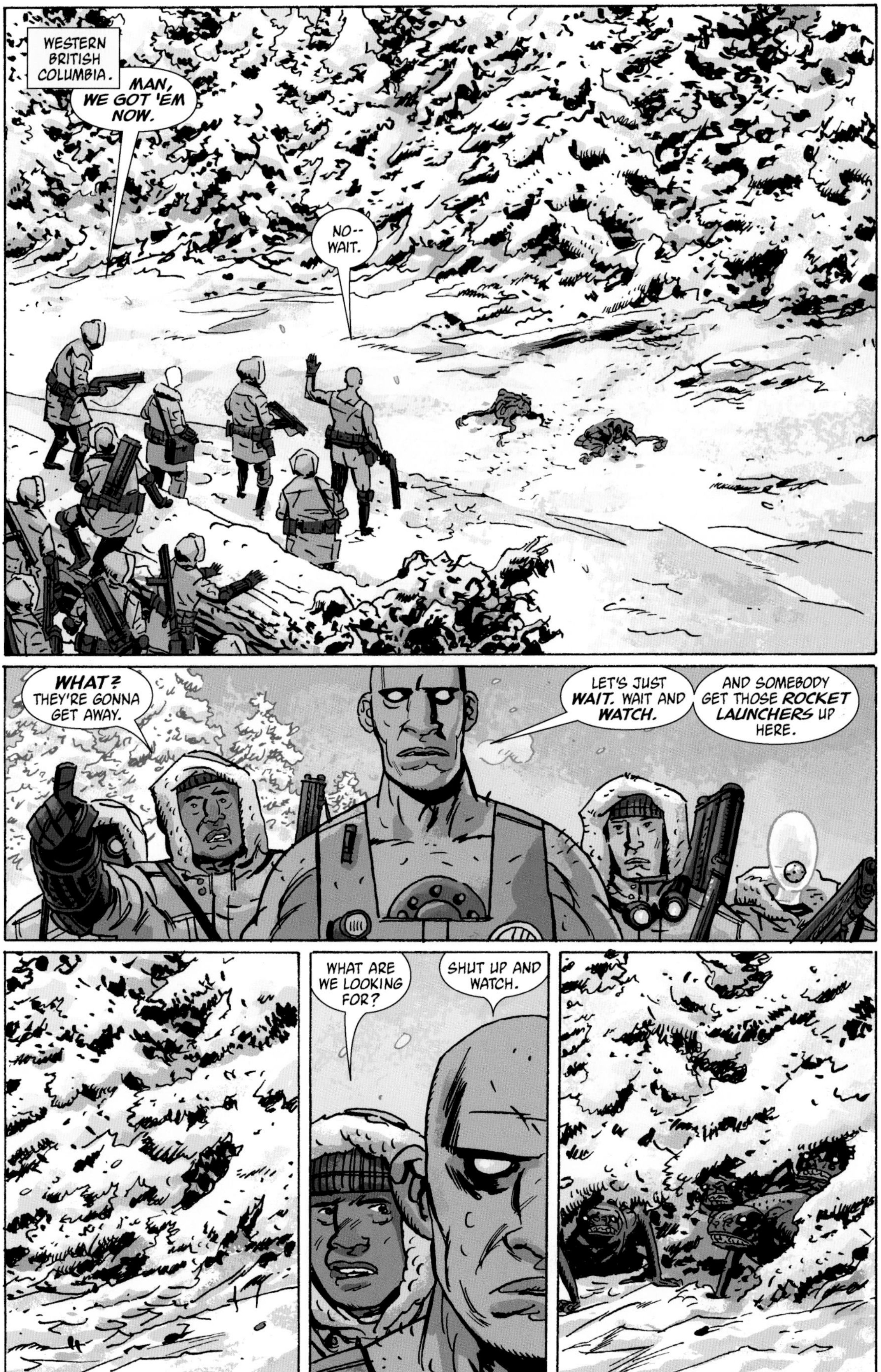
WESTERN BRITISH COLUMBIA.
MAN, WE GOT 'EM NOW.
NO-- WAIT.
WHAT? THEY'RE GONNA GET AWAY.
LET'S JUST WAIT. WAIT AND WATCH.
AND SOMEBODY GET THOSE ROCKET LAUNCHERS UP HERE.
WHAT ARE WE LOOKING FOR?
SHUT UP AND WATCH.

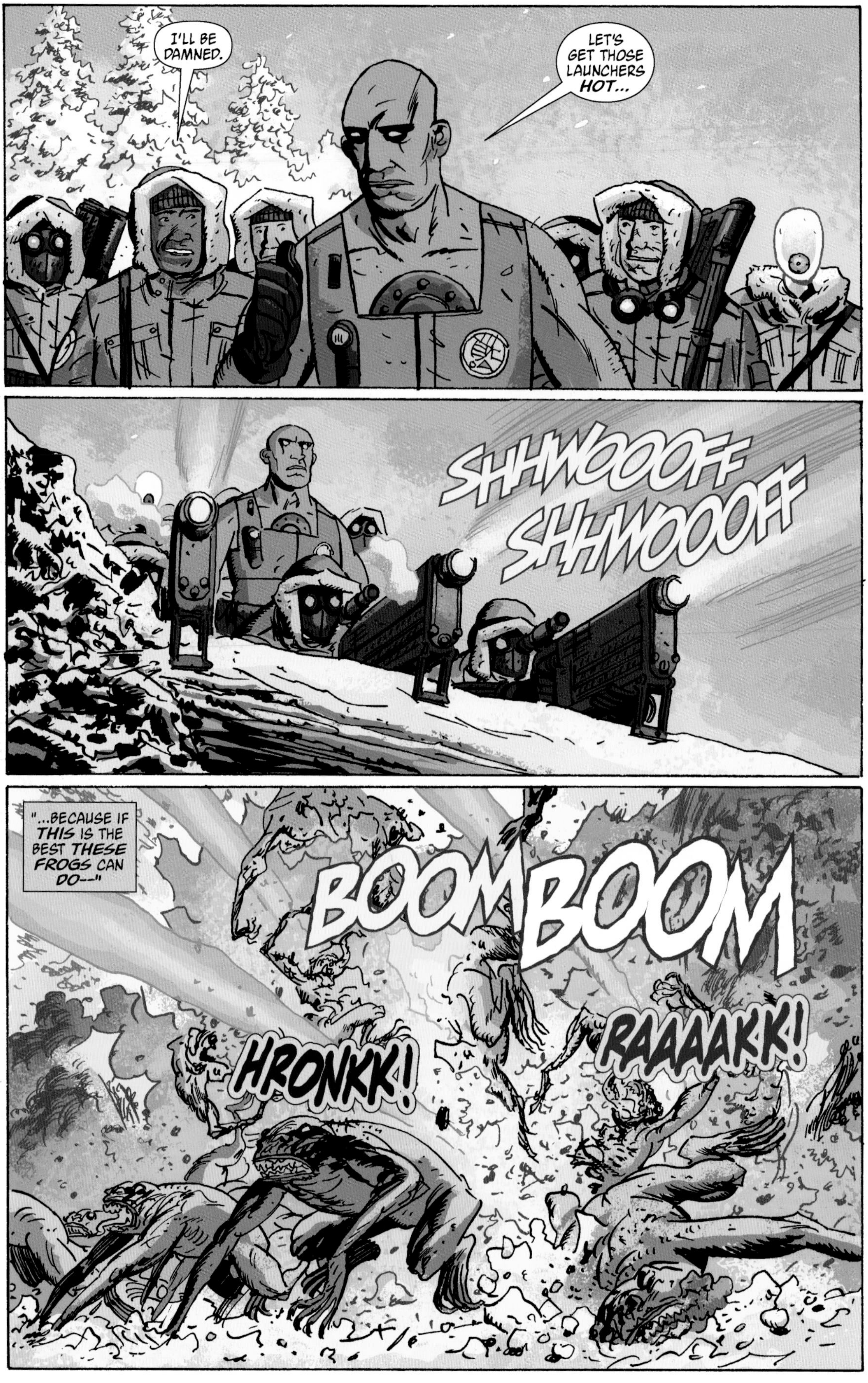
I'LL BE DAMNED.
LET'S GET THOSE LAUNCHERS HOT...
SHHWOOOFF
SHHWOOOFF
"...BECAUSE IF THIS IS THE BEST THESE FROGS CAN DO--"
BOOM
BOOM
HRONKK!
RAAAAKK!

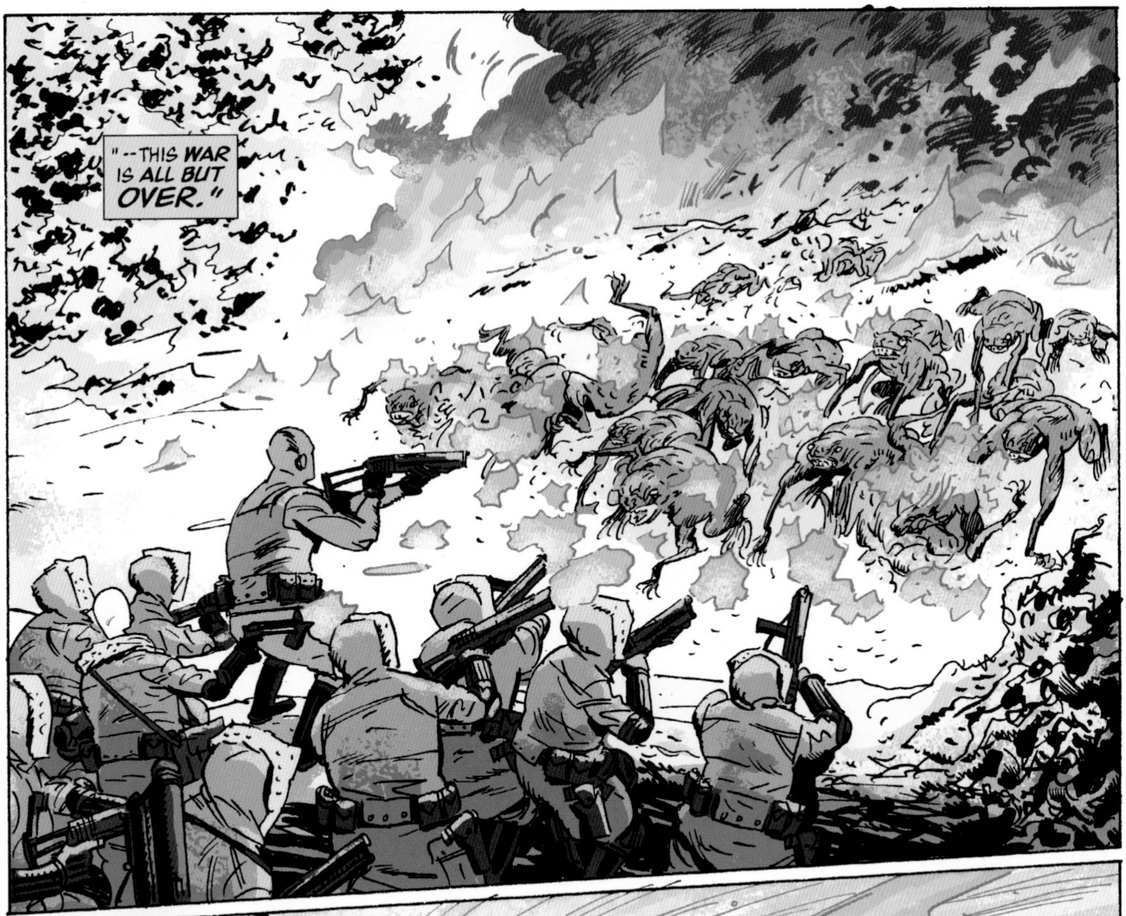
"--THIS WAR IS ALL BUT OVER."

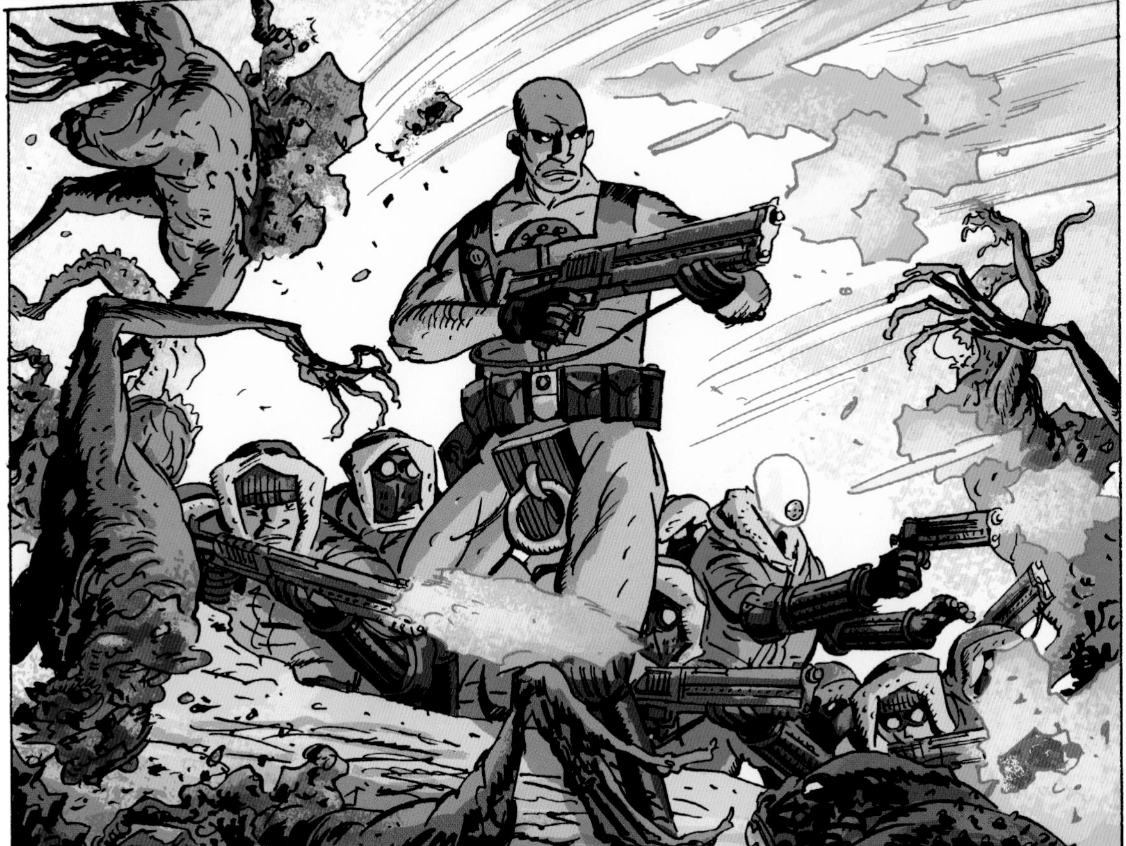

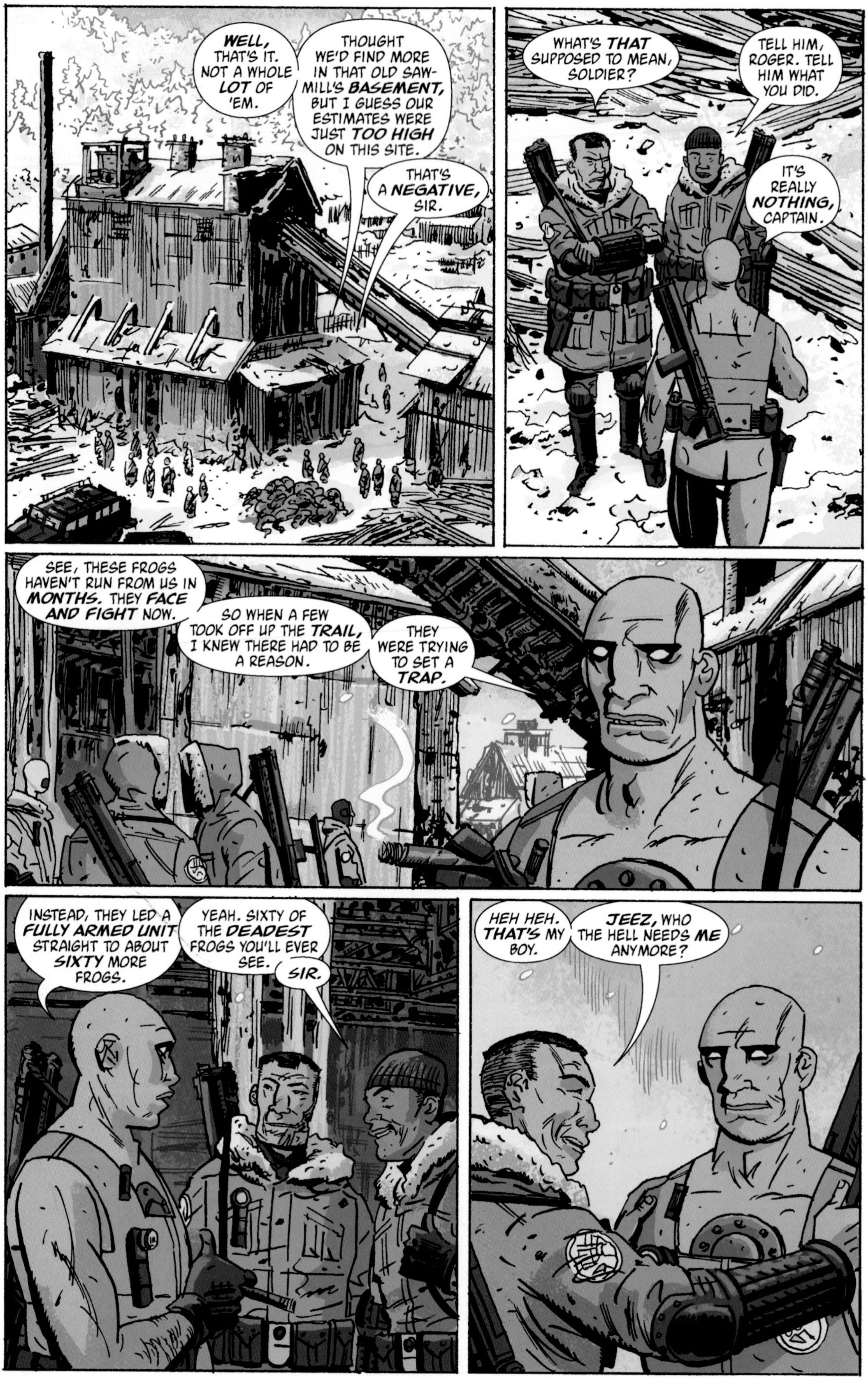
WELL, THAT'S IT. NOT A WHOLE LOT OF 'EM.
THOUGHT WE'D FIND MORE IN THAT OLD SAW-MILL'S BASEMENT, BUT I GUESS OUR ESTIMATES WERE JUST TOO HIGH ON THIS SITE.
THAT'S A NEGATIVE, SIR.
WHAT'S THAT SUPPOSED TO MEAN, SOLDIER?
TELL HIM, ROGER. TELL HIM WHAT YOU DID.
IT'S REALLY NOTHING, CAPTAIN.
SEE, THESE FROGS HAVEN'T RUN FROM US IN MONTHS. THEY FACE AND FIGHT NOW.
SO WHEN A FEW TOOK OFF UP THE TRAIL, I KNEW THERE HAD TO BE A REASON.
THEY WERE TRYING TO SET A TRAP.
INSTEAD, THEY LED A FULLY ARMED UNIT STRAIGHT TO ABOUT SIXTY MORE FROGS.
YEAH. SIXTY OF THE DEADEST FROGS YOU'LL EVER SEE.
SIR.
HEH HEH. THAT'S MY BOY.
JEEZ, WHO THE HELL NEEDS ME ANYMORE?

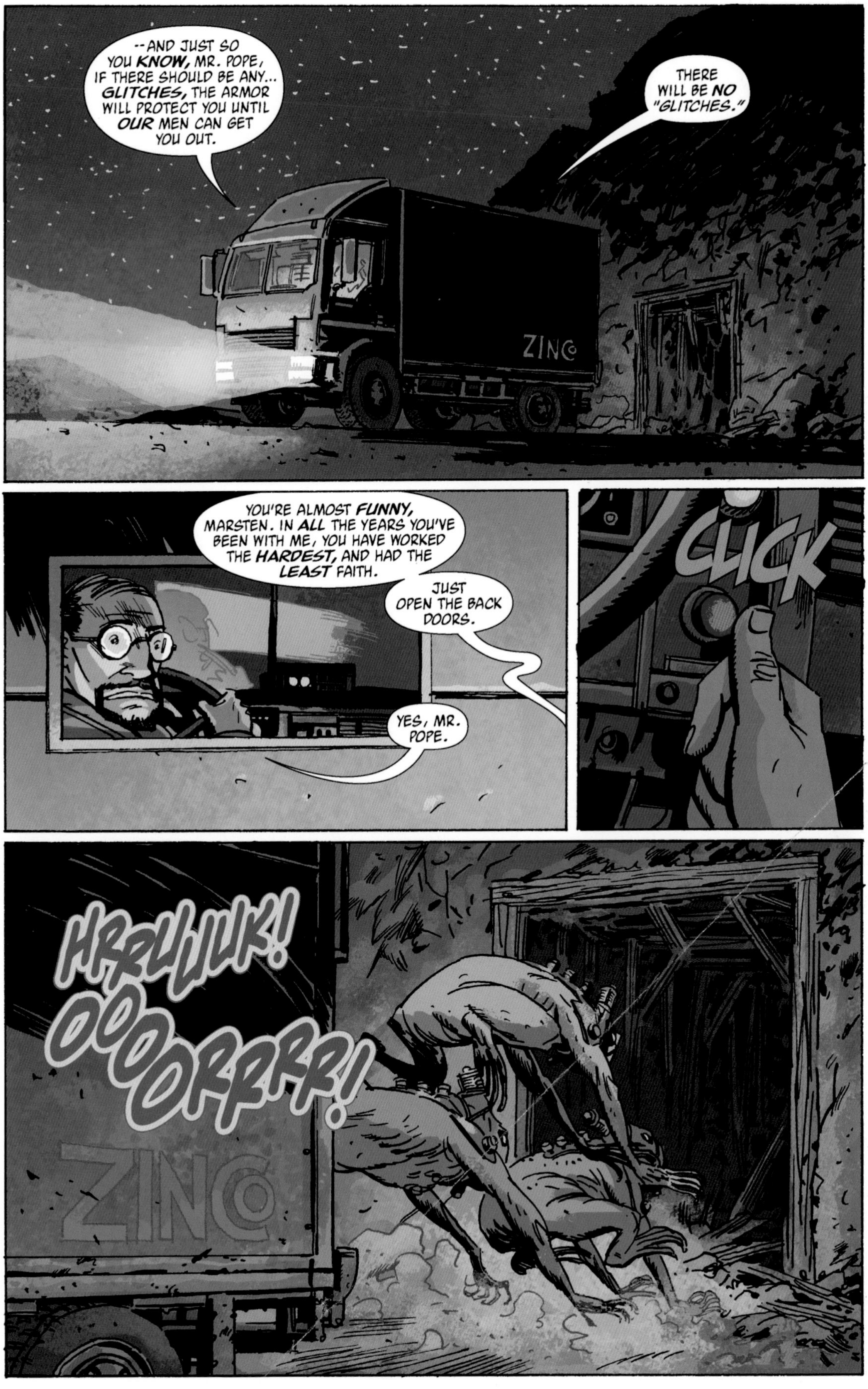
--AND JUST SO YOU KNOW, MR. POPE, IF THERE SHOULD BE ANY... GLITCHES, THE ARMOR WILL PROTECT YOU UNTIL OUR MEN CAN GET YOU OUT.
THERE WILL BE NO "GLITCHES."
ZINCO
YOU'RE ALMOST FUNNY, MARSTEN. IN ALL THE YEARS YOU'VE BEEN WITH ME, YOU HAVE WORKED THE HARDEST, AND HAD THE LEAST FAITH.
JUST OPEN THE BACK DOORS.
YES, MR. POPE.
CLICK
HRRULLK!
OOOORRRR!
ZINCO

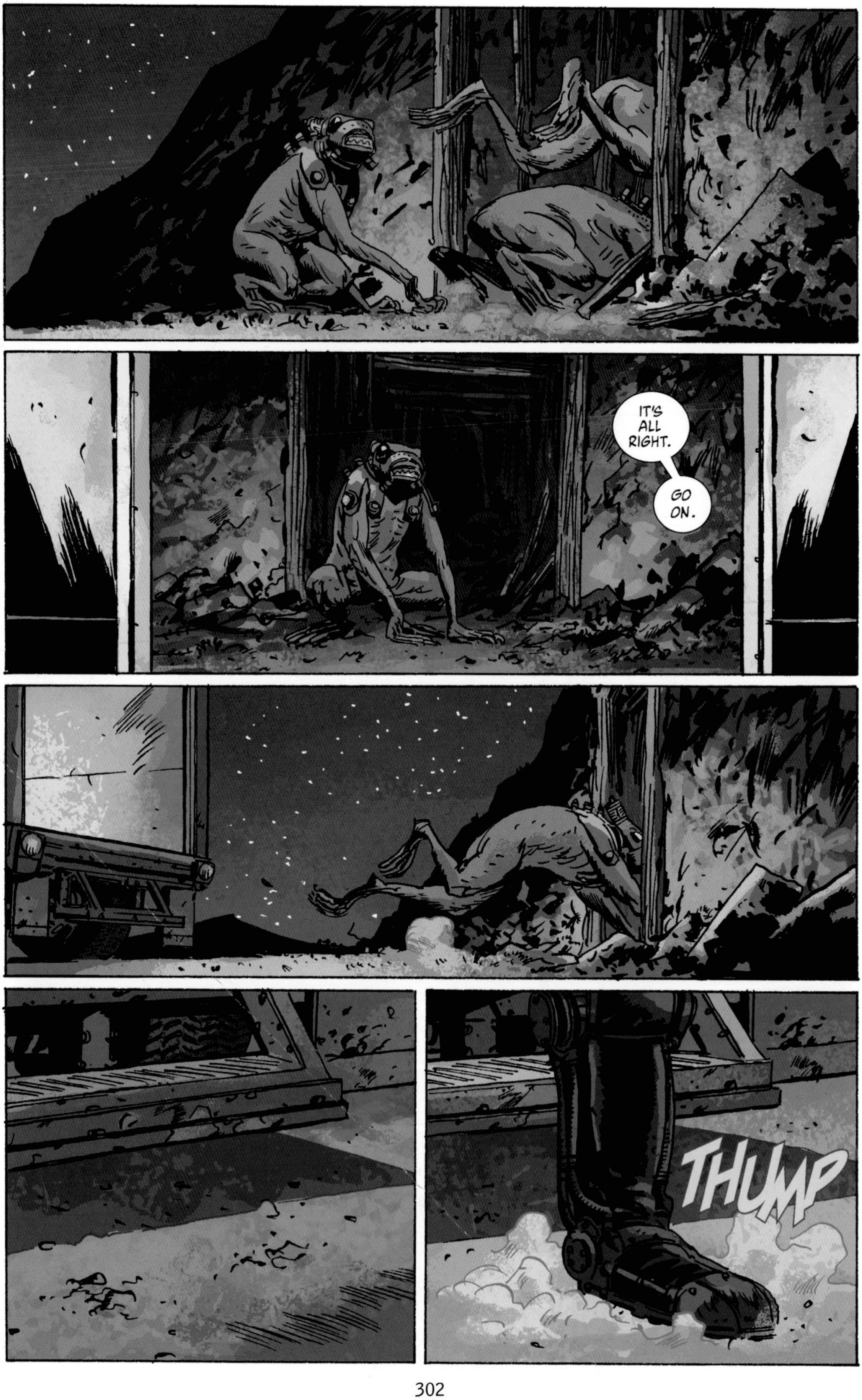
IT'S ALL RIGHT.
GO ON.
THUMP

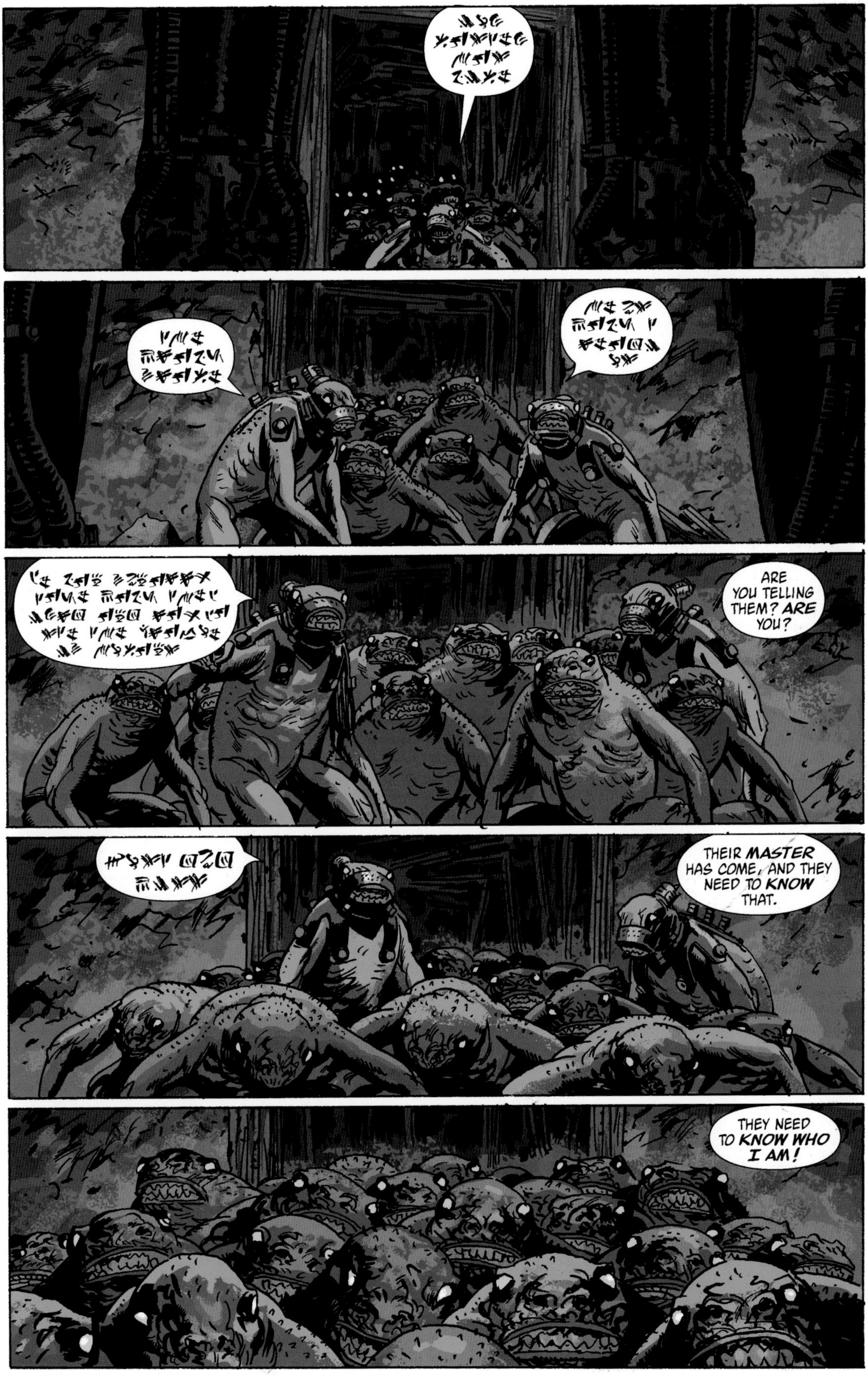
ARE YOU TELLING THEM? ARE YOU?
THEIR MASTER HAS COME, AND THEY NEED TO KNOW THAT.
THEY NEED TO KNOW WHO I AM!

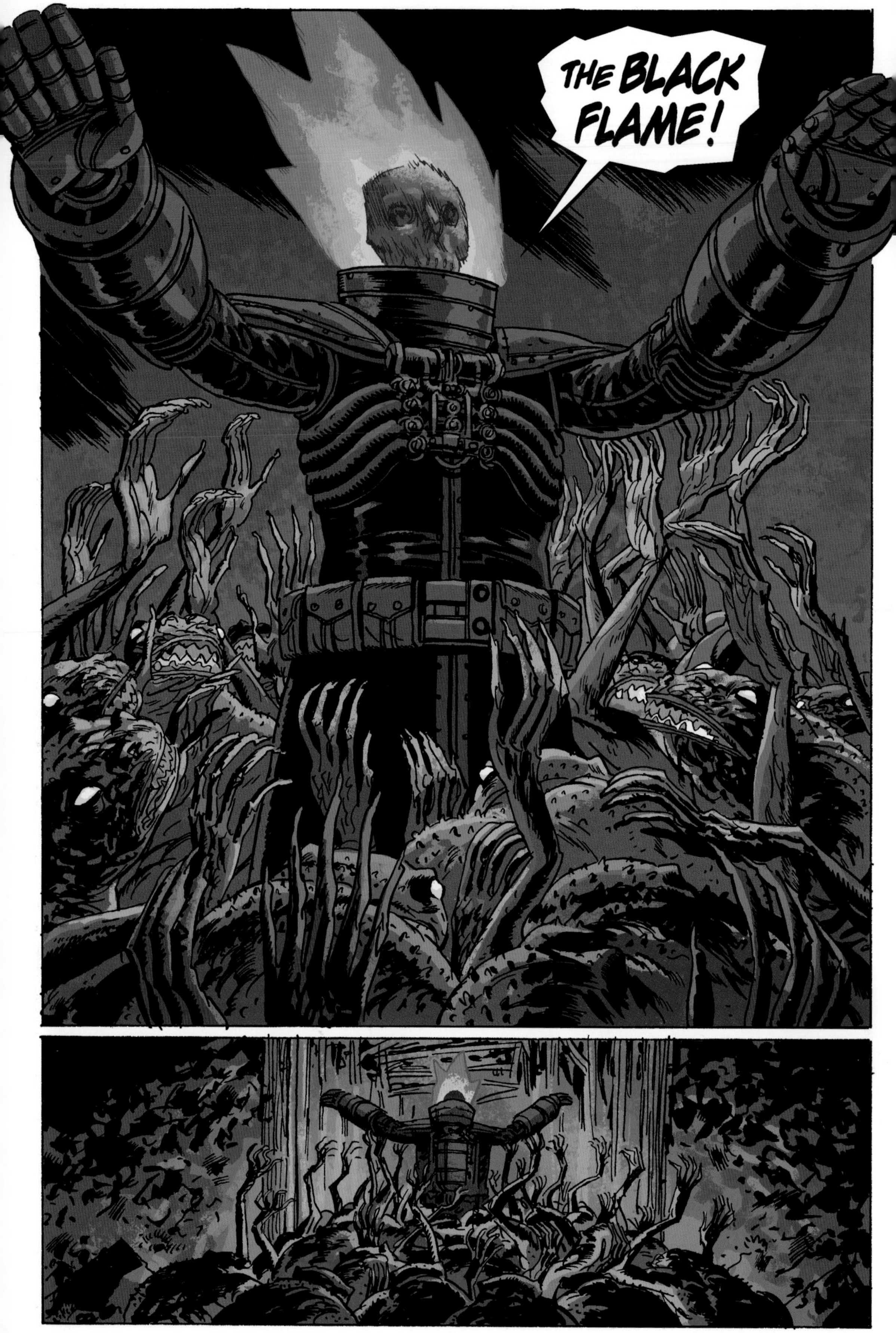
THE BLACK FLAME!

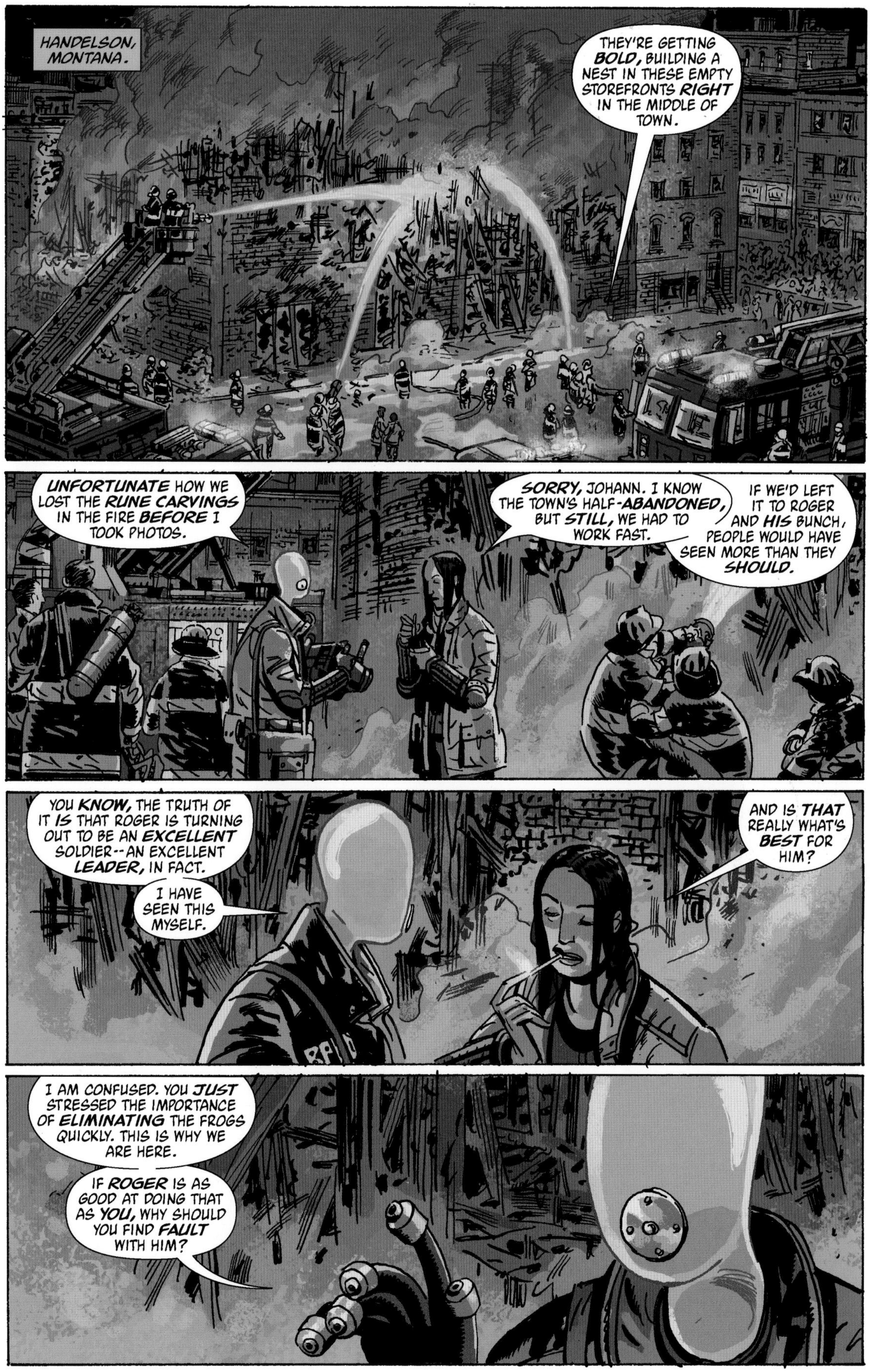

HANDELSON, MONTANA.
THEY'RE GETTING BOLD, BUILDING A NEST IN THESE EMPTY STOREFRONTS RIGHT IN THE MIDDLE OF TOWN.
UNFORTUNATE HOW WE LOST THE RUNE CARVINGS IN THE FIRE BEFORE I TOOK PHOTOS.
SORRY, JOHANN. I KNOW THE TOWN'S HALF-ABANDONED, BUT STILL, WE HAD TO WORK FAST.
IF WE'D LEFT IT TO ROGER AND HIS BUNCH, PEOPLE WOULD HAVE SEEN MORE THAN THEY SHOULD.
YOU KNOW, THE TRUTH OF IT IS THAT ROGER IS TURNING OUT TO BE AN EXCELLENT SOLDIER--AN EXCELLENT LEADER, IN FACT.
I HAVE SEEN THIS MYSELF.
AND IS THAT REALLY WHAT'S BEST FOR HIM?
I AM CONFUSED. YOU JUST STRESSED THE IMPORTANCE OF ELIMINATING THE FROGS QUICKLY. THIS IS WHY WE ARE HERE.
IF ROGER IS AS GOOD AT DOING THAT AS YOU, WHY SHOULD YOU FIND FAULT WITH HIM?

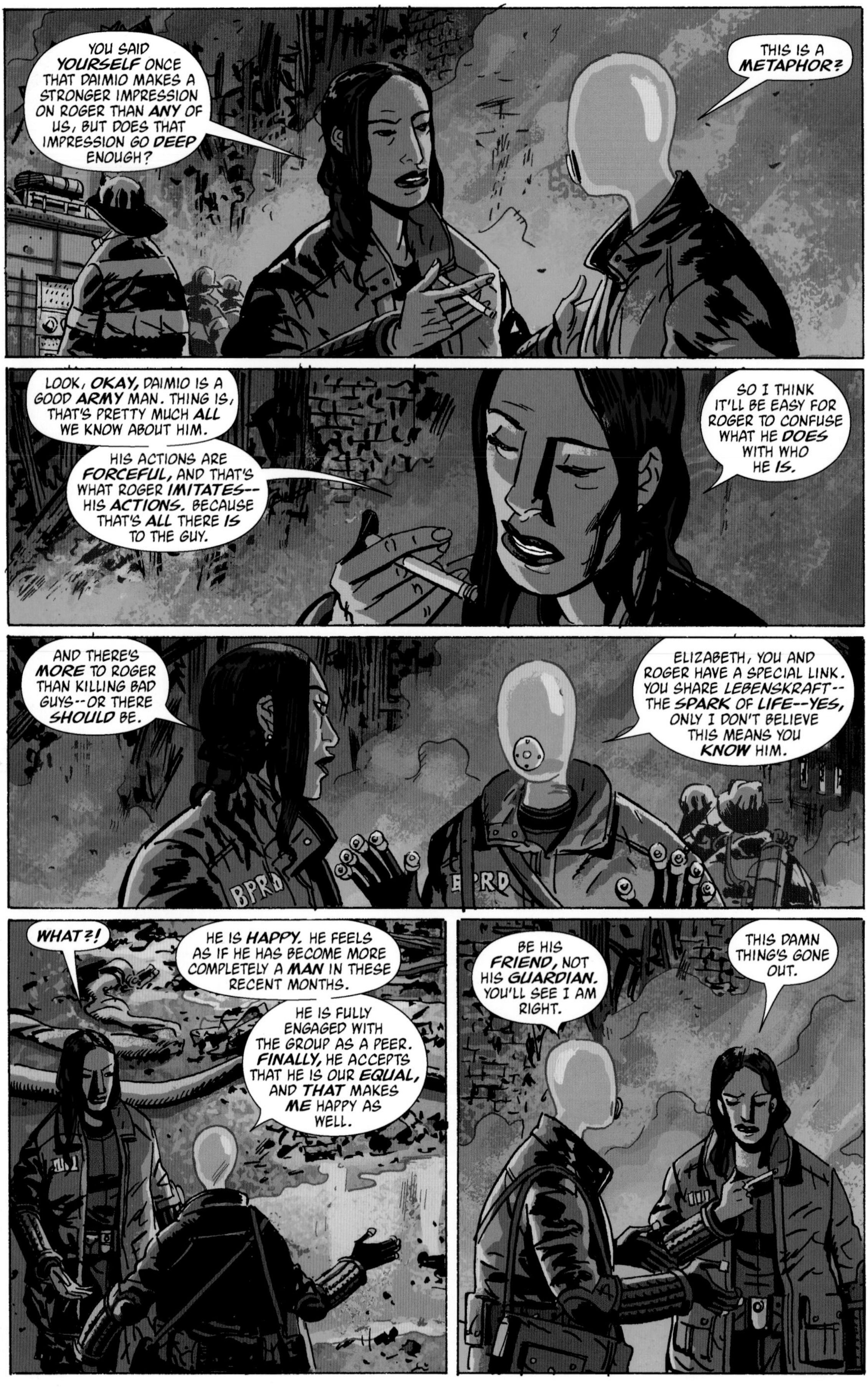
YOU SAID YOURSELF ONCE THAT DAIMIO MAKES A STRONGER IMPRESSION ON ROGER THAN ANY OF US, BUT DOES THAT IMPRESSION GO DEEP ENOUGH?
THIS IS A METAPHOR?
LOOK, OKAY, DAIMIO IS A GOOD ARMY MAN. THING IS, THAT'S PRETTY MUCH ALL WE KNOW ABOUT HIM.
HIS ACTIONS ARE FORCEFUL, AND THAT'S WHAT ROGER IMITATES-- HIS ACTIONS. BECAUSE THAT'S ALL THERE IS TO THE GUY.
SO I THINK IT'LL BE EASY FOR ROGER TO CONFUSE WHAT HE DOES WITH WHO HE IS.
AND THERE'S MORE TO ROGER THAN KILLING BAD GUYS--OR THERE SHOULD BE.
ELIZABETH, YOU AND ROGER HAVE A SPECIAL LINK. YOU SHARE LEBENSKRAFT-- THE SPARK OF LIFE--YES, ONLY I DON'T BELIEVE THIS MEANS YOU KNOW HIM.
BPRD
BPRD
WHAT?!
HE IS HAPPY. HE FEELS AS IF HE HAS BECOME MORE COMPLETELY A MAN IN THESE RECENT MONTHS.
HE IS FULLY ENGAGED WITH THE GROUP AS A PEER. FINALLY, HE ACCEPTS THAT HE IS OUR EQUAL, AND THAT MAKES ME HAPPY AS WELL.
BE HIS FRIEND, NOT HIS GUARDIAN. YOU'LL SEE I AM RIGHT.
THIS DAMN THING'S GONE OUT.

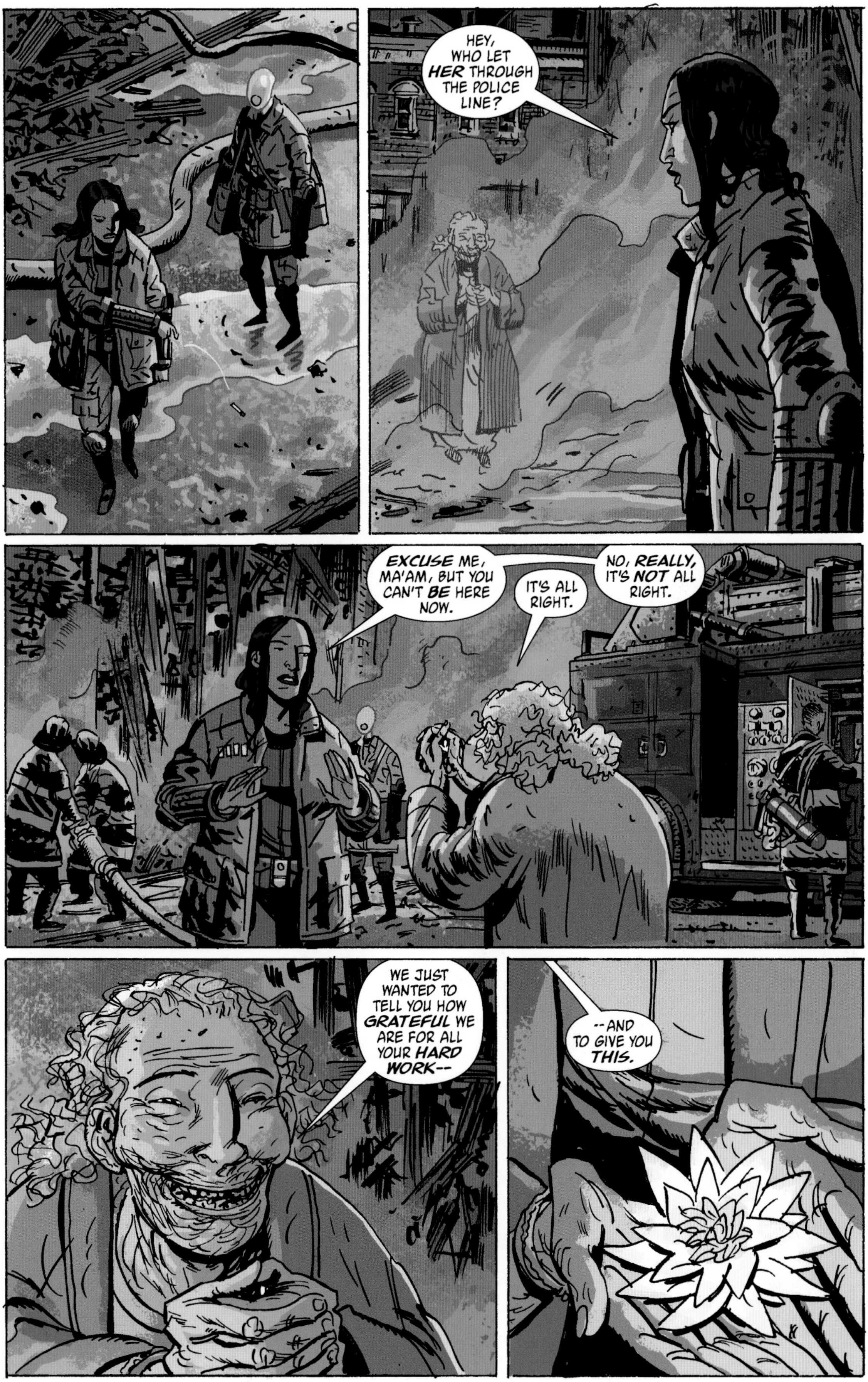
HEY, WHO LET HER THROUGH THE POLICE LINE?
EXCUSE ME, MA'AM, BUT YOU CAN'T BE HERE NOW.
IT'S ALL RIGHT.
NO, REALLY, IT'S NOT ALL RIGHT.
WE JUST WANTED TO TELL YOU HOW GRATEFUL WE ARE FOR ALL YOUR HARD WORK--
--AND TO GIVE YOU THIS.

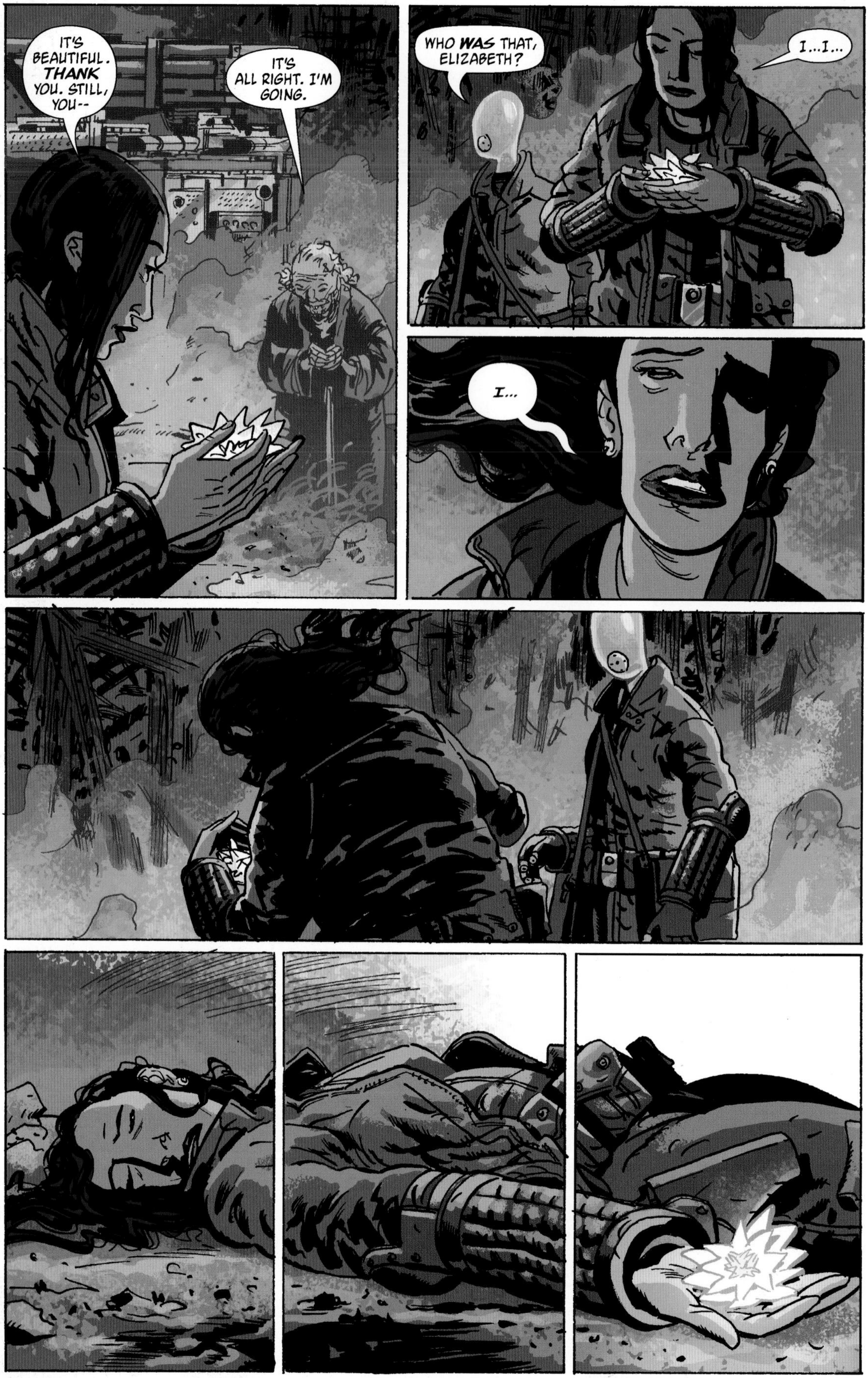
IT'S BEAUTIFUL. THANK YOU. STILL, YOU--
IT'S ALL RIGHT. I'M GOING.
WHO WAS THAT, ELIZABETH?
I...I...
I...

CHAPTER TWO

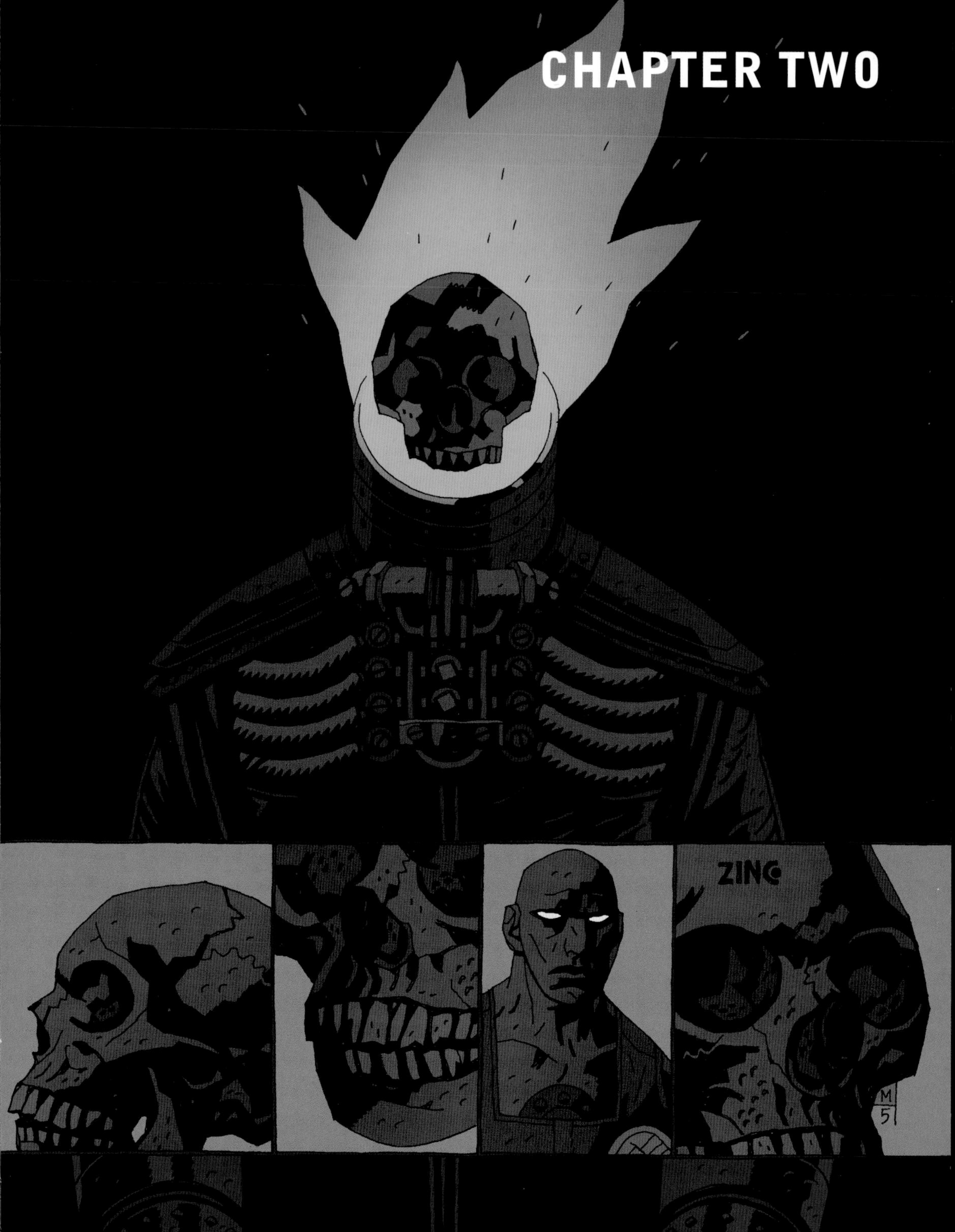
ZINC

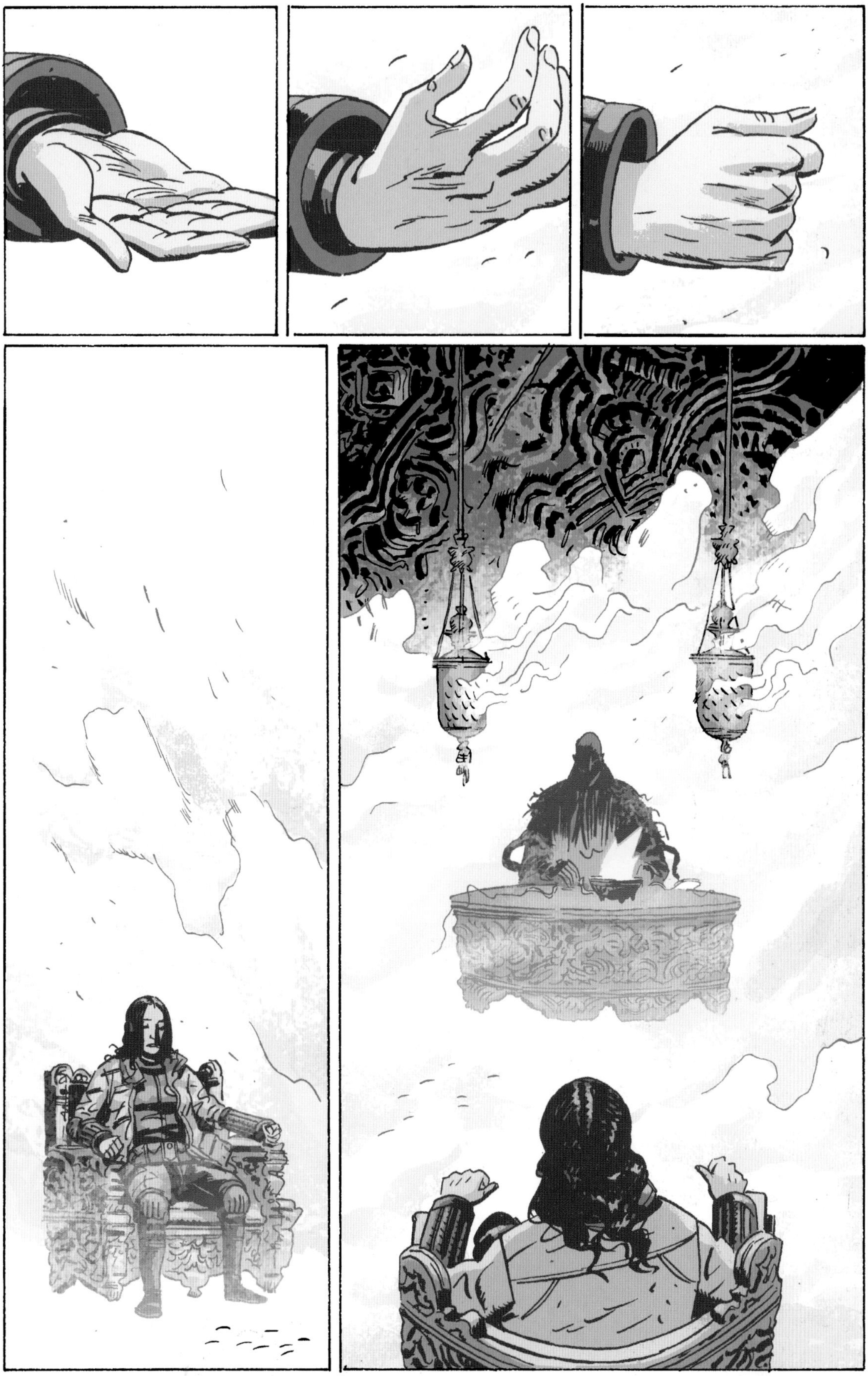

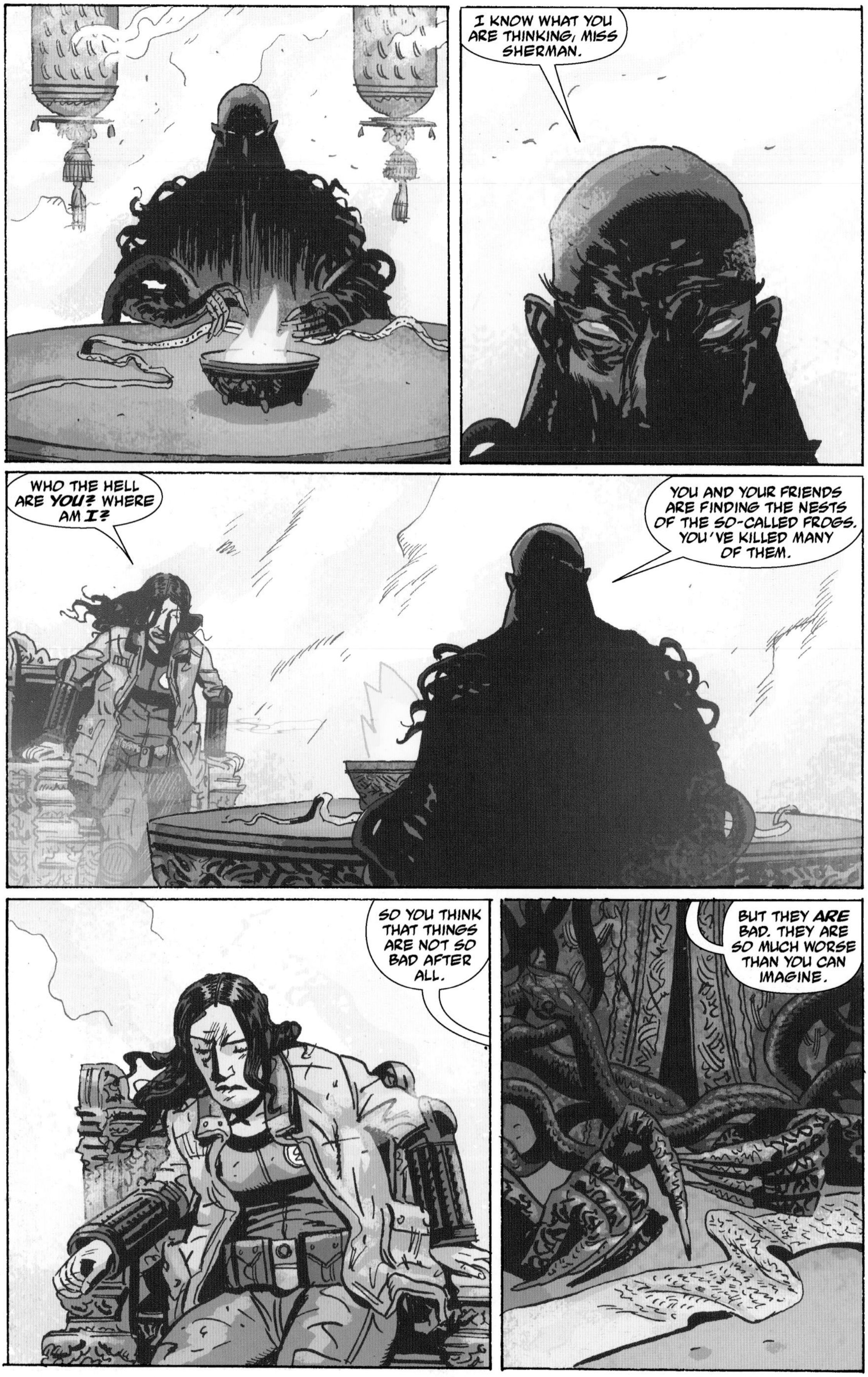
I KNOW WHAT YOU ARE THINKING, MISS SHERMAN.
WHO THE HELL ARE YOU? WHERE AM I?
YOU AND YOUR FRIENDS ARE FINDING THE NESTS OF THE SO-CALLED FROGS. YOU'VE KILLED MANY OF THEM.
SO YOU THINK THAT THINGS ARE NOT SO BAD AFTER ALL.
BUT THEY ARE BAD. THEY ARE SO MUCH WORSE THAN YOU CAN IMAGINE.

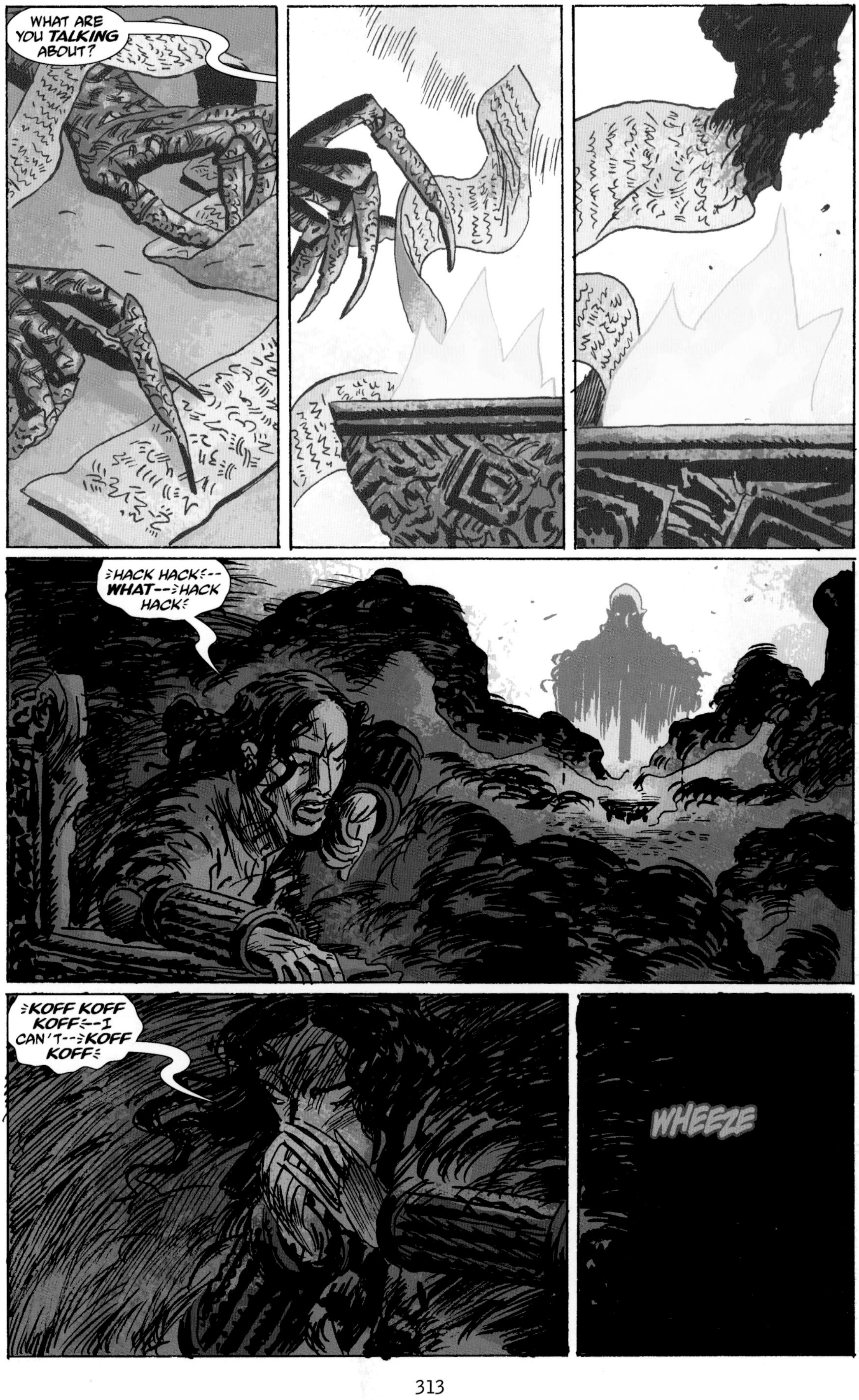
WHAT ARE YOU TALKING ABOUT?
HACK HACK-- WHAT--HACK HACK
KOFF KOFF KOFF--I CAN'T--KOFF KOFF
WHEEZE

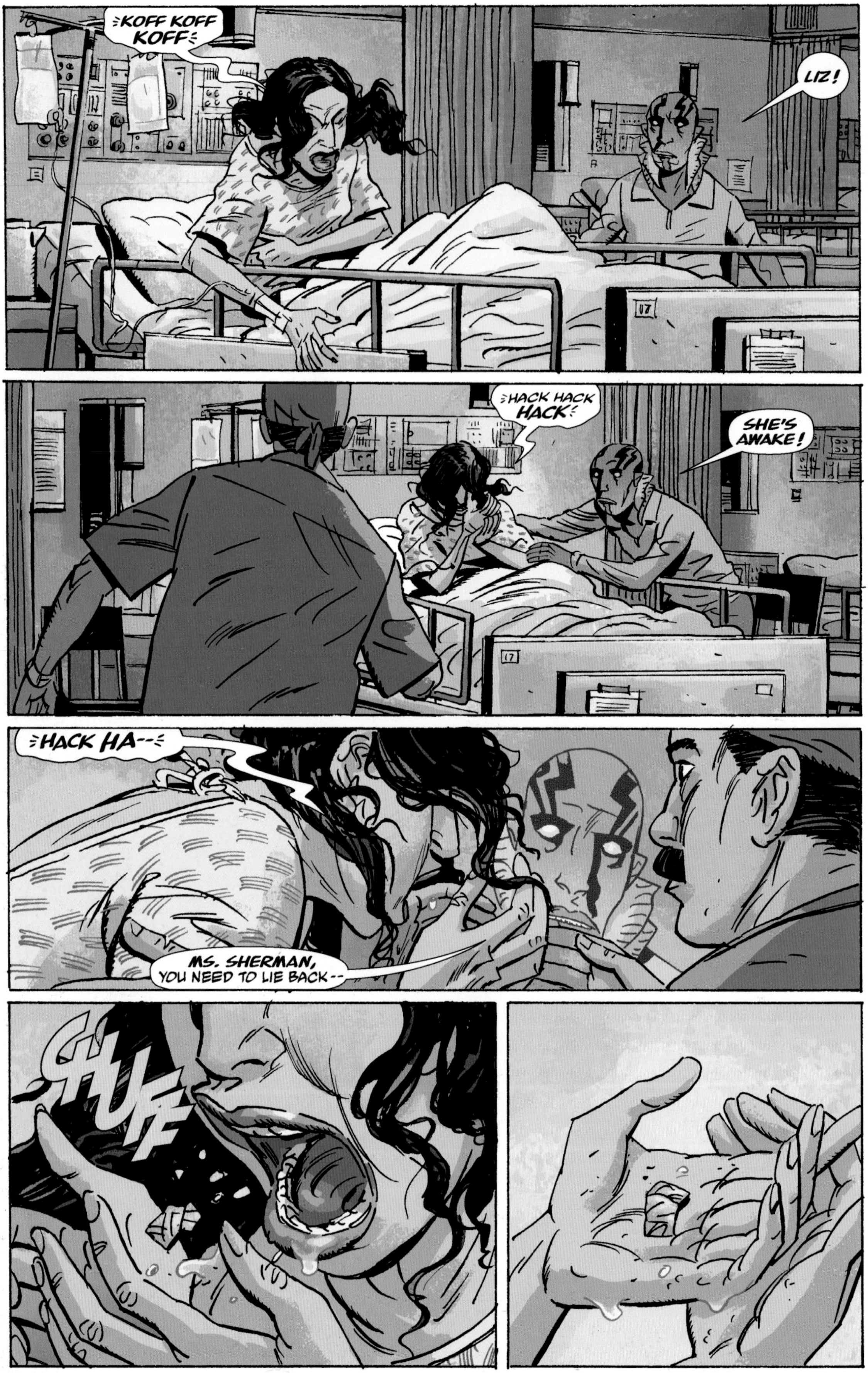
KOFF KOFF KOFF
LIZ!
HACK HACK HACK
SHE'S AWAKE!
HACK HA--
MS. SHERMAN, YOU NEED TO LIE BACK--
SHUFF

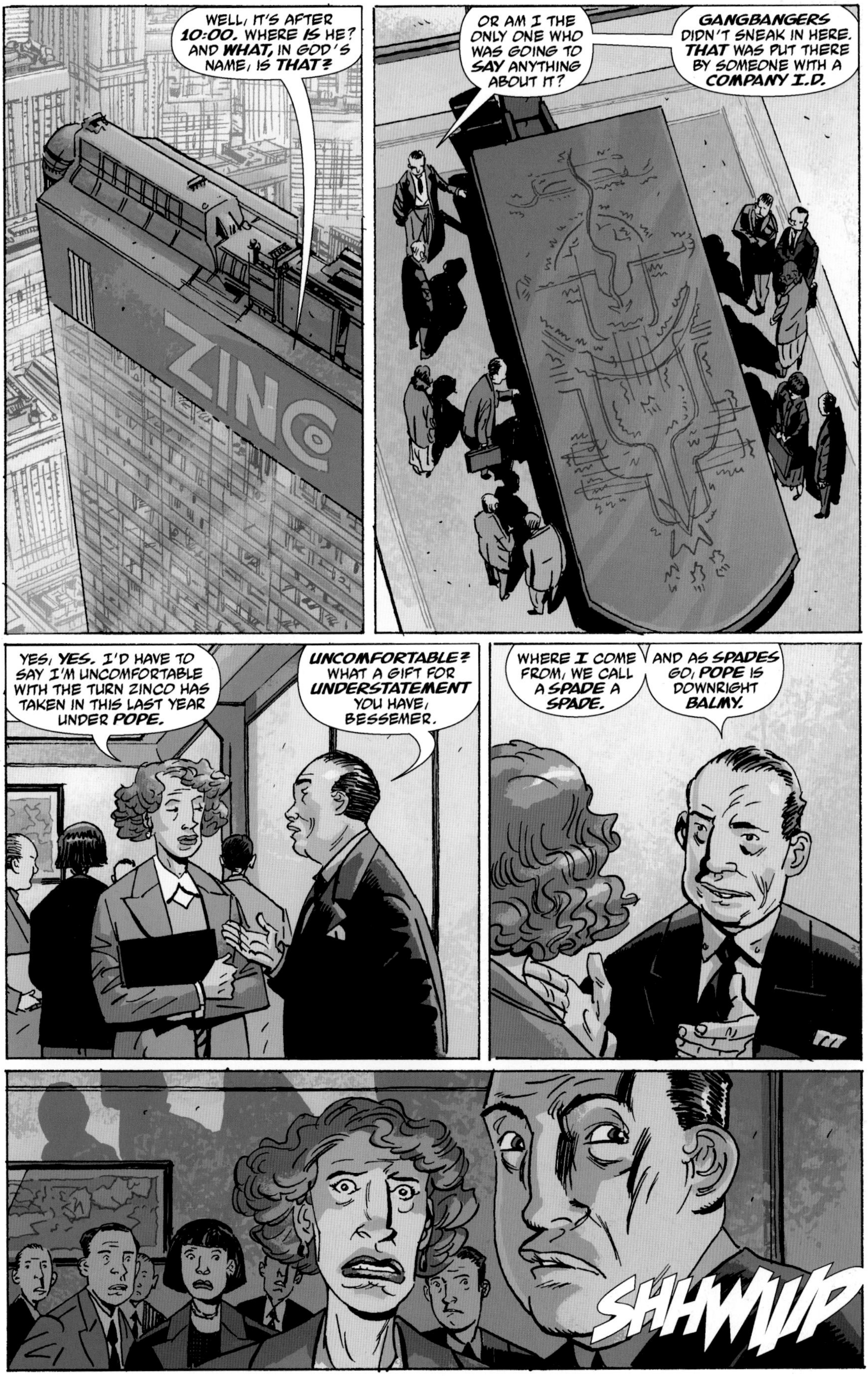
WELL, IT'S AFTER 10:00. WHERE IS HE? AND WHAT, IN GOD'S NAME, IS THAT?
OR AM I THE ONLY ONE WHO WAS GOING TO SAY ANYTHING ABOUT IT?
GANGBANGERS DIDN'T SNEAK IN HERE. THAT WAS PUT THERE BY SOMEONE WITH A COMPANY I.D.
ZINCO
YES, YES. I'D HAVE TO SAY I'M UNCOMFORTABLE WITH THE TURN ZINCO HAS TAKEN IN THIS LAST YEAR UNDER POPE.
UNCOMFORTABLE? WHAT A GIFT FOR UNDERSTATEMENT YOU HAVE, BESSEMER.
WHERE I COME FROM, WE CALL A SPADE A SPADE.
AND AS SPADES GO, POPE IS DOWNRIGHT BALMY.
SHHWIP

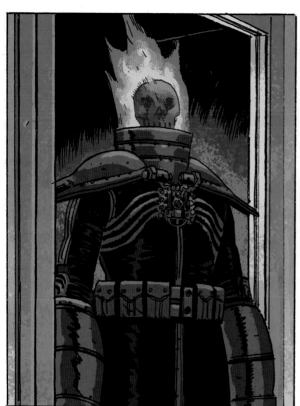

PUPUPUPUPUP

PUPUPUPUPUP

SPOKKT

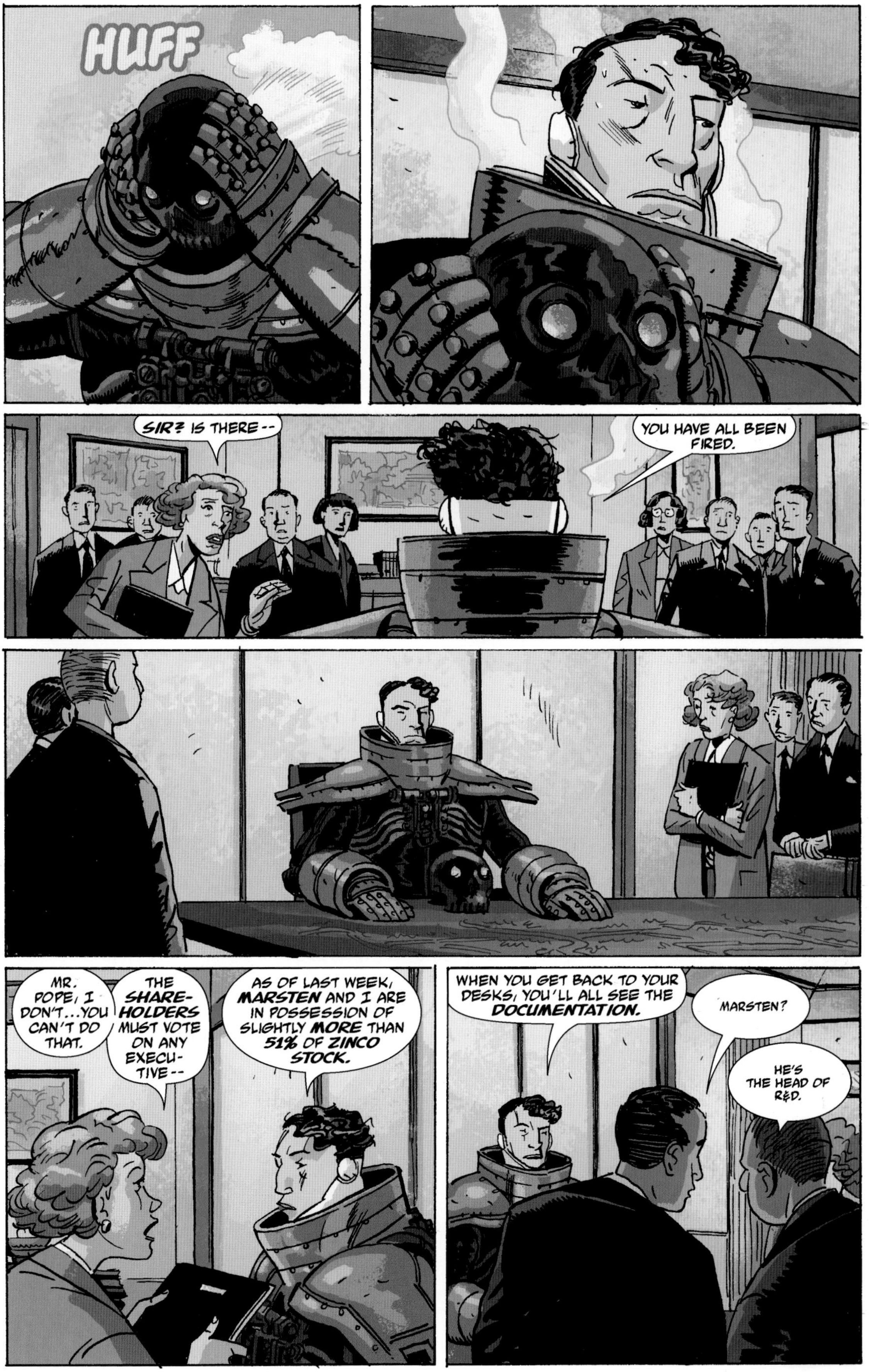
HUFF
SIR? IS THERE --
YOU HAVE ALL BEEN FIRED.
MR. POPE, I DON'T...YOU CAN'T DO THAT.
THE SHARE-HOLDERS MUST VOTE ON ANY EXECU-TIVE --
AS OF LAST WEEK, MARSTEN AND I ARE IN POSSESSION OF SLIGHTLY MORE THAN 51% OF ZINCO STOCK.
WHEN YOU GET BACK TO YOUR DESKS, YOU'LL ALL SEE THE DOCUMENTATION.
MARSTEN?
HE'S THE HEAD OF R&D.

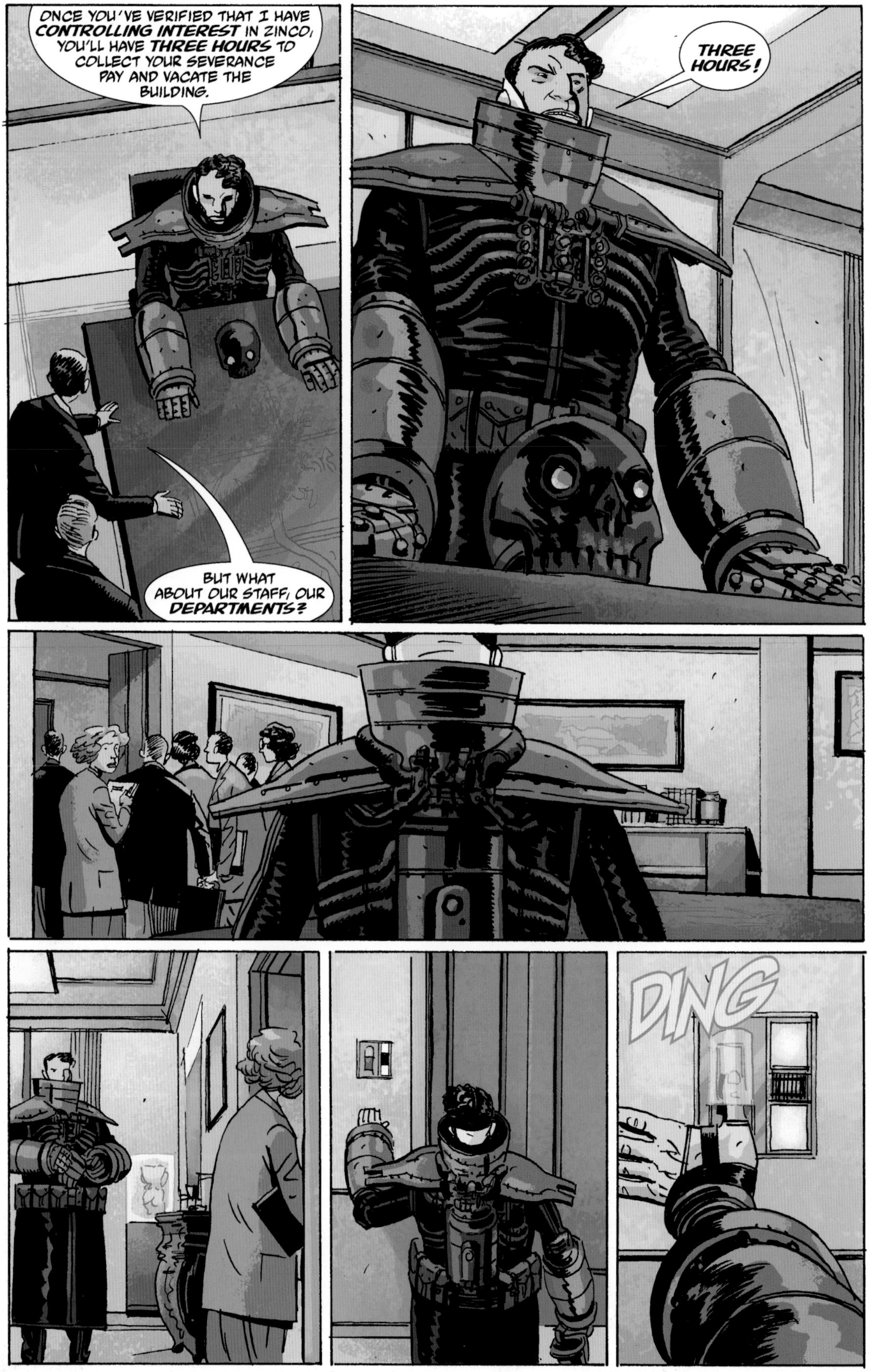
ONCE YOU'VE VERIFIED THAT I HAVE CONTROLLING INTEREST IN ZINCO, YOU'LL HAVE THREE HOURS TO COLLECT YOUR SEVERANCE PAY AND VACATE THE BUILDING.
BUT WHAT ABOUT OUR STAFF, OUR DEPARTMENTS?
THREE HOURS!
DING

SIR, IS THIS *REALLY* NECESSARY?

YOU MAKE IT SOUND AS IF I DON'T *WANT* TO DO IT, MARSTEN.

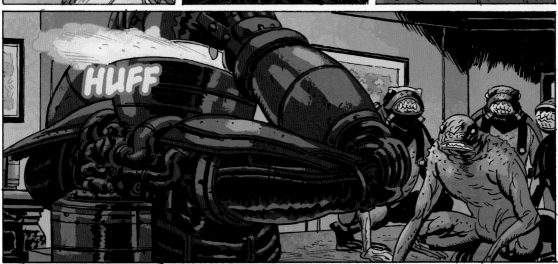

HUFF

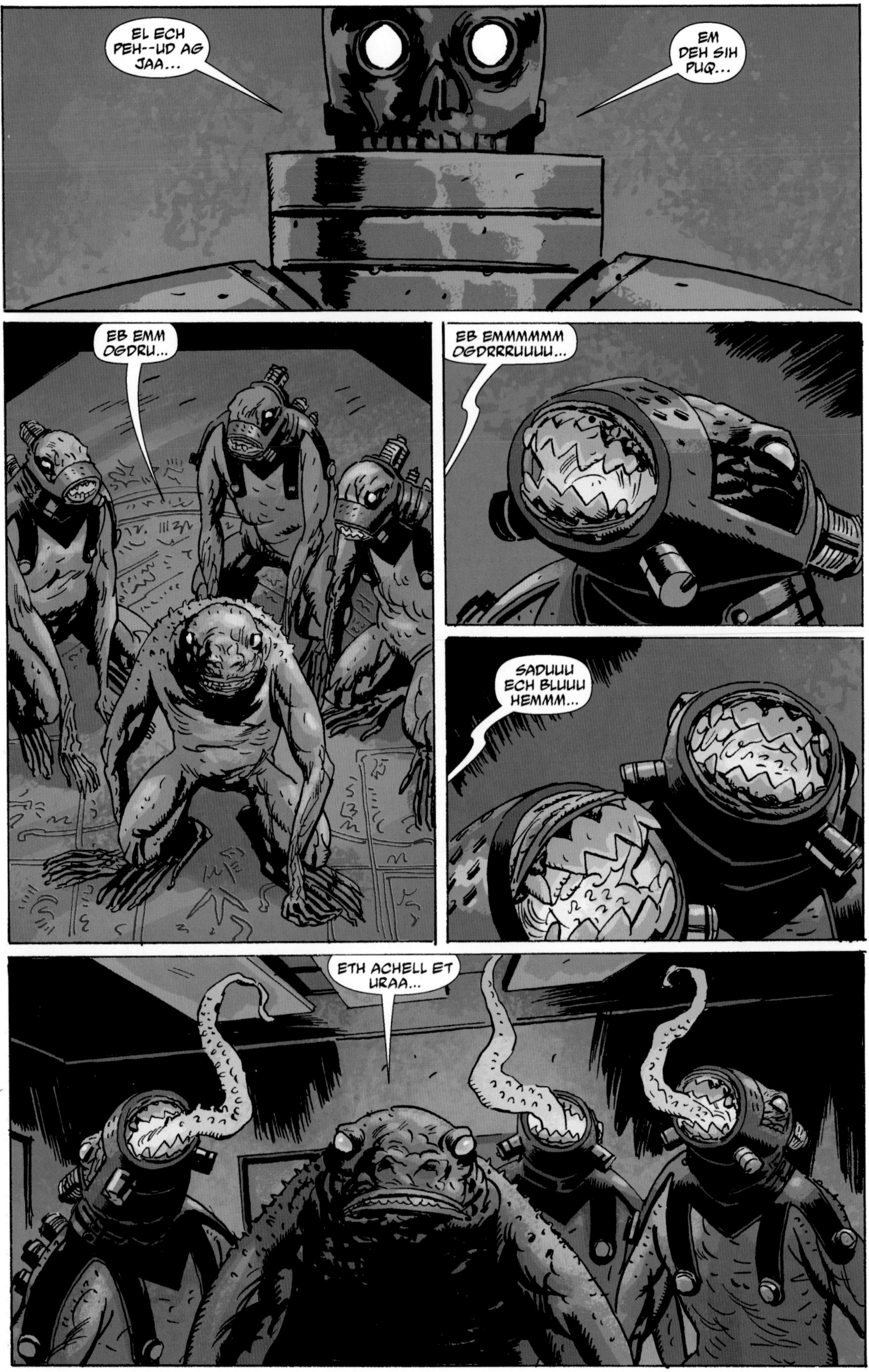
EL ECH PEH--UD AG JAA...
EM DEH SIH PUQ...
EB EMM OGDRU...
EB EMMMMMM OGDRRRUUUU...
SADUUU ECH BLUUU HEMMM...
ETH ACHELL ET URAA...

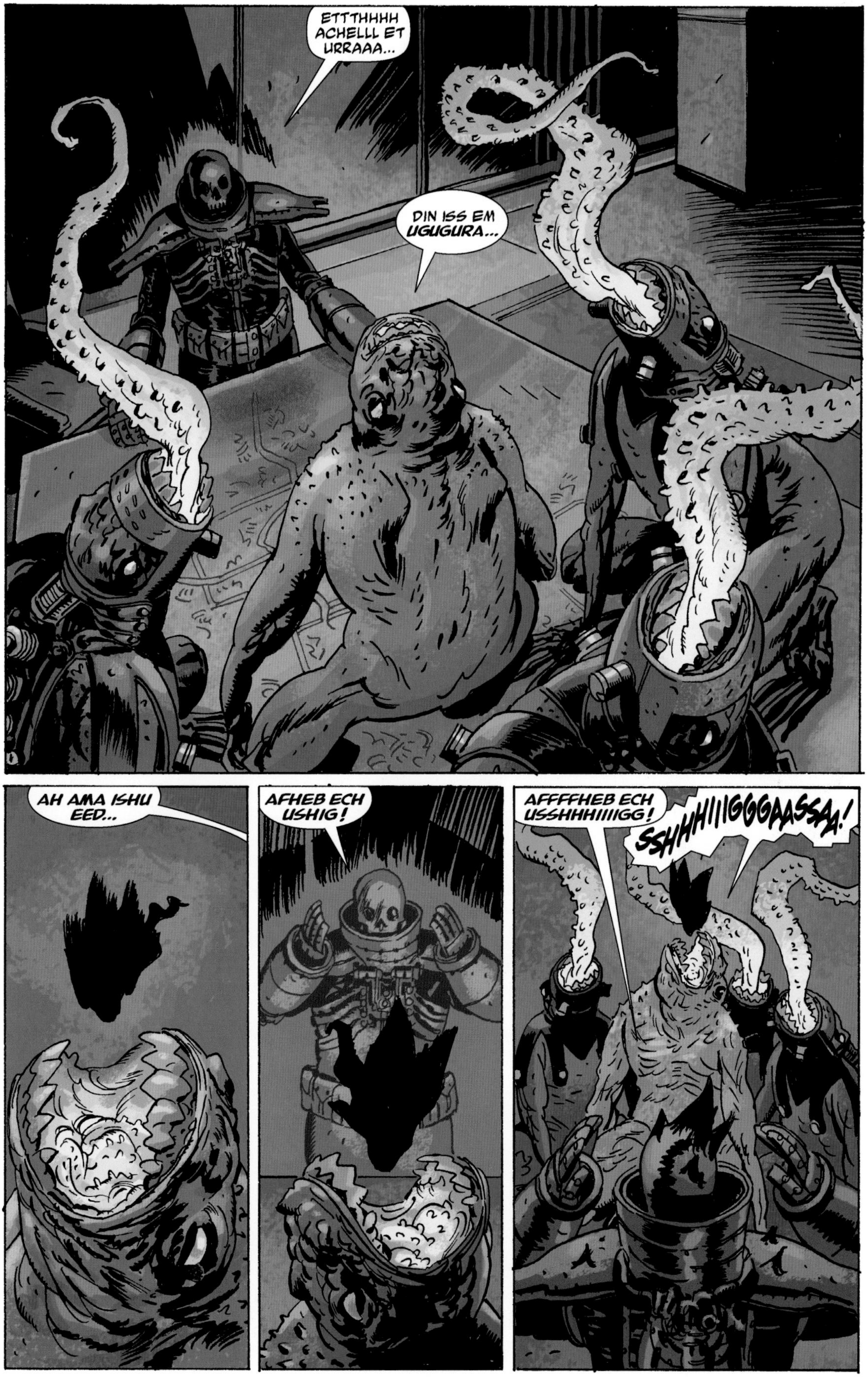
ETTTHHHH ACHELLL ET URRAAA...
DIN ISS EM UGUGURA...
AH AMA ISHU EED...
AFHEB ECH USHIG!
AFFFFHEB ECH USSHHHIIIIGG!
SSHHHIIIGGGAASSAA!

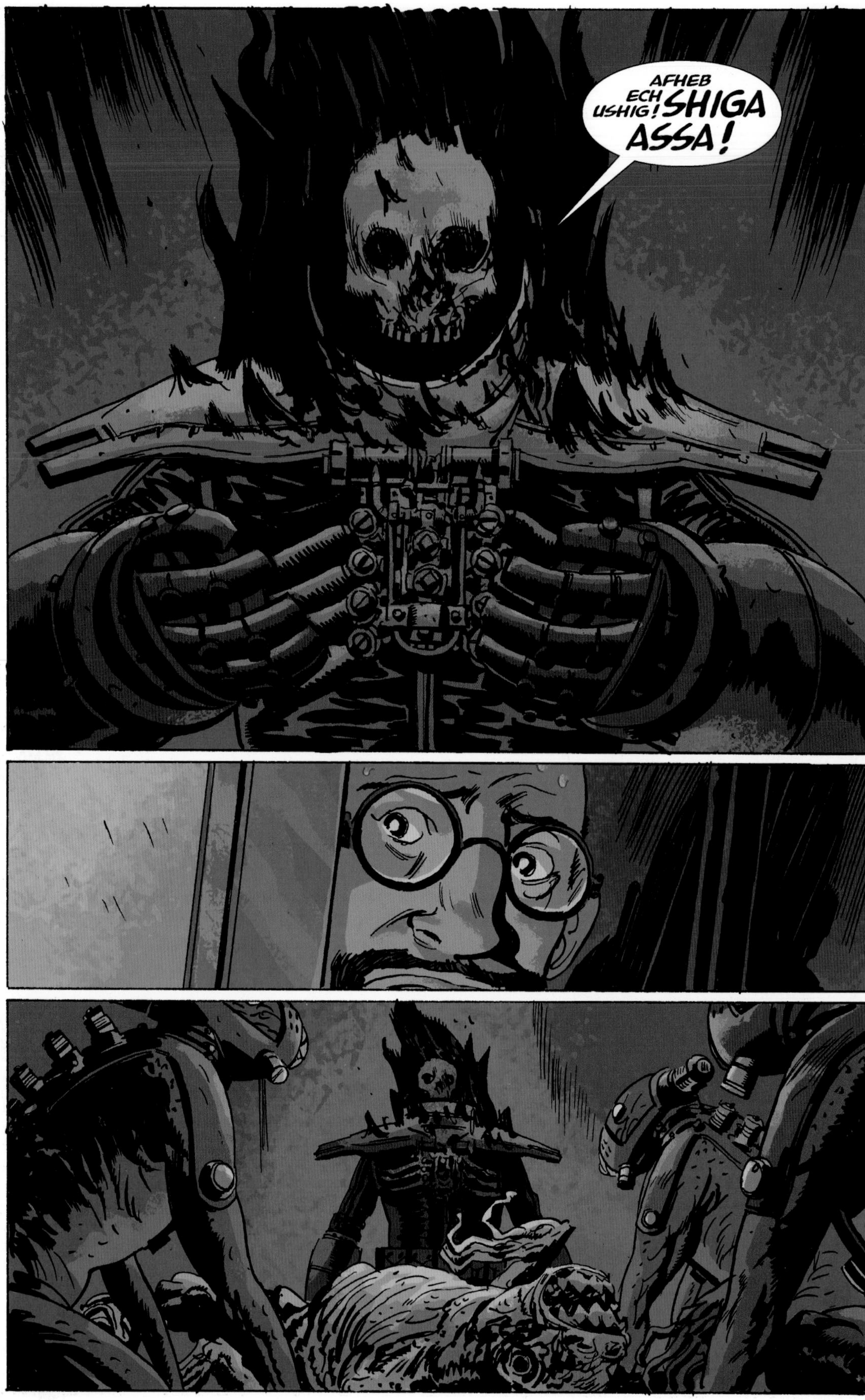
AFHEB ECH USHIG! SHIGA ASSA!

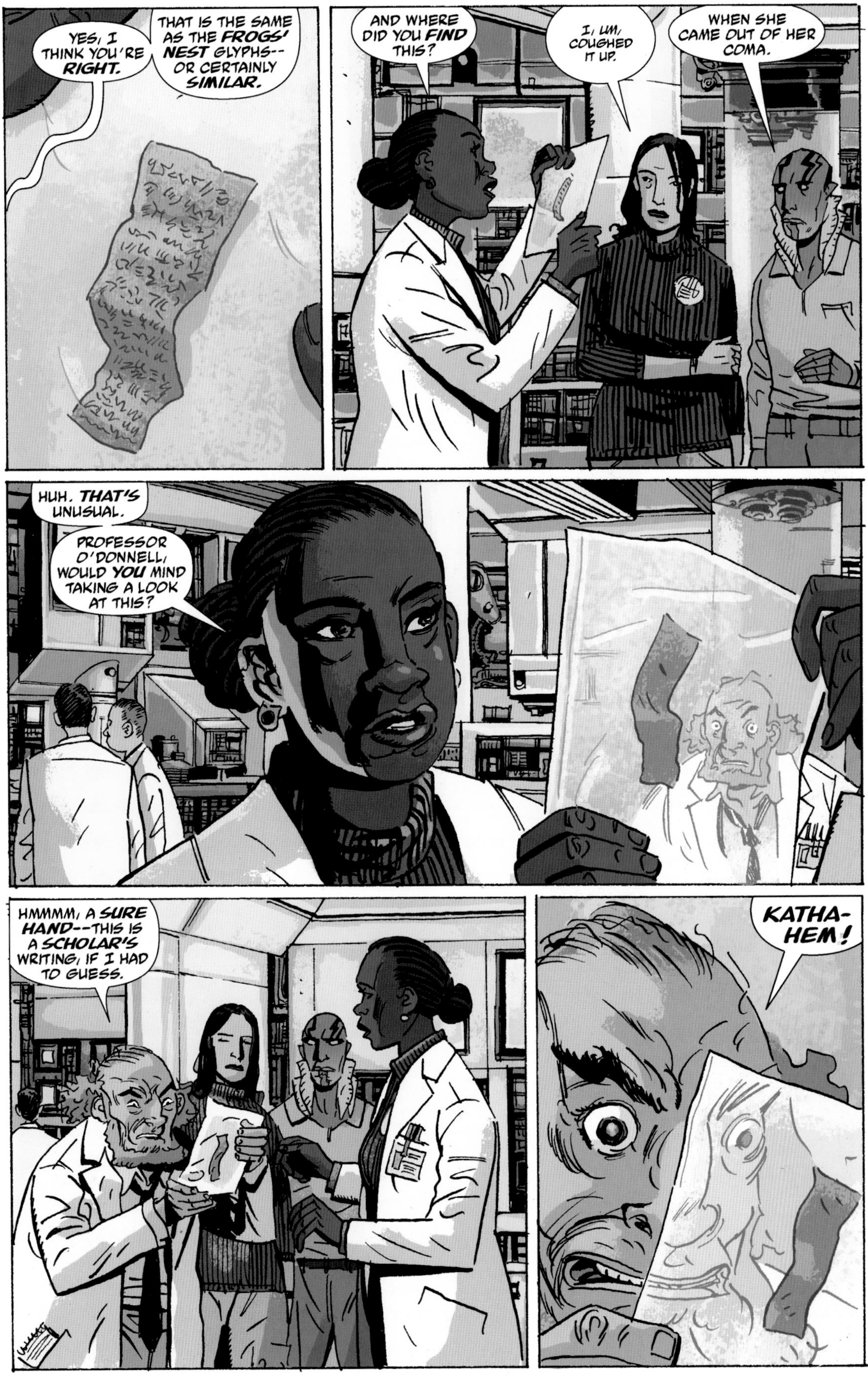
YES, I THINK YOU'RE RIGHT.
THAT IS THE SAME AS THE FROGS' NEST GLYPHS-- OR CERTAINLY SIMILAR.
AND WHERE DID YOU FIND THIS?
I, UM, COUGHED IT UP.
WHEN SHE CAME OUT OF HER COMA.
HUH. THAT'S UNUSUAL.
PROFESSOR O'DONNELL, WOULD YOU MIND TAKING A LOOK AT THIS?
HMMMM, A SURE HAND--THIS IS A SCHOLAR'S WRITING, IF I HAD TO GUESS.
KATHA-HEM!

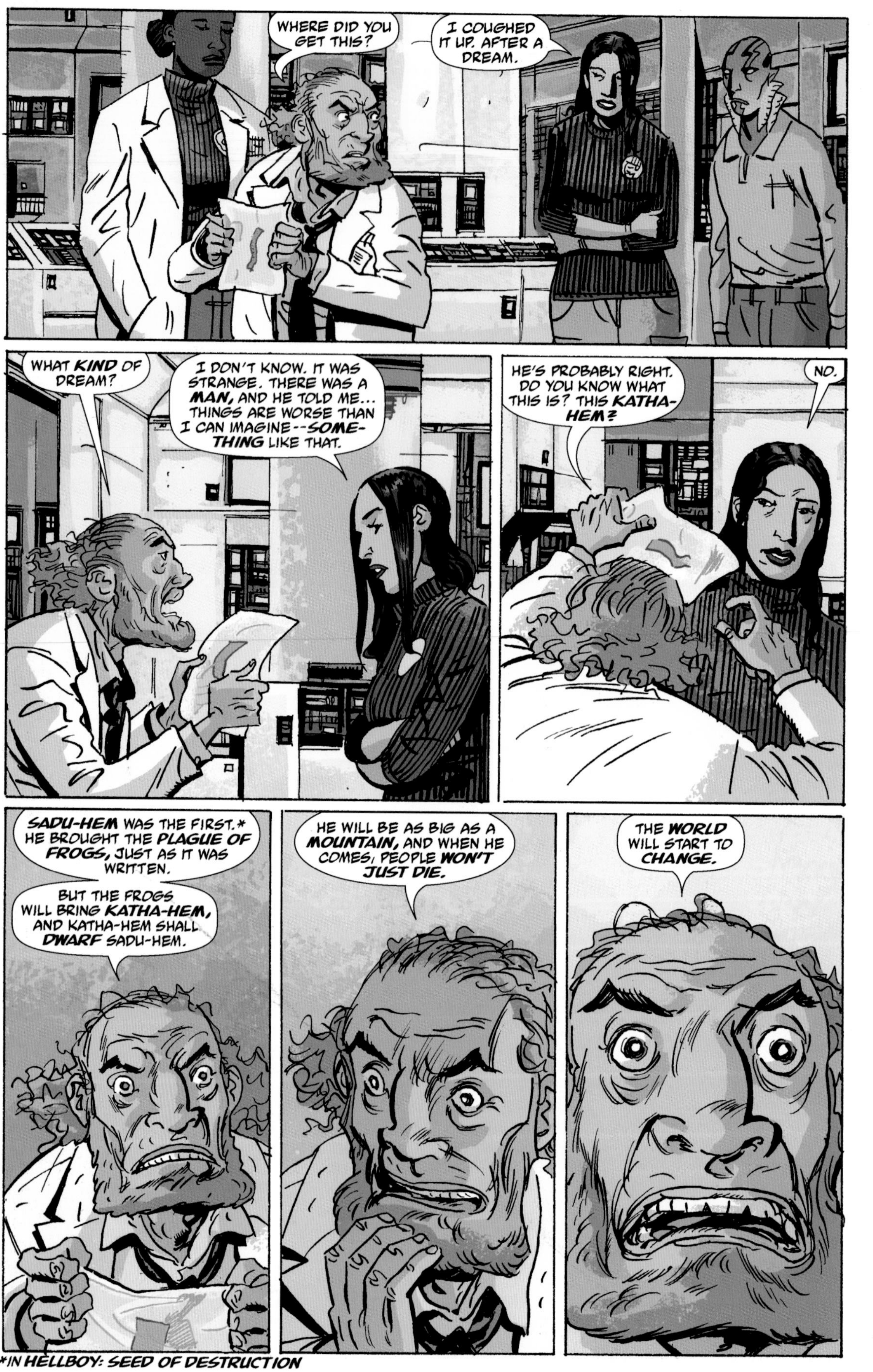
WHERE DID YOU GET THIS?
I COUGHED IT UP. AFTER A DREAM.
WHAT KIND OF DREAM?
I DON'T KNOW. IT WAS STRANGE. THERE WAS A MAN, AND HE TOLD ME... THINGS ARE WORSE THAN I CAN IMAGINE--SOMETHING LIKE THAT.
HE'S PROBABLY RIGHT. DO YOU KNOW WHAT THIS IS? THIS KATHA-HEM?
NO.
SADU-HEM WAS THE FIRST.* HE BROUGHT THE PLAGUE OF FROGS, JUST AS IT WAS WRITTEN.
BUT THE FROGS WILL BRING KATHA-HEM, AND KATHA-HEM SHALL DWARF SADU-HEM.
HE WILL BE AS BIG AS A MOUNTAIN, AND WHEN HE COMES, PEOPLE WON'T JUST DIE.
THE WORLD WILL START TO CHANGE.

*IN HELLBOY: SEED OF DESTRUCTION

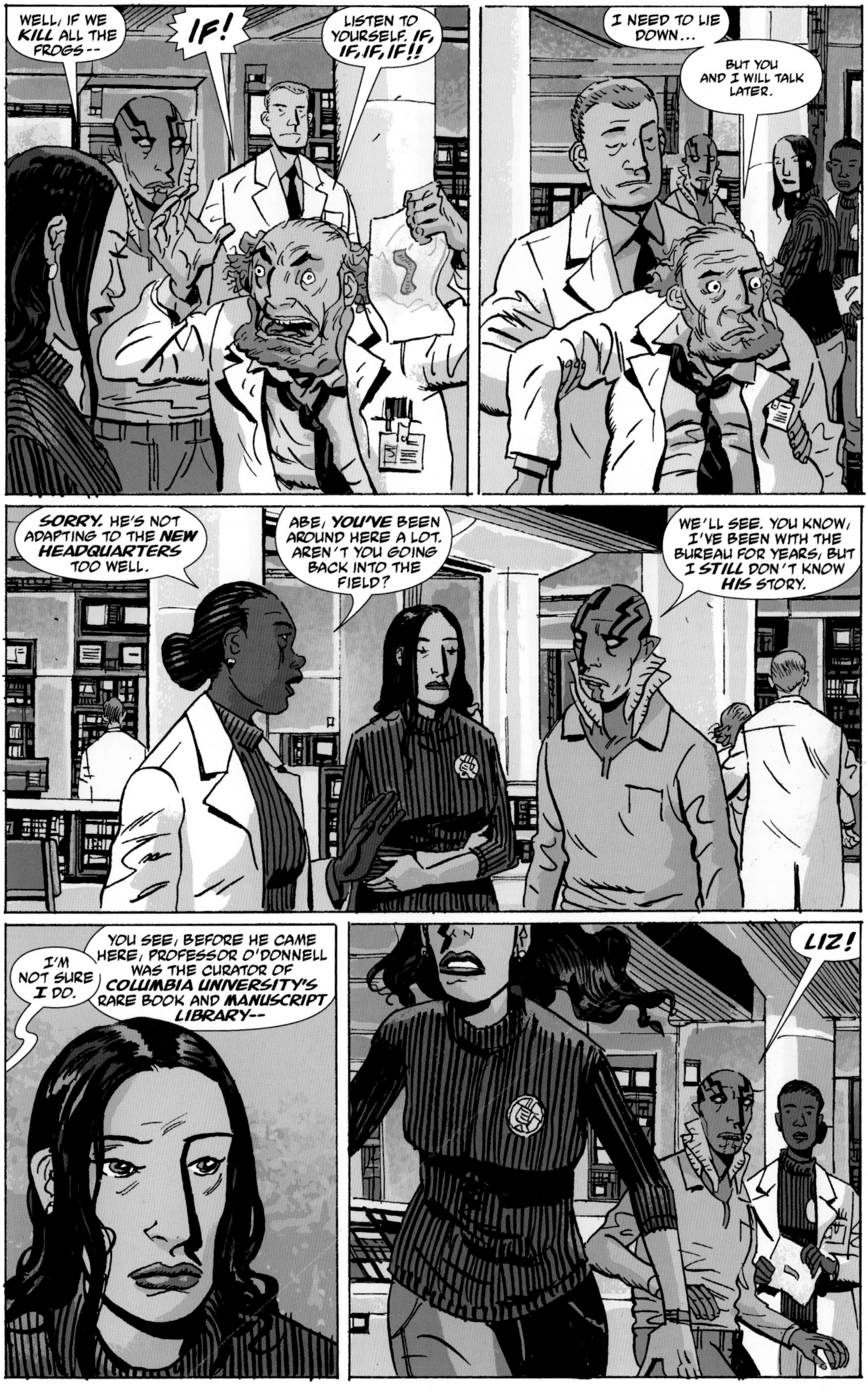

WELL, IF WE KILL ALL THE FROGS--
IF!
LISTEN TO YOURSELF. IF, IF, IF, IF!!
I NEED TO LIE DOWN...
BUT YOU AND I WILL TALK LATER.
SORRY. HE'S NOT ADAPTING TO THE NEW HEADQUARTERS TOO WELL.
ABE, YOU'VE BEEN AROUND HERE A LOT. AREN'T YOU GOING BACK INTO THE FIELD?
WE'LL SEE. YOU KNOW, I'VE BEEN WITH THE BUREAU FOR YEARS, BUT I STILL DON'T KNOW HIS STORY.
I'M NOT SURE I DO.
YOU SEE, BEFORE HE CAME HERE, PROFESSOR O'DONNELL WAS THE CURATOR OF COLUMBIA UNIVERSITY'S RARE BOOK AND MANUSCRIPT LIBRARY--
LIZ!

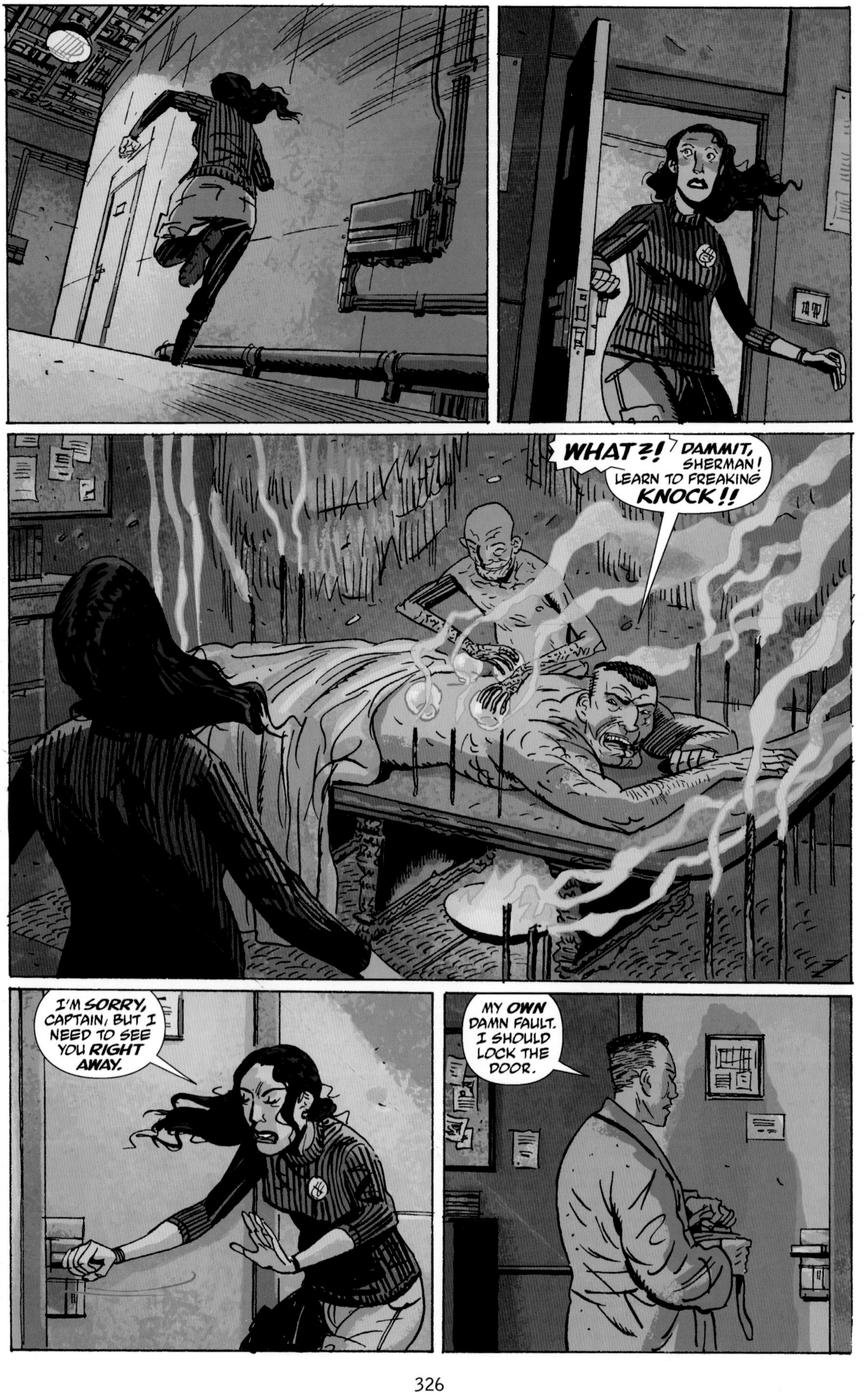
WHAT?! DAMMIT, SHERMAN! LEARN TO FREAKING KNOCK!!
I'M SORRY, CAPTAIN, BUT I NEED TO SEE YOU RIGHT AWAY.
MY OWN DAMN FAULT. I SHOULD LOCK THE DOOR.

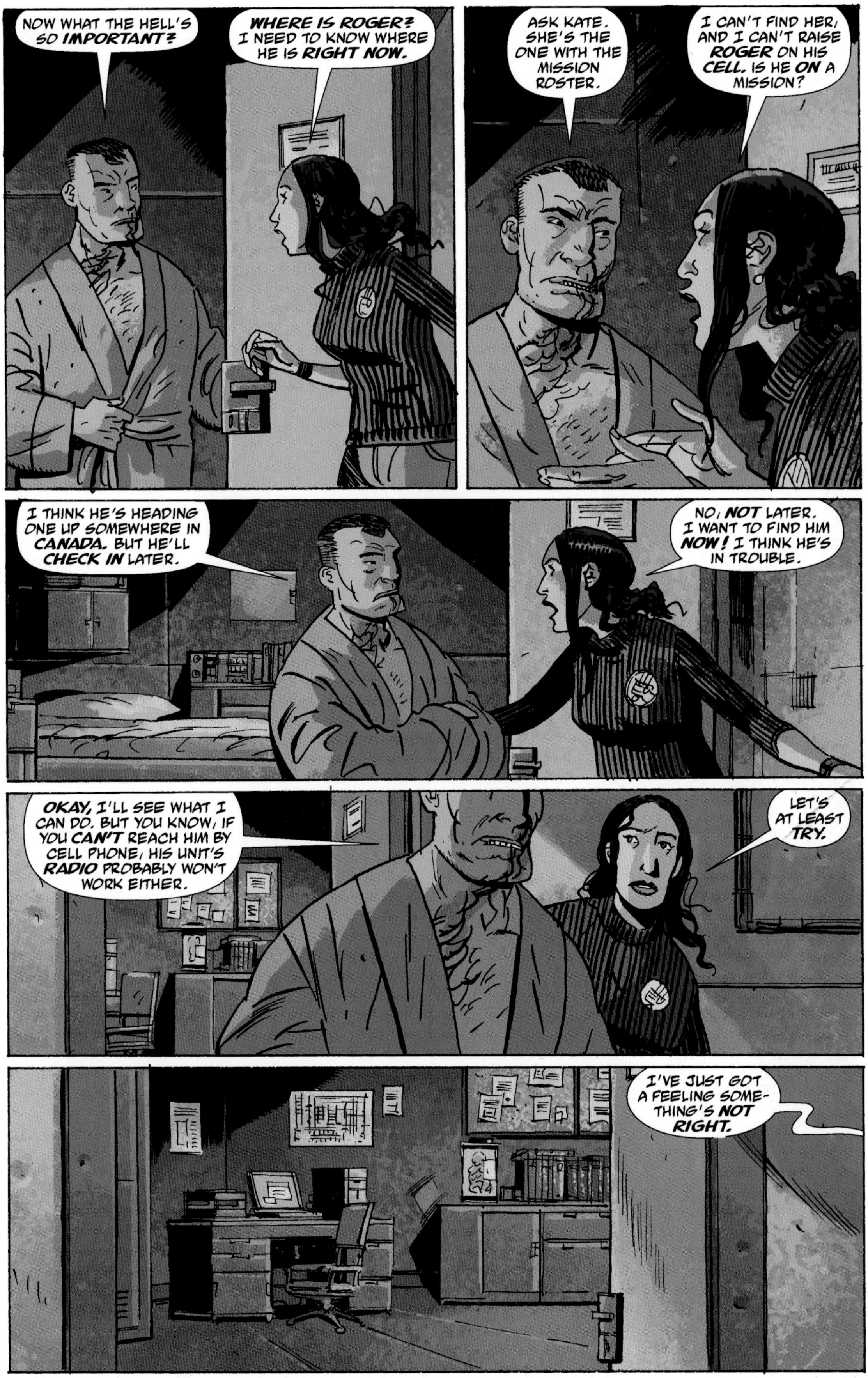

NOW WHAT THE HELL'S SO IMPORTANT?
WHERE IS ROGER? I NEED TO KNOW WHERE HE IS RIGHT NOW.
ASK KATE. SHE'S THE ONE WITH THE MISSION ROSTER.
I CAN'T FIND HER, AND I CAN'T RAISE ROGER ON HIS CELL. IS HE ON A MISSION?
I THINK HE'S HEADING ONE UP SOMEWHERE IN CANADA. BUT HE'LL CHECK IN LATER.
NO, NOT LATER. I WANT TO FIND HIM NOW! I THINK HE'S IN TROUBLE.
OKAY, I'LL SEE WHAT I CAN DO. BUT YOU KNOW, IF YOU CAN'T REACH HIM BY CELL PHONE, HIS UNIT'S RADIO PROBABLY WON'T WORK EITHER.
LET'S AT LEAST TRY.
I'VE JUST GOT A FEELING SOME-THING'S NOT RIGHT.

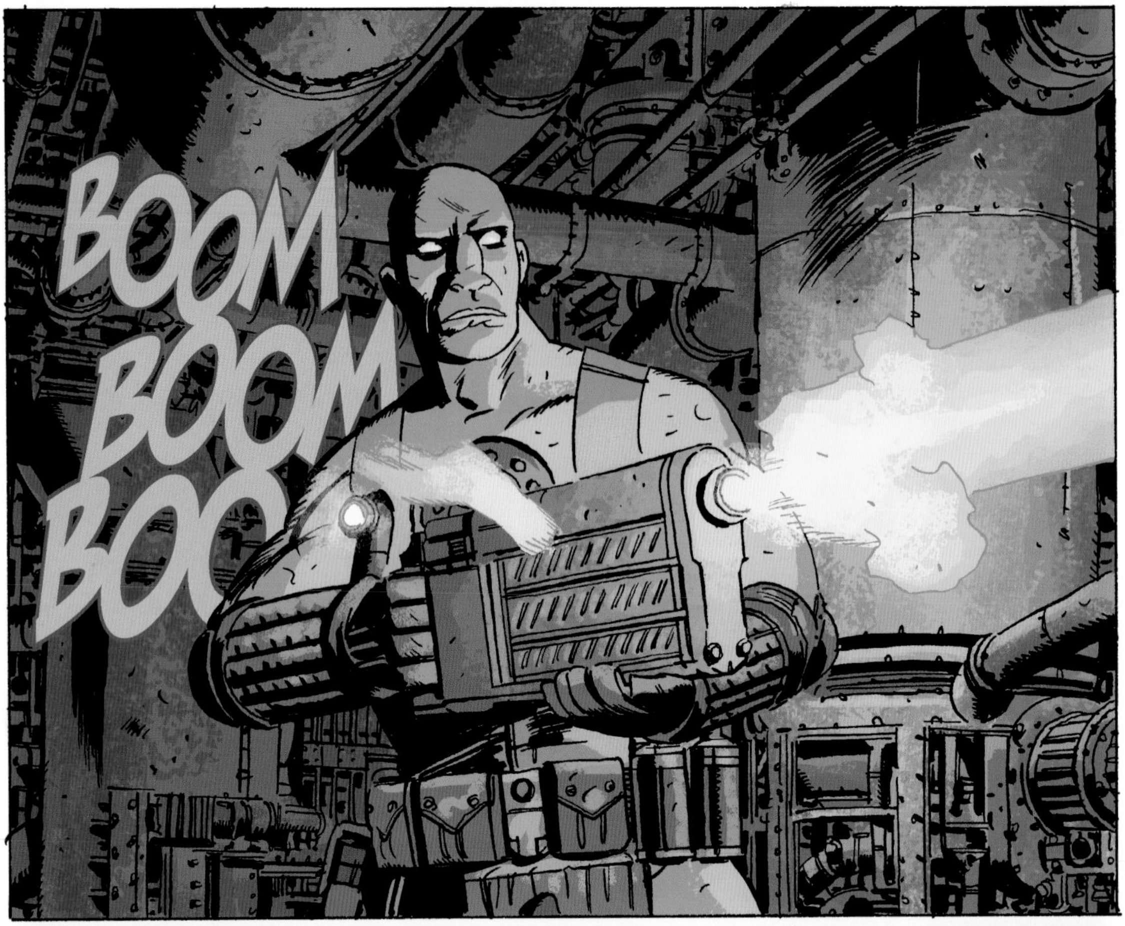
BOOM
BOOM
BOO

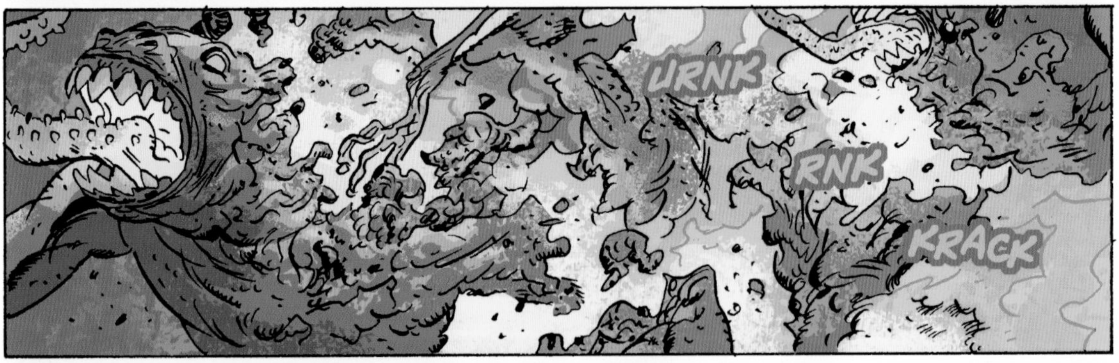
URNK
RNK
KRACK

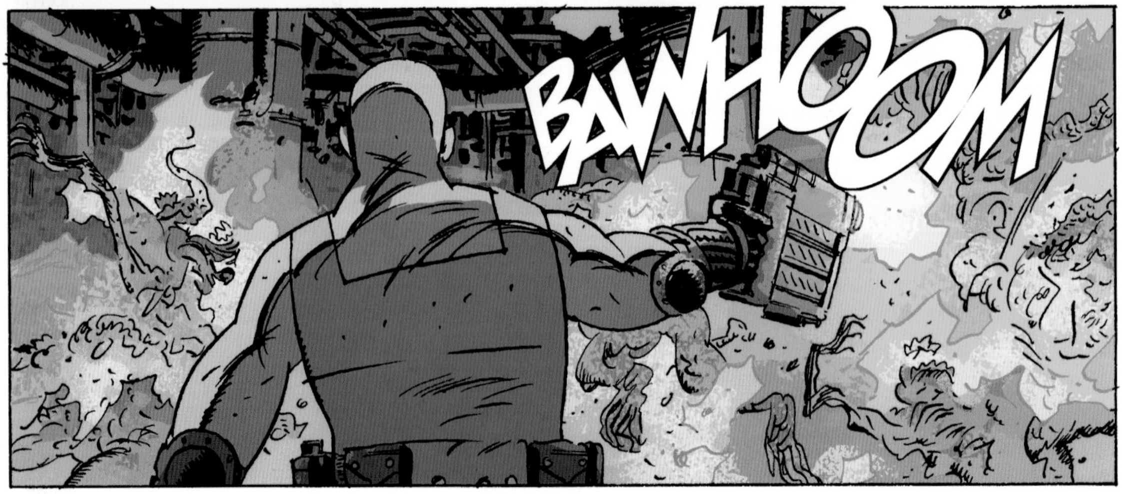
BAWHOOM

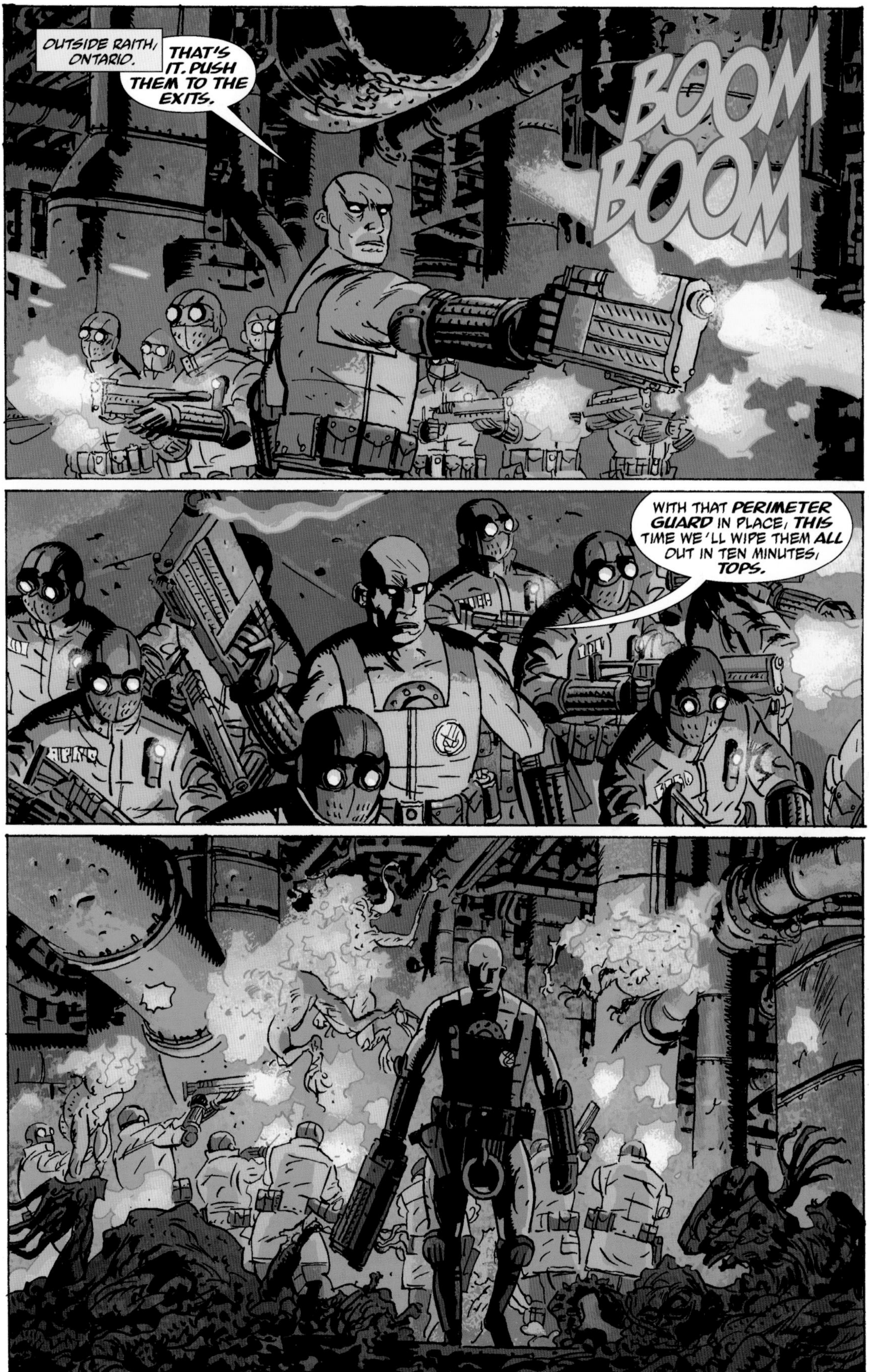
OUTSIDE RAITH, ONTARIO.
THAT'S IT. PUSH THEM TO THE EXITS.
BOOM BOOM
WITH THAT PERIMETER GUARD IN PLACE, THIS TIME WE'LL WIPE THEM ALL OUT IN TEN MINUTES, TOPS.

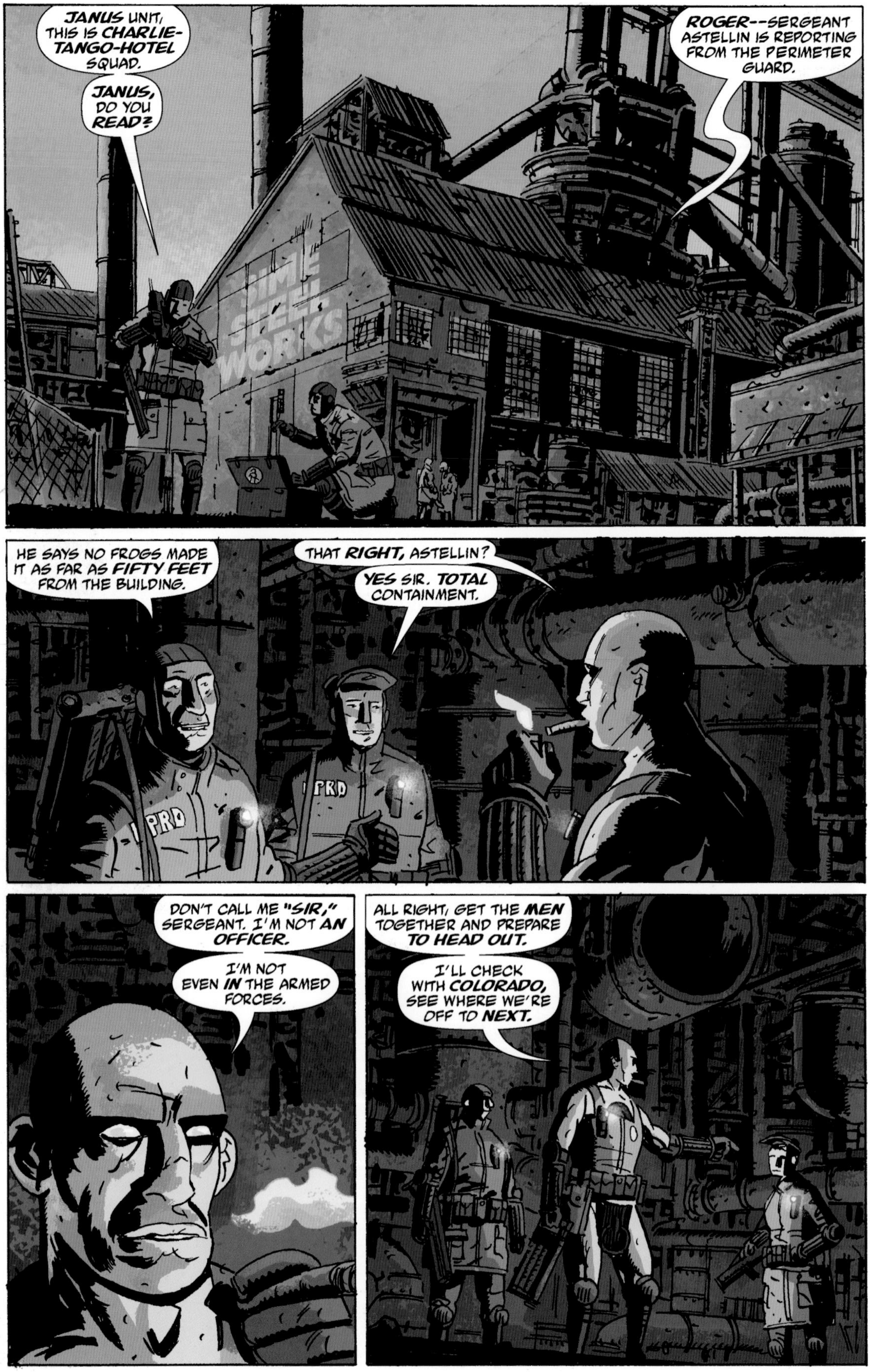
JANUS UNIT, THIS IS CHARLIE-TANGO-HOTEL SQUAD.
JANUS, DO YOU READ?
ROGER--SERGEANT ASTELLIN IS REPORTING FROM THE PERIMETER GUARD.
HE SAYS NO FROGS MADE IT AS FAR AS FIFTY FEET FROM THE BUILDING.
THAT RIGHT, ASTELLIN?
YES SIR. TOTAL CONTAINMENT.
DON'T CALL ME "SIR," SERGEANT. I'M NOT AN OFFICER.
I'M NOT EVEN IN THE ARMED FORCES.
ALL RIGHT, GET THE MEN TOGETHER AND PREPARE TO HEAD OUT.
I'LL CHECK WITH COLORADO, SEE WHERE WE'RE OFF TO NEXT.

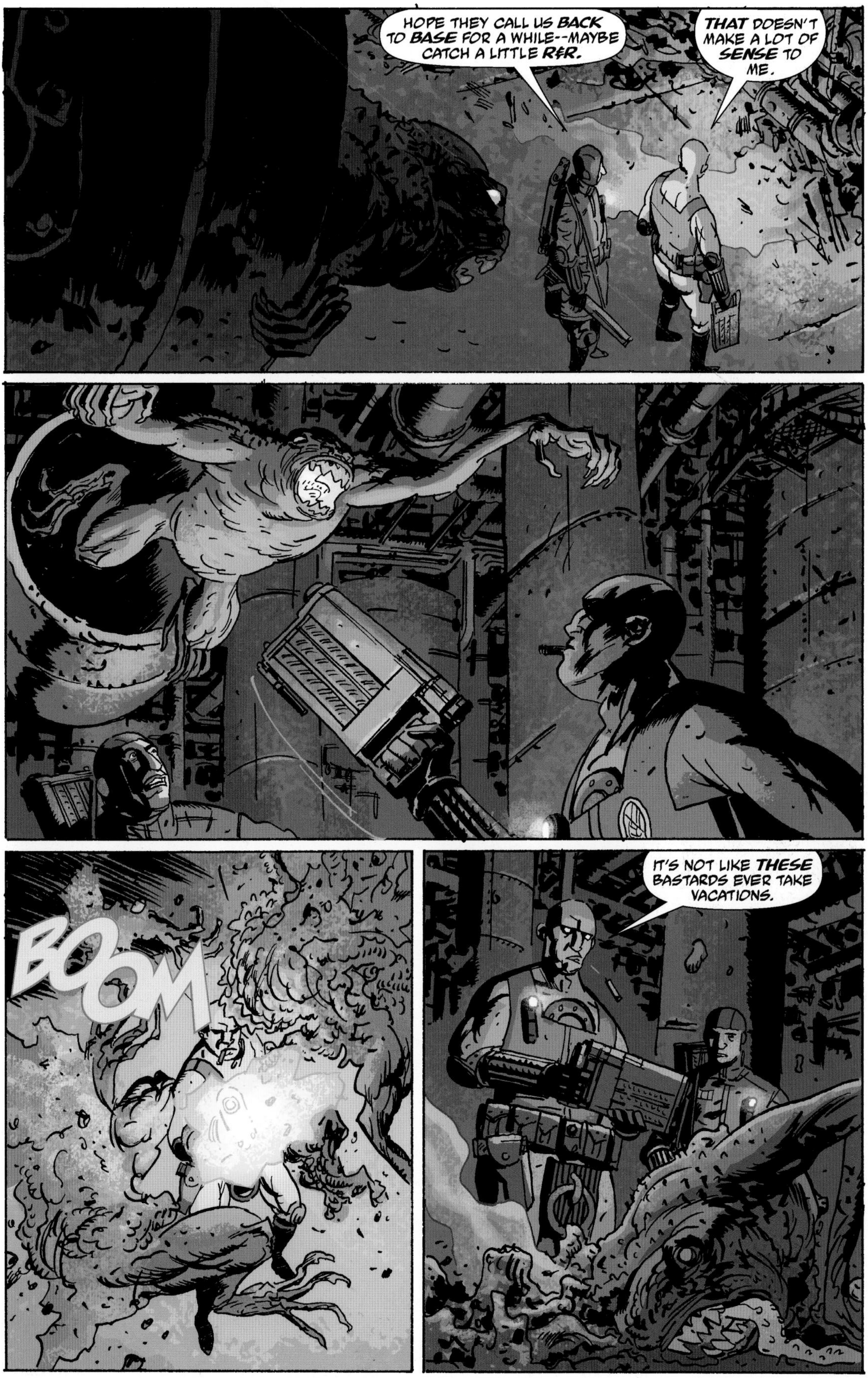
HOPE THEY CALL US BACK TO BASE FOR A WHILE--MAYBE CATCH A LITTLE R&R.
THAT DOESN'T MAKE A LOT OF SENSE TO ME.
BOOM
IT'S NOT LIKE THESE BASTARDS EVER TAKE VACATIONS.

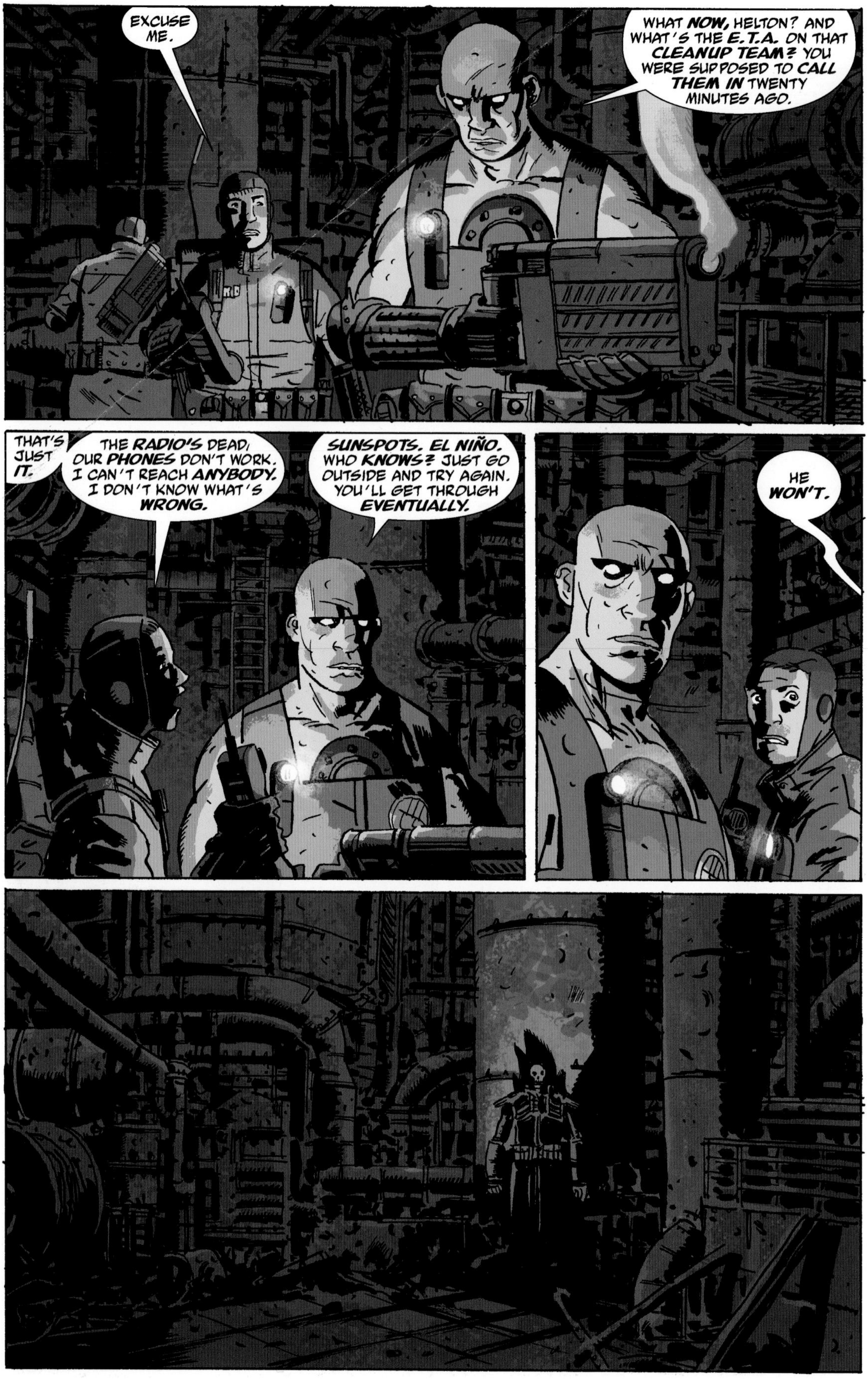
EXCUSE ME.
WHAT NOW, HELTON? AND WHAT'S THE E.T.A. ON THAT CLEANUP TEAM? YOU WERE SUPPOSED TO CALL THEM IN TWENTY MINUTES AGO.
THAT'S JUST IT.
THE RADIO'S DEAD, OUR PHONES DON'T WORK. I CAN'T REACH ANYBODY. I DON'T KNOW WHAT'S WRONG.
SUNSPOTS. EL NIÑO. WHO KNOWS? JUST GO OUTSIDE AND TRY AGAIN. YOU'LL GET THROUGH EVENTUALLY.
HE WON'T.

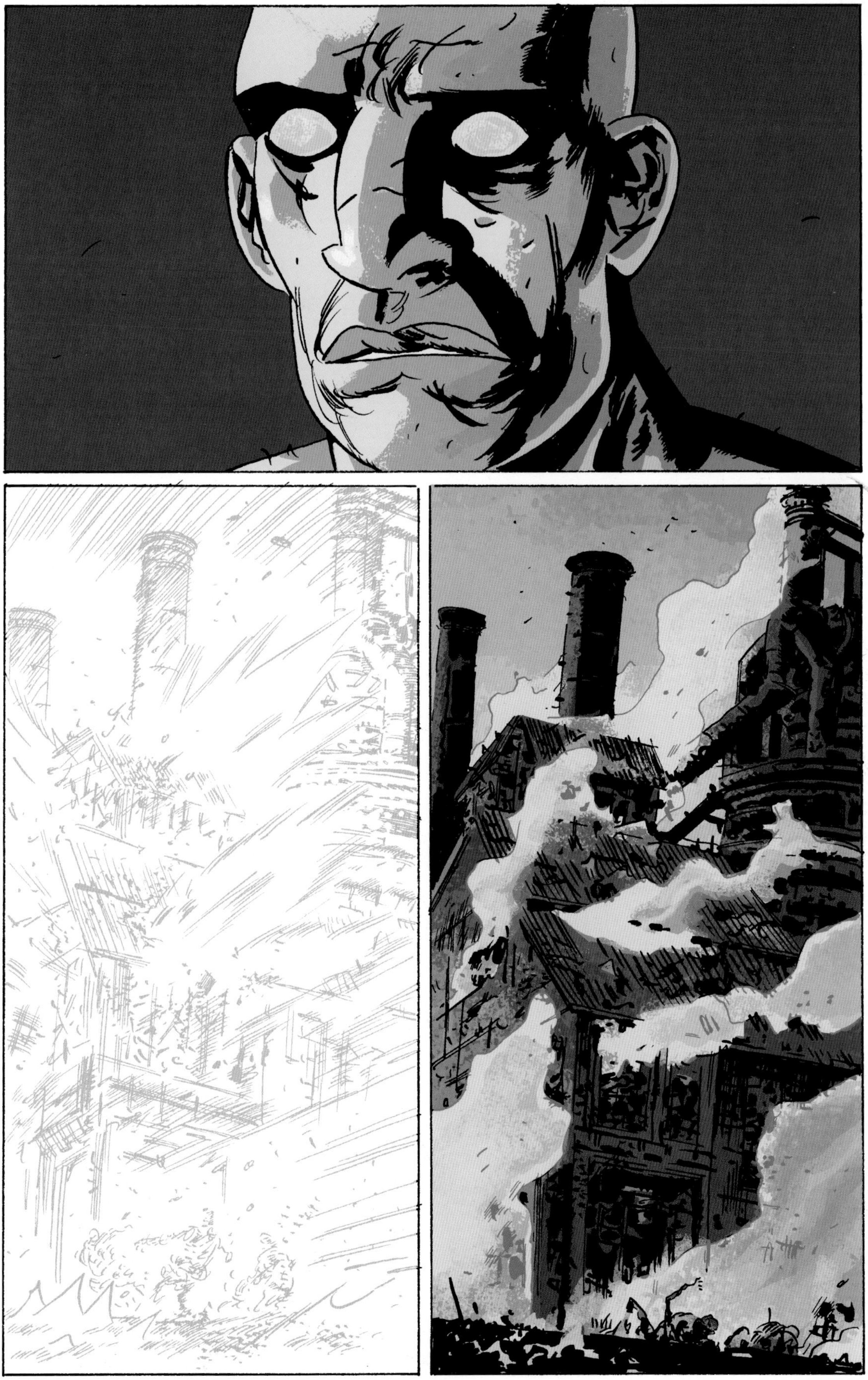

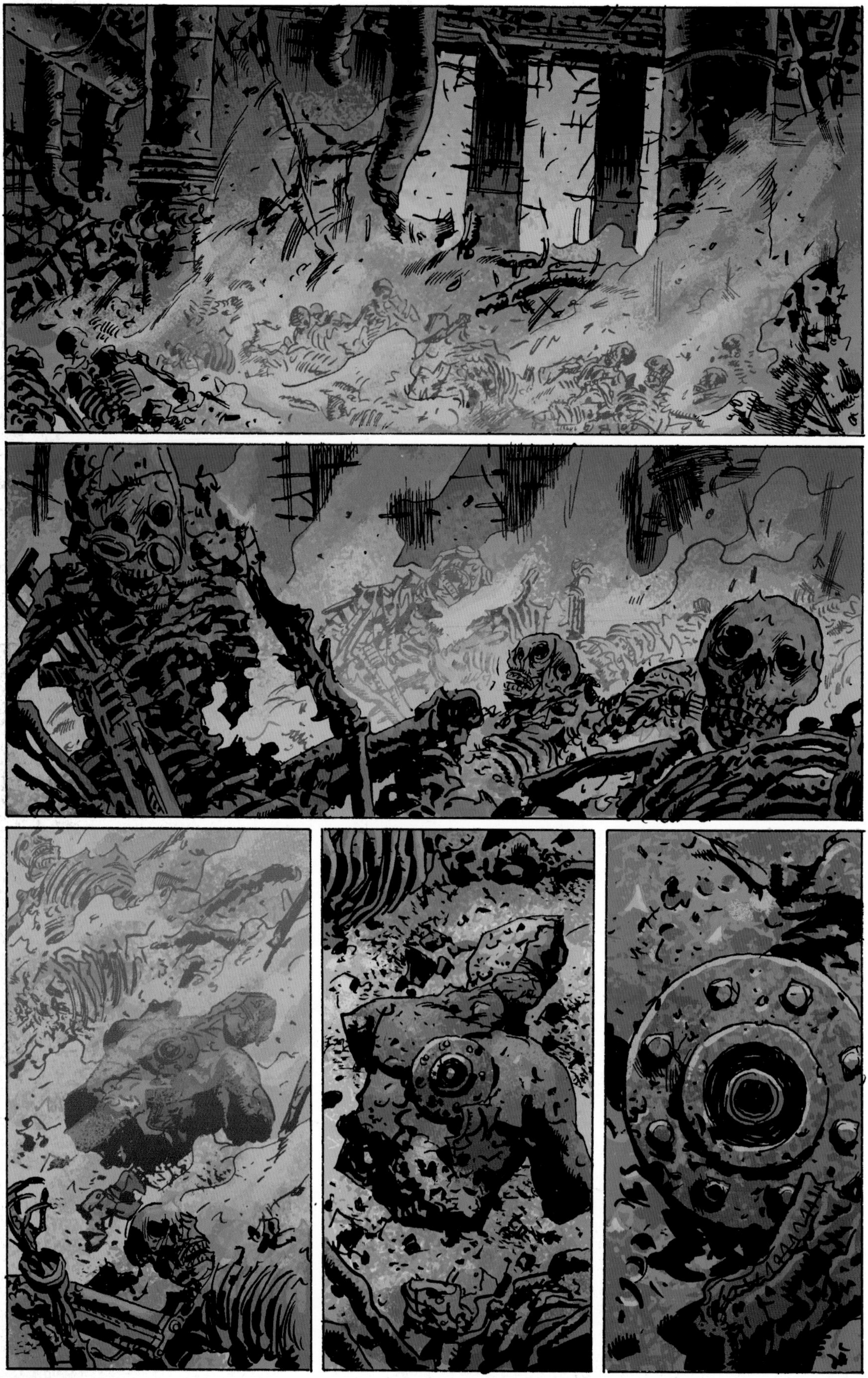

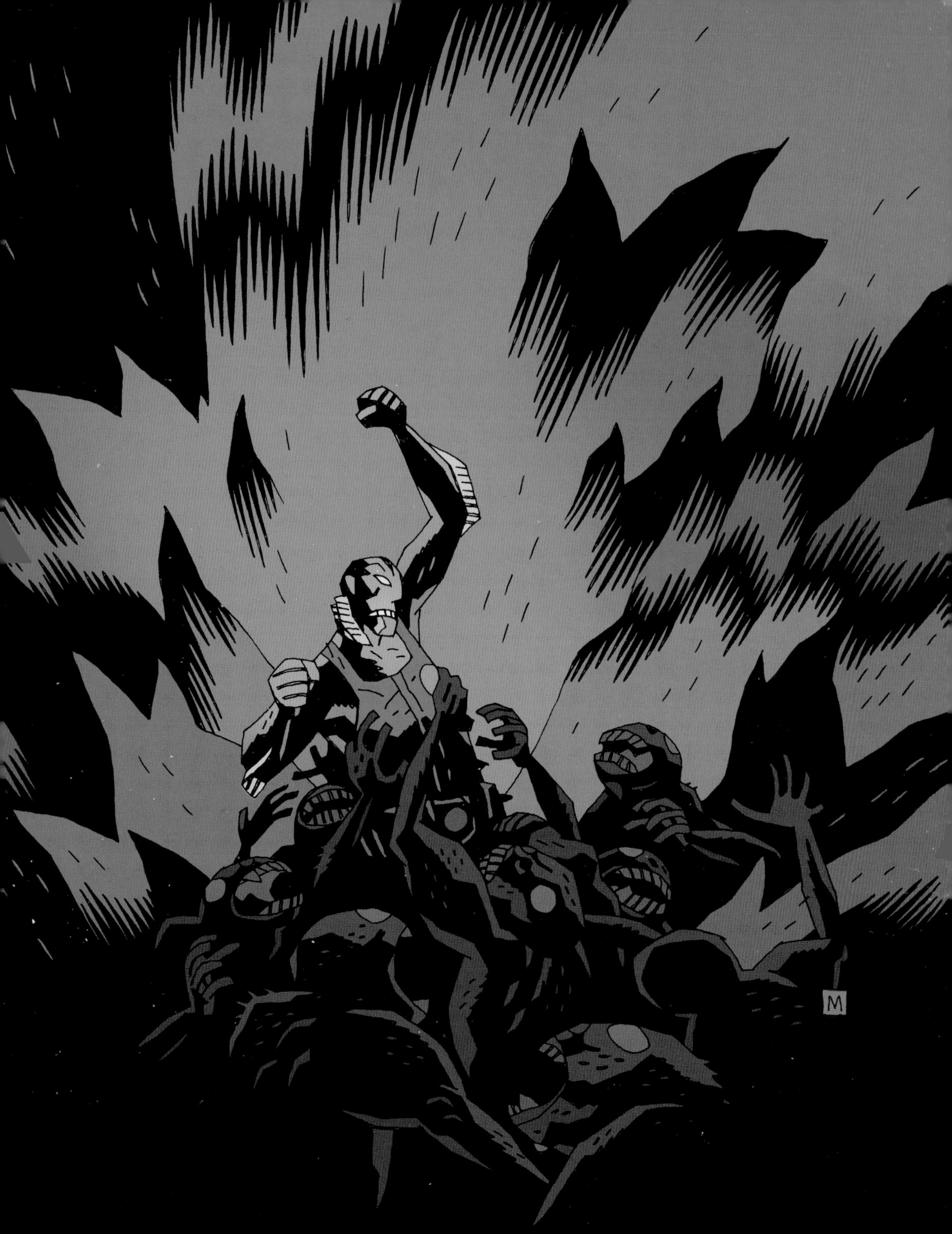

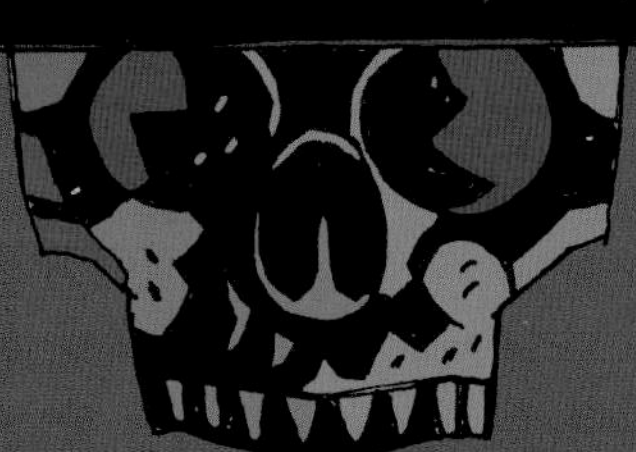

CHAPTER THREE

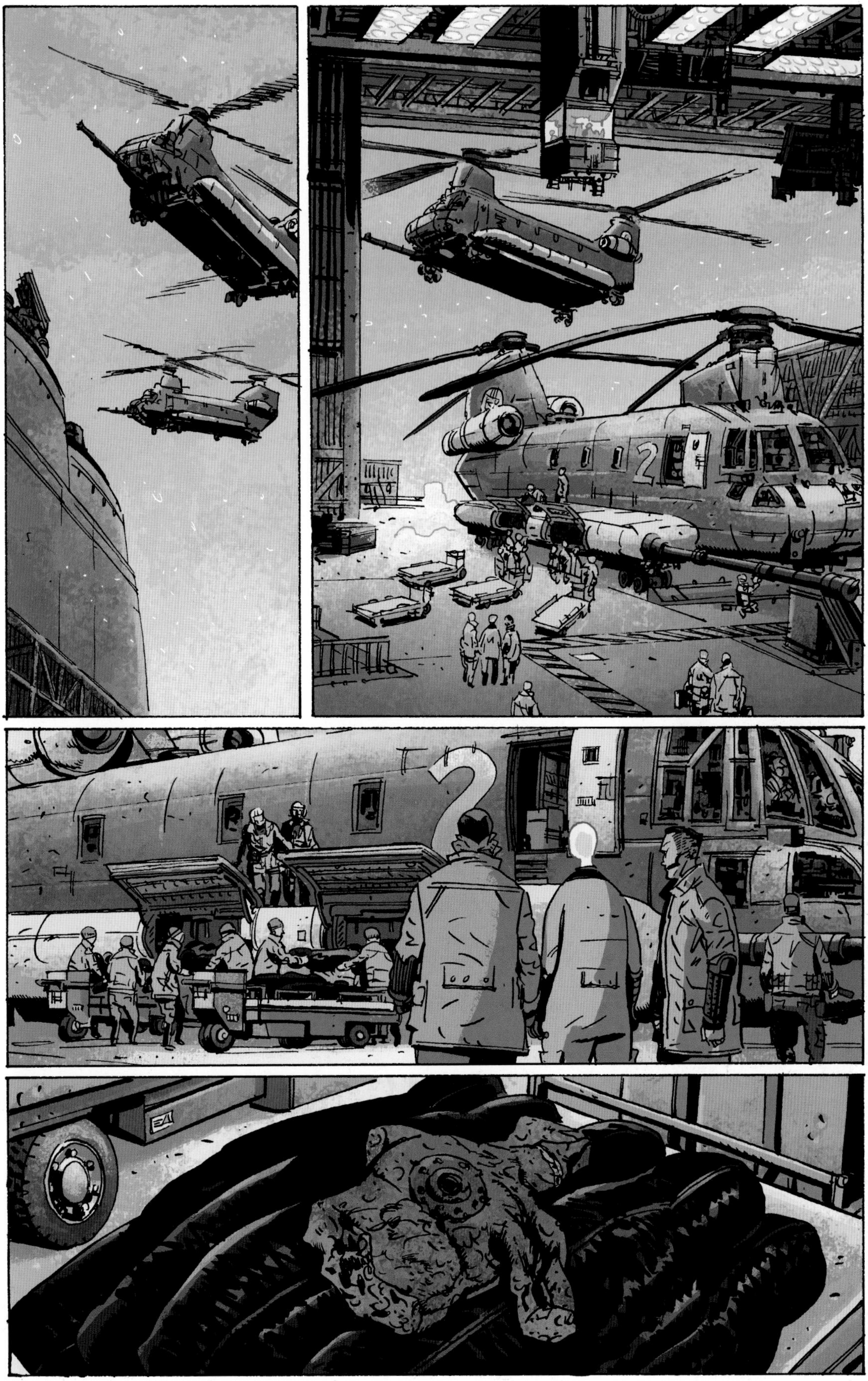

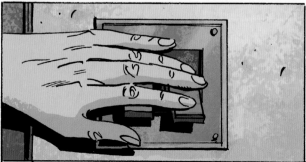

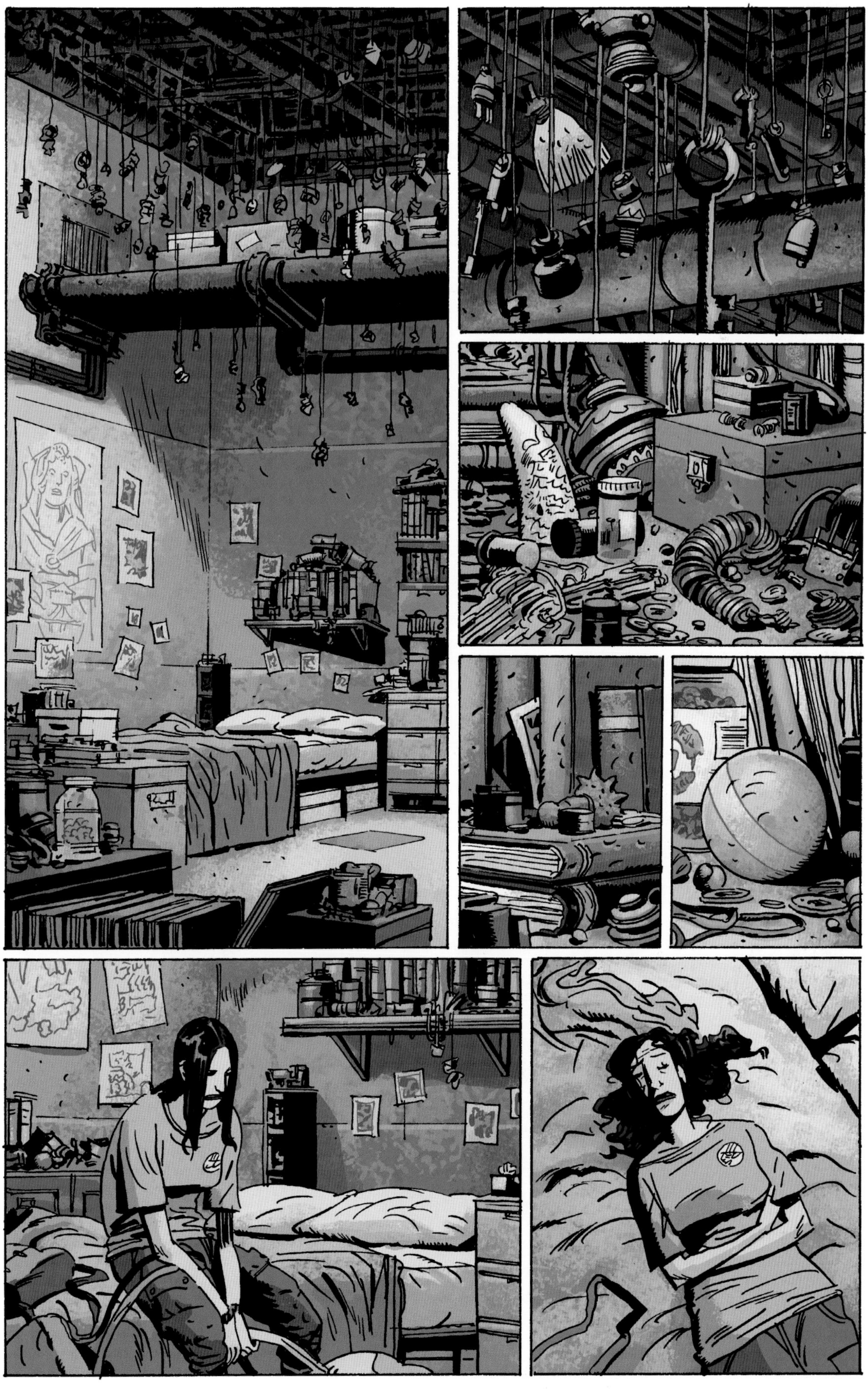

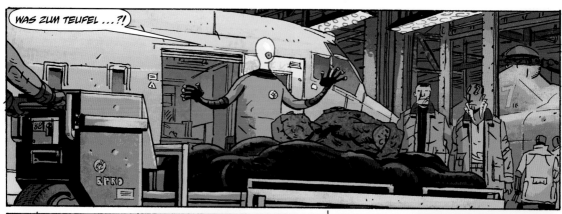

WAS ZUM TEUFEL ...?!

THE OTHERS YOU PUT IN *BODY BAGS*, BUT NOT *ROGER*?

YOU THINK HE IS *GARBAGE* YOU CAN *THROW JUST ANYWHERE*?

NOT MY *CALL*, AGENT KRAUS. THE *DIRECTOR* DOESN'T WANT HIM IN THE MORGUE.

THIS IS *WRONG*. HE WAS A *PERSON*!

HE WAS A *MENSCH*!

COME *ON*, JOHANN.

YEAH, LET'S TAKE IT EASY.

WHY?! WHY MUST I "TAKE IT EASY"?

AND WHO ARE THE TWO OF *YOU* TO TELL *ME* ANYTHING?

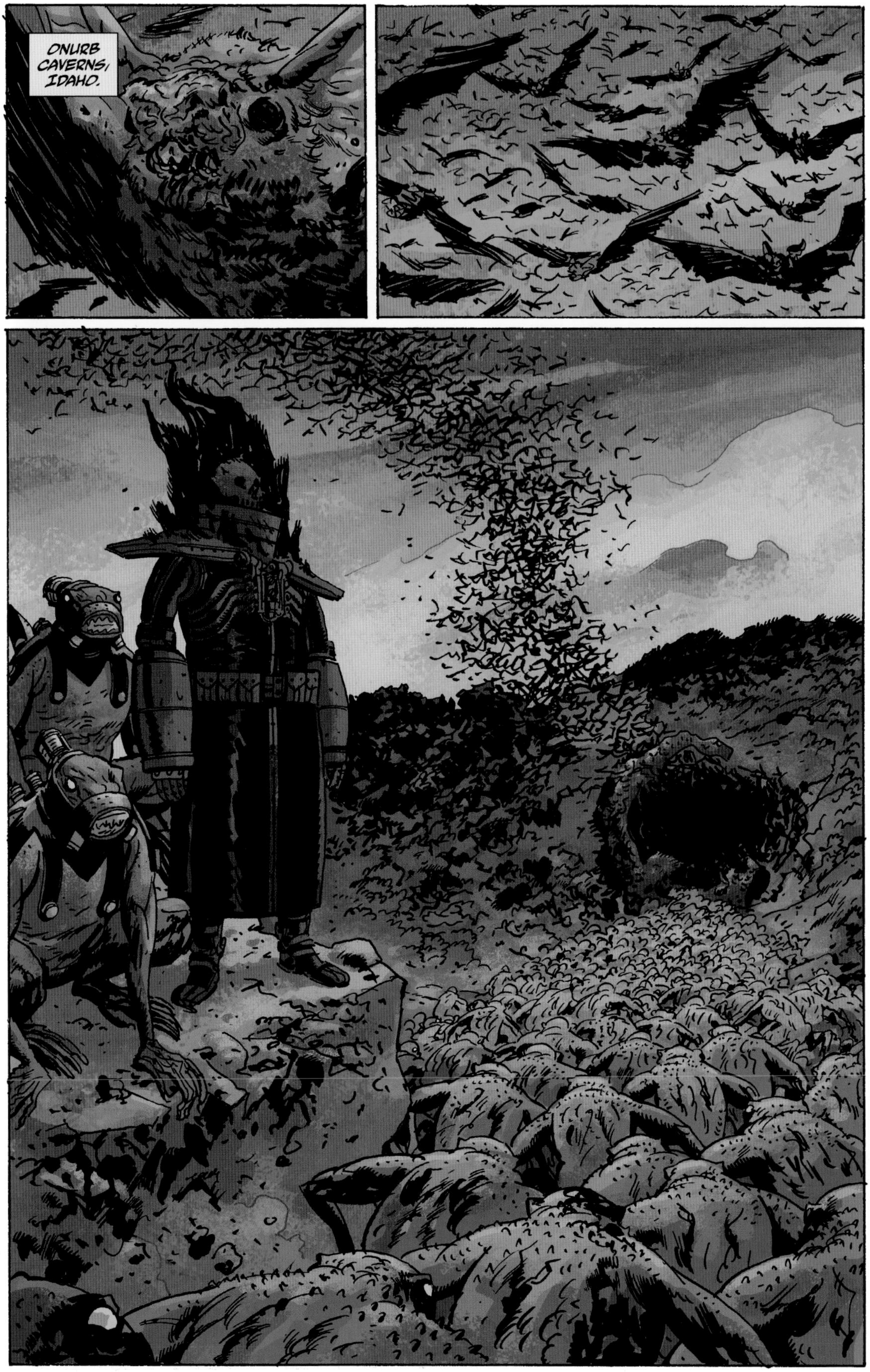
ONURB CAVERNS, IDAHO.

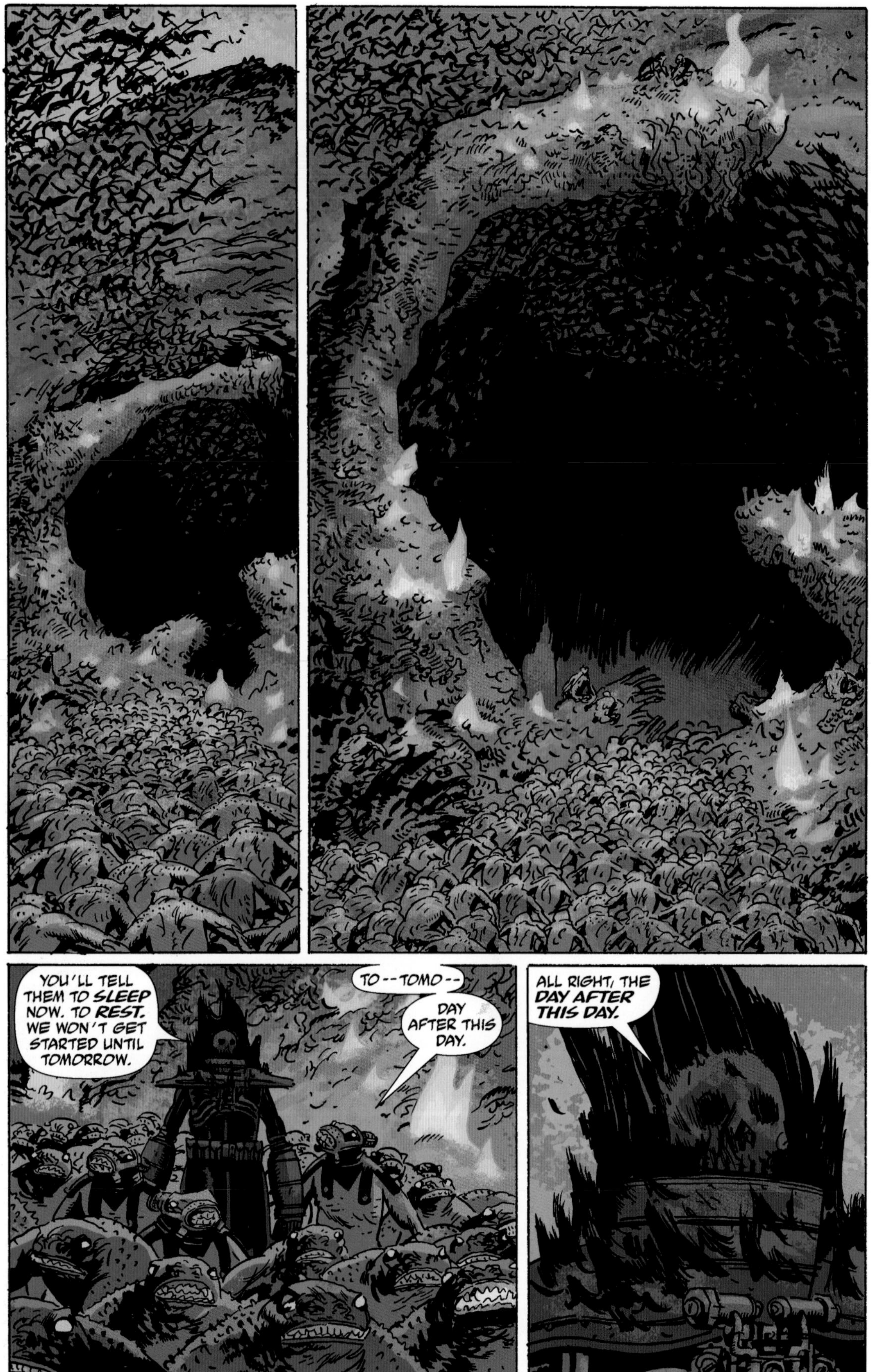
YOU'LL TELL THEM TO **SLEEP** NOW. TO **REST.** WE WON'T GET STARTED UNTIL TOMORROW.
TO--TOMO--
DAY AFTER THIS DAY.
ALL RIGHT, THE ***DAY AFTER THIS DAY.***

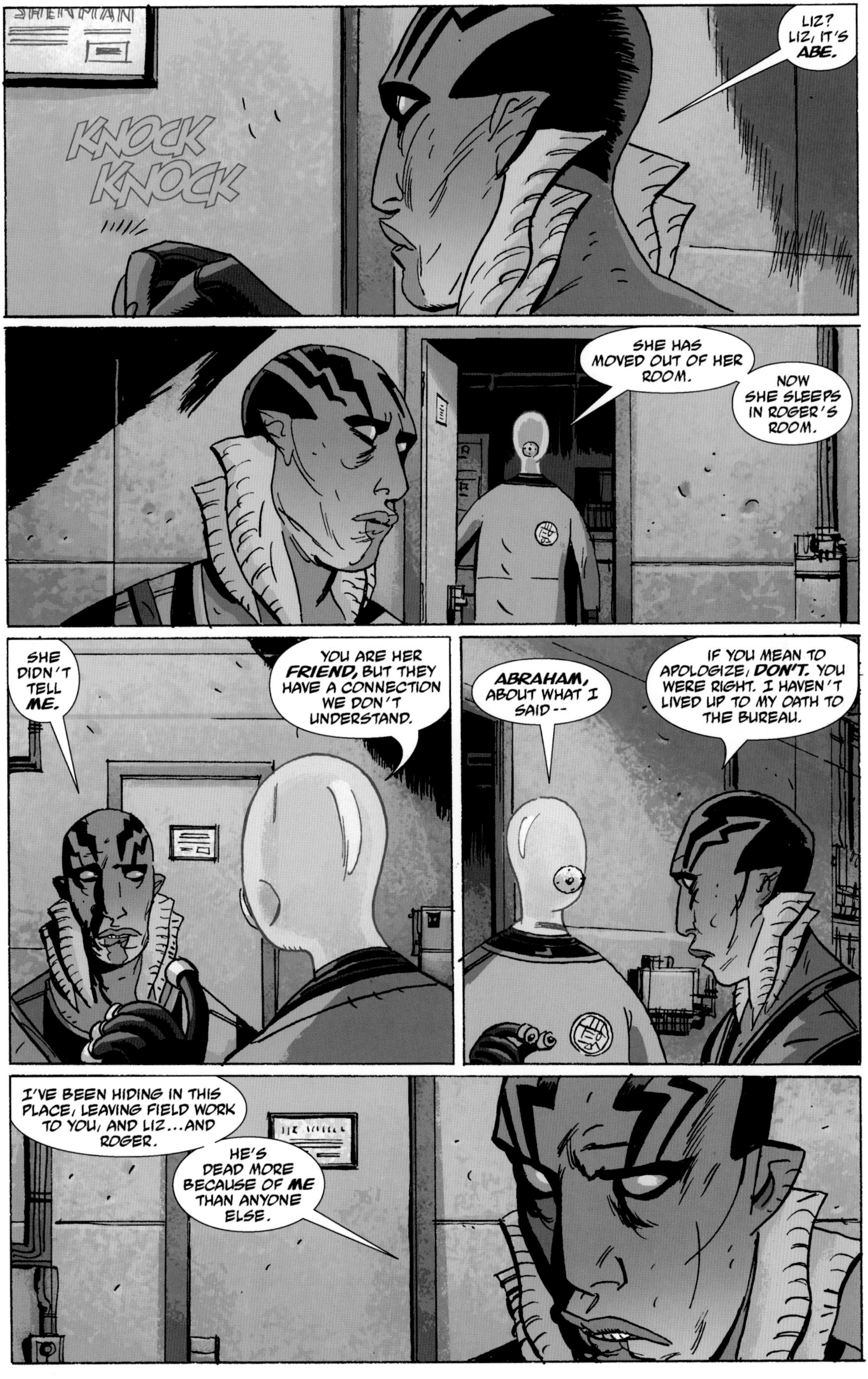
KNOCK KNOCK
LIZ? LIZ, IT'S **ABE.**
SHE HAS MOVED OUT OF HER ROOM.
NOW SHE SLEEPS IN ROGER'S ROOM.
SHE DIDN'T TELL **ME.**
YOU ARE HER **FRIEND,** BUT THEY HAVE A CONNECTION WE DON'T UNDERSTAND.
ABRAHAM, ABOUT WHAT I SAID --
IF YOU MEAN TO APOLOGIZE, **DON'T.** YOU WERE RIGHT. I HAVEN'T LIVED UP TO MY OATH TO THE BUREAU.
I'VE BEEN HIDING IN THIS PLACE, LEAVING FIELD WORK TO YOU, AND LIZ...AND ROGER.
HE'S DEAD MORE BECAUSE OF **ME** THAN ANYONE ELSE.

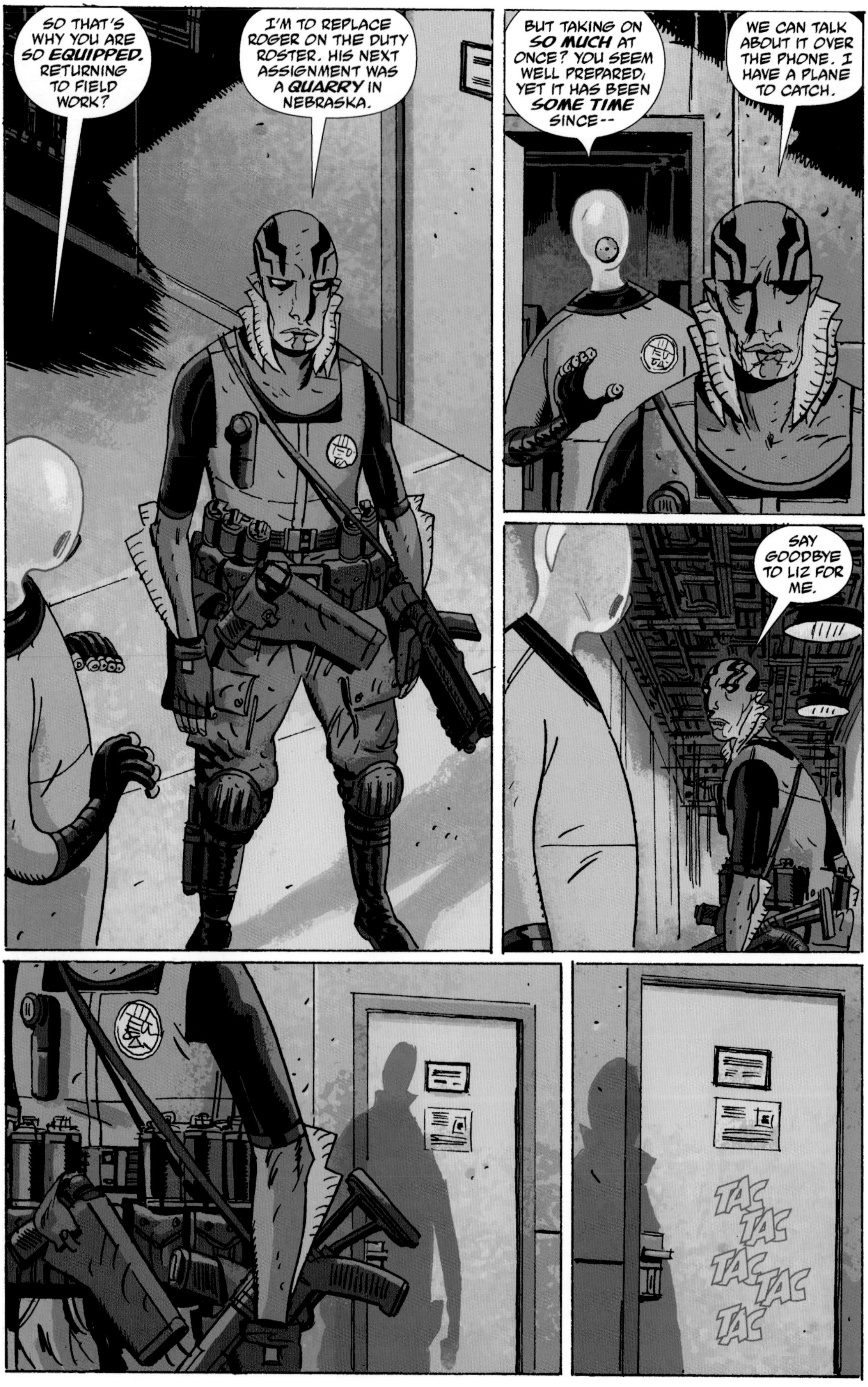
SO THAT'S WHY YOU ARE SO EQUIPPED. RETURNING TO FIELD WORK?
I'M TO REPLACE ROGER ON THE DUTY ROSTER. HIS NEXT ASSIGNMENT WAS A QUARRY IN NEBRASKA.
BUT TAKING ON SO MUCH AT ONCE? YOU SEEM WELL PREPARED, YET IT HAS BEEN SOME TIME SINCE--
WE CAN TALK ABOUT IT OVER THE PHONE. I HAVE A PLANE TO CATCH.
SAY GOODBYE TO LIZ FOR ME.
TAC TAC TAC TAC TAC

--cannot, in hindsight, truthfully say that under my command Agent Roger received all the training required of a platoon leader.

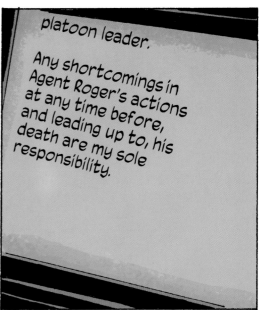

platoon leader.

Any shortcomings in Agent Roger's actions at any time before, and leading up to, his death are my sole responsibility.

IT IS TIME, CAPTAIN.

NOT *NOW*, CHINAMAN!

I am grateful for the opportunity the Bureau has offered me, but I must respectfully submit my resignation, effective immediately upon your receipt of this letter.

Captain Benjamin Daimio
cc: Dr. Kate Corrigan

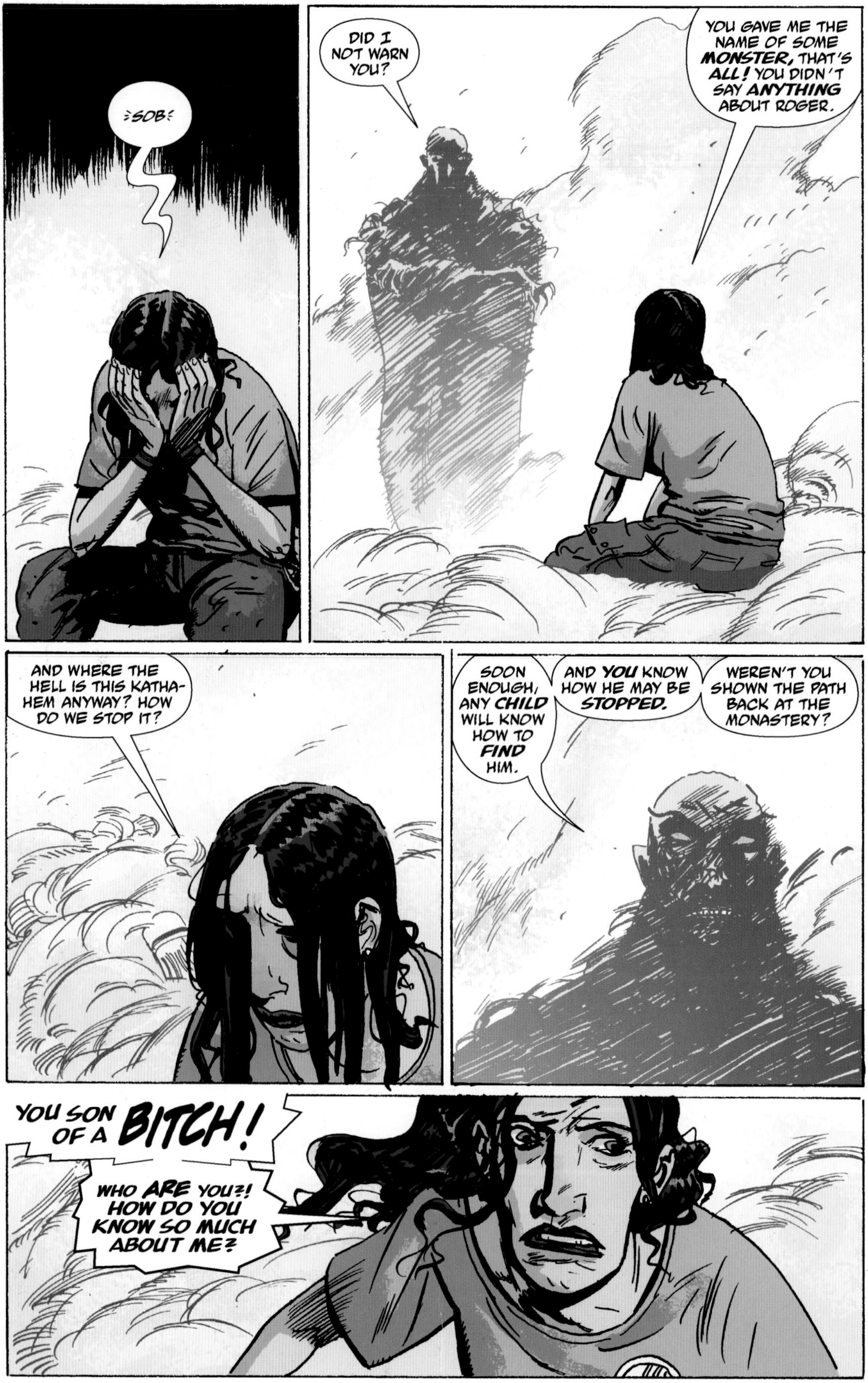
SOB
DID I NOT WARN YOU?
YOU GAVE ME THE NAME OF SOME MONSTER, THAT'S ALL! YOU DIDN'T SAY ANYTHING ABOUT ROGER.
AND WHERE THE HELL IS THIS KATHA-HEM ANYWAY? HOW DO WE STOP IT?
WEREN'T YOU SHOWN THE PATH BACK AT THE MONASTERY?
AND YOU KNOW HOW HE MAY BE STOPPED.
SOON ENOUGH, ANY CHILD WILL KNOW HOW TO FIND HIM.
YOU SON OF A BITCH!
WHO ARE YOU?! HOW DO YOU KNOW SO MUCH ABOUT ME?

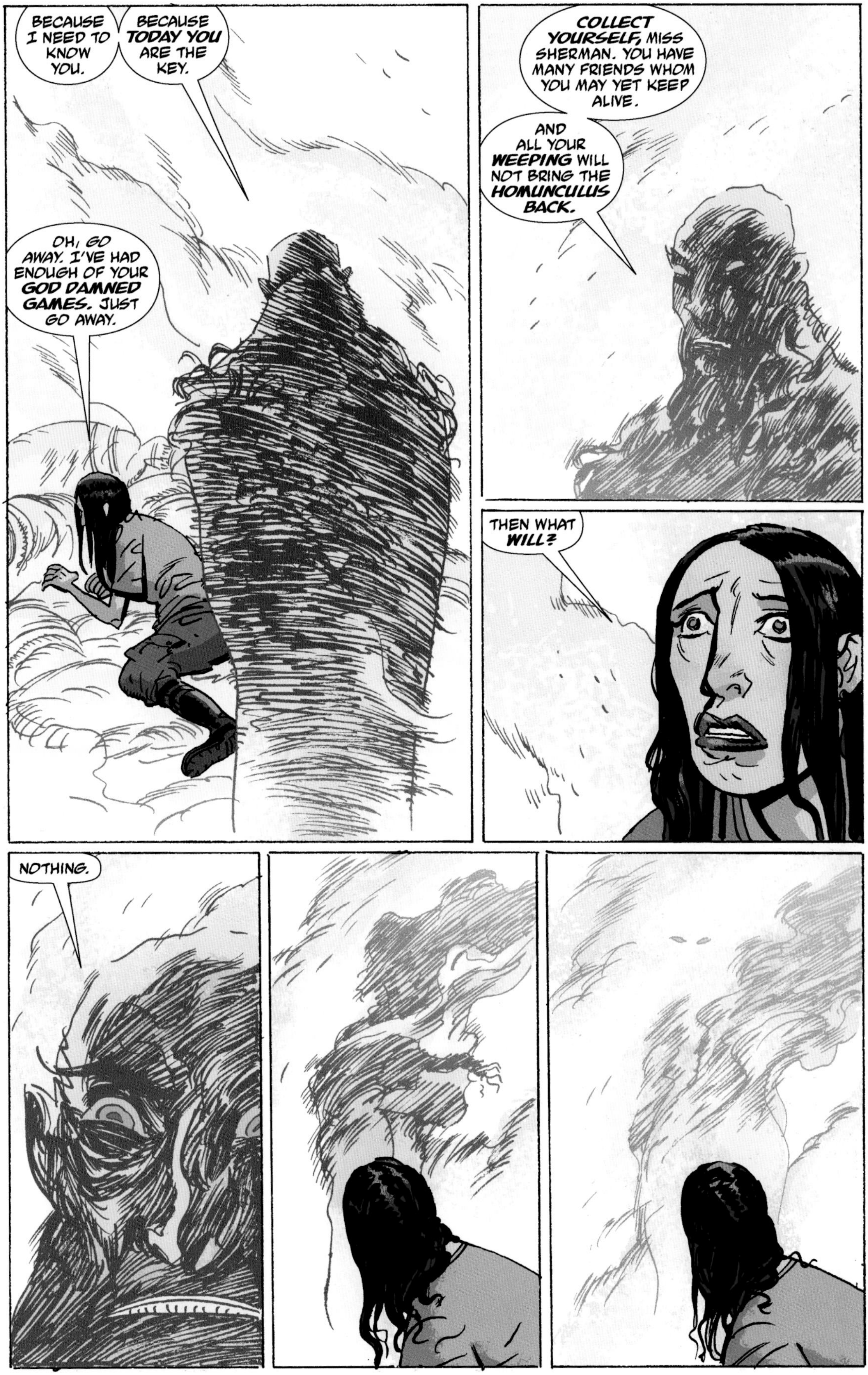
BECAUSE I NEED TO KNOW YOU.
BECAUSE TODAY YOU ARE THE KEY.
OH, GO AWAY. I'VE HAD ENOUGH OF YOUR GOD DAMNED GAMES. JUST GO AWAY.
COLLECT YOURSELF, MISS SHERMAN. YOU HAVE MANY FRIENDS WHOM YOU MAY YET KEEP ALIVE.
AND ALL YOUR WEEPING WILL NOT BRING THE HOMUNCULUS BACK.
THEN WHAT WILL?
NOTHING.

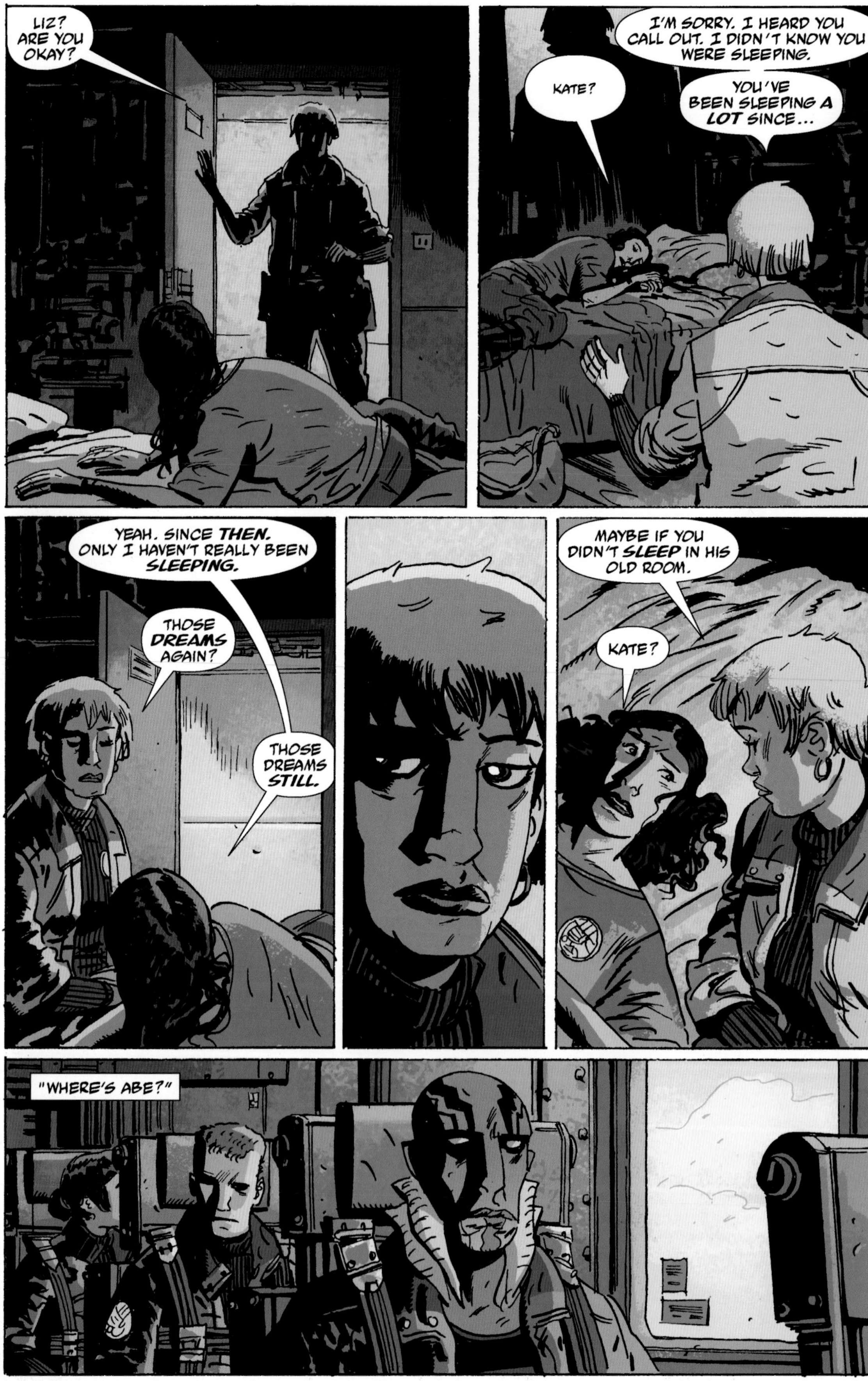
LIZ? ARE YOU OKAY?
KATE?
I'M SORRY. I HEARD YOU CALL OUT. I DIDN'T KNOW YOU WERE SLEEPING.
YOU'VE BEEN SLEEPING A LOT SINCE...
YEAH. SINCE THEN. ONLY I HAVEN'T REALLY BEEN SLEEPING.
THOSE DREAMS AGAIN?
THOSE DREAMS STILL.
MAYBE IF YOU DIDN'T SLEEP IN HIS OLD ROOM.
KATE?
"WHERE'S ABE?"

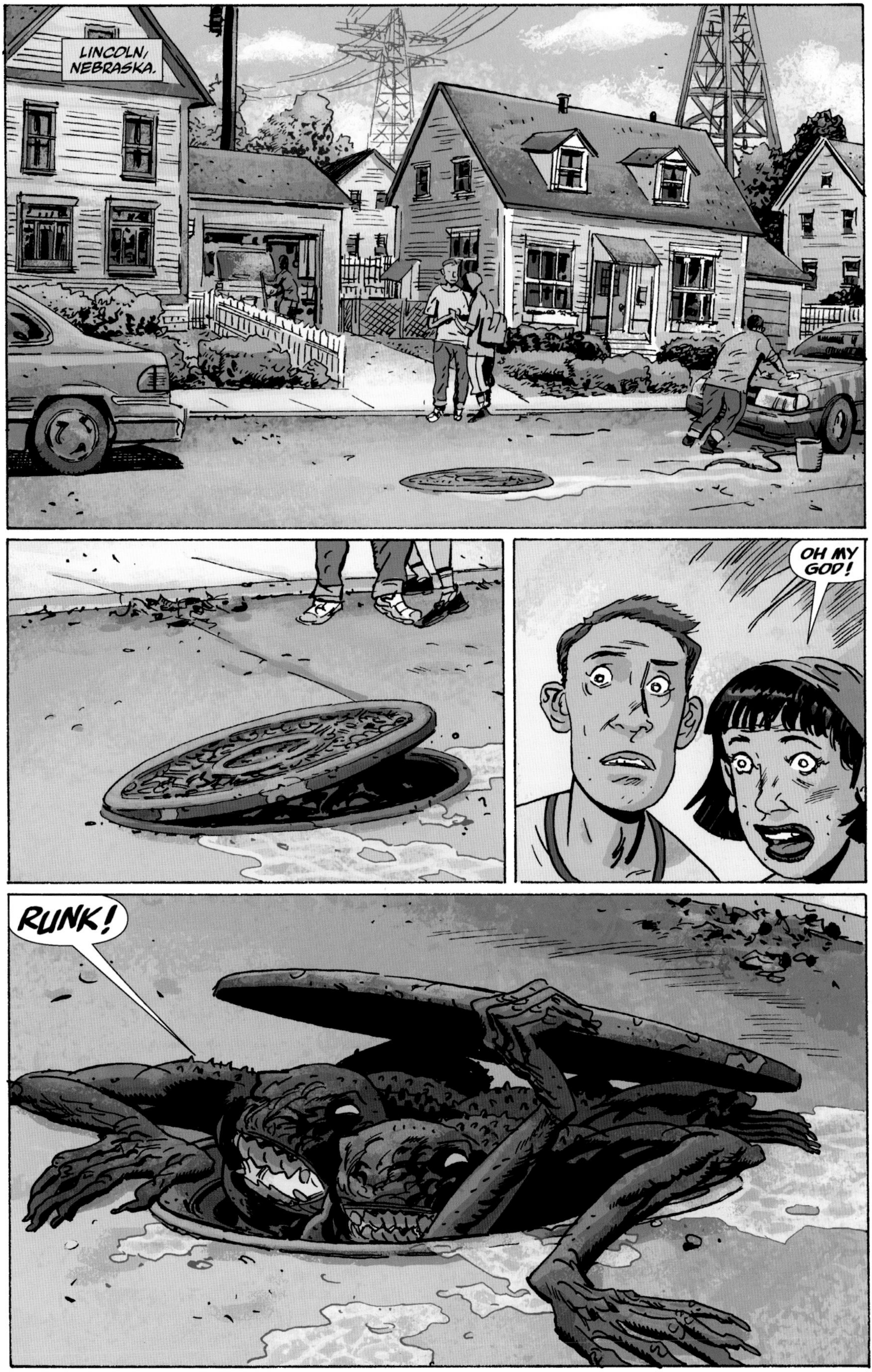
LINCOLN, NEBRASKA.
OH MY GOD!
RUNK!

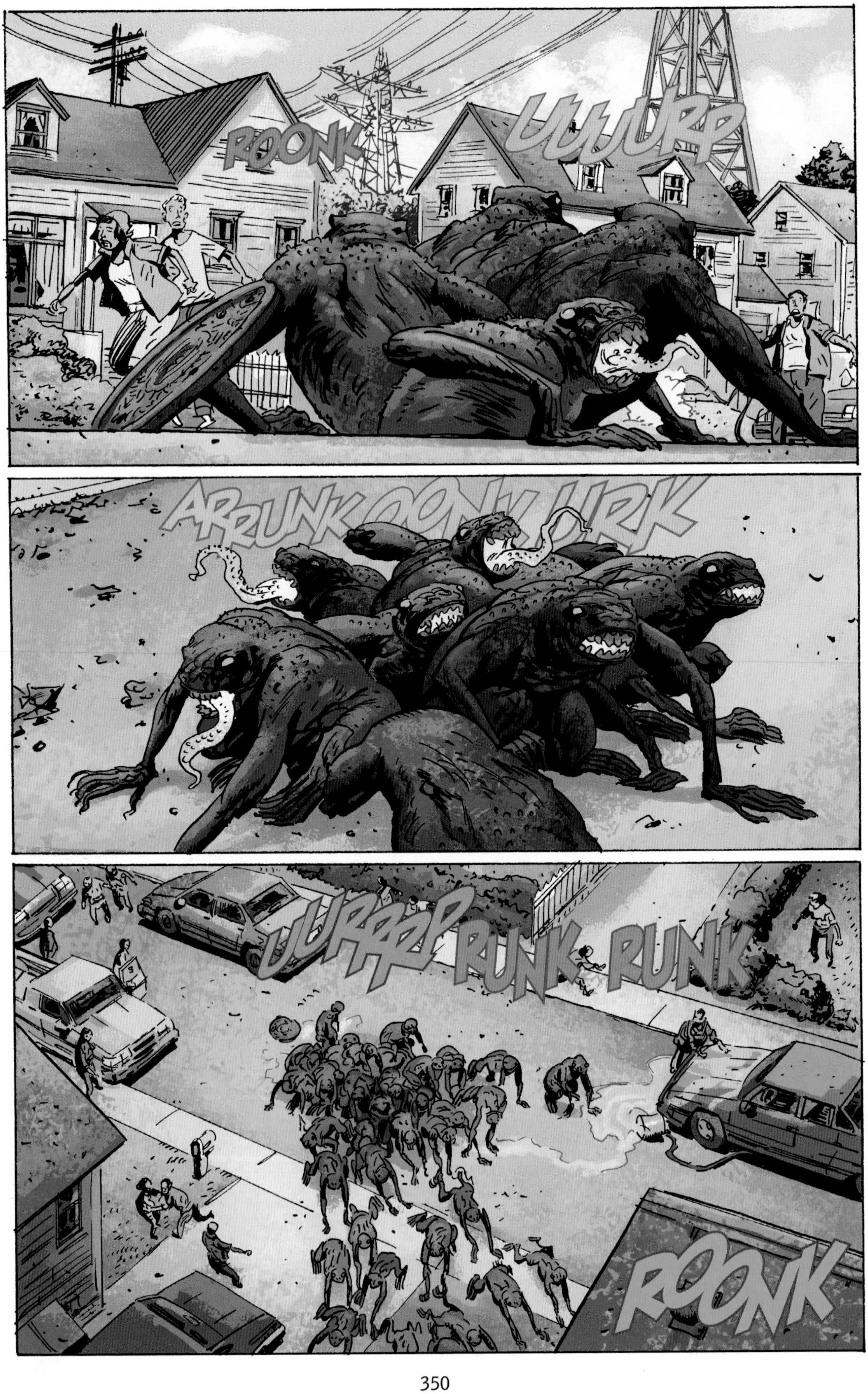
ROONK
UUUURP
ARRUNKOONKURK
UURRRP
RUNK RUNK
ROONK

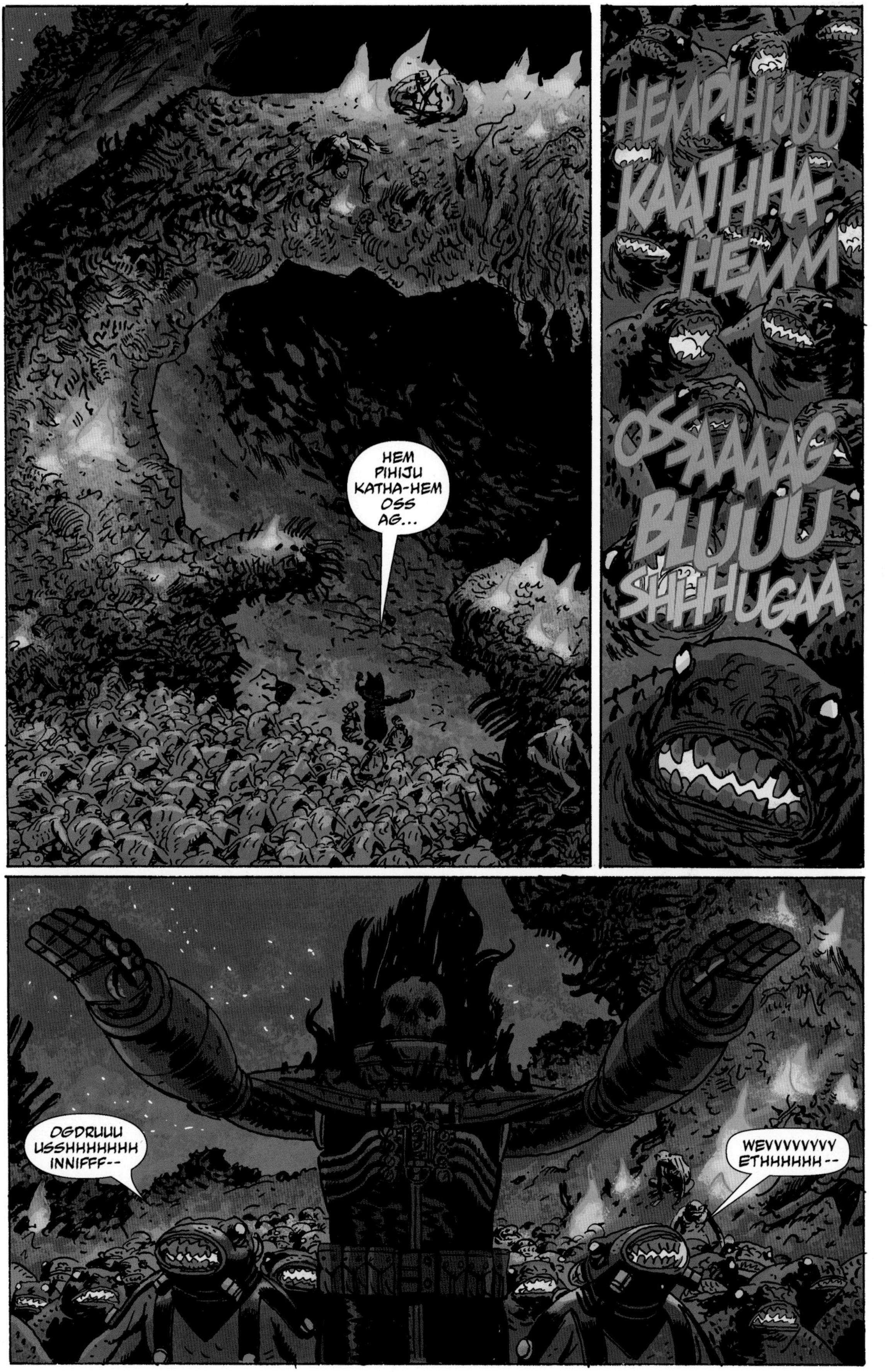
HEM PIHIJU KATHA-HEM OSS AG...
HEMPIHIJUU KAATHHA-HEMM
OSSAAAAG BLUUU SHHHUGAA
OGDRUUU USSHHHHHHH INNIFFF--
WEVVVVVVVY ETHHHHHH--

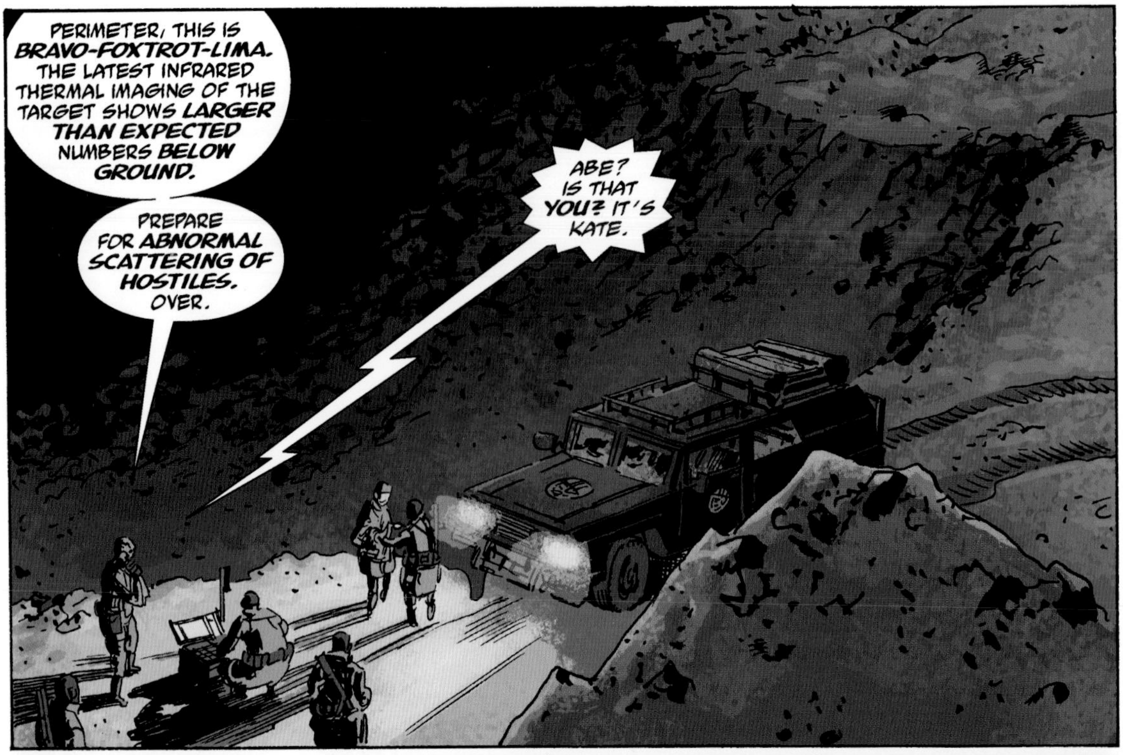
PERIMETER, THIS IS **BRAVO-FOXTROT-LIMA.** THE LATEST INFRARED THERMAL IMAGING OF THE TARGET SHOWS **LARGER THAN EXPECTED** NUMBERS **BELOW GROUND.**
PREPARE FOR **ABNORMAL SCATTERING OF HOSTILES.** OVER.
ABE? IS THAT **YOU?** IT'S KATE.

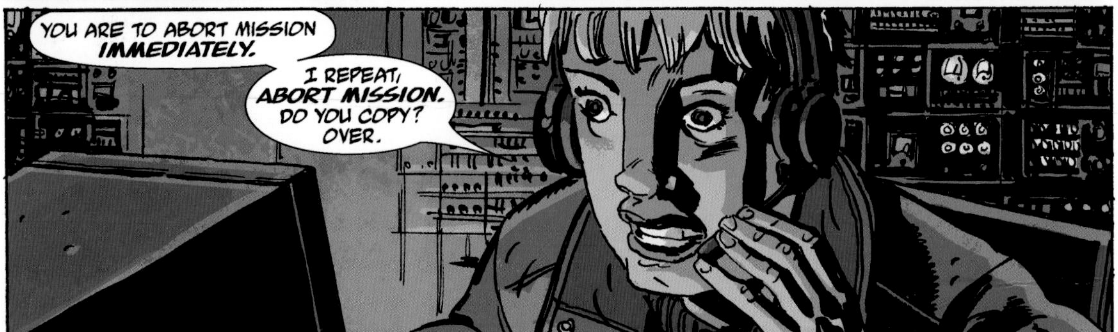
YOU ARE TO ABORT MISSION **IMMEDIATELY.**
I REPEAT, **ABORT MISSION.** DO YOU COPY? OVER.

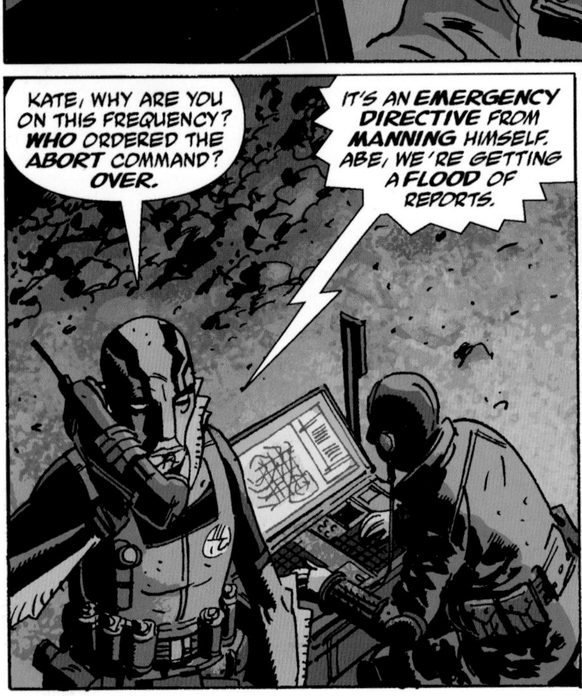
KATE, WHY ARE YOU ON THIS FREQUENCY? **WHO** ORDERED THE **ABORT** COMMAND? **OVER.**
IT'S AN **EMERGENCY DIRECTIVE** FROM **MANNING** HIMSELF. ABE, WE'RE GETTING A **FLOOD** OF REPORTS.

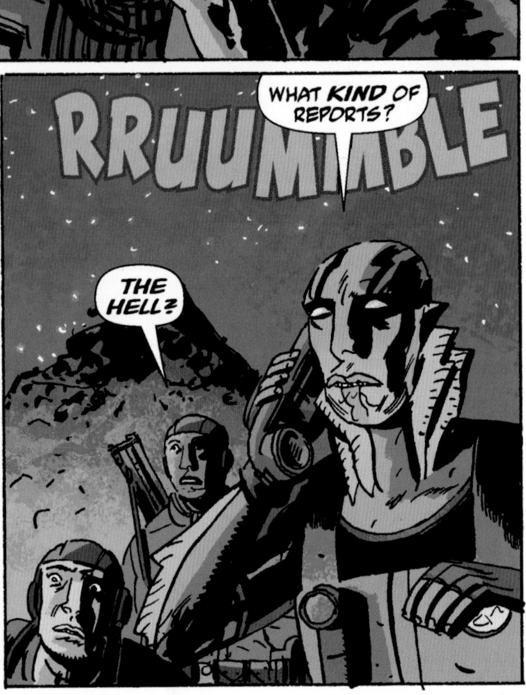
RRUUMMBLE
WHAT **KIND** OF REPORTS?
THE HELL?

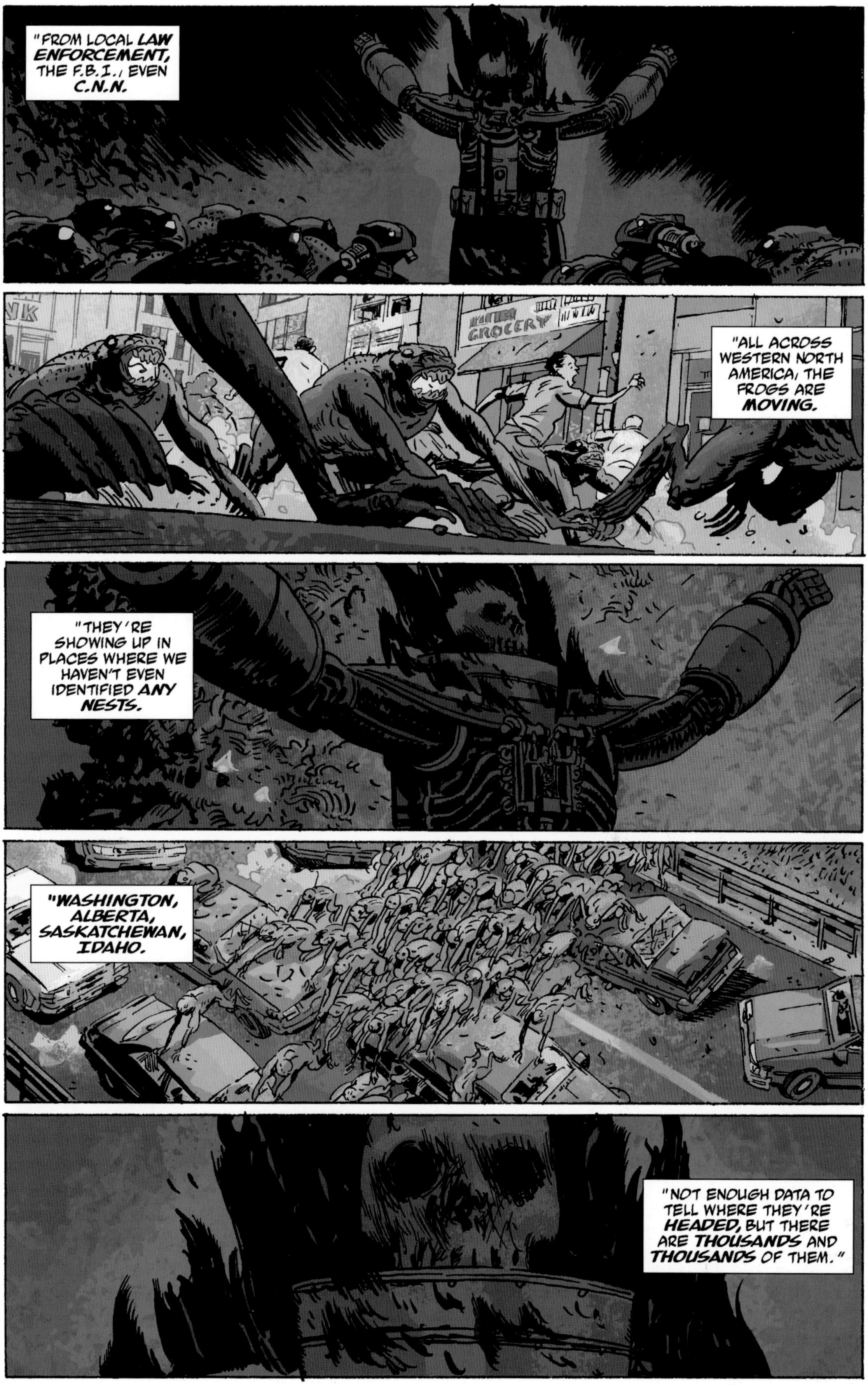
"FROM LOCAL LAW ENFORCEMENT, THE F.B.I., EVEN C.N.N.
GROCERY
"ALL ACROSS WESTERN NORTH AMERICA, THE FROGS ARE MOVING.
"THEY'RE SHOWING UP IN PLACES WHERE WE HAVEN'T EVEN IDENTIFIED ANY NESTS.
"WASHINGTON, ALBERTA, SASKATCHEWAN, IDAHO.
"NOT ENOUGH DATA TO TELL WHERE THEY'RE HEADED, BUT THERE ARE THOUSANDS AND THOUSANDS OF THEM."

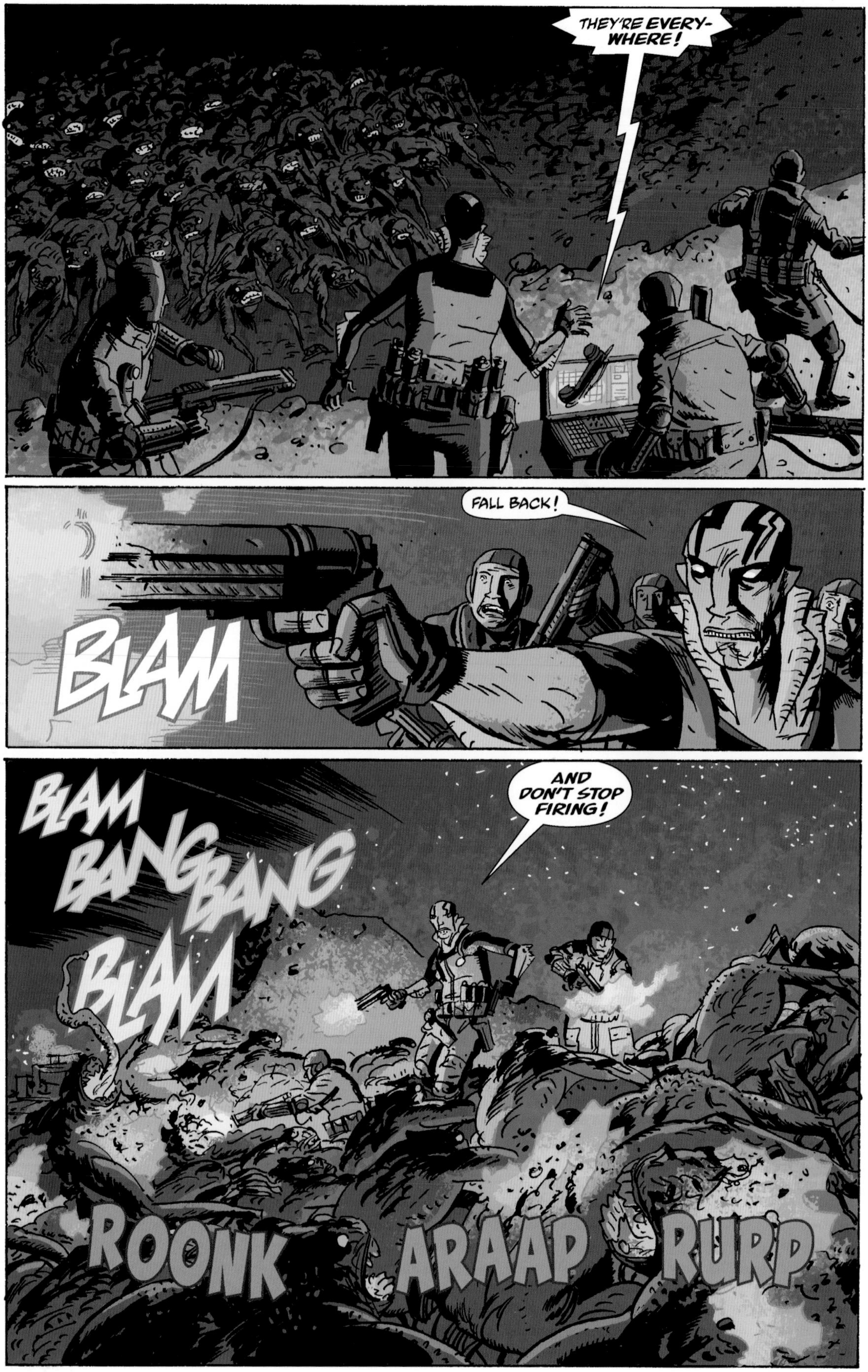
THEY'RE EVERY-WHERE!
FALL BACK!
BLAM
AND DON'T STOP FIRING!
BLAM
BANG BANG
BLAM
ROONK
ARAAP
RURP

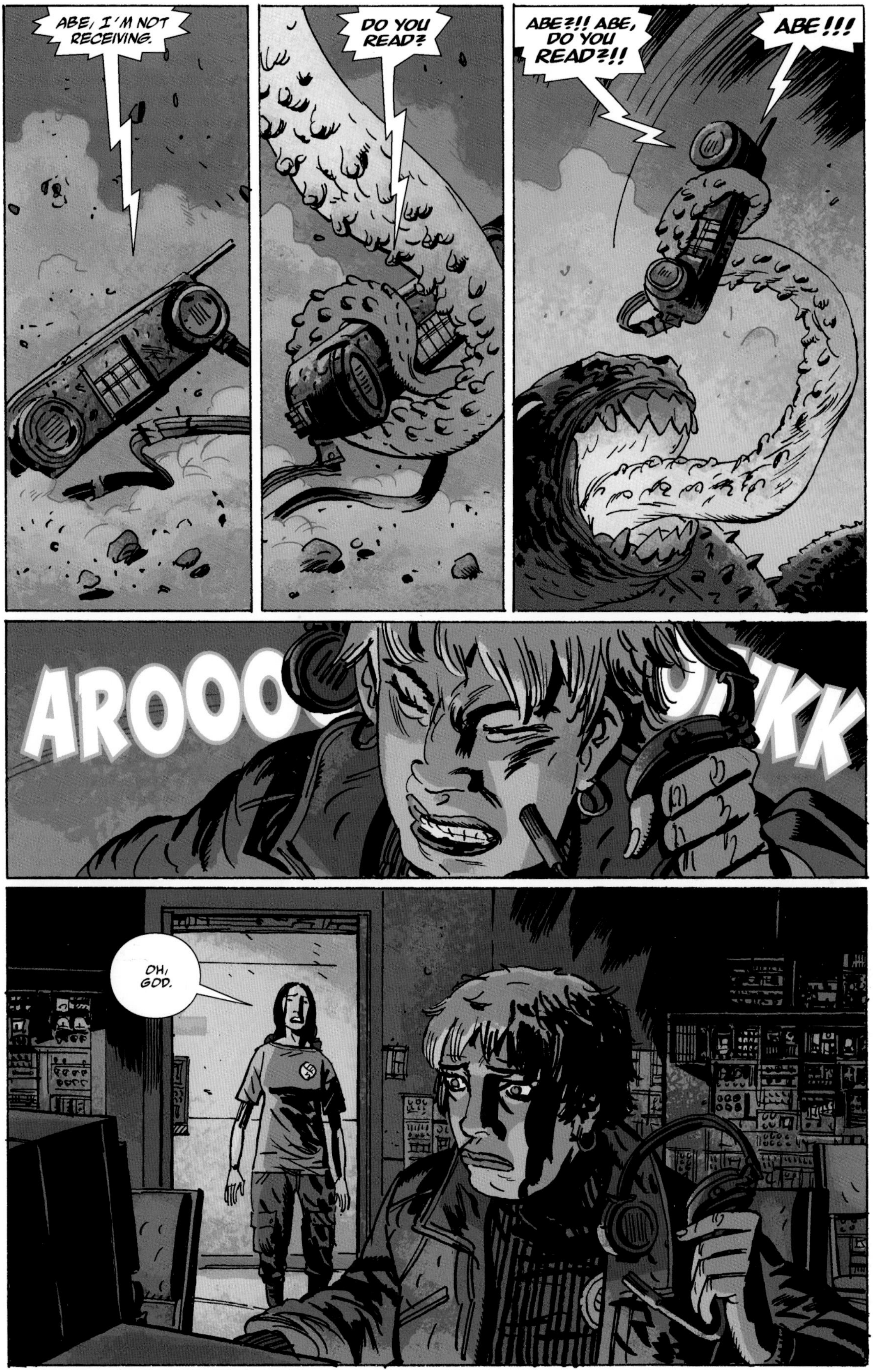
ABE, I'M NOT RECEIVING.
DO YOU READ?
ABE?!! ABE, DO YOU READ?!!
ABE!!!
AROOOO
KK
OH, GOD.

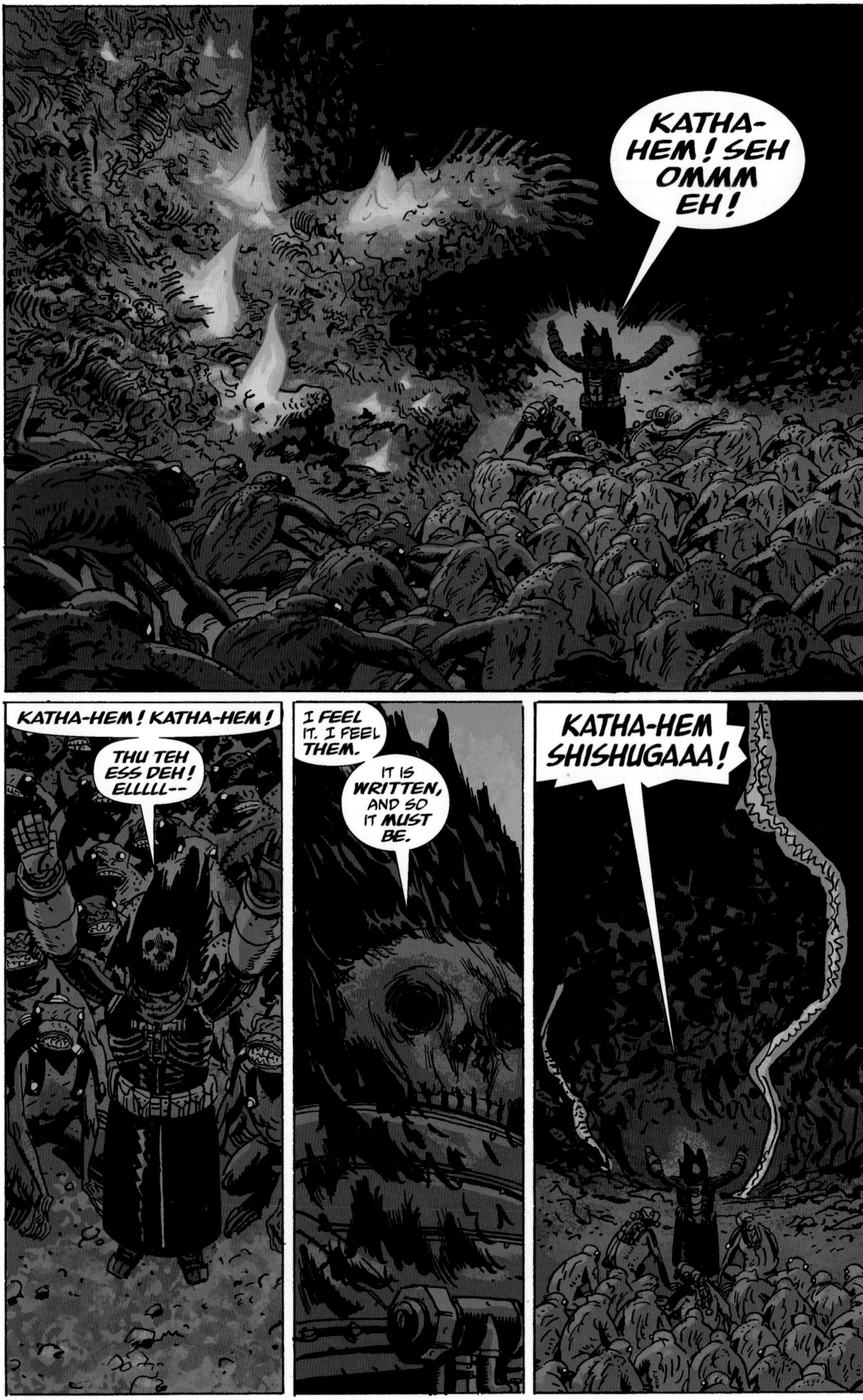
KATHA-HEM! SEH OMMM EH!
KATHA-HEM! KATHA-HEM!
THU TEH ESS DEH! ELLLLL--
I FEEL IT. I FEEL THEM.
IT IS WRITTEN, AND SO IT MUST BE.
KATHA-HEM SHISHUGAAA!

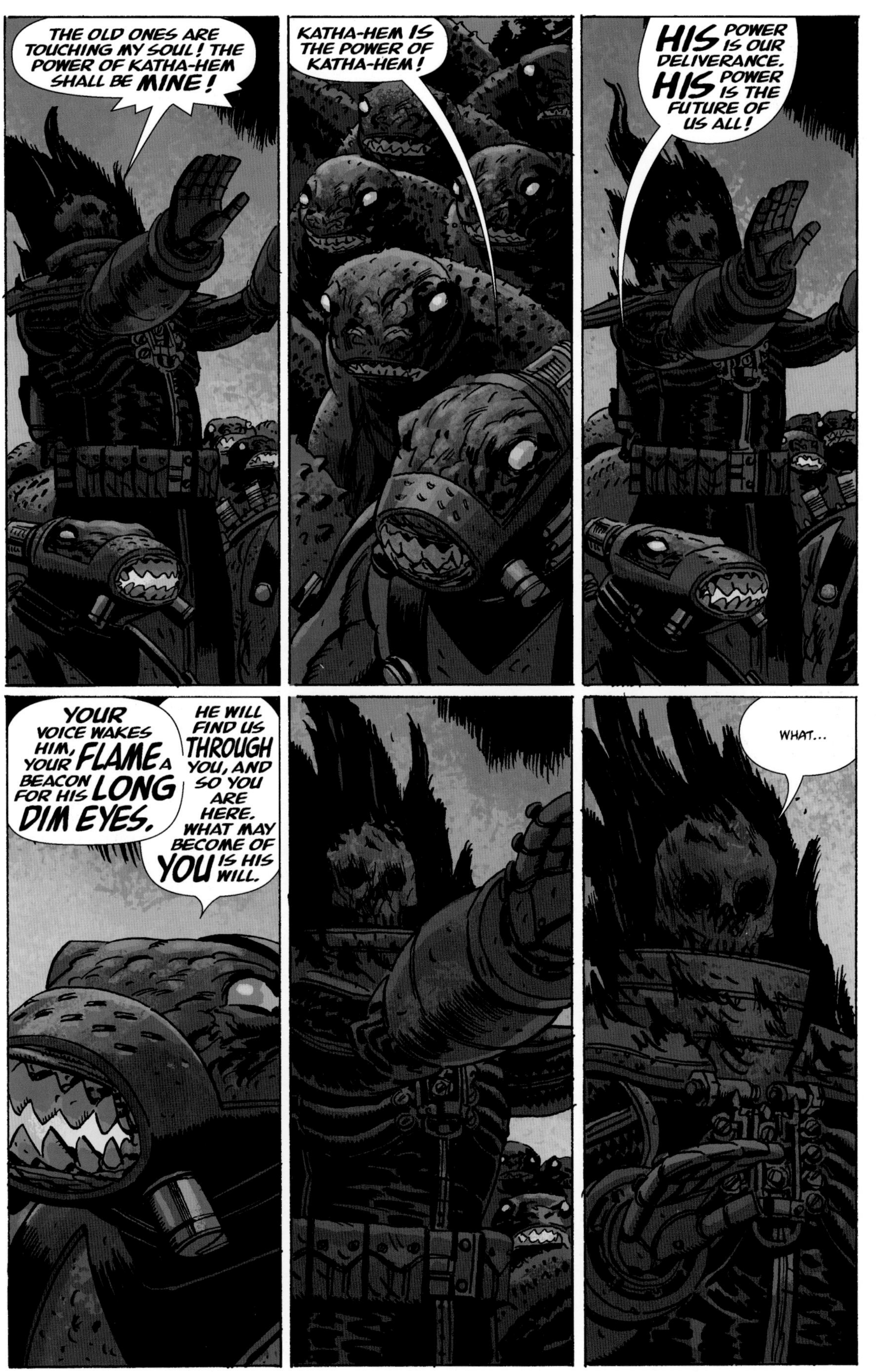
THE OLD ONES ARE TOUCHING MY SOUL! THE POWER OF KATHA-HEM SHALL BE MINE!
KATHA-HEM IS THE POWER OF KATHA-HEM!
HIS POWER IS OUR DELIVERANCE. HIS POWER IS THE FUTURE OF US ALL!
YOUR VOICE WAKES HIM, YOUR FLAME A BEACON FOR HIS LONG DIM EYES.
HE WILL FIND US THROUGH YOU, AND SO YOU ARE HERE. WHAT MAY BECOME OF YOU IS HIS WILL.
WHAT...

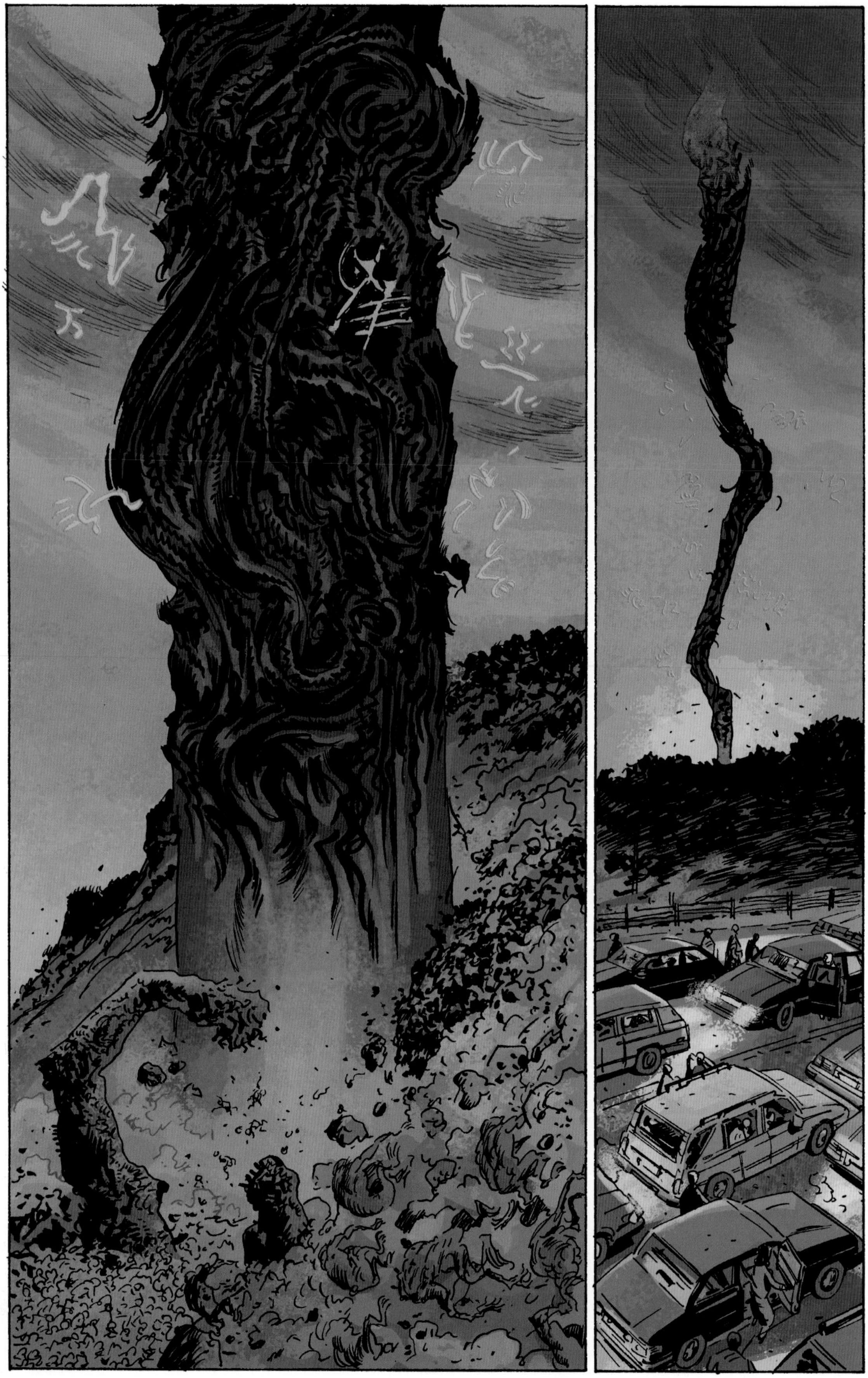

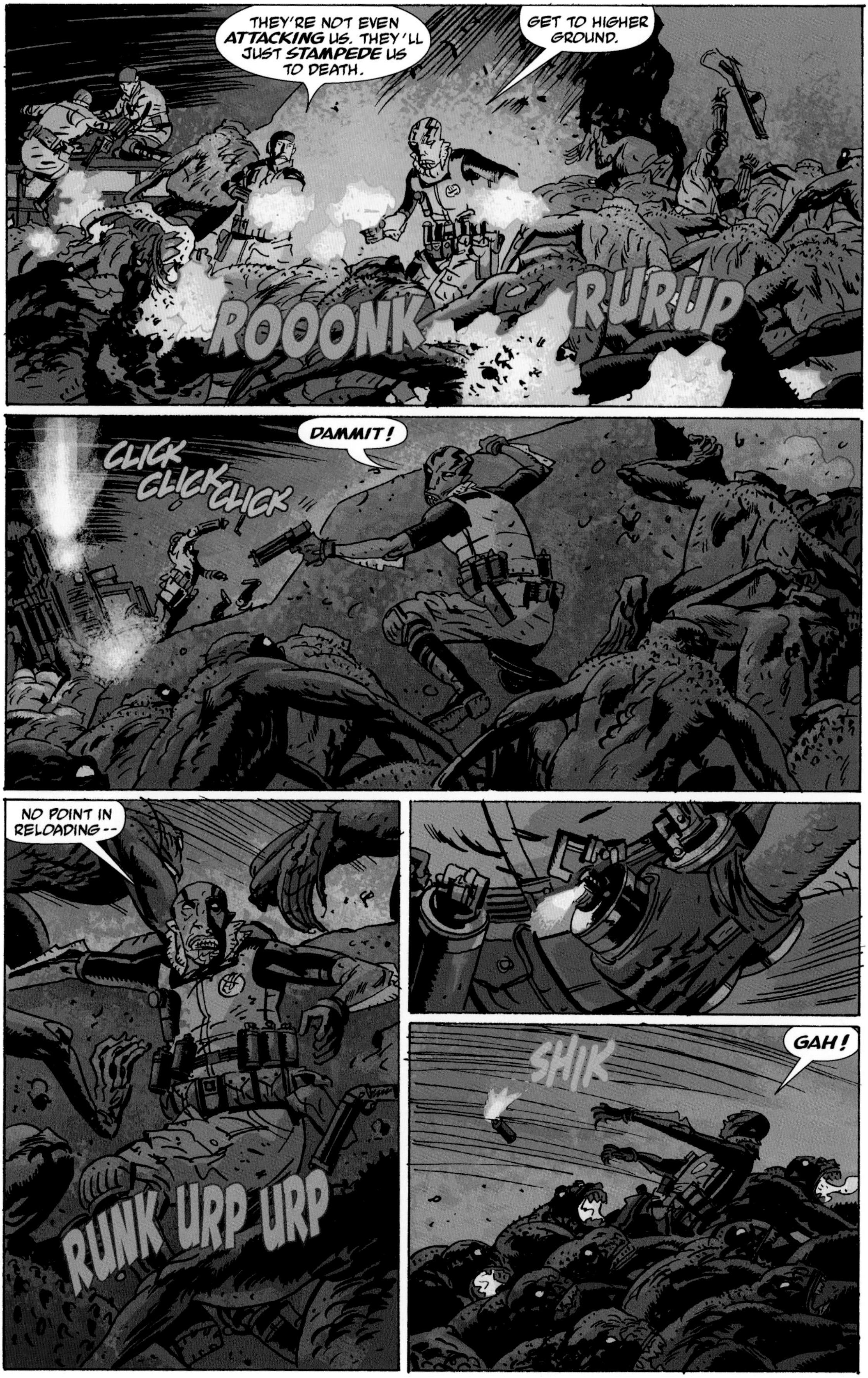
THEY'RE NOT EVEN ATTACKING US. THEY'LL JUST STAMPEDE US TO DEATH.
GET TO HIGHER GROUND.
ROOONK
RURUP
CLICK CLICK CLICK
DAMMIT!
NO POINT IN RELOADING--
RUNK URP URP
SHIK
GAH!

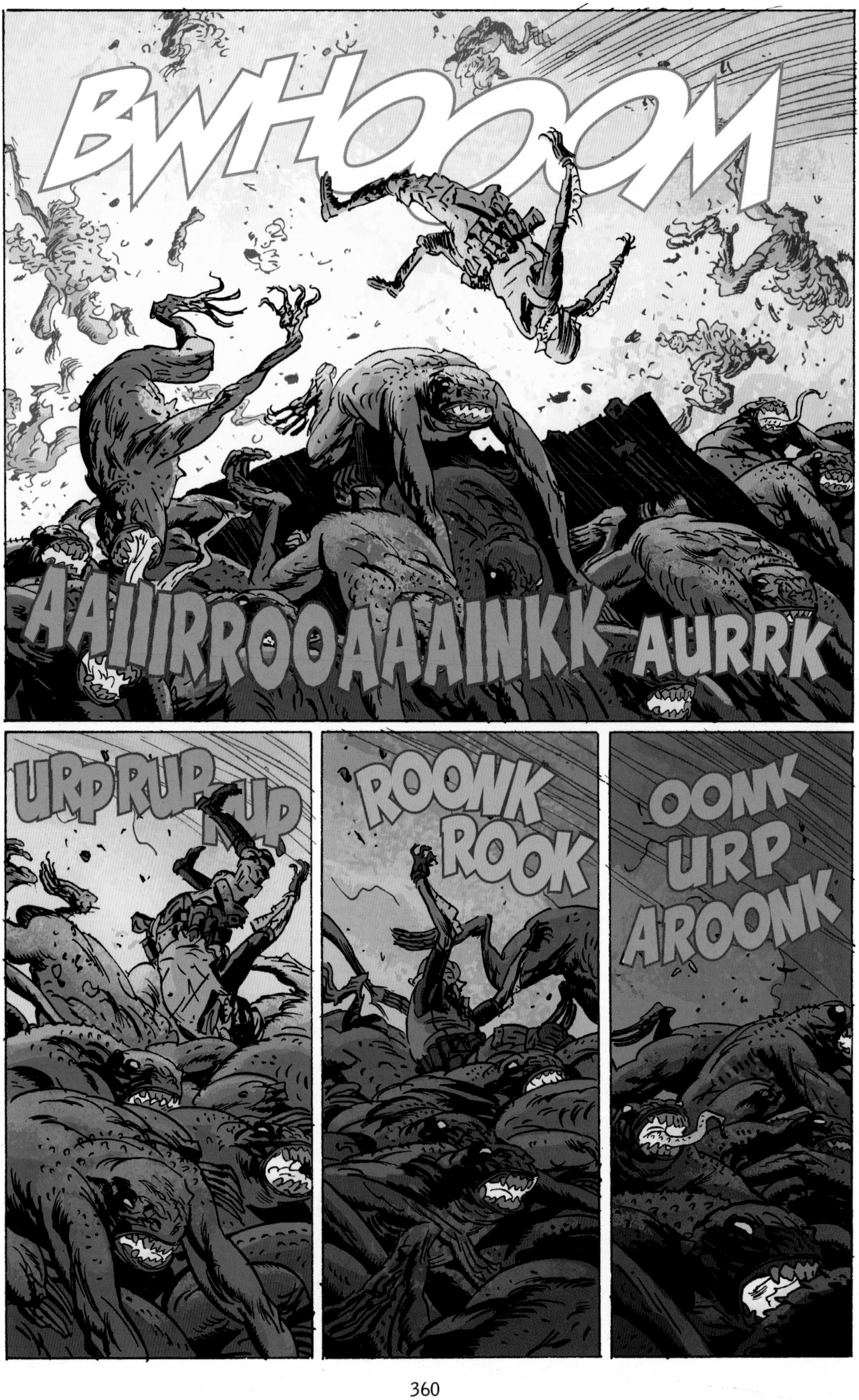
BWHOOOM
AAIIIRROOAAAINKK
AURRK
URPRUPRUP
ROONK
ROOK
OONK
URP
AROONK

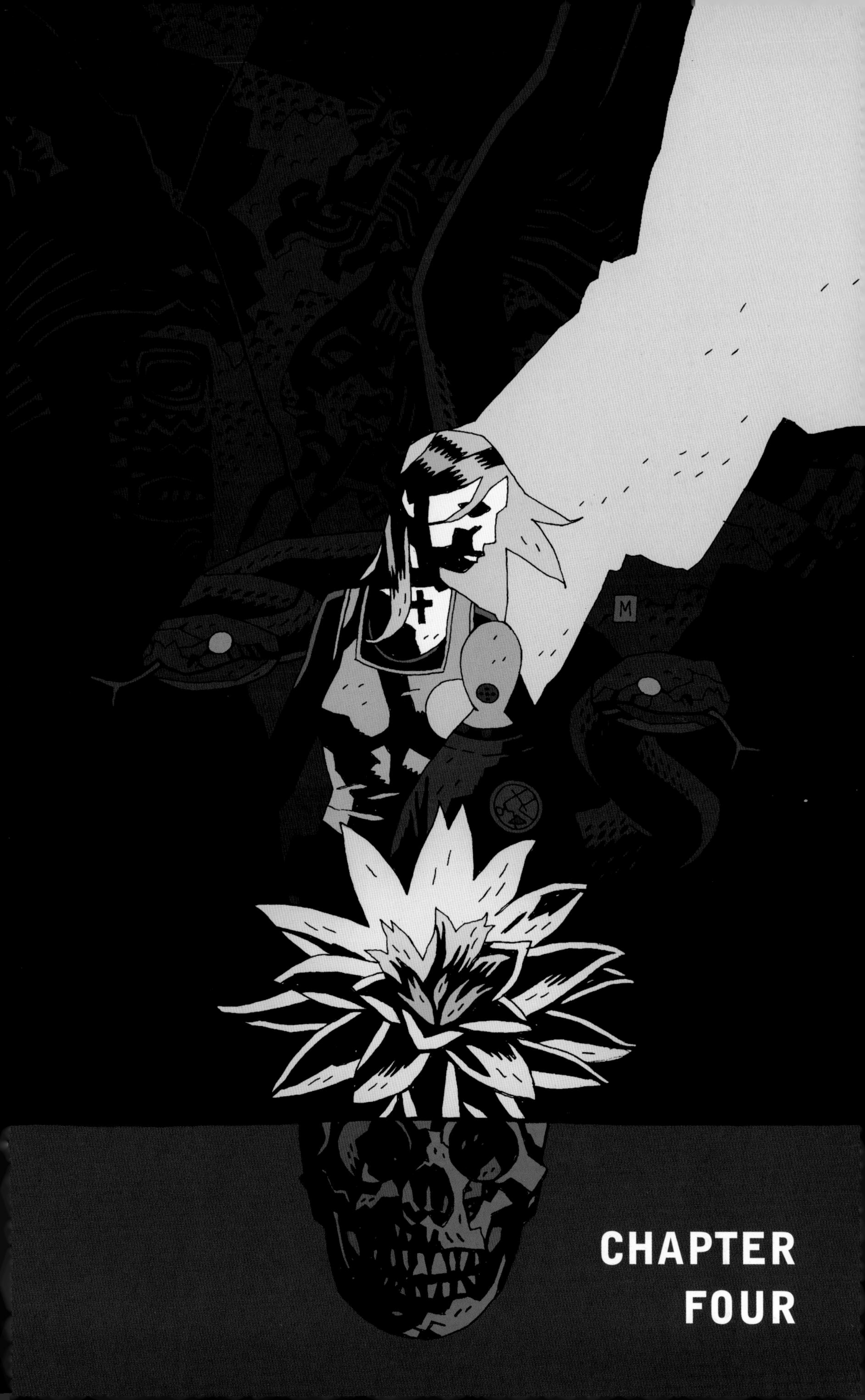

CHAPTER FOUR

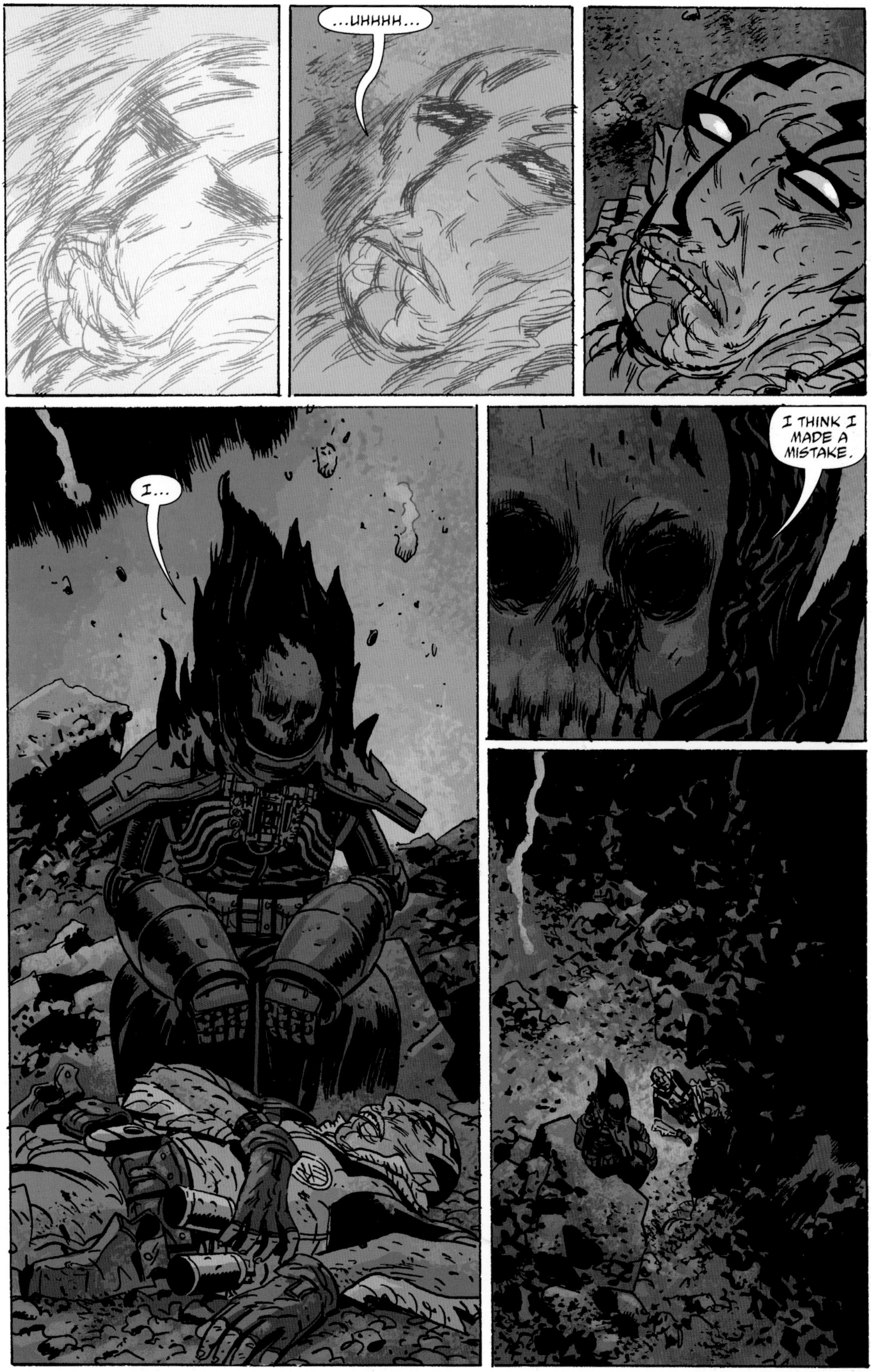
...UHHHH...
I...
I THINK I MADE A MISTAKE.

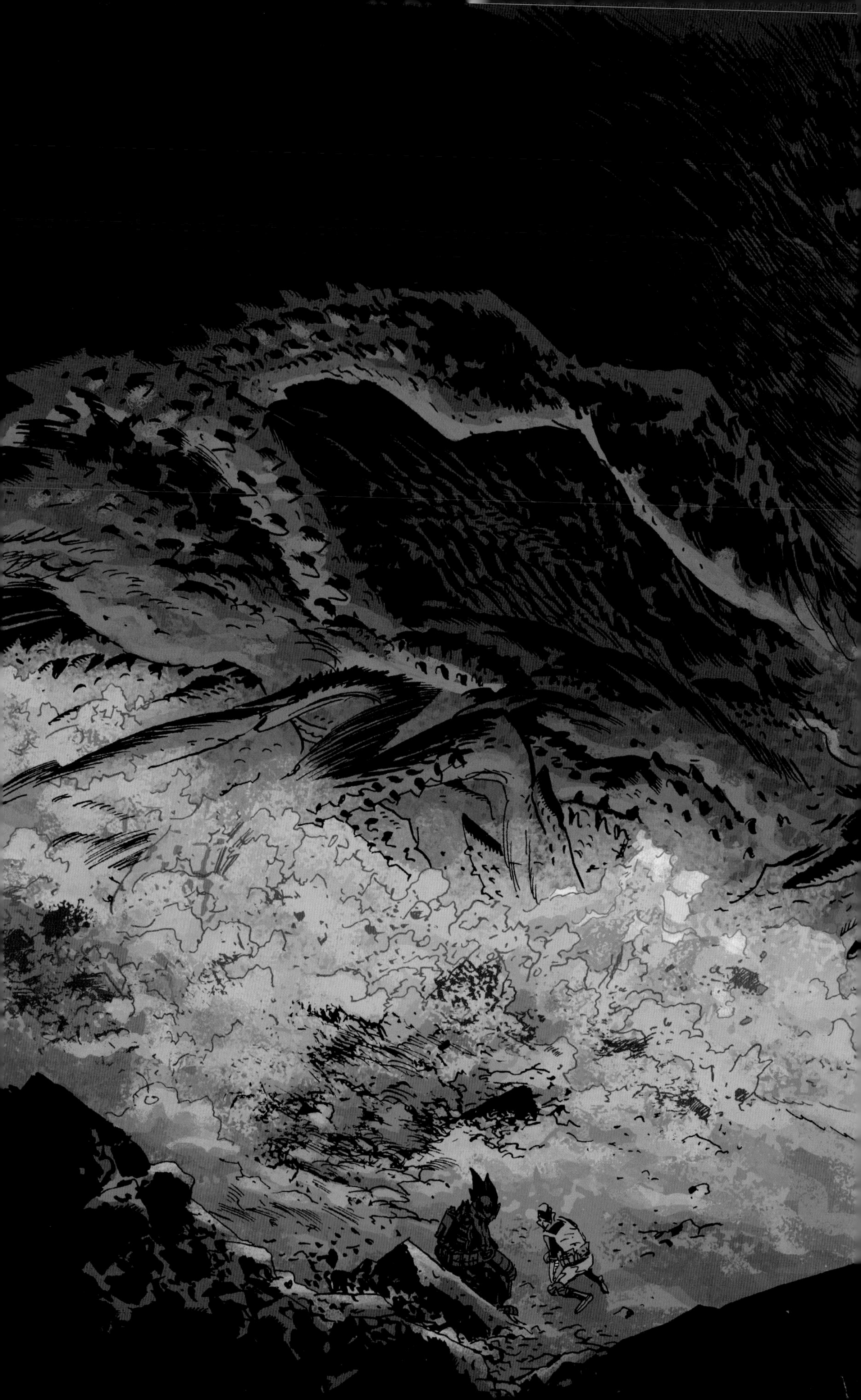

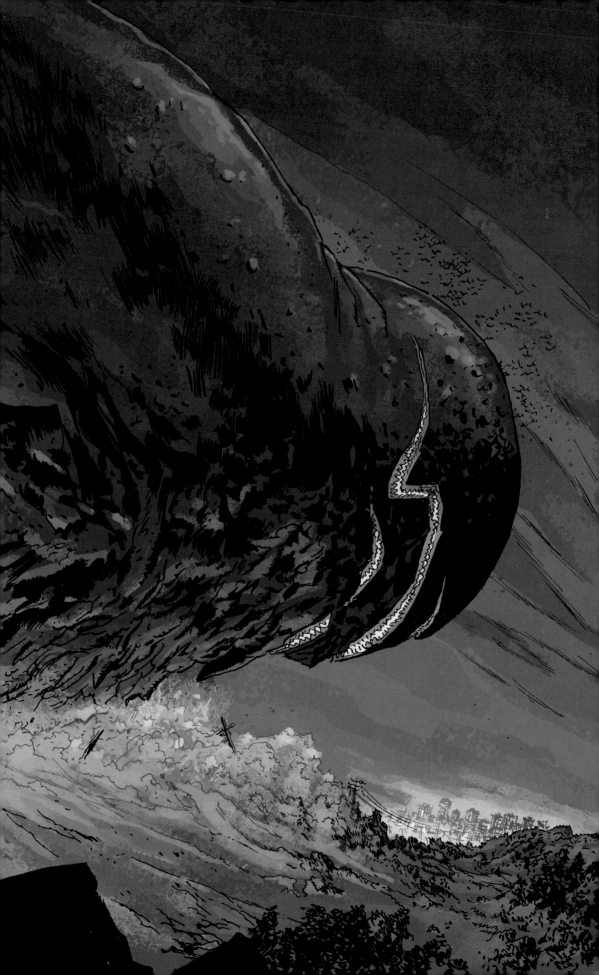

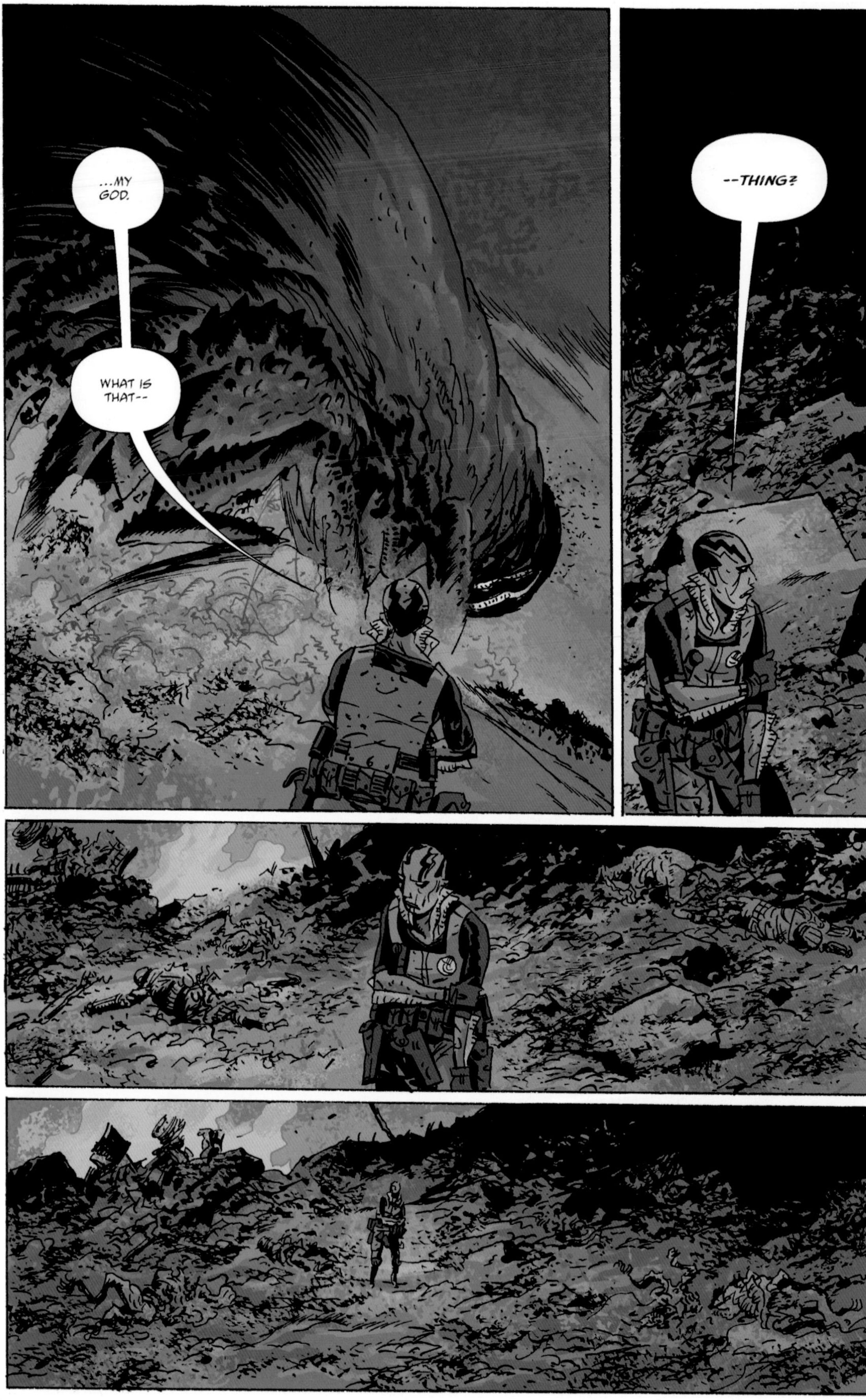
...MY GOD.
WHAT IS THAT--
--THING?

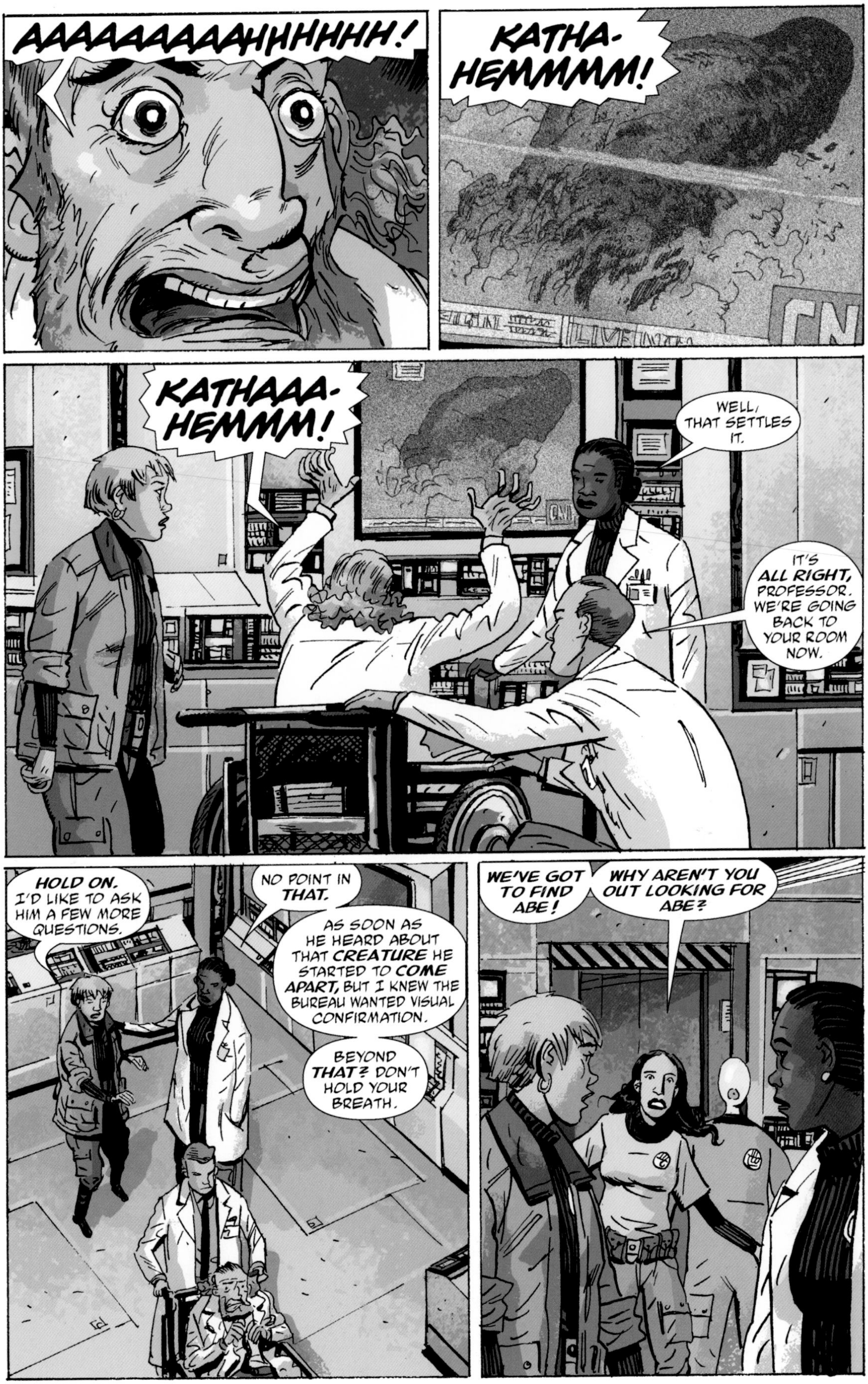
AAAAAAAAAHHHHHH!
KATHA-HEMMMM!
KATHAAA-HEMMM!
WELL, THAT SETTLES IT.
IT'S ALL RIGHT, PROFESSOR. WE'RE GOING BACK TO YOUR ROOM NOW.
HOLD ON. I'D LIKE TO ASK HIM A FEW MORE QUESTIONS.
NO POINT IN THAT.
AS SOON AS HE HEARD ABOUT THAT CREATURE HE STARTED TO COME APART, BUT I KNEW THE BUREAU WANTED VISUAL CONFIRMATION.
BEYOND THAT? DON'T HOLD YOUR BREATH.
WE'VE GOT TO FIND ABE!
WHY AREN'T YOU OUT LOOKING FOR ABE?

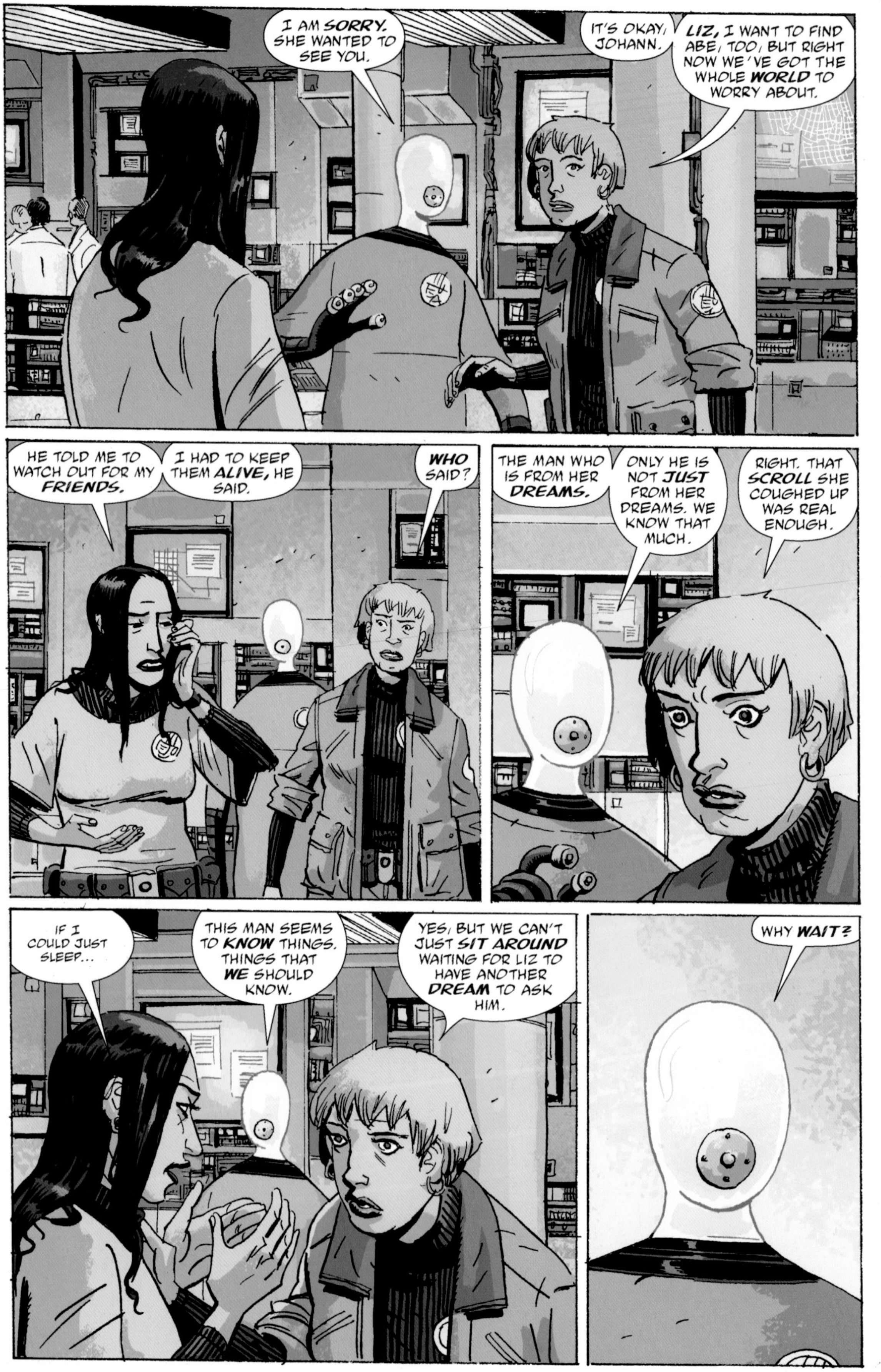
I AM SORRY. SHE WANTED TO SEE YOU.
IT'S OKAY, JOHANN.
LIZ, I WANT TO FIND ABE, TOO, BUT RIGHT NOW WE'VE GOT THE WHOLE WORLD TO WORRY ABOUT.
HE TOLD ME TO WATCH OUT FOR MY FRIENDS.
I HAD TO KEEP THEM ALIVE, HE SAID.
WHO SAID?
THE MAN WHO IS FROM HER DREAMS.
ONLY HE IS NOT JUST FROM HER DREAMS. WE KNOW THAT MUCH.
RIGHT. THAT SCROLL SHE COUGHED UP WAS REAL ENOUGH.
IF I COULD JUST SLEEP...
THIS MAN SEEMS TO KNOW THINGS. THINGS THAT WE SHOULD KNOW.
YES, BUT WE CAN'T JUST SIT AROUND WAITING FOR LIZ TO HAVE ANOTHER DREAM TO ASK HIM.
WHY WAIT?

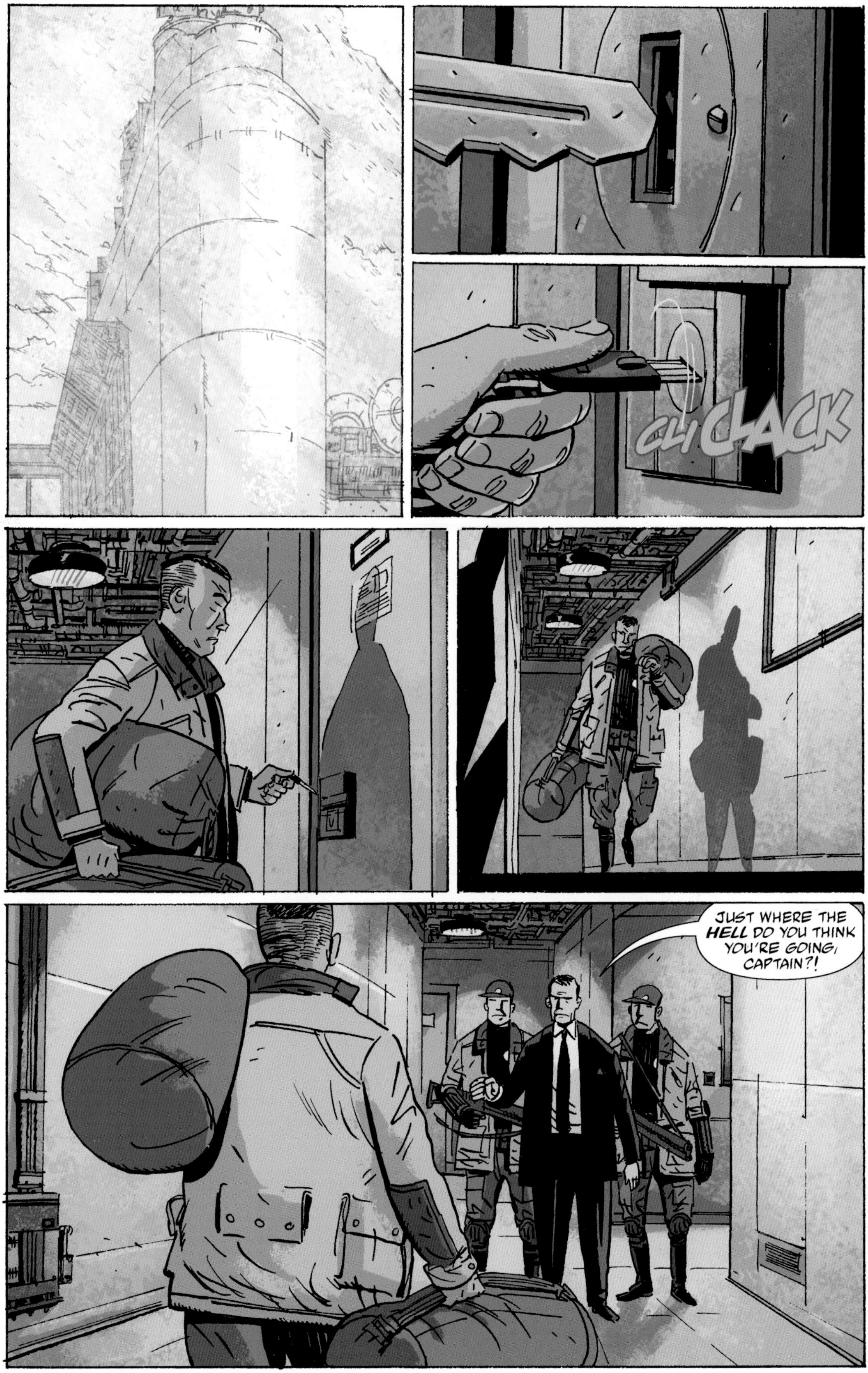
CLI CLACK
JUST WHERE THE HELL DO YOU THINK YOU'RE GOING, CAPTAIN?!

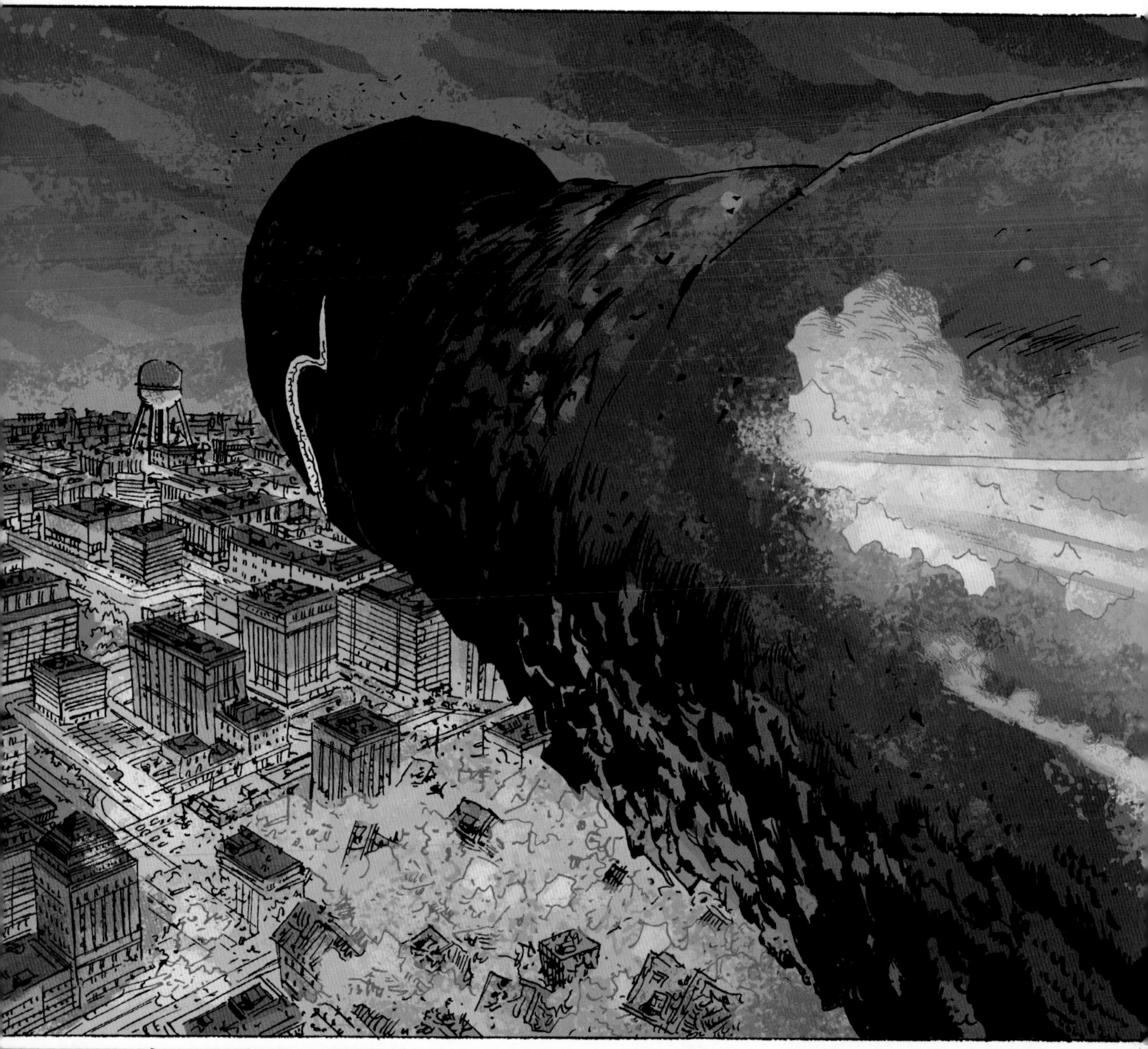

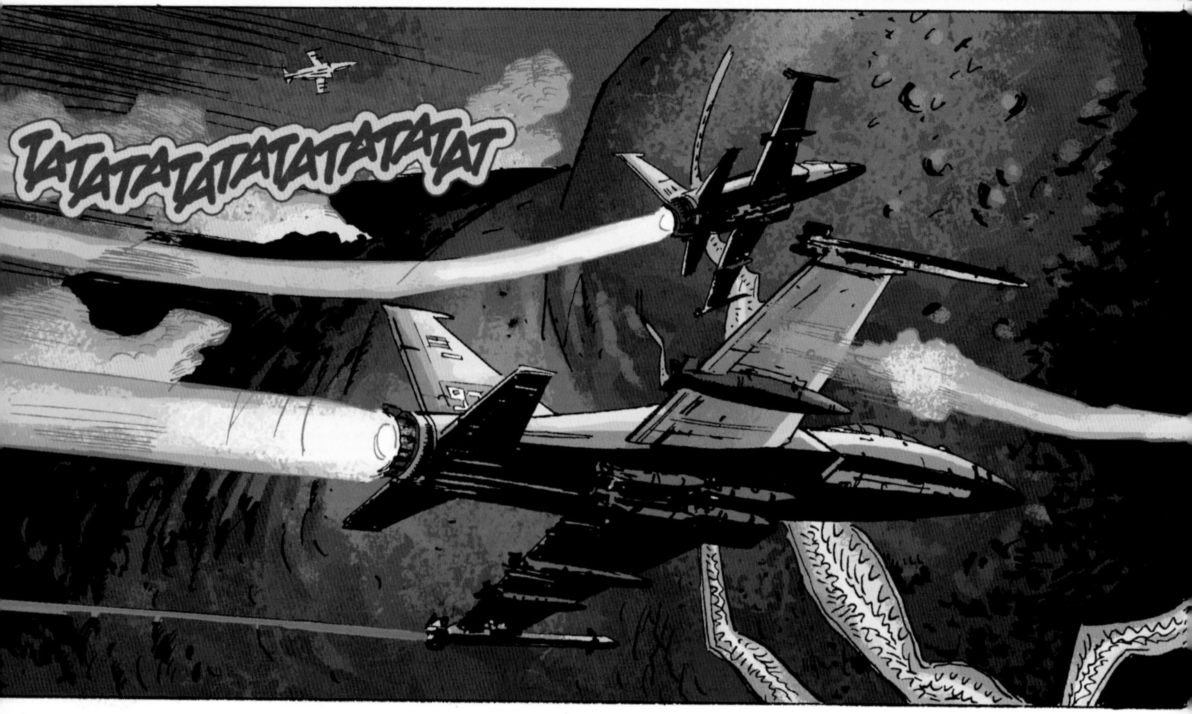
TATATATATATATATATAT

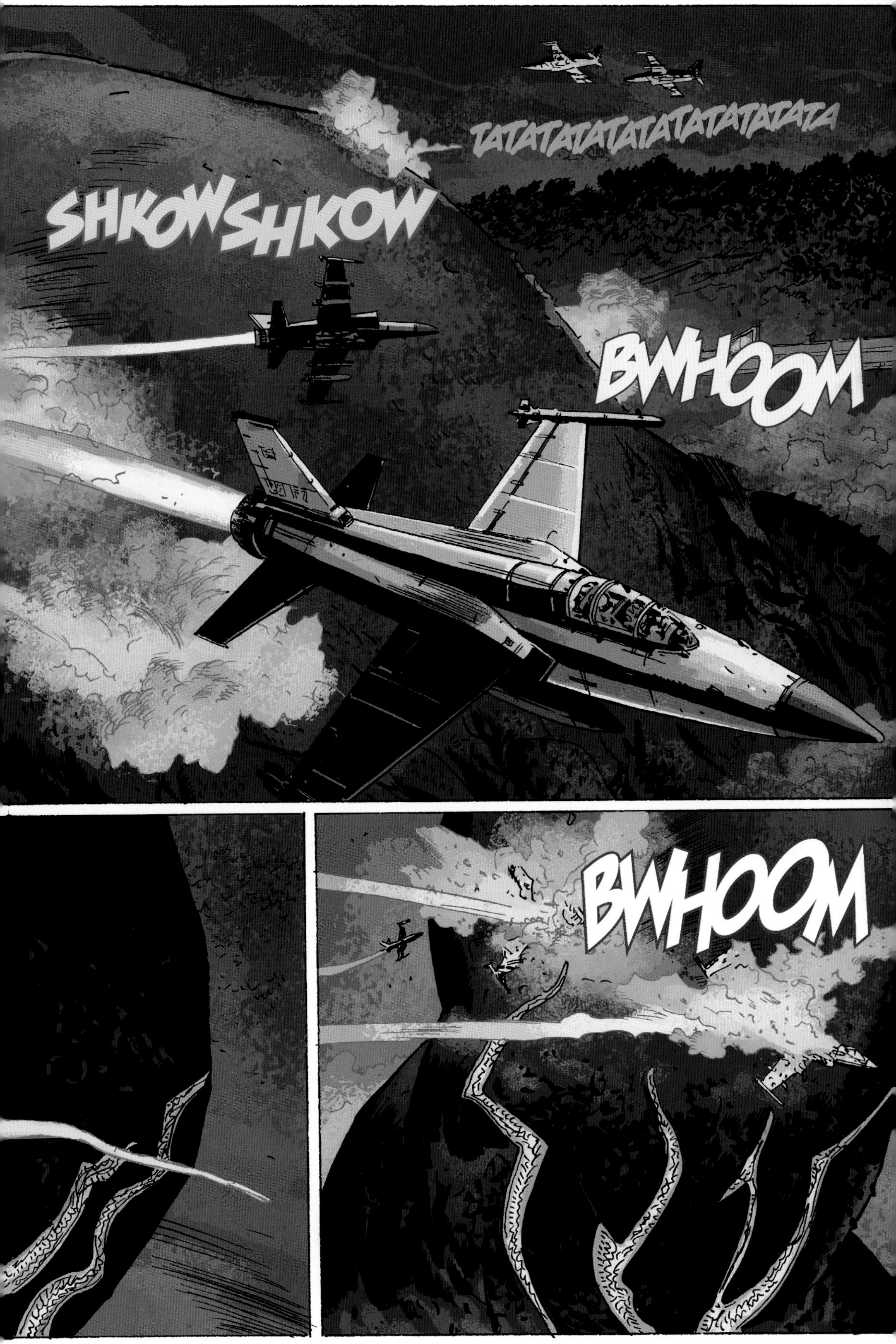
TATATATATATATATATATATATA
SHKOW SHKOW
BWHOOM
BWHOOM

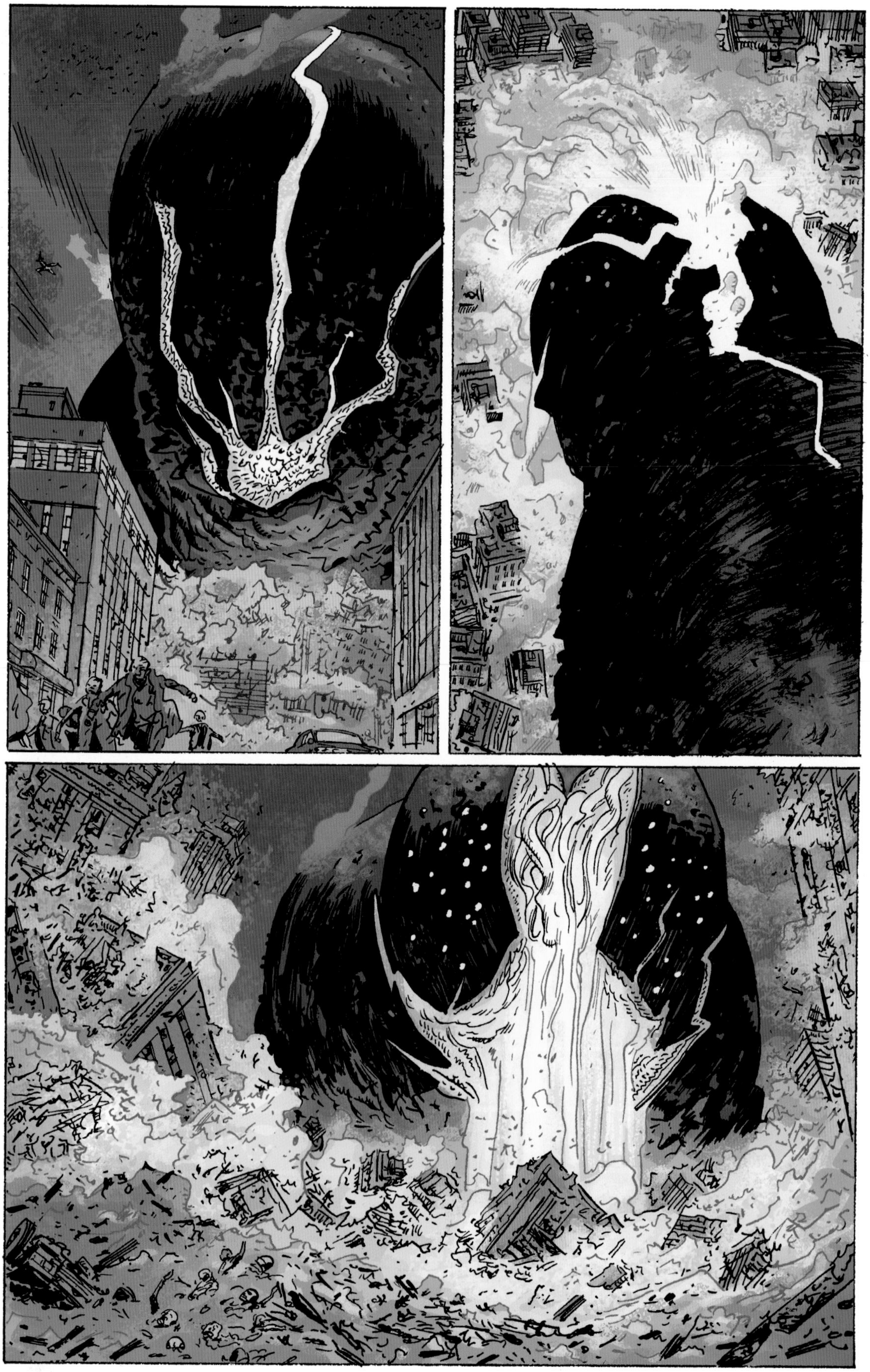

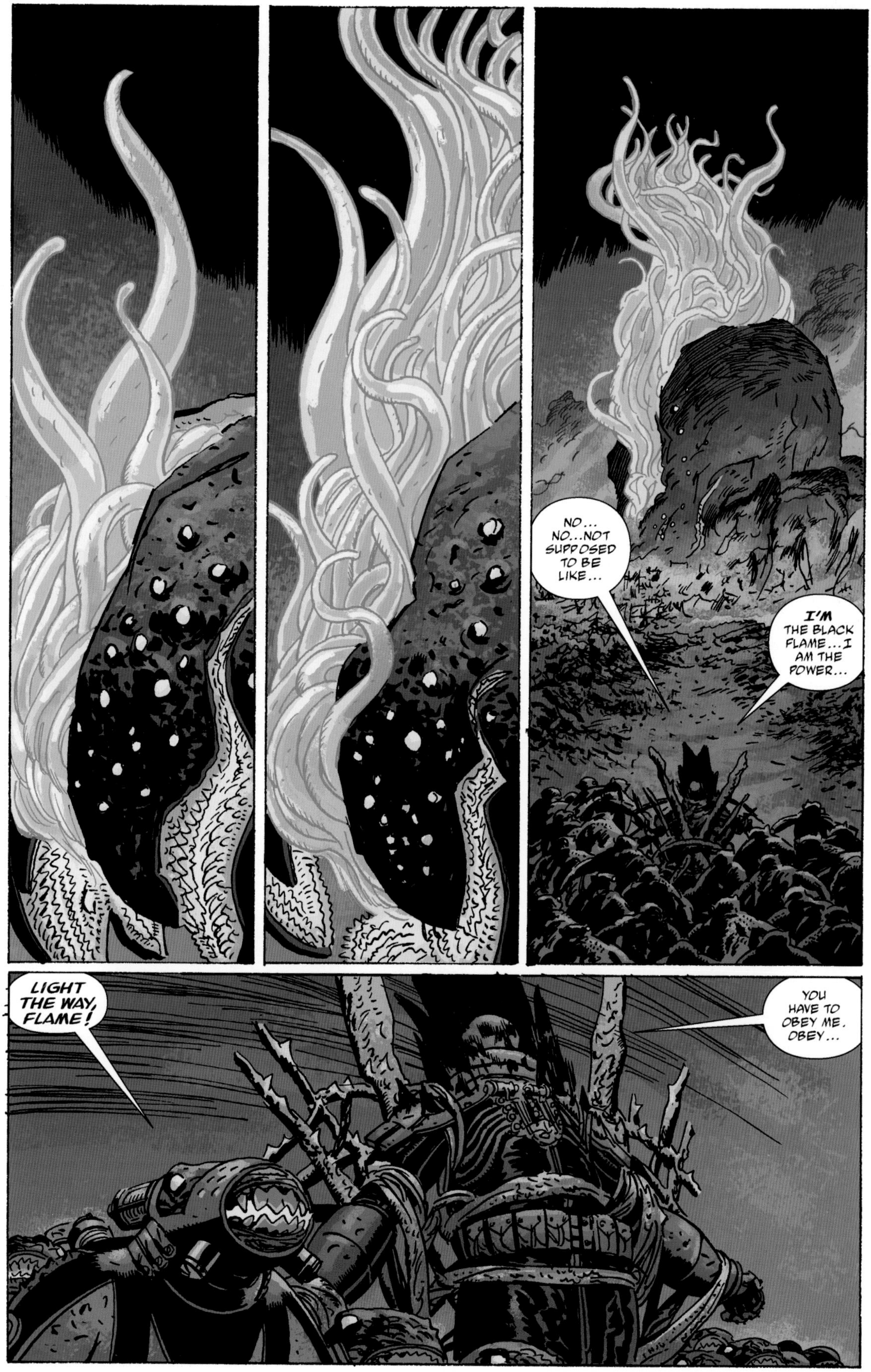
NO... NO...NOT SUPPOSED TO BE LIKE...
I'M THE BLACK FLAME...I AM THE POWER...
LIGHT THE WAY, FLAME!
YOU HAVE TO OBEY ME. OBEY...

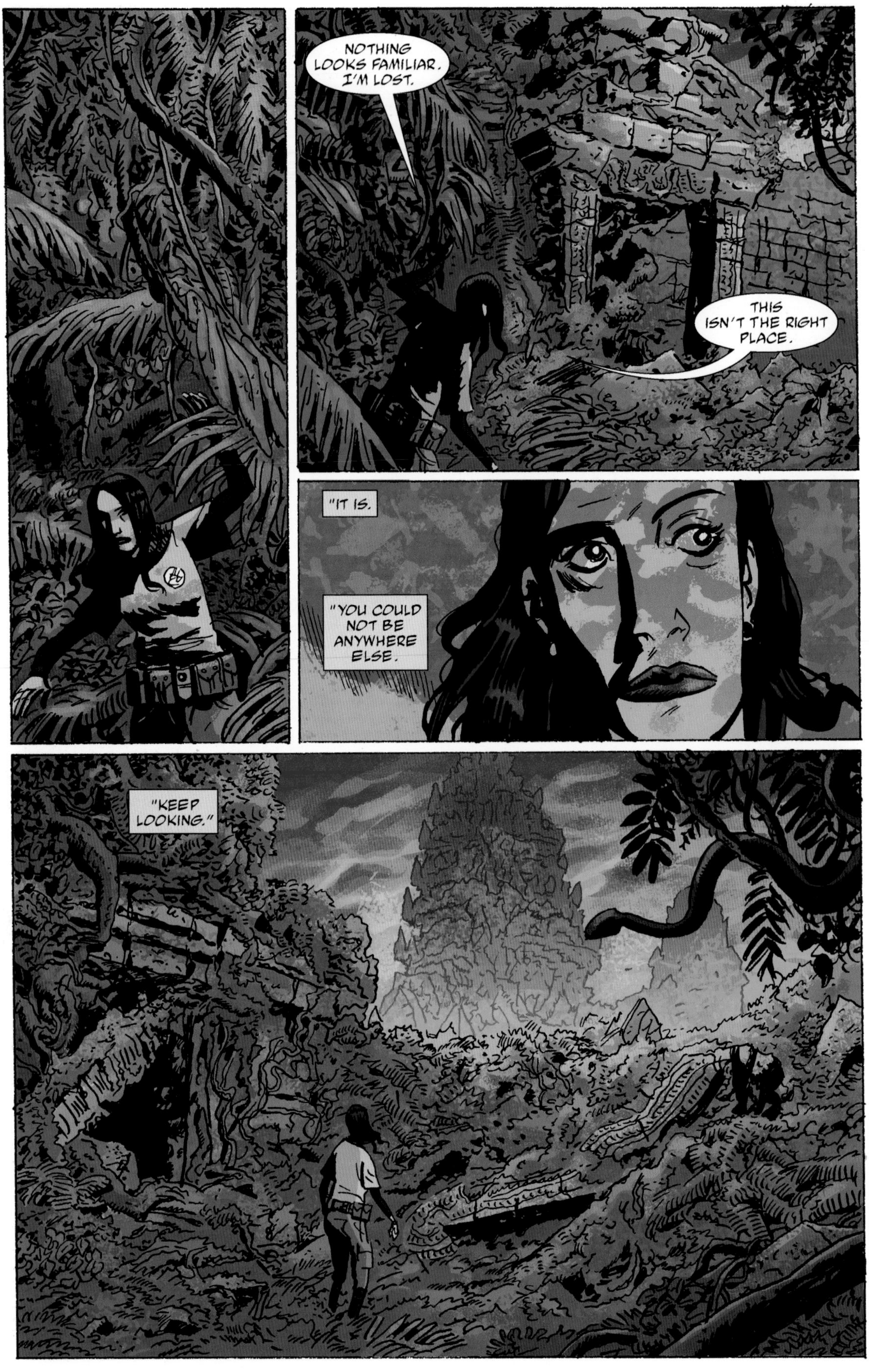
NOTHING LOOKS FAMILIAR. I'M LOST.
THIS ISN'T THE RIGHT PLACE.
"IT IS.
"YOU COULD NOT BE ANYWHERE ELSE.
"KEEP LOOKING."

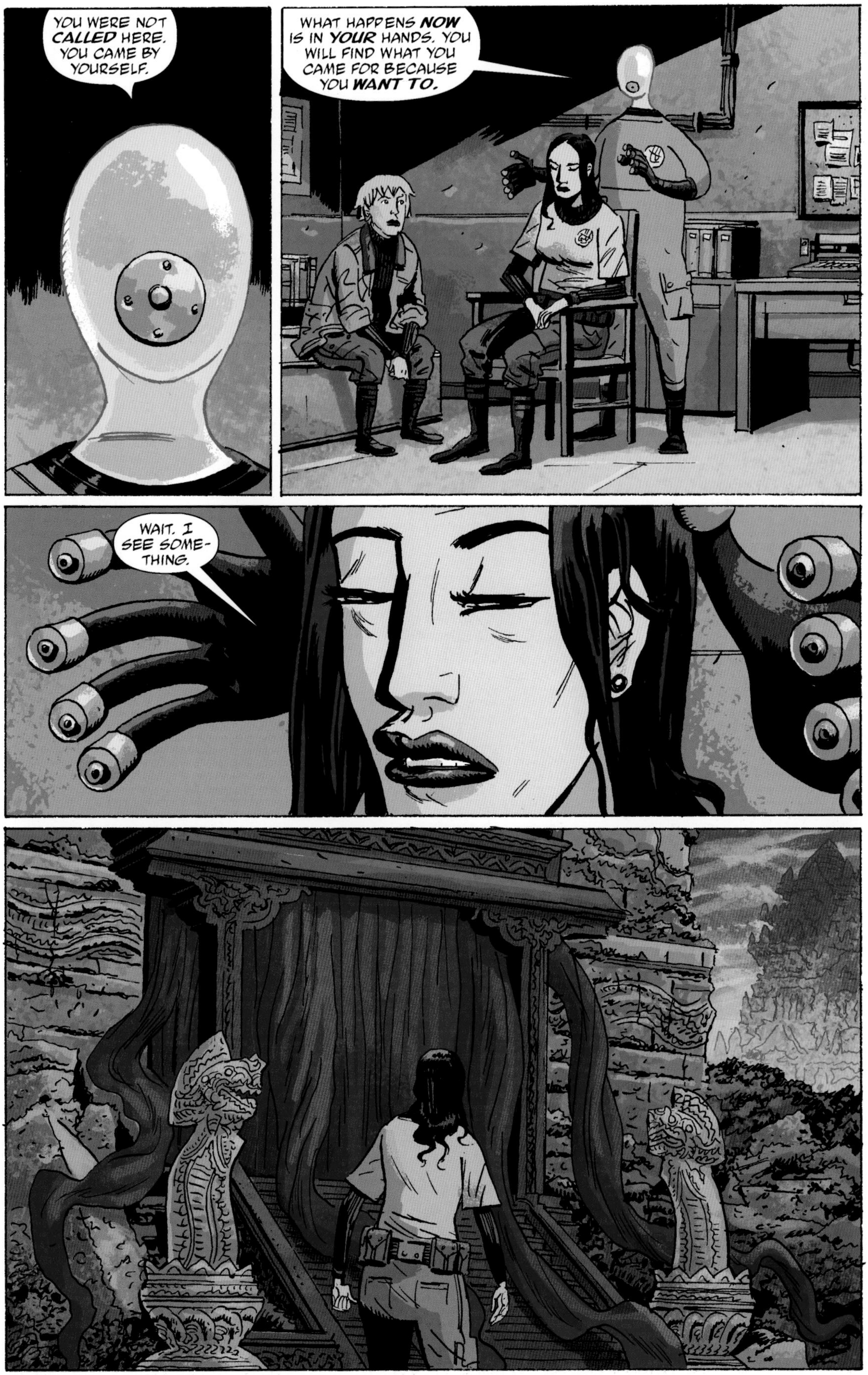
YOU WERE NOT CALLED HERE. YOU CAME BY YOURSELF.
WHAT HAPPENS NOW IS IN YOUR HANDS. YOU WILL FIND WHAT YOU CAME FOR BECAUSE YOU WANT TO.
WAIT. I SEE SOME-THING.

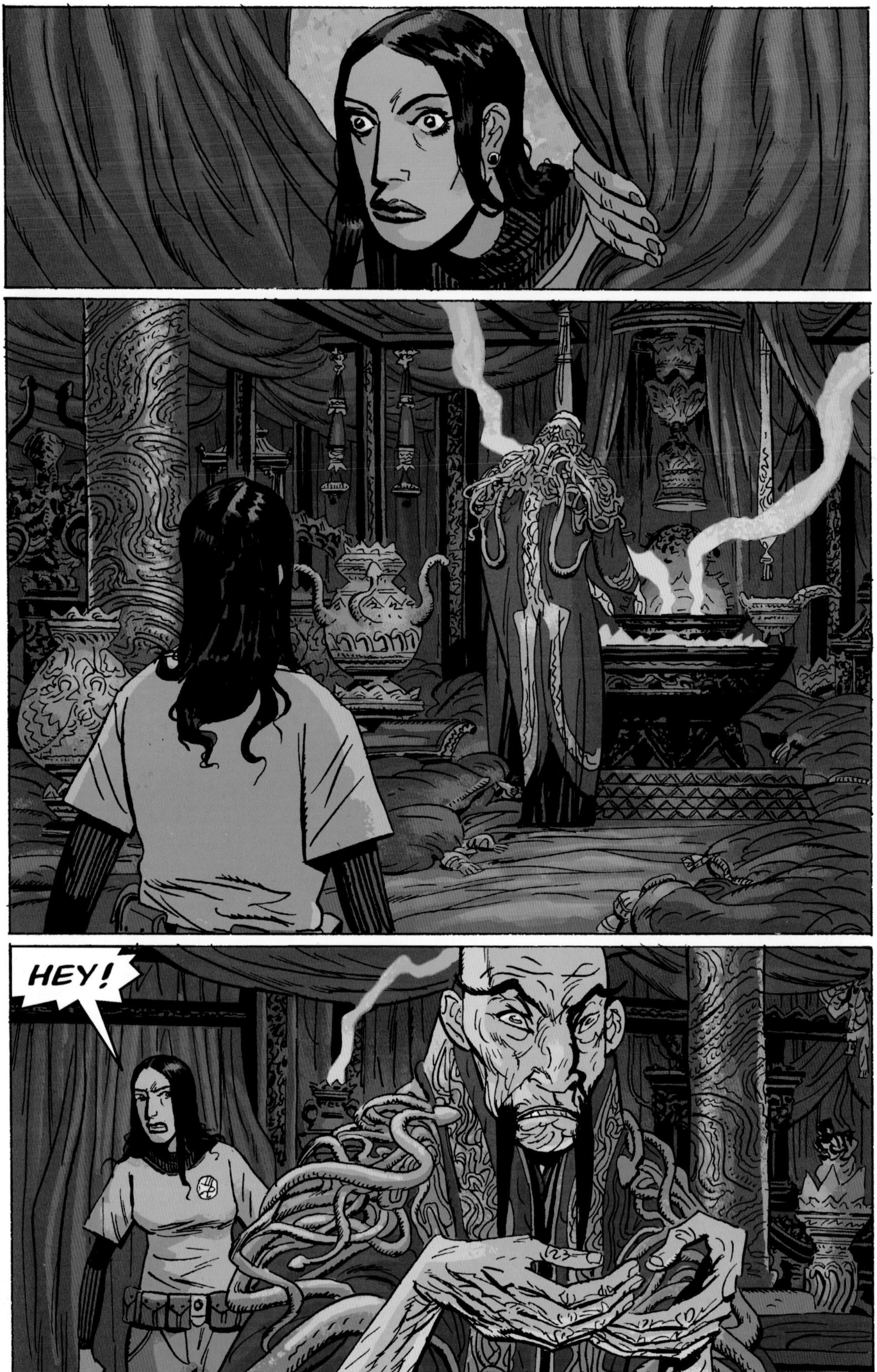
HEY!

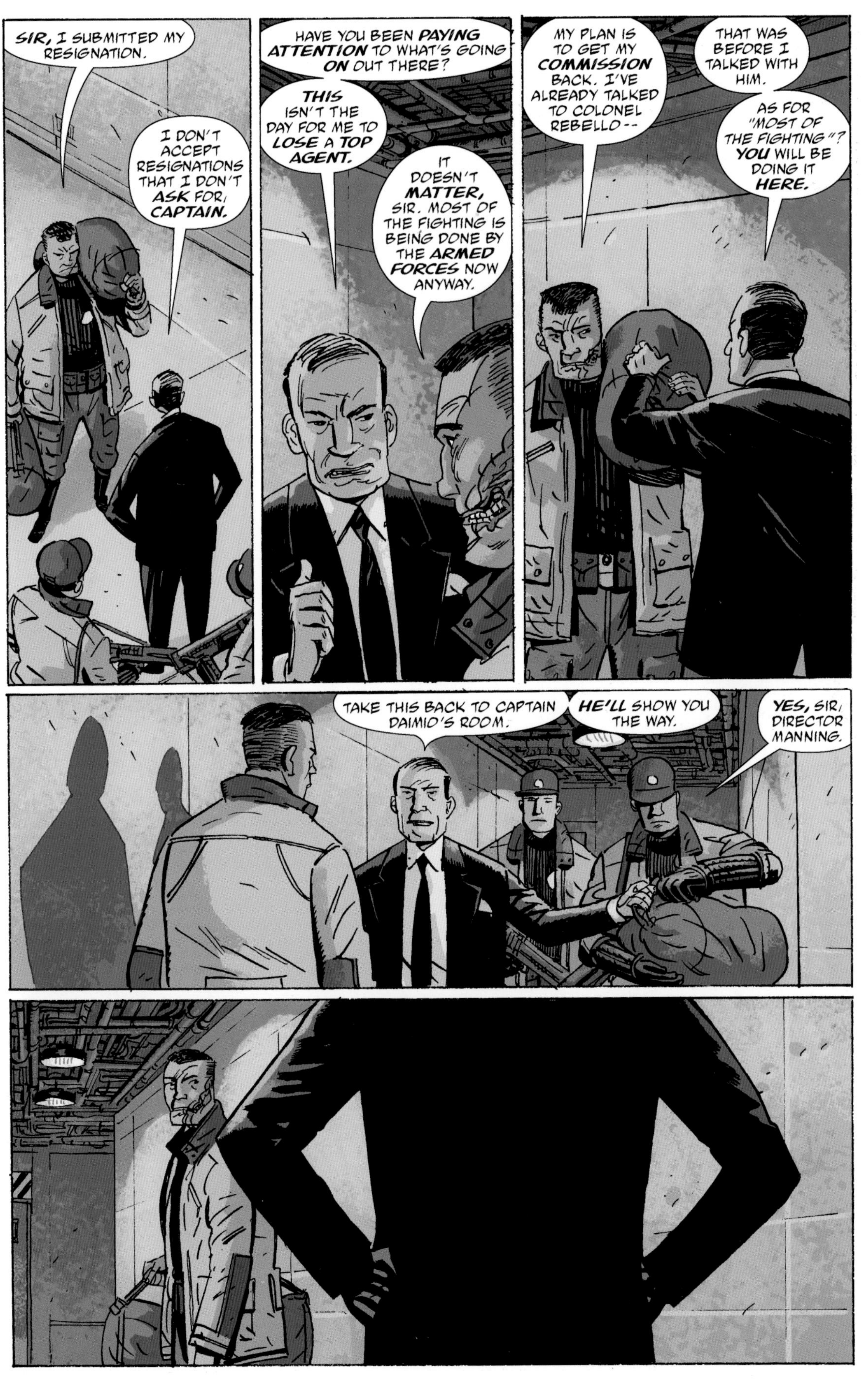
SIR, I SUBMITTED MY RESIGNATION.
I DON'T ACCEPT RESIGNATIONS THAT I DON'T ASK FOR, CAPTAIN.
HAVE YOU BEEN PAYING ATTENTION TO WHAT'S GOING ON OUT THERE?
THIS ISN'T THE DAY FOR ME TO LOSE A TOP AGENT.
IT DOESN'T MATTER, SIR. MOST OF THE FIGHTING IS BEING DONE BY THE ARMED FORCES NOW ANYWAY.
MY PLAN IS TO GET MY COMMISSION BACK. I'VE ALREADY TALKED TO COLONEL REBELLO--
THAT WAS BEFORE I TALKED WITH HIM.
AS FOR "MOST OF THE FIGHTING"? YOU WILL BE DOING IT HERE.
TAKE THIS BACK TO CAPTAIN DAIMIO'S ROOM.
HE'LL SHOW YOU THE WAY.
YES, SIR, DIRECTOR MANNING.

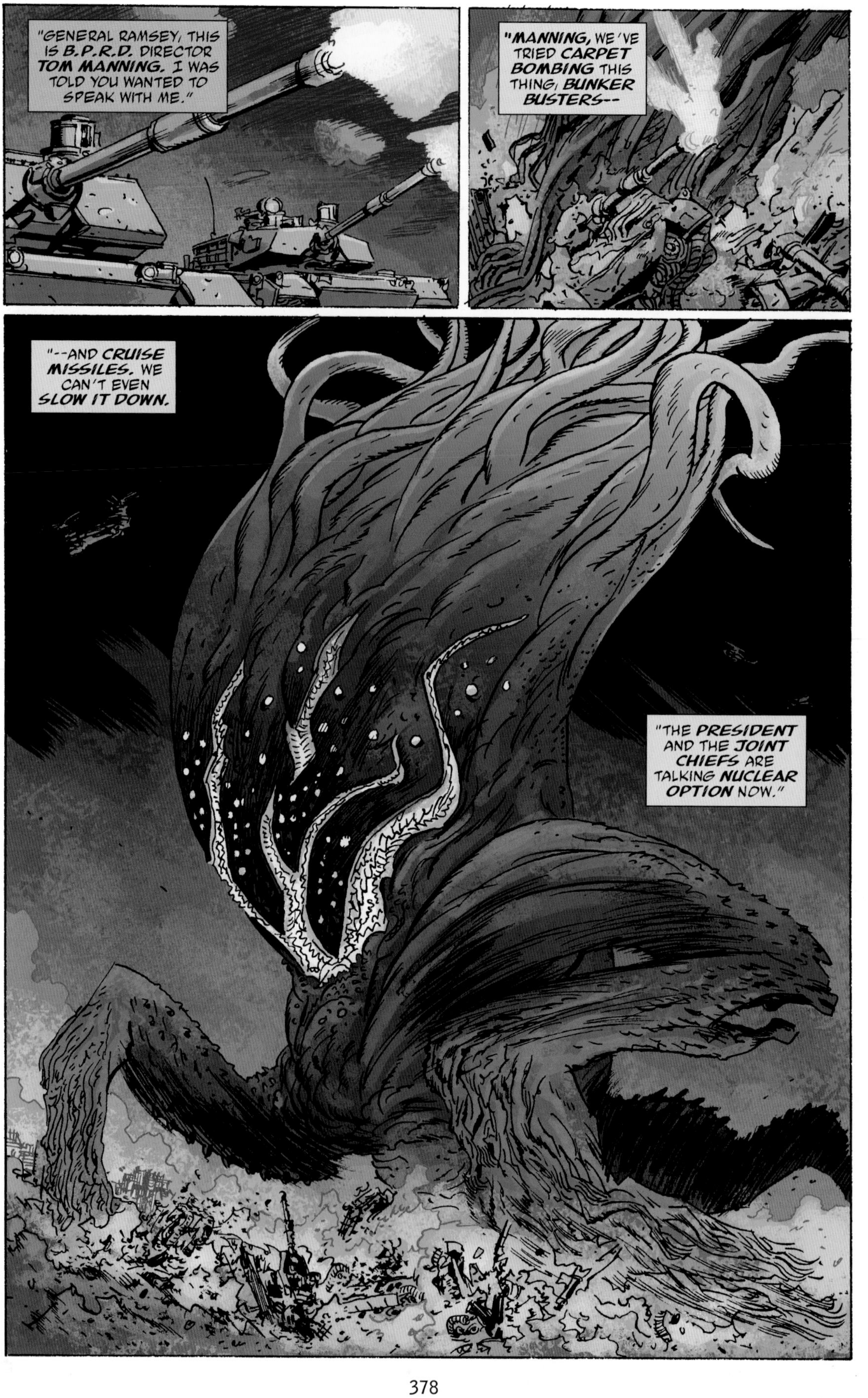
"GENERAL RAMSEY, THIS IS B.P.R.D. DIRECTOR TOM MANNING. I WAS TOLD YOU WANTED TO SPEAK WITH ME."
"MANNING, WE'VE TRIED CARPET BOMBING THIS THING, BUNKER BUSTERS--
"--AND CRUISE MISSILES. WE CAN'T EVEN SLOW IT DOWN.
"THE PRESIDENT AND THE JOINT CHIEFS ARE TALKING NUCLEAR OPTION NOW."

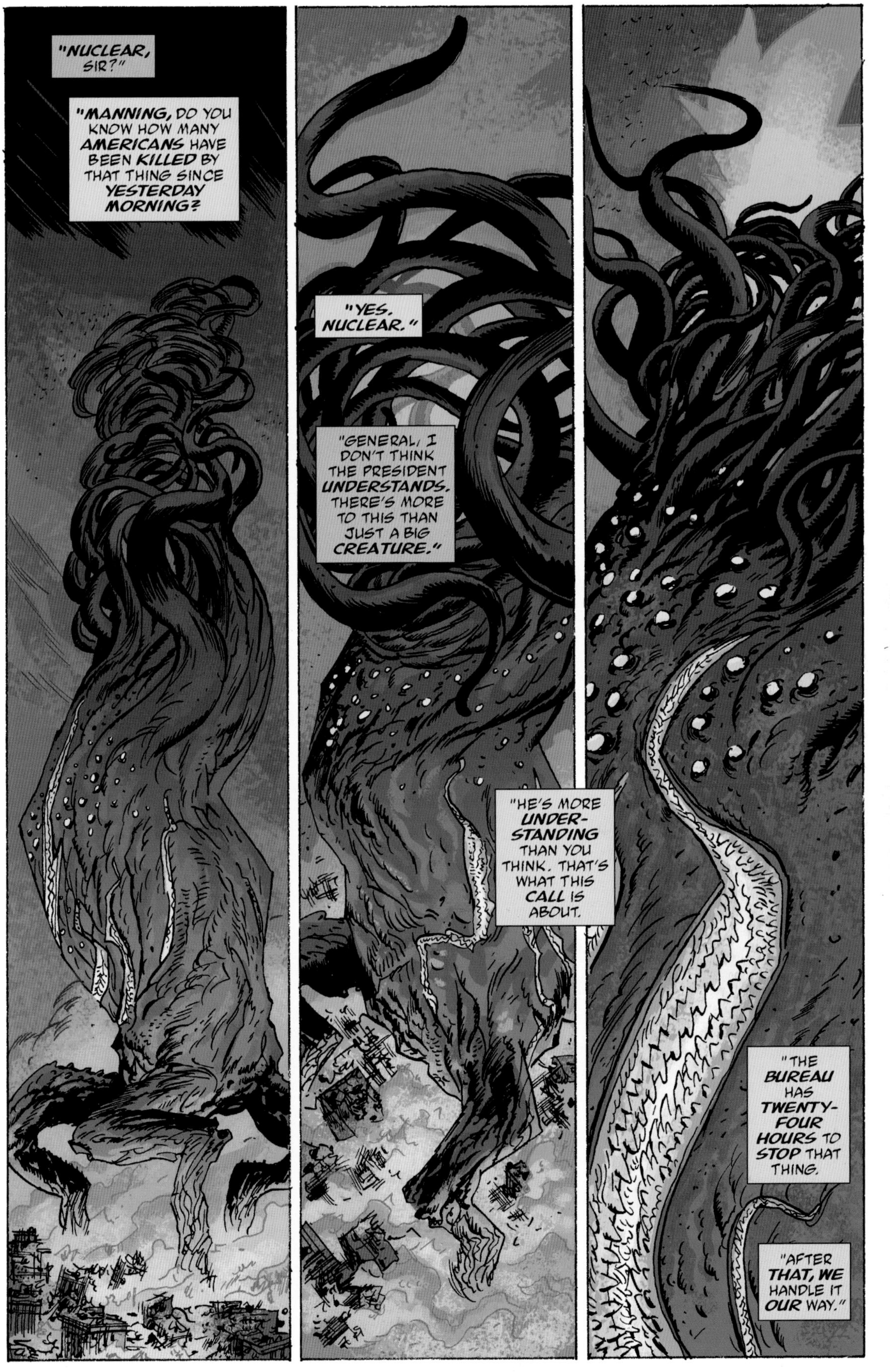
"NUCLEAR, SIR?"
"MANNING, DO YOU KNOW HOW MANY AMERICANS HAVE BEEN KILLED BY THAT THING SINCE YESTERDAY MORNING?
"YES. NUCLEAR."
"GENERAL, I DON'T THINK THE PRESIDENT UNDERSTANDS. THERE'S MORE TO THIS THAN JUST A BIG CREATURE."
"HE'S MORE UNDER-STANDING THAN YOU THINK. THAT'S WHAT THIS CALL IS ABOUT.
"THE BUREAU HAS TWENTY-FOUR HOURS TO STOP THAT THING.
"AFTER THAT, WE HANDLE IT OUR WAY."

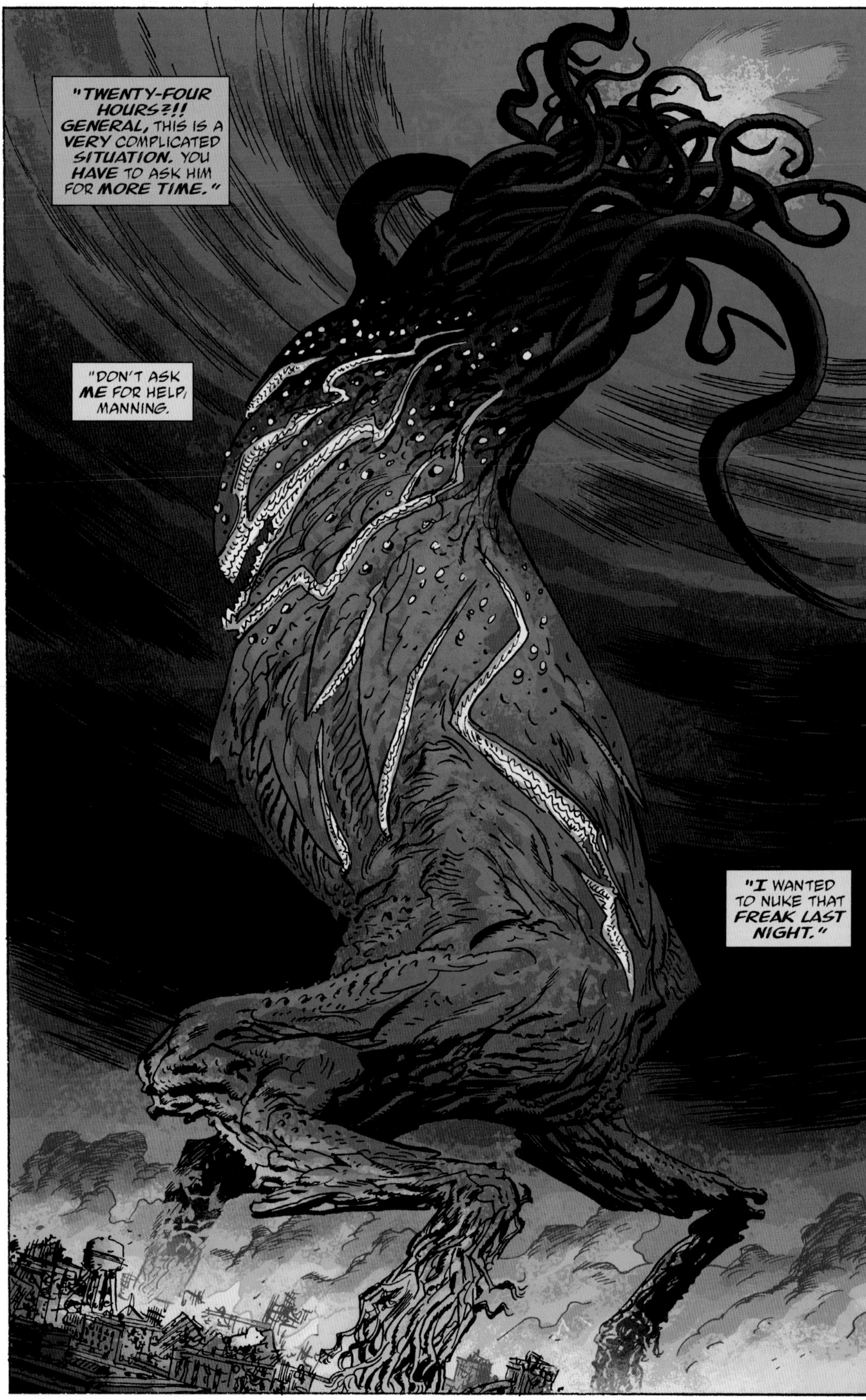
"TWENTY-FOUR HOURS?!! GENERAL, THIS IS A VERY COMPLICATED SITUATION. YOU HAVE TO ASK HIM FOR MORE TIME."
"DON'T ASK ME FOR HELP, MANNING.
"I WANTED TO NUKE THAT FREAK LAST NIGHT."

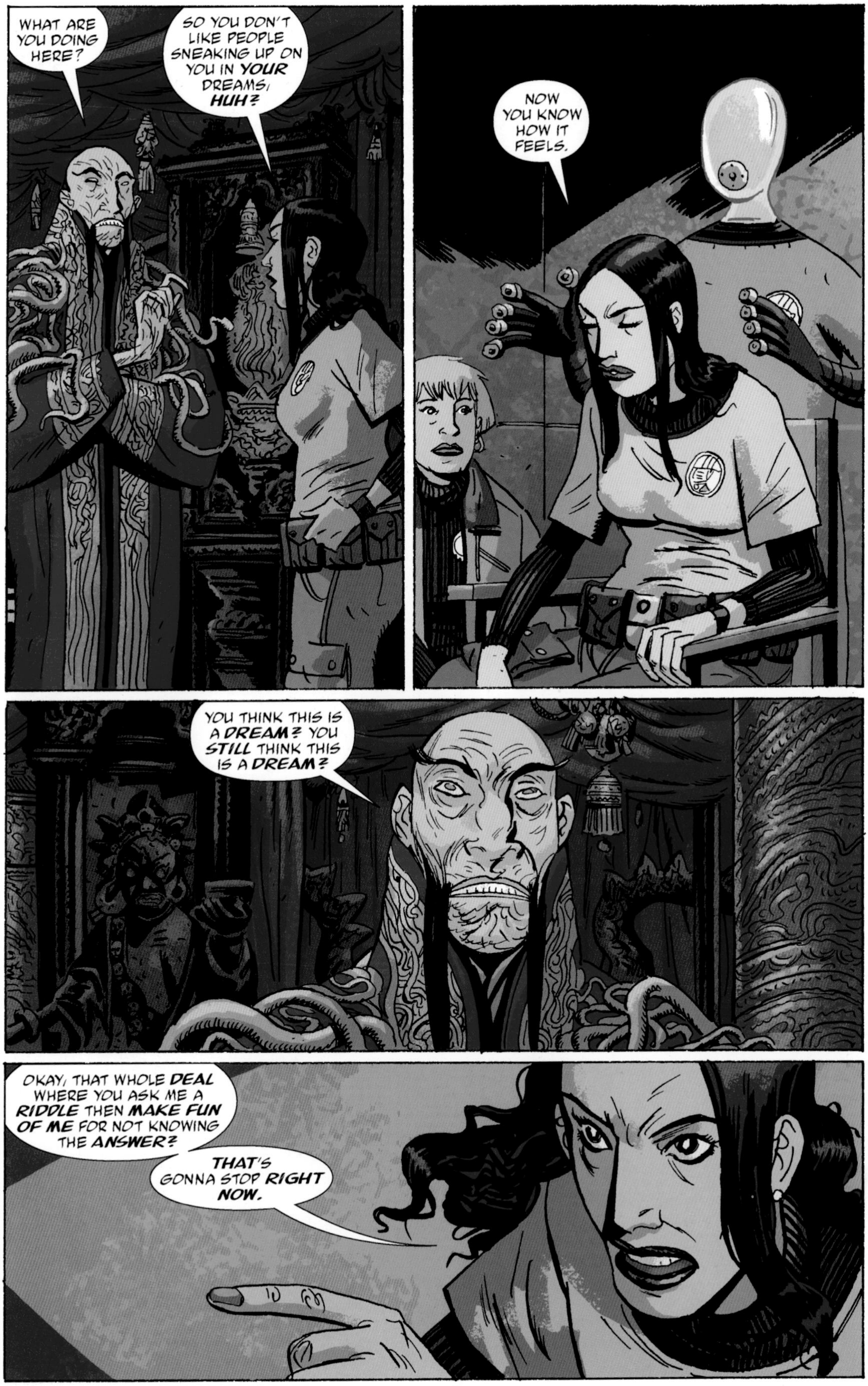
WHAT ARE YOU DOING HERE?
SO YOU DON'T LIKE PEOPLE SNEAKING UP ON YOU IN **YOUR** DREAMS, **HUH?**
NOW YOU KNOW HOW IT FEELS.
YOU THINK THIS IS A **DREAM?** YOU **STILL** THINK THIS IS A **DREAM?**
OKAY, THAT WHOLE **DEAL** WHERE YOU ASK ME A **RIDDLE** THEN **MAKE FUN OF ME** FOR NOT KNOWING THE **ANSWER?**
THAT'S GONNA STOP **RIGHT NOW.**

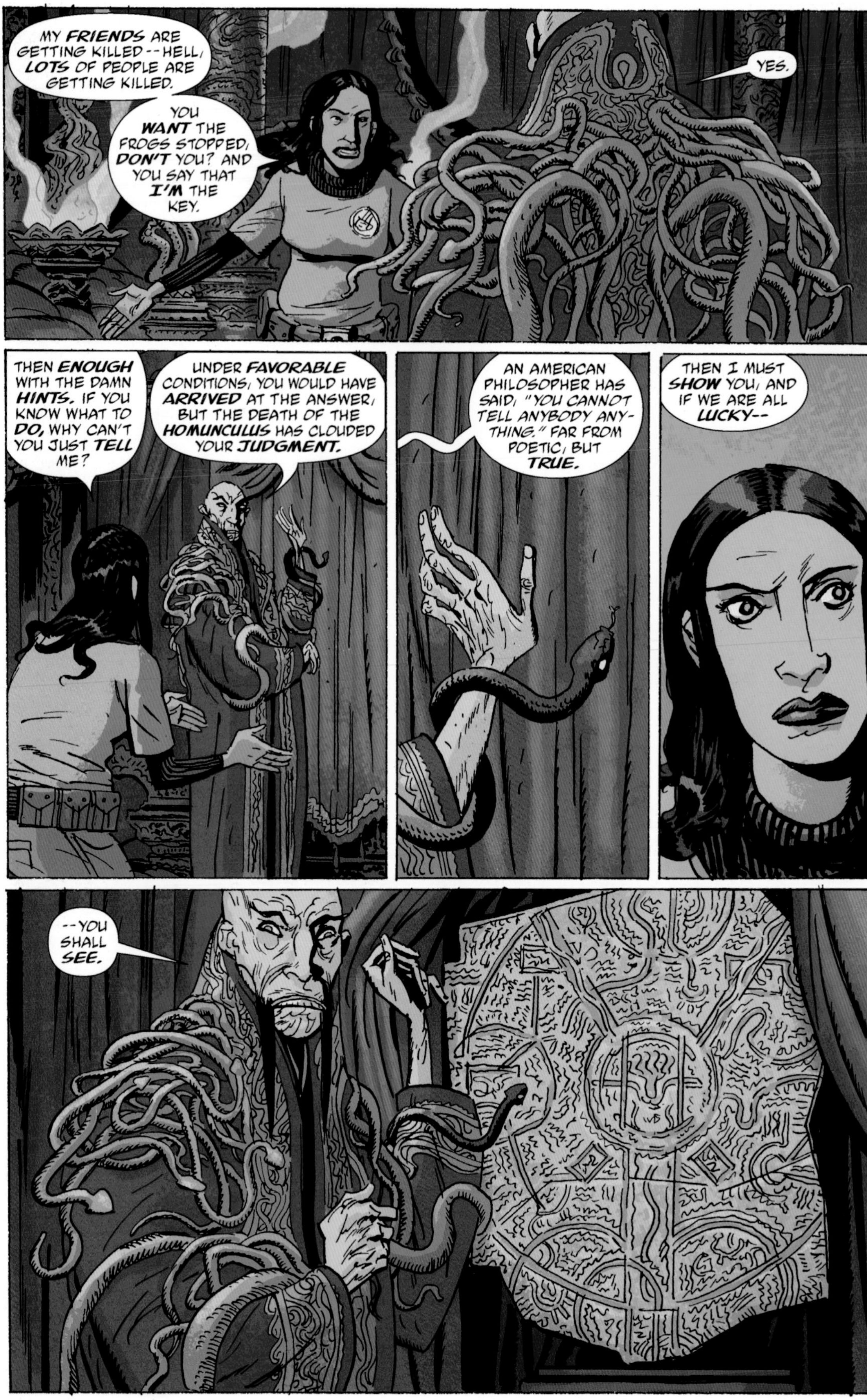
MY FRIENDS ARE GETTING KILLED--HELL, LOTS OF PEOPLE ARE GETTING KILLED.
YOU WANT THE FROGS STOPPED, DON'T YOU? AND YOU SAY THAT I'M THE KEY.
YES.
THEN ENOUGH WITH THE DAMN HINTS. IF YOU KNOW WHAT TO DO, WHY CAN'T YOU JUST TELL ME?
UNDER FAVORABLE CONDITIONS, YOU WOULD HAVE ARRIVED AT THE ANSWER, BUT THE DEATH OF THE HOMUNCULUS HAS CLOUDED YOUR JUDGMENT.
AN AMERICAN PHILOSOPHER HAS SAID, "YOU CANNOT TELL ANYBODY ANYTHING." FAR FROM POETIC, BUT TRUE.
THEN I MUST SHOW YOU, AND IF WE ARE ALL LUCKY--
--YOU SHALL SEE.

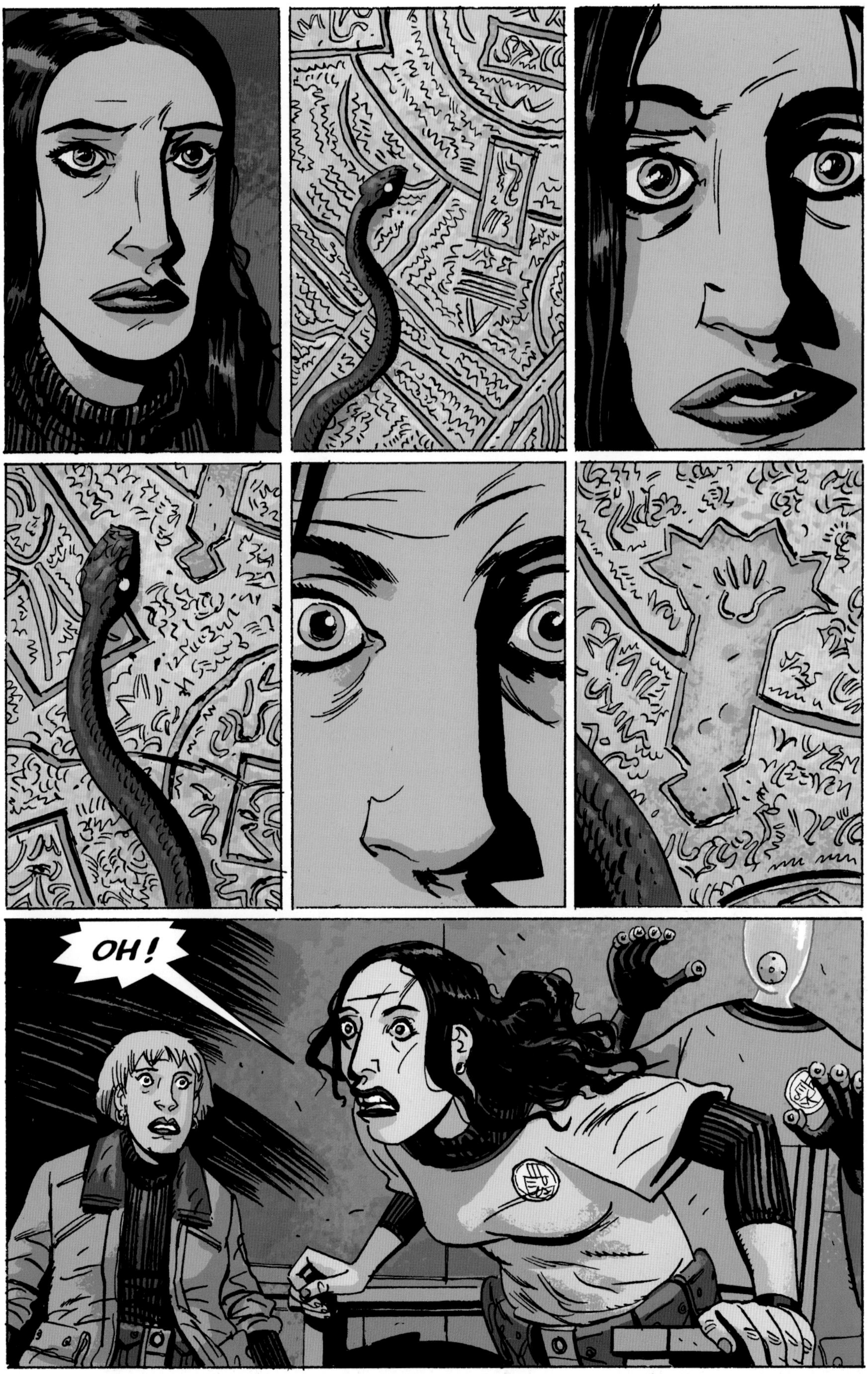
OH!

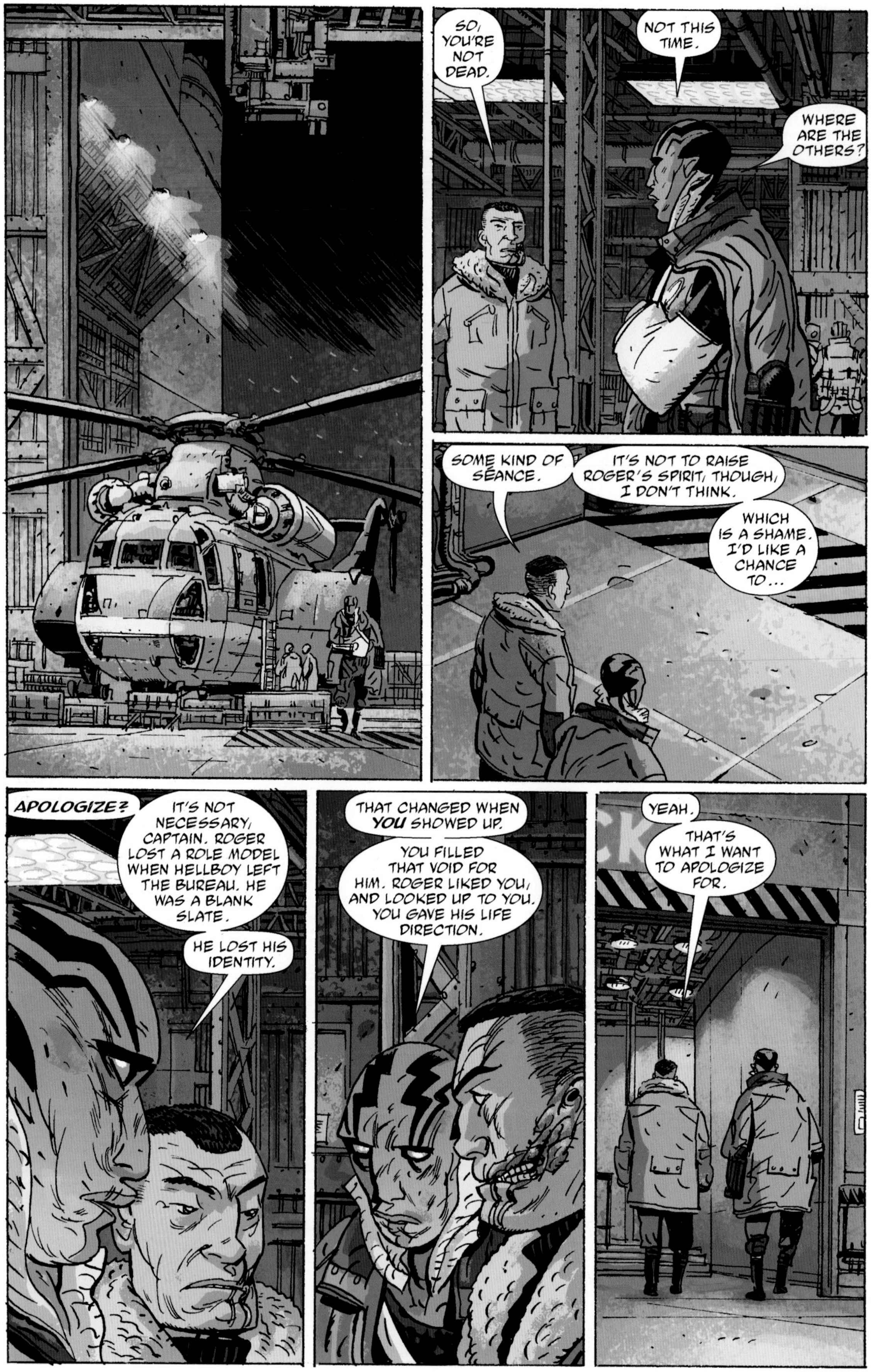
SO, YOU'RE NOT DEAD.
NOT THIS TIME.
WHERE ARE THE OTHERS?
SOME KIND OF SÉANCE.
IT'S NOT TO RAISE ROGER'S SPIRIT, THOUGH, I DON'T THINK.
WHICH IS A SHAME. I'D LIKE A CHANCE TO...
APOLOGIZE?
IT'S NOT NECESSARY, CAPTAIN. ROGER LOST A ROLE MODEL WHEN HELLBOY LEFT THE BUREAU. HE WAS A BLANK SLATE.
HE LOST HIS IDENTITY.
THAT CHANGED WHEN YOU SHOWED UP.
YOU FILLED THAT VOID FOR HIM. ROGER LIKED YOU, AND LOOKED UP TO YOU. YOU GAVE HIS LIFE DIRECTION.
YEAH.
THAT'S WHAT I WANT TO APOLOGIZE FOR.

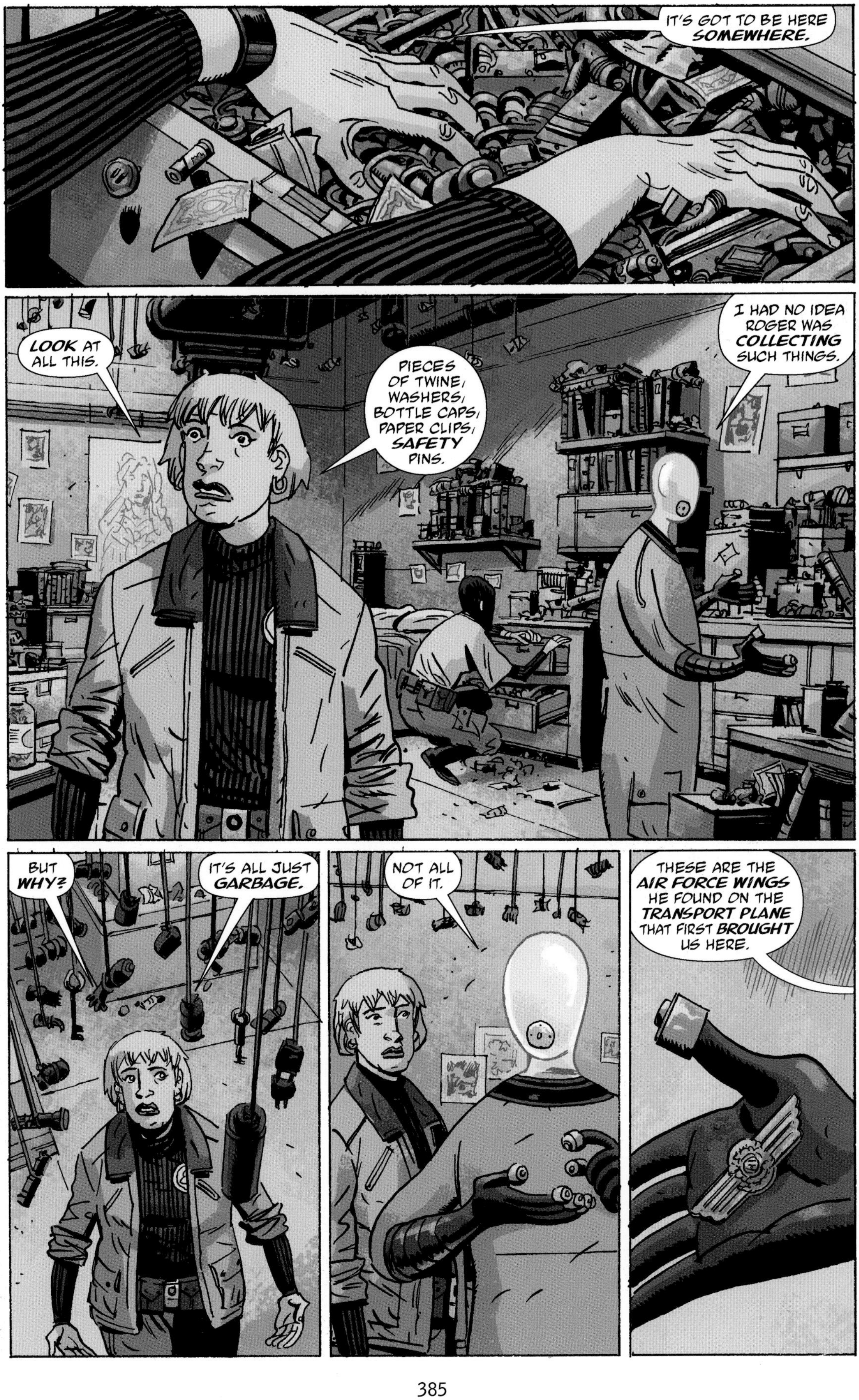
IT'S GOT TO BE HERE SOMEWHERE.
LOOK AT ALL THIS.
PIECES OF TWINE, WASHERS, BOTTLE CAPS, PAPER CLIPS, SAFETY PINS.
I HAD NO IDEA ROGER WAS COLLECTING SUCH THINGS.
BUT WHY?
IT'S ALL JUST GARBAGE.
NOT ALL OF IT.
THESE ARE THE AIR FORCE WINGS HE FOUND ON THE TRANSPORT PLANE THAT FIRST BROUGHT US HERE.

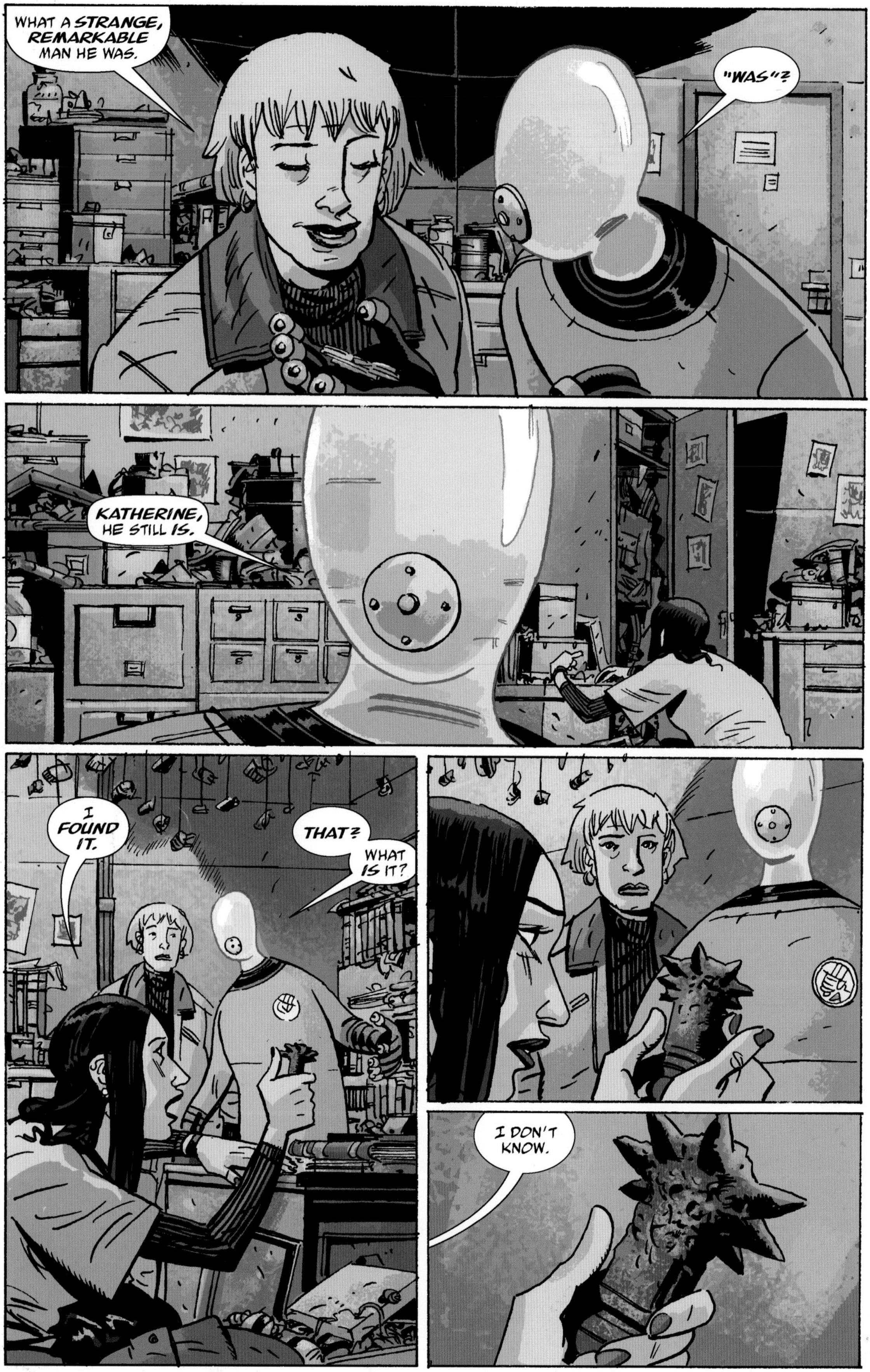
WHAT A STRANGE, REMARKABLE MAN HE WAS.
"WAS"?
KATHERINE, HE STILL IS.
I FOUND IT.
THAT? WHAT IS IT?
I DON'T KNOW.

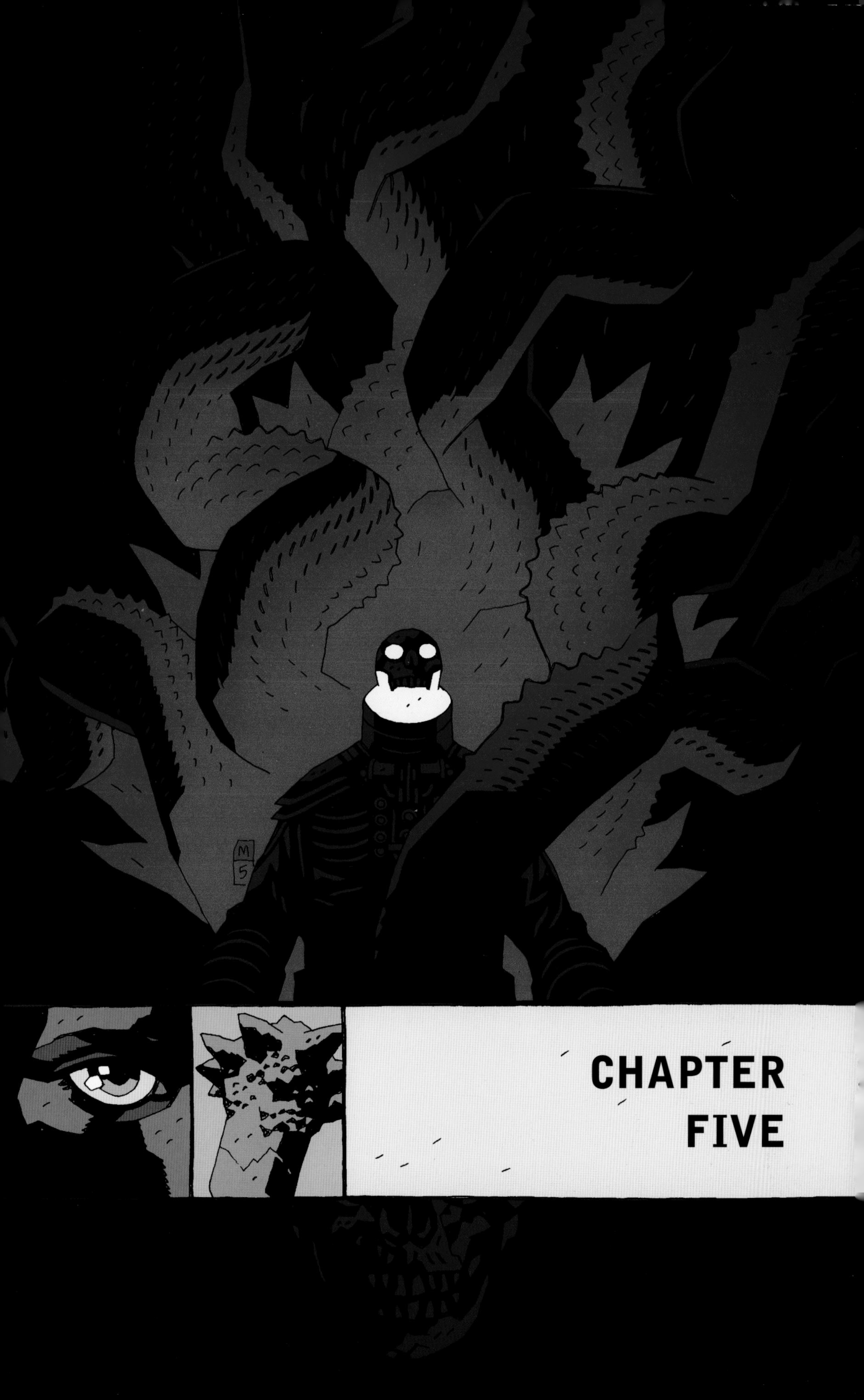
CHAPTER
FIVE

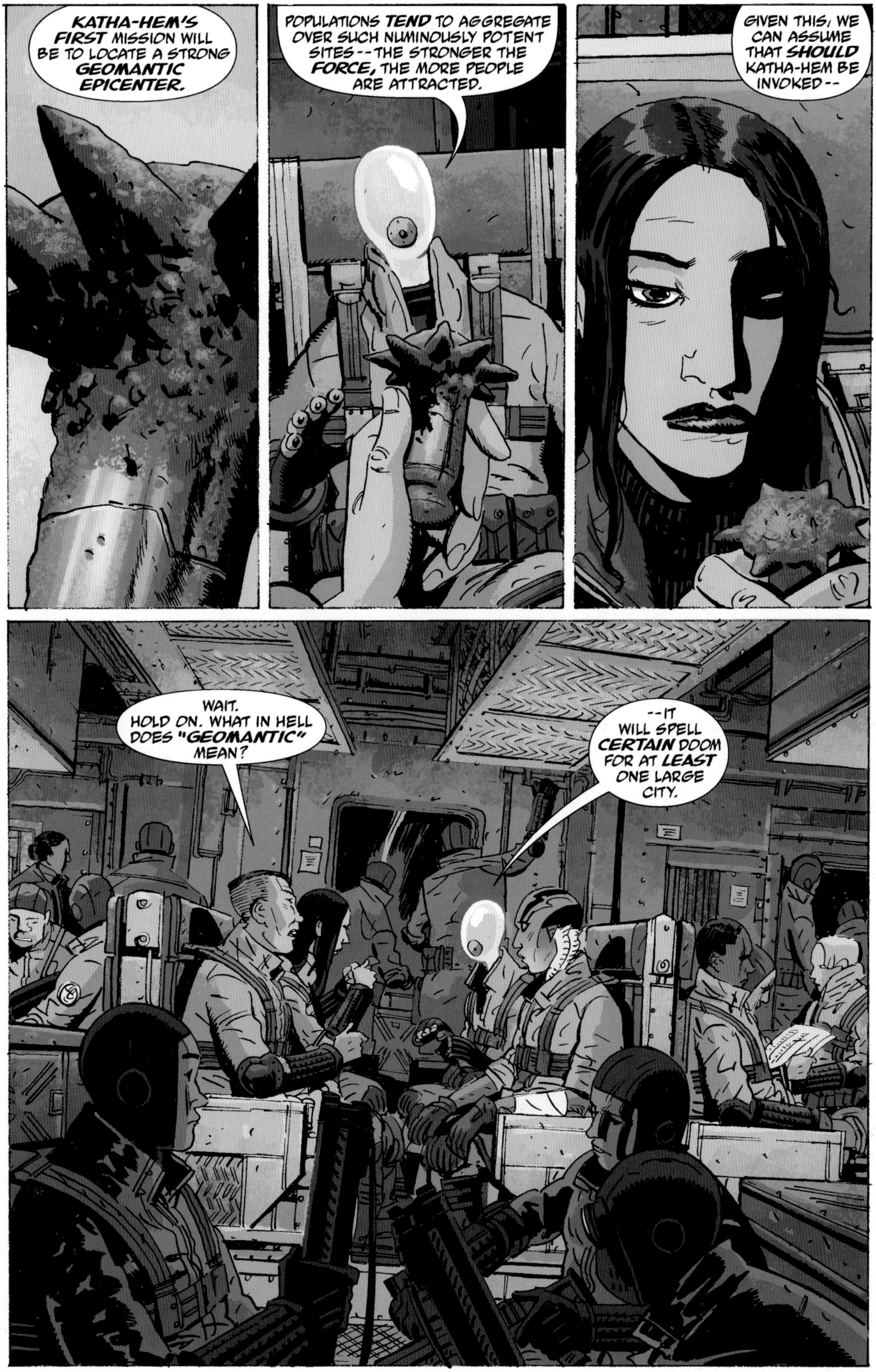
KATHA-HEM'S FIRST MISSION WILL BE TO LOCATE A STRONG GEOMANTIC EPICENTER.
POPULATIONS TEND TO AGGREGATE OVER SUCH NUMINOUSLY POTENT SITES--THE STRONGER THE FORCE, THE MORE PEOPLE ARE ATTRACTED.
GIVEN THIS, WE CAN ASSUME THAT SHOULD KATHA-HEM BE INVOKED--
WAIT. HOLD ON. WHAT IN HELL DOES "GEOMANTIC" MEAN?
--IT WILL SPELL CERTAIN DOOM FOR AT LEAST ONE LARGE CITY.

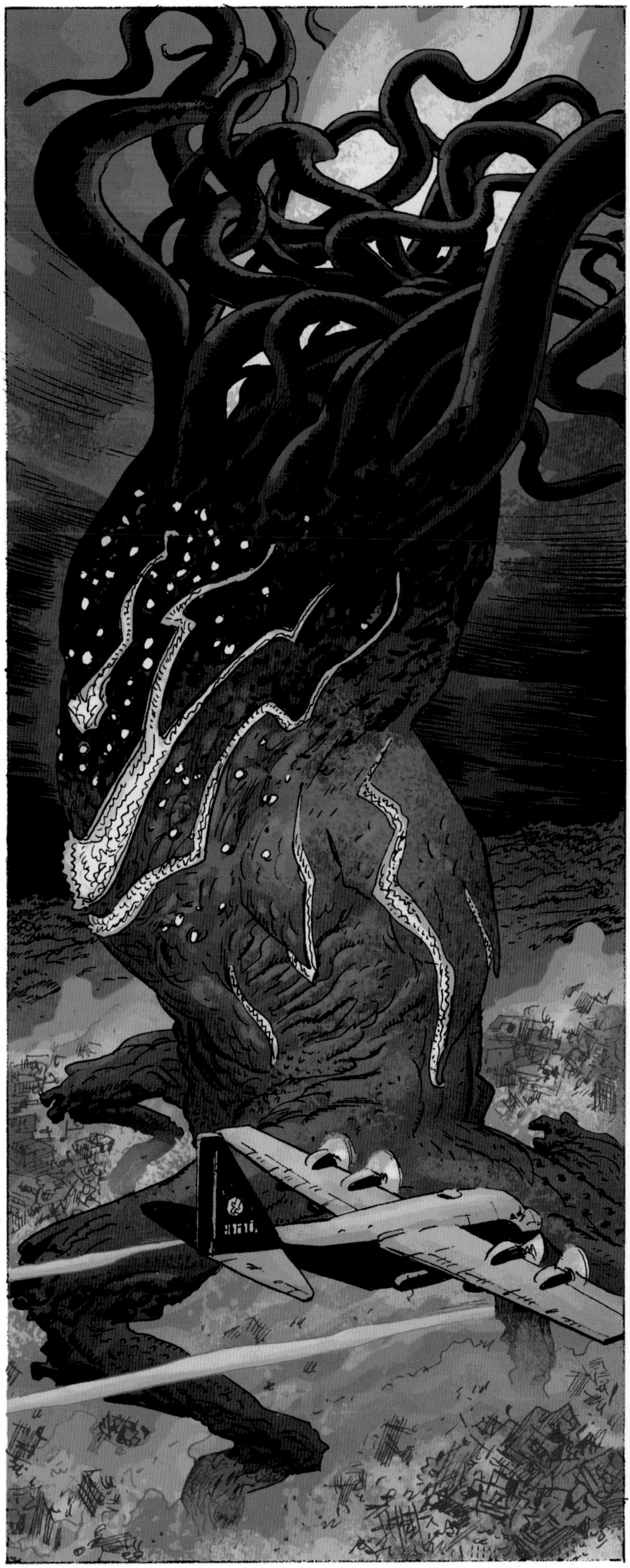

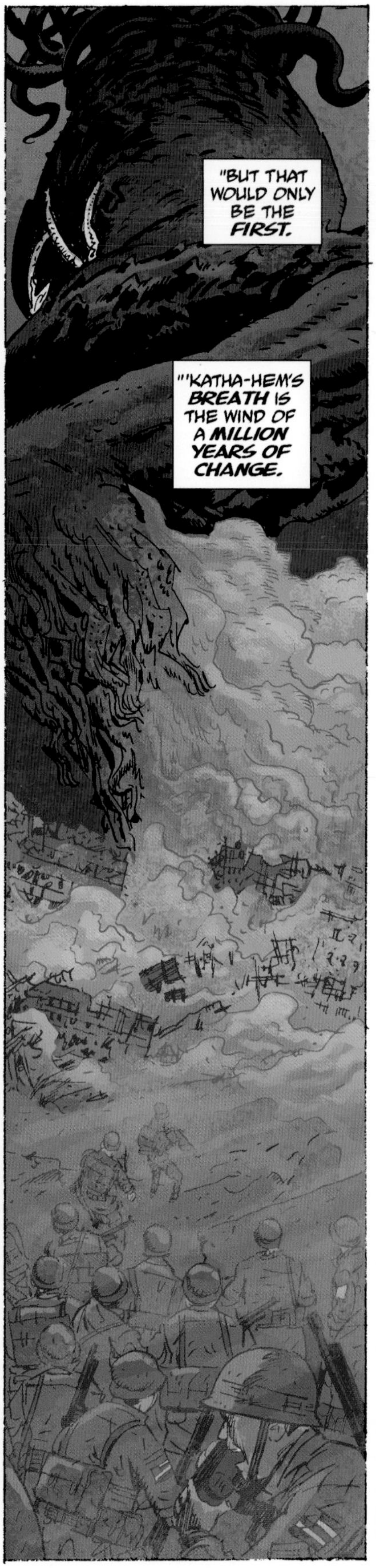
"BUT THAT WOULD ONLY BE THE FIRST.
"'KATHA-HEM'S BREATH IS THE WIND OF A MILLION YEARS OF CHANGE.

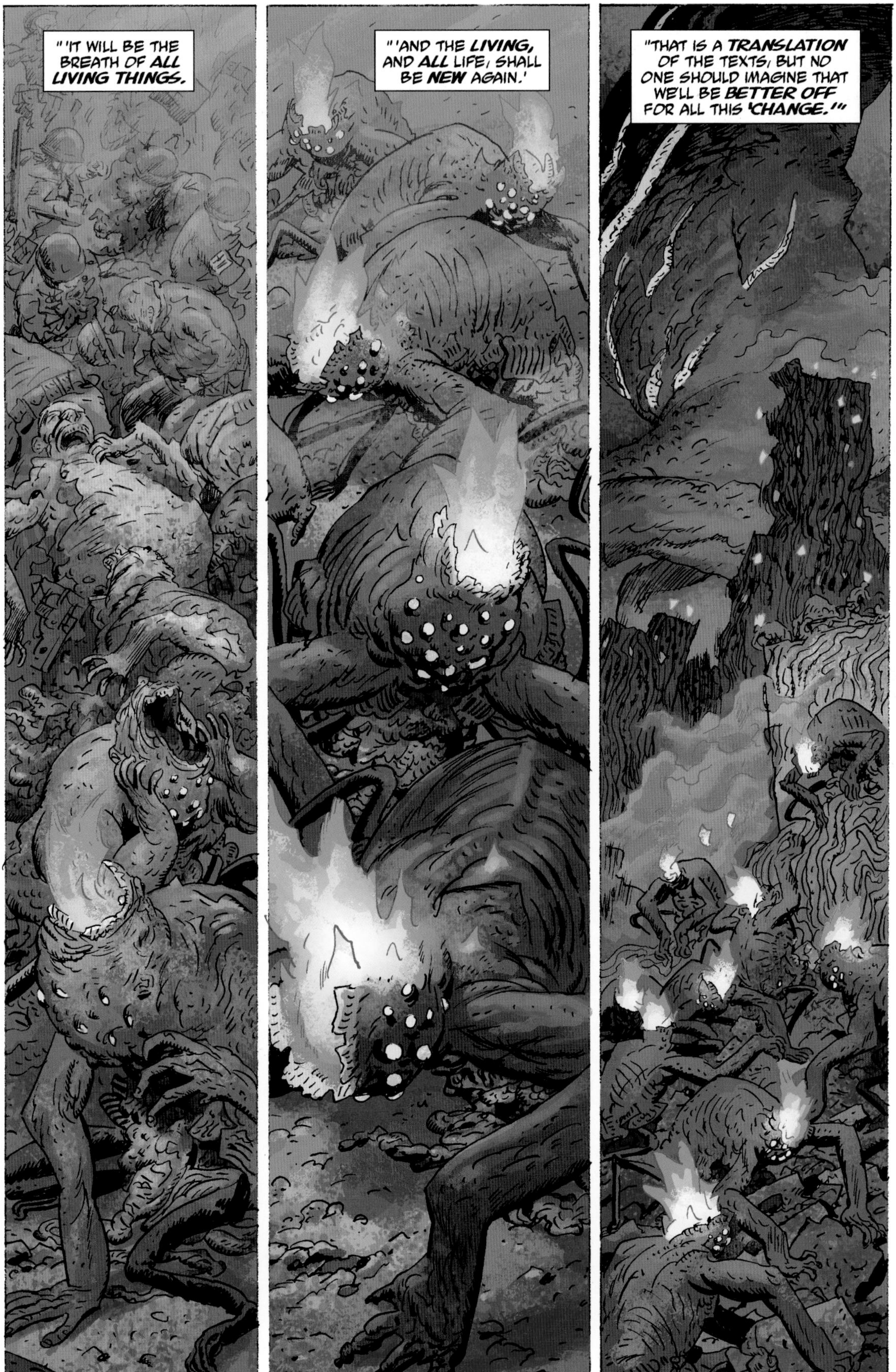
"'IT WILL BE THE BREATH OF ALL LIVING THINGS.
"'AND THE LIVING, AND ALL LIFE, SHALL BE NEW AGAIN.'
"THAT IS A TRANSLATION OF THE TEXTS, BUT NO ONE SHOULD IMAGINE THAT WE'LL BE BETTER OFF FOR ALL THIS 'CHANGE.'"

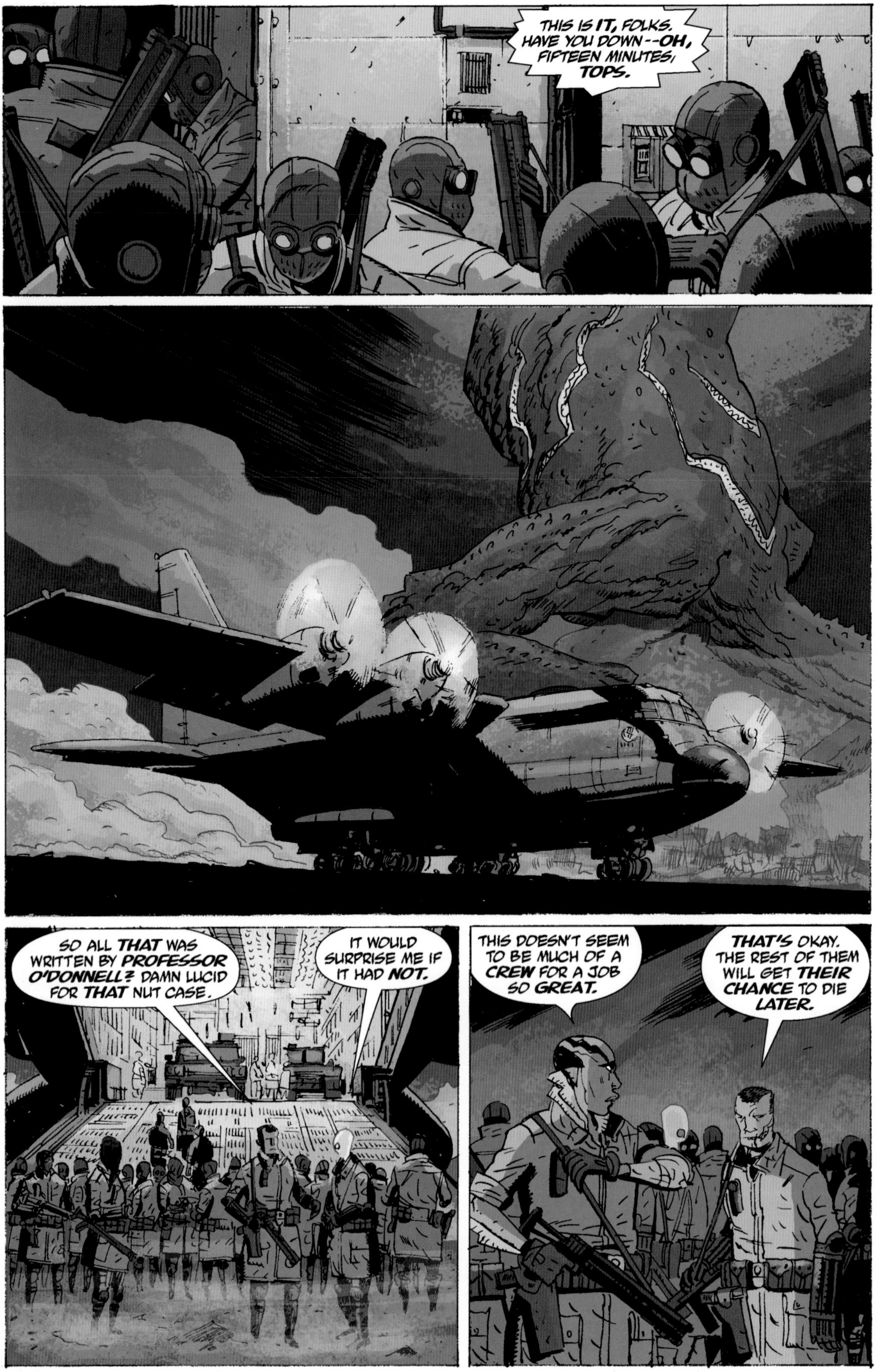
THIS IS IT, FOLKS. HAVE YOU DOWN--OH, FIFTEEN MINUTES, TOPS.
SO ALL THAT WAS WRITTEN BY PROFESSOR O'DONNELL? DAMN LUCID FOR THAT NUT CASE.
IT WOULD SURPRISE ME IF IT HAD NOT.
THIS DOESN'T SEEM TO BE MUCH OF A CREW FOR A JOB SO GREAT.
THAT'S OKAY. THE REST OF THEM WILL GET THEIR CHANCE TO DIE LATER.

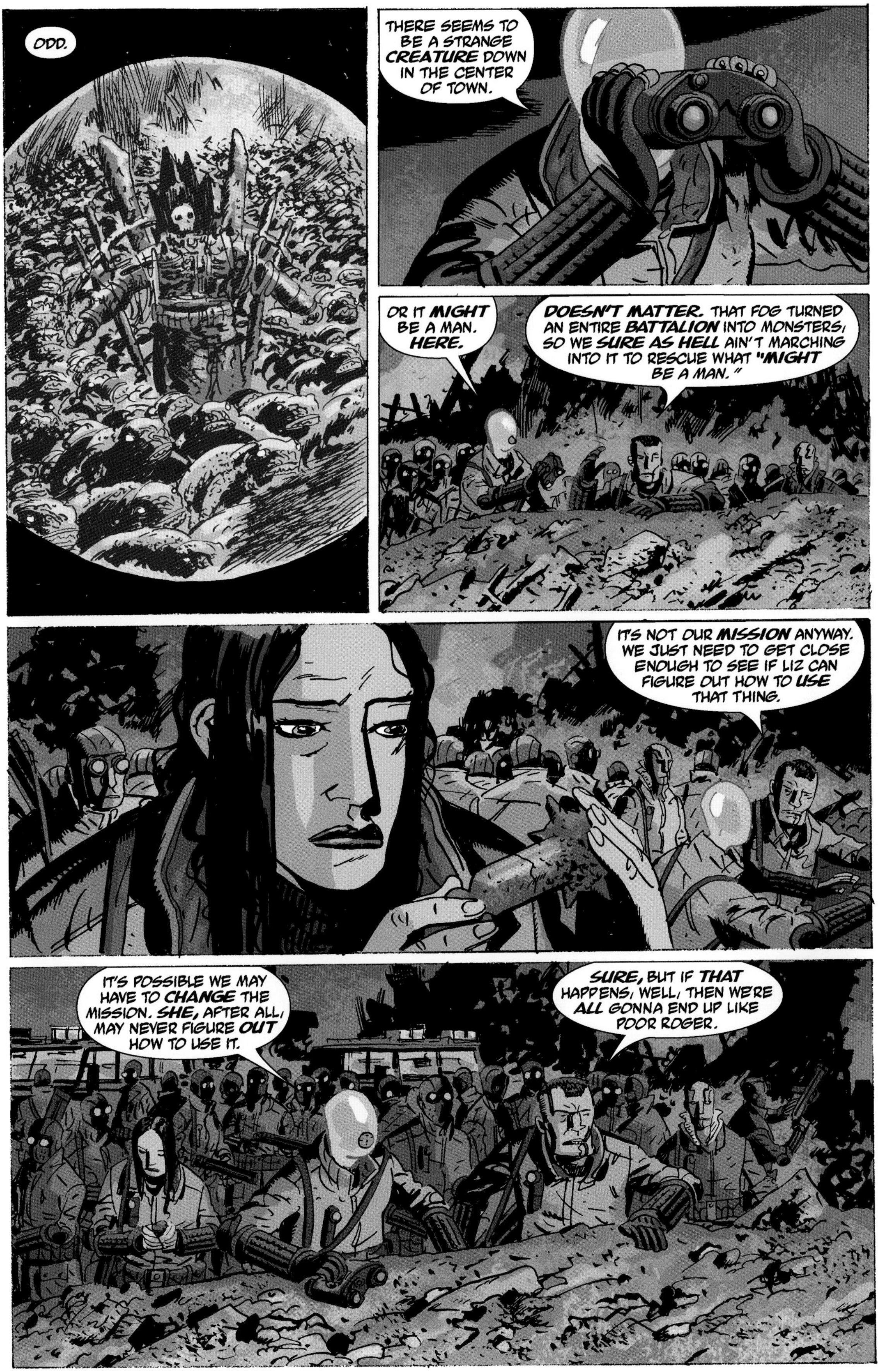
ODD.
THERE SEEMS TO BE A STRANGE CREATURE DOWN IN THE CENTER OF TOWN.
OR IT MIGHT BE A MAN. HERE.
DOESN'T MATTER. THAT FOG TURNED AN ENTIRE BATTALION INTO MONSTERS, SO WE SURE AS HELL AIN'T MARCHING INTO IT TO RESCUE WHAT "MIGHT BE A MAN."
IT'S NOT OUR MISSION ANYWAY. WE JUST NEED TO GET CLOSE ENOUGH TO SEE IF LIZ CAN FIGURE OUT HOW TO USE THAT THING.
IT'S POSSIBLE WE MAY HAVE TO CHANGE THE MISSION. SHE, AFTER ALL, MAY NEVER FIGURE OUT HOW TO USE IT.
SURE, BUT IF THAT HAPPENS, WELL, THEN WE'RE ALL GONNA END UP LIKE POOR ROGER.

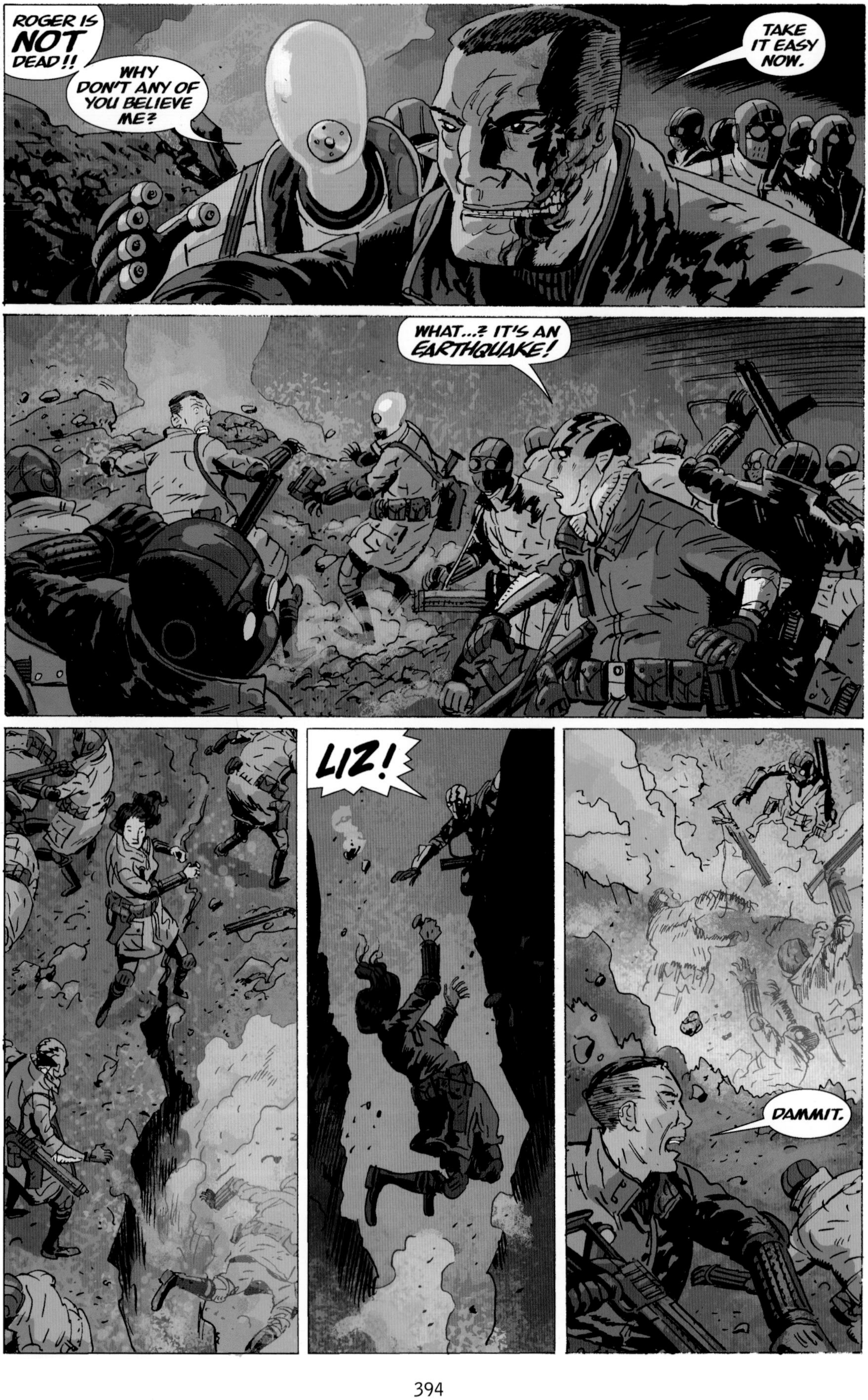
ROGER IS NOT DEAD!!
WHY DON'T ANY OF YOU BELIEVE ME?
TAKE IT EASY NOW.
WHAT...? IT'S AN EARTHQUAKE!
LIZ!
DAMMIT.

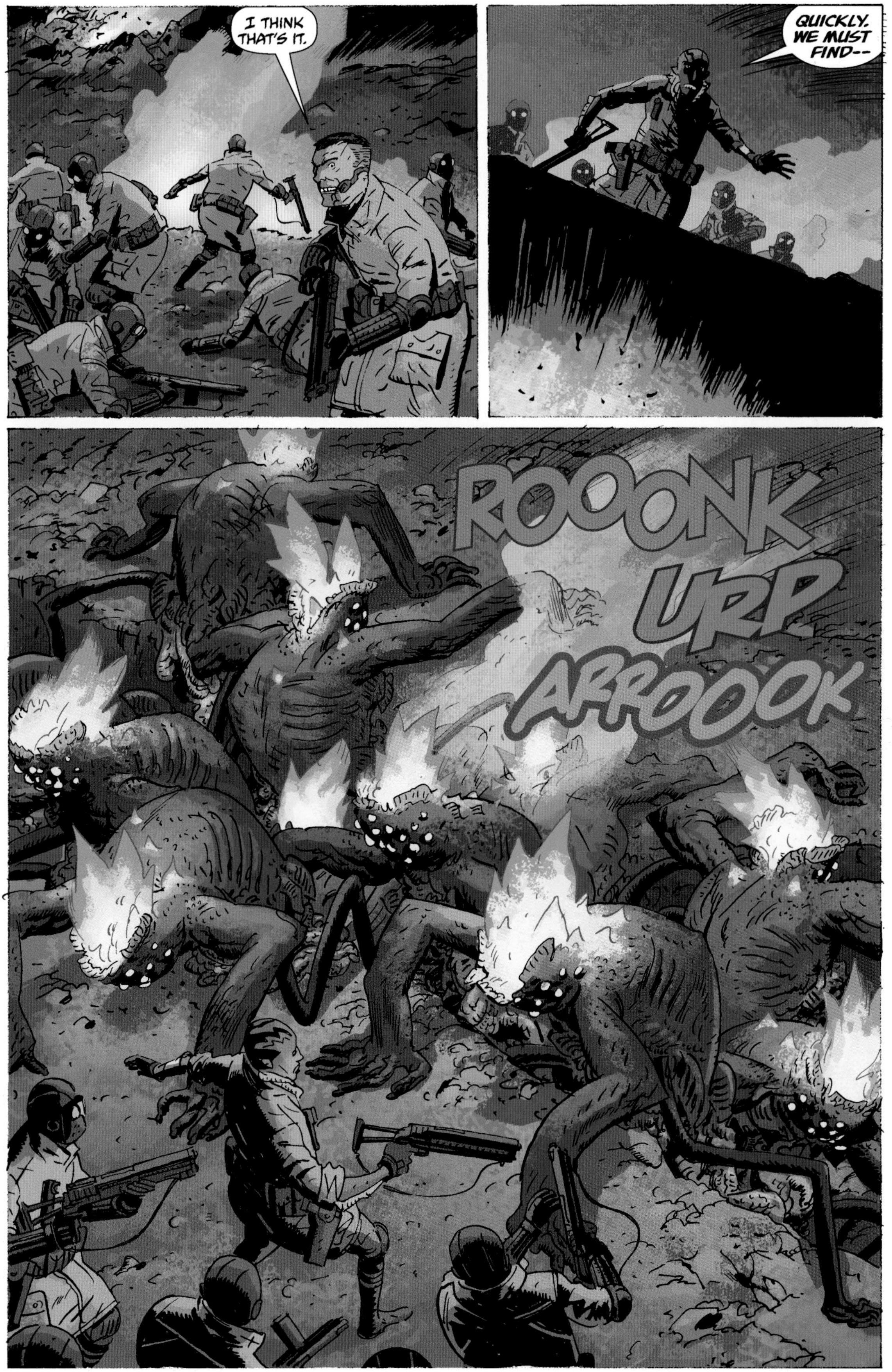
I THINK THAT'S IT.
QUICKLY. WE MUST FIND--
ROOONK
URP
ARROOOK

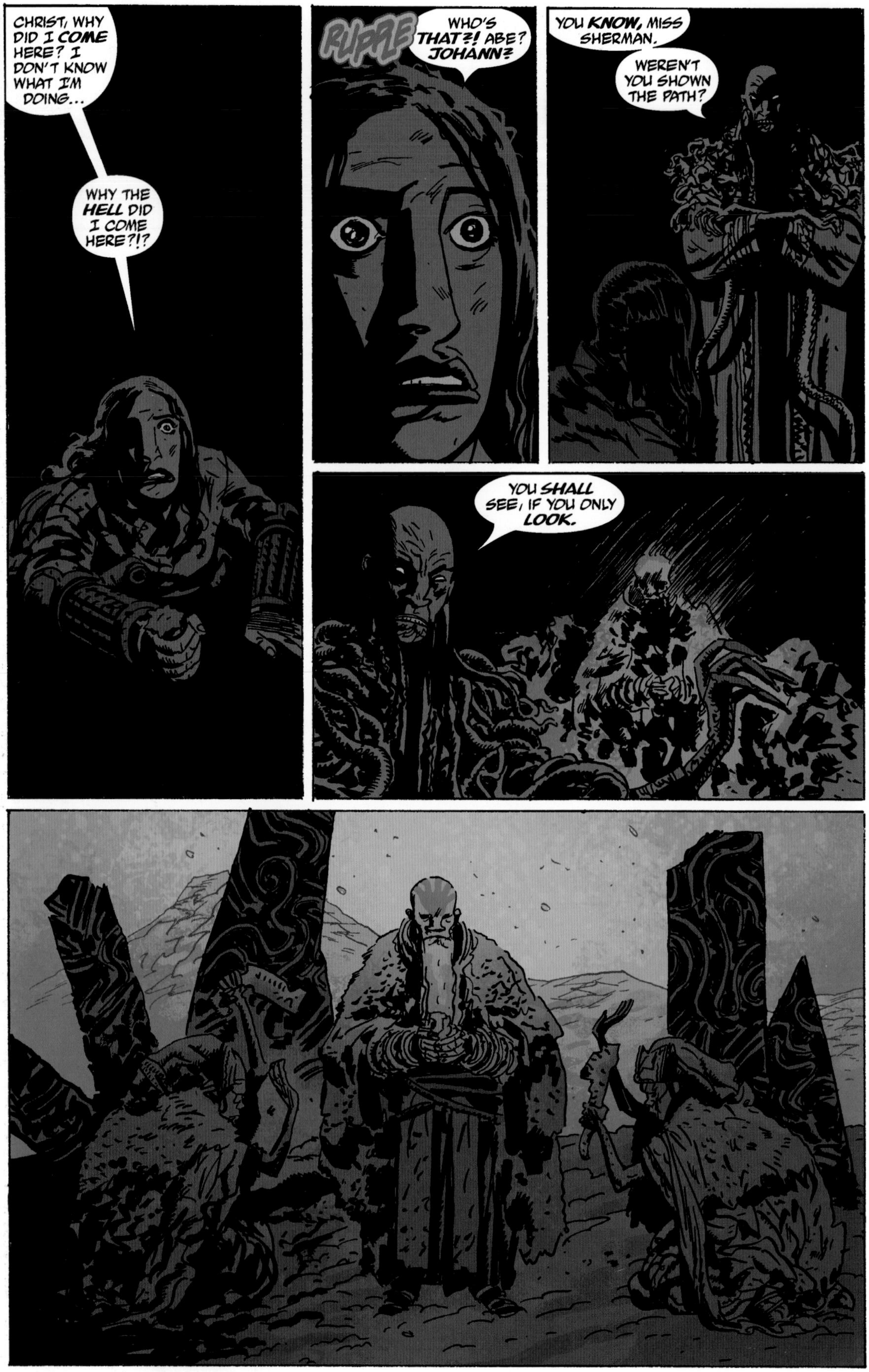
CHRIST, WHY DID I COME HERE? I DON'T KNOW WHAT I'M DOING...
WHY THE HELL DID I COME HERE?!?
RUPPLE
WHO'S THAT?! ABE? JOHANN?
YOU KNOW, MISS SHERMAN.
WEREN'T YOU SHOWN THE PATH?
YOU SHALL SEE, IF YOU ONLY LOOK.

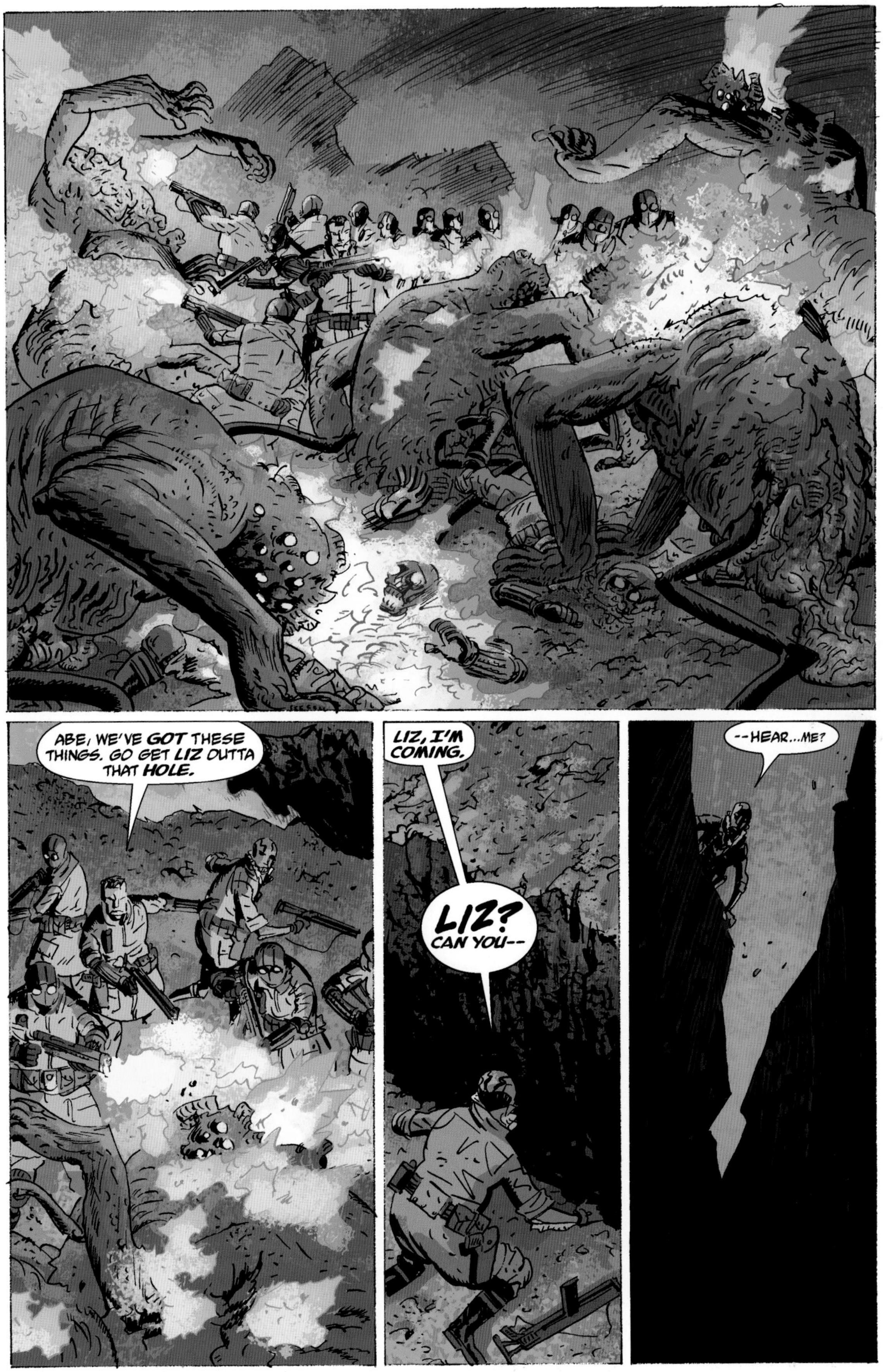
ABE, WE'VE GOT THESE THINGS. GO GET LIZ OUTTA THAT HOLE.
LIZ, I'M COMING.
LIZ? CAN YOU--
--HEAR...ME?

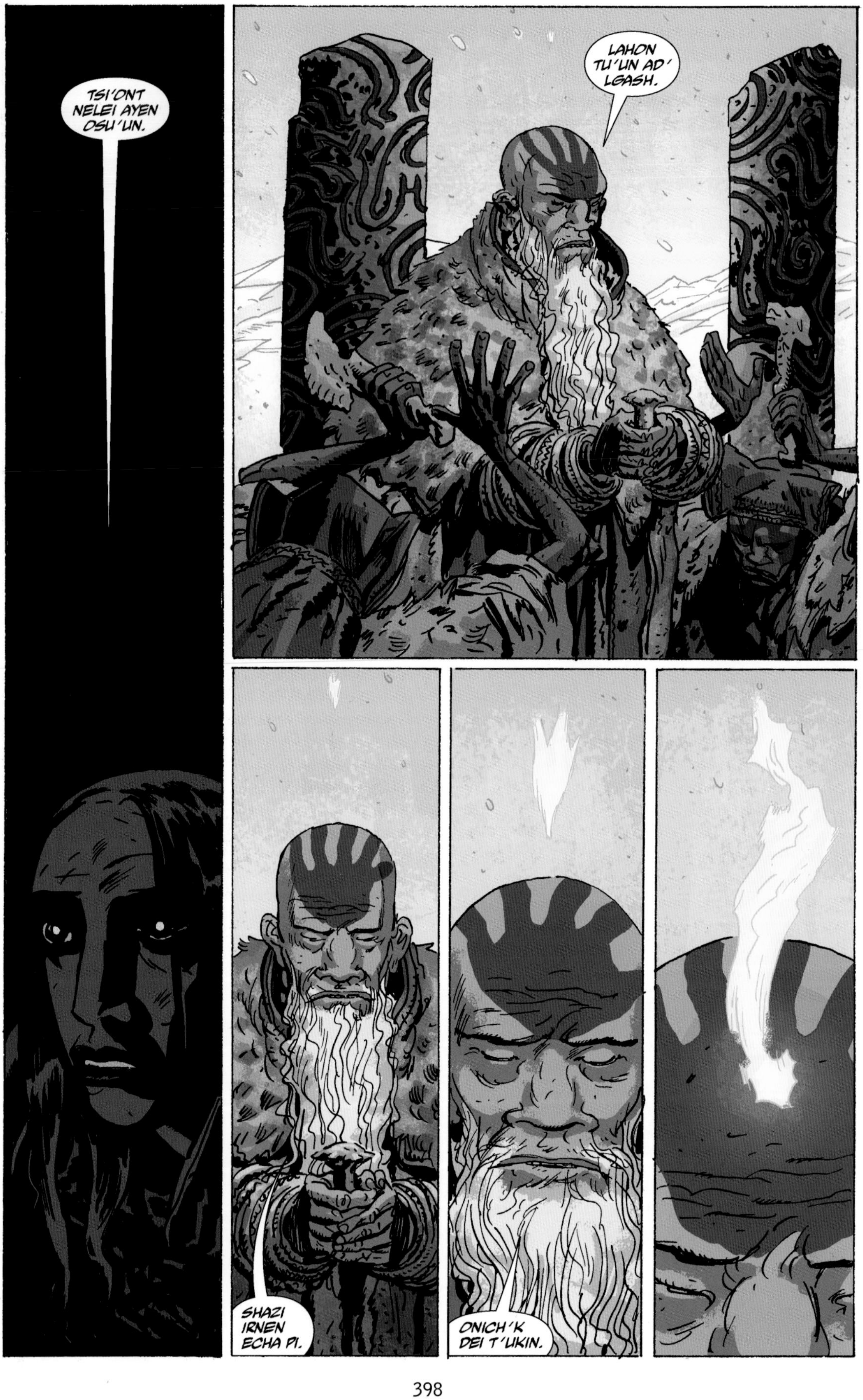
TSI'ONT NELEI AYEN OSU'UN.
LAHON TU'UN AD' LGASH.
SHAZI IRNEN ECHA PI.
ONICH'K DEI T'UKIN.

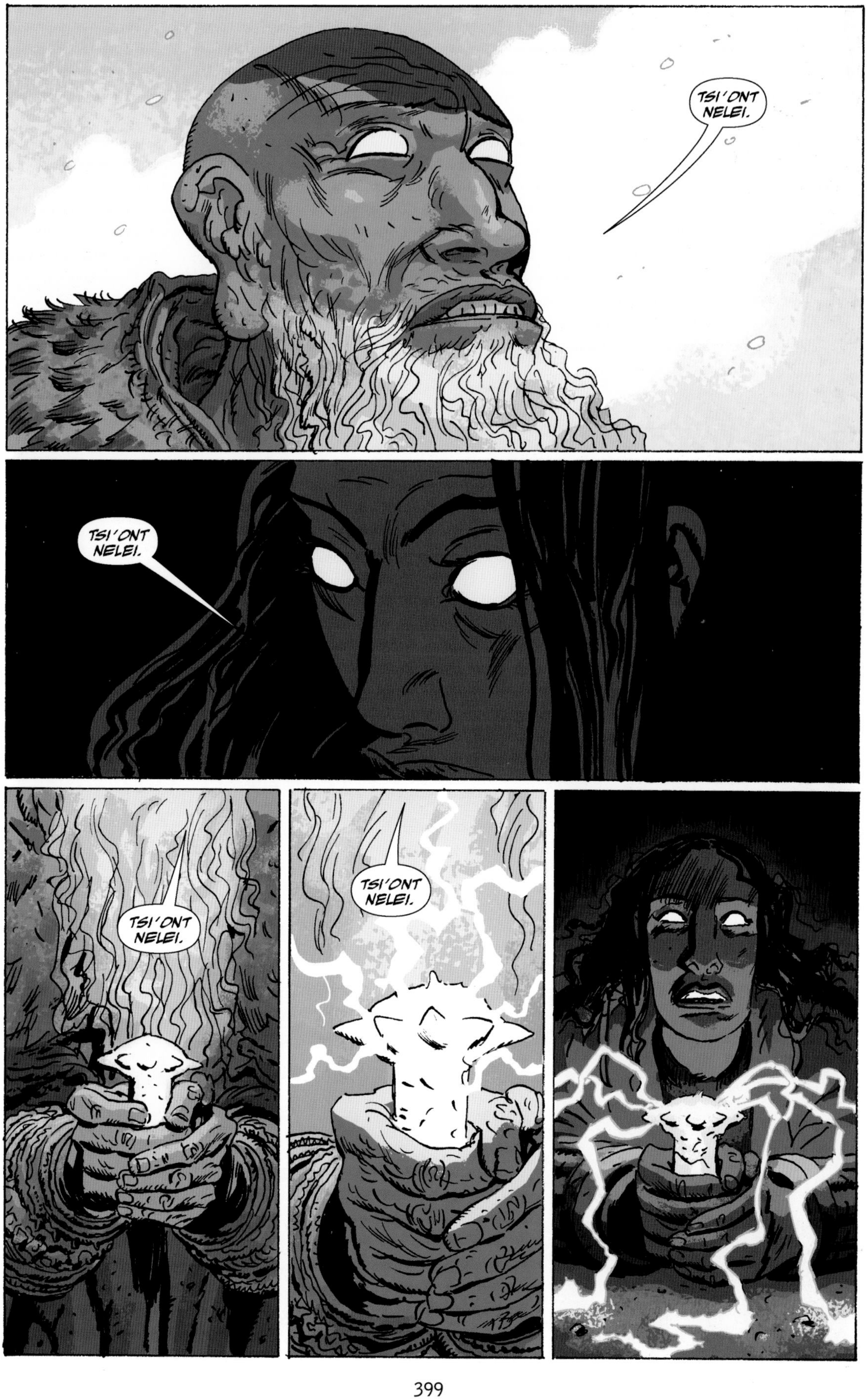
TSI'ONT NELEI.
TSI'ONT NELEI.
TSI'ONT NELEI.
TSI'ONT NELEI.

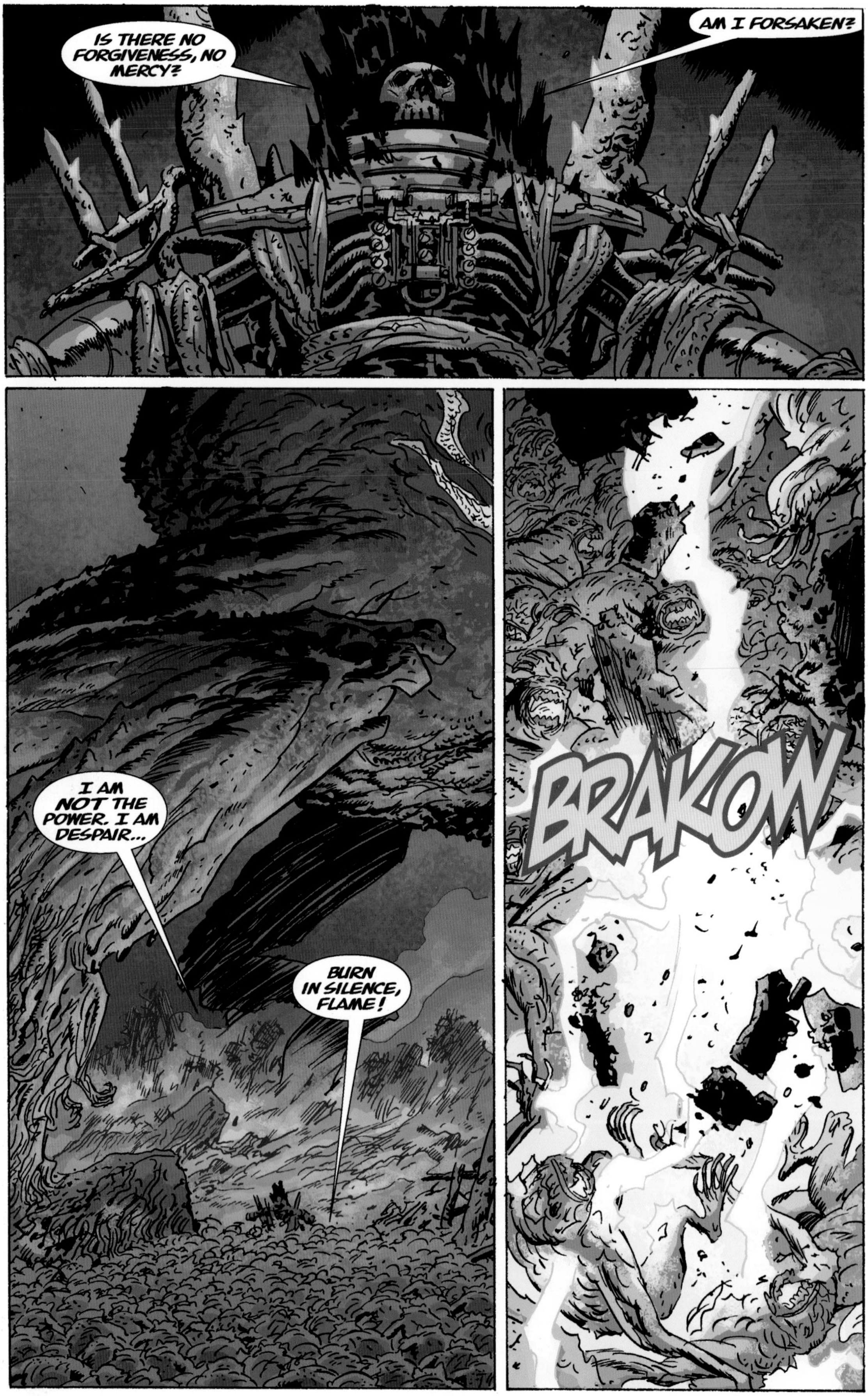
IS THERE NO FORGIVENESS, NO MERCY?
AM I FORSAKEN?
I AM NOT THE POWER. I AM DESPAIR...
BURN IN SILENCE, FLAME!
BRAKOW

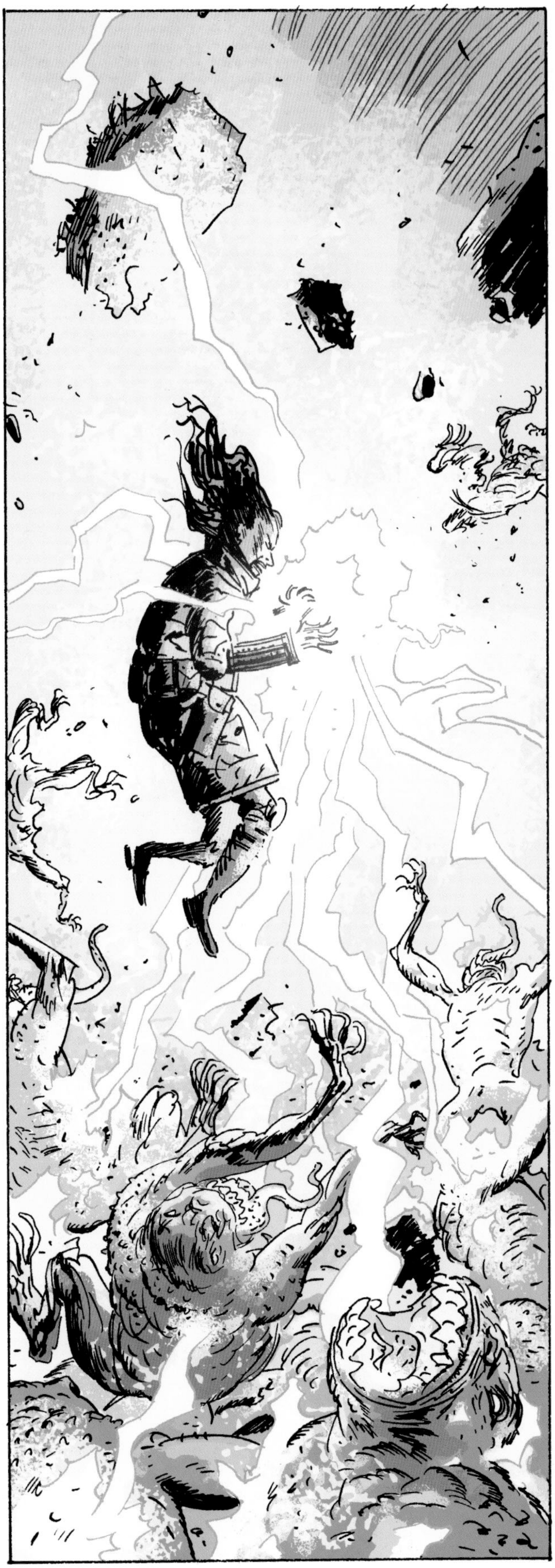

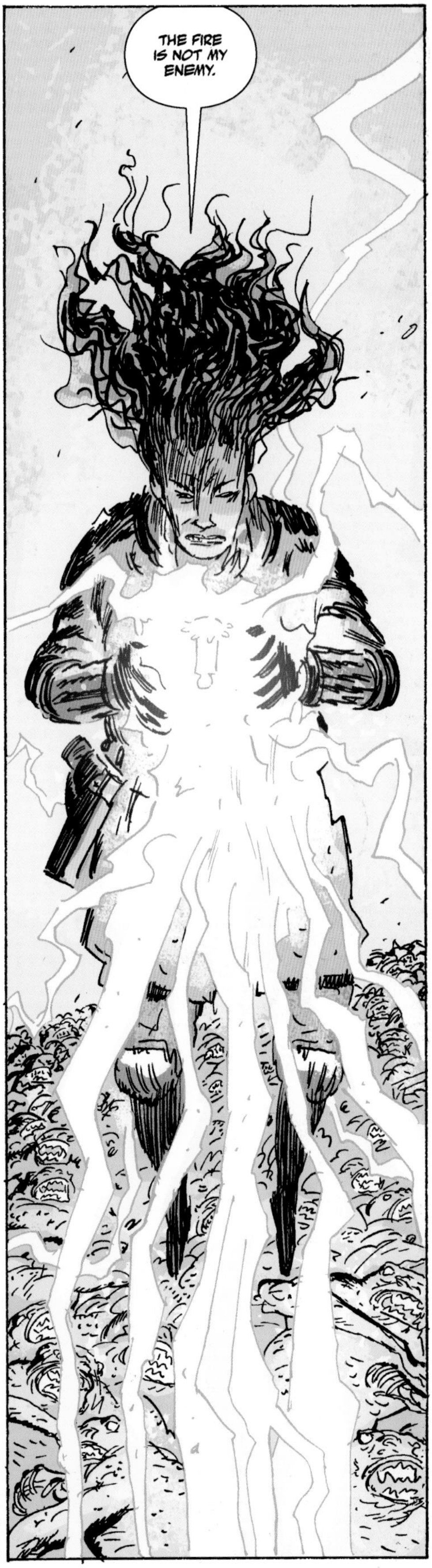
THE FIRE IS NOT MY ENEMY.

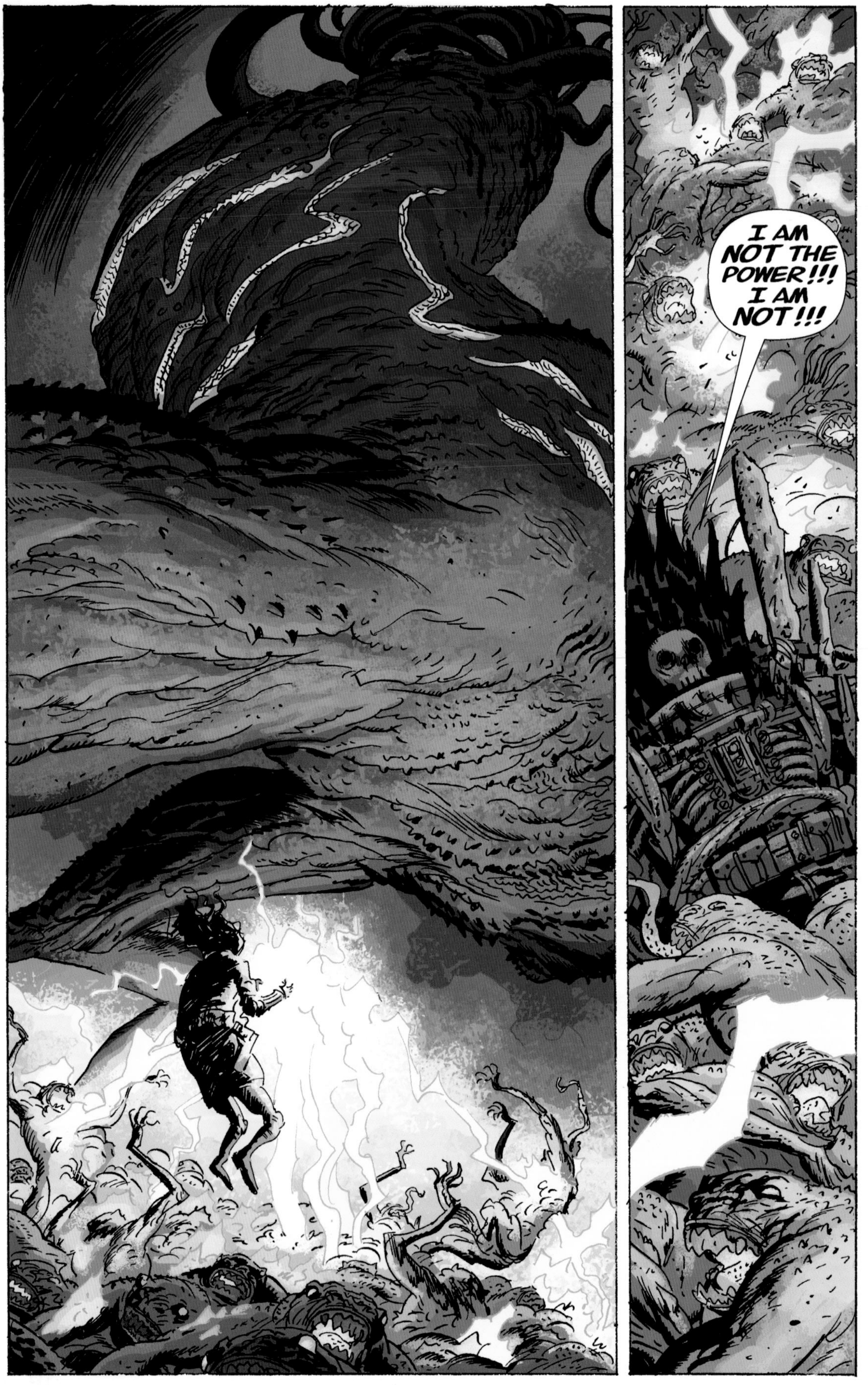
I AM NOT THE POWER!!! I AM NOT!!!

THE FIRE IS PART OF ME.

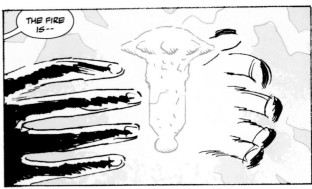

THE FIRE IS--

--MINE!

SHRAAAK

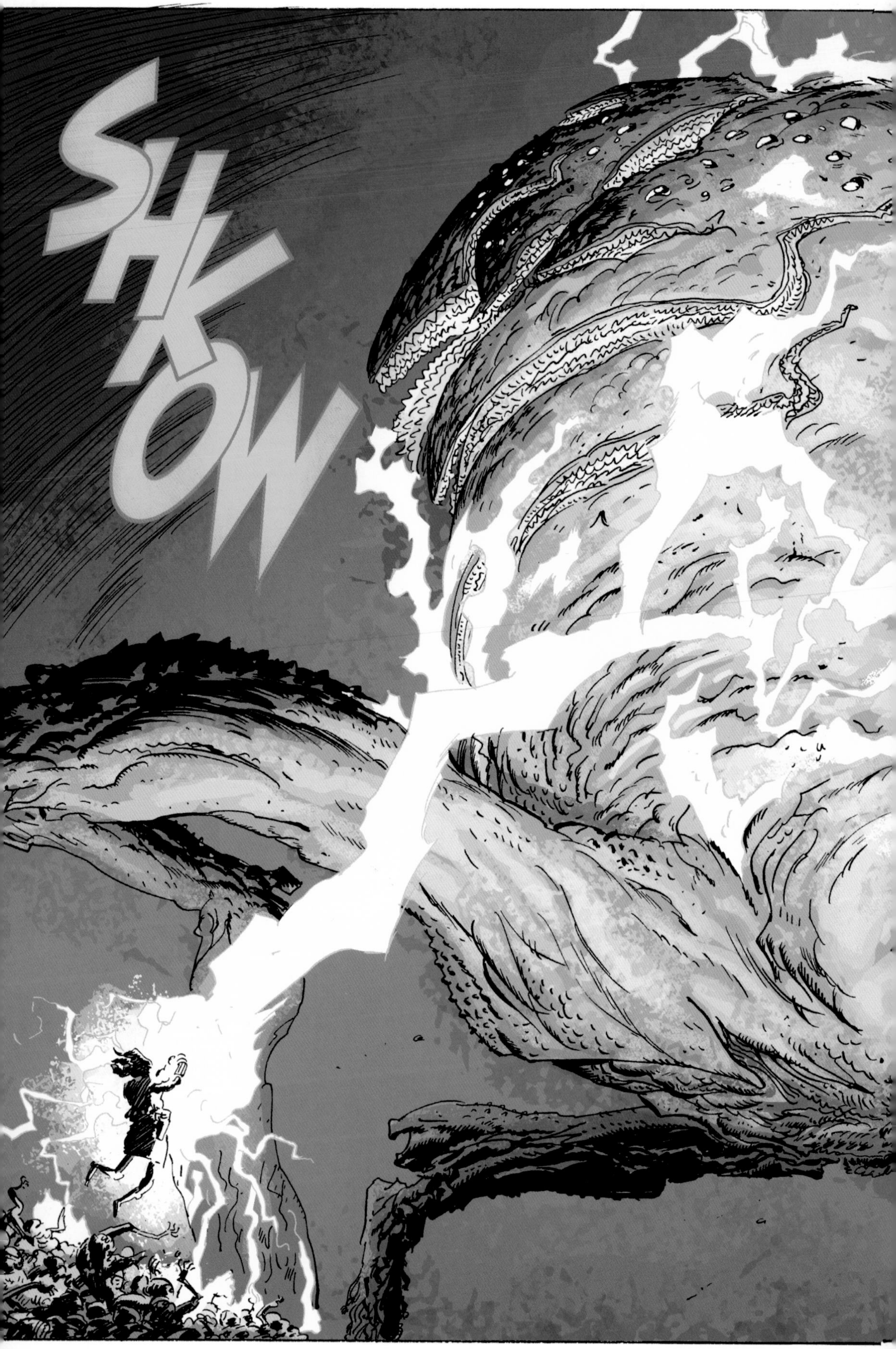
SHKOW

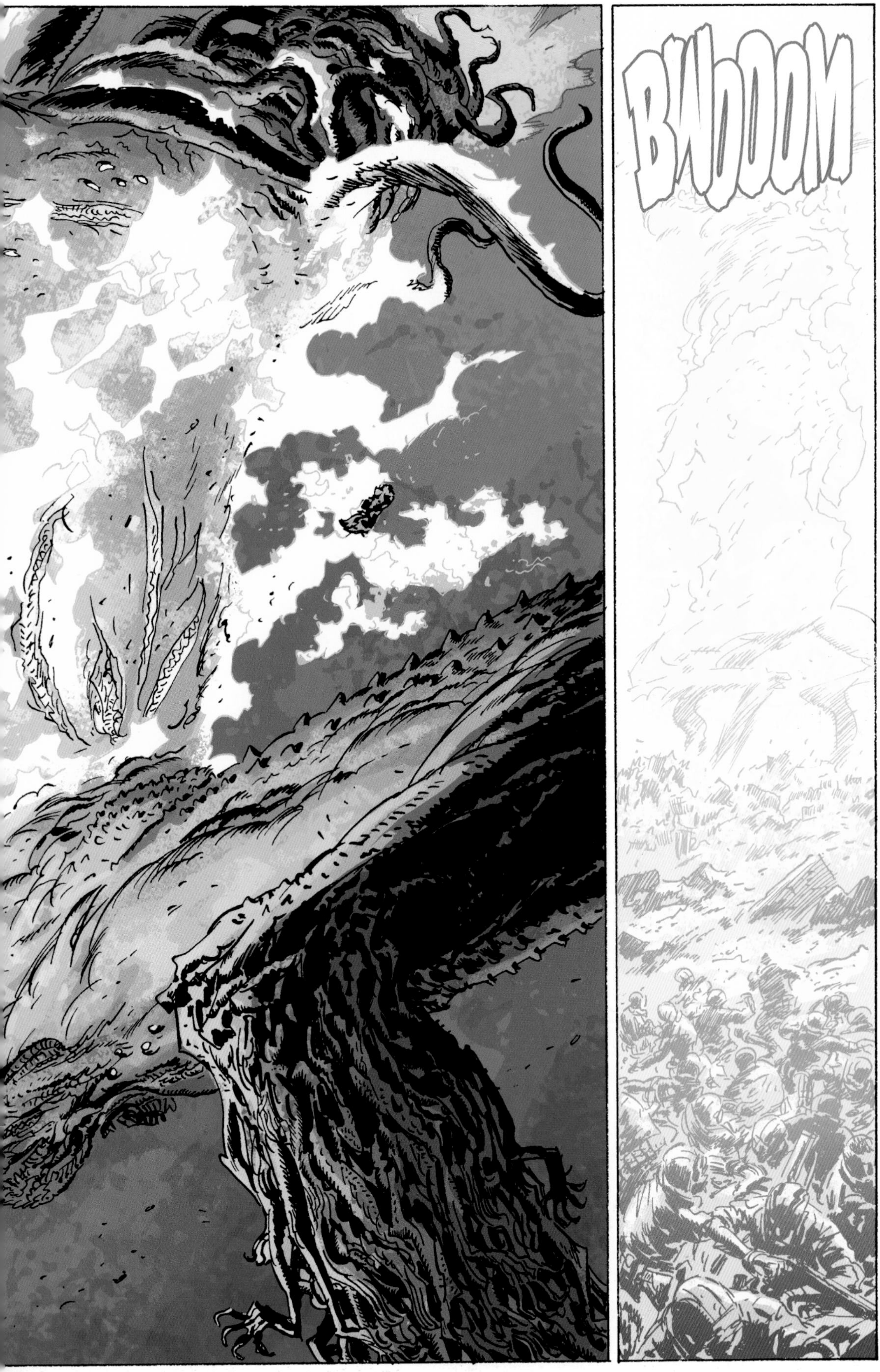
BWOOOM

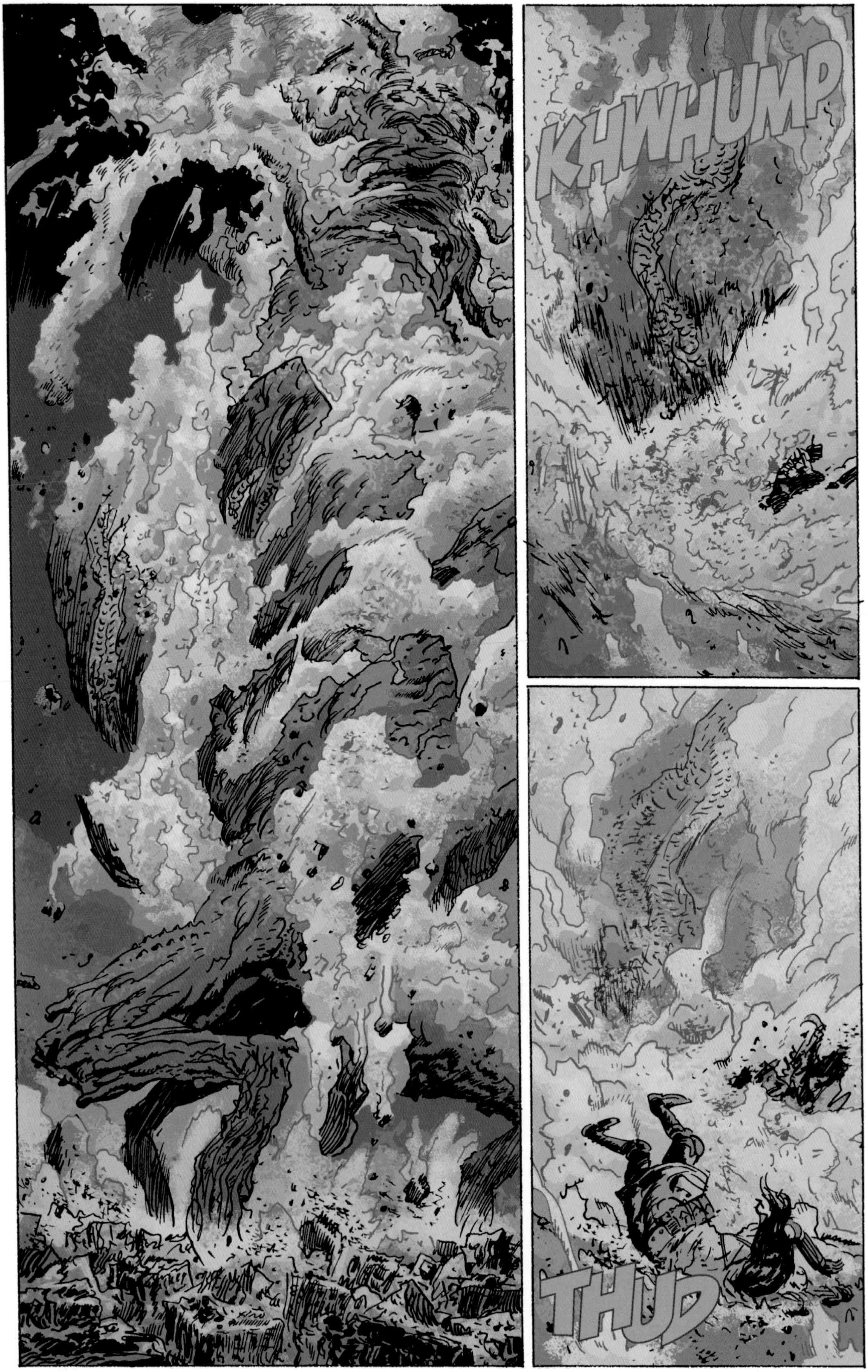
KHWHUMP
THUD

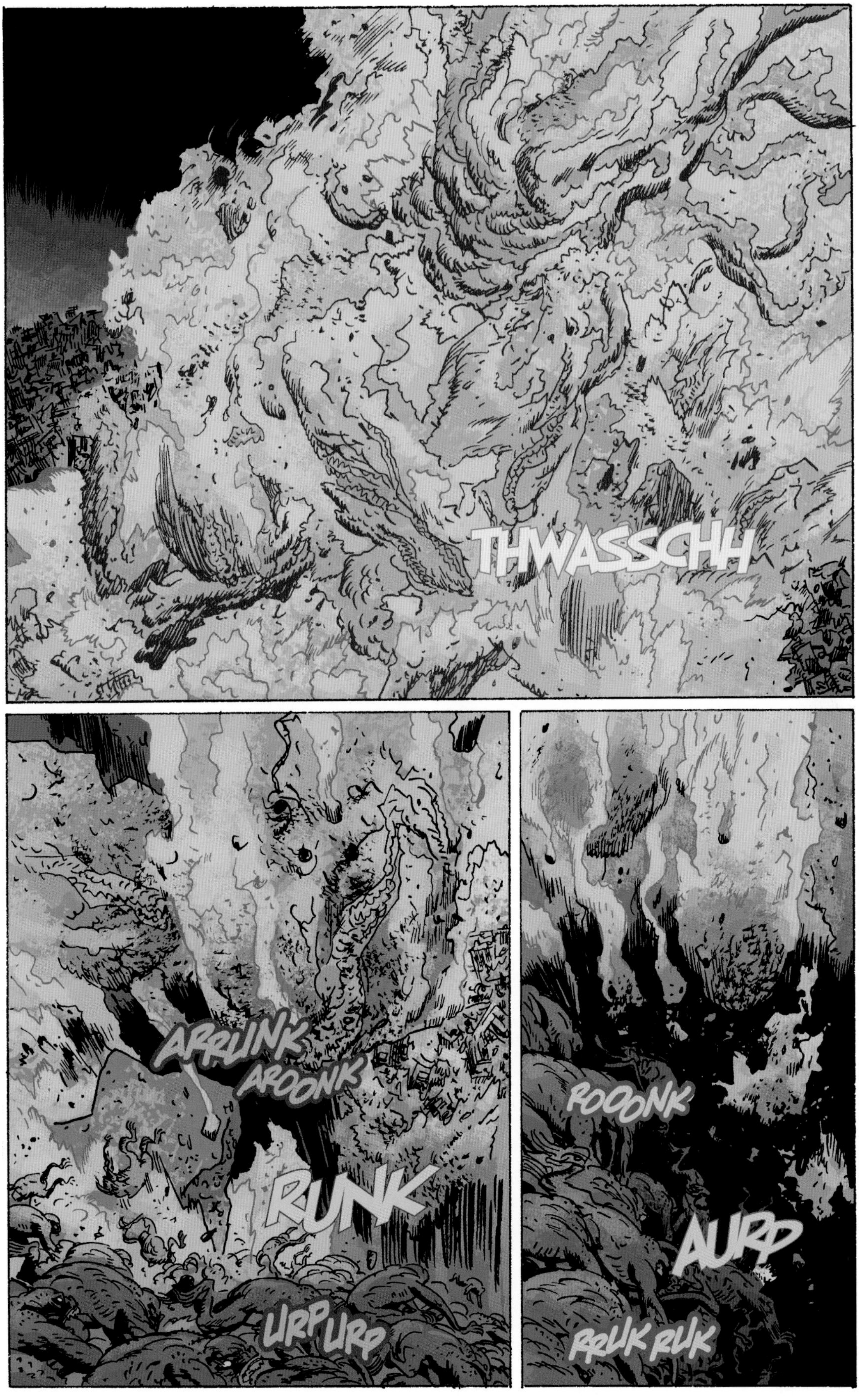
THWASSCHH
ARRUNK
AROONK
RUNK
URP URP
ROOONK
AURP
RRUK RUK

CHIK

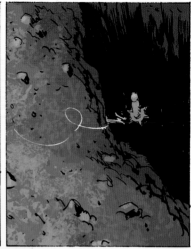

YOU'RE ALIVE!

I'M ALIVE!

HOW? HOW DID YOU DO THAT?

I DON'T--

THEY DID THIS TO ME. I CAN'T GET OUT OF THIS *SUIT.* HELP ME.

I'LL TRY--

I'M SORRY ABOUT YOUR FRIEND -- THE GRAY MAN.

IT WAS *WRONG* OF ME TO DO THAT. I *AM* SORRY...

ROGER?

YOU... KILLED ROGER?

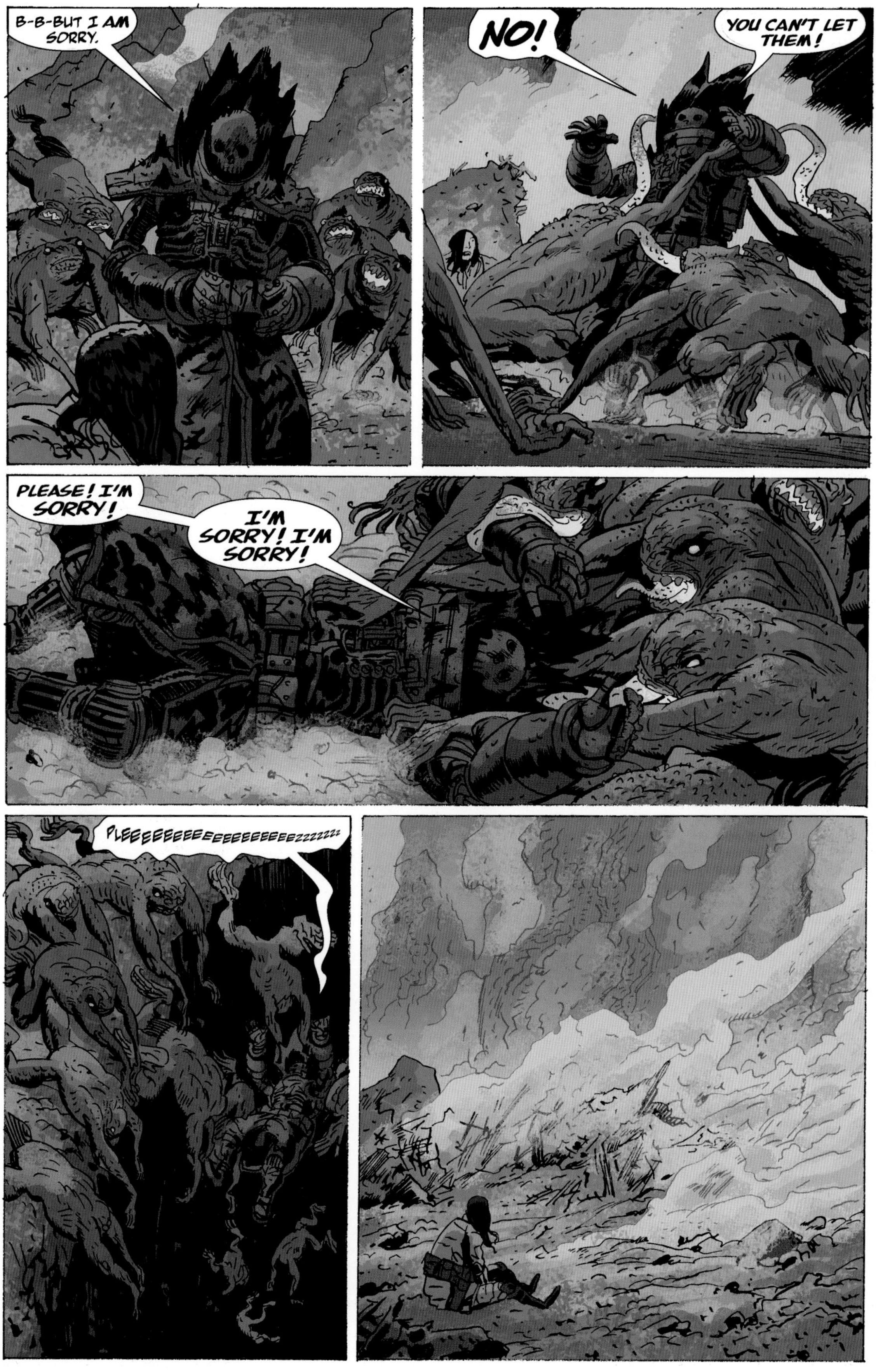
B-B-BUT I AM SORRY.
NO!
YOU CAN'T LET THEM!
PLEASE! I'M SORRY!
I'M SORRY! I'M SORRY!
PLEEEEEEEEEEEEEEEEEEEzzzzzzz

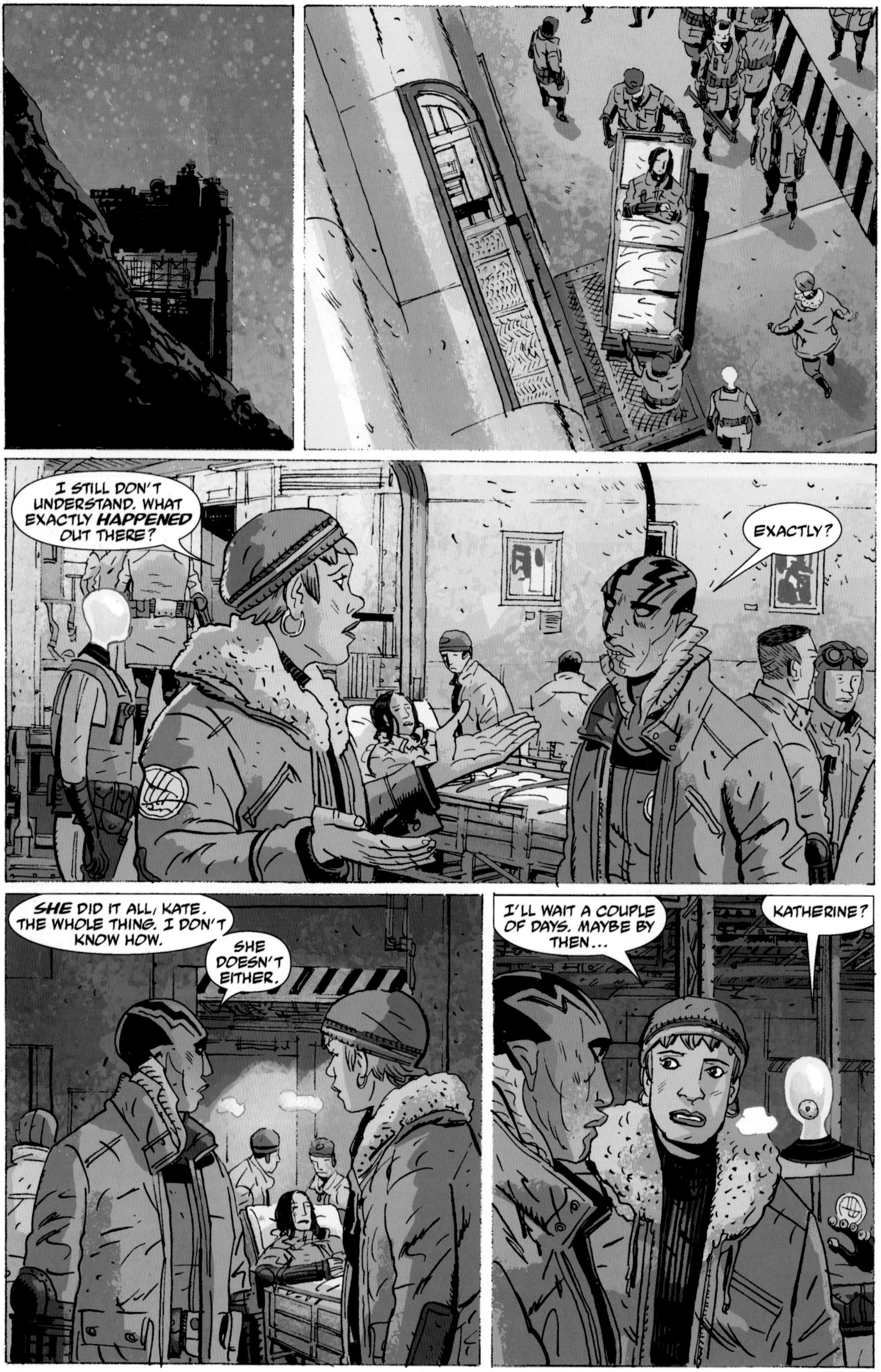
I STILL DON'T UNDERSTAND. WHAT EXACTLY HAPPENED OUT THERE?
EXACTLY?
SHE DID IT ALL, KATE. THE WHOLE THING. I DON'T KNOW HOW.
SHE DOESN'T EITHER.
I'LL WAIT A COUPLE OF DAYS. MAYBE BY THEN...
KATHERINE?

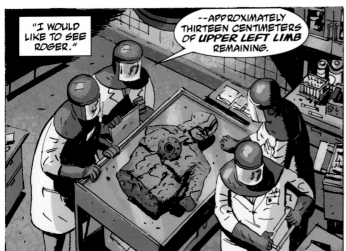

"I WOULD LIKE TO SEE ROGER."

--APPROXIMATELY THIRTEEN CENTIMETERS OF UPPER LEFT LIMB REMAINING.

INCISION BEGUN SEVEN CENTIMETERS BELOW SHOULDER.

TISSUE IS REMARKABLY HARD AND RESISTANT TO BLADE.

UNKNOWN WHETHER THIS IS DUE TO TRAUMA OR--

STOP!!

MY GOD, WHAT ARE YOU DOING IN HERE?!

GET OUT, MONSTERS!

HERAUS!

HOW COULD YOU LET THIS HAPPEN?! HOW?!!

JOHANN, I DIDN'T--

SLAM

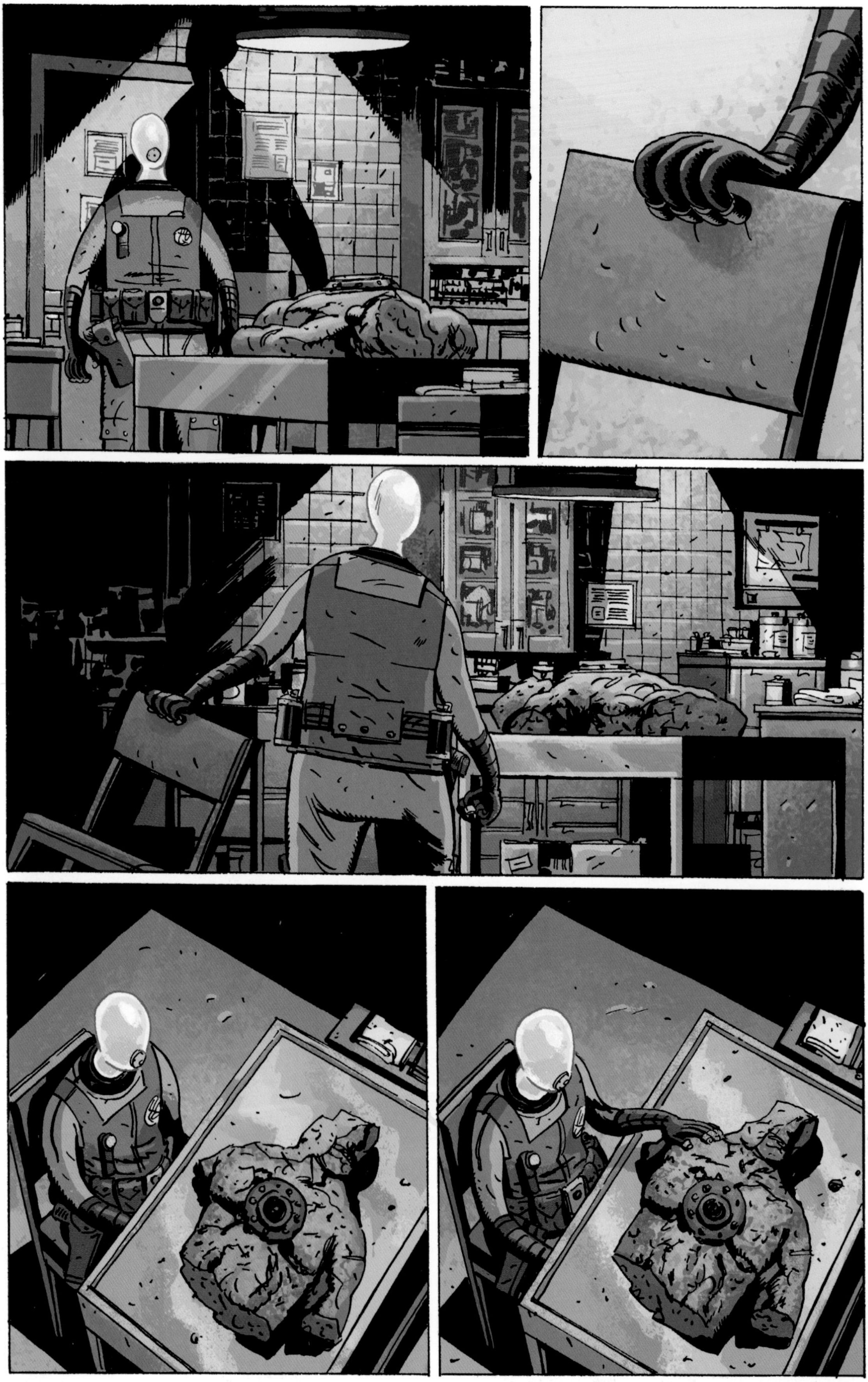

THE END

EPILOGUE

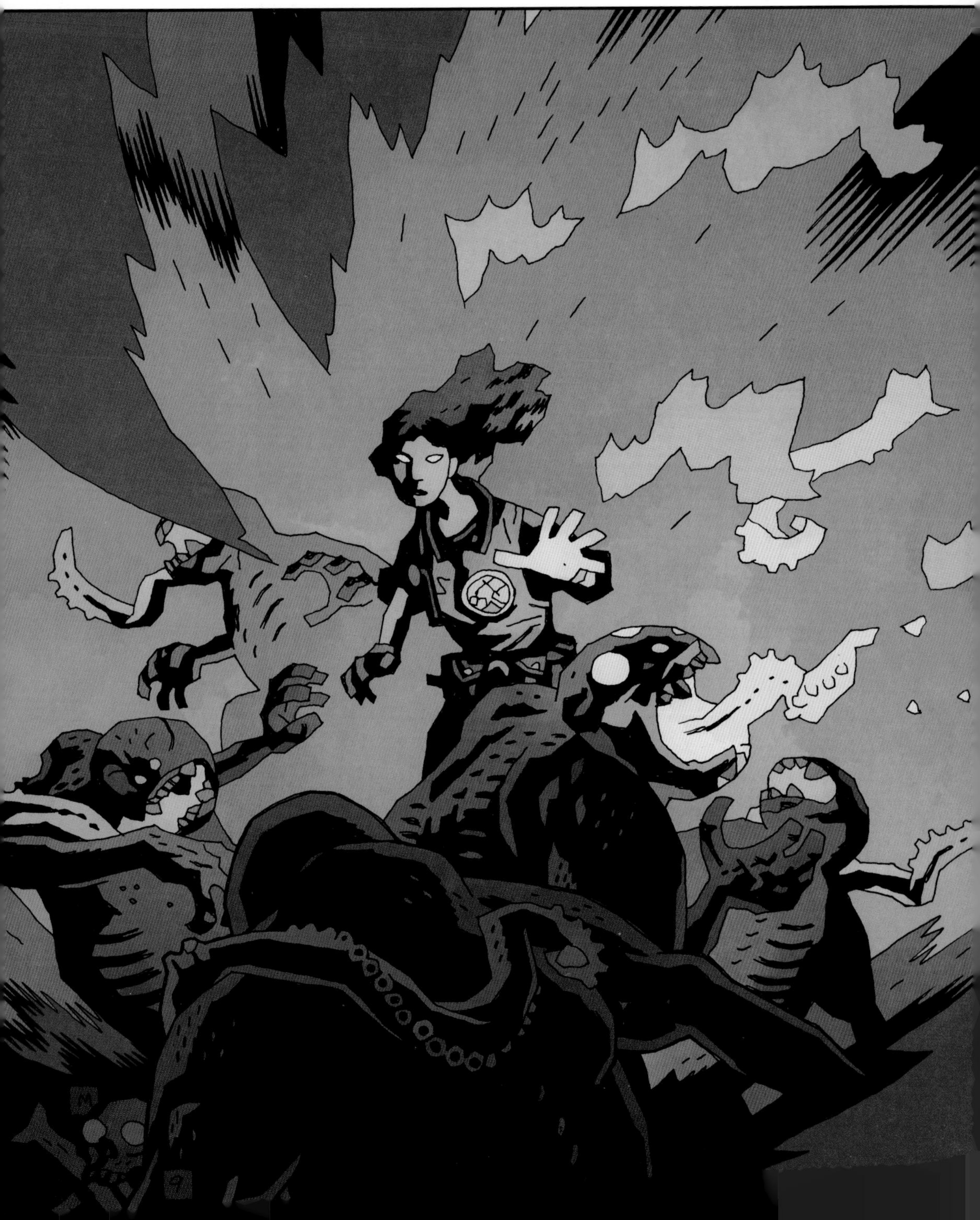

EPILOGUE

STORY BY JOHN ARCUDI

ART BY KARL MOLINE

COLORS BY DAVE STEWART

LETTERS BY CLEM ROBINS

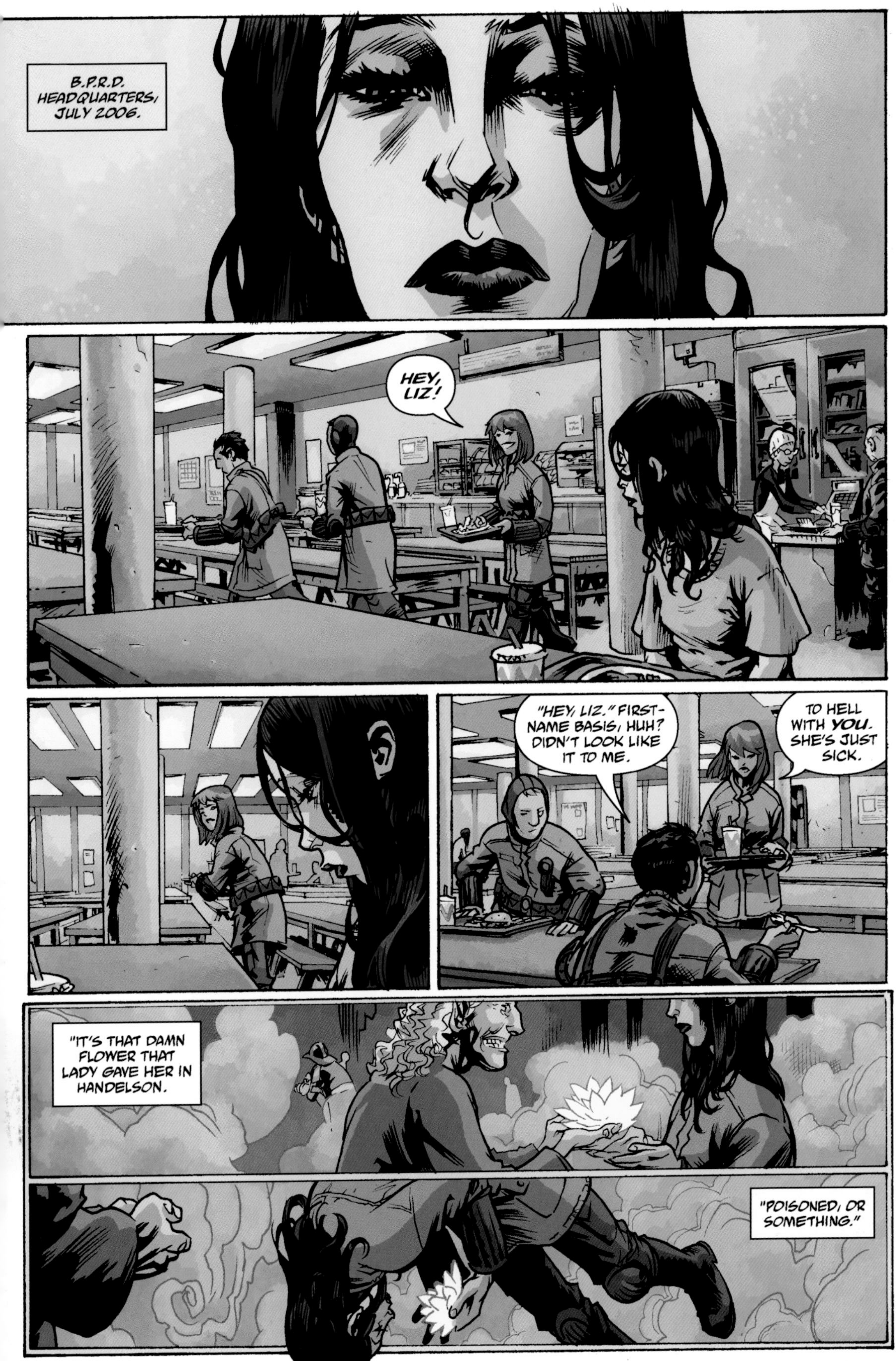

B.P.R.D. HEADQUARTERS, JULY 2006.
HEY, LIZ!
"HEY, LIZ." FIRST-NAME BASIS, HUH? DIDN'T LOOK LIKE IT TO ME.
TO HELL WITH YOU. SHE'S JUST SICK.
"IT'S THAT DAMN FLOWER THAT LADY GAVE HER IN HANDELSON.
"POISONED, OR SOMETHING."

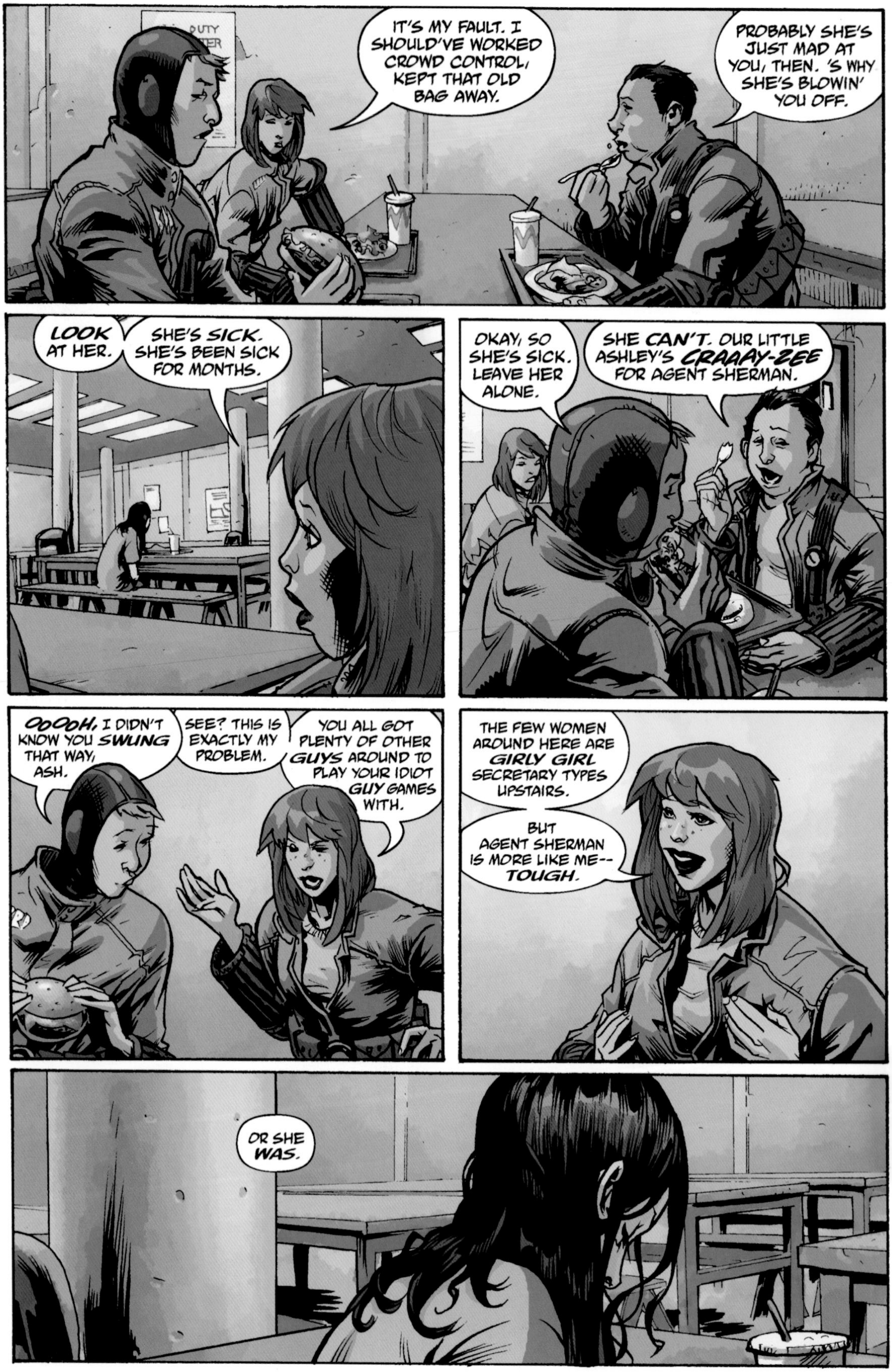
IT'S MY FAULT. I SHOULD'VE WORKED CROWD CONTROL, KEPT THAT OLD BAG AWAY.
PROBABLY SHE'S JUST MAD AT YOU, THEN. 'S WHY SHE'S BLOWIN' YOU OFF.
LOOK AT HER.
SHE'S SICK. SHE'S BEEN SICK FOR MONTHS.
OKAY, SO SHE'S SICK. LEAVE HER ALONE.
SHE CAN'T. OUR LITTLE ASHLEY'S CRAAAY-ZEE FOR AGENT SHERMAN.
OOOOH, I DIDN'T KNOW YOU SWUNG THAT WAY, ASH.
SEE? THIS IS EXACTLY MY PROBLEM.
YOU ALL GOT PLENTY OF OTHER GUYS AROUND TO PLAY YOUR IDIOT GUY GAMES WITH.
THE FEW WOMEN AROUND HERE ARE GIRLY GIRL SECRETARY TYPES UPSTAIRS.
BUT AGENT SHERMAN IS MORE LIKE ME-- TOUGH.
OR SHE WAS.

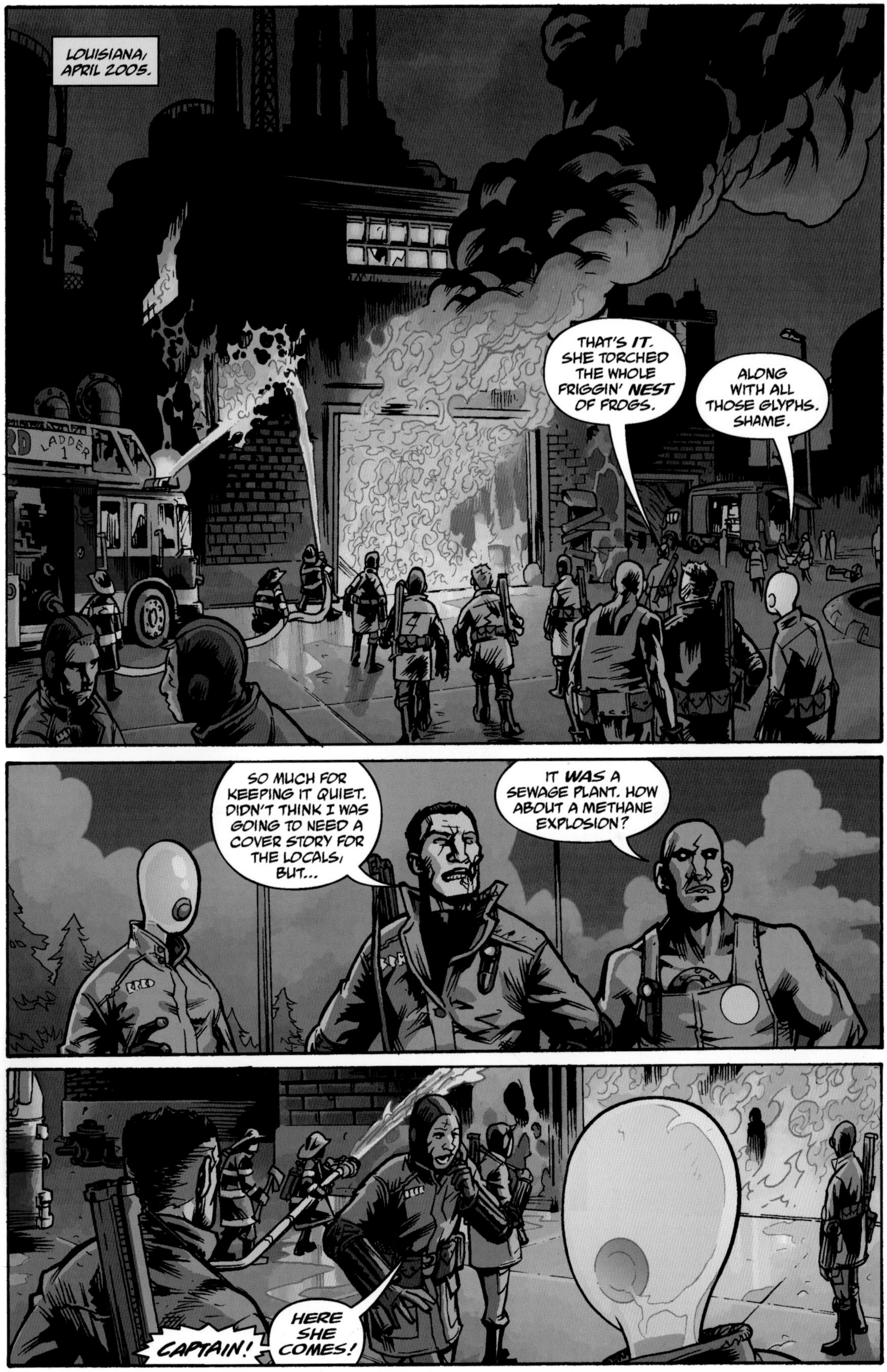
LOUISIANA, APRIL 2005.
THAT'S IT. SHE TORCHED THE WHOLE FRIGGIN' NEST OF FROGS.
ALONG WITH ALL THOSE GLYPHS. SHAME.
SO MUCH FOR KEEPING IT QUIET. DIDN'T THINK I WAS GOING TO NEED A COVER STORY FOR THE LOCALS, BUT...
IT WAS A SEWAGE PLANT. HOW ABOUT A METHANE EXPLOSION?
CAPTAIN!
HERE SHE COMES!

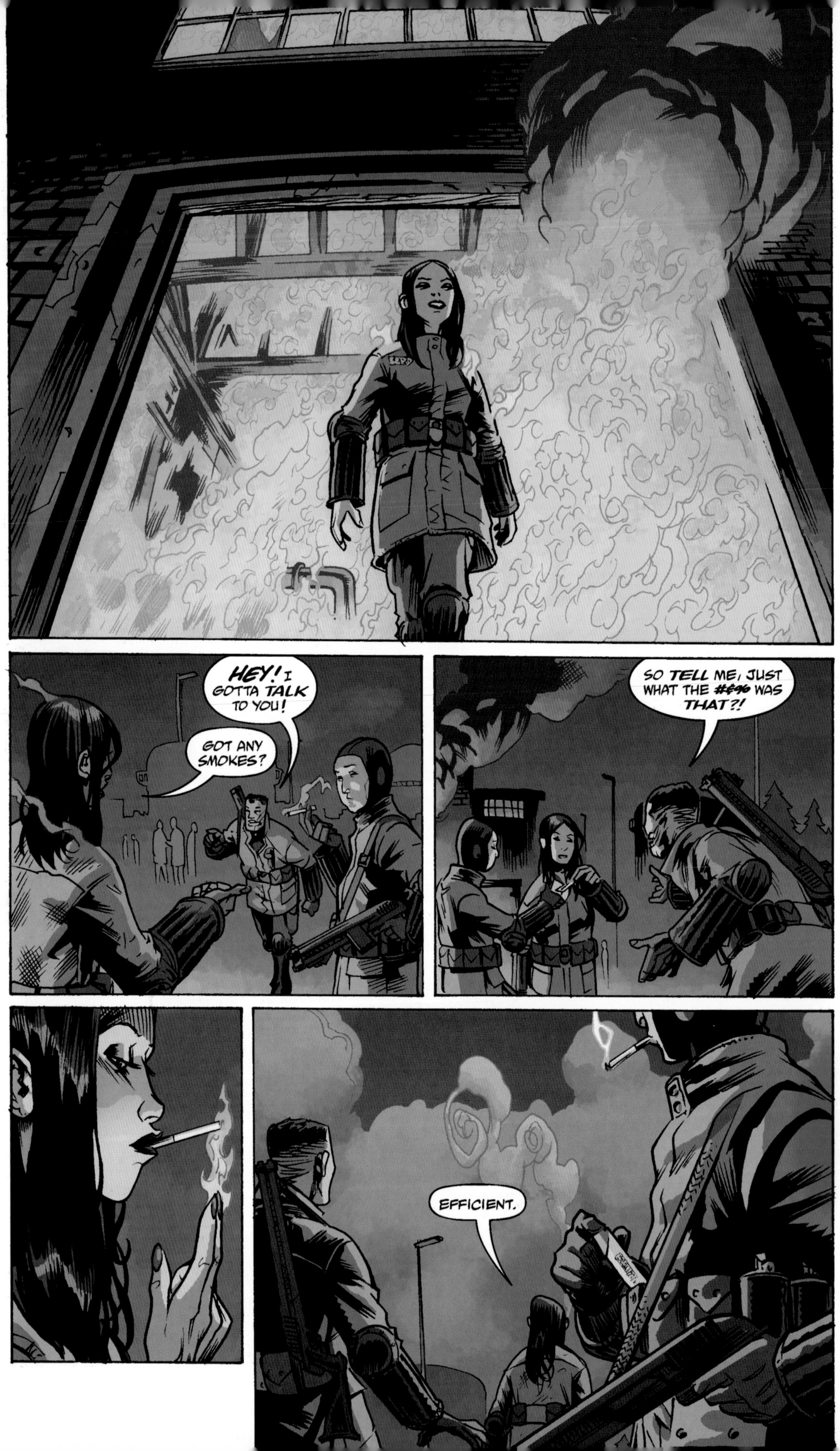
HEY! I GOTTA TALK TO YOU!
GOT ANY SMOKES?
SO TELL ME, JUST WHAT THE #€%! WAS THAT?!
EFFICIENT.

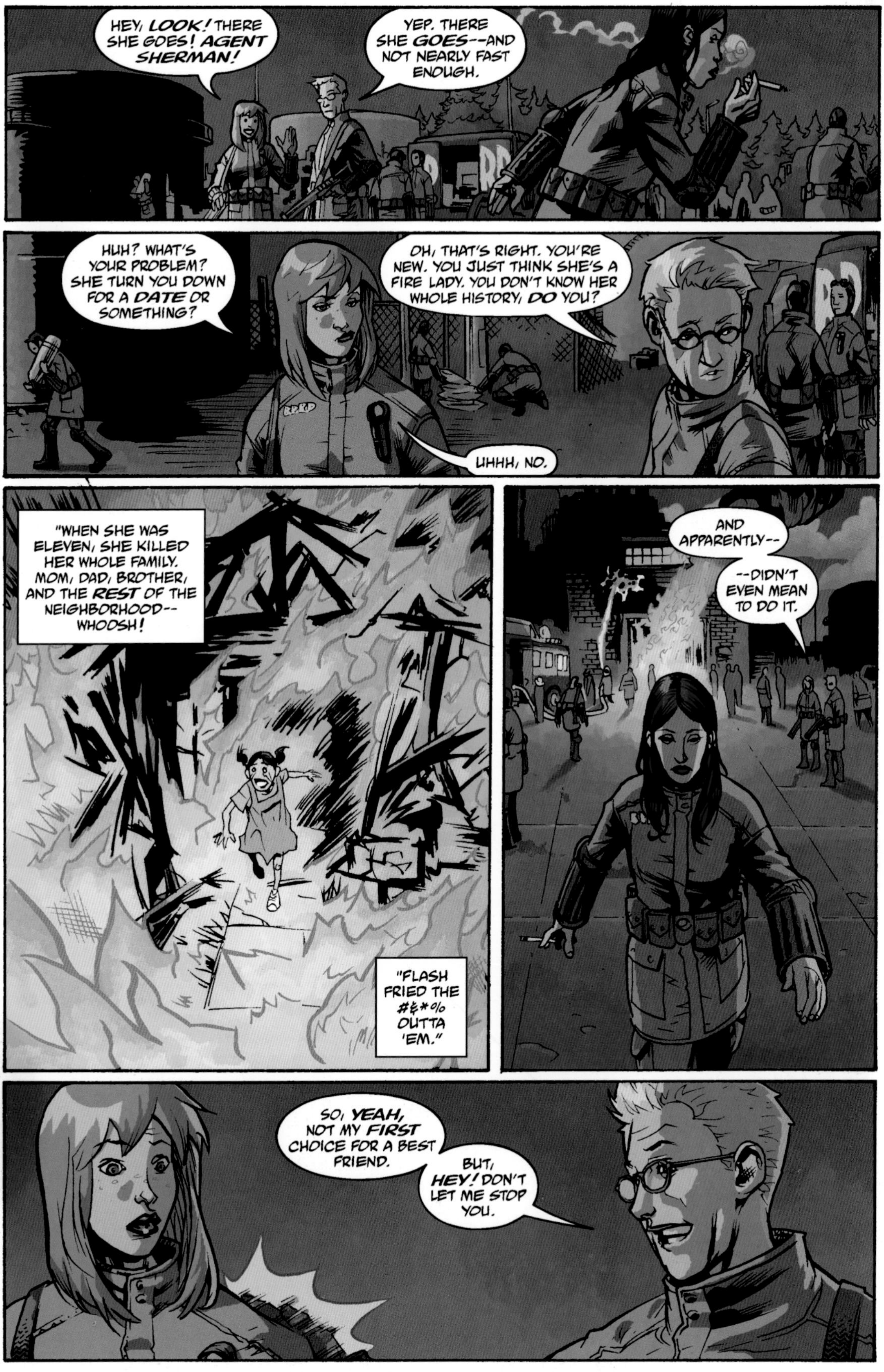
HEY, LOOK! THERE SHE GOES! AGENT SHERMAN!
YEP. THERE SHE GOES--AND NOT NEARLY FAST ENOUGH.
HUH? WHAT'S YOUR PROBLEM? SHE TURN YOU DOWN FOR A DATE OR SOMETHING?
OH, THAT'S RIGHT. YOU'RE NEW. YOU JUST THINK SHE'S A FIRE LADY. YOU DON'T KNOW HER WHOLE HISTORY, DO YOU?
UHHH, NO.
"WHEN SHE WAS ELEVEN, SHE KILLED HER WHOLE FAMILY. MOM, DAD, BROTHER, AND THE REST OF THE NEIGHBORHOOD--WHOOSH!
"FLASH FRIED THE #&*% OUTTA 'EM."
AND APPARENTLY--
--DIDN'T EVEN MEAN TO DO IT.
SO, YEAH, NOT MY FIRST CHOICE FOR A BEST FRIEND.
BUT, HEY! DON'T LET ME STOP YOU.

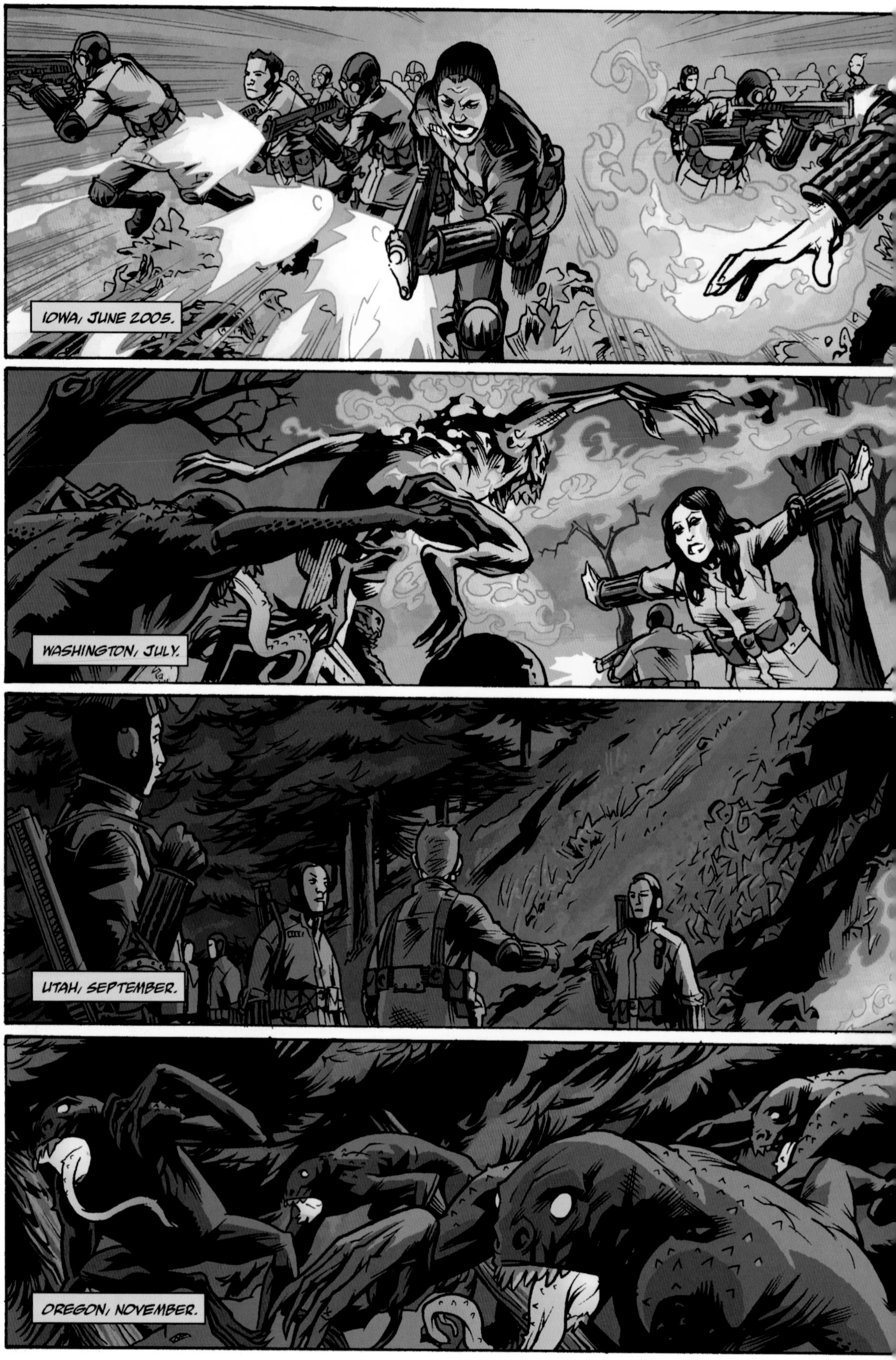
IOWA, JUNE 2005.
WASHINGTON, JULY.
UTAH, SEPTEMBER.
OREGON, NOVEMBER.

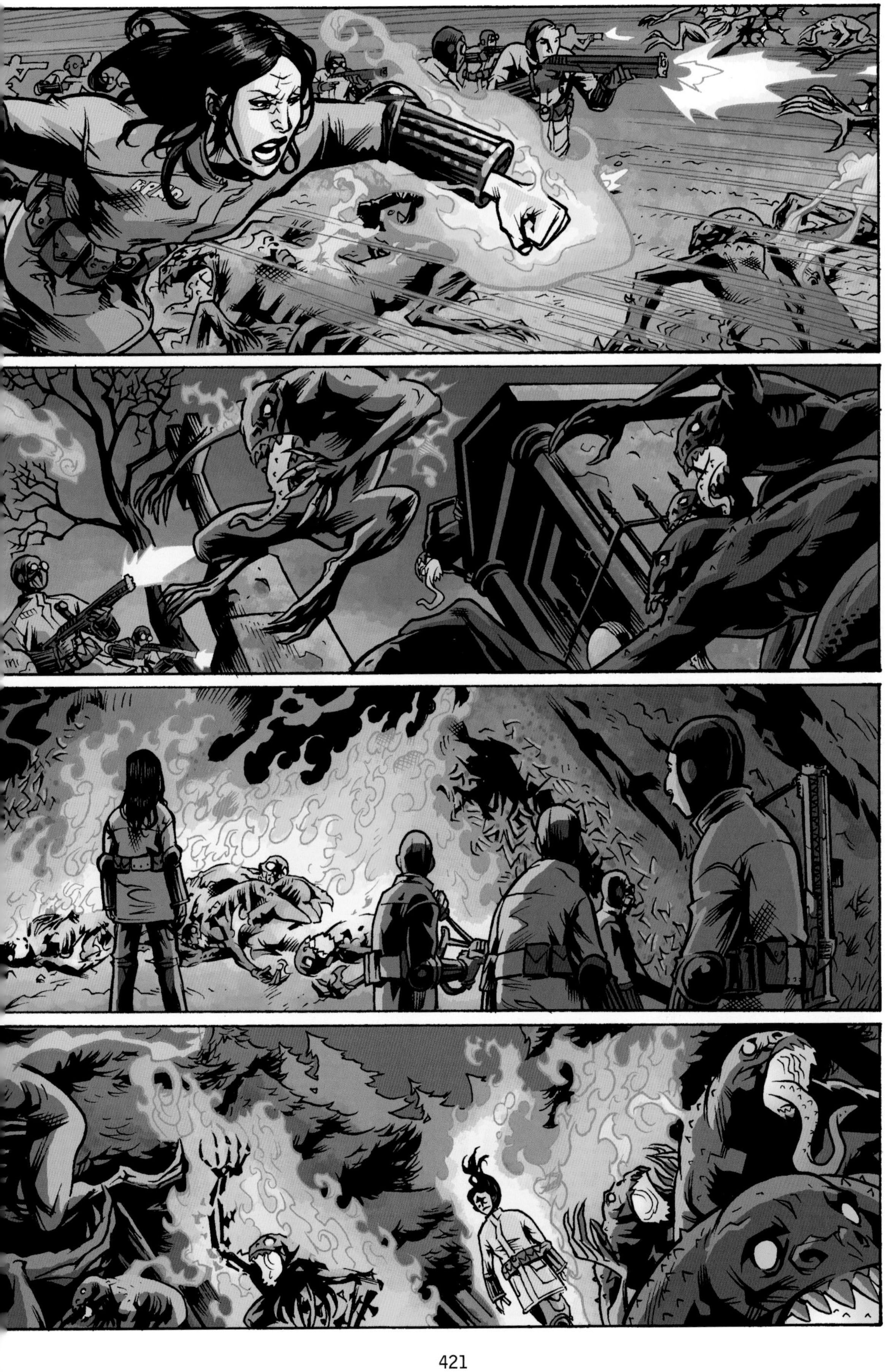

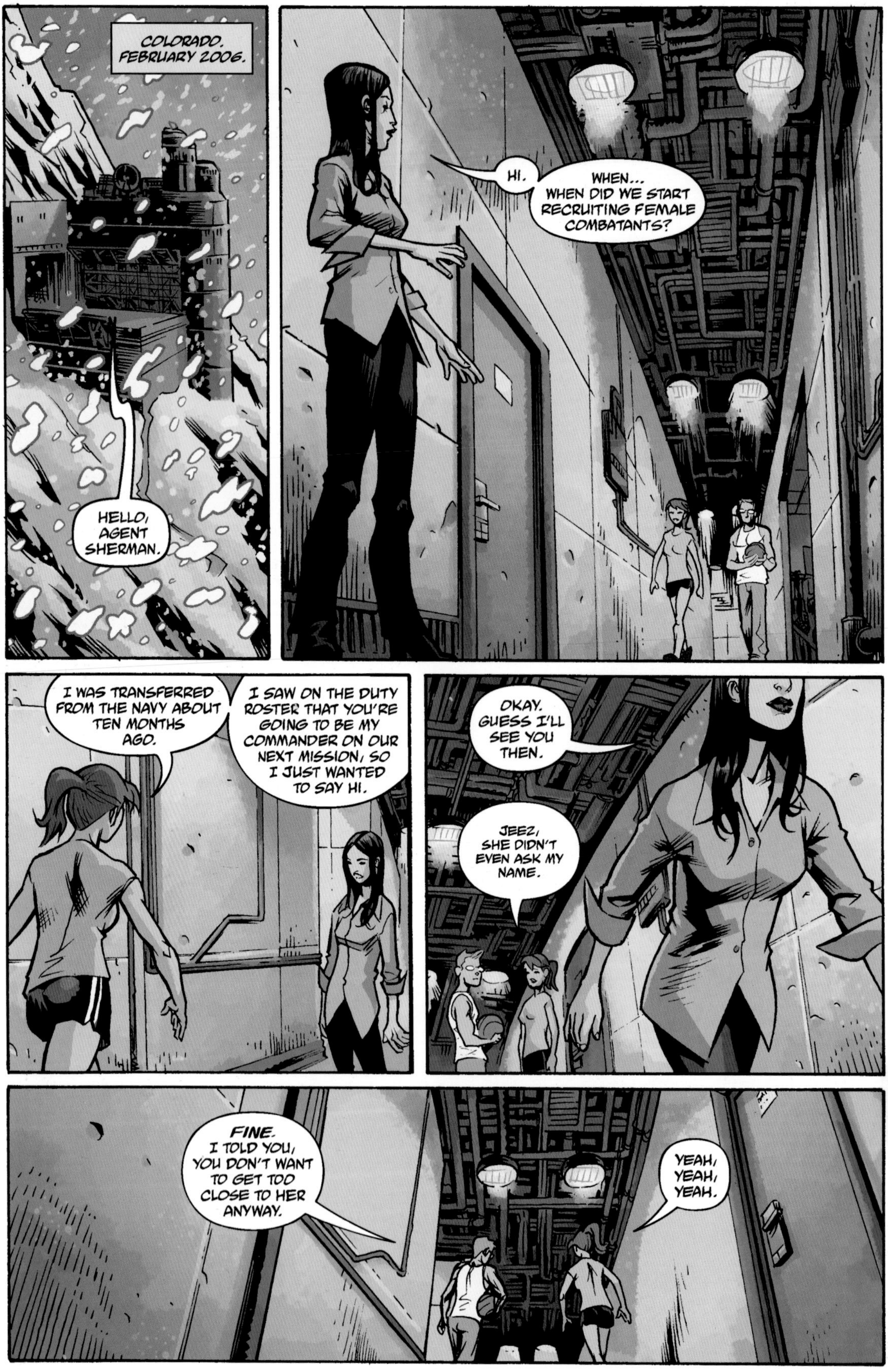
COLORADO, FEBRUARY 2006.
HELLO, AGENT SHERMAN.
HI.
WHEN... WHEN DID WE START RECRUITING FEMALE COMBATANTS?
I WAS TRANSFERRED FROM THE NAVY ABOUT TEN MONTHS AGO.
I SAW ON THE DUTY ROSTER THAT YOU'RE GOING TO BE MY COMMANDER ON OUR NEXT MISSION, SO I JUST WANTED TO SAY HI.
OKAY. GUESS I'LL SEE YOU THEN.
JEEZ, SHE DIDN'T EVEN ASK MY NAME.
FINE. I TOLD YOU, YOU DON'T WANT TO GET TOO CLOSE TO HER ANYWAY.
YEAH, YEAH, YEAH.

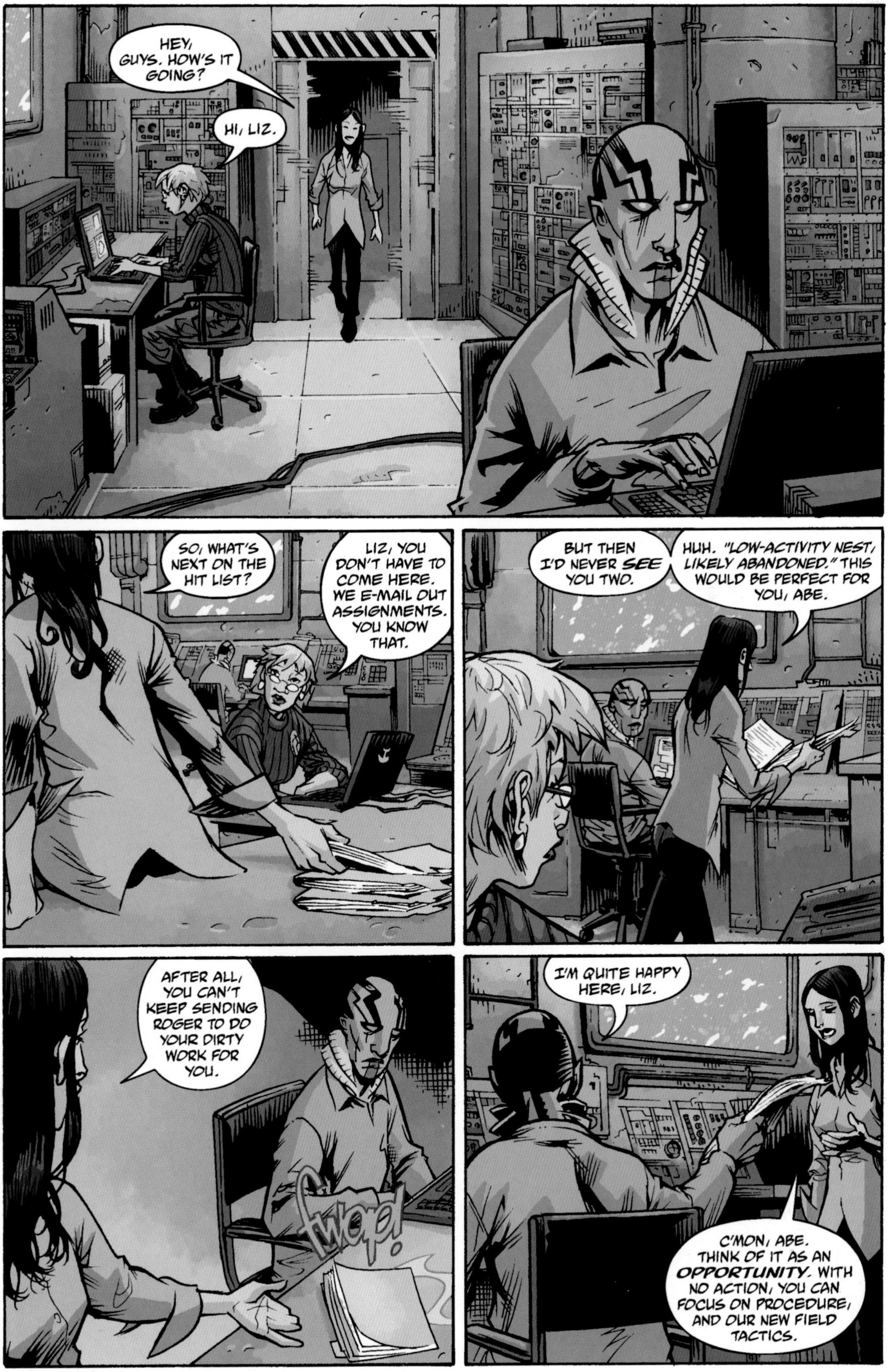
HEY, GUYS. HOW'S IT GOING?
HI, LIZ.
SO, WHAT'S NEXT ON THE HIT LIST?
LIZ, YOU DON'T HAVE TO COME HERE. WE E-MAIL OUT ASSIGNMENTS. YOU KNOW THAT.
BUT THEN I'D NEVER SEE YOU TWO.
HUH. "LOW-ACTIVITY NEST, LIKELY ABANDONED." THIS WOULD BE PERFECT FOR YOU, ABE.
AFTER ALL, YOU CAN'T KEEP SENDING ROGER TO DO YOUR DIRTY WORK FOR YOU.
fwop!
I'M QUITE HAPPY HERE, LIZ.
C'MON, ABE. THINK OF IT AS AN OPPORTUNITY. WITH NO ACTION, YOU CAN FOCUS ON PROCEDURE, AND OUR NEW FIELD TACTICS.

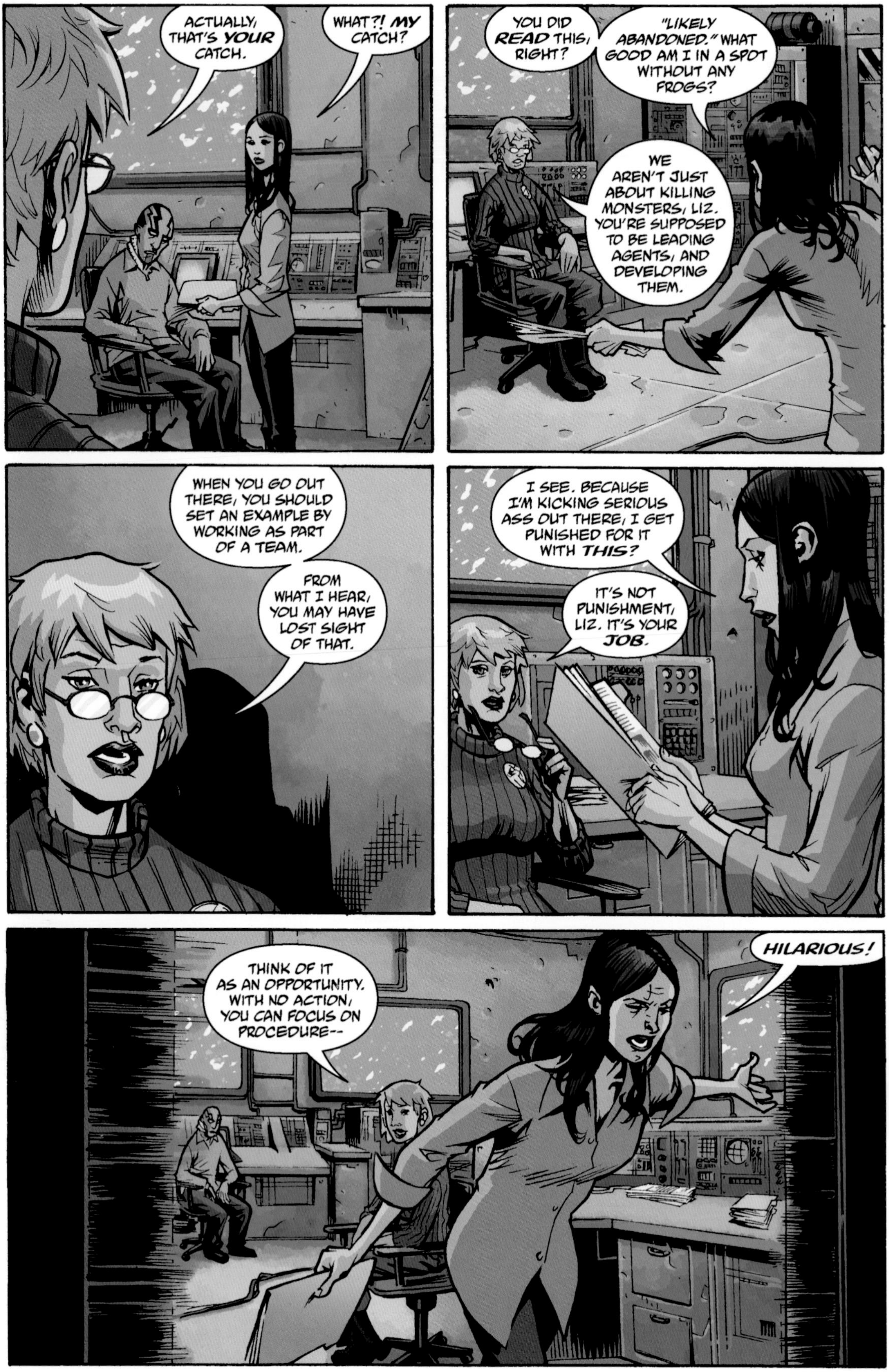
ACTUALLY, THAT'S YOUR CATCH.
WHAT?! MY CATCH?
YOU DID READ THIS, RIGHT?
"LIKELY ABANDONED." WHAT GOOD AM I IN A SPOT WITHOUT ANY FROGS?
WE AREN'T JUST ABOUT KILLING MONSTERS, LIZ. YOU'RE SUPPOSED TO BE LEADING AGENTS, AND DEVELOPING THEM.
WHEN YOU GO OUT THERE, YOU SHOULD SET AN EXAMPLE BY WORKING AS PART OF A TEAM.
FROM WHAT I HEAR, YOU MAY HAVE LOST SIGHT OF THAT.
I SEE. BECAUSE I'M KICKING SERIOUS ASS OUT THERE, I GET PUNISHED FOR IT WITH THIS?
IT'S NOT PUNISHMENT, LIZ. IT'S YOUR JOB.
THINK OF IT AS AN OPPORTUNITY. WITH NO ACTION, YOU CAN FOCUS ON PROCEDURE--
HILARIOUS!

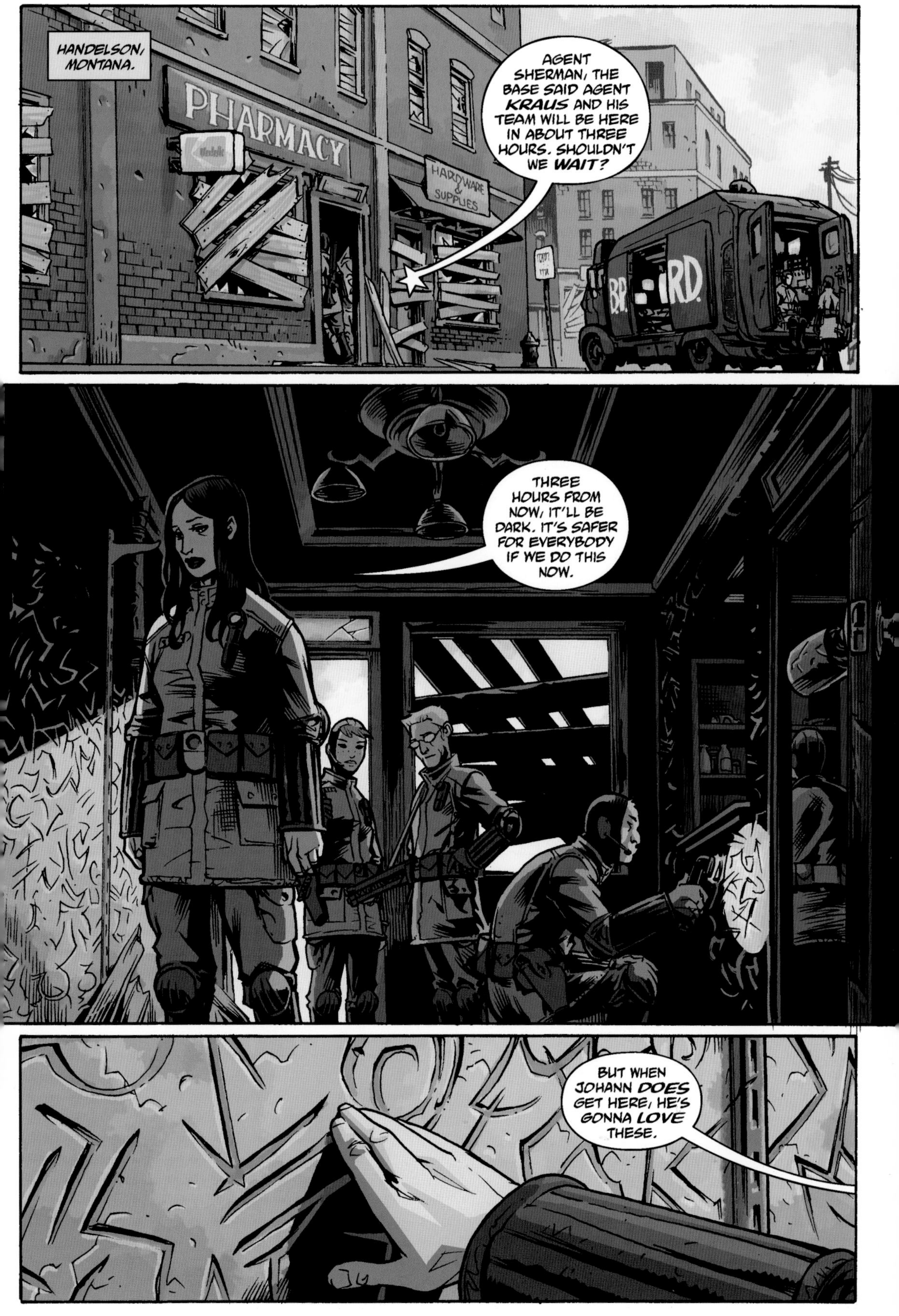
HANDELSON, MONTANA.
PHARMACY
HARDWARE & SUPPLIES
AGENT SHERMAN, THE BASE SAID AGENT KRAUS AND HIS TEAM WILL BE HERE IN ABOUT THREE HOURS. SHOULDN'T WE WAIT?
B.P.R.D.
THREE HOURS FROM NOW, IT'LL BE DARK. IT'S SAFER FOR EVERYBODY IF WE DO THIS NOW.
BUT WHEN JOHANN DOES GET HERE, HE'S GONNA LOVE THESE.

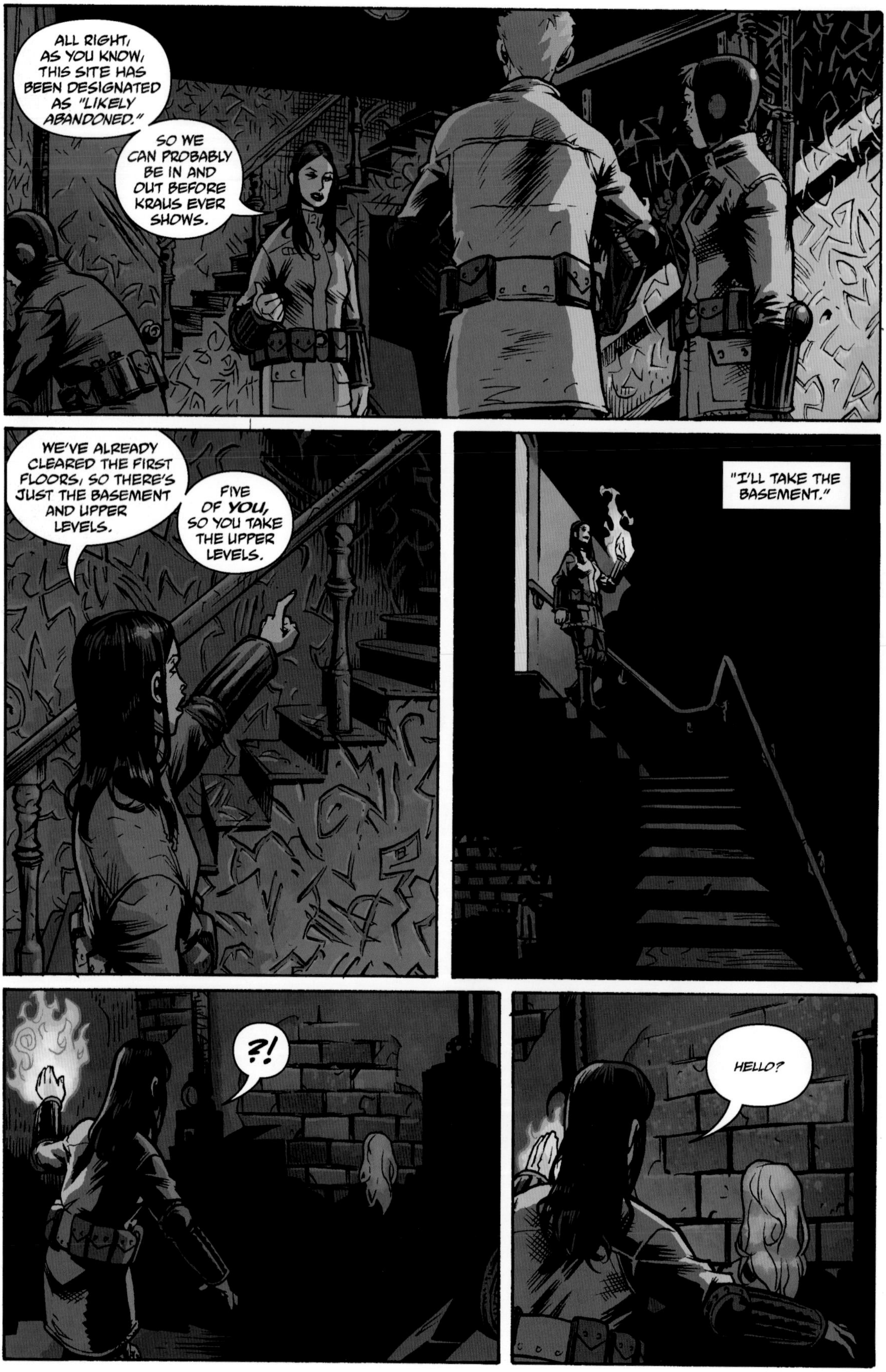
ALL RIGHT, AS YOU KNOW, THIS SITE HAS BEEN DESIGNATED AS "LIKELY ABANDONED."
SO WE CAN PROBABLY BE IN AND OUT BEFORE KRAUS EVER SHOWS.
WE'VE ALREADY CLEARED THE FIRST FLOORS, SO THERE'S JUST THE BASEMENT AND UPPER LEVELS.
FIVE OF YOU, SO YOU TAKE THE UPPER LEVELS.
"I'LL TAKE THE BASEMENT."
?!
HELLO?

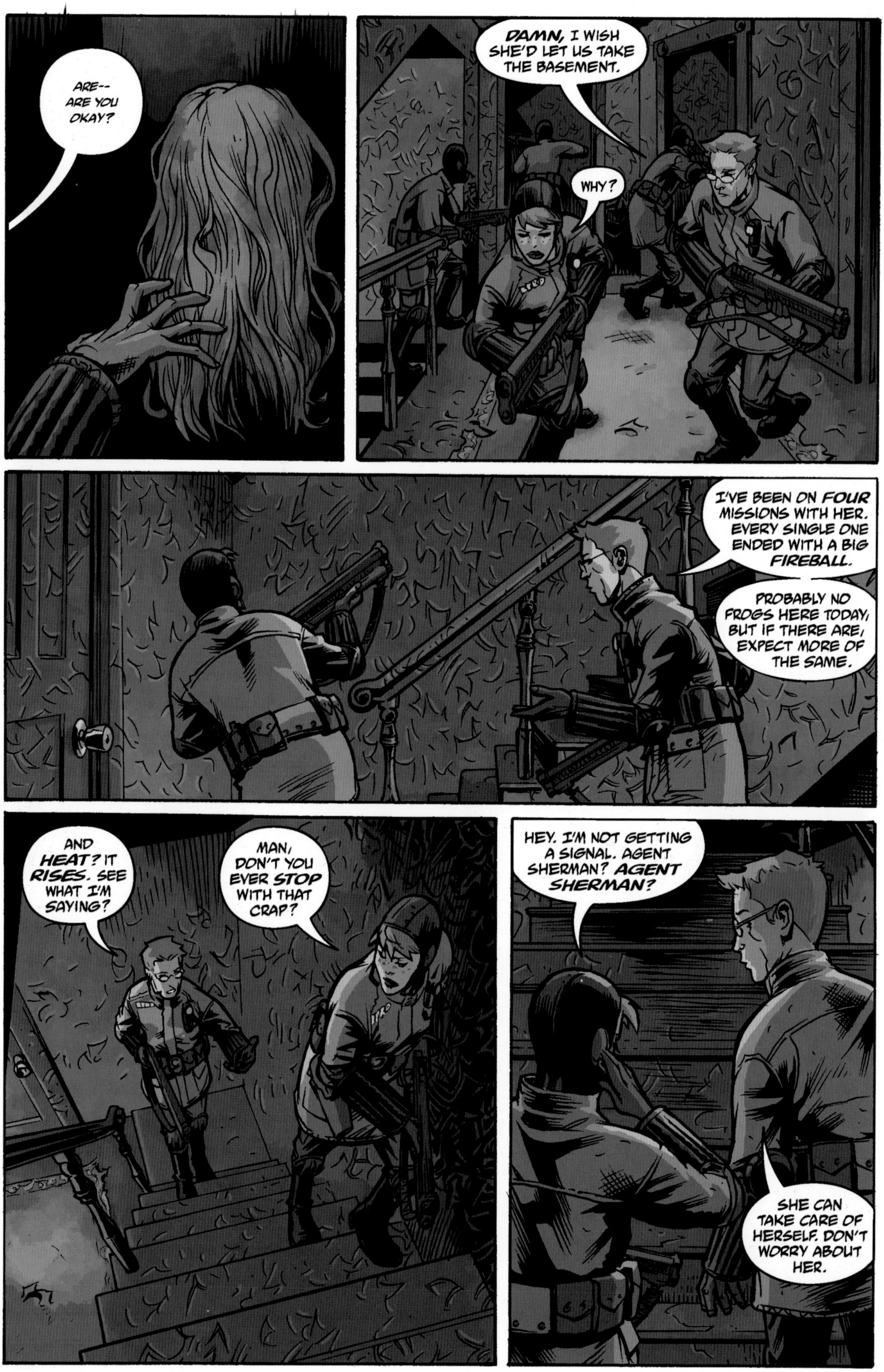
ARE--
ARE YOU OKAY?
DAMN, I WISH SHE'D LET US TAKE THE BASEMENT.
WHY?
I'VE BEEN ON FOUR MISSIONS WITH HER. EVERY SINGLE ONE ENDED WITH A BIG FIREBALL.
PROBABLY NO FROGS HERE TODAY, BUT IF THERE ARE, EXPECT MORE OF THE SAME.
AND HEAT? IT RISES. SEE WHAT I'M SAYING?
MAN, DON'T YOU EVER STOP WITH THAT CRAP?
HEY. I'M NOT GETTING A SIGNAL. AGENT SHERMAN? AGENT SHERMAN?
SHE CAN TAKE CARE OF HERSELF. DON'T WORRY ABOUT HER.

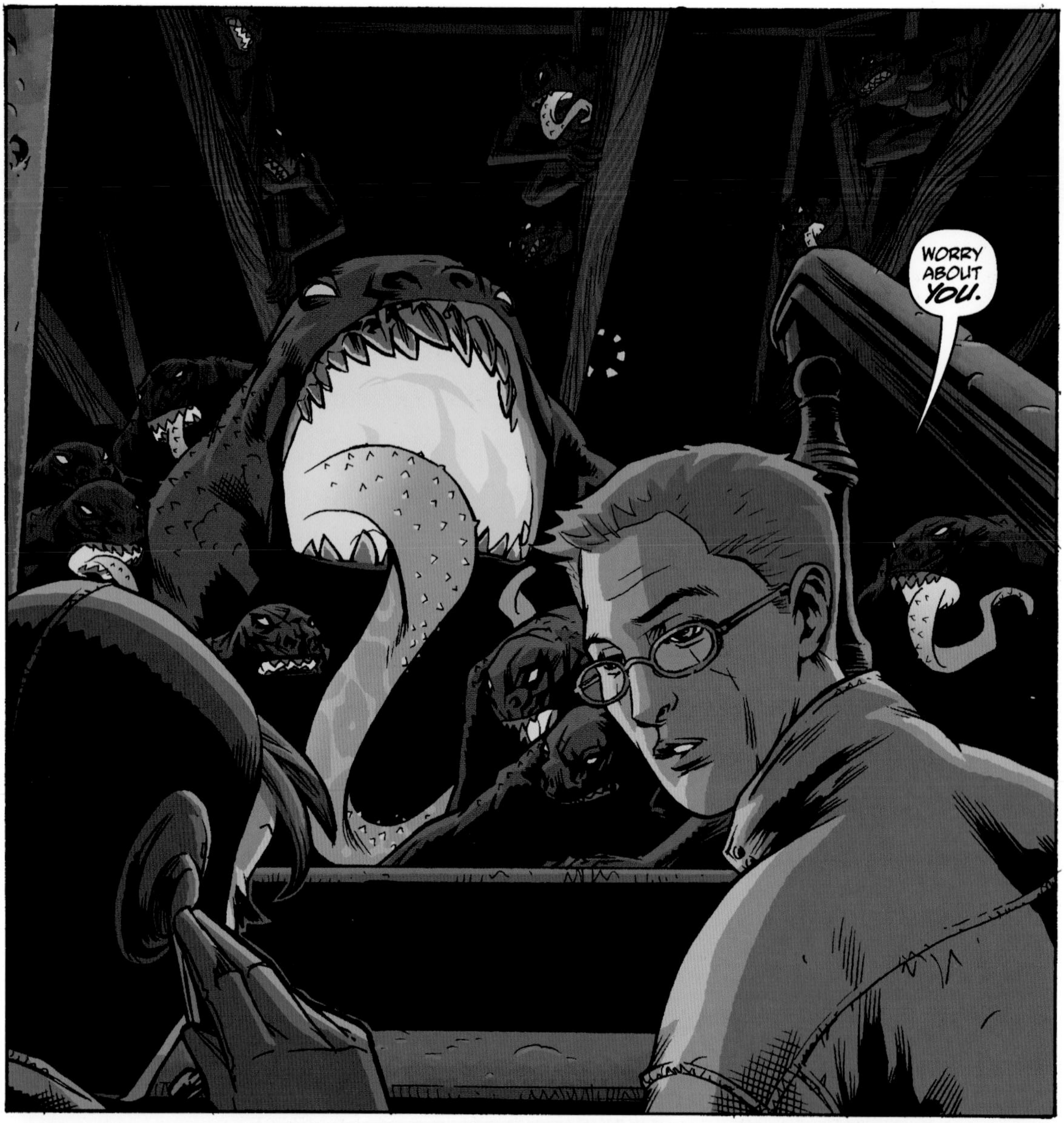
WORRY ABOUT YOU.

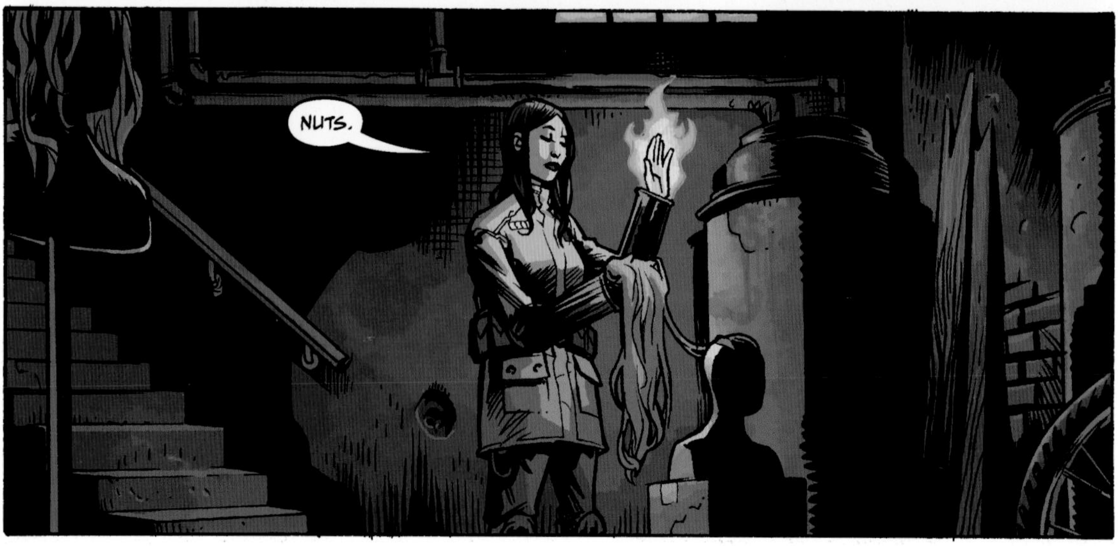
NUTS.

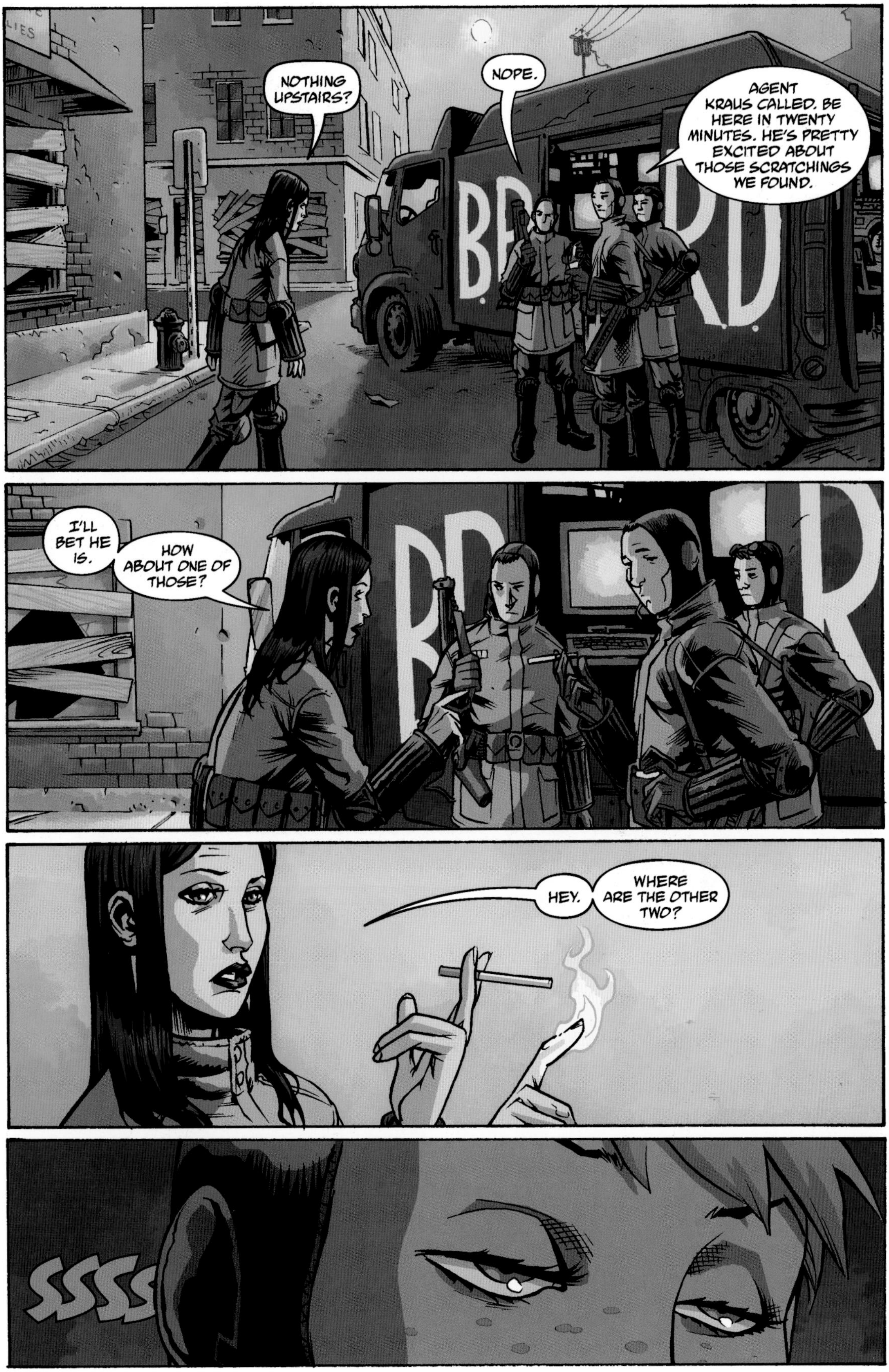
NOTHING UPSTAIRS?
NOPE.
AGENT KRAUS CALLED. BE HERE IN TWENTY MINUTES. HE'S PRETTY EXCITED ABOUT THOSE SCRATCHINGS WE FOUND.
I'LL BET HE IS.
HOW ABOUT ONE OF THOSE?
HEY.
WHERE ARE THE OTHER TWO?
SSSS

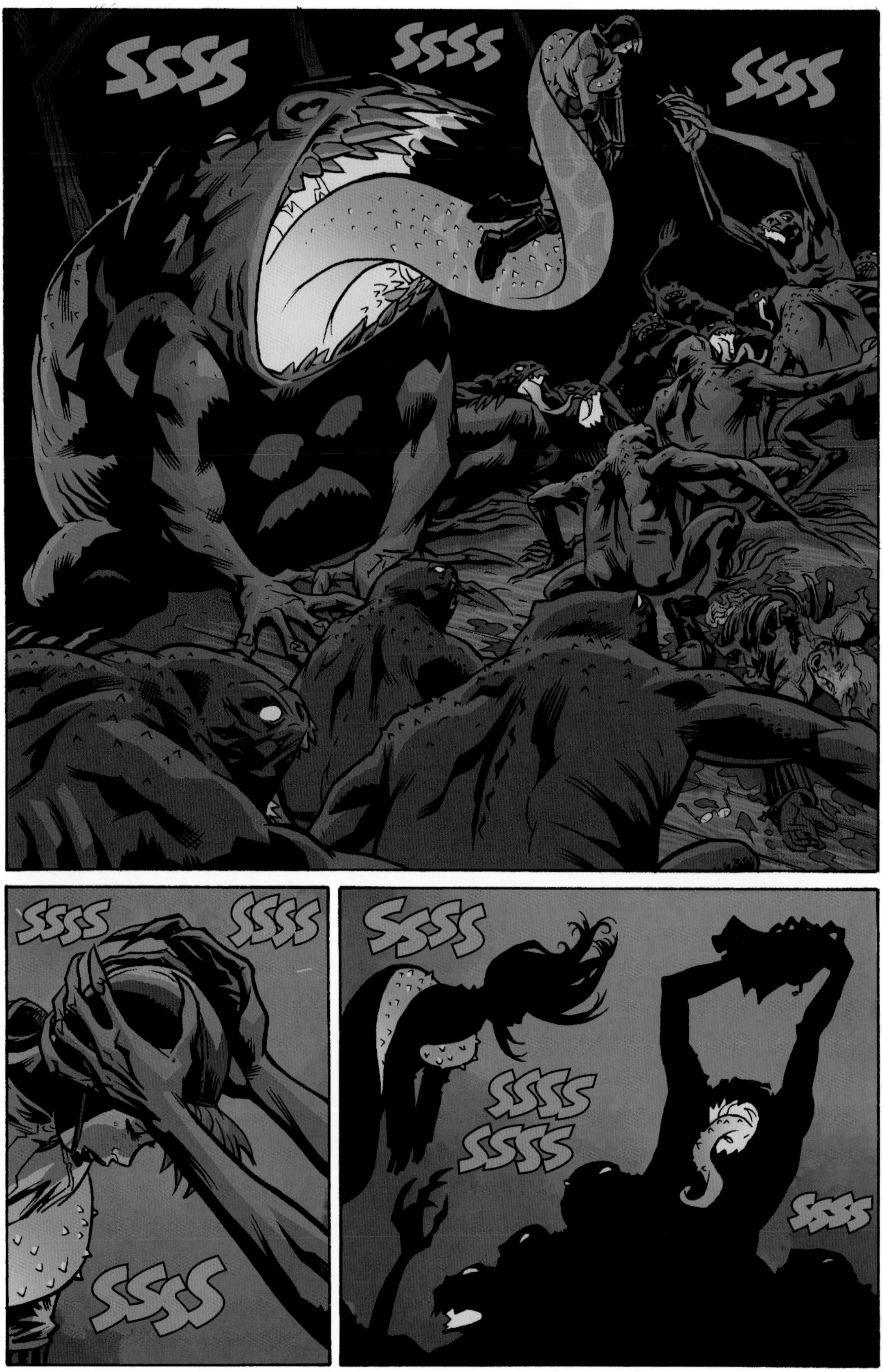
SSSS
SSSS
SSSS
SSSS
SSSS
SSSS
SSSS
SSSS
SSSS
SSSS
SSSS

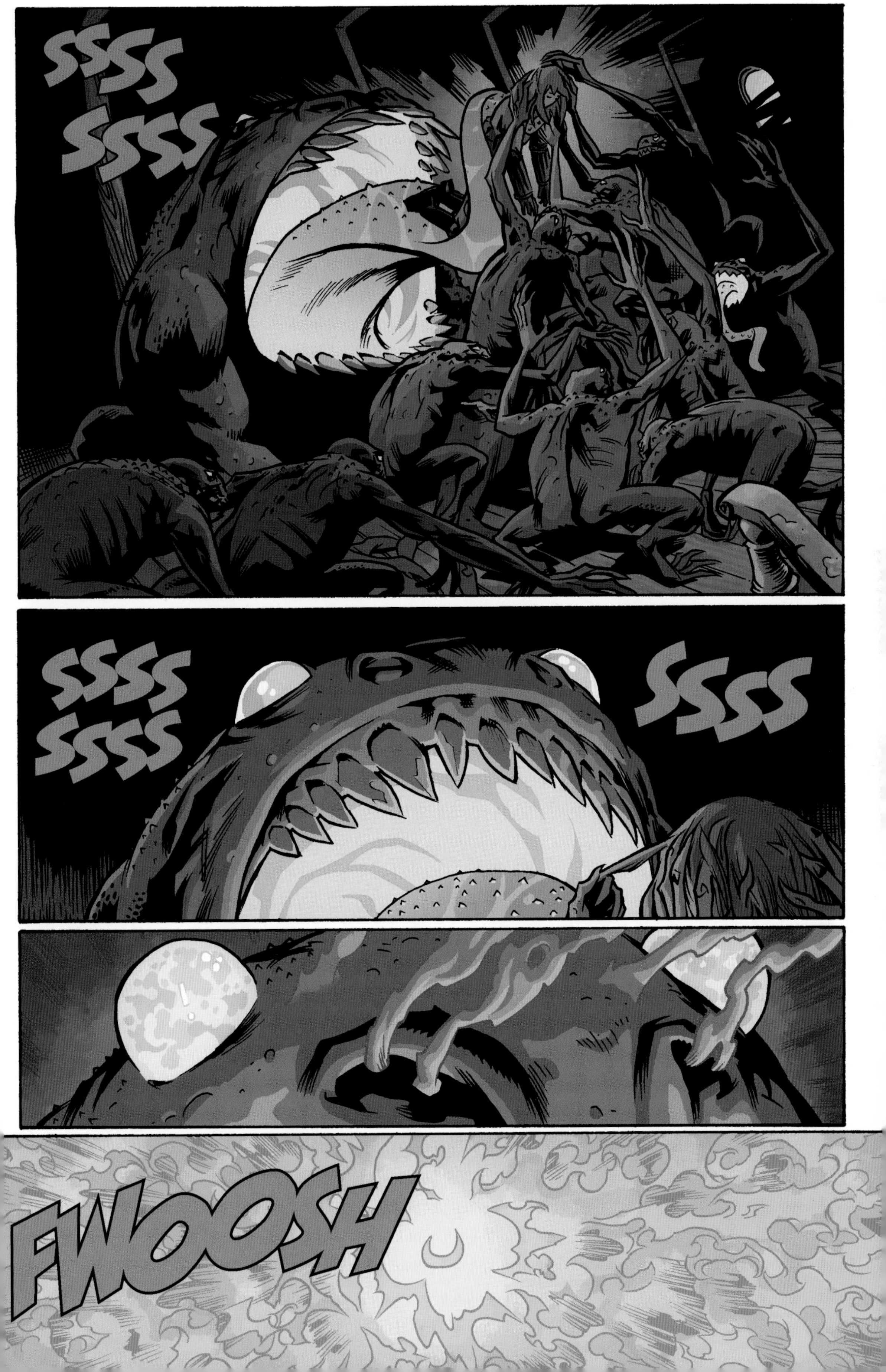
SSSS
SSSS
SSSS
SSSS
SSSS
FWOOSH

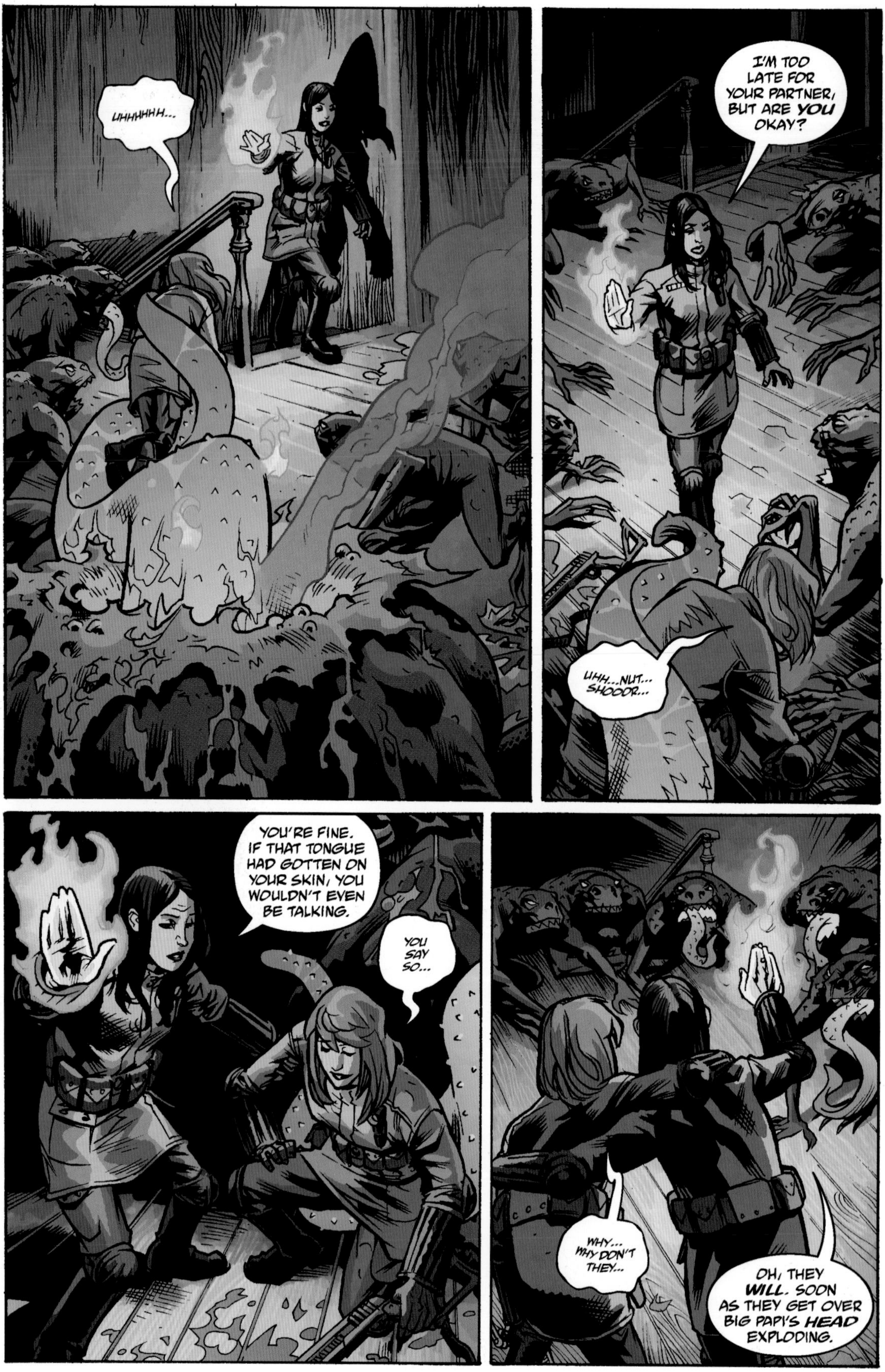
UHHHHHH...
I'M TOO LATE FOR YOUR PARTNER, BUT ARE YOU OKAY?
UHH...NUT... SHOOOR...
YOU'RE FINE. IF THAT TONGUE HAD GOTTEN ON YOUR SKIN, YOU WOULDN'T EVEN BE TALKING.
YOU SAY SO...
WHY... WHY DON'T THEY...
OH, THEY WILL. SOON AS THEY GET OVER BIG PAPI'S HEAD EXPLODING.

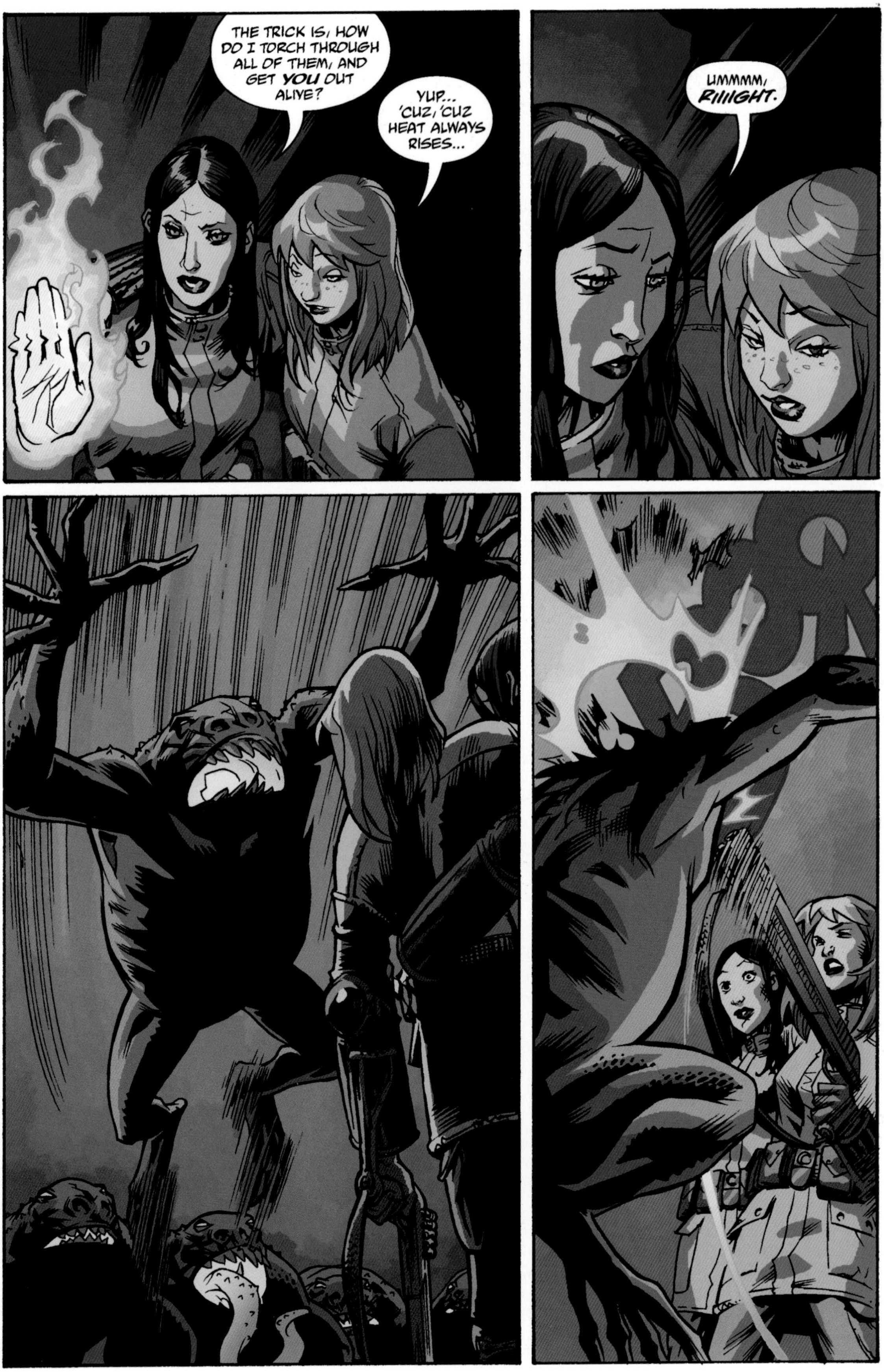
THE TRICK IS, HOW DO I TORCH THROUGH ALL OF THEM, AND GET YOU OUT ALIVE?
YUP... 'CUZ, 'CUZ HEAT ALWAYS RISES...
UMMMM, RIIIGHT.

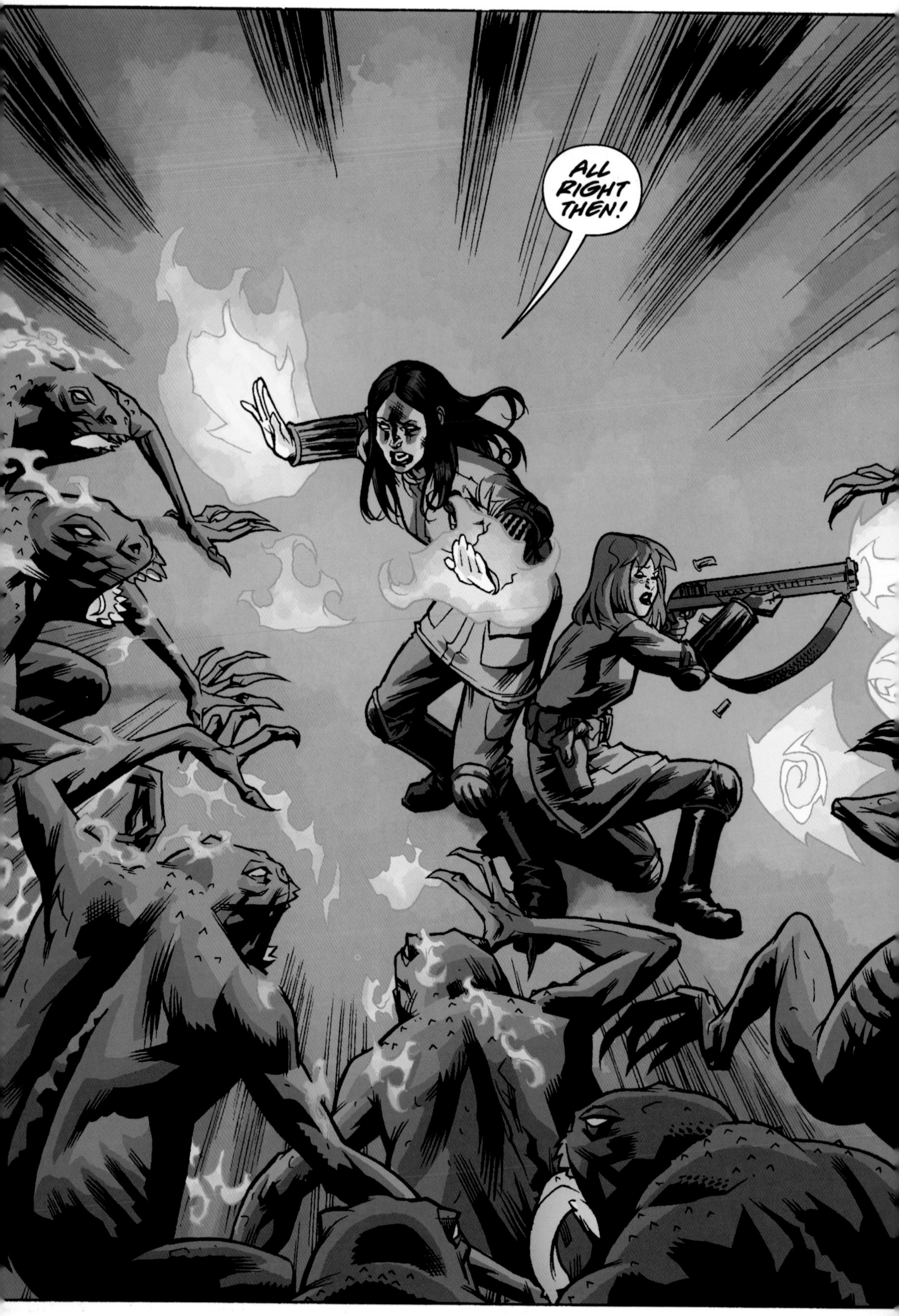
ALL RIGHT THEN!

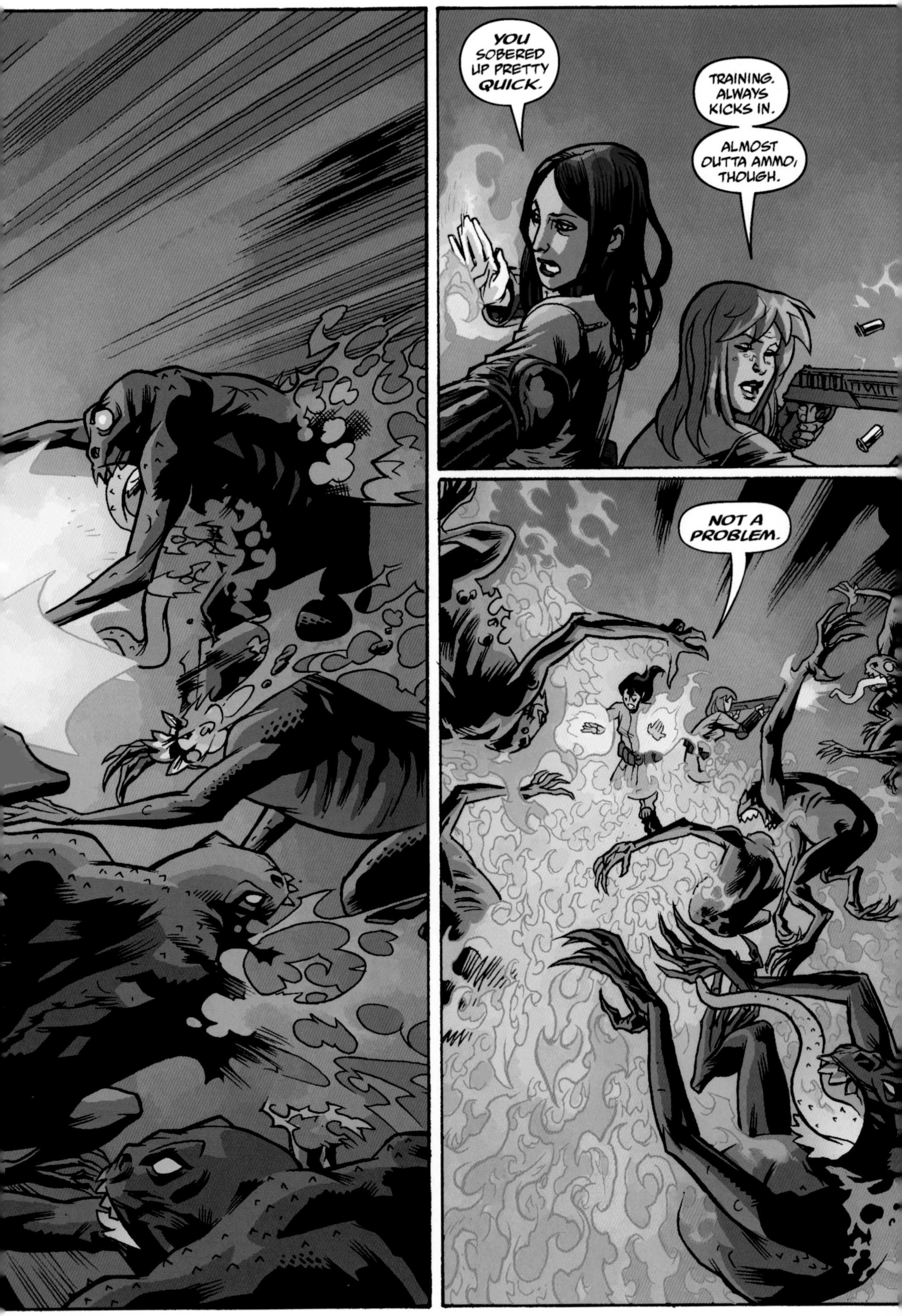
YOU SOBERED UP PRETTY QUICK.
TRAINING. ALWAYS KICKS IN.
ALMOST OUTTA AMMO, THOUGH.
NOT A PROBLEM.

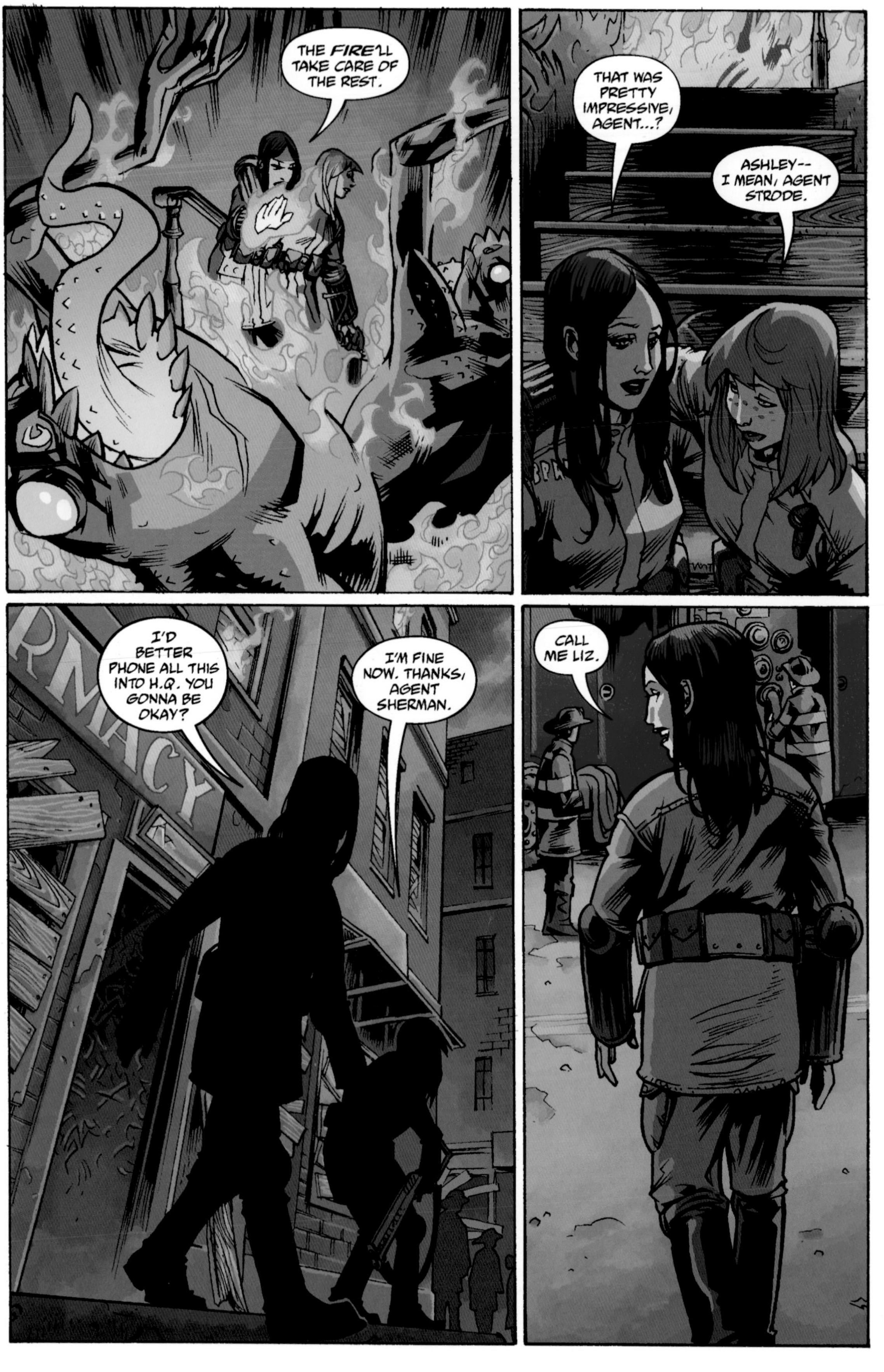
THE FIRE'LL TAKE CARE OF THE REST.
THAT WAS PRETTY IMPRESSIVE, AGENT...?
ASHLEY-- I MEAN, AGENT STRODE.
I'D BETTER PHONE ALL THIS INTO H.Q. YOU GONNA BE OKAY?
I'M FINE NOW. THANKS, AGENT SHERMAN.
CALL ME LIZ.

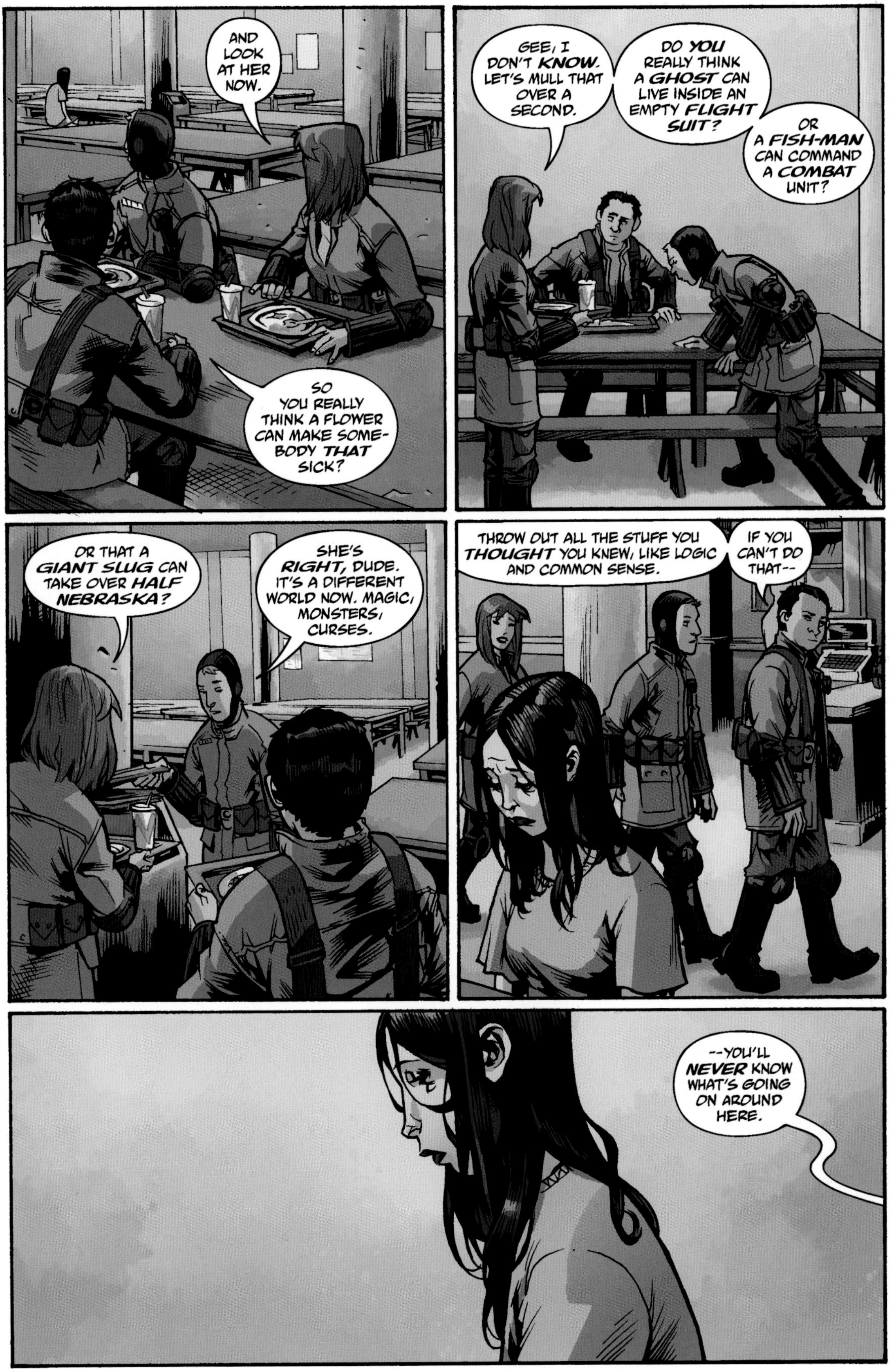
AND LOOK AT HER NOW.
SO YOU REALLY THINK A FLOWER CAN MAKE SOME-BODY THAT SICK?
GEE, I DON'T KNOW. LET'S MULL THAT OVER A SECOND.
DO YOU REALLY THINK A GHOST CAN LIVE INSIDE AN EMPTY FLIGHT SUIT?
OR A FISH-MAN CAN COMMAND A COMBAT UNIT?
OR THAT A GIANT SLUG CAN TAKE OVER HALF NEBRASKA?
SHE'S RIGHT, DUDE. IT'S A DIFFERENT WORLD NOW. MAGIC, MONSTERS, CURSES.
THROW OUT ALL THE STUFF YOU THOUGHT YOU KNEW, LIKE LOGIC AND COMMON SENSE.
IF YOU CAN'T DO THAT--
--YOU'LL NEVER KNOW WHAT'S GOING ON AROUND HERE.

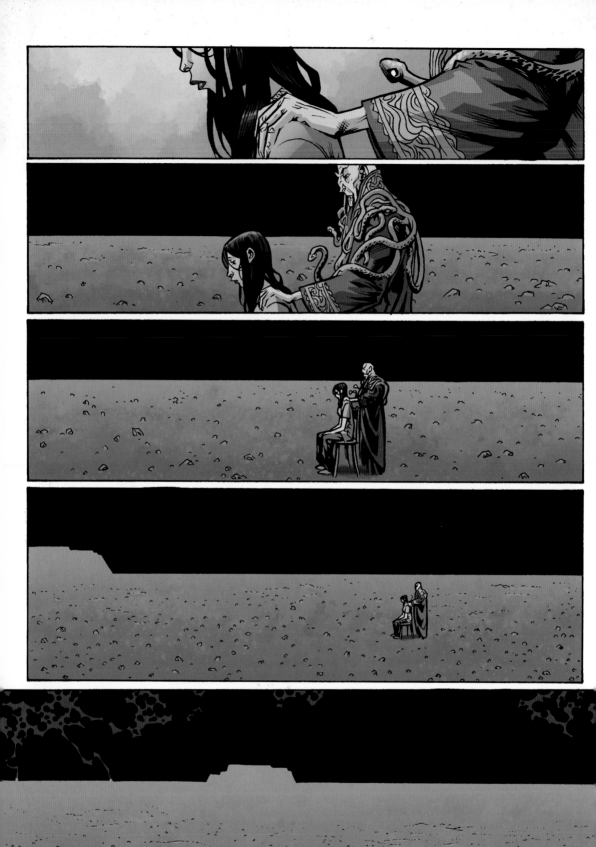

THE
END

ENTER JOHN ARCUDI

When I decided that I wanted someone to cowrite *B.P.R.D.* with me, John was the only name on my list. I'd known him for years, knew we spoke the same language when it comes to old comics and monsters. Most importantly, he is not only a great writer, but he's also a master of combining humor (my kind of humor) and horror. When I asked him to come onboard, he said yes right away. If he'd said no . . . Well, I don't like to think about that. If he'd said no, there's a good chance you wouldn't be holding a second collection of *B.P.R.D.* stories. It almost certainly wouldn't be this good.

After writing *Plague of Frogs*, I knew I wanted to push the B.P.R.D. in a new direction. I wanted to relocate them into a mountain, and, as is so often the case when you move into a mountain, I knew something bad would happen there. I also wanted to introduce a new, hard-ass, formerly dead, military-type character. Over a couple of lunches and a lot of phone calls, John and I hammered out the basic plot for *The Dead*. He then wrote everything that happens in the new headquarters, and I wrote the sequences with Abe and his dead wife. It was a clean, simple, and organized way to work—and we have never done anything like it since.

The Black Flame came together really fast, and it's pretty hard to remember who came up with what. Early on John suggested that we create some kind of old-school supervillain. I grew up reading Stan Lee and Jack Kirby Marvel comics, so I was all for it. We both loved the Black Flame character briefly introduced in *The Dead*, recognizing him as the Red Skull of our *B.P.R.D.* universe. So what if the Red Skull made himself into Doctor Doom and then, slowly . . . turned into something else? Add the escalating of the frog problem and Liz Sherman's mysterious "friend," and there you go. I'm pretty sure we cobbled the plot together over a single lunch, and then John went home and did all the "real" writing.

I think *The Black Flame* established how John and I work *most* of the time on this series—*we* talk and *he* writes. I hate typing and can't spell, but I like going to lunch and I don't mind talking on the phone. Also John is a much better writer than I am, so the more I stay out of his way and let him do what he does, and the more he makes the characters his own, the better the book is. The five standalone stories that make up *War on Frogs* (rearranged chronologically for this collection) are actually almost entirely John's. He picked up on a couple of things I established (the little-girl frog monster from the original *Plague of Frogs* story and the original frog monsters from the first *Hellboy* book, *Seed of Destruction*), and I might have had a few suggestions along the way (though right now I'll be damned if I can remember any), but these stories are definitely his.

In this collection you see *B.P.R.D.* really turn into the series that continues today, thanks to both John and the great Guy Davis (helped along by some wonderful guest artists). I am very proud of this series and increasingly embarrassed about taking any of the credit for it.

There you go—

MIKE MIGNOLA

THE DEAD

SKETCHBOOK

Notes by Guy Davis

While most of the design work for the B.P.R.D. was already done before I started on the *Plague of Frogs* story line, *The Dead* would bring a lot of new designs for the B.P.R.D. team. But first there were the sketches for the short story "Born Again"—below are some early drawings for the living fossil.

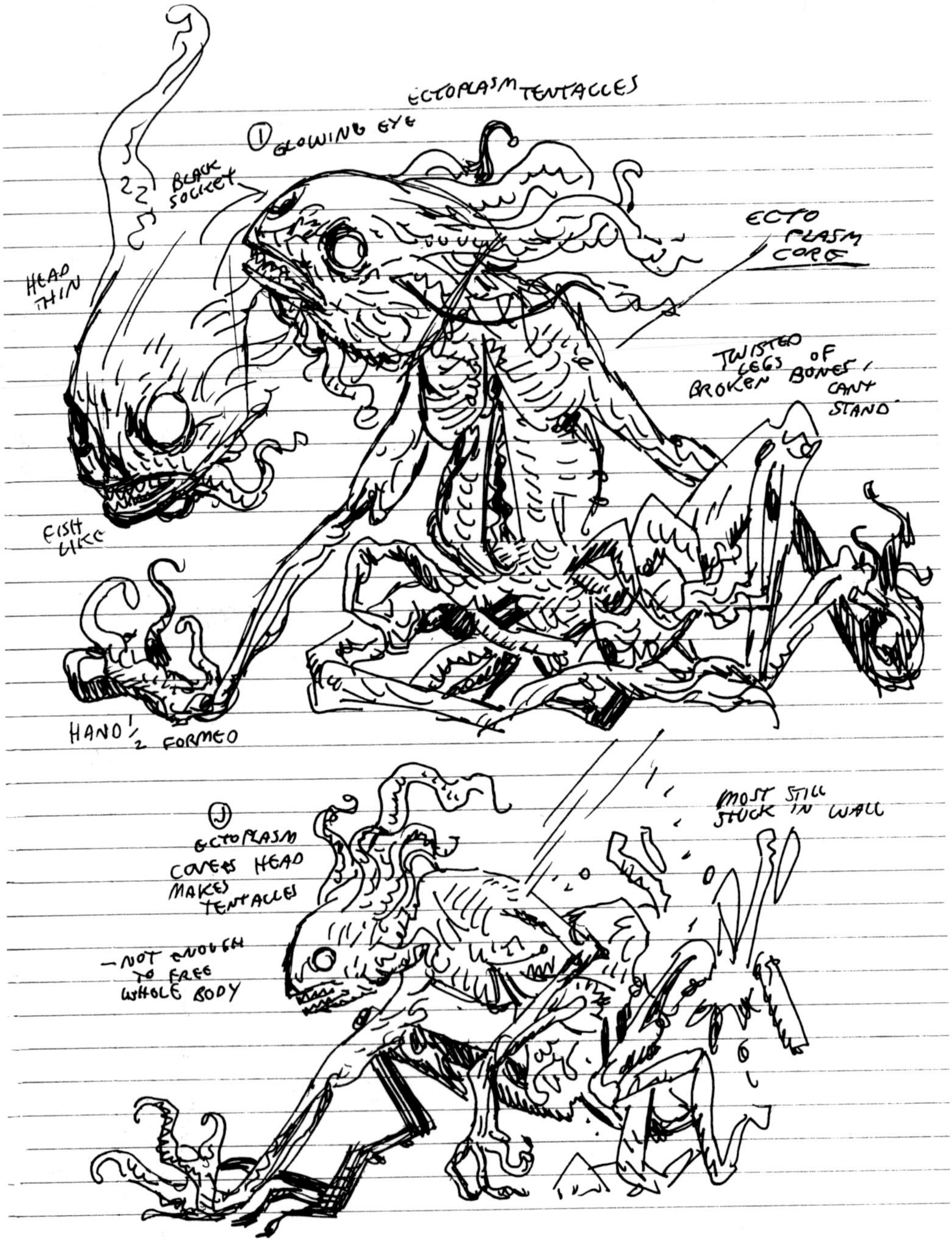
ECTOPLASM TENTACLES
① GLOWING EYE
BLACK SOCKET
ECTO PLASM CORE
HEAD THIN
TWISTED LEGS OF BROKEN BONES / CANT STAND
FISH LIKE
HAND ½ FORMED
② ECTOPLASM COVERS HEAD MAKES TENTACLES
—NOT ENOUGH TO FREE WHOLE BODY
MOST STILL STUCK IN WALL

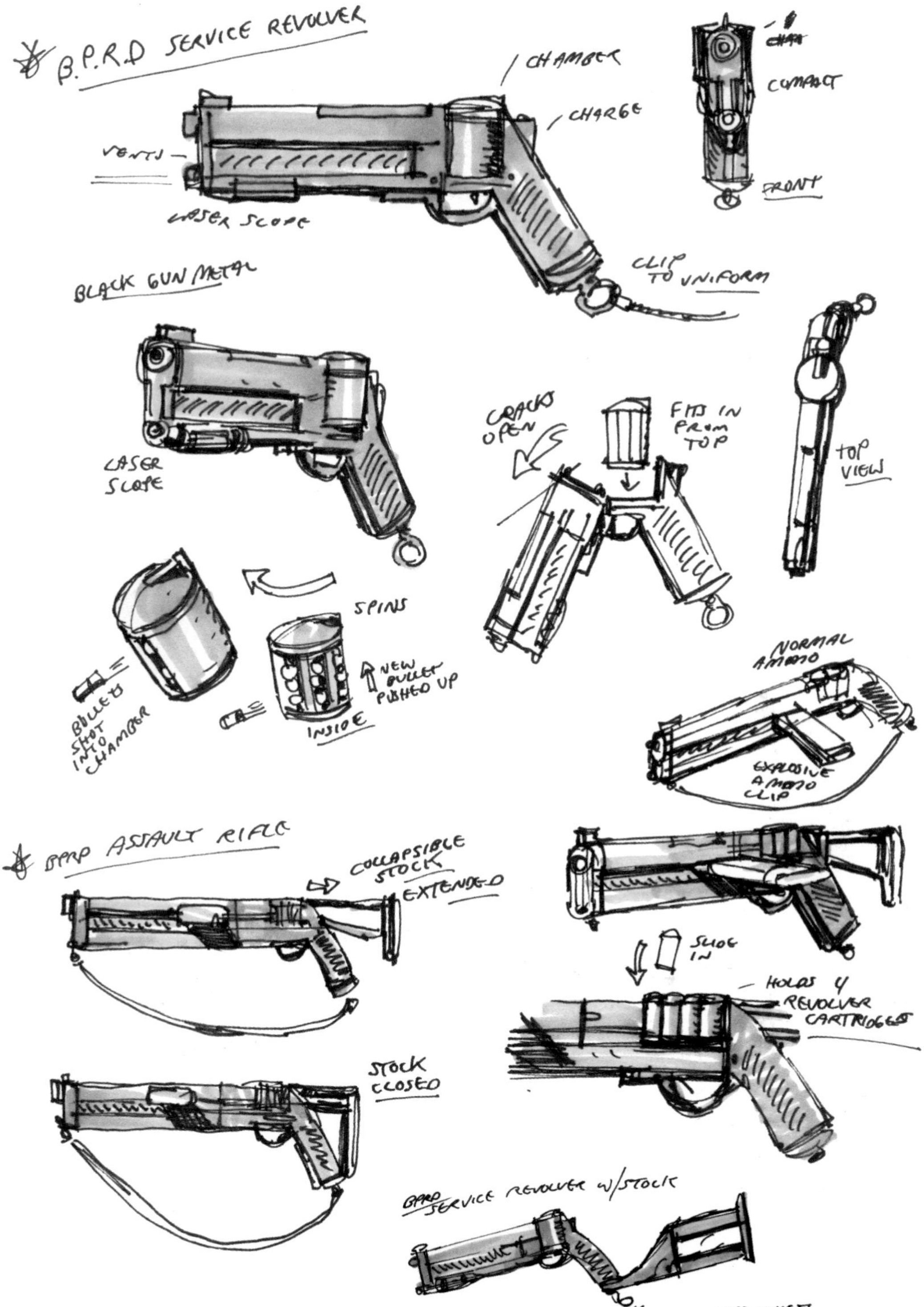
B.P.R.D SERVICE REVOLVER
CHAMBER
CHARGE
VENTS
LASER SCOPE
COMPACT
FRONT
CLIP TO UNIFORM
BLACK GUN METAL
LASER SCOPE
CRACKS OPEN
FITS IN FROM TOP
TOP VIEW
SPINS
NEW BULLET PUSHED UP
INSIDE
BULLETS SHOT INTO CHAMBER
NORMAL AMMO
EXPLOSIVE AMMO CLIP
BPRD ASSAULT RIFLE
COLLAPSIBLE STOCK
EXTENDED
SLIDE IN
HOLDS 4 REVOLVER CARTRIDGES
STOCK CLOSED
BPRD SERVICE REVOLVER W/STOCK
PISTOL STOCK

Mike reworked the new uniforms of the B.P.R.D. team to reflect a more organized, utilitarian feel, and I wanted the guns to match that.

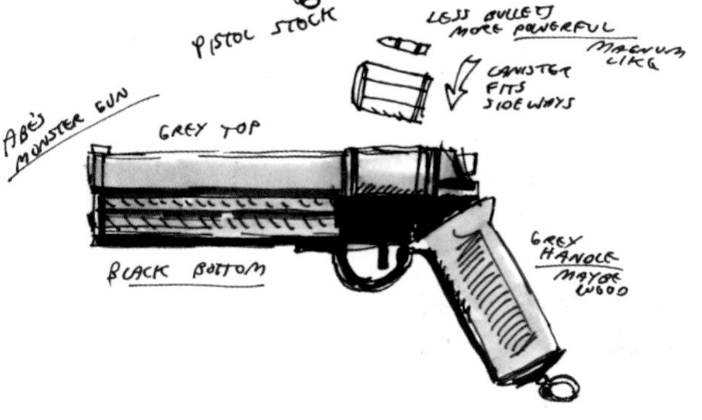
LESS BULLETS MORE POWERFUL
MAGNUM LIKE
CANISTER FITS SIDEWAYS
ABE'S MONSTER GUN
GREY TOP
GREY HANDLE
MAYBE WOOD
BLACK BOTTOM

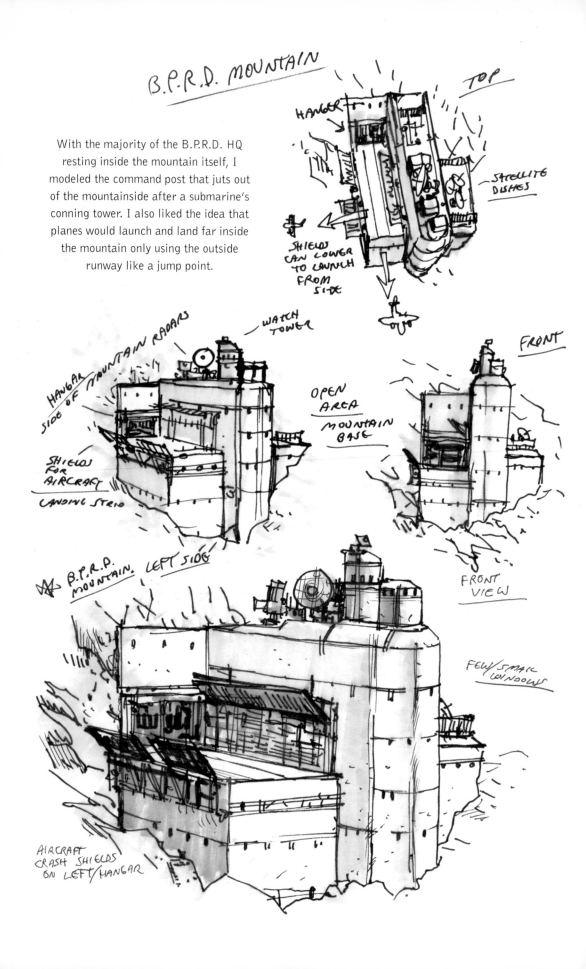

B.P.R.D. MOUNTAIN

With the majority of the B.P.R.D. HQ resting inside the mountain itself, I modeled the command post that juts out of the mountainside after a submarine's conning tower. I also liked the idea that planes would launch and land far inside the mountain only using the outside runway like a jump point.

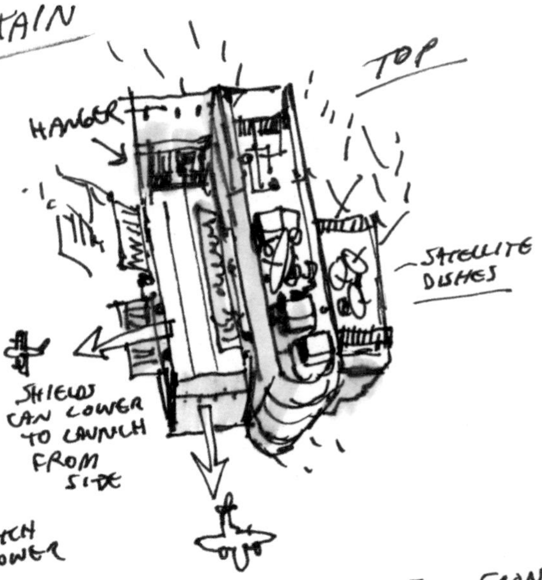
TOP
HANGER
SATELLITE DISHES
SHIELDS CAN LOWER TO LAUNCH FROM SIDE

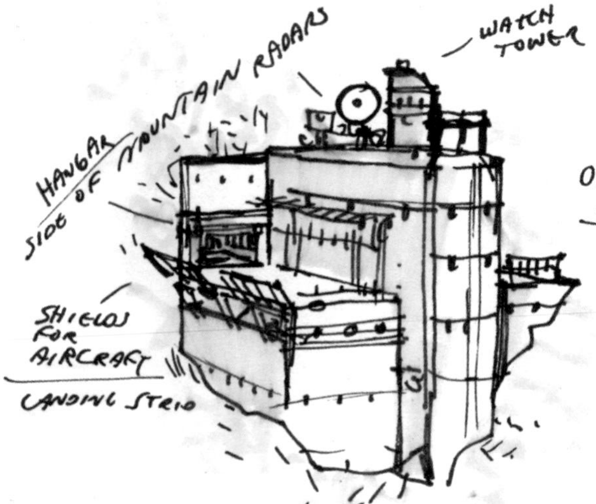
WATCH TOWER
HANGAR SIDE OF MOUNTAIN RADARS
SHIELDS FOR AIRCRAFT
LANDING STRIP
OPEN AREA
MOUNTAIN BASE

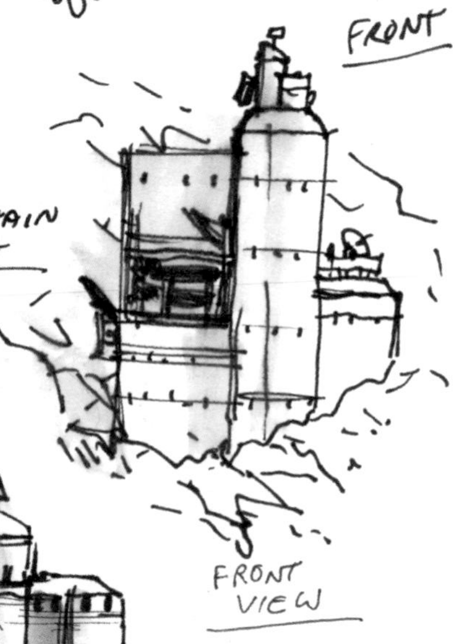
FRONT
FRONT VIEW

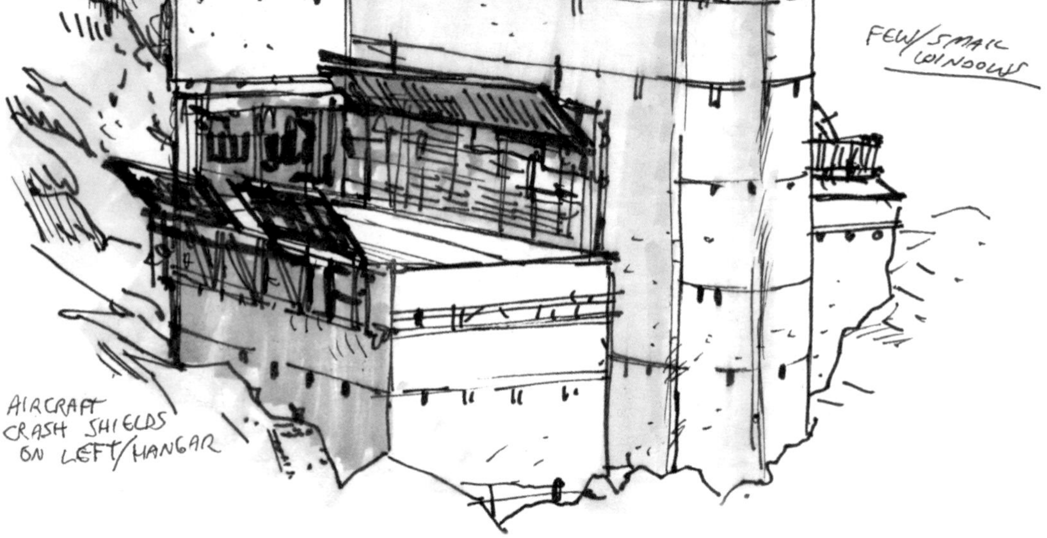
B.P.R.D. MOUNTAIN, LEFT SIDE
FEW/SMALL WINDOWS
AIRCRAFT CRASH SHIELDS ON LEFT/HANGAR

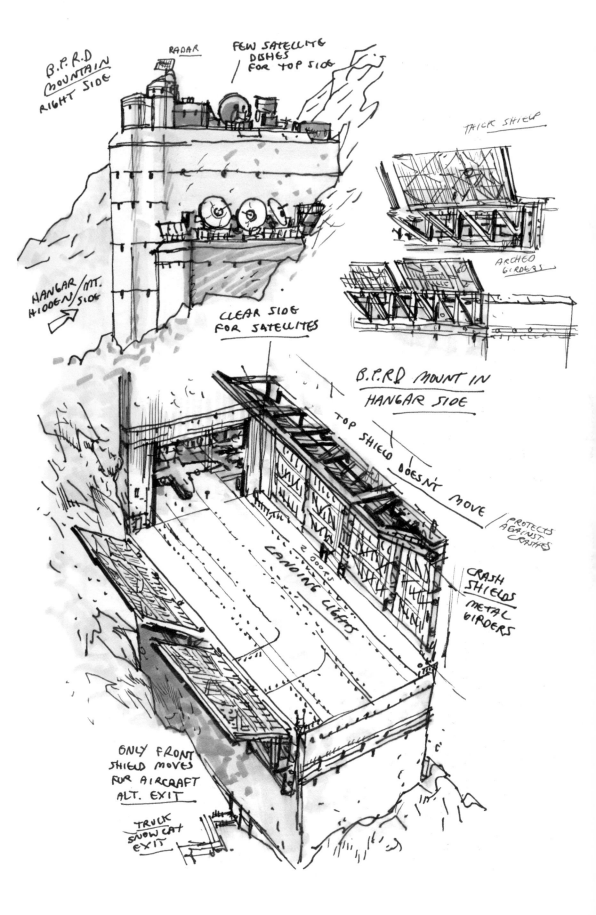

B.P.R.D MOUNTAIN RIGHT SIDE

RADAR

FEW SATELLITE DISHES FOR TOP SIDE

HANGAR / MT. HIDDEN / SIDE

CLEAR SIDE FOR SATELLITES

THICK SHIELD

ARCHED GIRDERS

B.P.R.D MOUNTIN HANGAR SIDE

TOP SHIELD DOESN'T MOVE

PROTECTS AGAINST CRASHES

LANDING CLIFFS

CRASH SHIELDS

METAL GIRDERS

ONLY FRONT SHIELD MOVES FOR AIRCRAFT ALT. EXIT

TRUCK SNOW CAT EXIT

A lot of times designs come out as first imagined after reading the script—Abe's corpse wife was one of them. I wanted her to be a dark mass of hair and gunk, almost a silhouette until seen up close.

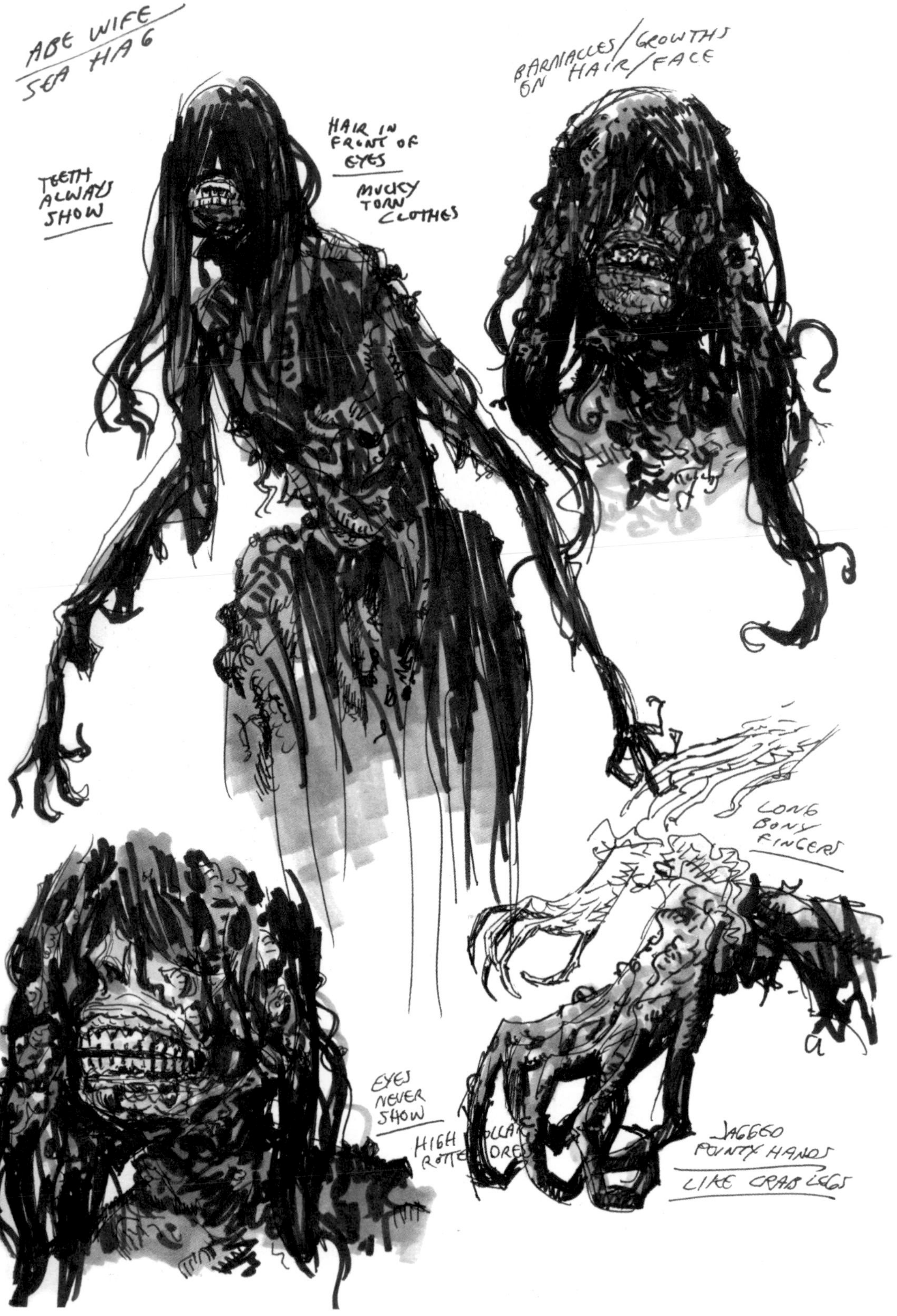

ABE WIFE
SEA HAG
BARNACLES/GROWTHS ON HAIR/FACE
HAIR IN FRONT OF EYES
MUCKY TORN CLOTHES
TEETH ALWAYS SHOW
LONG BONY FINGERS
EYES NEVER SHOW
HIGH
JAGGED POINTY HANDS
LIKE CRAB LEGS

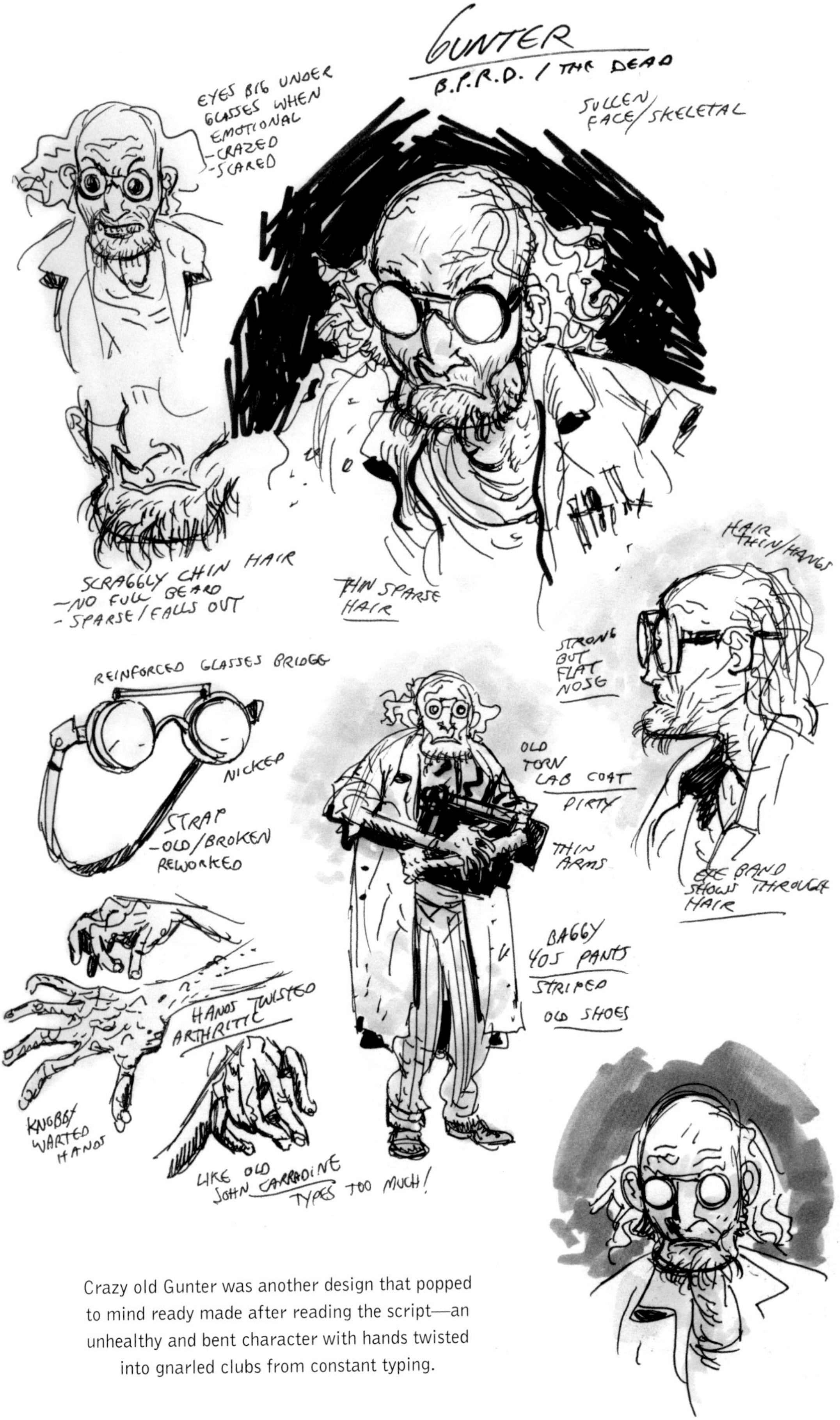
GUNTER
B.P.R.D. / THE DEAD
EYES BIG UNDER GLASSES WHEN EMOTIONAL
-CRAZED
-SCARED
SULLEN FACE/SKELETAL
SCRAGGLY CHIN HAIR
-NO FULL BEARD
-SPARSE/FALLS OUT
THIN SPARSE HAIR
HAIR THIN/HANGS
STRONG BUT FLAT NOSE
REINFORCED GLASSES BRIDGE
NICKED
STRAP
-OLD/BROKEN
REWORKED
OLD TORN LAB COAT
DIRTY
THIN ARMS
EYE BAND SHOWS THROUGH HAIR
BAGGY 40S PANTS
STRIPED
OLD SHOES
HANDS TWISTED ARTHRITIC
KNOBBY WARTED HANDS
LIKE OLD JOHN CARRADINE TYPES TOO MUCH!

Crazy old Gunter was another design that popped to mind ready made after reading the script—an unhealthy and bent character with hands twisted into gnarled clubs from constant typing.

We wanted Johann's giant power pack to make him look like some sort of debris-covered hermit crab.

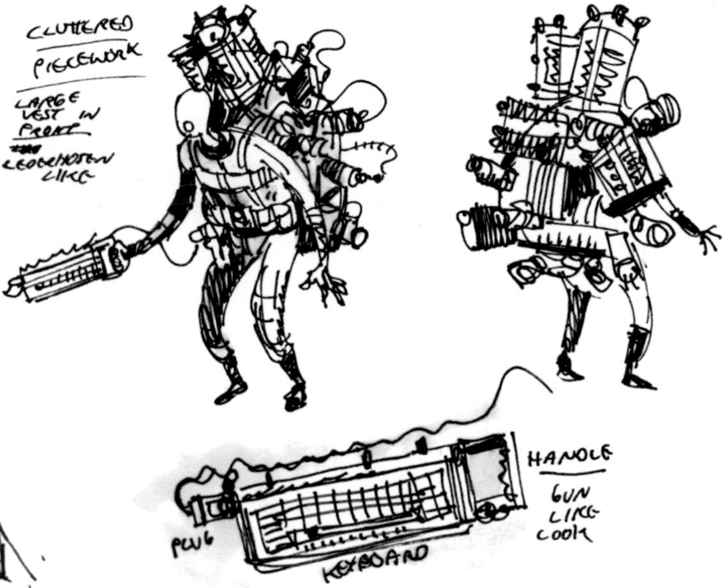
CLUTTERED
PIECEWORK
LARGE VEST IN FRONT
LEDERHOSEN LIKE
HANDLE
PLUG
KEYBOARD

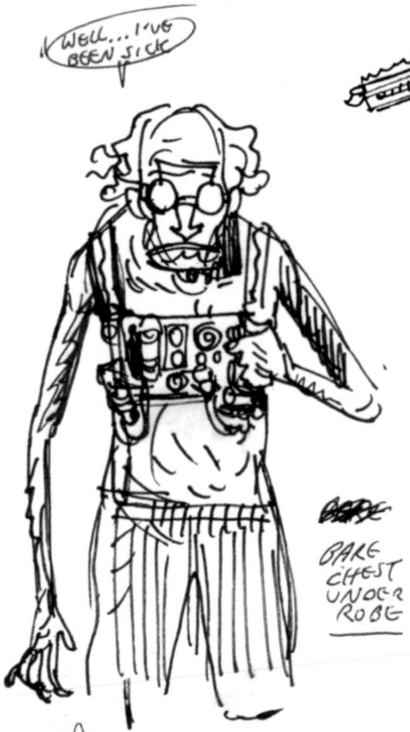
WELL... I'VE BEEN SICK
BARE CHEST UNDER ROBE

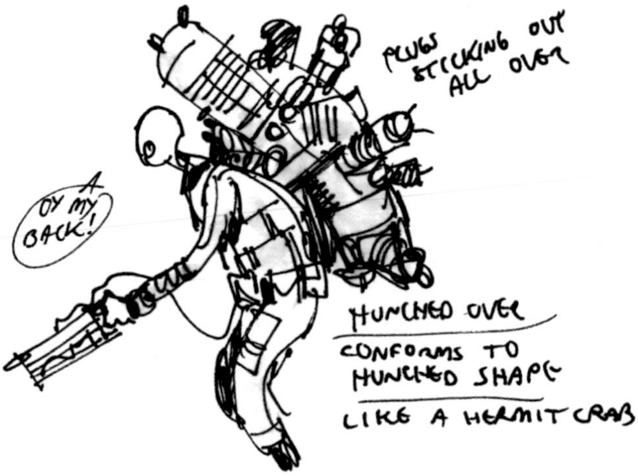
PLUGS STICKING OUT ALL OVER
OY MY BACK!
HUNCHED OVER
CONFORMS TO HUNCHED SHAPE
LIKE A HERMIT CRAB

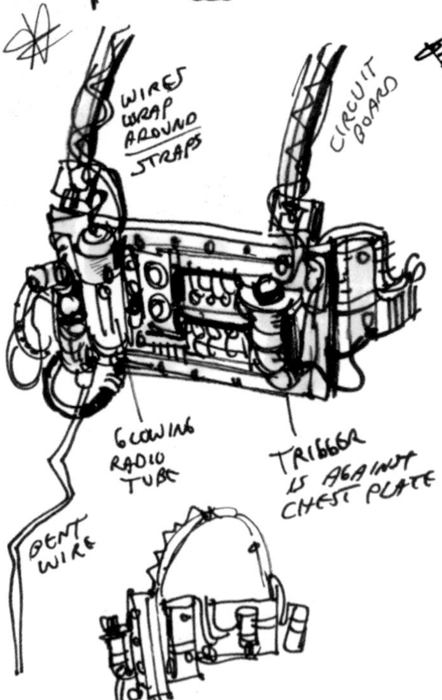
WIRES WRAP AROUND STRAPS
CIRCUIT BOARD
GLOWING RADIO TUBE
TRIGGER IS AGAINST CHEST PLATE
BENT WIRE

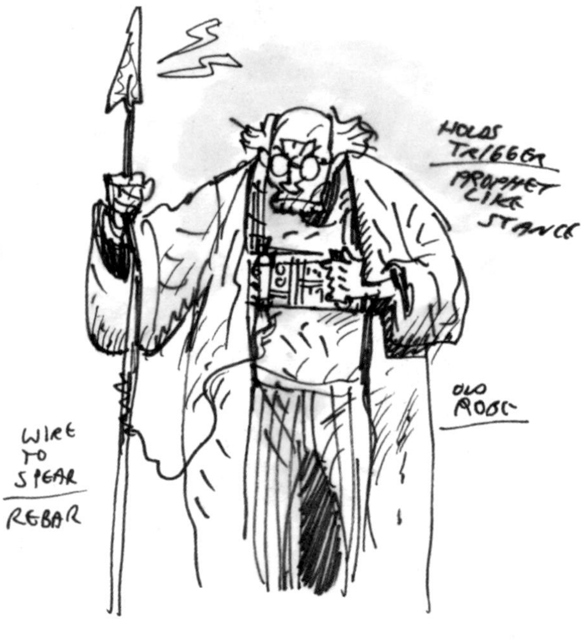
HOLDS TRIGGER
PROPHET LIKE STANCE
OLD ROBE
WIRE TO SPEAR
REBAR

Gunter's more stylish and less cumbersome power pack unfortunately made it look like he was wearing a sports bra.

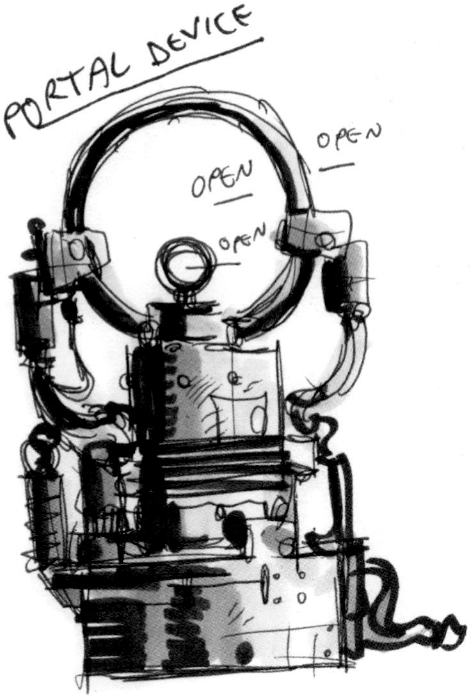
PORTAL DEVICE
OPEN
OPEN
OPEN

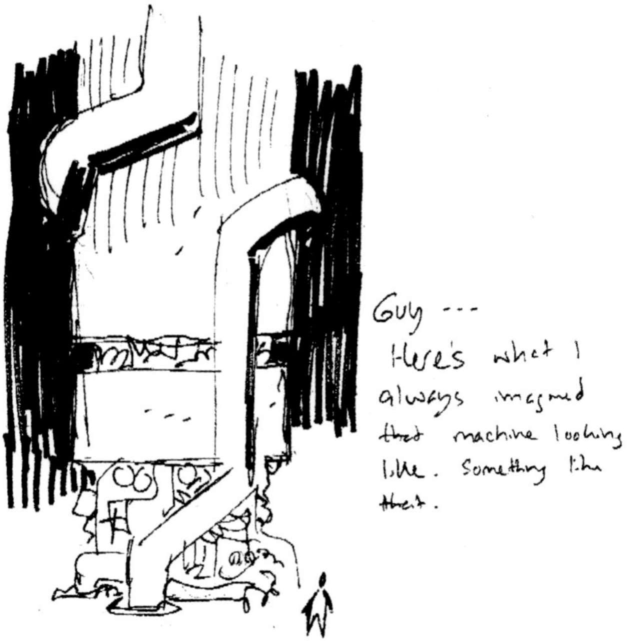
Guy ---
Here's what I always imagined that machine looking like. Something like that.

Above, the first design of the portal machine was too close in design to the "hellhole generator" from the *Hellboy* movie. Upper right is Mike's sketch of a blast-furnace-type design that I redrew into the final version, below.

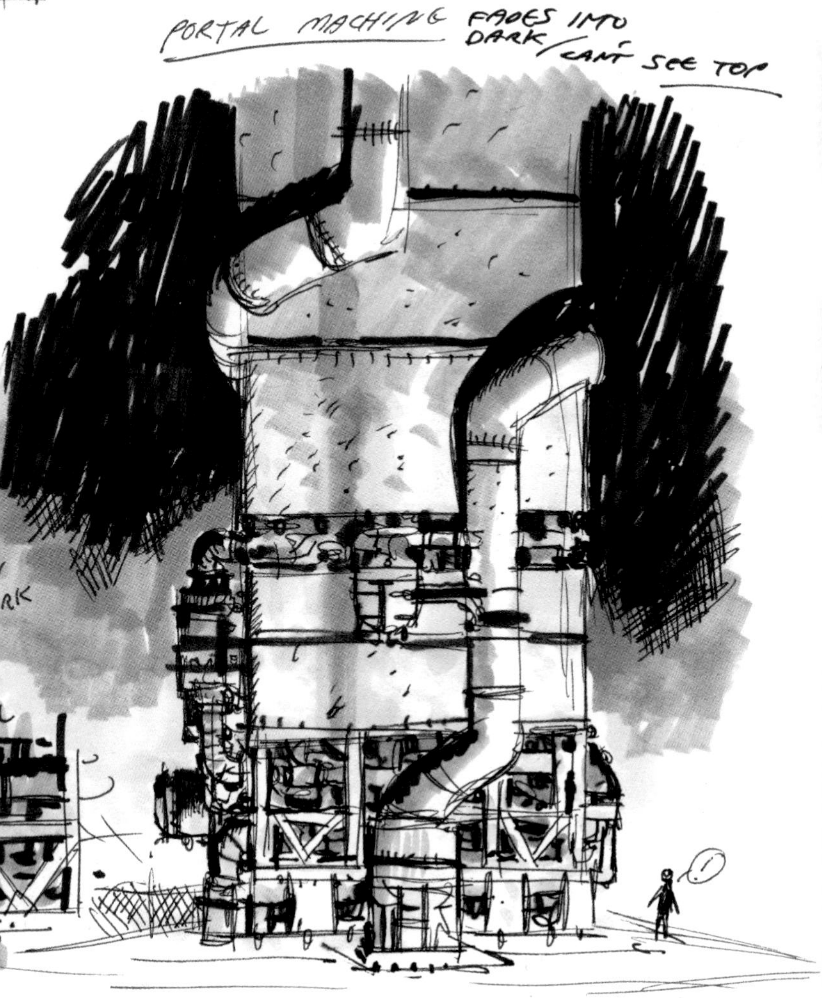
PORTAL MACHINE FADES INTO DARK / CAN'T SEE TOP
!

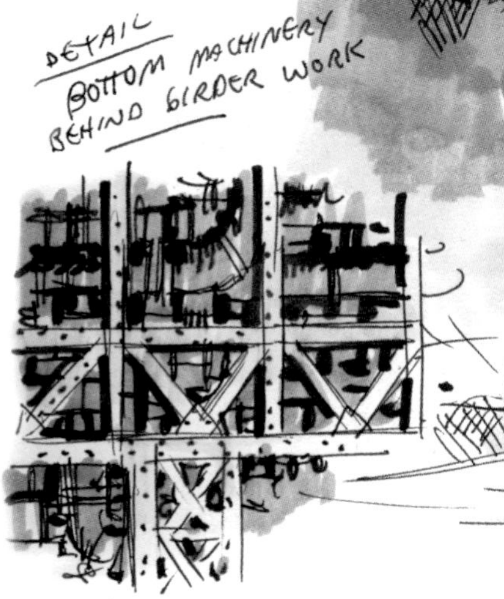
DETAIL
BOTTOM MACHINERY BEHIND GIRDER WORK

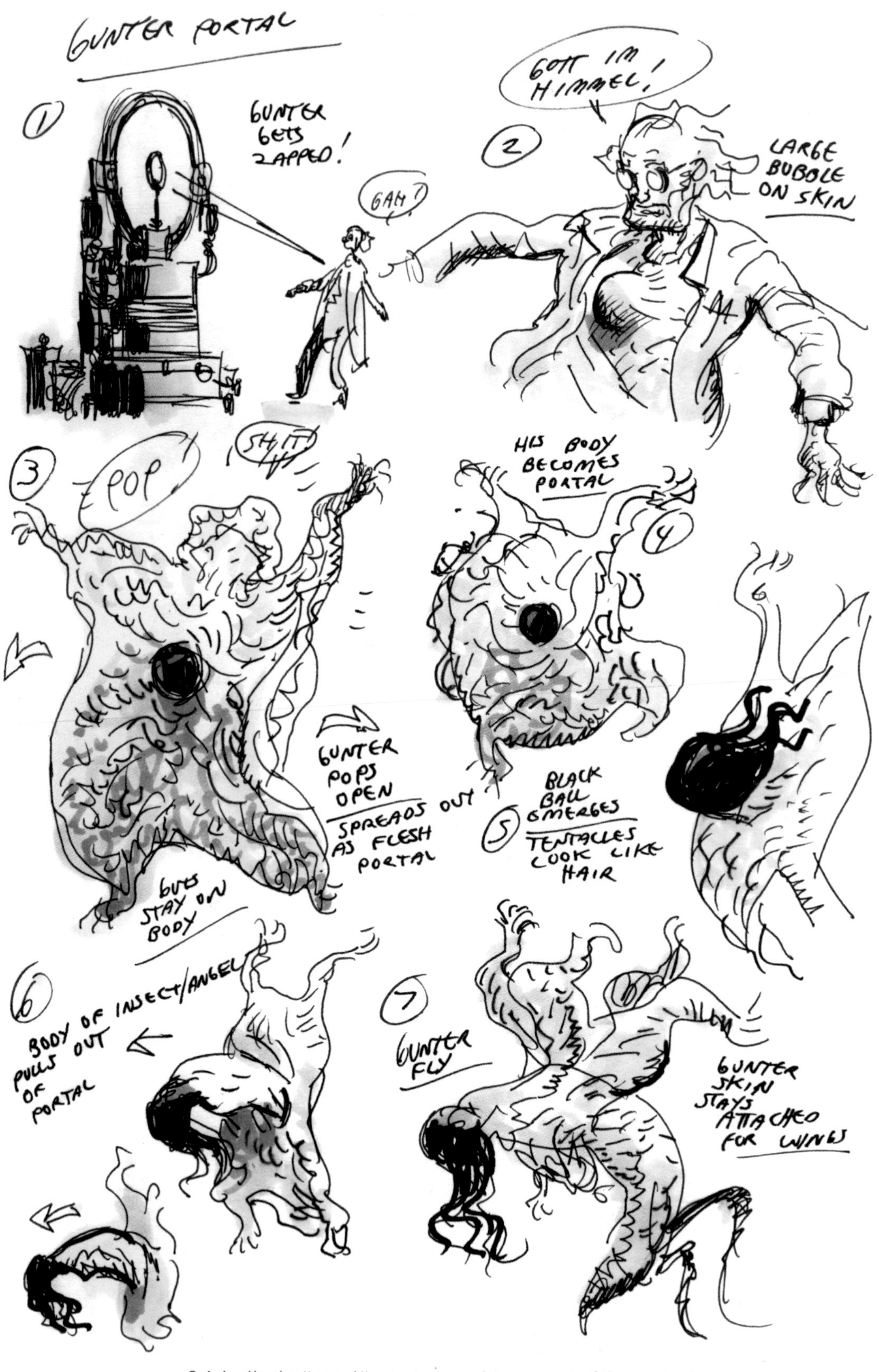
GUNTER PORTAL
1
GUNTER GETS ZAPPED!
GAH!
GOTT IM HIMMEL!
2
LARGE BUBBLE ON SKIN
3
POP!
SHIT!
HIS BODY BECOMES PORTAL
4
GUNTER POPS OPEN
SPREADS OUT AS FLESH PORTAL
BLACK BALL EMERGES
5
TENTACLES LOOK LIKE HAIR
GUTS STAY ON BODY
6
BODY OF INSECT/ANGEL PULLS OUT OF PORTAL
7
GUNTER FLY
GUNTER SKIN STAYS ATTACHED FOR WINGS

Originally the "angel" was supposed to pop out of Gunter's chest, making him the portal—but I wanted to have him be part of the monster, with his body opening up to a skinned sheet that would form the angel's wings as a nice, horrific transformation.

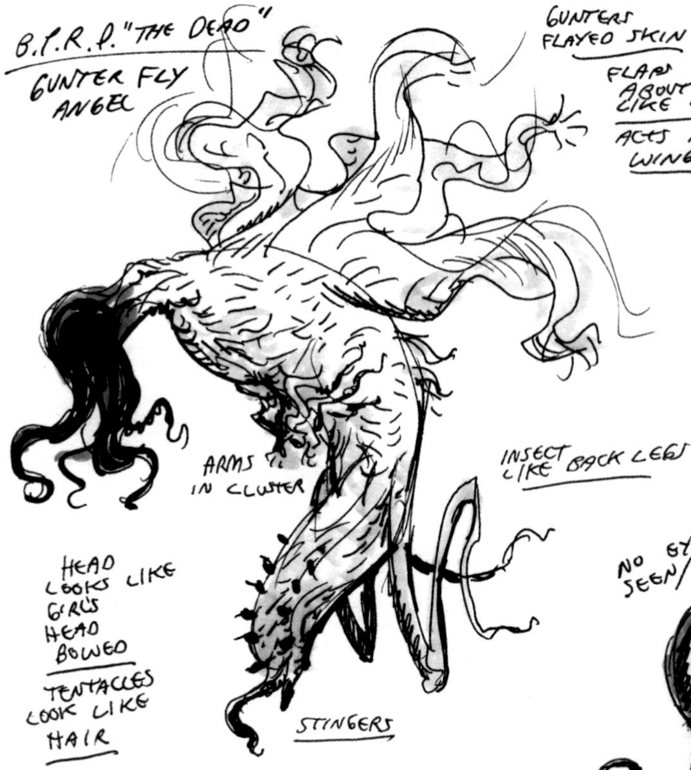
B.P.R.D. "THE DEAD"
GUNTER FLY ANGEL
GUNTERS FLAYED SKIN
FLAPS ABOUT LIKE CLOTH
ACTS AS WINGS
ARMS IN CLUSTER
INSECT LIKE BACK LEGS
HEAD LOOKS LIKE GIRL'S HEAD BOWED
TENTACLES LOOK LIKE HAIR
STINGERS

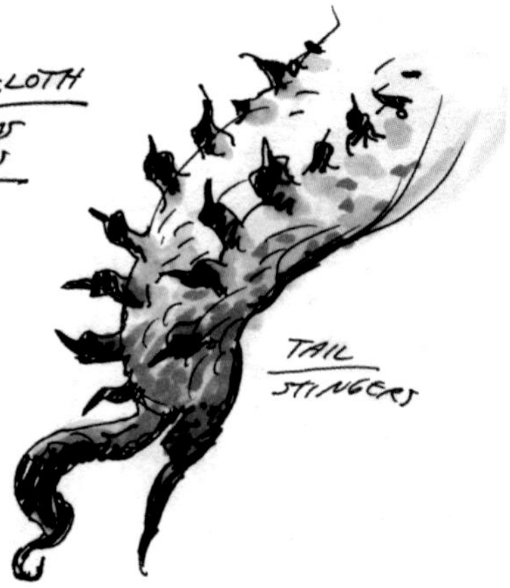
TAIL STINGERS

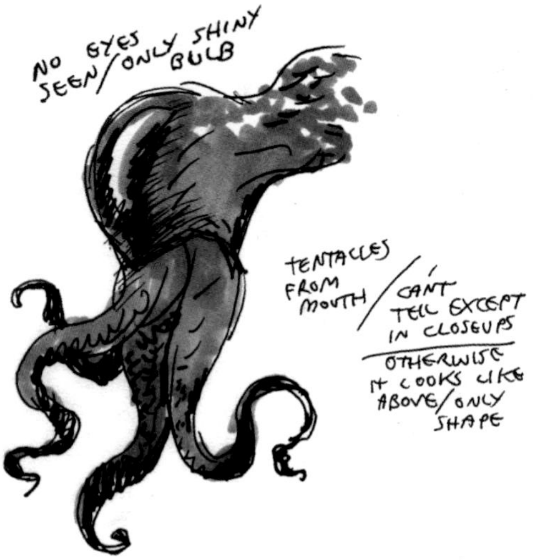
NO EYES SEEN/ONLY SHINY BULB
TENTACLES FROM MOUTH/CAN'T TELL EXCEPT IN CLOSEUPS
OTHERWISE IT LOOKS LIKE ABOVE/ONLY SHAPE

The angel was the design in this series that went through the most reworking—while the basic body shape remained the same, the head went through a lot of redesigns. Originally it was a black mass of tentacles, but that was considered too close in feel to the design for Abe's wife, with her matted, black hair.

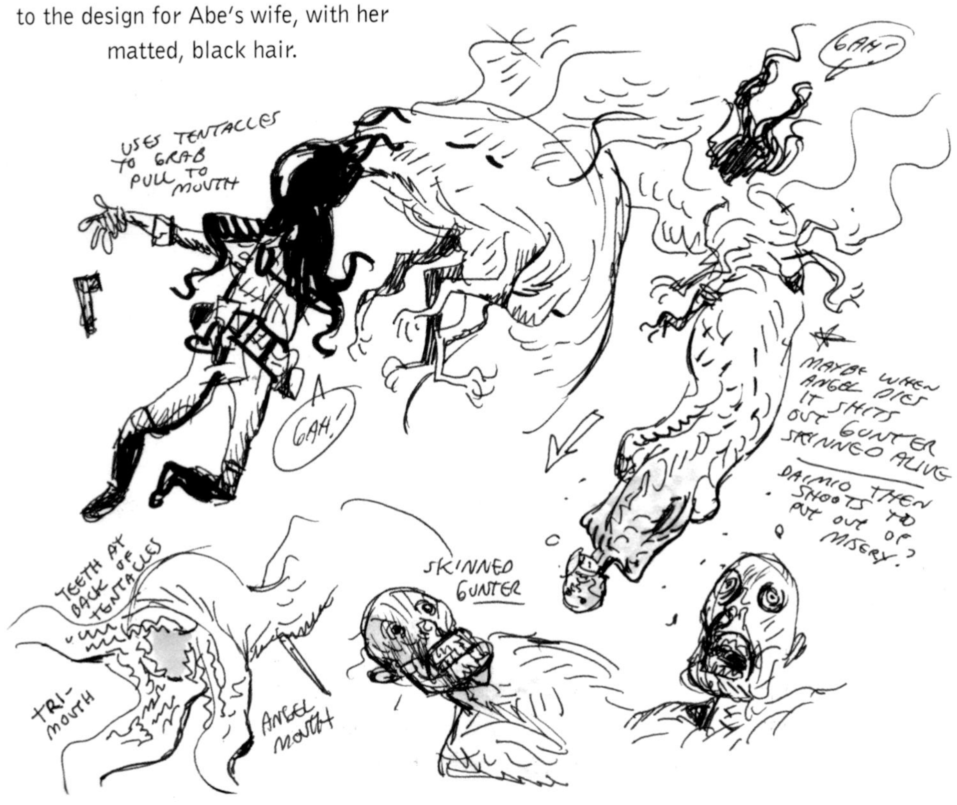
GAH!
USES TENTACLES TO GRAB PULL TO MOUTH
GAH!
MAYBE WHEN ANGEL DIES IT SHITS OUT GUNTER SKINNED ALIVE
DAIMIO THEN SHOOTS TO PUT OUT OF MISERY?
TEETH AT BACK OF TENTACLES
TRI-MOUTH
ANGEL MOUTH
SKINNED GUNTER

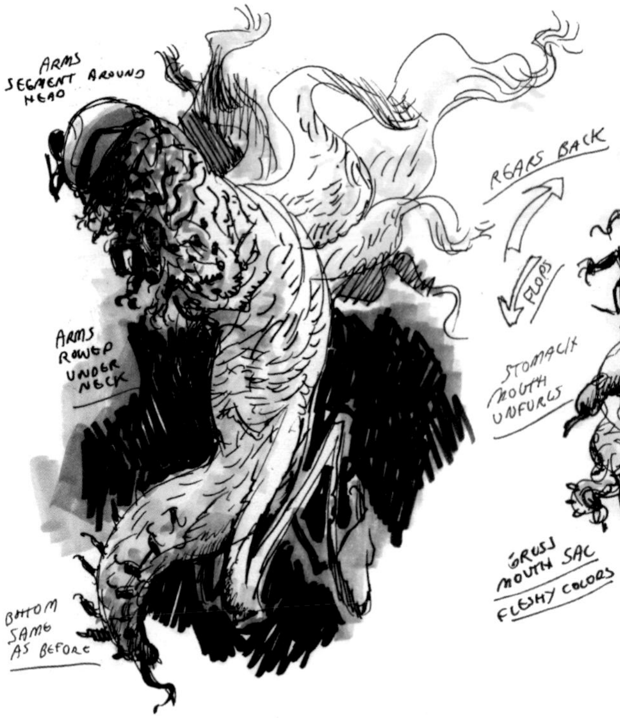
ARMS SEGMENT AROUND HEAD
ARMS ROWED UNDER NECK
BOTTOM SAME AS BEFORE
REARS BACK
FLOPS
STOMACH MOUTH UNFURLS

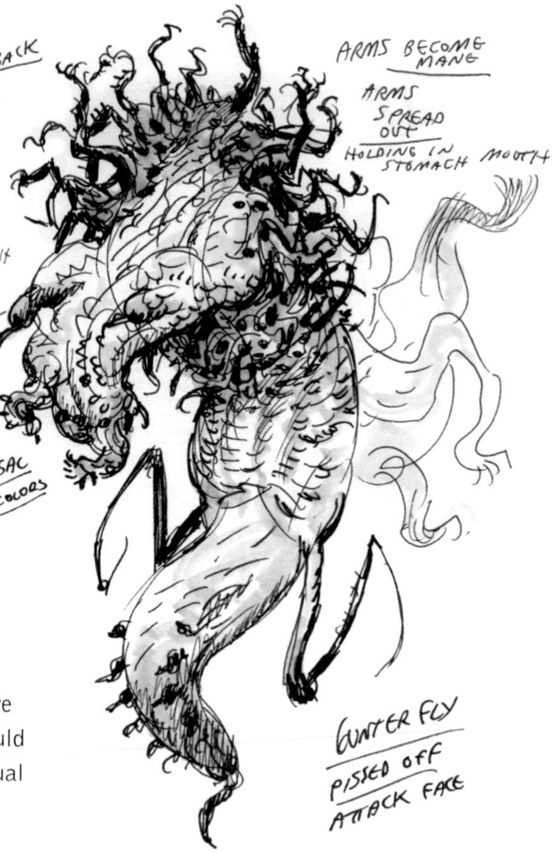
ARMS BECOME MANE
ARMS SPREAD OUT
HOLDING IN STOMACH MOUTH
GROSS MOUTH SAC
FLESHY COLORS
COUNTER FLY
PISSED OFF
ATTACK FACE

The final direction for the angel's head was inspired by a "Heike crab," where the top of the head would be a shell that would resemble a stylized tribal face while the actual mouth and face would be hidden under the mass of arms.

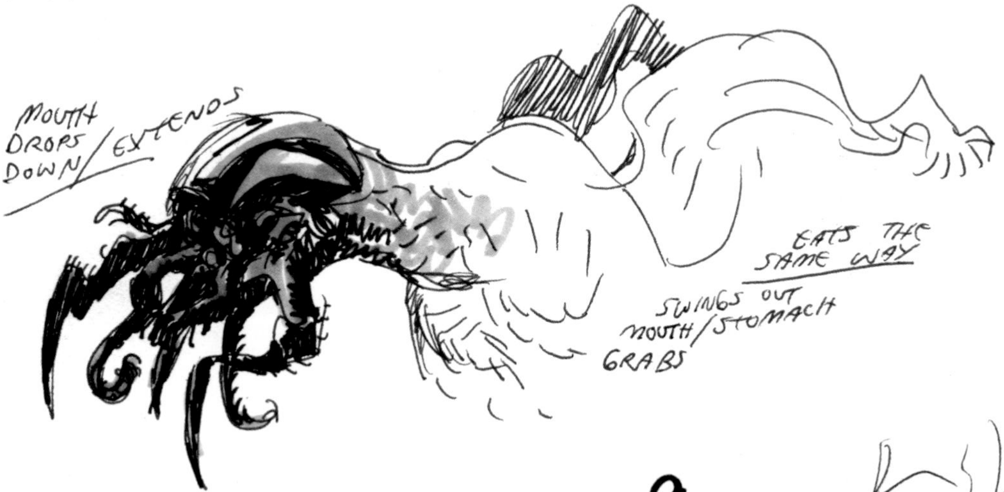
MOUTH DROPS DOWN/EXTENDS
EATS THE SAME WAY
SWINGS OUT MOUTH/STOMACH
GRABS

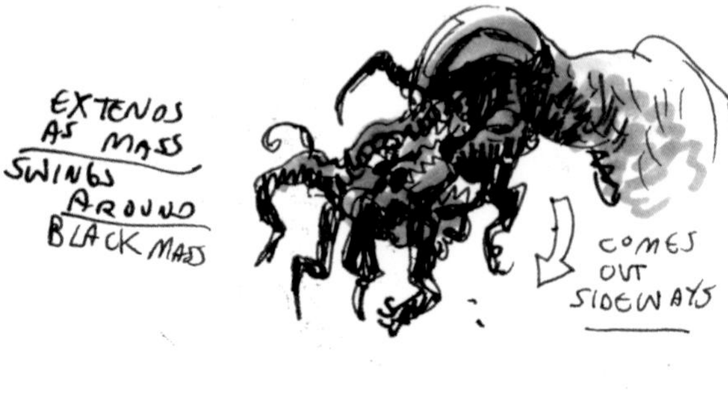
EXTENDS AS MASS
SWINGS AROUND
BLACK MASS
COMES OUT SIDEWAYS

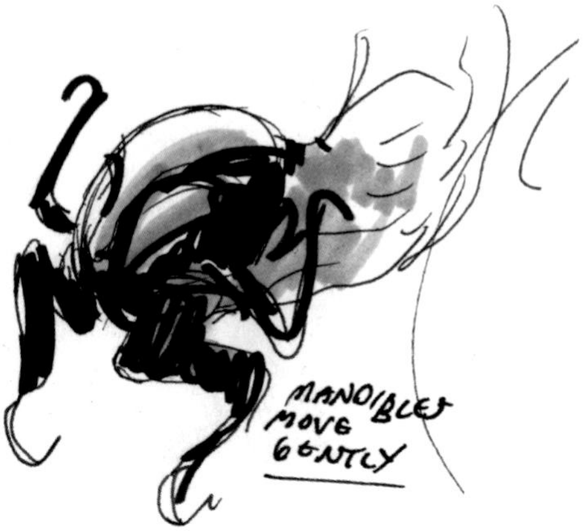
MANDIBLES MOVE GENTLY

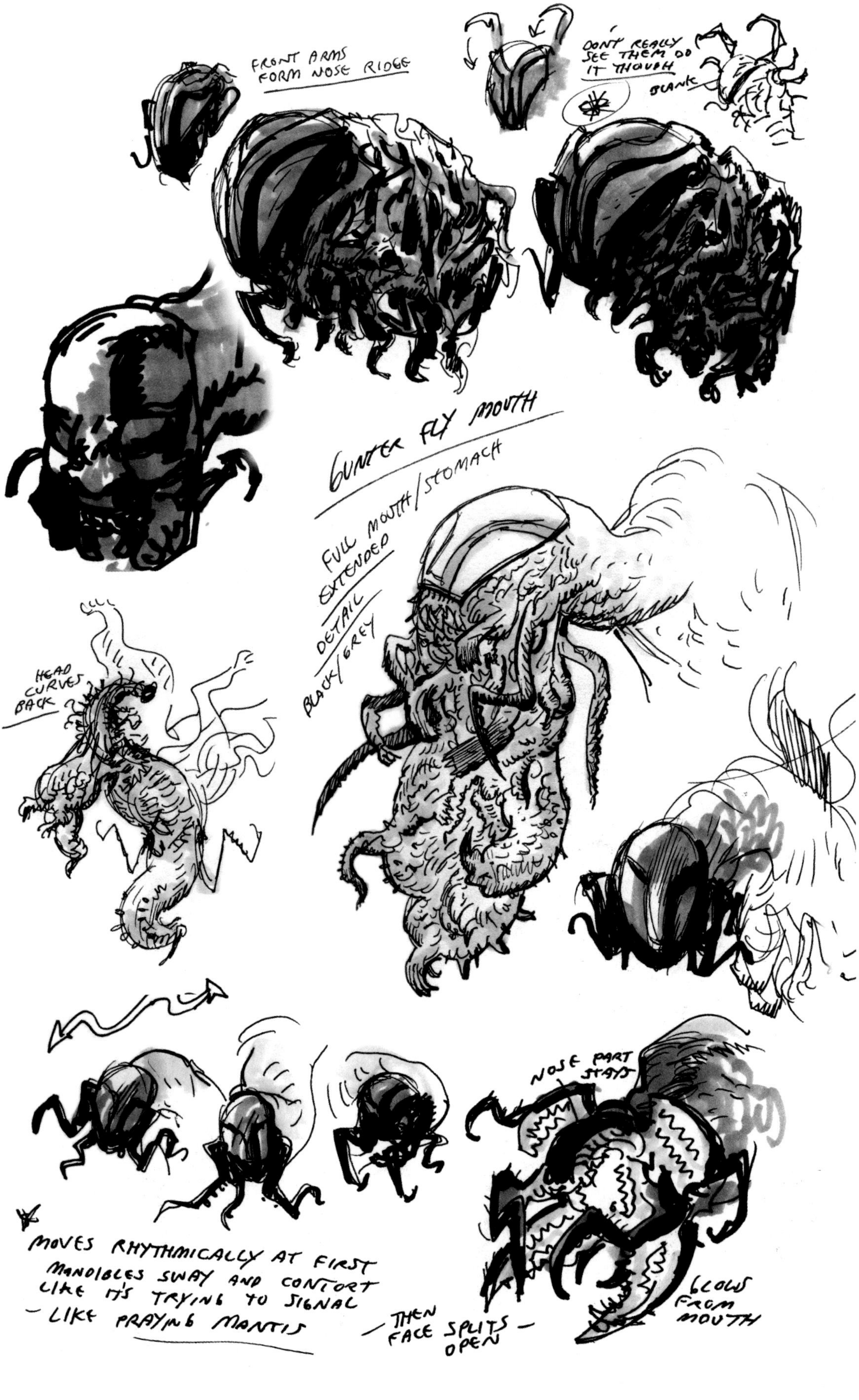
FRONT ARMS FORM NOSE RIDGE
DON'T REALLY SEE THEM DO IT THOUGH
BLANK
GUNNER FLY MOUTH
FULL MOUTH/STOMACH EXTENDED
DETAIL
BLACK/GREY
HEAD CURVES BACK
NOSE PART STAYS
MOVES RHYTHMICALLY AT FIRST
MANDIBLES SWAY AND CONTORT
LIKE IT'S TRYING TO SIGNAL
- LIKE PRAYING MANTIS
- THEN FACE SPLITS OPEN -
GLOWS FROM MOUTH

One of the best parts of *The Dead* was getting to design all the weird old villains for the folder Johann found. John Arcudi called one afternoon, and we went back and forth on some names and ideas for the characters. Even though you only get a glimpse of them in the comic, we wanted to flesh them out as much as possible beforehand.

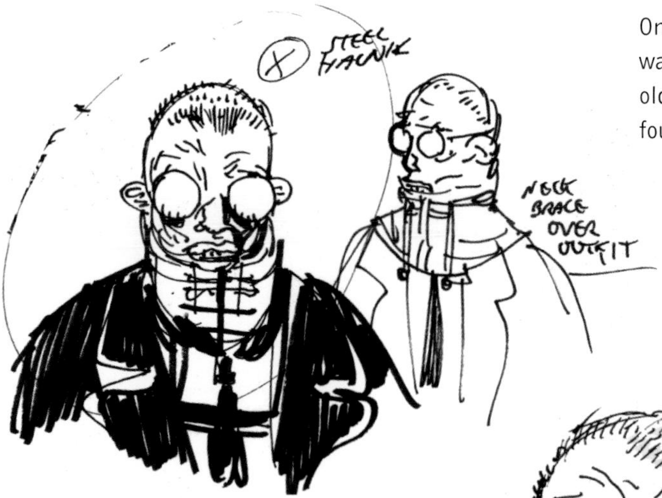

STEEL HAWK
NECK BRACE OVER OUTFIT

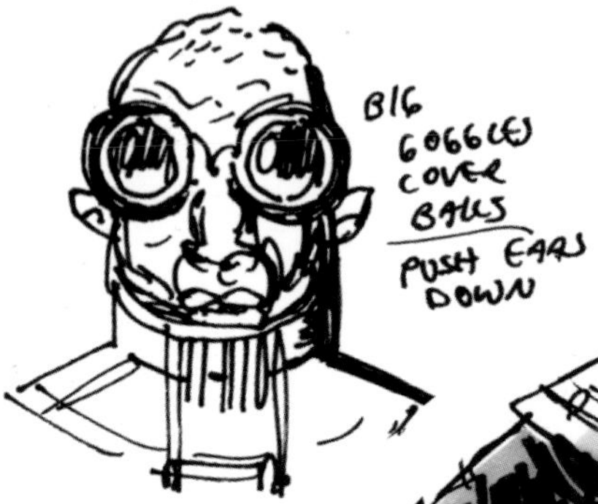

BIG GOGGLES COVER BALLS
PUSH EARS DOWN

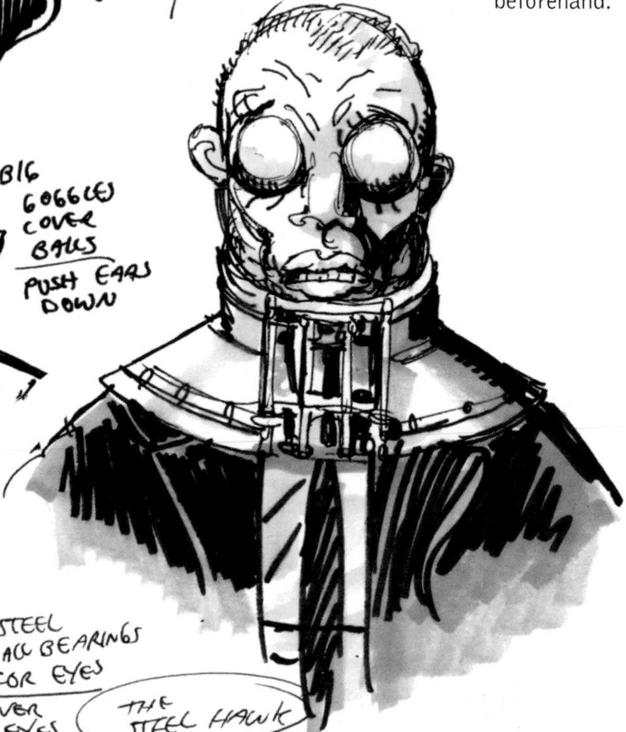

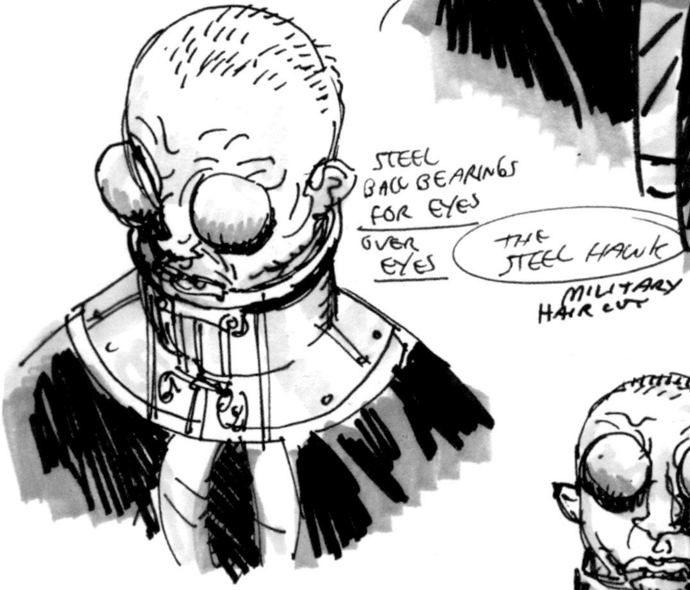

STEEL BALL BEARINGS FOR EYES
OVER EYES
THE STEEL HAWK
MILITARY HAIR CUT

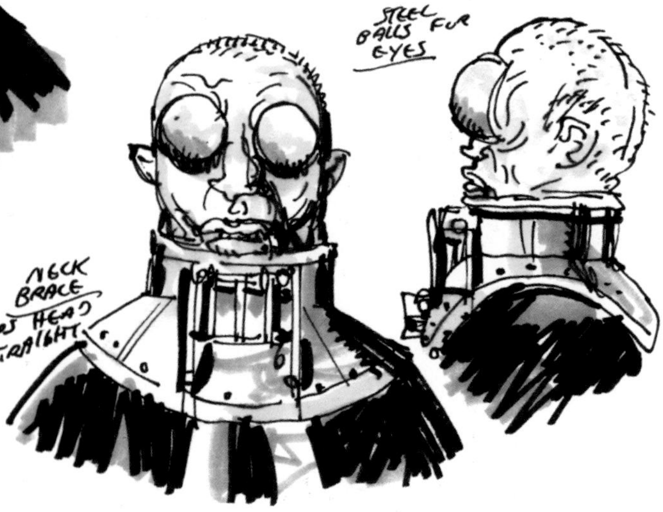

STEEL BALLS FOR EYES
NECK BRACE
KEEPS HEAD UP/STRAIGHT

First up was one of my favorites to design, the Steel Hawk! The neck brace was an homage to one of my favorite Peter Lorre films, *Mad Love*.

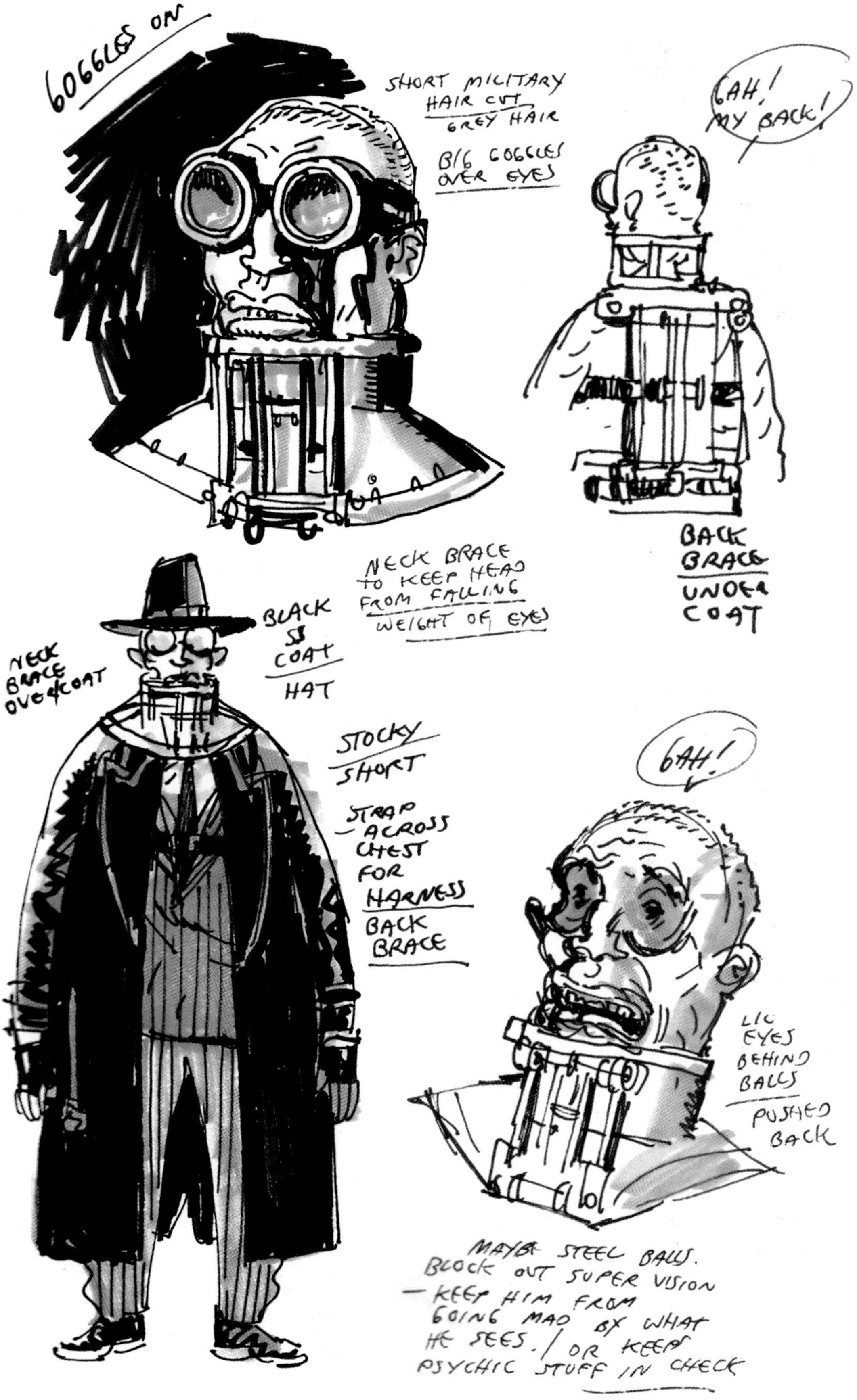
GOGGLES ON
SHORT MILITARY HAIR CUT
GREY HAIR
BIG GOGGLES OVER EYES
GAH! MY BACK!
BACK BRACE
UNDER COAT
NECK BRACE TO KEEP HEAD FROM FALLING
WEIGHT OF EYES
BLACK SS COAT
HAT
NECK BRACE OVERCOAT
STOCKY
SHORT
STRAP ACROSS CHEST FOR HARNESS
BACK BRACE
GAH!
EYES BEHIND BALLS
PUSHED BACK
MAYBE STEEL BALLS. BLOCK OUT SUPER VISION
— KEEP HIM FROM GOING MAD BY WHAT HE SEES. / OR KEEP PSYCHIC STUFF IN CHECK

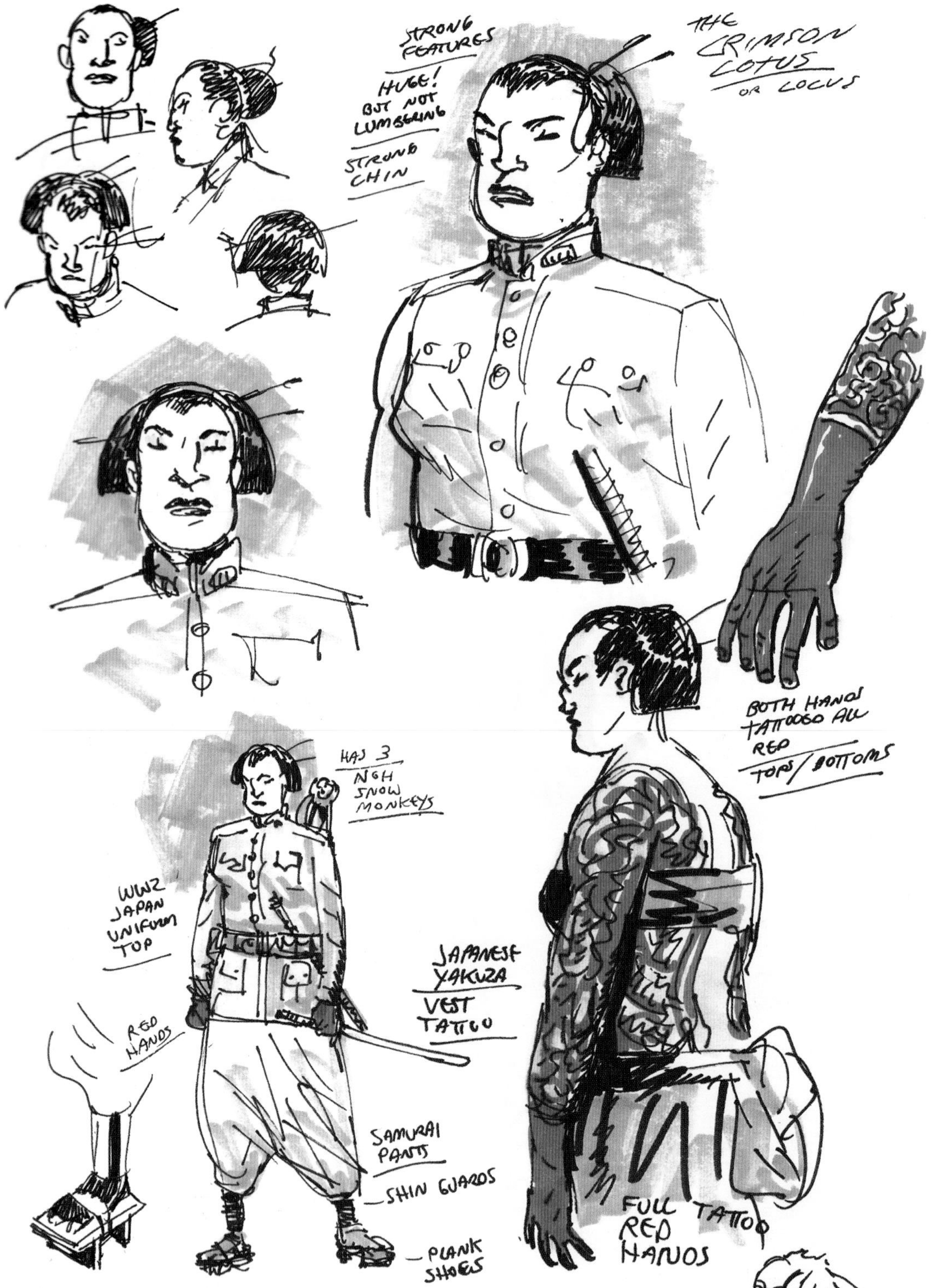
STRONG FEATURES
HUGE! BUT NOT LUMBERING
STRONG CHIN
THE CRIMSON LOTUS OR LOCUS
BOTH HANDS TATTOOED ALL RED TOPS/BOTTOMS
HAS 3 NOH SNOW MONKEYS
WW2 JAPAN UNIFORM TOP
RED HANDS
JAPANESE YAKUZA
VEST TATTOO
SAMURAI PANTS
SHIN GUARDS
PLANK SHOES
FULL TATTOO RED HANDS

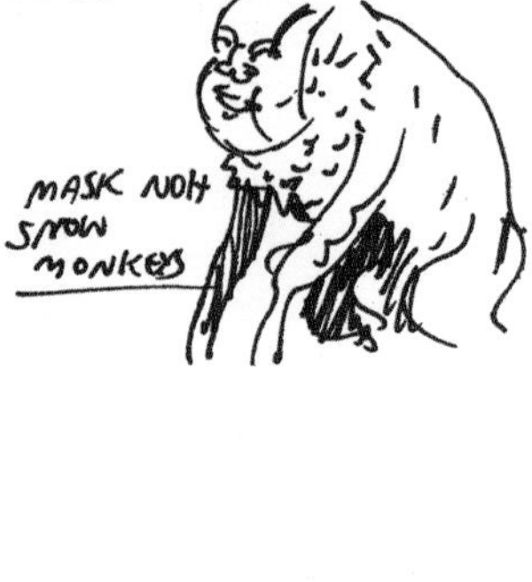
MASK NOH SNOW MONKEYS

For the first time you can see how the Crimson Lotus got her name—it's because of the red-tattooed hands. John talked about having gorillas as her henchmen. But I liked the idea of smaller snow monkeys with Noh-mask faces. Opposite: Some ideas for the Noh monkeys—I'm sure we haven't seen the end of these pests!

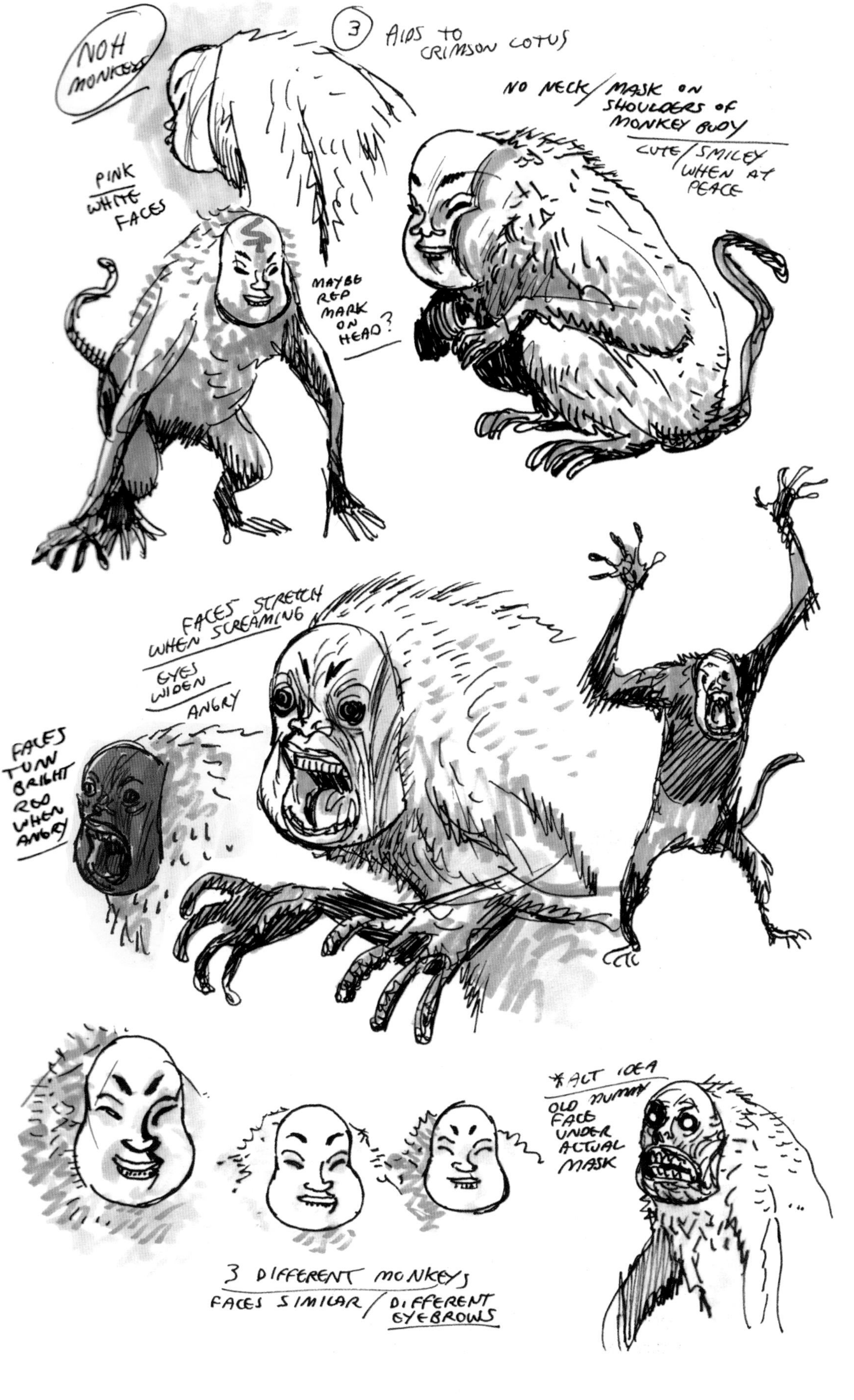
NOH MONKEYS
3 AIDS TO CRIMSON LOTUS
NO NECK / MASK ON SHOULDERS OF MONKEY BODY
CUTE / SMILEY WHEN AT PEACE
PINK / WHITE FACES
MAYBE RED MARK ON HEAD?
FACES STRETCH WHEN SCREAMING
EYES WIDEN
ANGRY
FACES TURN BRIGHT RED WHEN ANGRY
*ALT IDEA
OLD MUMMY FACE UNDER ACTUAL MASK
3 DIFFERENT MONKEYS
FACES SIMILAR / DIFFERENT EYEBROWS

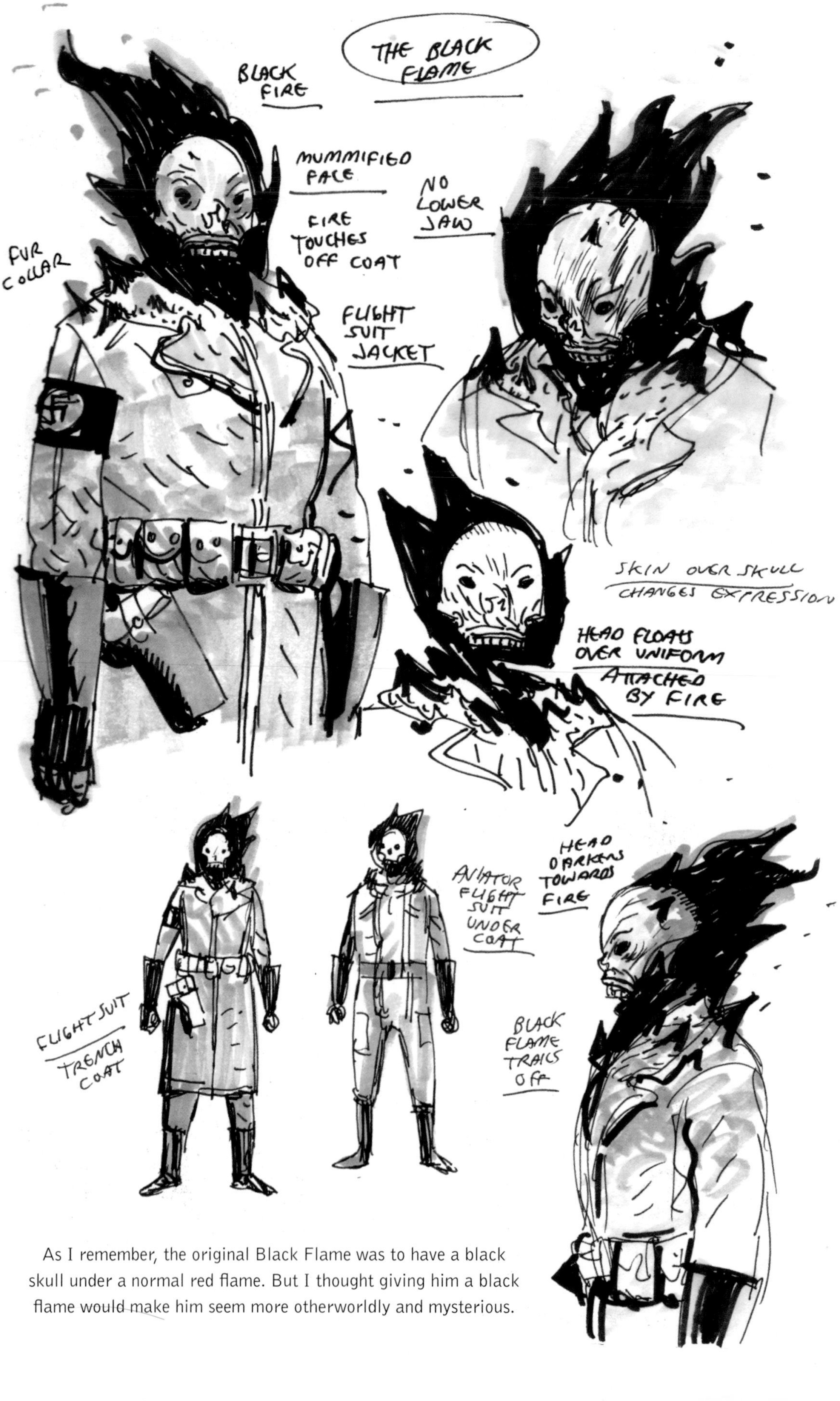
THE BLACK FLAME
BLACK FIRE
MUMMIFIED FACE
NO LOWER JAW
FIRE TOUCHES OFF COAT
FUR COLLAR
FLIGHT SUIT JACKET
SKIN OVER SKULL
CHANGES EXPRESSION
HEAD FLOATS OVER UNIFORM
ATTACHED BY FIRE
HEAD DARKENS TOWARDS FIRE
AVIATOR FLIGHT SUIT UNDER COAT
FLIGHT SUIT
TRENCH COAT
BLACK FLAME TRAILS OFF

As I remember, the original Black Flame was to have a black skull under a normal red flame. But I thought giving him a black flame would make him seem more otherworldly and mysterious.

You only get a glimpse of the original Black Flame's plane, *The Iron Bat,* in the offices of Zinco. For a while we were thinking the Black Flame might be like a gremlin (as seen in the folder) and wouldn't need a flying machine—but I couldn't pass up the chance to design his 1940s-style transport.

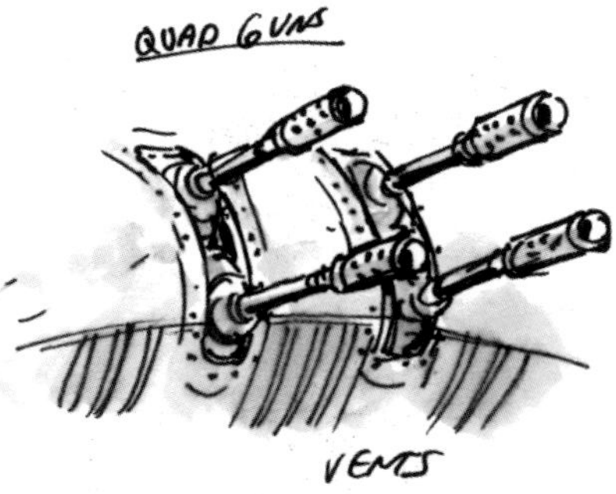
QUAD GUNS
VENTS

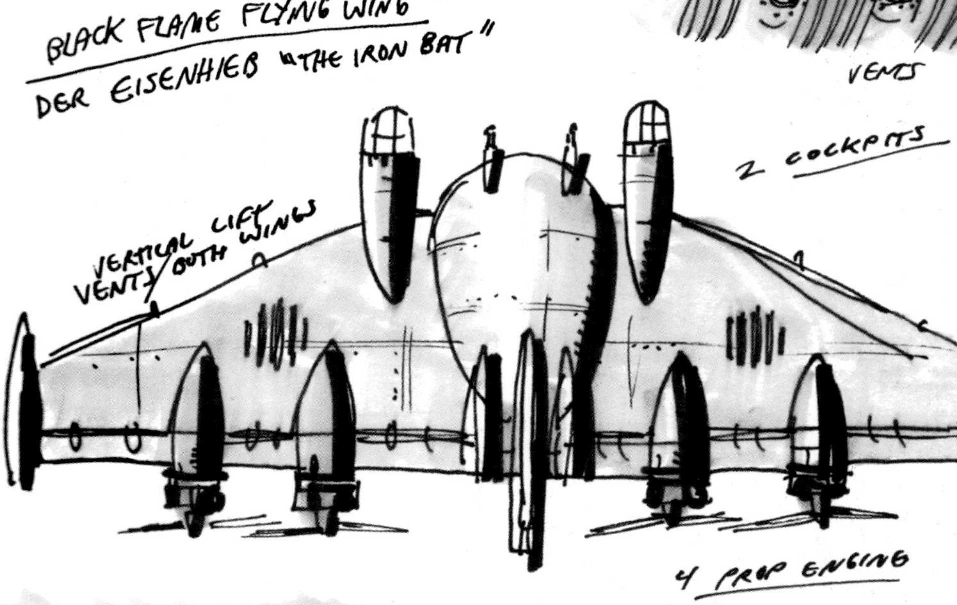
BLACK FLAME FLYING WING
DER EISENHIEB "THE IRON BAT"
2 COCKPITS
VERTICAL LIFT VENTS/BOTH WINGS
4 PROP ENGINE

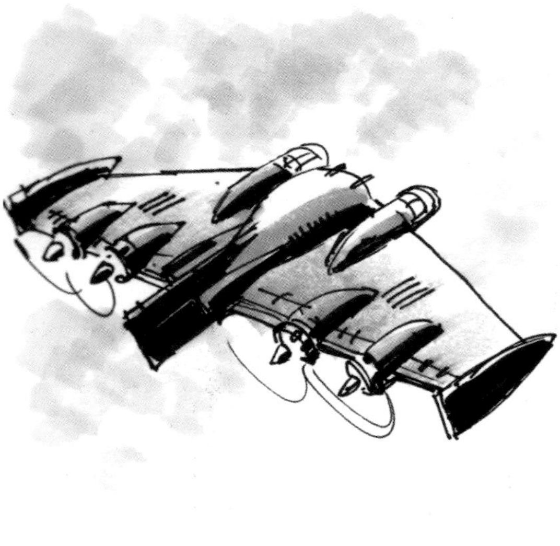

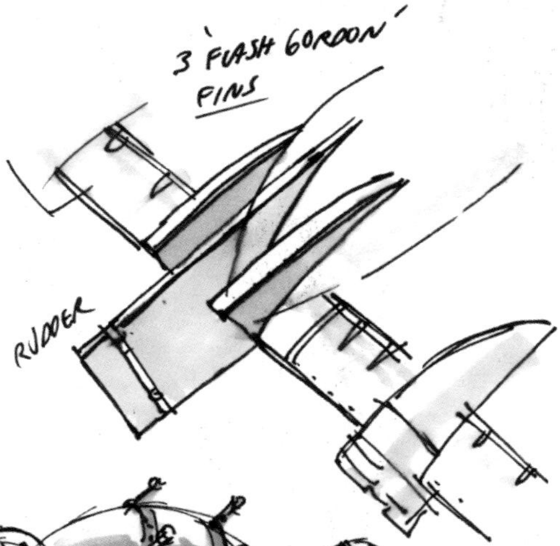
3 'FLASH GORDON' FINS
RUDDER

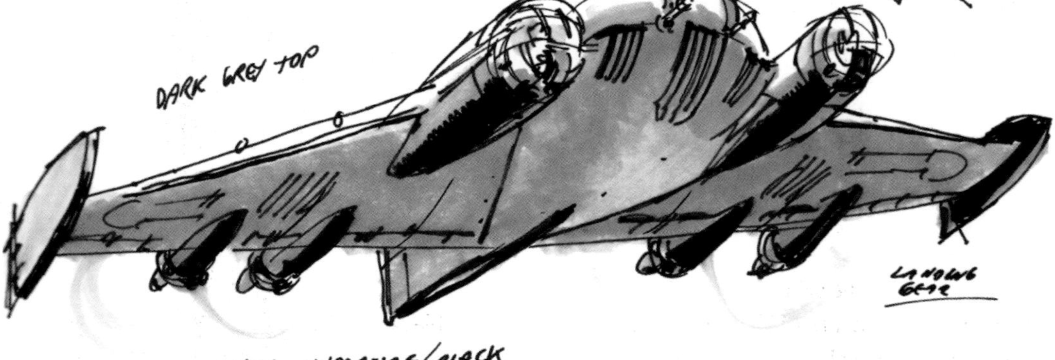
DARK GREY TOP
LANDING GEAR
DARKER UNDERSIDE/BLACK

Kalski was based on one of John's favorite sculptors, Stanislav Szukalski. At first we were designing him as a homunculus—like Roger, except evil.

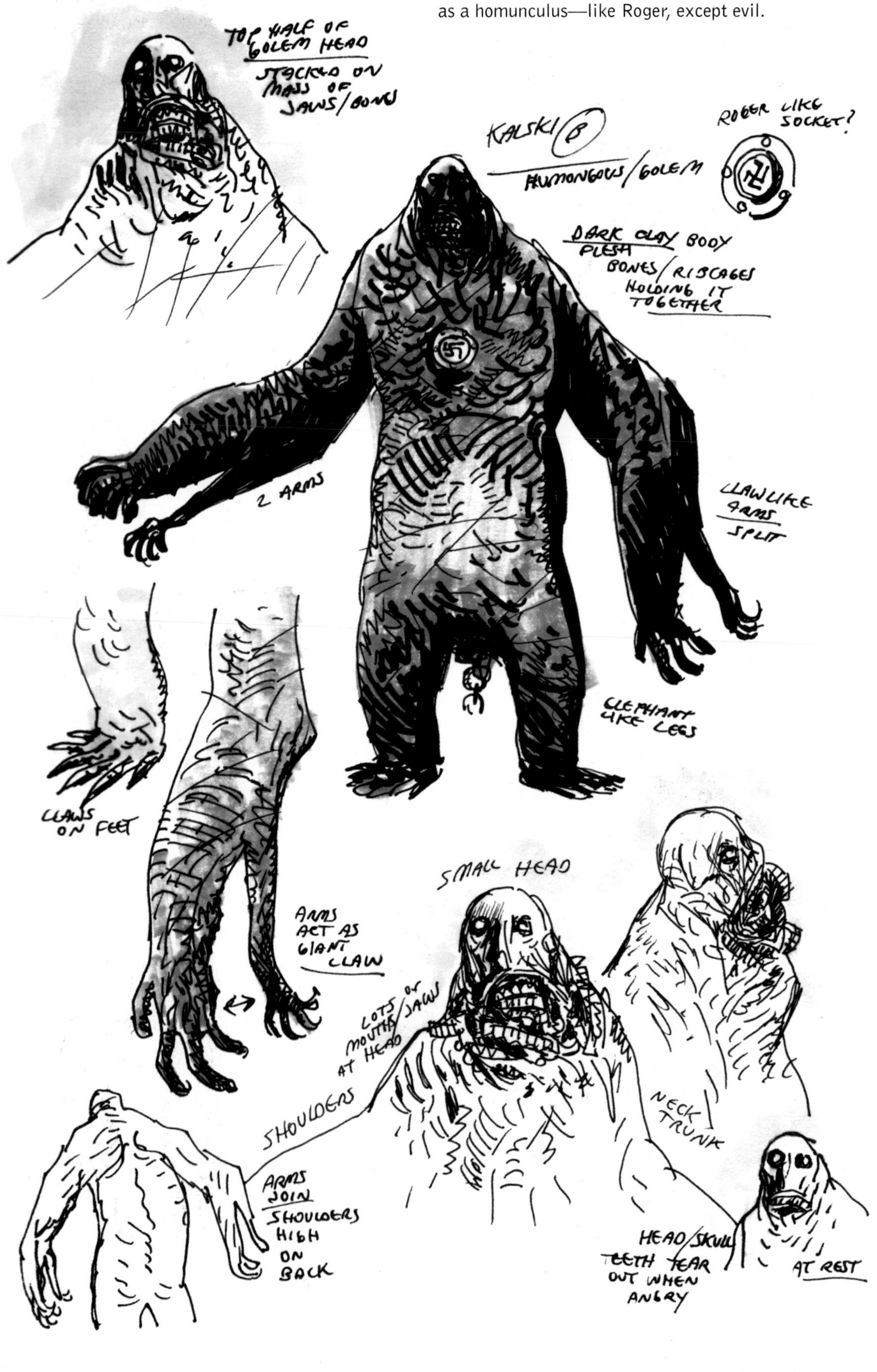

TOP HALF OF GOLEM HEAD
STACKED ON MASS OF JAWS/BONES
KALSKI B
HUMONGOUS/GOLEM
ROGER LIKE SOCKET?
DARK CLAY BODY FLESH
BONES/RIBCAGES HOLDING IT TOGETHER
2 ARMS
CLAWLIKE ARMS
SPLIT
ELEPHANT LIKE LEGS
CLAWS ON FEET
SMALL HEAD
ARMS ACT AS GIANT CLAW
LOTS OF MOUTHS/JAWS AT HEAD
SHOULDERS
NECK TRUNK
ARMS JOIN
SHOULDERS HIGH ON BACK
HEAD/SKULL
TEETH TEAR OUT WHEN ANGRY
AT REST

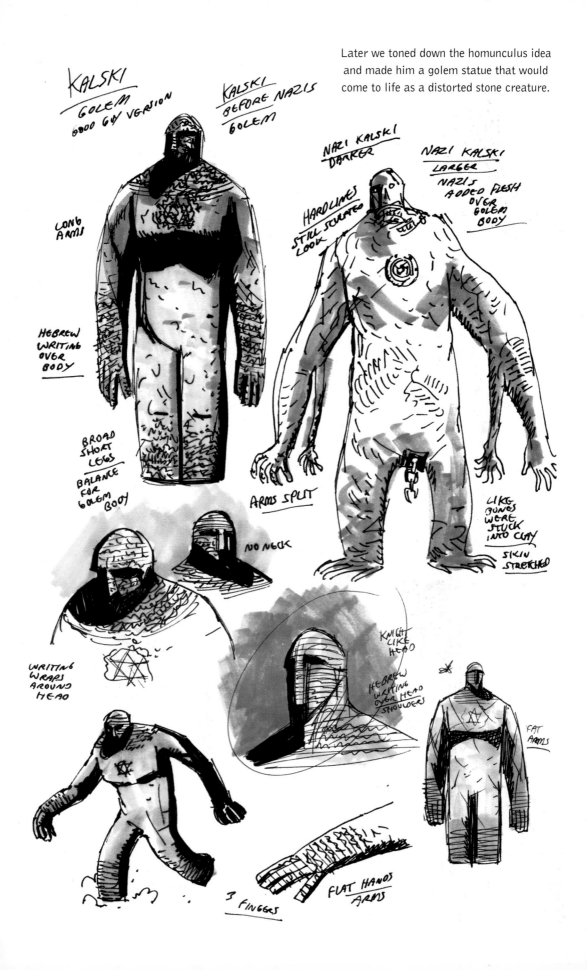

Later we toned down the homunculus idea and made him a golem statue that would come to life as a distorted stone creature.

KALSKI
GOLEM GOOD GUY VERSION

KALSKI
BEFORE NAZIS
GOLEM

LONG ARMS

HEBREW WRITING OVER BODY

BROAD SHORT LEGS
BALANCE FOR GOLEM BODY

NAZI KALSKI
DARKER

HARDLINES
STILL SCULPTED
LOOK

NAZI KALSKI
LARGER
NAZIS ADDED FLESH OVER GOLEM BODY

ARMS SPLIT

LIKE BONES WERE STUCK INTO CLAY

SKIN STRETCHED

NO NECK

WRITING WRAPS AROUND HEAD

KNIGHT LIKE HEAD

HEBREW WRITING OVER HEAD SHOULDERS

FAT ARMS

3 FINGERS

FLAT HANDS ARMS

THE BLACK FLAME

SKETCHBOOK

Notes by Guy Davis

During work on the *B.P.R.D.: The Dead* story line, Mike and John had already told me what was in store for the upcoming *The Black Flame*, so designs were jump-started a little earlier for both the title character and Katha-Hem. The new Black Flame himself pretty much took final form from the beginning: below is the first sketch I did of him after talking to Mike about the idea of a Doctor Doom–styled villain in a blast-furnace suit and flaming skull mask. Opposite are a couple of drawings of the original Black Flame for Pope's office scene, and more designs refining the details of the power suit, with Mike himself designing the chest plate when he drew the cover to *The Black Flame* #3.

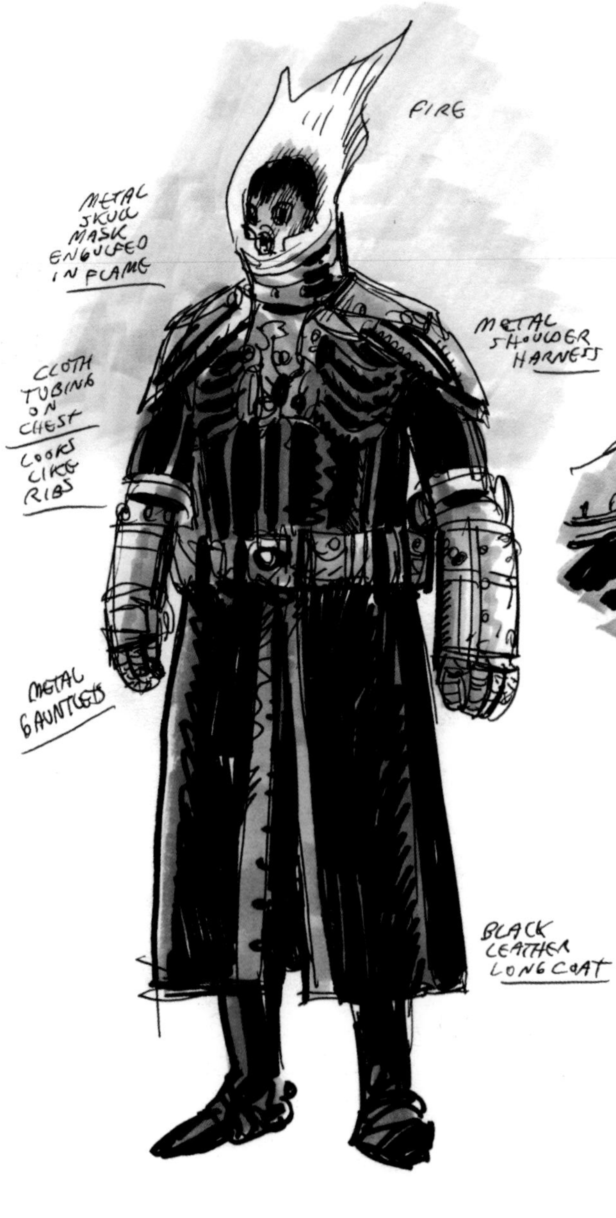
FIRE
METAL SKULL MASK ENGULFED IN FLAME
METAL SHOULDER HARNESS
CLOTH TUBING ON CHEST
LOOKS LIKE RIBS
METAL GAUNTLETS
BLACK LEATHER LONG COAT

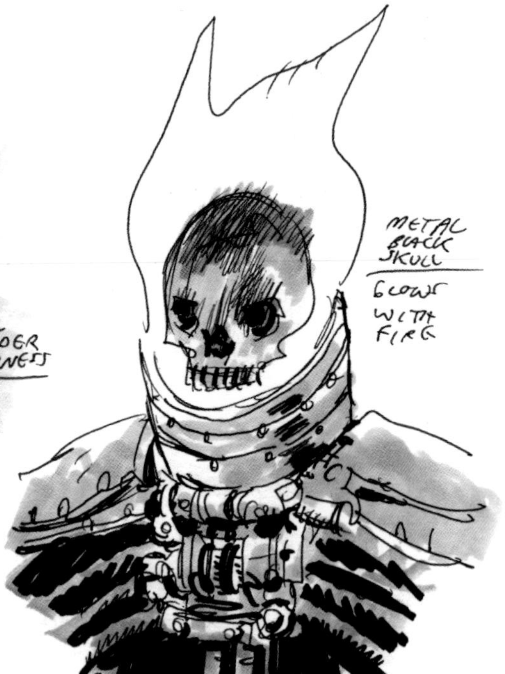
METAL BLACK SKULL
GLOWS WITH FIRE

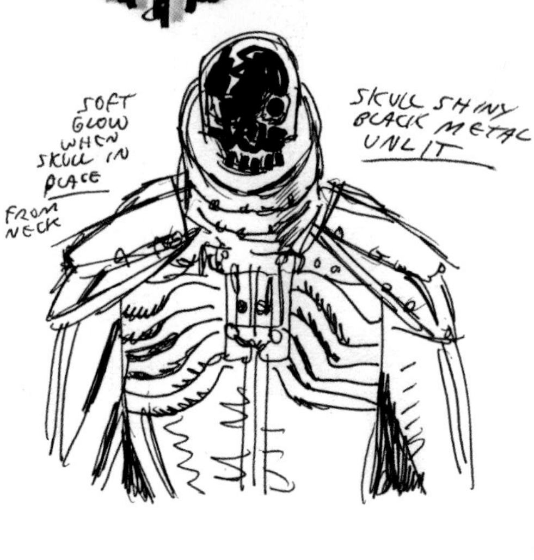
SOFT GLOW WHEN SKULL IN PLACE
FROM NECK
SKULL SHINY BLACK METAL UNLIT

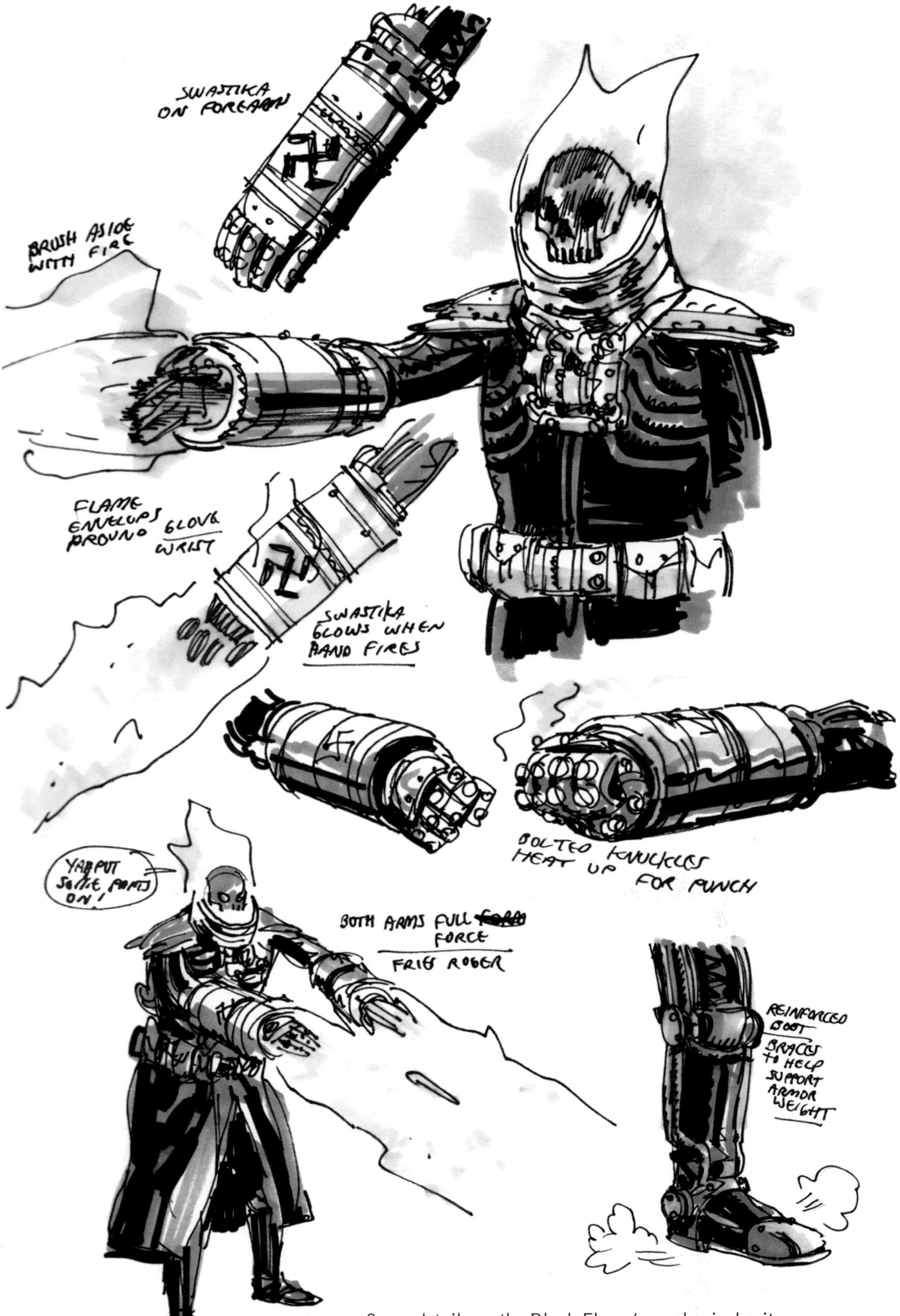
SWASTIKA ON FOREARM
BRUSH ASIDE WITH FIRE
FLAME ENVELOPS AROUND GLOVE WRIST
SWASTIKA GLOWS WHEN HAND FIRES
BOLTED KNUCKLES HEAT UP FOR PUNCH
YA PUT SOME PANTS ON!
BOTH ARMS FULL FORCE
REINFORCED BOOT
BRACES TO HELP SUPPORT ARMOR WEIGHT

Some details on the Black Flame's mechanical suit. Mike wanted to lose the swastika symbols to make it clear that Pope's infatuation with the character was occult in nature and not just the result of his Nazi ties.

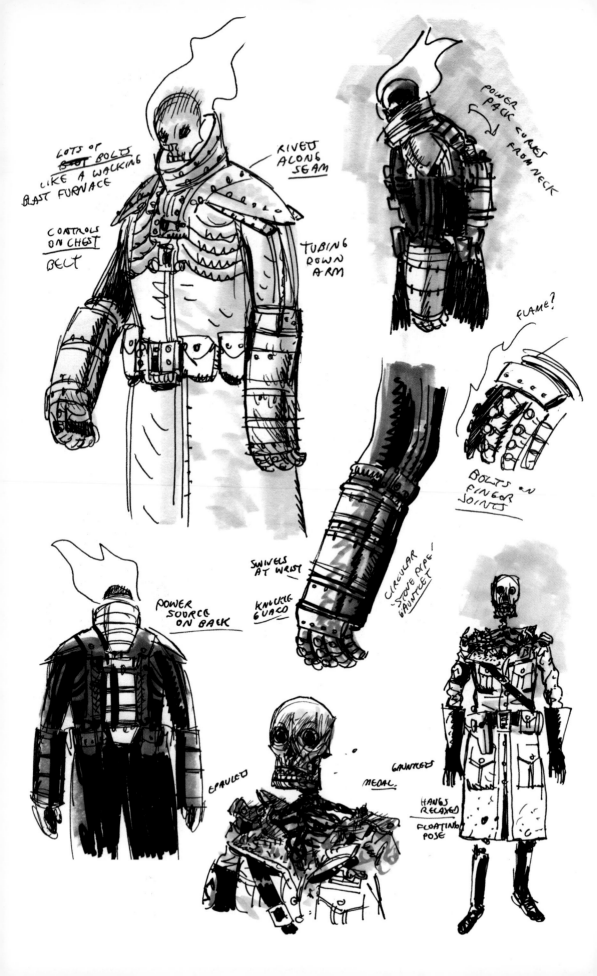

LOTS OF ~~BOLT BOLT~~ BOLTS
LIKE A WALKING
BLAST FURNACE

CONTROLS
ON CHEST
BELT

RIVET
ALONG
SEAM

TUBING
DOWN
ARM

POWER
PACK COMES
FROM NECK

FLAME?

BOLTS ON
FINGER
JOINTS

SWIVELS
AT WRIST

KNUCKLE
GUARD

POWER
SOURCE
ON BACK

CIRCULAR
'STOVE PIPE'
GAUNTLET

EPAULET

MEDAL

GAUNTLET

HANGS
RELAXED

FLOATING
POSE

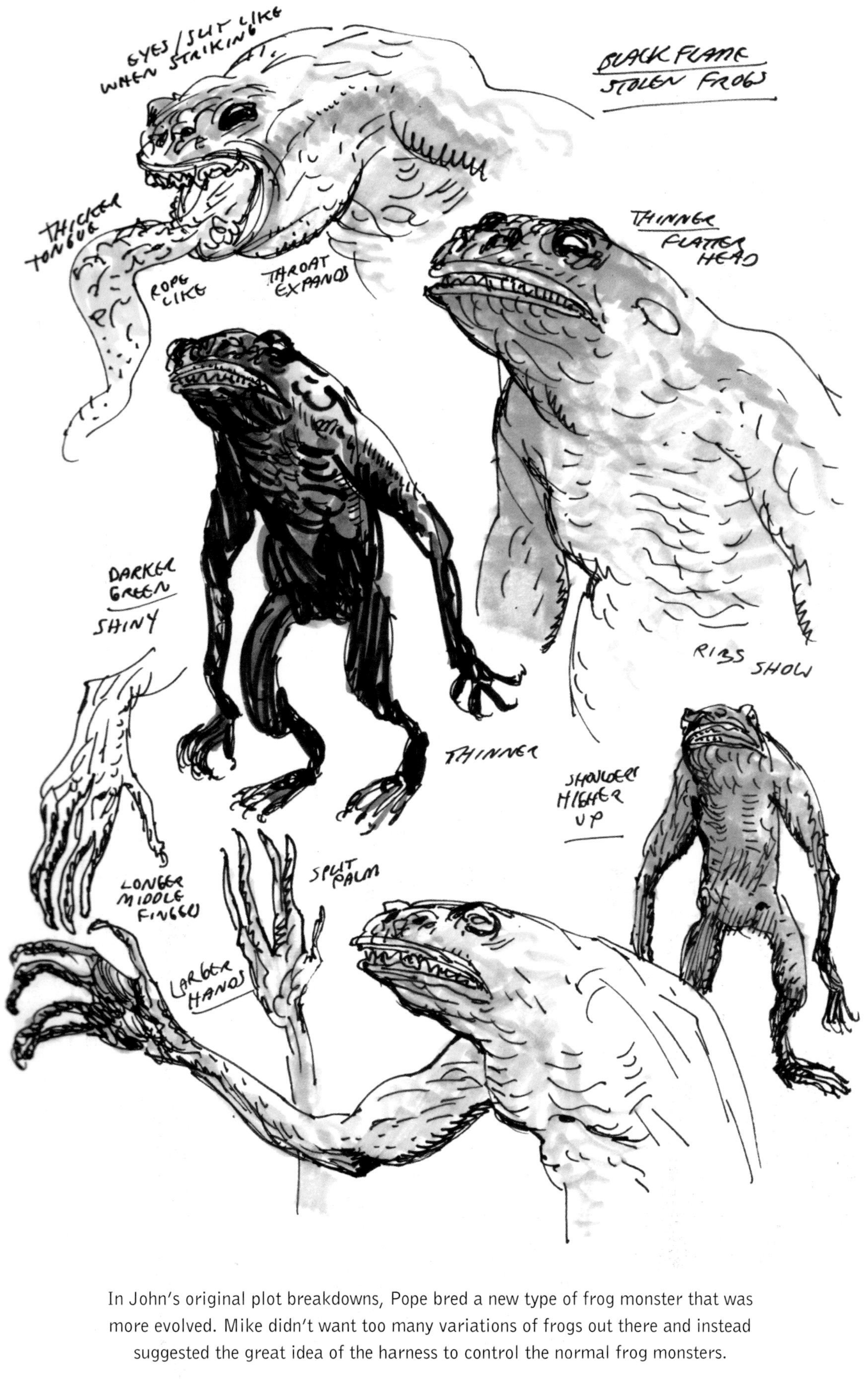

EYES/SLIT LIKE WHEN STRIKING
BLACK FLAME STOLEN FROGS
THICKER TONGUE
ROPE LIKE
THROAT EXPANDS
THINNER FLATTER HEAD
DARKER GREEN SHINY
RIBS SHOW
THINNER
SHOULDERS HIGHER UP
LONGER MIDDLE FINGER
SPLIT PALM
LARGER HANDS

In John's original plot breakdowns, Pope bred a new type of frog monster that was more evolved. Mike didn't want too many variations of frogs out there and instead suggested the great idea of the harness to control the normal frog monsters.

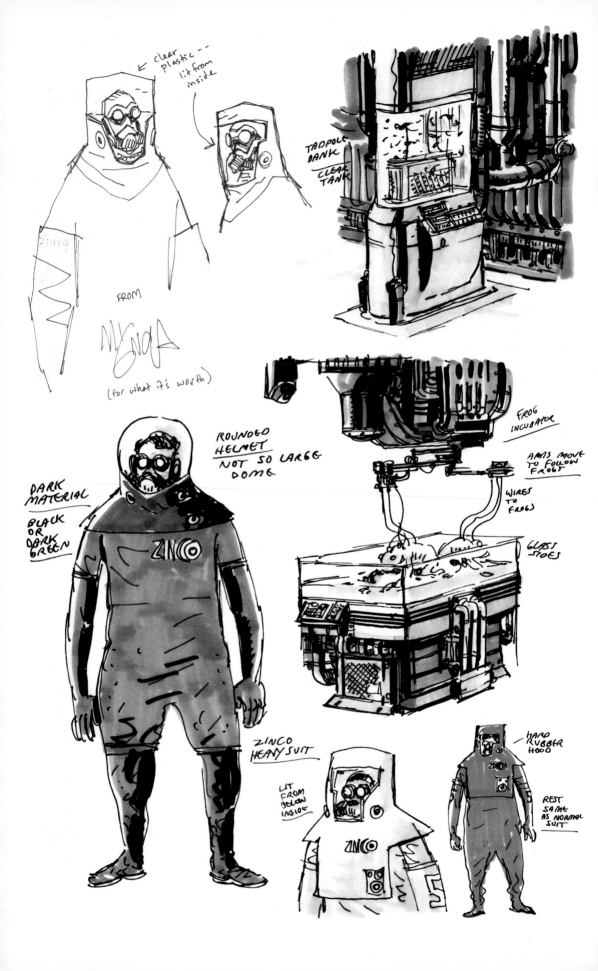

← clear plastic -- lit from inside

TADPOLE BANK

CLEAR TANK

FROM

NYSNGA

(for what it's worth)

FROG INCUBATOR

ARMS MOVE TO FOLLOW FROG

WIRES TO FROG

ROUNDED HELMET NOT SO LARGE DOME

DARK MATERIAL

BLACK OR DARK GREEN

GLASS SIDES

ZINCO

ZINCO HEAVY SUIT

LIT FROM BELOW INSIDE

ZINCO

HARD RUBBER HOOD

REST SAME AS NORMAL SUIT

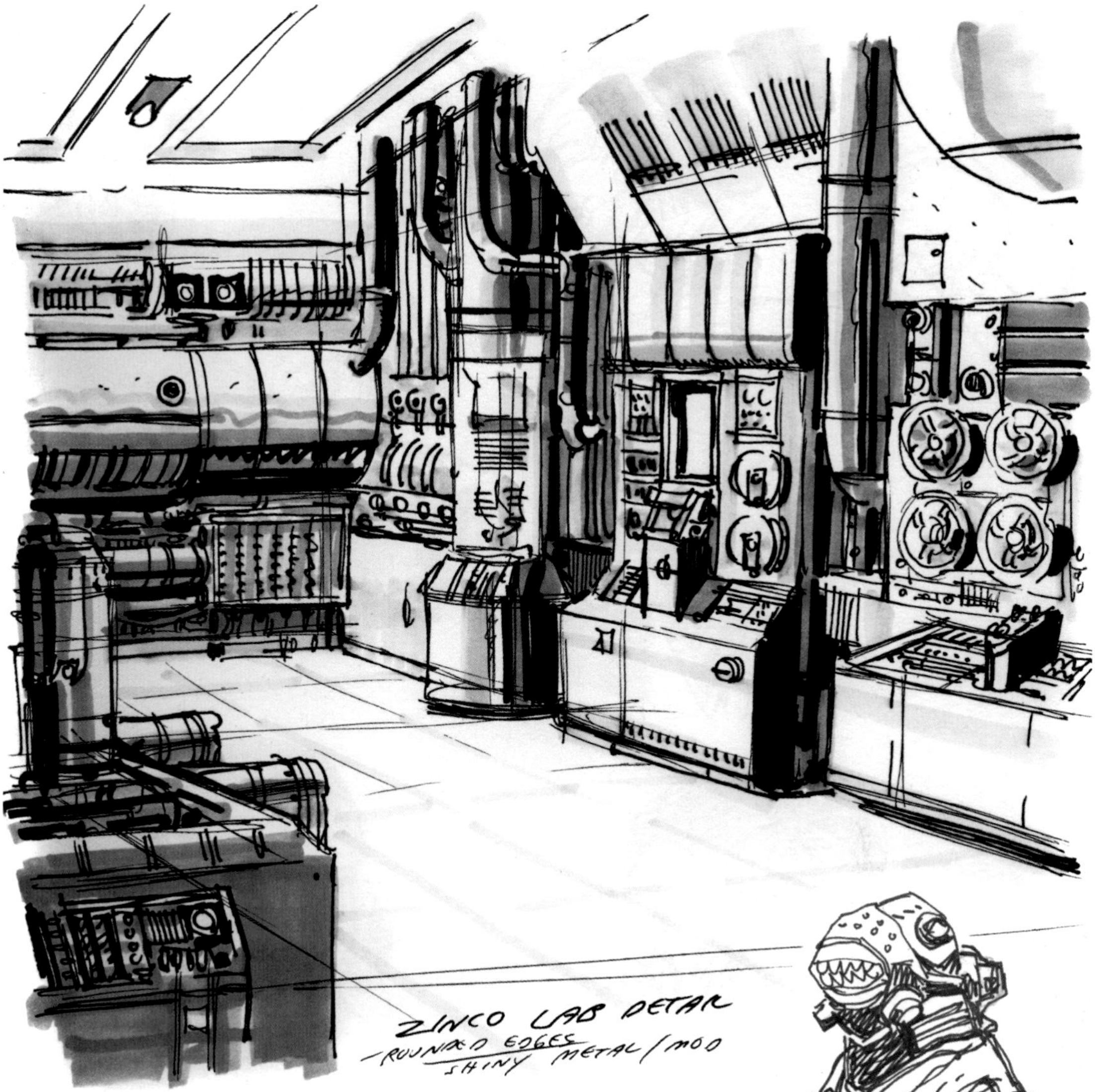
ZINCO LAB DETAIL
-ROUNDED EDGES
SHINY METAL/MOD

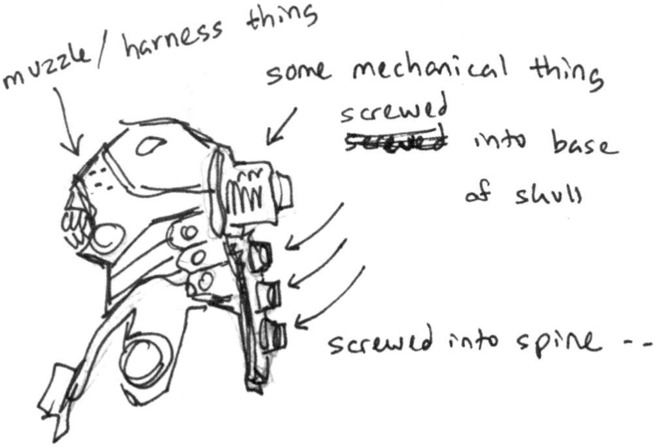
muzzle/ harness thing
some mechanical thing
screwed into base of skull
screwed into spine --

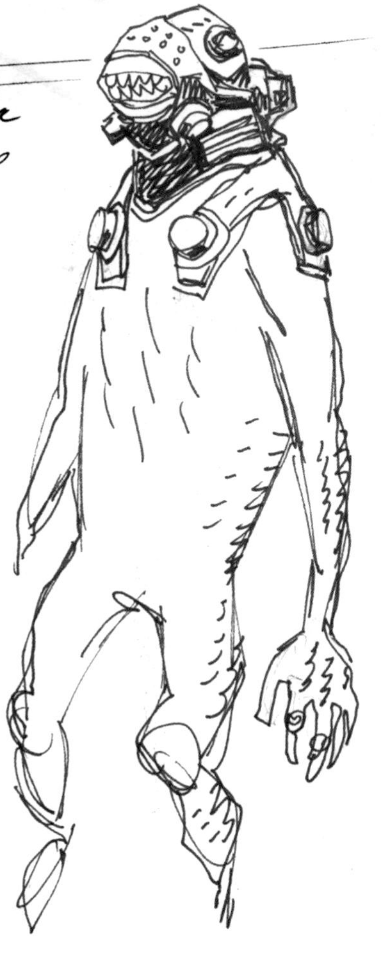

Mike wanted the Zinco lab to be an homage to Jack Kirby, all shiny metal and mod design to set it off from the B.P.R.D. utilitarian look. On this page is an early design done to get the feel of the lab, along with Mike's designs for the frog harness. On the previous page are his Zinco lab suit notes along with my take on his designs and some details for various lab equipment.

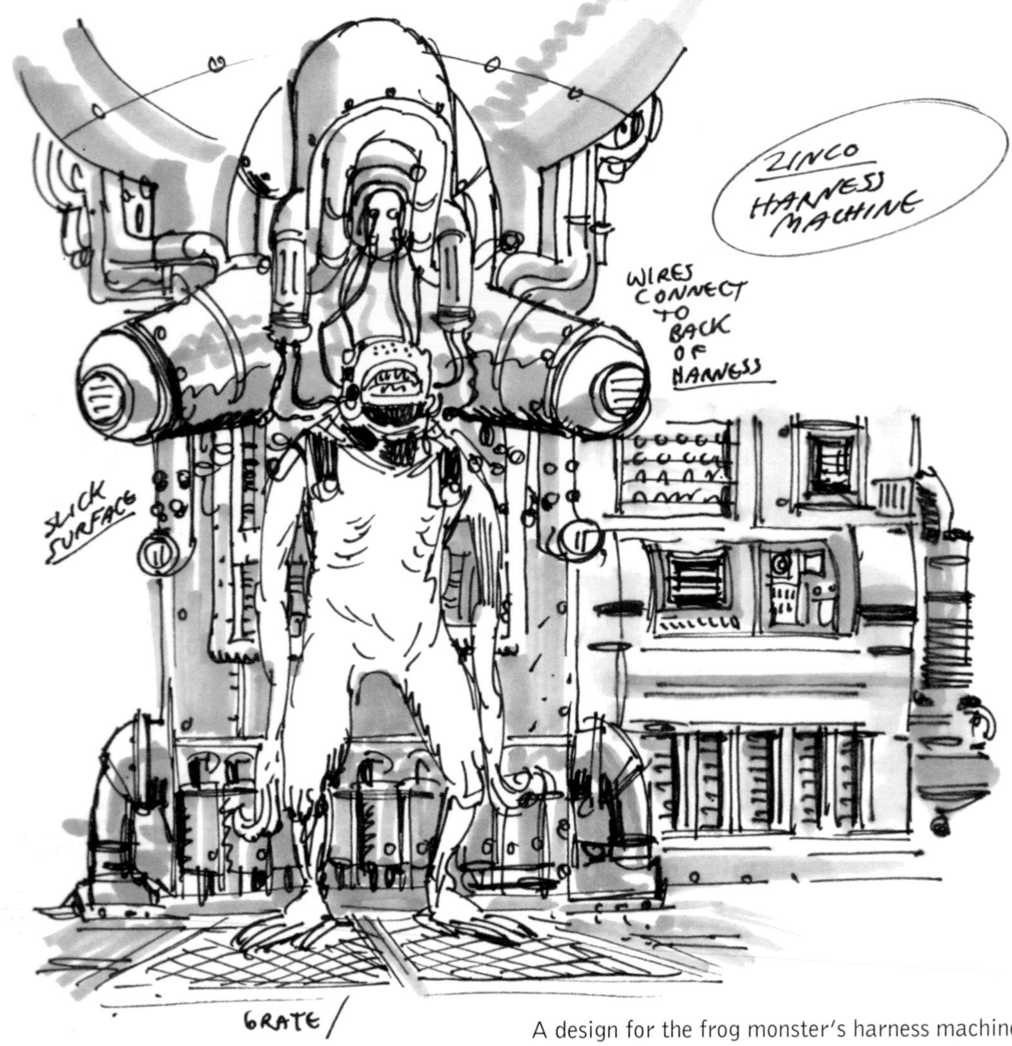
ZINCO HARNESS MACHINE
WIRES CONNECT TO BACK OF HARNESS
SLICK SURFACE
GRATE

A design for the frog monster's harness machine in the Zinco labs. Below: A couple of ideas for Pope's transformation into the true Black Flame. The machine-generated fire becomes a sort of tentacled Katha-Hem flame.

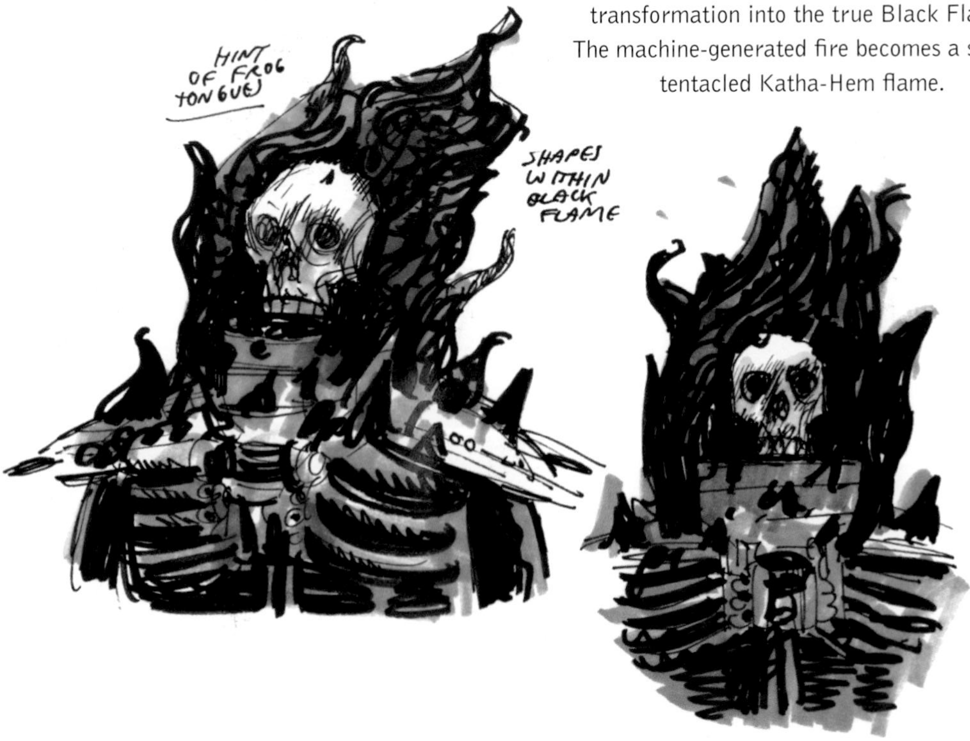
HINT OF FROG TONGUES
SHAPES WITHIN BLACK FLAME

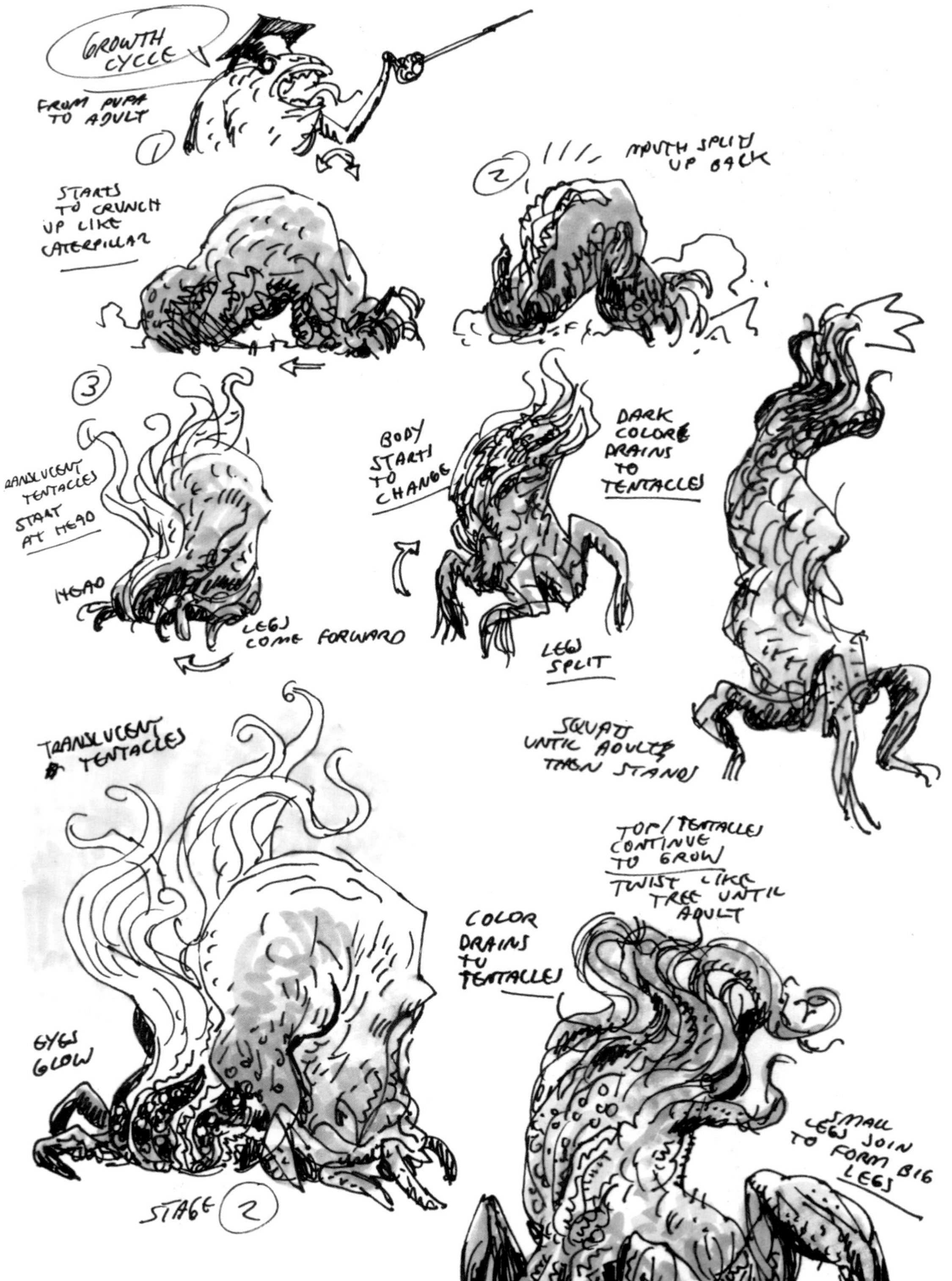
GROWTH CYCLE
FROM PUPA TO ADULT
1
2
MOUTH SPLITS UP BACK
STARTS TO CRUNCH UP LIKE CATERPILLAR
3
TRANSLUCENT TENTACLES START AT HEAD
HEAD
LEGS COME FORWARD
BODY STARTS TO CHANGE
DARK COLORS DRAINS TO TENTACLES
LEGS SPLIT
SQUATS UNTIL ADULTS THEN STANDS
TRANSLUCENT TENTACLES
TOP/TENTACLES CONTINUE TO GROW
TWIST LIKE TREE UNTIL ADULT
COLOR DRAINS TO TENTACLES
EYES GLOW
SMALL LEGS JOIN TO FORM BIG LEGS
STAGE 2

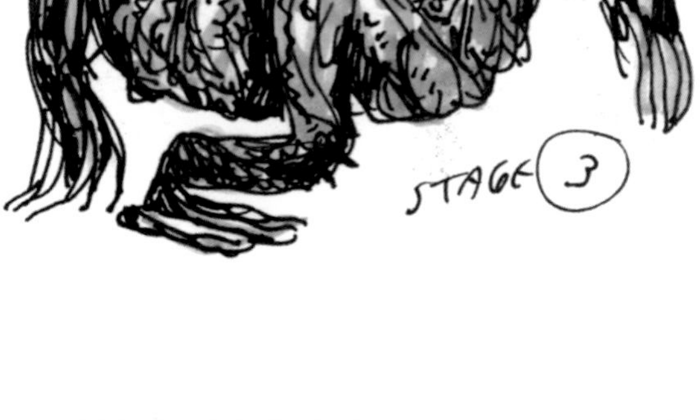
STAGE 3

Even though we don't fully see it in the actual story, I wanted to work out the different stages of the rampaging larva that transforms into Katha-Hem.

Some more ideas on the details for the Katha-Hem larval stage. The floating eye made him seem more evolved and didn't fit with the early stage, which we wanted to be more like a rampaging caterpillar.

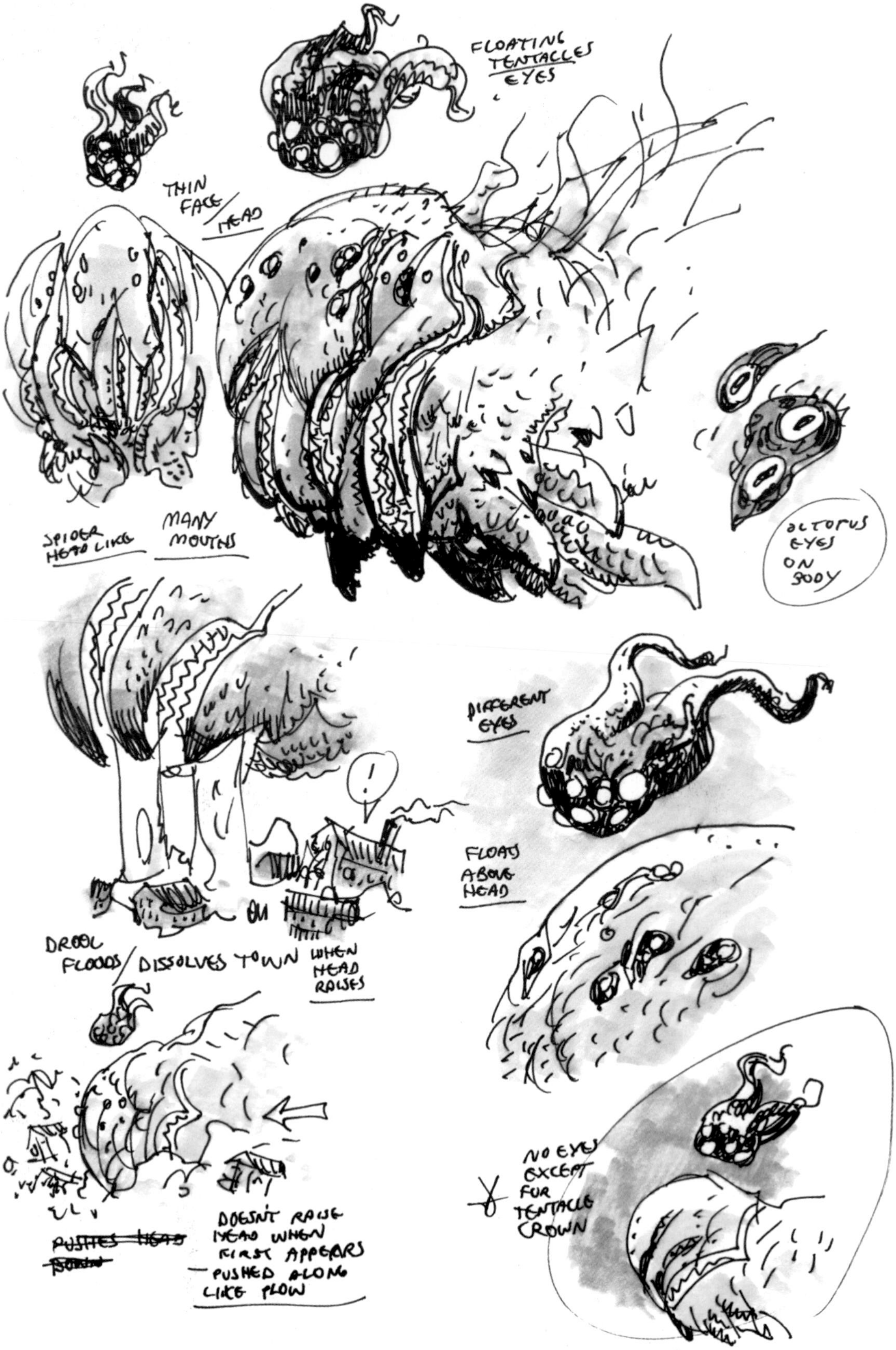
FLOATING TENTACLES EYES
THIN FACE/HEAD
SPIDER HEAD LIKE
MANY MOUTHS
OCTOPUS EYES ON BODY
DIFFERENT EYES
FLOATS ABOVE HEAD
DROOL FLOODS/DISSOLVES TOWN WHEN HEAD RAISES
~~PUSHES HEAD DOWN~~
DOESN'T RAISE HEAD WHEN FIRST APPEARS
– PUSHED ALONG LIKE PLOW
NO EYES EXCEPT FOR TENTACLE CROWN

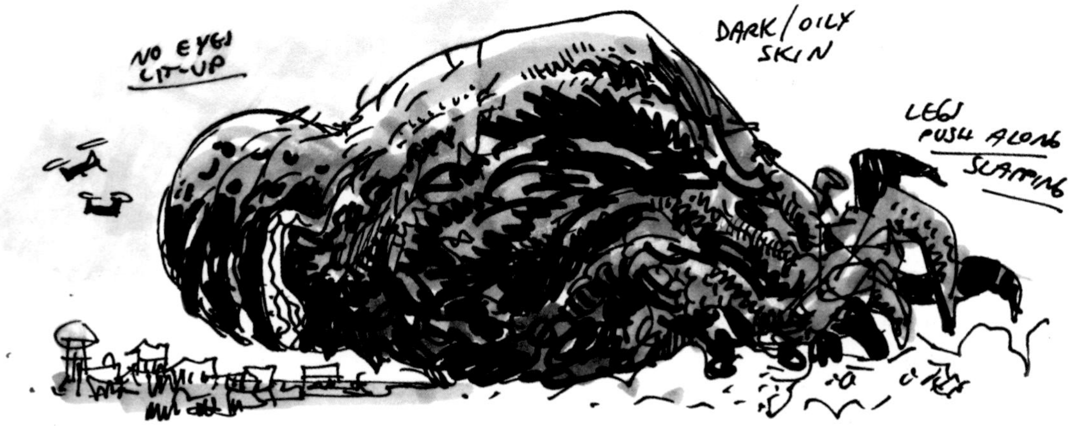
NO EYES
LIT-UP
DARK / OILY
SKIN
LEGS
PUSH ALONG
SLAMMING

Above is one of the final sketches to the larval state of Katha-Hem that was inspired by *Moby Dick*—below is the first take on his adult form that I did during work on *The Dead*. The basic shape would remain the same but the details would change to fit him into the Hellboy universe.

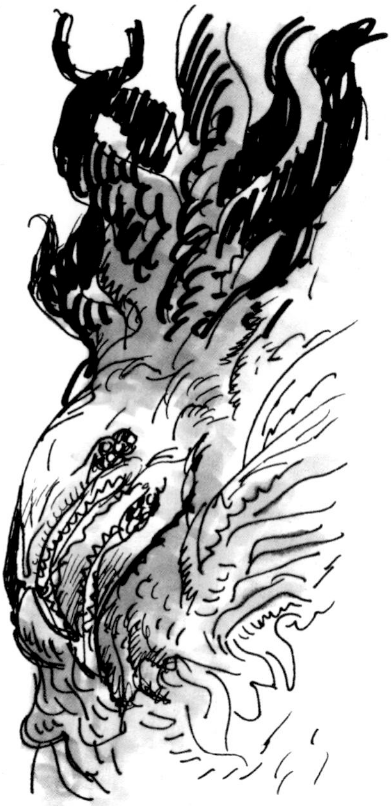

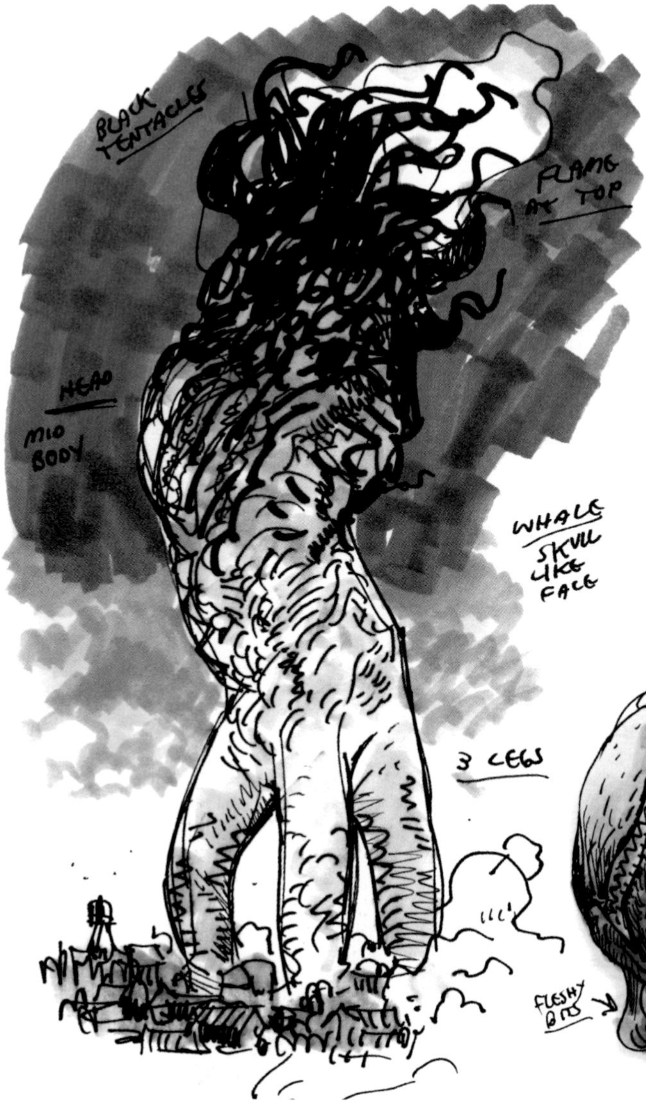
BLACK
TENTACLES
FLAME
AT TOP
HEAD
MID
BODY
WHALE
SKULL
LIKE
FACE
3 LEGS

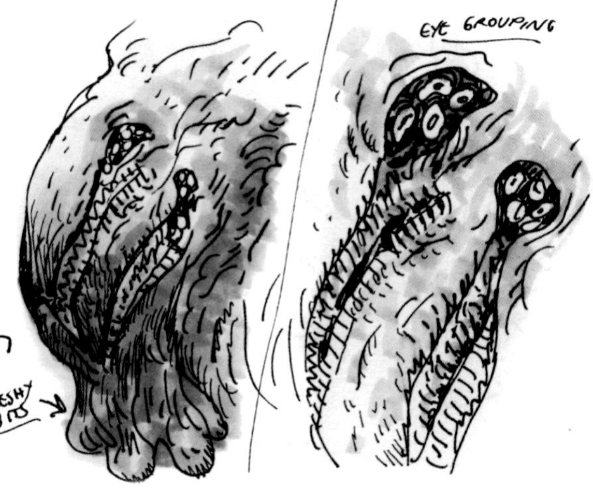
EYE GROUPING
FLESHY
BITS

The final take on Katha-Hem was to be more insect-like to tie him into the Ogdru Hem shown in *Hellboy: The Island.* The whale-like mouth remained from the original design, but the elephant tree-like legs became the insect-like limbs made out of twisted root-like arms.

—Guy Davis
Crab Point, Michigan

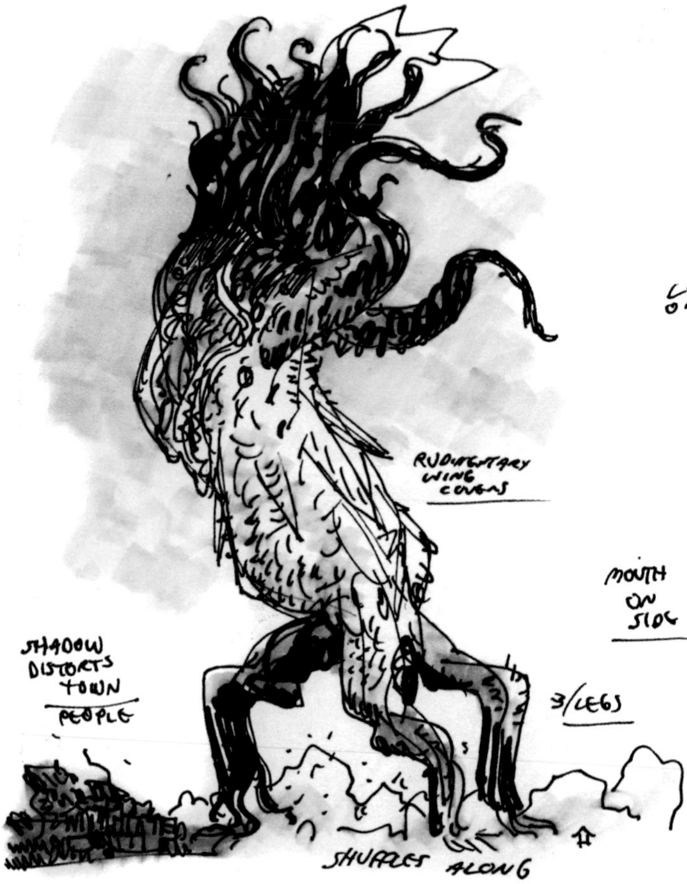
RUDIMENTARY WING COVERS
SHADOW DISTORTS TOWN PEOPLE
3/LEGS
SHUFFLES ALONG

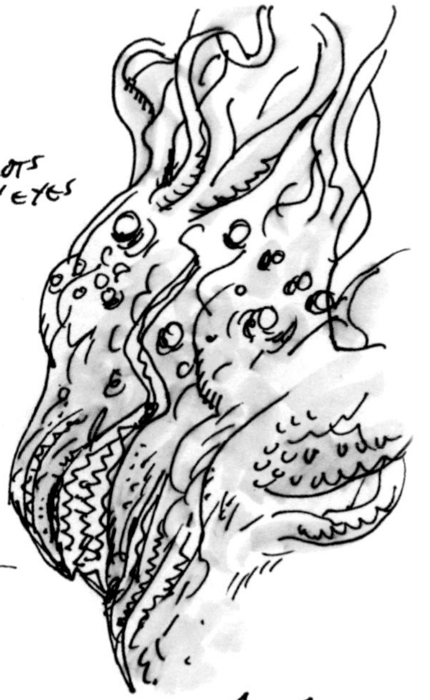
LOTS O' EYES
MOUTH ON SIDE

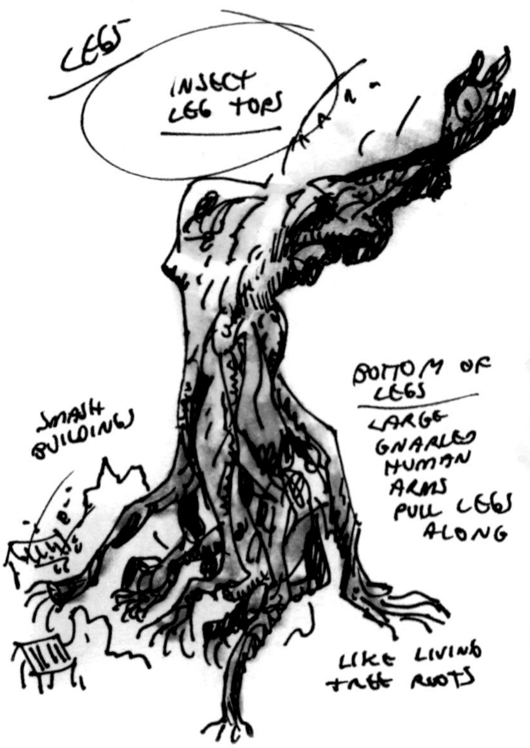
LEGS
INSECT LEG TOPS
BOTTOM OF LEGS
LARGE GNARLED HUMAN ARMS PULL LEGS ALONG
SMASH BUILDINGS
LIKE LIVING TREE ROOTS

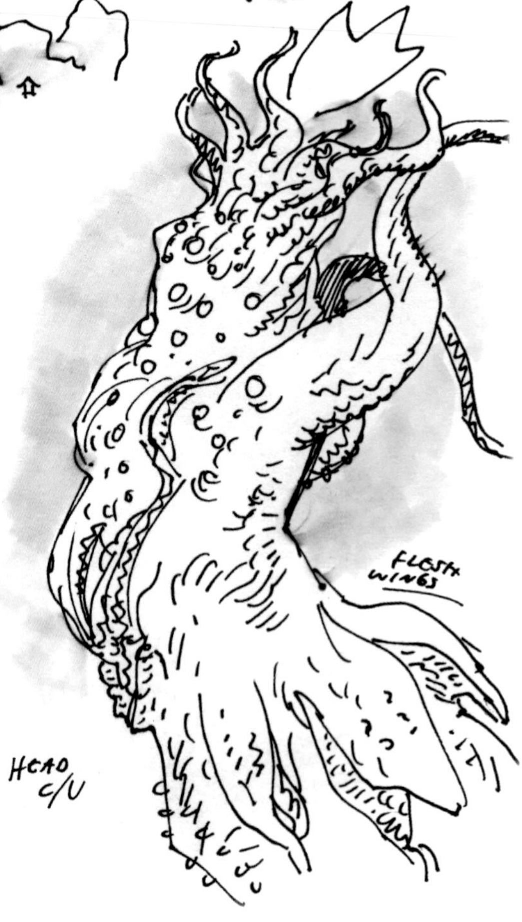
FLESH WINGS
HEAD C/U

WAR ON FROGS

SKETCHBOOK

Notes by Scott Allie

War on Frogs came about through a phone call between John Arcudi and me during a Christmas vacation when I was at my parents' home in Massachusetts in 2007. We were working with Herb Trimpe on an eight-page *Goon* story that would run on *MySpace Dark Horse Presents* the following month, and we wanted to do something else with Herb. Since we work most extensively together on *B.P.R.D.*, we realized that would be the quickest thing to pull together. John started musing about Herb Trimpe doing a Nick Fury war comic starring the Hulk—if you know Herb's history at Marvel, you'll see that this was a good fit. Roger, by then already dead, and the ongoing war on frogs was the perfect match, and it was a great opportunity to do another Roger story without bringing him back from the dead. As the idea grew over the phone, we realized *War on Frogs* would be a great way to do a bunch of one-shots with different artists, and so we called Mignola and got him onboard.

Herb ran into trouble schedulewise, so we pulled Guy Davis in to ink him, leading to a bizarre hybrid of their very different styles. Above are Herb's pencils, with Guy and Dave finishing up for him. The following page presents another comparison, with a couple panels Herb inked before realizing the schedule had gotten away from him. For consistency, Guy re-inked those panels.

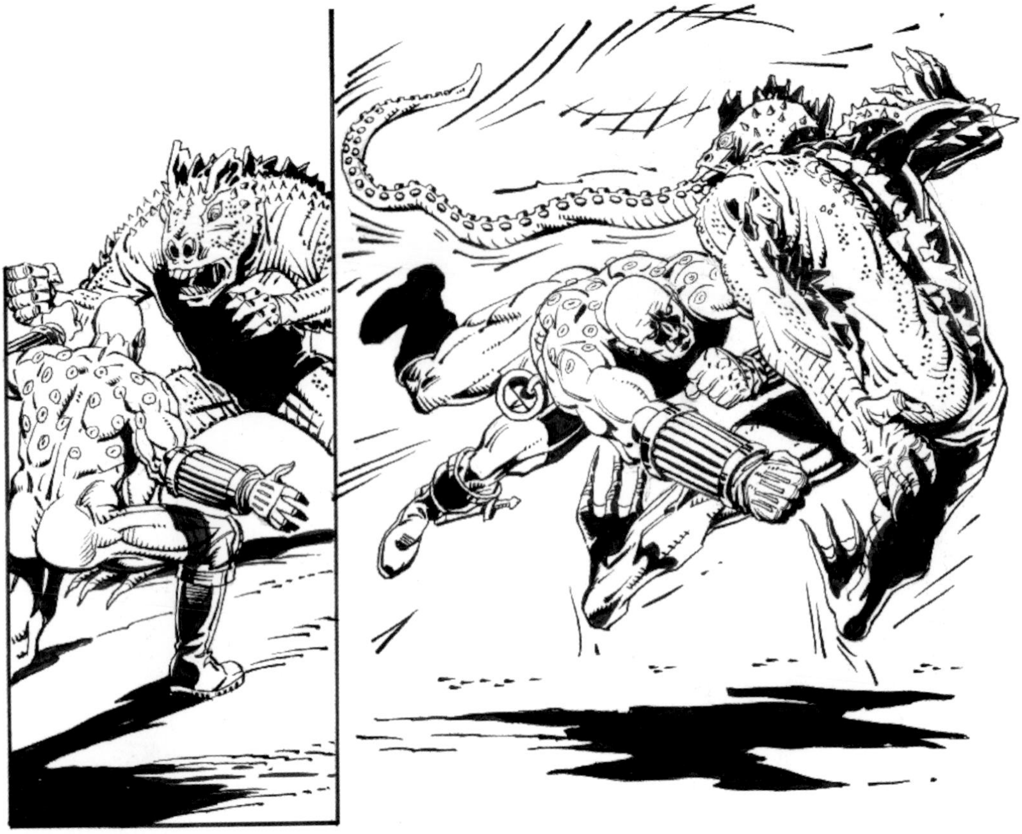

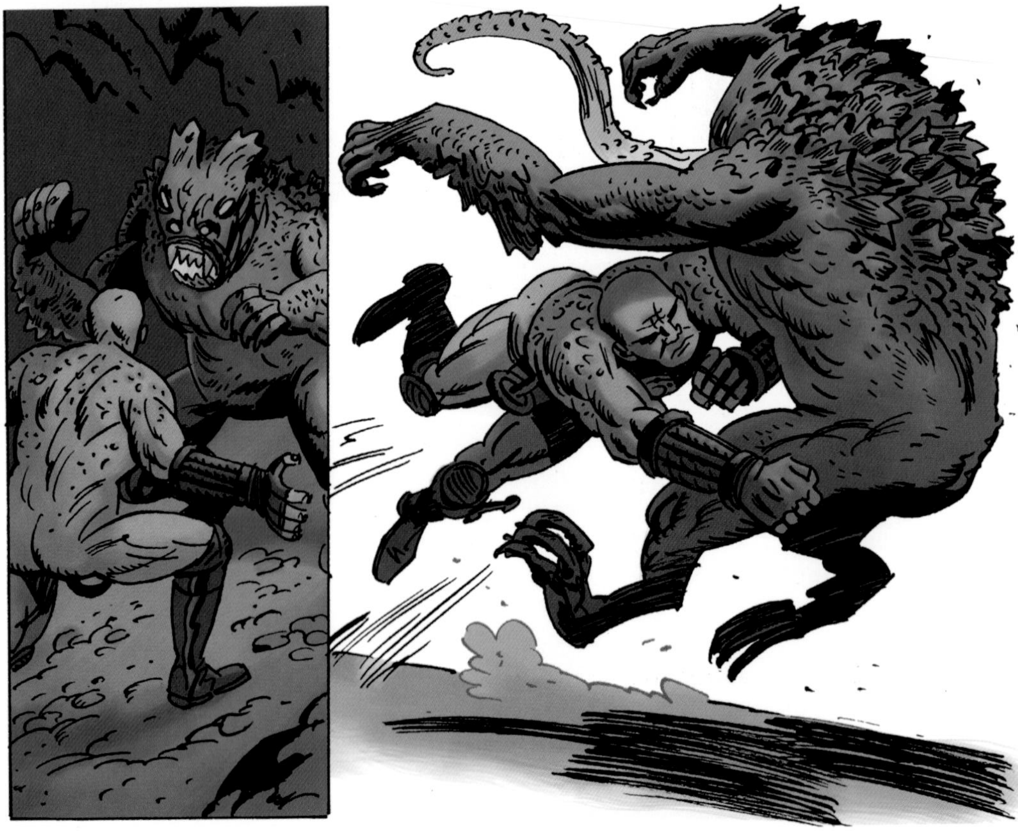

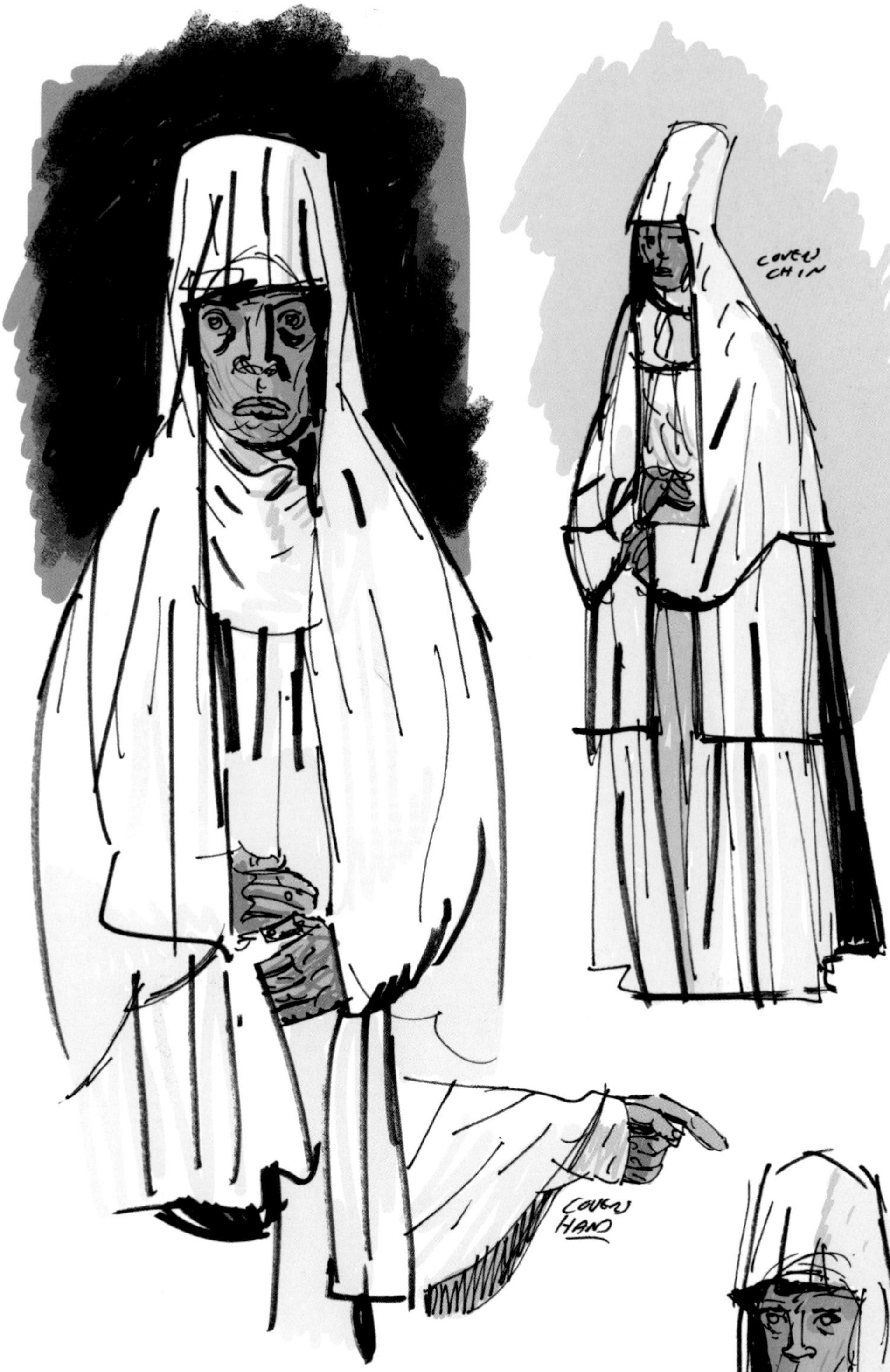
COVERED CHIN
COVERED HAND

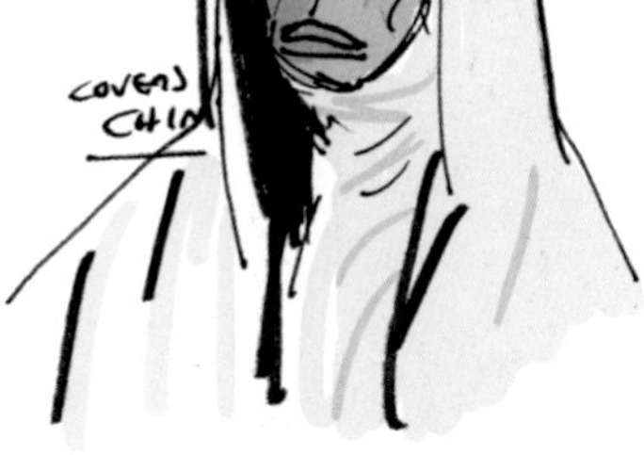
COVERED CHIN

Since *B.P.R.D.* is as much Guy's book as John's, we brought him in for a two-part story which ran in *MySpace Dark Horse Presents*.

Before Herb had started his one-shot, Mignola designed the monster frog for that issue.

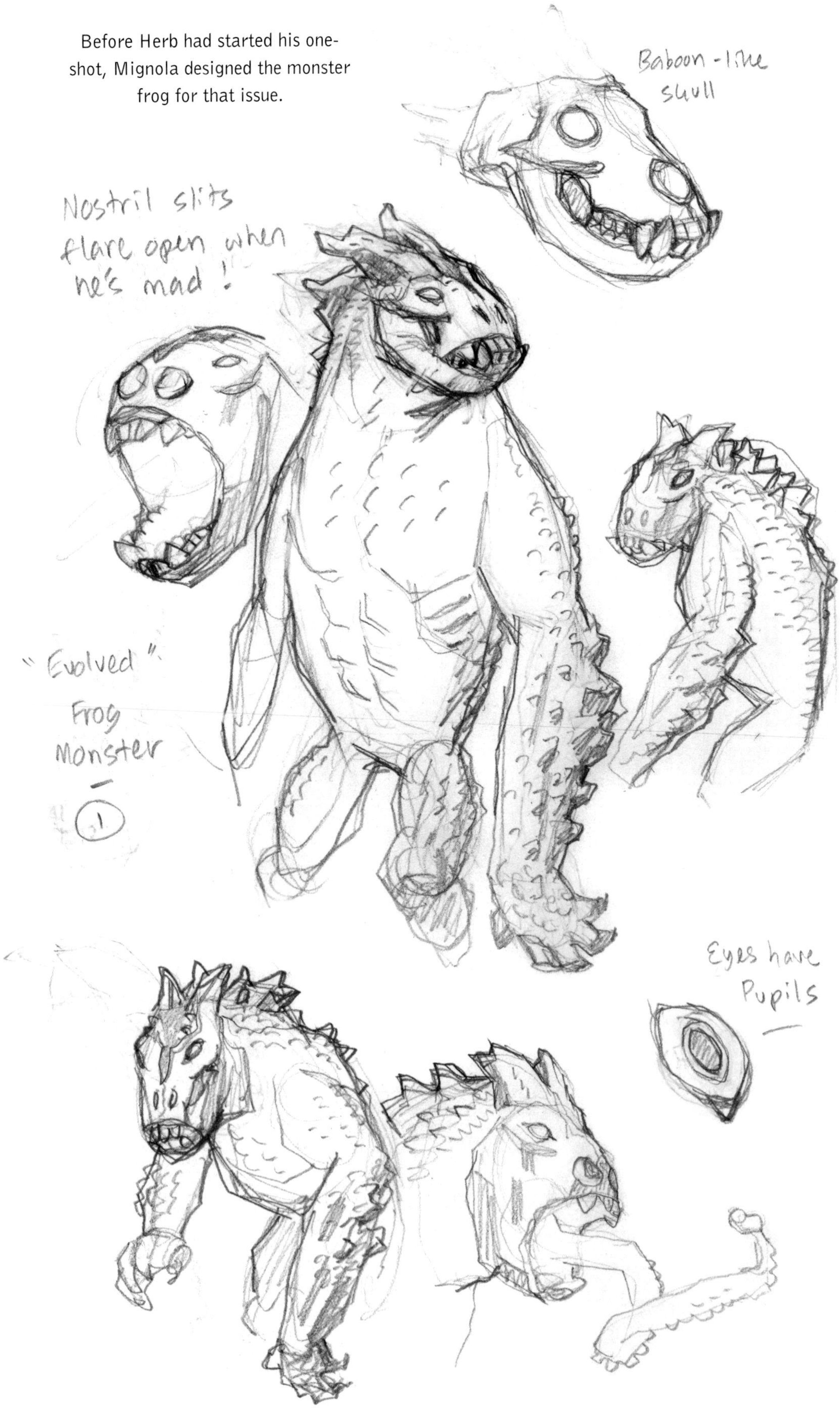
Baboon-like skull
Nostril slits flare open when he's mad!
"Evolved" Frog Monster
Eyes have Pupils

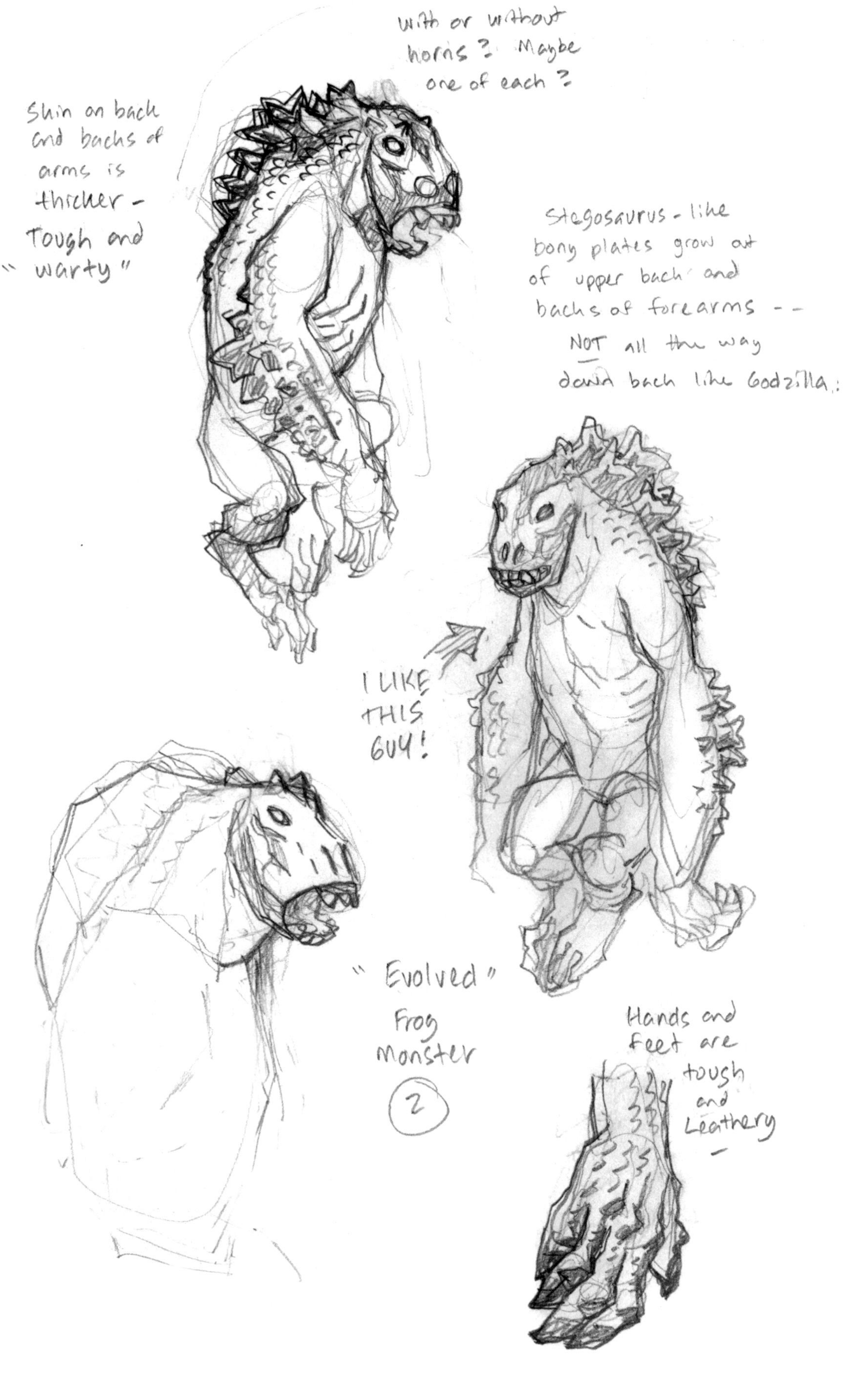
With or without horns? Maybe one of each?
Skin on back and backs of arms is thicker - Tough and "warty"
Stegosaurus-like bony plates grow out of upper back and backs of forearms -- NOT all the way down back like Godzilla.
I LIKE THIS GUY!
"Evolved" Frog Monster
2
Hands and feet are tough and Leathery

John Severin and Peter Snejbjerg didn't have much to design for their issues, or did their designing on the page, which is why they're not represented on these pages. Karl Moline, however, is a devout sketchbook artist, working out his take on the characters before starting the book itself. His layouts (following spread) also pack a lot of energy.

Thanks to all of the great artists who joined the team for this look back at the war.

—Scott Allie

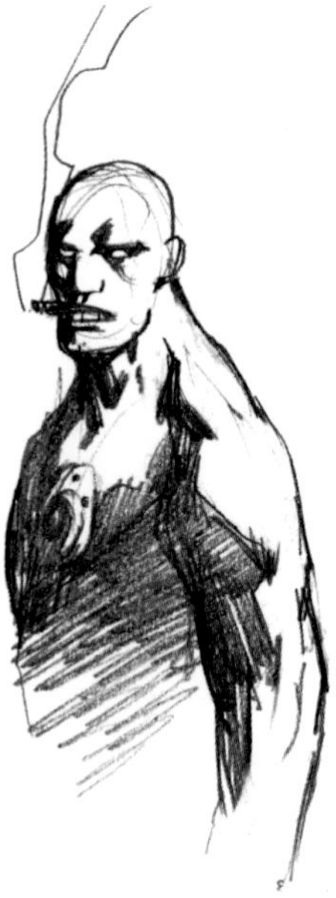

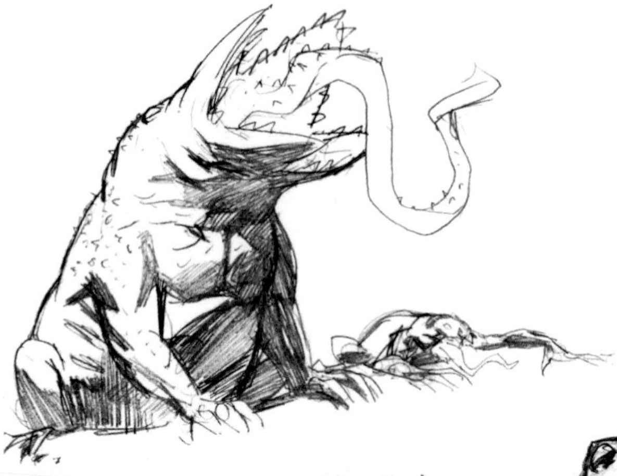

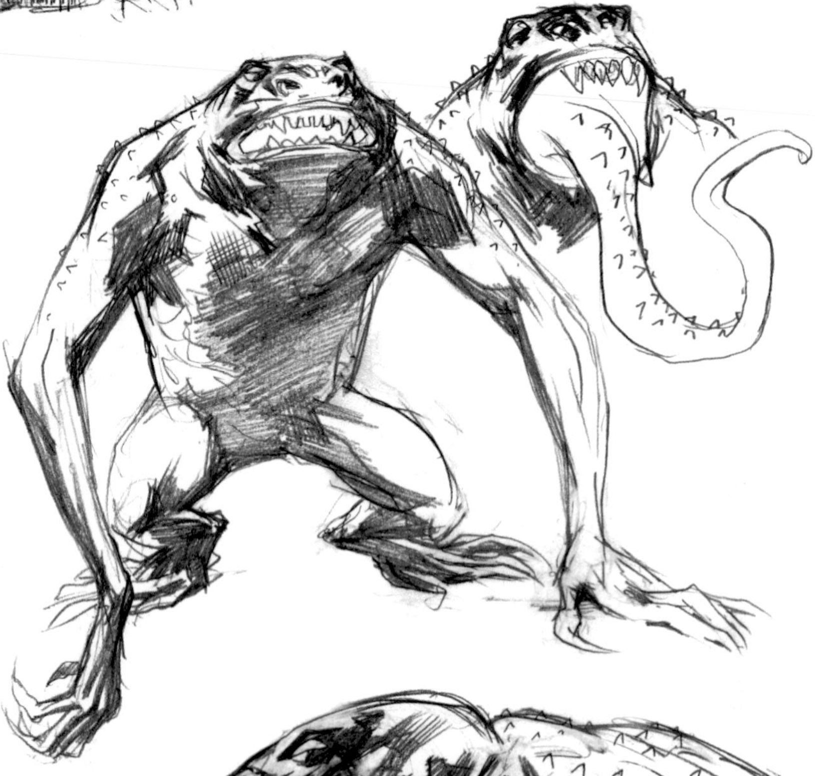

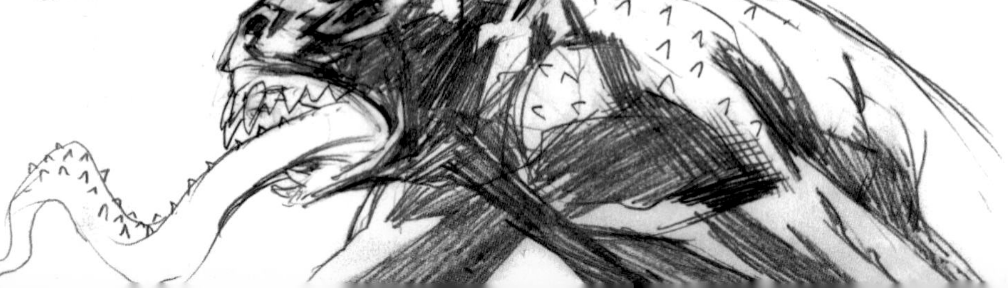

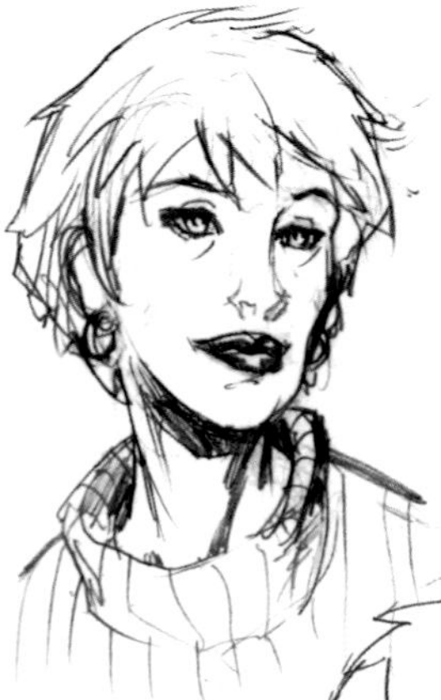

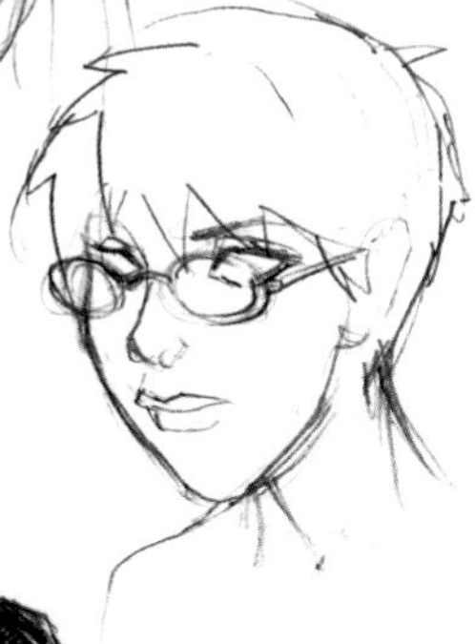

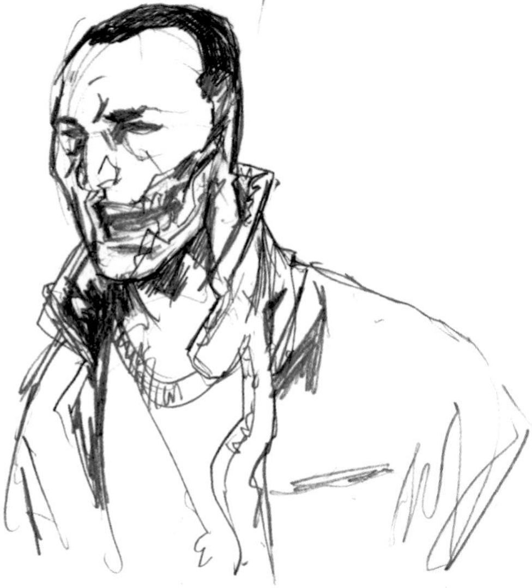

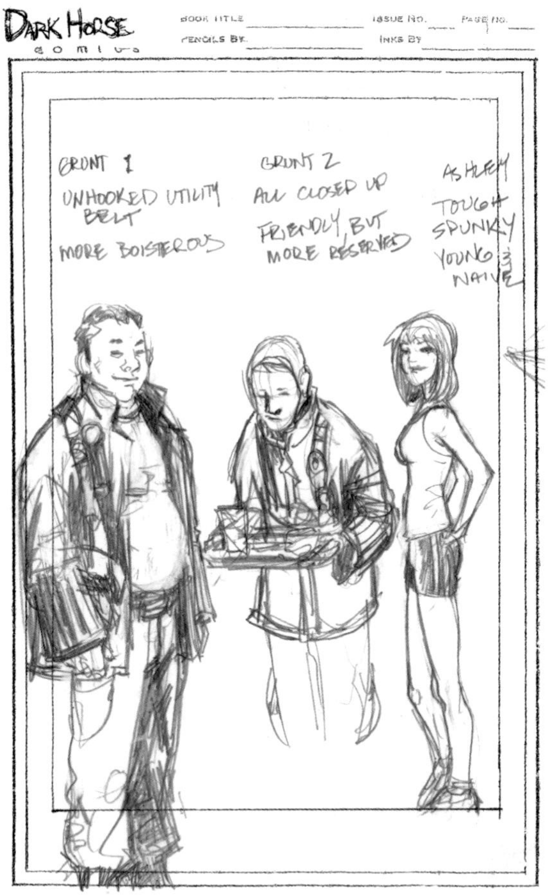
DARK HORSE COMICS
BOOK TITLE
ISSUE NO.
PAGE NO.
PENCILS BY
INKS BY
GRUNT 1
UNHOOKED UTILITY BELT
MORE BOISTEROUS
GRUNT 2
ALL CLOSED UP
FRIENDLY, BUT MORE RESERVED
ASHLEY
TOUGH
SPUNKY
YOUNG & NAIVE

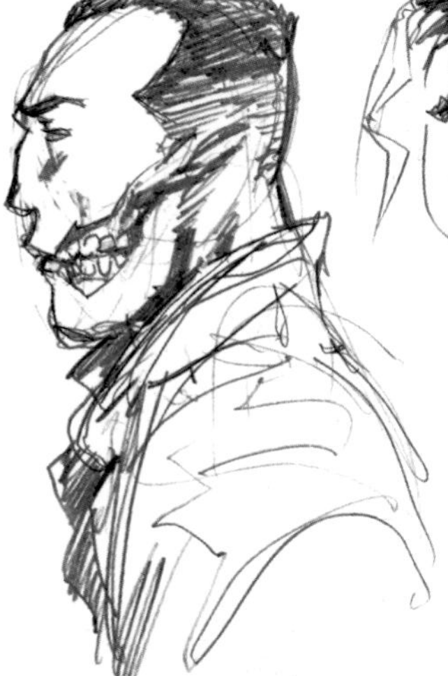

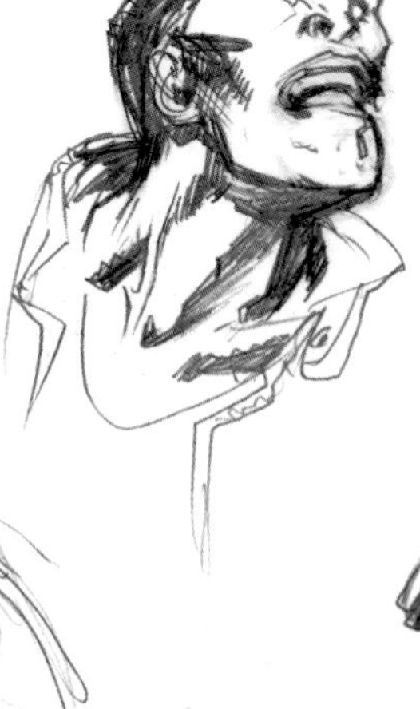

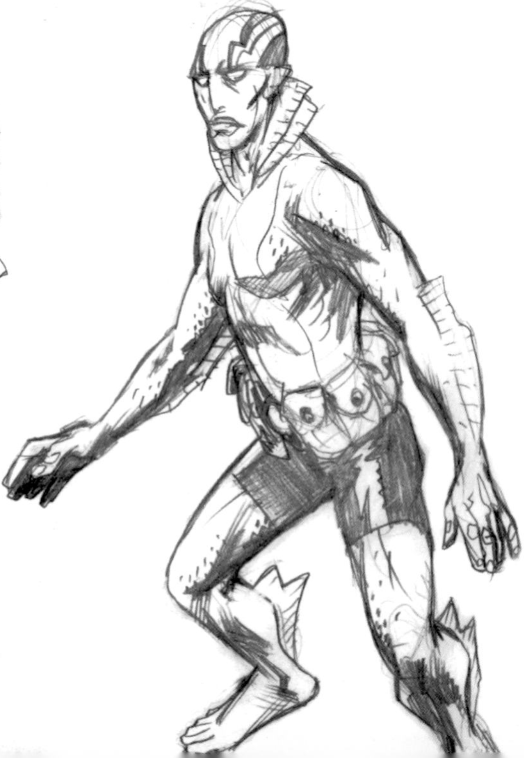

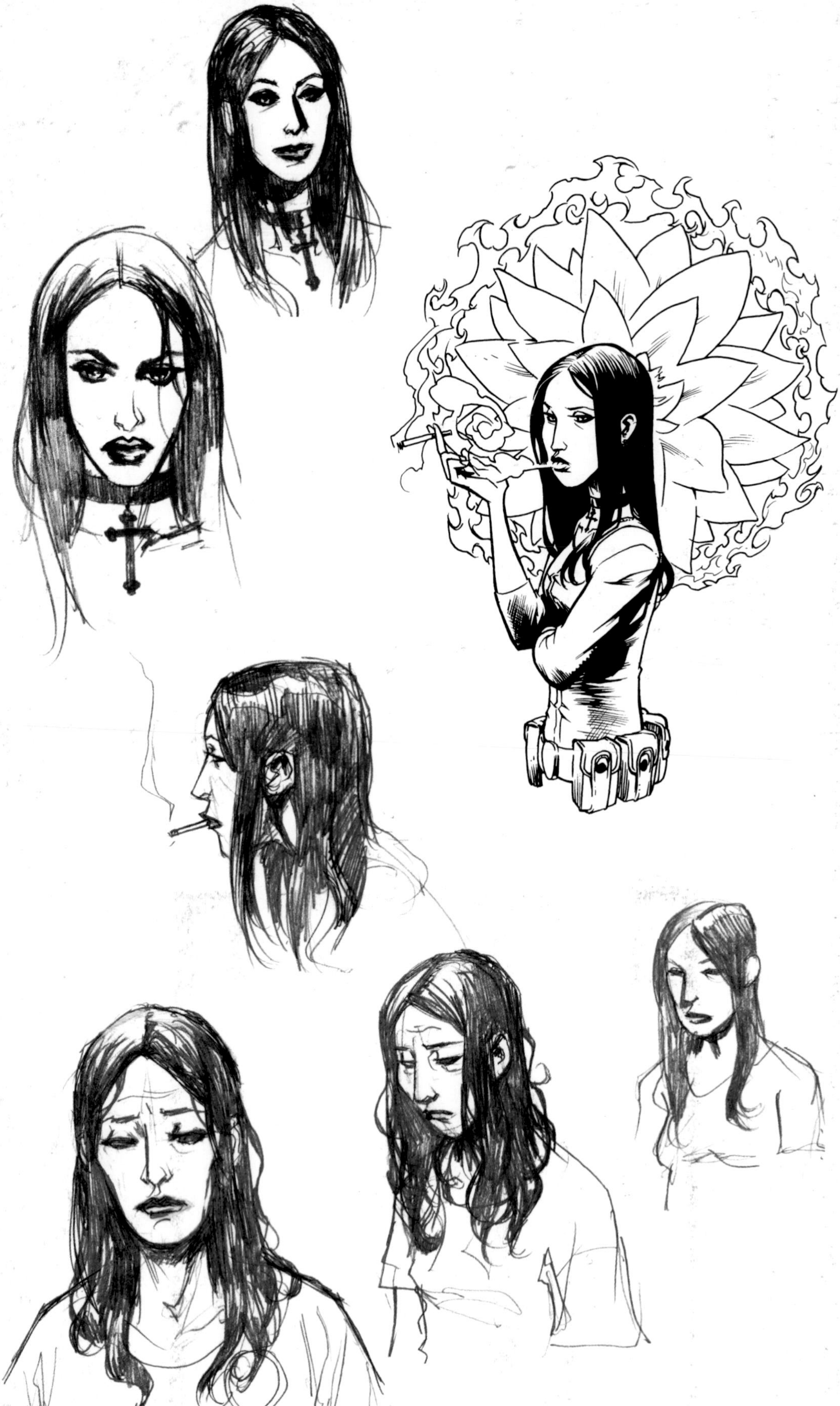

RECOMMENDED DARK HORSE READING

THE COMPLETE
MAJOR BUMMER SUPER SLACKTACULAR
JOHN ARCUDI DOUG MAHNKE

THE COMPLETE MAJOR BUMMER SUPER SLACKTACULAR!

John Arcudi, Doug Mahnke

Lou Martin has been granted incredible powers and has the potential to become the world's greatest superhero. Too bad he just wants to watch TV, play video games, eat all the junk food he can find, and keep his superpowered self firmly planted on the couch. (Go figure—a slipshod alien college student would get *Louis Martin*, slacker extraordinaire, and *Martin Lewis*, promising young lawyer and philanthropist, confused, and send the Extreme Enhancement Module to the wrong guy!) Now Lou's got to contend with an outlandish host of superheroes, and one *very* enthusiastic superfan, all trying to get him out of the house so he can . . . *ugh . . . contribute to society*. And that's not to mention the supervillains, monsters, and aliens out to make a name for themselves by bringing him down!

$29.99 | ISBN 978-1-59582-534-6

GUY DAVIS
THE MARQUIS
INFERNO

THE MARQUIS: INFERNO

Guy Davis

In eighteenth-century Venisalle, faith governs life and death, and the guilty hide their shame behind masks, showing their faces only in the secret rites of the confessional. It is to this stronghold of the Inquisition that the souls of hell have escaped to possess the living, spreading sin, murder, and chaos. Amid the carnage, one man is blessed with the clarity to recognize the demons that prey on his countrymen—and the means to return them to the fires of hell. But as the stakes rise, the lines separating good and evil begin to blur, and the Marquis—the dark avenger whom even demons fear to cross—finds himself torn between the blind faith that has defined his life and the bitter truths exposed under his new sight.

$24.99 | ISBN 978-1-59582-368-7

From the creator of BUFFY THE VAMPIRE SLAYER and the major motion picture SERENITY
joss whedon
karl moline
andy owens
FRAY

FRAY: FUTURE SLAYER

Joss Whedon, Karl Moline, Andy Owens

Hundreds of years in the future, Manhattan has become a deadly slum, run by mutant crime lords and disinterested cops. Stuck in the middle is a young girl who thought she had no future but learns she has a great destiny. In a world so poisoned that it doesn't notice the monsters on its streets, how can a street kid like Fray unite a fallen city against a demonic plot to consume mankind? Joss Whedon, the celebrated creator of *Buffy the Vampire Slayer*, brings his vision to the future in this unique tale.

$19.99 | ISBN 978-1-56971-751-6

THE
MASK
OMNIBUS
VOLUME 1

THE MASK OMNIBUS VOLUME 1

Doug Mahnke, John Arcudi

It has all the makings of an epic adventure: an ancient artifact has been rediscovered—a mask of unknown origins, with unforeseen power and magic. But who knew that after donning this mask even the wimpiest geek would become an indestructible, shape-changing supertornado with a mind for mischief and an appetite for destruction?

$24.99 | ISBN 978-1-59307-927-7

AVAILABLE AT YOUR LOCAL COMICS SHOP OR BOOKSTORE! • To find a comics shop in your area, call 1-888-266-4226.

For more information or to order direct visit DarkHorse.com or call 1-800-862-0052 Mon.–Fri. 9 AM to 5 PM Pacific Time. Prices and availability subject to change without notice.

DARK HORSE BOOKS *drawing on your nightmares*
DarkHorse.com

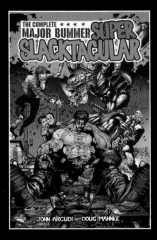

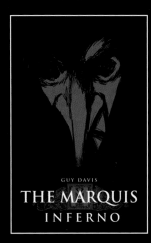

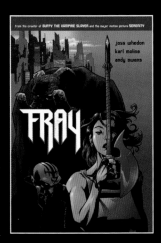

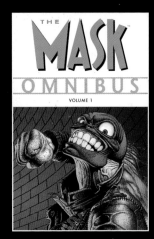

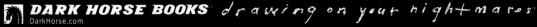

HELLBOY

by MIKE MIGNOLA

HELLBOY LIBRARY EDITION VOLUME 1:
SEED OF DESTRUCTION AND WAKE THE DEVIL
ISBN 978-1-59307-910-9 | $49.99

HELLBOY LIBRARY EDITION VOLUME 2:
THE CHAINED COFFIN AND THE RIGHT HAND OF DOOM
ISBN 978-1-59307-989-5 | $49.99

HELLBOY LIBRARY EDITION VOLUME 3:
CONQUEROR WORM AND STRANGE PLACES
ISBN 978-1-59582-352-6 | $49.99

SEED OF DESTRUCTION
WITH JOHN BYRNE
ISBN 978-1-59307-094-6 | $17.99

WAKE THE DEVIL
ISBN 978-1-59307-095-3 | $17.99

THE CHAINED COFFIN AND OTHERS
ISBN 978-1-59307-091-5 | $17.99

THE RIGHT HAND OF DOOM
ISBN 978-1-59307-093-9 | $17.99

CONQUEROR WORM
ISBN 978-1-59307-092-2 | $17.99

STRANGE PLACES
ISBN 978-1-59307-475-3 | $17.99

THE TROLL WITCH AND OTHERS
ISBN 978-1-59307-860-7 | $17.99

DARKNESS CALLS
WITH DUNCAN FEGREDO
ISBN 978-1-59307-896-6 | $19.99

THE WILD HUNT
WITH DUNCAN FEGREDO
ISBN 978-1-59582-352-6 | $19.99

THE CROOKED MAN AND OTHERS
WITH RICHARD CORBEN
ISBN 978-1-59582-477-6 | $17.99

THE ART OF HELLBOY
ISBN 978-1-59307-089-2 | $29.99

HELLBOY II: THE ART OF THE MOVIE
ISBN 978-1-59307-964-2 | $24.99

HELLBOY: THE COMPANION
ISBN 978-1-59307-655-9 | $14.99

HELLBOY: WEIRD TALES
VOLUME 1
ISBN 978-1-56971-622-9 | $17.99
VOLUME 2
ISBN 978-1-56971-953-4 | $17.99

HELLBOY: MASKS AND MONSTERS
WITH JAMES ROBINSON AND SCOTT BENEFIEL
ISBN 978-1-59582-567-4 | $17.99

B.P.R.D.
WITH JOHN ARCUDI AND GUY DAVIS

PLAGUE OF FROGS HARDCOVER COLLECTION VOLUME 1
ISBN 978-59582-609-1 | $34.99

THE DEAD
ISBN 978-1-59307-380-0 | $17.99

THE BLACK FLAME
ISBN 978-1-59307-550-7 | $17.99

WAR ON FROGS
ISBN 978-1-59582-480-6 | $17.99

THE UNIVERSAL MACHINE
ISBN 978-1-59307-710-5 | $17.99

THE GARDEN OF SOULS
ISBN 978-1-59307-882-9 | $17.99

KILLING GROUND
ISBN 978-1-59307-956-7 | $17.99

THE WARNING
ISBN 978-1-59582-304-5 | $17.99

THE BLACK GODDESS
ISBN 978-1-59582-411-0 | $17.99

KING OF FEAR
ISBN 978-1-59582-564-3 | $17.99

1946
WITH JOSHUA DYSART AND PAUL AZACETA
ISBN 978-1-59582-191-1 | $17.99

1947
WITH JOSHUA DYSART, FÁBIO MOON, AND GABRIEL BÁ
ISBN 978-1-59582-478-3 | $17.99

ABE SAPIEN: THE DROWNING
WITH JASON SHAWN ALEXANDER
ISBN 978-1-59582-185-0 | $17.99

LOBSTER JOHNSON: THE IRON PROMETHEUS
WITH JASON ARMSTRONG
ISBN 978-1-59307-975-8 | $17.99

WITCHFINDER: IN THE SERVICE OF ANGELS
WITH BEN STENBECK
ISBN 978-1-59582-483-7 | $17.99

NOVELS

HELLBOY: EMERALD HELL
BY TOM PICCIRILLI
ISBN 978-1-59582-141-6 | $12.99

HELLBOY: THE ALL-SEEING EYE
BY MARK MORRIS
ISBN 978-1-59582-141-6 | $12.99

HELLBOY: THE FIRE WOLVES
BY TIM LEBBON
ISBN 978-1-59582-204-8 | $12.99

HELLBOY: THE ICE WOLVES
BY MARK CHADBOURN
ISBN 978-1-59582-205-5 | $12.99

LOBSTER JOHNSON: THE SATAN FACTORY
BY THOMAS E. SNIEGOSKI
ISBN 978-1-59582-203-1 | $12.99

SHORT STORIES
ILLUSTRATED BY MIKE MIGNOLA

HELLBOY: ODD JOBS
BY POPPY Z. BRITE, GREG RUCKA, AND OTHERS
ISBN 978-1-56971-440-9 | $14.99

HELLBOY: ODDER JOBS
BY FRANK DARABONT, GUILLERMO DEL TORO, AND OTHERS
ISBN 978-1-59307-226-1 | $14.99

HELLBOY: ODDEST JOBS
BY JOE R. LANSDALE, CHINA MIÉVILLE, AND OTHERS
ISBN 978-1-59307-944-4 | $14.99

ALSO

THE AMAZING SCREW-ON HEAD AND OTHER CURIOUS OBJECTS HARDCOVER COLLECTION
BY MIKE MIGNOLA
ISBN 978-1-59582-501-8 | $17.99

BALTIMORE: THE PLAGUE SHIPS
WITH CHRISTOPHER GOLDEN AND BEN STENBECK
ISBN 978-1-59582-673-2 | $24.99

DARK HORSE BOOKS
DarkHorse.com

AVAILABLE AT YOUR LOCAL COMICS SHOP OR BOOKSTORE! • To find a comics shop in your area, call 1-888-266-4226.
For more information or to order direct visit DarkHorse.com or call 1-800-862-0052 Mon.–Fri. 9 A.M. to 5 P.M. Pacific Time.
Prices and availability subject to change without notice.